# Holt Online Assessment

## Let the POWER of Holt technology work for you– and make the MOST of your day!

## 1 ASSESS

- Use Holt's pre-made tests with built-in audio links to assess all skill areas including listening comprehension.
- Create and administer your own tests online with **ExamView® Version 5 Assessment Suite**.

## 2 GRADE

- Select guidelines for automated scoring and save countless hours.

## 3 REPORT

- Generate reports for students, parents or administrators with ease.
- Track academic progress to focus instruction.

## 4 REMEDIATE

- Access additional activities and resources to help each and every student succeed.

**Contact your Holt sales representative for more information.**

INDIANA

HOLT

# SPANISH 3 ¡EXPRÉSATE!

correlated to

## *Indiana*

### Academic Standards for World Languages, Grade 11

CONTENTS

Printed in the United States of America



ISBN-13: 978-0-55-400472-3
ISBN-10: 0-55-400472-0
123 048 09 08 07

**Explanation of Correlation** The following document is a correlation of ***Holt Spanish 3 ¡Exprésate!*** to the 2007 Indiana Academic Standards for World Languages, Grade 11. The format for this correlation follows the same basic format established by the Academic Standards, modified to accommodate the addition of page references. The correlation provides a cross-reference between the skills in the Academic Standards and representative page numbers where those skills are taught or assessed.

The references contained in this correlation reflect Holt, Rinehart and Winston's interpretation of the Spanish objectives outlined in the Indiana curriculum.

**Key to References**

| PREFIX | EXPLANATION |
|---|---|
| SE | *Student Edition* |
| ATE | *Annotated Teacher's Edition* |

**Detailed correlation of**
**Holt *Spanish 3 ¡Exprésate!* to the**

# Indiana Academic Standards for World Languages, Grade 11

**STANDARD 1 COMMUNICATION:**
**Write and speak in a language other than English**
***Learners engage in written and spoken conversations on a variety of topics. (Interpersonal)***

| | | | |
|---|---|---|---|
| **11.1.1** | Initiate, sustain, and close conversations in limited yet varied situations. | **SE** | 11, 13, 15, 17, 19, 27, 29, 31, 47, 53, 55, 67, 69, 89, 103, 115, 121, 137, 177, 179, 192, 206, 213, 227, 235, 248, 267, 283, 297, 299, 317, 323, 327, 345, 359, 371, 373, 375, 387, 407, 413, 415, 419, 427, 429, 431, 433, 439, 449 |
| | | **ATE** | 8, 12, 19, 22, 26, 31, 50, 54, 64, 68, 98, 100, 102, 112, 116, 132, 158, 202, 206, 230, 234, 244, 278, 282, 292, 296, 320, 324, 327, 334, 336, 338, 345, 359, 372, 386, 407, 414, 424, 428, 439, 449 |
| **11.1.2** | Exchange detailed information and opinions orally on a variety of topics. | **SE** | 47, 53, 63, 67, 89, 103, 111, 115, 121, 153, 177, 192, 201, 206, 213, 317, 234, 237, 239, 243, 247, 267, 282, 296, 299, 323, 327, 331, 333, 359, 371, 373, 381, 386, 407, 415, 419, 423, 427, 429, 431, 433, 439, 449 |
| | | **ATE** | 46, 53, 62, 67, 88, 103, 111, 115, 121, 132, 136, 152, 178, 192, 200, 206, 234, 242, 248, 267, 282, 290, 296, 299, 316, 323, 327, 332, 358, 372, 380, 386, 406, 414, 422, 427, 429, 431, 433, 439, 448 |
| **11.1.3** | Exchange detailed information and opinions in written form on a variety of topics. | **SE** | 41, 83, 131, 173, 221, 263, 311, 353, 401, 443 |
| | | **ATE** | 13, 23, 29, 59, 65, 67, 83, 121, 129, 195, 209, 249, 255, 287, 289, 295, 301, 351, 354, 385 |

| | | |
|---|---|---|
| **11.1.4** | Make requests and ask different types of questions in a variety of social situations. | **SE** 11, 17, 59, 61, 143, 147, 149, 157, 195, 199, 235, 247, 249, 339, 419, 431<br>**ATE** 8, 23, 54, 154, 188, 192, 338 |
| **11.1.5** | Recognize and use situation-appropriate non-verbal communication. | **SE** 34, 35, 47, 89, 145, 147, 151, 179, 197, 205, 209, 303, 379, 449<br>**ATE** 17, 25, 34, 55, 75, 76, 124, 161, 166, 205, 211, 214, 256, 304, 305, 327, 346, 394, 436 |
| **11.1.6** | Use speaking and listening strategies to facilitate communication.<br>Examples: Circumlocution, synonyms and antonyms | **SE** 15, 17, 19, 29, 31, 33, 71, 73, 75, 105, 107, 109, 195, 197, 199, 237, 239, 241, 285, 287, 289, 327, 329, 331, 375, 389, 417, 419, 421<br>**ATE** 37, 56, 118, 298, 340, 388, 415, 430 |

**STANDARD 2 COMMUNICATION:**
**Interpret information in a language other than English**
***Learners interpret written and spoken language on a variety of topics. (Interpretive)***

| | | |
|---|---|---|
| **11.2.1** | Respond accurately to everyday requests, commands, and directions. | **SE** 55, 61, 207<br>**ATE** T64-T67, 9, 23, 47C, 51, 65, 99, 113, 141, 155, 189, 203, 231, 279, 293, 321, 335, 369, 383, 411 |
| **11.2.2** | Demonstrate comprehension of both authentic and non-authentic written and spoken language through developmentally appropriate tasks.<br>Example: Provide a brief summary of the material in the target language | **SE** 21, 35, 37, 40, 63, 77, 79, 82, 125, 127, 130, 153, 167, 169, 215, 217, 220, 257, 259, 262, 305, 307, 352, 347, 349, 371, 395, 397, 400, 439, 441<br>**ATE** 1, 3, 5, 20, 34, 36, 38, 62, 76, 78, 80, 91, 93, 95, 110, 124, 126, 128, 152, 166, 168, 181, 183, 185, 200, 214, 216, 218, 242, 256, 258, 260, 271, 273, 275, 290, 304, 308, 350, 351, 380, 394, 396, 398, 436, 438, 440 |
| **11.2.3** | Make educated guesses about meaning in unfamiliar written and spoken contexts. | **SE** xvi, 34, 76, 80, 124, 128, 166, 170, 214, 218, 256, 260, 304, 308, 346, 350, 394, 398, 436, 440<br>**ATE** xvi, 38, 76, 80, 124, 128, 166, 170, 214, 218, 256, 260, 304, 308, 346, 350, 394, 398, 436, 440 |

**STANDARD 3 COMMUNICATION:**
**Present information in a language other than English**
***Learners present to an audience of listeners or readers on a variety of topics. (Presentational)***

| | | |
|---|---|---|
| **11.3.1** | Recite rhymes, proverbs, and poetry or sing songs of the target language and cultures. | **SE** 221<br>**ATE** 226, 397, 441 |
| **11.3.2** | Produce and present creative material on a variety of topics.<br>Examples: Reports, student-written plays, etc. | **SE** 37, 41, 47, 89, 137, 147, 179, 373, 377, 379, 387, 393, 407<br>**ATE** 5C, 41, 46, 47C, 52, 83, 95C, 111, 125, 136, 137C, 178, 185C, 191, 201, 205, 207, 226, 227C, 261, 268, 275C, 287, 307, 316, 317C, 325, 339, 358, 365C, 393, 406, 407C, 419, 431, 448 |

| | | | |
|---|---|---|---|
| **11.3.3** | Read passages aloud to demonstrate improving intonation and pronunciation. | **SE** | 41, 263 |
| | | **ATE** | 34, 69, 192, 214, 216, 219, 256, 262, 290, 332, 441 |
| **11.3.4** | Compose cohesive written information using appropriate formats and more varied vocabulary and structures. | **SE** | 41, 83, 131, 173, 221, 263, 311, 353, 401, 443 |
| | | **ATE** | 5C, 40, 41,47C, 82, 83, 95C, 130, 131, 137C, 172, 173, 185C, 220, 221, 227C, 262, 263, 275C, 310-311, 317C, 352, 353, 365C, 400, 401, 407C, 442, 443 |

**STANDARD 4 CULTURES:**
**Develop awareness of other cultures**
***Learners examine, experience, and reflect on the relationships among the practices, products, and perspectives of the cultures studied.***

| | | | |
|---|---|---|---|
| **11.4.1** | Analyze and reflect on cultural practices of the target cultures. | **SE** | 37, 47, 79, 89, 111, 127, 153, 169, 179, 201, 217, 220, 243, 259, 262, 269, 274, 291, 333, 349, 381, 397, 407, 423, 439 |
| | | **ATE** | 3, 5, 20, 36, 47, 62, 78, 88, 91, 93, 95, 110, 126, 136, 137D, 152, 168, 178, 181, 183, 185, 185D, 200, 216, 218, 258, 260, 269, 271, 273, 275, 290, 306, 316, 332, 348, 358, 361, 363, 380, 396, 407, 422, 438, 448 |
| **11.4.2** | Describe products, perspectives, and symbols of the target cultures. | **SE** | 21, 37, 47, 63, 79, 89, 111, 127, 153, 169, 179, 184, 185, 201, 217, 220, 243, 259, 262, 269, 291, 307, 333, 349, 381, 397, 407, 423, 439 |
| | | **ATE** | 3, 5, 20, 36, 46, 47D, 62, 78, 88, 91, 93, 95, 110, 126, 136, 137C, 152, 168, 178, 181, 183, 185, 200, 216, 218, 226, 227D, 242, 258, 260, 269, 271, 273, 275, 290, 306, 316, 332, 348, 358, 361, 363, 365, 380, 396, 407, 422, 438, 448 |
| **11.4.3** | Discuss factors that influence practices, products, and perspectives.<br>Examples: Health, technology, social issues, gender equality, etc. | **SE** | 21, 37, 47, 63, 79, 89, 111, 127, 153, 169, 179, 201, 217, 243, 259, 262, 269, 291, 307, 333, 349, 362, 363, 381, 397, 407, 423, 439 |
| | | **ATE** | 3, 5, 20, 36, 46, 47D, 62, 78, 88, 91, 93, 95, 110, 126, 136, 152, 168, 178, 181, 183, 185, 200, 216, 218, 226, 242, 258, 260, 269, 271, 273, 275, 290, 306, 316, 332, 348, 358, 361, 363, 365, 380, 396, 407, 422, 438, 448 |
| **11.4.4** | Recognize the interrelations among the practices, products, and perspectives of the target cultures. | **SE** | 21, 37, 47, 63, 79, 89, 95, 111, 127, 153, 169, 179, 182-185, 201, 217, 220, 243, 259, 291, 307, 333, 349, 362, 363, 381, 397, 407, 423, 439 |
| | | **ATE** | 3, 5, 20, 36, 46, 47D, 62, 78, 88, 91, 93, 95, 110, 126, 136, 152, 168, 178, 185, 200, 216, 218, 226, 242, 258, 260, 269, 271, 273, 275, 306, 316, 332, 348, 358, 361, 363, 365, 380, 396, 407C, 422, 438, 448 |
| **11.4.5** | Explain contributions from other cultures. | **SE** | 37, 47, 79, 89, 127, 169, 179, 201, 217, 259, 262, 264, 269, 307, 349, 397, 407, 439 |
| | | **ATE** | 3, 5, 36, 47, 47D, 78, 88, 91, 93, 95, 126, 136, 168, 178, 185C, 185, 216, 218, 226, 258, 260, 269, 271, 273, 275, 306, 316, 348, 358, 361, 363, 365, 396, 407, 438, 448 |
| **11.4.6** | Identify significant events unique to the target cultures. | **SE** | 37, 182, 183, 259, 272, 273, 362, 363, 396-397, 422 |
| | | **ATE** | 1, 3, 5, 37, 47D, 93, 153, 183, 263, 269, 275, 363, 396, 422 |

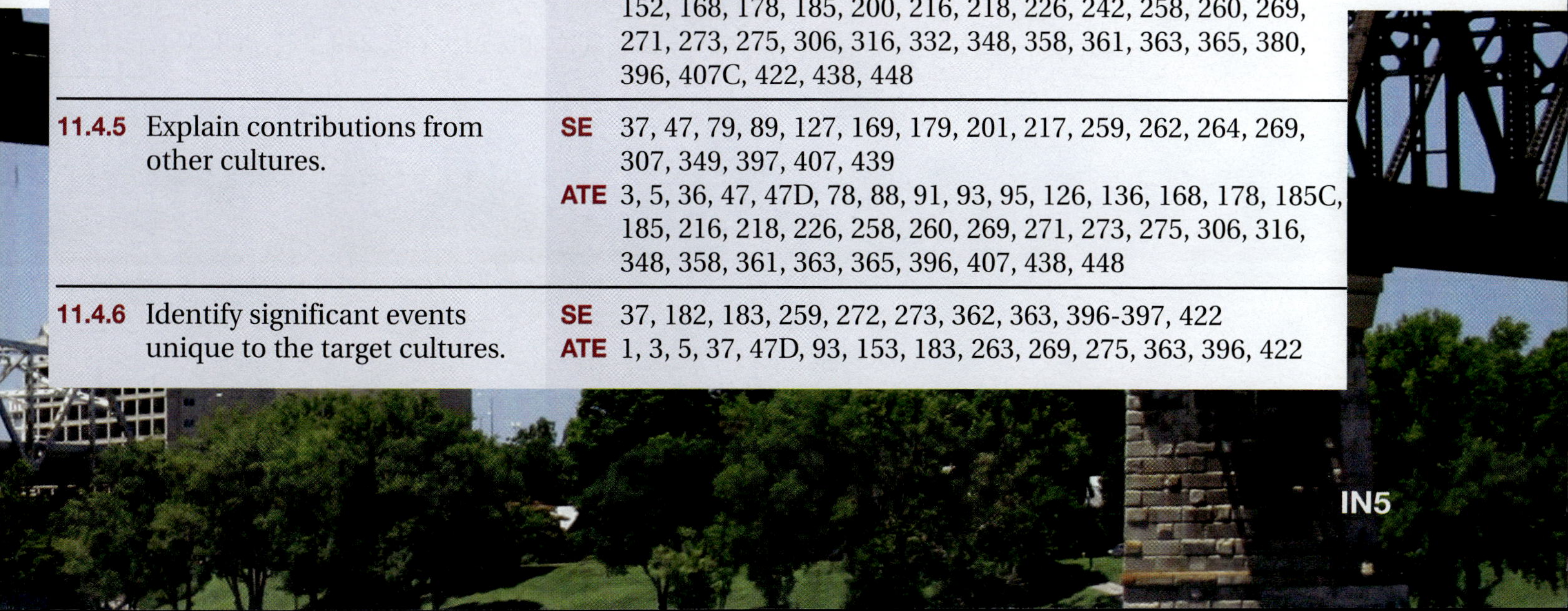

| | | |
|---|---|---|
| **STANDARD 5 CONNECTIONS: Make connections to other content areas** *Learners use the target language to expand their knowledge of and make connections among multiple content areas.* | | |
| **11.5.1** | Make connections with other content areas through resources intended for native speakers. | **SE** 37, 259<br>**ATE** 5C, 5D, 46, 88, 91, 136, 137C, 178, 181, 185C, 226, 227C, 268, 271, 316, 358, 361, 365C, 406, 448 |
| **11.5.2** | Design and share activities and materials that integrate the target language and cultures with concepts and skills from other content areas. Examples: Puzzles, games, cadet teaching, etc. | **SE** 51, 53, 73, 89, 137, 343, 359, 387, 391, 427, 429<br>**ATE** T64-T67, 5C, 45, 47C, 47D, 47, 87, 95C, 135, 137C, 177, 185C, 225, 227C, 267, 275C, 315, 317C, 317D, 357, 365C, 405, 407C, 447 |
| **STANDARD 6 CONNECTIONS: Access and connect information through various media** *Learners strengthen language proficiency and cultural knowledge by using current digital media and authentic resources.* | | |
| **11.6.1** | Use digital media and culturally authentic resources to build vocabulary and improve receptive and productive language skills. Examples: RSS feeds/Podcasts, streaming audio, streaming video, etc. | **SE** 10, 16, 20, 42, 43, 46, 52, 56, 99, 100, 101, 116, 120, 124, 142, 145, 146, 148, 150, 152, 218, 226, 270, 280, 286, 302, 303, 324, 354, 360, 402, 406, 434, 436, 438<br>**ATE** 5E, 5E, 47E, 47F, 95E, 95F, 137F, 185E, 185F, 227E, 227F, 275E, 285F, 317E, 317F, 365E, 365F, 407E, 407F |
| **11.6.2** | Use digital media and culturally authentic resources to study target cultures. Examples: News broadcasts, online newspapers, virtual environments, etc. | **SE** 1, 20, 34, 62, 76, 90, 110, 124, 152, 166, 180, 200, 214, 242, 256, 290, 304, 332, 346, 380, 394, 422, 436<br>**ATE** 1, 79, 91, 181, 203, 205, 245, 249, 271, 361, 387 |
| **11.6.3** | Identify and evaluate resources intended for native speakers. | **SE** 1, 20, 34, 62, 76, 90, 110, 124, 152, 166, 180, 200, 214, 220, 256, 290, 304, 310, 332, 346, 352, 380, 394, 400, 422, 436, 442<br>**ATE** 1, 79, 91, 181, 203, 205, 219, 245, 249, 271, 309, 351, 361, 387, 399, 441 |

**STANDARD 7 COMPARISONS:**
**Investigate the nature of language and culture**
***Learners understand the nature of language and culture through comparisons of the languages and cultures studied and their own.***

| | | | |
|---|---|---|---|
| **11.7.1** | Use elements of word formation to expand vocabulary and derive meaning. Examples: Prefixes, suffixes, roots | **SE** | 29, 43, 57, 109, 119, 151, 161, 175, 195, 213, 241, 253, 264, 267, 286, 303, 327, 343, 374-389, 402, 419, 444 |
| | | **ATE** | 14, 28, 42, 56, 70, 84, 104, 118, 146, 160, 174, 194, 208, 222, 236, 252, 264, 267, 284, 298, 312, 326, 340, 354, 374, 388, 402, 416, 430, 444 |
| **11.7.2** | Recognize and use a variety of language structures. Example: Mood | **SE** | 14-19, 41, 47, 70-75, 83, 118-123, 131, 137, 174-177, 173, 208-213, 221, 222-225, 227, 264, 269, 268, 298-303, 311, 317, 326-331, 353, 354-357, 359, 401, 407, 416-421, 443, 449 |
| | | **ATE** | 28-33, 42-45, 56-61, 84-87, 104-109, 146-151, 160-165, 174-177, 194-199, 236-241, 250-255, 267, 284-289, 312-315, 340-347, 374-379, 402-405, 430-435, 444-447 |
| **11.7.3** | Compare and use idiomatic, colloquial, and proverbial expressions in the target language. | **SE** | 13, 47, 55, 89, 103, 137, 145, 179, 193, 227, 235, 269, 283, 317, 325, 359, 407, 415, 448, R21-R24 |
| | | **ATE** | 12, 54, 102, 144, 192, 234, 282, 324, 386, 414, R21-R24 |
| **11.7.4** | Compare and use authentic forms of address in familiar and unfamiliar social situations. | **SE** | 336, 337 |
| | | **ATE** | 317C, 348, 349 |
| **11.7.5** | Compare systems of other cultures and the learner's own culture. Examples: Educational, political, religious practices, etc. | **SE** | 3, 21, 63, 79, 90-95, 111, 153, 169, 183, 201, 216-217, 243, 259, 272, 291, 333, 349, 364, 381, 396-397, 423, 439 |
| | | **ATE** | 20, 62, 78, 79, 95, 110, 126, 127, 137D, 152, 168, 180-185, 200, 216-217, 220, 242, 259, 275, 290, 306, 316, 332, 348-349, 362, 363, 365, 380, 381, 396-397, 422, 438 |
| **11.7.6** | Compare and contrast elements that shape cultural identity in the learner's heritage and in the target cultures. | **SE** | 3, 21, 63, 79, 90-95, 111, 153, 169, 183, 201, 216-217, 243, 259, 272, 291, 333, 349, 364, 381, 396-397, 423, 439 |
| | | **ATE** | 20, 62, 78, 79, 95, 110, 126, 127, 152, 168, 180-185, 200, 216-217, 220, 242, 259, 275, 290, 306, 332, 348-349, 362, 363, 365, 380, 381, 396-397, 422, 438 |

| **STANDARD 8 COMMUNITIES:** **Become an active global citizen by experiencing languages and cultures in multiple settings** ***Learners use their knowledge of the target language and cultures both within and beyond the school setting for personal enrichment and civic engagement.*** | | |
|---|---|---|
| **11.8.1** | Share experiences from the world language classroom with others. | **SE** 126-127, 243, 333<br>**ATE** 46, 95C, 178, 226, 268, 316 |
| **11.8.2** | Investigate and share with others the influences of the target language and cultures on the community.<br>Examples: Architecture, special events, stores and shops, careers using the target language, etc. | **SE** 111, 126-127, 153, 227, 243, 333, 449<br>**ATE** 89, 136, 185D, 226, 268, 316, 358, 406 |
| **11.8.3** | Show evidence of becoming a life-long learner by using the target language and cultural knowledge for personal enrichment.<br>Examples: Watch movies in the target language, listen to songs in the target language, join a club, establish e-pal or pen pal connections with native speakers, investigate a local and/or global need that is identified as authentic by the cultures of the target language, travel abroad | **SE** 63, 111, 243, 252, 281, 349, 413, 415, 419, 427, 429, 431, 433, 435, 439, 449<br>**ATE** 11, 21, 47C, 79, 88, 95C, 95D, 136, 137C, 137D, 185D, 203, 226, 227D, 251, 275D, 281, 283, 317C, 317D, 349, 365D, 407D, 410, 419, 425, 426, 427, 431, 432, 433, 435, 438, 439, 448 |

TEACHER'S EDITION

HOLT SPANISH 3

# ¡Exprésate!®

Nancy Humbach

Sylvia Madrigal Velasco

HOLT, RINEHART AND WINSTON
A Harcourt Education Company
Orlando • Austin • New York • San Diego • London

# Holt Teacher Advisory Panel

As members of the **Holt World Languages Teacher Advisory Panel,** the following teachers made a unique and invaluable contribution to the ***¡Exprésate!*** Spanish program. They generously shared their experience and expertise in a collaborative group setting and helped refine early materials into the program design represented in this book. We wish to thank them for the many hours of work they put into the development of this program and for the many ideas they shared.

**¡Muchísimas gracias a todos!**

**Erick Ekker**
Bob Miller Middle School
Henderson, NV

**Dulce Goldenberg**
Miami Senior High School
Miami, FL

**Beckie Gurnish**
Ellet High School
Akron, OH

**Bill Heller**
Perry High School
Perry, NY

**MilyBett Llanos**
Westwood High School
Austin, TX

**Rosanna Perez**
Communications Arts
High School
San Antonio, TX

**Jo Schuler**
Central Bucks High School East
Doylestown, PA

**Leticia Schweigert**
Science Academy
Mercedes, TX

**Claudia Sloan**
Lake Park High School
Roselle, IL

**Judy Smock**
Gilbert High School
Gilbert, AZ

**Catriona Stavropoulos**
West Springfield High School
Springfield, VA

**Nina Wilson**
Burnet Middle School
Austin, TX

**Janet Wohlers**
Weston Middle School
Weston, MA



Acknowledgments and other credits appear on pages R106–R108, which are extensions of the copyright page.

Printed in the United States of America



ISBN-13: 978-0-03-045374-8

ISBN-10: 0-03-045374-7

1 2 3 4 5 6 7 032 09 08 07 06

# Authors

## Nancy Humbach

Nancy Humbach is Associate Professor and Coordinator of Languages Education at Miami University, Oxford, Ohio. She has authored or co-authored over a dozen textbooks in Spanish. A former Fulbright-Hayes Scholar, she has lived and studied in Colombia and Mexico and has traveled and conducted research throughout the Spanish-speaking world. She is a recipient of many honors, including the Florence Steiner Award for Leadership in the Foreign Language Profession and the Nelson Brooks Award for the Teaching of Culture.

## Sylvia Madrigal Velasco

Sylvia Madrigal Velasco was born in San Benito, Texas. The youngest of four siblings, she grew up in the Rio Grande Valley, between two cultures and languages. Her lifelong fascination with Spanish has led her to travel in many Spanish-speaking countries. She graduated from Yale University in 1979 and has worked for over 20 years as a textbook editor and author at various publishing companies. She has written bilingual materials, video scripts, workbooks, CD-ROMs, and readers.

## Contributing Writers

**Vivian Bosque, Ed.D.**
Nova Southeastern University
Miami, FL
Ms. Bosque wrote material for the Heritage Speakers suggestions.

**Marci Reed**
Austin, TX
Ms. Reed wrote material for the **Geocultura** pages.

## Field Test Participants

**We express our appreciation to the teachers and students who helped field test *¡Exprésate!* Levels 1–3.**

**Kathleen Neal Carroll**
Johnny G. Economedes High School
Edinburg, TX

**Inés Loveras**
Port Richmond High School
Staten Island, NY

**Jenny L. Wilton**
Roosevelt High School
St. Louis, MO

**Yadira Gonzáles**
Memorial High School
McAllen, TX

**Nitza T. Cochran**
Nathan B. Forrest MS
Jacksonville, FL

**Doris Muñoz Fuentes**
Fort Hamilton High School
Brooklyn, NY

**Diane Mackenzie**
Atherton High School
Louisville, KY

**Sara Kate Perkins**
Andrews High School
High Point, NC

**María E. Negrón**
John F. Kennedy High School
Richmond, VA

**Ms. Luz M. Vasquez**
Thomas Jefferson High School
San Antonio, TX

**Zulema Silva**
Dudley High School
Greensboro, NC

**Hank Cline**
Jamesville-Dewitt High School
Jamesville, NY

**Yvonne L. Harrell**
Englewood High School
Jacksonville, FL

## Reviewers

**We'd like to thank the following teachers for having reviewed one or more chapters of *¡Exprésate!***

**Elizabeth Baird**
Independence High School
Independence, OH

**Janet J. Bishop**
Pelham High School
Pelham, AL

**Laura Grable**
Riverhead Central School District
Riverhead, NY

**Manuel Hernández**
Presentation High School
San Jose, CA

**Christine M. Lord**
Dracut HS
Dracut, MA

**Pablo Oliva**
Arendell Parrott Academy
Kinston, NC

**Sharon Strait**
Mukwonago High School
Mukwonago, WI

**Dora Villani**
High School for American Studies
Bronx, NY

## Teacher's Edition

# Contenido

# To the Teacher

*¡Exprésate!*—a new program with real-world photos, on-location video, animated grammar, and solid pedagogy—is an exciting, motivational, and effective Spanish series that will appeal to all types of learners and keep them coming back for more. Based on the "five C's" of the national standards, this new program has an easy-to-use format that allows students to achieve success, and gives teachers a host of teaching tools to make sure all students can focus on each lesson's goals.

## Communication

*¡Exprésate!* engages students right from the start of each lesson and carefully leads them from structured practice to open-ended communication. Unique image-based **Vocabulario** presentations introduce a thematic context and provide a reason and motivation for using the language. Colorful **Gramática** presentations, accompanied by **animated grammar** explanations, help students achieve accuracy in their communication. You can feel confident that Holt's approach to grammar gives students exactly what they need for success. Additional information on grammar logic is highlighted in the Chapter Opener of the *Teacher's Edition*. At a glance, you will see how and why concepts are introduced and where they are re-entered.

## Cultures

The **Geocultura** feature that precedes each chapter, realia-based readings and activities, and culture notes in each chapter offer high-interest cultural information and a chance to learn about the **products**, **practices**, and **perspectives** of the target cultures.

## Connections

Links to other subject areas, such as social studies, math, language arts, music, and fine arts are found throughout each chapter of *¡Exprésate!*. Additional opportunities for connections are found at point of use in the *Teacher's Edition*.

## Comparisons

To enable students to acquire a broader and a deeper understanding of language and culture *¡Exprésate!* offers them multiple opportunities to compare the new language and culture with their own.

## Communities

The ultimate goal of learning to communicate in a new language should be the ability to function in an increasingly diverse community and an increasingly demanding world market. *¡Exprésate!* is built on the theory that the global community has its roots in the second language classroom. If learning language and culture is enjoyable and accessible, all students will become productive members of their community.

For any language program to be successful, the needs of teachers and students have to be the primary consideration. From suggestions for differentiated instruction to the latest in technology products, *¡Exprésate!* provides an abundance of teacher support and learning tools to help ensure success for all teachers and students.

# Contenido en breve

# Castilla-La Mancha

## Capítulo 1 ¡Adiós al verano!



**OBJETIVOS**

In this chapter, you will learn to
- talk about the past
- talk about what you liked and used to do
- ask for and give advice
- talk about the future

**Geocultura**

Molinos de viento en las llanuras de Castilla-La Mancha

**En video**

Geocultura GeoVisión
Gramática 1 y 2 GramaVisión
Cultura VideoCultura
VideoNovela Clara perspectiva
Variedades

**OBJETIVOS**

**In this chapter, you will learn to**
- express interest and displeasure
- invite someone to do something
- describe the ideal friend
- express happiness and unhappiness

Vista de las famosas casas colgadas en Cuenca, Castilla-La Mancha

**En video**

Geocultura **GeoVisión**
Gramática 1 y 2 **GramaVisión**
Cultura **VideoCultura**
VideoNovela **Clara perspectiva**
**Variedades**

# El Caribe

## Capítulo 3 Todo tiene solución



**OBJETIVOS**

In this chapter, you will learn to
- complain
- express an opinion and disagree
- make suggestions
- apologize

**Geocultura**

Vista de la ciudad de La Habana, Cuba

**En video**

Geocultura **GeoVisión**
Gramática 1 y 2 **GramaVisión**
Cultura **VideoCultura**
VideoNovela **Clara perspectiva**
**Variedades**

# Capítulo 4 Entre familia ............................... 138

## Chapter Interleaf with Teaching Resources



### OBJETIVOS

In this chapter, you will learn to
- ask about the latest news
- react to news
- comment on food
- explain and give excuses

Zona agrícola en el oeste de Cuba

### En video

| | |
|---|---|
| Geocultura | GeoVisión |
| Gramática 1 y 2 | GramaVisión |
| Cultura | VideoCultura |
| VideoNovela | Clara perspectiva |
| | Variedades |

# El Suroeste y el Norte de México

## Capítulo 5 El arte y la música



**OBJETIVOS**

In this chapter, you will learn to

- ask for and give opinions
- introduce and change a topic of conversation
- make suggestions and recommendations
- turn down an invitation

**Geocultura**

El Álamo, San Antonio, Texas

**En video**

Geocultura **GeoVisión**
Gramática 1 y 2 **GramaVisión**
Cultura **VideoCultura**
VideoNovela **Clara perspectiva**
**Variedades**

# Capítulo 6 ¡Ponte al día!



## OBJETIVOS

In this chapter, you will learn to
- express certainty
- express doubt and disbelief
- ask about information and explain where you found it
- talk about what you know and don't know

Vista del Río Grande, Suroeste y Norte de México

## En video

Geocultura **GeoVisión**
Gramática 1 y 2 **GramaVisión**
Cultura **VideoCultura**
VideoNovela **Clara perspectiva**
**Variedades**

# Los Andes

## Capítulo 7 Mis aspiraciones 

### Chapter Interleaf with Teaching Resources



**OBJETIVOS**

In this chapter, you will learn to
- talk about challenges
- talk about accomplishments
- talk about future plans
- express cause and effect

**Geocultura**

Iglesia de San Francisco, Quito, Ecuador

**En video**

Geocultura GeoVisión
Gramática 1 y 2 GramaVisión
Cultura VideoCultura
VideoNovela Clara perspectiva
Variedades

# Capítulo 8 ¿A qué te dedicas?



**OBJETIVOS**

**In this chapter, you will learn to**
- say what you can and can not do
- talk about what you do and do not understand
- write a formal letter
- talk about your plans

Vista del cañón del Colca, Perú

**En video**

Geocultura **GeoVisión**
Gramática 1 y 2 **GramaVisión**
Cultura **VideoCultura**
VideoNovela **Clara perspectiva**
**Variedades**

# El Cono Sur

## Capítulo 9 Huellas del pasado



### Chapter Interleaf with Teaching Resources



### OBJETIVOS

In this chapter, you will learn to

- set the scene for a story
- continue and end a story
- talk about your hopes and wishes
- express regret and gratitude

### Geocultura

Vista de la ciudad de Buenos Aires, capital de Argentina

### En video

Geocultura **GeoVisión**
Gramática 1 y 2 **GramaVisión**
Cultura **VideoCultura**
VideoNovela **Clara perspectiva**
**Variedades**

# Capítulo 10 El mundo en que vivimos .....408



## OBJETIVOS

In this chapter, you will learn to
- talk about past events
- express and support a point of view
- make predictions and give warnings
- express assumptions

Picos del cerro Aconcagua en la cordillera de los Andes, Argentina

## En video

Geocultura **GeoVisión**
Gramática 1 y 2 **GramaVisión**
Cultura **VideoCultura**
VideoNovela **Clara perspectiva**
**Variedades**

# Pacing

## Base your pacing on your schedule...

If you are teaching on a traditional schedule, base your instruction on the following plan.

### Traditional Schedule

**Days of Instruction: 180**

| | | |
|---|---|---|
| **Geocultura** | 2 days of instruction for **Geocultura: La historia** (preceding first chapter in the unit); 2 days of instruction for **Geocultura: El Arte** (preceding second chapter in the unit) x 5 Geoculturas | 20 days |
| **Chapter** | 16 days per chapter (including assessment) x 10 | 160 days |
| **Total days of instruction using ¡Exprésate!:** | | **180 days** |

### Block Schedule

**Blocks of instruction: 90**

| | | |
|---|---|---|
| **Geocultura** | 1 block of instruction per **Geocultura: La historia** and 1 block of instruction per **Geocultura: El Arte** x 5 Geoculturas | 10 blocks |
| **Chapter** | 8 blocks per chapter (including assessment) x 10 | 80 blocks |
| **Total blocks of instruction using ¡Exprésate!:** | | **90 blocks** |

If you are teaching on a block schedule, spend two blocks on each **Geocultura** and eight blocks on each chapter.

## ...and plan your lessons to fit.

| Suggested pacing: | Traditional Schedule | Block Schedule |
|---|---|---|
| Vocabulario 1/Gramática 1 | 5 1/2 days | 2 1/2 blocks |
| Cultura | 1/2 day | 1/2 block |
| Vocabulario 2/Gramática 2 | 5 1/2 days | 2 1/2 blocks |
| Novela | 1/2 day | 1/2 block |
| Lectura informativa | 1 day | 1/2 block |
| Leamos y escribamos | 1 day | 1/2 block |
| Prepárate para el examen | 1/2 day | 1/4 block |
| Chapter Test | 1 day | 1/2 block |
| Integración | 1/2 day | 1/4 block |

# Planning

## One-Stop Planner® CD-ROM

### Use the One-Stop Planner to make *¡Exprésate!* work for you...

- **Calendar planning tool** for both short-term and long-term planning
- Interactive *Teacher's Edition* with direct links to print and media resources
- **ExamView® 5 Assessment Suite**
- **Clip art Library**

### ...or customize lesson plans to suit your style or individual classes.

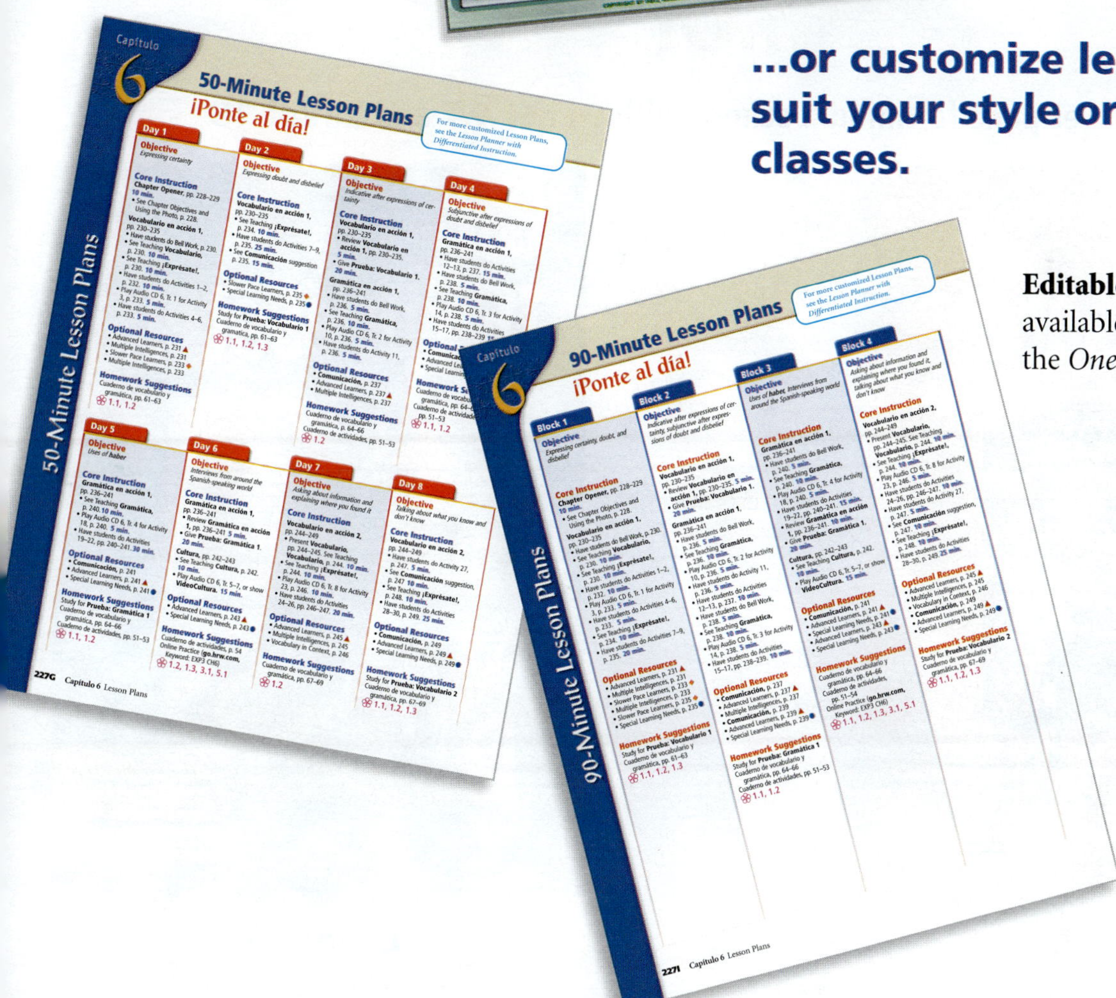


**Editable lesson plans** are available for all chapters on the *One-Stop Planner*.

# Articulation Across Levels

## From Middle School through Advanced Placement

**Level 1**

Begin the learning experience with **Level 1** ...

**...or**

set a slower pace for middle school with **Level 1A** and **Level 1B**

**Level 1A**

\+

**Level 1B**

**Level 2** thoroughly reviews the basics and continues to build a solid foundation for communication.

**Level 3** begins with a review of the major points covered in Level 2, then builds student skills to the Intermediate Proficiency level.

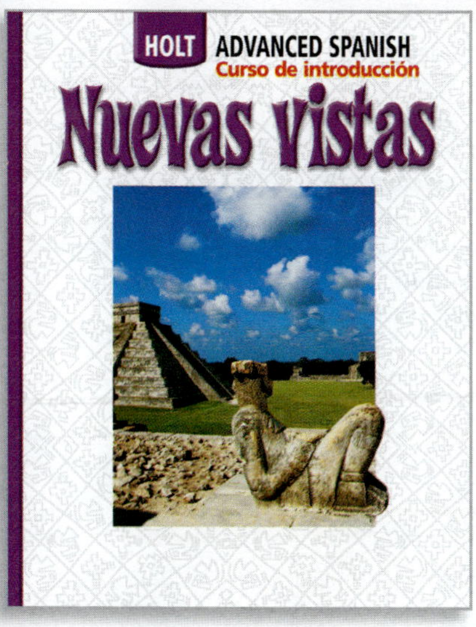


**NUEVAS VISTAS**
**Curso de introducción**
**(Level 4)**

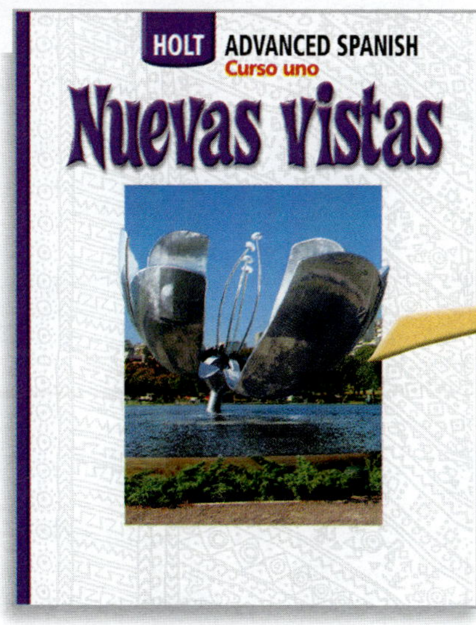


**NUEVAS VISTAS**
**Curso uno**
**(Level 5)**

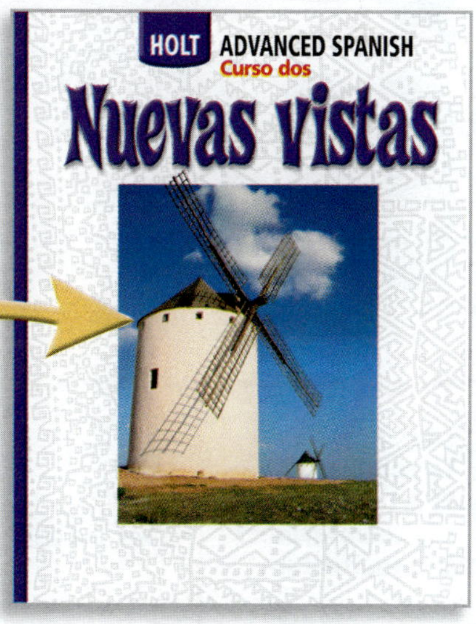


**NUEVAS VISTAS**
**Curso dos**
**(Level 6)**

**Nuevas Vistas** will prepare your students for the AP* exams. It is especially effective in preparing Heritage Speakers for the challenges they will face in the workplace and as members of the global Spanish-speaking community.

*Advanced Placement Program and AP are registered trademarks of the College Entrance Examination Board, which was not involved in the production of, and does not endorse, this product.

# Scope and Sequence

# ¡Exprésate! Level 1

## Capítulo 1 ¡Empecemos! pp. 4–37

**España**

**La geografía**
**Las celebraciones**
**La comida**
**La arquitectura**
**El arte**

| Vocabulary | Functions | Grammar | Culture | Strategies |
|---|---|---|---|---|
| • Greetings and goodbyes | • Asking someone's name<br>• Asking how someone is<br>• Introducing someone<br>• Saying where you and others are from | • Subjects and verbs in sentences<br>• Subject pronouns | • Diminutives and nicknames<br>• How students address teachers<br>• **Comparaciones:** Greetings and goodbyes<br>• **Comunidad:** Spanish clubs and associations | • **Video Strategy:** Making connections<br>• **Reading Strategy:** Recognizing cognates<br>• **Writing Strategy:** Making lists |
| • Numbers 0–31<br>• Telling time<br>• Days of the week and months of the year<br>• Alphabet | • Giving phone numbers<br>• Giving the time, the date, and the day<br>• Spelling words and giving e-mail addresses | • Present tense of the verb **ser**<br>• Punctuation marks and written accents | FINE ART<br>• ***La persistencia de la memoria,*** Salvador Dalí | |

**Review/Re-Entry** • **Integración,** pp. 36–37

## Capítulo 2 A conocernos pp. 42–75

**Puerto Rico**

**La geografía**
**La comida**
**El arte**
**Las celebraciones**
**La arquitectura**

| Vocabulary | Functions | Grammar | Culture | Strategies |
|---|---|---|---|---|
| • Describing friends<br>• Numbers 32–100 | • Describing people<br>• Asking someone's age and birthday | • **Ser** with adjectives<br>• Gender and adjective agreement<br>• Question formation | • Ways to describe people<br>• Legal driving and voting age<br>• **Comparaciones:** Describing yourself and your best friend<br>• **Comunidad:** Customer surveys in Spanish | • **Video Strategy:** Drawing conclusions<br>• **Reading Strategy:** Making inferences<br>• **Writing Strategy:** Cluster diagrams |
| • Likes and dislikes | • Talking about what you and others like<br>• Describing things | • Nouns and definite articles<br>• The verb **gustar, ¿Por qué?** and **porque**<br>• The preposition **de** | • Puerto Rican musicians<br>FINE ART<br>• ***Día lluvioso en El Viejo San Juan,*** Orlando Santiago Correa | |

**Review/Re-Entry** • **ser** • **Integración,** pp. 74–75

## Capítulo 3 ¿Qué te gusta hacer? pp. 80–113

### Texas

**La geografía**
**La arquitectura**
**El arte**
**La comida**
**Las celebraciones**

| Vocabulary | Functions | Grammar | Culture | Strategies |
| --- | --- | --- | --- | --- |
| • Sports and leisure activities | • Talking about what you and others like to do<br>• Talking about what you want to do | • **Gustar** with infinitives<br>• Pronouns after prepositions<br>• Present tense of **querer** with infinitives | • Team sports in Latin America<br>• Introducing friends to parents<br>• **Comparaciones:** Weekends activities<br>• **Comunidad:** Volunteering in your community | • **Video Strategy:** Understanding subtext<br>• **Reading Strategy:** Making predictions<br>• **Writing Strategy:** Arranging ideas chronologically |
| • Weekend activities | • Talking about every-day activities<br>• Saying how often you do things | • Present tense of regular **-ar** verbs<br>• Present tense of **ir** and **jugar**<br>• Weather expressions | • Who pays when going out with friends<br>FINE ART<br>• ***La feria en Reynosa,*** Carmen Lomas Garza | |
| **Review/Re-Entry** | • Subject pronouns | • **Integración,** pp. 112–113 | | |

## Capítulo 4 La vida escolar pp. 118–151

### Costa Rica

**La geografía**
**Las celebraciones**
**El arte**
**La comida**
**Las criaturas**

| Vocabulary | Functions | Grammar | Culture | Strategies |
| --- | --- | --- | --- | --- |
| • School supplies and items needed for school<br>• Classes | • Saying what you have and what you need<br>• Talking about classes | • Indefinite articles; **¿cuánto?, mucho,** and **poco**<br>• Present tense of **tener** and **tener** idioms<br>• **Venir** and **a** + time | • Beginning of the school year<br>• Electives and tracking<br>• **Comparaciones:** A typical day at school<br>• **Comunidad:** Exchange students | • **Video Strategy:** Comparing and contrasting<br>• **Reading Strategy:** Who, what, where, when, and why questions<br>• **Writing Strategy:** Using drawings |
| • School events<br>• Places at school | • Talking about plans<br>• Inviting others to do something | • **Ir a** + infinitives<br>• Present tense of **-er** and **-ir** verbs and tag questions<br>• **-er**/**-ir** verbs with irregular **yo** forms | • Passing and failing courses<br>• School schedules and sessions in Costa Rica<br>FINE ART<br>• ***Domingueando,*** Tomás Povedano de Arcos | |
| **Review/Re-Entry** | • **los** + days of the week | • **Integración,** pp. 150–151 | | |

## Capítulo 5 En casa con la familia pp. 156–189

### Chile

**La geografía**
**La arquitectura**
**La comida**
**Las celebraciones**
**Las bellas artes**

| Vocabulary | Functions | Grammar | Culture | Strategies |
| --- | --- | --- | --- | --- |
| • Family members<br>• Describing people (physical and personality) | • Describing people and family relationships | • Possessive adjectives<br>• Stem-changing verbs **o → ue**<br>• Stem-changing verbs **e → ie** | • Hispanic surnames<br>• Extended families<br>• **Comparaciones:** Describing family<br>• **Comunidad:** Surnames and family trees | • **Video Strategy:** Understanding humor<br>• **Reading Strategy:** Scanning<br>• **Writing Strategy:** Graphic organizers |
| • Rooms in the house<br>• Furniture and accessories | • Talking about where you and others live<br>• Talking about your responsibilities | • **Estar** with prepositions<br>• Negation<br>• **Tocar** and **parecer** | • Climate and houses<br>FINE ART<br>• ***Esperando a los pescadores,*** Isidoro Molleda | |
| **Review/Re-Entry** | • **querer** and **tener** | • Negation | • **Integración,** pp. 188–189 | |

## México

La geografía
El arte
La arquitectura
Las celebraciones
La comida

### Capítulo 6 ¡A comer! pp. 194–227

| Vocabulary | Functions | Grammar | Culture | Strategies |
|---|---|---|---|---|
| • Lunch foods<br>• Foods you might order in a restaurant<br>• Describing food<br>• Table setting | • Commenting on food<br>• Taking an order and making polite requests | • **Ser** and **estar**<br>• **Pedir** and **servir**<br>• **Preferir, poder,** and **probar** | • Mexican food; **atole**<br>• Corn as a staple food<br>• **Comparaciones:** Favorite dishes<br>• **Comunidad:** International restaurants | • **Video Strategy:** Recognizing a make-believe situation<br>• **Reading Strategy:** Considering genre<br>• **Writing Strategy:** Arranging your ideas in chronological order |
| • Breakfast and dinner foods | • Talking about meals<br>• Offering help and giving instructions | • Direct objects and direct object pronouns<br>• Affirmative informal commands<br>• Affirmative informal commands with pronouns | • Main meal of the day<br>• Snacks<br>FINE ART<br>• ***The Market of Cuernavaca in the Age of the Spanish Conquest,*** Diego Rivera | |

**Review/Re-Entry** • Stem-changing verbs • Definition of pronouns; subject pronouns • **Integración,** pp. 226–227

## Argentina

La geografía
La arquitectura
El arte
Las celebraciones
La comida

### Capítulo 7 Cuerpo sano, mente sana pp. 232–265

| Vocabulary | Functions | Grammar | Culture | Strategies |
|---|---|---|---|---|
| • Daily routine<br>• Personal items<br>• Parts of the body | • Talking about your daily routine<br>• Talking about staying fit and healthy | • Verbs with reflexive pronouns<br>• Using infinitives<br>• Stem-changing verbs | • Argentina's ski resorts<br>• **Comparaciones:** Keeping in shape<br>• **Comunidad:** Spanish in health care | • **Video Strategy:** Understanding a character's motives<br>• **Reading Strategy:** Using background knowledge<br>• **Writing Strategy:** Graphic organizers |
| • Telling how you feel<br>• More parts of the body<br>• Healthful advice | • Talking about how you feel<br>• Giving advice | • **Estar, sentirse,** and **tener**<br>• Negative informal commands<br>• Object and reflexive pronouns with commands | • Argentine food<br>• **Mate**<br>FINE ART<br>• ***Un alto en el campo,*** Prilidiano Pueyrredón | |

**Review/Re-Entry** • **querer, jugar, poder,** and **pedir** • Rules for written accents • **Integración,** pp. 264–265

## Florida

La geografía
La comida
El arte
La arquitectura
Las celebraciones

### Capítulo 8 Vamos de compras pp. 270–303

| Vocabulary | Functions | Grammar | Culture | Strategies |
|---|---|---|---|---|
| • Clothing<br>• Colors | • Asking for and giving opinions<br>• Asking for and offering help in a store | • **Costar** and numbers to 1 million<br>• Demonstrative adjectives and comparisons<br>• The verb **quedar** | • Clothing sizes<br>• **Guayaberas**<br>• **Comparaciones:** Shopping<br>• **Comunidad:** Clothes from around the globe | • **Video Strategy:** Recognizing different points of view<br>• **Reading Strategy:** Visualizing what you read<br>• **Writing Strategy:** Creating sharp, clear contrasts |
| • Stores and the things you buy there<br>• Expressions of time | • Saying where you went and what you did<br>• Talking on the phone | • Preterite of **-ar** verbs<br>• Preterite of **ir**<br>• Preterite of **-ar** verbs with reflexive pronouns | • Spanish speakers' buying power in the USA<br>• Open-air markets and bargaining<br>FINE ART<br>• ***Mercado caribeño,*** Dra. Dominica Alcántara | |

**Review/Re-Entry** • **parecer** • **Integración,** pp. 302–303

| | Vocabulary | Functions | Grammar | Culture | Strategies |
|---|---|---|---|---|---|

## Capítulo 9 ¡Festejemos! pp. 308–341

**La República Dominicana**

**La geografía**
**La arquitectura**
**El arte**
**Las celebraciones**
**La comida**

| Vocabulary | Functions | Grammar | Culture | Strategies |
|---|---|---|---|---|
| • Holidays<br>• Holiday activities | • Talking about your plans<br>• Talking about past holidays | • Preterite of **-er** and **-ir** verbs<br>• Review of the preterite<br>• **Pensar que** and **pensar** with infinitives | • Dominican **carnaval**<br>• **Pasteles en hoja**<br>• **Comparaciones:** Holidays and celebrations<br>• **Comunidad:** Hispanic celebrations in the U.S. | • **Video Strategy:** Predicting<br>• **Reading Strategy:** Using context and grammatical clues<br>• **Writing Strategy:** Using descriptive details |
| • Party foods<br>• Party activities<br>• Getting ready for a party | • Preparing for a party<br>• Greetings, introducing others, and saying goodbye | • Review of direct object pronouns<br>• **Conocer** and personal **a**<br>• Present progressive | • Special birthdays: **quinceañeras**<br>• Dancing at parties<br>FINE ART<br>• ***Merengue,*** Jaime Colson | |

**Review/Re-Entry**
- Preterite of regular **-ar** verbs
- Third person direct object pronouns
- Greetings
- **Integración,** pp. 340–341

## Capítulo 10 ¡A viajar! pp. 346–379

**Perú**

**La geografía**
**La arquitectura**
**El arte**
**Las celebraciones**
**La comida**

| Vocabulary | Functions | Grammar | Culture | Strategies |
|---|---|---|---|---|
| • Airport and travel terms | • Asking for and giving information<br>• Reminding and reassuring | • Review of the preterite<br>• Preterite of **-car, -gar, -zar** verbs<br>• Preterite of **hacer** | • Uros islands<br>• Quinoa<br>• **Comparaciones:** Traveling<br>• **Comunidad:** Tourism and Spanish | • **Video Strategy:** Summarizing<br>• **Reading Strategy:** Reading with a purpose<br>• **Writing Strategy:** Using transitional phrases |
| • Vacation activities<br>• Transportation<br>• Reacting to news | • Talking about a trip<br>• Expressing hopes and wishes | • Informal commands of spelling-change and irregular verbs<br>• Review of direct object pronouns<br>• Review of verbs with infinitives | • Traveling by train in Peru<br>• Peru's Manu rainforest<br>FINE ART<br>• ***La vendedora de anticuchos,*** Juan de la Cruz Machicado | |

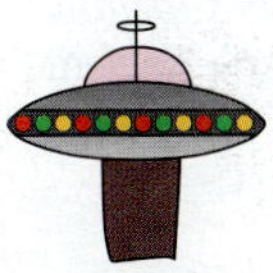

**Review/Re-Entry**
- Preterite of **ir**
- Informal affirmative and negative commands
- **Integración,** pp. 378–379

# Scope and Sequence

# ¡Exprésate! Level 2

## Ciudad de México

**La geografía**
**El arte**
**Las celebraciones**
**La historia**
**La arqueología**

### Capítulo 1 Familiares y amigos pp. 4–39

| Vocabulary | Functions | Grammar | Culture | Strategies |
|---|---|---|---|---|
| • Describing friends and family members | • Asking about people, routines, and activities<br>• Expressing likes and dislikes | • Nouns, adjectives, and **gustar**<br>• Present tense of regular and stem-changing verbs<br>• Present tense of **e → i** stem-changing verbs and irregular verbs<br>• Reflexive pronouns | • Xochimilco gardens<br>• Mexico's Independence Day, September 16<br>• **Comparaciones:** Studying world languages<br>• **Comunidad:** Studying world languages in the U.S. | • **Video Strategy:** Looking for clues<br>• **Reading Strategy:** Looking for key words<br>• **Writing Strategy:** Using a prewriting list |
| • Celebrations and preparations<br>• Parts of the house<br>• Household chores<br>• Family members<br>• Travel plans and activities | • Offering help and talking about chores<br>• Talking about plans and places | • Idioms with **tener**<br>• Verbs followed by infinitives<br>• Present progressive<br>• **Ir a** with infinitives<br>• Direct object pronouns<br>• Affirmative and negative informal commands | • Shopping in Mexico City<br>• Aztec ruins in Mexico City<br>FINE ART<br>• ***Mis sobrinas,*** María Izquierdo | |

**Review/Re-Entry**
• Family and home • **gustar, ir,** and **ser** • Nouns • Adjectives • Present tense • Question words • Informal commands • **Integración,** pp. 38–39

## Cuzco

**La geografía**
**Las celebraciones**
**La arqueología**
**El arte y la artesanía**
**La arquitectura**

### Capítulo 2 En el vecindario pp. 44–79

| Vocabulary | Functions | Grammar | Culture | Strategies |
|---|---|---|---|---|
| • Professions<br>• Work-related verbs | • Talking about what people do for a living<br>• Introducing people | • Indirect objects and indirect object pronouns;<br>• **dar**<br>• **decir**<br>• **Saber** and **conocer**<br>• Uses of **ser** | • Terrace farming in Peru<br>• Llamas<br>• **Comparaciones:** Preparing for a profession<br>• **Comunidad:** Bilingualism in the workplace | • **Video Strategy:** Resolving problems<br>• **Reading Strategy:** Looking for cognates<br>• **Writing Strategy:** Creating a clear setting |
| • Parts of the house<br>• Furniture<br>• Chores | • Describing a house<br>• Saying what needs to be done and complaining | • **Ser** and **estar**<br>• Expressions followed by infinitives<br>• Preterite of regular verbs, **hacer,** and **ir** | • Incan architecture<br>• Potatoes and **el chuño**<br>FINE ART<br>• ***La caserita*** Gladys Martínez Nosiglia | |

**Review/Re-Entry**
• Personal **a** • Uses of **ser** • Adjectives of nationality • **tocar** • Preterite of regular verbs, **hacer,** and **ir** • **Integración,** pp. 78–79

## Capítulo 3 Pueblos y ciudades pp. 84–119

## Santo Domingo

**La geografía**
**La comida**
**Las artes**
**La naturaleza**
**La historia**

| Vocabulary | Functions | Grammar | Culture | Strategies |
|---|---|---|---|---|
| • Names of stores<br>• Places around town | • Asking for information<br>• Asking where someone went and what he or she did | • Impersonal **se** and passive **se**<br>• Preterite of **-car, -gar,** and **-zar** verbs and **conocer**<br>• Irregular verbs in the preterite: **andar, tener, venir, dar, ver** | • **Bachata** music<br>• **Comparaciones:** Plazas and other gathering places<br>• **Comunidad:** Spanish in the community | • **Video Strategy:** Gathering information<br>• **Reading Strategy:** Focusing on ideas<br>• **Writing Strategy:** Using dialog |
| • Places in the city<br>• Ordinal numbers | • Asking for and giving directions<br>• Asking for clarification | • Formal commands<br>• Irregular formal commands<br>• Commands with pronouns and review of informal commands | • Santo Domingo<br>• **Merengue**<br>FINE ART<br>• ***Merengue en el pueblo,*** José Morillo | |

**Review/Re-Entry**
- Present tense of **conocer**
- **hay que, deber,** and **tener que**
- Preterite tense of **hacer** and **ir**
- **Integración,** pp. 118–119
- **haber**
- Informal commands

## Capítulo 4 ¡Mantente en forma! pp. 124–159

## Miami

**La geografía**
**Las bellas artes**
**Las celebraciones**
**La vida latina**
**Los deportes**

| Vocabulary | Functions | Grammar | Culture | Strategies |
|---|---|---|---|---|
| • Competitions<br>• Emotional reactions | • Talking about how something turned out<br>• Talking about and reacting to events | • Irregular preterites **ponerse**, **decir**, **ser** and **estar**<br>• Preterite of stem-changing **-ir** verbs | • **Calle Ocho** festival<br>• **Jai-alai**<br>• **Comparaciones:** School/club sports<br>• **Comunidad:** Spanish in the medical professions | • **Video Strategy:** Asking questions<br>• **Reading Strategy:** Using graphic organizers<br>• **Writing Strategy:** Providing specific details |
| • Parts of the body<br>• Injuries<br>• Illnesses<br>• Treatments and advice | • Talking about getting hurt<br>• Asking for and giving advice | • Verbs with reflexive pronouns and direct objects<br>• Past participles used as adjectives<br>• Preterite of **caerse** | • Latin American Art<br>• Tourism in Miami<br>FINE ART<br>• ***La zumba, el mamey y otras frutas tropicales,*** Tere Pastoriza | |

**Review/Re-Entry**
- Reflexive pronouns
- Preterite of **-ar** and **-er** verbs and **dar**

## Capítulo 5 Día a día pp. 164–199

## San José

**La geografía**
**Los museos**
**Los parques**
**Los festivales**
**Las bellas artes**

| Vocabulary | Functions | Grammar | Culture | Strategies |
|---|---|---|---|---|
| • Routine activities<br>• Getting ready | • Telling someone to hurry<br>• Reminding someone to do something | • Preterite of **poder** and **traer**<br>• More verbs with reflexive pronouns<br>• Possessive pronouns | • African heritage<br>• **Quetzal** bird<br>• **Comparaciones:** Being on time<br>• **Comunidad:** Spanish in advertising | • **Video Strategy:** Understanding relationships<br>• **Reading Strategy:** Making predictions<br>• **Writing Strategy:** Transitional phrases |
| • Pastimes and interests<br>• Time expressions | • Expressing interest and disinterest<br>• Talking about how long something has been going on | • Negative expressions<br>• **Hace** with time expressions<br>• **Pero** and **sino** | • Costa Rican oxcarts<br>• Music in San José<br>FINE ART<br>• ***Casa de adobes,*** Ezequiel Jiménez | |

**Review/Re-Entry**
- Preterite of **decir**
- Possessive adjectives
- Reflexive pronouns
- **no** in negative expressions
- **Integración,** pp. 198–199

| | Vocabulary | Functions | Grammar | Culture | Strategies |
|---|---|---|---|---|---|
| **Capítulo 6 Recuerdos pp. 204–239** | | | | | |
| **Segovia** | • Childhood activities<br>• Toys and games | • Talking about what you used to like and dislike<br>• Saying what you used to do and what you wanted to be | • Imperfect tense<br>• Imperfect of **ir** and **ver**<br>• Verbs with reciprocal actions | • Segovia's **Alcázar**<br>• Outdoor cafes<br>• Winter sports in the Guadarrama Mountains<br>• **Comparaciones:** Childhood likes and dislikes<br>• **Comunidad:** Researching the past | **Video Strategy:** Comparing attitudes<br>**Reading Strategy:** Using context<br>**Writing Strategy:** Avoiding repetition |
| La geografía<br>La historia<br>La arquitectura<br>Más geografía<br>La moneda | • Adjectives to describe people<br>• Life events | • Describing people and things in the past<br>• Talking about an emotional reaction | • Imperfect of **ser** and **haber**<br>• Preterite with mental and emotional states<br>• Preterite of **creer, leer, construir,** and **oír; caerle a uno** | • Roman aqueduct<br>FINE ART<br>• ***Clotilde y Elena en las rocas, Jávea,*** Joaquín Sorolla Y Bastida | |
| **Review/Re-Entry** | • **hay**<br>• Preterite of **estar** and **ponerse** | | • Present of **oír**<br>• **Integración,** pp. 238–239 | | |

| | Vocabulary | Functions | Grammar | Culture | Strategies |
|---|---|---|---|---|---|
| **Capítulo 7 ¡Buen provecho! pp. 244–279** | | | | | |
| **San Juan** | • Menu words<br>• Restaurant terms<br>• Foods<br>• Adjectives to describe food | • Ordering in a restaurant<br>• Talking about how food tastes | • Double object pronouns<br>• Commands with double object pronouns<br>• Adverbs | • Puerto Rican cooking<br>• **Comparaciones:** Festivals and holidays<br>• **Comunidad:** Spanish in culinary schools | **Video Strategy:** Understanding subtext<br>**Reading Strategy:** Looking for organizational clues<br>**Writing Strategy:** Using adjectives that focus on the senses |
| La geografía<br>La arquitectura<br>La vida cultural<br>La vida contemporánea<br>La historia | • Food terms<br>• Measurements<br>• More adjectives to describe food | • Talking about your diet<br>• Describing the preparation of food | • More uses of the imperfect<br>• Review of the imperfect<br>• Past participles used as adjectives | • **El gofio,** a Puerto Rican sweet<br>FINE ART<br>• ***El pan nuestro,*** Ramón Frade | |
| **Review/Re-Entry** | • Direct and indirect object pronouns<br>• Pronouns with affirmative and negative commands<br>• Using the imperfect in descriptions | | | • Adjective agreement<br>• **Integración,** pp. 278–279 | |

| | Vocabulary | Functions | Grammar | Culture | Strategies |
|---|---|---|---|---|---|
| **Capítulo 8 Tiendas y puestos pp. 284–319** | | | | | |
| **Santiago** | • Buying and selling terms<br>• Adjectives to describe clothing | • Talking about trying on clothes and how they fit<br>• Talking about shopping for clothes | • Imperfect and preterite<br>• Using the imperfect of **ir a** + infinitive<br>• Comparatives and superlatives | • Europeans in Chile<br>• **Arpilleras**<br>• **Comparaciones:** Dressing up to go out<br>• **Comunidad:** Spanish in the fashion industry | **Video Strategy:** Following the plot<br>**Reading Strategy:** Using background knowledge<br>**Writing Strategy:** Comparing and contrasting |
| La geografía<br>La historia<br>La arquitectura<br>Los barrios<br>Más geografía | • Handicrafts<br>• Jewelry<br>• Materials | • Bargaining in a market<br>• Stating preferences | • **Por** and **para**<br>• Demonstrative adjectives **ese** and **aquel;** adverbs of place<br>• Adjectives as nouns | • Chilean handicrafts<br>• Foods from Chile<br>FINE ART<br>• ***El mercado,*** Ana Cortés | |
| **Review/Re-Entry** | • Comparison with adjectives<br>• Irregular comparatives | | • **este** and **ese**<br>• **Integración,** pp. 318–319 | | |

## Capítulo 9 A nuestro alrededor pp. 324–359

**El Paso**

**La geografía**
**El arte**
**La arquitectura**
**Las celebraciones**
**La economía**

| Vocabulary | Functions | Grammar | Culture | Strategies |
|---|---|---|---|---|
| • Nature<br>• Animals and plants<br>• Weather and natural events | • Talking about a place and its climate<br>• Telling a story | • Comparing quantities; adjectives as nouns<br>• Preterite and imperfect to begin a story<br>• Preterite and imperfect to continue and end a story | • Museum of Archaeology in El Paso<br>• Ysleta and Spanish missions<br>• **Comparaciones:** How climate and geography affect a region<br>• **Comunidad:** Spanish and the sciences | **Video Strategy:** Making deductions<br><br>**Reading Strategy:** Taking notes<br><br>**Writing Strategy:** Establishing the tone and mood |
| • Camping terms<br>• Outdoor activities | • Talking about what you and others will do<br>• Wondering out loud | • Subjunctive mood for hopes and wishes<br>• Subjunctive of stem-changing **-ir** and irregular verbs<br>• Future tense | • Conserving water in El Paso<br>• Hueco Tanks<br>FINE ART<br>• ***El Paso antes de su fundación,*** José Cisneros | |

| Review/Re-Entry | | |
|---|---|---|
| | • **tanto** | • Weather expressions |
| | • Infinitives after **querer** and **poder** | • **Integración,** pp. 358–359 |

## Capítulo 10 De vacaciones pp. 364–399

**Buenos Aires**

**La geografía**
**Gente famosa**
**Las costumbres**
**Las compras**
**La música**

| Vocabulary | Functions | Grammar | Culture | Strategies |
|---|---|---|---|---|
| • Travel words<br>• Methods of payment | • Asking for and making recommendations<br>• Asking for and giving information | • Present perfect<br>• Irregular past participles<br>• Subjunctive for giving advice and opinions<br>• Subjunctive of **-car, -gar, -zar, -ger,** and **-guir** verbs | • Mar del Plata and Bariloche in Argentina<br>• Vacations in the Spanish-speaking world<br>• **Comparaciones:** Popular tourist attractions<br>• **Comunidad:** Spanish and tourism | **Video Strategy:** Putting the story together<br><br>**Reading Strategy:** Making inferences<br><br>**Writing Strategy:** Using conjunctions and transitional phrases |
| • Places to visit<br>• Things to do<br>• Writing a letter or e-mail | • Talking about where you went and what you did<br>• Talking about the latest news | • Review of preterite and imperfect<br>• Review of present progressive and future<br>• Review of the subjunctive | • Eva Perón<br>• Origins of the **tango**<br>FINE ART<br>• ***Libertad,*** Marilyn Itrat | |

| Review/Re-Entry | | |
|---|---|---|
| | • Past participles | • Present progressive and future |
| | • Subjunctive | • **Integración,** pp. 398–399 |

# Scope and Sequence

# ¡Exprésate! Spanish Level 3

**Castilla-La Mancha**

**La geografía**
**La historia**
**El arte**

## Capítulo 1 ¡Adiós al verano! pp. 6–47

| Vocabulary | Functions | Grammar | Culture | Strategies |
|---|---|---|---|---|
| • Vacation activities and destinations<br>• Weather | • Talking about the past<br>• Saying what you liked and used to do | • Preterite and imperfect<br>• **Ser** and **estar**<br>• Subjunctive mood | • Geography of Castilla-La Mancha<br>• Culture and folklore of Castilla-La Mancha<br>• The town of Cuenca<br>• **Comparaciones:** Summer trips<br>• **Comunidad:** Spanish-speaking tourists in the U.S. | • **Video Strategy:** Analyzing the opening<br>• **Reading Strategy:** Determining the point of view<br>• **Writing Strategy:** Using point of view in a story |
| • Activities<br>• Advice | • Asking for and giving advice<br>• Asking about the future | • Pronouns<br>• Comparisons, demonstrative adjectives, and demonstrative pronouns<br>• Negative words and time constructions | • How Castilla-La Mancha was named<br>• **Mazapán** and **queso manchego**<br>• Languages in Spain<br>FINE ART<br>• ***Torero y toro,*** Óscar Domínguez | |

**Review/Re-Entry**
• **Ser** and **estar** • Preterite and imperfect • Past participles • Subjunctive mood
• Pronouns • Reciprocal actions • Negative words • **Integración,** pp. 46–47

## Capítulo 2 ¡A pasarlo bien! pp. 48–89

| Vocabulary | Functions | Grammar | Culture | Strategies |
|---|---|---|---|---|
| • Pastimes<br>• Sports | • Expressing interest and displeasure<br>• Inviting someone to do something and responding | • Imperfect<br>• **Ir a** + infinitive in the imperfect<br>• **Nosotros** commands | • Hiking in Spain<br>• **El jai-alai**<br>• **Comparaciones:** Friendships<br>• **Comunidad:** Television programming in Spanish | • **Video Strategy:** Looking for personality traits<br>• **Reading Strategy:** Looking for the main idea<br>• **Writing Strategy:** Writing an outline |
| • Friendships and relationships<br>• Adjectives to describe friends | • Describing the ideal friend<br>• Expressing happiness and unhappiness | • Object pronouns<br>• Subjunctive with the unknown or nonexistent<br>• Subjunctive with expressions of feelings | • **La Ruta de Don Quijote**<br>FINE ART<br>• ***Feria de Santiponce,*** Manuel Rodríguez de Guzmán | |

**Review/Re-Entry**
• Imperfect • **Ir a** + infinitive in the imperfect • **Integración,** pp. 88–89
• Subjunctive **nosotros** forms of **-zar, -gar, -car** verbs • Subjunctive endings
• Verbs used with indirect object pronouns • Object pronouns

## El Caribe

La geografía
La historia
El arte

| | Vocabulary | Functions | Grammar | Culture | Strategies |
|---|---|---|---|---|---|
| **Capítulo 3 Todo tiene solución pp. 96–137** | | | | | |
| | • Attitudes and opinions<br>• School courses | • Complaining<br>• Expressing an opinion and disagreeing | • Verb + infinitive<br>• Subjunctive with will or wish<br>• Subjunctive with negation or denial | • Schools in Puerto Rico<br>• Schools in Cuba<br>• **Comparaciones:** Family conflicts<br>• **Comunidad:** Spanish at U.S. universities | • **Video Strategy:** Making deductions<br>• **Reading Strategy:** Paraphrasing<br>• **Writing Strategy:** Brainstorming |
| | • Relationship problems and solutions | • Making suggestions<br>• Apologizing | • Future tense<br>• Conditional | • **Telenovelas** in Latin America<br>FINE ART<br>• ***Cometas y habitantes,*** José Morillo | |
| **Review/Re-Entry** | • Verb + infinitive<br>• Future tense | • Subjunctive with will or wish<br>• Irregular stems in the future | • **Saber** and **haber** in the subjunctive<br>• **Integración,** pp. 136–137 | | |
| **Capítulo 4 Entre familia pp. 138–179** | | | | | |
| | • Family members and relationships<br>• Family events | • Asking about and responding to the latest news<br>• Reacting to news | • Present progressive<br>• Present perfect indicative<br>• Present perfect subjunctive | • Caribbean family ties<br>• Weddings in Latin America<br>• **Comparaciones:** Keeping in touch with relatives<br>• **Comunidad:** Imported food in the U.S. | • **Video Strategy:** Connecting the dots<br>• **Reading Strategy:** Using context<br>• **Writing Strategy:** Using rhyme in poetry |
| | • Foods | • Commenting on food<br>• Explaining and giving excuses | • Preterite<br>• **Se** + indirect object pronouns<br>• Past progressive | • Caribbean dishes<br>• **Sancocho**<br>• Typical Cuban dishes<br>FINE ART<br>• ***Baile en la playa,*** Julio Marcano | |
| **Review/Re-Entry** | • Present progressive<br>• Imperfect of **estar** | • Present perfect indicative<br>• Object pronouns and participles | • Irregular past participles<br>• **Integración,** pp. 178–179 | • Preterite | |

## El Suroeste y el Norte de México

La geografía
La historia
El arte

| | Vocabulary | Functions | Grammar | Culture | Strategies |
|---|---|---|---|---|---|
| **Capítulo 5 El arte y la música pp. 186–227** | | | | | |
| | • Arts and architecture<br>• Adjectives to describe art | • Asking for and giving opinions<br>• Introducing and changing a topic of conversation | • Comparatives of equality and superlatives<br>• Passive **se** and impersonal **se**<br>• Passive voice with **ser** | • Spanish influence in Mexican architecture<br>• **Comparaciones:** Art and architecture in Mexico and Costa Rica<br>• **Comunidad:** Hispanic art in the U.S. | • **Video Strategy:** Getting confirmation<br>• **Reading Strategy:** Drawing inferences<br>• **Writing Strategy:** Making a writing plan |
| | • Music and dramatic arts<br>• Adjectives to describe art | • Making suggestions and recommendations<br>• Inviting someone to do something and turning down an invitation | • Subjunctive with hopes and wishes<br>• Past perfect | • **Norteña** music<br>• Frida Kahlo<br>FINE ART<br>• ***Unidad panamericana,*** Diego Rivera | |
| **Review/Re-Entry** | • Comparatives of equality<br>• Passive **se**, impersonal **se**<br>• Subjunctive with hopes and wishes | • Superlatives<br>• Past participles<br>• Demonstrative adjectives | • **Integración,** pp. 226–227 | | |

### Capítulo 6 ¡Ponte al día! pp. 228–269

| Vocabulary | Functions | Grammar | Culture | Strategies |
|---|---|---|---|---|
| • Electronic media terms<br>• Adjectives to describe media | • Expressing certainty<br>• Expressing doubt and disbelief | • Indicative after expressions of certainty<br>• Subjunctive after expressions of doubt and disbelief<br>• Uses of **haber** | • Programs in Spanish<br>• Latin American news<br>• **Comparaciones:** Means of communication<br>• **Comunidad:** Spanish-language news programming | • **Video Strategy:** Analyzing viewpoints<br>• **Reading Strategy:** Determining chronological order<br>• **Writing Strategy:** Putting events in order |
| • Print media terms | • Asking about information and explaining where you found it<br>• Talking about what you know and don't know | • Indefinite expressions<br>• Gender of nouns<br>• Indicative in compound sentences | • Latin American game shows<br>Fine Art<br>• ***Códice Mendoza*** | |

**Review/Re-Entry**
• Present perfect subjunctive • **Haber** • **Integración,** pp. 268–269
• **Decir** with the subjunctive • Indefinite expressions

## Los Andes: Ecuador, Perú y Bolivia

**La geografía**
**La historia**
**El arte**

### Capítulo 7 Mis aspiraciones pp. 276–317

| Vocabulary | Functions | Grammar | Culture | Strategies |
|---|---|---|---|---|
| • Challenges<br>• Cultural heritage | • Talking about challenges<br>• Talking about accomplishments | • Preterite and imperfect of stative verbs<br>• Grammatical reflexives<br>• **Lo** and **lo que** | • Indigenous words<br>• Otavalo<br>• **Comparaciones:** Future plans<br>• **Comunidad:** Hispanics in the U.S. | • **Video Strategy:** Separating the essential from the non-essential<br>• **Reading Strategy:** Making inferences<br>• **Writing Strategy:** Leading readers to make inferences |
| • Hopes and plans | • Talking about future plans<br>• Expressing cause and effect | • Subjunctive after adverbial conjunctions<br>• Subjunctive with future actions<br>• Indicative with habitual or past actions | • Andean peoples and artifacts<br>• Incan roads<br>Fine Art<br>• ***Benito's Village,*** Benito Huillcahuaman | |

**Review/Re-Entry**
• **Conocer, saber,** and **querer** • Preterite and imperfect • Reflexive actions
• Subjunctive • Indicative • **Integración,** pp. 316–317

### Capítulo 8 ¿A qué te dedicas? pp. 318–359

| Vocabulary | Functions | Grammar | Culture | Strategies |
|---|---|---|---|---|
| • Jobs and business terms<br>• Volunteerism<br>• Technology | • Saying what you can and cannot do<br>• Talking about what you do and do not understand | • Verbs with indirect object pronouns<br>• Verbs that express "to become"<br>• Uses of **se** | • Business hours<br>• Internet in Peru<br>• **Comparaciones:** Using technology<br>• **Comunidad:** Hispanics in the business world | • **Video Strategy:** Evaluating choices<br>• **Reading Strategy:** Determining the author's purpose<br>• **Writing Strategy:** Using dialogue |
| • Professions<br>• Workplace terms | • Writing a formal letter<br>• Talking about your plans | • Conditional<br>• Past subjunctive with hypothetical statements<br>• Past subjunctive (with past tense) | • **La licenciatura**<br>Fine Art<br>• *A women at a fruit stall,* ***Mollendo, Perú,*** A.S. Forrest | |

**Review/Re-Entry**
• Indirect object pronouns • Conditional
• Subjunctive uses • **Integración,** pp. 358–359

## El Cono Sur

**La geografía**
**La historia**
**El arte**

### Capítulo 9 Huellas del pasado pp. 366–407

| Vocabulary | Functions | Grammar | Culture | Strategies |
|---|---|---|---|---|
| • Legends, folk tales and fairy tales | • Setting the scene for a story<br>• Continuing and ending a story | • Preterite and imperfect in storytelling<br>• Preterite and imperfect contrasted<br>• **Por** and **para** | • Indigenous peoples in Argentina<br>• Iguazú National Park<br>• **Comparaciones:** Legends<br>• **Comunidad:** Spanish explorers and U.S. place names | • **Video Strategy:** Predicting<br>• **Reading Strategy:** Determining the main idea<br>• **Writing Strategy:** Using detailed descriptions |
| • Historical events | • Talking about your hopes and wishes<br>• Expressing regret and gratitude | • Uses of subjunctive<br>• Sequence of tenses | • Chilean political history<br>• Chilean flag<br>FINE ART<br>• ***Revista de Rancagua,*** Juan Manuel Blanes | |

**Review/Re-Entry**
• Preterite and imperfect
• Verbs with special meanings in the preterite
• **Por** and **para**
• Subjunctive
• Impersonal expressions
• **Integración,** pp. 406–407

### Capítulo 10 El mundo en que vivimos pp. 408–449

| Vocabulary | Functions | Grammar | Culture | Strategies |
|---|---|---|---|---|
| • Natural disasters | • Talking about a past event<br>• Expressing and supporting a point of view | • Present and past progressive<br>• **Haber**<br>• Expressions of time | • Argentina's economy<br>• Buenos Aires<br>• Natural disasters in Chile<br>• **Comparaciones:** Experiencing historical events<br>• **Comunidad:** The use of pesticides in Latin America | • **Video Strategy:** Tying together all the events<br>• **Reading Strategy:** Understanding figures of speech and dialect<br>• **Writing Strategy:** Using rhetorical devices |
| • Environment | • Making predictions and giving warnings<br>• Expressing assumptions | • Future tense<br>• Subjunctive with doubt, denial, and feelings<br>• Subjunctive and indicative with adverbial clauses | • Natural resources of Argentina<br>• Environmental issues in Argentina<br>• Buenos Aires<br>• Chile's business relationship with the U.S.<br>FINE ART<br>• ***Mirando un paracaídas,*** Patricia Figueroa | |

**Review/Re-Entry**
• Present and past progressive
• Expressions of time
• Subjunctive use
• Present participles
• Ordinal numbers
• Indicative
• **Haber**
• Future tense
• **Integración,** pp. 448–449
• Perfect tense

# Scope and Sequence

# Nuevas vistas Curso de introducción

## Colección 1 ¡Así somos! Págs. xx–47

| Lectura | Cultura | Comunicación | Escritura |
| --- | --- | --- | --- |
| "Yo soy, tú eres, él es..."<br><br>**Julio Cortázar**<br>"Viajes"<br><br>"...Y así nos distraemos"<br><br>**Estrategias**<br>Comparing and contrasting<br>Text impressions | ***Contigo en la distancia:*** Telenovela<br>¿Qué hicisteis en México? (Episode 1)<br><br>Por una vida sana (Episode 2)<br><br>**Cultura y comparaciones**<br>Music and dance of the Spanish-speaking world | **Vocabulario**<br>Synonyms<br>Antonyms<br><br>**Gramática**<br>Uses and conjugation of the present indicative<br>**Ser, estar,** and **gustar**<br>Adjectives<br>Present progressive<br>Present perfect<br>Comparatives | **Ortografía**<br>Stress<br>The letter **h**<br>The */y/* sound (letters **y** and **ll**)<br><br>**Taller del escritor**<br>Informal letter-writing<br>Formal letter-writing<br><br>**Así se dice**<br>Writing letters: greeting, body, and closing |

## Colección 2 La niñez Págs. 48–95

| Lectura | Cultura | Comunicación | Escritura |
| --- | --- | --- | --- |
| **Carmen Kurtz**<br>"El nacimiento de Veva"<br><br>**Elena Poniatowska**<br>"Los juegos de Lilus"<br><br>**Estrategias**<br>Thinking aloud<br>Making inferences | ***Contigo en la distancia:*** Telenovela<br>El mundo es un balón de fútbol (Episode 3)<br>¡Qué sabroso! (Episode 4)<br><br>**Cultura y comparaciones**<br>Milestones in the history of the Spanish-speaking world | **Vocabulario**<br>Contextual clues<br>Register<br><br>**Gramática**<br>Past indicative tenses: Preterite, imperfect, past progressive, past perfect<br>Pronouns: Direct and indirect object pronouns | **Ortografía**<br>Written accent: words with final and penultimate stress<br>The letters **b** and **v,** the letters **m** and **n**<br><br>**Taller del escritor**<br>A biographical sketch<br>Autobiographical writing<br><br>**Así se dice**<br>Writing about a person's life<br>Writing a description |

## Colección 3 El mundo en que vivimos Págs. 96–147

| Lectura | Cultura | Comunicación | Escritura |
| --- | --- | --- | --- |
| "Tecnología: Rumbo al futuro"<br><br>"Protejamos nuestra tierra"<br><br>**Estrategias**<br>Looking for visual clues<br>Identifying the chain of events | ***Contigo en la distancia:*** Telenovela<br>El poder del amor (Episode 5)<br><br>La obra maestra (Episode 6)<br><br>**Cultura y comparaciones**<br>The varied landscapes of the Spanish-speaking world | **Vocabulario**<br>Neologisms<br>Cognates and false cognates<br><br>**Gramática**<br>Future<br>Future perfect<br>Conditional<br>Reflexive verbs<br>Imperative mood<br>Combined use of direct and indirect object pronouns<br>Simple and compound sentences | **Ortografía**<br>Diphthongs and hiatus<br>The */s/* sound (letters **s, c,** and **z**)<br><br>**Taller del escritor**<br>An advertisement<br>An expository essay<br><br>**Así se dice**<br>Writing an advertisement<br>Discussing cause and effect |

# For Beginning Heritage Speakers or Level 4

## Colección 4 El misterio y la fantasía Págs. 148–199

| Lectura | Cultura | Comunicación | Escritura |
|---|---|---|---|
| **Guillermo Samperio**<br>"Tiempo libre"<br><br>**Carlos Fuentes**<br>"Chac Mool"<br><br>**Estrategias**<br>Looking for key words<br>Anticipation guide | ***Contigo en la distancia:*** Telenovela<br>¡Mira, tienes una carta! (Episode 7)<br><br>Al mundo le hace falta más romance (Episode 8)<br><br>**Cultura y comparaciones**<br>Architecture of the Spanish-speaking world | **Vocabulario**<br>Word families<br>Word formation: prefixes and suffixes<br><br>**Gramática**<br>Subjunctive mood: uses and conjugation of the present subjunctive<br>Subjunctive in noun clauses: expressions of will and emotion, of doubt and judgment<br>Present perfect subjunctive<br>Subjunctive in adjectival clauses<br>Prepositions and adverbs | **Ortografía**<br>Written accent: words with antepenultimate or prior stress<br>The */k/* sound (letters **c**, **qu**, and **k**)<br><br>**Taller del escritor**<br>A fantasy tale<br>An informative article<br><br>**Así se dice**<br>Expressing surprise<br>Presenting information |

## Colección 5 El amor Págs. 200–255

| Lectura | Cultura | Comunicación | Escritura |
|---|---|---|---|
| **Laura Esquivel**<br>"Enero: tortas de Navidad" de *Como agua para chocolate*<br><br>**Horacio Quiroga**<br>"El hijo"<br><br>**Estrategias**<br>Making predictions based on quotes from the text<br>Reading, evaluating, and rereading | ***Contigo en la distancia:*** Telenovela<br>En casa del tío Guadalupe (Episode 9)<br><br>Cuando sea mayor… (Episode 10)<br><br>**Cultura y comparaciones**<br>Food from around the Spanish-speaking world | **Vocabulario**<br>More prefixes and suffixes<br><br>**Gramática**<br>Adverbial clauses: indicative and subjunctive in adverbial clauses of manner, place, time, cause, condition, and purpose<br>Relative clauses<br>Imperfect subjunctive use in noun, adjectival, and adverbial clauses<br>Conditional sentences | **Ortografía**<br>Diacritic accent marks<br>The */x/* sound (letters **j** and **g**)<br><br>**Taller del escritor**<br>A persuasive essay<br>A script<br><br>**Así se dice**<br>Persuading or convincing your reader<br>Writing a script |

## Colección 6 El poder de la palabra Págs. 256–305

| Lectura | Cultura | Comunicación | Escritura |
|---|---|---|---|
| **Julia de Burgos**<br>"A Julia de Burgos"<br><br>**Miguel de Cervantes**<br>de *Don Quijote de la Mancha*<br><br>**Estrategias**<br>Contrasting<br>Using contextual clues | ***Contigo en la distancia:*** Telenovela<br>Si yo fuera presidenta (Episode 11)<br><br>El tiempo vuela, ¿no? (Episode 12)<br><br>**Cultura y comparaciones**<br>Art of the Spanish-speaking world: murals | **Vocabulario**<br>Figurative language: metaphors and comparisons<br>Symbols and hyperbole<br><br>**Gramática**<br>Past perfect subjunctive in noun clauses and in conditional sentences<br>Passive voice and impersonal **se**<br>Infinitives, gerunds, and participles<br>Sequence of tenses | **Ortografía**<br>Punctuation marks<br>The */r/* and */rr/* sounds<br><br>**Taller del escritor**<br>Poetry<br>Short story<br><br>**Así se dice**<br>Writing comparisons<br>Linking events and ideas |

# Scope and Sequence

# Nuevas vistas Curso uno

## Colección 1 ¡Viva la juventud! Págs. xxii–57

| Lectura | Cultura | Comunicación | Escritura |
|---|---|---|---|
| **Rubén Darío**<br>"Mis primeros versos"<br>**Gary Soto**<br>"Primero de secundaria"<br>**Gabriel García Márquez**<br>"Un cuentecillo triste"<br><br>**Estrategia para leer**<br>Comparing and contrasting<br><br>**Elementos de literatura**<br>Biographies, autobiographies, essays, and articles | **Cultura y lengua**<br>Nicaragua<br><br>**Panorama cultural**<br>What do you do to get the attention of a boy or girl you like?<br><br>**Comunidad y oficio**<br>Spanish speakers in the United States | **Así se dice**<br>Expressing feelings<br>Talking about causes and effects<br>Narrating an experience in the past<br>Combining sentences<br>Evaluating a written work<br>Reflecting about a written work<br>**Vocabulario**<br>Prefixes and suffixes<br>**Gramática**<br>Nouns<br>Definite and indefinite articles<br>Adjectives<br>**Comparación y contraste**<br>Definite and indefinite articles in Spanish and English | **Prepara tu portafolio**<br>Writing notebook<br>Creative writing<br>Speaking and listening<br>Art<br><br>**Ortografía**<br>The letter **h**<br>The */y/* sound<br>Diacritics<br><br>**Taller del escritor**<br>Autobiographical writing |

## Colección 2 Habla con los animales Págs. 58–125

| Lectura | Cultura | Comunicación | Escritura |
|---|---|---|---|
| **Horacio Quiroga**<br>"La guerra de los yacarés"<br>**Juan Ramón Jiménez**<br>de *Platero y yo*<br>**Rigoberta Menchú**<br>de *Me llamo Rigoberta Menchú*<br><br>**Estrategia para leer**<br>Using context clues<br><br>**Elementos de literatura**<br>Plot, characterization, setting, point of view, irony, and theme | **Cultura y lengua**<br>Uruguay<br><br>**Panorama cultural**<br>In your country, how are animals treated? Are there laws that protect them?<br><br>**Comunidad y oficio**<br>Spanish and preservation of the environment | **Así se dice**<br>Giving a description<br>Comparing and contrasting<br>Talking about what one should do<br>Combining sentences<br>Evaluating a written work<br>**Vocabulario**<br>Word families<br>**Gramática**<br>Verbs<br>Present tense<br>Imperfect tense<br>Preterite tense<br>Uses of the preterite and imperfect<br>**Comparación y contraste**<br>The past in Spanish and English | **Prepara tu portafolio**<br>Writing notebook<br>Investigation<br>Speaking and listening<br>Drawing<br>Creative writing<br><br>**Ortografía**<br>The letters **b** and **v**<br>Division of words into syllables<br><br>**Taller del escritor**<br>Writing a short story |

## Colección 3 Fábulas y leyendas Págs. 126–183

| Lectura | Cultura | Comunicación | Escritura |
|---|---|---|---|
| **Ana María Shua**<br>"Posada de las Tres Cuerdas"<br>**Antonio Landaura**<br>"La puerta del infierno"<br>**Ciro Alegría**<br>"Güeso y Pellejo"<br><br>**Estategia para leer**<br>Making predictions<br><br>**Elementos de literatura**<br>Myths, legends, folktales, and fables | **Cultura y lengua**<br>Argentina<br><br>**Panorama cultural**<br>Have you ever heard a chilling story? Can you tell it to us?<br><br>**Comunidad y oficio**<br>Protecting the cultural heritage of the Americas | **Así se dice**<br>Expressing certainty<br>Presenting and connecting ideas<br>Expressing certainty or doubt<br>Talking about cause and effect<br>Evaluating a written work<br>**Vocabulario**<br>Synonyms and antonyms<br>**Gramática**<br>Mood<br>Forms of the present subjunctive<br>Present subjunctive in noun and adverbial clauses<br>**Comparación y contraste**<br>Infinitives and noun clauses in Spanish and English | **Prepara tu portafolio**<br>Writing notebook<br>Creative writing<br>Speaking and listening<br>Investigation<br><br>**Ortografía**<br>The */s/* sound<br>The tonic accent<br><br>**Taller del escritor**<br>Writing an essay |

# For Intermediate Heritage Speakers or Level 5

| Lectura | Cultura | Comunicación | Escritura |
|---|---|---|---|
| **Colección 4 Dentro del corazón Págs. 184–243**  | | | |
| **Serafín y Joaquín Álvarez Quintero**<br>"Mañana de sol"<br>**Isabel Allende**<br>de *Paula*<br>**José Martí**<br>de *Versos sencillos*<br>**Antonio Cabán Vale**<br>"Verde luz"<br><br>**Estrategia para leer**<br>Recognizing cause and effect<br><br>**Elementos de literatura**<br>Drama | **Cultura y lengua**<br>Spain<br><br>**Panorama cultural**<br>When you feel overwhelmed by problems, what do you do to relax?<br><br>**Comunidad y oficio**<br>Pioneer Latino artists in the United States | **Así se dice**<br>Talking about the past<br>Asking for and clarifying an opinion<br>Talking about hypothetical situations<br>Combining sentences<br>Evaluating a written work<br>**Vocabulario**<br>Idiomatic expressions<br>**Gramática**<br>Imperfect subjunctive; Conditional; Future<br>**Comparación y contraste**<br>Future<br>Modals in Spanish and English | **Prepara tu portafolio**<br>Writing notebook<br>Creative writing<br>Dramatization<br>Art<br><br>**Ortografía**<br>The /*k*/ sound<br>Tonic stress<br><br>**Taller del escritor**<br>Persuasive writing |
| **Colección 5 Caminos Págs. 244–303**  | | | |
| **Alfonso Quijada Urías**<br>"Hay un naranjo ahí"<br>**Pablo Neruda** "La tortuga"<br>**Sabine R. Ulibarrí**<br>"El forastero gentil"<br>**Jorge Manrique**<br>de *Coplas por la muerte de su padre*<br>**Antonio Machado**<br>de *Soledades* y de *Campos de Castilla*<br><br>**Estrategia para leer**<br>Evaluating<br><br>**Elementos de literatura**<br>Poetry: rhyme, imagery, and similes | **Cultura y lengua**<br>Chile<br><br>**Panorama cultural**<br>Have you ever felt like a stranger in the midst of people you know?<br><br>**Comunidad y oficio**<br>Traveling in a multilingual world | **Así se dice**<br>Talking about poetry<br>Presenting and supporting an opinion<br>Talking about someone in the past<br>Evaluating a written work<br>**Vocabulario**<br>Specialized vocabulary<br>**Gramática**<br>Present perfect indicative<br>Present perfect subjunctive<br>Past perfect indicative<br>Past perfect subjunctive<br>Sequence of verb tenses<br>**Comparación y contraste**<br>Infinitives and tenses in Spanish and English | **Prepara tu portafolio**<br>Writing notebook<br>Speaking and listening<br>Investigation<br>Creative revising<br>Art<br><br>**Ortografía**<br>The /*x*/ sound<br>Accentuation<br><br>**Taller del escritor**<br>Persuasive writing |
| **Colección 6 Tierra, sol y mar Págs. 304–363**  | | | |
| **Alejandro Balaguer**<br>de "Valle del Fuego"<br>**Jordi Sierra i Fabra**<br>de *Aydin*<br>**Federico García Lorca**<br>"Romance sonámbulo"<br><br>**Estrategia para leer**<br>Writing a summary<br><br>**Elementos de literatura**<br>The novel | **Cultura y lengua**<br>Peru<br><br>**Panorama cultural**<br>Is there any place that you will always remember, either for its beauty or for the significance it has for you?<br><br>**Comunidad y oficio**<br>Spanish in the media | **Así se dice**<br>Expressing similarities and differences<br>Combining sentences<br>Evaluating a written work<br>Reflecting about a written work<br>**Vocabulario**<br>Cognates<br>**Gramática**<br>Infinitives<br>Gerunds<br>Prepositions<br>**Comparación y contraste**<br>Gerunds, infinitives, and prepositions in Spanish and English | **Prepara tu portafolio**<br>Writing notebook<br>Creative revising<br>Investigation<br>Speaking and listening<br><br>**Ortografía**<br>The sounds /*r*/ and /*rr*/<br>Diphthongs and hiatuses<br><br>**Taller del escritor**<br>Informative writing |

# Scope and Sequence

# Nuevas vistas Curso dos

## Colección 1 Esfuerzos heroicos Págs. xxii–73

| Lectura | Cultura | Comunicación | Escritura |
|---|---|---|---|
| **Juan Francisco Manzano**<br>de *Autobiografía de un esclavo*<br>**Horacio Quiroga**<br>"En la noche"<br>**Rose del Castillo Guilbault**<br>"Trabajo de campo"<br>**Sor Juana Inés de la Cruz**<br>"Soneto 149"<br><br>**Estrategia para leer**<br>Using context clues<br><br>**Elementos de literatura**<br>Biographies, autobiographies, essays, and articles<br><br>**Enlaces**<br>La prosa didáctica medieval | **Cultura y lengua**<br>Cuba<br><br>**Panorama cultural**<br>Have you ever done something heroic or witnessed an act of heroism?<br><br>**Comunidad y oficio**<br>Humanitarian services for refugees | **Así se dice**<br>Talking about feelings and actions in the past<br>Talking about causes and effects<br>Describing in the past<br>Expressing your point of view<br>Evaluating a written work<br>Reflecting on a written work<br>**Vocabulario**<br>Synonyms; Tone and register<br>**Gramática**<br>Personal pronouns<br>Direct and indirect object pronouns<br>Prepositional pronouns<br>Reflexive pronouns<br>Possessive pronouns<br>Demonstrative pronouns<br>**Comparación y contraste**<br>The indirect object in Spanish and English | **Prepara tu portafolio**<br>Research and oral report<br>Adventure story<br>Creative writing<br><br>**Ortografía**<br>Capitalization<br>Diacritical marks; Dieresis<br><br>**Taller del escritor**<br>Autobiographical writing |

## Colección 2 Lazos de amistad Págs. 80–139

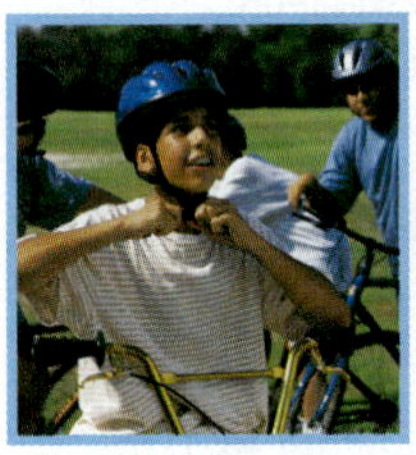

| Lectura | Cultura | Comunicación | Escritura |
|---|---|---|---|
| **Gary Soto**<br>"Cadena rota," "Naranjas"<br>**Gregorio López y Fuentes**<br>"Una carta a Dios"<br>**Nicolás Guillén**<br>"La muralla"<br><br>**Estrategia para leer**<br>Drawing conclusions<br><br>**Elementos de literatura**<br>Short story: plot, characterization, and setting<br><br>**Enlaces**<br>El soneto del Siglo de Oro | **Cultura y lengua**<br>The Mexican Americans<br><br>**Panorama cultural**<br>Have you ever done a generous deed anonymously, or known someone who has?<br><br>**Comunidad y oficio**<br>Spanish in emergency services | **Así se dice**<br>Relating physical appearance to personality<br>Presenting and supporting an opinion<br>Writing a letter of apology<br>Reflecting on a written work<br>**Vocabulario**<br>Anglicisms: loanwords, calques, and false cognates<br>**Gramática**<br>Adjectives<br>Adverbs<br>Comparatives<br>**Comparación y contraste**<br>Diminutives and augmentatives in Spanish | **Prepara tu portafolio**<br>Writing/Solving a problem<br>Creative writing<br><br>**Ortografía**<br>The */r/* and */rr/* sounds<br>The */y/* sound<br>Accent marks<br><br>**Taller del escritor**<br>Biographical sketch |

## Colección 3 El frágil medio ambiente Págs. 146–215

| Lectura | Cultura | Comunicación | Escritura |
|---|---|---|---|
| **Lecturas**<br>**Mistral:** de "La fiesta del árbol"<br>**Paz:** "Arbol adentro"<br>**García Lorca:** "Paisaje"<br>**Mistral:** "Meciendo"<br>**Denevi:** "Las abejas de bronce"<br>**de Castro:** "Dicen que no hablan las plantas"<br>**Estategia para leer**<br>Distinguishing fact and opinion<br>**Elementos de literatura**<br>Poetry; Rhetorical devices; style<br>**Enlaces**<br>La poesía del siglo XIX | **Cultura y lengua**<br>Chile<br><br>**Panorama cultural**<br>Where are you from? What do you think of your city? Is it an ideal place to live and work?<br><br>**Comunidad y oficio**<br>Business opportunities in the national and international markets | **Así se dice**<br>Explaining a point of view<br>Talking about nature using comparisons<br>Contrasting two ideas<br>Talking about what should be done<br>Reflecting on a written work<br>**Vocabulario**<br>Figurative language<br>**Gramática**<br>The uses of **se**<br>Passive voice<br>**Comparación y contraste**<br>Passive and active voice in Spanish and English | **Prepara tu portafolio**<br>Research and presentation<br>Publication and poetry<br>Dramatization<br><br>**Ortografía**<br>The letters **b** and **v**<br>Diphthongs and hiatuses<br><br>**Taller del escritor**<br>Informative report |

# For Advanced Heritage Speakers or Level 6

## Colección 4 Pruebas Págs. 222–295

| Lectura | Cultura | Comunicación | Escritura |
|---|---|---|---|
| **Josefina Niggli**<br>"El anillo del general Macías"<br>**Francisco Jiménez**<br>"Cajas de cartón"<br>**Jorge Luis Borges**<br>"Los dos reyes y los dos laberintos"<br><br>**Estrategia para leer**<br>Writing a summary<br><br>**Elementos de literatura**<br>Drama<br><br>**Enlaces**<br>La poesía latinoamericana del siglo XX | **Cultura y lengua**<br>Mexico<br><br>**Panorama cultural**<br>Have you ever been faced with a dilemma where you had to make a difficult decision?<br><br>**Comunidad y oficio**<br>Achievement through education | **Así se dice**<br>Talking about how things really are<br>Taking about the consequences of an historical event<br>Talking about hypothetical situations<br>Reflecting on a written work<br>**Vocabulario**<br>Regionalisms<br>**Gramática**<br>Relative clauses and relative pronouns<br>The use of relative pronouns<br>**Comparación y contraste**<br>Relative clauses in Spanish and English | **Prepara tu portafolio**<br>Journalism<br>Literature and history<br><br>**Ortografía**<br>The letters **m** and **n**<br>Accent marks and suffix-es<br><br>**Taller del escritor**<br>Persuasive Writing |

## Colección 5 Mitos Págs. 302–363

| Lectura | Cultura | Comunicación | Escritura |
|---|---|---|---|
| Versión de **Jorge Luis Arriola**<br>*El Popol Vuh*<br>Versión de **Douglas Gifford**<br>"Tres mitos latinoamericanos"<br>Versión de **Américo Paredes**<br>"El corrido de Gregorio Cortez"<br><br>**Estrategia para leer**<br>Evaluating<br><br>**Elementos de literatura**<br>Myths, legends, and folktales<br><br>**Enlaces**<br>La nueva narrative latinoameri-cana del siglo XX | **Cultura y lengua**<br>The Mayans<br><br>**Panorama cultural**<br>If you could put some-thing in a time capsule to show the progress of our civilization, what would it be?<br><br>**Comunidad y oficio**<br>Preserving oral traditions | **Así se dice**<br>Evaluating a literary text<br>Making conjectures<br>Making comparisons<br>Evaluating a written work<br>Reflecting on a written work<br>**Vocabulario**<br>Loanwords from indigenous American languages<br>**Gramática**<br>Review of relative clauses<br>Mood with relative clauses<br>The subjunctive in adverbial clauses<br>**Comparación y contraste**<br>Relative clauses with indefinite antecedents in Spanish and English | **Prepara tu portafolio**<br>Art<br>Posters<br><br>**Ortografía**<br>The */s/* sound<br>Verb forms and accent marks<br><br>**Taller del escritor**<br>Persuasive Writing |

## Colección 6 Perspectivas humorísticas Págs. 376–427

| Lectura | Cultura | Comunicación | Escritura |
|---|---|---|---|
| **Miguel de Cervantes**<br>de *Don Quijote de la Mancha*<br>**Pedro Antonio de Alarcón**<br>"El libro talonario"<br>**Lope de Vega**<br>"*El soneto*"<br><br>**Estrategia para leer**<br>Cause and effect<br><br>**Elementos de literatura**<br>The novel<br><br>**Enlaces**<br>El teatro latinoamericano del siglo XX | **Cultura y lengua**<br>Spain<br><br>**Panorama cultural**<br>Have you ever done something that was embarrassing at the time but that now makes you laugh?<br><br>**Comunidad y oficio**<br>Bilingualism in law | **Así se dice**<br>Talking about hypothetical situations in the past<br>Talking about the arts<br>Making conjectures<br>Evaluating a written work<br>**Vocabulario**<br>Learned words<br>**Gramática**<br>Aspect<br>Perfective aspect<br>Imperfective aspect<br>Progressive aspect<br>**Comparación y contraste**<br>The imperfect and the preterite progressive in Spanish | **Prepara tu portafolio**<br>Creative writing and drawing<br>Creative writing<br><br>**Ortografía**<br>Verbs that end in **-ear**<br>Minimal pairs<br><br>**Taller del escritor**<br>Writing an essay |

# Student Edition

## *¡Exprésate!* gives students the confidence to express themselves!

With ever-growing class sizes and more ability levels than ever before in the Spanish classroom, it takes a special Spanish program to engage your students. ***¡Exprésate!*** immerses students in the Spanish-speaking world and makes them want to communicate!

### Cross-curricular connections make material relevant to students

The ***Geocultura*** pages that come before each chapter introduce students to a new country. Students make connections with geography, art, architecture, food, and celebrations.

The **GeoVisión** video brings each location to life.

# Colorful and vivid presentations that hold students' attention

Objetivos
• Expressing certainty
• Expressing doubt and disbelief

## Vocabulario en acción 1

### Los medios electrónicos

Me gusta **estar al tanto** de las noticias. Siempre leo el periódico y veo **los noticieros** en la televisión.

Leo a menudo **las noticias en línea**. Estoy convencida de que los que navegamos mucho por Internet **estamos bien informados.**

Este **reportero** nunca está bien informado. No **trata los temas muy a fondo**. El año pasado, por ejemplo, **investigó la crisis ambiental** y **el reportaje** que hizo fue muy superficial. **Pasó por alto** muchos detalles importantes.

En cambio, **la locutora** del **canal** 13 es mi favorita. Sus reportajes son **detallados** e **informativos**. Siempre presenta las noticias **de modo** muy **imparcial**, sobre todo los asuntos **controvertidos**. Por eso **me inspira confianza**.

Este señor **reseña** las últimas películas. Es evidente que sa muchísimo de cinematograf

230 doscientos treinta Capítulo 6 • ¡Pont

***Vocabulary*** and functional phrases are the foundation of meaningful communication. The large, real-life photos in the vocabulary sections help students connect learning Spanish to their world.

**Listening Practice** is available throughout the program. Don't miss the listening opportunities found in: the Audio CD Program, the **Online Student Edition** listening activities, the **Interactive CD-ROM,** and *Pre-AP Instructional Resources.*

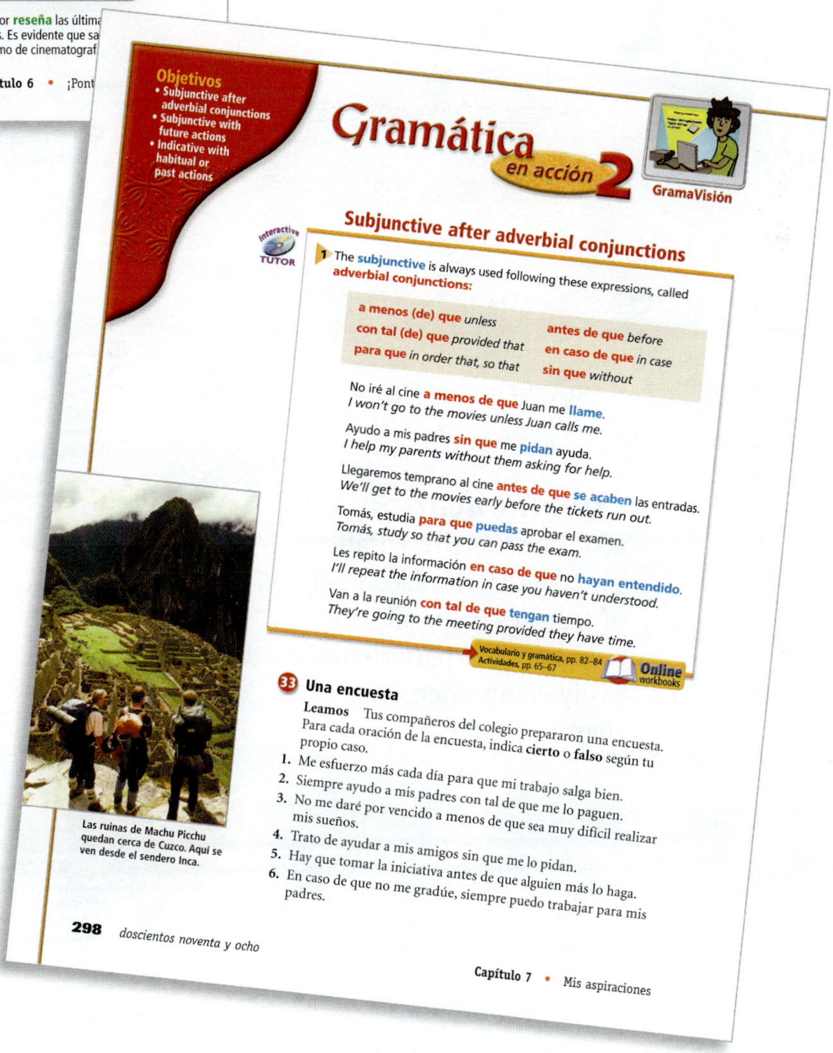

Objetivos
• Subjunctive after adverbial conjunctions
• Subjunctive with future actions
• Indicative with habitual or past actions

## Gramática en acción 2

GramaVisión

Interactive TUTOR

### Subjunctive after adverbial conjunctions

1 The **subjunctive** is always used following these expressions, called **adverbial conjunctions:**

| | |
|---|---|
| **a menos (de) que** *unless* | **antes de que** *before* |
| **con tal (de) que** *provided that* | **en caso de que** *in case* |
| **para que** *in order that, so that* | **sin que** *without* |

No iré al cine **a menos de que** Juan me **llame**.
*I won't go to the movies unless Juan calls me.*

Ayudo a mis padres **sin que** me **pidan** ayuda.
*I help my parents without them asking for help.*

Llegaremos temprano al cine **antes de que se acaben** las entradas.
*We'll get to the movies early before the tickets run out.*

Tomás, estudia **para que puedas** aprobar el examen.
*Tomás, study so that you can pass the exam.*

Les repito la información **en caso de que** no **hayan entendido**.
*I'll repeat the information in case you haven't understood.*

Van a la reunión **con tal de que tengan** tiempo.
*They're going to the meeting provided they have time.*

Vocabulario y gramática, pp. 82–84 Actividades, pp. 65–67 Online workbooks

Las ruinas de Machu Picchu quedan cerca de Cuzco. Aquí se ven desde el sendero Inca.

**33 Una encuesta**

**Leamos** Tus compañeros del colegio prepararon una encuesta. Para cada oración de la encuesta, indica **cierto** o **falso** según tu propio caso.

1. Me esfuerzo más cada día para que mi trabajo salga bien.
2. Siempre ayudo a mis padres con tal de que me lo paguen.
3. No me daré por vencido a menos de que sea muy difícil realizar mis sueños.
4. Trato de ayudar a mis amigos sin que me lo pidan.
5. Hay que tomar la iniciativa antes de que alguien más lo haga.
6. En caso de que no me gradúe, siempre puedo trabajar para mis padres.

298 doscientos noventa y ocho Capítulo 7 • Mis aspiraciones

***Grammar*** presentations are color-coded with graphics and highlighting to emphasize the important points.

***GramaVisión*** animated presentation makes even the most abstract concepts accessible to all students.

**Listening Practice** is available throughout the program. The listening opportunities are found in: the Audio CD Program, the **Online Student Edition** listening activities, the **Interactive CD-ROM,** and *Pre-AP Instructional Resources.*

Student Edition

*Student Edition* *continued*

## A consistent lesson format balances grammar and communication

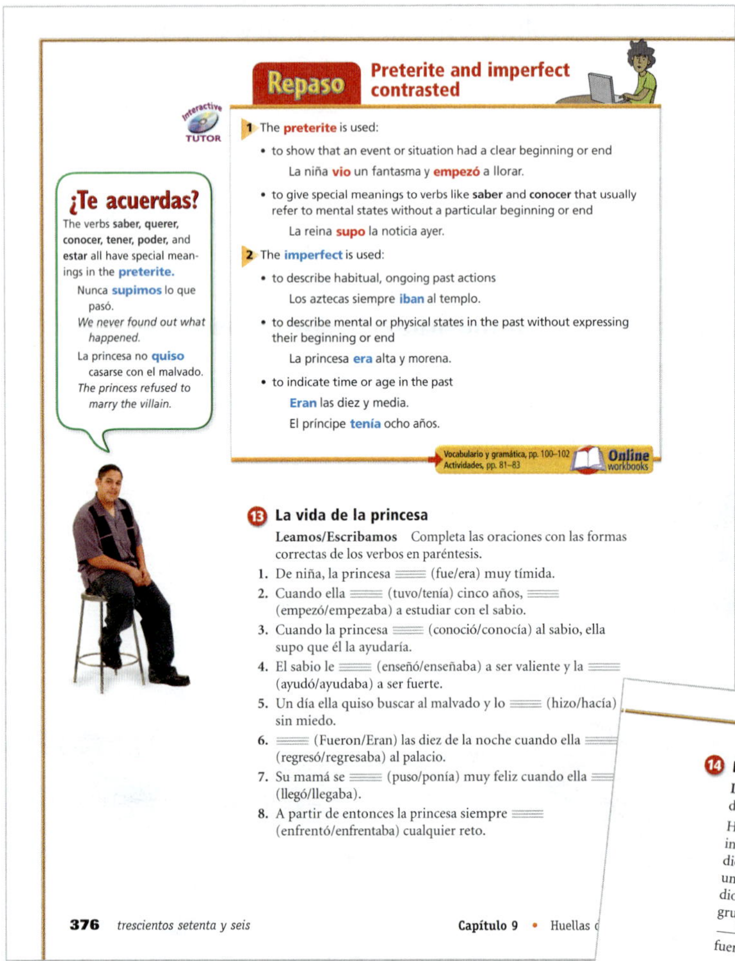

**Repaso** Preterite and imperfect contrasted

Interactive TUTOR

**1** The **preterite** is used:

- to show that an event or situation had a clear beginning or end

  La niña **vio** un fantasma y **empezó** a llorar.

- to give special meanings to verbs like **saber** and **conocer** that usually refer to mental states without a particular beginning or end

  La reina **supo** la noticia ayer.

**2** The **imperfect** is used:

- to describe habitual, ongoing past actions

  Los aztecas siempre **iban** al templo.

- to describe mental or physical states in the past without expressing their beginning or end

  La princesa **era** alta y morena.

- to indicate time or age in the past

  **Eran** las diez y media.

  El príncipe **tenía** ocho años.

Vocabulario y gramática, pp. 100–102 Actividades, pp. 81–83 Online workbooks

**¡Te acuerdas?**

The verbs **saber, querer, conocer, tener, poder,** and **estar** all have special meanings in the **preterite.**

Nunca **supimos** lo que pasó.

*We never found out what happened.*

La princesa no **quiso** casarse con el malvado.

*The princess refused to marry the villain.*

**13 La vida de la princesa**

**Leamos/Escribamos** Completa las oraciones con las formas correctas de los verbos en paréntesis.

1. De niña, la princesa ═══ (fue/era) muy tímida.
2. Cuando ella ═══ (tuvo/tenía) cinco años, ═══ (empezó/empezaba) a estudiar con el sabio.
3. Cuando la princesa ═══ (conoció/conocía) al sabio, ella supo que él la ayudaría.
4. El sabio le ═══ (enseñó/enseñaba) a ser valiente y la ═══ (ayudó/ayudaba) a ser fuerte.
5. Un día ella quiso buscar al malvado y lo ═══ (hizo/hacía) sin miedo.
6. ═══ (Fueron/Eran) las diez de la noche cuando ella ═══ (regresó/regresaba) al palacio.
7. Su mamá se ═══ (puso/ponía) muy feliz cuando ella ═══ (llegó/llegaba).
8. A partir de entonces la princesa siempre ═══ (enfrentó/enfrentaba) cualquier reto.

376 *trescientos setenta y seis* Capítulo 9 • Huellas d

Each ***Grammar*** section leads students from closed-ended, structured practice through open-ended communication. This format allows students to learn the grammar rules using the thematic vocabulary they need to participate actively in a communicative situation.

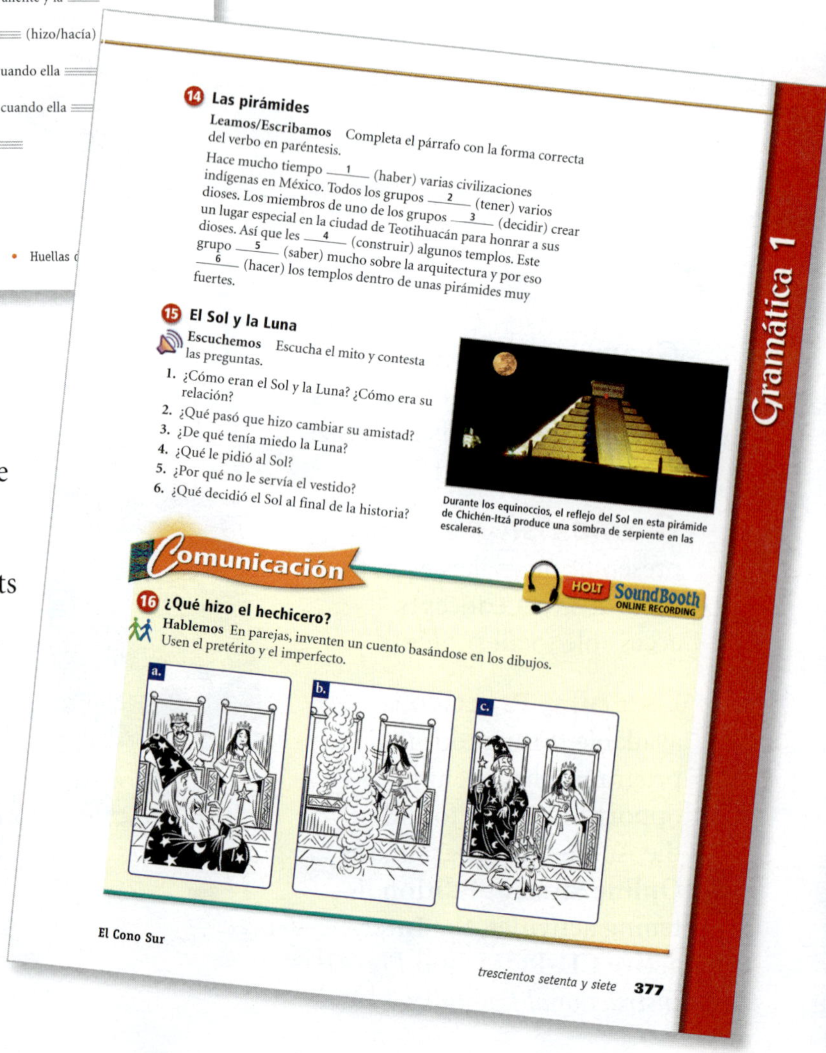

**14 Las pirámides**

**Leamos/Escribamos** Completa el párrafo con la forma correcta del verbo en paréntesis.

Hace mucho tiempo __1__ (haber) varias civilizaciones indígenas en México. Todos los grupos __2__ (tener) varios dioses. Los miembros de uno de los grupos __3__ (decidir) crear un lugar especial en la ciudad de Teotihuacán para honrar a sus dioses. Así que les __4__ (construir) algunos templos. Este grupo __5__ (saber) mucho sobre la arquitectura y por eso __6__ (hacer) los templos dentro de unas pirámides muy fuertes.

**15 El Sol y la Luna**

**Escuchemos** Escucha el mito y contesta las preguntas.

1. ¿Cómo eran el Sol y la Luna? ¿Cómo era su relación?
2. ¿Qué pasó que hizo cambiar su amistad?
3. ¿De qué tenía miedo la Luna?
4. ¿Qué le pidió al Sol?
5. ¿Por qué no le servía el vestido?
6. ¿Qué decidió el Sol al final de la historia?

Durante los equinoccios, el reflejo del Sol en esta pirámide de Chichén-Itzá produce una sombra de serpiente en las escaleras.

**Comunicación**

HOLT SoundBooth ONLINE RECORDING

**16 ¿Qué hizo el hechicero?**

**Hablemos** En parejas, inventen un cuento basándose en los dibujos. Usen el pretérito y el imperfecto.

a. b. c.

Gramática 1

El Cono Sur *trescientos setenta y siete* 377

***Communication*** is the goal of every presentation. The consistent placement of features helps all students recognize the pattern and easily comprehend the chapter format.

## Cultural interviews introduce students to people from around the Spanish-speaking world

Cultura

VideoCultura

Comparaciones

**A la cama no te irás sin saber una cosa más**

Hoy en día, la radio y la televisión llegan hasta el último rincón de América Latina. Las grandes ciudades tienen una gran oferta de medios de comunicación, como televisión por cable y por satélite, que sin embargo son servicios algo caros. Los noticieros incluyen noticias del país, y también bastantes noticias internacionales. También cada vez más, la gente se informa por medio de Internet. ¿Ves tú los noticieros de la televisión? ¿Te gustaría poder ver canales de otros países por televisión? ¿Has visto las páginas Web de algún periódico extranjero?

Un quiosco en el centro de la Ciudad de México

**Sumitsuki**
El Paso, Texas

*Vamos a hablar sobre los medios de comunicación de El Paso, Texas. ¿Estás bien informada sobre los eventos de tu país?*
Sí, estoy muy bien informada.
*¿Cómo te pones al tanto?*
Yo veo las noticias, escucho el radio, y leo el periódico.
*¿Cuántas veces por semana ves las noticias?*
Cinco veces.

Nuevo México
Oklahoma
El Paso
TEXAS
México
Golfo de México

Visit Holt Online
go.hrw.com
KEYWORD: EXP3 CH6
Online Edition

**Octavio**
Santiago, Chile

*¿Tú crees que las imágenes violentas en la televisión, el cine o las noticias nos afectan de modo negativo y por qué?*
Yo creo que sí nos afectan, deberían no afectarnos, pero la mentalidad de los hombres, parece que no está preparada para recibir imágenes tan fuertes. Yo creo que el ejemplo claro está en los niños. Cuando un niño ve [a] dos hombres peleando, van con su amigo y lo repiten, lo recrean. Yo creo que todos tenemos algo de niño y todo lo hacemos recreándolo.
*¿Tú crees que es verdad que los periodistas siempre tratan de dar informes de un modo imparcial? ¿Por qué sí or por qué no?*
No, yo creo que es imposible que un periodista tenga una visión imparcial por muy profesional que sea, porque es humano y siente y se apasiona y tal como siente y se apasiona, se apasiona con ciertos temas. Es imposible que una persona que crea esto diga imparcialmente lo contrario.

Bolivia
Santiago
CHILE
Argentina

**Para comprender**
1. ¿Qué hace Sumitsuki para estar al tanto?
2. ¿Con qué frecuencia ve Sumitsuki las noticias?
3. Según Octavio, ¿cómo reaccionan los niños y adultos después de ver imágenes violentas en la televisión?
4. ¿Por qué no cree Octavio que los periodistas traten siempre los temas de un modo imparcial?

**Para pensar y hablar**
En tu opinión, ¿hay una relación entre la violencia y los medios de comunicación y de entretenimiento? ¿Crees que las imágenes que se ven en la televisión, el cine o los periódicos deben ser controladas por la comunidad o el gobierno? ¿Por qué sí o por qué no?

**Comunidad y oficio**
**Los medios de comunicación en español**

En este país, hay varias emisoras que ofrecen programación en español. Haz una investigación sobre una emisora de radio o de televisión en tu comunidad o en otra parte del país que tenga programación en español. Habla con alguien que trabaje allí y pregúntale sobre la importancia de ofrecer esos servicios a los hispanohablantes de la zona y sobre cómo escogen la programación. También investiga la demanda de programación en español en tu comunidad.

Jorge Ramos es un locutor de noticias en Univisión.

Cultura

242 *doscientos cuarenta y dos* Capítulo 6 • ¡Ponte al día!

El Suroeste y el norte de México *doscientos cuarenta y tres* 243

In every ***Cultura*** section, students meet people from different countries and learn more about culture in the Spanish-speaking world.

**VideoCultura** presents interviews shot on location and helps students become accustomed to different accents.

**Listening Practice** is available throughout the program. The listening opportunities are found in: the Audio CD Program, the **Online Student Edition** listening activities, the **Interactive CD-ROM,** and the cultural interviews found in *Pre-AP Instructional Resources.*

## Integrated technology puts language in context for students

***Clara perspectiva***, an intriguing video story, will have students guessing all year long. While trying to predict what will happen next, students learn the language in context as the story progresses with each chapter.

**Novela en video** provides optional Spanish captions if you choose to give students some "text support" as they watch the story unfold.

**Listening Practice** is available throughout the program. The listening opportunities are found in: the Audio CD Program, the **Novela en video** suggested listening activities in the *Teacher's Edition* wrap, and the **Online Student Edition** listening activities.

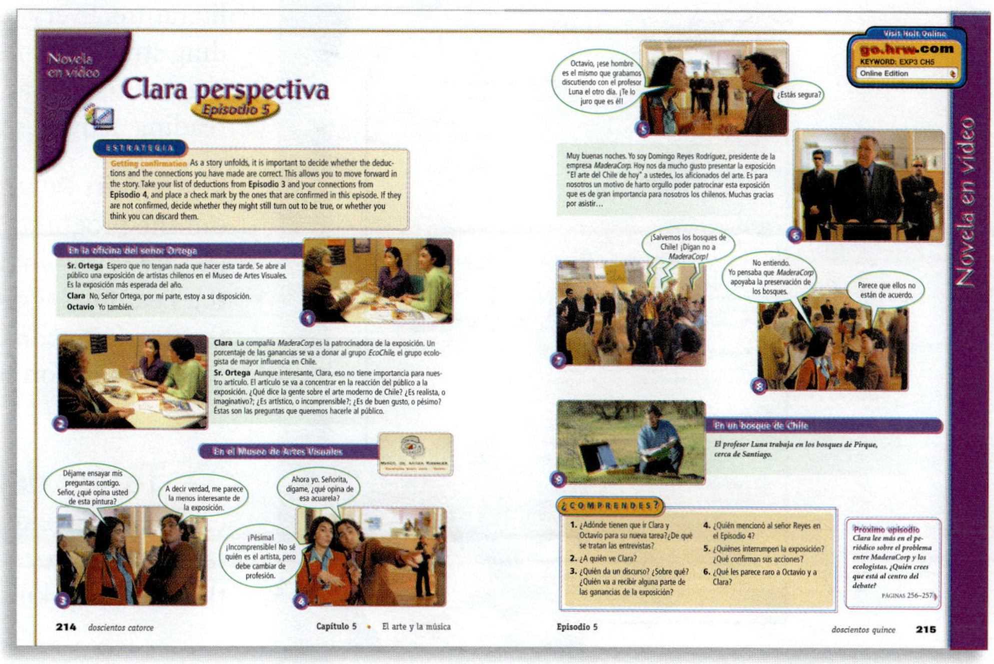
Novela en video

**Clara perspectiva**
*Episodio 5*

ESTRATEGIA

**Getting confirmation** As a story unfolds, it is important to decide whether the deductions and the connections you have made are correct. This allows you to move forward in the story. Take your list of deductions from **Episodio 3** and your connections from **Episodio 4**, and place a check mark by the ones that are confirmed in this episode. If they are not confirmed, decide whether they might still turn out to be true, or whether you think you can discard them.

**En la oficina del señor Ortega**

**Sr. Ortega** Espero que no tengan nada que hacer esta tarde. Se abre al público una exposición de artistas chilenos en el Museo de Artes Visuales. Es la exposición más esperada del año.
**Clara** No, Señor Ortega, por mi parte, estoy a su disposición.
**Octavio** Yo también.

1

**Clara** La compañía *MaderaCorp* es la patrocinadora de la exposición. Un porcentaje de las ganancias se va a donar al grupo *EcoChile*, el grupo ecologista de mayor influencia en Chile.
**Sr. Ortega** Aunque interesante, Clara, eso no tiene importancia para nuestro artículo. El artículo se va a concentrar en la reacción del público a la exposición. ¿Qué dice la gente sobre el arte moderno de Chile? ¿Es realista, o imaginativo?; ¿Es artístico, o incomprensible?; ¿Es de buen gusto, o pésimo? Éstas son las preguntas que queremos hacerle al público.

2

**En el Museo de Artes Visuales**

Déjame ensayar mis preguntas contigo. Señor, ¿qué opina usted de esta pintura?
A decir verdad, me parece la menos interesante de la exposición.

3

Ahora yo. Señorita, dígame, ¿qué opina de esa acuarela?
¡Pésima! ¡Incomprensible! No sé quién es el artista, pero debe cambiar de profesión.

4

Visit Holt Online
go.hrw.com
KEYWORD: EXP3 CH5
Online Edition

Octavio, ¡ese hombre es el mismo que grabamos discutiendo con el profesor Luna el otro día. ¡Te lo juro que es él!
¿Estás segura?

5

Muy buenas noches. Yo soy Domingo Reyes Rodríguez, presidente de la empresa *MaderaCorp*. Hoy nos da mucho gusto presentar la exposición "El arte del Chile de hoy" a ustedes, los aficionados del arte. Es para nosotros un motivo de harto orgullo poder patrocinar esta exposición que es de gran importancia para nosotros los chilenos. Muchas gracias por asistir…

6

¡Salvemos los bosques de Chile! ¡Digan no a *MaderaCorp*!

7

No entiendo. Yo pensaba que *MaderaCorp* apoyaba la preservación de los bosques.
Parece que ellos no están de acuerdo.

8

**En un bosque de Chile**

*El profesor Luna trabaja en los bosques de Pirque, cerca de Santiago.*

9

**¿COMPRENDES?**
1. ¿Adónde tienen que ir Clara y Octavio para su nueva tarea? ¿De qué se tratan las entrevistas?
2. ¿A quién ve Clara?
3. ¿Quién da un discurso? ¿Sobre qué? ¿Quién va a recibir alguna parte de las ganancias de la exposición?
4. ¿Quién mencionó al señor Reyes en el Episodio 4?
5. ¿Quiénes interrumpen la exposición? ¿Qué confirman sus acciones?
6. ¿Qué les parece raro a Octavio y a Clara?

**Próximo episodio**
*Clara lee más en el periódico sobre el problema entre MaderaCorp y los ecologistas. ¿Quién crees que está al centro del debate?*
PÁGINAS 256–257

Novela en video

214 *doscientos catorce* Capítulo 5 • El arte y la música

Episodio 5 *doscientos quince* 215

*Student Edition* continued

# Reading and writing practice build student comprehension and written communication

Visit Holt Online
go.hrw.com
KEYWORD: EXP3 CH6
Online Edition

## Leamos y escribamos

**ESTRATEGIA**

**para leer** When you read a story like the *Popol Vuh*, it's important to know the order in which the events happened. The best way to follow and understand a story is to make a list of events in chronological order. This will help you keep track of events from the beginning to the end of the story.

**Antes de leer**

A El *Popol Vuh* es el libro sagrado maya que explica la creación del mundo y el desarrollo de la naturaleza y de los seres humanos. La selección que vas a leer trata de los hermanos Xbalamqué y Junajpú, que con la ayuda de la naturaleza y de poderes sobrehumanos, logran vencer el mal. Los hermanos llamaron la atención de los Señores del Infierno *(hell)* con su juego de pelota *(ball)* y por eso tuvieron que someterse a desafíos *(challenges)* imposibles. Mientras lees, escribe en orden cronológico los desafíos que enfrentaron los hermanos y las otras cosas que hicieron los Señores para hacerles daño, y cuáles fueron los resultados.

### del Popol Vuh

Los muchachos dijeron a los Señores del Infierno, los Ajawab de Xibalbá:

—A los dos primeros no los saludamos porque son muñecos[1] hechos de madera y trapos[2], pero a vosotros sí: Jun Camé, y Wukub Camé, Xiquiripat y Cuchumaquic, Ajalpuj y Ajalk'aná, Ajalmez y Ajaltok'ob, Chamiabac y Chamiajolom, Quicxic y Patán, Quicré y Quicrixcac[3]. Y tú, Jolomán, que estás sentado en un banco.

Nada gustaron de esto[4] los Ajawab y los invitaron a sentarse.

—Eso no, dijeron los muchachos, ese asiento es piedra que está quemando; no nos sentamos en ella.

—Ea, pues, dijeron los Señores, vayan a descansar a la posada[5].

Por orden de los Señores fueron conducidos[6] a la Casa Oscura, donde les llevaron dos ocotes[7] y dos cigarros y les advirtieron[8] que, ardiendo[9] toda la noche, los habían de devolver[10] enteros por la mañana. Ellos tomaron dos plumas[11] de la cola de la guacamaya y las pusieron en el ocote y en las puntas de los cigarros pusieron dos luciérnagas[12]. Así estuvieron haciendo como[13] que ardían toda la noche.

Los señores quedaron muy admirados de ver los cigarros y los ocotes enteros e invitaron a los muchachos a jugar a la pelota. Primero jugaron con una cabeza de puma y después con la pelota de hule[14] de Junajpú e Xbalamqué.

Otra noche los metieron[15] en la Casa del Fuego, pero éste no les hizo daño alguno sino salieron muy hermosos por la mañana.

1 figures, dolls 2 rags, cloth 3 *names of the lords of hell* 4 didn't like that at all 5 guest house 6 were taken/led 7 sliver of ocote pine 8 warned, advised 9 (keeping them) burning 10 they were to return them 11 feathers 12 glow worms, fireflies 13 pretending 14 rubber ball 15 put them

260 *doscientos sesenta* **Capítulo 6** • ¡Ponte al día!

A la noche siguiente llevaron a los muchachos a la Casa de los Murciélagos[16], donde había infinidad de ellos.

Junajpú e Xbalamqué se metieron dentro de sus cerbatanas a dormir, y aunque los murciélagos revoloteaban a su alrededor, no pudieron morderlos[17]. Junajpú quiso ver si ya había amanecido[18] y al sacar[19] la cabeza para certificarlo se la cortó[20] Camazotz, el Murciélago, quedando[21] sólo el cuerpo.

Los murciélagos fueron a poner la cabeza de Junajpú al atrio donde se jugaba a la pelota.

Xbalamqué llamó al pizote[22], al puerco y a todos los grandes y pequeños animales, para que lo ayudaran a remendar[23] a Junajpú y todos acudieron[24].

A lo último vino Coc, la Tortuga, balanceándose y dando vueltas a un lado y otro para caminar. Tomóla Xbalamqué[25] y labró de ella[26] la cabeza de Junajpú, la cual salió perfecta después de hacerle boca y ojos.

Esto fue hecho con mucha sabiduría[27] porque así lo dispuso Uc'ux Caj, el Corazón del Cielo.

Al terminar la cabeza se la pusieron al cuerpo de Junajpú y éste pudo hablar.

Puesta la cabeza de Junajpú en el atrio, los Señores fueron a celebrar el vencimiento[28] de los muchachos y se pusieron a jugar a la pelota.

Xbalamqué rebatió fuertemente la pelota que fue a caer junto a un tomatal[29] donde estaba un conejo, aconsejado por Xbalamqué, que salió corriendo y los Señores detrás de él creyendo que era la pelota.

Quedó solo todo el atrio e Xbalamqué tomó la cabeza de Junajpú y se la puso al cuerpo cambiándola por la cabeza de tortuga, la que colocó[30] en su lugar en el atrio.

Los Señores estaban admirados de ver el prodigo[31] que sucedía con Junajpú.

16 bats 17 bite them 18 if the sun had come up 19 upon sticking out 20 (the bat) cut it off 21 leaving behind 22 coati, a raccoon-like animal 23 to fix, to mend 24 came to help 25 Xbalamqué took her 26 made out of her 27 wisdom 28 defeat 29 tomato patch 30 put 31 *prodigio* wonder, miracle

**El Suroeste y el norte de México** *doscientos sesenta y uno* 261

Leamos y escribamos

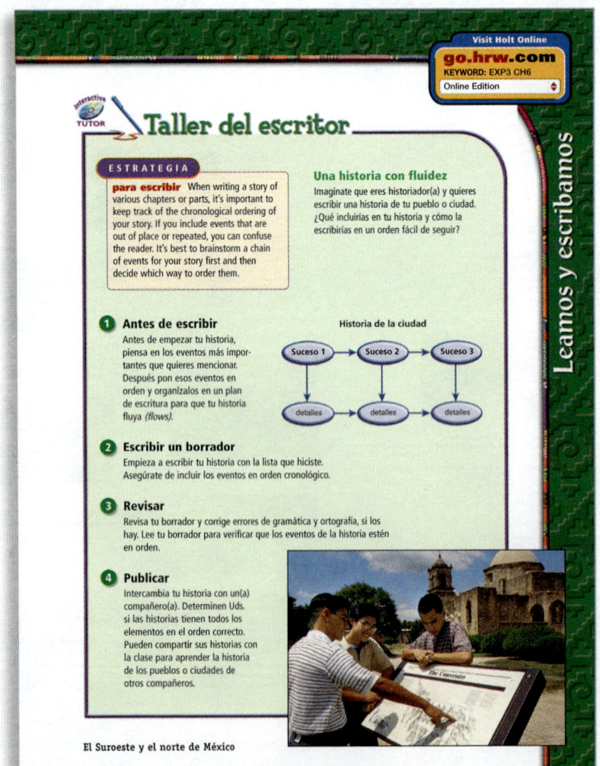

Visit Holt Online
go.hrw.com
KEYWORD: EXP3 CH6
Online Edition

interactive TUTOR

## Taller del escritor

**ESTRATEGIA**

**para escribir** When writing a story of various chapters or parts, it's important to keep track of the chronological ordering of your story. If you include events that are out of place or repeated, you can confuse the reader. It's best to brainstorm a chain of events for your story first and then decide which way to order them.

**Una historia con fluidez**

Imagínate que eres historiador(a) y quieres escribir una historia de tu pueblo o ciudad. ¿Qué incluirías en tu historia y cómo la escribirías en un orden fácil de seguir?

1 **Antes de escribir**
Antes de empezar tu historia, piensa en los eventos más importantes que quieres mencionar. Después pon esos eventos en orden y organízalos en un plan de escritura para que tu historia fluya *(flows).*

Historia de la ciudad
Suceso 1 → Suceso 2 → Suceso 3
detalles → detalles → detalles

2 **Escribir un borrador**
Empieza a escribir tu historia con la lista que hiciste. Asegúrate de incluir los eventos en orden cronológico.

3 **Revisar**
Revisa tu borrador y corrige errores de gramática y ortografía, si los hay. Lee tu borrador para verificar que los eventos de la historia estén en orden.

4 **Publicar**
Intercambia tu historia con un(a) compañero(a). Determinen Uds. si las historias tienen todos los elementos en el orden correcto. Pueden compartir sus historias con la clase para aprender la historia de los pueblos o ciudades de otros compañeros.

**El Suroeste y el norte de México**

Leamos y escribamos

The ***Leamos*** section provides students with readings from informational texts to literature. Every reading has a corresponding strategy to help students tackle reading confidently as well as pre-and post-reading activities.

**Listening Practice** is available throughout the program. The listening opportunities are found in: the Audio CD Program, the **Leamos** suggested listening activities in the *Teacher's Edition* wrap, and the **Online Student Edition** listening activities.

**Taller del escritor** follows each reading and steps students through the writing process, gradually building their writing skills in Spanish.

Student Edition

# Two types of review boost students' retention

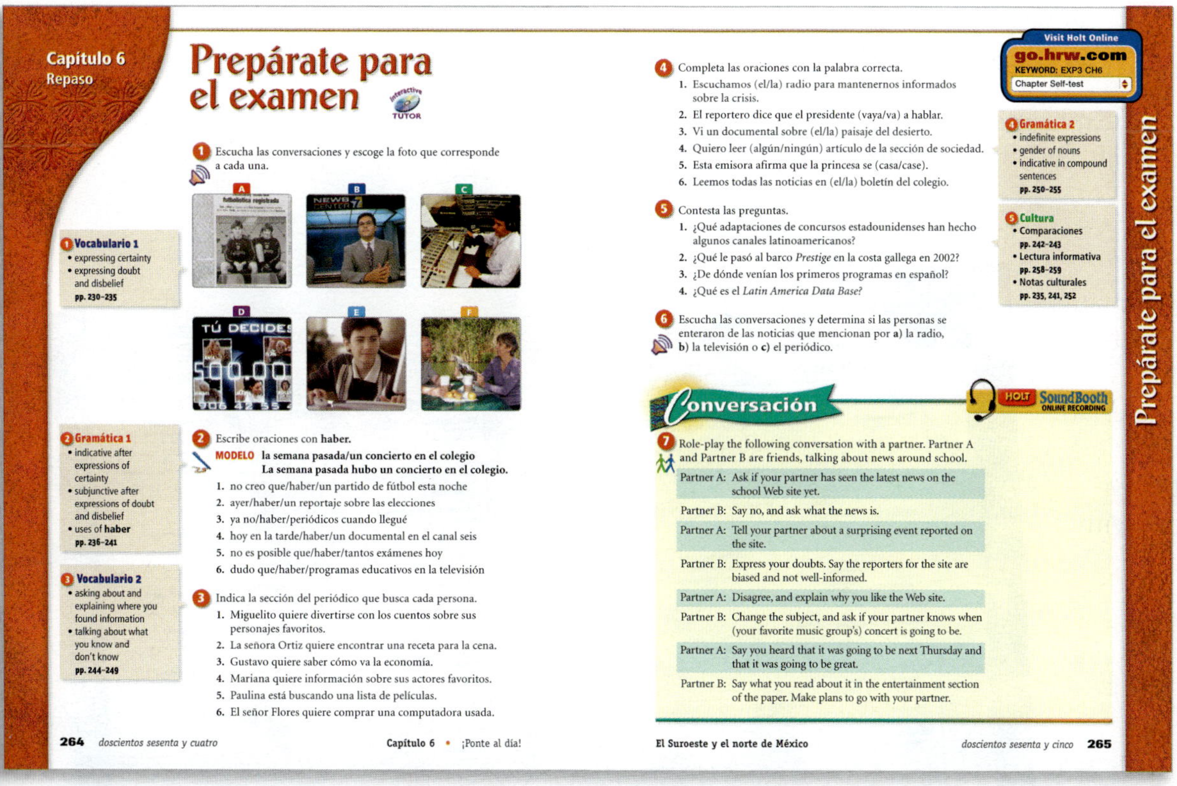

Capítulo 6 Repaso

Prepárate para el examen

1 Escucha las conversaciones y escoge la foto que corresponde a cada una.

1 Vocabulario 1 • expressing certainty • expressing doubt and disbelief pp. 230–235

2 Escribe oraciones con **haber**.

**MODELO** la semana pasada/un concierto en el colegio
La semana pasada hubo un concierto en el colegio.

1. no creo que/haber/un partido de fútbol esta noche
2. ayer/haber/un reportaje sobre las elecciones
3. ya no/haber/periódicos cuando llegué
4. hoy en la tarde/haber/un documental en el canal seis
5. no es posible que/haber/tantos exámenes hoy
6. dudo que/haber/programas educativos en la televisión

2 Gramática 1 • indicative after expressions of certainty • subjunctive after expressions of doubt and disbelief • uses of **haber** pp. 236–241

3 Indica la sección del periódico que busca cada persona.

1. Miguelito quiere divertirse con los cuentos sobre sus personajes favoritos.
2. La señora Ortiz quiere encontrar una receta para la cena.
3. Gustavo quiere saber cómo va la economía.
4. Mariana quiere información sobre sus actores favoritos.
5. Paulina está buscando una lista de películas.
6. El señor Flores quiere comprar una computadora usada.

3 Vocabulario 2 • asking about and explaining where you found information • talking about what you know and don't know pp. 244–249

4 Completa las oraciones con la palabra correcta.

1. Escuchamos (el/la) radio para mantenernos informados sobre la crisis.
2. El reportero dice que el presidente (vaya/va) a hablar.
3. Vi un documental sobre (el/la) paisaje del desierto.
4. Quiero leer (algún/ningún) artículo de la sección de sociedad.
5. Esta emisora afirma que la princesa se (casa/case).
6. Leemos todas las noticias en (el/la) boletín del colegio.

4 Gramática 2 • indefinite expressions • gender of nouns • indicative in compound sentences pp. 250–255

5 Contesta las preguntas.

1. ¿Qué adaptaciones de concursos estadounidenses han hecho algunos canales latinoamericanos?
2. ¿Qué le pasó al barco *Prestige* en la costa gallega en 2002?
3. ¿De dónde venían los primeros programas en español?
4. ¿Qué es el *Latin America Data Base*?

5 Cultura • Comparaciones pp. 242–243 • Lectura informativa pp. 258–259 • Notas culturales pp. 235, 241, 252

6 Escucha las conversaciones y determina si las personas se enteraron de las noticias que mencionan por **a)** la radio, **b)** la televisión o **c)** el periódico.

Visit Holt Online go.hrw.com KEYWORD: EXP3 CH6 Chapter Self-test

Conversación

7 Role-play the following conversation with a partner. Partner A and Partner B are friends, talking about news around school.

Partner A: Ask if your partner has seen the latest news on the school Web site yet.
Partner B: Say no, and ask what the news is.
Partner A: Tell your partner about a surprising event reported on the site.
Partner B: Express your doubts. Say the reporters for the site are biased and not well-informed.
Partner A: Disagree, and explain why you like the Web site.
Partner B: Change the subject, and ask if your partner knows when (your favorite music group's) concert is going to be.
Partner A: Say you heard that it was going to be next Thursday and that it was going to be great.
Partner B: Say what you read about it in the entertainment section of the paper. Make plans to go with your partner.

Prepárate para el examen

264 doscientos sesenta y cuatro Capítulo 6 • ¡Ponte al día! El Suroeste y el norte de México doscientos sesenta y cinco 265

The ***Prepárate para el examen*** review section offers **discrete, chapter-specific practice** with references back into the chapter if students need further review.

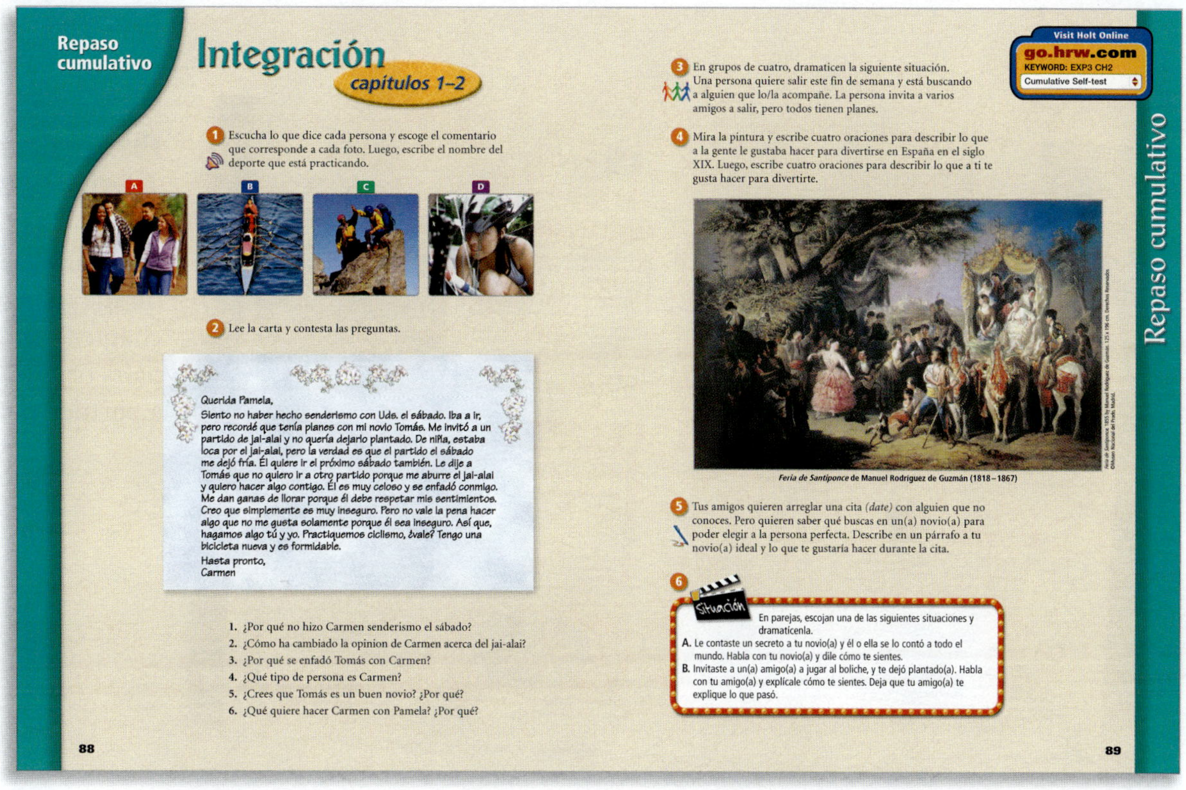

Repaso cumulativo

Integración capítulos 1–2

1 Escucha lo que dice cada persona y escoge el comentario que corresponde a cada foto. Luego, escribe el nombre del deporte que está practicando.

2 Lee la carta y contesta las preguntas.

Querida Pamela,
Siento no haber hecho senderismo con Uds. el sábado. Iba a ir, pero recordé que tenía planes con mi novio Tomás. Me invitó a un partido de jai-alai y no quería dejarlo plantado. De niña, estaba loca por el jai-alai, pero la verdad es que el partido el sábado me dejó fría. El quiere ir el próximo sábado también. Le dije a Tomás que no quiero ir a otro partido porque me aburre el jai-alai y quiero hacer algo contigo. Él es muy celoso y se enfadó conmigo. Me dan ganas de llorar porque él debe respetar mis sentimientos. Creo que simplemente es muy inseguro. Pero no vale la pena hacer algo que no me gusta solamente porque él sea inseguro. Así que, hagamos algo tú y yo. Practiquemos ciclismo, ¿vale? Tengo una bicicleta nueva y es formidable.
Hasta pronto,
Carmen

1. ¿Por qué no hizo Carmen senderismo el sábado?
2. ¿Cómo ha cambiado la opinión de Carmen acerca del jai-alai?
3. ¿Por qué se enfadó Tomás con Carmen?
4. ¿Qué tipo de persona es Carmen?
5. ¿Crees que Tomás es un buen novio? ¿Por qué?
6. ¿Qué quiere hacer Carmen con Pamela? ¿Por qué?

3 En grupos de cuatro, dramaticen la siguiente situación. Una persona quiere salir este fin de semana y está buscando a alguien que lo/la acompañe. La persona invita a varios amigos a salir, pero todos tienen planes.

4 Mira la pintura y escribe cuatro oraciones para describir lo que a la gente le gustaba hacer para divertirse en España en el siglo XIX. Luego, escribe cuatro oraciones para describir lo que a ti te gusta hacer para divertirte.

*Feria de Santiponce* de Manuel Rodríguez de Guzmán (1818–1867)

5 Tus amigos quieren arreglar una cita (*date*) con alguien que no conoces. Pero quieren saber qué buscas en un(a) novio(a) para poder elegir a la persona perfecta. Describe en un párrafo a tu novio(a) ideal y lo que te gustaría hacer durante la cita.

6 Situación

En parejas, escojan una de las siguientes situaciones y dramatícenla.

A. Le contaste un secreto a tu novio(a) y él o ella se lo contó a todo el mundo. Habla con tu novio(a) y dile cómo te sientes.
B. Invitaste a un(a) amigo(a) a jugar al boliche, y te dejó plantado(a). Habla con tu amigo(a) y explícale cómo te sientes. Deja que tu amigo(a) te explique lo que pasó.

Visit Holt Online go.hrw.com KEYWORD: EXP3 CH2 Cumulative Self-test

Repaso cumulativo

88 89

The ***Integración*** section provides students with **cumulative practice after every chapter.** Students are ready for a cumulative test at any time.

Student Edition

# Teacher's Edition

## Using the Chapter Interleaf

Each chapter of the *¡Exprésate! Teacher's Edition* includes interleaf pages to help you plan, teach, and expand your lessons.

***Planning Guide*** at the beginning of each chapter provides a snapshot of the material presented and the resources available for additional practice with each chapter section.

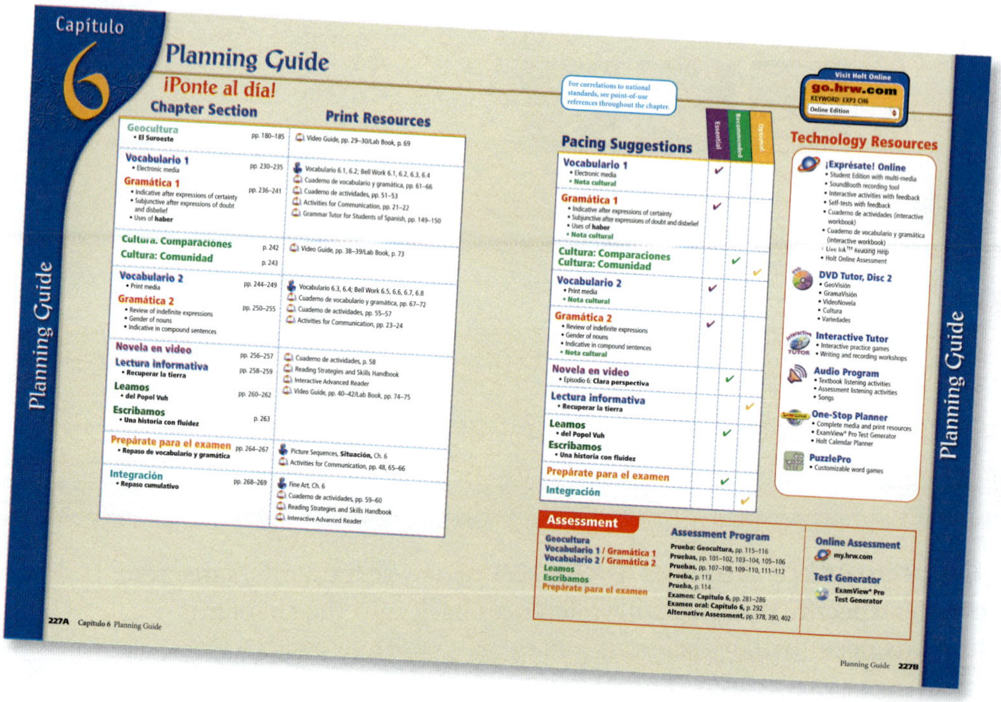


***Projects and Traditions*** allow students to work at several different levels to expand on the information in the chapter—individually, in pairs or groups, or with a partner class.

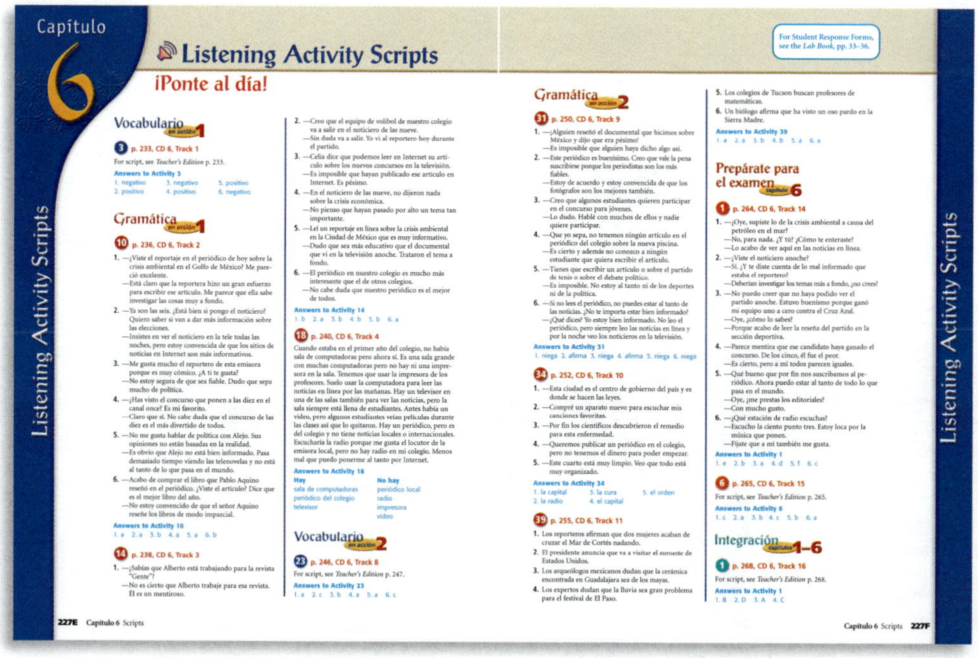


***Textbook Listening Activity Scripts*** are placed at point of use throughout each chapter. In addition, all scripts and answers for listening activities are found on these pages for easy reference. The activity masters for listening activities are found in the Lab Book.

***Suggested Lesson Plans*** provide a logical sequence of instruction along with suggestions for optional practice and homework. Both **50-minute** and **90-minute block** plans are provided.

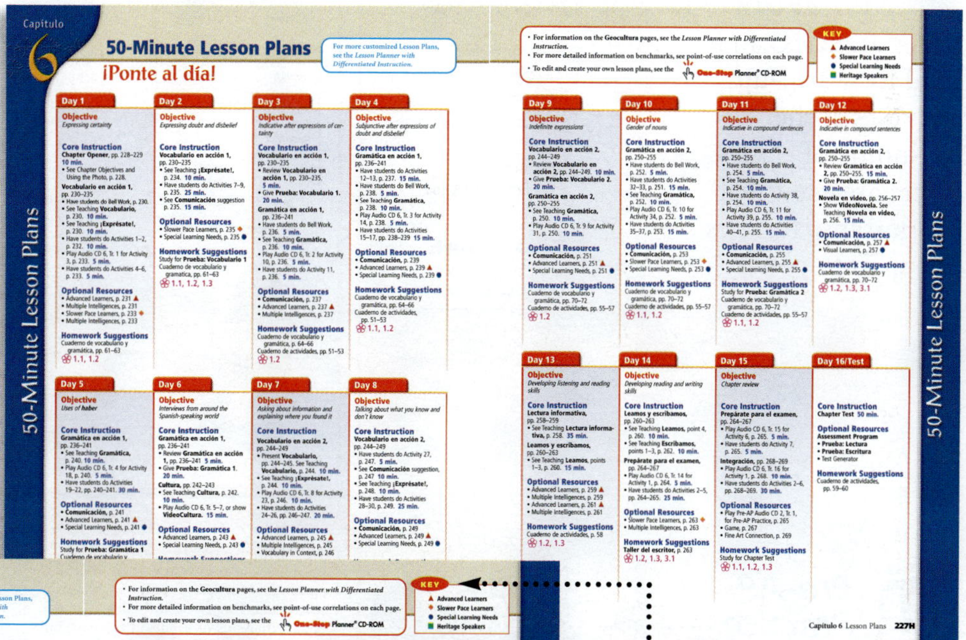


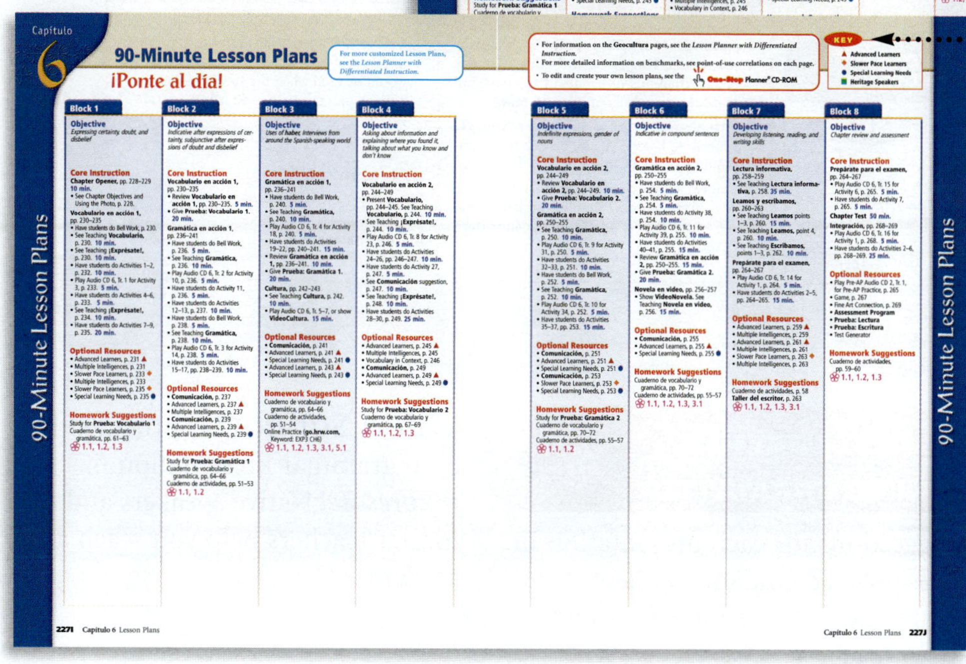


**KEY**

- ▲ Advanced Learners
- ◆ Slower Pace Learners
- ● Special Learning Needs
- ■ Heritage Speakers

Ideas and suggestions for differentiated instruction are noted with these icons ▲◆●■.

# *Teacher's Edition* continued

## Using the Wrap-Around Teacher Text

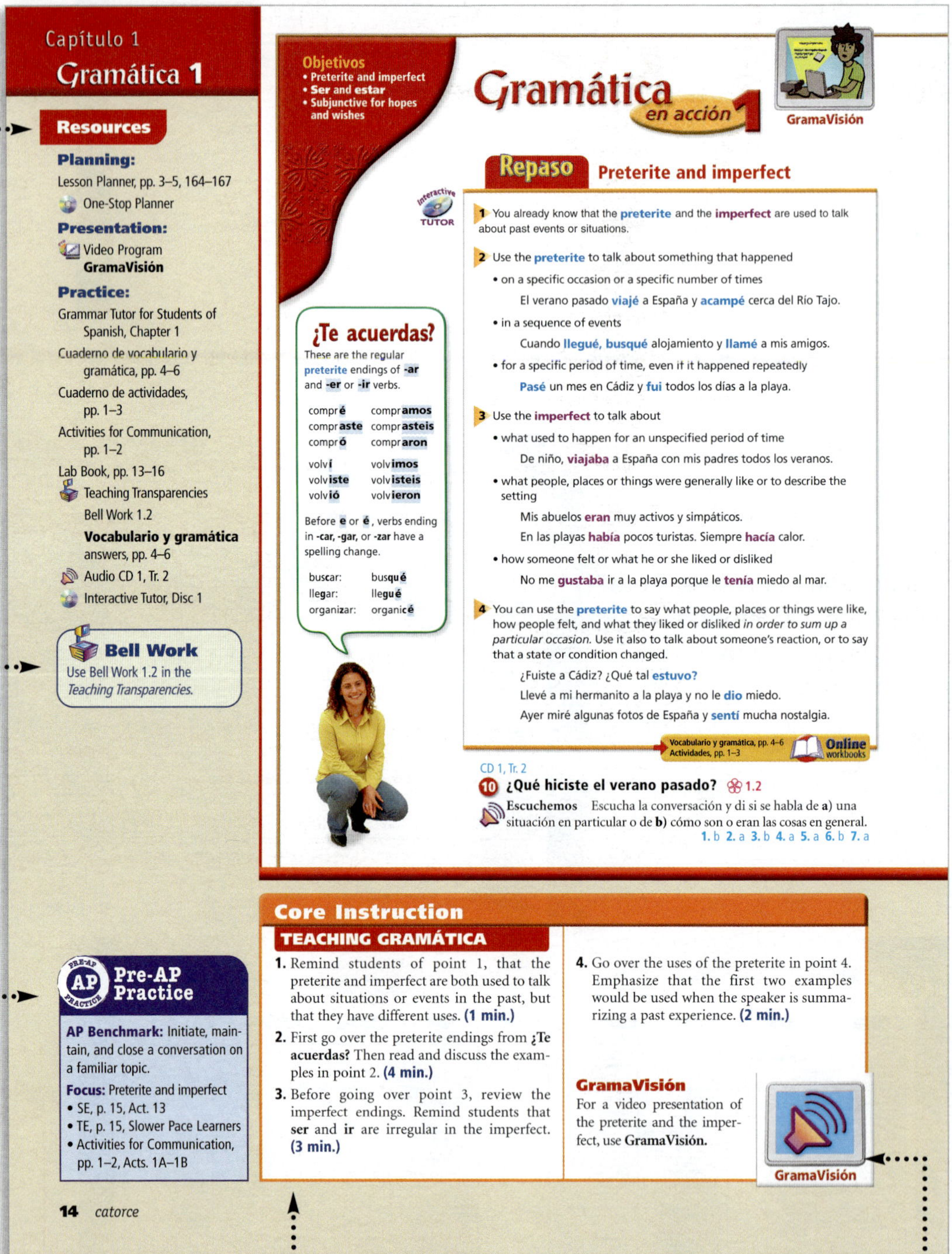

Capítulo 1

Gramática 1

**Resources**

**Planning:**
Lesson Planner, pp. 3–5, 164–167
One-Stop Planner

**Presentation:**
Video Program
**GramaVisión**

**Practice:**
Grammar Tutor for Students of Spanish, Chapter 1
Cuaderno de vocabulario y gramática, pp. 4–6
Cuaderno de actividades, pp. 1–3
Activities for Communication, pp. 1–2
Lab Book, pp. 13–16
Teaching Transparencies
Bell Work 1.2
**Vocabulario y gramática** answers, pp. 4–6
Audio CD 1, Tr. 2
Interactive Tutor, Disc 1

**Bell Work**
Use Bell Work 1.2 in the *Teaching Transparencies.*

**Pre-AP Practice**

**AP Benchmark:** Initiate, maintain, and close a conversation on a familiar topic.
**Focus:** Preterite and imperfect
- SE, p. 15, Act. 13
- TE, p. 15, Slower Pace Learners
- Activities for Communication, pp. 1–2, Acts. 1A–1B

**Objetivos**
- Preterite and imperfect
- **Ser and estar**
- Subjunctive for hopes and wishes

**Gramática en acción 1**

GramaVisión

Interactive TUTOR

**Repaso** Preterite and imperfect

1 You already know that the **preterite** and the **imperfect** are used to talk about past events or situations.

2 Use the **preterite** to talk about something that happened
- on a specific occasion or a specific number of times
  El verano pasado **viajé** a España y **acampé** cerca del Río Tajo.
- in a sequence of events
  Cuando **llegué**, **busqué** alojamiento y **llamé** a mis amigos.
- for a specific period of time, even if it happened repeatedly
  **Pasé** un mes en Cádiz y **fui** todos los días a la playa.

3 Use the **imperfect** to talk about
- what used to happen for an unspecified period of time
  De niño, **viajaba** a España con mis padres todos los veranos.
- what people, places or things were generally like or to describe the setting
  Mis abuelos **eran** muy activos y simpáticos.
  En las playas **había** pocos turistas. Siempre **hacía** calor.
- how someone felt or what he or she liked or disliked
  No me **gustaba** ir a la playa porque le **tenía** miedo al mar.

4 You can use the **preterite** to say what people, places or things were like, how people felt, and what they liked or disliked *in order to sum up a particular occasion.* Use it also to talk about someone's reaction, or to say that a state or condition changed.
¿Fuiste a Cádiz? ¿Qué tal **estuvo**?
Llevé a mi hermanito a la playa y no le **dio** miedo.
Ayer miré algunas fotos de España y **sentí** mucha nostalgia.

**¿Te acuerdas?**
These are the regular **preterite** endings of **-ar** and **-er** or **-ir** verbs.

| | |
|---|---|
| compr**é** | compr**amos** |
| compr**aste** | compr**asteis** |
| compr**ó** | compr**aron** |
| volv**í** | volv**imos** |
| volv**iste** | volv**isteis** |
| volv**ió** | volv**ieron** |

Before **e** or **é**, verbs ending in **-car, -gar,** or **-zar** have a spelling change.

| | |
|---|---|
| buscar: | bus**qué** |
| llegar: | lle**gué** |
| organizar: | organi**cé** |

Vocabulario y gramática, pp. 4–6 Actividades, pp. 1–3 Online workbooks

CD 1, Tr. 2

**10** ¿Qué hiciste el verano pasado? 1.2

**Escuchemos** Escucha la conversación y di si se habla de **a)** una situación en particular o de **b)** cómo son o eran las cosas en general.
1. b 2. a 3. b 4. a 5. a 6. b 7. a

**Core Instruction**

**TEACHING GRAMÁTICA**

1. Remind students of point 1, that the preterite and imperfect are both used to talk about situations or events in the past, but that they have different uses. **(1 min.)**
2. First go over the preterite endings from **¿Te acuerdas?** Then read and discuss the examples in point 2. **(4 min.)**
3. Before going over point 3, review the imperfect endings. Remind students that **ser** and **ir** are irregular in the imperfect. **(3 min.)**
4. Go over the uses of the preterite in point 4. Emphasize that the first two examples would be used when the speaker is summarizing a past experience. **(2 min.)**

**GramaVisión**
For a video presentation of the preterite and the imperfect, use **GramaVisión.**

GramaVisión

**14** *catorce*

**Resources**
This feature provides a quick list of all the resources you can use for each chapter section.

***Bell Work***
transparencies can be used for warm-up activities at the beginning of class. There are eight Bell Work transparencies per chapter.

***Pre-AP Practice***
This feature provides suggestions for activities to practice one of the 12 AP Spanish Language benchmarks. The activities can come from the *Student Edition, Teacher's Edition,* and the ancillaries, and have a specific focus (a particular vocabulary topic or grammar point, for example). There are two to three Pre-AP Practice suggestions per chapter.

**Core Instruction**
**TEACHING GRAMÁTICA**
Timed suggestions for each presentation in the chapter provide guidance to newer teachers, and a quick reference for more experienced teachers.

***Video Support*** is provided for each grammar presentation in ***¡Exprésate!*** Native speakers and master teachers help you reach all students.

**4 Hablando del pasado** 1.2

**Leamos/Escribamos** Completa la conversación con las palabras del cuadro.

| | | |
|---|---|---|
| sucedió | aterradora | trágico |
| estalló | solidaridad | pánico |

—¿Te acuerdas cuando __1__ una bomba en los Juegos Olímpicos? **1.** estalló

—Sí, lo recuerdo. Fue una explosión __2__ y estaba muy asustado. **2.** aterradora

—¿Dónde estabas cuando __3__? **3.** sucedió

—Estaba entrando al estadio cuando sentí algo como un terremoto y todo el mundo sintió __4__. **4.** pánico

—Fue __5__, pero me impresionó la __6__ entre todos los países que se apoyaron para que continuaran los Juegos. **5.** trágico **6.** solidaridad

**5 Me acuerdo...** 1.3

**Leamos/Escribamos** Completa las oraciones según tus experiencias. Da tantos detalles como puedas.

1. Fui al estreno de...
2. En las últimas elecciones...
3. Me acuerdo cuando sucedió...
4. Un acontecimiento trágico del año pasado fue...
5. Fue emocionante el descubrimiento de...
6. Muchos refugiados vinieron a Estados Unidos porque...

*Nota cultural*

La década de los 90 fue marcada por crisis económicas en México, Asia y Brasil. Argentina fue también afectada por estos sucesos; los precios de los productos argentinos subieron, los productos de exportación bajaron, y a finales de los años 90, comenzó una crisis económica en Argentina. En 2001, las imágenes en la televisión eran escenas de caos y pánico en las ciudades de Argentina. El desempleo alcanzó niveles de más del 20%. ¿Por qué crees que una crisis económica en un país o región podría contribuir a crisis parecidas en otros países? 3.1

## Comunicación

HOLT SoundBooth ONLINE RECORDING

**6 ¿Dónde estabas cuando...?** 1.1, 1.2

**Hablemos** Con un(a) compañero(a), hablen de las cosas emocionantes que han pasado en el colegio este año. Pregúntense si recuerdan el acontecimiento y dónde estaban cuando sucedió. Usen las palabras de **Vocabulario** y las expresiones de **Exprésate.**

**MODELO** —**¿Te acuerdas cuando nuestro equipo de básquetbol ganó el campeonato?**

—**Lo recuerdo como si fuera ayer. ¡Qué emocionante!**

Capítulo 10

# Vocabulario 1

Vocabulario 1

### Heritage Speakers

Ask heritage speakers to talk about how their ancestors came to this country. Were they **refugiados** or **inmigrantes?**

***Heritage Speakers*** offers suggestions for activities to be done by native speakers, either individually or in pairs or groups.

### Connections

**Social Studies Link**

As an extension of the information in the **Nota cultural,** tell students that Argentina's fragile economy has been combined with a fragile government that at one point saw five presidents in two weeks! Ask students to do research to find out what the Argentinean government and citizens are doing today to try to improve their economy and strengthen their government. What solutions do students suggest? 3.1

***"Five-C's"*** suggestions that focus on the **national standards** for enhancing or extending the material on the student page.

### Comunicación

**Group Activity: Presentational**

Have groups of students talk about how they relate to events of the past. Are events far in the past something they experience best when seeing a film, reading essays or fiction with people's thoughts and observations from another time, seeing pictures, or visiting a historical museum with many artifacts and people in period costumes? Are there other mediums that they prefer? Ask groups of students to role-play a scene for the class to demonstrate how each medium helps them relate to or understand the past. 1.3

***Comunicación*** The activities suggested here focus on one of the three kinds of communication: **interpersonal, interpretative, or presentational.**

### Differentiated Instruction

**ADVANCED LEARNERS**

**Challenge** After reading the **Nota cultural,** have students conduct research by going to the Web sites of **La Nación, Clarín,** *The Washington Post,* and *The New York Times* on the roles of the **Fondo Monetario Internacional** and the **Banco Mundial** in Argentina. The **FMI** and **Banco Mundial** have their own Web sites as well. Ask them to focus on the conditions imposed on the country for foreign debt repayment and privatization, and their effects on unemployment. 3.1, 3.2

**MULTIPLE INTELLIGENCES**

**Intrapersonal** Have students think about how they would respond if they ever had to live through a natural disaster. How would they help others? Ask them to write a paragraph describing an imaginary, but conceivable disaster, and the role they would play. For example, the last of the sentences might read, **Ayudaría a los trabajadores a repartir provisiones de emergencia a los refugiados.** 1.3

**Differentiated Instruction** See the Differentiated Instruction CD-ROM.



**Differentiated Instruction** suggests ways to address the diversity of any classroom. The suggestions on the left are for either advanced or slower-paced learners, and those on the right are suggested actvities for special-needs learners or multiple intelligences.

# Technology Resources

## Any time, from any computer, access *¡Exprésate!* online.

### All Online Editions include

- All pages of *Student Edition* in interactive format
- All related audio and video at point of use
- Audio Recordings of all vocabulary and expressions
- Practice activities, Projects, and Self-tests
- Searchable Spanish-English/English-Spanish Glossaries
- Searchable Grammar Summary
- Photo Tour slide shows
- Photo Projects
- Four-skills Online Assessment

### Also available with each Online Edition

- Online Voice Recording
- Complete Video Program
- Online Workbooks
- Live Ink™ Reading Help

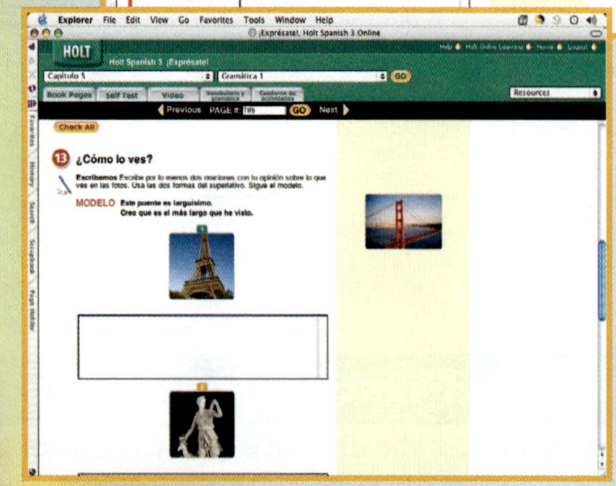

Technology Resources

# Video Takes You There!

GeoVisión

GramaVisión

VideoCultura

VideoNovela

## Video Program

Shot on location around the Spanish-speaking world, the Video Program provides video support for you and your students throughout the book

- **GeoVisión** Video tours of the Spanish-speaking world
- **GramaVisión** Animated grammar presentations explain and model all grammar topics
- **VideoCultura** Interviews with Spanish-speakers from around the world
- **VideoNovela** An exciting, ongoing story modeling vocabulary, functional expressions, and grammar in every chapter

# Tools to Increase Student Success!

## DVD Program

- The entire Video Program
- Optional captions for all video segments
- Additional cultural footage
- Additional scenes modeling language in context

## Interactive CD-ROM Tutor

- Simulated conversations for listening, speaking, and assessment (archivable)
- Varied writing activities archived for portfolio development
- Games to practice all chapter content
- Spanish-English and English-Spanish glossaries
- A grammar reference tool
- Teacher Management System

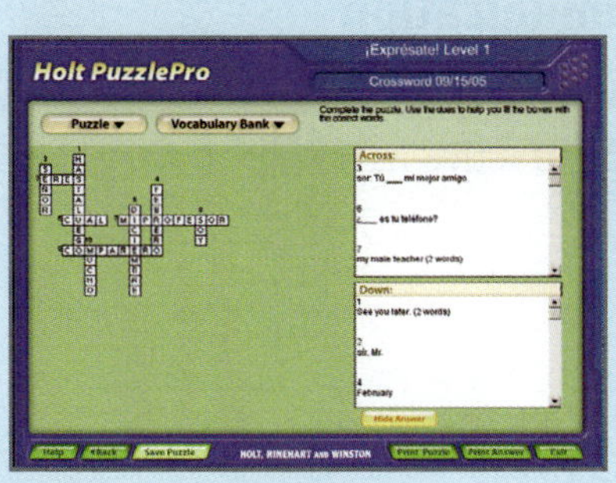


## Holt Puzzle Pro® CD-ROM

- Interactive crossword puzzles, jumbles, word searches to practice vocabulary
- Customization capabilty to allow you to choose which words to include
- Instant correction and feedback
- Print capability for traditional completion of puzzles

# Ancillaries

## *¡Exprésate!* offers a comprehensive ancillary package that meets the needs of today's classroom

## Review

### Puente: Customized Level 2 Review

- Diagnostic tests
- Review of vocabulary and grammar topics
- Listening activities

## Planning

### Teacher's One-Stop Planner with ExamView® 5 Assessment Suite

- Interactive **Teacher's Edition** with links to all print and media resources
- **Entire audio** and **video** programs
- **Clip art** library
- **Lesson Planner** with Differentiated Instruction

## Listening and Speaking

### Lab Book

- **Student Response Forms** for the listening activities
- Activity masters for video-related activities
- Online Resource Activities for every chapter

### Audio Compact Discs

Listening activities for the *Student Edition*, the *Assessment Program*, recorded reading selections, and songs

## Vocabulary & Grammar Practice

### Cuaderno de vocabulario y gramática

- Alternate presentations of major grammar points
- Differentiated practice for slower-paced and advanced learners

### Grammar Tutor for Students of Spanish

- Comparisons of basic grammar concepts in English and Spanish
- Comprehension-check activities in both languages

### Teaching Transparencies

- Colorful transparencies and blackline masters
- Fine art transparencies
- Suggested activities for using the transparencies

### Additional Listening Activities

For additional listening practice and lab work, use the audio CD and blackline masters in the *Pre-AP Instructional Resources* ancillary. (These additional listening activities are designed for use for all students.)

### Activities for Communication

- **Information gap activities** and **Situation cards**
- **Picture sequences** for practice narrating a story

## Reading and Writing

### Interactive Advanced Reader

- Two illustrated readings per chapter
- Vocabulary support and reading strategies

### Reading Strategies and Skills Handbook

- Explanations of reading strategies
- Activity masters for application of strategies

### Cuaderno de actividades

- Open-ended reading and writing activities

## Assessment Program

**Core Assessment:**

- Quizzes for vocabulary, grammar, skills-based, reading, writing, and **Geocultura**
- Chapter Tests, Midterm and Final Exams
- Differented assessment for slower-paced and advanced learners

**Alternative Assessment:**

- Suggestions for portfolio and performance assessment
- Rubrics, checklists, and evaluations forms

## Pre-AP Practice

### Pre-AP Instructional Resources

- Teaching suggestions, rubrics, and blackline masters
- An audio CD with listening activities, simulated conversations, and integrated skills practice
- Available for all three levels

Ancillaries

# Cultural References

*Page numbers referring to material in the Student Edition appear in regular type.*
*For material located in the Teacher's Edition, page numbers appear in* ***boldface type.***

## FOOD



## FRIENDS



## GEOGRAPHY AND MAPS

## HISTORY

## HOLIDAYS

## HOME AND FAMILY LIFE



## LANGUAGE



## PARKS

## PEOPLE



## POINTS OF INTEREST

# Implementing National Standards

**Paul Sandrock**
*World Language Consultant,*
*Wisconsin Department of Public Instruction*
*Madison, Wisconsin*

## RESEARCH

**National Standards in Foreign Language Education Project. (1999)** *Standards for Foreign Language Learning in the 21st Century.* Lawrence, KS: Allen Press.

**Phillips, June K., ed. (1999)** *Foreign Language Standards: Linking Research, Theories, and Practice.* Lincolnwood, IL: National Textbook Company. (ACTFL Foreign Language Education Series)

**Sandrock, Paul. (2002)** *Planning Curriculum for Learning World Languages.* Madison, WI: Wisconsin Department of Public Instruction.

**Shrum, Judith and Eileen Glisan. (2000)** *Teacher's Handbook: Contextualized Language Instruction,* 2nd Edition. Heinle & Heinle.

**Wiggins, Grant, and Jay McTighe. (1998)** *Understanding by Design.* Alexandria, VA: Association for Supervision and Curriculum Development.

*To implement the five goals of the national standards—communication, cultures, connections, comparisons, and communities—requires a shift from emphasizing the means to focusing on the ends.*

Instead of simply planning a series of activities, today's world language teacher focuses on what and how the student is learning. Rather than teaching and testing the four skills of listening, speaking, reading, and writing in isolation, teachers need to make their instructional decisions based on the three purposes directing the communication (interpersonal, interpretive, and presentational) and within a cultural context. Our standards answer why we are teaching various components of language.

Since the publication of the standards, many states have developed more specific performance standards that provide evidence of the application of the national content standards, and teachers have carried the standards into the classroom. Textbook writers and materials providers are also responding to the shift brought about by the standards, providing an organization, creating a context, and modeling the kind of instruction that leads students to successfully demonstrate the communication strategies envisioned in our standards. Textbooks can bring authentic materials into the classroom, real cultural examples that avoid stereotypes, and a broader exposure to the variety of people who speak the language being studied. Standards provide the ends; teachers use textbooks and materials to help students practice the means.

Assessment is the jigsaw puzzle that shows students what they can do with their new language. If we only test students on the means of vocabulary and grammar, students simply collect random puzzle pieces. We have to test, and students have to practice, putting the pieces together in meaningful and purposeful ways. When they are truly communicating, students will know they've achieved the standards.

| | |
|---|---|
| **Communication**<br>Communicate in Languages Other Than English | **Standard 1.1 Interpersonal** Students engage in conversations, provide and obtain information, express feelings and emotions, and exchange opinions.<br>**Standard 1.2 Interpretive** Students understand and interpret written and spoken language on a variety of topics.<br>**Standard 1.3 Presentational** Students present information, concepts, and ideas to an audience of listeners or readers on a variety of topics. |
| **Cultures**<br>Gain Knowledge and Understanding of Other Cultures | **Standard 2.1 Practices** Students demonstrate an understanding of the relationship between the practices and perspectives of the culture studied.<br>**Standard 2.2 Products** Students demonstrate an understanding of the relationship between the products and perspectives of the culture studied. |
| **Connections**<br>Connect with Other Disciplines and Acquire Information | **Standard 3.1 Across Disciplines** Students reinforce and further their knowledge of other disciplines through the foreign language.<br>**Standard 3.2 Added Perspective** Students acquire information and recognize the distinctive viewpoints that are only available through the foreign language and its cultures. |
| **Comparisons**<br>Develop Insight into the Nature of Language and Culture | **Standard 4.1 Language** Students demonstrate understanding of the nature of language through comparisons of the language studied and their own.<br>**Standard 4.2 Culture** Students demonstrate understanding of the concept of culture through comparisons of the cultures studied and their own. |
| **Communities**<br>Participate in Multilingual Communities at Home and Around the World | **Standard 5.1 Practical Applications** Students use the language both within and beyond the school setting.<br>**Standard 5.2 Personal Enrichment** Students show evidence of becoming life-long learners by using the language for personal enjoyment and enrichment. |

**Kylene Beers, PhD.**
*Clinical Associate Professor*
*University of Houston*
*Houston, Texas*

## RESEARCH

**Baumann, J. 1984**
"Effectiveness of a Direct Instruction Paradigm for Teaching Main Idea Comprehension." *Reading Research Quarterly,* 20: 93–108.

**Beers, K. 2002.**
*When Kids Can't Read—What Teachers Can Do.* Portsmouth: Heinemann.

**Dole, J., Brown, K., and Trathen, W. 1996.**
"The Effects of Strategy Instruction on the Comprehension Performance of At-Risk Students," *Reading Research Quarterly,* 31: 62–89.

**Duffy, G. 2002**
"The Case for Direct Explanation of Strategies." *Comprehension Instruction: Research-Based Best Practices.* Eds. C. Block and M. Pressley. New York: Guilford Press. 28–41.

**Pearson, P. D. 1984**
"Direct Explicit Teaching of Reading Comprehension." *Comprehension Instruction: Perspectives and Suggestions.* Eds. G. Duffy, L. Roehler, and J. Mason. New York: Longman, 222–233.

# Teaching Comprehension

*"Comprehension is both a product and a process, something that requires purposeful, strategic effort on the reader's part as he or she predicts, visualizes, clarifies, questions, connects, summarizes, and infers."*

**—Kylene Beers**

## When the Text is Tough

"Comprehension is only tough when you can't do it," explained the eleventh grader. I almost dismissed his words until I realized what truth they offered. We aren't aware of all the thinking we do to comprehend a text until faced with a difficult text. Then, all too clearly, we're aware of what words we don't understand, what syntax seems convoluted, what ideas are beyond our immediate grasp. As skilled readers, we know what to do; we slow our pace, re-read, ask questions, connect whatever we do understand to what we don't understand, summarize what we've read thus far, make inferences about what the author is saying. In short, we make that invisible act of comprehension visible as we consciously push our way through the difficult text. At those times, we realize that, indeed, comprehension is tough.

## Reading Strategies for Struggling Readers

It's even tougher if you lack strategies that would help you through the difficult text. Many struggling readers believe they aren't successful readers because that's just the way things are (Beers, 2002); they believe successful readers know some secret that they haven't been told (Duffy, 2002). While we don't mean to keep comprehension a secret, at times we do. For instance, though we tell students to "re-read," we haven't shown them how to alter their reading. We tell them to "make inferences," or "make predictions," but we haven't taught them how to do such things. In other words, we tell them what to do, but don't show them how to do it, in spite of several decades of research showing the benefit of direct instruction in reading strategies to struggling readers. (Baumann, 1984; Pearson, P.D., 1984; Dole, et al., 1996; Beers, 2002).

## Direct Instruction

Direct instruction means telling students what you are going to teach them, modeling it for them, providing assistance as they practice it, then letting them practice it on their own. It's not saying, "Visualize while you read," but, instead, explaining, "Today, I'm going to read this part aloud to you. I'm going to focus on seeing some of the action in my mind as I read. I'm going to stop occasionally and tell you what I'm seeing and what in the text helped me see that." When we directly teach comprehension strategies to students via modeling and repeated practice, we show students that good readers don't just get it. They work hard to get it. ***¡Exprésate!*** takes the secret out of comprehension as it provides teachers the support they need to reach struggling readers.

ol Ann
linson
University
f Virginia

Cindy Strickland
*The University of Virginia*

## RESEARCH

**Tomlinson, C., and Eidson, C.** *Design for Differentiation: Curriculum for the Differentiated Classroom,* Grades 5–9. Alexandria, VA: Association for Supervision and Curriculum Development (in press).

**Tomlinson, C. 2001.** *How to Differentiate Instruction in Mixed-Ability Classrooms,* 2/e. Alexandria, VA: Association for Supervision and Curriculum Development

**Tomlinson, C. and Allan, S. 2001.** *Leadership for Differentiating Schools and Classrooms.* Alexandria, VA: Association for Supervision and Curriculum Development, 2000.

**Winebrenner, S. 1996.** *Teaching Kids with Learning Difficulties in the Regular Classroom.* Minneapolis, MN: Free Spirit, 1996.

# Differentiated Instruction

*Teachers who differentiate their instruction recognize that students are at different points in their learning journeys, will grow at different rates, and will need different kinds and amounts of support to reach their goals.*

## Differentiation and Varied Approaches

Differentiated classrooms offer varied approaches to **content** (what students learn), **process** (how students go about making sense of essential knowledge and practicing essential skills), **product** (how students demonstrate what they have learned), and **learning environment** (the setting in which students learn). Differentiation is based on an ongoing diagnosis of student interest, learning profile, and readiness.

## Differentiation and the World-Language Teacher

World language teachers are natural differentiators for learning profile. We provide opportunities for students to acquire proficiency in the target language through a variety of means: speaking, listening, writing, and reading. Through this variety of approaches, we recognize that students' proficiency in each of these skill areas will vary. Good language teachers work hard to help students improve in areas in which they struggle, and revel in areas of strength.

Systematic differentiation for readiness provides many world-language teachers with a bit more of a challenge. Students come to us with a huge range in amount and type of language experience, including, for example, first-year students who have had no exposure to the target language, who have had an exploratory class, who have studied another target language, or who are native speakers.

## Key Principles of Differentiated Instruction

There are several key principles to follow when differentiating instruction in the language classroom. First, start by clearly defining what is most essential for students to know, understand, and be able to do in the target language. Second, hold high expectations for all students and make sure that they are engaged in **respectful work**. Third, use **flexible grouping,** an excellent tool to ensure that all students learn to work independently, cooperatively and collaboratively in a variety of settings and with a variety of peers.

A final principle of differentiated instruction is **ongoing assessment**. To this end, the teacher constantly monitors student interest, learning profile, and readiness in order to adjust to the growing and changing learner. Teachers must not assume that a student will have the same readiness or interest in every unit of study or in every skill area. Preassessment is a must, particularly in the areas of knowledge and facility with vocabulary and grammatical constructions.

## The Role of the Teacher in Academically Diverse Classrooms

Good teachers have always recognized that "one size fits all" instruction does not serve students well. To be effective, teachers must find ways consistently to **reach more kinds of learners more often**—by recognizing and responding to students' varied readiness levels, by honoring their diverse interests, and by understanding their preferences for how they learn information and practice new skills.

# Technology and Foreign Language Instruction

**Robert Ponterio,** *Professor of French, SUNY Cortland*

**Jean W. LeLoup,** *Professor of Spanish, SUNY Cortland*

*New technologies make it possible for foreign language teachers to bring the world into their classroom as never before and to make direct connections between their students and the speakers and culture of the target language.*

## From the World to the Classroom

Communication technologies are of prime interest to foreign language professionals because communication is the main thrust in foreign language teaching (Omaggio Hadley, 2001; Phillips, 1998). The present emphasis on *using* language, not just *learning about* language, calls for materials that prepare students for authentic communicative situations and lead them quickly to work with real information in the target language. In addition, the ready access to authentic materials, native speakers, and rich target language input that these new media can provide facilitates the creation of lessons that have tremendous potential in the foreign language classroom for directly addressing many of the goal areas of the national Standards for Foreign Language Learning (Shrum & Glisan, 2000).

## The Standards, Cultural Knowledge, and Multimedia

The Standards stress the importance of cultural knowledge as an integral part of language learning; the tri-part examination of cultural products, practices and the perspectives underlying them is greatly enhanced by using Internet materials that help students better connect with different cultural realities (Standards, 1999). Multimedia— mixing together realia, photos, video, and sounds from the native environment— contributes significantly to creating a culturally and linguistically authentic context for language learning. Multimedia visual materials also offer a window to nonlinguistic cues that are vital to second language comprehension and learning (Binkley, 2003).

## Technology Is a Tool

Technology is a powerful tool when properly integrated in the curriculum (LeLoup & Ponterio, 2003). Computers, audio, and video are an adjunct to language learning objectives and not an end in themselves; they offer many benefits for expanding options in the instructional process. Access to the materials through Internet sites can significantly increase the time spent working with the language as well as the quality of homework activities. Electronic materials are easily updated for continued accuracy and adapted to correspond to current lesson topics and themes. Computer-based exercises that offer immediate feedback to the learner reflect a student-centered approach to language instruction that can help reinforce accuracy in the written language and provide for self-paced learning. For example, the use of hypertext allows an individual to find clarification of meaning or to examine an idea in more depth by connecting to additional materials beyond the text. It puts the power to control this exploration squarely in the student's hands. Current writing tools, both assisted writing environments and word processors, help develop the skills needed for communication in the real world (Scott, 1996). Finally, because of its flexibility and ease of use, technology provides the optimal vehicle for creating authentic assessments, which parallels the use of authentic materials and complements a proficiency-based orientation (Terry, 1998).

### RESEARCH

**Binkley, S. C. (2004).** "Using digital video of native speakers to enhance listening comprehension and cultural competence." In Lomicka, L., & Cooke-Plagwitz, J., Eds. *Teaching with Technology.* Boston, MA: Heinle & Heinle; 115–120.

**LeLoup, J. W. & Ponterio, R. (2003).** *Second Language Acquisition and Technology: A Review of the Research.* ERIC Digest EDO-FL-03-11.

**Omaggio Hadley, A. (2001).** *Teaching language in context.* Boston, MA: Heinle & Heinle.

**Phillips, J. K. (1998).** "Changing teacher/learner roles in Standards-driven contexts." In Harper, J., Lively, M., & Williams, M., Eds. *The coming of age of the profession: Issues and emerging ideas for the teaching of foreign languages.* Boston, MA: Heinle & Heinle; 3–14.

**Scott, V. M. (1996).** *Rethinking foreign language writing.* Boston, MA: Heinle & Heinle.

**Shrum, J. L., & Glisan, E. W. (2000).** *Teacher's Handbook: Contextualized Language Instruction.* Boston, MA: Heinle & Heinle.

*Standards for foreign language learning in the 21st century.* (1999). Lawrence, KS: Allen Press, Inc.

**Terry, R. M. (1998).** Authentic tasks and materials for testing in the foreign language classroom. In Harper, J., Lively, M., & Williams, M., Eds. *The coming of age of the profession: Issues and emerging ideas for the teaching of foreign languages.* Boston, MA: Heinle & Heinle; 277-290.

Nancy Humbach

# Classroom Management

*Successful classes are created by teachers who are motivated, have high expectations, demonstrate enthusiasm for their students and for content, and who maintain organization, flexibility, and the ability to mediate.*

## Managing Your Class Successfully

Managing the classroom so that students stay on task, understand the concepts being taught, and have their needs addressed is one of the most daunting challenges facing a teacher. The beginning of the year is the best time to let students know what you expect of them and what they can expect of you. Inform students what they will need to bring to class and discuss with them required behaviors, such as respect for others. For more effective participation, allow students to brainstorm behaviors that would help them learn.

Present your expectations in writing and on your website, if you have one, keeping rules and regulations simple and clear. State them in positive terms, such as "Come to class with textbook, paper, etc.," instead of "Don't come to class without…"

## Plans and Organization

To keep your class running smoothly, create lesson plans that have a variety of activities, plans for transitions between activities, a varied pace, and attention to time-on-task. Effective lesson plans take into account the ability level of the students. They present a challenge that is within reach of the students but holds their interest, and they include advance organizers, presentations, checks, and evaluations.

Begin class on a positive note by having an activity (some type of advance organizer) on the board, the overhead, or on paper. Such an activity will allow you to take attendance and check homework and still be ready to begin class as the bell rings.

Task-based activities enlist the creativity of students and may be done either alone, in pairs, or in groups. Problem-solving tasks with time limits allow students to be involved actively in learning, as do those that require students to discover solutions or outcomes.

## Pair and Group Work

Group work is important in a language class. If you plan well, train students to work in groups, and have a sound evaluation plan, group work can be rewarding and a highly productive part of the learning process. No matter how you establish your groups, the process of moving into groups must be rapid and cause as little disruption as possible. Systematic monitoring is essential for successful pair and group work, evaluation, and teacher feedback.

## Be Prepared—But Stay Flexible

No two teaching situations are alike. What works for one teacher or one class may not work in all situations. However, motivation, preparation, interest in the students and in the content, and sensible ground rules for such things as pair and group work can help you maintain a successful class.

### RESEARCH


**Cangelosi, James (1997).** *Classroom Management Strategies: Gaining and Maintaining Students' Cooperation.* New York: Addison Wesley Longman. Third Edition.

**Danforth, Scot and Joseph R. Boyle (2000).** *Cases in Behavior Management.* Upper Saddle River: Pearson Education (Merrill Prentice Hall).

**McEwan Landau, Barbara (2004).** *The Art of Classroom Management: Building Equitable Learning Communities.* Pearson Education (Merrill Prentice Hall).

**McEwan, Barbara (2000).** *The Art of Classroom Management: Effective Practices for Buiding Equitable Learning Communities.* Upper Saddle River: Pearson Education (Merrill Prentice Hall).

**Palmer, Parker (1998).** *The Courage to Teach: Exploring the Inner Landscape of a Teacher's Life.* San Francisco: Jossey-Bass Publishers.

**Schmuck, Richard A. and Patricia A. Schmuck (2001).** *Group Processes in the Classroom.* Boston: McGraw Hill. Eighth Edition.

**Shrum, Judith and Eileen Glisan.** *Teachers' Handbook: Contextualized Language Instruction.* Boston: Heinle and Heinle. Any edition.

# Game Bank

## ¡Ponga!

*This game, played much like Bingo, lets students practice numbers, colors, body parts, clothing, or other objects in Spanish.*

**Materials** Index cards (or paper) and markers

**Procedure** Students prepare their own Ponga card by drawing a card similar to a Bingo card with four horizontal and vertical spaces. Students write a number, color a square a certain color, or draw a body part, piece of clothing, or other object in each space. Read a number or one of the other themed vocabulary words in Spanish and record it. Students cover or cross off the spaces as the items in them are called until a player has filled an entire row or column. He or she then says **¡Ponga!** The student who reads the vocabulary back correctly wins. You may laminate the cards for later use with water-based markers, or use paper scraps to cover the numbers.

## Cerebro

*This game, played like Concentration®, helps students learn and review through concentration and recall. This game can be used to reinforce vocabulary, questions and answers, and verbs.*

**Materials** Index cards

**Procedure** Have students make three pairs of cards. On a card have them write a question, a verb, or a vocabulary word. On the card's mate, the student writes the answer to the question, draws the action of the verb, or draws the vocabulary item. Divide the class into pairs or small groups. Have one student combine and shuffle all the group's cards together and then lay them out in a grid on the desk, blank side up. Players take turns turning over two cards each. If they match, the player takes them. If they don't, they are returned, face down, to their original place. Play continues until all the cards are paired. The player with the most matches wins.

## Categorías

*This game is patterned after the game Scattergories®. It should be played in teams and is good for reinforcing vocabulary from various categories.*

**Materials** A timer, index cards, and pencils and paper for scoring

**Procedure** Make index cards with the letters of the alphabet on them. Write a list of three categories on the board that the class has learned: classes, school supplies, names, descriptive adjectives or other themed vocabulary. Have teams prepare a paper with three columns, one for each category. One team chooses a letter from the stack of index cards and calls out the letter to be used in this round. The timer is set for one minute and the round begins. For each category, teams quickly fill in the answer sheet with vocabulary words that begin with the key letter. When the timer rings, students must stop writing. Have one team read its answers. If any other team has that word, everyone crosses it off their list. The next team reads any words remaining on their lists, and again any duplicates are crossed off all lists. Repeat this process for the remaining teams. The winning team is the one with the highest number of unique, unduplicated words.

## Arreglar palabras

*Similar to Scrabble®, this game is excellent for review of all learned vocabulary and verbs.*

**Materials** Heavy paper or card stock.

**Procedure** Cut the paper into one-inch squares. Leave a third of them blank and write the Spanish alphabet on the rest. Make extra squares with the most common letters: vowels, s, t, etc. A blank may serve as any letter. Place the letters face down in one pile and the blanks in another pile. Each student picks ten letters and five blanks. Using learned vocabulary, students arrange letters and blanks to form as many words as possible on their desk. The student with the most words, and the student with the longest word, are the winners. This game may be played in pairs with students taking turns and building their words off of the already played words on the desk.

## Mímica

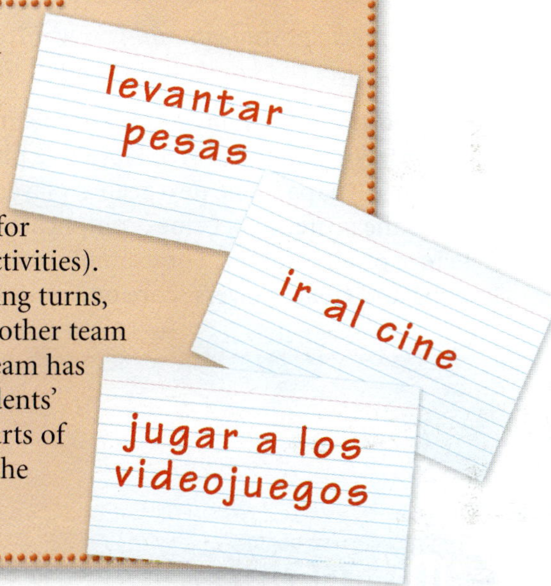


*Played like charades, this game reviews active verbs. It is an excellent activity for kinesthetic learners.*

**Materials** Index cards

**Procedure** Write action verbs or phrases from chapter themes on index cards, (things you like to do, school activities, preparing for a party, preparing and serving food, staying healthy, or vacation activities). Divide the class into teams and give one card to each student. Taking turns, students act out their word or phrase without speaking, while the other team guesses in Spanish. You may consider limiting the time that each team has to guess. As a challenge, have the teams combine a number of students' cards to created sentences, assigning nouns and other necessary parts of speech to individuals. The team acts out its string of words while the other team tries to figure out the sentence that is being presented.

## La papa caliente

*This exciting game quickly practices vocabulary and phrases while getting the entire class involved.*

**Materials** A small box, a wind up timer or battery operated alarm clock

**Procedure** Make a **papa caliente** by placing an alarm clock or a timer in a small box. Be sure the alarm or timer ticks loudly. Have students sit in a circle. Call out a category based on a vocabulary category, (**frutas, comida del desayuno,** etc.). As you name the category hand the **papa** to a student who must then say a related vocabulary word. After saying a word, that student then passes the **papa** to the student to the right, who is to name a different item from the category. If a student is left holding the **papa** when the timer goes off, they are out of the game. You decide when a category has been exhausted and change it accordingly. The winner is the last student remaining who could think of new vocabulary, and pass the **papa** on with out getting caught by the buzzer.

## Palabras revueltas

*This game is good for tactile learners. The goal is for students to construct Spanish vocabulary words from scrambled letters.*

**Materials** Small squares of paper for each student

**Procedure** Divide the class into two teams. Each person on the team finds a different Spanish vocabulary word from the chapter and writes each letter of that word on one of the pieces of paper. After everyone is finished, team members exchange their letters with a person on the other team. Students quickly try to arrange the letters to form the word. The student who unscrambles a word before his or her counterpart wins a point for his or her team.

## Una palabra más

*This game helps students build on words and ideas to make complete sentences. The sentences can be odd or funny, but they should be grammatically correct.*

**Procedure** Create any number of teams. Begin a sentence on the board with a word. For example, (**Mi**). Have one player write a word to continue the sentence, (**papá**). The next team's player writes another word, (**tiene**). Once the sentence becomes complicated, students may add words before or after others. For example, **inteligente** could go between **papá** and **tiene**. Players score one point for each logical contribution.

## ¡Dibújalo!

*This game provides a thorough review of nouns, verbs, and adjectives and creates team spirit within the class.*

**Materials** Index cards and colored markers

**Procedure** Divide the class into five equal groups of students. Each group selects 10 vocabulary items from a chapter or various chapters already learned and writes one vocabulary word on each card. A more challenging version can be played with phrases or short sentences. Combine all cards from each group and shuffle. Divide the class into two teams. You will need one scorekeeper and one timekeeper. Give the first team a card with the Spanish word written on it. That team member goes to the board and must illustrate the word within 15 seconds. The next three people in line from that person's team are allowed one guess each. If one of the three people guesses correctly, the team scores a point. If they cannot guess, the question goes to the next person on the other team. The other team is allowed only one guess. If the student shown the card does not know what the Spanish word means, the team defaults its turn, and the opportunity to play the word goes to the other team. *¡Dibújalo!* can be played by the whole class, or a small group for vocabulary review.

## De sílabas a palabras

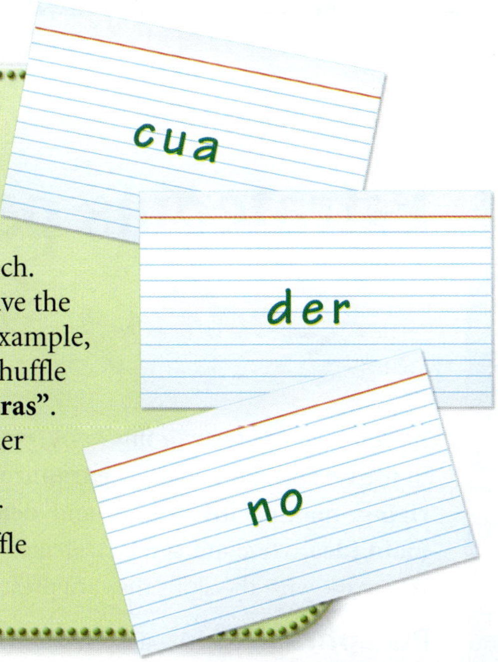


*This game provides an opportunity to practice pronunciation and can be used to review vocabulary from any chapter.*

**Materials** Index cards and pens or markers

**Procedure** Review the definition of a syllable as a short unit of speech. Break up the vocabulary words from the chapter into syllables and have the students write each syllable on an index card using large letters. For example, make three cards for **cua** – **der** – **no,** two cards for **com** – **prar,** etc. Shuffle the cards and pass them out among students. Say **"De sílabas a palabras"**. Give the students a specific amount of time (one minute), to find other people with whom they can form a word. Tell students to call out **"¡Palabra!"** when they have formed a word. The group must say their word in unison as you point to them. Collect all the index cards, shuffle them, and redistribute to play again.

## Béisbol con palabras

*With this game students will practice the new vocabulary words and expressions and review previously learned vocabulary.*

**Preparation** Develop a list of questions whose answers require the students to use words and phrases from the current and previous chapters. (Examples: **Para evitar el estrés yo practico _______. Para tener músculos grandes hay que levantar ______. Debes dormir para no estar _______. Antes de hacer ejercicio hay que _______.**)

**Procedure** Divide the class into two teams. Assign a student scorekeeper. Draw a baseball diamond with bases on the board. Set a number of innings for playing. The batter is the first player on Team A. You serve as the pitcher and ask the batter a question. If the batter gives a correct answer, he or she moves to first base. The scorekeeper places a mark on first base. If the batter cannot answer, he or she is out. You then ask a question of the second batter on Team A. If the second batter answers correctly, he or she goes to first base. If there is a player on first base, he or she advances to second base and the scorekeeper places a mark on second base. A team scores a run by advancing a player to home plate. Team A continues batting until it has three outs. Then Team B goes to bat. When Team B has three outs, the first inning is over. Teams get one point for each run, and the team with the most points wins.

## Cadena

*This game, which helps students review vocabulary, is good for auditory learners.*

**Procedure** Have all students stand up. Announce a vocabulary theme, (school classes, clothing, housing items, etc.). Say a sentence with one word from the theme. For example, **En el colegio estudio matemáticas**. The first student then repeats the sentence saying what you said and adding another word that follows the theme, (**En el colegio estudio matemáticas y español**). When someone says the "chain" incorrectly, he or she sits down. This sequence continues until no one can add any more words to the sentence. At this time you might select another theme. The winners are the last three students to be left standing.

# Estrategias para leer

## Reading Strategies

As you read the texts in this book, you will be asked to use certain skills, such as **paraphrasing, summarizing, making inferences,** and **determining the main idea.** Here are some strategies that may help you work with the skills that are presented.

**Paraphrasing** A paraphrase is a summary in which the author's ideas are restated in the reader's own words. Paraphrasing is a good way to check your understanding; if you can state someone else's ideas in your own words, then you have understood what you read.

**Summarizing** is similar to paraphrasing. While paraphrasing is retelling a story in your own words, summarizing is retelling the most important information or details of a text.

After you have read a story, for example, practice retelling it to a partner. Before you retell it, make a checklist of the things to include in the retelling, such as title, setting, main characters and their relationship to each other, main events, conflict, and resolution of the conflict.

**Making inferences** As readers, we make inferences when we combine information in the text with what we already know in order to understand things the writer has not stated directly. Understanding a text or story well enough to be able to make such connections can be a matter of reading the text several times, focusing each time on what you didn't understand with the previous reading. Here are some steps that may help.

1. Read the text one time through, rate your understanding on a scale of 1–10, and write down any questions you have. Discuss your questions with a partner and see if he or she understood some things that you did not.
2. Read the text again, rate your understanding, and see if you find the answers to some of your questions.

3. If you still have questions, read the text a third time, rate your understanding, and discuss any remaining questions with your partner.

**Determining the main idea** The main idea is what the writer wants readers to remember about the topic—the message, opinion, insight, or lesson that is the focus or key idea of the text. Sometimes the main idea is directly stated; at other times, it is implied.

One way to figure out the main idea is to break the reading into small chunks, and then decide what one word conveys the message of that chunk. Discuss your decisions with a partner or small group. Your group may come to a consensus about what the most important word is.

Finding the most important word in each of the passages, and putting all of these words together, will help you figure out the most important word, and thought, of the entire passage.

There are many other strategies that will help you develop the skills you need to become a good reader. As a general rule, re-reading a text and breaking it down into smaller pieces will make it easier to use these skills.

Estrategias para leer

# Sugerencias para continuar tus estudios

## Tips for studying Spanish

Do you remember everything you learned last year? It's easy to forget your Spanish when you don't use it for a while. Here are some tips to help you in Spanish class this year.

### ¡Escucha!

When someone else is speaking, ask yourself what that person is saying. Listen for specific words or phrases that either support or do not support your guess. If you don't hear or understand a word, don't panic or give up. Try to figure out its meaning from the sentences that follow it.

### ¡Habla!

Have you ever tried to say something in English, but then you forgot a certain word? Chances are you did not let that stop you. You simply thought of another way of saying the same thing. Use that same trick when speaking Spanish.

With a classmate, practice short conversations on topics you learned about last year. If you can't remember how to say something in Spanish, look in the glossary or ask someone, **"¿Cómo se dice...?"** You can also try using words you do know or gestures to explain what you mean.

### ¡Lee!

Sometimes you might feel anxious when you read in Spanish, because understanding the entire text seems to be an overwhelming task. One easy way to reduce this anxiety is to break the reading up into parts. With the reading divided into small sections, you can focus all your attention on one section at a time.

If you look up specific words or phrases in an English-Spanish dictionary, be careful about choosing the meaning. Many words can have several different meanings in English or in Spanish. Be sure to look closely at the context, if one is given, before choosing a word.

### ¡Escribe!

Before you begin writing, organize your ideas. Write a sentence that states the main ideas. Then choose the details that support them. List them in an order that makes sense to you. After you have listed all of your ideas, you can write about the ones that appeal to you most.

One way to make the task of writing easier is to make sure you know most of the words you will need to use. With a classmate, make a list of the words you will probably need to complete your task. Then look up the words you don't know in the dictionary. Look at the charts in the back of this book to refresh your memory on important grammar points.

Learning a foreign language is like any other long-term project, such as getting into shape or taking up a new sport: it will take some time to see the results you want. Remember, knowing another language is a valuable asset, and you've already come a long way. Keep up your Spanish and . . . **¡Exprésate!**

**Resources**

**Planning:**
Lesson Planner, p. xv
One-Stop Planner

**Presentation:**
Teaching Transparencies **Mapa 1**
Video Program, Videocassette 1
DVD Program, Disc 1
**GeoVisión**

**Practice:**
Video Guide, pp. 1–2
Lab Book, pp. 1, 55
Interactive Tutor, Disc 1

**VIDEO OPTIONS**
- **VideoCultura**
- **VideoNovela**
- **Variedades**
- **GramaVisión**

**Pre-AP Practice**

**AP Benchmark:** Recognize cultural elements implicit in oral and written texts.
**Focus:** Cultural Practice (**historia**)
- SE, p. 3, **1936–1939**
- TE, p. 3, **La historia,** History Link
- TE, p. 4, Connections: Thinking Critically

GeoVisión

**Capítulos 1 y 2**

# Geocultura Castilla-La Mancha

▲ **La ciudad de Toledo** está ubicada en un precipicio a orillas del río Tajo. La ciudad es testigo de la rica historia de una región en la que los cristianos, musulmanes y judíos se han entremezclado, dejando cada uno sus huellas.

Talavera de la Reina
Montes

▼ **Las extensas llanuras de Castilla-La Mancha** son el escenario perfecto para los molinos de viento en uso desde el siglo XVI, en los tiempos de Miguel de Cervantes. En su obra *El ingenioso hidalgo don Quijote de la Mancha,* el héroe, don Quijote, ataca a los molinos, confundiéndolos con gigantes. El castillo es de origen musulmán.

## Almanaque

**Provincias de la comunidad autónoma**
Guadalajara, Toledo, Cuenca, Ciudad Real, Albacete

**Idioma** castellano

**Industrias importantes**
turismo, agricultura, ganadería

**Nota de interés**
Durante mucho tiempo el azafrán valió su peso en oro. Hoy sigue siendo la especia más cara del mundo.

**¿Sabías que...?**
**Toledo, la capital de Castilla-La Mancha, también fue la capital de España hasta 1561.**

## Background Information

### History

The region of Castilla-La Mancha has been witness to repeated invading forces and occupations. The Romans were the first organized occupants of this region, building cities and imposing their language and laws. The Romans were followed by the Visigoths, a Germanic tribe also known as the West Goths. Berbers and Arabs, later known as Moors, invaded later and occupied Spain from the eighth century until 1492, when the last Muslim stronghold of Granada was taken.

### Geography

**Castilla-La Mancha** is an autonomous region in Spain located to the south and east of Madrid. Castilla-La Mancha is divided into five provinces and Toledo is the capital.

**Las llanuras** are dry, extensive flatlands located in the heart of the region which cover parts of Cuenca, Toledo, Ciudad Real, and Albacete.

The largest mountain ranges in the region are the **Montes de Toledo** in the east, and the **Serranía de Cuenca** in the west.

# Castilla-La Mancha

▲ **El azafrán,** uno de los importantes productos agrícolas de Castilla-La Mancha, viene de una pequeña flor de color lila. Para obtener un kilo de azafrán hay que recoger a mano los estigmas de casi 85.000 flores.

▲ **El Parque Nacional de las Tablas de Daimiel,** en la provincia de Ciudad Real, acoge una cantidad enorme de aves acuáticas.

▲ **Las Casas Colgadas,** en la ciudad de Cuenca, fueron construidas al borde de un precipicio. Durante el siglo XIV servían de lugar de veraneo para la Familia Real.

◀ **El Centro Astronómico de Yebes,** en la provincia de Guadalajara, es una de las diez instituciones más grandes de investigación científica en España.

## Atlas INTERACTIVO MUNDIAL

Have students use the interactive atlas at **go.hrw.com**.

### Map Activities

1. Have students look at the map of Spain and locate the five provinces in Castilla-La Mancha. **(Guadalajara, Cuenca, Albacete, Ciudad Real, Toledo)**
2. Have students locate and name the river that runs through Toledo. **(Río Tajo)**
3. Ask students to locate the highest mountain in Castilla-La Mancha. **(Calderina, 1.208m.)**
4. Ask students to name the two largest bodies of water in the region. **(Embalse de Buendía, Embalse de Alarcón)**

3.1

## Language Note

The official language of Spain is **castellano,** which is commonly known as modern Spanish. It was once a dialect spoken in Cantabria. Different languages are spoken in other regions of Spain. The most common languages are **euskera, catalán,** and **gallego.** The modern Spanish language as well as the dialects spoken in Spain have had Arabic influence. It is estimated that roughly 4,000 words in modern Spanish have Arabic roots. For example, **almohada** and **ojalá** come directly from Arabic, but have undergone spelling changes. English has also adopted Arabic words such as alcohol, algebra, adobe, and sugar. Have students research other ways that the Arabic language has influenced the languages of the world.

## ¿Sabías que... ?

Students might be interested in knowing the following facts about Castilla-La Mancha.

- Castilla-La Mancha is the third-largest region in Spain and covers 80,000 square kilometers.
- The province of Madrid was once part of Castilla-La Mancha.
- Albacete became part of Castilla-La Mancha in 1978. Albacete had originally been part of Murcia.
- Castilla-La Mancha has a population of nearly 1,800,000.

## Preguntas 1.2, 3.1

1. **¿Desde cuándo se han utilizado los molinos de viento? (Desde el siglo XVI)**
2. **¿Cuántas flores se necesitan para obtener un kilo de azafrán? (85.000 flores)**
3. **¿En qué provincia está el Parque Nacional de las Tablas de Daimiel? (En la provincia de Ciudad Real)**
4. **¿Para qué servían las casas colgadas durante el siglo XIV? (Como lugar de veraneo de la Familia Real)**
5. **¿Qué es el Centro Astronómico de Yebes? (Un centro de investigación)**

# *La historia* de Castilla-La Mancha

100 | 200 | 300 | 400 | 500 | 600 | 700 | 800 | 900 | 1000

### Cultures

**Practices and Perspectives**

Castilla-La Mancha has a strong agricultural economy. A wide variety of crops such as wheat, oats, saffron, olives, grapes, garlic, and potatoes are grown in this region. Castilla-La Mancha is also well known for its **manchego** sheep cheese, and is a producer of wine. About 2.8 million pounds of grapes per year are produced in the region. Have students research some other crops in this region. How long have the crops been planted in the region? Why are they important? What is the benefit of planting a wide variety of crops? 2.1, 2.2

### Answers

**Siglos II a.C.–III d.C.:** Madrid, Sagunto, Tarragona, Segovia, Valeria, entre otros
**Siglos V–VIII:** Los visigodos dominaron España por tres siglos.
**Siglos VIII–XI:** Se muestran las influencias en la arquitectura, el idioma, las costumbres culturales.
**1085:** Answers will vary.
**1561:** Answers will vary.
**1808–1814:** Era importante porque fue una de las primeras victorias de las fuerzas aliadas contra Napoleón.
**1936–1939:** Franco mantuvo el poder por 35 años.
**1982–presente:** La ejecutiva, la legislativa, la jurídica

**Siglos II a.C.–III d.C.** 3.1
**La ciudad romana de Segóbriga** sirve como testigo de la ocupación romana en España. Las ruinas de un anfiteatro y baños públicos atraen a cantidades de turistas a este pequeño pueblo cada año. **Investiga qué otros sitios en España tienen ruinas romanas.**

**Siglos V–VIII**
**La tribu germánica de los visigodos** invadió la península y nombró Toledo su capital. *La Corona de Recesvinto* es uno de los tesoros que queda de los tiempos de ocupación visigoda en España. **¿Cuánto tiempo dominaron España los visigodos?** 3.1

**Siglos VIII–XI** 2.2, 3.1
**Los musulmanes** expulsaron a los visigodos y ocuparon el terreno de Castilla-La Mancha durante cuatro siglos. Construyeron mezquitas elaboradas y fundaron **escuelas superiores** de matemáticas y lenguas. Hoy día usamos el sistema numérico árabe. **Investiga qué otras influencias dejaron los árabes en España.**

3.1 **1085**
**Alfonso VI «el Bravo»** (antes de 1040–1109) encabezó la reconquista cristiana de España contra los musulmanes, capturando Toledo en 1085. Su vasallo Rodrigo Díaz de Vivar, «el Cid», capturó Valencia en 1094. **En tu opinion, ¿por qué se llamó «el Bravo»?**

### Core Instruction

**TEACHING LA HISTORIA**

1. Point out that this region has a well-recorded history from the first century. Have students look at the dates covered in the timeline. **(2 min.)**
2. Mention that Spain's early-recorded history begins with occupations by other cultures. Spain was occupied by three different groups, beginning in the first and ending in the fifteenth century. **(3 min.)**
3. Have students read captions individually or as a group. Help students with any unfamiliar vocabulary. **(8 min.)**
4. Call on volunteers to read the questions at the end of each caption to the class. **(5 min.)**
5. Have students answer the questions for each caption as a class. Help students as needed. **(10 min.)**

**¿Sabías que...?**
José Bonaparte, el hermano de Napoleón, fue el rey de España durante la ocupación francesa.

Visit Holt Online
go.hrw.com
KEYWORD: EXP3 CH1
Photo Tour

1100 1200 1300 1400 1500 1600 1700 1800 1900 2000

**3.1 1561**
**Felipe II** (1527–1598) trasladó la capital de España de Toledo a Madrid en 1561. Debido a esto y a la inflación causada por la abundancia de oro traído desde las Américas, Toledo dejó de ser un centro intelectual y artístico para convertirse en provincia agrícola. **¿Conoces una región en Estados Unidos que se transformó drásticamente como Toledo?**

**3.1 1808–1814**
**La Guerra de la Independencia**
Napoleón Bonaparte controló la mayoría de Europa, incluyendo España, Italia, Alemania y Austria, entre 1804 y 1814. **La Batalla de Talavera,** en La Mancha, constituyó una de las primeras victorias de las fuerzas españolas aliadas con las de Gran Bretaña contra Napoleón. **¿Por qué fue importante para España la Batalla de Talavera?**

**3.1 1936–1939**
**El Alcázar de Toledo** fue el lugar de una batalla clave en la **Guerra Civil de España** en 1936. El General Francisco Franco marchó a Madrid después de la victoria de sus tropas nacionalistas en Toledo. **¿Cuánto tiempo estuvo en el poder el dictador Franco?**

**3.1 1982–presente**
**Castilla-La Mancha** se convirtió en región autónoma en 1982. Las Cortes de Castilla-La Mancha, con sede en este monasterio, tienen función legislativa. Las Cortes, el Presidente de la Junta y el Consejo de Gobierno forman las **tres ramas administrativas** del gobierno de Castilla-La Mancha. **¿Cuáles son las ramas administrativas de tu estado?**

## Teaching Suggestion

La **Ciudad Encantada** is a memorable place in Cuenca for tourists to visit. It is a complex of rock formations that have been shaped over thousands of years of erosion. On a tour of the **Ciudad Encantada,** the traveler will see rock formations that look like people, monuments, and buildings. Ask students if they know of a place like **Ciudad Encantada** in their communities. What is the legend or history behind it that makes it attractive to tourists?

## ¿Comprendes?

You can use the following questions to check students' comprehension of the **Geocultura.**

1. **¿Dónde hay ruinas romanas? (Segóbriga)**
2. **¿Qué construyeron los musulmanes en Castilla-La Mancha? (mezquitas y escuelas superiores)**
3. **¿Qué ciudad fue la capital de los visigodos? (Toledo)**
4. **¿Qué logró Alfonso VI en 1085? (la captura de Toledo)**
5. **¿Cuál ha sido la capital de España después de 1561? (Madrid)**
6. **¿Qué hicieron las tropas de Franco desde la victoria en Toledo? (Marcharon a Madrid.)**
7. **¿Cuáles son las ramas administrativas de Castilla-La Mancha? (Las cortes, el Presidente de la Junta, el Consejo del Gobierno)** 1.2, 3.1

## Interdisciplinary Links

### La historia 4.2

**History Link** The **Alcázar de Toledo** witnessed the victory of Francisco Franco and his troops in a key battle of the Spanish civil war, which claimed the lives of more than 350,000 people in its fierce battles. Franco's victory marked the beginning of his 35-year dictatorship in Spain. Franco ruled until 1975, when he picked his successor. The first democratic elections were held in 1977, and a new constitution was drafted in 1978. Have students compare Spain's current form of government with the U.S. government. How is Spain's government different?

### Las matemáticas

**Math Link** The Moors had great influence on Spanish culture during their occupation of Spain. They were the first to build institutions of higher learning in the country. Among other contributions in math, science, art, and architecture was the concept of zero in mathematics and the number system. Have students research the concept of zero and its introduction in Europe. Challenge students to find another culture that developed this same concept independently.

# El arte de Castilla-La Mancha

100 a.C. | 1200 | 1300 | 1400

**Siglo I a.C.** 4.2

**Los romanos** reconocieron la alta calidad de la elaboración del acero en Toledo y llevaron su fama a Roma. La belleza y calidad de las **espadas y puñales de Toledo** tienen fama mundial. **¿Hay alguna artesanía famosa en tu región o comunidad?**

3.1
**1226–1493**

La construcción de la **Catedral de Toledo** duró de 1226 hasta 1493. Por eso el monumento refleja varios estilos de arquitectura. El exterior es un ejemplo de arquitectura gótica francesa, mientras los estilos mudéjar y barroco decoran la mayoría de su interior. **¿Por qué crees que tardaron tanto en construir la catedral?**

3.1 **Siglo XIV**

En **la Sinagoga del Tránsito** los arcos y los diseños geométricos son típicos del arte mudéjar. **Mudéjar** se refiere a los árabes que permanecieron en España después de la reconquista y su arte es preponderante en muchos edificios en Castilla-La Mancha. **¿Quién hizo el arte mudéjar?**

2.2
**Siglo XV–presente**

El arte del **damasquinado** es el arte de origen árabe de incrustar hilo de oro, plata o cobre sobre acero. Los platos, broches, pulseras y anillos damasquinados de Toledo son famosos por todo el mundo. **¿Qué materiales se usan para este arte?**

3.1 **Siglo XV**

**El Castillo de Belmonte** fue construido en el siglo XV. Es uno de los castillos mejor preservados de la región. Es principalmente gótico en estilo, con arte mudéjar y renacentista. **Investiga en Internet quién construyó el castillo.**

## Connections

### Thinking Critically

In 1977, soon after the end of the Franco dictatorship, Spanish lawmakers wrote a new constitution. Since then, the country has enjoyed relative political stability. Spain joined the European Union in 1986 and has benefited from commercial ties with member states. Spain elected José María Aznar as president in 1996 and again in 2000. Aznar's monetary policies were able to sustain the growth of Spain's economy at nearly 4 percent per year. Despite the continued growth, in March of 2004 José Luis Rodríguez Zapatero was elected president, rejecting Aznar's hand-picked successor. Spain stopped using the peseta in January of 2002 and switched to the euro. Ask students to use Spanish resources to research the economic effects of Spain joining the European union and using the euro. 3.1

## Answers

**Siglo I:** Answers will vary.
**1226–1493:** Por las guerras de la reconquista española
**Siglo XIV:** Los árabes que permanecieron en España después de la reconquista
**Siglo XV–presente:** Acero, oro, plata, cobre
**Siglo XV:** Don Juan Pacheco, el primer marqués de Villena, construyó el castillo.
**Siglo XVI–presente:** Answers will vary.
**1597:** El Greco vino de Grecia.
**1620:** Answers will vary.
**Siglo XVIII:** Answers will vary.

## Core Instruction

### TEACHING EL ARTE

1. Have students compare the types of architecture pictured. Ask students how each building is different. **(3 min.)**
2. Have students look at the **damasquinado** and the **Talavera** works. Ask students which style is older. **(2 min.)**
3. Have students compare the El Greco painting with his student's painting. Call on volunteers to point out similarities. **(5 min.)**
4. Have students look at each piece of artwork while volunteers read the captions. **(5 min.)**
5. Call on volunteers to read the caption questions and as a class have students answer the questions. **(10 min.)**

# Castilla-La Mancha

### ¿Sabías que...?

Hasta hoy día algunos países usan las espadas de Toledo en sus uniformes militares.

Visit Holt Online
**go.hrw.com**
KEYWORD: EXP3 CH1
Photo Tour

1600 · 1700 · 1800

2.2
**Siglo XVI–presente**
**La cerámica y los azulejos de Talavera** han decorado las casas ilustres de la región. **¿Crees que la cerámica fue fabricada para usar o para decorar?**

**Siglo XVIII** 3.1
**El altar de la Catedral de Toledo** fue elaborado entre 1721 y 1732. Es un buen ejemplo del estilo barroco del siglo XVIII, el cual se caracteriza por líneas onduladas y el contraste entre la luz y la oscuridad. **¿Por qué crees que muchas obras de arte tienen motivo religioso?**

**1620** 1.3
Un discípulo de El Greco, **Luis Tristán** (1586–1624) sigue las tradiciones de la Escuela de Arte de Toledo. En *Adoración de Los Reyes Magos* (1620) su uso predominante del claroscuro refleja la influencia de su maestro. **¿Te gustaría ser discípulo de un artista? ¿Con quién te gustaría estudiar?**

**1597** 3.1
**El Greco,** Domenikos Theotocopoulos (1541–1614), llegó a Toledo en 1577. Se enamoró de la ciudad y se quedó en Toledo hasta su muerte en 1614. Es considerado el primer genio de la escuela española de pintura. *Vista de Toledo* (1597) demuestra colores intensos y contrastes dramáticos de luz. **¿De qué país vino El Greco?**

## History Link

Castilla-La Mancha hosts evidence of pre-historic inhabitants. **El Parque Cultural de Arte Rupestre** in Cuenca has more than 200 figures depicting pre-historic hunters, fauna, and animals. **La Cueva de los Casares** in Guadalajara has over 100 figures painted on its walls. They depict large game animals and pre historic hunters. **La cueva de la Vieja** and **La cueva del Queso** in Albacete show how pre-historic hunters lived in the Castilla-La Mancha region. Have students find pictures from these sites on the Internet. Why do they think pre-historic hunters painted these figures, and what do the figures tell us about them?

## ¿Comprendes?

Use the following questions to check students' comprehension.

1. **¿Quiénes apreciaron la calidad de las espadas de Toledo? (los romanos)**
2. **¿Qué estilos se pueden ver en la Catedral de Toledo? (gótico francés, mudéjar, barroco)**
3. **¿Cuál es el origen del arte damasquinado? (árabe)**
4. **¿Cuál es el estilo principal del Castillo de Belmonte? (gótico)**
5. **¿En qué año llegó El Greco a Toledo? (en 1577)**
6. **Nombra una característica del arte barroco del siglo XVIII. (líneas onduladas)** 1.2, 3.1

## Interdisciplinary Links

### El arte

**Art Link** The city of Toledo was once an artistic and cultural center in Spain. Toledo-based artist El Greco is now world-famous. The Toledo school of art instructed painters in the baroque style, which was popular in the late sixteenth century. Ask students to find information on the art and culture of Toledo today. Which city is currently the center of artistic expression and trends in Spain? 2.2, 3.1

### La historia

**History link** The Toledo sword-making tradition began in the fifth century B.C. when Iberian blacksmiths made the **falcata,** an early version of the sword. The Roman legions as well as the Christian armies of the **reconquista** used Toledo swords, which are still made today with nearly the same techniques used over 1,000 years ago. Ask students to relate this practice to **damasquinado** art. Have them find pictures of and information on how **damasquinado** art is made. 2.1, 2.2

## Assess

**Assessment Program**
**Prueba: Geocultura,** pp. 15–16, 35–36

**Online Assessment**
**my.hrw.com**

**Test Generator**

**Assess** **Differentiated Assessment** See the Differentiated Assessment CD-ROM.

Capítulo 1

# Planning Guide

## ¡Adiós al verano!

| Chapter Section | | Print Resources |
|---|---|---|
| **Geocultura**<br>• **Castilla-La Mancha** | pp. T72–5 | Video Guide, pp. 1–2/Lab Book, p. 55 |
| **Vocabulario 1**<br>• This past summer . . . | pp. 8–13 | Vocabulario 1.1, 1.2; Bell Work 1.1, 1.2, 1.3, 1.4<br>Cuaderno de vocabulario y gramática, pp. 1–6<br>Cuaderno de actividades, pp. 1–3<br>Activities for Communication, pp. 1–2<br>Grammar Tutor for Students of Spanish, pp. 113–114 |
| **Gramática 1**<br>• Repaso: Preterite and imperfect<br>• **Ser** and **estar**<br>• Repaso: Subjunctive Mood | pp. 14–19 | |
| **Cultura: Comparaciones** | p. 20 | Video Guide, pp. 4, 5/Lab Book, p. 56 |
| **Cultura: Comunidad** | p. 21 | |
| **Vocabulario 2**<br>• Some advice | pp. 22–27 | Vocabulario 1.3, 1.4; Bell Work 1.5, 1.6, 1.7, 1.8<br>Cuaderno de vocabulario y gramática, pp. 7–12<br>Cuaderno de actividades, pp. 5–7<br>Activities for Communication, pp. 3–4<br>Grammar Tutor for Students of Spanish, pp. 115–120 |
| **Gramática 2**<br>• Repaso: Pronouns<br>• Repaso: Comparisons, demonstrative adjectives and pronouns<br>• Negative words and time constructions | pp. 28–33 | |
| **Novela en video** | pp. 34–35 | Cuaderno de actividades, p. 8<br>Reading Strategies and Skills Handbook<br>Interactive Advanced Reader<br>Video Guide, pp. 6–8/Lab Book, pp. 57–58 |
| **Lectura informativa**<br>• **Una visita a Castilla-La Mancha** | pp. 36–37 | |
| **Leamos**<br>• **El árbol de oro** | pp. 38–40 | |
| **Escribamos**<br>• **El punto de vista** | p. 41 | |
| **Prepárate para el examen**<br>• **Repaso de vocabulario y gramática** | pp. 42–45 | Picture Sequences, Situación, Ch. 1<br>Activities for Communication, pp. 43, 55–56 |
| **Integración**<br>• **Repaso cumulativo** | pp. 46–47 | Fine Art, Ch. 1<br>Cuaderno de actividades, pp. 9–10<br>Reading Strategies and Skills Handbook<br>Interactive Advanced Reader |

Planning Guide

Visit Holt Online
**go.hrw.com**
KEYWORD: EXP3 CH1
Online Edition

For correlations to national standards, see point-of-use references throughout the chapter.

## Pacing Suggestions

| | Essential | Recommended | Optional |
|---|---|---|---|
| **Vocabulario 1**<br>• This past summer . . .<br>• **Nota cultural** | ✔ | | |
| **Gramática 1**<br>• Repaso: Preterite and imperfect<br>• **Ser** and **estar**<br>• Repaso: Subjunctive Mood<br>• **Nota cultural** | ✔ | | |
| **Cultura: Comparaciones** | | ✔ | |
| **Cultura: Comunidad** | | | ✔ |
| **Vocabulario 2**<br>• Some advice<br>• **Nota cultural** | ✔ | | |
| **Gramática 2**<br>• Repaso: Pronouns<br>• Repaso: Comparisons, demonstrative adjectives and pronouns<br>• Negative words and time constructions<br>• **Nota cultural** | ✔ | | |
| **Novela en video**<br>• Episodio 1: **Clara perspectiva** | | ✔ | |
| **Lectura informativa**<br>• **Una visita a Castilla-La Mancha** | | | ✔ |
| **Leamos**<br>• **El árbol de oro**<br>**Escribamos**<br>• **El punto de vista** | | ✔ | |
| **Prepárate para el examen** | | ✔ | |
| **Integración** | | | ✔ |

## Technology Resources

### ¡Exprésate! Online
- Student Edition with multi-media
- SoundBooth recording tool
- Interactive activities with feedback
- Self-tests with feedback
- Cuaderno de actividades (interactive workbook)
- Cuaderno de vocabulario y gramática (interactive workbook)
- Live Ink™ Reading Help
- Holt Online Assessment

### DVD Tutor, Disc 1
- GeoVisión
- GramaVisión
- VideoNovela
- Cultura
- Variedades

### Interactive Tutor
- Interactive practice games
- Writing and recording workshops

### Audio Program
- Textbook listening activities
- Assessment listening activities
- Songs

### One-Stop Planner
- Complete media and print resources
- ExamView® Pro Test Generator
- Holt Calendar Planner

### PuzzlePro
- Customizable word games

## Assessment

**Geocultura**
**Vocabulario 1 / Gramática 1**
**Vocabulario 2 / Gramática 2**
**Leamos**
**Escribamos**
**Prepárate para el examen**

### Assessment Program

**Prueba: Geocultura,** pp. 15–16
**Pruebas,** pp. 1–2, 3–4, 5–6
**Pruebas,** pp. 7–8, 9–10, 11–12
**Prueba,** p. 13
**Prueba,** p. 14
**Examen: Capítulo 1,** pp. 205–212
**Examen oral: Capítulo 1,** p. 216
**Alternative Assessment,** pp. 373, 385, 397

### Online Assessment

**my.hrw.com**

### Test Generator

**ExamView® Pro Test Generator**

# Projects

## ¡Adiós al verano!

### Actividades del verano

In this activity, students will use all four skills as they create magazine advertisements for summer activities and vacations, present them, and read and listen to those of others. Have students discuss seasonal advertising, how advertising influences them, and how it targets certain consumers. Have them say what kinds of ads they prefer.

**SUGGESTED SEQUENCE**

1. Have students work individually or in groups. They will need pictures of vocabulary items; they can use photos found in magazines or illustrations. (Encourage artistic students to create their own.) Each item should include a price in **euros** reflecting the current exchange rate, which they can find in the newspaper or on the Internet.
2. Remind students to use the chapter vocabulary in both a written and an oral context. Encourage them to be creative yet accurate in their ads.
3. Assign due dates for the rough draft, the completed ad, and the oral presentation. The rough draft may be a sketch with drawings labeled in Spanish.
4. Allow for peer review after completion of the first draft.
5. Collect rough drafts from the students.
6. Have them do the final draft and present their ad to the class. 1.3, 3.1

### Partner Class Project

Have students find advertisements online for vacation activities in Spain. What kinds of activities did they find? What are some of the catchphrases used? Ask students to print out the best advertisements and present them to the class, explaining why they like them. 3.2

### Grading the projects

Suggested point distribution (100 points total)

**Travel activities**

| | |
|---|---|
| Vocabulary use in ad | 45 |
| Creativity and appearance | 25 |
| **Oral presentation** | |
| Comprehensibility | 10 |
| Vocabulary use | 10 |
| Delivery | 10 |

### Game Bank

For game ideas, see pages T64–T67.

### e-community

**e-mail forum:**

Post the following questions on the classroom e-mail forum:

**¿Qué hiciste este verano?**

All students will contribute to the list and then share the items. 1.3

# ¡Adiós al verano!

## El arte

Explain to students that Spanish artists have contributed to many art movements throughout history. At the beginning of the twentieth century in Europe, one of the most important and revolutionary art movements was born: cubism. Cubism is an abstract style in which paintings and sculptures are portrayed by geometric forms (such as the intersection of cubes and cones). Pablo Picasso, a Spanish painter, and the French artist Georges Braque created this style. These artists influenced other European and Latin American painters such as Juan Gris and Diego Rivera.

Divide the class into teams of four to do research and create posters of the artists who used this technique and their famous works. The drawings can be used to decorate the room. Discuss with students that changing the traditional forms of painting and perspective alters the depiction of reality. 2.1, 3.1

## Receta

Spanish **empanadas** are large baked pies made of pork, chicken, sardines, tuna, or even **anguilas** *(eels)*. Latin American **empanadas** are small shaped pies, fried or baked, with meat or fruit. The following recipe can also be made with salmon or cod.

### Empanada gallega

**para 4 personas**

4 tazas de harina
½ taza de aceite de oliva o de girasol
½ taza de leche entera
¼ cucharadita de sal
⅓ taza de aceite de oliva o de girasol
1 cebolla grande, rajada
¼ pimiento rojo y ¼ pimiento verde, en trozos pequeños

4 onzas de pasas sin pepita
4 libras de tomates, pelados y en trozos pequeños
8 onzas de atún en conserva y desmenuzado
1 huevo batido

Mezcle bien la harina, el aceite y la sal en una sopera grande. Luego ponga la mezcla sobre papel encerado ligeramente enharinado y amásela hasta que quede lisa. Cúbrala con un trapo de cocina limpio y ponga la masa en el refrigerador por media hora.

Caliente el aceite en una sartén grande y fría la cebolla a fuego lento por 10 minutos y los pimientos por 10 minutos más. Añada las pasas y los tomates y cocínelos por 20 minutos. Saque la masa del refrigerador y divida la masa en dos partes iguales. Estírelas en otro papel enharinado y ponga una de las mitades en una placa. Añada el relleno a la masa, luego el atún y luego la otra mitad de la masa. Cierre bien los bordes de la empanada y pinte la superficie con el huevo batido. Cocine al horno a 425° durante los primeros 15 minutos y luego a 400° minutos por otros 30 minutos. Córtela en trozos y sírvala caliente.

2.2, 3.1

# Listening Activity Scripts

## ¡Adiós al verano!

### Vocabulario en acción 1

**1** p. 10, CD 1, Track 1

1. Tuvimos que esperar una hora en la estación de trenes. Jugamos naipes hasta que llegó el tren.
2. Patiné en el paseo al lado del río. La temperatura estaba a 35 grados centígrados. ¡Qué calor!
3. Montamos a caballo por la playa. Íbamos lentamente para poder disfrutar de la vista.
4. Vimos la catedral de la ciudad. ¡Es impresionante!

**Answers to Activity 1**

1. c 2. a 3. b 4. d

### Gramática en acción 1

**10** p. 15, CD 1, Track 2

1. —Hola Gilberto, ¿qué planes tienes para el verano?
   —No sé. Casi siempre viajo por toda Europa. Es fácil y barato viajar por tren.
2. —¿Qué hiciste el verano pasado?
   —Fui a Francia. Me quedé en París.
3. —¿Conoces a alguien allí?
   —Sí, en París tengo algunos amigos. De niño viajaba a París con mis padres que eran comerciantes y tenían una galería de arte allí.
4. —¿Y tú? ¿Qué planes tienes?
   —Me gustaría conocer París. El año pasado fui a Argentina. Me encontré con una amiga en Buenos Aires y recorrimos toda la ciudad.
5. —¿Aprendieron a bailar tango?
   —No, pero sí asistimos a un concierto de música clásica en el Teatro Colón.
6. —¿Te gusta la música clásica?
   —Sí, ahora me fascina. Antes me aburría.
7. —Pues a mí también me gusta. Pero prefiero escuchar y ver bailar el tango.
   —Bueno, entonces tienes que viajar a Argentina. Si quieres te ayudo a organizar un tour.
   —¡De acuerdo!

**Answers to Activity 10**

1. b 2. a 3. b 4. a 5. a 6. b 7. b

### Vocabulario en acción 2

**20** p. 24, CD 1, Track 6

1. Soy muy tímida y no me gusta hacer presentaciones en la clase. ¿Cómo puedo resolver este problema?
2. Prefiero hacer mis trabajos en casa porque tengo mucha información útil en mi computadora. Pero según la profesora, tenemos que hacer los trabajos en las computadoras del colegio. ¿Qué debo hacer?
3. Quiero practicar algún deporte este año, pero el problema es que no me gusta correr. Tampoco me gusta hacer deportes en el gimnasio del colegio. ¿Qué me recomiendas?
4. A mí me gusta coleccionar monedas y pósters pero no tengo con quien intercambiarlos. ¿Qué consejos tienes?
5. No me gustan los deportes pero me encanta escribir.
6. Necesito ocuparme con algún deporte tranquilo. ¿Puedes darme algún consejo?

**Answers to Activity 20**

a. 3 b. 2 c. 6 d. 1 e. 4 f. 5

### Gramática en acción 2

**38** p. 32, CD 1, Track 7

1. Hace diez años, vinimos a este pueblo.
2. Hace seis años que ayudo a mis padres en nuestra tienda familiar.
3. Conocí a Alejandra, mi mejor amiga, cuando empecé el colegio hace cuatro años.
4. Hace dos semestres que estudio el chino.
5. Hace un mes, mi familia y yo fuimos a Taiwán de vacaciones, y pude practicar el chino con la gente.
6. Cuando volvimos hace una semana, decidí asistir a la universidad.

**Answers to Activity 38**

1. c 2. a 3. b 4. e 5. d 6. f

For Student Response Forms, see the *Lab Book*, pp. 13–16.

## Prepárate para el examen capítulo 1

**1** p. 42, CD 1, Track 9

1. Nosotros fuimos a la ciudad y lo pasamos de película.
2. Fernando fue a un lago con sus amigos y nadaron mucho.
3. Sara y sus hermanos dieron una caminata por el bosque.
4. Lorena y su familia acamparon en las montañas y se aburrieron mucho.

**Answers to Activity 1**

1. a  2. c  3. d  4. b

**6** p. 43, CD 1, Track 10

RAMÓN Oye, Patricia, hace una semana llegaste de España, ¿verdad? ¿Te gusta este colegio?

PATRICIA Sí, pero quiero participar en actividades para poder conocer a más gente. ¿Puedes darme algún consejo?

RAMÓN Pues, hace dos años que soy miembro de la banda escolar y es genial. Te aconsejo que vengas conmigo al ensayo hoy.

PATRICIA Gracias, pero no toco ningún instrumento.

RAMÓN Entonces te recomiendo que participes en el club de debate. Lo paso de maravilla con ese grupo, y nos hace falta la perspectiva de una extranjera.

PATRICIA La verdad es que me aburro en los debates. Prefiero hacer algo más activo.

RAMÓN ¿Por qué no vas al centro recreativo para hacer ejercicios aeróbicos?

PATRICIA Prefiero practicar un deporte en un equipo.

RAMÓN En ese caso, debes hablar con Maribel. Ella sabe más que yo sobre los deportes. Pero te sugiero que practiques el atletismo porque nuestro equipo es el mejor.

PATRICIA Ay, no. No me gusta correr tanto.

RAMÓN Entonces el golf puede ser el deporte para ti.

PATRICIA Eso sí me interesa. Hablaré con Maribel a ver qué dice. ¡Gracias!

**Answers to Activity 6**

la banda escolar, el club de debate, los ejercicios aeróbicos, el atletismo, el golf

## Integración capítulo 1

**1** p. 46, CD 1, Track 11

1. —Este verano fui al campo con mi familia y montamos a caballo.
2. —Quiero practicar el atletismo con el equipo de mi colegio este año.
3. —¿Alguien quiere ver mi colección de estampillas? Tengo algunas de España.
4. —Me interesa jugar al golf para poder hacerme amigo de los chicos del equipo.

**Answers to Activity 1**

1. B  2. C  3. A  4. D

# 50-Minute Lesson Plans

# ¡Adiós al verano!

For more customized Lesson Plans, see the *Lesson Planner with Differential Instruction.*

## Day 1

**Objective**
*Talking about the past*

**Core Instruction**
**Chapter Opener,** pp. 6–7
**10 min.**
- See Chapter Objectives, p. 6.
- See Using the Photo and **Más vocabulario,** p. 6.

**Vocabulario en acción 1,** pp. 8–13
- Have students do Bell Work, p. 8.
- See Teaching **Vocabulario,** p. 8. **10 min.**
- See Teaching **¡Exprésate!,** p. 8. **5 min.**
- Play Audio CD 1, Tr. 1 for Activity 1, p. 10. **5 min.**
- Have students do Activities 2–5, pp. 10–11. **20 min.**

**Optional Resources**
- Slower Pace Learners, p. 9 ◆
- Multiple Intelligences, p. 9
- **Comunicación,** p. 11
- Heritage Speakers, p. 11 ■
- Advanced Learners, p. 11 ▲
- Multiple Intelligences, p. 11

**Homework Suggestions**
Cuaderno de vocabulario y gramática, pp. 1–3
❀ 1.2, 2.2

## Day 2

**Objective**
*Talking about what you liked to do*

**Core Instruction**
**Vocabulario en acción 1,** pp. 8–13
- Have students do Activity 6, p. 11. **10 min.**
- See Teaching **¡Exprésate!,** p. 12. **10 min.**
- Have students do Activities 7–9, p. 13. **30 min.**

**Optional Resources**
- **Comunicación,** p. 13
- Advanced Learners, p. 13 ▲
- Special Learning Needs, p. 13 ●

**Homework Suggestions**
Study for **Prueba: Vocabulario 1**
❀ 1.1, 1.2, 1.3

## Day 3

**Objective**
*Ser and estar*

**Core Instruction**
**Vocabulario en acción 1,** pp. 8–13
- Review **Vocabulario en acción 1,** pp. 8–13. **5 min.**
- Give **Prueba: Vocabulario 1. 20 min.**

**Gramática en acción 1,** pp. 14–19
- See Teaching **Gramática,** p. 14. **10 min.**
- Play Audio CD 1 for Activity 10, Tr. 2, p. 14. **5 min.**
- Have students do Activities 11–12, p. 15. **10 min.**

**Optional Resources**
- **Comunicación,** p. 15
- Slower Pace Learners, p. 15 ◆
- Advanced Learners, p. 15 ▲

**Homework Suggestions**
Cuaderno de vocabulario y gramática, pp. 4–6
Cuaderno de actividades, pp. 1–3
❀ 1.2

## Day 4

**Objective**
*Present perfect*

**Core Instruction**
**Gramática en acción 1,** pp. 14–19
- Have students do Activity 13, p. 15. **10 min.**
- See Teaching **Gramática,** p. 16. **10 min.**
- Have students do Activities 14A–16, pp. 16–17. **30 min.**

**Optional Resources**
- **Comunicación,** p. 17
- Slower Pace Learners, p. 17 ◆
- Multiple Intelligences, p. 17

**Homework Suggestions**
Cuaderno de vocabulario y gramática, pp. 4–6
Cuaderno de actividades, pp. 1–3
❀ 1.1, 1.2, 1.3

## Day 5

**Objective**
*Subjunctive mood*

**Core Instruction**
**Gramática en acción 1,** pp. 14–19
- See Teaching **Gramática,** p. 18. **10 min.**
- Have students do Activities 18–19, p. 19. **25 min.**
- Review **Gramática en acción 1,** pp. 14–19. **15 min.**

**Optional Resources**
- Slower Pace Learners, p. 19 ◆
- Multiple Intelligences, p. 19

**Homework Suggestions**
Study for **Prueba: Gramática 1**
Cuaderno de vocabulario y gramática, pp. 4–6
Cuaderno de actividades, pp. 1–3
❀ 1.1, 1.2, 1.3

## Day 6

**Objective**
*Interviews from around the Spanish-speaking world*

**Core Instruction**
**Gramática en acción 1,** pp. 14–19
- Give **Prueba: Gramática 1. 20 min.**

**Cultura,** pp. 20–21
- See Teaching **Cultura,** p. 20. **15 min.**
- Play Audio CD 1, Tr. 3–5, p. 20, or show **VideoCultura. 15 min.**

**Optional Resources**
- Advanced Learners, p. 21 ▲
- Multiple Intelligences, p. 21

**Homework Suggestions**
Cuaderno de actividades, p. 14
Online Practice (**go.hrw.com,** Keyword: EXP3 CH1)
❀ 1.2, 1.3, 4.2

## Day 7

**Objective**
*Asking for advice*

**Core Instruction**
**Vocabulario en acción 2,** pp. 22–27
- See Teaching **Vocabulario,** p. 22. **10 min.**
- See Teaching **¡Exprésate!,** p. 22. **10 min.**
- Play Audio CD 1, Tr. 6 for Activity 20, p. 24. **5 min.**
- Have students do Activities 21–25, pp. 24–25. **25 min.**

**Optional Resources**
- Advanced Learners, p. 23 ▲
- Special Learning Needs, p. 23 ●

**Homework Suggestions**
Cuaderno de vocabulario y gramática, pp. 7–9
❀ 1.1, 1.2

## Day 8

**Objective**
*Asking about the future and responding*

**Core Instruction**
**Vocabulario en acción 2,** pp. 22–27
- See Teaching **¡Exprésate!,** p. 26. **10 min.**
- Have students do Activities 26–29, p. 27. **30 min.**
- Review **Vocabulario en acción 2,** pp. 22–27. **10 min.**

**Optional Resources**
- **Comunicación,** p. 27
- Advanced Learners, p. 27 ▲
- Multiple Intelligences, p. 27

**Homework Suggestions**
Study for **Prueba: Vocabulario 2**
Cuaderno de vocabulario y gramática, pp. 7–9
❀ 1.1, 1.2, 1.3

- For information on the **Geocultura** pages, see the *Lesson Planner with Differentiated Instruction.*
- For more detailed information on benchmarks, see point-of-use correlations on each page.
- To edit and create your own lesson plans, see the **One-Stop** Planner® CD-ROM

**KEY**
- ▲ Advanced Learners
- ◆ Slower Pace Learners
- ● Special Learning Needs
- ■ Heritage Speakers

## Day 9

### Objective
*Pronouns*

### Core Instruction
**Vocabulario en acción 2,** pp. 22–27
- Give **Prueba: Vocabulario 2.** **20 min.**

**Gramática en acción 2,** pp. 28–33
- See Teaching **Gramática,** p. 28. **10 min.**
- Have students do Activities 30–32, pp. 28–29. **20 min.**

### Optional Resources
- **Comunicación,** p. 29
- Advanced Learners, p. 29 ▲
- Special Learning Needs, p. 29 ●

### Homework Suggestions
Cuaderno de vocabulario y gramática, pp. 10–12
Cuaderno de actividades, pp. 5–7
1.2

## Day 10

### Objective
*Comparisons, demonstrative adjectives and pronouns*

### Core Instruction
**Gramática en acción 2,** pp. 28–33
- Have students do Activity 33, p. 29. **5 min.**
- See Teaching **Gramática,** p. 30. **10 min.**
- Have students do Activities 34–37, pp. 30–31. **35 min.**

### Optional Resources
- **Comunicación,** p. 31
- Advanced Learners, p. 31 ▲
- Multiple Intelligences, p. 31

### Homework Suggestions
Cuaderno de vocabulario y gramática, pp. 10–12
Cuaderno de actividades, pp. 5–7
1.1, 1.2, 1.3

## Day 11

### Objective
*Negative words and time constructions*

### Core Instruction
**Gramática en acción 2,** pp. 28–33
- See Teaching **Gramática,** p. 32. **10 min.**
- Play Audio CD 1, Tr. 7 for Activity 38, p. 32. **5 min.**
- Have students do Activities 39–41, p. 33. **25 min.**
- Review **Gramática en acción 2,** pp. 28–33. **10 min.**

### Optional Resources
- **Comunicación,** p. 33
- Slower Pace Learners, p. 33 ◆
- Special Learning Needs, p. 33 ●

### Homework Suggestions
Study for **Prueba: Gramática 2**
Cuaderno de vocabulario y gramática, pp. 10–12
Cuaderno de actividades, pp. 5–7
1.1, 1.2, 1.3

## Day 12

### Objective
*Developing listening and reading skills*

### Core Instruction
**Gramática en acción 2,** pp. 28–33
- Give **Prueba: Gramática 2.** **20 min.**

**Novela en video,** pp. 34–35
- Show **VideoNovela.** See Teaching **Novela en video,** p. 34. **30 min.**

### Optional Resources
**Assessment Program**
- Skills Quiz: **Vocabulario y gramática 2**

### Homework Suggestions
Cuaderno de vocabulario y gramática, pp. 10–12
1.2, 1.3

## Day 13

### Objective
*Developing reading and writing skills*

### Core Instruction
**Lectura informativa,** pp. 36–37
- See Teaching **Lectura informativa,** p. 36. **40 min.**

**Leamos y escribamos,** pp. 38–41
- See Teaching **Leamos,** points 1–2, p. 38. **10 min.**

### Optional Resources
- Heritage Speakers, p. 37 ■
- Advanced Learners, p. 37 ▲
- Special Learning Needs, p. 37 ●
- Slower Pace Learners, p. 39 ◆
- Multiple Intelligences, p. 39

### Homework Suggestions
Cuaderno de actividades, p. 8
1.1, 1.2, 3.1

## Day 14

### Objective
*Developing reading and writing skills*

### Core Instruction
**Leamos y escribamos,** pp. 38–41
- See Teaching **Leamos,** points 3–4, p. 38. **35 min.**
- See Teaching **Escribamos,** p. 40. **5 min.**

**Prepárate para el examen,** pp. 42–45
- Play Audio CD 1, Tr. 9 for Activity 1, p. 42. **5 min.**
- Have students do Activities 2–3, p. 42. **5 min.**

### Optional Resources
- Advanced Learners, p. 41 ▲
- Special Learning Needs, p. 41 ●

### Homework Suggestions
**Taller del escritor,** p. 41
1.2, 3.1

## Day 15

### Objective
*Chapter review*

### Core Instruction
**Prepárate para el examen,** pp. 42–45
- Have students do Activities 4–5, p. 43. **10 min.**
- Play Audio CD 1, Tr. 10 for Activity 6, p. 43. **5 min.**
- Have students do Activity 7, p. 43. **5 min.**

**Integración,** pp. 46–47
- Play Audio CD 1, Tr. 11 for Activity 1, p. 46. **5 min.**
- Have students do Activities 2–6, pp. 46–47. **25 min.**

### Optional Resources
- Play Pre-AP Audio CD 1, Tr. 1, for Pre-AP Practice, p. 43
- Game, p. 45
- Fine Art Connection, p. 47

### Homework Suggestions
Study for Chapter Test
1.1, 1.2, 1.3

## Day 16/Test

### Core Instruction
**Chapter Test** **50 min.**

### Optional Resources
**Assessment Program**
- **Prueba: Lectura**
- **Prueba: Escritura**
- Test Generator

### Homework Suggestions
Cuaderno de actividades, pp. 9–10

# Indiana
## The Hoosier State

State capitol, Indianapolis

Indiana covered bridge

Autumn in Northern Indiana

### Chapter 1

The following chart presents *¡Exprésate!* Chapter 1 correlations to the Indiana Academic Standards for World Languages, Grade 11. The correlations here are to the *Student Edition* (SE) and *Teacher's Edition* (TE) only. For additional teaching resources, see pages 5A-5B

| INDIANA ACADEMIC STANDARDS | | | CHAPTER 1 SE/TE CORRELATIONS |
|---|---|---|---|
| **Standard 1 COMMUNICATION:** | | | |
| **Write and speak in a language other than English** | 11.1.1 | Initiate, sustain, and close conversations in limited yet varied situations. | SE: 11, 13, 15, 17, 19, 27, 29, 31, 47<br>TE: 8, 12, 19, 22, 26, 31 |
| | 11.1.2 | Exchange detailed information and opinions orally on a variety of topics. | SE: 47<br>TE: 46 |
| | 11.1.3 | Exchange detailed information and opinions in written form on a variety of topics. | SE: 41<br>TE: 13, 23, 29 |
| | 11.1.4 | Make requests and ask different types of questions in a variety of social situations. | SE: 11, 17<br>TE: 8, 23 |
| | 11.1.5 | Recognize and use situation-appropriate non-verbal communication. | SE: 34, 35, 47<br>SE: 17, 25, 34 |
| | 11.1.6 | Use speaking and listening strategies to facilitate communication. | SE: 15, 17, 19, 29, 31, 33<br>TE: 37 |
| **Standard 2 COMMUNICATION:** | | | |
| **Interpret information in a language other than English** *Learners interpret written and spoken language on a variety of topics. (Interpretive)* | 11.2.1 | Respond to everyday requests, commands, and directions. | SE: T64-T67, 9, 23 |
| | 11.2.2 | Demonstrate comprehension of both authentic and non-authentic written and spoken language through developmentally appropriate tasks. | SE: 21, 35, 37, 40<br>TE: 1, 3, 5, 20, 34, 36, 38 |
| | 11.2.3 | Make educated guesses about meaning in unfamiliar written and spoken contexts. | SE: xvi, 34<br>TE: xvi, 38 |
| **Standard 3 COMMUNICATION:** | | | |
| **Present information in a language other than English** *Learners present to an audience of listeners or readers on a variety of topics. (Presentational)* | 11.3.2 | Produce and present creative material on a variety of topics. | SE: 37, 41, 47<br>TE: 5C, 41, 46 |
| | 11.3.3 | Read passages aloud to demonstrate improving intonation and pronunciation. | SE: 41<br>TE: 34 |
| | 11.3.4 | Compose cohesive written information using appropriate formats and more varied vocabulary and structures. | SE: 41<br>TE: 5C, 40, 41 |
| **Standard 4 CULTURES:** | | | |
| **Develop awareness of other cultures.** *Learners examine, experience, and reflect on the relationships among the practices, products, and perspectives of the cultures studied.* | 11.4.1 | Analyze and reflect on cultural practices of the target cultures. | SE: 37, 47<br>TE: 3, 5, 20, 36, 47 |
| | 11.4.2 | Describe products, perspectives, and symbols of the target cultures. | SE: 21, 37, 47<br>TE: 3, 5, 20, 36, 46 |
| | 11.4.3 | Discuss factors that influence practices, products, and perspectives. | SE: 21, 37, 47<br>TE: 3, 5, 20, 36, 46 |

| | | | |
|---|---|---|---|
| | 11.4.4 | Recognize the interrelations among the practices, products, and perspectives of the target cultures. | SE: 21, 37, 47<br>TE: 3, 5, 20, 36, 46 |
| | 11.4.5 | Explain contributions from other cultures. | SE: 37, 47<br>TE: 3, 5, 36, 47 |
| | 11.4.6 | Identify significant events unique to the target cultures. | SE: 37<br>TE: 1, 3, 5, 37 |
| **Standard 5 CONNECTIONS:** | | | |
| **Make connections to other content areas** *Learners use the target language to expand their knowledge of and make connections among multiple content areas.* | 11.5.1 | Make connections with other content areas through resources intended for native speakers. | SE: 37<br>TE: 5C, 5D, 46 |
| | 11.5.2 | Design and share activities and materials that integrate the target language and cultures with concepts and skills from other content areas. | SE: T64-T67, 5C, 45 |
| **Standard 6 CONNECTIONS:** | | | |
| **Access and connect information through various media** *Learners strengthen language proficiency and cultural knowledge by using current digital media and authentic resources.* | 11.6.1 | Use digital media and culturally authentic resources to build vocabulary, improve reading ability, and encourage cultural awareness. | SE: 10, 16, 20, 42, 43, 46<br>TE: 5E |
| | 11.6.2 | Use digital media and culturally authentic resources to study target cultures. | SE: 1, 20, 34<br>TE: 1 |
| | 11.6.3 | Identify and evaluate resources intended for native speakers. | SE: 1, 20, 34<br>TE: 1 |
| **Standard 7 COMPARISONS:** | | | |
| **Investigate the nature of language and culture** *Learners understand the nature of language and culture through comparisons of the languages and cultures studied and their own.* | 11.7.1 | Use elements of word formation to expand vocabulary and derive meaning. | SE: 29, 43<br>TE: 14, 28, 42 |
| | 11.7.2 | Recognize and use a variety of language structures. | SE: 14-19, 41, 47<br>TE: 28-33, 42-45 |
| | 11.7.3 | Compare and use idiomatic, colloquial, and proverbial expressions in the target language. | SE: 13, 47<br>TE: 12 |
| | 11.7.5 | Compare systems of other cultures and the learner's own culture. | SE: 3, 21<br>TE: 20 |
| | 11.7.6 | Compare and contrast elements that shape cultural identity in the learner's heritage and in the target cultures. | SE: 3, 21<br>TE: 20 |
| **Standard 8 COMMUNITIES:** | | | |
| **Become an active global citizen by experiencing languages and cultures in multiple settings** | 11.8.1 | Share experiences from the world language classroom with others. | TE: 46 |
| | 11.8.3 | Show evidence of becoming a life-long learner by using the target language and cultural knowledge for personal enrichment. | TE: 11, 21 |

## Meeting the National Standards

**Communication**
Comunicación, pp. 11, 13, 15, 17, 19, 25, 27, 29, 31, 33
Game, p. 45
Situación, p. 47

**Cultures**
El arte, p. 5D
Practices and Perspectives, pp. 12, 35
Products and Perspectives, p. 19
Nota cultural, p. 27
Heritage Speakers, p. 37
Culture Project, p. 46

**Connections**
Atlas Interactivo Mundial, pp. 1, 21
Interdisciplinary Links, p. 5
Receta, p. 5D
Nota cultural, pp. 10, 24, 31
Geography Link, pp. 17, 37
History Link, p. 31
Art Link, p. 37

**Comparisons**
Language to Language, p. 9
Comparing and Contrasting, pp. 12, 21, 35
Nota cultural, pp. 13, 16
Comparaciones, p. 20

**Communities**
Comunidad y oficio, p. 21

## Using the Photo

Tell students that this photograph was taken in Consuegra, a town of Castilla-La Mancha. The windmill called **Caballero del Verde Gabán** contains editions of Don Quijote in various languages. Have students discuss what these windmills may have been used for (to grind grain) and compare them to modern wind generators.

## Más vocabulario

**el molino de viento** *windmill*
**el gigante** *giant*
**el aspa** *arm (of a windmill)*

# Capítulo 1

# ¡Adiós al verano!

### OBJETIVOS

**In this chapter you will learn to**
- talk about the past
- talk about what you liked and used to do
- ask for and give advice
- talk about the future

**And you will use**
- preterite and imperfect
- **ser** and **estar**
- subjunctive for hopes and wishes
- pronouns
- comparisons, demonstrative adjectives and pronouns
- negative words and time constructions

### ¿Qué ves en la foto?

- ¿Qué hacen los jóvenes en la foto?
- ¿Cómo es el clima en este lugar?
- ¿Te gustaría viajar a un lugar como éste? ¿Por qué?

| Suggested pacing: | Traditional Schedule | Block Schedule |
|---|---|---|
| Vocabulario 1/Gramática 1 | 5 1/2 days | 2 1/2 blocks |
| Cultura | 1/2 day | 1/2 block |
| Vocabulario 2/Gramática 2 | 5 1/2 days | 2 1/2 blocks |
| Novela | 1/2 day | 1/2 block |
| Lectura informativa | 1 day | 1/2 block |
| Leamos y escribamos | 1 day | 1/2 block |
| Prepárate para el examen | 1/2 day | 1/4 block |
| Chapter Test | 1 day | 1/2 block |
| Integración | 1/2 day | 1/4 block |

Los molinos de viento de Consuegra

## Chapter Opener

### Holt Grammar Logic
**CHAPTER 1**

In each chapter of *¡Exprésate!*, the communicative contexts of the theme determine what grammar topics are covered. In this chapter students will:

- *Talk about the past, and talk about what they liked to do and used to do.* Students will need to review and contrast preterite and imperfect, and **ser** and **estar.** They will review the concept of the subjunctive, and will use it to express hopes and wishes and give advice and opinions.
- *Ask for and give advice, and talk about the future.* Students will review subject and object pronouns, comparisons, demonstrative adjectives and pronouns, negative words, and time constructions with **hacer.**

### Puente: Customized Level 2 Review

Use *Puente: Customized Level 2 Review* to help your students review basic grammar, vocabulary, and culture topics. Grammar topics with practice include: present tense, verbs like **gustar,** reflexives, commands, object pronouns, preterite and imperfect, and demonstratives.

### LISTENING PRACTICE — Language Lab and Classroom Activities

**Vocabulario**
Activity 1, p. 10, CD 1, Tr. 1
Activity 20, p. 24, CD 1, Tr. 6

**Gramática**
Activity 10, p. 15, CD 1, Tr. 2
Activity 38, p. 32, CD 1, Tr. 7

**Cultura**
**Comparaciones,** pp. 20–21, CD 1, Tr. 3–5

**Novela**
**Novela en video,** Escuchemos, p. 34

**Leamos**
Escuchemos, p. 38

**Lectura informativa**
pp. 36–37, CD 1, Tr. 8

**Repaso**
Activity 1, p. 42, CD 1, Tr. 9
Activity 6, p. 43, CD 1, Tr. 10
**Variedades,** Lab Book, p. 56

**Integración**
Activity 1, p. 46, CD 1, Tr. 11

**Assessment Program**
CD 1, Tr. 12–15

**Additional Listening**
Pre-AP CD 1, Trs. 1–4

**Resources**

**Planning:**

Lesson Planner, pp. 1–2, 162–163

One-Stop Planner

**Presentation:**

Teaching Transparencies
**Vocabulario** 1.1, 1.2

**Practice:**

Cuaderno de vocabulario y gramática, pp. 1–3

Activities for Communication, pp. 1–2

Teaching Transparencies
Bell Work 1.1
**Vocabulario y gramática** answers, pp. 1–3

Interactive Tutor, Disc 1

**Bell Work**

Use Bell Work 2.1 in the *Teaching Transparencies*, or write this activity on the board.

**Completa las oraciones con tus propias experiencias.**

1. Hace cinco años...
2. Hace una semana...
3. Hace un mes...
4. Hace dos días...
5. Hace diez años.... 1.2

**Objetivos**
- Talking about the past
- Talking about what you liked and used to do

# Vocabulario en acción 1

## Hice muchas cosas en España este verano.

Archivo Editar Ver Herramientas Ayuda
Atrás Adelante Actualizar Detener Página inicial Buscar Favoritos Correo Imprimir
Dirección:

Mis vacaciones
Mi familia
Mis amigos

**Di una caminata** con mi familia cerca de Toledo. Almorzamos en un lugar con una vista hermosa a **la ciudad.** Luego **acampamos** en **el bosque.**

Pasamos un fin de semana muy bueno en Toledo. Tomamos un autobús desde **la estación de autobuses** hasta la Plaza Zocodover. Visitamos **la catedral** y varios **monumentos. Paseamos** por **el río** Tajo y **nos divertimos** mucho.

**Hacía calor** en Toledo y no había **brisa.** Pero el sábado **llovió a cántaros,** cayeron **relámpagos** y escuché **truenos.** Luego, cuando solamente caía una **llovizna,** fuimos a un concierto al aire libre.

Toda la familia **disfrutó de** las vacaciones porque hicimos actividades interesantes. Un día todos **montamos a caballo** y ¡hasta intentamos **el patinaje en línea!**

## Core Instruction

### TEACHING VOCABULARIO

1. Use transparencies **1.1** and **1.2** to introduce vocabulary to students. Read each caption, placing emphasis on the targeted vocabulary words. **(5 min.)**
2. Ask students questions to monitor comprehension. **¿Qué actividades se pueden practicar en el mar? (2 min.)**
3. Go over **Más vocabulario** and model each word in a sentence. Ask more comprehension questions. **¿Practicas natación durante una tormenta? (3 min.)**

### TEACHING ¡EXPRÉSATE!

1. Model both sides of a conversation using the **¡Exprésate!** expressions to talk about the past and to respond. **(2 min.)**
2. Hand out photographs of people doing the activities described in **Vocabulario 1,** or pictures of specific places. Ask questions and have individual students hold up their photographs. For example, ask: **¿Qué hiciste el verano pasado?** If a student holds up a photograph of Ecuador, you might respond: **Viajé a Ecuador. (3 min.)**

**Más vocabulario...**

**Actividades**

| | |
|---|---|
| trotar | *to jog* |

**Tiempo**

| | |
|---|---|
| los grados Fahrenheit/centígrados | *degrees Fahrenheit/centigrade* |
| la tormenta | *storm* |

Visit Holt Online
**go.hrw.com**
KEYWORD: EXP3 CH1
Vocabulario 1 practice

Al día siguiente fuimos a **la estación de trenes** para regresar a Madrid.

**Nos aburrimos** un poco en el tren. Mamá **hizo crucigramas,** papá y yo **jugamos naipes** y mi hermana **conversó** con una chica que también viajaba a Madrid. Vimos **las montañas** por la ventanilla.

Pasamos dos semanas en **la costa. Coleccioné caracoles** e **hice windsurf.** Cuando **me cansé de hacer windsurf,** practiqué el **esquí acuático** y **la natación.**

## ¡Exprésate!

| To talk about the past | To respond |
|---|---|
| **¿Qué hiciste el verano pasado?** *What did you do last summer?* | **Viajé a...** *I traveled to . . .* |
| **¿Qué tal lo pasaste?** *Did you have a good time?* | **Lo pasé de película/de maravilla.** *I had a great time.* |
| **¿Adónde fuiste?** *Where did you go?* | **Fui a...** *I went to . . .* |
| **¿Qué te pareció...?** *How was . . . ?* | **Lo/La encontré muy interesante.** *I found it very interesting.* |

Interactive TUTOR

Vocabulario y gramática, pp. 1–3 — Online workbooks

▶ **Vocabulario adicional** — Los viajes, p. R15

## Differentiated Instruction

### SLOWER PACE LEARNERS

**Additional Practice** Have students work in groups to write sentences about a summer vacation using the vocabulary words. Ask them to separate the sentences into four or five sections and illustrate each section. Have groups present their stories for the class. 1.2, 1.3

### MULTIPLE INTELLIGENCES

**Kinesthetic** Have small groups of students act out scenes to show what they did this summer. The rest of the class should describe what each person did, based on the presentation. Tell students to be sure to exaggerate facial expressions and body language so their classmates can include the **¡Exprésate!** phrases in their descriptions. (**Lo pasó de película/de maravilla. Lo/La encontró muy interesante.**) 1.2



### TPR
**TOTAL PHYSICAL RESPONSE**

Bring to class the following items: a crossword puzzle, playing cards, an umbrella, roller blades, and shells. Have individual students respond to the following commands:

**Pásame algo que necesitas durante una tormenta.**

**Señala algo que puedas coleccionar en la playa.**

**Busca un naipe con el número 7.**

**Pásame el crucigrama.**

**Ponte algo para hacer patinaje en línea.** 1.2

### COMMON ERROR ALERT
**¡OJO!**

Students often misuse the term **afuera** to talk about an outdoor event. Tell them that the phrase **al aire libre** is used in Spanish. Point out the use of this phrase in the photo caption on page 8.

### Comparisons

**Language to Language**

Tell students that **llover a cántaros**, literally "to rain pitchers", is the Spanish equivalent of "to rain cats and dogs". Have students look up other Spanish idioms and try to find an English equivalent. 4.1

### También se puede decir...

Tell students that **la equitación** can also be used to refer to horseback riding. Also, in the region of Santander, they might hear the terms **calabobos** or **chirimiri** used for **llovizna.**

**Differentiated Instruction** See the Differentiated Instruction CD-ROM.

## Resources

**Planning:**

Lesson Planner, pp. 1–2, 162–163

One-Stop Planner

**Presentation:**

Teaching Transparencies
**Vocabulario** 1.1, 1.2

**Practice:**

Cuaderno de vocabulario y gramática, pp. 1–3

Activities for Communication, pp. 1–2

Lab Book, pp. 13–16

Teaching Transparencies
**Vocabulario y gramática** answers, pp. 1–3

Audio CD 1, Tr. 1

Interactive Tutor, Disc 1

## Teacher to Teacher

**Christine Lord**
Dracut High School
Dracut, MA

To review the preterite, I give each student two sets of cards, one containing the roots of various verbs (at least fifteen), including the irregular preterite ones, and the other containing all the verb endings possible in the preterite. I ask the students to form a verb in the preterite using one card from each set, giving them, for example, a pronoun and an infinitive **(yo, hacer).** They race to match the appropriate roots and endings. 1.2

CD 1, Tr. 1

### 1 ¿Quién es? 1.2

**Escuchemos** Escucha los comentarios y escoge la foto que corresponde a cada comentario. **1.** c **2.** a **3.** b **4.** d

A

B

C

D

### 2 ¿Qué significa? 1.2

**Leamos/Escribamos** Escribe la palabra de **Vocabulario** que corresponde a cada definición.

1. Cuando esto ocurre, hay lluvia, viento y relámpagos. la tormenta
2. Para hacer esta actividad necesitas una silla especial. montar a caballo
3. Un lugar con muchos edificios y calles. la ciudad
4. En este lugar se puede nadar y coleccionar caracoles. la costa
5. Correr lentamente como ejercicio. trotar
6. Un edificio donde se celebran ritos religiosos. la catedral

### Nota cultural

La región de Castilla-La Mancha está dominada por una extensa llanura, pero también tiene montañas como la Cordillera Central al norte, el Sistema Ibérico al noreste, la Sierra Morena y los Montes de Toledo al sur. Hay muchas lagunas, como las lagunas de Ruidera y de Cañada del Hoyo, y dos ríos grandes, el Tajo y el Guadiana.

¿Cómo se compara la geografía variada de Castilla-La Mancha con la de tu región? 3.1

**El Lago Una en la Reserva Nacional de la Serranía de Cuenca**

### 3 ¿Lo pasaron bien? 1.2

**Leamos/Escribamos** Completa el diálogo con las palabras del cuadro.

| | | | |
|---|---|---|---|
| la catedral | divertimos | Fahrenheit | qué tal |
| hiciste | tormenta | bosque | una caminata |

CARMEN ¡Hola Miguel! ¿Qué ___1___ este verano? **1.** hiciste
MIGUEL Acampé en el ___2___ con mi familia. **2.** bosque
CARMEN ¿Hizo mucho calor?
MIGUEL Sí. Hizo mucho calor... cien grados ___3___. **3.** Fahrenheit
CARMEN ¿Y ___4___ lo pasaron? **4.** qué tal
MIGUEL Bueno, la primera noche hubo una ___5___ y llovió a cántaros. **5.** tormenta
CARMEN ¡Qué desastre! ¿Qué hicieron el segundo día?
MIGUEL Decidimos ir a un hotel en la ciudad. Fuimos a un concierto y nos ___6___ mucho. Al día siguiente dimos ___7___ por la ciudad y tomamos fotos de ___8___.
CARMEN Me parece que disfrutaron su viaje a la ciudad.

**6.** divertimos **7.** una caminata **8.** la catedral

## Core Instruction

### VOCABULARY IN CONTEXT

Ask students to write a short essay or story using ten words from **Vocabulario 1.** For each vocabulary word used, students should draw a picture or cut one out of a magazine to represent the word instead of writing it. Students then exchange their work with a partner who replaces each drawing or picture with the correct vocabulary word. When finished, students give the essay or story back to the writer for correction.

### 4 Guía turística ❀ 1.2

**Escribamos** Escribe lo que se puede ver o hacer en cada lugar de Castilla-La Mancha, según las fotos.

**MODELO** **En Talavera de la Reina, puedes ver la famosa cerámica, pintada de muchos colores.**

Talavera de la Reina

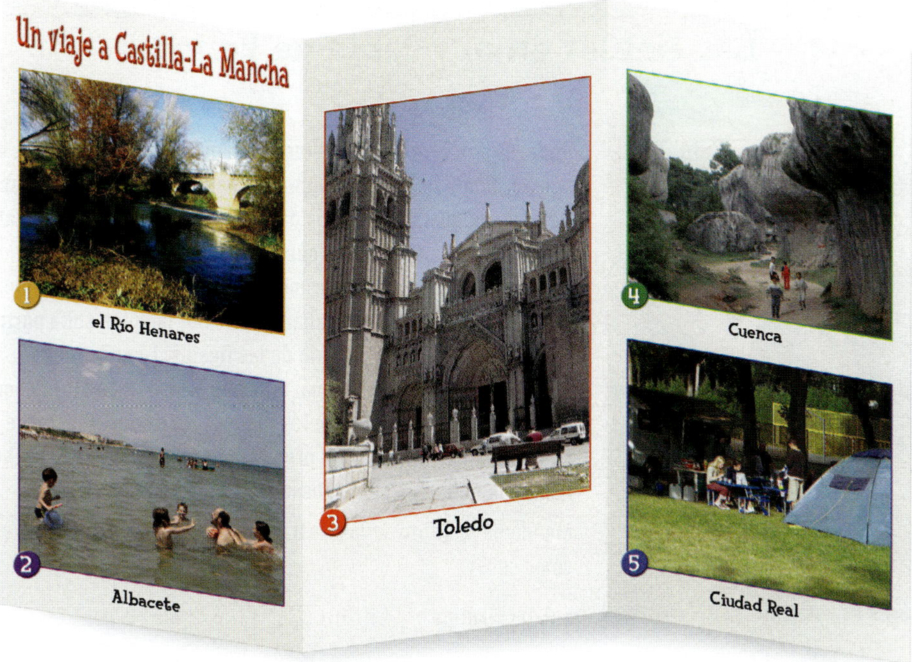


### 5 Adivina la pregunta ❀ 1.2

**Leamos/Hablemos** Lee las siguientes respuestas y haz una pregunta para cada una.

1. Viajé por Europa con mis papás.
2. Fuimos a España, Francia e Inglaterra.
3. Lo pasé de película.
4. ¿España? Lo encontré fascinante.
5. Comimos muchos mariscos.
6. Viajamos en tren.

## Comunicación

HOLT SoundBooth ONLINE RECORDING

### 6 ¿Qué hiciste el verano pasado? ❀ 1.1, 1.2

**Hablemos** Túrnense tú y un(a) compañero(a) para hablar de lo que hicieron el verano pasado. Usen las palabras y las expresiones de **Vocabulario** y **Exprésate.**

Vocabulario 1

### 1 Script

1. Tuvimos que esperar una hora en la estación de trenes. Jugamos naipes hasta que llegó el tren.
2. Patiné en el paseo al lado del río. La temperatura estaba a 35 grados centígrados. ¡Qué calor!
3. Montamos a caballo por la playa. Íbamos lentamente para poder disfrutar de la vista.
4. Vimos la catedral de la ciudad. ¡Es impresionante!

### 4 Possible Answers

1. Puedes pasear por el Río Henares.
2. Puedes nadar (jugar) en las playas de Albacete.
3. En Toledo, puedes visitar la catedral de arquitectura gótica.
4. Puedes dar una caminata en las afueras de Cuenca.
5. Puedes acampar en Cuidad Real.

### 5 Possible Answers

1. ¿Qué hiciste el verano pasado?
2. ¿Adónde fueron?
3. ¿Qué tal lo pasaste?
4. ¿Qué te pareció España?
5. ¿Qué comieron?
6. ¿Qué medio de transporte usaron?

### Heritage Speakers

Have heritage speakers name other favorite summer activities that are not included in **Vocabulario 1.** Ask them to describe each activity as you write the names of the activities on the board or on a transparency.

## Comunicación

### Group Activity: Presentational

Divide the class into small groups. Have students imagine their ideal vacation. Ask them to take turns describing what they did on this ideal vacation, without saying where they went. They should be sure to include details that will give their classmates clues about where they went on this imaginary trip. The rest of the group must guess the location.

❀ 1.3

## Differentiated Instruction

### ADVANCED LEARNERS

**3 Challenge** Have students write a travel brochure like the one in Activity 4. They can write a guide for their own community or one for a favorite place. Ask them to draw or find pictures to use in the brochure. Under each picture, they should write a description of the activity. ❀ 1.3

### MULTIPLE INTELLIGENCES

**Naturalist** Have students imagine they are taking a tour on horseback through Castilla-La Mancha. Ask them to use a map and research information to decide where their tour will go and what they will see along the way. Encourage them to describe the landscape and the flora and fauna of the region. What are the advantages of touring the region on horseback? Have them convince their classmates that this is the best way to see the countryside. ❀ 1.3, 3.1

**Differentiated Instruction** See the Differentiated Instruction CD-ROM.

## Resources

**Planning:**

Lesson Planner, pp. 1–2, 162–163

One-Stop Planner

**Presentation:**

Teaching Transparencies
**Vocabulario** 1.1, 1.2

**Practice:**

Cuaderno de vocabulario y gramática, pp. 1–3

Activities for Communication, pp. 1–2

Teaching Transparencies
**Vocabulario y gramática** answers, pp. 1–3

Interactive Tutor, Disc 1

## Comparisons

### Comparing and Contrasting

Tell students that Castilla-La Mancha and other regions of Spain are famous for their **fiestas.** Ask students to find information on some Spanish festivals and compare them to the festivals they grew up with. Are the activities similar? What are the major differences? 2.1, 4.2

## Cultures

### Practices and Perspectives

After students have read the **Nota cultural** on page 13, have them think about the traditions in their family or community. Are the traditions historical or religious? Are they based on the industry of the community? Have students further investigate one of the traditions of Castilla-La Mancha and describe its significance. 2.1

Archivo Editar Ver Herramientas Ayuda

Atrás Adelante Actualizar Detener Página Inicial Buscar Favoritos Correo Imprimir

Dirección:

# Las fiestas en el pueblo de Felipe

Querido Jorge:

Aquí ves una foto de las fiestas de mi pueblo. Son del 4 al 11 de agosto, todos los años. Siempre me han encantado estas fiestas. De niño me gustaba ver a los payasos y comer tortilla de patata. Ahora me gustan los bailes que dan por la noche, pero de niño me gustaba jugar con mis primos en la plaza. Jugábamos todo tipo de juegos y nos lo pasábamos bomba. También solía participar en el desfile el primer día de las fiestas. Lo encontraba genial. Usaba ropa tradicional y tocaba la flauta. La última noche de las fiestas, disfrutaba de los fuegos artificiales. Esa noche, solía dormir en casa de mis primos, y pasábamos toda la noche hablando de lo que habíamos hecho.

Mándame una foto de las fiestas de tu pueblo. Me gustaría ver cómo son.

Saludos, Felipe

## ¡Exprésate!

**To talk about what you liked and used to do**

Interactive TUTOR

| | |
|---|---|
| **De niño(a), me gustaba...** *As a child, I liked to . . .* | **Cuando tenía diez años, me encantaba...** *When I was ten, I loved to . . .* |
| **Cuando era joven, solía...** *When I was young, I usually . . .* | **Siempre disfrutaba de...** *I always enjoyed . . .* |
| **De pequeño, me lo pasaba bomba...** *When I was little, I had a great time . . .* | **Lo encontraba genial...** *I thought . . . was great . . .* |

Vocabulario y gramática, pp. 1–3 Online workbooks

## Core Instruction

### TEACHING ¡EXPRÉSATE!

1. Read the letter aloud as a class and discuss what Jaime used to like to do at the festivals and what he likes to do now. **(3 min.)**
2. Model the sentences from **¡Exprésate!**, completing each one with activities that you liked to do as a child. **(2 min.)**
3. Have volunteers say activities from **Vocabulario 1** for you to model in a sentence. Provide variations of the **¡Exprésate!** sentences to demonstrate that students can use the expressions in different ways. **(montar a caballo) De niño me encantaba montar a caballo. (hacer crucigramas) Cuando tenía quince años, disfrutaba mucho haciendo crucigramas. (5 min.)**

**7** **¿Cierto o falso?** 1.2

**Leamos/Escribamos** Di si cada oración es **cierta** o **falsa** según la carta de Felipe. Corrige las oraciones falsas.

1. De niño, a Felipe le gustaban los bailes que daban por la noche.
2. Felipe nunca comía tortilla de patata durante las fiestas.
3. Cuando era pequeño, Felipe disfrutaba de las fiestas.
4. A Felipe no le gustaba participar en el desfile.
5. Felipe encontraba geniales los fuegos artificiales.
6. De joven, a Felipe le encantaba jugar con sus primos durante las fiestas.

**8** **Haz el cuento** 1.2

**Leamos/Escribamos** Completa el diálogo con las palabras del cuadro.

| | | |
|---|---|---|
| genial | aburría | bomba |
| disfrutaba | solía | gustaba |

MARTÍN De niño, me __1__ dar caminatas por el bosque o acampar en las montañas. gustaba

TERESA ¿De verdad? A mí no me gustaba el bosque. Mi familia __2__ ir a la playa. solía

MARTÍN Me __3__ mucho en la playa de joven. No había nada que hacer. aburría

TERESA Pues, yo lo encontraba __4__. Cuando tenía cinco años, me encantaba coleccionar caracoles. genial

MARTÍN Es que yo nunca __5__ de la natación. disfrutaba

TERESA ¡Yo tampoco! Pero me lo pasaba __6__ practicando el esquí acuático. bomba

**Nota cultural**

Castilla-La Mancha es una comunidad rica en cultura y folclor. La región tiene muchas tradiciones populares: fiestas, romerías *(pilgrimages)*, bailes y carreras para celebrar los ciclos agrícolas, momentos históricos, milagros o acontecimientos religiosos. En el Baile de la Soldadesca en Toledo (abajo), la gente se viste con ropa típica y baila danzas folclóricas, llamadas animeros, en la plaza.

¿Conoces algo de las tradiciones y el folclor de tu región? 4.2

## Comunicación

HOLT SoundBooth ONLINE RECORDING

**9** **Lo que me gustaba hacer** 1.1, 1.3

**Hablemos** Túrnense tú y un(a) compañero(a) para hablar de lo que les gustaba hacer de niños. Luego, resuman para la clase lo que le gustaba hacer a su compañero(a).

**MODELO** —**Cuando tenía siete años, me encantaba patinar.**
—**Yo solía jugar al escondite con mis amigos.**

**7** **Answers**

1. falsa; Le gustaba ver a los payasos y comer tortilla de patata.
2. falsa; Siempre comía tortilla de patata.
3. cierta
4. falsa; Solía participar en los desfiles del primer día de las fiestas.
5. cierta
6. cierta

## Comunicación

**Pair Activity: Interpretive**

Have students cut out photographs from magazines that show an activity they used to like to do when they were small. Have them attach the photo to a piece of construction paper or card stock and write an expression below it, using a sentence from **¡Exprésate!** Display the photos around the classroom and have students guess who used to do each activity. Keep the cards and re-use them to review for chapter and semester exams.

**MODELO**
**—De niña, a Patricia le gustaba jugar con animales de peluche.**
1.2

## Differentiated Instruction

**ADVANCED LEARNERS**

**Personalization** Have students write a letter like the one from Jaime to Jorge on page 12. They should describe a festival, fair, holiday, or other activity that they have been attending every year since they were children. Ask them to tell what they used to like to do during the occasion as compared to what they like to do now. Have students exchange letters with a partner and discuss them. 1.3

**SPECIAL LEARNING NEEDS**

**Students with Learning Disabilities** Before students do the activities on page 13, you may want to remind them that the imperfect is used to talk about things they used to do. Review conjugations of the following verbs in the imperfect: **soler, hacer, ir, gustar.** Then write sample sentences on the board or on a transparency using the **¡Exprésate!** phrases, and underline the verbs in the imperfect.

**Assess**

**Assessment Program**
**Prueba: Vocabulario 1,** pp. 1–2
Alternative Assessment, pp. 373, 385, 397

**Online Assessment**
**my.hrw.com**

**Test Generator**

**Assess** **Differentiated Instruction** See the Differentiated Instruction CD-ROM.

## Resources

**Planning:**

Lesson Planner, pp. 3–5, 164–167

One-Stop Planner

**Presentation:**

Video Program
**GramaVisión**

**Practice:**

Grammar Tutor for Students of Spanish, Chapter 1

Cuaderno de vocabulario y gramática, pp. 4–6

Cuaderno de actividades, pp. 1–3

Activities for Communication, pp. 1–2

Lab Book, pp. 13–16

Teaching Transparencies
Bell Work 1.2
**Vocabulario y gramática** answers, pp. 4–6

Audio CD 1, Tr. 2

Interactive Tutor, Disc 1

**Bell Work**

Use Bell Work 1.2 in the *Teaching Transparencies.*

**Pre-AP Practice**

**AP Benchmark:** Initiate, maintain, and close a conversation on a familiar topic.

**Focus:** Preterite and imperfect
- SE, p. 15, Act. 13
- TE, p. 15, Slower Pace Learners
- Activities for Communication, pp. 1–2, Acts. 1A–1B

**Objetivos**
- Preterite and imperfect
- **Ser** and **estar**
- Subjunctive for hopes and wishes

# Gramática en acción 1

GramaVisión

Interactive TUTOR

## Repaso Preterite and imperfect

**1** You already know that the **preterite** and the **imperfect** are used to talk about past events or situations.

**2** Use the **preterite** to talk about something that happened
- on a specific occasion or a specific number of times

  El verano pasado **viajé** a España y **acampé** cerca del Río Tajo.
- in a sequence of events

  Cuando **llegué, busqué** alojamiento y **llamé** a mis amigos.
- for a specific period of time, even if it happened repeatedly

  **Pasé** un mes en Cádiz y **fui** todos los días a la playa.

**3** Use the **imperfect** to talk about
- what used to happen for an unspecified period of time

  De niño, **viajaba** a España con mis padres todos los veranos.
- what people, places or things were generally like or to describe the setting

  Mis abuelos **eran** muy activos y simpáticos.

  En las playas **había** pocos turistas. Siempre **hacía** calor.
- how someone felt or what he or she liked or disliked

  No me **gustaba** ir a la playa porque le **tenía** miedo al mar.

**4** You can use the **preterite** to say what people, places or things were like, how people felt, and what they liked or disliked *in order to sum up a particular occasion.* Use it also to talk about someone's reaction, or to say that a state or condition changed.

¿Fuiste a Cádiz? ¿Qué tal **estuvo?**

Llevé a mi hermanito a la playa y no le **dio** miedo.

Ayer miré algunas fotos de España y **sentí** mucha nostalgia.

Vocabulario y gramática, pp. 4–6
Actividades, pp. 1–3
Online workbooks

### ¿Te acuerdas?

These are the regular **preterite** endings of **-ar** and **-er** or **-ir** verbs.

| | |
|---|---|
| compr**é** | compr**amos** |
| compr**aste** | compr**asteis** |
| compr**ó** | compr**aron** |
| volv**í** | volv**imos** |
| volv**iste** | volv**isteis** |
| volv**ió** | volv**ieron** |

Before **e** or **é**, verbs ending in **-car, -gar,** or **-zar** have a spelling change.

| | |
|---|---|
| buscar: | bus**qué** |
| llegar: | lle**gué** |
| organizar: | organi**cé** |

CD 1, Tr. 2

**10** **¿Qué hiciste el verano pasado?** 1.2

**Escuchemos** Escucha la conversación y di si se habla de **a)** una situación en particular o de **b)** cómo son o eran las cosas en general.

**1.** b **2.** a **3.** b **4.** a **5.** a **6.** b **7.** a

## Core Instruction

### TEACHING GRAMÁTICA

**1.** Remind students of point 1, that the preterite and imperfect are both used to talk about situations or events in the past, but that they have different uses. **(1 min.)**

**2.** First go over the preterite endings from **¿Te acuerdas?** Then read and discuss the examples in point 2. **(4 min.)**

**3.** Before going over point 3, review the imperfect endings. Remind students that **ser** and **ir** are irregular in the imperfect. **(3 min.)**

**4.** Go over the uses of the preterite in point 4. Emphasize that the first two examples would be used when the speaker is summarizing a past experience. **(2 min.)**

**GramaVisión**

For a video presentation of the preterite and the imperfect, use **GramaVisión.**

GramaVisión

Visit Holt Online
**go.hrw.com**
KEYWORD: EXP3 CH1
Gramática 1 practice

**11 Cuéntame más** 1.2

**Escribamos** Completa la conversación con el pretérito o imperfecto de los verbos según el contexto.

MATEO ¿Qué tal las vacaciones? ¿Adónde __1__ (ir)? fuiste
SONIA Mi familia y yo __2__ (visitar) a mis abuelos en Santander, en la playa. visitamos
MATEO ¿Y qué tal __3__ (estar)? estuvo
SONIA Genial. Fíjate que de niña no me __4__ (gustar) ir a la playa, pero ahora me encanta. __5__ (Venir) mis primos y nos lo __6__ (pasar) bomba. gustaba, Vinieron, pasamos
MATEO ¿Por qué no te __7__ (gustar) ir a la playa de niña? gustaba
SONIA __8__ (Preferir) jugar en casa de mis abuelos. __9__ (Haber) muchas cosas antiguas—muebles, pinturas, muñecas, libros. __10__ (Fascinarme) los dibujos en los libros. Y tú, ¿qué hiciste? Prefería, Había, Me fascinaban
MATEO Pues…

**12 ¿Qué hicieron?** 1.2

**Escribamos** Escribe dos o tres oraciones acerca de cada foto. Explica adónde fueron las personas y qué hicieron. Luego describe qué había en el lugar y cómo era.

**MODELO** **Adriana fue al campo y montó a caballo. El caballo era grande y hermoso. El campo estaba verde.**

Adriana

1. Sergio

2. Clara y sus amigos

3. Mis amigos y yo

## Comunicación

HOLT SoundBooth ONLINE RECORDING

**13 Tus vacaciones de verano** 1.1, 1.3

**Leamos/Hablemos** Pregúntale a tu compañero(a) qué hizo durante sus vacaciones de verano. Luego pregúntale adónde iba de vacaciones de niño y qué hacía. Túrnense.

### 10 Script

1. —Hola Gilberto, ¿qué planes tienes para el verano?
—No sé. Casi siempre viajo por toda Europa. Es fácil y barato viajar por tren.
2. —¿Qué hiciste el verano pasado?
—Fui a Francia. Me quedé en París.
3. —¿Conoces a alguien allí?
—Sí, en París tengo algunos amigos. De niño viajaba a París con mis padres que eran comerciantes y tenían una galería de arte allí.
4. —¿Y tú? ¿Qué planes tienes?
—Me gustaría conocer París. El año pasado fui a Argentina. Me encontré con una amiga en Buenos Aires y recorrimos toda la ciudad.
5. —¿Aprendieron a bailar tango?
—No, pero sí asistimos a un concierto de música clásica en el Teatro Colón.
6. —¿Te gusta la música clásica?
—Sí, ahora me fascina. Antes me aburría.
7. —Pues a mí también me gusta. Pero prefiero escuchar y ver bailar el tango.
—Bueno, entonces tienes que viajar a Argentina. Si quieres te ayudo a organizar un tour.
—¡De acuerdo!

## Comunicación

### Pair Activity: Interpretive

Have students write a brief narrative of a real or imaginary worst vacation. Tell them to use the preterite and the imperfect to talk about what happened, who was there and what they were like, what the conditions were like, and so on. Instruct them to highlight the verbs in the preterite and imperfect and to rewrite their narrative with those verbs replaced by their infinitive in parentheses. Have them exchange their narrative with a partner and to replace the infinitives in parentheses with a conjugated verb in the preterite or imperfect.

1.2, 1.3

## Differentiated Instruction

### SLOWER PACE LEARNERS

**Additional Practice** Have students work with a partner to conduct a poll about how many students did certain activities and whether they used to do them all the time. Provide sample questions in the preterite and imperfect. **¿De niño(a), fuiste a la playa alguna vez? ¿Ibas a la playa todos los veranos?** Students should give the survey to their classmates and present the results to the class. **Tres estudiantes, de niños, montaron a caballo. Uno(a) montaba a caballo casi todos los fines de semana.** 1.1, 1.3

### ADVANCED LEARNERS

**Extension** Write pairs of sentences on the board, one using the preterite and another using the imperfect. Use the same verb for each sentence. Have students refer to points 2, 3 and 4 to give their opinions of the difference in meaning between each pair. Ask them to write a sentence to go with each one to clarify the context. **Ayer mi profesora estaba contenta./¿Qué tal estuvo?//No me gustaba acampar./ No me gustó hacer windsurf.** 1.2

**Differentiated Instruction** See the Differentiated Instruction CD-ROM.

# Gramática 1

## Resources

**Planning:**

Lesson Planner, pp. 3–5,164–167

One-Stop Planner

**Presentation:**

Video Program
**GramaVisión**

**Practice:**

Grammar Tutor for Students of Spanish, Chapter 1

Cuaderno de vocabulario y gramática, pp. 4–6

Cuaderno de actividades, pp. 1–3

Activities for Communication, pp. 1–2

Teaching Transparencies
Bell Work 1.3
**Vocabulario y gramática** answers, pp. 4–6

Interactive Tutor, Disc 1

### Bell Work

Use Bell Work 1.3 in the *Teaching Transparencies,* or write this activity on the board.

**Completa las oraciones con la forma correcta de *ir* o *ser* en el pretérito o en el imperfecto.**

1. Ayer después de clases, nosotros ____ al cine, pero la película ____ aburrida.
2. Todos los veranos, Raquel ____ a las montañas.
3. El domingo, yo ____ primero a la iglesia y después con mi familia al restaurante.
4. Cuando estaba en Perú, Iván ____ a Machu Picchu tres veces.
5. De niña, mi abuela ____ rubia y delgada.

1.2

## Repaso Ser and estar

Interactive TUTOR

**1** As you have learned, both **ser** and **estar** have specific uses and cannot be used interchangeably.

**2** **Ser** is used:

- to describe or identify people, places, or things
  Tomás y Elena **son** listos.
- to tell time
  **Son** las dos y media.
- to say what someone's profession is
  Mario **es** bombero.
- to talk about nationality and origin
  **Soy** de España, pero mi mamá **es** francesa.

**3** **Estar** is used:

- to say where something or someone is located
  Luis **está** en Cuenca.
- to describe physical conditions, emotions or feelings, or how something tastes
  Marta **estuvo** enferma la semana pasada.
  Hernán **estaba** preocupado por el examen.
  El bistec **está** un poco salado.
- with the present participle to form the present or past progressive
  Ellos **están** esperando el autobús.
  ¿Qué **estabas** haciendo cuando te llamé?

**Vocabulario y gramática**, pp. 4–6
**Actividades**, pp. 1–3
**Online** workbooks

### Nota cultural

Cuenca es un pueblo pequeño en Castilla-La Mancha, construido sobre los acantilados *(cliffs)* de una montaña. Es famoso por sus Casas Colgadas (abajo), que fueron construidas en los acantilados y están situadas de tal forma que parecen estar colgantes. Este pueblo antiguo, establecido durante el imperio romano, está tan bien conservado que Cuenca ha sido nombrado Patrimonio de la humanidad *(World Heritage Site).*

¿Qué sitios históricos hay en tu ciudad o pueblo? 4.2

### 14 A Cuando estoy de vacaciones... 1.2

**Leamos/Escribamos** Completa las oraciones según tus propias experiencias. Después explica por qué se utiliza **ser** o **estar** en cada oración.

1. Mi lugar preferido para ir de vacaciones es ____.
2. Durante las últimas vacaciones de verano, mis amigos y yo estuvimos en ____.
3. Cuando estoy de viaje con mi familia, me gusta ____.
4. Mi playa favorita está en ____.
5. El año pasado, viajé a ____ y estuve allí por ____ días.
6. Antes de salir para un viaje, casi siempre estoy ____.
7. Para mis próximas vacaciones, estoy pensando en ir a ____.

## Core Instruction

### TEACHING GRAMÁTICA

1. Remind students that they have already learned the uses of **ser** and **estar.**
2. Go over the uses of **ser** in point 2 and read the examples. **(3 min.)**
3. Provide more examples of **ser** and ask students to identify its uses. For example: **¡Ya son las seis!** (to tell time) **(2 min.)**
4. Go over the uses of **estar** in point 3 and read the examples. **(3 min.)**
5. Provide more examples and ask students to identify the use of **estar.** For example: **Mi hermano está leyendo un libro.** (to form the present progressive) **(2 min.)**

### GramaVisión

For a video presentation of **ser** and **estar,** use **GramaVisión.**

GramaVisión

14 B **De vacaciones** 1.2

**Leamos/Escribamos** Completa el diálogo con la forma correcta de **ser** o **estar.**

GRACIELA ¿Adónde vas de vacaciones? **1.** Es **2.** es

ANDRÉS Siempre vamos a la costa. ¡__1__ un lugar muy hermoso! La playa a la que vamos __2__ muy grande.

GRACIELA ¿Te lo pasas bien allí? **3.** es **4.** son **5.** están

ANDRÉS Sí. Allí conocí a Begoña, una chica española. Ella __3__ de Sevilla. La vi en la playa y la saludé. Ella me presentó a sus hermanos. Ellos __4__ estudiantes. Los dos __5__ estudiando medicina.

GRACIELA ¡Qué bien! ¿Qué pasó cuando tuviste que regresar a casa?

ANDRÉS Mira, cuando terminaron las vacaciones, Begoña regresó a Sevilla, donde __6__ su familia. Pero nosotros estamos en contacto por correo electrónico. Me dice que ahora ella __7__ de nuevo en el colegio.

GRACIELA ¿Me la presentas? **6.** estaba **7.** está

ANDRÉS ¡Claro!

15 **¿Ser o estar?** 1.2

**Escribamos** Describe lo que ves en cada foto. Usa **ser** o **estar**.

# Comunicación

HOLT SoundBooth ONLINE RECORDING

16 **¿Qué está pasando?** 1.1, 1.2

**Hablemos** Dile a tu compañero(a) algo que ves y algo que está pasando en el salón de clase. Describe algo verdadero y algo falso. Tu compañero(a) debe corregir lo falso. Sigan el modelo y túrnense.

**MODELO** **—Son las doce. El profesor no está en el salón de clase.**
**—El profesor sí está en el salón de clase. Está escribiendo algo en la pizarra.**



## Connections

### Geography Link

After students have read the **Nota cultural** on page 16, tell them that Spain is one of the countries with the largest number of World Heritage sites. Spain joined UNESCO's World Heritage List in 1982 when it ratified a convention to protect its cultural and natural heritage sites. In 1993 it also formed the Group of World Heritage Cities, which promotes the cultural heritage of 11 cities in Spain. Tell students that Cuenca is one of the cities and have them investigate other World Heritage cities and sites in Spain. Students should find out what cultural or historical features of that city allowed it to qualify as a World Heritage City. 3.1

## Comunicación

### Class Activity: Presentational

Have students take turns describing items in the classroom using **ser** and **estar** without identifying the item. The rest of the class must guess what object is being described. **Es un gran dibujo de todos los países del mundo. Está colgado cerca de la pizarra. (el mapa)** 1.3

## Differentiated Instruction

### SLOWER PACE LEARNERS

**Additional Practice** Have students write a sentence for each use of **ser** and **estar** listed on page 14. Tell them to leave a blank space for the verb. Ask them to exchange sentences with a partner and write the answers. They should pass the sentences back to their partner to correct, and discuss the answers. 1.2

### MULTIPLE INTELLIGENCES

**Mathematical** Have students form mathematical sentences with **ser.** For example: **Dos y dos son ____. Cinco millas son ____ kilómetros.** Have them quiz a partner on the answers. If they do not know an answer, have them look it up. Ask volunteers to write their completed sentences on the board. 3.1

**Differentiated Instruction** See the Differentiated Instruction CD-ROM.

## Resources

**Planning:**

Lesson Planner, pp. 3–5, 164–167

One-Stop Planner

**Presentation:**

Video Program
**GramaVisión**

**Practice:**

Grammar Tutor for Students of Spanish, Chapter 1

Cuaderno de vocabulario y gramática, pp. 4–6

Cuaderno de actividades, pp. 1–3

Activities for Communication, pp. 1–2

Teaching Transparencies
Bell Work 1.4
**Vocabulario y gramática** answers, pp. 4–6

Interactive Tutor, Disc 1

### Bell Work

Use Bell Work 1.4 in the *Teaching Transparencies,* or write this activity on the board.

**Completa las oraciones con la forma correcta de *ser* o *estar* en el presente.**

1. Ana ______ cansada.
2. Paco ______ de Toledo.
3. ______ las diez y media.

1.2

### 17 Answers

1. vayamos
2. hagamos
3. practicar
4. dar
5. sea

# Repaso Subjunctive for hopes and wishes

Interactive TUTOR

### ¿Te acuerdas?

To form the present subjunctive, add these endings to the **yo**-form stem of regular verbs.

| -AR VERBS | -ER / -IR VERBS |
|---|---|
| habl**e** | le**a** |
| habl**es** | le**as** |
| habl**e** | le**a** |
| habl**emos** | le**amos** |
| habl**éis** | le**áis** |
| habl**en** | le**an** |

**1** You already know that the subjunctive mood is used to express hopes and wishes with **esperar que, querer que,** and **preferir que,** and to give advice and opinions with **es mejor que, es buena idea que, es importante que, aconsejar que, recomendar que,** and **sugerir que.**

**2** In Spanish the **subjunctive** usually appears in the **dependent** or **subordinate clause,** and is introduced by the conjunction **que** after the **main clause.**

*Main clause* — *Subordinate clause*

**Espero que el viaje a Toledo sea divertido.**
*I hope the trip to Toledo is fun.*

*Main clause* — *Subordinate clause*

**Te recomiendo que des una caminata por la ciudad.**
*I recommend you take a walk around the city.*

**3** The **subjunctive** is used when the subjects of the **main clause** and the **subordinate clause** are different.

*different subjects*

**Espero que Carmen pueda acompañarnos a Guadalajara.**
*I hope Carmen can come with us to Guadalajara.*

*different subjects*

**Óscar sugiere que nosotros llevemos un picnic al lago.**
*Oscar suggests we bring a picnic to the lake.*

**4** When there is no change of subject, an **infinitive** follows the verb in the **main clause.**

**Gloria prefiere ir** al bosque.

Vocabulario y gramática, pp. 4–6
Actividades, pp. 1–3
**Online** workbooks

### 17 Otros planes 1.2

**Leamos/Escribamos** Completa las oraciones con la forma correcta del verbo en paréntesis.

1. Fabián y Lorenzo quieren que nosotros ==== (ir) al lago con ellos.
2. Ellos nos recomiendan que ==== (hacer) windsurf en el lago.
3. Quiero ==== (practicar) el esquí acuático también.
4. Mis amigos prefieren ==== (dar) caminatas por el bosque.
5. Esperamos que el viaje al lago ==== (ser) divertido.

## Core Instruction

### TEACHING GRAMÁTICA

1. Review the information in **¿Te acuerdas?** with students, then go over point 1 and use five phrases in a sentence. **(3 min.)**
2. Go over point 2. Write more examples and have students identify the main and subordinate clauses and circle the word **que: El profesor nos aconseja que estudiemos mucho. (3 min.)**
3. Go over point 3. Write more examples and have students identify the subject of the main clause and the subject of the subordinate clause. **Alejo espera que tú vengas pronto. (Alejo/tú) (3 min.)**
4. Go over point 4 with paired sentences: **Quieren llegar temprano./Quieren que llegues temprano. (1 min.)**

### GramaVisión

For a video presentation of the subjunctive mood for hopes and wishes, use **GramaVisión.**

GramaVisión

## 18A Te recomiendo que... 1.2

**Leamos/Hablemos** Lee las oraciones y da una recomendación u opinión a cada persona. Usa las expresiones del cuadro.

| | |
|---|---|
| Te recomiendo que... | Te aconsejo que... |
| (No) Es una buena idea que... | Es mejor que... |
| Es importante que... | Te sugiero que... |

1. Ana quiere aprender a patinar pero no tiene patines.
2. Gabriela quiere montar a caballo pero no sabe hacerlo.
3. Tus amigos quieren ir al bosque pero hay una tormenta.
4. Margarita quiere saber si es mejor viajar en autobús o en tren.
5. Marcos quiere ir a un lugar donde se pueda acampar.
6. Tus padres quieren ir a un lugar histórico.

## 18B ¡Nuestra clase va a España! 1.3

**Escribamos** La clase de español ha planeado un viaje a Castilla-La Mancha. Escribe ocho oraciones sobre las recomendaciones, preferencias y sugerencias de todos acerca del viaje.

**MODELO** **El profesor recomienda que vayamos primero a Toledo. Marta y yo sugerimos que...**

## Comunicación

HOLT SoundBooth ONLINE RECORDING

## 19 ¿Qué les recomiendas? 1.1, 1.2

**Hablemos** Con un(a) compañero(a), inventa un cuento basándote en los dibujos. Incluyan por lo menos tres recomendaciones, usando el subjuntivo.

## Answers

Use the Chapter 1 *Picture Sequences Transparency.*

**19 Sample Answer**

Los amigos quieren que Roberto nade con ellos pero él no no quiere. Está nervioso. Roberto piensa que viene una tormenta y les aconseja que salgan del agua. Pedro recomienda que vayan a otro lugar a jugar naipes y Roberto está de acuerdo.

## Comunicación

### Class Activity: Presentational

Have students think of things they hope will happen in the world. Ask each student to prepare five sentences in the subjunctive about their hopes. Have them take turns presenting their sentences to the class. 1.3

## Cultures

### Products and Perspectives

Tell students that almonds are used in many Spanish recipes. They are used to make **turrón,** the typical candy eaten during **Navidad.** Have students find out what other typical Spanish recipes include almonds. 2.2

## Differentiated Instruction

### SLOWER PACE LEARNERS

**18 Additional Practice** Have students work in small groups to practice making recommendations using the subjunctive. Students should invent a problem like those listed in Activity 18, and the other members of the group should make recommendations. 1.1

### MULTIPLE INTELLIGENCES

**Interpersonal** Tell students to imagine they are tutoring students in Level 1 Spanish. Since they have already studied two levels, they should be able to understand the difficulties of students just beginning to learn a language. Have them write a short paragraph with recommendations about what new Spanish students should do to get the most out of their classes. You may wish to have some students visit a Spanish 1 class to present their recommendations. 1.3

## Assess

**Assessment Program**

**Prueba: Gramática 1,** pp. 3–4

**Prueba: Aplicación 1,** pp. 5–6

Audio CD 3, Tr. 12

Alternative Assessment, pp. 373, 385, 397

**Online Assessment**
**my.hrw.com**

**Test Generator**

**Resources**

**Planning:**
Lesson Planner, pp. 6, 166–167
One-Stop Planner

**Presentation:**
Audio CD 1, Trs. 3–5
Video Program, Videocassette 1
DVD Program
**VideoCultura**

**Practice:**
Cuaderno de actividades, p. 4
Video Guide, pp. 4–5
Lab Book, p. 56
Interactive Tutor, Disc 1

# Cultura

VideoCultura

## Comparaciones

Interactive TUTOR

CD 1, Tr. 3-5

La playa y la bahía de Tamariu, Costa Brava, España

### El trabajo sin reposo convierte al hombre en un soso 4.2

En algunos países de habla hispana, muchas familias dejan la ciudad y van a la playa o al campo a pasar las vacaciones de verano. Muchas familias de clase media compran una segunda vivienda en estos lugares, o si no, la alquilan por un mes. Los chicos hacen amigos allí que ven todos los veranos. A veces, la vida en la ciudad se paraliza durante todo el mes, y las tiendas y bancos tienen horarios reducidos. Compara esto con el efecto que tienen las vacaciones en tu ciudad, en tu vida y la de tus compañeros.

### María
**Madrid, España**

***¿En tu país es común hacer un viaje durante el verano?***
Sí, nosotros nos solemos ir de vacaciones sobre el julio y agosto.

***¿Hay un lugar que sea muy popular?***
Sí, casi todo el mundo suele ir a las playas.

***De niña, ¿qué hacías durante las vacaciones de verano?***
Yo me iba sobre julio con mis padres a la playa y luego en agosto me venía, me bañaba en la piscina.

***¿Qué hiciste durante el verano el año pasado?***
El año pasado estuve en Galicia haciendo una visita turística, y luego me vine aquí a la playa.

***¿Qué planes tienes para el verano que viene?***
El verano que viene pienso irme con mis tías y con mi prima al Caribe y Disneyworld®.

**Pre-AP Practice**

**AP Language Examination:** Have students first listen to the interviews with books closed to help prepare them for Section I, Part A: **Listening—Short Dialogues and Narratives.** Point out that María, like many Spanish speakers, uses the present tense of the helping verb **soler (solemos, suele).** Students have learned the imperfect of **soler** to talk about what they used to do.

## Core Instruction

### TEACHING CULTURA

1. Read and discuss the introductory paragraph as a class. **(3 min.)**
2. Ask students where they think Spaniards and Argentines would spend their summer vacations. Then have volunteers read the interviews. Were students' predictions correct? **(3 min.)**
3. Have students answer the **Para comprender** questions. Then have them work in pairs to discuss **Para pensar y hablar. (5 min.)**

### VideoCultura

For a video presentation of the interviews as well as for an additional interview, see Chapter 1 **VideoCultura** on Videocassette or on DVD.

VideoCultura

Visit Holt Online
**go.hrw.com**
KEYWORD: EXP3 CH1
Online Edition

## Brando
**Buenos Aires, Argentina**

***En tu país, ¿es común hacer un viaje durante el verano?***
Sí, durante el verano se va a las costas del mar argentino: Mar de Tuyú, Villa Gesell, Miramar, Mar de Plata.

***¿Hay un lugar popular?***
Sí, mayormente se va a Mar de Plata, que es una de las costas que tiene el centro más grande acá en Buenos Aires.

***De niño, ¿qué hacías durante las vacaciones de verano?***
Construía castillitos en la arena, salía con mis primos.

***¿Qué hiciste durante el verano el año pasado?***
Estuve en las costas de lo que es el Mar de Tuyú.

***¿Y qué planes tienes para el verano que viene?***
Pienso hacer unos tours de Mendoza en febrero y en enero ir a una costa.

### Para comprender 1.2

1. Según María, ¿adónde van muchos españoles durante el verano?
2. Cuando María era niña, ¿cómo pasaba los meses de julio y agosto? ¿Hizo algo parecido el año pasado?
3. ¿Adónde van los argentinos durante el verano? De niño, ¿qué hacía Brando durante las vacaciones?
4. María y Brando hablan de ir a la playa. ¿Adónde va la gente de tu ciudad durante el verano?

### Para pensar y hablar 1.3

Para ti, ¿es el viajar una manera de reunirse con la familia y conocer nuevos amigos o lugares? ¿Cómo te diviertes durante las vacaciones? Compara lo que haces hoy con lo que hacías de niño. ¿Qué te gustaría hacer en unas vacaciones futuras?

## Comunidad y oficio 1.3, 5.1

### Turistas hispanohablantes

Cada año, millones de turistas hispanohablantes vienen a Estados Unidos, principalmente de México, Latinoamérica y el Caribe. Ya que el turismo internacional es una de las bases de la economía, muchos lugares de interés turístico e histórico promueven el turismo entre los visitantes hispanohablantes proporcionando publicidad e información en español. Investiga los principales sitios turísticos de tu región y averigua el porcentaje de hispanohablantes que los visita anualmente. ¿Cuáles de estos lugares tienen guías o folletos en español? Utiliza la información que encontraste en tus investigaciones para diseñar y redactar una guía turística de tu región para visitantes hispanohablantes.

**El centro de visitantes de la ciudad de Nueva York**

## Differentiated Instruction

### ADVANCED LEARNERS

**Challenge** Have students use the same questions to interview a classmate. Ask them to write a paragraph comparing the answers given by María, Brando, and their classmate. 1.1

### MULTIPLE INTELLIGENCES

**Spatial** Tell students to imagine that they work for a travel agency that needs Spanish speakers. Have them draw a map of Spain or Argentina and mark where the most popular beaches are located. Have them research possible beach trips from Madrid or from Buenos Aires. What route would they take by car? What cities would they pass through? What train lines are available? Ask them to prepare a short presentation for the class as if they were selling a vacation package to clients. 3.1

## Atlas
### INTERACTIVO MUNDIAL

Have students use the interactive atlas at **go.hrw.com**.

**Map Activities**

1. Have students locate Spain on a map of Europe. Ask them what countries border Spain. Then have them locate the capital of Spain.
2. Have students locate Argentina and name the bordering countries. Ask them to locate the capital of Argentina. What do they notice about the location of the capital?
3. What characteristics do Spain and Argentina have in common with respect to their location? 3.1

### Answers

1. Van a las playas.
2. Iba a la playa en junio; Sí, hizo una visita turística a Galicia y luego fue a la playa.
3. Van a las costas del mar argentino. Construía castillitos en la arena, salía con sus primos.
4. Answers will vary.

### Comparisons

**Comparing and Contrasting**

Ask students to discuss the activities mentioned by Brando and María in their interviews. Were their summer activities similar to what people do in the U.S.? 4.2

### Career Path

Have groups of students brainstorm a list of ideas for careers in tourism. In which jobs would knowledge of Spanish be an advantage? Have groups share their ideas with the class.

## Resources

**Planning:**

Lesson Planner, pp. 7–8, 168–169

One-Stop Planner

**Presentation:**

Teaching Transparencies
**Vocabulario** 1.3, 1.4

**Practice:**

Cuaderno de vocabulario y gramática, pp. 7–9

Activities for Communication, pp. 3–4

Teaching Transparencies
Bell Work 1.5
**Vocabulario y gramática** answers, pp. 7–9

Interactive Tutor, Disc 1

### Bell Work

Use Bell Work 1.5 in the *Teaching Transparencies.*

### Pre-AP Practice

**AP Benchmark:** Formulate questions to seek clarification or further information.

**Focus:** Asking about the future
- SE, p. 27, Act. 29
- TE, p. 27, **Comunicación**
- Activities for Communication, p. 56, **Repaso**

**Objetivos**
- Asking for and giving advice
- Talking about the future

# Vocabulario en acción 2

## ¡Ayúdame, Amparo!

## Querida Amparo

**Querida Amparo:**

Necesito su ayuda. Voy a empezar un nuevo año escolar y quiero que este año sea el mejor. El año pasado **tenía ganas de participar** en las actividades del colegio, pero no lo hice. Mi vida es **solitaria** y muy **aburrida.** ¿Qué puedo hacer para cambiar esto?

Joaquín

**Querido Joaquín:**

No te preocupes, hay una solución. **¿Te interesa** discutir ideas? Debes participar en **el club de debate.** ¿Te gusta correr? Debes **practicar atletismo.** ¿Te gusta la música? Debes participar en **la banda escolar**. ¿Eres creativo? ¿Por qué no **haces diseño por computadora** o **diseñas páginas Web?** En fin, hay muchas cosas que puedes hacer para tener una vida más interesante.

Amparo

**Querida Amparo:**

Sé que necesito **mantenerme en forma** pero no sé cómo empezar. Sigo **una dieta balanceada** pero, ¡no tengo tiempo para hacer nada! ¿Qué consejos me da?

Ana Luisa

**Querida Ana Luisa:**

No necesitas tener mucho tiempo para mantenerte en forma. Busca una actividad que puedas hacer con una amiga, como los **ejercicios aeróbicos**, para que te diviertas más. Puedes **saltar a la cuerda** por unos minutos todos los días o ir a un **centro recreativo** y **hacer gimnasia.**

Amparo

## Core Instruction

### TEACHING VOCABULARIO

1. Use transparencies **Vocabulario 1.3** and **1.4** to present the vocabulary. Read each letter, pointing to the words as you read. **(4 min.)**
2. After reading each letter, ask questions to monitor comprehension. **¿Joaquín participó en las actividades de su colegio el año pasado? (no) ¿Ana Luisa sigue una dieta balanceada? (sí) (3 min.)**
3. Go over **Más vocabulario** and model each word in a sentence. **(3 min.)**

### TEACHING ¡EXPRÉSATE!

1. Read the sentences in **¡Exprésate!** aloud to model pronunciation. **(1 min.)**
2. Model both sides of a conversation using the sentences from **¡Exprésate!** First, present a problem. **—Me gusta montar a caballo pero no me gusta salir a montar solo.** Then ask for advice. **—¿Qué consejos tienes?** Finally, give advice. **—Te aconsejo que te hagas amigo de alguien que pueda montar a caballo contigo. (4 min.)**

Visit Holt Online
go.hrw.com
KEYWORD: EXP3 CH1
Vocabulario 2 practice

# Querida Amparo

**Querida Amparo:**

Soy una persona bastante **nerviosa** e **impaciente.** Me siento muy ansioso todo el tiempo y no sé por qué. ¿Qué puedo hacer para llevar una vida más calmada?

Fernando

**Querido Fernando:**

¡Hay mucho que puedes hacer! Algunas personas **coleccionan estampillas, observan la naturaleza** o se ocupan con una actividad tranquila como **jugar al golf.** Vas a ver cómo cambia tu vida.

Amparo

**Más vocabulario...**

| | |
|---|---|
| **coleccionar pósters/monedas** | *to collect posters/coins* |
| **crear (quemar) CDs** | *to make (burn) CDs* |
| **escribir poemas y cuentos** | *to write poems and stories* |
| **hacerse amigo(a) de alguien** | *to make a friend* |
| **la oratoria** | *speech (class)* |

Vocabulario 2

## ¡Exprésate!

| To ask for advice | To give advice |
|---|---|
| **¿Qué consejos tienes?** *What advice do you have?* | **Hay que...** *One has to . . .* |
| **¿Puedes darme algún consejo?** *Can you give me some advice?* | **Te aconsejo que...** *I advise you to . . .* |
| **¿Qué debo hacer?** *What should I do?* | **Debes...** *You should . . .* |
| **¿Qué me recomiendas?** *What do you recommend (to me)?* | **Te recomiendo que...** *I recommend that you . . .* |

Interactive TUTOR

Vocabulario y gramática, pp. 7–9 Online workbooks

## TPR
### Total Physical Response

Have students respond to the following commands.

**Señala a alguien que participa en la banda escolar.**

**Haz ejercicios aeróbicos.**

**Pon una cara que muestre que estás aburrido(a).**

**Busca un libro que te interese en el salón.**

1.2

### Common Error Alert ¡OJO!

Students often have trouble with usage of **tener** expressions in Spanish. Point out that **tener ganas de (hacer)** means *to feel like (doing).* Model the phrase in a sentence and then remind them of other **tener** expressions such as **tener hambre, tener sueño, tener razón.**

### También se puede decir...

In Spain, the word **sellos** is commonly used instead of **estampillas.** You may also see the word **timbres** used.

### Circumlocution

For additional practice, have students choose activities from **Vocabulario 1** and describe them without using the vocabulary word. The rest of the class must guess the activity they are describing. 1.1

## Differentiated Instruction

### ADVANCED LEARNERS

**Challenge** Have students write their own **Querida Amparo** letters asking for advice about a problem, real or imaginary. Ask them to exchange letters with a partner and respond with a letter giving advice. 1.1

### MULTIPLE INTELLIGENCES

**Students with AD(H)D** Some students may not be able to focus on the meaning of the vocabulary words in the letters. You may wish to review the vocabulary words separately after reading the letters. List words on the board or on a transparency and have students tell what each word means. If they do not know the meaning of a particular word, allow them to look it up. 1.2

**Differentiated Instruction** See the Differentiated Instruction CD-ROM.

## Resources

**Planning:**

Lesson Planner, pp. 7–8, 168–169

One-Stop Planner

**Presentation:**

Teaching Transparencies
**Vocabulario** 1.3, 1.4

**Practice:**

Cuaderno de vocabulario y gramática, pp. 7–9

Activities for Communication, pp. 3–4

Lab Book, pp. 13–16

Teaching Transparencies
**Vocabulario y gramática** answers, pp. 7–9

Audio CD 1, Tr. 6

Interactive Tutor, Disc 1

### 20 Script

1. Soy muy tímida y no me gusta hacer presentaciones en la clase. ¿Cómo puedo resolver este problema?
2. Prefiero hacer mis trabajos en casa porque tengo mucha información útil en mi computadora. Pero según la profesora, tenemos que hacer los trabajos en las computadoras del colegio. ¿Qué debo hacer?
3. Quiero practicar algún deporte este año, pero el problema es que no me gusta correr. Tampoco me gusta hacer deportes en el gimnasio del colegio. ¿Qué me recomiendas?
4. A mí me gusta coleccionar monedas y pósters pero no tengo con quien intercambiarlos. ¿Qué consejos tienes?
5. No me gustan los deportes pero me encanta escribir.
6. Necesito ocuparme con algún deporte tranquilo. ¿Puedes darme algún consejo?

### Nota cultural

La primera parte del nombre Castilla-La Mancha viene de la palabra "castillo". Los expertos creen que la palabra "Mancha" viene de la palabra árabe "Mantxa" *(dry land)*, aunque algunos dicen que es una contracción de la frase "La más ancha" *(the widest)*. Las dos interpretaciones son aptas para describir esta región ancha, seca y llena de castillos.

¿Qué regiones de Estados Unidos tienen extensas llanuras y un clima seco, como Castilla-La Mancha? 3.1

Vista de las murallas de Alarcón

CD 1, Tr. 6

### 20 ¿Qué me aconsejas? 1.2

**Escuchemos** Escucha los problemas y escoge el consejo que corresponde a cada uno.

**a.** Te recomiendo que participes en el equipo de golf. 3
**b.** Debes quemar CDs con la información y llevarlos al colegio. 2
**c.** Mi consejo es que aprendas a jugar al golf. Así puedes relajarte. 6
**d.** Si estás nerviosa durante una presentación, toma clases de oratoria. 1
**e.** Te aconsejo que te hagas amigo de alguien que coleccione las mismas cosas. 4
**f.** Debes escribir cuentos o poemas en tu tiempo libre. 5

### 21 ¿Se relaciona? 1.2

**Leamos** Indica la palabra o frase que no se relaciona lógicamente con las otras dos.

| | | | |
|---|---|---|---|
| 1. | diseñar páginas Web | hacer diseño por computadora | jugar al golf |
| 2. | quemar CDs | hacer gimnasia | practicar atletismo |
| 3. | el club de debate | mantenerse en forma | la oratoria |
| 4. | saltar a la cuerda | escribir cuentos | escribir poemas |
| 5. | las estampillas | las monedas | la banda |
| 6. | hacer gimnasia | los ejercicios aeróbicos | la naturaleza |

**1.** jugar al golf **2.** quemar CDs **3.** mantenerse en forma **4.** saltar a la cuerda **5.** la banda **6.** la naturaleza

### 22 Un discurso 1.2

**Leamos/Escribamos** Completa el diálogo con las palabras del cuadro.

| | | |
|---|---|---|
| impaciente | poemas | mantenerme |
| recomiendas | naturaleza | aeróbicos |

MÓNICA Quiero __1__ en forma este año, pero no tengo ganas de practicar atletismo. mantenerme aeróbicos
FERNANDO Debes hacer algo divertido, como los ejercicios __2__.
MÓNICA Tampoco sé cómo estar más tranquila. Es que soy una persona muy __3__. impaciente
FERNANDO Puedes ir al bosque y observar la __4__. naturaleza
MÓNICA ¿Y qué me __5__ si no me gusta dar caminatas? recomiendas
FERNANDO Pues, te gusta escribir. Te aconsejo que escribas __6__ o cuentos en un lugar tranquilo. poemas
MÓNICA ¡Buena idea!

## Core Instruction

### VOCABULARY IN CONTEXT

Divide the vocabulary words among four groups of students. Students are to make one set of note cards with a synonym, definition, or drawing for each word assigned to their group. Then they are to make another set of note cards with the vocabulary words written on them. Groups shuffle their cards, then pass them to another group. Give students three minutes to match the new sets of cards. The original group then checks that the second group has matched the cards correctly. Cards are shuffled again and passed to a third group. Play continues in this manner until all the vocabulary words have been practiced by each group.

## 23 ¿Qué les recomiendas? 1.2

**Leamos/Escribamos** Vas a ser un(a) "hermano(a) mayor" de varios estudiantes del primer año en el colegio. Dales consejos sobre qué deben hacer, según lo que les interese.

**MODELO** **Guille/la literatura**
**Guille, te recomiendo que escribas poemas para la revista del colegio.**

1. Sara/correr
2. José/tocar música
3. Fátima/hablar en público
4. Jorge/mantenerse en forma
5. Alicia/practicar español
6. Andrés/aprender a usar la computadora
7. Emilio/conocer a más gente
8. Luisa/buscar un pasatiempo

## 24 ¿Qué le aconsejas? 1.2

**Leamos/Hablemos** Mira las fotos y da un consejo o una recomendación a cada persona. Usa las palabras de **Vocabulario** y las expresiones de **Exprésate.**

1

2

3

4

## Comunicación

HOLT SoundBooth ONLINE RECORDING

## 25 ¿Qué debo hacer? 1.1, 1.2

**Hablemos** Hablen tú y un(a) compañero(a) de dos actividades que les guste hacer. Luego, pídanse consejos sobre otras actividades que puedan hacer para pasar el tiempo o para mantenerse en forma.

**MODELO** **—A mí me gusta jugar al golf para relajarme.**
**—A mí me relaja hacer gimnasia. Te la recomiendo.**

Vocabulario 2

### 23 Possible Answers

1. Sara, te aconsejo que corras con el equipo de atletismo.
2. José, debes tocar música durante el almuerzo.
3. Fátima, te recomiendo que tomes una clase de oratoria.
4. Jorge, debes practicar algún deporte.
5. Alicia, te aconsejo que estudies en España.
6. Andrés, debes comprar una computadora.
7. Emilio, te recomiendo que participes en los clubes de la escuela.
8. Luisa, debes hablar con tus amigos sobre sus pasatiempos.

## Comunicación

### Class Work: Interpersonal

Have students create a short conversation about an exchange student who is having trouble adapting to life in the United States. The student asks for advice and other members of the group ask questions about his or her likes and dislikes in order to make recommendations. 1.1

## Differentiated Instruction

### SLOWER PACE LEARNERS

24 Before students do Activity 24, describe the scenes in the photographs as a class. Have students tell what they think each person's problem is. Then have volunteers give advice using words from **Vocabulario** and expressions from **¡Exprésate!** Ask the rest of the class whether they agree with the advice. 1.2

### MULTIPLE INTELLIGENCES

**Interpersonal** Have students work in pairs to role-play a conversation for each item in Activity 23. This will give them an opportunity to ask the new student more questions about his or her interests and to give more specific advice. 1.1

**Resources**

**Planning:**

Lesson Planner, pp. 7–8, 168–169

One-Stop Planner

**Presentation:**

Teaching Transparencies
**Vocabulario** 1.3, 1.4

**Practice:**

Cuaderno de vocabulario y gramática, pp. 7–9

Activities for Communication, pp. 3–4

Teaching Transparencies
**Vocabulario y gramática** answers, pp. 7–9

Interactive Tutor, Disc 1

**Más práctica**

Have students imagine they are running for president. Divide the class into pairs and have them take turns interviewing each other about what they plan to do as president. Tell them to take notes on their partner's answers so they can then tell the class what he or she plans to do.
1.1

## Este año será diferente

ALBERTO Manuela, ganaste un campeonato importante de fútbol y todo el mundo quiere saber: ¿Qué vas a hacer ahora? ¿Vas a dedicarle todo tu tiempo al deporte? ¿Vas a dejar el colegio y entrenarte para los Juegos Olímpicos?

MANUELA No, voy a regresar al colegio. Tal vez en el futuro sí me entrenaré para los Juegos Olímpicos. Pero ahora lo más importante para mí es la educación.

ALBERTO ¿Y qué cambios vas a hacer este año?

MANUELA Pues, voy a estudiar más. También quiero participar en actividades como el club de debate y la banda escolar. El año pasado no hice más que hacer gimnasia y jugar al fútbol, y por eso no pude hacer otras cosas.

ALBERTO ¿Y cómo vas a mantenerte en forma para el próximo campeonato?

MANUELA Iré al gimnasio por las mañanas y así tendré tiempo por las tardes para participar en otras actividades y para estudiar. El año pasado siempre me entrenaba por las tardes también, y por eso no estudié lo suficiente.

ALBERTO ¿Qué piensas hacer cuando te gradúes del colegio?

MANUELA Pienso ir a la universidad. Si estudio más este año, creo que lo puedo lograr.

ALBERTO Bueno, te deseo mucha suerte.

### ¡Exprésate!

| To ask about the future | To respond |
|---|---|
| **¿Qué vas a hacer...?**<br>*What are you going to do . . .?* | **Voy a estudiar...**<br>*I'm going to study . . .* |
| **¿Adónde piensas ir...?**<br>*Where do you plan to go . . .?* | **Pienso ir...**<br>*I plan to go . . .* |
| **¿Qué cambios vas a hacer?**<br>*What will you do differently?* | **De hoy en adelante participaré en...**<br>*From now on I'll participate in . . .* |
| **¿Cómo vas a mantenerte en forma?**<br>*How will you stay in shape?* | **Voy a practicar...**<br>*I will practice . . .* |

Interactive TUTOR

Vocabulario y gramática, pp. 7–9 Online workbooks

## Core Instruction

### TEACHING ¡EXPRÉSATE!

1. Have volunteers read the conversation between Alberto and Manuela. Ask volunteers to tell what Manuela plans to do this year. **(3 min.)**
2. Use the expressions from **¡Exprésate!** to model both sides of a conversation, asking someone about the future and responding. You may want to role-play talking to a famous person to help students better understand the context of each response. **(2 min.)**
3. Ask volunteers to name activities they plan to do this year, for example, **escribir poemas.** Use the expressions to model a conversation with the student.

**—¿Qué va a hacer Tina después de clases?**

**—Va a escribir poemas. (5 min.)**

2. falsa; Manuela va a regresar al colegio.

## 26 Mis planes 1.2

**Leamos/Escribamos** Basándote en el diálogo, determina si cada oración es **cierta** o **falsa.** Corrige las oraciones falsas.

1. Manuela ganó un campeonato de gimnasia. falsa; de fútbol
2. Manuela va a dedicarle más tiempo al deporte.
3. A Manuela no le interesa participar en las actividades del colegio. falsa; Manuela quiere participar en más actividades este año.
4. Manuela piensa estudiar más este año. cierta
5. A Manuela le gustaría ir a la universidad. cierta
6. Manuela irá al gimnasio por las tardes. falsa; Irá al gimnasio por las mañanas.

## 27 ¿Qué harás? 1.2

**Leamos/Hablemos** Contesta las preguntas con las frases en paréntesis.

1. ¿Piensas participar en algún club este año? (participar en el club de debate)
2. ¿Qué van a hacer esta tarde? (hacer ejercicios aeróbicos)
3. ¿Cómo vas a sacar una A en historia? (estudiar todos los días)
4. ¿Adónde piensas ir para observar la naturaleza? (ir a las montañas)
5. ¿Qué harás en tu tiempo libre? (escribir cuentos)
6. ¿Qué harás cuando te gradúes del colegio? (ir a la universidad)

## 28 ¿Qué van a hacer? 1.2

**Escribamos** Escribe una oración con el tiempo futuro para decir lo que harán las personas en las fotos la próxima semana.

1

2

3

4

### Comunicación

HOLT SoundBooth ONLINE RECORDING

## 29 El mejor año 1.1, 1.3

**Hablemos** Túrnense tú y un(a) compañero(a) para entrevistarse sobre qué van a hacer este año para que sea el mejor año del colegio.

### Nota cultural

Una de las comidas típicas de Castilla-La Mancha es el **mazapán**, un dulce de almendra. Según una leyenda de Toledo, el mazapán se hizo en un convento cuando la ciudad estaba sitiada por los árabes en el siglo XIII. Hicieron una pasta con almendra y azúcar, los únicos alimentos que tenían, la hornearon y la llamaron "pan de maza". Otro alimento regional famoso de la región es el **queso manchego**.

¿Cuáles son las comidas típicas de tu región? 2.2

Vocabulario 2

### 27 Answers

1. Sí, pienso participar en el club de debate.
2. Vamos a hacer ejercicios aeróbicos.
3. De hoy en adelante estudiaré todos los días.
4. Pienso ir a las montañas.
5. Escribiré cuentos.
6. Iré a la universidad.

### Circumlocution

Read the following descriptions aloud and have volunteers tell which vocabulary word fits each description.

1. **En este deporte, algunos miembros del equipo corren en la carrera de cien metros.**
2. **Para seguir esto, tengo que comer bien.**
3. **En esta clase, hay que dar discursos.**
4. **En este lugar hago gimnasia.** 1.2

### Comunicación

**Class Activity: Interpersonal**

Have students imagine they are famous teenagers such as actors or athletes. Ask them to interview each other about their plans for the future. 1.1

## Differentiated Instruction

### ADVANCED LEARNERS

**Challenge** Have students write a paragraph about what they plan to do this year to make it the best year yet. Ask them to exchange paragraphs with a partner to peer-edit. Then have them give their partners advice on how best to accomplish their goals. 1.3

### MULTIPLE INTELLIGENCES

**27 Intrapersonal** You may want to modify Activity 27 to have students give their own answers to each question. Have students work in pairs to ask each other the questions and to respond. Then ask them to write their answers in their notebooks. 1.1

### Assess

**Assessment Program**

**Prueba: Vocabulario 2,** pp. 7–8

Alternative Assessment, pp. 373, 385, 397

**Online Assessment** my.hrw.com

**Test Generator**

**Assess** **Differentiated Instruction** See the Differentiated Instruction CD-ROM.

## Resources

**Planning:**

Lesson Planner, pp. 9–11, 170–173

One-Stop Planner

**Presentation:**

Video Program, **GramaVisión**

**Practice:**

Grammar Tutor for Students of Spanish, Chapter 1

Cuaderno de vocabulario y gramática, pp. 10–12

Cuaderno de actividades, pp. 5–7

Activities for Communication, pp. 3–4

Teaching Transparencies Bell Work 1.6

**Vocabulario y gramática** answers, pp. 10–12

Interactive Tutor, Disc 1

### Bell Work

Use Bell Work 1.6 in the *Teaching Transparencies*, or write this activity on the board.

**Escribe cuatro oraciones sobre lo que vas a hacer este año.** 1.3

**Objetivos**
- Pronouns
- Comparisons, demonstrative adjectives and pronouns
- Negative words and time constructions

Interactive TUTOR

# Gramática en acción 2

GramaVisión

## Repaso Pronouns

**1** In Spanish, as in English, the **subject (sujeto)** of a verb does the action and the **object (complemento)** of a verb receives the action.

**María** llama a **Juan.** **Alberto** lleva una **mochila.**

**2** Spanish speakers don't often use **subject pronouns** because the verb ending usually indicates the subject. However, the pronoun may be used to clarify or emphasize the subject.

**Yo** iré al concierto, no Paco. ¡**Tú** tienes que hacerlo!

**3** Pronouns used after prepositions such as **a, de,** and **para** are known as **objects of prepositions.** They have the same form as subject pronouns, except for **mí** and **ti,** which are used instead of **yo** and **tú.** These pronouns join **con** to form **conmigo** and **contigo**.

Carlos me habló **de usted.** Tienes un regalo **para mí?**

**4** **Direct objects** receive the action of the verb. **Indirect objects** usually stand for people who *receive the direct object* or who *experience* the action of the verb. Before **lo(s)** and **la(s), le(s)** changes to **se.**

Mi hermano compró **un boleto** extra y **se lo** regaló a **su novia** en vez de a mí. **Me** parece injusto.

Vocabulario y gramática, pp. 10–12
Actividades, pp. 5–7
Online workbooks

### ¿Te acuerdas?

The pronoun **se** can also refer back to the subject **(reflexive pronoun)** or stand for people doing something to or for each other **(reciprocal actions).**

Irma trota por la mañana para mantener**se** en forma.

Ángel y Gabriela **se** escriben poemas todos los días.

### 30 Sujeto y complemento 1.2

**Leamos/Hablemos** Indica el **sujeto** y el **complemento** de cada oración. Luego, vuelve a decir cada una utilizando pronombres.

1. Paulina y Ana ven a Nacho.
2. Ricardo ayuda a sus amigos.
3. Carolina trae la comida.
4. Mi amiga y yo llamamos al director.
5. Tú y Roberto leen los libros para mañana.
6. Mi profesor tiene los exámenes.

## Core Instruction

### TEACHING GRAMÁTICA

**1.** Go over point 1 with students. Write more sentences and have students identify the subject and object. **Lisa come un taco. Alberto ve un perro. (3 min.)**

**2.** Go over point 2. Ask students to think of times when they might want to emphasize the subject by using a subject pronoun. **(2 min.)**

**3.** Go over point 3. Point out the accent on **mí.** Remind students that the accent differentiates the pronoun used as an object of a preposition (**para mí**) from the possessive pronoun (**mi libro**). **(3 min.)**

**4.** Go over point 4. Provide an example with each type of pronoun. **Luisa me llamó ayer. Le regalé un libro a Juan. Se lo regalé por la mañana.** Lastly, review the information in **¿Te acuerdas? (3 min.)**

### GramaVisión

For a video presentation of pronouns, use **GramaVisión.**

GramaVisión

Visit Holt Online
**go.hrw.com**
KEYWORD: EXP3 CH1
Gramática 2 practice

## 31 Pronombres 1.2

**Leamos/Escribamos** Completa el diálogo con los pronombres correctos.

JORGE Oye, Carmen, ¡ __1__ (ella/tú) llegaste tarde hoy!
CARMEN Ya lo sé, Jorge. ¡ __2__ (Nos/Me) levanté muy tarde hoy porque no sonó el despertador *(alarm)*!
JORGE Pues, tengo algo para __3__ (ti/nosotros). Es un libro de matemáticas que puedes usar en la clase.
CARMEN ¡Gracias, Jorge! Esto __4__ (me/te) va a ayudar mucho.
JORGE De nada. ¿Tú y Alejandra van a ir al ensayo para el club de drama esta tarde?
CARMEN __5__ (Ustedes/Yo) sí voy a ir, pero Alejandra no puede. __6__ (Él/Ella) tiene que cuidar a sus hermanos. Voy a ayudarla después.
JORGE Ustedes siempre __7__ (se/les) ayudan con todo. Qué suerte que sean tan buenas amigas. ¿Puedo ir __8__ (contigo/conmigo) a su casa?

## 32 ¿Qué pasa? 1.2

**Escribamos** Describe en una oración lo que pasa en cada foto. Usa por lo menos un pronombre en cada oración.

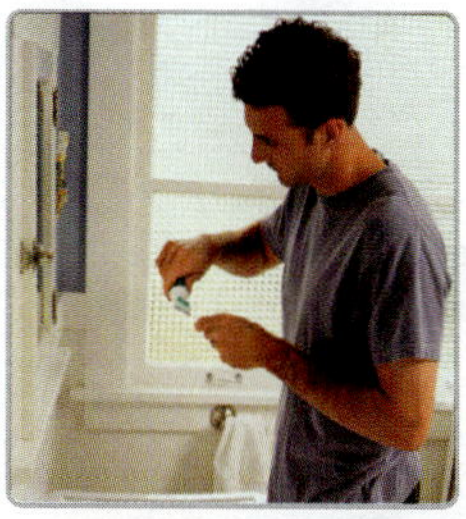
1. Víctor

2. Fernanda y yo

3. Cristina y Tito

4. Rosa y Andrea

## Comunicación

HOLT SoundBooth ONLINE RECORDING

## 33 Adivina quién 1.1, 1.3

**Hablemos** Túrnense tú y un(a) compañero(a) para describir a las personas de tu colegio y adivinar a quién se describe. Usen pronombres en su descripción para no decir quién es.

**MODELO** **—La ves todos los días y está en el club de debate.**
**—¿Es María Eugenia?**
**—¡Exactamente!**

### 30 Answers

1. sujeto: Paulina y Ana; complemento: Nacho; Ellas lo ven.
2. sujeto: Ricardo; complemento: sus amigos; Él los ayuda.
3. sujeto: Carolina; complemento: la comida; Ella la trae.
4. sujeto: Mi amiga y yo; complemento: el director; Nosotros(as) lo llamamos.
5. sujeto: Tú y Roberto; complemento: los libros; Ustedes los leen.
6. sujeto: Mi profesor; complemento: los exámenes; Él los tiene.

### Más práctica

To further review pronouns, you may wish to have students identify the underlined words in each of the following sentences as reflexive, direct object, or indirect object pronouns. If students have trouble distinguishing direct object pronouns from indirect object pronouns, tell them they will have more practice with both types of pronouns in Chapter 2.

1. **Me acosté a las once.** (reflexive pronoun)
2. **Le di el libro a Marta.** (indirect object pronoun)
3. **¿Has visto a Sara? La llamé, pero no está en casa.** (direct object pronoun)
4. **Marcos nos vio en el parque.** (direct object pronoun)
5. **Mi mamá les regaló unos libros.** (indirect object pronoun)
6. **¿Te lavaste la cara?** (reflexive pronoun) 1.2

## Differentiated Instruction

### ADVANCED LEARNERS

**Challenge** Have students write a paragraph about their summer vacation without using subject pronouns. Ask them to exchange paragraphs with a partner, and have the partner rewrite the paragraph, adding subject pronouns where appropriate. Remind them that the subject pronoun is not always necessary in Spanish. 1.3

### SPECIAL LEARNING NEEDS

**31 Students with AD(H)D** Before students do Activity 31, have them write down the verbs in each sentence. Tell them to look at the verb ending to help them decide which subject pronoun to use. For example, they would write **llegaste** in the first sentence. The ending **-aste** tells them that the subject pronoun is **tú.** 1.2

## Comunicación

### Group Activity: Presentational

Have students take turns describing famous people. Tell them they should not use names, only pronouns. The rest of the class has to guess who they are describing. The person who guesses correctly describes the next person. 1.3

**Differentiated Instruction** See the Differentiated Instruction CD-ROM.

# Gramática 2

## Resources

**Planning:**

Lesson Planner, pp. 9–11, 170–173

One-Stop Planner

**Presentation:**

Video Program
**GramaVisión**

**Practice:**

Grammar Tutor for Students of Spanish, Chapter 1

Cuaderno de vocabulario y gramática, pp. 10–12

Cuaderno de actividades, pp. 5–7

Activities for Communication, pp. 3–4

Teaching Transparencies

Bell Work 1.7
**Vocabulario y gramática** answers, pp. 10–12

Interactive Tutor, Disc 1

### Bell Work

Use Bell Work 1.7 in the *Teaching Transparencies*, or write this activity on the board.

**Vuelve a escribir cada oración, reemplazando la(s) palabra(s) subrayada(s) con un pronombre.**

1. Paulina y yo vamos a dar una caminata.
2. Vi a Francisco en el parque.
3. Creo que Sara tiene mi mochila.
4. Tina y Lola van al colegio.
5. Mis papás me esperan en casa. 1.2

## Repaso Comparisons, demonstrative adjectives and pronouns

Interactive TUTOR

**1** To compare two unequal things, actions, or quantities, use the constructions **más** (+ noun/adjective/adverb +) **que** and **menos** (+ noun/adjective/adverb +) **que.**

Tengo **más** planes **que** Fernanda para este año.
Seremos **menos** perezosos **que** el año pasado.
Tú llegaste al colegio **más** tarde **que** Sara.
Berta nada **más que** nadie.

**2** Use a form of the demonstrative adjective that agrees in gender and number with what the speaker is pointing out and shows how far someone or something is in distance or in time.

| | *this* | *these* | *that* | *those* | *that* (*farther away*) | *those* |
|---|---|---|---|---|---|---|
| masculine | **este** | **estos** | **ese** | **esos** | **aquel** | **aquellos** |
| feminine | **esta** | **estas** | **esa** | **esas** | **aquella** | **aquellas** |

¿Te gusta **este** centro recreativo?
Voy a hacer gimnasia con **esas** chicas que entraron.
¿Te acuerdas de **aquel** chico que trabajaba aquí?

**3** You can also use a demonstrative pronoun with an accent mark on the stressed syllable **(éste, ése, aquél)** to avoid repeating a noun. Use the neutral forms **(esto, eso, aquello)** to refer to an idea or to something that was said or done.

Ese diseño para el póster es mejor que **aquél** (aquel diseño). *(agrees with)*

Vocabulario y gramática, pp. 10–12
Actividades, pp. 5–7
Online workbooks

### ¿Te acuerdas?

The following comparisons are irregular.

más + bueno → **mejor**
más + malo → **peor**
más + joven → **menor**
más + viejo → **mayor**

Soy **mayor que** mi prima.
Cantan **peor que** mi perro.

El Cine Callao en la Gran Vía de Madrid tiene pósters que miden más de veinte pies.

### 34 ¿Quieres ver mi colección? 1.2

**Leamos** Completa cada oración con las palabras correctas.

1. Tere, ¿qué opinas de (esta/aquél) estampilla?
2. ¿(Ésa/Este) que está en la primera página de tu álbum?
3. No, (esta/ésta) que acabo de sacar.
4. Es muy bonita. Pero prefiero (aquélla/ésta) que me enseñaste ayer.
5. Te la doy por (esas/éstas) estampillas de España que tú tienes.
6. Vale. ¿Quieres ver (aquellos/aquél) pósters que te mencioné?

## Core Instruction

### TEACHING GRAMÁTICA

1. Go over point 1. **(2 min.)**
2. Have students read point 2 and the chart examples. Practice using the demonstrative adjectives by talking about items in the classroom. Use the appropriate adjective depending on where the item is with respect to your position. **¿Leíste este libro?** (to refer to a book in your hands) **Tráeme esos libros.** (to refer to books at the back of the classroom) **¿Se acuerdan de aquel libro que usaron el año pasado?** **(4 min.)**
3. Go over point 3. Write more examples, using demonstrative adjectives and demonstrative pronouns. Have students identify whether each is an adjective or a pronoun. **(4 min.)**

### GramaVisión

For a video presentation of comparisons, demonstrative adjectives and pronouns, use **GramaVisión.**

GramaVisión

**35 ¿Cierto o falso?** 1.2

**Leamos/Escribamos** Indica si cada oración es **cierta** o **falsa** en tu caso. Corrige las oraciones falsas.

1. Este año, tengo mucho más tarea que el año pasado.
2. Me interesan más los deportes en equipo que los deportes que se practican individualmente.
3. Hago menos actividades ahora que hace dos años.
4. Para mí, es más difícil seguir una dieta balanceada que mantenerme en forma.
5. Saco mejores notas en oratoria que en matemáticas.
6. Estudiar mucho es más importante que hacer amigos.

**36 Tus comparaciones** 1.2

**Escribamos** Escribe una oración para comparar cada par de cosas que se menciona abajo. Usa **más que** y **menos que** en tus oraciones. Sigue el modelo.

**MODELO** **la natación/el esquí acuático**
**Me gusta más la natación que el esquí acuático.**

1. la música rock/la música clásica
2. diseñar páginas Web/coleccionar estampillas
3. el golf/el atletismo
4. la clase de inglés/la clase de matemáticas
5. los poemas/las novelas
6. el club de debate/el club de español
7. el centro recreativo/el colegio
8. observar la naturaleza/participar en un deporte

### Nota cultural

El idioma oficial de España es el español, pero varias regiones españolas tienen sus propios idiomas además del español. En Galicia se habla *gallego,* un idioma parecido al portugués, en Cataluña se habla *catalán* y en el País Vasco se habla *euskera,* un idioma que no tiene nada que ver con ningún idioma europeo. El español moderno, el idioma oficial de toda España, se conoce como *castellano.*

¿En qué otros países se habla más de un idioma? 3.1

Letrero en catalán y castellano

## Comunicación

HOLT SoundBooth ONLINE RECORDING

**37 Comparte tus opiniones** 1.1, 1.2

**Hablemos** Con un(a) compañero(a), comenta y compara varios libros, películas o programas de televisión que hayan leído o visto recientemente. Usen adjetivos o pronombres demostrativos para describirlos, y compárenlos utilizando **más que** y **menos que.**

**MODELO** **—Ayer vi la nueva película "El terror", y hace un mes vi "Una boda en el campo". "El terror" me gustó más que "Una boda en el campo" porque tiene más suspenso.**
**—A mí esas películas no me gustan. Prefiero las películas cómicas...**

## Gramática 2

### Connections

#### History Link

Tell students that when Francisco Franco's authoritarian regime ruled Spain, regional languages such as **catalán** were prohibited. Ask students to research the current conflict between **castellano** and regional languages, especially **catalán.** Do they think the past prohibition of these languages by Franco led to the intense pride in regional languages that we see in Spain today? 3.1

#### Heritage Speakers

If you have any heritage speakers from Spain in your class, ask them to tell what they know about the different languages spoken in Spain.

### Comunicación

#### Pair Activity: Interpersonal

Have students work in pairs. Ask them to use the information from **Geocultura** on Castilla-La Mancha to generate several comparisons between their region and Castilla-La Mancha. Tell them to discuss their ideas and then write five comparative sentences to share with the class. 1.1, 3.1

## Differentiated Instruction

### ADVANCED LEARNERS

**Challenge** Have students research an activity that interests them and write a paragraph comparing details about the activity in Spain and the United States. For example, if a student chooses windsurfing, he or she may want to tell in which country the activity is most popular and where there are more places to windsurf. Ask them to include at least four comparisons in their paragraphs. 1.3, 4.2

### MULTIPLE INTELLIGENCES

**Logical/Mathematical** Have students write a five-question survey about students' habits. The questions should be quantitative: **¿Cuántas horas de tarea haces cada noche? ¿Cuántos libros llevas a casa? ¿Cuántos días de la semana participas en un club?** Ask students to give the survey to two classmates. Then have them draw charts to show the results. Under each chart, they should write a sentence of comparison. **David tiene más horas de tarea que Diana.** 1.1, 3.1

**Differentiated Instruction** See the Differentiated Instruction CD-ROM.

## Resources

**Planning:**

Lesson Planner, pp. 9–11, 170–173

One-Stop Planner

**Presentation:**

Video Program **GramaVisión**

**Practice:**

Grammar Tutor for Students of Spanish, Chapter 1

Cuaderno de vocabulario y gramática, pp. 10–12

Cuaderno de actividades, pp. 5–7

Activities for Communication, pp. 3–4

Lab Book, pp. 13–16

Teaching Transparencies Bell Work 1.8

**Vocabulario y gramática** answers, pp. 10–12

Audio CD 1, Tr. 7

Interactive Tutor, Disc 1

### Bell Work

Use Bell Work 1.8 in the *Teaching Transparencies,* or write this activity on the board.

**Completa las oraciones con la palabra correcta.**

1. **¿Quieres (esta/este) libro?**
2. **No, prefiero (aquél/aquel).**
3. **¿Me pasas (esa/esta) hoja de papel que tienes en la mano?**
4. **Me encantó (este/aquel) ensayo que leímos el año pasado.**
5. **¿Puedes leer (aquel/aquella) oración en el letrero?** 1.2

### 38 Script

See script on page 5E.

Interactive TUTOR

## Repaso Negative words and time constructions

### ¿Te acuerdas?

Other negative words include **nada, nadie, tampoco,** and **ni.**

**No** quiero hacer **nada.**
Yo **tampoco.**
**Nadie** quiere ir al centro recreativo.
**No** quiero hacer gimnasia **ni** saltar la cuerda.

**1** Negative words can go before or after the verb. If they go after the verb, **no** is used before the verb. Use **ninguno(a)** to say *none, not (a single) one.* It is generally used only in the singular and matches the noun it describes in gender. It can stand alone or go in front of a noun. **Ninguno** changes to **ningún** before a masculine singular noun.

> **Ninguno** de ellos me saludó.
> **No** tenemos **ningún** examen mañana.
> Jaime **no** quiere practicar atletismo **jamás.**
> Ella **nunca** llega a tiempo a **ninguna** parte.

**2** The time construction **hacer + time + que + verb** is used to describe an event that began in the past and is still going on.

> **Hace un año que participo** en el club de debate.
> *I have been participating in the debate club for a year.*

For an event that *has not happened* for a period of time up to the present, put **no** in front of the verb.

> **Hace un año que no participo** en el coro.
> *I haven't participated in choir for a year.*

**3** **Hacer + time** can also be used to describe how long ago an event or situation took place.

> **Hace dos años,** me hice amigo de Juan.
> *Two years ago, I became friends with Juan.*
> Vi a Ricardo **hace dos días.**
> *I saw Ricardo two days ago.*

Vocabulario y gramática, pp. 10–12
Actividades, pp. 5–7
Online workbooks

CD 1, Tr. 7

### 38 ¿Hace cuánto tiempo? 1.2

**Escuchemos** Coloca estas actividades en orden cronológico según las oraciones que vas a escuchar. **1.** c **2.** a **3.** b **4.** e **5.** d **6.** f

- **a.** ayudar en la tienda familiar
- **b.** conocer a mi mejor amiga
- **c.** venir a este pueblo
- **d.** ir a Taiwán
- **e.** estudiar chino
- **f.** decidir asistir a la universidad

## Core Instruction

### TEACHING GRAMÁTICA

1. Go over the first part of point 1. Write more examples with **ninguno, ninguna,** and **ningún. (3 min.)**
2. Go over the second part of point 1. Write more examples, placing the negative word before the verb and then after, and have students underline the negative words. **Jamás he corrido cinco millas. No he hecho windsurfing jamás. (3 min.)**
3. Go over point 2. Ask students how long they have been doing certain activities and then use the time construction to restate their responses to the class. **¿Cuánto tiempo hace que practicas atletismo? (1 año) Hace un año que practico atletismo. (2 min.)**
4. Go over point 3. Use the **hacer** + time construction to tell how long ago certain events happened at your school. **Hace una semana empezamos el año escolar. (2 min.)**

### GramaVisión

For a video presentation of negative words and time constructions, use **GramaVisión.**

GramaVisión

**39** **Por favor, necesito...** 1.2

**Escribamos** Imagina que es tu primera semana en la universidad y hay varias cosas que no tienes. Escribe una oración para cada imagen, usando las expresiones de **Gramática.**

**MODELO** **No tengo microondas. Mi compañero de cuarto tampoco tiene uno. (Ni mi compañero de cuarto ni yo tenemos microondas.)**

1

2

3

4
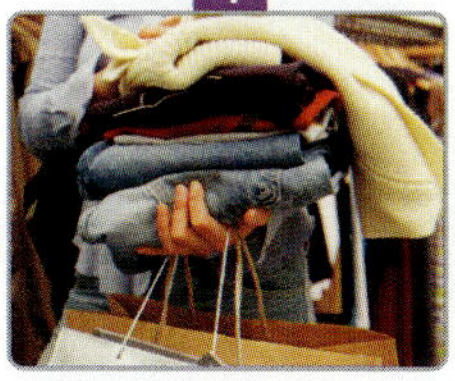

5

6

**40** **Mi vida** 1.3

**Escribamos** Completa las oraciones con algo importante o interesante que hiciste o que sucedió.

1. Hace quince años...
2. Hace diez años...
3. Hace un año...
4. Hace un mes...
5. Hace una semana...
6. Hace una hora...

## Comunicación

HOLT SoundBooth ONLINE RECORDING

**41** **¿Qué quieres hacer?** 1.1, 1.2

**Hablemos** Dramatiza la siguiente conversación. Tú y tu compañero(a) quieren hacer algo juntos, pero a ti no te interesa hacer lo que él o ella sugiere. Responde con expresiones negativas hasta que ustedes lleguen a un acuerdo.

**MODELO** **—¿Por qué no participamos en el club de debate?**
**—No quiero participar en ese club jamás.**

Gramática 2

### Más práctica

Have students rephrase the following sentences using the **hacer** + time construction.

1. **Hoy es jueves. El lunes vi a Elena.**
2. **Estamos en septiembre. En julio fui a España.**
3. **Son las tres. A las dos y media llamé a Sara.**
4. **Estamos en el siglo XXI. En el siglo XV, Colón llegó a las Américas.** 1.2

## Comunicación

### Pair Activity: Interpersonal

Have students work with a partner to discuss activities they have done in past school years and activities they still participate in. Ask them to use the time constructions on page 32 in their conversations.

**MODELO**
**—Hace cuatro años que participo en el club de drama.**
**—Pues yo participé hace dos años, pero ahora no tengo tiempo.**
1.1

## Differentiated Instruction

### SLOWER PACE LEARNERS

**Additional Practice** Have students practice negative words by writing ten sentences about activities they have never done. Ask them to exchange sentences with a partner and underline the negative words. 1.2

### SPECIAL LEARNING NEEDS

**38** **Students with Auditory Impairments** You may wish to have students do Activity 38 on their own, using headphones to listen to the script at their own volume and speed.

## Assess

**Assessment Program**
**Prueba: Gramática 2,** pp. 9–10
**Prueba: Aplicación 2,** pp. 11–12
Audio CD 1, Tr. 13
Alternative Assessment, pp. 373, 385, 397

**Online Assessment**
**my.hrw.com**

**Test Generator**

**Assess** **Differentiated Instruction** See the Differentiated Instruction CD-ROM.

# Capítulo 1
# Novela

## Resources

**Planning:**

Lesson Planner, pp. 12, 172–173

One-Stop Planner

**Presentation:**

Video Program, Videocassette 1

DVD Program

**VideoNovela**

**Practice:**

Video Guide, pp. 6–8

Lab Book, pp. 57–58

### Visual Learners

As a class, arrange the video information in a graphic organizer. List the events that are unexplained and brainstorm conclusions about who else might be a part of the story and why. 1.2

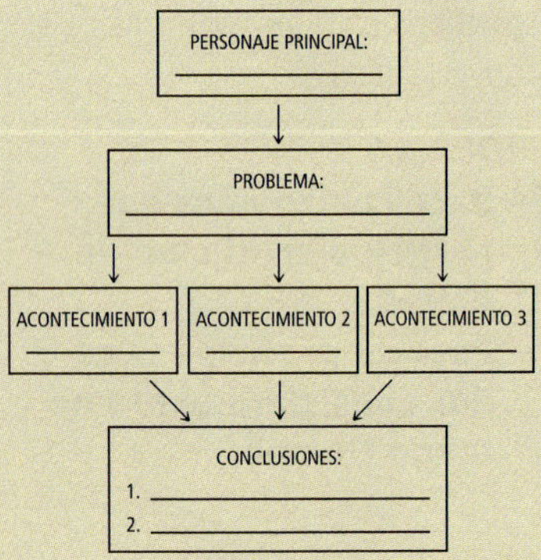


Novela en video

# Clara perspectiva
## Episodio 1

**ESTRATEGIA**

**Analyzing the opening** Usually in any story, an incident at the beginning gets the plot going. The main character is faced with a problem that sets him or her off on some sort of journey. As you go through **Episodio 1,** decide who you think the main character is and why. What is that character's problem? What does the character see on the journey to solving the problem? What events in the episode are unexplained? Can you tell from these unexplained events who else might be a central part of the story? Why? 1.2

**En la universidad**

**En el café una semana después**

**Clara** Le pedí la recomendación al profesor Luna hace una semana. Y todavía no la escribe.
**Graciela** ¿Cuándo la tienes que entregar?
**Clara** En dos días. De todos los puestos que solicité, éste, el de la revista *Chile en la Mira,* es el que más quiero.

**Graciela** Sí, entiendo por qué. Es una revista buenísima. El otro día leí allí un artículo súper interesante sobre el medio ambiente.
**Clara** ¡No sé qué voy a hacer!

**Graciela** ¿Por qué no le pides la recomendación a la profesora del Valle? O pídesela al profesor Matías.
**Clara** Tienes razón. Los llamo apenas llegue a mi casa, pero no te he contado lo más interesante.

## Core Instruction

### TEACHING NOVELA EN VIDEO

1. Have students scan the **Novela en video** text to familiarize themselves with the names of the characters. **(1 min.)**
2. Play the video, stopping periodically to ask comprehension questions. **(20 min.)**
3. Have volunteers play the parts of the characters and read the video text aloud. **(3 min.)**
4. Ask students to tell who they think the main character is in this episode and have them discuss the character's problem. **(2 min.)**
5. Have students work in pairs to answer the **¿Comprendes?** questions on page 35. **(5 min.)**

### Escuchemos

As students watch the **Novela,** have them tally the number of times they hear someone give Clara advice, or tell her what to do or not do. (four times) Then have them summarize the story.

**Novela en video**

Visit Holt Online
**go.hrw.com**
KEYWORD: EXP3 CH1
Online Edition

Novela en video

5

6

7

**Graciela** Bueno y entonces, ¿qué pasó?
**Clara** No, nada. Se separaron sin despedirse. El profesor Luna se fue por un lado y el hombre por otro.
**Graciela** Clara, Clara, Clara. ¿Qué voy a hacer contigo?

**En la universidad**

***Dos personas le dan un sobre al profesor Luna.***

8

**¿COMPRENDES?**

1. ¿Qué quiere Clara con el profesor Luna? ¿Es importante? ¿Cómo lo sabes?
2. ¿Qué le pide Clara al profesor Luna? ¿Para qué es? ¿Él se la da?
3. ¿Qué dice Graciela de la revista?
4. ¿Qué más le cuenta Clara a Graciela sobre el profesor Luna?
5. ¿Qué cree Clara del incidente? ¿Qué cree Graciela?
6. ¿Crees que las dos personas que le dieron el sobre al profesor Luna al final tienen algo que ver con el hombre de traje oscuro? ¿Por qué sí o por qué no?

1.2, 1.3

**Próximo episodio**
*Clara empieza a trabajar en la revista* Chile en la Mira*. ¿Crees que va a olvidarse del asunto con el profesor Luna?*
PÁGINAS 76–77

**Clara perspectiva, Episodio 1**

In **Episodio 1**, we meet Clara de la Rosa and her friend Graciela. While on campus, Clara goes to see her Environmental Studies professor, Armando Luna. When she finds him, he's in a big hurry and rushes off. Because she thinks his behavior is strange, she decides to follow him to see where he goes. She sees an ominous man approach him and speak to him in a threatening manner. A week later, she meets her friend Graciela at a café, where she talks about her plans to apply for an internship at *Chile en la Mira,* a popular Chilean magazine. She tells Graciela about the professor and the strange man. Graciela makes fun of Clara's sleuthing. Later, we see Professor Luna on campus approached by two young people who give him an envelope.

### Gestures

Have students note the gestures used by the actors. What gestures do they use to show emotion? Do students use the same types of gestures to show emotion? Have students note what gestures are used in the rest of the video to show the same emotions.

### ¿Comprendes? Answers

1. Clara quiere hablar con él. Sí; dice que es urgente.
2. Clara le pide una recomendación para un puesto en la revista *Chile en la Mira.* No.
3. Graciela dice que es buenísima.
4. Clara le cuenta que lo vio discutiendo con un señor de traje oscuro.
5. Clara cree que fue algo importante porque los dos discutieron un buen rato. Graciela cree que probablemente sólo se peleó con un amigo.
6. Answers will vary.

### Cultures

#### Practices and Perspectives

Have students note the difference between the way Clara speaks to the professor and the way she speaks to Graciela. Point out that she addresses the professor as **usted** and Graciela as **tú.** What formalities do students use in the United States to show respect to teachers?

2.1, 4.2

### Comparisons

#### Comparing and Contrasting

Have students look up information about popular magazines in Chile, such as **Qué Pasa.** Are they similar to magazines in the United States? What kinds of topics do they cover?

4.2

**Resources**

**Planning:**

Lesson Planner, pp. 13, 174–175

One-Stop Planner

**Presentation:**

Audio CD 1, Tr. 8

**Practice:**

Cuaderno de actividades, p. 8

Reading Strategies and Skills Handbook, Chapter 1

Interactive Advanced Reader

# Lectura informativa

CD 1, Tr. 8

# Una visita a Castilla-La Mancha

El azafrán se recolecta de pequeñas flores color lila.

**Los castillos de Castilla-La Mancha**

Durante siglos, varios ejércitos lucharon por el control de la región de Castilla-La Mancha. En la Edad Media, Castilla-La Mancha era una zona neutral entre los cristianos del norte de lo que hoy es España y los musulmanes del sur, por lo tanto, construyeron muchos castillos fortificados. Hoy en día estos castillos son un recuerdo impresionante de la historia de la región, y todos los años los turistas siguen la "Ruta de los castillos" para verlos.

**Arte y arquitectura de Toledo**

Toledo, una ciudad de Castilla-La Mancha muy popular entre los turistas, es un centro importante de la historia medieval de Europa. Su arquitectura incluye edificios de muchas épocas, de estilos morisco, mudéjar, gótico y del renacimiento[1]. También tiene una tradición artística importante; el famoso pintor El Greco vivió allí desde 1577 hasta su muerte en 1604.

A lo largo de la historia las espadas de Toledo eran reconocidas como las mejores del mundo y fueron usadas por Aníbal y su ejército, los romanos, los ejércitos musulmanes e incluso los samurai japoneses.

**El azafrán de Consuegra**

El mes de octubre es buen momento para visitar Castilla-La Mancha. Ésta es la época de la cosecha de la uva[2] y no solamente los viñedos[3] están llenos de colores, sino que la tierra al sur de Toledo está cubierta de crocos[4]. Los moros trajeron a España esta flor que produce una de las especias más caras del mundo, el azafrán[5]. Esta especia es la que se usa en la famosa paella de España y la que le da el color amarillo intenso. La mayor cosecha de azafrán se realiza alrededor del pueblo de Consuegra. Una vez al año se celebra el Día de la Rosa de Azafrán y una chica es elegida para presidir el festival. La llaman Dulcinea de La Mancha, por la enamorada de Don Quijote en el libro de Cervantes.

La Crestería Manchega

1 *de estilos...* Moorish, Mudejar, Gothic, and Renaissance styles 2 grape harvest 3 vineyards 4 crocus flowers 5 saffron

## Core Instruction

**TEACHING LECTURA INFORMATIVA**

Before beginning the reading, ask students what they know about Spain or if anyone has traveled there. Have students think about what Castilla-La Mancha offers tourists. Ask students what attracts them to the region by looking at the photos. Have them also look back at the Castilla-La Mancha **Geocultura** on pages 1–5.

1. Call on volunteers to read the photo captions. **(2 min.)**
2. Have students read the boldface text before each paragraph. **(3 min.)**
3. Have students read each paragraph individually or in pairs. **(10 min.)**
4. Ask students to help you summarize the reading. **(5 min.)**
5. Have students do the **Comprensión** activities with a partner. **(10 min.)**
6. Have students do the **Actividad** and share their answers with the class. **(10 min.)**

**Pre-AP Practice**

**AP Language Examination: Lectura informativa** helps students prepare for Section I, Part B: **Reading Comprehension.** The audio recording helps them prepare for Part A: **Listening–Short Narratives.**

Para la Fiesta de la Endiablada, en Almonacid del Marquesado, los jóvenes se cuelgan cencerros *(cow-bells)* del cuello y corren por el pueblo.

**Los festivales de La Mancha**

Otro festival importante en la región es la Fiesta del Olivo[6], en Mora. Las aceitunas[7] son uno de los productos más importantes de la región. También están el Festival de San Isidro que se celebra en Talavera de la Reina entre mayo y junio y la Fiesta de la Amistad[8] que se celebra en Polán en el mes de junio.

**La cerámica de Talavera de la Reina**

Talavera de la Reina tiene una rica tradición artesanal. Hay muchos talleres[9] que producen trabajos en cuero, entre los que se destacan las sillas de montar. También hay talleres que producen velas y figuras de cera[10] y otros que se especializan en la elaboración de muebles y la talla de madera[11]. Pero los talleres más importantes son los de cerámica. Por la cantidad, calidad y variedad de su producción cerámica, Talavera de la Reina es conocida en toda España como la Ciudad de la cerámica. La gente viene de todas partes del mundo para comprar azulejos[12], platos, jarrones[13], candelabros, cuencos[14] y otras piezas elaboradas y pintadas a mano.

6 Olive Festival 7 olives 8 Festival of Friendship 9 workshops 10 wax 11 wood carving 12 tiles 13 vases 14 bowls

## Comprensión

**A Cierto o falso** Basándote en lo que leíste, contesta **cierto** o **falso.** 1.2

1. En la Edad Media, los musulmanes vivían en el norte de España. falso
2. Se puede encontrar arquitectura mudéjar en Toledo. cierto
3. Toledo es famoso por sus espadas. cierto
4. La cosecha de la uva se realiza en Castilla-La Mancha en junio. falso
5. Las aceitunas y el azafrán son productos importantes de Castilla-La Mancha. cierto
6. El Festival de San Isidro se celebra en Talavera de la Reina. cierto

**B Detalles importantes** Contesta las preguntas. 1.2

1. ¿Qué pintor famoso vivía en Toledo en el siglo XVI? El Greco
2. ¿De qué planta se obtiene el azafrán? el croco
3. ¿Quiénes trajeron el azafrán a España? los moros
4. ¿Cuándo se celebra la Fiesta de la Amistad? junio
5. ¿Qué festivales rinden honores a productos importantes de Castilla-La Mancha? La Fiesta del Olivo y El Día de la Rosa de Azafrán

**Actividad** 1.1, 3.1

**Un viaje** ¿Qué parte de Castilla-La Mancha te interesa ver? ¿A qué festival quieres ir? Habla con un(a) compañero(a) sobre qué hacer en un viaje a Castilla-La Mancha. Busquen más información por Internet para compartir con la clase.



# Lectura informativa

### Heritage Speakers

Ask heritage speakers if they know of particular celebrations or customs in a Spanish-speaking country. Ask them what the history of the celebration is and why it is still important today. 2.1

### Connections

**Geography Link**

Have students refer to the map of Castilla-La Mancha in **Geocultura.** In small groups, have students give a tour of the region to tourists. They can use the Internet to find at least one activity for each region and point it out on the map. 3.1

**Art Link**

Tell students that archaeologists working on Toledo's Carranque recently uncovered a 4th-century Roman basilica, Spain's oldest. Have students research more information about Toledo to find specific examples of its impressive architecture. You might suggest that they investigate the **Alcázar,** the two synagogues, the **Iglesia de Santo Tomé,** or the **Museo de Santa Cruz.** 3.1

### Post-Reading Activities

Ask students to think about what would attract tourists to their community. Have them make a short list of attractions such as historical sites, food, or festivals that would be interesting to a visitor and ask volunteers to share their lists with the class. How are the attractions different in Castilla-La Mancha and the students' communities? 2.1, 4.2

## Differentiated Instruction

**ADVANCED LEARNERS**

**Extension** Have students continue the Geography Link by connecting each of the points on the tour map they prepared, and providing the distance in kilometers between each point using a map key. They should also make a short list of expressions in Spanish to help the tourist. 3.1

**SPECIAL LEARNING NEEDS**

**Students with Learning Disabilities** Have students listen to the audio recording of the reading. Play one paragraph at a time, stopping at the end of each. Have students tell you the main idea of each paragraph. Once students have summarized each paragraph, have them make an overall summary of the reading as a group. 1.2

### Assess

**Assessment Program**
**Prueba: Lectura,** p. 13

**Online Assessment**
**my.hrw.com**

**Test Generator**

**Assess** **Differentiated Instruction** See the Differentiated Instruction CD-ROM.

**Resources**

**Planning:**

Lesson Planner, pp. 13–14, 174–175

One-Stop Planner

**Practice:**

Cuaderno de actividades, p. 8

Reading Strategies and Skills Handbook, Chapter 1

Interactive Advanced Reader

**Escuchemos**

Play the recording of the reading, and have students listen with their books closed for the tense used when someone's appearance or personality is being described in the story. (the imperfect)

**Pre-AP Practice**

**AP Language Examination:** **Leamos** helps students prepare for Section I, Part B: **Reading Comprehension.**

# Leamos y escribamos

**ESTRATEGIA**

**para leer** Determining the narrator's point of view is an important strategy. When the story is told in the first person, the narrator tells the events from his or her point of view. When the story is told in the third person, the narrator describes the actions of the characters from a distance. Before reading the story, scan the verbs in the first paragraph to determine the point of view of the narrator. 1.2, 3.1



## Antes de leer 1.2

**A** Ana María Matute nació en Barcelona en 1926 y su juventud fue marcada por la Guerra Civil española. En 1984 Matute obtuvo el Premio Nacional de Literatura Infantil con la obra *Sólo un pie descalzo.* El cuento "El árbol de oro" es uno de los cuentos más populares de la colección *Historias de la Artámila.* Mientras lees el cuento, determina quién es el narrador y considera por qué la autora escogió a este personaje para narrar el cuento. ¿Cuántos años tiene el (la) narrador(a)? ¿Qué papel *(role)* tiene este personaje en el cuento?

# El árbol de oro

*de Ana María Matute*

Asistí durante un otoño a la escuela de la señorita Leocadia, en la aldea, porque mi salud no andaba bien y el abuelo retrasó mi vuelta a la ciudad. Como era el tiempo frío y estaban los suelos embarrados y no se veía rastro de muchachos, me aburría dentro de la casa, y pedí al abuelo asistir a la escuela. El abuelo consintió, y acudí a aquella casita alargada y blanca de cal, a las afueras del pueblo.

La señorita Leocadia era alta y gruesa, tenía el carácter más bien áspero. Las clases en la escuela, con la lluvia rebotando en el tejado y en los cristales, tenían su atractivo. Recuerdo especialmente a un muchacho de unos diez años, hijo de un aparcero[1] muy pobre, llamado Ivo. Era un muchacho delgado, de ojos azules, que bizqueaba[2] ligeramente al hablar. Todos los muchachos y muchachas de la escuela admiraban y envidiaban un poco a Ivo, por el don que poseía de atraer la atención sobre sí, en todo momento. No es que fuera ni inteligente ni gracioso, y, sin embargo, había algo en él, en su voz quizás, en las cosas que contaba, que conseguía cautivar a quien le escuchase. También la señorita Leocadia se dejaba prender de aquella red de plata que Ivo tendía a cuantos atendían sus enrevesadas[3] conversaciones, y —yo creo que muchas veces contra su voluntad— la señorita Leocadia le confiaba a Ivo tareas deseadas por todos, o distinciones que merecían alumnos más estudiosos y aplicados.

1 tenant farmer 2 to squint, to be cross-eyed 3 intricate, complicated

## Core Instruction

### TEACHING LEAMOS

Before beginning the reading, ask students if they had a teacher in elementary school that assigned tasks to students. What tasks did the teacher assign? (erase the board, sharpen pencils) Have students describe a typical morning in elementary school in the first person to a partner.

1. Read **Antes de leer** to students and tell students that this story is set in a small town in Spain. **(5 min.)**
2. Read the first paragraph aloud to the class and summarize the setting. **(5 min.)**
3. Have students read the rest of the story. Stop and monitor comprehension as needed. **(20 min.)**
4. Have students complete the **Comprensión** activities on page 40 with a partner. **(15 min.)**

Quizá lo que más se envidiaba de Ivo era la posesión de la codiciada[4] llave de *la torrecita*. Ésta era, en efecto, una pequeña torre situada en un ángulo de la escuela, en cuyo interior se guardaban los libros de lectura. Allí entraba Ivo a buscarlos, y allí volvía a dejarlos, al terminar la clase.

Ivo estaba muy orgulloso de esta distinción, y por nada del mundo la hubiera cedido. Un día, Mateo Heredia, el más aplicado y estudioso de la escuela, pidió encargarse de la tarea —a todos nos fascinaba el misterioso interior de la torrecita, donde no entramos nunca—, y la señorita Leocadia pareció acceder. Pero Ivo se levantó, y acercándose a la maestra empezó a hablarle en su voz baja, bizqueando los ojos y moviendo mucho las manos, como tenía por costumbre. La maestra dudó un poco, y al fin dijo:

—Quede todo como estaba. Que siga encargándose Ivo de la torrecita.

A la salida de la escuela le pregunté:

—¿Qué le has dicho a la maestra?

Ivo me miró de través y vi relampaguear sus ojos azules.

—Le hablé del árbol de oro.

Sentí una gran curiosidad.

—¿Qué árbol?

—Si no se lo cuentas a nadie...

—Te lo juro, que a nadie se lo diré.

Entonces Ivo me explicó:

—Veo un árbol de oro. Un árbol completamente de oro: ramas, tronco, hojas... ¿sabes? Las hojas no se caen nunca. En verano, en invierno, siempre. Resplandece[5] mucho; tanto, que tengo que cerrar los ojos para que no me duelan.

—¡Qué embustero[6] eres! —dije, aunque con algo de zozobra[7]. Ivo me miró con desprecio.

—No te lo creas —contestó—. Me es completamente igual que te lo creas o no... ¡Nadie entrará nunca en la torrecita, y a nadie dejaré ver mi árbol de oro! ¡Es mío! La señorita Leocadia lo sabe, y no se atreve a darle la llave a Mateo Heredia, ni a nadie... ¡Mientras yo viva, nadie podrá entrar allí y ver mi árbol!

Lo dijo de tal forma que no pude evitar el preguntarle:

—¿Y cómo lo ves...?

—¡Ah, no es fácil —dijo, con aire misterioso—. Cualquiera no podría verlo. Yo sé la rendija[8] exacta. Una que hay corriendo el cajón de la derecha: me agacho y me paso horas y horas... ¡Cómo brilla el árbol! ¡Cómo brilla! Fíjate que si algún pájaro se le pone encima también se vuelve de oro. Eso me digo yo: si me subiera a una rama, ¿me volvería acaso de oro también?

No supe qué decirle, pero, desde aquel momento, mi deseo de ver el árbol creció de tal forma que me desasosegaba[9]. Todos los días, al acabar la clase de lectura, Ivo se acercaba al cajón de la maestra, sacaba la llave y se dirigía a la torrecita. Cuando volvía, le preguntaba:

—¿Lo has visto?

—Sí —me contestaba. Y, a veces, explicaba alguna novedad:

—Le han salido unas flores raras. Mira: así de grandes, como mi mano lo menos, y con los pétalos alargados.

Ocurrió entonces algo que secretamente yo deseaba; me avergonzaba sentirlo, pero así era: Ivo enfermó, y la señorita Leocadia encargó a otro la llave de la torrecita. Primeramente, la disfrutó Mateo Heredia. Yo espié su regreso, el primer día, y le dije:

4 much desired, coveted 5 shines 6 liar 7 anxiety 8 crack 9 made me uneasy

# Leamos y escribamos

## Active Reading Questions

1. **¿Por qué los muchachos del colegio envidiaban a Ivo?**
2. **¿Qué es *la torrecita?* ¿Para qué se usa?**
3. **¿Qué siente Ivo con respecto al árbol de oro?**
4. **¿Por qué la señorita Leocadia encargó la llave a otra persona?**

1.2, 3.2

## Connections

### Thinking Critically

Tell students that many of Ana María Matute's stories reflect her experiences as a pre-adolescent during the Spanish Civil War. She often writes of isolation and suffering, using humble children as characters. Ask students to discuss how **El árbol de oro** reflects these themes. 3.1

## Teaching Suggestion

Have students create a character sketch of the narrator. Ask them to provide passages from the reading to support their ideas. 3.1

## Differentiated Instruction

### SLOWER PACE LEARNERS

**Additional Practice** If students have trouble understanding the story, have them reread it one paragraph at a time with a partner. As they read, have them make a list of words they do not understand. As students finish each paragraph, go over their lists as a class and help students determine the meaning by using the context in the story. 1.2

### MULTIPLE INTELLIGENCES

**Linguistic** Ask students to think about a memorable day from their childhood. Ask them to narrate this day in the first person and include details that made it memorable. The narration can include something from real life or it could be fictional. 1.3

**B Answers**

1. Ivo era un compañero de la narradora. Tenía diez años, era pobre, delgado, de ojos azules que bizqueaba al hablar.
2. Tenía un don de atraer la atención sobre sí en todo momento.
3. Veía un árbol de oro.
4. Ivo se enfermó y la profesora le dio la llave a otro niño. La narradora se la pidió y el niño se la dio.
5. No vio nada.
6. Descubrió un árbol de oro al lado de una crucecilla de hierro con el nombre de Ivo.

### Thinking Critically

Have students go to **BBCMUNDO.com** on the Internet and look over the articles. Ask them to choose an article that interests them, print it out, and read it. Have them take turns summarizing their articles for the class and giving their opinions. Suggest that they keep a list of unknown words from the article on a separate sheet of paper with the title of the article at the top. Ask them to try to determine the meaning of the words using context clues. Have them use a dictionary to check their answers. 1.2

### Post-Reading Activity

Have students think about the role of the tree for Ivo in the story. Ask them why they think Ivo told the other children about what he saw in the **torrecita.** Ask students why they think the narrator didn't feel sad for Ivo at the end of the story. 1.2

### Pre-AP Practice

**AP Language Examination: Leamos and Escribamos** help students prepare for Section I, Part B: **Reading Comprehension** and Section II, Part A: **Informal Writing.**

—¿Has visto un árbol de oro?

—¿Qué andas graznando[10]? —me contestó de malos modos, porque no era simpático, y menos conmigo. Unos días después, me dijo:

—Si me das algo a cambio, te dejo un ratito la llave y vas durante el recreo. Nadie te verá...

Vacié mi hucha[11], y, por fin, conseguí la codiciada llave. Mis manos temblaban de emoción cuando entré en el cuartito de la torre. Allí estaba el cajón. Lo aparté y vi brillar la rendija en la oscuridad. Me agaché y miré.

Cuando la luz dejó de cegarme, mi ojo derecho sólo descubrió una cosa: la seca tierra de la llanura alargándose hacia el cielo. Nada más. Tuve una gran decepción y la seguridad de que me habían estafado[12].

Olvidé la llave y el árbol de oro. Antes de que llegaran las nieves regresé a la ciudad.

Dos veranos más tarde volví a las montañas. Un día, pasando por el cementerio — era ya tarde y se anunciaba la noche en el cielo: el sol, como una bola roja, caía a lo lejos — vi algo extraño. De la tierra pedregosa[13], entre las cruces caídas, nacía un árbol grande y hermoso, con las hojas anchas de oro: encendido y brillante todo él, cegador[14]. Algo me vino a la memoria, como un sueño, y pensé: "Es un árbol de oro". Busqué al pie del árbol, y no tardé en dar con una crucecilla de hierro negro, mohosa[15] por la lluvia. Mientras la enderezaba[16], leí: IVO MÁRQUEZ, DE DIEZ AÑOS DE EDAD.

Y no daba tristeza alguna, sino, tal vez, una extraña y muy grande alegría.

**10** squawking about **11** piggy bank **12** cheated, tricked **13** rocky **14** blinding **15** moldy **16** straightened

## Comprensión 1.2

**B Los acontecimientos** Contesta las preguntas.

1. ¿Quién era Ivo? ¿Cómo era?
2. ¿Qué tenía Ivo que les daba envidia a los demás?
3. ¿Qué veía Ivo en la torrecita?
4. ¿Cómo entró la narradora por fin a la torrecita?
5. ¿Qué vio la narradora en la torrecita?
6. Cuando la narradora volvió después de varios años, ¿qué descubrió?

## Pasó así 1.2

**C ¿Es cierto?** Determina si cada oración es **cierta** o **falsa.**

1. La narradora estaba en las montañas porque había estado enferma. cierta
2. Ivo era de una familia pobre. cierta
3. Los estudiantes admiraban a Ivo. cierta
4. Muchas personas habían visto el árbol de oro. falsa
5. La narradora siempre creía en el árbol de oro. falsa
6. Ivo quería que la narradora entrara a la torrecita. falsa

## Después de leer 1.2

**D** Repasa el cuento y busca las descripciones de la casa de la narradora, del colegio, de la señorita Leocadia y del cementerio. Escribe los adjetivos en una lista. ¿Cómo es el ambiente? ¿Cuál es el efecto del árbol de oro en este ambiente? Comenta la importancia de la fantasía en este cuento.

## Core Instruction

### TEACHING ESCRIBAMOS

1. Discuss **Estrategia para escribir** as a class. **(2 min.)**
2. Have students brainstorm a list of characters to be included in their narration before they do step 1. **(5 min.)**
3. Have students write their narration and revise it with a partner (steps 2 and 3). **(20 min.)**
4. Have students exchange their completed narration with a partner and do step 4. **(6 min.)**

# Taller del escritor 1.3

**ESTRATEGIA**

**para escribir** When writing a story, it's important to decide what point of view will best communicate your ideas. If you want readers to feel a closer connection with one character, you may want to use the first person. If you'd like to communicate the thoughts of all of the characters, the third person omniscient narrator may be the best choice. The word *omniscient* means all-knowing; the narrator knows what all of the characters say, do, and think.

## El punto de vista

Vas a escribir un cuento sobre algo que te pasó de niño(a) o algo que le pasó a otro(a) niño(a). Puedes escribir un cuento realista o puedes añadir algunos elementos de fantasía.

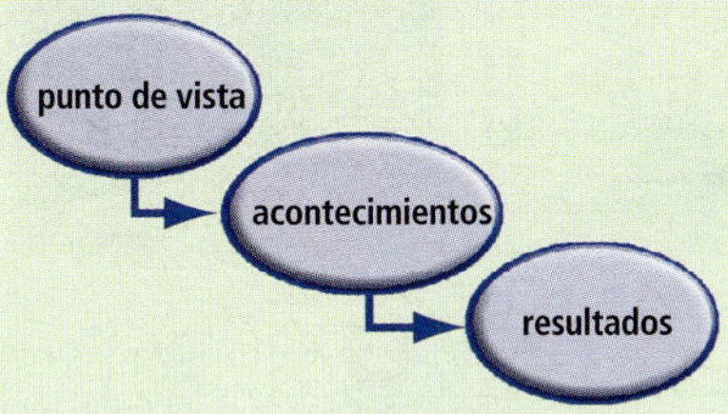


**1 Antes de escribir**

Antes de empezar tu cuento, decide quiénes van a ser los personajes. Determina qué acontecimientos vas a describir y qué personajes vas a incluir. Escribe una lista de los personajes y sus características y decide qué punto de vista vas a usar.

**2 Escribir un borrador**

Empieza a escribir el cuento. Describe a los personajes y sus acciones desde el punto de vista que escogiste.

**3 Revisar**

Revisa tu borrador y corrige los errores de gramática y ortografía si los hay. Lee tu borrador para ver si se mantiene el mismo punto de vista a través de todo el cuento. ¿Están bien descritos los personajes? ¿Está claro el orden de los sucesos?

**4 Publicar**

Comparte tu cuento con un(a) compañero(a) para que lo lea. Túrnense para comentar los puntos de vista que escogieron para sus cuentos. Da tu opinión de los personajes. Compartan sus cuentos con la clase y comparen el efecto de la primera persona con el de la tercera persona.

Leamos y escribamos

## Process Writing

Ask students to think about what their narration might include. Have them think about the events they would like to narrate and make a list. Have them use the graphic organizer to present the events in order. They should also think about whether the story should be narrated in the first or third person. For example, if the narrator was not present for certain events in the story, students might want to narrate in the third person.

## Writing Assessment

To assess the **Taller del escritor,** you can use the following rubric.

| Writing Rubric | 4 | 3 | 2 | 1 |
|---|---|---|---|---|
| **Content** (Complete—Incomplete) | | | | |
| **Comprehensibility** (Comprehensible—Seldom comprehensible) | | | | |
| **Accuracy** (Accurate—Seldom accurate) | | | | |
| **Organization** (Well-organized—Poorly organized) | | | | |
| **Effort** (Excellent effort—Minimal effort) | | | | |

18–20: A 16–17: B 14–15: C 12–13: D Under 12: F

## Differentiated Instruction

### ADVANCED LEARNERS

**Variation** Have students create a narration in the third person about an event of their choosing. First have students use the graphic organizer to outline the narration. Students should include various elements and characters in their narration. 1.3

### SPECIAL LEARNING NEEDS

**Students with Visual Impairments/ Learning Disabilities** Students may have a difficult time visualizing the graphic organizer in the book. You may want to create an additional graphic organizer on the board or on a transparency and have volunteers provide information to fill it in. Students may copy the organizer into their notebooks and use it as a reference to do the writing exercises.

### Assess

**Assessment Program**
**Prueba: Lectura,** p. 13
**Prueba: Escritura,** p. 14
**Online Assessment**
**my.hrw.com**
**Test Generator**

**Assess** **Differentiated Instruction** See the Differentiated Instruction CD-ROM.

# Prepárate para el examen

## Resources

**Planning:**

Lesson Planner, pp. 14–15, 174–177

One-Stop Planner

**Presentation:**

Video Program, Videocassette 1

DVD Program

**Variedades**

**Practice:**

Activities for Communication, pp. 43, 55–56

Video Guide, pp. 1, 2

Lab Book, pp. 1, 13–16, 56

Audio CD 1, Trs. 9–10

Pre-AP Instructional Resources

Pre-AP Audio CD 1, Trs. 1–4

Interactive Tutor, Disc 1

Teaching Transparencies

**Situación, Capítulo 1**

Picture Sequences, Chapter 1

## 1 Script

1. Nosotros fuimos a la ciudad y lo pasamos de película.
2. Fernando fue a un lago con sus amigos y nadaron mucho.
3. Sara y sus hermanos dieron una caminata por el bosque.
4. Lorena y su familia acamparon en las montañas y se aburrieron mucho.

---

Capítulo 1
Repaso

# Prepárate para el examen

Interactive TUTOR

CD 1, Tr. 9

**1** Escucha los comentarios y escoge la foto que corresponde a cada uno. 1.2  **1.** a **2.** c **3.** d **4.** b

A

B

C

D

**1 Vocabulario 1**
- talking about the past
- talking about what you liked and used to do

**pp. 8–13**

**2 Gramática 1**
- preterite and imperfect
- **ser** and **estar**
- subjunctive for hopes and wishes

**pp. 14–19**

**3 Vocabulario 2**
- asking for and giving advice
- talking about the future

**pp. 22–27**

**2** Completa las oraciones con la forma correcta de los verbos. 1.2

1. Yo (fui/iba) con mi amigo Julio a España en junio.
2. Julio (conocía/conoció) a su novia en España.
3. Él dice que su novia española (es/está) muy bonita.
4. Espero que (puedo/pueda) conocerla algún día.
5. Julio quiere que ella (viene/venga) a visitarnos aquí.
6. Parece que ellos (están/son) la pareja perfecta.

**3** Completa el diálogo con las palabras del cuadro. 1.2

| consejo | coleccionar | interesa | aburrida | hacerte | atletismo |
|---|---|---|---|---|---|

TINA: Siempre estoy muy __1__ después del colegio. No tengo nada que hacer. aburrida

CARMELA: A mí me encanta correr, y pienso practicar __2__ este año. ¿Por qué no lo practicas también? atletismo

TINA: No me gusta correr. ¿Qué otro __3__ me puedes dar? consejo

CARMELA: Pues, también me gusta __4__ cosas, y tengo un álbum lleno de estampillas. Si quieres, te ayudo a empezar un álbum. coleccionar

TINA: Gracias, Carmela, pero la verdad es que no me __5__. Pero sí me gusta hacer diseño por computadora. interesa

CARMELA: Entonces debes __6__ amiga de Emilio; él sabe diseñar páginas Web y te puede enseñar. hacerte

## Oral Assessment

### Speaking Rubric

To assess the speaking activities in this section, you might use the following rubric. For additional speaking rubrics, see the Alternative Assessment section of the *Assessment Program.*

| Speaking Rubric | 4 | 3 | 2 | 1 |
|---|---|---|---|---|
| **Content** (Complete—Incomplete) | | | | |
| **Comprehension** (Total—Little) | | | | |
| **Comprehensibility** (Comprehensible—Incomprehensible) | | | | |
| **Accuracy** (Accurate—Seldom Accurate) | | | | |
| **Fluency** (Fluent—Not Fluent) | | | | |

18–20: A  16–17: B  14–15: C  12–13: D  Under 12: F

Visit Holt Online
go.hrw.com
KEYWORD: EXP3 CH1
Chapter Self-test

4 Completa las oraciones con la palabra correcta. 1.2

1. (Hace/Hacemos) una semana que estamos en Toledo.
2. Mamá (se/le) regaló una espada de Toledo a mi hermano.
3. Nunca he visto una espada más bonita que (aquélla/aquél).
4. Luego mi papá (nos/se) invitó a comer.
5. Mi hermano comió mucho más (de/que) yo.
6. (Nunca/Ninguno) de nosotros dejó nada en el plato.

5 Contesta las preguntas. 1.2

1. ¿En qué ciudad de Castilla-La Mancha vivía El Greco? Toledo
2. ¿Qué especia que se usa en las paellas se produce en Castilla-La Mancha? el azafrán
3. ¿Por qué es famosa la ciudad de Cuenca? por las Casas Colgadas
4. ¿Cómo se llama el famoso dulce de almendra de Toledo? el mazapán

CD 1, Tr. 10 1.2

6 Escucha el diálogo entre Ramón y Patricia y escribe una lista de las actividades que Ramón le sugiere a ella. la banda escolar el club de debate los ejercicios aeróbicos el atletismo el golf

**4 Gramática 2**
- pronouns
- comparisons, demonstrative adjectives and pronouns
- negative words and time constructions

pp. 28–33

**5 Cultura**
- Comparaciones pp. 20–21
- Lectura informativa pp. 36–37
- Notas culturales pp. 10, 13, 16, 24, 27, 31

## Conversación

HOLT SoundBooth ONLINE RECORDING

7 Role-play the following conversation with a partner. Partner A and Partner B are classmates talking about their summer vacations. 1.1, 1.2

| | |
|---|---|
| Partner A: | Ask what your partner did on vacation. |
| Partner B: | Say what you did and what it was like. Ask if your partner visited his or her grandparents this summer. |
| Partner A: | Say you used to visit them, but that this summer, you all went on a family trip. |
| Partner B: | Ask where your partner went and about the trip. |
| Partner A: | Say you learned how to ride horseback and play golf. Compare the trip to another one you've taken. |
| Partner B: | Say you've been golfing for a few years. Ask if your partner is planning on being on the golf team this year. |
| Partner A: | Explain your plans for school activities this year. Ask what your partner is going to do. |
| Partner B: | Describe your plans for school activities, and end the conversation. |

**6 Script**

See script on page 5F.

**7 Answers**

Below is a sample student conversation.

(A)—Hola, Miguel, ¿cómo estás? ¿Qué tal las vacaciones? ¿Qué hiciste?
(B)—Hola, Andrés, ¿qué tal? Pues, hice varias cosas. En julio fui a la playa con mis primos. La pasé de maravilla. ¿Y tú? ¿Fuiste a visitar a tus abuelos este verano?
(A)—Pues, antes sí, en el verano íbamos al pueblo de mis abuelos, pero este verano, decidimos hacer un viaje con toda la familia.
(B)—Ah, ¿sí? Dime... ¿adónde fueron, entonces? ¿Qué hicieron?
(A)—Fuimos a Asturias, a las montañas. Estuvo fenomenal. Aprendí a montar a caballo y jugar al golf. El viaje me pareció mucho más interesante que el del verano pasado.
(B)—No sabía que te gustaba el golf. Hace tres años que juego al golf, y me gusta mucho. ¿Piensas participar en el equipo de golf este año?
(A)—No sé. Quiero participar en la banda escolar, como el año pasado. No sé si voy a tener tiempo para el golf también. ¿Y tú?
(B)—Pues, yo sí voy a estar en el equipo de golf, y tal vez en el club de computación. ¿Por qué no vas conmigo a la primera reunión del equipo de golf? Tengo que irme ahora, pero te llamo más tarde, ¿vale?

## Conversación

### Additional Speaking Practice

For additional speaking practice, use the *Picture Sequences Transparency* for Chapter 1. Use the Speaking Rubric on the preceding page to evaluate their performance. You may also wish to use the Interviews and Role-Plays in the *Activities for Communication* book.

### Pre-AP Practice

7 In the Level 3 *Pre-AP Instructional Resources* you will find an alternative version of Activity 7. The following resources in that book will help you prepare students for the AP Language Exam:

- Blackline master, pp. 27, 37, 47
- Pre-AP Audio CD 1, Trs. 1–4
- Scripts and answers, pp. 57–75

Capítulo 1

# Prepárate para el examen

## Grammar Review

For more practice with the grammar topics in this chapter, see the *Grammar Tutor,* the *Interactive Tutor,* or the *Cuaderno de vocabulario y gramática.*

**GramaVisión**

## Heritage Speakers

Remind your heritage speakers that irregular preterite verbs will often have the letters *y, v,* or *j* near the end of the word. Some examples are **creyó, estuvo and trajo.** Working in pairs, have them come up with a list of other irregular preterites that have *y, v,* or *j* in similar position. Whenever they misspell any such words, remind students in Spanish: **i griega, uve, jota.**

1.2

## Más práctica

For additional practice with demonstrative pronouns and adjectives, write these sentences on the board or on a transparency and have volunteers choose the correct word to complete each item.

1. **A mí me gusta (ésta/esta) blusa.**
2. **Yo prefiero (aquélla/ aquel).**
3. **Póntela con (estas/estos) pantalones.**
4. **¿Pero no te gustan (éstos/estos)?**
5. **Sí, pero no con (esa/ese) blusa.**
6. **Bueno, tráeme (aquél/ este) cinturón que vimos al otro lado de la tienda.**

1.2

**Gramática 1**

- preterite and imperfect **pp. 14–15**
- **ser** and **estar** **pp. 16–17**
- subjunctive for hopes and wishes **pp. 18–19**

## Repaso de Gramática 1

For the uses of the preterite and imperfect, see page 14.

For the uses of **ser** and **estar,** see page 16.

The **subjunctive** mood is used to express hopes and wishes or to give advice and opinions. The **subjunctive** is used when the subjects of the **main clause** and the **subordinate clause** are different. The **subjunctive** is introduced by the conjunction **que.**

**Te recomiendo que vayas al lago.**　　**¿Prefieres que hagamos un crucigrama?**

**Gramática 2**

- pronouns **pp. 28–29**
- comparisons, demonstrative adjectives and pronouns **pp. 30–31**
- negative words and time constructions **pp. 32–33**

## Repaso de Gramática 2

For a review of pronouns, see page 28.

To compare two unequal things, actions, or quantities, use the constructions **más** (+ noun/adjective/adverb +) **que** and **menos** (+ noun/adjective/adverb +) **que.**

Soy **más alta que** Ernesto.

Marisa corre **más rápido que** Ana.

Use a form of the demonstrative adjective **este** to say *this,* a form of **ese** to say *that,* and a form of **aquel** to indicate a person or thing that is even farther away from the speaker.

**¿Estos** pósters son tus favoritos?

You can also use a demonstrative pronoun (**éste, ése, aquél**) to avoid repeating a noun. The neutral forms (**esto, eso, aquello**) refer to an idea or to something that was said or done.

Yo prefiero **aquéllos.**

For negative constructions, see page 32.

The time construction **hacer + time + que + verb** is used to describe an event that began in the past and is still going on.

**Hace un año que estudio** español.

**Hacer + time** can also be used to describe how long ago something happened.

**Hace dos días,** regresé de España.

## Chapter Review

**Teacher Management System**

To access, launch the program, type "admin" in the password area, and press RETURN. For more details, log on to www.hrw.com/CDROMTUTOR.

Create a variety of puzzles to review chapter vocabulary.

**DVD Program**

**Interactive Tutor**

**PuzzlePro**

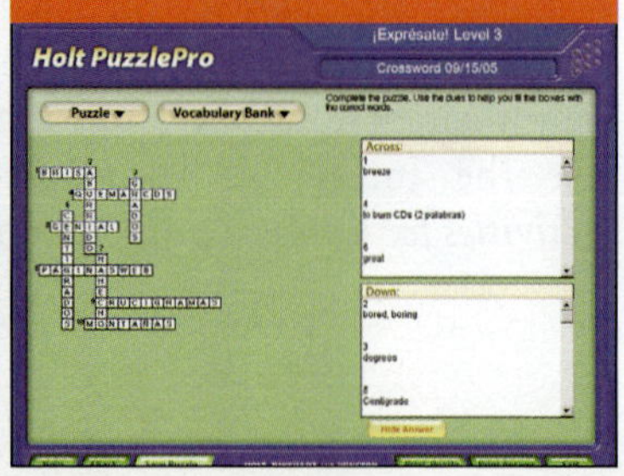

# Repaso de Vocabulario 1

**Talking about the past**

| | |
|---|---|
| aburrirse | *to get bored* |
| acampar | *to camp* |
| ¿Adónde fuiste? | *Where did you go?* |
| el bosque | *woods/forest* |
| la brisa | *breeze* |
| cansarse de | *to get tired of* |
| la catedral | *cathedral* |
| la ciudad | *city* |
| coleccionar caracoles | *to collect seashells* |
| conversar | *to converse* |
| la costa | *coast* |
| dar una caminata | *to take a walk* |
| disfrutar de | *to enjoy* |
| divertirse | *to have fun* |
| el esquí acuático | *water skiing* |
| la estación de trenes/ autobuses | *train/bus station* |
| Fui a... | *I went to . . .* |
| los grados Fahrenheit/ centígrados | *degrees Fahrenheit/centigrade* |
| hacer calor | *to be hot* |
| hacer crucigramas | *to do crossword puzzles* |
| hacer windsurf | *to windsurf* |
| jugar naipes | *to play cards* |
| Lo/La encontré muy interesante. | *I found it very interesting* |
| Lo pasé de película/ de maravilla. | *I had a great time.* |
| llover a cántaros | *to pour rain* |
| la llovizna | *drizzle* |
| las montañas | *mountains* |
| los monumentos | *monuments* |
| montar a caballo | *(to go) horseback riding* |
| la natación | *swimming* |
| pasear | *to go for a walk* |
| el patinaje (en línea) | *(inline) skating* |
| ¿Qué hiciste el verano pasado? | *What did you do last summer?* |
| ¿Qué tal lo pasaste? | *Did you have a good time?* |
| ¿Qué te pareció...? | *How was . . . ?* |
| el relámpago | *lightning* |
| el río | *river* |
| la tormenta | *storm* |
| trotar | *to jog* |
| el trueno | *thunder* |
| Viajé a... | *I traveled to . . .* |

**Talking about what you liked and used to do . . . . . . . . . . . . . . . . . . . . See p. 12.**

# Repaso de Vocabulario 2

**Asking for and giving advice**

| | |
|---|---|
| aburrido(a) | *bored, boring* |
| la banda escolar | *school band* |
| el centro recreativo | *recreation center* |
| el club de debate | *debate club* |
| coleccionar estampillas/ pósters/monedas | *to collect stamps/posters/coins* |
| crear (quemar) CDs | *to make (burn) CDs* |
| Debes... | *You should . . .* |
| la dieta balanceada | *balanced diet* |
| diseñar páginas Web | *to design Web pages* |
| escribir poemas y cuentos | *to write poems and stories* |
| los ejercicios aeróbicos | *aerobic exercise* |
| hacer diseño por computadora | *to do design on the computer* |
| hacer gimnasia | *to do gymnastics* |
| hacerse amigo(a) de alguien | *to become friends with someone* |
| Hay que... | *One has to . . .* |
| impaciente | *impatient* |
| interesar | *to interest* |
| jugar al golf | *to play golf* |
| mantenerse en forma | *to stay in shape* |
| nervioso(a) | *nervous* |
| observar la naturaleza | *to observe nature* |
| la oratoria | *speech (class)* |
| participar | *to participate* |
| practicar atletismo | *to do track and field* |
| ¿Puedes darme algún consejo? | *Can you give me some advice?* |
| ¿Qué consejos tienes? | *What advice do you have?* |
| ¿Qué debo hacer? | *What should I do?* |
| ¿Qué me recomiendas? | *What do you recommend (to me)?* |
| saltar la cuerda | *to jump rope* |
| solitario(a) | *lonely* |
| Te aconsejo que... | *I advise you to . . .* |
| Te recomiendo que... | *I recommend that you . . .* |
| tener ganas de (hacer) | *to feel like (doing)* |

**Talking about the future . . . . . . . . . . . . . . See p. 26.**

Capítulo 1

# Prepárate para el examen

Prepárate para el examen

## Vocabulary Review

For more practice with the vocabulary in this chapter, see the *Interactive Tutor* or the *Cuaderno de vocabulario y gramática.*

## Online Edition

Use the online textbook to hear the **Vocabulario** items.

## Game

**¿Cómo te diré?**

Write vocabulary words from the chapter on index cards. Arrange four desks so that two sets of partners face each other. Place the cards face down. Divide the class into two teams and appoint a scorekeeper and a timekeeper. Have two players from each team sit at the four desks. A player from Team A takes a card and shows it to one of the players from Team B. Using circumlocution, the Team A player describes the word to his or her partner without saying the word itself. If the partner guesses the word, Team A receives five points. If not, the Team B player gives a clue to his or her partner. If the partner guesses correctly, Team B receives four points. Play alternates between the two teams, with the points earned dropping off by one after each incorrect guess. 1.2

**Online Edition**

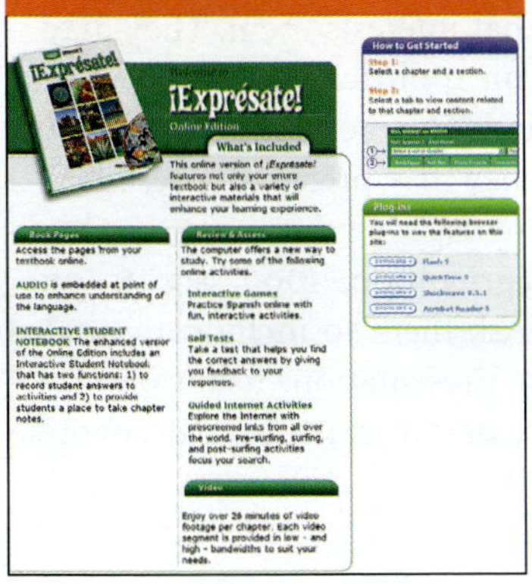


**Transparency: Vocabulario**

**Transparency: Situación**

## Assess

**Assessment Program**

**Examen: Capítulo 1,** pp. 205–210

Audio CD 1, Trs. 14–15

**Examen oral: Capítulo 1,** p. 216

Alternative Assessment, pp. 373, 385, 397

**Online Assessment**
**my.hrw.com**

**Test Generator**

**Assess** **Differentiated Instruction** See the Differentiated Instruction CD-ROM.

Capítulo 1

# Integración

## Resources

**Planning:**

Lesson Planner, pp. 15, 176–177

One-Stop Planner

**Presentation:**

Teaching Transparencies
Fine Art, Chapter 1

**Practice:**

Cuaderno de actividades, pp. 9–10

Lab Book pp. 1, 13–16

Audio CD 1, Tr. 11

### 1 Script

1. Este verano fui al campo con mi familia y montamos a caballo.
2. Quiero practicar el atletismo con el equipo de mi colegio este año.
3. ¿Alguien quiere ver mi colección de estampillas? Tengo algunas de España.
4. Me interesa jugar al golf para poder hacerme amigo de los chicos del equipo.

### Teacher to Teacher

**Debbie Chraibi**
**William R. Boone High School**
**Orlando, FL**

First, have student pairs write and illustrate a story of unfortunate events using verbs in the present tense. State that their grade will be based on specific grammar points you wish to review. (noun-adjective agreement, present tense verb forms, etc.) Students present their illustrated story to the class. After the class has reviewed the preterite and imperfect, return the stories to student pairs to be rewritten in the past tense. The focus at this time is on choosing the correct form of past tense for each verb. It's a fun way of reviewing and students enjoy revising their original creations from the present to the past tense. 1.2, 1.3

Repaso cumulativo

# Integración capítulo 1

CD 1, Tr. 11

**1** Escucha lo que dice cada persona y escoge la foto que corresponde. 1.2 **1.** B **2.** C **3.** A **4.** D

A

B

C

D

**2** Cristóbal viajó a España este verano y trajo una guía turística para mostrársela a sus amigos. Léela y contesta las siguientes preguntas. 1.2

**Viaja a España, el país del sol, donde hay algo para todos.**

**¿Te gusta la playa?** Visita la Costa del Sol y disfruta de actividades como el esquí acuático y el windsurf. **Si prefieres las montañas,** la Sierra Nevada es el lugar para ti. Se puede acampar o dar una caminata por sus pequeños pueblos, blancos como la nieve. Aquí hace menos calor que en la costa. Siempre ha sido uno de los lugares preferidos de los turistas. Te recomiendo que pases algunos días también en **Castilla-La Mancha.** Puedes viajar desde una estación de trenes tan bonita como la de Toledo o ver unas casas tan impresionantes como las de Cuenca. Haz un viaje que no vas a olvidar nunca. ¡Ven a España!

1. ¿Adónde puedes ir si te gusta la playa? la Costa del Sol
2. ¿Qué región se recomienda a las personas que prefieren las montañas? la Sierra Nevada
3. ¿Qué se puede hacer en las montañas? (3. acampar, dar una caminata por los pueblos blancos como la nieve)
4. ¿Dónde hace más calor, en las montañas o en la costa? (4. en la costa)
5. ¿Dónde está la estación de trenes que se menciona en el anuncio? Toledo

### Culture Project

Remind students that, as stated in **Geocultura,** Castilla-La Mancha became an autonomous region in 1982. Explain that the autonomous regions of Spain are very different from one another. Just like different regions of the United States, they all have unique personalities and traditions. Ask students to research the autonomous regions of Spain and prepare a presentation comparing and contrasting each region with Castilla-La Mancha. Tell them to focus on a topic that interests them. They may wish to focus on politics, and how the autonomous regions interact with the central government. Or they may prefer to investigate topics such as language, environment, architecture, music, agriculture, food, sports or other traditions. Ask them to include a visual display with their presentation, using photographs, timelines, or other items that correspond to their topic. 2.1, 2.2

Visit Holt Online
**go.hrw.com**
KEYWORD: EXP3 CH1
Cumulative Self-test

## Repaso cumulativo

3 En grupos, hablen de lo que les gustaba hacer de niños durante el verano. Luego, expliquen lo que hicieron este verano pasado y lo que piensan hacer este año. **1.1, 1.3**

4 Observa la pintura y escribe por lo menos ocho oraciones sobre la obra. ¿Qué ves en la pintura? ¿Qué pasa o qué va a pasar? ¿Has visto un toro alguna vez? Si no, ¿es algo que deseas ver? En tu opinión, ¿cómo son los toreros y los toros? **1.3, 2.1**

***Torero y toro*** de Óscar Domínguez

5 Imagina que eres el (la) director(a) del colegio. Escribe una carta a los estudiantes de primer año para explicarles todas las actividades que se ofrecen en el colegio. Explica lo que vas a hacer para que este año sea el mejor y dales recomendaciones para el nuevo año escolar. **1.3**

6 **Situación**

Acabas de conocer a un(a) estudiante español(a) en una fiesta. En parejas, dramaticen una conversación. Los dos deben hablar un poco sobre cómo son y qué les gusta hacer. Luego el (la) estudiante español(a) puede explicar lo que desea hacer en Estados Unidos y tú puedes darle consejos. **1.1, 1.3**

### Fine Art Connection

Tell students that this painting, ***Torero y toro,*** is by Óscar Domínguez (1906–1957). Domínguez was born in La Laguna on the island of Tenerife, Spanish Canary Islands. He spent his formative years in Tacoronte and then moved to Paris in 1927, where he spent the rest of his life. A surrealist painter and friend of Pablo Picasso, Domínguez created several paintings with bulls as the main focus.

### Analyzing

Have students look at the bull and the bullfighter in the painting. Ask students what they think about the distortions in the bodies of both the bull and the bullfighter. Call on volunteers to describe what they see. **2.2, 3.1**

### Extension

Have students carefully look at all of the elements in the painting. Have them describe the crowd, the bullring, the colors, and so on. Have students investigate the bull-fighting tradition in Spain. They could include information such as its history, its significance in Spanish culture, and the controversies of bullfighting in present-day Spain. **2.1**

### ACTFL Performance Standards

The activities in this Chapter 1 target the different communicative models as described in the Standards.

| | | |
|---|---|---|
| **Interpersonal** | Two-way communication using receptive skills and productive skills | **Comunicación (SE),** pp. 11, 13, 15, 17, 19, 25, 27, 29, 31, 33<br>**Comunicación (TE),** pp. 25, 27, 31, 33<br>**Conversación,** p. 43<br>**Situación,** p. 47 |
| **Interpretive** | One-way communication using receptive skills | **Comunicación (SE),** pp. 11, 17, 19, 25, 31, 33<br>**Comunicación (TE),** pp. 13, 15<br>**Novela en video,** pp. 34–35<br>**Leamos,** pp. 38–40<br>**Conversación,** p. 43 |
| **Presentational** | One-way communication using productive skills | **Comunicación (SE),** pp. 13, 15, 27, 29<br>**Comunicación (TE),** pp. 11, 15, 17, 19, 29<br>**Taller del escritor,** p. 41 |

Capítulo 2

# Planning Guide

## ¡A pasarlo bien!

| Chapter Section | | Print Resources |
|---|---|---|
| **Geocultura**<br>• **Castilla-La Mancha** | pp. T72–5 | Video Guide, pp. 1–2/Lab Book, p. 55 |
| **Vocabulario 1**<br>• Hobbies and sports<br>**Gramática 1**<br>• Repaso: Imperfect<br>• Repaso: **Ir a** + infinitive in the imperfect<br>• **Nosotros** command | pp. 50–55<br>pp. 56–61 | Vocabulario 2.1, 2.2; Bell Work 2.1, 2.2, 2.3, 2.4<br>Cuaderno de vocabulario y gramática, pp. 13–18<br>Cuaderno de actividades, pp. 11–13<br>Activities for Communication, pp. 5–6<br>Grammar Tutor for Students of Spanish, pp. 121–124 |
| **Cultura: Comparaciones**<br>**Cultura: Comunidad** | p. 62<br>p. 63 | Video Guide, pp. 10, 11/Lab Book, p. 59 |
| **Vocabulario 2**<br>• Friendship<br>**Gramática 2**<br>• Repaso: Object pronouns<br>• Subjunctive with the unknown or nonexistent<br>• Subjunctive with expressions of feelings | pp. 64–69<br>pp. 70–75 | Vocabulario 2.3, 2.4; Bell Work 2.5, 2.6, 2.7, 2.8<br>Cuaderno de vocabulario y gramática, pp. 19–24<br>Cuaderno de actividades, pp. 15–17<br>Activities for Communication, pp. 7–8<br>Grammar Tutor for Students of Spanish, pp. 125–128 |
| **Novela en video**<br>**Lectura cultural**<br>• **Una noche en España**<br>**Leamos**<br>• **Un oso y un amor**<br>**Escribamos**<br>• **La amistad es para siempre** | pp. 76–77<br>pp. 78–79<br>pp. 80–82<br>p. 83 | Cuaderno de actividades, p. 18<br>Reading Strategies and Skills Handbook<br>Interactive Advanced Reader<br>Video Guide, pp. 12–14/Lab Book, pp. 60–61 |
| **Prepárate para el examen**<br>• **Repaso de vocabulario y gramática** | pp. 84–87 | Picture Sequences, Situación, Ch. 2<br>Activities for Communication, pp. 44, 57–58 |
| **Integración**<br>• **Repaso cumulativo** | pp. 88–89 | Fine Art, Ch. 2<br>Cuaderno de actividades, pp. 19–20<br>Reading Strategies and Skills Handbook<br>Interactive Advanced Reader |

For correlations to national standards, see point-of-use references throughout the chapter.

Visit Holt Online
**go.hrw.com**
KEYWORD: EXP3 CH2
Online Edition

# Pacing Suggestions

| | Essential | Recommended | Optional |
|---|---|---|---|
| **Vocabulario 1**<br>• Hobbies and sports<br>• **Nota cultural** | ✔ | | |
| **Gramática 1**<br>• Repaso: Imperfect<br>• Repaso: **Ir a** + infinitive in the imperfect<br>• **Nosotros** command<br>• **Nota cultural** | ✔ | | |
| **Cultura: Comparaciones**<br>**Cultura: Comunidad** | | ✔ | ✔ |
| **Vocabulario 2**<br>• Friendship<br>• **Nota cultural** | ✔ | | |
| **Gramática 2**<br>• Repaso: Object pronouns<br>• Subjunctive with the unknown or nonexistent<br>• Subjunctive with expressions of feelings<br>• **Nota cultural** | ✔ | | |
| **Novela en video**<br>• Episodio 2: **Clara perspectiva** | | ✔ | |
| **Lectura cultural**<br>• **Una noche en España** | | | ✔ |
| **Leamos**<br>• **Un oso y un amor**<br>**Escribamos**<br>• **La amistad es para siempre** | | ✔ | |
| **Prepárate para el examen** | | ✔ | |
| **Integración** | | | ✔ |

# Technology Resources

### ¡Exprésate! Online
- Student Edition with multi-media
- SoundBooth recording tool
- Interactive activities with feedback
- Self-tests with feedback
- Cuaderno de actividades (interactive workbook)
- Cuaderno de vocabulario y gramática (interactive workbook)
- Live Ink™ Reading Help
- Holt Online Assessment

### DVD Tutor, Disc 1
- GeoVisión
- GramaVisión
- VideoNovela
- Cultura
- Variedades

### Interactive Tutor
- Interactive practice games
- Writing and recording workshops

### Audio Program
- Textbook listening activities
- Assessment listening activities
- Songs

### One-Stop Planner
- Complete media and print resources
- ExamView® Pro Test Generator
- Holt Calendar Planner

### PuzzlePro
- Customizable word games

# Assessment

| | Assessment Program |
|---|---|
| Geocultura | **Prueba: Geocultura,** pp. 35–36 |
| Vocabulario 1 / Gramática 1 | **Pruebas,** pp. 21–22, 23–24, 25–26 |
| Vocabulario 2 / Gramática 2 | **Pruebas,** pp. 27–28, 29–30, 31–32 |
| Leamos | **Prueba,** p. 33 |
| Escribamos | **Prueba,** p. 34 |
| Prepárate para el examen | **Examen: Capítulo 2,** pp. 217–224 |
| | **Examen oral: Capítulo 2,** p. 228 |
| | **Alternative Assessment,** pp. 374, 386, 398 |

### Online Assessment
**my.hrw.com**

### Test Generator
**ExamView® Pro Test Generator**

Planning Guide

# Projects

## ¡A pasarlo bien!



### Un itinerario

In this project, students work in groups to create a week-long itinerary for a group of Spanish-speaking exchange students, evaluate each group's itinerary, and present theirs for an oral grade.

**SUGGESTED SEQUENCE**

1. Tell students they are in charge of creating an itinerary for a group of Spanish-speaking high-school students visiting their city for a week during summer vacation. Their itineraries should include fun, useful information about their city.
2. Assign students to work in groups of three or four to work on each itinerary.
3. Have students work together to write the itinerary in the form of a daily schedule. They should plan several activities, meals, and free times throughout each day.
4. When students have created the itinerary, they should copy it onto plain white paper and illustrate it with pictures from local brochures, personal pictures, or drawings.
5. Have students evaluate all of the itineraries, awarding 1st, 2nd, and 3rd place to the best three schedules.
6. Each group presents its itinerary in Spanish for an oral grade.

❀ 1.3

### Partner Class Project

Have students plan sports-themed vacations to Spanish-speaking countries. They should contact a travel agency that employs Spanish-speaking agents and do online research about appropriate places for skiing, diving, climbing, hiking, or any other sport they might be interested in. Have them suggest activities to do at each destination. Then ask students to use the information to create a bilingual Web site promoting a vacation for travelers who want to take part in sporting events around the world. ❀ 3.2

### e-community

**e-mail forum:**

Post the following question on the classroom e-mail forum:

**¿Has visto algún programa sobre deportes en otro país? Explica.**

All students will contribute to the list and then share the items. ❀ 1.3

### Grading the projects

Suggested point distribution (100 points total)

| | |
|---|---|
| Content | 20 |
| Language use | 20 |
| Creativity/Originality | 20 |
| Appearance | 20 |
| Oral presentation | 20 |

### Game Bank

For game ideas, see pages T64–T67.

# ¡A pasarlo bien!

## La historia

For nearly 800 years (from their arrival in 711 until their expulsion in 1492), the Arabic-speaking people in Spain, **los moros,** cultivated the most sophisticated culture in medieval Europe. Mathematics, science, architecture and the decorative arts flourished throughout the region. Moorish architecture in Sevilla, Córdoba, and Granada is characterized by ornate geometrical patterns and arches. Spanish music was heavily influenced by **los moros,** and the language has borrowed many Arabic words, often beginning with the prefix *al-*, such as **álgebra, alfombra, almohada,** and **algodón.** The Moors also contributed to Spanish cuisine, especially desserts; the use of almonds, egg yolks and honey is attributed to them. Have students research Moorish influences on Spanish architecture, language, music, and customs, and create a poster that reflects their research, then present their poster in Spanish for an oral activity. **2.2, 3.1**

## Receta

You might have students make the following recipe as a class project or for extra credit.

### Tortilla de patatas

**para 4 personas**

6 huevos medianos

4 patatas grandes (de preferencia patatas blancas)

1 cebolla mediana, bien picada

1 taza de aceite de oliva

sal al gusto

Se pelan las patatas y se cortan en trocitos de 1/8 de pulgada de grosor. En una sartén antiadherente, se calienta el aceite a fuego mediano y luego se añaden las patatas. Se cocinan hasta que estén blandas, y se añade la cebolla picada. Se cocina todo hasta que la cebolla esté transparente. Mientras tanto se baten los huevos en un plato hondo. Se saca la mezcla de las patatas y la cebolla del aceite con una espumadera y se incorpora al plato hondo con los huevos. Se mezcla todo y se añade sal al gusto. Se saca el aceite de la sartén dejando sólo lo suficiente para cubrir el fondo. Se vuelve la sartén al fuego y cuando esté caliente el aceite se añade la mezcla de patatas, huevos y cebolla. Se distribuye bien y se cocina a fuego lento hasta que los huevos estén casi cocinados. Se pone un plato grande encima de la sartén y se le da vuelta a la tortilla para luego cocinar el otro lado. Se cocina hasta que los huevos estén cocinados. Se coloca en un plato para servir. Se corta en trozos como una torta. **2.2, 3.1**

Capítulo 2

# Listening Activity Scripts

## ¡A pasarlo bien!

### Vocabulario en acción 1

**1** p. 52, CD 2, Track 1

1. Soy un fanático de las artes marciales. Este año estoy tomando clases de kárate y me gustan mucho.
2. Me la paso practicando ciclismo. Voy en bicicleta a todas partes.
3. Estoy loca por la escalada deportiva. Me gusta escalar en un lugar seguro.
4. Soy un gran aficionado al tiro con arco. Lo practico con el equipo de mi colegio.
5. Creo que el dominó es genial. Juego con mi amigo en el café.
6. Me encanta el senderismo. Voy a las montañas todos los fines de semana.
7. Soy muy buena para el remo. Participo en muchas competencias.
8. Estoy aprendiendo la esgrima. Estoy tomando clases y tengo un profesor muy bueno.

**Answers to Activity 1**

1. d 2. e 3. h 4. f 5. b 6. a 7. c 8. g

### Gramática en acción 1

**9** p. 56, CD 2, Track 2

1. Soy Elena. De niña, me la pasaba haciendo rompecabezas.
2. Me llamo Juan Luis. Juego al fútbol a veces con mis amigos, pero la verdad es que no soy gran aficionado.
3. Me llamo Victoria. Recuerdo que tenía que practicar el tenis todo el tiempo. ¡Cómo me fastidiaba!
4. Soy Alejandro. Mis amigos y yo éramos fanáticos del tiro con arco.
5. Soy Carolina. Recuerdo que era muy buena para el remo y practicaba siempre que podía.
6. Me llamo José Miguel. Mi padre y yo vamos juntos a las clases de kárate. A él le gusta mucho, pero a mí me deja frío.
7. Soy Sara. Hago senderismo con mi familia todos los fines de semana. ¡Es genial!
8. Soy Guillermo. Recuerdo que estaba loco por el boliche. De niño jugaba con un equipo.

**Answers to Activity 9**

1. pasado 3. pasado 5. pasado 7. presente
2. presente 4. pasado 6. presente 8. pasado

**13** p. 58, CD 2, Track 3

1. Ay, perdóname. De veras, quería ir al partido, pero no pude. Tuve que lavar el carro y limpiar el garaje.
2. Lo siento mucho. Iba a ir al partido, pero tenía mucha tarea para la clase de química.
3. Quería ir al partido, pero tuve que cortar el césped. ¡Cómo me molestan los quehaceres!
4. Oye, discúlpame. Quería ir al partido, pero tuve que cuidar a mis hermanas.
5. Ay, lo siento. Iba a ir, pero tuve que cocinar para el cumpleaños de mi abuela.
6. Qué pena. Te dije que iba al partido, pero mis padres no me permitieron ir. Tuve que practicar el piano.

**Answers to Activity 13**

1. b 2. a 3. f 4. e 5. d 6. c

**17** p. 60, CD 2, Track 4

1. —¿Estás aburrida, Laura? Ve al partido de volibol.
—¡Qué buena idea! No sabía que había uno hoy.
2. —Manuel, va a hacer sol el sábado. ¡Practiquemos ciclismo por la tarde!
—¡Estupendo! Estaré en tu casa con mi bicicleta a las dos.
3. —¿No estás preparada para el examen? Pues, estudia más.
—Sí, tienes razón. Esta noche voy a estudiar.
4. —Mamá, no tengo tarea esta noche. ¿Por qué no vamos al cine?
—¡Buena idea! Veamos la película de las siete.
5. —Lola, tengo una nueva tienda de acampar. ¡Acampemos este fin de semana!
—¡Genial! Invitemos a Marta también.
6. —Felipe, no veas tanto la televisión. ¿Por qué no practicas un deporte?
—Ya me apunté para clases de esgrima.

**Answers to Activity 17**

1. b 2. a 3. b 4. a 5. a 6. b

### Vocabulario en acción 2

**21** p. 66, CD 2, Track 8

1. Mi amiga Laura siempre me dice lo que realmente opina, aún cuando no esté de acuerdo conmigo. Me gusta que ella me diga la verdad, sin problemas.
2. Sergio, mi compañero de clase, tiene una opinión muy alta de sí mismo. Siempre se está mirando en el espejo y cada cinco minutos tiene que arreglarse el pelo para estar perfecto.
3. Mi vecino Tomás guarda los secretos que le cuento. Yo sé que él no se los contará a nadie. Tiene muy buena reputación.
4. Mi tía Claudia siempre les pregunta a las personas qué piensan. Ella no puede hacer nada sin pedir una opinión. Es muy inteligente, pero ella no tiene confianza en sí misma.

For Student Response Forms, see the *Lab Book,* pp. 17–20.

5. Juan Pablo era amigo de mi hermana Susana, pero ya no. No le gustaba cuando Susana hablaba con otros chicos, y ella rompió con él.
6. Mi prima Marisa siempre me da un abrazo cuando me ve. Es muy simpática con todo el mundo, y les sonríe a todos.
7. Mónica me decía que era mi amiga, pero entonces les dijo mentiras acerca de mí a otras personas. A ella no le pienso contar más secretos.
8. David es un compañero que siempre comparte sus cosas conmigo. Me presta su chaqueta si llueve, o me da medio sándwich si olvido mi almuerzo.

**Answers to Activity 21**

1. c 3. f 5. e 7. d
2. h 4. b 6. g 8. a

## Gramática en acción 2

### 34 p. 73, CD 2, Track 9

1. Conozco a un chico que es muy chismoso.
2. No hay nada que me moleste más que una mentira.
3. Busco una solución que sea justa.
4. No hay nada que alegre a mi hermano.
5. ¿Hay alguien aquí que sepa por qué Diana se ve tan decepcionada?
6. Ella tiene un novio que es muy mentiroso.
7. Pues, en nuestra clase no hay nadie que sea tan malo.
8. Ella necesita un novio que respete sus sentimientos.

**Answers to Activity 34**

1. a 2. b 3. b 4. b 5. b 6. a 7. b 8. b

### 37 p. 74, CD 2, Track 10

1. —¿Sabías que Teresa y Mateo hicieron las paces?
—Pues, creo que forman una buena pareja.
2. —¿Dónde está Samuel? No me digas que nos ha dejado plantados otra vez.
—No me gusta que la gente sea tan descortés.
3. —Oye, me dijeron que se canceló el examen de química hoy.
—Parece que nos dan un día más para estudiar.
4. —¿Has visto las noticias? Nuestro equipo no avanza a los finales del campeonato.
—¡Qué pena! Es triste que otra vez pierdan la oportunidad de ganarlo.
5. —Fíjate que todavía no puedo encontrar la llave del apartamento.
—Siento que no puedas encontrarla.
6. —He oído que Ángel rompió con Isabel ayer por teléfono.
—¡Ay, qué lástima que se separen así de rápido! ¡Qué grosero es Ángel!
7. —Se dice que Silvia tiene un nuevo novio. ¡Está muy contenta!
—¡Qué bien! Pienso que ella merece ser feliz.
8. —Gregorio me ha dejado de hablar. Estoy muy frustrado con él.
—Me decepciona que haga eso. No lo entiendo.

**Answers to Activity 37**

1. b 2. a 3. b 4. a 5. a 6. a 7. b 8. a

## Prepárate para el examen capítulo 2

### 6 p. 85, CD 2, Track 13

MARIBEL Es difícil encontrar un novio. Yo estoy buscando a alguien que sea muy abierto y muy leal.

ALEJANDRO Pues, yo también. Todo el mundo quiere alguien así. Pero además quiero una novia que respete mis sentimientos. Tiene que ser muy paciente conmigo porque sé que a veces soy muy terco.

MARIBEL Está bien. Yo busco a un novio que practique ciclismo, porque yo me la paso practicando ciclismo.

ALEJANDRO Yo también quiero una novia que sea atlética, porque me encantan los deportes.

MARIBEL Para mí, es importante tener un novio que siempre me diga la verdad.

ALEJANDRO Pues, yo quiero una novia que sea muy generosa. Me gustan los regalos.

MARIBEL ¡Ja, ja! Por lo menos eres honesto, Alejandro.

**Answers to Activity 6**

Maribel: abierto, leal, honesto, que practique ciclismo
Alejandro: paciente, atlética, generosa

## Integración capítulos 1–2

### 1 p. 88, CD 2, Track 14

1. Iba muy rápido por el río en mi bote y les gané a los otros competidores.
2. Quería llegar hasta el lago, pero tuve que ponerle más aire a la llanta de mi bicicleta.
3. Hicimos una caminata muy larga por el bosque.
4. Escalamos una montaña muy alta y había una vista preciosa en la cima.

**Answers to Activity 1**

1. b, el remo (remar) 3. a, el senderismo
2. d, el ciclismo 4. c, la escalada deportiva

# 50-Minute Lesson Plans

## ¡A pasarlo bien!

For more customized Lesson Plans, see the *Lesson Planner with Differentiated Instruction.*



### Day 1

**Objective**
*Expressing interest and displeasure*

**Core Instruction**
**Chapter Opener**, pp. 48–49
**10 min.**
- See Chapter Objectives, p. 48.
- See Using the Photo, p. 48.

**Vocabulario en acción 1,** pp. 50–55
- Have students do Bell Work, p. 50.
- See Teaching **Vocabulario 1,** p. 50. **10 min.**
- See Teaching **¡Exprésate!,** p. 50. **10 min.**
- Play Audio CD 2, Tr. 1 for Activity 1, p. 52. **5 min.**
- Have students do Activities 2–5, pp. 52–53. **10 min.**
- See **Comunicación,** p. 53. **5 min.**

**Optional Resources**
- Advanced Learners, p. 51 ▲
- Multiple Intelligences, p. 51
- Vocabulary in Context, p. 52
- Slower Pace Learners, p. 53 ◆
- Special Learning Needs, p. 53 ●

**Homework Suggestions**
Cuaderno de vocabulario y gramática, pp. 13–15
❀ 1.1, 1.2, 1.3

### Day 2

**Objective**
*Inviting someone to do something*

**Core Instruction**
**Vocabulario en acción 1,** pp. 50–55
- See Teaching **¡Exprésate!,** p. 54. **15 min.**
- Have students do Activities 6–8, p. 55. **20 min.**
- See **Comunicación,** p. 55. **15 min.**

**Optional Resources**
- Advanced Learners, p. 55 ▲
- Special Learning Needs, p. 55 ●

**Homework Suggestions**
Study for **Prueba: Vocabulario 1**
❀ 1.1, 1.2, 1.3

### Day 3

**Objective**
*Imperfect*

**Core Instruction**
**Vocabulario en acción 1,** pp. 50–55
- Review **Vocabulario en acción 1,** pp. 50–55. **5 min.**
- Give **Prueba: Vocabulario 1.** **20 min.**

**Gramática en acción 1,** pp. 56–61
- Have students do Bell Work, p. 56. **5 min.**
- See Teaching **Gramática,** p. 56. **15 min.**
- Play Audio CD 2, Tr. 2 for Activity 9, p. 56. **5 min.**

**Optional Resources**
- Heritage Speakers, p. 57 ■
- Slower Pace Learners, p. 57 ◆
- Special Learning Needs, p. 57 ●

**Homework Suggestions**
Cuaderno de vocabulario y gramática, pp. 16–18
Cuaderno de actividades, pp. 11–13
❀ 1.2

### Day 4

**Objective**
*Ir a + infinitive in the imperfect*

**Core Instruction**
**Gramática en acción 1,** pp. 56–61
- Have students do Activities 10–12, p. 57. **15 min.**
- Have students do Bell Work, p. 58. **5 min.**
- See Teaching **Gramática,** p. 58. **10 min.**
- Play Audio CD 2, Tr. 3 for Activity 13, p. 58. **5 min.**
- Have students do Activities 14–16, p. 59. **15 min.**

**Optional Resources**
- **Comunicación,** p. 59
- Advanced Learners, p. 59 ▲
- Special Learning Needs, p. 59 ●

**Homework Suggestions**
Cuaderno de de vocabulario y gramática, pp. 16–18
Cuaderno de actividades, pp. 11–13
❀ 1.1, 1.2, 1.3

### Day 5

**Objective**
***Nosotros** commands*

**Core Instruction**
**Gramática en acción 1,** pp. 56–61
- Have students do Bell Work, p. 60. **5 min.**
- See Teaching **Gramática,** p. 60. **15 min.**
- Play Audio CD 2, Tr. 4 for Activity 17, p. 60. **5 min.**
- Have students do Activities 18–20, pp. 60–61. **25 min.**

**Optional Resources**
- **Comunicación,** p. 61
- Slower Pace Learners, p. 61 ◆
- Special Learning Needs, p. 61 ●

**Homework Suggestions**
Study for **Prueba: Gramática 1**
Cuaderno de vocabulario y gramática, pp. 16–18
Cuaderno de actividades, pp. 11–13
❀ 1.1, 1.2

### Day 6

**Objective**
*Interviews from around the Spanish-speaking world*

**Core Instruction**
**Gramática en acción 1,** pp. 56–61
- Review **Gramática en acción 1,** pp. 56–61 **5 min.**
- Give Prueba: **Gramática 1.** **20 min.**

**Cultura,** pp. 62–63
- See Teaching **Cultura,** p. 62. **10 min.**
- Play Audio CD 2, Tr. 5–7, p. 62, or show **VideoCultura.** **15 min.**

**Optional Resources**
- Advanced Learners, p. 63 ▲
- Multiple Intelligences, p. 63
- Communities, p. 63

**Homework Suggestions**
Cuaderno de actividades, p. 14
Online Practice (**go.hrw.com,** Keyword: EXP3 CH2)
❀ 1.2, 1.3, 4.2, 5.1, 5.2

### Day 7

**Objective**
*Describing the ideal friend*

**Core Instruction**
**Vocabulario en acción 2,** pp. 64–69
- See Teaching **Vocabulario 2,** p. 64. **10 min.**
- See Teaching **¡Exprésate!** p. 64. **10 min.**
- Play Audio CD 2, Tr. 8 for Activity 21, p. 66. **5 min.**
- Have students do Activity 22, p. 66. **10 min.**
- Have students do Activities 23–24, p. 67. **15 min.**

**Optional Resources**
- Advanced Learners, p. 65 ▲
- Multiple Intelligences, p. 65
- Circumlocution, p. 68

**Homework Suggestions**
Cuaderno de vocabulario y gramática, pp. 19–21
❀ 1.1, 1.2, 1.3

### Day 8

**Objective**
*Expressing happiness and unhappiness*

**Core Instruction**
**Vocabulario en acción 2,** pp. 64–69
- Have students do Activity 25, p. 67. **10 min.**
- See Teaching **¡Exprésate!,** p. 68. **15 min.**
- Have students do Activities 26–28, p. 69. **25 min.**

**Optional Resources**
- Heritage Speakers, p. 69 ■
- **Comunicación,** p. 69
- Advanced Learners, p. 69 ▲
- Multiple Intelligences, p. 69

**Homework Suggestions**
Study for **Prueba: Vocabulario 2**
Cuaderno de vocabulario y gramática, pp. 19–21
❀ 1.1, 1.2

- For information on the **Geocultura** pages, see the *Lesson Planner with Differentiated Instruction.*
- For more detailed information on benchmarks, see point-of-use correlations on each page.
- To edit and create your own lesson plans, see the **One-Stop** Planner® CD-ROM

**KEY**

- ▲ Advanced Learners
- ◆ Slower Pace Learners
- ● Special Learning Needs
- ■ Heritage Speakers

## Day 9

### Objective
*Object pronuns*

### Core Instruction
**Vocabulario en acción 2,** pp. 64–69
- Review **Vocabulario en acción 2,** pp. 64–69. **10 min.**
- Give **Prueba: Vocabulario 2. 20 min.**

**Gramática en acción 2**, pp. 70–75
- See Teaching **Gramática,** p. 70. **15 min.**
- Have students do Activity 29, p. 70. **5 min.**

### Optional Resources
- **Comunicación,** p. 71
- Slower Pace Learners, p. 71 ◆
- Special Learning Needs, p. 71 ●

### Homework Suggestions
Cuaderno de vocabulario y gramática, pp. 22–24

Cuaderno de actividades, pp. 15–17

1.2

## Day 10

### Objective
*Subjunctive with the unknown or nonexistent*

### Core Instruction
**Gramática en acción 2,** pp. 70–75
- Have students do Activities 30–32, p. 71. **15 min.**
- Have students do Bell Work, p. 72. **5 min.**
- See Teaching **Gramática,** p. 72. **10 min.**
- Have students do Activity 33, p. 72. **5 min.**
- Play Audio CD 2, Tr. 9, for Activity 34, p. 73. **5 min.**
- Have students do Activities 35–36, p. 73. **10 min.**

### Optional Resources
- Slower Pace Learners, p. 73 ◆
- Special Learning Needs, p. 73 ●
- **Comunicación,** p. 73

### Homework Suggestions
Cuaderno de vocabulario y gramática, pp. 22–24

Cuaderno de actividades, pp. 15–17

1.1, 1.2, 1.3

## Day 11

### Objective
*Subjunctive with expressions of feelings*

### Core Instruction
**Gramática en acción 2,** pp. 70–75
- Have students do Bell Work, p. 74. **5 min.**
- See Teaching **Gramática,** p. 74. **15 min.**
- Play Audio CD 2, Tr. 10, for Activity 37, p. 74. **10 min.**
- Have students do Activities 38–41, pp. 74–75. **20 min.**

### Optional Resources
- **Comunicación,** p. 75
- Slower Pace Learners, p. 75 ◆
- Multiple Intelligences, p. 75

### Homework Suggestions
Study for **Prueba: Gramática 2**

Cuaderno de vocabulario y gramática, pp. 22–24

Cuaderno de actividades, pp. 15–17

1.1, 1.2

## Day 12

### Objective
*Subjunctive with expressions of feelings*

### Core Instruction
**Gramática en acción 2,** pp. 70–75
- Review **Gramática en acción 2,** pp. 70–75. **15 min.**
- Give **Prueba: Gramática 2. 20 min.**

**Novela en video,** pp. 76–77
- Show **VideoNovela.** See Teaching **Novela en video,** p. 76. **15 min.**

### Optional Resources
- **Comunicación,** p. 77
- Cultures, p. 76

### Homework Suggestions
Cuaderno de vocabulario y gramática, pp. 22–24

1.2, 1.3

## Day 13

### Objective
*Developing listening and reading skills*

### Core Instruction
**Lectura cultural,** pp. 78–79
- See Teaching **Lectura cultural,** p. 78. **35 min.**

**Leamos y escribamos,** pp. 80–83
- See Teaching **Leamos,** items 1–3, p. 80. **15 min.**

### Optional Resources
- Advanced Learners, p. 79 ▲
- Multiple Intelligences, p. 79
- Slower Pace Learners, p. 81 ◆
- Special Learning Needs, p. 81 ●

### Homework Suggestions
Cuaderno de actividades, p. 18

1.2, 1.3

## Day 14

### Objective
*Developing reading and writing skills*

### Core Instruction
**Leamos y escribamos,** pp. 80–83
- See Teaching **Leamos,** items 4–5, p. 80. **20 min.**
- See Teaching **Escribamos,** p. 82. **15 min.**

**Prepárate para el examen,** pp. 84–87
- Have students do Activities 1–4, pp. 84–85. **15 min.**

### Optional Resources
- Advanced Learners, p. 83 ▲
- Multiple Intelligences, p. 83

### Homework Suggestions
**Taller del escritor,** p. 83

1.2, 1.3

## Day 15

### Objective
*Chapter review*

### Core Instruction
**Prepárate para el examen,** pp. 84–87
- Have students do Activity 5, p. 85. **5 min.**
- Play Audio CD 2, Tr. 13 for Activity 6, p. 85. **5 min.**
- Have students do Activity 7, p. 85. **5 min.**

**Integración,** pp. 88–89
- Play Audio CD 2, Tr. 14 for Activity 1, p. 88. **5 min.**
- Have students do Activities 2–6, pp. 88–89. **30 min.**

### Optional Resources
- Play Pre-AP Audio CD 1, Tr. 5, for Pre-AP Pratice, p. 85
- Game, p. 87
- Fine Art Connection, p. 89

### Homework Suggestions
Study for Chapter Test

1.1, 1.2, 1.3

## Day 16/Test

### Core Instruction
**Chapter Test 50 min.**

### Optional Resources
Assessment Program
- **Prueba: Lectura**
- **Prueba: Escritura**
- Test Generator

### Homework Suggestions
Cuaderno de actividades, pp. 19–20

# Indiana
## The Hoosier State

Ohio River Bridge

Rocky Hollow Turkey Run State Park

Indianapolis skyline

### Chapter 2

The following chart presents *¡Exprésate!* Chapter 2 correlations to the Indiana Academic Standards for World Languages, Grade 11. The correlations here are to the *Student Edition* (SE) and *Teacher's Edition* (TE) only. For additional teaching resources, see pages 47A-47B

| INDIANA ACADEMIC STANDARDS | | | CHAPTER 2 SE/TE CORRELATIONS |
|---|---|---|---|
| **Standard 1 COMMUNICATION:** | | | |
| **Write and speak in a language other than English** | 11.1.1 | Initiate, sustain, and close conversations in limited yet varied situations. | SE: 53, 55, 67, 69, 89<br>TE: 50, 54, 64, 68 |
| | 11.1.2 | Exchange detailed information and opinions orally on a variety of topics. | SE: 53, 63, 67, 89<br>TE: 53, 62, 67, 88 |
| | 11.1.3 | Exchange detailed information and opinions in written form on a variety of topics. | SE: 83<br>TE: 59, 65, 67, 83 |
| | 11.1.4 | Make requests and ask different types of questions in a variety of social situations. | SE: 59, 61<br>TE: 54 |
| | 11.1.5 | Recognize and use situation-appropriate non-verbal communication. | SE: 89<br>TE: 55, 75, 76 |
| | 11.1.6 | Use speaking and listening strategies to facilitate communication. | SE: 71, 73, 75<br>TE: 56 |
| **Standard 2 COMMUNICATION:** | | | |
| **Interpret information in a language other than English** *Learners interpret written and spoken language on a variety of topics. (Interpretive)* | 11.2.1 | Respond to everyday requests, commands, and directions. | SE: 55, 61<br>TE: 47C, 51, 65 |
| | 11.2.2 | Demonstrate comprehension of both authentic and non-authentic written and spoken language through developmentally appropriate tasks. | SE: 63, 77, 79, 82<br>TE: 62, 76, 78, 80, 91, 93, 95 |
| | 11.2.3 | Make educated guesses about meaning in unfamiliar written and spoken contexts. | SE: 76, 80<br>TE: 76, 80 |
| **Standard 3 COMMUNICATION:** | | | |
| **Present information in a language other than English** *Learners present to an audience of listeners or readers on a variety of topics. (Presentational)* | 11.3.2 | Produce and present creative material on a variety of topics. | SE: 89<br>TE: 47C, 52, 83 |
| | 11.3.3 | Read passages aloud to demonstrate improving intonation and pronunciation. | SE: 69 |
| | 11.3.4 | Compose cohesive written information using appropriate formats and more varied vocabulary and structures. | SE: 83<br>TE: 47C, 82, 83 |
| **Standard 4 CULTURES:** | | | |
| **Develop awareness of other cultures.** *Learners examine, experience, and reflect on the relationships among the practices, products, and perspectives of the cultures studied.* | 11.4.1 | Analyze and reflect on cultural practices of the target cultures. | SE: 79, 89<br>TE: 62, 78, 88, 91, 93, 95 |
| | 11.4.2 | Describe products, perspectives, and symbols of the target cultures. | SE: 63, 79, 89<br>TE: 47D, 62, 78, 88, 91, 93, 95 |
| | 11.4.3 | Discuss factors that influence practices, products, and perspectives. | SE: 63, 79, 89<br>TE: 47D, 62, 78, 88, 91, 93, 95 |

| | | | |
|---|---|---|---|
| | **11.4.4** | Recognize the interrelations among the practices, products, and perspectives of the target cultures. | **SE:** 63, 79, 89, 95<br>**TE:** 47D, 62, 78, 88, 91, 93, 95 |
| | **11.4.5** | Explain contributions from other cultures. | **SE:** 79, 89<br>**TE:** 47D, 78, 88, 91, 93, 95 |
| | **11.4.6** | Identify significant events unique to the target cultures. | **TE:** 47D, 93 |

## Standard 5 CONNECTIONS:

| | | | |
|---|---|---|---|
| **Make connections to other content areas** *Learners use the target language to expand their knowledge of and make connections among multiple content areas.* | **11.5.1** | Make connections with other content areas through resources intended for native speakers. | **SE:** 88, 91 |
| | **11.5.2** | Design and share activities and materials that integrate the target language and cultures with concepts and skills from other content areas. | **SE:** 51, 53, 73, 89<br>**TE:** 47C, 47D, 47, 87 |

## Standard 6 CONNECTIONS:

| | | | |
|---|---|---|---|
| **Access and connect information through various media** *Learners strengthen language proficiency and cultural knowledge by using current digital media and authentic resources.* | **11.6.1** | Use digital media and culturally authentic resources to build vocabulary, improve reading ability, and encourage cultural awareness. | **SE:** 52, 56<br>**TE:** 47E, 47F |
| | **11.6.2** | Use digital media and culturally authentic resources to study target cultures. | **SE:** 62, 76, 90<br>**TE:** 79, 91 |
| | **11.6.3** | Identify and evaluate resources intended for native speakers. | **SE:** 62, 76, 90<br>**TE:** 79, 91 |

## Standard 7 COMPARISONS:

| | | | |
|---|---|---|---|
| **Investigate the nature of language and culture** *Learners understand the nature of language and culture through comparisons of the languages and cultures studied and their own.* | **11.7.1** | Use elements of word formation to expand vocabulary and derive meaning. | **SE:** 57<br>**TE:** 56, 70, 84 |
| | **11.7.2** | Recognize and use a variety of language structures. | **SE:** 70-75, 83<br>**TE:** 56-61, 84-87 |
| | **11.7.3** | Compare and use idiomatic, colloquial, and proverbial expressions in the target language. | **SE:** 55, 89<br>**TE:** 54 |
| | **11.7.5** | Compare systems of other cultures and the learner's own culture. | **SE:** 63, 79, 90-95<br>**TE:** 62, 78, 79, 95 |
| | **11.7.6** | Compare and contrast elements that shape cultural identity in the learner's heritage and in the target cultures. | **SE:** 63, 79, 90-95<br>**TE:** 62, 78, 79, 95 |

## Standard 8 COMMUNITIES:

| | | | |
|---|---|---|---|
| **Become an active global citizen by experiencing languages and cultures in multiple settings** *Learners use their knowledge of the target language and cultures both within and beyond the school setting for personal enrichment and civic engagement.* | **11.8.2** | Investigate and share with others the influences of the target language and cultures on the community. | **TE:** 89 |
| | **11.8.3** | Show evidence of becoming a life-long learner by using the target language and cultural knowledge for personal enrichment. | **SE:** 63<br>**TE:** 47C, 79, 88 |

## Meeting the National Standards

**Communication**
Comunicación, pp. 53, 55, 57, 59, 61, 67, 69, 71, 75, 77
Game, p. 87
Situación, p. 89

**Cultures**
Practices and Perspectives, pp. 52, 53, 54, 76
Nota cultural, p. 61
Culture Project, p. 88

**Connections**
La historia, p. 47D
Receta, p. 47D
History Link, p. 55
Atlas Interactivo Mundial, p. 63
Nota cultural, p. 74
Multiple Intelligences, p. 79
Advanced Learners, p. 79
Language Arts Link, p. 81
Analyzing, p. 89
Extension, p. 89

**Comparisons**
Comparaciones, p. 62
Language to Language, pp. 71, 86
Comparing and Contrasting, pp. 77, 79
Post-Reading Activities, p. 79
Culture Project, p. 88

**Communities**
Community Link, p. 57
Comunidad y oficio, p. 63
Multicultural Link, p. 88

# Capítulo 2

# ¡A pasarlo bien!

## OBJETIVOS

**In this chapter you will learn to**
- express interest and displeasure
- invite someone to do something
- describe the ideal friend
- express happiness and unhappiness

**And you will use**
- imperfect
- **ir a** + infinitive in the imperfect
- **nosotros** commands
- object pronouns
- subjunctive with the unknown or nonexistent
- subjunctive with expressions of feelings

### ¿Qué ves en la foto?

- ¿Qué hacen estos chicos?
- ¿Qué están mirando?
- ¿Te gustaría hacer una excursión a esta ciudad? ¿Por qué?

### Using the Photo

Have students look at the photo and describe the scene. Then have them discuss the questions on page 48 as a class. Tell them that Toledo, set on a mountain and kept isolated by the Tajo river, has always been well-protected. The structure at the top of the hill is the Alcázar, Charles V's fortified palace.

### Más vocabulario

**la muralla** *wall*
**medieval** *medieval*
**la vista** *view*

| Suggested pacing: | Traditional Schedule | Block Schedule |
|---|---|---|
| Vocabulario 1/Gramática 1 | 5 1/2 days | 2 1/2 blocks |
| Cultura | 1/2 day | 1/2 block |
| Vocabulario 2/Gramática 2 | 5 1/2 days | 2 1/2 blocks |
| Novela | 1/2 day | 1/4 block |
| Lectura cultural | 1/2 day | 1/2 block |
| Leamos y escribamos | 1 day | 1/2 block |
| Prepárate para el examen | 1 day | 1/2 block |
| Chapter Test | 1 day | 1/2 block |
| Integración | 1/2 day | 1/4 block |

Dos chicos disfrutan la vista en Toledo, España.

# Chapter Opener

## Holt Grammar Logic

### CHAPTER 2

- *To express interest and displeasure, and to invite someone to do something,* students will need to review the imperfect, including **ir a** + *infinitive* in the imperfect, and they will need to use **nosotros** commands.
- *To describe the ideal friend, and to express happiness and unhappiness,* students will need to review direct and indirect object pronouns, and they will need to use the subjunctive with the unknown or nonexistent, and with expressions of feelings.

## Learning Tips

Have students look up information about Toledo in Spanish on the Internet. Have them practice discussing the information they learn with classmates. Remind them that their classmates are just learning too, so everyone will make mistakes. 1.1, 3.2

## DVD VIDEO OPTIONS

- VideoCultura
- VideoNovela
- Variedades
- GramaVisión

## LISTENING PRACTICE — Language Lab and Classroom Activities

**Vocabulario**
Activity 1, p. 52, CD 2, Tr. 1
Activity 21, p. 66, CD 2, Tr. 8

**Gramática**
Activity 9, p. 56, CD 2, Tr. 2
Activity 13, p. 58, CD 2, Tr. 3
Activity 17, p. 60, CD 2, Tr. 4
Activity 34, p. 73, CD 2, Tr. 9
Activity 37, p. 74, CD 2, Tr. 10

**Cultura**
**Comparaciones,** pp. 62–63, CD 2, Tr. 5–7

**Novela**
**Novela en video,** Escuchemos, p. 76

**Lectura cultural**
pp. 78–79, CD 2, Tr. 11

**Leamos**
pp. 80–81, CD 2, Tr. 12
**Escuchemos,** p. 80

**Repaso**
Activity 6, p. 85, CD 2, Tr. 13
**Variedades,** Lab Book, p. 59

**Integración**
Activity 1, p. 88, CD 2, Tr. 14

**Assessment Program**
CD 2, Tr. 15–18

**Additional Listening**
Pre-AP CD 1, Trs. 5–8

**Resources**

**Planning:**

Lesson Planner, pp. 17–18, 178–179

One-Stop Planner

**Presentation:**

Teaching Transparencies
**Vocabulario** 2.1, 2.2

**Practice:**

Cuaderno de vocabulario y gramática, pp. 13–15

Activities for Communication, pp. 5–6

Teaching Transparencies
Bell Work 2.1
**Vocabulario y gramática** answers, pp. 13–15

Interactive Tutor, Disc 1

**Bell Work**

Use Bell Work 2.0 in the *Teaching Transparencies.*

**Objetivos**
- Expressing interest and displeasure
- Inviting someone to do something

# Vocabulario en acción 1

## En España

## Los pasatiempos y los deporte

Soy un **fanático** de los deportes. El fútbol, el béisbol, el volibol... me gustan casi todos los deportes. Por ejemplo, **practico ciclismo** a menudo con un grupo de amigos. ¡Es **genial!**

La **escalada deportiva** es **estupenda.** Voy a **escalar** este fin de semana con unos amigos.

El verano pasado aprendí a **esgrimir** con un amigo. **Me lo paso bien** practicando **esgrima.**

Hay unos deportes que, francamente, **me aburren. No aguanto el boliche.** Pero tengo que confesar que cuando hace mal tiempo y quiero estar adentro con los amigos, no es tan malo.

Me gusta **remar** con el club de **remo** de mi ciudad. Como ejercicio para todo el cuerpo, es formidable.

**Más vocabulario...**

| | |
|---|---|
| el jai-alai | *jai-alai* |
| jugar al boliche | *to bowl* |
| el senderismo | *hiking* |
| el tiro con arco | *archery* |

**También se puede decir...**

You may hear **la arquería** for **el tiro con arc** and **pista y campo** instead of **el atletismo**.

**Pre-AP Practice**

**AP Benchmark:** Use language that is semantically and grammatically accurate according to a given context.

**Focus:** Inviting someone to do something and to respond
- SE, p. 55, Act. 7
- TE, p. 55, **Comunicación**
- **Cuaderno de vocabulario y gramática,** p. 15, Act. 7

## Core Instruction

### TEACHING VOCABULARIO

1. Introduce the vocabulary on pages 50 and 51 and model the pronunciation of each word by reading the captions as students look at the photos. Then go over the words in **Más vocabulario.** **(4 min.)**
2. Ask students questions to prompt them to use vocabulary words. **¿Qué deporte se puede hacer en las montañas? ¿en un lago? ¿dentro de un edificio?** **(2 min.)**
3. Pantomime the activities in **Vocabulario 1** and have students tell which one you are representing. **(4 min.)**

### TEACHING ¡EXPRÉSATE!

1. Model the **¡Exprésate!** expressions for students. Use the expression **dejar frío** with **le** or **les** and point out that it takes an indirect object pronoun. **(2 min.)**
2. Have students respond as you ask the questions included in the **¡Exprésate!** presentation. **¿Qué deporte te gusta a ti? Eres muy bueno para el kárate, ¿verdad?** **(4 min.)**
3. Ask volunteers to tell about the sports they like and dislike, using expressions from **¡Exprésate!** **(4 min.)**

Visit Holt Online
**go.hrw.com**
KEYWORD: EXP3 CH2
Vocabulary 1 practice

No practico **el atletismo** pero es algo que me gusta ver, por ejemplo, durante los Juegos Olímpicos. Me gusta sobre todo **el salto de altura.**

Pienso tomar clases de **kárate** algún día. **Las artes marciales** te enseñan mucha disciplina.

Claro, uno no puede pasar todo el tiempo practicando deportes. Hay pasatiempos que me interesan mucho, como, por ejemplo, …

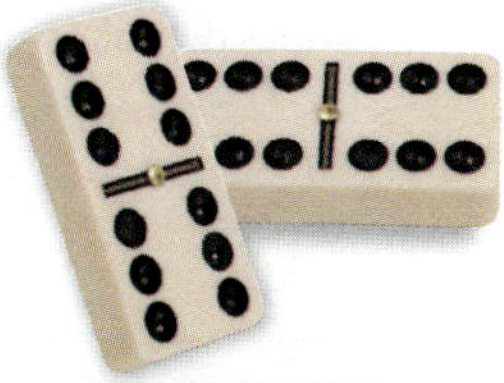

**el dominó**

**los juegos de computadora**

**los rompecabezas**

## ¡Exprésate!

| To express interest and displeasure | To respond |
|---|---|
| **Soy un(a) gran aficionado(a) a... ¿Qué deporte te gusta a ti?** *I'm a big . . . fan. What sport do you like?* | **Pues, la verdad es que...** *Well, the truth is that . . .* |
| **Eres muy bueno(a) para... ¿verdad?** *You're really good at . . . aren't you?* | **Sí, me la paso... Estoy loco(a) por...** *Yes, I'm always doing . . . I'm crazy about . . .* |
| **Los/Las... me dejan frío(a).** *The . . . don't do anything for me.* | **¿Ah, sí? Pues, yo creo que...** *Really? Well, I think . . .* |

Interactive TUTOR

Vocabulario y gramática, pp. 13–15 Online workbooks

▶ Vocabulario adicional — Los deportes, p. R15

Vocabulario 1

## TPR
### Total Physical Response

Bring to class or have students bring to class items used for each activity listed in **Vocabulario:** dominoes, puzzle pieces, computer games, karate belt, bathing suit, oar, bowling shoes. Spread the items in front of the classroom and have individual students respond to the following commands. Modify the commands as needed depending on the items you have.

**Dame el juego de computadora.**

**Ponte el cinturón que se usa para el kárate.**

**Saca las fichas de dominó de la caja.**

**Busca algo que alguien se pone para hacer windsurf.**

**Ponte algo que se necesita para jugar al boliche.**

**Agarra el arco que se usa para el tiro con arco.**

**Muéstrame cómo remar.** 1.2

### Common Error Alert
### ¡OJO!

Students may try to translate sports names such as *climbing* or *bowling* using the gerund form of the verb as in English. Remind them that in Spanish the gerund form is not as common; *bowling* is **jugar al boliche** rather than **jugando al boliche;** *climbing* is **la escalada deportiva,** not **escalando,** and *fencing* is **la esgrima,** not **esgrimiendo.**

### También se puede decir...

Students may also hear **el tiro con arco** or **arco y flecha** used to describe *archery.*

## Differentiated Instruction

### Advanced Learners

**Extension** Give students a closed-book dictation and have them check their spelling when they have finished. (**Soy un fanático de los deportes acuáticos. Me encanta remar y el windsurf es genial. Los deportes que se pueden hacer en las montañas también son formidables. Soy un gran aficionado a la escalada deportiva.**) 1.2

### Multiple Intelligences

**Kinesthetic** Have students act out the sports and pastimes in **Vocabulario 1.** The rest of the class must guess the activity. The person who guesses correctly acts out the next word.

**Differentiated Instruction** See the Differentiated Instruction CD-ROM.

## Resources

**Planning:**

Lesson Planner, pp. 17–18, 178–179

One-Stop Planner

**Presentation:**

Teaching Transparencies **Vocabulario** 2.1, 2.2

**Practice:**

Cuaderno de vocabulario y gramática, pp. 13–15

Activities for Communication, pp. 5–6

Lab Book, pp. 17–20

Teaching Transparencies **Vocabulario y gramática** answers, pp. 13–15

Interactive Tutor, Disc 1

### 1 Script

See script on page 47E.

### Cultures

**Practices and Perspectives**

Tell students that winter sports are quite popular in Spain, as are mountain climbing, cycling, swimming, and surfing. Remind them that soccer is, by far, the most popular sport. Ask students to compare these sports with those that are popular in the United States.

2.1, 4.2

CD 2, Tr. 1

### 1 ¿A quién le gusta? 1.2

**Escuchemos** Mira las fotos y escucha los comentarios. Decide qué comentario corresponde a cada foto.

A

B

C

D

E

F

G

H

1. d 2. e 3. h 4. f 5. b 6. a 7. c 8. g

**Nota cultural**

Para los aficionados al senderismo, los Pirineos en el norte de España son las montañas preferidas. Otros destinos populares para los senderistas son los Picos de Europa al norte de Santander o la Sierra Nevada, en el sur. El llano en el sur y la meseta central presentan otros paisajes bonitos para ir de excursión.

¿Dónde te gusta hacer senderismo? 1.2

### 2 Los deportes preferidos 1.2

**Leamos/Escribamos** Completa la conversación entre Sonia y Ernesto con las palabras y expresiones del cuadro.

| | | | |
|---|---|---|---|
| escalar | remo | fanático | geniales |
| me deja | bueno para | juegos de computadora | senderismo |
| aficionada | me la paso | | |

1. bueno para SONIA Ernesto, eres muy __1__ la natación, ¿no?

ERNESTO No, la natación __2__ frío. Pero estoy loco por otros deportes acuáticos, como el esquí acuático y el __3__. 2. me deja 3. remo

SONIA Yo también prefiero los deportes al aire libre. Me encanta hacer __4__ en el bosque y en las montañas. 4. senderismo

ERNESTO ¿Ah, sí? El senderismo me aburre, pero soy un __5__ de la escalada deportiva. Me encanta __6__. 5. fanático 6. escalar

SONIA No soy una gran __7__ a la escalada deportiva. Me da miedo. ¿Lo haces a menudo? 7. aficionada

ERNESTO Sí, __8__ escalando durante el verano. 8. me la paso

SONIA ¿Y qué vas a hacer esta tarde? Está lloviendo.

ERNESTO Voy a quedarme en casa jugando a los __9__. ¿Te gustan? 9. juegos de computadora

SONIA ¡Claro que sí! Creo que son __10__. 10. geniales

## Core Instruction

### VOCABULARY IN CONTEXT

Ask students to write a short story about a summer vacation, using ten words from **Vocabulario 1.** For each vocabulary word used, students should draw a picture or cut one out of a magazine to represent the word instead of writing it. Students then exchange their work with a partner who replaces each drawing or picture with the correct vocabulary word. When finished, students give the essay or story back to the writer for correction. Have volunteers read their stories for the class. You might have them write their stories on transparencies and place the pictures as they would on paper to help the rest of the class follow along. Ask students to vote on the most interesting or most unusual summer vacation.

### 3 Es lo opuesto ❀ 1.2

**Leamos/Escribamos** Escribe las oraciones de nuevo para comunicar el sentido opuesto. Utiliza las expresiones de **Exprésate.**

**MODELO** **Bernardo cree que los programas de deportes en la tele son geniales.**
**A Bernardo le dejan frío los programas de deportes en la tele.**

1. A mi hermano le aburren los juegos de computadora.
2. Marta, eres una gran aficionada al senderismo, ¿verdad?
3. Luis es muy bueno para el jai-alai.
4. Mi amiga Catarina es una fanática de los rompecabezas.
5. Paulina se la pasa jugando al boliche.
6. Pablo cree que la esgrima es genial.

### 4 Las actividades preferidas ❀ 1.2

**Escribamos** Usa una palabra o expresión de cada columna para escribir seis oraciones completas sobre tus propias experiencias.

**MODELO** **Mi hermano se la pasa practicando el kárate.**

| | | | |
|---|---|---|---|
| yo | (no) ser bueno(a) para | el ciclismo | el senderismo |
| mi mejor amigo(a) | estar loco(a) por | la escalada deportiva | el kárate |
| el profesor/la profesora | (no) ser aficionado(a) a | el remo | la esgrima |
| mi hermano(a) | pasársela practicando | la pelota | los juegos de computadora |
| mis compañeros de clase | | el boliche | el tiro con arco |

## Comunicación

HOLT SoundBooth ONLINE RECORDING

### 5 Los gustos de la clase ❀ 1.1, 1.3

**Hablemos/Escribamos** Con un(a) compañero(a), haz una encuesta de cuatro o cinco preguntas sobre los gustos en cuanto a los deportes. En grupos, túrnense para hacer las preguntas y contestarlas. Después, hagan una gráfica o tabla con los resultados de la encuesta.

**MODELO** **—¿Qué deporte te gusta más?**
**—Pues, el deporte que más me gusta es la escalada deportiva.**

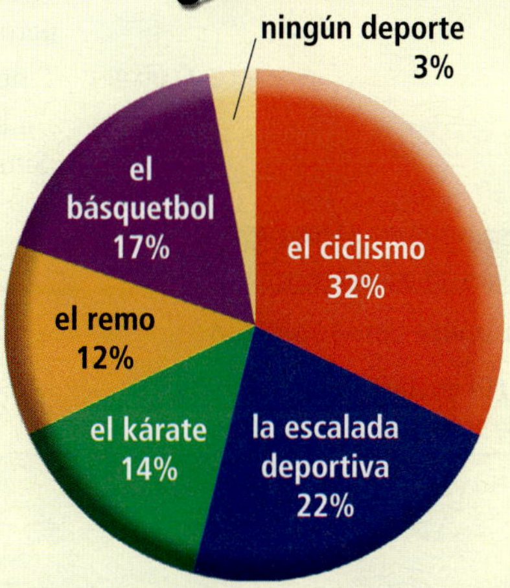


## Differentiated Instruction

### SLOWER PACE LEARNERS

2 Before students do Activity 2, have them close their books. Read the entire conversation aloud with the answers included, and tell them to simply focus on understanding what is going on. Ask volunteers to summarize what happened in the conversation. Then have them open their books and complete Activity 2. ❀ 1.2

### SPECIAL LEARNING NEEDS

4 **Students with AD(H)D** Some students may have trouble figuring out which elements to combine from the boxes. You may want to change the format of Activity 4 to sentence completion. Create a handout that has the first part of the sentence already composed from a subject and a verb phrase from the first two boxes. Instruct students to complete the sentences with vocabulary chosen from the third box. ❀ 1.2

Vocabulario 1

## Cultures

### Practices and Perspectives

Bullfighting is another spectacle that is popular throughout Spain despite continued pressure from international animal-rights activists. Bullfighting began in village squares and became formalized with the building of the bullring in Ronda in the late 18th century. Since then, the bullfight has had specific individuals who participate in the spectacle: the bull, the **picador,** the **banderilleros,** and the **matador.** Have students research information about bullfighting in Spain. They may wish to focus their research on famous bullfighters, bullfighting traditions, important bullrings, or another aspect of the sport that interests them. Have them share their findings with the class. ❀ 2.1

## Comunicación

### Class Activity: Presentational

Have pairs of students present their graphs from Activity 5 to the class and explain the results. Then allow the class to discuss what they observe about the results. You might start them off with some questions. **¿Hay muchos aficionados al ciclismo en esta clase? ¿Muchos estudiantes creen que el dominó es genial?** ❀ 1.3

**Differentiated Instruction** See the Differentiated Instruction CD-ROM.

## Resources

**Planning:**

Lesson Planner, pp. 17–18, 178–179

One-Stop Planner

**Presentation:**

Teaching Transparencies
**Vocabulario** 2.1, 2.2

**Practice:**

Cuaderno de vocabulario y gramática, pp. 13–15

Activities for Communication, pp. 5–6

Teaching Transparencies
**Vocabulario y gramática** answers, pp. 13–15

Interactive Tutor, Disc 1

## Cultures

### Practices and Perspectives

The **Tour de France, Giro d'Italia,** and **Vuelta a España** make up the "Big Three" world road cycling competitions. The **Vuelta a España,** in which the world's greatest cyclists have competed (or compete), takes place in Spain. Each stage of the 3-week race covers more than 200 kilometers, including up to 7 mountain passes, though the course is always changing. Many cycling fans find that following the **Vuelta** is an excellent way to tour Spain. Have students check the tour's official Web site or do research in the library or on the Internet. They should find information on the final leg of the **Vuelta a España** and make a short presentation about the sights the cyclists or fans might see along the way. 2.1

## Teaching Suggestion

You may wish to have students rewrite the dialog substituting **ustedes** verbal forms for the **vosotros** forms. 1.2

En el Parque del Retiro, Madrid

## ¿Qué planes tenéis?

| | |
|---|---|
| ROSALÍA | ¿Qué planes tenéis vosotros para este fin de semana? |
| CARMEN | Pues, la verdad es que no tengo planes. ¿Por qué? |
| ROSALÍA | ¿Os gustaría ver la Vuelta a España en la tele? Va a ir mucha gente a casa de Marisol a verla. |
| ANTONIO | No, gracias. Iba a remar con unos amigos. Además, el ciclismo me aburre. |
| ROSALÍA | ¿En serio? ¡Pero es genial! Estoy loca por el ciclismo. |
| CARMEN | No veamos la Vuelta a España. No aguanto estar sentada sin hacer nada los sábados. Si vamos a estar sentados, mejor me quedo en casa jugando al dominó con mi hermanito. |
| ROSALÍA | Bueno, no seas dramática. ¿Sabes? Podríamos ver el campeonato de kárate o la competencia de atletismo, pero no... seríamos espectadores nada más. |
| CARMEN | Tengo una idea. ¿Por qué no jugamos al boliche? |
| ROSALÍA | ¿Al boliche? Bueno, como quieras. Me da lo mismo. ¡Simplemente no quiero quedarme en casa! |

### ¡Exprésate!

| To invite someone to do something | To respond |
|---|---|
| **¿Te gustaría...? Yo te invito.**<br>*Would you like to . . . ? My treat.* | **No, gracias. Iba a...**<br>*No, thanks. I was going to . . .* |
| **No vayamos a... No aguanto...**<br>*Let's not go to . . . I can't stand . . .* | **Como quieras. Me da lo mismo.**<br>*Whatever you want. It's all the same to me.* |

Interactive TUTOR

Vocabulario y gramática, pp. 13–15 Online workbooks

## Core Instruction

### TEACHING ¡EXPRÉSATE!

1. Read the conversation aloud with students. **(2 min.)**
2. Ask students to tell what happened in the conversation, and allow them to ask questions about the parts they do not understand. **(3 min.)**
3. Model the **¡Exprésate!** functions for students. Then ask individuals to do various activities and have them respond using expressions from **¡Exprésate!** **(2 min.)**
4. Reverse roles. Have students use expressions from **¡Exprésate!** to invite you to do an activity, and respond to their invitations. **(4 min.)**

### 6 ¿Qué hacemos? 1.2

**Leamos/Escribamos** Basándote en la conversación en la página 54, contesta **cierto** o **falso.** Corrige las oraciones falsas.

1. Carmen ya tiene muchos planes para el fin de semana. falso. Carmen no tiene ningún plan para el fin de semana.
2. Antonio es un gran aficionado al ciclismo. falso. A Antonio le aburre el ciclismo.
3. Antonio va a remar con unos amigos. cierto.
4. A Rosalía le deja fría el ciclismo. falso. Rosalía está loca por el ciclismo.
5. Carmen no quiere quedarse sentada el sábado. cierto.
6. Rosalía está loca por el boliche. falso. A Rosalía le da igual. Simplemente no quiere quedarse en casa.

### 7 ¿Aceptarás la invitación? 1.2

**Leamos/Escribamos** Responde a cada invitación, según tus propios gustos. En algunas respuestas, explica por qué no puedes aceptar la invitación. Usa las frases de **Exprésate** en tus respuestas.

MODELO **—Voy a ir a un partido de fútbol mañana. ¿Quieres ir?**
**—Gracias, pero no puedo. Iba a ir al lago.**
**—(Sí, gracias. Me fascina el fútbol.)**

1. ¿Te gustaría ver la nueva película española conmigo este viernes?
2. ¿Por qué no jugamos al dominó?
3. ¿Te gustaría ver el campeonato de básquetbol en la tele con nosotros este domingo?
4. ¿Quieres hacer un rompecabezas conmigo este sábado?
5. ¿Te gustaría ir a un concierto el viernes? Yo te invito.
6. ¿Te gustaría acompañarme a la competencia de esgrima el sábado?
7. ¿Te gustaría hacer senderismo conmigo este fin de semana?
8. ¿Por qué no hacemos windsurf hoy?

El equipo Real Madrid celebra después del partido contra Barcelona.

## Comunicación

HOLT SoundBooth ONLINE RECORDING

### 8 ¿Qué vamos a hacer? 1.1, 1.3

**Hablemos** Haz una lista de cuatro actividades que te gustaría hacer con un(a) amigo(a). Luego, invita a un(a) compañero(a) a acompañarte. Tu compañero(a) debe aceptar dos de las invitaciones y rechazar *(turn down)* dos. Si tu compañero(a) rechaza la invitación, entonces debe ofrecer una explicación o alternativa.

MODELO **—¿Te gustaría remar conmigo esta semana?**
**—No gracias, el remo me aburre. ¿Por qué no...?**

▶ **Vocabulario adicional** — Los deportes, p. R15

## Connections

### History Link

Madrid's soccer team, Real Madrid, benefited from government assistance and preferential treatment for years, in large part due to the actions of dictator Francisco Franco, who favored Real Madrid. The team was able to secure the best players, field the best teams, and win championships for years. Today, one of the greatest sports rivalries in Spain is between Real Madrid and FC Barcelona. Have students research information about the two teams. You may also wish to have students research Franco. 3.1

## Comunicación

### Group Activity: Interpersonal

Have students think of an activity they would like to do over the weekend and tell them to invite someone to go with them. Their classmates will respond by accepting or rejecting the invitation. Once someone has accepted an invitation, that person must reject further invitations by explaining that he or she already has plans. Continue until everyone has a partner for a weekend activity. 1.1

## Differentiated Instruction

### ADVANCED LEARNERS

**Challenge** Have students design ads for activities they could do in Castilla-La Mancha. Collect their work and pass them out to different students. Group students in threes. One student will invite another to do the activity in the ad, and he or she will turn down the invitation. The third student will try to convince the second student to accept the invitation using words like: **buena idea, divertido, disfrutar, genial, formidable, estupendo.** Students take turns playing each role. 1.1

### SPECIAL LEARNING NEEDS

**6 Students with Learning Disabilities** Before students answer the questions in Activity 6, have three volunteers act out the parts of Rosalía, Carmen, and Antonio. Give each student a nametag so the rest of the class can clearly identify the characters. Then go over the true/false statements together. If students are uncertain of the answer, have the volunteers reread the appropriate sections and decide on the answers as a class. 1.1

## Assess

**Assessment Program**
**Prueba: Vocabulario 1,** pp. 21–22
Alternative Assessment, pp. 374, 386, 398

**Online Assessment**
**my.hrw.com**

**Test Generator**

**Assess Differentiated Instruction** See the Differentiated Instruction CD-ROM.

## Resources

**Planning:**

Lesson Planner, pp. 19–21, 180–183

One-Stop Planner

**Presentation:**

Video Program
**GramaVisión**

**Practice:**

Grammar Tutor for Students of Spanish, Chapter 2

Cuaderno de vocabulario y gramática, pp. 16–18

Cuaderno de actividades, pp. 11–13

Activities for Communication, pp. 5–6

Lab Book, pp. 17–20

Teaching Transparencies
Bell Work 2.2
**Vocabulario y gramática** answers, pp. 16–18

Audio CD 2, Tr. 2

Interactive Tutor, Disc 1

### Bell Work

Use Bell Work 2.2 in the *Teaching Transparencies,* or write this activity on the board.

**Usa las expresiones de ¡Exprésate! para escribir cuatro invitaciones a un amigo.** 1.2

**Objetivos**
- Imperfect
- **Ir a** + infinitive in the imperfect
- **Nosotros** commands

# Gramática en acción 1

GramaVisión

Interactive TUTOR

## Repaso Imperfect

**1** The **imperfect** tense is used to talk about past events. It tells what one used to do, how things used to be, or what happened in general.

De niño, me **fascinaban** los rompecabezas.
*When I was a boy, puzzles used to fascinate me.*

En la escuela primaria, las niñas **jugaban** al fútbol cada día.
*In elementary school, the girls would play soccer every day.*

En esos días, **teníamos** más tiempo libre.
*Back in those days, we had more free time.*

**2** The verb endings in the **imperfect** are:

| -ar verbs | |
|---|---|
| -aba | -ábamos |
| -abas | -abais |
| -aba | -aban |

| -er/-ir verbs | |
|---|---|
| -ía | -íamos |
| -ías | -íais |
| -ía | -ían |

**3** **Ir, ver,** and **ser** are the only verbs that are irregular in the imperfect.

De niño, David **iba** a clases de kárate todos los lunes.
Cuando **era** joven, María practicaba el atletismo.
Silvia **veía** los partidos de básquetbol en la tele todos los sábados.

**4** The imperfect is often used with expressions such as **muchas veces, a veces, (casi) siempre,** and **todos los años/días.**

Vocabulario y gramática, pp. 16–18
Actividades, pp. 11–13
Online workbooks

### ¿Te acuerdas?

The **present tense** is often used to say what happens *on a regular basis.*

**Juego** al fútbol los lunes.

The **present progressive** is used with most verbs to say what is *going on at the moment.*

Marcelo **está estudiando.**

With **ir** and *verbs that refer to states or conditions,* use the **present tense** instead of the present progressive.

Ana **va** al centro recreativo.

Me **fascinan** los trenes.

CD 2, Tr. 2 See script on p. 47E.

### 9 ¿Les gustaba o no? 1.2

**Escuchemos** Escucha mientras varias personas hablan de las cosas que hacían de niño o que hacen ahora. Escribe el nombre de la persona y escribe **presente** si la persona hace la actividad ahora o **pasado** si la hacía de niño(a).

1. Elena pasado
2. Juan Luis presente
3. Victoria pasado
4. Alejandro pasado
5. Carolina pasado
6. José Miguel presente
7. Sara presente
8. Guillermo pasado

## Core Instruction

### TEACHING GRAMÁTICA

1. Go over point 1 with students and read the examples. **(2 min.)**
2. Go over point 2 and ask students to help you conjugate the verbs **remar, esgrimir,** and **hacer** in the imperfect. Write the conjugations on the board. **(3 min.)**
3. Go over point 3 and model sentences using the imperfect conjugations of the verbs **ir, ver,** and **ser** in sentences. Use different forms by varying the subject: **nosotros, ustedes, tú, yo, mi amigo(a). (4 min.)**
4. Go over point 4 with students and provide sample sentences. **De niña, iba muchas veces a las montañas. A veces hacía senderismo con mi papá. Mi hermano casi siempre se quejaba. Todos los años hacíamos un viaje a los Pirineos en España. (6 min.)**

### GramaVisión

For a video presentation of the imperfect, use **GramaVisión.**

GramaVisión

### 10 ¿Qué hacían todos? 1.2

**Escribamos** Basándote en los dibujos, escribe qué actividad hacía cada persona de niño y qué opinaba de la actividad.

**MODELO** **De niño, Jaime tenía que practicar el violín todos los días. No le gustaba para nada.**

Jaime

1. mi hermano y yo

2. Emilio y Marcos

3. Martín

4. mi familia y yo

5. Teresa y su abuelo

6. mi mejor amigo(a) y yo

### 11 Antes y ahora 1.2

**Escribamos** Escribe dos oraciones para cada número. La primera oración debe decir qué hacía la persona de niño(a) y qué opinaba de la actividad, y la segunda oración debe decir qué opina ahora de esta actividad.

**MODELO** **yo/nadar**
**Cuando era niña, no me gustaba nadar porque...**
**Ahora creo que...**

1. mi mejor amigo/tomar clases de piano
2. mi hermano(a)/trepar a los árboles
3. mis amigos y yo/ver dibujos animados en la televisión
4. tú/jugar al béisbol
5. mis primos/montar en bicicleta
6. mi mamá/coleccionar animales de peluche

## Comunicación

HOLT SoundBooth ONLINE RECORDING

### 12 Yo hacía lo mismo 1.1, 1.3

**Hablemos** Piensa en cuatro actividades que te gustaba hacer o que odiabas hacer de niño. En grupos de tres, traten de encontrar a alguien con los mismos gustos que tú de niño(a). Túrnense para hacerse preguntas sobre sus gustos.

### Heritage Speakers

Have students work in pairs to create a short conversation about what they used to do as children. Encourage them to share their conversations with the class and allow their classmates to ask questions. 1.1

### Communities

#### Community Link

Have students interview older members of their community about what they used to do as teenagers. How did they spend their free time? What did they do at home and at school? Ask students to conduct the interviews in Spanish. Have volunteers share their responses with the class. 1.1, 5.2

### Comunicación

#### Group Activity: Interpretive

Tell students to imagine they are a famous person. Have each student write the name of the celebrity on a piece of paper. Collect the papers and write all of the names on the board. Have students then imagine what that person used to do before becoming famous and ask them to prepare four sentences using the imperfect. Students will take turns presenting their sentences to the class, while the rest of the class tries to guess who they are. 1.2

## Differentiated Instruction

### SLOWER PACE LEARNERS

9 If students have difficulty completing Activity 9, tell them to listen for verbs in the imperfect versus the present, and also for the word **recuerdo,** which signals that the people are talking about their past. After playing each item, have students repeat what they heard. Then answer the questions as a class. 1.2

### SPECIAL LEARNING NEEDS

10 **Students with Visual Impairments** For students with visual impairments, you might want to describe aloud the art for Activity 10. You may wish to use circumlocution to describe each activity without naming it and include a description of each character's facial expression.

**Differentiated Instruction** See the Differentiated Instruction CD-ROM.

## Resources

**Planning:**

Lesson Planner, pp. 19–21, 180–183

One-Stop Planner

**Presentation:**

Video Program
**GramaVisión**

**Practice:**

Grammar Tutor for Students of Spanish, Chapter 2

Cuaderno de vocabulario y gramática, pp. 16–18

Cuaderno de actividades, pp. 11–13

Activities for Communication, pp. 5–6

Lab Book, pp. 17–20

Teaching Transparencies
Bell Work 2.3
**Vocabulario y gramática** answers, pp. 16–18

Audio CD 2, Tr. 3

Interactive Tutor, Disc 1

### Bell Work

Use Bell Work 2.3 in the *Teaching Transparencies,* or write this activity on the board.

**Completa las oraciones con la forma correcta del verbo entre paréntesis.**

1. Todos los veranos, nosotros _____ (ir) a la playa.
2. De niño, siempre me _____ (gustar) jugar al dominó.
3. Ahora el dominó _____ (aburrirme).
4. De joven, mi hermano _____ (practicar) atletismo.

1.2

### 13 Script

See script on p. 47E.

## Repaso Ir a + infinitive in the imperfect

Interactive TUTOR

**1** Use **ir a + infinitive** in the **imperfect** to state what someone *was going to do.*

**Iba a estudiar,** pero...
*I was going to study, but . . .*

**2** **Ir a + infinitive** is followed by a verb in the **preterite** when the second verb refers to a completed action or to a condition that ended.

**Iba a llamarte,** pero se me **olvidó.**

Mis padres **iban a ver** la película, pero **llegaron** tarde.

**3** **Ir a + infinitive** is followed by another verb in the **imperfect** when the second verb refers to an ongoing state or condition in the past.

Nosotros **íbamos a jugar** al fútbol, pero **teníamos** mucha tarea.

Eduardo **iba a salir,** pero se **sentía** muy cansado.

Vocabulario y gramática, pp. 16–18
Actividades, pp. 11–13
**Online** workbooks

CD 2, Tr. 3

### 13 ¿Por qué no fuiste? 1.2

**Escuchemos** Escucha mientras las personas de los dibujos explican por qué no fueron a tu partido de béisbol. Identifica a cada persona según lo que dice. **1.** b **2.** a **3.** f **4.** e **5.** d **6.** c

a.

b.

c.

d.

e.

f.

## Core Instruction

### TEACHING GRAMÁTICA

1. Review **ir a** + infinitive in the present tense by asking students **¿Qué vas a hacer este fin de semana?** **(2 min.)**
2. Go over point 1 with students. Say what you were going to do last weekend but didn't do. **El fin de semana pasado, iba a ir al cine pero no fui.** Then ask students **¿Qué ibas a hacer el fin de semana pasado?** **(2 min.)**
3. Go over point 2. Point out that object pronouns are often attached to the end of the infinitive as in the first example. Have volunteers provide more examples of **ir a** + infinitive followed by the **preterite.** **(3 min.)**
4. Go over point 3. Have volunteers provide alternative endings to each example using verbs in the **imperfect** that describe different conditions. **(3 min.)**

### GramaVisión

For a video presentation of **ir a** + infinitive, use **GramaVisión.**

GramaVisión

## 14 Un fin de semana muy movido 1.2

**Leamos/Escribamos** Lee el diario de José y contesta las preguntas.

Tenía muchos planes para este fin de semana pero no tuve el tiempo suficiente para hacerlo todo. El sábado por la mañana iba a ir al parque a jugar al fútbol, pero me desperté tarde. Me quedé en casa jugando juegos de computadora. Por la tarde mis padres querían hacer senderismo, pero mi mamá se enfermó. Así que fui al parque a jugar al básquetbol. Luego, iba a ver una película con mis primos, pero ellos tuvieron que ayudar a mi tía en casa. El domingo por la tarde Marcos y yo queríamos ver un partido de fútbol, pero llegamos tarde y ya no había boletos. Fuimos a un restaurante a comer. Después, regresé a casa para hacer la tarea. ¡Los fines de semana pasan demasiado rápido!

1. ¿Qué iba a hacer José temprano el sábado? ¿Por qué no lo hizo?
2. ¿Qué querían hacer los padres de José? ¿Qué pasó?
3. Después de jugar al básquetbol, ¿que iban a hacer José y sus primos? ¿Por qué no pudieron ir sus primos?
4. ¿Qué iban a hacer José y Marcos el domingo? ¿Qué hicieron?

## 15 Excusas y más excusas 1.2

**Escribamos** Todos en la familia Mercado iban a hacer varias cosas ayer, pero no las hicieron. Explica por qué.

MODELO **La señora Mercado/hacer las compras/tener que llevar a la bebé al médico**
**La señora Mercado iba a hacer las compras, pero tuvo que llevar a la bebé al médico.**

1. Daniel y Rita/organizar sus cuartos/tener mucha tarea
2. El señor Mercado/lavar el carro/sentirse muy cansado
3. Fernanda y yo/preparar la cena/(yo) cortarme con el cuchillo
4. Yo/jugar al dominó con mi abuelo/tener que estudiar
5. La señora Mercado/tomar una siesta/no tener tiempo
6. La abuela/leer un libro/no poder encontrar los anteojos

1. Daniel y Rita iban a organizar sus cuartos, pero tenían mucha tarea.
2. El señor Mercado iba a lavar el carro, pero se sentía muy cansado.
3. Fernanda y yo íbamos a preparar la cena, pero me corté con el cuchillo.
4. Iba a jugar al dominó con mi abuelo, pero tuve que estudiar.
5. La señora Mercado iba a tomar una siesta, pero no tuvo tiempo.
6. La abuela iba a leer un libro, pero no pudo encontrar los anteojos.

## Comunicación

HOLT SoundBooth ONLINE RECORDING

## 16 ¿Qué les pasó? 1.1, 1.3

**Hablemos** Hiciste una fiesta el sábado, pero dos de tus amigos no vinieron. En grupos de tres, creen una conversación en que uno de Uds. les pregunta a los otros dos qué pasó. Los dos amigos deben explicar por qué no fueron a la fiesta. Después, hagan planes para reunirse en otro momento.

### 14 Answers

1. Iba a ir al parque a jugar al fútbol. Se despertó tarde.
2. Querían hacer senderismo. Su mamá se enfermó.
3. Iba a ver una película con ellos. Ellos tuvieron que ayudar en casa.
4. Iban a ver un partido de fútbol. Fueron a un restaurante a comer.

### Más práctica

Have students use the following subjects and verbs to tell what each person was going to do last weekend.

1. **Marta/hacer senderismo**
2. **Tú/practicar atletismo**
3. **Nosotros/remar**
4. **Yo/jugar al boliche**
5. **Juan y Carlos/escalar**

1.2

### Comunicación

**Pair Activity: Interpersonal**

Have students work in pairs to talk about the things they were going to do last year but never did. They should take turns telling what they were going to do and why they didn't do it. Then they can talk about what activities they are going to do this year.

MODELO
**El año pasado iba a practicar atletismo, pero tenía miedo. Este año voy a hablar con el entrenador y probar el salto de altura.** 1.1

## Differentiated Instruction

### ADVANCED LEARNERS

**14 Challenge** Have students write their own journal entries about their weekend. Have them tell what they were going to do but didn't, and what activities they did do. Ask students to share their journal entries with the class. 1.3

### SPECIAL LEARNING NEEDS

**13 Students with Auditory Impairments** You may want to modify Activity 13 for students with auditory impairments. Instead of listening to the audio script, have students come up with their own sentences for each illustration. Have volunteers write their sentences on the board and ask the rest of the class to decide which illustration corresponds to each sentence. 1.2

Differentiated Instruction See the Differentiated Instruction CD-ROM.

## Resources

**Planning:**

Lesson Planner, pp. 19–21, 180–183

One-Stop Planner

**Presentation:**

Video Program
**GramaVisión**

**Practice:**

Grammar Tutor for Students of Spanish, Chapter 2

Cuaderno de vocabulario y gramática, pp. 16–18

Cuaderno de actividades, pp. 11–13

Activities for Communication, pp. 5–6

Lab Book, pp. 17–20

Teaching Transparencies

Bell Work 2.4

**Vocabulario y gramática** answers, pp. 16–18

Audio CD 2, Tr. 4

Interactive Tutor, Disc 1

### Bell Work

Use Bell Work 2.4 in the *Teaching Transparencies*, or write this activity on the board.

**Completa las siguientes oraciones.**

1. Iba a jugar al boliche pero…
2. Mis papás iban a salir pero…
3. Mi amigo iba a correr pero…
4. Nosotros íbamos a descansar pero…

1.2

### Teaching Suggestion

Have partners create a prioritized list of ten **nosotros** commands about what students should do as a class to make this school year the best it can be. Have them create posters with the commands to display in the classroom. 1.3

## Nosotros commands

Interactive TUTOR

### ¿Te acuerdas?

Verbs ending in **-car, -gar,** and **-zar** have the same spelling change in **nosotros commands** as in the present subjunctive.

sacar → **saquemos**
llegar → **lleguemos**
organizar → **organicemos**

Verbs having irregular present subjunctive forms will have the same irregular **nosotros command** forms.

dar → **demos**
ser → **seamos**

**1** You've used **vamos a + infinitive** to say what a group of people is going to do. To suggest that a group of people do or not do something *(Let's [not] . . .)*, use **nosotros commands.**

**No hablemos** con el director; **hablemos** con Sergio mejor.

*Let's not speak to the principal; let's speak to Sergio instead.*

**2** Use the **nosotros** form of the present subjunctive for **nosotros commands.** The verb **ir** has an irregular affirmative form: **vamos.**

**No vayamos** al lago hoy; que está lloviznando. **Vamos** al cine.

*Let's not go to the lake today; it's drizzling. Let's go to the movies.*

**3** **Object** or **reflexive pronouns** are attached to the end of a verb in affirmative commands or go between **no** and the verb in negative commands.

—¿Hacemos la fiesta esta semana? ¿Invitamos a los vecinos?

—Sí, **hagámosla** el viernes. No, **no los invitemos** esta vez.

Note that the final **-s** is dropped before adding **nos**.

**No nos preocupemos** por eso. **Vámonos** ya.

Vocabulario y gramática, pp. 16–18
Actividades, pp. 11–13
Online workbooks

CD 2, Tr. 4

### 17 Sugerencias 1.2

**Escuchemos** Escucha las conversaciones y determina si la persona que habla primero sugiere **a)** hacer algo con la otra persona o **b)** que la otra persona haga algo solo(a).

**1.** b **2.** a **3.** b **4.** a **5.** a **6.** b

### 18 Un buen equipo 1.2

**Escribamos** Eres el capitán del equipo de volibol de tu colegio. Escribe las metas *(goals)* del equipo. Anima a todos a hacer las siguientes cosas.

**MODELO** **practicar con el equipo de la universidad (sí)**
**Practiquemos con el equipo de la universidad.**

| *Sí* | *No* |
|---|---|
| 1. llegar a tiempo a los partidos | 5. ser maleducados durante los partidos |
| 2. invitar a los nuevos estudiantes a participar | 6. olvidarnos de darle las gracias al director |
| 3. organizar un campeonato para abril | 7. faltar a los entrenamientos |
| 4. hacer una fiesta o un baile en mayo | 8. sacar malas notas en clase |

## Core Instruction

### TEACHING GRAMÁTICA

1. Provide some examples to review formal and informal commands. **(2 min.)**
2. Go over point 1. Have volunteers use these verbs in **nosotros** commands: **hacer, cantar, salir, jugar, escalar. (2 min.)**
3. Go over point 2 with more examples you and the students create, such as **No vayamos a la oficina, vamos a la playa. (4 min.)**
4. Go over point 3. Ask volunteers to write on the board the affirmative and negative **nosotros** command form of these verbs: **irse, acostarse, sentarse. (4 min.)**
5. Go over **¿Te acuerdas?** Have students use other **-zar, -gar,** and **-car** verbs in a **nosotros** command. **(3 min.)**

### GramaVisión

For a video presentation of the **nosotros** commands, use **GramaVisión.**

GramaVisión

**19 Tú eres el líder** 1.2

**Leamos/Escribamos** Contesta las preguntas con mandatos afirmativos o negativos.

**MODELO** **—No hay nada interesante que hacer este fin de semana. ¿Qué hacemos?**
**—Hagamos una excursión al lago el sábado y alquilemos un bote.**

1. Estoy harto de ver televisión todas las tardes. ¿Por qué no hacemos algo más interesante?
2. Dicen que no va a haber un club de español el año que viene porque no hay suficientes estudiantes interesados. ¿Qué podemos hacer?
3. No me gusta practicar escalada deportiva en esta montaña porque es peligroso. ¿Adónde podemos ir?
4. El jai-alai es un deporte genial. ¿Qué podemos hacer para ver un partido?
5. El club de ajedrez tiene muy poca publicidad en el colegio. ¿Crees que podemos hacer algo para mejorarla?
6. Vamos a hacer senderismo el sábado, pero hay gente de diferentes niveles en el grupo. ¿Cómo podemos organizar la excursión?

### Nota cultural

El **jai-alai,** o la pelota vasca, es un deporte típico del norte de España. En el idioma vasco, jai-alai significa «fiesta alegre». Los vascos jugaban a la pelota durante los festivales de los pueblos y usaban las paredes de las iglesias como cancha. Hoy en día, hay canchas de pelota, llamadas **frontones,** en todas las ciudades grandes del norte de España. Se juega al jai-alai entre octubre y junio.

¿En qué parte de Estados Unidos hay partidos de jai-alai también? 2.1

## Comunicación

HOLT SoundBooth ONLINE RECORDING

1.1, 1.2

**20 ¿Qué hacemos este fin de semana?**

**Leamos /Hablemos** En parejas, escojan actividades que les interesen de la guía de ocio. Creen una conversación en que Uds. hablen de qué van a hacer. Túrnense para sugerir dos actividades y respondan a ellas con mandatos afirmativos o negativos.

**MODELO** **—Vamos al Museo del Prado, ¿quieres?**
**—No, gracias. Vamos al cine mejor.**

| | | |
|---|---|---|
| Películas: | Cine Alcalá<br>Cine Méndez | pág. 2<br>pág. 3 |
| Restaurantes: | italianos<br>chinos | pág. 4<br>pág. 5 |
| Exposiciones de arte: | Museo del Prado<br>Museo Reina Sofía | pág. 6<br>pág. 6 |
| Conciertos: | Guitarra clásica<br>Flamenco | pág. 8<br>pág. 8 |
| Deportes: | Fútbol<br>Jai-alai | pág. 9<br>pág. 9 |
| Teatro: | Centro cultural<br>Bellas Artes | pág. 10<br>pág. 10 |



**17 Script**

See script on page 47E.

**18 Answers**

1. Lleguemos a tiempo a los partidos.
2. Invitemos a los nuevos estudiantes.
3. Organicemos un campeonato para abril.
4. Hagamos una fiesta o un baile en mayo.
5. No seamos maleducados durante los partidos.
6. No nos olvidemos de darle las gracias al director.
7. No faltemos a los entrenamientos.
8. No saquemos malas notas en clase.

## Comunicación

**Group Activity: Presentational**

Have the class plan a field trip. Divide the class into small groups, and have each group come up with three suggestions. Ask each group to write their suggestions on the board using a **nosotros** command. Then allow the class to discuss the suggestions and decide together on the top three choices.

1.3

## Differentiated Instruction

### SLOWER PACE LEARNERS

**17 Building on Previous Skills** Before students do Activity 17, review formal and informal commands. Tell them that informal commands have the same form as the third person singular form of the present indicative. **Habla con tu profesor. Juega conmigo. Come las verduras.** Tell them that formal commands are formed by using the third person singular form of the present subjunctive. List the irregular informal commands on the board: **dar: dé, decir: di, hacer: haz, ir: ve, poner: pon, salir: sal, ser: sé, tener: ten, venir: ven.**

### SPECIAL LEARNING NEEDS

**18 Students with Visual Impairments** Students with visual impairments may have trouble reading the text for Activity 18. You may want to complete this activity orally as a class. You can list the items aloud or have students come up with their own ideas about what the volleyball team should and should not do.

## Assess

**Assessment Program**

**Prueba: Gramática 1,** pp. 23–24

**Prueba: Aplicación 1,** pp. 25–26

Audio CD 2, Tr. 15

Alternative Assessment, pp. 374, 386, 398

**Online Assessment** **my.hrw.com**

**Test Generator**

## Resources

**Planning:**

Lesson Planner, pp. 22, 182–183

One-Stop Planner

**Presentation:**

Audio CD 2, Trs. 5–7

Video Program, Videocassette 1

DVD Program

**VideoCultura**

**Practice:**

Cuaderno de actividades, p. 14

Video Guide, pp. 10–11

Lab Book, p. 59

Interactive Tutor, Disc 1

### Language Note

Point out that both Lucía and Pamela use the subjunctive to tell what they look for in a boyfriend. Explain to students that the subjunctive is used to talk about the unknown or nonexistent, and tell them they will learn more about this use of the subjunctive in **Gramática 2.**

# Cultura

VideoCultura

## Comparaciones

Interactive TUTOR

CD 2, Tr. 5-7

Un grupo de jóvenes en Toledo, España

1.3, 4.2

### A buen amigo, buen abrigo

En muchas partes del mundo hispano, muchas amistades que se hacen en el colegio duran toda la vida. La gente no cambia tanto de ciudad, y se mantiene en contacto con sus amigos y amigas de la escuela o del colegio. Crecen juntos y tienen experiencias parecidas que los unen para el resto de sus vidas. Compara esto con la experiencia de tu pueblo o ciudad. ¿Crees que seguirás en contacto con todos tus amigos? ¿Cómo crees que será la vida de tus amigos dentro de 10 años?

### Lucía
**Madrid, España**

***Para ti, ¿qué es un buen amigo?***

Es una persona con la que compartir diversiones, una persona que te escucha, es una persona que está ahí en todo momento.

***¿Qué haces para no tener un malentendido con un amigo?***

Intento ser siempre yo, comunicar todo lo que pienso y lo que siento.

***¿Alguna vez has tenido un malentendido con un amigo?***

Sí, una vez una amiga me contó algo importante para ella y yo no pude juzgarlo de esa manera, y entonces yo se lo conté a otra amiga, y a ella le sentó muy mal.

***¿Cómo lo resolvieron?***

Hablando. Ella me dijo que le había sentado mal y yo le pedí disculpas.

***¿Qué buscas en un novio?***

Una persona que te escuche, que comparta diversiones, que comparta malos ratos, que te acepte como eres.

### Pre-AP Practice

**AP Language Examination:** Have students first listen to the interviews with books closed to help prepare them for Section I, Part A: **Listening—Short Dialogues and Narratives.** Point out that Lucía, like many Spanish speakers, may combine adjacent vowels pronouncing them together **(una amiga, …conté a otra…).**

## Core Instruction

### TEACHING CULTURA

1. Read and discuss the introductory paragraph as a class. **(2 min.)**
2. Have students listen to the audio recording or watch the video and take notes. Then have them look over the interview questions and discuss with a partner how they would answer each question. **(4 min.)**
3. Have students answer the questions in **Para comprender** and then discuss the questions in **Para pensar y hablar** as a class. **(4 min.)**

### VideoCultura

For a video presentation of the interviews above as well as an additional interview for this chapter, see Chapter 2 **VideoCultura** on Videocassette or on DVD.

VideoCultura

Visit Holt Online
**go.hrw.com**
KEYWORD: EXP3 CH2
Online Edition

## Pamela
**Santo Domingo, República Dominicana**

***Para ti, ¿qué es un buen amigo?***
Es una persona que me comprenda, que sea sincera, que esté conmigo en los buenos y los malos momentos.

***¿Qué haces para no tener un malentendido con un amigo?***
Pues, nos tenemos una muy buena comunicación y si hay algo que nos molesta, nos hablamos.

***¿Alguna vez has tenido un malentendido con un buen amigo?***
Sí, [un amigo y yo] tuvimos un malentendido porque se suponía que debía de decirle algo y no lo hice. Entonces se sintió traicionado.

***¿Qué buscas en un novio?***
Una persona sincera y honesta, y que tenga buenos sentimientos hacia mí.

Cultura

### Para comprender 1.2

1. Busca cinco palabras que describan un buen amigo para Lucía. ¿Y un novio?
2. ¿Lucía hizo bien o mal al contarle a otra persona lo que le dijo la amiga? Explica.
3. Busca cinco palabras que describan un buen amigo para Pamela. ¿Y un novio?
4. ¿El amigo de Pamela tenía derecho a sentirse traicionado por lo que no hizo Pamela? Explica.
5. ¿Estás de acuerdo con Lucía y Pamela en que la mejor manera de resolver un malentendido es hablando? ¿Qué pasa si uno guarda para sí los sentimientos?

### Para pensar y hablar 1.3

¿Crees que es muy difícil encontrar amigos que cumplan con los requisitos de Lucía y Pamela? ¿Qué buscas tú en un amigo y qué no aguantas? ¿Cómo es un buen amigo tuyo en comparación con los de Pamela y Lucía?

## Comunidad y oficio 5.1, 5.2

### Programación en español

En Estados Unidos, hay cada vez más canales de televisión y emisoras con programación en español. Busca los canales y emisoras que tengan programas en español y escucha un partido deportivo o ve una telenovela *(soap opera)*. Fíjate en las expresiones que usan. ¿Cuáles de las expresiones ya conoces? ¿Cuáles son nuevas? Escribe las expresiones que aprendiste sobre los deportes (si viste un partido) o sobre las relaciones personales (si viste una telenovela). Ponte en contacto con la persona que dirige la programación en un canal de televisión o una emisora de habla hispana. Pregúntale cómo decide qué programas televisar o poner en la radio, y quiénes ven y escuchan los programas.

Jim Talamonti anuncia los juegos de los Laredo Bucks en inglés y en español a la vez.

## Atlas INTERACTIVO MUNDIAL

Have students use the interactive atlas at **go.hrw.com**.

**Map Activities**

1. Have students locate Spain on a world map and ask them to name the islands of Spain. **(las Islas Baleares, las Islas Canarias)** In what bodies of water are the islands located? **(el mar Mediterráneo, el océano Atlántico)**
2. Then have them locate the Dominican Republic and identify its neighboring countries. In what body of water is the Dominican Republic located? **(el mar Caribe)**
3. What do Spain and the Dominican Republic have in common? What are some differences?

3.1

## Answers

1. un buen amigo: solidario, abierto, amigable, confiable, divertido; un novio: leal, solidario, amigable, confiable, divertido
2. No hizo mal porque no sabía que era un secreto.
3. un buen amigo: sincero, solidario, leal, confiable, honesto; un novio: sincero, solidario, leal, confiable, honesto
4. Answers will vary.
5. Answers will vary.

## Differentiated Instruction

### ADVANCED LEARNERS

**Challenge** Have students work in pairs to participate in the same interview that Lucía and Pamela participated in. Students will take turns being interviewer and interviewee. The student conducting the interview should take notes in order to summarize his or her partner's answers for the class. 1.1

### MULTIPLE INTELLIGENCES

**Intrapersonal** Have students tell whether they think they are a good friend to others. Have them share the qualities that make them a good friend as well as mistakes they have made in the past that may have caused misunderstandings. How did they resolve the conflicts? What qualities do they look for in a friend?

## Career Path

After students have read the **Comunidad y oficio** text, ask them to discuss the possibilities for a career in sports using the Spanish language. Have volunteers tell whether or not this is a job that might interest them.

## Resources

**Planning:**

Lesson Planner, pp. 23–24, 184–185

One-Stop Planner

**Presentation:**

Teaching Transparencies
**Vocabulario** 2.3, 2.4

**Practice:**

Cuaderno de vocabulario y gramática, pp. 19–21

Activities for Communication, pp. 7–8

Teaching Transparencies
Bell Work 2.5
**Vocabulario y gramática** answers, pp. 19–21

Interactive Tutor, Disc 1

### Bell Work

Use Bell Work 2.5 in the *Teaching Transparencies.*

**Objetivos**
- Describing the ideal friend
- Expressing happiness and unhappiness

# Vocabulario en acción 2

## En Toledo La amistad

¿Cómo debe ser un buen amigo? Pues, te voy a dar un ejemplo de cómo es un buen amigo o una buena amiga. (¡Y te voy a dar un ejemplo de alguien que no es un buen amigo!)

Ésta es mi amiga Pilar. Es una buena amiga y **tenemos mucho en común.** Es **generosa.** Comparte sus discos compactos conmigo, y si necesito algo, lo que sea, me lo presta.

A veces me ayuda a **resolver problemas.** No siempre está de acuerdo conmigo pero **respeta mis sentimientos** y es completamente **honesta** conmigo.

Es muy **leal** a sus amigos. Sé que puedo **contar con** ella para todo.

Pilar es **abierta** y **amigable.** Se lleva bien con todo el mundo; es muy **solidaria.**

**Más vocabulario...**

| | |
|---|---|
| **atento(a)** | *helpful* |
| **confiar en** | *to trust* |
| **un(a) conocido(a)** | *acquaintance* |
| **grosero(a)** | *rude, vulgar* |
| **maleducado(a)** | *rude* |
| **mentir (ie, i)** | *to lie* |
| **querer (ie) a** | *to love (someone)* |
| **seco(a)** | *cold, unfriendly* |
| **tolerante** | *tolerant* |
| **(no) valer la pena** | *to (not) be worth it* |

## Core Instruction

### TEACHING VOCABULARIO

1. Have students look at the photos on pages 64 and 65 as you read the captions aloud. Check understanding of the target vocabulary by asking questions such as: **Nombra a un amigo(a) con quien tienes mucho en común. ¿Qué tienen en común? ¿Qué hace una persona abierta? ¿Una persona leal guarda secretos?** **(5 min.)**
2. Go over **Más vocabulario** with students and have volunteers use each word in a sentence. **(5 min.)**

### TEACHING ¡EXPRÉSATE!

1. Read the **¡Exprésate!** expressions aloud to model pronunciation. **(2 min.)**
2. Act out both sides of a short conversation in which one person asks the questions in the left column and a second person responds using the answers in the right column. **(3 min.)**
3. Then ask the questions in the left column and have volunteers answer using **Vocabulario** and expressions from **¡Exprésate!** **(5 min.)**

### Pre-AP Practice

**AP Benchmark:** Interpret linguistic cues to infer social relationships.

**Focus:** Expressing happiness and unhappiness
- SE, p. 69, Act. 27
- TE, p. 69, Advanced Learners
- TE, p. 69, Multiple Intelligences

Visit Holt Online
**go.hrw.com**
KEYWORD: EXP3 CH2
Vocabulario 2 practice

Y éste es Julio. Fuimos amigos por un tiempo pero siempre tuvimos problemas. Él dice que sólo **«tuvimos malentendidos».**

Podía ser muy **terco.** Además, **tenía fama de ser creído,** de considerarse superior a todo el mundo. La verdad es que era bastante **inseguro.**

Era bastante **chismoso** también. No me gustaba como **chismeaba** sobre nuestros amigos; eso me pareció muy **desleal.** Nunca sabías si iba a **guardar los secretos** de uno o no.

¡Y qué **celoso** era! Una vez **rompió con** una novia porque la vio hablando con otro chico. Hasta **tenía celos de** sus amigos.

Julio no era nada **confiable.** Muchas veces **me dejaba plantado** en un café o en el cine. Al final me cansé de su actitud y no lo volví a llamar. Todavía no **hemos hecho las paces.**

## ¡Exprésate!

**To describe the ideal friend**

Interactive TUTOR

| | |
|---|---|
| **¿Cómo debe ser un(a) buen(a) amigo(a)?** *What should a good friend be like?* | **Un(a) buen(a) amigo(a) debe apoyarme y... No debe...** *A good friend should support me and . . . He/She shouldn't . . .* |
| **¿Qué buscas en un(a) novio(a)?** *What do you look for in a boyfriend (girlfriend)?* | **Busco a alguien a quien le guste(n)... y que sepa algo de...** *I'm looking for someone who likes . . . and who knows something about . . .* |

Vocabulario y gramática, pp. 19–21 Online workbooks

## TPR
### Total Physical Response

Have individual students respond by pantomiming the following commands.

**Señala a un(a) compañero(a) amigable.**

**Haz las paces con el (la) compañero(a) que está a tu lado.**

**Busca a alguien a quien le gusten los deportes.**

**Siéntate al lado de alguien que sepa algo de música.**

1.2

## Teacher to Teacher

**Angie Rhymes**
Goodson Middle School
Cypress, TX

I have students use Inspiration® software to create a web as a pre-writing activity. For example, when writing a description of a friend, I have students create a web of themselves or a person close to them. I also have students work in groups of three to five to brainstorm about a celebrity. They place the person being described in the center, then add circles containing adjectives in the webbing process. Students then search for pictures to represent each description.

## Differentiated Instruction

### Advanced Learners

**Challenge** Have students write a short paragraph describing a good friend. Ask them to read the paragraph to the class, and then have the class come up with five adjectives to describe the person based on the paragraph.
1.2, 1.3

### Multiple Intelligences

**Kinesthetic** Have students work in groups to act out situations between friends based on the vocabulary on pages 64 and 65. Their classmates should then use the vocabulary to describe what happened in each presentation.
1.3

**Differentiated Instruction** See the Differentiated Instruction CD-ROM.

**Resources**

**Planning:**

Lesson Planner, pp. 23–24, 184–185

One-Stop Planner

**Presentation:**

Teaching Transparencies
**Vocabulario** 2.3, 2.4

**Practice:**

Cuaderno de vocabulario y gramática, pp. 19–21

Activities for Communication, pp. 7–8

Lab Book, pp. 17–20

Teaching Transparencies
**Vocabulario y gramática** answers, pp. 19–21

Audio CD 2, Tr. 8

Interactive Tutor, Disc 1

**21 Script**

See script on pages 47E–47F.

**Teacher to Teacher**

**Kassie Harshman**
Lafayette High School
St. Joseph, MO

**Imaginary Friends** When working on descriptions, I have the kids create an imaginary friend using construction paper. Their friend can be any kind of creature. Students name them, give them an age, and write a description of physical and personality traits. Finally, the students introduce their friend to the rest of the class, and we display the friends in the classroom. 1.3

Un joven de Buenos Aires observa la variedad de revistas internacionales.

CD 2, Tr. 8

### 21 ¿Cómo son? 1.2

**Escuchemos** Escucha a Pilar describir a unos conocidos y decide qué adjetivo corresponde a cada persona.

| | |
|---|---|
| 1. Laura c. | a. generoso |
| 2. Sergio h. | b. insegura |
| 3. Tomás f. | c. honesta |
| 4. Tía Claudia b. | d. desleal |
| 5. Juan Pablo e. | e. celoso |
| 6. Marisa g. | f. confiable |
| 7. Mónica d. | g. amigable |
| 8. David a. | h. creído |

### 22 ¿Qué tal se llevan Uds.? 1.2

**Leamos** Evalúa la relación que tienes con tu mejor amigo(a) o novio(a) por medio de la siguiente encuesta *(poll)*. Escoge **A** si estás de acuerdo, **B** para decir "a veces" y **C** si no estás de acuerdo.

**¿Qué tal se llevan Uds.?**

**Encuesta**

1. Mi amigo(a) y yo tenemos mucho en común. A B C
2. Podemos resolver problemas y hacer las paces fácilmente. A B C
3. Respetamos los sentimientos de la otra persona. A B C
4. Puedo contar con mi amigo(a). A B C
5. Tenemos malentendidos frecuentes, sobre cosas pequeñas. A B C
6. Mi amigo(a) chismea sobre mis asuntos personales. A B C
7. Tengo celos de los otros amigos de él/ella. A B C
8. Me deja plantado(a) con frecuencia. A B C

**Evaluación**

Preguntas 1 a 4

**Mayoría de respuestas A:** ¡Felicidades! Tienes una amistad verdadera. Guárdala como un tesoro.
**Mayoría de respuestas B:** Parece que Uds. tienen que cambiar algunos hábitos si quieren mejorar su relación.
**Mayoría de respuestas C:** ¡Ojo! Es hora de buscar otro(a) amigo(a).

Preguntas 5 a 8

**Mayoría de respuestas A:** ¿Qué pasa? Parece que esta relación no funciona bien en absoluto.
**Mayoría de respuestas B:** Mmmm... si Uds. de verdad quieren seguir siendo amigos, hay que analizar qué deben hacer para llevarse mejor.
**Mayoría de respuestas C:** ¡Muy bien! Uds. tienen una relación muy buena. Sigan así.

## Core Instruction

### VOCABULARY IN CONTEXT

**Cooperative Learning** Divide the class into groups of four to create a vocabulary "dictionary" about friendships. Have students divide the list of words from **Vocabulario 1** evenly among themselves. Each entry should have the part of speech of the word, a definition, and a sentence using the word in context. When they have finished with the entries assigned to them, have students compile their work into a dictionary to be copied for each member of their group. Students then work as a group to check and verify each entry in the dictionary.

## 23 Avísame, por favor 1.2

**Leamos/Escribamos** Completa la carta que escribió Marta al periódico, pidiendo ayuda con una relación problemática. Usa las formas correctas de las palabras del cuadro.

| | | | |
|---|---|---|---|
| abierto | celoso | confiar en | dejar plantado |
| malentendido | resolver un problema | valer la pena | desleal |

Querida Elena:

Te escribo porque quiero __1__ que tengo con una amiga. Recientemente parece que no puedo __2__ ella. Ayer quedamos en tomar café después del trabajo, pero ella me __3__. Luego descubrí que estaba con otra amiga, y ahora estoy __4__ de ella. ¿Crees que todo fue un __5__, o crees que ella es __6__? Quiero ser __7__ con ella y explicarle mis emociones, pero no sé si __8__ hacerlo. ¿Qué debo hacer?

1. resolver un problema
2. confiar en
3. dejó plantada
4. celosa
5. malentendido
6. desleal
7. abierta
8. vale la pena

## 24 ¿Qué opinas tú? 1.3

**Leamos/Escribamos** Imagínate que vas a contestarle la carta a Marta. Escribe una carta de ocho oraciones en la que analices el problema y le des consejos.

## Comunicación

HOLT SoundBooth ONLINE RECORDING

## 25 Un buen amigo es... 1.1, 1.2

**Escribamos/Hablemos** Completa las oraciones según tus opiniones sobre cómo debe ser un(a) buen(a) amigo(a). Después, compara tus respuestas con las de un(a) compañero(a). ¿Son similares o muy distintas sus opiniones?

**MODELO** Un buen amigo es ==.
—**Para mí, un buen amigo es leal y amigable.**
—**Para mí, un buen amigo es honesto y respeta mis sentimientos.**

Un(a) buen(a) amigo(a)...
es ==.
me ayuda a ==.
sabe ==.
(no) tiene ==.
puede ==.

### Heritage Speakers

Organize your heritage speakers in groups of three or four students. Can they think of slang words related to **pasatiempos, deportes,** or **amistad?** In what country or region are those words used? What is the context in which they are used? You can give them the example of **chama,** which is used in Venezuela when referring to a friend. Have the groups share their words and explanations with the rest of the class. 1.3

### Connections

### Thinking Critically

Bring in Spanish language magazines or newspapers and pass them out to groups of students or have students read them online. Ask them to read the advice column. Have them list any words or phrases they recognize from **Vocabulario 2.** Then have them list any new words and phrases they find in the column. Allow groups to discuss the advice and to suggest new ways to solve the problems mentioned in the letters. 3.2

### Comunicación

### Class Activity: Presentational

Have students work in pairs to prepare a conversation about a problem between friends. The friends will be invented characters. Pairs will take turns presenting their conversations. The class will then talk about what happened and tell what kind of person they think each of the characters is. 1.3

## Differentiated Instruction

### SLOWER PACE LEARNERS

**Additional Practice** For more practice on describing the ideal friend, have groups of students work together to talk about characters from a popular movie or television show. Ask them to describe the characters and to tell whether each character would be an ideal friend. Have them explain why or why not. 1.1

### SPECIAL LEARNING NEEDS

**24 Students with Dyslexia** Students with dyslexia may have difficulty writing a letter for Activity 24. You may want to change this activity to a speaking activity. As a class, discuss how Elena might answer Marta's letter. You can compose a letter on the board or on a transparency as students provide ideas. 1.2

**Differentiated Instruction** See the Differentiated Instruction CD-ROM.

## Resources

**Planning:**

Lesson Planner, pp. 23–24, 184–185

One-Stop Planner

**Presentation:**

Teaching Transparencies
**Vocabulario** 2.3, 2.4

**Practice:**

Cuaderno de vocabulario y gramática, pp. 19–21

Activities for Communication, pp. 7–8

Teaching Transparencies
**Vocabulario y gramática** answers, pp. 19–21

Interactive Tutor, Disc 1

## Teacher Note

Tell students that the word **ganas** is used in many phrases related to desire or wish: **comer con ganas** (to eat heartily), **quedarse con las ganas** (to have to do without), **quitar las ganas** (to stop wanting), **tener ganas de** (to want to). In the **¡Exprésate!** sentence, the phrase **darle ganas a uno de...** means *to make one feel like doing something.*

## Circumlocution

Have each student write a sentence on an index card using one of the vocabulary words from pp. 64–65 that describes a friend. Ask them to underline the vocabulary word on the card. Collect the cards. Pass one card to a volunteer, who must describe the person without using the vocabulary word on the card. Students must guess the word. For example, the card reads: **Este amigo me deja plantado.** The student might say: **Este amigo siempre hace planes conmigo y luego no aparece en el lugar donde deberíamos encontrarnos. A veces se olvida y a veces simplemente no va.** 1.1

Dos amigas en Toledo

# ¿Qué puedo hacer?

LUZ MARÍA ¿Qué te pasa, Fernanda? Te ves muy dolida. ¿Has estado llorando?

FERNANDA La verdad es que sí. Estoy completamente decepcionada con José Manuel. Ayer me mintió y...

LUZ MARÍA ¡Otra vez! Ay, chica, no entiendo por qué lo quieres tanto. Es grosero y además creidísimo. Bueno, ¿qué te dijo?

FERNANDA Que había estado estudiando en casa por la tarde, pero cuando lo llamé a las tres, su hermanita me dijo que estaba con Laura. Cada vez que lo pienso, me dan ganas de llorar.

LUZ MARÍA ¿Estaba con Laura? Pero ella es la persona más seca que he conocido en mi vida y tiene fama de ser desleal. Mira, no vale la pena estar celosa ni perder el tiempo llorando. Tienes que romper con él lo más pronto posible.

FERNANDA Tienes toda la razón. Lo he pensado bien y voy a llamarlo esta noche.

LUZ MARÍA Así tiene que ser.

FERNANDA Bueno, hablemos de algo menos trágico. Hoy te vi de buen humor.

LUZ MARÍA ¿Cuándo, en el colegio? Ah sí, estaba entusiasmada porque al fin voy a poder terminar mi proyecto para la clase de historia.

FERNANDA ¿No estabas haciendo ese proyecto con Hernán?

LUZ MARÍA Sí, aunque Hernán es poco confiable, ¿sabes? Estaba haciendo yo casi toda la investigación. Pero resolvimos el problema y vamos a trabajar juntos de nuevo.

FERNANDA ¿Cuál fue el problema?

LUZ MARÍA Me acusó de ser criticona, ¿te puedes imaginar? ¡Yo, criticona! Soy la persona más tolerante del mundo.

## ¡Exprésate!

| To express happiness and unhappiness | Interactive TUTOR |
|---|---|
| **¿Qué te pasa? ¿Estás dolido(a)?**<br>*What's the matter? Are you upset?* | **Sí, estoy decepcionado(a) porque...**<br>**Me dan ganas de llorar.**<br>*Yes, I'm disappointed because . . .*<br>*It makes me feel like crying.* |
| **Te veo de buen humor.**<br>*I see you're in a good mood.* | **Sí, estoy entusiasmado(a) porque...**<br>*Yes, I'm excited because . . .* |

Vocabulario y gramática, pp. 19–21 Online workbooks

## Core Instruction

### TEACHING ¡EXPRÉSATE!

1. Model both sides of a conversation using the questions and responses from **¡Exprésate!** Be sure to show how you are feeling by making a happy or a sad face, depending on the expression. **(2 min.)**
2. Read the exchanges with students and have them identify the phrases that express happiness or unhappiness. **(10 min.)**
3. Then have students make either a happy face or a sad face. Depending on the face each student makes, ask: **¿Qué te pasa? ¿Estás dolida?** Or say: **Te veo de buen humor.** Have students respond using words from **Vocabulario 2** and expressions from **¡Exprésate! (3 min.)**

**26 ¿Qué les pasa a las dos amigas?** 1.2

**Leamos/Escribamos** Basándote en la conversación entre Fernanda y Luz María, contesta las preguntas.

1. ¿Por qué llora Fernanda? Está decepcionada de José Manuel.
2. ¿Cómo le parece Fernanda a Luz María? Le parece dolida.
3. ¿Quién es José Manuel? El novio de Fernanda.
4. ¿Cómo es José Manuel, según Luz María? Es grosero y creidísimo.
5. ¿Qué va a hacer Fernanda esta noche? Va a llamarlo para romper con él.
6. ¿Cómo es Hernán, según Luz María? Es poco confiable.
7. ¿Cómo es Luz María, según Hernán? Es criticona.
8. En la opinión de Luz María, ¿cómo es ella? Es la persona más tolerante del mundo.

**27 ¿Qué debo hacer?** 1.2

**Leamos/Hablemos** Lee lo que varios amigos te cuentan sobre sus problemas. ¿Qué le dirías *(would you say)* a cada uno? Utiliza las expresiones del diálogo y de **Exprésate.**

1. Me siento fastidiado porque mi amiga y yo tenemos muchos malentendidos. La quiero mucho y no quiero dejar de ser amigos. ¿Qué debo hacer?
2. ¡Ese Fernando! Últimamente estoy muy decepcionada con él. Me dejó plantada ayer por la tarde y no creo que siempre me diga la verdad. ¿Qué puedo hacer?
3. Ayer Laura me contó algo sobre Verónica, mi mejor amiga, pero no sé si es mentira o no. No me parece verdad, pero es posible. ¿A quién le debo preguntar?
4. Santiago me pasó una nota que dice que Jorge salió con otra chica anoche que no es su novia. ¿Debo decirle algo a Jorge? ¿O a su novia?

Los amigos tienen mucho que contarse.

## Comunicación

HOLT SoundBooth ONLINE RECORDING

**28 ¿En qué momentos te sientes así?** 1.1, 1.2

**Hablemos** Júntate con dos o tres compañeros y pregúntales cuándo experimentan *(experience)* las siguientes emociones.

**MODELO** —¿En qué momentos te sientes fastidiada?
—Me siento fastidiada si tengo que esperar mucho.

| | | |
|---|---|---|
| decepcionado(a) | fastidiado(a) | dolido(a) |
| nervioso(a) | entusiasmado(a) | de buen humor |

### Heritage Speakers

Ask heritage speakers to share other ways of expressing happiness or unhappiness. Have them describe a situation and tell what expression they would use, or have them model both sides of a conversation. 1.3

## Comunicación

### Class Activity: Interpretive

Write different situations on separate index cards. Hand the cards out to students. Have them take turns reading their cards to the class and acting out how they would feel in that situation. Volunteers will then tell how the person feels.

**MODELO**
**—Eva se siente nerviosa cuando tiene que hacer una presentación delante de la clase.** 1.2, 1.3

## Differentiated Instruction

### ADVANCED LEARNERS

26 **Challenge** Have volunteers read the conversation on page 68 aloud. Then have them close their books and try to answer the questions in Activity 26. When they have finished answering the questions, have them open their books to check their answers. 1.2

### MULTIPLE INTELLIGENCES

**Interpersonal** Have students summarize what happened in the conversation on page 68. Ask them to explain how Luz María feels and why. Ask them if they think she has a right to feel the way she does. What would they advise her to do? 1.2

### Assess

**Assessment Program**
**Prueba: Vocabulario 2,** pp. 27–28
Alternative Assessment, pp. 374, 386, 398

**Online Assessment**
**my.hrw.com**

**Test Generator**

## Resources

**Planning:**

Lesson Planner, pp. 25–27, 186–189

One-Stop Planner

**Presentation:**

Video Program
**GramaVisión**

**Practice:**

Grammar Tutor for Students of Spanish, Chapter 2

Cuaderno de vocabulario y gramática, pp. 22–24

Cuaderno de actividades, pp. 15–17

Activities for Communication, pp. 7–8

Teaching Transparencies
Bell Work 2.6
**Vocabulario y gramática** answers, pp. 22–24

Interactive Tutor, Disc 1

### Bell Work

Use Bell Work 2.6 in the *Teaching Transparencies,* or write this activity on the board.

**¿Cómo te sientes cuando un(a) amigo(a) hace las siguientes cosas?**

1. te deja plantado(a)
2. te ayuda a resolver un problema
3. te miente
4. dice que te quiere mucho
5. es maleducado(a) 1.3

**Objetivos**
- Object pronouns
- Subjunctive with the unknown or nonexistent
- Subjunctive with expressions of feelings

# Gramática en acción 2

GramaVisión

Interactive TUTOR

## Repaso Object pronouns

**1** The **direct object (complemento directo)** is the noun on which an action is being performed. A direct object may be replaced by a **direct object pronoun (pronombre del complemento directo): me, te, lo, la, nos, os, los, las.** The direct object pronoun goes before the conjugated verb or is attached to the infinitive.

| | |
|---|---|
| Susana busca **el nuevo libro.** | Susana **lo** busca. |
| Susana quiere ver **la película.** | Susana quiere ver**la**. |
| | (Susana **la** quiere ver.) |

**2** The **indirect object (complemento indirecto)** is the person for whom or to whom an action is performed. The indirect object is used with a pronoun that refers to the noun, and is called the **indirect object pronoun (pronombre del complemento indirecto): me, te, le, nos, os, les.**

| | |
|---|---|
| Susana **nos** regala el libro a **nosotros.** | Susana **nos** regala el libro. |

**3** When both a direct object pronoun and an indirect object pronoun are used in the same sentence, the indirect object pronoun goes first.

| | |
|---|---|
| Susana **nos** regala **el libro** a **nosotros.** | Susana **nos lo** regala. |

**4** If the indirect object pronoun **le** or **les** comes before the direct object pronouns **la, lo, las,** or **los,** the indirect object pronoun changes to **se.**

| | |
|---|---|
| Nosotros **le** regalamos **flores** a **Clara.** | Nosotros **se las** regalamos. |

Vocabulario y gramática, pp. 22–24
Actividades, pp. 15–17
Online workbooks

### ¿Te acuerdas?

These verbs are commonly used with **indirect object pronouns:** **comprar, contar, contestar, dar, decir, dejar, enviar, explicar, hablar, mandar, mentir, pagar, pasar, pedir, preguntar, prestar,** and **regalar.**

¿**Me** prestas ese disco compacto?
¿Qué **te** dijo Anabel?

### 29 ¿Cuándo lo haces? 1.2

**Escribamos** Escribe una oración que explique cuándo hiciste estas actividades. Usa pronombres del complemento directo.

**MODELO** **hacer la tarea**
**¿La tarea? La hice después de regresar a casa.**

1. ver el partido
2. llamar a tu amigo(a)
3. visitar a tus abuelos
4. organizar tu cuarto
5. regar las plantas
6. leer el periódico

## Core Instruction

### TEACHING GRAMÁTICA

1. Go over points 1 and 2 with students and read the examples. Check comprehension by writing the following sentence on the board and asking volunteers to underline the direct object and circle the indirect object. **Yo le mando una carta a Enrique.** **(5 min.)**
2. Go over points 3 and 4 with students. Then have them repeat the sentence you wrote on the board, but using only direct and indirect object pronouns. Write the new sentence on the board. **(5 min.)**
3. Go over **¿Te acuerdas?** with students and have volunteers use the verbs in sentences with indirect object pronouns. Write the sentences on the board as students say them. **(5 min.)**

### GramaVisión

For a video presentation of object pronouns, use **GramaVisión.**

GramaVisión

Visit Holt Online
go.hrw.com
KEYWORD: EXP3 CH2
Gramática 2 practice

**30 ¿Qué? ¿A quién?** 1.2

**Leamos/Escribamos** Escribe cada oración de nuevo, reemplazando los sustantivos con pronombres del complemento directo y del complemento indirecto.

**MODELO** **Yo les digo la verdad a mis amigos.**
**Yo se la digo.**

1. Mis padres me van a dar el regalo a mí. Mis padres me lo van a dar. *or* Mis padres van a dármelo.
2. Mi hermano nunca le presta sus discos compactos a mi hermana. Mi hermano nunca se los presta.
3. La profesora nos pidió la tarea. La profesora nos la pidió.
4. Mi compañero le pasó el balón al entrenador. Mi compañero se lo pasó.
5. Yo le pagué cuarenta dólares al cajero. Yo se los pagué.
6. Mis tíos le regalaron la bicicleta a mi primo. Mis tíos se la regalaron.
7. Mis tíos nos enviaron las fotos a mi familia y a mí. Mis tíos nos las enviaron.
8. Mi mejor amiga dejó la nota para mí. Mi mejor amiga me la dejó.

Un grupo de jóvenes camina por una calle de Toledo, España.

**31 En tu experiencia** 1.3

**Leamos/Escribamos** Contesta las preguntas basándote en tus experiencias.

1. ¿A quién le prestas tus cosas? ¿A quién no le prestas nada?
2. Cuando sales, ¿tienes que pedirles permiso a tus padres?
3. ¿Siempre les dices la verdad a tus amigos?
4. ¿Quién te compra los mejores regalos de cumpleaños?
5. ¿Vas a ver a tus amigos hoy después de clase?
6. ¿Cuándo conociste a tu mejor amigo(a)? ¿Recuerdas dónde lo(la) conociste?
7. ¿Quién te da buenos consejos? ¿Qué te dice esa persona?

## Comunicación

HOLT SoundBooth ONLINE RECORDING

**32 ¿Cómo pueden resolverlo?** 1.1, 1.2

**Hablemos** Con un(a) compañero(a), dramatiza una conversación sobre un problema que tienes. Tu compañero(a) debe proponer una resolución. Usen por lo menos cuatro pronombres de complemento directo o indirecto.

**MODELO** **—Tengo una amiga que me llama sólo cuando necesita algo.**
**—Pues, dile que...**

### COMMON ERROR ALERT ¡OJO!

When the direct object is a person, students often mistakenly use the indirect object pronoun. Remind them that verbs such as **ver, ayudar** and **llamar** take direct object pronouns. **Vi a Ana. (La vi.) Ayudé a mis amigos. (Los ayudé.)**

### Comparisons

#### Language to Language

Students often find object pronouns difficult to determine. Show them that both Spanish and English verbs frequently need objects to complete their meaning. My friend found (what?). My friend found it. **Mi amigo encontró (¿qué?). Mi amigo lo encontró.** (The teacher chooses (whom?). The teacher chooses us. **El profesor escoge (¿a quién?). El profesor nos escoge.** Finding the pronouns to complement the verbs becomes easier when students ask the questions *whom?* or *what?* Write these sentences on the board and have students ask the questions *whom?* and *what?* to find the object pronouns. **Mi mamá me regaló un vestido. Lola te llamó.**

4.1

## Differentiated Instruction

### SLOWER PACE LEARNERS

29 Before students do Activity 29, write the direct object pronouns on the board or on a transparency. For each item, give students an answer shell so that they only have to provide the direct object pronoun to complete each one. **1. ______ vi después de clase. 2. ______ llamé por la tarde. 3. ______ visité todos los veranos. 4. ______ compré por la mañana. 5. ______ lavé el sábado. 6. ______ leí anoche.**
1.2

### SPECIAL LEARNING NEEDS

30 **Students with Dyslexia** To help students remember the correct pronoun order, write the direct object pronouns on blue cards and the indirect object pronouns on red cards. Write an example on the board, taping the cards in the appropriate places: **Ella me lo regala.** Write the sentence shells on the board leaving spaces. Have volunteers place the correct direct and indirect object pronouns in the spaces. Then have them copy the completed sentences in their notebooks. 1.2

## Comunicación

#### Pair Activity: Interpersonal

Have pairs of students come up with problems that elicit double object pronouns with verbs such as **dar, regalar, mandar, decir,** and **contar.** Each pair trades their problems with another pair and prepares a response. Have pairs present their exchanges to the class. Allow other students to add their own comments or advice for each problem.

1.1

**Differentiated Instruction** See the Differentiated Instruction CD-ROM.

## Resources

**Planning:**

Lesson Planner, pp. 25–27, 186–189

One-Stop Planner

**Presentation:**

Video Program
**GramaVisión**

**Practice:**

Grammar Tutor for Students of Spanish, Chapter 2

Cuaderno de vocabulario y gramática, pp. 22–24

Cuaderno de actividades, pp. 15–17

Activities for Communication, pp. 7–8

Lab Book, pp. 17–20

Teaching Transparencies
Bell Work 2.7
**Vocabulario y gramática** answers, pp. 22–24

Audio CD 2, Tr. 9

Interactive Tutor, Disc 1

### Bell Work

Use Bell Work 2.7 in the *Teaching Transparencies.*

### Más práctica

Have students prepare two pictures, one of a girl imagining her "ideal boyfriend" and one of a girl on a date with her boyfriend. Have a volunteer show the first picture and model several sentences that contrast the use of the subjunctive and the indicative. For example, say **Elena busca un novio que sea** ______. Then show the second picture and say **Marta tiene un novio que es** ______. Ask students to explain why each verb form is used. 1.2

## Subjunctive with the unknown or nonexistent

Interactive TUTOR

**1** You already know that the **indicative** is generally used to talk about ***what is;*** whereas the **subjunctive** is often used to talk about ***what should be,*** or ***what people think/feel about what is.***

*speaker talks about what is*

Alonso **puede** ser muy terco, pero **es** generoso y leal también.

*what speaker thinks/feels about what is*

Espero que Alonso **sea** generoso y leal conmigo.
No es bueno que Alonso **sea** tan terco.

**2** In certain situations, the **subjunctive** is used to talk about ***what is not.*** It is used after expressions like **No hay nadie/nada que...** when the person or thing referred to, the **antecedent,** is ***nonexistent.***

*nonexistent: according to the speaker, such a person does not exist*

No hay **nadie** que **confíe** en Marcos.
No hay **nada** que me **fastidie** más que un chiste grosero.

**3** In other situations, the speaker ***doesn't know what is.*** He or she may be looking for someone or something with certain qualities, without having anyone or anything particular in mind. The **antecedent** is ***unknown.***

*unknown: the speaker doesn't know of anyone in particular with those qualities*

Busco **una novia** que **sea** abierta y amigable.
¿Conoces a **alguien** que **hable** francés?
Quiero comprarte **algo** que te **guste.**

Vocabulario y gramática, pp. 22–24
Actividades, pp. 15–17
Online workbooks

### ¡Te acuerdas?

The **indicative** is used to talk about **someone** or **something** that the speaker *does know about.*

Conozco a muchas **personas** que **hablan** francés. (Mi amigo Luc es de Francia. La mamá de Anne es francesa.)

Busco a **la señora** que **cuida** las plantas. ¿La han visto?

### 33 ¿Existe o no? 1.2

**Leamos** Completa cada oración con la forma correcta del verbo.

1. ¿Conoces a alguien que (está/esté) de buen humor hoy?
2. Tengo un novio que (guarda/guarde) mis secretos.
3. No hay nada que me (alegra/alegre) más que la amistad.
4. Quiero confiar en alguien que (puede/pueda) resolver mis problemas.
5. Mi hermano quiere una novia que no (es/sea) criticona.
6. Cristina es muy graciosa; los chistes que (cuenta/cuente) son excelentes.
7. No conozco a nadie que (confía/confíe) completamente en Marcos.

## Core Instruction

### TEACHING GRAMÁTICA

1. Discuss point 1. Have students provide pairs of sentences about the same topic. In the first sentence, they use the indicative; and in the second, the subjunctive. **(4 min.)**
2. Go over point 2. Write more examples and have students identify what is nonexistent. **No veo a nadie que lleve un sombrero rojo. No están pasando ninguna película que me interese. (4 min.)**
3. Ask students to read the examples in **¿Te acuerdas?** and identify what is known. **(2 min.)**
4. Go over point 3. Have students compare the examples in point 3 with those in **¿Te acuerdas?** As a class, write pairs of sentences about something or someone that is known and unknown. **Tengo un profesor que sabe español. Busco un profesor que sepa español. (5 min.)**

### GramaVisión

For a video presentation of the subjunctive with the unknown or nonexistent, use **GramaVisión.**

GramaVisión

CD 2, Tr. 9 See script on p. 47F.

**34** **¿Existe o no?** 1.2

**Escuchemos** Escucha las oraciones y di si el narrador se refiere a algo o a alguien que **a)** sabe que existe o conoce o **b)** no sabe si existe o a no existe en absoluto. **1.** a **2.** b **3.** b **4.** b **5.** b **6.** a **7.** b **8.** b

**35** **¿Cómo es el (la) novio(a) ideal?** 1.2

**Escribamos** Basándote en los dibujos, escribe ocho oraciones sobre cómo son las personas ideales para Pilar y Miguel.

**MODELO** **Pilar quiere salir con alguien que le dé regalos.**

## Comunicación

HOLT SoundBooth ONLINE RECORDING

**36** **¿Conoces a alguien que...?** 1.1, 1.2

**Hablemos** Pregúntale a tu compañero si conoce a alguien que corresponda a la frase de uno de los cuadros. Si él o ella contesta que sí, puedes rellenar el cuadro. Si no, le toca a él o a ella hacerte una pregunta.

**MODELO** **—¿Conoces a alguien que sepa guardar un secreto?**

**—Sí, conozco a alguien que sabe guardar un secreto. ¡Es mi hermana!**

| | | |
|---|---|---|
| ser de otro país | saber guardar un secreto | querer romper con su novio(a) |
| saber cocinar bien | tener problemas con sus amigos | tener dos novios(as) |
| tener mucho en común contigo | dejarte plantado(a) a veces | llevarse bien con todo el mundo |

## Teacher to Teacher

**Alejandro Avendaño**
Eastside High School
IB Program
Gainesville, FL

This chart uses the word *wedding* to help students remember the uses of the subjunctive in Spanish. I always tell my students that since the **subjuntivo** deals with the unknown, gray area of subjectivity, it is similar to the "cold feet" experienced before a wedding. Therefore, "Wedding? **Ojalá.**"

***"Wedding" Conditions Chart***

| | |
|---|---|
| Wish / want | **Quiero que vengas a EPCOT.** |
| Emotion | **Sentimos mucho que estés enfermo.** |
| Desire | **¿Deseas que yo te lleve a la playa de Clearwater?** |
| Doubt | **Mis padres dudan que yo estudie cuando vaya a UF.** |
| Insistence | **La madre de Luis insiste en que él limpie su cuarto.** |
| Negation | **La Srta. Pérez niega que sus estudiantes sean perezosos.** |
| Gustar | **Me gusta que vengas de compras conmigo al Florida Mall.** |
| Ojalá | **Ojalá que el subjuntivo no sea un dolor de cabeza.** |

## Differentiated Instruction

### SLOWER PACE LEARNERS

**35** Some students may have trouble remembering the correct vocabulary to form complete sentences in Activity 35. Before students do the activity, work together as a class to describe what is happening in each drawing. Write each verb on the board for students to use as a reference as they complete the activity.
1.2

### SPECIAL LEARNING NEEDS

**34** **Students with Auditory Impairments**
For students with auditory impairments, you may want to print out a copy of the script for Activity 34. Once students have done the activity, have them underline the phrase that indicates whether each item mentions something that is known or unknown/nonexistent.
1.2

## Comunicación

### Pair Activity: Interpersonal

Have students work in pairs to talk about their ideal boyfriend or girlfriend. They might want to use the ideas from the bingo game in Activity 36 to start. Once both students have had a chance to describe their ideal boyfriend or girlfriend, students can summarize their partner's responses for the class.
1.1

## Resources

**Planning:**

Lesson Planner, pp. 25–27, 186–189
One-Stop Planner

**Presentation:**

Video Program
**GramaVisión**

**Practice:**

Grammar Tutor for Students of Spanish, Chapter 2
Cuaderno de vocabulario y gramática, pp. 22–24
Cuaderno de actividades, pp. 15–17
Activities for Communication, pp. 7–8
Lab Book, pp. 17–20
Teaching Transparencies
Bell Work 2.8
**Vocabulario y gramática** answers, pp. 22–24
Audio CD 2, Tr. 10
Interactive Tutor, Disc 1

### Bell Work

Use Bell Work 2.8 in the *Teaching Transparencies,* or write this activity on the board.

**Completa las oraciones. Usa la forma correcta del verbo entre paréntesis.**

1. Busco un(a) novio(a) que (ser)...
2. No conozco a nadie que (tener)...
3. ¿Tienes algún amigo que (saber)...?
4. Nunca he visto un perro que (bailar)...
5. ¿Conoces a alguien que (viajar)...? 1.2

### 37 Script

See script on page 47F.

## Subjunctive with expressions of feelings

Interactive TUTOR

**1** The **subjunctive** is used in the subordinate clause after certain **expressions of feelings** in the main clause, when there is a change of subject.

*expression of feelings*
**Me alegra que vengan** mis amigos a nuestra fiesta.

*expression of feelings*
**Siento que lleguemos** tan tarde.

**2** However, if the main clause states a **fact or belief,** the **indicative** is used in the subordinate clause. If there is no change of subject, an **infinitive** is used.

*fact or belief*
**Pienso que** mi novia **va** a romper conmigo.

*no change of subject*
**Me molesta llegar** tarde.

Vocabulario y gramática, pp. 22–24
Actividades, pp. 15–17
Online workbooks

**Some expressions of feelings followed by the subjunctive**

| | |
|---|---|
| me frustra que | me preocupa que |
| me gusta que | me sorprende que |
| me irrita que | siento que |
| me molesta que | |

### Nota cultural

Hay mucha variedad geográfica en Castilla-La Mancha, y gran parte de la región está dedicada a parques y reservas naturales donde se puede ir de excursión. Una excursión popular en Castilla-La Mancha es la "Ruta de Don Quijote", que sigue los pasos del famoso personaje a los molinos de viento y a otros lugares de la obra maestra de Cervantes.

¿Conoces una obra literaria que represente sitios de interés de tu región? 3.1

Molino de viento, Consuegra

CD 2, Tr. 10

### 37 ¿Cómo reaccionan? 1.2

**Escuchemos** Basándote en lo que oyes, decide si **a)** la segunda persona reacciona con una emoción, o si **b)** reacciona diciendo lo que cree. Presta atención al uso del subjuntivo.

1. b 2. a 3. b 4. a 5. a 6. a 7. b 8. a

### 38 ¿Subjuntivo o no? 1.2

**Leamos/Escribamos** Completa las oraciones con la forma correcta del verbo entre paréntesis.

1. Me parece que tú no ═══ (comer) mucho hoy. comes
2. No me sorprende que el profesor ═══ (dar) un examen hoy. dé
3. ¿Por qué no te gusta que tu hermano ═══ (hacer) eso? haga
4. Siento mucho que mi perro te ═══ (molestar). moleste
5. ¿No ves que ═══ (haber) tres figuras en esa pintura? hay
6. A Laura le encanta que sus padres ═══ (viajar) a París este verano. viajen
7. Notamos que el carro no ═══ (marchar) bien. marcha
8. Mis padres temen que los resultados de la prueba no ═══ (ser) muy buenos. sean

## Core Instruction

### TEACHING GRAMÁTICA

1. Go over point 1 with students and read the examples. **(3 min.)**
2. Go over point 2 with students. Have volunteers use each phrase in a sentence. **(4 min.)**
3. Go over point 3 with students. Remind them that they have already practiced the subjunctive and the indicative in expressions of the unknown versus expressions of known facts. **(4 min.)**
4. Have students practice using the subjunctive with the expressions of feelings listed in the grammar presentation. **(4 min.)**

### GramaVisión

For a video presentation of the subjunctive with expressions of feelings, use **GramaVisión.**

GramaVisión

**39** **Mezcla de oraciones** 1.2

**Escribamos** Usa una palabra o frase de cada columna para escribir ocho oraciones completas.

**MODELO** **A mis padres no les gusta que yo llegue tarde.**

| | | | |
|---|---|---|---|
| a mí | (no) molestar | que | mis amigos |
| a mis amigos | (no) preocupar | | los profesores |
| al (a la) profesor(a) | (no) gustar | | las clases |
| a mis padres | (no) frustrar | | los adultos |
| a mi hermano(a) | (no) sorprender | | los jóvenes |
| a los jóvenes | | | yo |

## Comunicación

HOLT SoundBooth ONLINE RECORDING

**40** **¿Qué me cuentas?** 1.1, 1.2

**Hablemos** Inventen tú y un(a) compañero(a) dos o tres chismes sobre algún actor o alguna actriz. Luego, dramaticen una conversación o llamada telefónica en que uno le cuenta el chisme al otro, y el otro reacciona. Usen las palabras de **Vocabulario.**

**MODELO** **—Fíjate, me han dicho que...**
**—¡No me digas! ¿Es verdad que...?**
**—Oye, ¿has oído que...?**
**—Ay, pero no puede ser...**

**41** **Describe la situación** 1.1, 1.2

**Hablemos** Describan tú y un(a) compañero(a) lo que pasa en cada dibujo. Expliquen cómo reacciona o cómo se siente cada persona.

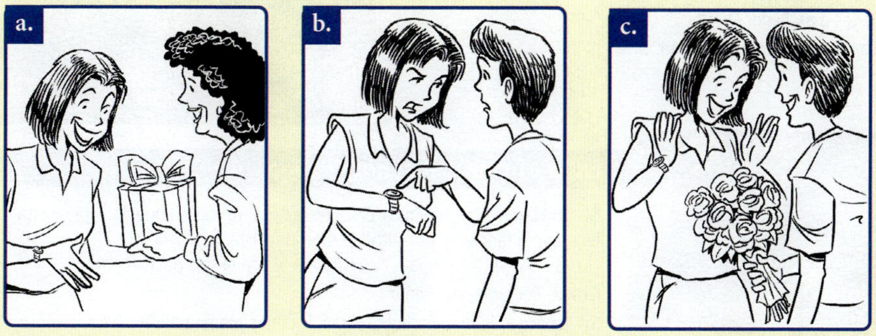


## Gramática 2

### Heritage Speakers

Heritage speakers sometimes are surprised when they learn the subjunctive. Colloquial Spanish speakers often use it incorrectly. Explain to students that the correct use of the subjunctive is studied in school in countries where Spanish is spoken and that they will also learn it in this class.

### Answers

Use the Chapter 2 *Picture Sequences Transparency.*

**41** Sample Answer

**A Rosa le hace feliz que su amiga le regale algo para su cumpleaños. A ella le molesta que su amigo llegue tarde el día de su cumpleaños. Le sorprende que su amigo le traiga flores y se pone feliz.**

### Comunicación

**Class Activity: Presentational**

Have pairs of students act out scenes similar to those in Activity 41. They should clearly express an emotion in their skits. The rest of the class uses the expressions from page 74 to tell how each person feels. 1.3

## Differentiated Instruction

### SLOWER PACE LEARNERS

**37** **Additional Practice** To give students additional practice with subjunctive versus indicative, pass out the script for Activity 37. Have students work in pairs to rewrite each response. If it contains an expression of feelings and the subjunctive, students should rewrite the response in the indicative using a clause that states fact or belief. For example, the first response is **Me alegra que estén contentos.** Students might write **Creo que forman una buena pareja.** 1.2

### MULTIPLE INTELLIGENCES

**Linguistic** Write several situations on the board using words and expressions from **Vocabulario 2.** Have students take turns telling how each situation makes them feel. You might include the following situations: **Tu amigo(a) es muy inseguro(a). Tu amigo(a) te deja plantado(a). Tu amigo(a) es muy generoso(a). Crees que tu amigo(a) no guarda tus secretos. Tu compañero(a) es muy grosero(a).** 1.2

### Assess

**Assessment Program**

**Prueba: Gramática 2,** pp. 29–30

**Prueba: Aplicación 2,** pp. 31–32

Audio CD 2, Tr. 16

Alternative Assessment, pp. 374, 386, 398

**Online Assessment**

**my.hrw.com**

**Test Generator**

## Resources

**Planning:**

Lesson Planner, pp. 28, 188–189

One-Stop Planner

**Presentation:**

Video Program, Videocassette 1

DVD Program

**Video Novela**

**Practice:**

Video Guide, pp. 12–14

Lab Book, p. 60

### Visual Learners

To help students identify the personality traits of the characters, have them complete a word web for each character. Have students tell what actions made them choose each character trait.

1.2

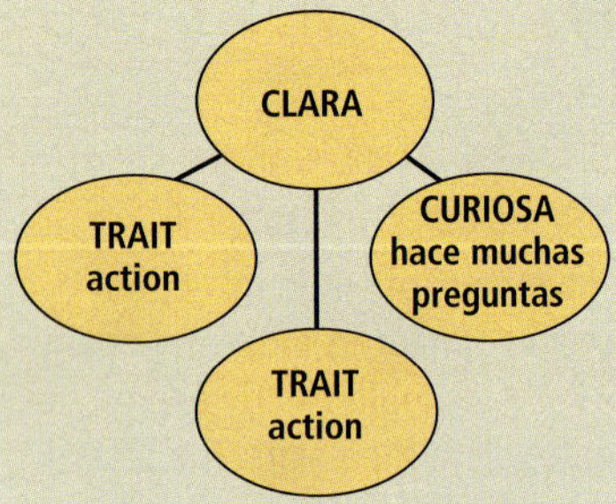


## Cultures

### Practices and Perspectives

Have students discuss the way Clara and Octavio interact with their boss in the workplace. Is the scene similar to something they might see in the United States? Have them explain their ideas.

2.1, 4.2

Novela en video

# Clara perspectiva

## Episodio 2

**ESTRATEGIA**

**Looking for personality traits** Character is best illustrated through behavior. What are Clara, Octavio, and Señor Ortega like? What actions do they take that make you think so? What a character is like may give you clues about what actions he or she might take in the future. Do you think Clara is curious? Do you think she's just going to let go of this matter with the professor? Do you think Octavio will help her? Why or why not? 1.2

### En las oficinas de *Chile en la Mira*

**Clara** Hola. Yo soy Clara de la Rosa.
**Octavio** Mucho gusto, Clara. Yo me llamo Octavio Medina.
**Clara** ¿Llevas mucho tiempo trabajando acá?
**Octavio** No, al contrario. Es mi primer día en la oficina.
**Clara** Ah, ¿tú también? ¡Qué alivio! No me voy a sentir tan sola.

1

2

**Clara** ¿Sabes algo del señor Ortega, nuestro jefe?
**Octavio** No mucho, pero mi compañero que trabajó acá el verano pasado me dijo que era un poco seco, pero muy atento.
**Clara** Menos mal. No me gustaría tener un jefe seco...

**Sr. Ortega** Buenos días, Señorita de la Rosa, Señor Medina.
**Octavio** Buenos días, Señor Ortega.
**Clara** Muy buenos días, Señor Ortega.
**Sr. Ortega** Por favor, pasen a mi oficina.

3

4

### En la oficina del señor Ortega

**Sr. Ortega** Bienvenidos a *Chile en la Mira*. Ya sabrán que en esta revista tenemos estándares muy altos. Somos la revista de mayor circulación de todo el país. Necesito gente con la que pueda contar.
**Clara** Por supuesto, Señor Ortega.
**Sr. Ortega** Bien. Su primera tarea. Estamos preparando un artículo sobre la vida del universitario chileno.
**Clara** ¡Genial! Nosotros sabemos algo de ese tema.

## Core Instruction

### TEACHING NOVELA EN VIDEO

1. Have students review what happened in **Episodio 1.** **(1 min.)**
2. Have students scan the **Novela en video** text. **(1 min.)**
3. Play the video. If students have trouble understanding any segment of the video, you might want to use the captioned version of the episode. **(5 min.)**
4. Play the video a second time and have students describe the personality of each character. **(5 min.)**
5. Have students work in pairs to answer the questions on page 77. **(5 min.)**

### Escuchemos

As students watch the **Novela,** have them listen for the interview where the student describes his pastimes. What expressions for pastimes are used by the interviewer and the student?

Novela en video

5

**Sr. Ortega** Bien. Quiero que vayan a sitios típicos de universitarios. Allí quiero que hagan unas 30 entrevistas y que las graben con esta grabadora.

**Octavio** ¿Qué clase de preguntas debemos hacerles?

**Sr. Ortega** Buena pregunta, Octavio. La idea del artículo es identificar los pasatiempos o deportes más comunes entre los universitarios y los sitios de Santiago que se consideran más "en la onda" hoy día. Recuerden, el periodista es mitad detective. Queremos identificar pasatiempos, deportes y sitios que no se hayan mostrado jamás en nuestra competencia.

**Octavio** Sí señor, por supuesto.

**Sr. Ortega** Aunque yo sea un poco "seco", no quiero que los artículos de la revista lo sean. Los espero ver aquí a las cinco de la tarde, con las cintas en mano.

Visit Holt Online
**go.hrw.com**
KEYWORD: EXP3 CH2
Online Edition

6

### En la universidad

**Octavio** ¿Cuál es tu pasatiempo favorito?

**Joven** No tengo tiempo para pasatiempos, con mis estudios, y el trabajo, y mi polola, y mis amigos, y mi familia…

**Octavio** ¿Eres gran aficionado a los deportes?

**Joven** Sólo por televisión, nada más. Aunque soy muy bueno para la pelota.

**Octavio** ¿Hay algún sitio en Santiago que frecuentes con tus amigos?

**Joven** Sí.—"Café Tecno". Vamos allí a jugar videojuegos y a…

**Octavio** ¡¿Clara?!

7

8

9

### ¿COMPRENDES?

1. ¿A quién se presenta Clara? ¿Para quién van a trabajar?
2. ¿Sabe Octavio algo del señor Ortega? ¿Qué sabe? ¿Cómo lo sabe?
3. ¿Sabe el señor Ortega que Clara cree que es "seco"? ¿Cómo lo sabes?
   1.2, 1.3
4. ¿Qué pasa durante la entrevista? ¿Qué hace Octavio? ¿Cómo se siente el hombre?
5. ¿Qué quiere hacer Clara? ¿Qué le dice Octavio?
6. Con base en sus acciones de Episodios 1 y 2, ¿cómo son las personalidades de Clara y de Octavio?

**Próximo episodio**
*Clara, Graciela y Octavio se juntan para analizar la situación del profesor Luna. ¿Qué crees que grabó Clara en la cinta?*
PÁGINAS 124–125



Novela en video

### Gestures

Have students note the gestures used by the speakers. What gestures do they use to show emotion? Do students use the same types of gestures to show emotion?

### ¿Comprendes? Answers

1. A Octavio. Van a trabajar para el señor Ortega.
2. Su compañero, que trabajó allí el verano pasado, le dijo que era un poco seco pero muy atento.
3. Sí. Estaba entrando cuando Clara dijo que no le gustaría tener un jefe seco.
4. Clara interrumpe porque quiere escuchar la cinta. Octavio le dice a Clara que no les queda mucho tiempo.
5. Quiere escuchar la cinta. Octavio le dice que no les queda mucho tiempo.
6. **Possible answers:** Clara es muy habladora y curiosa. Octavio es muy serio.

### Comparisons

#### Comparing and Contrasting

Octavio's interviewee says that he doesn't have time for pastimes because of the time he devotes to his studies, friends, and family. Do students in the U.S. feel this way? Do they have places to go to play video games like the Café Tecno that the student mentions in his interview?

4.2

### Clara perspectiva, Episodio 2

In **Episodio 2,** Clara has her first day of work at ***Chile en la Mira.*** She meets another intern, Octavio, also starting his first day at work. While pondering what their new boss Señor Ortega will be like, he surprises them and catches Clara making fun of him, which immediately starts Clara off on the wrong foot. Señor Ortega gives them their first assignment: to find a popular hangout for young people and record interviews about current popular pastimes and hobbies. While conducting interviews, Clara sees Professor Luna talking to two men, one of whom is the strange man she saw threatening him before. She breaks away from Octavio, taking the tape recorder, and surreptitiously records the conversation between Professor Luna and the two men. Octavio convinces her that she should put away the tape and get back to their assignment.

### Comunicación

#### Group Activity: Interpersonal

Have student pairs prepare an interview similar to the one Clara and Octavio had to conduct. They interview other student pairs to find out about the latest sports and pastimes and where they are held. Each pair prepares a short presentation to share their interview results.

1.1

# Lectura cultural

**Resources**

**Planning:**

Lesson Planner, pp. 29, 190–191

One-Stop Planner

**Presentation:**

Audio CD 2, Tr. 11

**Practice:**

Cuaderno de actividades, p. 18

Reading Strategies and Skills Handbook

Interactive Advanced Reader

**Pre-Reading Activity**

Ask students to talk about what they do when they go out at night. What time do they usually go out? Where do they go? What do they eat? What kind of music do they listen to? Tell them that they are going to read about nightlife in Spain. As they read, have them think about the similarities and differences between the nightlife for young people in the U.S. and Spain. 2.1, 4.2

**Pre-AP Practice**

**AP Language Examination:** **Lectura informativa** helps students prepare for Section I, Part B: **Reading Comprehension.** The audio recording helps them prepare for Part A: **Listening–Short Narratives.**

# Lectura cultural

CD 2, Tr. 11

## Una noche en España

*A los españoles les encanta salir de noche. Lee este artículo sobre la vida nocturna en España y luego haz las actividades que siguen.*

Se dice que de todos los europeos, los españoles son los que menos duermen. En España, se cena alrededor de las diez o las once. Sin embargo, después de comer a esta hora, los españoles no se acuestan. Muchos jóvenes, especialmente los que viven en la ciudad, salen para reunirse con sus amigos y disfrutar de los varios restaurantes y clubes de su barrio. De esta manera se puede decir que los españoles tienen más tiempo para disfrutar de cada día. ¡Y lo pasan bien!

En España, hay muchos establecimientos que puedes visitar durante la noche. Los jóvenes españoles suelen salir en grupos e ir a tantos clubes o restaurantes como pueden, porque se considera descortés estar en un lugar toda la noche. Es preferible comer un poco en un lugar, tomar una bebida en otro, bailar un rato en un club y luego cambiar de lugar para relajarse un poco. Esto es lo que en España se llama la 'movida', porque muchas personas van de un solo lugar a otro durante una noche típica.

**Estudiantes españoles e internacionales se reúnen con sus amigos en la Plaza Mayor de Salamanca.**

La música forma una parte importante de la vida española. Probablemente ya conoces el flamenco, que es la música más famosa de España. Pero los adolescentes escuchan todo tipo de música, incluso la música norteamericana y de otras partes del mundo.

Hay pocos conciertos de grupos internacionales en España, pero siempre se puede escuchar la música. Por la noche, especialmente en el sur, se pueden escuchar las tunas, grupos de estudiantes

**Core Instruction**

**TEACHING LECTURA CULTURAL**

1. Read the introductory paragraph with students and ask them what they think the nightlife is like in Spain. **(2 min.)**
2. Read the first paragraph aloud. Ask students why it is said that Spaniards sleep less than other Europeans. **(3 min.)**
3. Have students read the rest of the selection on their own. Ask them to comment on the information they found interesting or surprising. **(10 min.)**
4 Have students do Activity A under **Comprensión.** Then have them work in pairs to do Activity B. **(10 min.)**
5. Have students make the travel brochure in **Actividad. (10 min.)**

La gente comparte varios platos de tapas cuando sale. Las tapas más populares son la tortilla de patatas, las gambas, las alcachofas y las sardinas.

universitarios que andan por las calles y las plazas cantando y tocando guitarras, laúdes y otros instrumentos tradicionales. Y más tarde se puede escuchar música y bailar en los clubes, donde se tocan canciones populares europeas y de todo el mundo.

Después de tanto bailar uno tiene hambre. Las tapas son perfectas para calmar el hambre y socializar, y además hay cientos de variedades de tapas. Por lo general, las tapas se pueden comer con las manos. Casi todos los clubes o restaurantes en España ofrecen tapas como algo de picar mientras uno conversa con amigos. Cada persona típicamente compra un plato de tapas durante la noche, y así todos comparten el dinero y la comida.

## Comprensión

**A Los pasatiempos** ¿Sí o no? 1.2

1. Los españoles duermen más horas que los otros europeos.
2. A los españoles no les gusta la música norteamericana.
3. La cena se come muy tarde.
4. Las tapas son un tipo de bebida.
5. Es normal quedarse en un solo lugar toda la noche.
6. Las tunas tocan música tradicional.

**B La noche** Contesta las preguntas. 1.2

1. ¿Qué hacen los jóvenes después de cenar?
2. ¿Qué es "la movida"? ¿Por qué se llama así?
3. ¿De dónde es la música que se escucha en los clubes?
4. ¿Cuál es la música más famosa de España?
5. ¿Dónde se pueden escuchar las tunas?
6. ¿Cuándo se comen las tapas? ¿Cuántos platos de tapas compra cada persona del grupo?

### Actividad 1.3

**Folleto de viaje** Prepara un folleto de viaje para tu pueblo o ciudad que tenga una lista de restaurantes y clubes. Describe lo que puedes comer, beber o hacer en estos establecimientos y añade tus recomendaciones de lugares favoritos.

Lectura cultural

# Lectura cultural

## Comparisons

### Comparing and Contrasting

Ask students if they have places in their community where friends get together, like the Spanish plaza shown in the photograph on page 78. Then have them look at the photograph of **tapas** on page 79. Do these foods look familiar? Has anyone in the class tried **tapas?** Can they name the **tapas** in the photograph? Ask students to compare these dishes to appetizers or snacks they eat when they go out with their friends. 2.1, 4.2

### Post-Reading Activities

Ask students to compare the hour that young people go out in Spain to how late they stay out. Then have students compare the type of music mentioned in the reading with the music they usually listen to. 4.2

### A Answers

1. no
2. no
3. sí
4. no
5. no
6. sí

### B Answers

1. Salen para reunirse con sus amigos.
2. Es la costumbre de los españoles de ir de un lugar a otro durante una noche típica.
3. Es de todas partes del mundo.
4. Es el flamenco.
5. …en los barrios, …en el sur.
6. …durante la noche, después de bailar, mientras uno conversa con amigos. Cada persona compra un plato.

## Differentiated Instruction

### ADVANCED LEARNERS

**Challenge** Have students work in pairs to create a conversation in which they plan a night out in Spain. They can use the information from the selection as a start, and may wish to look up more specific information on the Internet about Spanish nightlife. Encourage them to use the **¡Exprésate!** functions from **Vocabulario 1** to invite each other out and to respond, and words from **Vocabulario 2** to talk about what other friends they would like to invite and why. 1.3, 3.2

### MULTIPLE INTELLIGENCES

**Musical/Rhythmic** Bring to class different types of music listed in the selection: **flamenco, música de las tunas,** and popular Spanish music. Play each type for students and tell them what it is. Then play a game. Every time you play flamenco music during the class, students must write a Spanish food item in their notebooks. Every time you play classic **tunas** music, they must write down a word to describe a friend, and every time you play popular Spanish music, they must write a pastime in Spanish. 3.1

### Assess

**Assessment Program**
**Prueba: Lectura,** p. 33
Standardized Assessment Tutor, pp. 7–10
**Online Assessment**
**my.hrw.com**
**Test Generator**

# Leamos y escribamos

## Resources

**Planning:**

Lesson Planner, pp 29–30, 190–191

One-Stop Planner

**Presentation:**

Audio CD 2, Tr. 12

**Practice:**

Cuaderno de actividades, p. 18

Reading Strategies and Skills Handbook, Chapter 2

Interactive Advanced Reader

### AP Reading Suggestion

Have students analyze the reading by looking at the symbolism of the bear and how it holds the story together. Encourage them to think about the reaction of the children when they see the bear, and what the narrator does with the bear. Ask them to write a short paragraph focusing on the role of the bear in the story.

### Applying the Strategies

For more practice with finding the main idea, you might have students use the "Read, rate, reread" strategy from the *Reading Strategies and Skills Handbook.*

### Escuchemos

Play the recording of the reading, and have students listen, with their books closed, for at least two things the writer and his girlfriend used to do together as children.

### Pre-AP Practice

**AP Language Examination:** **Leamos** helps students prepare for Section I, Part B: **Reading Comprehension.** The audio recording helps them prepare for Part A: **Listening—Short Narratives.**

# Leamos y escribamos

**ESTRATEGIA**

**para leer** One important strategy in understanding a story is to look for the main idea of the text. Remember that you do not always have to understand every word in a text to get the main idea of the story.

CD 2, Tr. 12

**Antes de leer** 1.2

**A** Prepara una hoja de papel con el título "Idea principal del cuento". Cuando leas el cuento, apunta los detalles que te parezcan importantes para entender mejor la idea principal.

# Un oso y un amor

*de Sabine Ulibarrí*

Era ya fines de junio. Ya había terminado el ahijadero[1] y la trasquila[2]. El ganado iba subiendo la sierra. Abrán apuntando, dirigiendo. Yo, adelante con seis burros cargados. De aquí en adelante la vida sería lenta y tranquila.

Hallé un sitio adecuado. Descargué los burros. Puse la carpa[3]. Corté ramas para las camas. Me puse a hacer de comer para cuando llegara Abrán. Ya las primeras ovejas estaban llegando. De vez en cuando salía a detenerlas, a remolinarlas, para que fueran conociendo su primer rodeo.

El pasto alto, fresco y lozano. Los tembletes[4] altos y blancos, sus hojas agitadas temblando una canción de vida y alegría. Los olores y las flores. El agua helada y cristalina del arroyo. Todo era paz y harmonía. Por eso los dioses viven en la sierra. La sierra es una fiesta eterna.

Las ollitas hervían. Las ovejas pacían o dormían. Yo contemplaba la belleza y la grandeza de la naturaleza.

De pronto oí voces y risas conocidas. Lancé un alarido[5]. Eran mis amigos de Tierra Amarilla. Abelito Sánchez, acompañado de Clorinda Chávez y Shirley Cantel. Los cuatro estábamos en tercer año de secundaria. Teníamos quince años.

Desensillamos y persogamos[6] sus caballos. Y nos pusimos a gozar el momento. Había tanto que decir. Preguntas. Bromas. Tanta risa que reanudar.

1 sheep breeding season 2 sheep shearing 3 tent
4 aspen trees 5 a shout 6 we tied up

## Core Instruction

### TEACHING LEAMOS

1. Read the **Estrategia para leer** with students. **(2 min.)**
2. Go over the introductory paragraph and have students prepare a sheet of paper on which to record the main idea and important details. **(3 min.)**
3. Read the first page aloud with students. Ask them what details they think are important so far. Remind them that the illustrations can also help them figure out important details. **(10 min.)**
4. Have students read the rest of the selection to themselves and allow them to ask questions about the parts they did not understand. **(10 min.)**
5. Answer the questions in Activity B as a class. Then have students work with a partner to answer the questions in Activities C and D. **(10 min.)**

Ahora al recordarlo me estremezco[7]. ¡Qué hermoso era aquello! Éramos jóvenes. Sabíamos querer y cantar. Sin licor, sin drogas, sin atrevimientos soeces[8].

Cuando llegó Abrán comimos. Yo tenía un sabroso y oloroso costillar de corderito[9] asado sobre las brasas. Ellos habían traído golosinas que no se acostumbran en la sierra. La alegría y la buena comida, la amistad y el sitio idílico convirtieron aquello en un festín para recordar siempre.

Shirley Cantel y yo crecimos juntos. Desde niños fuimos a la escuela juntos. Yo cargaba con sus libros. Más tarde íbamos a traer las vacas todas las tardes. Jugábamos en las caballerizas o en las pilas de heno. Teníamos carreras de caballo. En las representaciones dramáticas en la escuela ella y yo hacíamos los papeles importantes. Siempre competimos a ver quién sacaba las mejoras notas. Nunca se nos ocurrió que estuviéramos enamorados. Este año pasado, por primera vez, lo descubrimos, no sé cómo. Ahora la cosa andaba en serio. Verla hoy fue como una ilusión de gloria.

Shirley tenía una paloma[10] blanca que llamaba mucho la atención. Siempre la sacaba cuando montaba a caballo. La paloma se le posaba en un hombro, o se posaba en la crin[11] o las ancas del caballo. Llegó a conocerme y a quererme a mí también. A veces la paloma andaba conmigo. Volaba y volvía. La paloma era otro puente sentimental entre nosotros dos. Hoy me conoció. De inmediato se posó en mi hombro. Su cucurucú[12] sensual en mi oído era un mensaje de amor de su dueña.

Era gringa Shirley pero hablaba el español igual que yo. Esto era lo ordinario en Tierra Amarilla. Casi todos los gringos de entonces hablaban español. Eramos una sola sociedad. Nos llevábamos muy bien.

Chistes y bromas. Risas y más risas. Coqueteos[13] fugaces. Preguntas intencionadas. Contestaciones inesperadas. La fiesta en su apogeo[14].

De pronto el ganado se asusta. Se azota de un lado a otro. Se viene sobre nosotros como en olas. Balidos de terror. Algo está espantando al ganado.

Cojo[15] el rifle. Le digo a Shirley, "Ven conmigo." Vamos de la mano. Al doblar un arbusto nos encontramos con un oso. Ha derribado una oveja. Le ha abierto las entrañas. Tiene el hocico ensangrentado. Estamos muy cerca.

Ordinariamente el oso huye cuando se encuentra con el hombre. Hay excepciones: cuando hay cachorros, cuando está herido, cuando ha probado sangre. Entonces se pone bravo. Hasta un perro se pone bravo cuando está comiendo.

Éste era un oso joven. Tendría dos o tres años. Éstos son más atrevidos y más peligrosos. Le interrumpimos la comida. Se enfureció. Se nos vino encima[16].

Los demás se habían acercado. Estaban contemplando el drama. El oso se nos acercaba lentamente. Se paraba. Se sacudía la cabeza y gruñía[17]. Nosotros reculábamos[18] poco a poco. Hasta que topamos con un árbol caído. No había remedio. Tendríamos que confrontarnos con el bicho[19].

Nadie hizo por ayudarme. Nadie dijo nada. Las muchachas calladas. Nada de histeria. Quizás si hubiera estado solo habría estado muerto de miedo. Pero allí estaba mi novia a mi lado. Su vida dependía de mí. Los otros me estaban mirando.

Nunca me he sentido tan dueño de mí mismo. Nunca tan hombre, nunca tan macho. Me sentí primitivo, defendiendo a mi mujer. Ella y los demás tenían confianza en mí.

7 I shudder 8 vulgarities 9 side of lamb 10 dove 11 mane 12 cooing 13 flirtations 14 peak 15 I grab 16 charged us 17 was growling 18 backed up 19 animal

# Leamos y escribamos

## Active Reading Questions

1. **¿Por qué dice el narrador al principio de la página 81: "Ahora al recordarlo me estremezco."?**
2. **¿Qué hicieron el narrador y Shirley de niños?**
3. **¿Cuál es la importancia de la paloma de Shirley? ¿Qué mensaje le da al narrador?**
4. **¿Era extraño que Shirley hablara español? Explica.**
5. **¿Cuándo se pone bravo un oso?**
6. **¿Cómo se sintió el narrador cuando tuvo que enfrentar al oso? ¿Por qué?** 1.2, 3.2

## Finding the Main Idea

As students read the selection, have them stop periodically to summarize what they have read by identifying the main idea and supporting details in each section. Have them write their notes on a separate piece of paper. Remind them that they do not have to understand every word in the text in order to figure out the main idea. Once they have finished reading, they will use their notes and graphic organizers to summarize the story for the class. 3.1, 3.2

## Connections

### Language Arts Link

Sabine Ulibarrí, the author of **Un oso y un amor,** was born in 1919 in Tierra Amarilla, N.M. Have students research more information on Ulibarrí. They may wish to investigate his childhood, some of his other writings, his service in World War II, or his contributions to the promotion of better cultural understanding in multiethnic societies. 3.1

## Differentiated Instruction

### SLOWER PACE LEARNERS

**Additional Practice** Help students understand the story structure by asking them to skim the verbs in the first paragraph. Ask them what verb tense is used most often and why. (the imperfect, to set the stage) Then have them skim through the verbs on the rest of the page. What verb tense is used most often? (the preterite, to narrate the action in the past) 1.2

### SPECIAL LEARNING NEEDS

**Students with AD(H)D** Students may not be able to focus on reading the story from start to finish. You might divide it into four parts (first page, first column of second page, second column of second page, last page). Read the first part aloud with students. Then have volunteers summarize what happened. Have students read the second part to themselves and allow them to ask questions. Read the third part as a class. Ask students what they think will happen next. Then have them read the last part to themselves. Ask them to comment on the main idea of the story. 1.2

**C Answers**
1. Tenían quince años.
2. Comieron y hablaron.
3. Crecieron juntos.
4. Tenía hambre y no temía a los humanos.
5. Sí, porque conservaba la piel del oso en su casa.
6. Se fueron a universidades diferentes y hubo una guerra. Se compara con un río que se bifurca.

### Teaching Suggestion

Have students analyze the symbolism of the bear in the story. Encourage them to think about the reaction of the children when they see the bear, and what the narrator does with the bear. Have them write a short paragraph focusing on the role of the bear in the story. 1.2

### Post-Reading Strategy

After students have read the selection, have them share their notes with the class. Did everyone choose the same main idea and important details? Have students use their organizers to summarize the story for the class. Then have students explain the significance of the bear rug at the end of the story. 1.2

Alcé[20] el rifle. Apunté. Firme, seguro. Disparé. El balazo entró por la boca abierta y salió por la nuca. El balazo retumbó por la sierra. El oso cayó muerto a nuestros pies. Shirley me abrazó. Quise morirme de felicidad.

Desollé[21] al animal yo mismo. Sentí su sangre caliente en mis manos, y en mis brazos. Me sentí conquistador.

En una ocasión le había regalado yo a Shirley un anillo que mi madre me había dado a mí. En otra una caja de bombones. En esta ocasión le regalé la piel de un oso que ella conoció en un momento espantoso. Cuando se fue se llevó la piel bien atada en los tientos de la silla.

Pasaron los años. Yo me fui a una universidad, ella, a otra. Eso nos separó. Después vino una guerra que nos separó más. Cuando un río se bifurca en dos, no hay manera que esos dos ríos se vuelvan a juntar.

No la he vuelto a ver desde esos días. De vez en vez[22] alguien me dice algo de ella. Sé que se casó, que tiene familia y que vive muy lejos de aquí. Yo me acuerdo con todo cariño de vez en vez de la hermosa juventud que compartí con ella.

Recientemente un viejo amigo me dijo que la vio allá donde vive y conoció a su familia. Me dijo que en el suelo, delante de la chimenea tiene ella una piel de oso. También ella se acuerda.

**20** I raised **21** I skinned **22** once in a while

### Comprensión 1.2

**B** Contesta las preguntas basándote en lo que leíste.
1. ¿Cuántos años tenían los personajes del cuento?
2. ¿Qué hicieron cuando llegaron los amigos al campamento?
3. ¿Dónde conoció el narrador a su novia Shirley?
4. ¿Por qué no huyó el oso al ver al narrador con el rifle?
5. ¿Por qué se separaron el narrador y Shirley? ¿Con qué compara el narrador las vidas de estos jóvenes separados?
6. ¿Recordó Shirley esta experiencia años después?

### Pasó así 1.2

**C** Contesta **cierto** o **falso.**
1. Abrán y el narrador guiaban caballos por la sierra. falso
2. Los amigos de Abrán y del narrador fueron a visitarlos en la sierra. cierto
3. Shirley era la novia del narrador. cierto
4. Shirley no hablaba español. falso
5. Un oso mató una oveja para comérsela. cierto
6. El narrador lanzó piedras al oso y huyó. falso

### Después de leer 1.3

**D** ¿Te has separado poco a poco de un(a) amigo(a) alguna vez? ¿Cómo ocurrió? ¿Cómo te sentiste? Compara tus experiencias con un(a) compañero(a). Revisen sus apuntes del cuento y hagan un resumen de la historia juntos.

**Pre-AP Practice**

**AP Language Examination:** **Leamos and Escribamos** help students prepare for Section I, Part B: **Reading Comprehension** and Section II, Part A: **Informal Writing.**

## Core Instruction

### TEACHING ESCRIBAMOS

1. Read the **Estrategia para escribir** with students. Tell them they may wish to use an outline similar to the sample on page 83. **(5 min.)**
2. Have students read the introductory paragraph and use the questions as a guide to brainstorm ideas for their essay. **(5 min.)**
3. For homework, have students organize their ideas in outline form using the example on the page as a model.
4. During the next class, have students follow steps 1 through 3 to write their essays using their outlines to guide their writing.
5. After sharing the essays in step 4, allow students to discuss the essays as a class. Did students have similar experiences? How did students narrate their stories? **(5 min.)**

Visit Holt Online
**go.hrw.com**
KEYWORD: EXP3 CH2
Online Edition

Interactive TUTOR

# Taller del escritor 1.3

**ESTRATEGIA**

**para escribir** When writing an essay, write an outline first. Your outline should include a topic and subtopics. In an outline, subtopics are labeled with Roman numerals. The points you want to mention within these subtopics can be outlined with numerals or letters.

## La amistad es para siempre

¿Has tenido que separarte de un(a) amigo(a) alguna vez? ¿Qué pasó? ¿Cuál fue la razón por la que se dejaron de hablar o de verse? ¿Cómo te sentiste? ¿Has vuelto a ver a tu amigo(a) desde entonces? Escribe un ensayo de dos o tres párrafos sobre tus experiencias.

Amistades perdidas
I. ¿Por qué se separan los amigos?
  1. la familia se muda
  2. forman nuevas amistades
  3. se van a la universidad/cambian de colegio
II. ¿Cómo me sentí?
  1. extraño
  2. triste
III. El futuro
  1. no he vuelto a saber de mi amigo(a)
  2. me gustaría volver a ver a mi amigo(a)

### 1 Antes de escribir

Antes de empezar, haz una lista de las razones por las que se pueden separar los amigos. Después anota cómo te sentiste cuando te separaste de tu amigo(a). Luego apunta tus ideas sobre el futuro de tu amistad con él o ella.

### 2 Escribir un borrador

Empieza a escribir tu ensayo. Asegúrate de que tu ensayo tenga párrafos definidos y detalles relacionados a los temas.

### 3 Revisar

Revisa tu ensayo y corrige los errores de gramática u ortografía. Verifica que tus párrafos estén bien formados y que contengan las ideas de tu borrador.

### 4 Publicar

Comparte tu ensayo con tus compañeros de clase. Comparen sus experiencias y hablen de lo que aprendieron de su experiencia.

## Leamos y escribamos

### Process Writing

Explain to students that an outline is a good way to organize their information before writing an essay. To help them practice using an outline, write one together as a class or go over the one on page 83. 3.1

### Writing Assessment

To assess **Taller del escritor,** you can use the following rubric.

| Writing Rubric | 4 | 3 | 2 | 1 |
|---|---|---|---|---|
| **Content** (Complete—Incomplete) | | | | |
| **Comprehensibility** (Comprehensible—Seldom comprehensible) | | | | |
| **Accuracy** (Accurate—Seldom accurate) | | | | |
| **Organization** (Well-organized—Poorly organized) | | | | |
| **Effort** (Excellent effort—Minimal effort) | | | | |

18–20: A  14–15: C  Under 12: F
16–17: B  12–13: D

## Differentiated Instruction

### ADVANCED LEARNERS

**Extension** You might have students create a character list for their essays. Have them list the characters and write a short description for each, telling what the person looks like and describing the character's personality. Have them share their descriptions with the class. 1.3

### MULTIPLE INTELLIGENCES

**Kinesthetic** Divide the class into small groups and have them exchange essays. Each group will prepare a presentation to dramatize a classmate's essay. Then the author of the essay will tell whether or not the dramatization was an accurate representation of what happened. If not, the author might want to add more detail or important events to the essay in order for readers to clearly visualize what happened. 1.2, 1.3

### Assess

**Assessment Program**
**Prueba: Lectura,** p. 33
**Prueba: Escritura,** p. 34
**Online Assessment**
my.hrw.com
**Test Generator**

**Assess** **Differentiated Instruction** See the Differentiated Instruction CD-ROM.

## Resources

**Planning:**

Lesson Planner, pp. 30–31, 190–193

One-Stop Planner

**Presentation:**

Video Program, Videocassette 2

DVD Program

**Variedades**

**Practice:**

Activities for Communication, pp. 44, 57–58

Video Guide, pp. 10–11

Lab Book, pp. 2, 17–20, 59

Audio CD 2, Tr. 13

Pre-AP Instructional Resources

Pre-AP Audio CD 1, Trs. 5–8

Interactive Tutor, Disc 1

Teaching Transparencies

**Situación, Capítulo 2**

Picture Sequences, Chapter 2

### 5 Possible Answers

1. alrededor de las diez o las once; alimentos que se pueden comer con las manos
2. Suelen salir para reunirse con sus amigos y disfrutar de los restaurantes y clubes de su barrio.
3. todo tipo de música
4. los Pirineos, los Picos de Europa
5. del norte

### 6 Answers

Maribel: abierto, leal, que practique ciclismo, que diga la verdad

Alejandro: que respete sus sentimientos, paciente, atlética, generosa

Capítulo 2
Repaso

# Prepárate para el examen

Interactive TUTOR

**1 Vocabulario 1**
- expressing interest and displeasure
- inviting someone to do something

pp. 50–55

**2 Gramática 1**
- imperfect
- **ir a** + infinitive in the imperfect
- **nosotros** commands

pp. 56–61

**3 Vocabulario 2**
- describing the ideal friend
- expressing happiness and unhappiness

pp. 64–69

**1** Di si a cada persona le gusta la actividad que está haciendo. Escribe una oración para cada foto. 1.2

1. Manolo

2. Olga

3. Emilio y Felipe

**2** Completa cada oración con la forma correcta del imperfecto. 1.2

1. De niña, me la ═══ (pasar) jugando al volibol. pasaba
2. Iba a jugar ayer, pero ═══ (estar) muy cansada. estaba
3. Nosotros ═══ (ver) los partidos de fútbol todos los días. veíamos
4. A veces nosotros ═══ (ir) a ver los partidos en vivo. íbamos
5. De niño yo ═══ (hacer) senderismo de vez en cuando. hacía
6. Cuando tú ═══ (tener) cinco años, estabas loca por los rompecabezas. tenías

**3** Completa las oraciones con una palabra o una frase del cuadro. 1.2

| | | |
|---|---|---|
| celoso | tenemos mucho en común | creído |
| dejó plantado | tuvimos un malentendido | chismosa |

1. A Lorenzo no le gustan las mismas películas ni las mismas actividades que a mí. Nosotros no ═══. tenemos mucho en común
2. Tenía planes con Rosa el sábado. Íbamos a ver una película a las siete pero ella nunca llegó. Me ═══. dejó plantado
3. María siempre le está contando los secretos de otras personas a todo el mundo. Ella es muy ═══. chismosa
4. Pablo discute mucho con Diana porque no le gusta cuando sale con otros amigos. Creo que él es demasiado ═══. celoso
5. Eduardo solamente habla de sí mismo y piensa que siempre tiene la razón. Es muy ═══. creído
6. Nancy estaba enojada porque pensó que no la invité a mi fiesta. Pero ═══. Yo pensé que ella no quería venir. tuvimos un malentendido

## Oral Assessment

### Speaking Rubric

To assess the speaking activities in this section, you might use the following rubric. For additional speaking rubrics, see the Alternative Assessment section of the *Assessment Program.*

| Speaking Rubric | 4 | 3 | 2 | 1 |
|---|---|---|---|---|
| **Content** (Complete—Incomplete) | | | | |
| **Comprehension** (Total—Little) | | | | |
| **Comprehensibility** (Comprehensible—Incomprehensible) | | | | |
| **Accuracy** (Accurate—Seldom Accurate) | | | | |
| **Fluency** (Fluent—Not Fluent) | | | | |

18–20: A 16–17: B 14–15: C 12–13: D Under 12: F

# Prepárate para el examen



4 Completa cada oración con la palabra correcta. 1.2

1. (La/Le) quiero regalar algo a Julia para su cumpleaños.
2. Pero no hay nada en esta tienda que me (guste/gusta).
3. Me molesta que Andrés no me (ayude/ayuda) a buscar el regalo.
4. (Le/Lo) llamé hoy y me dijo que no tenía tiempo.
5. Tengo que buscarme un novio que (sea/es) más solidario.
6. (Le/Lo) voy a decir que no quiero seguir en esta relación.

**4 Gramática 2**
- object pronouns
- subjunctive with the unknown or non-existent
- subjunctive with expressions of feelings

pp. 70–75

5 Contesta las preguntas. 1.2

1. ¿A qué hora suelen cenar los españoles? ¿Qué suelen hacer cuando salen por la noche?
2. ¿Qué son las tapas?
3. ¿Qué es la Ruta de Don Quijote?
4. ¿Dónde se puede hacer senderismo en España?
5. ¿En qué parte de España se origina el jai-alai?

**5 Cultura**
- Comparaciones pp. 62–63
- Lectura cultural pp. 78–79
- Notas culturales pp. 52, 61, 74

CD 2, Tr. 13 1.2

6 Escucha mientras Maribel y Alejandro hablan sobre lo que buscan en un(a) novio(a). Escribe una lista de las cualidades que busca Maribel, y otra lista de las que busca Alejandro.

## Conversación

HOLT SoundBooth ONLINE RECORDING

7 Role-play the following conversation with a partner. Partner A and Partner B are classmates, talking about weekend plans. 1.1, 1.2

Partner A: Tell your partner he or she looks excited. Ask what's up.

Partner B: Say you're in a great mood, but it's a secret.

Partner A: Say you aren't a gossip and your partner can trust you.

Partner B: Say you're excited because you asked Julio (Julia) to go out with you, and he (she) accepted.

Partner A: Say you know Julio (Julia); list some of his (her) good qualities. Explain that he (she) is a big fan of bowling. Suggest they go bowling together.

Partner B: Say really? Explain that bowling doesn't do anything for you.

Partner A: Suggest that your partner and Julio (Julia) do a different sports activity.

Partner B: Agree, thank your partner for the idea, and end the conversation.

### 5 Answers

1. En España se cena alrededor de las diez o las once. Las tapas son comidas para picar que se pueden comer con las manos.
2. Suelen salir en grupos y van a tantos restaurantes como pueden.
3. el flamenco, la música norteamericana, la música popular mundial, música tradicional que tocan las tunas
4. any two of these places: los Pirineos. los Picos de Europa, la Sierra Nevad, el llano, la meseta central
5. El jai-alai se origina en el norte de España; en regiones vascas.

### 6 Script

See script and answers on p. 47F.

### 7 Answers

Below is a sample student conversation.

(A) —Hola, Antonio, ¿qué tal? Oye, te veo muy entusiasmado. ¿Qué pasa?
(B) —Hola, Susana. Sí, estoy de muy buen humor, pero es un secreto.
(A) —¿!Un secreto!? Pero, Antonio... ya sabes que no soy una chismosa. Soy tu amiga; puedes confiar en mí.
(B) —Bueno, no sé... pues, sí, estoy entusiasmado porque invité a Julia a salir conmigo este sábado, y me dijo que sí.
(A) —¡A Julia! Qué bien. Conozco a Julia y es una chica estupenda—abierta, amigable, generosa. ¿Sabías que ella es una gran aficionada al boliche? ¿Por qué no van a jugar al boliche juntos el sábado?
(B) —¿Al boliche? ¿De veras? Pues, la verdad es que a mí el boliche me deja frío. ¿Qué debo hacer?
(A) —Pues, entonces te aconsejo que vayan al partido de baloncesto. Julia es atlética y le encanta cualquier deporte.
(B) —Gracias, muy buena idea. Voy a hablar con Julia ahora. Por favor, recuerda que es un secreto, ¿de acuerdo? Bueno, tengo que irme. Hasta pronto.

## Conversación

### Additional Speaking Practice

For additional speaking practice, use the *Picture Sequences Transparency* for Chapter 2. Use the Speaking Rubric on the preceding page to evaluate their performance. You may also wish to use the Interviews and Role-Plays in the *Activities for Communication* book.

### Pre-AP Practice

7 In the Level 3 *Pre-AP Instructional Resources* you will find an alternative version of Activity 7. The following resources in that book will help you prepare students for the AP Language Exam:

- Blackline masters, pp. 28, 38, 48
- Pre-AP Audio CD 1, Trs. 5–8
- Scripts and answers, pp. 57–75

# Prepárate para el examen

## Grammar Review

For more practice with the grammar topics in this chapter, see the *Grammar Tutor,* the *Interactive Tutor,* or the *Cuaderno de vocabulario y gramática.*

GramaVisión

## Language Note

When students review direct and indirect object pronouns, remind them that the pronoun **os** is used in Spain for **vosotros.** In Latin America the **vosotros** form is not used, and therefore the pronoun **os** is not used.

Tell students that they might hear Spanish speakers using **le** or **les** as direct object pronouns. This use of the object pronouns is called **leísmo** and is quite common, especially in Spain.

## Comparisons

### Language to Language

Have students translate the sample sentences for the subjunctive review in **Gramática 2.** What do they notice about the tense of the verbs in English? How does this differ from the verbs in Spanish?

1.2, 4.1

**Gramática 1**

- imperfect **pp. 56–57**
- **ir a** + infinitive in the imperfect **pp. 58–59**
- **nosotros** commands **pp. 60–61**

## Repaso de Gramática 1

Use the imperfect to talk about what someone used to do, how things used to be, or what happened in general. The only verbs with irregular forms are **ir, ser,** and **ver.**

| -ar verbs | | -er/-ir verbs | |
|---|---|---|---|
| habl**aba** | habl**ábamos** | sal**ía** | sal**íamos** |
| habl**abas** | habl**abais** | sal**ías** | sal**íais** |
| habl**aba** | habl**aban** | sal**ía** | sal**ían** |

Use **ir a + infinitive** in the **imperfect** to state what someone *was going to do.* **Ir a + infinitive** is followed by a verb in the preterite when the second verb describes a specific completed action in the past, and by the imperfect when the second verb describes an ongoing condition or state in the past.

**Íbamos a caminar** pero **empezó** a llover.

**Iba a salir** pero **estaba** cansada.

Use the **nosotros** form of the present subjunctive for nosotros commands. When **nos** is attached to the end of a command form, drop the **-s** from the **-amos** or **-emos** ending and add an accent mark.

**Veamos** la película primero y **almorcemos** luego en alguna parte.

Tenemos que salir temprano mañana. **Despertémonos** a las seis.

The verb **ir** has an irregular affirmative nosotros command form, vamos, and a regular negative command form, no vayamos.

**Gramática 2**

- object pronouns **pp. 70–71**
- subjunctive with the unknown or nonexistent **pp. 72–73**
- subjunctive with expressions of feelings **pp. 74–75**

## Repaso de Gramática 2

For a review of object pronouns, see page 70.

The subjunctive is used when the person or thing being referred to (the antecedent) is unknown or nonexistent.

Busco un **profesor** que **sepa** inglés.

No hay **nadie** en la clase que **entienda** la tarea.

¿Conoces a **unos chicos** que **tengan** tiempo para ayudarnos?

The subjunctive is used with expressions that convey feelings: me alegra que, temo que, es triste que, siento que, me molesta que, me frustra que, me sorprende que, me preocupa que, me irrita que.

**Es triste que** Paula **esté** enferma.

**Me alegra que vayamos** todos juntos.

## Chapter Review

**Teacher Management System**

To access, launch the program, type "admin" in the password area, and press RETURN. For more details, log on to www.hrw.com/CDROMTUTOR.

Create a variety of puzzles to review chapter vocabulary.

**DVD Program**

**Interactive Tutor**

**PuzzlePro**

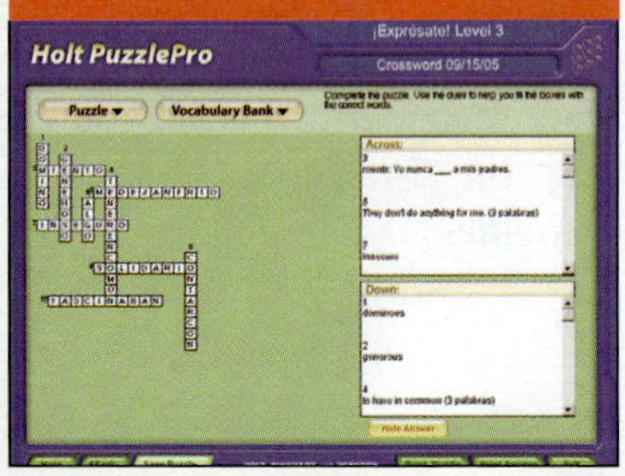

HOLT SoundBooth ONLINE RECORDING

## Repaso de Vocabulario 1

### Expressing interest and displeasure

| | |
|---|---|
| aburrir | to bore |
| aguantar | to stand, to tolerate |
| ¿Ah, sí? Pues, yo creo que... | Really? Well, I think . . . |
| las artes marciales | martial arts |
| el atletismo | track and field |
| el boliche (jugar al boliche) | bowling (to bowl) |
| el ciclismo (practicar ciclismo) | biking (to bike) |
| el dominó | dominoes |
| Eres muy bueno(a) para... ¿verdad? | You're really good at . . . aren't you? |
| la escalada deportiva | rock climbing |
| escalar | to climb |
| la esgrima | fencing |
| esgrimir | to fence |
| estar loco(a) por | to be crazy about |
| estupendo(a) | marvelous |
| fanático(a) | fan |
| genial | great |
| el jai-alai | jai-alai |
| los juegos de computadora | computer games |
| el kárate | karate |
| Los/Las... me (te, le...) dejan frío(a). | The . . . don't do anything for me (you, him/her . . .) |
| Pues, la verdad es que... | Well, the truth is that . . . |
| pasarlo bien/mal | to have a good/bad time |
| remar | to row |
| el rompecabezas | puzzle |
| el remo (remar) | rowing (to row) |
| el salto de altura | high jump |
| el senderismo (hacer senderismo) | hiking (to hike) |
| Sí, me la paso... Estoy loco(a) por... | Yes, I'm always doing . . . I'm crazy about . . . |
| Soy un(a) gran aficionado(a) a... | I'm a big . . . fan. |
| ¿Qué deporte te gusta a ti? | What sport do you like? |
| el tiro con arco | archery |

**Inviting someone to do something** . . . . . . . . . . . . . . . . . . . . . . . . *See p. 54.*

## Repaso de Vocabulario 2

### Describing the ideal friend

| | |
|---|---|
| abierto(a) | open |
| amigable | friendly |
| la amistad | friendship |
| atento(a) | helpful |
| apoyar | to support |
| Busco a alguien a quien le guste(n)... y que sepa algo de... | I'm looking for someone who likes . . . and knows something about . . . |
| celoso(a) | jealous |
| chismear | to gossip |
| chismoso(a) | gossipy |
| un(a) conocido(a) | acquaintance |
| confiable | reliable |
| confiar en | to trust |
| ¿Cómo debe ser un(a) buen(a) amigo(a)? | What should a good friend be like? |
| contar (ue) con | to count on (someone) |
| creído(a) | arrogant |
| criticón, criticona | critical, judgmental |
| dejar plantado(a) a alguien | to stand someone up |
| desleal | disloyal |
| generoso(a) | generous |
| grosero(a) | rude, vulgar |
| guardar los secretos | to keep secrets |
| hacer las paces | to make up |
| honesto(a) | honest |
| inseguro(a) | insecure |
| leal | loyal |
| maleducado(a) | rude, ill-bred |
| mentir (ie, i) | to lie |
| ¿Qué buscas en un(a) novio(a)? | What do you look for in a boyfriend/girlfriend? |
| querer (ie) a | to love (someone) |
| resolver (ue) un problema | to resolve a problem |
| respetar | to respect |
| romper con | to break up with |
| seco(a) | cold, unfriendly |
| los sentimientos | feelings |
| solidario(a) | supportive |
| tener celos de | to be jealous of |
| tener fama de ser | to be known to be |
| tener un malentendido | to have a misunderstanding |
| tener mucho/algo/nada en común | to have much/something/nothing in common |
| terco(a) | stubborn |
| tolerante | tolerant |
| Un(a) buen(a) amigo(a) debe apoyarme y... No debe... | A good friend should support me and . . . He/She shouldn't . . . |
| (no) valer la pena | to (not) be worth it |

**Expressing happiness and unhappiness** . . . . . . . . . . . . . . . . . . . . . . . *See p. 68.*

Preparate para el examen

Capítulo 2

# Prepárate para el examen

### Vocabulary Review

For more practice with the vocabulary in this chapter, see the *Interactive Tutor* or the *Cuaderno de vocabulario y gramática.*

### Online Edition

Students might use the online textbook to hear the **Vocabulario** items.

### Teaching Suggestion

Have students write a short poem using the vocabulary to learn about alliteration.

### Game

**¡Dibújalo!** Have students make preliminary sketches of vocabulary items so they will be ready to draw them on the board when called. Divide the class into two teams. Ask the first player from Team 1 to go to the board. Show the student a vocabulary word. The student draws a picture of the word and Team 1 has one minute to guess the word, including the article, before the opposing team may try. The team who guesses correctly gets a point. Repeat with the other team.

1.2

### Online Edition

### Transparency: Vocabulario

### Transparency: Situación

### Assess

**Assessment Program**

**Examen: Capítulo 2,** pp. 217–222

Audio CD 2, Trs. 17–18

**Examen oral: Capítulo 2,** p. 228

Alternative Assessment, pp. 374, 386, 398

**Online Assessment**
**my.hrw.com**

**Test Generator**

**Assess** **Differentiated Instruction** See the Differentiated Instruction CD-ROM.

## Resources

**Planning:**

Lesson Planner, pp. 31, 192–193

One-Stop Planner

**Presentation:**

Teaching Transparencies
Fine Art, Chapter 2

**Practice:**

Cuaderno de actividades, pp. 19–20

Lab Book, pp. 2, 17–20

Audio CD 2, Tr. 14

### 1 Script

1. Iba muy rápido por el río en mi bote y les gané a los otros competidores.
2. Quería llegar hasta el lago, pero tuve que ponerle más aire a la llanta de mi bicicleta.
3. Hicimos una caminata muy larga por el bosque.
4. Escalamos una montaña muy alta y había una vista preciosa en la cima.

### 2 Answers

1. Tenía planes con su novio.
2. De niña estaba loca por el jai-alai, pero ahora el deporte la aburre.
3. Tomás se enfadó porque ella no quiere ir a otro partido y prefiere hacer algo con Pamela. Es muy celoso.
4. Answers will vary.
5. Answers will vary.
6. Quiere practicar ciclismo porque tiene una bicicleta nueva.

### Communitites

**Multicultural Link**

Assign students to visit a nearby museum, speak with a Spanish-speaking tour guide, and write a critique in Spanish of one piece of art. The critique answers these questions: What movement does this art piece represent; who is the artist; what is his or her country of origin; and how does this piece compare to other art that I have evaluated? Encourage students to look at different pieces of art as well as artists, and to write on a particular style that they enjoy. 3.1, 5.1

**Repaso cumulativo**

# Integración

## capítulos 1–2

CD 2, Tr. 14

**1** Escucha lo que dice cada persona y escoge el comentario que corresponde a cada foto. Luego, escribe el nombre del deporte que está practicando. 1.2

**A**

3, el senderismo

**B**

1, el remo

**C**

4, la escalada deportiva

**D**

2, el ciclismo

**2** Lee la carta y contesta las preguntas. 1.2

Querida Pamela,

Siento no haber hecho senderismo con Uds. el sábado. Iba a ir, pero recordé que tenía planes con mi novio Tomás. Me invitó a un partido de jai-alai y no quería dejarlo plantado. De niña, estaba loca por el jai-alai, pero la verdad es que el partido el sábado me dejó fría. Él quiere ir el próximo sábado también. Le dije a Tomás que no quiero ir a otro partido porque me aburre el jai-alai y quiero hacer algo contigo. Él es muy celoso y se enfadó conmigo. Me dan ganas de llorar porque él debe respetar mis sentimientos. Creo que simplemente es muy inseguro. Pero no vale la pena hacer algo que no me gusta solamente porque él sea inseguro. Así que, hagamos algo tú y yo. Practiquemos ciclismo, ¿vale? Tengo una bicicleta nueva y es formidable.

Hasta pronto,
Carmen

1. ¿Por qué no hizo Carmen senderismo el sábado?
2. ¿Cómo ha cambiado la opinion de Carmen acerca del jai-alai?
3. ¿Por qué se enfadó Tomás con Carmen?
4. ¿Qué tipo de persona es Carmen?
5. ¿Crees que Tomás es un buen novio? ¿Por qué?
6. ¿Qué quiere hacer Carmen con Pamela? ¿Por qué?

### Culture Project

Students know that jai-alai originated in northern Spain. Have them research the history and development of the sport and how it became popular in other countries. They should include information about some famous players of the sport and should also compare the popularity of the sport in Spain and in the U.S. What parts of the U.S. have jai-alai courts, or **frontones?** Do Spanish players play on U.S. teams? Encourage them to watch a jai-alai game on television. 2.1, 4.2

Visit Holt Online
go.hrw.com
KEYWORD: EXP3 CH2
Cumulative Self-test

**3** En grupos de cuatro, dramaticen la siguiente situación. Una persona quiere salir este fin de semana y está buscando a alguien que lo/la acompañe. La persona invita a varios amigos a salir, pero todos tienen planes. 1.1, 1.3

**4** Mira la pintura y escribe cuatro oraciones para describir lo que a la gente le gustaba hacer para divertirse en España en el siglo XIX. Luego, escribe cuatro oraciones para describir lo que a ti te gusta hacer para divertirte. 1.2, 1.3

*Feria de Santiponce*, 1855 by Manuel Rodríguez de Guzmán. 125 x 196 cm. Derechos Reservados ©Museo Nacional del Prado, Madrid.

***Feria de Santiponce*** **de Manuel Rodríguez de Guzmán (1818–1867)**

**5** Tus amigos quieren arreglar una cita *(date)* con alguien que no conoces. Pero quieren saber qué buscas en un(a) novio(a) para poder elegir a la persona perfecta. Describe en un párrafo a tu novio(a) ideal y lo que te gustaría hacer durante la cita. 1.3

**6** **Situación**

En parejas, escojan una de las siguientes situaciones y dramatícenla.

**A.** Le contaste un secreto a tu novio(a) y él o ella se lo contó a todo el mundo. Habla con tu novio(a) y dile cómo te sientes.

**B.** Invitaste a un(a) amigo(a) a jugar al boliche, y te dejó plantado(a). Habla con tu amigo(a) y explícale cómo te sientes. Deja que tu amigo(a) te explique lo que pasó. 1.1, 1.3

## Fine Art Connection

Tell students this painting, ***Feria de Santiponce,*** was done by the Spanish artist Rodríguez de Guzmán in the nineteenth century. The **Feria de Santiponce** began in the small southern Spanish town of Santiponce in 1691, and is celebrated annually. The artist was born in Sevilla in 1818 and studied art at the **Escuela de Bellas Artes.** In 1854 he moved to Madrid, where he painted many scenes of Spanish **fiestas** for Isabel II. The ***Feria de Santiponce*** is now part of the collection of the **Museo del Prado** in Madrid.

### Analyzing

Have students describe what they see in the painting. Ask them to comment on the clothing, the setting, and the activities taking place in the painting. Then have them compare the **fiesta** depicted in the painting with a modern-day **fiesta.** 3.1

### Extension

Have students research work by Rodríguez de Guzmán. Ask them to find another painting of a Spanish **fiesta** and to research the history of the **fiesta.** Then have them compare the painting they found with the ***Feria de Santiponce.*** Ask students to share their findings with the class. 3.1

## ACTFL Performance Standards

The activities in Chapter 2 target the different communicative modes as described in the Standards.

| | | |
|---|---|---|
| **Interpersonal** | Two-way communication using receptive skills and productive skills | **Comunicación (SE),** pp. 53, 55, 57, 59, 61, 67, 69, 71, 73, 75<br>**Comunicación (TE),** pp. 55, 59, 71, 73, 77<br>**Conversación,** p. 85<br>**Situación,** p. 89 |
| **Interpretive** | One-way communication using receptive skills | **Comunicación (SE),** pp. 61, 67, 69, 71, 73, 75<br>**Comunicación (TE),** pp. 57, 69<br>**Novela en video,** pp. 76–77<br>**Leamos,** pp. 80–82<br>**Conversación,** p. 85 |
| **Presentational** | One-way communication using productive skills | **Comunicación (SE),** pp. 53, 55, 57, 59, 75<br>**Comunicación (TE),** pp. 53, 61, 67, 75 |

**Resources**

**Planning:**
Lesson Planner, p. xv
One-Stop Planner

**Presentation:**
Teaching Transparencies
**Mapa 4**
Video Program,
Videocassette 2
DVD Program
**Geovisión**

**Practice:**
Video Guide, pp. 15–16
Lab Book, p. 3, 62
Interactive Tutor, Disc 1

**VIDEO OPTIONS**

- **VideoCultura**
- **VideoNovela**
- **Variedades**
- **GramaVisión**

**Pre-AP Practice**

**AP Benchmark:** Recognize cultural elements implicit in oral and written texts.

**Focus:** Cultural Product (**arte, los taínos**)

- SE, p. 94, **Precolombino**
- TE, p. 94, Cultures: Products and Perspectives
- TE, p. 95D, **Los taínos**

GeoVisión

Capítulos 3 y 4

▲ **El observatorio de Arecibo,** en Puerto Rico, es el telescopio de un solo plato más grande del mundo. Mide 305 metros de diámetro. Con la ayuda del telescopio, los científicos han descubierto planetas. 2

# Geocultura
## *El Caribe*

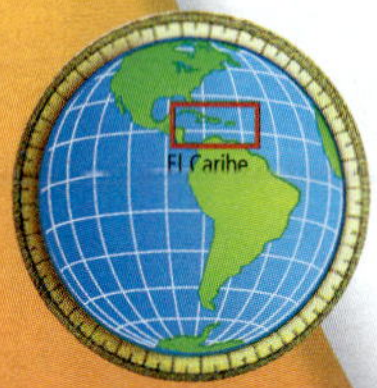


► **La costa de La Habana, Cuba,** está llena de hoteles modernos y rascacielos, mientras las edificaciones y calles de la Vieja Habana están en necesidad de reparación para conservar su historia colonial. Este contraste entre lo moderno y lo antiguo es común en las islas del Caribe. 1

### Almanaque

**Países y territorios caribeños de habla hispana**
Puerto Rico, 3.916.632 (San Juan)
Cuba, 11.346.670 (La Habana)
La República Dominicana, 8.950.034 (Santo Domingo)

**Industrias principales**
café, azúcar, plátanos, cacao, fármacos y químicos, textiles, turismo

### ¿Sabías que...?

**Durante enero y marzo las ballenas jorobadas emigran a la costa este de Samaná, República Dominicana, para la reproducción y el nacimiento de sus crías.**

◄ **Las aguas del mar Caribe** son perfectas para una gran variedad de deportes acuáticos, como navegar en barcos de vela, bucear, pescar o esquiar. Millones de turistas, de Estados Unidos y Europa principalmente, llegan a las islas del Caribe cada año.

## Background Information

### History

The island of **La Española,** known today as Hispaniola, was established as the center of the first Spanish colonial government shortly after the arrival of Christopher Columbus. Santo Domingo, the capital of the Dominican Republic, is the oldest city established by Europeans in the Western Hemisphere. For nearly 400 years, the islands of the Caribbean were of the utmost strategic importance to Spain, since they served as a port of exit and entry to the rest of Spanish colonial America.

### Geography

**The Greater Antilles** is part of the Antilles archipelago, which extends from the southern tip of Florida to the coast of Venezuela. Cuba, the Dominican Republic, and Puerto Rico are mountainous countries. Crops like coffee and bananas are grown in mountainous regions of these countries.

**La Habana** is the Cuban capital. The buildings in historic Havana are reminiscent of colonial times. The ocean boardwalk, or **malecón,** which extends for about three kilometers, is a popular spot for Havana residents and tourists alike.

# El Caribe

▲ **El Alcázar de Colón** se construyó en 1509 con la llegada a Santo Domingo del gobernador Diego Colón, hijo de Cristóbal Colón. Hoy el Alcázar sirve de museo. Cada uno de los veintidós cuartos está amueblado con piezas históricas y antigüedades. 3

▼ La rana más pequeña del hemisferio norte, el **Eleutherodactylus iberia,** se descubrió en el bosque tropical de Cuba en 1996. Sólo mide un centímetro, lo que hace que su nombre sea tres veces más largo que su cuerpo. 4

▲ **Huracanes** Cada año la gente del Caribe vive con la posibilidad de gran destrucción causada por las tormentas tropicales. Inundaciones, fallos de electricidad y la destrucción de casas ocurren con frecuencia, como se ve aquí en La Habana. 1

▼ Tradicionalmente, los productos agrícolas, como el plátano, la piña, el azúcar y el café que ves en esta foto del oeste de Cuba, eran las exportaciones principales del Caribe. Hoy **la economía de las islas** se ha diversificado para incluir productos tecnológicos, textiles y equipo médico. 5

## ¿Sabías que... ?

Students might be interested in knowing the following facts about the Caribbean.

- **El Alcázar de Colón** was originally built with 55 rooms and took four years to complete.
- **La Sierra del Escambray** in central Cuba was not officially named until 1959, following the Cuban revolution.
- **Pico Duarte** in the Dominican Republic has an elevation of 10,416 feet and is the highest point in the Caribbean.
- **The Puerto Rican coat of arms** dates from 1511 and is one of the oldest coat of arms still in use in the Western Hemisphere.

## Preguntas 1.2, 3.1

1. **¿Dónde está el Alcázar de Colón? (en Santo Domingo)**
2. **¿Cómo se llama la pequeña rana descubierta en Cuba en 1996? (Eleutherodactylus iberia)**
3. **¿De dónde son los turistas que llegan al Caribe? (de Estados Unidos y Europa)**
4. **¿Cuáles son los peligros de vivir en el Caribe? (tormentas tropicales, inundaciones, fallos de electricidad)**
5. **¿Cuáles son algunos productos que se hacen en el Caribe hoy en día? (productos tecnológicos, textiles, equipos médicos)**

## Atlas INTERACTIVO MUNDIAL

Have students use the interactive atlas at **go.hrw.com** to complete the map activities below.

### Map Activities

1. Have students look at the map of the Caribbean on page R7. Have them locate and name the three Spanish-speaking countries in the Caribbean. **(Cuba, La República Dominicana, Puerto Rico)**
2. Point out that there are several non-Spanish speaking countries or territories in the Caribbean. Have students identify two of them. **(Haití, Jamaica)**
3. Have students identify the capital of the Dominican Republic and its closest neighbors. **(Santo Domingo, Haití, Puerto Rico)**

3.1

## Cultures

### Products and Perspectives

**Music** Rhythms like the **danzón** originated in Matanzas, Cuba. Other Cuban music styles are the **guaracha** and **punto guajiro,** popular in the Cuban countryside. The **plena** and **jíbaro** rhythms are from Puerto Rico, and **bachata** originated in the Dominican Republic. The term **bachata** meant *get together* or *gathering*. This music is played with a guitar, a bass, **maracas,** bongo drums, or a **güiro,** a percussion instrument made from a hollow gourd. **Merengue** is also Caribbean, possibly derived from Haitian *mereng* and heavily influenced by African music. **Merengue** is popular throughout the Caribbean and in some parts of the U.S. Ask students why they think African culture has influence in the Caribbean and the United States.

2.2

# La historia del Caribe

ÉPOCA PRECOLOMBINA | 1400 | 1500

### Época precolombina 3.1

**Los taínos** se establecieron en las Grandes Antillas hace más de dos milenios. Cazaban pequeños animales y cultivaban cosechas como la yuca, el maíz, la calabaza y los cacahuetes. Los caribes, una tribu más agresiva que había conquistado las Pequeñas Antillas, atacaban a los taínos con frecuencia. **Investiga la distancia que hay entre las Grandes y las Pequeñas Antillas.**

### 3.1 1492

**Cristóbal Colón** llegó a la isla de San Salvador en las Bahamas en 1492 y tomó posesión del archipiélago en nombre de los Reyes de España. **¿Qué significaba esto para España?**

### Siglo XVI 3.1

En el siglo XVI los españoles construyeron **fortalezas** en Puerto Rico, Cuba, la Hispaniola y Cartagena de Indias para protegerse de los ataques de Holanda, Inglaterra, Francia y de varios grupos de piratas. Los marineros de barcos cargados con oro se reunían en La Habana, y como medida de seguridad, cruzaban el Océano Atlántico en caravanas. **¿Por qué crees que era más seguro viajar en caravana?**

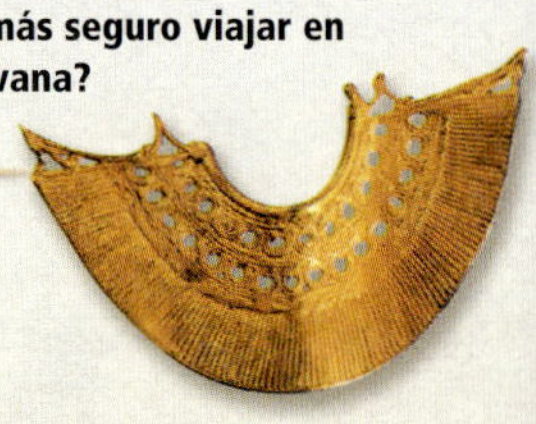

### 1500–1880 3.1

Barcos llenos de esclavos provenientes del continente africano cruzaron el Océano Atlántico y llegaron a las islas del Caribe, cambiando la demografía de las islas. **La herencia africana** transformó la expresión artística, literaria y cultural de la región. **Investiga cómo se ve esta influencia hoy día en el Caribe.**

## Teaching Suggestion

The Spanish maintained political and cultural dominance over the Caribbean for nearly four centuries through a central colonial authority ruling from Spain. Spanish dominance of the region came to an end with the Spanish American War in 1898. In contrast, the first settlers arrived in what is now the United States more than a century after Columbus landed in the Caribbean, and the United States won its independence in 1783. Have students think about why the situations in these two territories were so different. What factors contributed to such a long period of Spanish dominance of the region?

## Answers

**Época precolombina:** La distancia entres las Grandes y Pequeñas Antillas es aproximadamente 250 millas.
**1492:** Significaba que España se convirtió en un poder colonial.
**Siglo XVI:** Viajar en caravana era más seguro para poder protegerse de un ataque.
**1500–1880:** Esta influencia se ve en la música y la comida del Caribe.
**1822:** La isla se llama Hispaniola.
**1898:** España y Estados Unidos lucharon en la Guerra Hispano-norteamericana.
**1899–1953:** Porque creían en la causa anti-fascista y la anti-comunista.
**1959:** Cambiaron la cultura artística con música de Cuba. Introdujeron platillos cubanos a la Florida.

## Core Instruction

### TEACHING LA HISTORIA

1. Show students the timeline at the top of the page and point out the amount of time covered. Tell students that **Época precolombina** means, "time before the arrival of Columbus." Have students look at **¿Sabías que… ?** to point out how long the islands were inhabited before Columbus arrived. **(4 min.)**
2. Have students look at the photos and drawings in chronological order. Have them pay particular attention to the first and second illustrations. Point out that the colonial period lasted for nearly 400 years. **(2 min.)**
3. Have volunteers read the captions individually or in groups. Help students with any unfamiliar vocabulary. **(8 min.)**
4. Call on volunteers to read the questions at the end of each caption to the class. **(3 min.)**
5. Have students answer the questions for each caption as a class. Help students as needed. **(10 min.)**

## ¿Sabías que...?

Los primeros habitantes de la Hispaniola llegaron a la isla en piraguas desde Sudamérica alrededor de 2.600 a.C., aprovechando la corriente del Atlántico.

Visit Holt Online
**go.hrw.com**
KEYWORD: EXP3 CH3
Photo Tour

1800 — 1900 — 2000

**3.1 1822**
En 1822 los haitianos invadieron la República Dominicana y mantuvieron control de toda la isla durante veintidós años. La Trinitaria, un movimiento revolucionario encabezado por **Juan Pablo Duarte,** fue esencial en lograr la independencia de la República Dominicana en 1844. **¿Cómo se llama la isla que comparten Haití y la República Dominicana?**

**3.1 1898**
España perdió las islas de Puerto Rico y Cuba a Estados Unidos en la **Guerra Hispano-norteamericana** de 1898. El acorazado de España, la Infanta María Teresa, salió derrotado del puerto de Santiago de Cuba, marcando el fin de la época colonial de España. **¿Qué países lucharon en la Guerra Hispano-norteamericana?**

**1959** 2.1, 3.1
Después de la toma de poder de Fidel Castro en 1959, miles de cubanos se refugiaron en Estados Unidos. Entre 1965 y 1973 más de 260.000 refugiados cubanos llegaron a Estados Unidos. En la década de los ochenta de nuevo hubo un éxodo de gente en embarcaciones. **La flotilla de Mariel** trajo a más de 125.000 cubanos a las costas de la Florida. **¿Cómo cambiaron los refugiados cubanos la cultura de la Florida? Busca ejemplos.**

**1899–1953** 3.1
**El Regimiento 65,** fundado en 1899, fue un grupo de infantería compuesto de puertorriqueños que lucharon voluntariamente en **la Primera Guerra Mundial** al lado de Estados Unidos. También participó en campañas importantes de **la Guerra de Corea.** Cuatro soldados del regimiento recibieron la Cruz de Servicio Distinguido y 124 de ellos recibieron la Estrella de Plata. **¿Por qué crees que los soldados puertorriqueños se hicieron voluntarios estadounidenses en la Primera Guerra Mundial?**

## Connections

### Social Studies Link

After students have read the sections 1898 and 1959 on page 93, divide the class into two groups. One will research the economic, political, and social links between the U.S. and Puerto Rico, and the other those between the U.S. and Cuba, using sources from the library as well as from the Internet. Each group writes a two-page synopsis, peer-corrects it, and presents its findings to the class. You may wish to score each group on its written work. 3.1

## Cultures

### Practices and Perspectives

**El carnaval** is generally held on the last week of February before Lent. This event is deeply rooted in tradition and represents a mixture of Catholic, African, and native Caribbean elements. Have students work in groups to research this celebration and trace its roots. They can make masks, costumes, or food typical of the celebration and present them in a class culture fair. Have students compare these celebratory practices to those of Mardi Gras celebrations in the U.S. 2.1, 4.2

## Interdisciplinary Links

### El arte

**Music Link** The Puerto Rican **bomba** is a type of music deeply rooted in African tradition. This rhythm is typically heard in the northern coastal region near San Juan. The term **bomba** is the name of the drums and the pattern used to play this music accompanied by **maracas.** This style of music has made its way into the mainstream of Puerto Rican dance music. Have students find a type of music influenced by African rhythms in the U.S. What similarities does it have with Afro-Caribbean music forms? 4.2

### La arquitectura

**Architecture Link** The Spanish built the first strategic fortifications in the Americas on the islands of the Caribbean. They are impressive structures with thick stone walls and cannon positions built into them. The walls of the fortifications were usually built in a zigzag pattern, which was important for defense. Have students examine some historic forts in their region. Have them look at the building materials and the defense mechanisms built into them and compare these with Spanish forts.

## ¿Comprendes?

1. **¿Quiénes atacaban a los taínos frecuentemente? (los caribes)**
2. **¿Dónde construyeron sus fortalezas los españoles durante el siglo XVI? (en Puerto Rico, Cuba, Hispaniola, Cartagena)**
3. **¿Qué transformó la herencia africana en el Caribe? (la expresión artística, literaria y cultural)**
4. **¿Qué territorios caribeños perdió España en la Guerra Hispano-norteamericana? (Puerto Rico y Cuba)** 1.2, 3.1

### Language Note

Generally, Caribbean Spanish-speakers do not pronounce the "s" sound in a word unless it is the initial sound and tend to pronounce certain vowels nasally. In Puerto Rico and in the Dominican Republic, speakers will pronounce "l" instead of "r" when this sound does not appear at the beginning of a word. Speakers in Cuba tend not to pronounce the "r" sound in some words.

### Cultures

#### Products and Perspectives

**Taíno art** was very closely linked to ceremonial or religious purposes. The **Taíno** people made idols called *zemi,* out of stone, wood, shell or bone of different shapes and sizes. The *zemi* were a symbol of power and the **Taíno** used them to honor their many gods and ancestors during religious ceremonies. The **Taíno** culture also carved ceremonial stools, called *dujos,* out of wood. The *dujos* were used by chiefs and shamans exclusively and symbolized control over nature and society. Ask students to discuss what they know about other Native American art and the ceremonial purpose it served in the culture.

2.2

### Answers

**Época precolombina:** Usaban este mueble en ceremonias religiosas.
**Artesanía colonial:** La madera se usa mucho en la artesanía porque ha tenido un valor especial desde los tiempos precolombinos.
**1880:** El paisaje, la naturaleza
**1893:** Hay tristeza por la muerte de un niño, pero la muerte se celebra en algunas culturas como parte del ciclo de vida.
**1940:** La cabeza del gallo, las flores, los hierros, etc.
**1950:** En el uso de los colores café y blanco, las líneas, las formas de las personas, etc.
**2000:** Hay movimiento vertical y horizontal hacia los cuatro "vientos".
**2002:** Answers will vary.

# El arte del Caribe

ÉPOCA PRECOLOMBINA | 1850 | 19

### Precolombino 2.2, 3.1

**Los taínos** impresionaron a los españoles con su compleja y rica cultura. Ollas, joyas, muebles y otros artefactos precolombinos se encuentran en el Museo del Hombre Dominicano en Santo Domingo. **¿Para qué crees que los taínos usaban este mueble?**

Santos Figurines by Mariem Dalel

### 2.2 Artesanía colonial

Las esculturas elaboradas de madera fina son muy típicas de la isla de Puerto Rico. **¿Por qué crees que la madera es tan usada en la artesanía de Puerto Rico?**

### 2.2, 3.1 1880

*Jungla Cubana* fue pintado por el artista cubano **Esteban Chartrand** (1840–1884). Educado en Francia, Chartrand era un pintor muy de moda por sus paisajes tropicales reflejando el romanticismo europeo. **¿Qué te parece «romántico» en este cuadro?**

### 1893 2.1

En *El Velorio,* pintado en 1893 por el puertorriqueño **José Francisco Oller y Cesteros,** se celebra la muerte de un niño con bailes. Pero también se ve la tristeza profunda de la familia. **¿Por qué crees que hay celebración y tristeza al mismo tiempo?**

## Presentation

### TEACHING EL ARTE

1. Have students look at the time line at the top of the page and the dates in the timeline. **(2 min.)**
2. Point out the difference between the artistic styles on pages 94–95 and point out the time elapsed between them. **(2 min.)**
3. Have students take a look at each piece of artwork while you read the caption for each one. **(5 min.)**
4. Have students look at the painting *El velorio* at the bottom of page 94. Have them describe as a class what they see. **(5 min.)**
5. Read the questions following each caption. Call on volunteers to answer the questions. **(10 min.)**

Visit Holt Online
**go.hrw.com**
KEYWORD: EXP3 CH3
Photo Tour

## ¿Sabías que...?

*La mañana verde* (1943), obra de Wifredo Lam, alcanzó un precio de $1.267.500 en una subasta de Sotheby's en 1998.

1950 — 2000

**1940**
*El gallo* es uno de muchos cuadros con el mismo protagonista, el gallo, pintado por el artista cubano **Mariano Rodríguez** (1912–1990) en los años 1940. Mariano, como se le conoce, considera que sus obras son más expresionistas que abstractas porque al empezar sus obras observa la realidad de los objetos. **¿Qué detalles de *El gallo* te parecen tomados de la realidad?** 3.1

1.3, 3.1 **2000**
El cuadro *Cuatro Vientos* del pintor dominicano **Ramón Oviedo** (1924–) es un ejemplo del arte abstracto contemporáneo. **Describe el movimiento que ves en *Cuatro Vientos*.**

3.1 **1950**
El artista cubano **Wifredo Lam** (1902–1982) estudió arte en Madrid, España. Se ve la influencia del surrealismo de Pablo Picasso en esta obra, *Rumblings of the Earth* (1950). **Compara el estilo de este cuadro con *Guernica* de Picasso. Busca la obra de Picasso en la biblioteca. ¿En qué se parecen?**

1.2 **2002**
**Óscar de la Renta,** oriundo de la República Dominicana, ganó fama en el mundo de la moda trabajando en la casa de Elizabeth Arden en Nueva York. **Investiga qué elementos de una educación artística son necesarios en la carrera de diseño de modas.**

## Connections

### Thinking Critically

Caribbean artists have used many different artistic styles from Europe and around the world throughout history. Their work also reflects elements from their local culture. Have students investigate artistic styles used by artists in the United States such as pop art, abstract, expressionist, and so on, from 1940 to 2000. Have them compare the works by U.S. artists with *El gallo, Rumblings of the Earth,* and *Cuatro Vientos.* Have them point out the similarities and differences they see. What do they see in these paintings that clearly reflect the culture of the artist? 3.1, 4.2

## ¿Comprendes?

1. **Nombra algunos artefactos taínos. (ollas, joyas, muebles)**
2. **¿De qué están hechas las esculturas coloniales de Puerto Rico? (madera)**
3. **¿De dónde es Esteban Chartrand? (Cuba)**
4. **¿Qué está celebrando la gente en *El Velorio?* (la muerte de un niño)**
5. **¿Qué opina Mariano Rodríguez de sus obras? (Opina que son más expresionistas que abstractas.)**
6. **¿Qué influencia hay en la obra de Wilfredo Lam? (surrealismo)**
7. **¿Cuál es el estilo de *Cuatro Vientos* de Ramón Oviedo? (abstracto)**

1.2, 3.1

## Interdisciplinary Links

### El arte

**Literature Link** Fray Bartolomé de las Casas was one of the first religious figures to arrive in the Americas. He was interested in the native peoples of the Caribbean. De las Casas wrote a chronicle called *La brevísima historia de la destrucción de las Indias,* in which he defended the rights of the indigenous people of the Caribbean. Ask students what they know about chronicles describing U.S. Native American cultures and how they lived.

### El arte

**History Link** Colonial art in the Caribbean was heavily influenced by artistic styles from Europe. Many colonial-era artists were romanticists and painted landscapes or scenes that captured the feeling of the times. Colonial-era art was also religious in nature. Artists portrayed Jesus Christ, Catholic saints, and other religious figures in paintings, sculptures, and drawings. Ask students to find examples of colonial-era art from the Caribbean and share their findings with the class.

## Assess

**Assessment Program**
**Prueba: Geocultura,** pp. 55–56, 75–76

**Online Assessment**
**my.hrw.com**

**Test Generator**

**Assess** **Differentiated Instruction** See the Differentiated Instruction CD-ROM.

Capítulo 3

# Planning Guide

## Todo tiene solución

| Chapter Section | | Print Resources |
|---|---|---|
| **Geocultura**<br>• El Caribe | pp. 90–95 | Video Guide, pp. 15–16/Lab Book, p. 62 |
| **Vocabulario 1**<br>• Opinions about people and classes<br>**Gramática 1**<br>• Repaso: Verb + infinitive<br>• Repaso: Subjunctive with will or wish<br>• Subjunctive with negation or denial | pp. 98–103<br>pp. 104–109 | Vocabulario 3.1, 3.2; Bell Work 3.1, 3.2, 3.3, 3.4<br>Cuaderno de vocabulario y gramática, pp. 25–30<br>Cuaderno de actividades, pp. 21–23<br>Activities for Communication, pp. 9–10<br>Grammar Tutor for Students of Spanish, pp. 129–132 |
| **Cultura: Comparaciones**<br>**Cultura: Comunidad** | p. 110<br>p. 111 | Video Guide, pp. 18, 19/Lab Book, p. 63 |
| **Vocabulario 2**<br>• Relationships<br>**Gramática 2**<br>• Repaso: Future tense<br>• Conditional<br>• More uses of the conditional | pp. 112–117<br>pp. 118–123 | Vocabulario 3.3, 3.4; Bell Work 3.5, 3.6, 3.7, 3.8<br>Cuaderno de vocabulario y gramática, pp. 31–36<br>Cuaderno de actividades, pp. 25–27<br>Activities for Communication, pp. 11–12<br>Grammar Tutor for Students of Spanish, pp. 133–134 |
| **Novela en video**<br>**Lectura informativa**<br>• América en Español<br>**Leamos**<br>• El eclipse<br>**Escribamos**<br>• La impresión equivocada | pp. 124–125<br>pp. 126–127<br>pp. 128–130<br>p. 131 | Cuaderno de actividades, p. 28<br>Reading Strategies and Skills Handbook<br>Interactive Advanced Reader<br>Video Guide, pp. 20–22/Lab Book, pp. 64–65 |
| **Prepárate para el examen**<br>• Repaso de vocabulario y gramática | pp. 132–135 | Picture Sequences, Situación, Ch. 3<br>Activities for Communication, pp. 45, 59–60 |
| **Integración**<br>• Repaso cumulativo | pp. 136–137 | Fine Art, Ch. 3<br>Cuaderno de actividades, pp. 29–30<br>Reading Strategies and Skills Handbook<br>Interactive Advanced Reader |

For correlations to national standards, see point-of-use references throughout the chapter.

Visit Holt Online
**go.hrw.com**
KEYWORD: EXP3 CH3
Online Edition

## Pacing Suggestions

| | Essential | Recommended | Optional |
|---|---|---|---|
| **Vocabulario 1**<br>• Opinions about people and classes<br>• **Nota cultural** | ✔ | | |
| **Gramática 1**<br>• Repaso: Verb + infinitive<br>• Repaso: Subjunctive with will or wish<br>• Subjunctive with negation or denial<br>• **Nota cultural** | ✔ | | |
| **Cultura: Comparaciones** | | ✔ | |
| **Cultura: Comunidad** | | | ✔ |
| **Vocabulario 2**<br>• Relationships<br>• **Nota cultural** | ✔ | | |
| **Gramática 2**<br>• Repaso: Future tense<br>• Conditional<br>• More uses of the conditional<br>• **Nota cultural** | ✔ | | |
| **Novela en video**<br>• Episodio 3: **Clara perspectiva** | | ✔ | |
| **Lectura informativa**<br>• **América en Español** | | | ✔ |
| **Leamos**<br>• **El eclipse**<br>**Escribamos**<br>• **La impresión equivocada** | | ✔ | |
| **Prepárate para el examen** | | ✔ | |
| **Integración** | | | ✔ |

## Technology Resources

### ¡Exprésate! Online
- Student Edition with multi-media
- SoundBooth recording tool
- Interactive activities with feedback
- Self-tests with feedback
- Cuaderno de actividades (interactive workbook)
- Cuaderno de vocabulario y gramática (interactive workbook)
- Live Ink™ Reading Help
- Holt Online Assessment

### DVD Tutor, Disc 1
- GeoVisión
- GramaVisión
- VideoNovela
- Cultura
- Variedades

### Interactive Tutor
- Interactive practice games
- Writing and recording workshops

### Audio Program
- Textbook listening activities
- Assessment listening activities
- Songs

### One-Stop Planner
- Complete media and print resources
- ExamView® Pro Test Generator
- Holt Calendar Planner

### PuzzlePro
- Customizable word games

## Assessment

**Geocultura**
**Vocabulario 1 / Gramática 1**
**Vocabulario 2 / Gramática 2**
**Leamos**
**Escribamos**
**Prepárate para el examen**

### Assessment Program
**Prueba: Geocultura,** pp. 55–56
**Pruebas,** pp. 41–42, 43–44, 45–46
**Pruebas,** pp. 47–48, 49–50, 51–52
**Prueba,** p. 53
**Prueba,** p. 54
**Examen: Capítulo 3,** pp. 229–234
**Examen oral: Capítulo 3,** p. 240
**Alternative Assessment,** pp. 375, 387, 399

### Online Assessment
**my.hrw.com**

### Test Generator
**ExamView® Pro Test Generator**

Planning Guide

# Projects

## Todo tiene solución

### Los estereotipos

Students will research stereotypes that students in Spanish-speaking countries have of students in the United States. They should find out what the stereotypes are based on (movies, books, exchange student experiences) and suggest ways to combat these stereotypes.

**SUGGESTED SEQUENCE**

1. Students interview a native speaker of Spanish, such as an exchange student or an e-mail buddy in another country, to find out what stereotypes people have of students in the United States. They can also research information on the Internet if they are not able to personally speak with a foreign student.
2. Students list the stereotypes that foreign students have of U.S. students.
3. Students gather specific information about why these stereotypes exist and what they are based on.
4. Students prepare a short presentation for the class in which they list stereotypes and reasons for them, and suggest ways to combat these stereotypes. 3.2

### Partner Class Project

Students will create and carry out a survey about the issue of stereotypes. Because stereotypes are a sensitive issue, you may wish to monitor or modify the topics discussed in the survey. Students will work in pairs to prepare a five-question survey, conduct the survey, and compile the results to present to the class. Have students prepare five questions with quantifiable answers. (How often do you base your opinions of people on stereotypes? 1-Often, 2-Sometimes, 3-Seldom, 4-Never). One question should relate to stereotypes of Spanish speakers. Each student should interview five people, including at least one native speaker of Spanish, and then pairs can get together to compile the results and prepare a chart and a presentation on the computer to present the results to the class. 1.1

### e-community

**e-mail forum:**

Post the following questions on the classroom e-mail forum:

**¿Qué estereotipos tenemos que combatir en nuestro colegio?**

All students will contribute to the list and then share the items. 1.3

### Grading the projects

Suggested point distribution (100 points total)

Accuracy of information .......30

Written documentation ........30

Presentation to class ..........40

### Game Bank

For game ideas, see pages T64–T67.

# Todo tiene solución

## Los taínos

The original inhabitants of many Caribbean islands were the **Taínos,** a branch of the Arawak-speaking peoples who dominated the region. They were peaceful, skilled farmers with little interest in warfare. The **Taínos** enjoyed a developed culture which included playing ceremonial ball games similar to those of the Aztec and earlier Mayan cultures. Columbus had a peaceful encounter with the **Taínos** in 1492 on the island of Hispaniola (now comprising Haiti and the Dominican Republic), and he described them in utopian terms, claiming they lived in Edenic innocence. Unfortunately, European diseases for which the **Taínos** had no natural defense reduced the entire population to an estimated 500 people within fifty years of Columbus's arrival. Chapter 1 of the book *Caribbean,* by James Michener, has a fact-based

fictional record of **Taíno** life before Columbus. Have students research information about the **Taínos** and prepare a short presentation for the class about how the **Taínos** lived. 1.3, 3.1

## Receta

Cuban sandwiches are delicious and simple to prepare. Cubans in Florida usually call this dish **tortas** or **sándwiches a la plancha.** You might have students make the following recipe as a class project or for extra credit.

### Sándwiches cubanos

**para 2 personas**

un trozo mediano de pan *(French or Italian bread or hard-crust loaf)*

mantequilla

mostaza

1 rebanada de carne de puerco asada

1 o 2 rebanadas de jamón

2 rebanadas pequeñas de queso suizo

varias rodajas de pepino encurtido *(pickle)*

Caliente una sartén o si tiene una waflera *(waffle iron)* es mejor. Corte en dos partes el pan. Embarre la mantequilla (y la mostaza y mayonesa, si quiere) en cada una de las mitades. En una de las mitades, coloque las rebanadas de puerco y de jamón junto con el queso y el pepino encurtido. Después junte las dos partes y colóquelas en la sartén caliente o en la waflera y presione de tres a cuatro minutos hasta que quede dorado el pan. 2.2, 3.1

# Listening Activity Scripts

## Todo tiene solución



### Vocabulario en acción 1

**1** p. 100, CD 3, Track 1

Me llamo Kim y soy asiática. Me choca la actitud de muchos estudiantes hacia los asiáticos. Muchos de mis amigos creen que los asiáticos somos muy tímidos y sólo nos gusta estudiar el cálculo o el álgebra. Estos son estereotipos, y no son ciertos. Yo soy muy abierta y sociable y mi pasión es la literatura. Mis compañeros no son malas personas, simplemente tienen una impresión equivocada a causa de su ignorancia. Muchas veces la gente tiene prejuicios sobre las cosas que no conoce. Es importante conocer a personas de diferentes culturas para combatir la discriminación en este país.

**Answers to Activity 1**

| | | |
|---|---|---|
| 1. falsa | 3. cierta | 5. falsa |
| 2. falsa | 4. falsa | 6. cierta |

**4** p. 101, CD 3, Track 2

Mi clase favorita este semestre es la de literatura latinoamericana. Estamos leyendo cuentos de Gabriel García Márquez y ¡son geniales! Estoy seguro que voy a aprobar el curso. Por otro lado, no me gusta nada la clase de geometría. Las pruebas son demasiado difíciles. Y aunque las pruebas de ciencias sociales son fáciles, el profesor nos da tres horas de tarea cada noche y no tengo tiempo para hacerla. ¡No aguanto más! Voy a hablar con el consejero a ver si puedo dejar esa clase. Así tendré más tiempo para estudiar para el examen de álgebra. Me encanta la clase de álgebra y quiero sacar una buena nota porque quiero tomar un curso avanzado el próximo semestre. Además, tengo mucho que hacer para la clase de geografía. Tengo que dar una presentación la próxima semana, y ahora la profesora dice que tenemos un examen también. ¡Esto es el colmo! Ella nos da demasiado trabajo y la clase es muy aburrida.

**Answers to Activity 4**

| | |
|---|---|
| literatura | le gusta |
| geometría | no le gusta |
| ciencias sociales | no le gusta |
| álgebra | le gusta |
| geografía | no le gusta |

**8** p. 103, CD 3, Track 3

1. —A mi parecer, las mujeres no deben practicar deportes como el kárate y la esgrima.
   —¡Al contrario! Las mujeres pueden hacer todas las actividades que hacen los hombres.
2. —Me parece que los estudiantes que practican deportes no sacan buenas notas en clase.
   —¡Qué va! Mi amigo juega al fútbol americano y tiene las mejores notas de la clase. Y muchos otros practican deportes y aprueban todos los cursos.
3. —Creo que es difícil para los extranjeros asistir a nuestro colegio porque la gente tiene muchos prejuicios.
   —Bueno, es que por su ignorancia, muchos estudiantes maltratan a los extranjeros.
4. —¿Sabías que el director va a enseñar geometría? Será genial, ¿no?
   —No me parece buena idea que el director enseñe geometría.
5. —Mi horario este semestre es demasiado difícil. Tengo cinco clases y nunca tengo tiempo para descansar. ¡No aguanto más!
   —Tienes razón. Cinco clases es demasiado. Creo que el consejero te puede ayudar.
6. —Los estudiantes del colegio tienen una actitud negativa hacia la universidad.
   —No estoy de acuerdo contigo para nada. Todos mis amigos piensan asistir a la universidad.

**Answers to Activity 8**

1. b 2. b 3. a 4. b 5. a 6. b

### Gramática en acción 1

**15** p. 106, CD 3, Track 4

1. Espera estudiar la literatura de Latinoamérica.
2. Dice que le gusta viajar y conocer otros países.
3. Sus padres prefieren que se quede en casa.
4. Ellos dicen que es necesario que se enfoque en sus estudios.
5. Antonio quiere graduarse de la universidad y ser profesor.
6. Su hermano le pide que trabaje con él en su negocio.
7. Antonio piensa que puede ser una buena idea.

**Answers to Activity 15**

1. a 2. a 3. b 4. b 5. a 6. b 7. a

For Student Response Forms, see the *Lab Book,* pp. 21–24.

**18** p. 108, CD 3, Track 5

1. —¡Huy! ¡La tarea de geografía es muy difícil!
   —Pues no creo que sea tan difícil.
2. —El profesor cree que no somos aplicados.
   —Es cierto que él tiene una impresión equivocada de nosotros.
3. —No es justo que nos quite tantos puntos por errores pequeños.
   —No es verdad que no sea justo. Los errores que él encuentra son cosas que tenemos que saber.
4. —Me parece que sería buena idea hablar con él y pedirle más ayuda antes del próximo examen.
   —Estoy de acuerdo en que debemos hablar con él.
5. —Pero es tan antipático que me da miedo hablar con él.
   —No es cierto que sea antipático. Simplemente es estricto.
6. —Él se va a poner feliz si sabe que nos preocupan nuestras notas.
   —Creo que tienes razón.

**Answers to Activity 18**
1. b 2. a 3. b 4. a 5. b 6. a

## Vocabulario en acción 2

**23** p. 114, CD 3, Track 9

1. Ángela vio a Jorge y a Julia juntos ayer. Ahora Ángela cree que Jorge le es infiel.
2. Enrique admitió su error y le pidió perdón a Margarita.
3. Qué bueno que mis hermanas se comuniquen todos los días.
4. Andrés intentó disculparse, pero Pedro no le hizo caso.
5. Diana y Cristina son buenas amigas. Siempre se abrazan cuando se ven.
6. Eduardo le compró un regalo a Laura para su cumpleaños. Él nunca olvida esa fecha.

**Answers to Activity 23**
1. d 2. a 3. c 4. f 5. e 6. b

## Gramática en acción 2

**32** p. 118, CD 3, Track 10

1. Marta y Leticia se conocieron en la escuela primaria.
2. Ahora las dos están en el último año de colegio, y todavía son muy buenas amigas.
3. Siempre serán amigas, aún después de graduarse.
4. El año que viene, Marta irá a California y Leticia asistirá a la universidad de Nueva York, pero podrán visitarse de vez en cuando.
5. Hace poco decidieron hacer un viaje en el verano.
6. Harán un viaje en bicicleta por dos o tres semanas y acamparán en los parques de noche.
7. El último viaje que hicieron juntas fue un desastre.
8. Seguramente este viaje será mucho mejor porque lo planearán bien.

**Answers to Activity 32**
1. pasado 2. presente 3. futuro 4. futuro 5. pasado 6. futuro 7. pasado 8. futuro

**41** p. 122, CD 3, Track 11

1. Si yo pudiera hablar con el presidente de nuestro país, le preguntaría qué podría hacer él para mejorar la actitud de muchos jóvenes hacia la educación.
2. Si yo fuera tu hermana, estoy segura de que me pelearía contigo todos los días.
3. Si yo tuviera más dinero, le compraría una bicicleta a mi novio.
4. Si yo fuera profesor de álgebra, les haría caso a todos los estudiantes.
5. Si yo pudiera tomar un curso de literatura clásica, leería sin parar.
6. Si yo tuviera la oportunidad de hablar con mi ex-novia, le pediría perdón y le daría un abrazo.

**Answers to Activity 41**
1. b 2. d 3. f 4. e 5. c 6. a

## Prepárate para el examen capítulo 3

**1** p. 132, CD 3, Track 14

For script, see *Teacher's Edition,* p. 132.

**6** p. 133, CD 3, Track 15

For script, see *Teacher's Edition,* p. 133.

## Integración capítulos 1–3

**1** p. 136, CD 3, Track 16

For script, see *Teacher's Edition,* p. 136.

# 50-Minute Lesson Plans

For more customized Lesson Plans, see the *Lesson Planner with Differentiated Instruction.*

## Todo tiene solución

### Day 1

**Objective**
*Complaining*

**Core Instruction**
**Chapter Opener**, pp. 96–97
**10 min.**
- See Chapter Objectives, p. 96, and Using the Photo, p. 97.

**Vocabulario en acción 1,** pp. 98–103
- Have students do Bell Work, p. 98
- See Teaching **Vocabulario,** p. 98. **10 min.**
- See Teaching **¡Exprésate!,** p. 98. **5 min.**
- Play Audio CD 3, Tr. 1 for Activity 1, p. 100. **5 min.**
- Have students do Activities 2–3, p. 100. **10 min.**
- Play Audio CD 3, Tr. 2 for Activity 4, p. 101. **10 min.**

**Optional Resources**
- Advanced Learners, p. 99 ▲
- Multiple Intelligences, p. 99
- Slower Pace Learners, p. 101 ◆
- Multiple Intelligences, p. 101

**Homework Suggestions**
Cuaderno de vocabulario y gramática, pp. 25–27
❀ 1.2

### Day 2

**Objective**
*Expressing an opinion*

**Core Instruction**
**Vocabulario en acción 1,** pp. 98–103
- Have students do Activities 5–6, p. 101. **10 min.**
- See Teaching **¡Exprésate!,** p. 102. **10 min.**
- Have students do Activities 7–9, p 103. **20 min.**
- See **Comunicación** suggestion p. 103. **10 min.**

**Optional Resources**
- Advanced Learners, p. 103 ▲
- Special Learning Needs, p. 103 ●

**Homework Suggestions**
Study for **Prueba: Vocabulario 1**
❀ 1.1, 1.2, 1.3

### Day 3

**Objective**
*Verb + infinitive*

**Core Instruction**
**Vocabulario en acción 1,** pp. 98–103
- Review **Vocabulario en acción 1,** pp. 98–103. **5 min.**
- Give **Prueba: Vocabulario 1. 20 min.**

**Gramática en acción 1,** pp. 104–109
- Have students do Bell Work, p. 104. **5 min.**
- See Teaching **Gramática,** p. 104. **10 min.**
- Have students do Activities 10–13, pp. 104–105. **10 min.**

**Optional Resources**
- Slower Pace Learners, p. 105 ◆
- Special Learning Needs, p. 105 ●

**Homework Suggestions**
Cuaderno de vocabulario y gramática, pp. 28–30
Cuaderno de actividades, pp. 21–23
❀ 1.1, 1.2

### Day 4

**Objective**
*Subjunctive with will or wish*

**Core Instruction**
**Gramática en acción 1,** pp. 104–109
- Have students do Bell Work, p. 106. **5 min.**
- See Teaching **Gramática,** p. 106. **10 min.**
- Have students do Activity 14, p. 106. **10 min.**
- Play Audio CD 3, Tr. 4 for Activity 15, p. 106. **10 min.**
- Have students do Activities 16–17B, p. 107. **15 min.**

**Optional Resources**
- Advanced Learners, p. 107 ▲
- Special Learning Needs, p. 107 ●

**Homework Suggestions**
Cuaderno de vocabulario y gramática, pp. 28–30
Cuaderno de actividades, pp. 21–33
❀ 1.1, 1.2, 1.3

### Day 5

**Objective**
*Subjunctive with negation or denial*

**Core Instruction**
**Gramática en acción 1,** pp. 104–109
- Have students do Bell Work, p. 108. **5 min.**
- See Teaching **Gramática,** p. 108. **10 min.**
- Play Audio CD 3, Tr. 5 for Activity 18, p. 108. **5 min.**
- Have students do Activities 19–22, pp. 108–109. **30 min.**

**Optional Resources**
- Slower Pace Learners, p. 109 ◆
- Multiple Intelligences, p. 109

**Homework Suggestions**
Study for **Prueba: Gramática 1**
Cuaderno de vocabulario y gramática, pp. 28–30
Cuaderno de actividades, pp. 21–23
❀ 1.1, 1.2, 1.3

### Day 6

**Objective**
*Interviews from around the Spanish-speaking world*

**Core Instruction**
**Gramática en acción 1,** pp. 104–109
- Review **Gramática en acción 1,** pp. 104–109. **5 min.**
- Give **Prueba: Gramática 1. 20 min.**

**Cultura,** pp. 110–111
- See Teaching **Cultura,** p. 110. **10 min.**
- Play Audio CD 3, Tr. 6–8, p. 110, or show **VideoCultura. 15 min.**

**Optional Resources**
- Advanced Learners, p. 111 ▲
- Multiple Intelligences, p. 111

**Homework Suggestions**
Cuaderno de actividades, p. 24
Online Practice (**go.hrw.com,** Keyword: EXP3 CH3)
❀ 1.2, 4.2, 5.1

### Day 7

**Objective**
*Making suggestions*

**Core Instruction**
**Vocabulario en acción 2,** pp. 112–117
- See Teaching **Vocabulario,** p. 112. **10 min.**
- See Teaching **¡Exprésate!** p. 112. **10 min.**
- Play Audio CD 3, Tr. 9 for Activity 23, p. 114. **5 min.**
- Have students do Activities 24–27, pp. 114–115. **25 min.**

**Optional Resources**
- Heritage Speakers, p. 113 ■
- Advanced Learners, p. 113 ▲
- Special Learning Needs, p. 113 ●
- Advanced Learners, p. 115 ▲
- Special Learning Needs, p. 115 ●

**Homework Suggestions**
Cuaderno de vocabulario y gramática, pp. 31–33
❀ 1.1, 1.2

### Day 8

**Objective**
*Apologizing*

**Core Instruction**
**Vocabulario en acción 2,** pp. 112–117
- See Teaching **¡Exprésate!,** p. 116. **10 min.**
- Have students do Activities 28–31, p. 117. **30 min.**
- See **Comunicación** suggestion, p. 117. **10 min.**

**Optional Resources**
- Slower Pace Learners, p. 117 ◆
- Multiple Intelligences, p. 117

**Homework Suggestions**
Study for **Prueba: Vocabulario 2**
Cuaderno de vocabulario y gramática, pp. 31–33
❀ 1.1, 1.2

- For information on the **Geocultura** pages, see the *Lesson Planner with Differentiated Instruction.*
- For more detailed information on benchmarks, see point-of-use correlations on each page.
- To edit and create your own lesson plans, see the **One-Stop** Planner® CD-ROM

**KEY**
- ▲ Advanced Learners
- ◆ Slower Pace Learners
- ● Special Learning Needs
- ■ Heritage Speakers

## Day 9

**Objective**
*Future tense*

**Core Instruction**
**Vocabulario en acción 2,** pp. 112–117
- Review **Vocabulario en acción 2,** pp.112–117. **5 min.**
- Give **Prueba: Vocabulario 2. 20 min.**
- **Gramática en acción 2**, pp. 118–123
- See Teaching **Gramática,** p. 118. **10 min.**
- Play Audio CD 3, Tr. 10 for Activity 32, p. 118. **5 min.**
- Have students do Activities 33–34, pp. 118–119. **10 min.**

**Optional Resources**
- Advanced Learners, p. 119 ▲
- Special Learning Needs, p. 119 ●

**Homework Suggestions**
Cuaderno de vocabulario y gramática, pp 34–36
Cuaderno de actividades, pp. 25–27
1.2

## Day 10

**Objective**
*Conditional tense*

**Core Instruction**
**Gramática en acción 2,** pp. 118–123
- Have students do Activities 35–36, p. 119. **15 min.**
- Have students do Bell Work, p. 120. **5 min.**
- See Teaching **Gramática,** p. 120. **10 min.**
- Have students do Activities 37–40, pp. 120–121. **20 min.**

**Optional Resources**
- Advanced Learners, p. 121 ▲
- Multiple Intelligences, p. 121

**Homework Suggestions**
Cuaderno de vocabulario y gramática, pp. 34–36
Cuaderno de actividades, pp. 25–27
1.1, 1.2, 1.3

## Day 11

**Objective**
*More uses of the conditional*

**Core Instruction**
**Gramática en acción 2,** pp. 118–123
- Have students do Bell Work, p. 122. **5 min.**
- See Teaching **Gramática,** p. 122. **10 min.**
- Play Audio CD 3, Tr. 11 for Activity 41, p. 122. **5 min.**
- Have students do Activities 42–44, p. 123. **30 min.**

**Optional Resources**
- **Comunicación,** p. 123
- Slower Pace Learners, p. 123 ◆
- Special Learning Needs, p. 123 ●

**Homework Suggestions**
Study for **Prueba: Gramática 2**
Cuaderno de vocabulario y gramática, pp. 34–36
Cuaderno de actividades, pp. 25–27
1.1, 1.2, 1.3

## Day 12

**Objective**
*More uses of the conditional*

**Core Instruction**
**Gramática en acción 2,** pp. 118–123
- Review **Gramática en acción 2,** pp. 118–123. **10 min.**
- Give **Prueba: Gramática 2. 20 min.**

**Novela en video,** pp. 124–125
- Show **VideoNovela.** See Teaching **Novela en video,** p. 124. **20 min.**

**Optional Resources**
- **Comunicación,** p. 125

**Assessment Program:**
- **Prueba: Aplicación 2**

**Homework Suggestions**
Cuaderno de vocabulario y gramática, pp. 34–36
1.2, 3.1

## Day 13

**Objective**
*Developing listening and reading skills*

**Core Instruction**
**Lectura informativa,** pp. 126–127
- See Teaching **Lectura informativa,** p. 126. **25 min.**

**Leamos y escribamos,** pp. 128–131
- See Teaching **Leamos,** p. 128. **25 min.**

**Optional Resources**
- Slower Pace Learners, p. 127 ◆
- Special Learning Needs, p. 127 ●
- Advanced Learners, p. 129 ▲
- Multiple Intelligences, p. 129

**Homework Suggestions**
Cuaderno de actividades, p. 28
1.2, 1.3, 3.2

## Day 14

**Objective**
*Developing reading and writing skills*

**Core Instruction**
**Leamos y escribamos,** pp. 128–131
- See Teaching **Escribamos,** p. 130. **35 min.**

**Prepárate para el examen,** pp. 132–135
- Play Audio CD 3, Tr. 14 for Activity 1, p. 132. **5 min.**
- Have students do Activities 2–3, p. 132. **10 min.**

**Optional Resources**
- Slower Pace Learners, p. 131 ◆
- Special Learning Needs, p. 131 ●

**Homework Suggestions**
**Taller del escritor,** p. 131
1.2, 1.3

## Day 15

**Objective**
*Chapter review*

**Core Instruction**
**Prepárate para el examen,** pp. 132–135
- Have students do Activities 4–5, p. 133. **15 min.**
- Play Audio CD 3, Tr. 15 for Activity 6, p. 133. **5 min.**
- Have students do Activity 7, p. 133. **5 min.**

**Integración,** pp. 136–137
- Play Audio CD 3, Tr. 16 for Activity 1, p. 136. **5 min.**
- Have students do Activities 2–6, pp. 136–137. **20 min.**

**Optional Resources**
- Play Pre-AP Audio CD 1, Tr. 9, for Pre-AP Practice, p. 133
- Game, p. 135
- Fine Art Connection, p. 137

**Homework Suggestions**
Study for Chapter Test
1.1, 1.2, 1.3

## Day 16/Test

**Core Instruction**
**Chapter Test 50 min.**

**Optional Resources**
**Assessment Program**
- **Prueba: Lectura**
- **Prueba: Escritura**
- Test Generator

**Homework Suggestions**
Cuaderno de actividades, pp. 29–30

50-Minute Lesson Plans

# Indiana
## The Hoosier State

Indianapolis at night

Indiana Dunes State Park

### Chapter 3

The following chart presents *¡Exprésate!* Chapter 3 correlations to the Indiana Academic Standards for World Languages, Grade 11. The correlations here are to the *Student Edition* (SE) and *Teacher's Edition* (TE) only. For additional teaching resources, see pages 95A-95B

| INDIANA ACADEMIC STANDARDS | | | CHAPTER 3 SE/TE CORRELATIONS |
|---|---|---|---|
| **Standard 1 COMMUNICATION:** | | | |
| **Write and speak in a language other than English** | 11.1.1 | Initiate, sustain, and close conversations in limited yet varied situations. | SE: 103, 115, 121, 137<br>TE: 98, 100, 102, 112, 116, 132 |
| | 11.1.2 | Exchange detailed information and opinions orally on a variety of topics. | SE: 103, 111, 115<br>TE: 103, 111, 115, 121, 132, 136 |
| | 11.1.3 | Exchange detailed information and opinions in written form on a variety of topics. | SE: 131<br>TE: 121, 129 |
| | 11.1.5 | Recognize and use situation-appropriate non-verbal communication. | TE: 124 |
| | 11.1.6 | Use speaking and listening strategies to facilitate communication. | SE: 105, 107, 109<br>TE: 118 |
| **Standard 2 COMMUNICATION:** | | | |
| **Interpret information in a language other than English** *Learners interpret written and spoken language on a variety of topics. (Interpretive)* | 11.2.1 | Respond to everyday requests, commands, and directions. | SE: 99, 113 |
| | 11.2.2 | Demonstrate comprehension of both authentic and non-authentic written and spoken language through developmentally appropriate tasks. | SE: 125, 127, 130<br>TE: 110, 124, 126, 128 |
| | 11.2.3 | Make educated guesses about meaning in unfamiliar written and spoken contexts. | SE: 124, 128<br>TE: 124, 128 |
| **Standard 3 COMMUNICATION:** | | | |
| **Present information in a language other than English** *Learners present to an audience of listeners or readers on a variety of topics. (Presentational)* | 11.3.2 | Produce and present creative material on a variety of topics. | SE: 137<br>TE: 95C, 111, 125, 136 |
| | 11.3.4 | Compose cohesive written information using appropriate formats and more varied vocabulary and structures. | SE: 131<br>TE: 95C, 130, 131 |
| **Standard 4 CULTURES:** | | | |
| **Develop awareness of other cultures.** *Learners examine, experience, and reflect on the relationships among the practices, products, and perspectives of the cultures studied.* | 11.4.1 | Analyze and reflect on cultural practices of the target cultures. | SE: 111, 127<br>TE: 110, 126, 136 |
| | 11.4.2 | Describe products, perspectives, and symbols of the target cultures. | SE: 111, 127<br>TE: 110, 126, 136 |
| | 11.4.3 | Discuss factors that influence practices, products, and perspectives. | SE: 111, 127<br>TE: 110, 126, 136 |
| | 11.4.4 | Recognize the interrelations among the practices, products, and perspectives of the target cultures. | SE: 111, 127<br>TE: 110, 126, 136 |

| | | | |
|---|---|---|---|
| | **11.4.5** | Explain contributions from other cultures. | **SE:** 127<br>**TE:** 126, 136 |
| **Standard 5 CONNECTIONS:** | | | |
| **Make connections to other content areas**<br>*Learners use the target language to expand their knowledge of and make connections among multiple content areas.* | **11.5.1** | Make connections with other content areas through resources intended for native speakers. | **SE:** 136 |
| | **11.5.2** | Design and share activities and materials that integrate the target language and cultures with concepts and skills from other content areas. | **SE:** 137<br>**TE:** 95C, 135 |
| **Standard 6 CONNECTIONS:** | | | |
| **Access and connect information through various media**<br>*Learners strengthen language proficiency and cultural knowledge by using current digital media and authentic resources.* | **11.6.1** | Use digital media and culturally authentic resources to build vocabulary, improve reading ability, and encourage cultural awareness. | **SE:** 99, 100, 101, 116, 120, 124<br>**TE:** 95E, 95F |
| | **11.6.2** | Use digital media and culturally authentic resources to study target cultures. | **SE:** 110, 124 |
| | **11.6.3** | Identify and evaluate resources intended for native speakers. | **SE:** 110, 124 |
| **Standard 7 COMPARISONS:** | | | |
| **Investigate the nature of language and culture**<br>*Learners understand the nature of language and culture through comparisons of the languages and cultures studied and their own.* | **11.7.1** | Use elements of word formation to expand vocabulary and derive meaning. | **SE:** 109, 119<br>**TE:** 104, 118 |
| | **11.7.2** | Recognize and use a variety of language structures. | **SE:** 118-123, 131, 137<br>**TE:** 104-109 |
| | **11.7.3** | Compare and use idiomatic, colloquial, and proverbial expressions in the target language. | **SE:** 103, 137<br>**TE:** 102 |
| | **11.7.5** | Compare systems of other cultures and the learner's own culture. | **SE:** 111<br>**TE:** 110, 126, 127 |
| | **11.7.6** | Compare and contrast elements that shape cultural identity in the learner's heritage and in the target cultures. | **SE:** 111<br>**TE:** 110, 126, 127 |
| **Standard 8 COMMUNITIES:** | | | |
| **Become an active global citizen by experiencing languages and cultures in multiple settings**<br>*Learners use their knowledge of the target language and cultures both within and beyond the school setting for personal enrichment and civic engagement.* | **11.8.1** | Share experiences from the world language classroom with others. | **SE:** 126-127<br>**TE:** 95C |
| | **11.8.2** | Investigate and share with others the influences of the target language and cultures on the community. | **SE:** 111, 126-127<br>**TE:** 136 |
| | **11.8.3** | Show evidence of becoming a life-long learner by using the target language and cultural knowledge for personal enrichment. | **SE:** 111<br>**TE:** 95C, 95D, 136 |

# Chapter Opener

## Meeting the National Standards

**Communication**
Comunicación, pp. 101, 103, 105, 107, 109, 115, 117, 119, 121, 123, 125
Game, p. 135
Situación, p. 137

**Cultures**
Products and Perspectives, pp. 91, 94, 117
Practices and Perspectives, pp. 93, 101, 107
Nota cultural, pp. 100, 106
Culture Project, p. 136

**Connections**
Atlas Interactivo Mundial, pp. 91, 111
Social Studies Link, p. 93
Thinking Critically, pp. 95, 100
Los taínos, p. 95D
Receta, p. 95D
Multiple Intelligences, p. 109
History Link, p. 129
Language Arts Link, p. 130
Heritage Speakers, p. 130
Analyzing, p. 137
Extension, p. 137

**Comparisons**
El arte, p. 93
En inglés, p. 106
Language to Language, pp. 107, 134
Comparaciones, p. 110

**Communities**
Comunidad y oficio, p. 111
Community Link, p. 127

## Learning Tips

To help students learn more words and phrases for complaining, disagreeing, making suggestions, and apologizing, encourage them to watch Spanish language programming and listen for the expressions used.

# Capítulo 3

# Todo tiene solución

**OBJETIVOS**

**In this chapter you will learn to**
- complain
- express an opinion and disagree
- make suggestions
- apologize

**And you will use**
- verb + infinitive
- subjunctive with will or wish
- subjunctive with negation or denial
- future tense
- conditional

**¿Qué ves en la foto?**
- ¿Cómo se sienten estas personas?
- ¿De qué están hablando?
- ¿Has tenido una experiencia similar? ¿Qué hiciste?

| Suggested pacing: | Traditional Schedule | Block Schedule |
|---|---|---|
| Vocabulario 1/Gramática 1 | 5 1/2 days | 2 1/2 blocks |
| Cultura | 1/2 day | 1/2 block |
| Vocabulario 2/Gramática 2 | 5 1/2 days | 2 1/2 blocks |
| Novela | 1/2 day | 1/2 block |
| Lectura informativa | 1/2 day | 1/2 block |
| Leamos y escribamos | 1 day | 1/2 block |
| Prepárate para el examen | 1 day | 1/4 block |
| Chapter Test | 1 day | 1/2 block |
| Integración | 1/2 day | 1/4 block |

Amigos discutiendo en la República Dominicana

Visit Holt Online
**go.hrw.com**
KEYWORD: EXP3 CH3
Project Help

# Chapter Opener

## Holt Grammar Logic
### CHAPTER 3

- *To complain, express an opinion, and to disagree,* students will need to review verbs with infinitives, and the subjunctive with will or wish. They will also need to use the subjunctive with negation or denial.
- *To make suggestions, and to apologize,* students will need to review the future tense, and they will need to use the conditional, including the conditional with some "if" statements.

## Using the Photo
Tell students this photo was taken at a school in Santo Domingo, the capital of the Dominican Republic. Ask them to compare this school with their school. Then have them comment on what they notice about the setting. What is the climate like?

## Más vocabulario
**enfadarse** *to get angry*
**enfadado(a)** *angry*
**quejarse** *to complain*

## LISTENING PRACTICE — Language Lab and Classroom Activities

**Vocabulario**
Activity 1, p. 100, CD 3, Tr. 1
Activity 4, p. 101, CD 3, Tr. 2
Activity 8, p. 103, CD 3, Tr. 3
Activity 23, p. 114, CD 3, Tr. 9

**Gramática**
Activity 15, p. 106, CD 3, Tr. 4
Activity 18, p. 108, CD 3, Tr. 5
Activity 32, p. 118, CD 3, Tr. 10
Activity 41, p. 122, CD 3, Tr. 11

**Cultura**
**Comparaciones,** pp. 110–111, CD 3, Tr. 6–8

**Novela**
**Novela en video,** Escuchemos, p. 124

**Lectura informativa**
pp. 126–127, CD 3, Tr. 12

**Leamos**
pp. 128–129, CD 3, Tr. 13
**Escuchemos,** p. 128

**Repaso**
Activity 1, p. 132, CD 3, Tr. 14
Activity 6, p. 133, CD 3, Tr. 15
**Variedades,** Lab Book, p. 63

**Integración**
Activity 1, p. 136, CD 3, Tr. 16

**Assessment Program**
CD 3, Tr. 17–20

**Additional Listening**
Pre-AP CD 1, Trs. 9–12

## Resources

**Planning:**

Lesson Planner, pp. 33–34, 194–195

One-Stop Planner

**Presentation:**

Teaching Transparencies
**Vocabulario** 3.1, 3.2

**Practice:**

Cuaderno de vocabulario y gramática, pp. 25–27

Activities for Communication, pp. 9–10

Teaching Transparencies
Bell Work 3.1
**Vocabulario y gramática** answers, pp. 25–27

Interactive Tutor, Disc 1

### Bell Work

Use Bell Work 3.1 in the *Teaching Transparencies,* or write this activity on the board.

**Completa las siguientes oraciones.**

1. Me alegra que mis amigos...
2. Me frustra que el profesor...
3. Me sorprende que los estudiantes...
4. Me preocupa que mis notas...
5. Me molesta que mis vecinos...

1.2

**Objetivos**
- Complaining
- Expressing an opinion
- Disagreeing

# Vocabulario en acción 1

## Lo que piensa la gente

Me molestan **los estereotipos** sobre la gente que estudia mucho; tenemos **fama** de ser todos muy serios y secos. Me parece que a veces algunas personas tienen **una impresión equivocada** de mí. En realidad, me gusta pasarlo bien como cualquier otro estudiante.

Uno de mis primos tenía **una actitud hacia** las mujeres que me chocaba. Pensaba que las chicas no debían ser atléticas. Imagínate... ¡qué **falta de respeto!** Le dije que eso era **un estereotipo** del pasado; para **combatirlo,** lo invité a jugar al tenis conmigo ¡y le gané 6 a 0! Ahora me **respeta** y no dice esas cosas.

Para mí, **la imagen** del latino en la televisión y el cine estadounidense es bastante negativa. Me parece que **la discriminación** y **el prejuicio** que hay contra nosotros en Estados Unidos se debe en parte a esto. Las personas que no conocen a ningún latino ven esas imágenes y por su **ignorancia,** ellos **juzgan** mal a todos los latinos.

## Core Instruction

### TEACHING VOCABULARIO

1. Introduce the vocabulary using transparencies **Vocabulario 3.1** and **3.2.** Model the pronunciation and point to target vocabulary as you read each paragraph. **(2 min.)**
2. Ask students: **¿Alguna vez alguien ha tenido una impresión equivocada de ti?** Continue with other vocabulary words and phrases. **(3 min.)**
3. Introduce students to names of courses using transparency **Vocabulario 3.2.** **(2 min.)**
4. Ask them what classes this student has and when: **¿Cuál es su horario?** **(3 min.)**

### TEACHING ¡EXPRÉSATE!

1. Briefly review the school subjects by asking students which classes they have now and which ones will be taught at the university level. **¿Qué clases tienen? ¿Qué clases tomarán en la universidad?** **(4 min.)**
2. Act out both sides of a conversation as you model the expressions from **¡Exprésate!** Use gestures and body language to convey the meaning of the expressions. For example, show that you are frustrated when you say **¡No aguanto más!** or **¡Esto es el colmo!** **(2 min.)**

## Mis cursos para este semestre

Este **semestre** me estoy preparando para ir a **la universidad**. Tengo **un horario** difícil, y **la consejera** me dice que no puedo **suspender** ningún **curso** si quiero entrar a **la universidad**.

| HORA | LUNES | MARTES | MIÉRCOLES | JUEVES |
|---|---|---|---|---|
| 8:00 — 9:00 | **cálculo** | cálculo | cálculo | cálculo |
| 9:00 —10:00 | **ciencias sociales** | **geografía** | ciencias sociales | geografía |
| 10:00 —11:00 | **física** | física | física | física |
| 11:00 —12:00 | música | arte | música | arte |
| 12:00 —12:30 | almuerzo | almuerzo | almuerzo | almuerzo |
| 12:30 — 1:30 | **literatura** caribeña | educación física | literatura caribeña | educación física |
| 1:30 — 2:30 | francés | francés | francés | francés |

Visit Holt Online
**go.hrw.com**
KEYWORD: EXP3 CH3
Vocabulario 1 Practice

**También se puede decir...**

There are different words for **suspender**. Hondurans might use **reprobar**, some Ecuadoreans prefer **fallar**, Puerto Ricans might say **colgar**, and among Venezuelans, you may hear **raspar**.

**Más vocabulario...**

| | |
|---|---|
| **el álgebra** *(f.)* | *algebra* |
| **aprobar (ue)** | *to pass (a test, a class)* |
| **el director, la directora** | *principal* |
| **la geometría** | *geometry* |
| **tomar apuntes** | *to take notes* |

### ¡Exprésate!

**To complain**

Interactive TUTOR

**Me choca la actitud de... hacia... ¡No aguanto más!**
*I can't stand the attitude of . . . towards . . . I can't take it anymore!*

**El (La) consejero(a) insiste en que tome... ¡No me gusta para nada!**
*The guidance counselor insists that I take . . . I don't like it at all!*

**¿Mañana vamos a tener otra prueba en...? ¡Esto es el colmo!**
*We're going to have another test in . . . tomorrow? This is the last straw!*

Vocabulario y gramática, pp. 25–27 Online workbooks

▶ Vocabulario adicional — Los estudios, p. R16

Vocabulario 1



### TPR
**TOTAL PHYSICAL RESPONSE**

Bring in textbooks for the course words taught in **Vocabulario 1.** Present and model the following commands. Ask individuals to respond to the commands.

**Tráeme el libro de cálculo.**

**Levanta la mano si tienes la clase de física.**

**Levántate si tienes ciencias sociales hoy.**

**Señala un libro de literatura en el salón.**

**Tráeme el libro de geometría.**

**Levanta la mano si aprobaste tu último examen.**

1.2

**COMMON ERROR ALERT**
**¡OJO!**

Students may confuse **ciencias sociales** with a science course, since the course is often called Social Studies in English rather than Social Sciences. You may also want to point out the difference between **física** and **educación física** and remind them to look at the entire name before deciding which class is being referred to.

### También se puede decir...

Students may hear the term **asesor(a)** for *guidance counselor.* You may also want to mention that the verb **apuntar** *(to write down)* may be used instead of **tomar apuntes** *(to take notes).*

### Circumlocution

Have students describe situations in which people's actions show prejudice, stereotyping, lack of respect, or other themes from **Vocabulario 1.** Tell them they should not use the targeted vocabulary word in their descriptions. The rest of the class will decide which vocabulary word best describes each situation.

1.1

## Differentiated Instruction

### ADVANCED LEARNERS

**Personalization** Have students work in pairs to talk about their classes this year. They can discuss the classes they like best, the workload, the tests, the materials they need, or any topic they can think of. Have volunteers tell the class about their partner's experience so far this school year. 1.1

### MULTIPLE INTELLIGENCES

**Interpersonal** Have students think about the sources of prejudice. How does prejudice affect them? They can list reasons for prejudice and how it occurs in the school setting. They might suggest ways to combat prejudice in their school in order to start a discussion with the class. 1.1

**Differentiated Instruction** See the Differentiated Instruction CD-ROM.

## Resources

**Planning:**

Lesson Planner, pp. 33–34, 194–195

One-Stop Planner

**Presentation:**

Teaching Transparencies **Vocabulario** 3.1, 3.2

**Practice:**

Cuaderno de vocabulario y gramática, pp. 25–27

Activities for Communication, pp. 9–10

Lab Book, pp. 21–24

Teaching Transparencies **Vocabulario y gramática** answers, pp. 25–27

Audio CD 3, Trs. 1–2

Interactive Tutor, Disc 1

**1 Script**

See script on page 95E.

## Connections

**Thinking Critically**

Have students talk about any movies from Spanish-speaking countries they have seen. Ask each student to give a brief synopsis of the movie and to say how he or she felt about the country after seeing the movie. Do students feel that most movies are accurate portrayals of a country or can they sometimes be misleading? Do they see any stereotyping? Have them explain their ideas.

3.2

**Answers to Activity 2:**

1. imagen negativa
2. equivocada
3. fama
4. estereotipo
5. respeto
6. juzga
7. ignorancia
8. prejuicios

**Nota cultural**

Desde 1898 hasta 1948, el gobierno de Estados Unidos insistió que en Puerto Rico sólo se dieran las clases en inglés. Hoy en día todos los estudiantes aprenden inglés y español en el colegio. Más del 20 por ciento de los puertorriqueños van a colegios privados, un porcentaje más alto que en Estados Unidos.

¿Es así donde tú vives?

2.1, 4.2

Estudiantes puertorriqueños, Guánica

CD 3, Tr. 1

### 1 Impresiones equivocadas 1.2

**Escuchemos** Escucha la opinión de Kim. Basándote en lo que dice, indica si cada oración es **cierta** o **falsa.**

1. Kim está de acuerdo con los estereotipos sobre los asiáticos. falsa
2. Los asiáticos tienen fama de ser muy extrovertidos. falsa
3. La gente suele tener prejuicios sobre las cosas que no conoce. cierta
4. Kim cree que sus compañeros tienen prejuicios porque son malas personas. falsa
5. A Kim sólo le gusta estudiar matemáticas. falsa
6. Kim cree que una manera de combatir la discriminación es conocer a personas de diferentes culturas. cierta

### 2 Los estereotipos 1.2

**Leamos/Escribamos** Un estudiante escribió este párrafo acerca de los estereotipos sobre los miembros de la banda. Completa el párrafo con las palabras del cuadro.

| | | | |
|---|---|---|---|
| ignorancia | prejuicios | imagen negativa | equivocada |
| fama | respeto | estereotipo | juzga |

No entiendo por qué los miembros de la banda tienen una __1__. Mucha gente tiene una impresión __2__ de ellos. Tienen __3__ de ser muy aburridos, pero esto es un __4__. Yo los __5__ mucho porque tienen un talento especial y pasan mucho tiempo ensayando *(rehearsing)*. Además, los miembros de la banda son los estudiantes más divertidos e interesantes que conozco. La gente también los __6__ mal y cree que no son deportistas, pero más de la mitad del grupo practica algún deporte. De hecho, ¡el capitán del equipo de béisbol está en la banda! Obviamente muchos estudiantes saben poco de los miembros de la banda y es por su __7__ que tienen estos __8__.

### 3 En mi opinión 1.2

**Escribamos/Hablemos** Completa las oraciones con tus opiniones, usando las palabras de **Vocabulario** y las expresiones de **Exprésate.**

1. El estereotipo que más me molesta es...
2. Creo que tenemos que combatir...
3. Me parece que la gente a veces juzga...
4. Me choca la actitud de... hacia...
5. Es muy importante respetar a...
6. Muchas veces los prejuicios son el resultado de...
7. Cuando alguien tiene una impresión equivocada de mí...
8. Si queremos evitar la discriminación, es necesario...

## Core Instruction

### VOCABULARY IN CONTEXT

Ask students questions using words from **Vocabulario 1.** Questions should require students to either use the vocabulary contextually in their answers or ask them to define the words within the context of the question. For example, **¿Cuál es un efecto de la ignorancia? ¿Cómo se comportan o qué hacen las personas que tienen prejuicios contra ciertos grupos? ¿Qué tema estás estudiando en la clase de literatura? ¿Qué has aprendido en la clase de geografía?** Continue by having partners interview each other about their classes this semester using the expressions they learned in **¡Exprésate!** Ask them to comment on any stereotypes they may have encountered in their classes or in their extracurricular activities.

CD 3, Tr. 2

**4 Mis cursos este semestre** 1.2

**Escuchemos** Escucha lo que dice Roberto sobre los cursos que tiene este semestre. Escribe el nombre de los cinco cursos que menciona e indica si le gusta cada uno o no.

literatura; le gusta
geometría; no le gusta
ciencias sociales; no le gusta
álgebra; le gusta
geografía; no le gusta

**5 ¿Qué pasa aquí?** 1.2

**Leamos/Hablemos** Mira los dibujos y decide qué comentario va con cada uno.

a.

b.

c.

d.

e.

f.

1. Aunque mucha gente crea que no, a mi parecer los jóvenes de hoy sí respetan a los mayores. d
2. Este rompecabezas es imposible. ¡No aguanto más! e
3. Es un estereotipo que las mujeres no pueden competir con los hombres en los deportes. c
4. Me choca la ignorancia de los estudiantes sobre la geografía. b
5. Nuestra universidad es la más vieja del estado. f
6. Tenemos cinco libros para la clase de literatura. ¡Esto es el colmo! a

## Comunicación

HOLT SoundBooth ONLINE RECORDING

**6 ¡No sólo para hombres!** 1.1, 1.3

**Hablemos** En parejas, dramaticen la siguiente situación. Una estudiante quiere tomar clases de cálculo, pero sus padres prefieren que tome clases de literatura porque ellos creen que las matemáticas son sólo para los hombres.

Vocabulario 1

### 4 Script

See script on page 95E.

### Cultures

**Practices and Perspectives**

Have students research information on the university system in Latin American countries. Ask them to look for information on the process of getting into college, the types of programs offered, and how many years of study are required. Have them compare the university system in Latin America with that in the United States. 2.1, 4.2

### Comunicación

**Pair Activity: Interpersonal**

Have students work in pairs to discuss the classes they have this semester. Instruct them to tell about the classes they like, and voice their complaints about the classes they don't like. Based on what the other student says about the class, the partner will fill out a chart. In the chart they should include the name of the class, a column to rate their partner's opinion of the class, and a column to rate how well the partner is doing in the class. Ratings should be from 1–10, with 10 being the highest score. Have students summarize their findings for their classmates. 1.1

## Differentiated Instruction

### SLOWER PACE LEARNERS

**6** Before doing Activity 6, allow students to first review the vocabulary and take notes on phrases that might be useful for their dialogue. Have them take turns acting out the part of the parent and the part of the student. If they have trouble with this conversation, allow them to use another situation from their own experience in which stereotypes have played a part. 1.1

### MULTIPLE INTELLIGENCES

**5 Linguistic** Before students do Activity 5, have volunteers describe what is happening in each illustration. Ask them to describe how the people in the illustrations feel. Have them take notes on key words that are mentioned in this discussion. Then have them use their notes to complete the activity. 1.2

**Differentiated Instruction** See the Differentiated Instruction CD-ROM.

**Resources**

**Planning:**

Lesson Planner, pp. 33–34, 194–195

One-Stop Planner

**Presentation:**

Teaching Transparencies **Vocabulario** 3.1, 3.2

**Practice:**

Cuaderno de vocabulario y gramática, pp. 25–27

Activities for Communication, pp. 9–10

Lab Book, pp. 21–24

Teaching Transparencies **Vocabulario y gramática** answers, pp. 25–27

Audio CD 3, Tr. 3

Interactive Tutor, Disc 1

**Thinking Critically**

Have students conduct a survey. Ask them to make a list of activities that some may consider to be only for males or only for females. They might include, for example, **invitar a un(a) chico(a) a salir, jugar al básquetbol, tejer, cocinar, ser científico(a).** Have them poll students about whether or not they think these activities are for both males and females. They should create a chart of the results to share with the class as a way to start a discussion and voice their opinions. Ask them to explain why they think people gave the answers they did. 1.1

Jóvenes de San Juan, Puerto Rico

## ¡Las chicas toman la iniciativa!

CARMEN Ofelia, ¿ya invitaste a Miguel a salir?
OFELIA Todavía no, lo iba a hacer esta tarde.
DANIEL A mi parecer, las chicas no deben llamar a los chicos.
CARMEN ¿Nunca, dices?
OFELIA No le hagas caso a mi hermano, Carmen; es un tonto en estos asuntos.
DANIEL Bueno, si son amigos o si ya son novios, está bien. Pero si la chica llama al chico para invitarlo a salir, da muy mala impresión.
OFELIA ¡Qué va! Eso no es cierto, Daniel. Hay muchas chicas que toman la iniciativa.
DANIEL Quizás, pero vuelvo a repetir, da muy mala impresión.
CARMEN No estoy de acuerdo contigo. Al contrario, según lo que me han dicho muchos amigos, les gusta que las chicas los llamen para invitarlos a salir.
DANIEL Pues, no me parece que digan la verdad.
OFELIA ¿Ah, sí? ¡Pues, me dijo tu novia que ella tomó la iniciativa y te llamó primero!

### ¡Exprésate!

| To express an opinion | To disagree |
|---|---|
| **A mi parecer, no hay igualdad entre...** *The way I see it, there's no equality between . . .* | **¡Qué va! Eso no es cierto.** *No way! That's not true.* |
| **No me parece que sea justo.** *I don't think it's fair.* | **¡Al contrario! No estoy de acuerdo.** *On the contrary! I disagree.* |

Interactive TUTOR

Vocabulario y gramática, pp. 25–27 Online workbooks

## Core Instruction

### TEACHING ¡EXPRÉSATE!

1. Have a volunteer summarize what happened in the conversation on page 102. Then ask students **¿Cuál es la opinión de Daniel? ¿Están de acuerdo con su opinión?** **(2 min.)**
2. Then express an opinion on another topic using the expressions from **¡Exprésate!** Model the expressions to disagree in **¡Exprésate!** **(2 min.)**
3. Have volunteers read aloud the phrases in the conversation that include expressing an opinion and disagreeing. Ask students if they agree more with Daniel or with Carmen and Ofelia. **(2 min.)**

**7** **¿Las chicas pueden llamar a los chicos?** 1.2

**Leamos/Escribamos** Basándote en la conversación entre Carmen, Ofelia y Daniel, contesta las preguntas.

1. ¿Cuál es la opinión de Daniel sobre las chicas que llaman a los chicos para invitarlos a salir?
2. ¿Carmen está de acuerdo con Daniel? ¿Qué piensa ella?
3. Según Daniel, ¿cuándo puede una chica llamar a un chico para invitarlo a salir?
4. ¿Por qué a Ofelia le choca la actitud de Daniel hacia las chicas que llaman a los chicos?
5. ¿Crees que Daniel tiene una impresión equivocada? ¿Por qué?

CD 3, Tr. 3

**8** **¿Estás de acuerdo?** 1.2

**Escuchemos** Escucha las conversaciones y decide si la segunda persona **a**) está de acuerdo o **b**) no está de acuerdo con lo que dice la primera persona. **1.** b **2.** b **3.** a **4.** b **5.** a **6.** b

## Comunicación

HOLT SoundBooth ONLINE RECORDING

**9** **¿Cómo respondes?** 1.1, 1.2

**Leamos/Hablemos** Mira las fotos y lee la opinión de cada persona. En grupos de tres, túrnense para responder a cada opinión usando las expresiones de **Exprésate.**

1

Me parece que los jóvenes de hoy no aprenden nada en el colegio. Su ignorancia es terrible. No hacen su tarea nunca y se la pasan en fiestas con sus amigos. Deben ser más responsables.

2

Hoy en día, los estudiantes no respetan a nadie. No escuchan a sus profesores y su actitud hacia los estudios es terrible. Es importante que ellos conozcan a chicos de otros países para que aprendan cómo son los estudiantes de otros lugares. Ellos sí respetan a sus profesores.

3

Los atletas son los peores estudiantes. Suspenden todos los exámenes y no les interesa ir a la universidad. Pienso que deben tomar cursos especiales y hablar con un consejero para que entiendan que la educación es muy importante.

### 7 Answers

1. Cree que da muy mala impresión.
2. No. Ella piensa que a los chicos les gusta que las chicas los llamen para invitarlos a salir.
3. Él dice que si ya son novios, o son amigos, está bien.
4. Le choca porque la novia de Daniel lo llamó primero.
5. Answers will vary.

### 8 Script

See script on page 95E.

## Comunicación

### Class Activity: Presentational

Present several topics focusing on the chapter theme or themes from previous chapters (relationships, sports and pastimes, stereotypes, classes). Have a volunteer express an opinion about the first topic, and give the rest of the class the opportunity to disagree. The student who disagrees will express his or her opinion and then voice an opinion about the next topic. Continue until everyone has had the chance to express an opinion. 1.1, 1.3

## Differentiated Instruction

### ADVANCED LEARNERS

**Challenge** Have groups of students participate in a debate. Provide topics or let students choose their own. Allow them to prepare some arguments before they begin. Then have them debate in front of the class. The class will have to decide which group has the stronger argument. 1.1

### SPECIAL LEARNING NEEDS

**8 Students with Auditory Impairments** If you have students with auditory impairments, you may want to provide them with a copy of the script for Activity 8. Have students read the conversation and answer the questions. 1.2

### Assess

**Assessment Program**

**Prueba: Vocabulario 1,** pp. 41–42

Alternative Assessment, pp. 375, 387, 399

**Online Assessment**

**my.hrw.com**

**Test Generator**

**Assess** **Differentiated Instruction** See the Differentiated Instruction CD-ROM.

## Resources

**Planning:**

Lesson Planner, pp. 35–37, 196–199

One-Stop Planner

**Presentation:**

Video Program **GramaVisión**

**Practice:**

Grammar Tutor for Students of Spanish, Chapter 3

Cuaderno de vocabulario y gramática, pp. 28–30

Cuaderno de actividades, pp. 21–23

Activities for Communication, pp. 9–10

Teaching Transparencies

Bell Work 3.2

**Vocabulario y gramática** answers, pp. 28–30

Interactive Tutor, Disc 1

### Bell Work

Use Bell Work 3.2 in the *Teaching Transparencies*, or write this activity on the board.

**Lee las siguientes opiniones y escribe una oración para expresar desacuerdo.**

1. Me parece que no hay discriminación en nuestra sociedad.
2. A mi parecer, las mujeres no deben ir a la universidad.
3. Creo que la clase de ciencias sociales es muy fácil.
4. Los hombres no saben cocinar.
5. Los estudiantes en este colegio nunca tienen tarea. 1.2

**Objetivos**
- Verb + infinitive
- Subjunctive with will or wish
- Subjunctive with negation or denial

# Gramática en acción 1

GramaVisión

Interactive TUTOR

## Repaso Verb + infinitive

**1** Some conjugated verbs are followed by a **preposition** plus an **infinitive.**

La señora Villalobos **sueña con viajar** por el mundo.

Rosa **va a trabajar** esta tarde a las cuatro.

Luis **acaba de regresar** de Italia.

**2** Other conjugated verbs do not require a preposition and are followed directly by an **infinitive.**

Mis tíos **piensan llegar** a las once en punto.

Yolanda **debe estudiar** más para mejorar sus notas.

**3** Even if the verb is normally followed by the subjunctive, if the subject does not change, the second verb remains in the **infinitive.** If the subject does change, the second verb is in the **subjunctive.**

*same subject*
Carlos **espera sacar** buenas notas el semestre que viene.

*first subject* *second subject*
Los profesores **esperan que** Carlos **saque** buenas notas.

Vocabulario y gramática, pp. 28–30
Actividades, pp. 21–23
Online workbooks

### ¿Te acuerdas?

The verb immediately following a **preposition** is *always* in the **infinitive.**

Elena necesita su libro **para estudiar.**

Van **a cenar** después **de terminar** su tarea de cálculo.

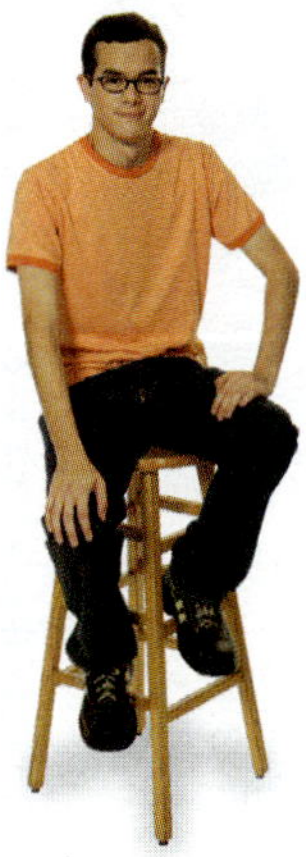

### 10 ¿Cómo será este semestre? 1.2

**Leamos** Completa el párrafo con las preposiciones correctas. Si el verbo no requiere preposición, escoge ∅.

Carolina está nerviosa por el comienzo del semestre. Mañana todos los estudiantes empezarán __1__ (a/de) inscribirse. Está nerviosa porque sus profesores suelen __2__ (∅/en) asignar muchas tareas difíciles. Carolina espera __3__ (a/∅) sacar muy buenas notas este semestre. Ella se pondrá __4__ (a/en) estudiar muy duro y piensa __5__ (de/∅) trabajar en las tardes. Este semestre, Carolina y su amiga Nancy insisten __6__ (de/en) estudiar juntas porque acaban __7__ (de/∅) escoger la misma clase de álgebra y van __8__ (con/a) comparar apuntes.

## Core Instruction

### TEACHING GRAMÁTICA

1. Give some examples of verb + preposition + infinitive. Practice this construction by asking students questions. **¿Qué vas a hacer esta noche? Esta noche voy a estudiar. ¿Necesitas zapatos nuevos? (¿para qué?) Los necesito para practicar atletismo. (3 min.)**
2. Have students think of other verb + preposition combinations that take the infinitive. If necessary, give them a list of prepositions. **(2 min.)**
3. Review **¿Te acuerdas?** Have volunteers talk about the chapter theme using **querer, necesitar, pensar, esperar,** and **deber** followed by the infinitive. **(3 min.)**
4. Go over point 3. Discuss the examples. Give more examples, if necessary. **(2 min.)**

### GramaVisión

For a video presentation of verbs followed by an infinitive, use **GramaVisión.**

GramaVisión

Visit Holt Online
**go.hrw.com**
KEYWORD: EXP3 CH3
Gramática 1 Practice

## 11 ¿Qué hicieron? 1.2

**Escribamos** Escribe dos oraciones para cada foto. Explica lo que hicieron esas personas y lo que hacen usando las siguientes frases.

**MODELO** **Fernando comenzó a correr después de clases.**

1. Fernando
comenzar a/dejar de

2. Eugenia
ponerse a/insistir en

3. Paula
aprender a/acabar de

4. Jaime
ayudar a/enseñar a

## 12 ¡Hagamos publicidad! 1.2

**Hablemos/Escribamos** Eres miembro del Club Internacional de tu colegio y estás trabajando en los letreros para la feria cultural. Escribe oraciones que puedan aparecer en los letreros usando las palabras del cuadro y el mandato de **nosotros.** ¿Se te olvidó? *Nosotros commands,* pp. 60–61

**MODELO** **luchar por**
**Luchemos por la diversidad en nuestra escuela.**

| | | |
|---|---|---|
| tratar de | ayudar a | soñar con |
| aprender a | dejar de | comenzar a |

## Comunicación

HOLT SoundBooth ONLINE RECORDING

## 13 Un cambio 1.1, 1.2

**Hablemos** Rodrigo está hablando con su hermano sobre su primer semestre de colegio. En parejas, dramaticen la conversación entre Rodrigo y su hermano. Sigan el modelo.

**MODELO** **—Este semestre me tiene muy preocupado. Quiero aprobar mis cursos pero son muy difíciles. ¿Qué hago?**
**—Tienes que...**

| | | | |
|---|---|---|---|
| insistir en | aprender a | tratar de | ir a |
| el horario | la literatura | la universidad | el semestre |
| aprobar | el/la consejero(a) | los cursos | empezar a |

### 11 Answers

Answers will vary. Possible answers:

1. Fernando comenzó a correr después de clases. Quiere dejar de ver tanta televisión.
2. Eugenia se puso a estudiar inmediatamente después de clases. Siempre insiste en hacer diez cosas a la vez.
3. Paula aprendió a patinar en línea. Paula acaba de caerse.
4. Jaime ayudó a su hermano a arreglar su bicicleta. Jaime enseña a su hermano a arreglar su bicicleta.

### Heritage Speakers

Have heritage speakers come up with their own phrases for Activity 12, without being restricted to using the words in the box or **nosotros** commands. Go over students' answers and write them on the board. Then have heritage speakers add their phrases to the list. 1.2

### Comunicación

### Group Activity: Interpersonal

Once students have had the chance to act out the conversation in Activity 13, have them work in groups to discuss their own plans for this semester. Each student should tell what he or she wants to do or hopes to do, and members of the group will express an opinion about each student's goals. 1.1

## Differentiated Instruction

### SLOWER PACE LEARNERS

**12 Extension** Before students do Activity 12, review **nosotros** commands. Write these common verb + preposition combinations on the board: **empezar a, ir a, ponerse a, soñar con.** Have them form sentences with each combination. Allow them to use the list as a reference as they do the activity. 1.2

### SPECIAL LEARNING NEEDS

**12 Students with AD(H)D** Draw several blank boxes on the board to represent the signs that students are making for the Cultural Fair. Quickly brainstorm some main ideas for the posters and the type of art that would be on each. Then have students work in pairs to come up with sentences and write them in the boxes so they can visualize the poster. 1.2

**Differentiated Instruction** See the Differentiated Instruction CD-ROM.

## Resources

**Planning:**

Lesson Planner, pp. 35–37, 196–199

One-Stop Planner

**Presentation:**

Video Program **GramaVisión**

**Practice:**

Grammar Tutor for Students of Spanish, Chapter 3

Cuaderno de vocabulario y gramática, pp. 28–30

Cuaderno de actividades, pp. 21–23

Activities for Communication, pp. 9–10

Lab Book, pp. 21–24

Teaching Transparencies

Bell Work 3.3

**Vocabulario y gramática** answers, pp. 28–30

Audio CD 3, Tr. 4

Interactive Tutor, Disc 1

### Bell Work

Use Bell Work 3.3 in the *Teaching Transparencies.*

### En inglés Answer

As a relative pronoun, specifically as an object: *The woman (that) you met yesterday was my teacher.*

### 15 Script

1. Espera estudiar la literatura de El Salvador.
2. Dice que le gusta viajar y conocer otros países.
3. Sus padres prefieren que se quede en casa.
4. Ellos dicen que es necesario que se enfoque en sus estudios.
5. Antonio quiere graduarse de la universidad y ser profesor.
6. Su hermano le pide que trabaje con él en su negocio.
7. Antonio piensa que puede ser una buena idea.

Interactive TUTOR

### En inglés

**In Spanish,** the word **que** is necessary to separate clauses.

Sé que el examen es hoy.

**In English,** however, the word *that* can be omitted.

I know (that) the exam is today.

Give another instance in English in which *that* can be omitted. 4.1

## Repaso: Subjunctive with will or wish

**1** Use the **subjunctive** in subordinate clauses when there is a change in subject between the main and subordinate clauses and when the main clause expresses **will** or **wish.**

*first subject* — *second subject*

Mis amigos **insisten en** que yo no **llegue** tarde a las juntas.

Alberto **necesita** que Alicia le **ayude** con la tarea.

El profesor nos **dice** que **trabajemos** en grupos.

La directora **pide** que los padres **hablen** con el consejero.

**2** As you know, when there is no change in subject with a **verb of will or wish,** the first verb is followed by the **infinitive.**

*same subject*

Mis amigos **insisten en llegar** temprano.

Alicia **necesita ayudar** a Alberto con la tarea.

Vocabulario y gramática, pp. 28–30
Actividades, pp. 21–23
Online workbooks

### Nota cultural

En Cuba, el colegio es obligatorio, pero gratis, desde los seis años hasta los quince años. Después de los quince años, los jóvenes deciden si quieren trabajar o seguir con sus estudios. Pero sigue siendo gratis, no importa cuántos años estudien. Uno puede graduarse de la universidad sin pagar ni un centavo.

¿Cómo se compara este sistema con el de Estados Unidos? 2.1, 4.2

### 14 El nuevo semestre 1.2

**Leamos/Escribamos** Completa las siguientes oraciones con la forma correcta del verbo entre paréntesis.

1. Los estudiantes esperan que sus horarios no ___ (ser) muy complicados. sean
2. Los profesores insisten en que los estudiantes ___ (tomar) buenos apuntes. tomen
3. Los estudiantes esperan que los profesores no ___ (dar) muchos exámenes. den
4. Los estudiantes piden que sus profesores ___ (tener) buen sentido del humor. tengan
5. Los padres quieren que sus hijos ___ (sacar) buenas notas. saquen
6. La directora espera que los alumnos ___ (ir) a la universidad después de graduarse. vayan

CD 3, Tr. 4

### 15 Hablando del futuro 1.2

**Escuchemos** Escucha las siguientes oraciones acerca de Antonio. Para cada oración, determina si se trata
**a)** de algo que Antonio quiere, espera o necesita, o
**b)** de algo que otra persona espera, quiere o necesita de Antonio.

**1.** a **2.** a **3.** b **4.** b **5.** a **6.** b **7.** a

## Core Instruction

### TEACHING GRAMÁTICA

1. Review the subjunctive conditions that students have learned so far: subjunctive with unknown or nonexistent, and subjunctive with expressions of feelings. **(2 min.)**
2. Go over point 1 and read the examples, indicating the main and subordinate clauses and the expressions of will or wish. Practice the use of the subjunctive with verbs of will or wish by asking students what their parents wish they would do: **¿Qué quieren tus padres que hagas? (3 min.)**
3. Go over point 2 and have students practice verbs of will or wish with the infinitive by asking what they prefer to do: **¿Qué prefieres hacer tú? (3 min.)**
4. Have students use these phrases in sentences followed by the correct verb form: **ojalá que, esperar que, decir que, recomendar que, pedir que. (2 min.)**

### GramaVisión

For a video presentation of the subjunctive with verbs of will or wish, use **GramaVisión.**

GramaVisión

**16 Un año nuevo** 1.2

**Escribamos** Escribe seis oraciones con las palabras de cada columna. Añade tus propios detalles.

**MODELO** **Mis amigos esperan que los profesores tengan paciencia.**

| | | | |
|---|---|---|---|
| los padres | querer | las clases | estudiar |
| los hijos | preferir | los padres | ayudar |
| los profesores | necesitar | los estudiantes | limpiar |
| los estudiantes | pedir | yo | tener |
| yo | recomendar | tú | preparar |
| mis amigos | esperar | los profesores | salir |
| mi abuela | decir | el director | ser |

## Comunicación

HOLT SoundBooth ONLINE RECORDING

**17 A Quiero que...** 1.1, 1.2

**Hablemos** En parejas, dramaticen una posible conversación entre Malena y su mamá basándose en los dibujos. Usen el subjuntivo en su conversación.

**MODELO** **—Malena, ¡mira este cuarto! ¡Es un desastre! Quiero que lo limpies ahora mismo.**

**17 B ¿Qué te piden a ti?** 1.1, 1.3

**Hablemos** Con un(a) compañero(a), hablen de lo que los demás piden, quieren y necesitan de ustedes dos. ¿Tienen ustedes alguna situación o queja en común?

**MODELO** **—Mi hermano menor siempre me pide que le ayude con su tarea de matemáticas. Es una lata.**

**—¡Qué pesado! No tengo que ayudar a mi hermana con su tarea, pero mis padres sí insisten en que...**



Gramática 1

### Cultures

**Practices and Perspectives**

Review the culture note with students. Have them compare the school system in Cuba with the school system in the United States. Ask them to comment on the benefits and disadvantages of each system. 2.1, 4.2

### Comparisons

**Language to Language**

Point out that often in cases where we would use the infinitive form in English, we use the subjunctive in Spanish. **Quiero que Laura salga conmigo** (I want Laura to go out with me). Write these sentences on the board and underline **salga** in the Spanish sentence and *to go out* in the English sentence. Have volunteers think of other examples. 4.1

### Comunicación

**Pair Activity: Interpersonal**

Have students interview their classmates about what they wish people would do to improve their community. Once the interviews are complete, have students present a summary to the class. 1.1

## Differentiated Instruction

### ADVANCED LEARNERS

**15 Extension** Once students have done Activity 15, hand out copies of the script. Have them underline the verbs in the subordinate clause and determine whether they are in the indicative or the subjunctive. Ask them to explain the reason for each. Then have them rewrite each sentence so that the opposite verb form is used in the subordinate clause. 1.2

### SPECIAL LEARNING NEEDS

**16 Students with Learning Disabilities** Before students do Activity 16, review the subjunctive endings. Then form sentences together. One volunteer will choose a noun from the first column, the next will conjugate a verb from the second column, the third will choose a noun from the third column, and the fourth will conjugate a verb from the fourth column. Write the sentences on the board as the volunteers provide fragments. Then read the completed sentence together. 1.2

**Differentiated Instruction** See the Differentiated Instruction CD-ROM.

## Resources

**Planning:**

Lesson Planner, pp. 35–37, 196–199

One-Stop Planner

**Presentation:**

Video Program **GramaVisión**

**Practice:**

Grammar Tutor, Chapter 3

Cuaderno de vocabulario y gramática, pp. 28–30

Cuad. de activ., pp. 21–23

Act. for Comm., pp. 9–10

Lab Book, pp. 21–24

Teaching Transparencies

Bell Work 3.4

**Vocabulario y gramática** answers, pp. 28–30

Audio CD 3, Tr. 5

Interactive Tutor, Disc 1

### Bell Work

Use Bell Work 3.4 in the *Teaching Transparencies.*

### Teacher to Teacher

**Patty Buzby**
William Penn High School
New Castle, DE

To practice the subjunctive with negation and denial, I use articles clipped from the tabloids, the more outlandish the better! Although these clippings are in English, I have students react to each one using an expression of negation or denial, and the correct form of the subjunctive. For example, **Dudo que el tabaco sea bueno para la salud,** etc. The headlines from the tabloid articles can be posted around the classroom along with students' sentences of negation and denial. 1.3

Interactive TUTOR

## Subjunctive with negation or denial

**1** The **subjunctive** is used when the main clause expresses a **negation** *(negación)* or **denial** and when there is a change of subject. Phrases that express negation or denial include: **no es verdad que, no es cierto que, no creer que, no estar de acuerdo (en) que,** and **negar que.**

**No es verdad que haya** tanta discriminación en nuestro país.
**No creo que** José **sea** muy chismoso.
**No es cierto que** él **tenga** una impresión equivocada de ti.

**2** If the main clause expresses **affirmation** *(afirmación)* or **agreement,** the **indicative** is used.

**Es verdad que hay** mucha discriminación en nuestro país.
**Creo que** José **es** muy chismoso.
**Es cierto que** él **tiene** una impresión equivocada de ti.

Vocabulario y gramática, pp. 28–30
Actividades, pp. 21–23
**Online** workbooks

### ¿Te acuerdas?

Remember that the verbs **saber** and **haber** are irregular in the subjunctive.

No creo que esa chica **sepa** que estoy en su clase de biología.
¿Niegas que **haya** alguien más inteligente que tú?

CD 3, Tr. 5 See script on p. 95F.

### 18 ¿Están de acuerdo? 1.2

**Escuchemos** Escucha las conversaciones e indica si lo que dice la segunda persona es
a) una **afirmación** o
b) una **negación**
de lo que dice la primera persona.

**1.** b **2.** a **3** b
**4.** a **5.** b **6.** a

### 19 La vida universitaria 1.2

**Leamos/Escribamos** Completa la conversación con la forma correcta del verbo entre paréntesis.

—Oye, ¿tú crees que los cursos en la universidad __1__ (ser) muy difíciles?
—No creo que __2__ (ser) difíciles. Si quieres sacar buenas notas en la universidad lo puedes __3__ (hacer).
—Los profesores están ocupados todo el tiempo y es cierto que __4__ (dar) mucha tarea. ¿Quién me podría __5__ (ayudar)?
—No creo que los profesores __6__ (estar) tan ocupados pero es verdad que dan mucha tarea.
—Primero tengo que __7__ (enfocarse) en los cursos que tengo ahora. ¡Mis padres no creen que __8__ (estudiar) suficiente!

**1.** son
**2.** sean
**3.** hacer
**4.** dan
**5.** ayudar
**6.** estén
**7.** enfocarme
**8.** estudie

## Core Instruction

### TEACHING GRAMÁTICA

**1.** Go over point 1. Have students indicate the main and subordinate clauses. **(2 min.)**

**2.** Go over point 2. Say a sentence that expresses affirmation and have a student disagree with a sentence that expresses negation. **Creo que va a nevar. No creo que vaya a nevar.** The student will then say a sentence that expresses affirmation, another volunteer will negate it, and so on. **(3 min.)**

**3.** Review **¿Te acuerdas?** with students and practice the verb forms in the subjunctive for **haber** and **saber.** Go over the examples in **¿Te acuerdas?,** as well as the following: **¿Hay tiempo para un examen? No creo que haya tiempo para un examen. ¿Tus compañeros saben la fecha de tu cumpleaños? No creo que sepan la fecha. (3 min.)**

### GramaVisión

For a video presentation of the subjunctive with negation or denial, use **GramaVisión.**

GramaVisión

**20 ¿Qué crees?** 1.3

**Escribamos** Completa las oraciones con tus opiniones.

**MODELO** **No creo que...**
**No creo que el álgebra sea tan difícil.**

1. No es cierto que...
2. No estoy de acuerdo en que...
3. Estoy seguro que...
4. No creo que...
5. Niego que...
6. Es verdad que...

Estudiantes dominicanos debaten sus opiniones después de clases.

## Comunicación

HOLT SoundBooth ONLINE RECORDING

**21 ¡No es cierto!** 1.1, 1.3

**Leamos/Hablemos** Con un(a) compañero(a), lee los recortes *(clippings)* del periódico. Después de leer, túrnense para decir si están de acuerdo o no con las siguientes opiniones. Expliquen por qué.

Los jóvenes de hoy son todos unos irresponsables.

Los jóvenes son unos perezosos y no ayudan en la casa.

¿Se debe jugar a los videojuegos en vez de ir al colegio?

Los colegios deben ampliar el día escolar a nueve horas.

**22 ¡Al debate!** 1.1, 1.3

**Hablemos** Dos estudiantes aspiran a ser presidente de su clase. En parejas, dramaticen el diálogo entre ellos. Una persona menciona por lo menos tres opiniones o afirmaciones y la otra explica por qué no está de acuerdo. Sigan el modelo.

**MODELO** **—Pienso que la directora debe darnos diez minutos más durante la hora del almuerzo.**
**—No estoy de acuerdo en que eso sea necesario, porque...**

Gramática 1

### Thinking Critically

Have students bring in an article or clipping about a Spanish-speaking country from a newspaper or magazine. Ask each student to summarize their article for the class and to tell whether they agree or disagree with the author. Discuss whether students feel that media reports are accurate or misleading. Do stereotypes or prejudice play a part? Have a native Spanish speaker guest visit the classroom for students to ask about her perception of stereotypes and prejudice.

### Comunicación

#### Pair Activity: Interpretive

Each student prepares ten statements about him or herself. Some statements should be true and some should be false. Next, pair students to tell their statements to each other. Each student listens and decides whether or not he thinks each statement is true. Students use the phrases they have just learned to express negation or affirmation. Students keep track of how many correct responses their partners make. Have pairs change partners and start again. 1.2

## Differentiated Instruction

### SLOWER PACE LEARNERS

**20 Variation** Have students work in pairs to do Activity 20. Provide several specific topics for them to comment on such as current events, school policies, class assignments, or sports. If necessary, express an opinion of your own about the topic and have them use one of the prompts listed in the Activity to write a response. 1.2

### MULTIPLE INTELLIGENCES

**20 Mathematical** Have each student ask these questions in Spanish of a native Spanish-speaking person: Where were you born; how long have you lived in the U.S.; what type of music do you like; how many people are in your family; what type of food do prefer? Have the class organize results based on country of origin and determine the percentage of the same answer to each question. (Thirty-five percent are from Cuba, fifty percent listen to **reggaetón,** etc.) 3.1

### Assess

**Assessment Program**

**Prueba: Gramática 1,** pp. 43–44

**Prueba: Aplicación 1,** pp. 45–46

Audio CD 3, Tr. 17

Alternative Assessment, pp. 375, 387, 399

**Online Assessment** **my.hrw.com**

**Test Generator**

**Resources**

**Planning:**

Lesson Planner, pp. 38, 198–199

One-Stop Planner

**Presentation:**

Audio CD 3, Trs. 6–8

Video Program, Videocassette 2

DVD Program

**VideoCultura**

**Practice:**

Cuaderno de actividades, p. 24

Video Guide, pp. 18–19

Lab Book, p. 63

Interactive Tutor, Disc 1

# Cultura

VideoCultura

## Comparaciones

Interactive TUTOR

CD 3, Tr. 6-8

Unos padres y su hijo se sientan para resolver un conflicto.

### Quien no oye consejos, no llega lejos 4.2

En América Latina y en España, naturalmente, los hijos también discuten con sus padres. Los padres se preocupan de lo que hacen sus hijos, y a veces intentan controlar su comportamiento. Quieren que sus hijos hagan la tarea, que lleguen temprano a casa, que se vistan bien, que sean responsables. Los hijos se resisten a este control, y a veces hay problemas. ¿Se parecen estos conflictos a los que tienen tus padres y tú?

### Zaida

**San Juan, Puerto Rico**

***¿Cuál es el problema más común que tiene Ud. con sus dos hijos?***

Bueno, el grande, el mayor tiene el problema de vestir desarreglado.

***¿Cómo quiere Ud. que se vista su hijo?***

Yo quiero que vista arreglado, que se vea bien, porque siempre está con los pantalones todos rotos y prefiero que vista mejor.

***¿Y con su hijo pequeño, ¿tiene Ud. algún problema?***

Sí, él siempre está pegado al televisor. Yo prefiero que haga ejercicio, que salga un rato porque a él le viene bien para la salud, [pero] no quiere.

***¿Y qué hacen ellos cuando Ud. les pide que estudien más o que vistan mejor, o que no vean tanto el televisor?***

Bueno, ellos se quejan y todo, pero terminan obedeciendo porque yo hablo con ellos y llegamos a un acuerdo, y ya hacen lo posible por obedecer.

## Pre-AP Practice

**AP Language Examination:** Have students first listen to the interviews with books closed to help prepare them for Section I, Part A: **Listening—Short Dialogues and Narratives.** Point out that Zaida, like many Spanish speakers from the Caribbean, may pronounce syllable final **r** as **l (acueldo).**

**AP Benchmark:** Identify and summarize the main points and details and predict outcomes from a conversation from a familiar topic.

**Focus:** Family relationships and conflicts

- SE, p. 111, **Para comprender**
- SE, p. 111, **Para pensar y hablar**
- TE, p. 111, Advanced Learners

## Core Instruction

### TEACHING CULTURA

1. Read and discuss the introductory paragraph as a class. **(1 min.)**
2. Have students listen to the audio recording or watch the video. Have them take notes on the key points that each interviewee makes and then compare notes with a partner. **(5 min.)**
3. Have students answer the questions in **Para comprender. (4 min.)**

### VideoCultura

For a video presentation of the interviews as well as for an additional interview, see Chapter 3 **VideoCultura** on Videocassette or on DVD.

VideoCultura

**Visit Holt Online**
**go.hrw.com**
KEYWORD: EXP3 CH3
Online Edition

## Rafael
**San José, Costa Rica**

***Tus padres y tú no siempre están de acuerdo, ¿no es cierto?***
Por supuesto, en todas familias siempre hay algunos conflictos.

***¿Me puedes decir cuál es el conflicto más común que tienen Uds.?***
Bueno, por lo general, siempre discutimos un poco por las horas de llegada a la casa.

***¿Qué quieren tus padres que hagas?***
Bueno, mis padres quieren que llegue a una hora determinada a la casa y yo, por supuesto, trato de extenderla.

***¿Qué hacen para resolver el problema?***
Bueno, lo más común es sentarnos a conversar, y comunicando solucionamos el problema lo más pronto posible.

Cultura

### Para comprender 1.2

1. ¿Qué conflictos tiene Zaida con sus hijos?
2. ¿Qué quiere Zaida que hagan sus hijos?
3. ¿Qué hace Zaida para que sus hijos le obedezcan al final?
4. ¿Por qué discuten Rafael y sus padres? ¿Qué hacen para resolver el problema?
5. ¿Te parece que Rafael y sus padres se llevan bien? ¿Por qué?
6. ¿Qué actitud tienen Rafael y Zaida hacia los conflictos entre familia?

### Para pensar y hablar 1.3

En tu opinión, ¿cuál es la causa más común de los conflictos entre padres e hijos? ¿Cómo se resuelven más fácil y rápidamente los conflictos? En tu opinión, ¿cómo se puede evitar algunos conflictos entre padres e hijos?

## Comunidad y oficio 5.1

### El español en la universidad

¿Sabías que puedes continuar con tus estudios de español en la universidad? Hay una gran variedad de programas disponibles para estudiantes que quieran sacar una especialización en español o combinar el estudio del español con otra disciplina. Existen, por ejemplo, programas de estudios latinoamericanos en los que se combinan las ciencias sociales (como historia, economía o ciencias políticas) con el español; también es posible combinar un programa de español con uno de educación, medicina o derecho. Investiga los programas de español de dos universidades de tu región. ¿Qué opciones hay para estudiantes que quieran combinar el estudio del español con otra disciplina? ¿Cuáles son tres profesiones en las que un conocimiento del español, en combinación con otros estudios, sería una ventaja?

**Póster sobre cursos de español para extranjeros, Salamanca, España**

## Atlas
### INTERACTIVO MUNDIAL

Have students use the interactive atlas at **go.hrw.com**.

**Map Activities**

1. Using the interactive atlas or Map Transparencies, have students locate San Juan and San José.
2. Have students discuss what they know about Puerto Rico and Costa Rica.

3.1

### Answers

1. No le gusta la manera de vestir del mayor y que el pequeño siempre esté pegado al televisor.
2. Quiere que su hijo mayor se vista arreglado y que el menor haga más ejercicio.
3. Habla con ellos para llegar a un acuerdo.
4. Discuten por las horas de llegada a la casa. Se sientan a conversar.
5. Answers may vary.
6. Se puede solucionar los problemas con buena comunicación.

### Career Path

Have students work in groups to discuss the career advantages they might gain from studying abroad in a Spanish-speaking country. Have groups share their ideas with the class. 1.1

## Differentiated Instruction

### ADVANCED LEARNERS

**Extension** Read the interviews aloud and have students summarize what you read, without referring to their books. Then have them compare the conflicts discussed in the interviews with those they have seen on television or in a movie. Ask them to talk about what certain characters want others to do. 1.2

### MULTIPLE INTELLIGENCES

**Kinesthetic** Give students time to read the interviews. Then have them work in groups to prepare a conversation to demonstrate the family conflicts mentioned in the interviews. Assign the first interview to half the class, and the second interview to the other half. Ask students to act out their conversations for the class. Then discuss the presentations together. 1.1, 1.3

## Resources

**Planning:**

Lesson Planner, pp. 39–40, 200–201

One-Stop Planner

**Presentation:**

Teaching Transparencies
**Vocabulario** 3.3, 3.4

**Practice:**

Cuaderno de vocabulario y gramática, pp. 31–33

Activities for Communication, pp. 11–12

Teaching Transparencies
Bell Work 3.5
**Vocabulario y gramática** answers, pp. 31–33

Interactive Tutor, Disc 1

### Bell Work

Use Bell Work 3.5 in the *Teaching Transparencies*, or write this activity on the board.

**Vuelve a escribir cada oración para expresar negación.**

1. **Es cierto que hay discriminación en nuestra comunidad.**
2. **Creo que debemos combatir la ignorancia.**
3. **Es verdad que los prejuicios son imposibles de evitar.**
4. **Estoy de acuerdo en que mucha gente tiene impresiones equivocadas.**

**1.2**

**Objetivos**
- Making suggestions
- Apologizing

# Vocabulario en acción 2

## En Puerto Rico

### ¿Qué hacemos?

MARTA ¿Vas a la fiesta este sábado con Esteban?
ANA No, **discutimos** esta mañana.
MARTA ¿Qué pasó? ¿Por qué **se pelearon?**
ANA **Me ofendió** mucho con un comentario que hizo sobre mi hermana. Dijo que ella era muy chismosa y que siempre le estoy contando lo que él y yo estamos haciendo.
MARTA ¿Y por eso **discutieron?**
ANA Bueno, me **hirió** mucho; **estoy resentida** con él. Nunca más le voy a hablar.
MARTA ¡No seas exagerada! Ya verás que pronto vas a **olvidar** esto y van a **reconciliarse.**

**Más vocabulario...**

| | |
|---|---|
| **besar** | *to kiss* |
| **cometer un error** | *to make a mistake* |
| **la comunicación** | *communication* |
| **darle un abrazo** | *to give (someone) a hug* |
| **dejar de hablarse** | *to stop speaking to one another* |
| **la disculpa** | *apology* |
| **maltratar** | *to mistreat* |
| **la reconciliación** | *reconciliation* |
| **ser (in)fiel** | *to be (un)faithful* |

## Core Instruction

### TEACHING VOCABULARIO

1. Introduce the vocabulary using transparencies **Vocabulario 3.3** and **3.4.** Have volunteers read the conversation between Marta and Ana and the text on page 113. **(3 min.)**
2. Ask students questions about the conversation, using vocabulary words: **¿Quiénes discutieron esta mañana? (2 min.)**
3. Present **Más vocabulario** and use each word in a sentence. **(2 min.)**
4. Have students comment on the situation between Ana and Esteban. **(3 min.)**

### TEACHING ¡EXPRÉSATE!

1. Introduce **¡Exprésate!** by modeling the pronunciation of each new expression. **(2 min.)**
2. Pretend that you are giving Esteban advice. Use the expressions to make suggestions about how he can win Ana over. **(2 min.)**
3. Then present several hypothetical problems to students and have volunteers use the expressions to make suggestions. For example: **Mi mejor amigo me insultó. ¿Me puedes dar un consejo?** Or: **Le ofendí a una amiga hoy y ahora ella está ofendida. ¿Qué sugieres que haga? (3 min.)**

¡Qué idiota soy! Creo que **insulté** a Ana esta mañana. Qué bueno que mi amigo Héctor me pueda dar **consejos.**

Me dijo: «Para **hacer las paces** es necesario comunicarse. **Admite tu error** y ella te **perdonará.**» Tiene toda la razón.

También me dijo: «**Yo que tú,** le cantaría una canción.» ¡Lástima que canto tan mal!

Al final me dijo: «Debes **pedirle perdón** a Ana y **comprarle un regalo.** Las rosas siempre son un bonito **detalle.**» ¡Pero ella es alérgica a las flores!

## ¡Exprésate!

### To make suggestions

Interactive TUTOR

| | |
|---|---|
| **No te olvides de...** *Don't forget to . . .* | **Sugiero que no hagas caso a los rumores.** *I suggest that you not pay attention to rumors.* |
| **¿Has pensado en...?** *Have you thought about . . . ?* | **No te conviene...** *It's not good for you . . .* |
| **Sería una buena/mala idea romper con...** *It would be a good/bad idea to break up with . . .* | **Date tiempo para pensarlo.** *Give yourself time to think it over.* |

Vocabulario y gramática, pp. 31–33 Online workbooks

Vocabulario 2

## TPR
### Total Physical Response

Tell pairs of students to imagine that they are in an argument. One student should play the part of Luis and one the part of Susana. Have them act out the following commands with gestures.

**Discutan.**

**Dejen de hablarse.**

**Luis, pídele perdón a Susana.**

**Hagan las paces.**

**Susana, perdónale a Luis.**

1.2

## Common Error Alert
### ¡OJO!

**¡OJO!** Remind students not to confuse **discúlpame** with **disculpe. Discúlpame** *(forgive me)* is the informal way to ask for forgiveness. **Disculpe** *(excuse me, pardon me)* is formal. Remind students not to confuse **discutir** with *discuss.* In Spanish, **discutir** implies an argument.

## Heritage Speakers

Have heritage speakers share other expressions for making suggestions and different phrases that they might use to talk about relationships. Have volunteers act out the expressions they present. Have the class say a word from **Vocabulario** most closely related to the new expression given by the heritage speakers. You may also want several heritage speakers to come to the front of the class and present a conversation using alternative expressions for those learned in **Vocabulario 2.** 1.1

## Differentiated Instruction

### Advanced Learners

**Personalization** Have students work in pairs to discuss what they believe are common problems with a boyfriend or girlfriend. Encourage them to use as much new vocabulary as possible. Tell them they can take turns talking about these problems and offering advice using the **¡Exprésate!** expressions. They can invent situations or use their own personal experience. 1.1

### Special Learning Needs

**Students with Visual Impairments** Students with visual impairments may have trouble seeing how the text relates to the photos in **Vocabulario 2.** Have volunteers read and act out the conversations, stressing the boldface vocabulary words. Then read the words from **Más vocabulario** aloud and have volunteers provide the English translations. 1.2

**Differentiated Instruction** See the Differentiated Instruction CD-ROM.

## Resources

**Planning:**

Lesson Planner, pp. 39–40, 200–201

One-Stop Planner

**Presentation:**

Teaching Transparencies
**Vocabulario** 3.3, 3.4

**Practice:**

Cuaderno de vocabulario y gramática, pp. 31–33

Activities for Communication, pp. 11–12

Lab Book, pp. 21–24

Teaching Transparencies
**Vocabulario y gramática** answers, pp. 31–33

Audio CD 3, Tr. 9

Interactive Tutor, Disc 1

### 23 Script

1. Ángela vio a Jorge y a Julia juntos ayer. Ahora Ángela cree que Jorge le es infiel.
2. Enrique admitió su error y le pidió perdón a Margarita.
3. Qué bueno que mis hermanas se comuniquen todos los días.
4. Andrés intentó disculparse, pero Pedro no le hizo caso.
5. Diana y Cristina son buenas amigas. Siempre se abrazan cuando se ven.
6. Eduardo le compró un regalo a Laura para su cumpleaños. Él nunca olvida esa fecha.

CD 3, Tr. 9

### 23 ¿Qué ocurrió aquí? 1.2

**Escuchemos** Mira las fotos y escucha las oraciones. Elige la foto que corresponde a cada oración.

**1.** d **2.** a **3.** c **4.** f **5.** e **6.** b

### 24 Rumores y desacuerdos 1.2

**Leamos/Escribamos** Completa las oraciones con la forma correcta de las palabras del cuadro.

| | | | |
|---|---|---|---|
| cometer un error | hacer(le) caso | hacer las paces | olvidar |
| comprarle un regalo | insultar | romper con | el rumor |

1. Después de un gran malentendido, Juan y Héctor intentaron ____ y dejar de pelear. hacer las paces
2. ¿Cómo pudiste ____ mi cumpleaños? ¡Te lo dije ayer! olvidar
3. Ana ____ Samuel después de tres años. Ahora se siente sola. rompió con
4. Quiero ____ a mi novia para el Día de San Valentín. ¿Qué me recomienda Ud., joyas o flores? comprarle un regalo
5. Oí ____ de que Verónica salió con Claudio anoche y no con Daniel. ¿Es verdad? el rumor
6. Todos creemos que Manuel ____ cuando se olvidó del cumpleaños de Lourdes. cometió un error
7. Leonardo trata de convencer a Natalia de que salga con él, pero ella no ____. le hace caso
8. No quería ____ a Catalina con lo que le dije; dile que lo siento mucho. insultar

## Core Instruction

### VOCABULARY IN CONTEXT

Use this activity to practice vocabulary words. Draw a chart on the board with the labels **El conflicto** and **La reconciliación.** One by one, have students go to the board and write a vocabulary word under the appropriate heading. For example, a student might write **darle un abrazo** under **La reconciliación.** Have students explain their reasoning and allow the rest of the class to tell whether they agree or disagree with the categorization. Then have students work in groups to prepare their own conversation about a conflict between friends and how they make up. They can use the chart as reference as they prepare their conversations. Have groups take turns presenting their conversations to the class. Ask students to raise their hands every time they hear a word or phrase from **Vocabulario** in the conversation.

**25 Se oye que...** 1.2

**Leamos** Se oyeron estos diálogos en el autobús del colegio, pero eran muy confusos *(mixed up)* por el ruido. Lee el comienzo de cada diálogo y decide qué respuesta lo completa mejor.

1. Ayer ofendí a Mónica, ¿sabes? La acusé de tomar un libro mío, pero más tarde lo encontré en mi mochila. c
2. ¿Oíste el último rumor? Dicen que Adela y Rafa se han reconciliado; él se disculpó por el error que cometió. d
3. Chica, ¿qué les pasó? ¿Por qué Vicente y tú dejaron de hablarse? a
4. ¿Todavía estás resentido con Carmen? ¿Qué te hizo? e
5. Pablo y yo siempre discutimos, pero luego me da un abrazo y me pide disculpas. Ya no confío en él. b

Estudiantes de preparatoria suben al autobús en Guánica, Puerto Rico.

a. Es que él me insultó ayer y todavía no me ha pedido perdón. Ya no puedo más.
b. Si Uds. siguen mis consejos, creo que se llevarán mejor, pero parece que te ha herido con sus comentarios.
c. Creo que debes admitir el error, y así hacer las paces.
d. ¡Qué bien! Si ella pudo perdonar ese error, es obvio que se dio tiempo para pensarlo.
e. Fíjate que ella y yo nos peleamos ayer por algo muy tonto, y ahora quiere romper conmigo.

**26 ¡Ayuda, por favor!** 1.2

**Escribamos** Escribe una carta a un(a) amigo(a) en la que describas un problema imaginario que tienes con otro(a) amigo(a). Pídele ayuda a tu amigo(a). Usa al menos seis expresiones del cuadro.

| | | | | |
|---|---|---|---|---|
| cometer un error | herir | la disculpa | discutir | olvidar |
| dejar de hablarse | insultar | ofender | pelearse | el rumor |

## Comunicación

HOLT SoundBooth ONLINE RECORDING

**27 Tus consejos** 1.1, 1.2

**Leamos/Hablemos** En parejas, intercambien las cartas que escribieron en la Actividad 26. Lee la carta de tu compañero(a) y luego ofrécele consejos. Usa las palabras de **Vocabulario** y las expresiones de **Exprésate** en la conversación.

### Más práctica

Have students write part of a conversation like those in Activity 25 using words from **Vocabulario 2.** Once students have written the beginning of the conversation, have them exchange papers with a partner. Students will then write the other part of the dialogue using vocabulary words and expressions. 1.1

### Comunicación

**Class Activity: Presentational**

Have students exchange letters with five other members of the class. They should take notes on the advice they receive from each person. Then have them prepare a short presentation for the class, telling what kinds of advice people gave them. Ask them to tell what they think was the best advice. 1.1, 1.3

## Differentiated Instruction

### ADVANCED LEARNERS

**25 Additional Practice** After doing Activity 25, have students create three conversations of their own using words from **Vocabulario** and expressions from **¡Exprésate!** They should write the beginning of each conversation on one piece of paper and the end of each conversation on a separate piece of paper, as in Activity 25. Have them exchange papers with a partner to match the beginning of each conversation with the correct ending. Then have them read the completed conversations aloud. 1.1

### SPECIAL LEARNING NEEDS

**25 Students with Learning Disabilities** Some students may have trouble matching the comments with their responses. Read them aloud one by one. After each one, ask students what type of response they would expect. Then read each of the choices and help students choose the best response by process of elimination. Have them cross out the sentences as they use them. Repeat this process until they have matched all the comments with the correct response.

**Differentiated Instruction** See the Differentiated Instruction CD-ROM.

## Resources

**Planning:**

Lesson Planner, pp. 39–40, 200–201

One-Stop Planner

**Presentation:**

Teaching Transparencies
**Vocabulario** 3.3, 3.4

**Practice:**

Cuaderno de vocabulario y gramática, pp. 31–33

Activities for Communication, pp. 11–12

Teaching Transparencies
**Vocabulario y gramática** answers, pp. 31–33

Interactive Tutor, Disc 1

## Heritage Speakers

Have heritage speakers share alternatives for ways to apologize with the class. If necessary, make a list of the alternative expressions on the board. Call on a heritage speaker to use the alternative expression with you in a conversation. 1.3

En una casa de San Juan, Puerto Rico

## La reconciliación

ESTEBAN Lo siento, Ana. No sé por qué dije esas cosas.

ANA No, no, lo siento yo. Fui muy tonta. Tienes razón, mi hermana puede ser un poco habladora y a veces le cuento información personal. No lo volveré a hacer.

ESTEBAN No, dije algo muy feo. No quise ofenderte. Mira, te traje unas flores.

ANA ¿Pero qué forma es ésta de pedirme perdón? ¿Se te ha olvidado que les tengo alergia a las flores?

ESTEBAN ¡Bueno, dáselas a tu hermana y te compro un helado!

### ¡Exprésate!

**To apologize**

Interactive TUTOR

| | |
|---|---|
| **Te juro que no lo volveré a hacer.** *I swear I'll never do it again.* | **No lo hice a propósito.** *I didn't do it on purpose.* |
| **Perdóname. No sé en qué estaba pensando.** *Forgive me. I don't know what I was thinking.* | **No quise hacerte daño.** *I didn't mean to hurt you.* |
| **Créeme que fue sin querer.** *Believe me, I didn't mean to do it.* | **No quise ofenderte.** *I didn't mean to offend you.* |

Vocabulario y gramática, pp. 31–33 Online workbooks

## Core Instruction

### TEACHING ¡EXPRÉSATE!

1. Briefly review new vocabulary by asking students about their relationships. **¿Te has sentido herido(a) alguna vez? ¿Cómo te sientes cuando una persona te ofende? (2 min.)**
2. Present several situations in which you might have to apologize to someone as you model expressions from **¡Exprésate!** to show what you might say in each situation. **(3 min.)**
3. Have students respond to hypothetical situations using the expressions from **¡Exprésate!** Use the following prompts: **Me ofendiste ayer. Lo que dijiste me insultó. Oí que empezaste un rumor. (3 min.)**

**28 ¿Cómo pasó?** 1.2

**Leamos** Pon las siguientes oraciones en orden cronológico según las conversaciones en las páginas 112, 113 y 116. 6, 5, 7, 3, 2, 1, 4

1. Esteban le da unas flores a Ana.
2. Ana admite su error en contarle cosas a su hermana.
3. Esteban le pide perdón a Ana.
4. Ana se ofende con Esteban por olvidar un detalle sobre ella.
5. Esteban le pide consejos a su amigo Héctor.
6. Ana se siente insultada por lo que dice Esteban sobre su hermana.
7. Héctor le da consejos a Esteban para que haga las paces con Ana.

**29 ¿Quién lo dijo?** 1.2

**Leamos/Hablemos** Basándote en las conversaciones, indica qué persona diría *(would say)* cada oración: **Ana, Marta, Esteban, Héctor** o **la hermana de Ana.** Una oración tiene más de una respuesta correcta.

1. Tal vez no le di buenos consejos a Esteban. Héctor
2. No puedo creer que no pueda confiar en mi hermana. Ana
3. Qué lastima que yo no cante mejor. Esteban
4. Creo que se van a reconciliar. Marta, Héctor
5. ¡No es cierto que yo no sepa guardar un secreto! la hermana de Ana
6. ¡Qué error cometí! Olvidé que Ana era alérgica a las flores. Esteban

**30 Tus reacciones** 1.2

**Leamos/Hablemos** ¿Qué expresión de **Exprésate** usarías *(would you use)* en las siguientes situaciones?

1. Un amigo te prestó unos discos compactos y los perdiste.
2. No le mandaste una tarjeta de cumpleaños a tu mejor amigo(a).
3. Un amigo te invitó a salir, pero te olvidaste de la hora y lo dejaste plantado.
4. Le contaste un rumor a otra persona acerca de un amigo. Tu amigo lo oyó, y se ofendió.

**Nota cultural**

Las telenovelas de Latinoamérica son muy famosas. A diferencia de las telenovelas estadounidenses, no duran más de un año. Por lo general, pasan las telenovelas más populares entre las siete y las nueve de la noche. En algunos hogares, ver una telenovela juntos es una manera de convivir con la familia y los amigos. Además, hay telenovelas hechas para adolescentes y para adultos.

¿Has visto una telenovela latinoamericana?
1.2, 5.2

Filmando un segmento de una telenovela mexicana, Ciudad de México

## Comunicación

HOLT SoundBooth ONLINE RECORDING

**31 Escena dramática** 1.1, 1.2

**Hablemos** En grupos de tres, dramaticen una escena de una telenovela *(soap opera)*. En la escena, unos amigos discutían, pero ya se están reconciliando. Expliquen qué causó el conflicto. Usen las palabras de **Vocabulario** y las expresiones de **Exprésate.**

### Cultures

**Products and Perspectives**

Discuss the **Nota cultural** with students. Ask whether anyone has seen Latin American soap operas, and have them share their opinions. Ask students if they have watched other Spanish-language programming. How do the programs compare with their English language counterparts? Suggest that students watch Spanish-language programming at home and then discuss the similarities and differences with the class.
2.2, 4.2

### Comunicación

**Group Activity: Interpersonal**

Have students work in groups of four to prepare the following presentation, like the one they read in **Vocabulario 2.** Two friends argue. Each asks another friend for advice, and then they reconcile. Have groups present their conversations to the class. The class should discuss which groups gave the best advice.
1.1

## Differentiated Instruction

**SLOWER PACE LEARNERS**

Some students might get confused trying to flip back to the conversations in order to complete Activities 28 and 29. Before they begin the Activities, help them summarize what happened in the story. Suggest that they write the names **Ana, Marta, Esteban, Héctor, la hermana de Ana** on a piece of paper and take notes next to each person's name as you summarize the story.

**MULTIPLE INTELLIGENCES**

**30 Linguistic** To modify Activity 30, have students present situations from their own personal experience in which they have had to apologize to someone, and have them use expressions from **¡Exprésate!** to demonstrate what they said. 1.2

### Assess

**Assessment Program**

**Prueba: Vocabulario 2,** pp. 47–48

Alternative Assessment, pp. 375, 387, 399

**Online Assessment** my.hrw.com

**Test Generator**

**Assess** **Differentiated Instruction** See the Differentiated Instruction CD-ROM.

## Resources

**Planning:**

Lesson Planner, pp. 41–43, 202–205

One-Stop Planner

**Presentation:**

Video Program **GramaVisión**

**Practice:**

Grammar Tutor for Students of Spanish, Chapter 3

Cuaderno de vocabulario y gramática, pp. 34–36

Cuaderno de actividades, pp. 25–27

Activities for Communication, pp. 11–12

Lab Book, pp. 21–24

Teaching Transparencies Bell Work 3.6

**Vocabulario y gramática** answers, pp. 34–36

Audio CD 3, Tr. 10

Interactive Tutor, Disc 1

### Bell Work

Use Bell Work 3.6 in the *Teaching Transparencies*, or write this activity on the board.

**Responde a cada situación con una expresión para pedir perdón.**

1. **Dijiste algo que le ofendió a tu amigo(a).**
2. **Es el cumpleaños de tu novio(a) y te olvidaste de comprarle un regalo.**
3. **Dejaste plantado(a) a tu amigo(a).**
4. **Fuiste infiel a tu pareja.**

1.2

**Objetivos**
- **Future tense**
- **Conditional**

# Gramática en acción 2

GramaVisión

Interactive TUTOR

## Repaso Future tense

**1** The **future tense** can be used to talk about future events. The regular endings, added to the infinitive form, are:

| | | | |
|---|---|---|---|
| yo | comer**é** | nosotros(as) | comer**emos** |
| tú | comer**ás** | vosotros(as) | comer**éis** |
| Ud., él, ella | comer**á** | Uds., ellos, ellas | comer**án** |

No lo **volveré** a hacer. **Hablaremos** sobre esto otro día.

**2** The future tense can be used to express the **probability** of something happening or being true. It can be used with the **present participle** to say what is probably going on.

—¿Qué hora es?
—No sé, **serán** las nueve más o menos.
—No oigo nada. Los niños **estarán durmiendo**.

Vocabulario y gramática, pp. 34–36
Actividades, pp. 25–27
Online workbooks

### ¡Te acuerdas?

The following verbs have irregular stems in the future tense. Add the future endings to the following stems:

| | |
|---|---|
| caber: **cabr-** | querer: **querr-** |
| decir: **dir-** | saber: **sabr-** |
| haber: **habr-** | salir: **saldr-** |
| hacer: **har-** | tener: **tendr-** |
| poder: **podr-** | valer: **valdr-** |
| poner: **pondr-** | venir: **vendr-** |

Marta no **querrá** pelear.

Los chicos **podrán** hacer las paces mañana.

CD 3, Tr. 10 See script on p. 95F.

**1.** pasado **2.** presente **3.** futuro **4.** futu
**5.** pasado **6.** futuro **7.** pasado **8.** futu

### 32 Pasado, presente y futuro 1.2

**Escuchemos** Escucha las siguientes oraciones y decide si describen algo que ya ocurrió (**pasado**), algo que ocurre ahora (**presente**) o algo que ocurrirá en el futuro (**futuro**).

### 33 ¿Qué pasará? 1.2

**Leamos/Escribamos** Lee las oraciones sobre qué va a pasar en tu colegio y en la sociedad. Indica si estás de acuerdo o no. Si no estás de acuerdo, escribe lo que tú crees que pasará.

1. Pondrán una pizzería y una heladería en la cafetería.
2. Empezarán un intercambio con estudiantes de otros países.
3. No usaremos libros, sólo computadoras.
4. Los estereotipos desaparecerán.
5. Todo el mundo irá a la universidad.
6. Las personas respetarán las culturas de personas de otros países.

## Core Instruction

### TEACHING GRAMÁTICA

1. Review the future tense by asking students what they will do when they graduate. **¿Qué harás? ¿Dónde vivirás? ¿Con qué frecuencia hablarás con tus padres? (2 min.)**
2. Go over point 2. Show several pictures of people students do not know and have them use the future of probability to say who they might be or what is probably happening. **¿Será este hombre el papá de la chica en la foto? ¿Qué estará haciendo el profesor? (3 min.)**
3. Go over **¿Te acuerdas?** with students and have them ask each other questions about the future using the irregular verbs. **(2 min.)**
4. Have volunteers act out what they will do on their next vacation while the class tries to guess what is being acted out. For example, a person pretends to pack a suitcase and get on a plane. The first student to guess **viajará** takes the next turn. **(3 min.)**

### GramaVisión

For a video presentation of the future tense, use **GramaVisión.**

GramaVisión

Visit Holt Online
**go.hrw.com**
KEYWORD: EXP3 CH3
Gramática 2 Practice

## 34 ¿Qué harán? 1.2

**Leamos/Escribamos** Escribe lo que cada persona hará cuando termine el año escolar.

1. los estudiantes/no estudiar Los estudiantes no estudiarán.
2. mis amigos y yo/hacer una fiesta Mis amigos y yo haremos una fiesta.
3. los profesores/poder viajar Los profesores podrán viajar.
4. la directora/descansar La directora descansará.
5. tú/no tomar clases de verano Tú no tomarás clases de verano.
6. nuestros padres/ponernos a trabajar en casa Nuestros padres nos pondrán a trabajar en casa.

## 35 ¿Quién será? 1.2

**Escribamos** Mira las fotos y describe lo que estará pasando.

MODELO **Andrés será el novio de Silvia. Silvia estará resentida porque Andrés no llegó a tiempo.**

Silvia y Andrés

1. Mónica y Gerardo

2. Lisa, Juan y Miguel

3. Emilio y Beatriz

4. Patricia y David

## Comunicación

HOLT SoundBooth ONLINE RECORDING

## 36 ¿Qué crees que haré? 1.1, 1.2

**Escribamos/Hablemos** Escribe cinco oraciones sobre lo que crees que hará tu compañero(a) en los próximos cinco años. Usa los verbos del cuadro. Después, trabaja con tu compañero(a) para compartir y responder a las predicciones.

MODELO **—Tú asistirás a la universidad después de graduarte.**
**—No, viajaré por el mundo durante un año.**

| | | | |
|---|---|---|---|
| asistir a | ir | salir | trabajar |
| hacer | ver | hacerse | vivir |
| viajar | tener | conocer | casarse |

Gramática 2

### COMMON ERROR ALERT ¡OJO!

Students often forget that the future tense can be used to express the probability of something happening. When they see the future tense, they assume the verb describes an action that will happen. Point out that in Activity 35 they are not talking about what will happen, but what is probably happening. Tell them that the sentences they write for this exercise will use the future of probability.

## Comunicación

### Class Activity: Interpersonal

As a class, talk about what you think famous people will do in the next few years. You might bring in a Spanish magazine such as ***¡Hola!*** or ***People en español*** to use as a conversation starter. You can look at the photos, share the captions together, and then prompt students to talk about what they will do in the future.

MODELO
**—¿Qué tipo de película hará este actor ahora?**
**—Creo que hará otra película de acción.**
1.1

## Differentiated Instruction

### ADVANCED LEARNERS

**35 Extension** After doing Activity 35, have students work in groups to present short skits to the class in which they play the parts of famous people. The rest of the class must guess who they are and what is going on in the skit. Have volunteers use the future of probability to say who they think the people might be and what is happening in each skit. 1.1

### SPECIAL LEARNING NEEDS

**34 Students with Dyslexia** Writing complete sentences can be challenging for students with dyslexia. For Activity 34, go over the sentences orally with students. Have them combine the subjects and verbs, conjugating the verbs as they go. As they say each sentence, write it on the board. Then have the class check the sentence to decide whether or not it is correct. Students may copy the correct sentences in their notebooks and have you check their work. 1.2

**Differentiated Instruction** See the Differentiated Instruction CD-ROM.

## Resources

**Planning:**

Lesson Planner, pp. 41–43, 202–205

One-Stop Planner

**Presentation:**

Video Program **GramaVisión**

**Practice:**

Grammar Tutor for Students of Spanish, Chapter 3

Cuaderno de vocabulario y gramática, pp. 34–36

Cuaderno de actividades, pp. 25–27

Activities for Communication, pp. 11–12

Teaching Transparencies

Bell Work 3.7

**Vocabulario y gramática** answers, pp. 34–36

Interactive Tutor, Disc 1

### Bell Work

Use Bell Work 3.7 in the *Teaching Transparencies*, or write this activity on the board.

**Completa las oraciones con la forma correcta del verbo en el futuro.**

1. Mi amiga y su novio _____ (dejar) de hablarse si él no le pide perdón.
2. Él le _____ (comprar) un regalo mañana.
3. Luego él _____ (admitir) su error.
4. Seguramente ella lo _____ (perdonar) y lo _____ (besar).

1.2

## The conditional

Interactive TUTOR

**1** The **conditional** is used to express what *would happen* or what someone *would do* in a given set of circumstances.

| | |
|---|---|
| En tu lugar, **estudiaría** más. | *In your place, I would study more.* |
| En esa situación, **pediría** más tiempo. | *In that situation, I would ask for more time.* |

**2** The endings, added to the infinitive form, are the same for **-er, -ar,** and **-ir** verbs.

| | | | |
|---|---|---|---|
| yo | habla**ría** | nosotros(as) | habla**ríamos** |
| tú | habla**rías** | vosotros(as) | habla**ríais** |
| Ud., él, ella | habla**ría** | Uds., ellos, ellas | habla**rían** |

**3** Some expressions that are often used with the conditional include **yo que tú, en tu lugar,** and **en esa situación.**

| | |
|---|---|
| Yo que tú, **trataría** de hacer las paces. | *If I were you, I would try to make up.* |
| En tu lugar, lo **llamaría** por teléfono. | *In your place, I would call him.* |

**4** Expressions that tell what you *would* or *would not like* are also used with the conditional.

| | |
|---|---|
| Me **gustaría** darle tiempo para pensar. | *I would like to give her time to think.* |
| Te **molestaría** oír el rumor. | *It would bother you to hear the rumor.* |

Vocabulario y gramática, pp. 34–36
Actividades, pp. 25–27
Online workbooks

### ¿Te acuerdas?

Verbs that have irregular stems in the future tense have the same irregular stems in the conditional:

| | |
|---|---|
| caber: **cabr-** | querer: **querr-** |
| decir: **dir-** | saber: **sabr-** |
| haber: **habr-** | salir: **saldr-** |
| hacer: **har-** | tener: **tendr-** |
| poder: **podr-** | valer: **valdr-** |
| poner: **pondr-** | venir: **vendr-** |

### 37 Después de graduarme... 1.2

**Hablemos/Escribamos** Completa las siguientes oraciones sobre lo que te gustaría hacer después de tu graduación.

1. En mi opinión, sería interesante trabajar en ____.
2. Creo que no me interesaría estudiar ____ en la universidad.
3. Algún día me gustaría ir a ____.
4. Allí podría ____.
5. Me gustaría vivir en ____.
6. Tendría una casa ideal, con ____.

## Core Instruction

### TEACHING GRAMÁTICA

1. Go over points 1 and 2. Practice the forms by asking students what they or other students would do in various situations. **¿Qué harían Pamela y David con cien dólares? Comprarían libros nuevos. (3 min.)**
2. Go over point 3 with students. Have them practice using the conditional with these phrases by asking their advice. **Discutí con mi amigo. ¿Qué me aconsejas? Yo que tú, hablaría con él. (2 min.)**
3. Go over point 4 with students. Practice the conditional by asking questions such as: **¿Qué te gustaría hacer hoy después de las clases? (2 min.)**
4. Review **¿Te acuerdas?** Have volunteers state a problem. Have students give them advice using the conditional form. The student giving the advice presents the next problem. **(3 min.)**

### GramaVisión

For a video presentation of the conditional, use **GramaVisión**.

GramaVisión

## 38 Lo pasaría bien 1.2

**Leamos/Escribamos** Completa el párrafo con la forma correcta del condicional de los verbos entre paréntesis.

Mi amigo Luis es muy tímido pero sé que le __1__ (gustar) salir con Cristina. Pienso que ella __2__ (aceptar) la invitación y que ellos lo __3__ (pasar) muy bien. En esa situación, yo le __4__ (escribir) una carta a la chica y la __5__ (invitar) al cine o a comer. Yo __6__ (ser) muy abierto con ella. Le __7__ (decir) que es bonita y que me __8__ (interesar) pasar tiempo con ella. ¡Seguramente ella __9__ (estar) encantada!

1. gustaría
2. aceptaría
3. pasarían
4. escribiría
5. invitaría
6. sería
7. diría
8. interesaría
9. estaría

## 39 En esa situación... 1.3

**Escribamos** Mira los dibujos y escribe lo que tú harías en cada situación.

**MODELO** **En esa situación, estudiaría más para el próximo examen.**

1.

2.

3.

4.

## Comunicación

HOLT SoundBooth ONLINE RECORDING

## 40 Como presidente... 1.1, 1.2

**Escribamos/Hablemos** ¿Qué harías como director(a) de tu colegio y como presidente del país? Escribe tres oraciones para cada situación. En parejas, comparen las respuestas.

**MODELO** **—Como presidente, combatiría la discriminación.**
**—¿Sí? Pues, yo trataría de resolver...**

| | | | |
|---|---|---|---|
| la discriminación | el estereotipo | la ignorancia | combatir |
| suspender | el horario | los cursos | el semestre |
| disculpar | respetar a | el/la consejero(a) | resolver |

### Más práctica

Have students write at least five sentences giving advice with the conditional. Have students choose a famous person, a friend, or a fictional character to whom they should give advice. Students should use expressions often used with the conditional, such as **yo que tú, en tu lugar,** and **en esa situación** in their sentences as well as words from **Vocabulario.** 1.2

### Comunicación

**Group Activity: Interpersonal**

Have students prepare four imaginary situations they would like advice on. Then have them take turns presenting their situations in small groups. Their classmates should each tell what they would do in that situation. Students should choose the responses they like best and share them with the class. 1.1

## Differentiated Instruction

### ADVANCED LEARNERS

**Additional Practice** Have students write a paragraph about where they would like to go on vacation. Ask them to describe all of the activities they would do, how they would dress, whom they would travel with, and other details. They should use as many verbs in the conditional as possible. Pairs of students exchange paragraphs and agree or disagree with their partner's ideas. If they disagree, have them make suggestions for how to improve the trip. 1.1, 1.3

### MULTIPLE INTELLIGENCES

**39 Bodily/Kinesthetic** Have groups of students come up with more situations like those in Activity 39. They should act out the situation for the class and show how they react to it. Have the rest of the students use the conditional to tell what each student or group of students would do in the situation, based on the presentation. 1.2, 1.3

## Resources

**Planning:**

Lesson Planner, pp. 41–43, 202–205

One-Stop Planner

**Presentation:**

Video Program **GramaVisión**

**Practice:**

Grammar Tutor for Students of Spanish, Chapter 3

Cuaderno de vocabulario y gramática, pp. 34–36

Cuaderno de actividades, pp. 25–27

Activities for Communication, pp. 11–12

Lab Book, pp. 21–24

Teaching Transparencies

Bell Work 3.8

**Vocabulario y gramática** answers, pp. 34–36

Audio CD 3, Tr. 11

Interactive Tutor, Disc 1

### Bell Work

Use Bell Work 3.8 in the *Teaching Transparencies*, or write this activity on the board.

**Completa las oraciones con la forma condicional del verbo en paréntesis.**

1. En esa situación, yo (tener) celos.
2. Yo que tú (hacer) las paces.
3. En tu lugar, (salir) con los amigos.
4. Yo le (decir) que fue un malentendido.
5. Yo no (saber) qué hacer en esa situación. 1.2

### 41 Script

See script on page 95F.

## More uses of the conditional

Interactive TUTOR

Use the **conditional** with the following **"if" statements** that express contrary-to-fact situations.

**Si yo fuera** la profesora, **daría** menos tarea.
*If I were the teacher, I would give less homework.*

**Si tú fueras** la profesora, ¿me **suspenderías?**
*If you were the teacher, would you fail me?*

**Si yo tuviera** más dinero, me **iría** de viaje.
*If I had more money, I would go on a trip.*

**Si tú tuvieras** más dinero, ¿**comprarías** una casa?
*If you had more money, would you buy a house?*

**Si yo pudiera** volver a presentar el examen, **estudiaría** más.
*If I could take the exam again, I would study more.*

**Si tú pudieras** volver a presentar el examen, **sacarías** una A.
*If you could take the exam again, you would get an A.*

You will learn more about this usage of the conditional in Chapter 8.

Vocabulario y gramática, pp. 24–36
Actividades, pp. 25–27
Online workbooks

CD 3, Tr. 11

### 41 ¿Quién lo dijo? 1.2

| | | |
|---|---|---|
| 1. b | 3. f | 5. c |
| 2. d | 4. e | 6. a |

**Escuchemos** Mira las fotos y escucha los comentarios. Escoge la foto que corresponde a cada comentario.

A

B

C

D

E

F

## Core Instruction

### TEACHING GRAMÁTICA

1. Introduce: **si yo fuera, si tú fueras, si yo tuviera, si tú tuvieras, si yo pudiera, si tú pudieras. (2 min.)**
2. Read through the examples. Explain that these examples describe what you *would do* or what *would happen* if the situation described were true. **(2 min.)**
3. Practice by telling what you would do in certain situations and then asking students what they would do in the same situation. **Si yo fuera el (la) presidente, combatiría la discriminación en este país. ¿Qué harías si fueras el (la) presidente?** Continue with **si yo tuviera, si yo pudiera. (3 min.)**
4. Have students state contrary-to-fact situations using the new phrases. Have them make a statement about what they would do in a certain situation and then ask a classmate what he or she would do. **(3 min.)**

### GramaVisión

For a video presentation of the conditional with contrary-to-fact situations, use **GramaVisión**.

GramaVisión

## 42 Mis sueños ❀ 1.2

**Escribamos** Usa una palabra o expresión de cada columna para escribir seis oraciones. Sigue el modelo.

**MODELO** **Si yo fuera famoso, iría a los premios Óscar.**

| | | |
|---|---|---|
| Si yo (no) fuera → | rico(a)<br>famoso(a)<br>presidente<br>estudiante → | hacer<br>tratar de<br>ir a<br>gustar<br>comprar<br>salir<br>jugar |
| Si yo (no) tuviera → | un millón de dólares<br>más tiempo<br>que hacer la tarea → | |

## 43 Si pudiera... ❀ 1.3

**Escribamos** Contesta las preguntas.

1. Si pudieras viajar, ¿adónde irías y por qué?
2. Si tuvieras la oportunidad de conocer a cualquier persona, ¿a quién te gustaría conocer y por qué?
3. Si pudieras resolver un problema de nuestra sociedad, ¿qué problema resolverías? ¿Qué harías?
4. Si pudieras viajar en el tiempo a cualquier década *(decade)* del pasado, ¿qué década escogerías y por qué? ¿Qué harías?

## Comunicación

HOLT SoundBooth ONLINE RECORDING

## 44 ¡Un millón de dólares! ❀ 1.1, 1.3

**Hablemos** Pregúntale a tu compañero(a) si él o ella haría lo que está haciendo la chica en cada uno de los dibujos. Si él o ella te dice que no, pregúntale «¿Qué harías en su lugar?» Túrnense.

a. b. c.

### Answers

Use the Chapter 3 *Picture Sequences Transparency.*

**44 Sample Answer**

**Si yo fuera rica, también compraría joyas para mí y para mis amigos. Y luego también compraría un carro nuevo para pasear con mis amigos. Por último, pagaría por un viaje ara ir a la playa con mis amigos.**

### Comunicación

**Class Activity: Presentational**

Have students circulate around the classroom to ask their classmates how they would answer the question: **¿Qué harías si fueras rico(a)?** Have them compile the results to prepare for the class in chart form. Ask them to present their charts and summarize their findings.

**MODELO**

**Tres personas irían de viaje. Una persona compraría una casa.**

❀ 1.1, 1.3

## Differentiated Instruction

### SLOWER PACE LEARNERS

**43 Variation** Before doing Activity 43, tell students that all of the sentences will be in the **yo** form. Review the **yo** form of the conditional for the verbs in the last column. If necessary, guide students on how to combine elements by asking them questions. **Si fueras rico(a), ¿qué comprarías?** Have students respond aloud before writing the response.
❀ 1.2

### SPECIAL LEARNING NEEDS

**42 Students with AD(H)D** If students have trouble focusing on how to combine the elements from the boxes, change the format to dehydrated sentences so that there is only one adjective and one verb for each sentence. That way, students can concentrate on conjugating the verb without being distracted by deciding which elements to combine.

### Assess

**Assessment Program**

**Prueba: Gramática 2,** pp. 49–50

**Prueba: Aplicación 2,** pp. 51–52

Audio CD 3, Tr. 18

Alternative Assessment, pp. 375, 387, 399

**Online Assessment**
**my.hrw.com**

**Test Generator**

## Resources

**Planning:**

Lesson Planner, pp. 44, 204–205

One-Stop Planner

**Presentation:**

Video Program, Videocassette 2

DVD Program

**VideoNovela**

**Practice:**

Video Guide, pp. 20–22

Lab Book, pp. 64–65

### Visual Learners

Have students create a graphic organizer in which they outline the information Clara and Octavio have gathered and the deductions they have made on their own.

| Situación | ① Alguien está siguiendo al profesor | ② ____ | ③ ____ |
|---|---|---|---|
| Clara and Octavio's deductions | | | |
| My deductions | | | |

1.2

Novela en video

# Clara perspectiva

## Episodio 3

DVD VIDEO

**ESTRATEGIA**

**Making deductions** Making deductions based on what unfolds in a story is an important skill. The characters themselves make deductions as they learn more about their situation. You may or may not agree with their deductions, because you may have information that they don't have. Think about the information you have gathered about the professor's situation up to now. Do you agree with Clara's and Octavio's deductions about his situation? Have you seen anything happen that they have not seen happen? Do you have anything to add to their deductions? 1.2, 3.1

### En el café

**Graciela** La cinta no se oye muy bien.
**Octavio** Tiene que ver con la región de Magallanes.
**Graciela** Sí, y el profesor tiene algo importante que ellos quieren.
**Clara** Y le ofrecen dinero para que se lo dé.

1

2

**Graciela** Pero, ¿qué es lo que quieren?
**Octavio** No está claro.
**Clara** La voz del profesor suena rara, ¿no? Parece que tenía mucho miedo, ¿no creen? Esos hombres lo insultaron.
**Octavio** A mi parecer, lo estaban amenazando. Pero el profesor no se dio por vencido.

**Clara** Pobre profesor Luna. ¿En qué se habrá metido?
**Graciela** ¿Quién sabe?

3

4

**Octavio** Perdóname Clara, pero me tengo que ir. Podemos hablar más de esto mañana.
**Clara** No tienes por qué disculparte, Octavio. Nos vemos mañana.
**Graciela** Mucho gusto, Octavio.
**Octavio** Igualmente, Graciela.

## Core Instruction

### TEACHING NOVELA EN VIDEO

1. Have students scan the **Novela en video** text and look at the photos from the episode. **(1 min.)**
2. Play the video, stopping periodically to ask comprehension questions. If students have trouble understanding any portion of the video, you might want to use the captioned version of the episode. **(5 min.)**
3. Ask students to discuss their deductions about the situation and compare them with Octavio and Clara's deductions. **(4 min.)**
4. Answer the questions on page 125 as a class. **(5 min.)**

### Escuchemos

As students watch the **Novela,** have them listen for one instance of Clara and Graciela disagreeing with each other. Have students say what they're disagreeing about.

Novela en video

Visit Holt Online
**go.hrw.com**
KEYWORD: EXP3 CH3
Online Edition

**Clara** No sé qué hacer sobre el profesor. No sé cómo ayudarlo.
**Graciela** Mira, el profesor se puede cuidar perfectamente solo. Así que te sugiero que no te preocupes por él.
**Clara** No sé. Sería una buena idea tratar de comunicarme con él, ¿no crees?

**Graciela** ¡Al contrario! Deja de meterte en líos que no te importan. No te conviene ser tan terca.
**Clara** ¿Yo, terca? Yo soy la primera en admitir un error.
**Graciela** Creo que tienes una impresión equivocada de la conversación que grabaste. Olvídalo, por favor.
**Clara** No estoy de acuerdo. Quizás debería hablar con él.

**Graciela** Octavio es bien simpático, ¿no? Yo que tú lo invitaría a tu almuerzo familiar el fin de semana que viene.
**Clara** ¡Graciela! ¿Cómo se te ocurre que lo voy a invitar a mi casa? Apenas lo conozco.
**Graciela** Era sólo una idea.

## En la universidad

**Hombre** Necesitamos ese estudio de impacto ambiental.
**Mujer** Sí. Pero no podemos entrar ahora. Pasa gente.
**Hombre** Tenemos que saber si el estudio favorece a la empresa *MaderaCorp*, o si nos favorece a nosotros.
**Mujer** Es verdad. Pero tenemos tiempo. No creo que el estudio se vaya a desaparecer dentro de 24 horas.

**Hombre 1** Tiene que tenerlo en la computadora.
**Hombre 2** Ése es un estereotipo.
**Hombre 1** Estereotipo o no, allí es donde tenemos que empezar a buscar.

Novela en video

## ¿COMPRENDES?

1. Nombra tres cosas que puedes deducir de la conversación de la cinta. ¿Qué cosas no puedes deducir?
2. ¿Cómo suena el profesor?
3. ¿Cómo analiza Octavio a los hombres?
4. ¿Qué quiere hacer Clara para el profesor? ¿Cómo reacciona Graciela?
5. ¿Qué piensa Graciela que debe hacer Clara para su reunión familiar? ¿Está de acuerdo Clara? ¿Por qué sí o por qué no?
6. ¿Qué buscan el hombre y la mujer? ¿Qué buscan los hombres de traje oscuro? ¿Lo encuentran? 1.2

**Próximo episodio**
*Octavio pasa por la casa de Clara durante su reunión familiar. ¿Crees que algo va a pasar en la reunión familiar que tenga que ver con el profesor Luna? ¿Quiénes serán las personas en la universidad?*

PÁGINAS 166–167

### Gestures

Ask students to note what kinds of gestures Clara, Graciela, and Octavio use when they are talking in the café. Are these gestures that they would also use in a formal situation, or would they only be used in a casual situation with friends? 2.1

### ¿Comprendes? Answers

1. Se puede deducir que el profesor tiene algo importante que los hombres quieren, que le ofrecen dinero para que se lo dé, y que tiene que ver con la región de Magallanes. No se puede deducir qué es lo que quieren del profesor.
2. Su voz suena rara. Creen que tiene mucho miedo y que los hombres lo insultaron.
3. Cree que los hombres lo estaban amenazando.
4. Quiere ayudarlo. Graciela cree que Clara no debe meterse en líos.
5. Cree que debe invitar a Octavio. Clara no está de acuerdo porque apenas lo conoce.
6. Buscan el estudio de impacto ambiental. Los hombres de traje oscuro buscan documentos del profesor. No los encuentran.

## Clara perspectiva, Episodio 3

In **Episodio 3,** Clara, Graciela, and Octavio meet to listen to the tape of the recorded conversation between Professor Luna and the two men. They are able to conclude that the professor was again being threatened because he apparently has something that the two men are interested in. They are able to make out mention of the region of Magallanes, an environmentally sensitive area in southern Chile. After Octavio leaves, Clara and Graciela continue their conversation. Back at Professor Luna's office, the two young people seen with the professor in **Episodio 1** try to sneak into the professor's office. Later, the two men seen with the professor in **Episodio 2** also try to break into the professor's office.

### Comunicación

**Pair Activity: Interpersonal**

Have students work in pairs to create a new scene for **Episodio 3.** One student will play Clara and the other will play her friend. Ask the friend to give Clara advice about what to do regarding the professor's situation. Have students present their conversations to the class. 1.1

# Lectura informativa

**Resources**

**Planning:**

Lesson Planner, pp. 45, 206–207

One-Stop Planner

**Presentation:**

Audio CD 3, Tr. 12

**Practice:**

Cuaderno de actividades, p. 28

Reading Strategies and Skills Handbook, Chapter 3

Interactive Advanced Reader

**Pre-Reading Activity**

Read the title of the informative reading with students and have them look at the photographs and captions. Ask them if they know of programs for Spanish speakers in their communities. Have them think about the importance of this type of program as they read the selection. Tell them they will have the opportunity to share their opinions when they have finished reading.

**About the Reading**

Tell students that this reading is from an article that appeared on **BBCMUNDO.com** entitled **"Educación sin fronteras".**

## Lectura informativa

CD 3, Tr. 12

# América en Español

*América en Español es una organización que ofrece cursos gratuitos de computación a los hispanos recién llegados a Chicago.*

**América en Español ayuda a los latinos a desarrollar conocimientos de computación.**

Más allá del sistema de educación formal, en Estados Unidos existe un sinnúmero[1] de organizaciones no gubernamentales[2] que promueven el aprendizaje de varias materias y oficios.

En particular, la comunidad latina es una de las más beneficiadas por este tipo de proyectos.

Un ejemplo es América en Español, una iniciativa sin fines de lucro[3] con sede en[4] Chicago, Illinois. Gracias a ella, cientos de latinos han aprendido nociones básicas de computación, por medio de cursos gratuitos en colegios comunitarios[5].

Los responsables de América en Español, Antonio Díaz y Rubén Legorreta, definen su actividad como una "misión y pasión" de tiempo completo, que iniciaron en 1999.

Antonio (39) nació en Los Ángeles de padres mexicanos. Lleva 20 años viviendo en Chicago.

Rubén (40) nació en Hidalgo, México, y llegó a Estados Unidos a los 18 años. Reanudó[6] sus estudios y se recibió de arquitecto.

No sólo procuran cerrar la brecha digital[7], sino que también aplican una buena dosis de motivación y participan en ferias de empleo para promover a sus alumnos.

América en Español se financia gracias a donaciones de comercios y otros benefactores que apuestan por su obra[8].

1 endless number
2 *organizaciones...* non-government organizations
3 *iniciativa...* non-profit initiative
4 *con...* based in
5 community schools
6 He resumed
7 *cerrar...*close the digital gap
8 believe in their work

**Pre-AP Practice**

**AP Language Examination: Lectura informativa** helps students prepare for Section I, Part B: **Reading Comprehension.** The audio recording helps them prepare for Part A: **Listening–Short Narratives.**

## Core Instruction

**TEACHING LECTURA INFORMATIVA**

1. Read and discuss the introductory paragraph as a class. Have students name any non-government organizations they know of that promote learning various skills. **(2 min.)**
2. Have students read the rest of the selection to themselves, and then have volunteers summarize the content. Give students the opportunity to ask questions about parts they do not understand and to express their opinions about this organization. **(15 min.)**
3. Have students answer the **Comprensión** questions. Then discuss **¿Qué piensas?** as a class. Ask volunteers to respond to the questions and allow students to explain why they agree or disagree with their classmates' ideas. **(8 min.)**

Dos estudiantes hablan sobre un proyecto de computación.

Pero, según Antonio Díaz y Rubén Legorreta, su mayor recompensa es cuando uno de sus alumnos llega a la meta y pone en práctica sus nuevos conocimientos.

Al pedirles un ejemplo, citaron la historia de Moisés García, un chico pandillero[9] que un día se interesó por uno de los cursos que América en Español ofrecía sobre construcción de sitios de Internet. Gracias a ese curso, Moisés descubrió su vocación por el diseño gráfico y de páginas web; ahora trabaja en esa área, con gran éxito.

"De nada nos sirve tener inteligencia, tener un título universitario, si no utilizamos lo que hemos aprendido; el ayudar a la gente tiene grandes recompensas", cuenta García.

Legorreta asiente: "Yo creo que en este país el latino va a tener un mayor alcance a todo nivel si nos educamos; esto a la larga[10] va a hacer que todos nuestros hijos desarrollen la misma mentalidad", afirma.

9 gang member
10 in the long run

## Comprensión

**A Los hechos** Basándote en lo que leíste, contesta las preguntas. 1.2

1. ¿Quiénes son Antonio Díaz y Rubén Legorreta?
2. ¿Cuándo se fundó América en Español?
3. ¿Dónde se ofrecen los cursos?
4. ¿De dónde viene el dinero para América en Español?
5. ¿Cuánto cuestan los cursos de América en Español?
6. ¿Qué opina Moisés García de la importancia de ayudar a los demás?

1.3

**B ¿Qué piensas?** Basándote en tus experiencias, contesta las preguntas.

1. ¿Cómo podría ayudar un programa como éste a cambiar la actitud de la gente hacia la tecnología?
2. ¿Por qué es importante enseñar computación?
3. ¿Qué otros tipos de cursos serían útiles para los inmigrantes?
4. ¿Conoces otros programas como América en Español?

## Actividad 1.3

**Anuncia tu programa** Imagina que eres el (la) director(a) de un programa como América en Español, y quieres comunicar tus nuevas ideas al público. Escribe un anuncio para las personas a quienes les interesaría tomar los cursos. Describe los cursos, el horario y otros detalles.

# Lectura informativa

### A Answers

1. Antonio Díaz y Rubén Legorreta son los fundadores de América en Español.
2. América en Español se fundó en 1999.
3. Se ofrecen los cursos en colegios comunitarios.
4. El dinero para América en Español viene de donaciones de comercios y otros benefactores.
5. Los cursos de América en Español son gratuitos.
6. Moisés García opina que ayudar a la gente tiene grandes recompensas.

## Communities

### Community Link

Ask students if they know of any non-governmental organization in their community that promotes learning of various skills. Are the organizations geared towards English-speakers? Do they think the community would benefit from organizations that provide classes or training for Spanish-speakers? Encourage students to find out more about the programs available in their community. They might want to volunteer at a program for immigrants as a way to practice their Spanish. If they find that no such programs exist in their community and there is a need for them, they may wish to write to local politicians to voice their concerns. 5.1

### Post-Reading Activities

Have students write a short summary outlining the main idea and important details in the selection. Have volunteers use their notes to summarize the selection for the class. 1.2

## Differentiated Instruction

### SLOWER PACE LEARNERS

**Additional Practice** For students who have trouble with reading comprehension in Spanish, have them complete a graphic organizer with the main idea of the selection and supporting details. You may want to draw a graphic organizer on the board with the following headers: **Organización, Personas que crearon la organización, Objetivo de la organización, Ejemplos.** Have students fill out the graphic organizer on a piece of paper and then use the information to answer the comprehension questions. 1.2

### SPECIAL LEARNING NEEDS

**Students with Dyslexia** It may be difficult for students with dyslexia to read and comprehend the selection. To assist these students, read the selection aloud. Then ask them to summarize the main points of the selection. If necessary, guide them with questions about the goals of the organization. Go back and read certain paragraphs again if they have trouble remembering the content. Then go over the comprehension questions with them orally before asking them to write the answers. 1.2

## Assess

**Assessment Program**
**Prueba: Lectura,** p. 53
**Online Assessment**
**my.hrw.com**
**Test Generator**

**Assess Differentiated Instruction** See the Differentiated Instruction CD-ROM.

## Resources

**Planning:**

Lesson Planner, pp. 45–46, 206–207

One-Stop Planner

**Presentation:**

Audio CD 3, Tr. 13

**Practice:**

Cuaderno de actividades, p. 28

Reading Strategies and Skills Handbook, Chapter 3

Interactive Advanced Reader

### Applying the Strategies

For more practice with paraphrasing, you might have students use the "Retellings" strategy from the *Reading Strategies and Skills Handbook.*

### Escuchemos

On the board write the following: **1. El fray creía que nada podría salvarlo., 2. El fray pensaba que descansaría un rato en un sofá., 3. Los indígenas no sabían que se produciría un eclipse ese día.** Play the recording of the reading and have students listen, with their books closed, to answer **cierto** or **falso** to each statement. (c, f, f)

### Pre-AP Practice

**AP Language Examination:** **Leamos** helps students prepare for Section I, Part B: **Reading Comprehension.** The audio recording helps them prepare for Part A: **Listening—Short Narratives.**

**AP Benchmark:** Identify and summarize the main points and details and make inferences and predictions from a written text.

**Focus:** Summarizing a text and making inferences

- SE, p. 130, Act. C
- SE, p. 130, Act. D
- TE, p. 129, Advanced Learners

# Leamos y escribamos

**ESTRATEGIA**

**para leer** A good way to improve your understanding of a text is to paraphrase each section. Paraphrasing is telling what happened in your own words. Even if you don't know the meaning of specific words, paraphrasing will help you understand the content of the text. Once you understand the content, it will be easier for you to figure out the meaning of unfamiliar words.

CD 3, Tr. 13

**Antes de leer** 1.2, 1.3

**A** Augusto Monterroso (1921–2003), escritor guatemalteco nacido en Tegucigalpa, Honduras, tuvo una carrera de más de cuatro décadas y es reconocido como uno de los grandes escritores de habla hispana. Monterroso escribió prosa *(prose)*, sobretodo cuentos cortos y ensayos. De hecho escribió el cuento más corto en la historia de la literatura latinoamericana. La obra completa es: "Cuando despertó, el dinosaurio todavía estaba allí." El cuento que vas a leer ahora se llama "El eclipse". Busca el pasaje en el que el fraile muestra su arrogancia, y vuelve a contarlo con tus propias palabras.

## El eclipse

*de Augusto Monterroso*

*La jornada.* México, 30 de diciembre.

Cuando fray Bartolomé Arrazola se sintió perdido aceptó que ya nada podría salvarlo. La selva poderosa de Guatemala lo había apresado[1], implacable y definitiva. Ante su ignorancia topográfica se sentó con tranquilidad a esperar la muerte. Quiso morir allí, sin ninguna esperanza, aislado[2], con el pensamiento fijo en la España distante, particularmente en el convento de los Abrojos, donde Carlos V condescendiera[3] una vez a bajar de su eminencia para decirle que confiaba en el celo religioso de su labor redentora[4].

1. taken him prisoner 2. isolated, alone 3. had condescended 4. redeeming

## Core Instruction

### TEACHING LEAMOS

1. Read the **Estrategia para leer** with students. Have them read the first paragraph and apply the strategy. **(3 min.)**
2. Read the following paragraphs as a class, stopping to have volunteers paraphrase each paragraph. **(5 min.)**
3. Have students look at the illustrations and paraphrase the part of the story depicted in each illustration. **(3 min.)**
4. Answer the **Comprensión** questions together. **(5 min.)**
5. Have students work in pairs to answer the **Pasó así** questions. **(5 min.)**
6. Allow students to work in small groups to discuss the **Después de leer** questions. **(5 min.)**

Visit Holt Online
**go.hrw.com**
KEYWORD: EXP3 CH3
Online Edition

Al despertar se encontró rodeado por un grupo de indígenas de rostro impasible que se disponían a sacrificarlo[5] ante un altar, un altar que a Bartolomé le pareció como el lecho en que descansaría, al fin, de sus temores, de su destino, de sí mismo.

Tres años en el país le habían conferido un mediano dominio[6] de las lenguas nativas. Intentó algo. Dijo algunas palabras que fueron comprendidas.

Entonces floreció en él una idea[7] que tuvo por digna de su talento y de su cultura universal y de su arduo conocimiento de Aristóteles. Recordó que para ese día se esperaba un eclipse total de sol. Y dispuso, en lo más íntimo, valerse de aquel conocimiento para engañar[8] a sus opresores y salvar la vida. —Si me matáis —les dijo— puedo hacer que el sol se oscurezca[9] en su altura.
Los indígenas lo miraron fijamente y Bartolomé sorprendió la incredulidad en sus ojos. Vio que se produjo un pequeño consejo, y esperó confiado, no sin cierto desdén.

Dos horas después el corazón de fray Bartolomé Arrazola chorreaba[10] su sangre vehemente sobre la piedra de los sacrificios (brillante bajo la opaca luz de un sol eclipsado), mientras uno de los indígenas recitaba sin ninguna inflexión de voz, sin prisa, una por una, las infinitas fechas en que se producirían eclipses solares y lunares, que los astrónomos de la comunidad maya habían previsto y anotado en sus códices sin la valiosa ayuda de Aristóteles.

---

**5.** sacrifice him **6.** mastery **7.** an idea came to him **8.** to trick **9.** make the sun dark **10.** was gushing



# Leamos y escribamos

## Active Reading Questions

1. ¿Cómo se sentía fray Bartolomé al principio del cuento?
2. ¿A qué se refiere el autor cuando menciona la "labor redentora" de fray Bartolomé en la página 128?
3. ¿Cúanto tiempo llevaba fray Bartolomé en Guatemala?
4. ¿Cuál es la impresión que tiene fray Bartolomé de los indígenas?

## Using Context

Divide the class into small groups. Assign each group one of the paragraphs from the selection. Have each group write down the words they do not know. Then ask them to use the context to paraphrase the paragraph for the class. Were they able to understand the basic content of the paragraph even though they did not know every word? What were some of the important context clues that helped them understand the meaning? 1.2

## Connections

### History Link

Tell students that Augusto Monterroso was a political activist from a young age, and often used his talent for writing to express his views. For political reasons he was exiled to Mexico in 1944. Have students research the political situation in Guatemala in the late 30's and early 40's and the reasons Monterroso was exiled. 3.1

## Differentiated Instruction

### ADVANCED LEARNERS

**Challenge** Have students write a summary of the story in their own words. Ask students to read their summaries to the class, and then discuss as a class the details each decided to include. Were the summaries similar? What do they think was the main idea? Allow students to share their ideas. 1.2

### MULTIPLE INTELLIGENCES

**Interpersonal** Have students work in pairs to discuss the events of **El eclipse** from the point of view of the indigenous tribe. Have them think about how the people perceived fray Bartolomé. What kind of image do they think the people had of him? Do they think that there were mistaken impressions on both parts? What do they think might have helped to resolve the situation? 1.1

## B Answers

1. Estaba perdido en la selva de Guatemala.
2. Un grupo de indígenas lo capturó.
3. Trató de asustarlos con noticias del eclipse.
4. Lo mataron.

## C Answers

1. b
2. b
3. a

### Post-Reading Strategy

Ask students to identify the main idea of the story. Have them find details that support the main idea. You might have pairs or groups of students work together to write an outline of the story using the main idea and details as the basis. They could write their outlines on transparencies to share with the class. 1.2

### Heritage Speakers

In ***El eclipse,*** students read about a priest who had very little respect for the indigenous people of Guatemala. Ask the heritage speakers in your class to work in groups of four and discuss any anecdotes that they might have heard about the way the indigenous people have been treated in their family's home country. How much of the attitude of fray Bartolomé de Arrazola is current today? Have them share these anecdotes with the rest of the class. The class as a whole can then discuss what individuals can personally do to change this attitude. 1.3, 3.2

### Connections

#### Language Arts Link

Have students find another story by Augusto Monterroso online or at the library. Ask them to read the story and take notes. Have each student paraphrase the story for the class. Then have the class discuss the themes and style of Monterroso's stories. 3.1, 3.2

### Comprensión 1.2

**B** **¿Comprendiste?** Contesta las preguntas.

1. ¿Dónde estaba fray Bartolomé y cuál era su problema?
2. ¿Quiénes capturaron a fray Bartolomé?
3. ¿Cómo trató de salvar su vida?
4. ¿Qué hicieron los indígenas con fray Bartolomé?

### Pasó así 1.2

**C** **Resumir** Indica cuál es el mejor resumen de los párrafos indicados.

1. **Párrafos 1 y 2**
   - a. Fray Bartolomé era un indígena. Conocía la selva de Guatemala, y quería morir allí, solo. Unos indígenas lo encontraron y él decidió irse con ellos.
   - b. Fray Bartolomé era un religioso español en Guatemala. No conocía la selva de Guatemala y se perdió. Unos indígenas lo encontraron y él sabía que lo iban a matar.
2. **Párrafos 3 y 4**
   - a. Fray Bartolomé no hablaba la lengua nativa. Se consideraba muy ignorante y sabía que los indígenas eran inteligentes. Pensaba que si podía mostrar que quería aprender, no lo matarían.
   - b. Fray Bartolomé sabía algunas palabras de la lengua nativa. Él pensó que los indígenas no sabían nada de los eclipses de sol, y quería asustarlos. Dijo que iba a haber un eclipse. Pensaba que con esta información no lo matarían.
3. **Párrafos 5 y 6**
   - a. Fray Bartolomé tenía una actitud superior hacia los indígenas. Pero ellos sabían cuándo iban a ocurrir los eclipses. Ellos lo mataron y luego, anunciaron todas las fechas en que ocurrirían los eclipses.
   - b. Fray Bartolomé respetaba mucho a los indígenas y les enseñó todo lo que sabía acerca de los eclipses. Después de aprender todo sobre los eclipses, lo mataron y repitieron todas las fechas en que ocurrirían los eclipses del futuro.

### Después de leer 1.3, 3.2

**D** ¿Qué quiere comunicar el autor acerca de los españoles que llegaron a las Américas y su actitud hacia los indígenas? ¿Tenían una impresión equivocada de los indígenas? Explica.

## Core Instruction

### TEACHING ESCRIBAMOS

1. Have students think about a time when they have had the wrong impression of someone. Have them share their experiences with the class. **(2 min.)**
2. Discuss **Estrategia para escribir** as a class. **(1 min.)**
3. Have students do prewriting Activity 1. Remind them that they should write down everything that comes to mind when they are brainstorming. **(3 min.)**
4. Have students do items 2 and 3. **(10 min.)**
5. Allow students to exchange drafts with a classmate to peer-edit. **(10 min.)**
6. Have students do item 4 and then share their paragraphs with the class. **(10 min.)**

Visit Holt Online
**go.hrw.com**
KEYWORD: EXP3 CH3
Online Edition

# Taller del escritor 1.3

**ESTRATEGIA para escribir** When recalling a memory to write about, it's best to brainstorm your ideas. This will help you think of all possible options. Make a list of your ideas and then narrow them down until you find your favorite.

## Una impresión equivocada

Es muy fácil tener una impresión equivocada de algo o de alguien. Hacemos observaciones de algo o de alguien y formulamos opiniones basadas en lo que suponemos. Escribe un párrafo sobre una impresión equivocada que hayas tenido de algo o de alguien y de cómo te diste cuenta de tu error.

Impresiones equivocadas

| | ropa | comida | personas |
|---|---|---|---|
| Idea 1 | | | |
| Idea 2 | | | |
| Idea 3 | | | |

### 1 Antes de escribir

Haz una lista de ocasiones en las que hayas tenido una impresión equivocada. En la lista, podrías tener varias categorías; por ejemplo, ropa, comida o personas. Apunta todo lo que puedas en cada categoría.

### 2 Escribir un borrador

Escoge tu tema favorito de la lista. Piensa en por qué tuviste una impresión equivocada y cómo te diste cuenta de tu error. Empieza a escribir tu borrador con esta información e incluye lo que aprendiste de esta experiencia.

### 3 Revisar

Revisa tu borrador y corrige los errores de gramática u ortografía. Verifica que tu borrador tenga toda la información necesaria.

### 4 Publicar

Intercambia tu párrafo con un(a) compañero(a) para que lo lea. Comparen sus experiencias y luego, con la clase, comenten las impresiones equivocadas que hayan tenido otros compañeros.

Leamos y escribamos

## Differentiated Instruction

### SLOWER PACE LEARNERS

You may want to have students work in pairs to facilitate the brainstorming process before they begin to work on their drafts. This will help them come up with more ideas, and pairs can help each other narrow down their options.

### SPECIAL LEARNING NEEDS

**Students with Learning Disabilities**
You may wish to add a step after step 2 to help students formulate their paragraphs. Have students share the ideas they have come up with in their drafts. With the help of the class, repeat these ideas in sentences that the students can use in their paragraphs, and help them expand on their ideas. Allow them to take notes as you go through each student's draft together. 1.2

# Leamos y escribamos

## Process Writing

Tell students that brainstorming ideas will help them find the best topic to write about. Remind them that they should write down everything that comes to mind before they begin to eliminate ideas.

## Writing Assessment

To assess the **Taller del escritor,** you can use the following rubric. For additional rubrics, see the *Alternative Assessment Guide.*

| Writing Rubric | 4 | 3 | 2 | 1 |
|---|---|---|---|---|
| **Content** (Complete—Incomplete) | | | | |
| **Comprehensibility** (Comprehensible—Seldom comprehensible) | | | | |
| **Accuracy** (Accurate—Seldom accurate) | | | | |
| **Organization** (Well-organized—Poorly organized) | | | | |
| **Effort** (Excellent effort—Minimal effort) | | | | |

18–20: A  14–15: C  Under
16–17: B  12–13: D  12: F

## Pre-AP Practice

**AP Language Examination: Leamos and Escribamos** help students prepare for Section I, Part B: **Reading Comprehension** and Section II, Part A: **Informal Writing.**

## Assess

**Assessment Program**
**Prueba: Lectura,** p. 53
**Prueba: Escritura,** p. 54
**Online Assessment**
**my.hrw.com**
**Test Generator**

# Capítulo 3
# Prepárate para el examen

## Resources

**Planning:**

Lesson Planner, pp. 46–47, 206–209

One-Stop Planner

**Presentation:**

Video Program, Videocassette 2

DVD Program

**Variedades**

**Practice:**

Activities for Communication, pp. 45, 59–60

Video Guide, pp. 18–19

Lab Book, pp. 3, 21–24, 63

Audio CD 3, Tr. 14–15

Pre-AP Instructional Resources

Pre-AP Audio CD 1, Trs. 9–12

Interactive Tutor, Disc 1

Teaching Transparencies
**Situación, Capítulo 3**
Picture Sequences, Chapter 3

### 1 Script

1. Me choca la actitud de Jimena hacia los estudios. Parece que no le importa sacar malas notas. Me molesta que no quiera trabajar con nosotros cuando hay que hacer un proyecto.
2. Todos piensan que no soy un estudiante aplicado solamente porque practico deportes. Pero yo estudio mucho y mis notas son bastante buenas. No me gustan los estereotipos de mis compañeros.
3. El examen de la semana pasada fue demasiado difícil. Todos mis compañeros de clase estaban muy nerviosos durante el examen. Espero que yo no lo haya suspendido.
4. La profesora me acusó de copiar el examen. Cuando todos se fueron después del examen, la profesora me dijo que quería hablar conmigo. Me dio un cero en el examen. ¡Esto es el colmo!

Capítulo 3
Repaso

# Prepárate para el examen

Interactive TUTOR

CD 3, Tr. 14 — 1.2

**1** Escucha los comentarios y escoge el dibujo que corresponde.

1. c
2. a
3. d
4. b

a.

b

c.

d.

**1 Vocabulario 1**
- complaining
- disagreeing

**pp. 98–103**

**2** Completa las oraciones con la forma correcta del verbo. — 1.2

1. Mis amigos van a ═══ (tener) una gran fiesta. tener
2. Esteban quiere ═══ (organizar) la fiesta. organizar
3. Él quiere que la fiesta ═══ (ser) una sorpresa. sea
4. Insiste en que todo el mundo ═══ (llegar) a tiempo. llegue
5. Prefiere que cada persona ═══ (traer) algo de comer. traiga
6. No creo que mucha gente ═══ (ir) a la fiesta. vaya

**2 Gramática 1**
- verb + infinitive
- subjunctive with will or wish
- subjunctive with negation or denial

**pp. 104–109**

**3** Completa las oraciones con la forma correcta de un verbo del cuadro. — 1.2

| | | |
|---|---|---|
| estar resentida | pedirle perdón | hacer las paces |
| dejar de hablarse | dar un abrazo | |

1. Celia y Manuel discutieron ayer y... dejaron de hablarse
2. María dijo algo que ofendió a Miguel y ahora debe...
3. Sandra y Roberto se reconciliaron. Vi que Roberto le...
4. Cuando dos personas se pelean, deben... hacer las paces
5. Juana ofendió a Eva y no se disculpó. Por eso, Eva...

2. pedirle perdón
3. dio un abrazo
5. está resentida

**3 Vocabulario 2**
- making suggestions
- apologizing

**pp. 112–117**

## Oral Assessment

### Speaking Rubric

To assess the speaking activities in this section, you might use this rubric. For additional speaking rubrics, see the Alternative Assessment section of the *Assessment Program*.

| Speaking Rubric | 4 | 3 | 2 | 1 |
|---|---|---|---|---|
| **Content** (Complete—Incomplete) | | | | |
| **Comprehension** (Total—Little) | | | | |
| **Comprehensibility** (Comprehensible—Incomprehensible) | | | | |
| **Accuracy** (Accurate—Seldom accurate) | | | | |
| **Fluency** (Fluent—Not fluent) | | | | |

18–20: A 16–17: B 14–15: C 12–13: D Under 12: F

Visit Holt Online
go.hrw.com
KEYWORD: EXP3 CH3
Chapter Self-test

4 Completa las oraciones con la forma correcta del verbo. 1.2

1. Si pudiera, esta noche ____ (ir) al cine con mis amigos. iría
2. Y a las nueve ____ (regresar) a mi casa. regresaría
3. Después de regresar, me ____ (poner) a estudiar geografía. pondría
4. Si no me pongo a estudiar ahora, mañana ____ (suspender) el examen. suspenderé
5. Si tuviera más tiempo, ____ (leer) todo el libro. leería
6. Ni modo. ¡Presentaré el examen y ____ (sacar) un diez! sacaré

4 Gramática 2
• future tense
• conditional
pp. 118–123

5 Contesta las preguntas. 1.3

1. ¿Qué es América en Español y qué hace?
2. ¿Te parece buena idea que los estudiantes de Puerto Rico aprendan el inglés y el español en el colegio? ¿Por qué?
3. ¿Hasta qué edad es obligatorio el colegio en Cuba?

1. Es una organización que les ofrece cursos de computación gratuitos a hispanos en Chicago. 2. Answers will vary. 3. Hasta los 15 años.

5 Cultura
• Comparaciones pp. 110–111
• Lectura informativa pp. 126–127
• Notas culturales pp. 100, 106, 117

CD 3, Tr. 15

6 Escucha la conversación entre Marcela y Teresa. Apunta en listas separadas las clases que las dos chicas tienen. 1.2

Marcela: cálculo, ciencias sociales, literatura
Teresa: álgebra, física, geografía, literatura

## Conversación

HOLT SoundBooth ONLINE RECORDING

7 Role-play the following conversation with a partner. Partner A and Partner B are talking about Partner A and his or her parents. 1.1, 1.2

Partner A: Complain about your parents. Say you can't take it anymore.

Partner B: Ask what's wrong and why your partner is so upset.

Partner A: Explain that your parents don't want you to play sports.

Partner B: Say that doesn't seem fair to you. Ask why.

Partner A: Say your parents insist that you take hard classes. They don't think you can play sports and get good grades.

Partner B: Say the image of athletes as bad students is a stereotype. Ask if your partner knows someone who is athletic and a good student.

Partner A: Say you've thought about talking to Lucho, a friend on the track team who gets goods grades.

Partner B: Say in your partner's place, you would introduce Lucho to your parents. Suggest your partner think it over, and end the conversation.

## Conversación

### Additional Speaking Practice

For additional speaking practice, use the *Picture Sequences Transparency* for Chapter 3. Use the Speaking Rubric on the preceding page to evaluate their performance. You may also wish to use the Interviews and Role-Plays in the *Activities for Communication* book.

### Pre-AP Practice

7 In the Level 3 *Pre-AP Instructional Resources* you will find an alternative version of Activity 7. The following resources in that book will help you prepare students for the AP Language Exam:

- Blackline masters, pp. 29, 39, 49
- Pre-AP Audio CD 1, Trs. 9–12
- Scripts and answers, pp. 57–75

### 6 Script

Marcela ¡Hola, Teresa! ¿Qué tal? ¿Cómo te va en el primer día de clases?
Teresa Ay, ¡qué horror! Mi horario es muy pesado y todos mis cursos son difíciles. Para empezar, tengo álgebra a las ocho de la mañana y para colmo, ya no hay más libros de texto. Por lo menos conseguí entrar a la clase de física que quería tomar.
Marcela A mí tampoco me gusta el álgebra, pero lo tomé el semestre pasado. Ahora comencé un curso de cálculo y me encanta. La clase que me deja completamente fría es la de ciencias sociales. No me gusta para nada, pero tengo que aprobarla.
Teresa Huy, qué mala suerte. Evité la clase de ciencias sociales y escogí la de geografía. Me gusta mucho este curso porque el profesor domina muy bien la materia.
Marcela ¿Qué clase tienes ahora?
Teresa Ahora empieza la clase de literatura en el salón 125.
Marcela ¿De veras? Yo también tengo literatura. ¡Qué bien!
Teresa Vámonos, ¡que ya se nos hizo tarde!

### 7 Answers

Below is a sample conversation.
(A) —¡Estoy tan frustrada con mis padres! ¡No aguanto más!
(B) —¿Qué te pasa? ¿Por qué te sientes tan enojada?
(A) —Es que mis padres no quieren que participe en ningún deporte este año. ¡Es el colmo!
(B) —No me parece que eso sea justo. ¿Por qué dicen eso?
(A) —Insisten en que tome cursos difíciles este año. No piensan que pueda jugar deportes y sacar buenas notas al mismo tiempo.
(B) —¡Qué va! La imagen de los atletas como malos estudiantes es un estereotipo. ¿Conoces a alguien que sea atlética y que también saque buenas notas?
(A) —Pues, sí. He pensado en hablar con Lucho, mi amigo del equipo de atletismo. Él saca buenas notas.
(B) —Yo que tú, le presentaría Lucho a mis padres. Date tiempo para pensarlo. ¡Suerte!

# Prepárate para el examen

## Grammar Review

For more practice with the grammar topics in this chapter, see the *Grammar Tutor,* the *Interactive Tutor,* or the *Cuaderno de vocabulario y gramática.*

GramaVisión

## Comparisons

### Language to Language

Ask students to translate the sample subjunctive sentences into English. What do they notice about the tense of the verb in English? What comparisons can they make between the use of the subjunctive in Spanish and in English?

4.1

## Teacher to Teacher

**Deborah Phillips**
Coppell High School
Coppell, TX

**Daily closure activity**
I have my students do their own closure at the end of class. One student stands in front of the class and shows laminated cards that say **cultura, tecnología, escuchar, escribir, hablar, ver, leer,** and **TPR** (total physical response). Students respond with **sí** or **no** depending on if the item on the card was covered in that day's lesson. Students get excited each day when they realize all of the ideas they have covered!

**Gramática 1**
- verb + infinitive
  pp. 104–105
- subjunctive with will or wish
  pp. 106–107
- subjunctive with negation or denial
  pp. 108–109

## Repaso de Gramática 1

Use a conjugated **verb** + **infinitive** in sentences where the subject for both verbs does not change, or after a **preposition.**

**Quiero ver** el partido el sábado. Carlos **insiste en ir** mañana.

Use the **subjunctive** in subordinate clauses when there is a change in subject between the main and subordinate clause and when the main clause expresses **will** or **wish.**

**Queremos** que las vacaciones **sean** divertidas.

Mis padres **insisten en** que yo **llegue** a tiempo.

Use the **subjunctive** when the main clause in a sentence expresses **negation** or **denial** and when there is a change of subject in the subordinate clause.

**No es cierto** que **vayan** a cambiar el horario.

If the main clause expresses **affirmation**, use the **indicative.**

**Es cierto** que **van** a cambiar el horario.

**Gramática 2**
- future tense
  pp. 118–119
- conditional
  pp. 120–123

## Repaso de Gramática 2

Add these endings to the infinitive form of regular verbs to form the **future tense: -é, -ás, -á, -emos, -éis, -án**. The future tense can be used not only to predict what will happen, but also to say what is probably going on.

Yo **seré** doctor y **ayudaré** a muchas personas.

Nosotros **comeremos** mucho en la fiesta.

Use the **conditional** to express what *would happen* or what someone *would do* in certain circumstances and in expressions that tell what you *would like* or *not like.* The conditional endings, added to the infinitive form, are: **-ía, -ías, -ía, -íamos, -íais, -ían**.

En su lugar yo **llamaría** a la policía. Me **gustaría** aprender otro idioma.

Use the **conditional** with the following **"if" statements** that express contrary-to-fact situations.

| | |
|---|---|
| **Si (yo) fuera** | **Si fuera** presidente, **combatiría** el crimen. |
| **Si (tú) fueras** | **Si fueras** el director, **planearías** más eventos. |
| **Si (yo) tuviera** | **Si tuviera** una lancha, **pescaría** en el lago. |
| **Si (tú) tuvieras** | **Si tuvieras** un carro, **vendrías** a mi casa. |
| **Si (yo) pudiera** | **Si pudiera** hablar francés, **viajaría** a París. |
| **Si (tú) pudieras** | **Si pudieras** cantar, me **cantarías** una canción. |

## Chapter Review

### Teacher Management System

To access, launch the program, type "admin" in the password area, and press RETURN. For more details, log on to www.hrw.com/CDROMTUTOR.

Create a variety of puzzles to review chapter vocabulary.

**DVD Program**

**Interactive Tutor**

**PuzzlePro**

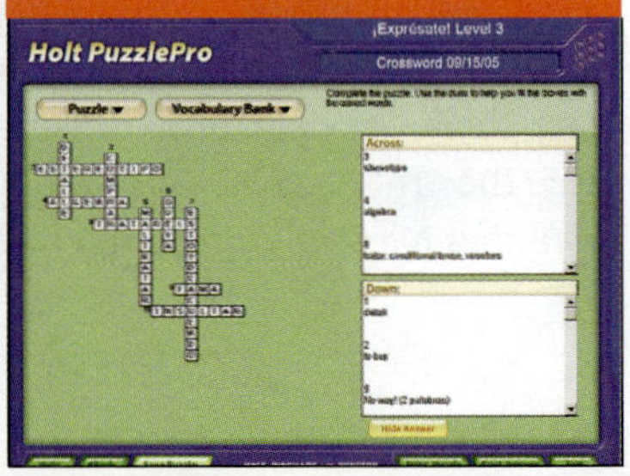

# Prepárate para el examen

## Repaso de Vocabulario 1

### Complaining

| | |
|---|---|
| el álgebra *(f.)* | *algebra* |
| aprobar | *to pass* |
| el (la) consejero(a) | *guidance counselor* |
| El (La) consejero(a) insiste en que tome... ¡No me gusta para nada! | *The guidance counselor insists that I take . . . I don't like it at all!* |
| el cálculo | *calculus* |
| las ciencias sociales | *social sciences* |
| combatir | *to combat* |
| los cursos | *classes* |
| el (la) director(a) | *principal* |
| la discriminación | *discrimination* |
| el estereotipo | *stereotype* |
| la falta de... | *lack of* |
| la fama | *reputation* |
| la física | *physics* |
| la geografía | *geography* |
| la geometría | *geometry* |
| el horario | *schedule* |
| la ignorancia | *ignorance* |
| la imagen (positiva/negativa) | *(positive/negative) image* |
| la impresión equivocada | *wrong impression* |
| juzgar | *to judge* |
| la literatura | *literature* |
| ¿Mañana vamos a tener otra prueba en...? ¡Esto es el colmo! | *We're going to have another test in . . . tomorrow? This is the last straw!* |
| Me choca la actitud de... hacia... ¡No aguanto más! | *I can't stand the attitude of . . . towards . . . I can't take it anymore!* |
| el prejuicio | *prejudice* |
| respetar (a alguien) | *to respect (someone)* |
| el respeto | *respect* |
| el semestre | *semester* |
| suspender | *to fail* |
| tomar apuntes | *to take notes* |
| la universidad | *university* |

### Expressing an opinion and disagreeing

| | |
|---|---|
| A mi parecer, no hay igualdad entre... | *The way I see it, there's no equality between . . .* |
| ¡Al contrario! No estoy de acuerdo. | *On the contrary! I disagree.* |
| No me parece que sea justo. | *I don't think it's fair.* |
| ¡Qué va! Eso no es cierto. | *No way! That's not true.* |

## Repaso de Vocabulario 2

### Making suggestions

| | |
|---|---|
| admitir un error | *to admit a mistake* |
| besar | *to kiss* |
| cometer un error | *to make a mistake* |
| comprarle un regalo | *to buy (someone) a gift* |
| la comunicación | *communication* |
| comunicarse | *to communicate* |
| el consejo | *advice* |
| darle un abrazo | *to give (someone) a hug* |
| Date tiempo para pensarlo. | *Give yourself time to think it over.* |
| dejar de hablarse | *to stop speaking to one another* |
| el detalle | *detail* |
| la disculpa | *apology* |
| disculparse | *to apologize* |
| discutir | *to argue* |
| estar resentido(a) | *to be resentful* |
| hacer las paces | *to make up* |
| ¿Has pensado en...? | *Have you thought about . . . ?* |
| herir (ie, i) | *to hurt (someone)* |
| insultar | *to insult* |
| maltratar | *to mistreat* |
| No te conviene... | *It's not good for you . . .* |
| No te olvides de... | *Don't forget to . . .* |
| ofender | *to offend* |
| olvidar | *to forget* |
| pedir perdón | *to ask for forgiveness* |
| pelearse | *to fight* |
| perdonar | *to forgive* |
| la reconciliación | *reconciliation* |
| reconciliarse | *to reconcile* |
| ser (in)fiel | *to be (un)faithful* |
| Sería una buena/mala idea romper con... | *It would be a good/bad idea to break up with . . .* |
| Sugiero que no hagas caso a los rumores. | *I suggest that you not pay attention to rumors.* |
| Yo que tú... | *If I were you . . .* |

### Apologizing

| | |
|---|---|
| Créeme que fue sin querer. | *Believe me, I didn't mean to do it.* |
| No lo hice a propósito. | *I didn't do it on purpose.* |
| No quise hacerte daño/ofenderte. | *I didn't mean to hurt/offend you.* |
| Perdóname. No sé en qué estaba pensando. | *Forgive me. I don't know what I was thinking.* |
| Te juro que no lo volveré a hacer. | *I swear I'll never do it again.* |

## Vocabulary Review

For more practice with the vocabulary in this chapter, see the *Interactive Tutor* or the *Cuaderno de vocabulario y gramática.*

## Online Edition

Students might use the online textbook to hear the **Vocabulario** items.

## Game

**Frases misteriosas** Select a word from **Vocabulario** or a phrase from **¡Exprésate!** On the board, draw blank lines for each letter in the word or phrase, leaving spaces between words. Give students one clue to the word or phrase, and then allow them to take turns as teams or individually asking if the word or phrase contains various letters. **(¿Hay una *p*?)** Allow them to continue until they guess a letter that is not used. The person or team that guesses the expression wins a point. 1.2

### Online Edition

### Transparency: Vocabulario

### Transparency: Situación

## Assess

**Assessment Program**

**Examen: Capítulo 3,** pp. 229–234

Audio CD 3, Trs. 19–20

**Examen oral: Capítulo 3,** p. 240

Alternative Assessment, pp. 375, 387, 399

**Online Assessment**

**my.hrw.com**

**Test Generator**

**Assess** **Differentiated Instruction** See the Differentiated Instruction CD-ROM.

**Resources**

**Planning:**

Lesson Planner, pp. 47, 208–209

One-Stop Planner

**Presentation:**

Teaching Transparencies
Fine Art, Chapter 3

**Practice:**

Cuaderno de actividades, pp. 29–30

Lab Book, pp. 3, 21–24

Audio CD 3, Tr. 16

### 1 Script

**1.** Cecilia: Voy a practicar ciclismo. ¿Alguien quiere acompañarme?
Alejandro: Por favor, Cecilia, el ciclismo no es para las mujeres.
Cecilia: ¡Qué va! Me ofendiste con tu comentario. Vamos juntos, Alejandro.
Alejandro: Está bien. Vamos… Oye, ¡espera! No vayas tan rápido… Perdóname por mi ignorancia… ¡ya veo que las mujeres sí pueden practicar ciclismo!

**2.** Sandra: Elvira, te veo de buen humor.
Elvira: Sí. Es que me cansé de pelear con Pedro, y hoy rompimos.
Sandra: ¿Y por qué estás de buen humor?
Elvira: Porque estoy buscando un novio que sea honesto y atento y Pedro no es así. Él quería hacer las paces, pero yo le dije que no. Ahora puedo buscar a alguien mejor.

**3.** Mateo: Juan, ¿tomaste la clase de álgebra este semestre?
Juan: Sí, fue muy difícil. Tuvimos que tomar muchos apuntes.
Mateo: ¿Suspendiste el examen?
Juan: ¡Al contrario! No solamente lo aprobé, sino que ¡saqué una A!

# Repaso cumulativo

# Integración
## capítulos 1–3

CD 3, Tr. 16 1.2

**1** Escucha lo que dice cada persona y escoge la foto que corresponde a cada conversación. **1.** a **2.** c **3.** b

a. Cecilia y Alejandro

b. Juan

c. Elvira y Pedro

**2** Escribe cuatro opiniones en una hoja de papel. En parejas, intercambien papeles y túrnense para negar lo que escribió tu compañero(a). 1.1, 1.2

MODELO —**Todas las mujeres son muy chismosas.**
—**¡Qué va! No es cierto que todas sean chismosas.**

**3** Lee la conversación y contesta las preguntas. 1.2

| | |
|---|---|
| FLOR | Julia, ¡estoy muy feliz de que me escribas desde Estados Unidos! |
| JULIA | Sí, qué bueno comunicarme al fin con mi amiga de Panamá. |
| FLOR | Supongo que eres alta, delgada y rica como todas las americanas. |
| JULIA | ¡Qué va! Ésos son estereotipos, nada más. De hecho, soy muy bajita y morena. ¿Y rica? ¡Para nada! Me imagino que Uds. se pasan todo el día en la playa. |
| FLOR | Eso no es cierto. ¡Vaya! ¡Las dos tenemos mucho que aprender! |
| JULIA | Tienes razón. Dime, ¿qué estudias en la universidad? |
| FLOR | Estoy tomando cuatro cursos ahora: literatura, geografía, física e historia. |
| JULIA | Yo quiero enseñar educación física. Practico muchos deportes. |
| FLOR | A mí me gusta practicar ciclismo. Iba a ir con mi novio hoy, pero nos peleamos y ahora él está resentido. Nunca admite sus errores. |

1. ¿De dónde es Flor? ¿Qué piensa de las americanas?
2. ¿Qué estereotipos tiene Julia sobre su amiga?
3. ¿Qué hace Julia en su tiempo libre?
4. ¿Qué cursos toma Flor en la universidad?
5. ¿Qué deporte practica Flor?

**Culture Project**

Have students rent a movie from a Spanish-speaking country. Ask them to think about the stereotypes projected by the movie. What images does the movie give them about the country where it takes place? Are the images true? Have them do some research on the country and compare the image projected by the movie to the facts. Then, have students think about any Hollywood movies they have seen recently that have stereotypes of Spanish-speaking countries. Tell students to compare these stereotypes with those in the Spanish-language movie they rented. Ask students to share their findings with the class, and then begin a discussion about the source of stereotypes. 2.1

Visit Holt Online
**go.hrw.com**
KEYWORD: EXP3 CH3
Cumulative Self-test

**4** En parejas, describan lo que están haciendo las personas en la pintura. Luego, lean el título de la pintura y comenten lo que significa. ¿Qué más observas? 1.1, 1.3

Cometas y habitantes, 30" × 24", painting by José Morillo. © José Morillo/Courtesy of De Bodden Buen Arte

***Cometas y habitantes*** **de José Morillo**

**5** Escribes una columna de consejos para un periódico. Recibiste una carta de una chica, Lola, que se ha peleado con su novio. Él es inseguro y se pone celoso cuando ella sale con sus amigas. Escríbele una carta a Lola y explica lo que tú harías en su lugar. 1.3

**6** **Situación** Trabajen en grupos pequeños e imaginen que uno de ustedes es el (la) nuevo(a) gobernador(a). El (la) gobernador(a) se describe a si mismo(a), y luego ustedes deben comentar lo que él (ella) hará como gobernador(a). 1.1, 1.3

### ACTFL Performance Standards

The activities in Chapter 3 target the different communicative modes as described in the Standards.

| | | |
|---|---|---|
| **Interpersonal** | Two-way communication using receptive skills and productive skills | **Comunicación (SE),** pp. 101, 103, 105, 107, 109, 115, 117, 119, 121, 123<br>**Comunicación (TE),** pp. 101, 105, 107, 117, 119, 121, 125<br>**Conversación,** p. 133<br>**Situación,** p. 137 |
| **Interpretive** | One-way communication using receptive skills | **Comunicación (SE),** pp. 103, 105, 107, 115, 117, 119, 121<br>**Comunicación (TE),** p. 109<br>**Novela en video,** pp. 124–125<br>**Leamos,** pp. 128–130 |
| **Presentational** | One-way communication using productive skills | **Comunicación (SE),** pp. 101, 107, 109, 123<br>**Comunicación (TE),** pp. 103, 115, 123, 125 |

### 3 Answers

1. Es de Panamá. Piensa que todas son altas, delgadas, y ricas.
2. Cree que se pasan todo el día en la playa.
3. Practica muchos deportes; quiere enseñar educación física.
4. Toma cuatro cursos: literatura geografía, física e historia.
5. Practica el ciclismo.

### Fine Art Connection

Tell students that this painting by José Morillo is titled ***Cometas y habitantes.*** Morillo is a Dominican artist who recreates scenes from his past and presents them on his canvases. Although he considers himself a shy person, he feels that his painting is just the opposite: very talkative and outgoing. His love for art, which began in his childhood, has become his greatest passion.

### Analyzing

Ask students to tell what kind of mood they think is portrayed in the painting. How do the colors affect the mood? Ask them if they would agree with Morillo that his painting is "talkative and outgoing" and have them explain why.

1. **¿Qué hacen las personas de la pintura?**
2. **¿Cómo son las personas?**
3. **¿Cuál es tu opinión de esta pintura?**
4. **Si fueras el pintor, ¿qué cambiarías?** 3.1

### Extension

Have students research another Dominican artist and compare his or her work to that of José Morillo. Ask them to prepare a short presentation for the class. 1.3

Capítulo 4

# Planning Guide

## Entre familia

| Chapter Section | | Print Resources |
| --- | --- | --- |
| **Geocultura**<br>• **El Caribe** | pp. 90–95 | Video Guide, pp. 15–16/Lab Book, p. 62 |
| **Vocabulario 1**<br>• Family news<br>**Gramática 1**<br>• Repaso: Present progressive<br>• Repaso: Present perfect indicative<br>• Present perfect subjunctive | pp. 140–145<br>pp. 146–151 | Vocabulario 4.1, 4.2; Bell Work 4.1, 4.2, 4.3, 4.4<br>Cuaderno de vocabulario y gramática, pp. 37–42<br>Cuaderno de actividades, pp. 31–33<br>Activities for Communication, pp. 13–14<br>Grammar Tutor for Students of Spanish, pp. 135–136 |
| **Cultura: Comparaciones**<br>**Cultura: Comunidad** | p. 152<br>p. 153 | Video Guide, pp. 24, 25/Lab Book, p. 66 |
| **Vocabulario 2**<br>• Home cooking<br>**Gramática 2**<br>• Repaso: Preterite<br>• **Se** + indirect object pronouns<br>• Past progressive | pp. 154–159<br>pp. 160–165 | Vocabulario 4.3, 4.4; Bell Work 4.5, 4.6, 4.7, 4.8<br>Cuaderno de vocabulario y gramática, pp. 43–48<br>Cuaderno de actividades, pp. 35–37<br>Activities for Communication, pp. 15–16<br>Grammar Tutor for Students of Spanish, pp. 137–142 |
| **Novela en video**<br>**Lectura cultural**<br>• **Los postres**<br>**Leamos**<br>• **de Epístola**<br>**Escribamos**<br>• **Tu comida favorita** | pp. 166–167<br>pp. 168–169<br>pp. 170–172<br>p. 173 | Cuaderno de actividades, p. 38<br>Reading Strategies and Skills Handbook<br>Interactive Advanced Reader<br>Video Guide, pp. 26–28/Lab Book, pp. 67–68 |
| **Prepárate para el examen**<br>• **Repaso de vocabulario y gramática** | pp. 174–177 | Picture Sequences, Situación, Ch. 4<br>Activities for Communication, pp. 46, 61–62 |
| **Integración**<br>• **Repaso cumulativo** | pp. 178–179 | Fine Art, Ch. 4<br>Cuaderno de actividades, pp. 39–40<br>Reading Strategies and Skills Handbook<br>Interactive Advanced Reader |

Visit Holt Online
**go.hrw.com**
KEYWORD: EXP3 CH4
Online Edition

For correlations to national standards, see point-of-use references throughout the chapter.

## Pacing Suggestions

| | Essential | Recommended | Optional |
|---|---|---|---|
| **Vocabulario 1**<br>• Family news<br>• **Nota cultural** | ✔ | | |
| **Gramática 1**<br>• Repaso: Present progressive<br>• Repaso: Present perfect indicative<br>• Present perfect subjunctive<br>• **Nota cultural** | ✔ | | |
| **Cultura: Comparaciones** | | ✔ | |
| **Cultura: Comunidad** | | | ✔ |
| **Vocabulario 2**<br>• Home cooking<br>• **Nota cultural** | ✔ | | |
| **Gramática 2**<br>• Repaso: Preterite<br>• **Se** + indirect object pronouns<br>• Past progressive<br>• **Nota cultural** | ✔ | | |
| **Novela en video**<br>• Episodio 4: **Clara perspectiva** | | ✔ | |
| **Lectura cultural**<br>• **Los postres** | | | ✔ |
| **Leamos**<br>• **de Epístola**<br>**Escribamos**<br>• **Tu comida favorita** | | ✔ | |
| **Prepárate para el examen** | | ✔ | |
| **Integración** | | | ✔ |

## Technology Resources

### ¡Exprésate! Online
- Student Edition with multi-media
- SoundBooth recording tool
- Interactive activities with feedback
- Self-tests with feedback
- Cuaderno de actividades (interactive workbook)
- Cuaderno de vocabulario y gramática (interactive workbook)
- Live Ink™ Reading Help
- Holt Online Assessment

### DVD Tutor, Disc 1
- GeoVisión
- GramaVisión
- VideoNovela
- Cultura
- Variedades

### Interactive Tutor
- Interactive practice games
- Writing and recording workshops

### Audio Program
- Textbook listening activities
- Assessment listening activities
- Songs

### One-Stop Planner
- Complete media and print resources
- ExamView® Pro Test Generator
- Holt Calendar Planner

### PuzzlePro
- Customizable word games

## Assessment

**Geocultura**
**Vocabulario 1 / Gramática 1**
**Vocabulario 2 / Gramática 2**
**Leamos**
**Escribamos**
**Prepárate para el examen**

### Assessment Program
**Prueba: Geocultura,** pp. 75–76
**Pruebas,** pp. 61–62, 63–64, 65–66
**Pruebas,** pp. 67–68, 69–70, 71–72
**Prueba,** p. 73
**Prueba,** p. 74
**Examen: Capítulo 4,** pp. 241–248
**Examen oral: Capítulo 4,** p. 252
**Alternative Assessment,** pp. 376, 388, 400

### Online Assessment
**my.hrw.com**

### Test Generator
**ExamView® Pro Test Generator**

Planning Guide

Capítulo 4

# Projects

## Entre familia



### Una degustación de comida caribeña

In this project students plan a tasting party of Caribbean dishes. They contact a person from a Caribbean country to obtain a recipe, prepare dishes at home, and sample them in class. During the party, students may speak only Spanish.

**SUGGESTED SEQUENCE**

1. Students work in small groups, each group representing a Caribbean country. The groups should make contact with a person from their chosen country, either in person or by e-mail, and request one or two typical recipes. Encourage them to use any available community resources such as a Latin American food market, both as a source of native speakers, and for ingredients. In order to encourage interaction with native speakers, you may wish to discourage Internet research for this project.
2. Students divide the responsibilities for preparing their dish and decide how they will accomplish the shopping, preparation, and cooking. Dishes are to be prepared outside of class. Students need to make only enough for everyone to have a taste. Make sure every group brings a different dish.
3. Each group prepares a small flag to represent its chosen country and places its dish(es) on the table by the flag. Each dish should be labeled with its name and a list of ingredients in Spanish.
4. At the **degustación,** each group serves its dish and answers questions about how it is made and what is in it. Students sample different dishes and discuss them with classmates.
5. If possible, videotape the **degustación** and play the tape later for the class. 2.2, 5.1

### Grading the projects

Suggested point distribution (100 points total)

Preparing food . . . . . . . . . . . .40

Recipe card, list of ingredients . . .20

Use of Spanish at **degustación** . . . . . . . . . . . .40

### Game Bank

For game ideas, see pages T64–T67.

### Partner Class Project

Have students work in pairs to create a menu for a Caribbean restaurant. They can research information on the Internet, make contact with a person from the chosen country for more information, and then prepare a menu on the computer with an attractive design. Suggest that they look for images in magazines or on the Internet that they can use in their menus. They should also include the price of each dish. Have partners present their menus to the class and ask the class to vote for the most enticing menu. 3.2

### e-community

**e-mail forum:**

Post the following questions on the classroom e-mail forum:

**¿Qué comidas caribeñas has probado? ¿Cuáles son tus favoritas?**

All students will contribute to the list and then share the items. 1.3

# Entre familia

## Las fiestas

New Year's Eve and Day are important holidays for families in Puerto Rico. Some people spend December 31 cleaning the house and the yard in preparation for the coming year. If all is in order as the New Year begins, one hopes that things will stay that way for the next 12 months. At midnight on New Year's Eve, Puerto Ricans traditionally practice the Spanish custom of eating 12 grapes, one with each stroke of the clock, to bring them good luck. Have students research New Year's celebrations around the Spanish-speaking world and compare the traditions with their own. 2.1, 4.2

## Receta

**Arroz con gandules** (rice with pigeon peas) is a popular dish made with typical Puerto Rican ingredients. You might have students make the following recipe as a class project or for extra credit.

### Arroz con gandules

**para 6 personas**

1 pimiento verde
1 tomate
2 dientes de ajo
1 cebolla pequeña
1 cucharadita de pimienta negra
2 onzas de salsa de tomate enlatada
2 tazas de gandules cocidos (se puede usar garbanzos)
2 tazas de arroz
2 tazas de aceitunas verdes, cortadas a la mitad
4 tazas de agua caliente
4 chiles
6 ramitas enteras de cilantro
4 cucharaditas de aceite de achiote
1 cucharadita de hojitas de orégano seco
sal al gusto

Lave, pele y corte todo, excepto la salsa de tomate, los gandules, el arroz y las aceitunas. No olvide quitar las semillas de los chiles y del pimiento. Mezcle los ingredientes en una licuadora hasta que se haga un puré. Caliente el aceite en una olla gruesa a fuego mediano. Vierta el puré en la olla y cocínelo, removiendo por 5 minutos. Agregue los gandules y después el arroz. Cocine y remueva hasta cubrir el arroz con el aceite. Añada la salsa de tomate, las aceitunas y la sal. Después baje la llama hasta que el agua se evapore. Voltee una o dos veces el arroz. Cúbralo y cocínelo a fuego lento durante 30 minutos. 2.2, 3.1

# Listening Activity Scripts

## Entre familia



### Vocabulario en acción 1

**1** p. 142, CD 4, Track 1

¿Qué tal? Me llamo Alfonso y les presento a mi familia. Primero les presento a mi papá. Se llama Enrique. Vivo con él, con mi madrastra Paulina y mi medio hermana Érica, en Santo Domingo. Érica y yo estudiamos en el mismo colegio. Mis abuelos viven en el mismo vecindario que nosotros. Mi abuelo se llama Eduardo y mi abuela se llama Roberta pero mi papá siempre les dice «suegro» y «suegra». Me alegra cuando nos visitan.

**Answers to Activity 1**
**Eduardo,** el suegro de Enrique
**Roberta,** la suegra de Enrique
**Paulina**, la madrastra de Alfonso
**Érica,** la medio hermana de Alfonso

**7** p. 145, CD 4, Track 2

1. —Mi primo Alejandro sigue estudiando medicina en la universidad.
—No me extraña. Él siempre decía que quería ser médico.
2. —¿Sabías que tu primo consiguió el puesto que quería en Suiza?
—¡No me lo puedo creer! ¿En serio?
3. —Fíjate que se han divorciado tía Lupe y tío Enrique.
—Sí, ya lo sabía. Me lo dijo abuela. Qué pena, ¿no?
4. —Tu tío cambió de trabajo. Ya no trabaja como mecánico.
—¡No me digas! ¿Y ahora a qué se dedica?
5. —Fíjate que mi hermano le dio un anillo de compromiso a su novia.
—Me has dejado boquiabierto. ¡Pensé que tu hermano jamás se casaría!
6. —El hijo de mi cuñada se graduó hace poco y se fue a Indonesia a trabajar.
—No me extraña. Los jóvenes de hoy trabajan en muchas partes.

**Answers to Activity 7**
1. b
2. a
3. b
4. a
5. a
6. b

### Gramática en acción 1

**9** p. 146, CD 4, Track 3

1. —¿Sigue buscando trabajo Marcos?
—Ya no. De hecho, ahora está trabajando en la compañía de su abuelo.
2. —¿Piensa viajar a Europa tu hermana?
—¡Claro! Ha soñado con hacerlo desde niña y está planeando viajar en junio.
3. —¿Qué tal el hijo menor de Josefina y Carlos? ¿Sigue enfermo?
—Sí, está tosiendo mucho y no se siente bien.
4. —¿Y a tu primo le gusta la nueva bicicleta?
—Pues, no tanto. Sigue cayéndose y se siente algo fastidiado.
5. —¿Ya dejó de llorar el bebé?
—Me parece que por fin está durmiendo.
6. —¿Le gusta a Celia su anillo de compromiso?
—¡Qué va! Si anda mostrándoselo a todo el mundo.

**Answers to Activity 9**
1. no
2. sigue pasando
3. sigue pasando
4. sigue pasando
5. no
6. sigue pasando

**13** p. 148, CD 4, Track 4

1. Mamá ha planeado una reunión familiar para julio.
2. En estos días, ella anda organizando todos los detalles.
3. Mi abuelo ha ofrecido su casa de la playa para la fiesta.
4. Papá ha hecho la lista de invitados.
5. Mamá y papá están consultando con las tías sobre el menú y el lugar para la fiesta.
6. Las tías han ayudado mucho en otras fiestas familiares y esperamos que puedan volver a ayudarnos.
7. Yo les estoy poniendo estampillas a los sobres.
8. Abuela está buscando recetas.

**Answers to Activity 13**

| | | |
|---|---|---|
| 1. a | 4. a | 7. b |
| 2. b | 5. b | 8. b |
| 3. a | 6. a | |

For Student Response Forms, see the *Lab Book,* pp. 25–28.

**17** p. 150, CD 4, Track 5

1. Me alegra que no tengamos que cancelar la boda.
2. Es una lástima que mi prima Martina no pueda venir.
3. Me gusta que la recepción sea en nuestra casa.
4. Me molesta que todavía no hayamos escogido un grupo musical.
5. Es bueno que pueda asistir tanta gente.
6. Es triste que la novia no haya encontrado un vestido apropiado.
7. Es maravilloso que haga tan buen tiempo este fin de semana.
8. Me encanta que por fin Alicia y Ernesto se hayan comprometido.

**Answers to Activity 17**

1. positiva 3. positiva 5. positiva 7. positiva
2. negativa 4. negativa 6. negativa 8. positiva

## Vocabulario en acción 2

**21** p. 156, CD 4, Track 9

1. —¿Qué tal si le echo un poco de apio a la ensalada?
   —Uy, qué asco. A mí no me gusta el apio.
2. —¿Quieres más bizcocho de chocolate?
   —Claro que sí. Sabe delicioso.
3. —¿Te gusta el puerco asado?
   —Se me hace la boca agua.
4. —¿No te gustaron los frijoles negros?
   —Pues, la verdad es que les falta sabor.
5. —¿Te gustaría probar el pavo?
   —Ya lo probé. Está demasiado seco.
6. —¿Te gustaron los camarones?
   —Ay, Silvia, están para chuparse los dedos.

**Answers to Activity 21**

1. e; no 2. d; sí 3. b; sí 4. a; no 5. f; no 6. c; sí

**27** p. 159, CD 4, Track 10

1. —Me parece que al pollo le falta algo pero no sé qué le falta.
   —Ya lo sé. Se me olvidó ponerle pimienta.
2. —Esta sopa está demasiada salada. No me la puedo comer.
   —Tienes razón. Es que se me fue la mano con la sal.
3. —El bizcocho está un poco seco, ¿no crees?
   —Sí, está seco. Lo que pasa es que se me acabó la mantequilla.
4. —La ensalada de pepinos no tiene mucho sabor.
   —Perdón, es que se me olvidó ponerle limón.
5. —Este sándwich está muy seco. ¿Qué pasó?
   —Es que se me acabó la mayonesa y no tuve tiempo de ir al supermercado.
6. —El flan está muy dulce.
   —Lo siento, es que se me fue la mano con el azúcar.

**Answers to Activity 27**

1. d 2. a 3. c 4. b 5. e 6. f

## Prepárate para el examen capítulo 4

**1** p. 174, CD 4, Track 13

1. —¿Qué anda haciendo tu hermana Faviola?
   —Fíjate que se acaba de graduar de la universidad.
2. —Fabián, te ves muy contento. Dame las buenas noticias.
   —Bueno, para empezar estoy disfrutando de una hamburguesa riquísima, pero sí, tengo buenas noticias: ¡me aceptaron en la universidad!
   —¡No me digas! Felicidades.
3. —¿Cómo te fue en la fiesta?
   —Estuvo muy bien. Hicimos salchichas a la parrilla y hablé con mis amigos. Y, ¿qué crees? La hermana de Andrés se va a casar.
   —¡No me lo puedo creer!

**Answers to Activity 1**

1. B 2. A 3. C

**6** p. 175, CD 4, Track 14

—¿Ya preparaste el plato que vas a llevar a la muestra de comida internacional?

—Sí, el plato que preparé sabe delicioso. Preparé un caldo de camarones. Traté de preparar un pollo frito pero se me quemó.

—¡Qué horror! Pues, fíjate que yo también tuve algunos problemas. Iba a llevar un plato de arroz con frijoles pero se me fue la mano con la sal, y la comida salió demasiado salada.

—¿Ah, sí?

—Sí. Y luego preparé una ensalada de calabacín, con pepino, lechuga y coliflor. Me salió muy bien la ensalada pero cuando fui a meterla en el refrigerador, se me fue el plato de la mano y se cayó al piso.

—¡No me digas!

—Entonces tuve que hacer algo rápido porque no tenía mucho tiempo. Así que preparé unas salchichas con queso.

**Answers to Activity 6**

caldo de camarones, pollo frito, arroz con frijoles, ensalada de calabacín, salchichas con queso

# 50-Minute Lesson Plans

## Entre familia

For more customized Lesson Plans, see the *Lesson Planner with Differentiated Instruction.*



### Day 1

**Objective**
*Asking about the latest news and responding*

**Core Instruction**
**Chapter Opener**, pp. 138–139 **10 min.**
- See Chapter Objectives, p. 138 and Using the Photo, p. 139.

**Vocabulario en acción 1,** pp. 140–145
- Have students do Bell Work, p. 140.
- See Teaching **Vocabulario 1,** p. 140. **10 min.**
- See Teaching **¡Exprésate!,** p. 140. **5 min.**
- Play Audio CD 4, Tr. 1 for Activity 1, p. 142. **5 min.**
- Have students do Activities 2–4, pp. 142–143. **20 min.**

**Optional Resources**
- Slower Pace Learners, p. 141 ◆
- Special Learning Needs, p. 141 ●
- Heritage Speakers, p. 143 ■
- Advanced Learners, p. 143 ▲
- Special Learning Needs, p. 143 ●

**Homework Suggestions**
Cuaderno de vocabulario y gramática, pp. 37–39

❀ 1.1, 1.3

### Day 2

**Objective**
*Reacting to news*

**Core Instruction**
**Vocabulario en acción 1,** pp. 140–145
- Have students do Activity 5, p. 143. **10 min.**
- See Teaching **¡Exprésate!,** p. 144. **10 min.**
- Have students do Activities 6–8, p. 145. **30 min.**

**Optional Resources**
- Advanced Learners, p. 145 ▲
- Special Learning Needs, p. 145 ●

**Homework Suggestions**
Study for **Prueba: Vocabulario 1**

❀ 1.1, 1.2, 1.3

### Day 3

**Objective**
*Present progressive*

**Core Instruction**
**Vocabulario en acción 1,** pp. 140–145
- Review **Vocabulario en acción 1,** pp. 140–145. **5 min.**
- Give **Prueba: Vocabulario 1. 20 min.**

**Gramática en acción 1,** pp. 146–151
- See Teaching **Gramática,** p. 146. **10 min.**
- Play Audio CD 4, Tr. 3 for Activity 9, p. 146. **5 min.**
- Have students do Activities 10–11, p. 147. **10 min.**

**Optional Resources**
- Heritage Sepakers, p. 147 ■
- Slower Pace Learners, p. 147 ◆
- Multiple Intelligences, p. 147

**Homework Suggestions**
Cuaderno de vocabulario y gramática, pp. 40–42
Cuaderno de actividades, pp. 31–33

❀ 1.2

### Day 4

**Objective**
*Present perfect indicative*

**Core Instruction**
**Gramática en acción 1,** pp. 146–151
- Have students do Activity 12, p. 147. **5 min.**
- See Teaching **Gramática,** p. 148. **10 min.**
- Play Audio CD 4, Tr. 4 for Activity 13, p. 148. **10 min.**
- Have students do Activities 14–16, p. 149. **25 min.**

**Optional Resources**
- **Comunicación,** p. 149
- Slower Pace Learners, p. 149 ◆
- Special Learning Needs, p. 149 ●

**Homework Suggestions**
Cuaderno de vocabulario y gramática, pp. 40–42
Cuaderno de actividades, pp. 31–33

❀ 1.1, 1.2

### Day 5

**Objective**
*Present perfect subjunctive*

**Core Instruction**
**Gramática en acción 1,** pp. 146–151
- See Teaching **Gramática,** p. 150. **10 min.**
- Play Audio CD 4, Tr. 5 for Activity 17, p. 150. **10 min.**
- Have students do Activities 18–20, p. 151. **30 min.**

**Optional Resources**
- **Comunicación,** p. 151
- Advanced Learners, p. 151 ▲
- Special Learning Needs, p. 151 ●

**Homework Suggestions**
Study for **Prueba: Gramática 1**
Cuaderno de vocabulario y gramática, pp. 40–42
Cuaderno de actividades, pp. 31–33

❀ 1.1, 1.2

### Day 6

**Objective**
*Interviews from around the Spanish-speaking world*

**Core Instruction**
**Gramática en acción 1,** pp. 146–151
- Review **Gramática en acción 1,** pp. 146–151 **5 min.**
- Give **Prueba: Gramática 1. 20 min.**

**Cultura,** pp. 152–153
- See Teaching **Cultura,** p. 152. **10 min.**
- Play Audio CD 4, Tr. 6–8, or show **VideoCultura. 15 min.**

**Optional Resources**
- Advanced Learners, p. 153 ▲
- Multiple Intelligences, p. 153

**Homework Suggestions**
Cuaderno de actividades, p. 34
Online Practice (**go.hrw.com,** Keyword: EXP3 CH4)

❀ 1.2, 1.3, 2.2, 4.2

### Day 7

**Objective**
*Commenting on food*

**Core Instruction**
**Vocabulario en acción 2,** pp. 154–159
- See Teaching **Vocabulario,** p. 154. **10 min.**
- See Teaching **¡Exprésate!** p. 154. **10 min.**
- Play Audio CD 4, Tr. 9 for Activity 21, p. 156. **5 min.**
- Have students do Activities 22–25, pp. 156–157. **25 min.**

**Optional Resources**
- Advanced Learners, p. 155 ▲
- Special Learning Needs, p. 155 ●
- Slower Pace Learners, p. 157 ◆
- Special Learning Needs, p. 157 ●

**Homework Suggestions**
Cuaderno de vocabulario y gramática, pp. 43–45

❀ 1.1, 1.2, 1.3

### Day 8

**Objective**
*Commenting on food, explaining and giving excuses*

**Core Instruction**
**Vocabulario en acción 2,** pp. 154–159
- See Teaching **¡Exprésate!,** p. 158. **10 min.**
- Have students do Activity 26, p. 159. **10 min.**
- Play Audio CD 4, Tr. 10 for Activity 27, p. 159. **10 min.**
- Have students do Activity 28, p. 159. **10 min.**
- Review **Vocabulario en acción 2,** pp. 154–159. **10 min.**

**Optional Resources**
- **Comunicación,** p. 159
- Advanced Learners, p. 159 ▲
- Multiple Intelligences, p. 159

**Homework Suggestions**
Study for **Prueba: Vocabulario 2**

❀ 1.1, 1.2, 1.3

- For information on the **Geocultura** pages, see the *Lesson Planner with Differentiated Instruction.*
- For more detailed information on benchmarks, see point-of-use correlations on each page.
- To edit and create your own lesson plans, see the **One-Stop** Planner® CD-ROM

**KEY**
- ▲ Advanced Learners
- ◆ Slower Pace Learners
- ● Special Learning Needs
- ■ Heritage Speakers

## Day 9

### Objective
*Preterite*

### Core Instruction
**Vocabulario en acción 2,** pp. 154–159
- Give **Prueba: Vocabulario 2.** **20 min.**

**Gramática en acción 2,** pp. 160–165
- See Teaching **Gramática,** p. 160. **10 min.**
- Have students do Activities 29–32, pp. 160–161. **20 min.**

### Optional Resources
- **Comunicación,** p. 161
- Advanced Learners, p. 161 ▲
- Special Learning Needs, p. 161 ●

### Homework Suggestions
Cuaderno de vocabulario y gramática, pp. 46–48
Cuaderno de actividades, pp. 35–37
1.1, 1.2, 1.3

## Day 10

### Objective
***Se** + indirect object pronouns, past progressive*

### Core Instruction
**Gramática en acción 2,** pp. 160–165
- See Teaching **Gramática,** p. 162. **10 min.**
- Have students do Activities 33–36, pp. 162–163. **30 min.**
- See Teaching **Gramática,** p. 164. **10 min.**

### Optional Resources
- **Comunicación,** p. 163
- Slower Pace Learners, p. 163 ◆
- Multiple Intelligences, p. 163

### Homework Suggestions
Cuaderno de vocabulario y gramática, pp. 46–48
Cuaderno de actividades, pp. 35–37
1.1, 1.2

## Day 11

### Objective
*Past progressive*

### Core Instruction
**Gramática en acción 2,** pp. 160–165
- Have students do Activities 37–40, pp. 164–165. **30 min.**
- Review **Gramática en acción 2,** pp. 160–165. **20 min.**

### Optional Resources
- **Comunicación,** p. 165
- Slower Pace Learners, p. 165 ◆
- Multiple Intelligences, p. 165

### Homework Suggestions
Study for **Prueba: Gramática 2**
Cuaderno de vocabulario y gramática, pp. 46–48
Cuaderno de actividades, pp. 35–37
1.1, 1.2, 1.3

## Day 12

### Objective
*Developing listening and reading skills*

### Core Instruction
**Gramática en acción 2,** pp. 160–165
- Give **Prueba: Gramática 2.** **20 min.**

**Novela en video,** pp. 166–167
- Show **VideoNovela.** See Teaching **Novela en video,** p. 166. **30 min.**

### Optional Resources
**Assessment Program**
- **Prueba: Aplicación 2**

### Homework Suggestions
Cuaderno de vocabulario y gramática, pp. 46–48
1.2

## Day 13

### Objective
*Developing listening and reading skills*

### Core Instruction
**Lectura cultural,** pp. 168–169
- See Teaching **Lectura cultural,** p. 168. **25 min.**

**Leamos y escribamos,** pp. 170–173
- See Teaching **Leamos,** p. 170. **25 min.**

### Optional Resources
- Slower Pace Learners, p. 169 ◆
- Special Learning Needs, p. 169 ●
- Advanced Learners, p. 171 ▲
- Multiple Intelligences, p. 171

### Homework Suggestions
Cuaderno de actividades, p. 38
1.2

## Day 14

### Objective
*Developing reading and writing skills*

### Core Instruction
**Leamos y escribamos,** pp. 170–173
- Have students do Activities B–C, p. 172. **15 min.**
- See Teaching **Escribamos,** p. 172.

**Prepárate para el examen,** pp. 174–177
- Play Audio CD 4, Tr. 13 for Activity 1, p. 174. **5 min.**
- Have students do Activities 2–5, pp. 174–175. **30 min.**

### Optional Resources
- Slower Pace Learners, p. 173 ◆
- Multiple Intelligences, p. 173

### Homework Suggestions
**Taller del escritor** p. 172
1.1, 1.2, 1.3, 3.1

## Day 15

### Objective
*Chapter review*

### Core Instruction
**Prepárate para el examen,** pp. 174–177
- Play Audio CD 4, Tr. 14 for Activity 6, p. 175. **5 min.**
- Have students do Activity 7, p. 175. **5 min.**

**Integración,** pp. 178–179
- Have students do Activities 1–6, pp. 178–179. **40 min.**

### Optional Resources
- Play Pre-AP Audio CD 1, Tr. 13, for Pre-AP Practice, p. 175
- Game, p. 177
- Fine Art Connection, p. 179

### Homework Suggestions
Study for Chapter Test
1.1, 1.2, 1.3, 4.2

## Day 16/Test

### Core Instruction
**Chapter Test** **50 min.**

### Optional Resources
**Assessment Program**
- **Prueba: Lectura**
- **Prueba: Escritura**
- Test Generator

### Homework Suggestions
Cuaderno de actividades, pp. 39–40

# Indiana
## The Hoosier State

The Indianapolis Canal

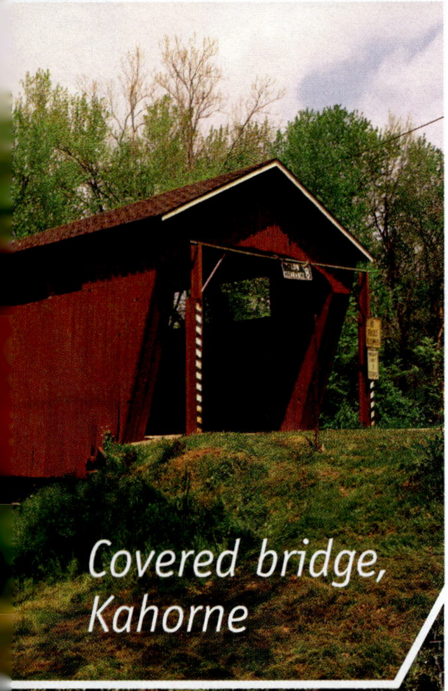
Covered bridge, Kahorne

Bloomington

### Chapter 4

The following chart presents *¡Exprésate!* Chapter 4 correlations to the Indiana Academic Standards for World Languages, Grade 11. The correlations here are to the *Student Edition* (SE) and *Teacher's Edition* (TE) only. For additional teaching resources, see pages 137A-137B

| INDIANA ACADEMIC STANDARDS | | | CHAPTER 4 SE/TE CORRELATIONS |
|---|---|---|---|
| **Standard 1 COMMUNICATION:** | | | |
| **Write and speak in a language other than English** | 11.1.1 | Initiate, sustain, and close conversations in limited yet varied situations. | SE: 177, 179<br>TE: 158 |
| | 11.1.2 | Exchange detailed information and opinions orally on a variety of topics. | SE: 121, 153, 177<br>TE: 152, 178 |
| | 11.1.3 | Exchange detailed information and opinions in written form on a variety of topics. | SE: 173 |
| | 11.1.4 | Make requests and ask different types of questions in a variety of social situations. | SE: 143, 147, 149, 157<br>TE: 154 |
| | 11.1.5 | Recognize and use situation-appropriate non-verbal communication. | SE: 145, 147, 151, 179<br>TE: 161, 166 |
| **Standard 2 COMMUNICATION:** | | | |
| **Interpret information in a language other than English** *Learners interpret written and spoken language on a variety of topics. (Interpretive)* | 11.2.1 | Respond accurately to everyday requests, commands, and directions. | SE: 141, 155 |
| | 11.2.2 | Demonstrate comprehension of both authentic and non-authentic written and spoken language through developmentally appropriate tasks. | SE: 153, 167, 169<br>TE: 152, 166, 168 |
| | 11.2.3 | Make educated guesses about meaning in unfamiliar written and spoken contexts. | SE: 166, 170<br>TE: 166, 170 |
| **Standard 3 COMMUNICATION:** | | | |
| **Present information in a language other than English** *Learners present to an audience of listeners or readers on a variety of topics. (Presentational)* | 11.3.2 | Produce and present creative material on a variety of topics. | SE: 147, 179<br>TE: 137C, 178 |
| | 11.3.4 | Compose cohesive written information using appropriate formats and more varied vocabulary and structures. | SE: 173<br>TE: 137C, 172, 173 |
| **Standard 4 CULTURES:** | | | |
| **Develop awareness of other cultures.** *Learners examine, experience, and reflect on the relationships among the practices, products, and perspectives of the cultures studied.* | 11.4.1 | Analyze and reflect on cultural practices of the target cultures. | SE: 153, 169, 179<br>TE: 137D, 152, 168, 178 |
| | 11.4.2 | Describe products, perspectives, and symbols of the target cultures. | SE: 153, 169, 179<br>TE: 137C, 152, 168, 178 |
| | 11.4.3 | Discuss factors that influence practices, products, and perspectives. | SE: 153, 169, 179<br>TE: 152, 168, 178 |
| | 11.4.4 | Recognize the interrelations among the practices, products, and perspectives of the target cultures. | SE: 153, 169, 179<br>TE: 152, 168, 178 |

| | | | |
|---|---|---|---|
| | 11.4.5 | Explain contributions from other cultures. | SE: 169, 179<br>TE: 168, 178 |
| | 11.4.6 | Identify significant events unique to the target cultures. | TE: 153 |

## Standard 5 CONNECTIONS:

| | | | |
|---|---|---|---|
| **Make connections to other content areas** *Learners use the target language to expand their knowledge of and make connections among multiple content areas.* | 11.5.1 | Make connections with other content areas through resources intended for native speakers. | TE: 137C, 178 |
| | 11.5.2 | Design and share activities and materials that integrate the target language and cultures with concepts and skills from other content areas. | TE: 137C, 177 |

## Standard 6 CONNECTIONS:

| | | | |
|---|---|---|---|
| **Access and connect information through various media** *Learners strengthen language proficiency and cultural knowledge by using current digital media and authentic resources.* | 11.6.1 | Use digital media and culturally authentic resources to build vocabulary, improve reading ability, and encourage cultural awareness. | SE: 142, 145, 146, 148, 150, 152<br>TE: 137F |
| | 11.6.2 | Use digital media and culturally authentic resources to study target cultures. | SE: 152, 166 |
| | 11.6.3 | Identify and evaluate resources intended for native speakers. | SE: 152, 166 |

## Standard 7 COMPARISONS:

| | | | |
|---|---|---|---|
| **Investigate the nature of language and culture** *Learners understand the nature of language and culture through comparisons of the languages and cultures studied and their own.* | 11.7.1 | Use elements of word formation to expand vocabulary and derive meaning. | SE: 151, 161, 175<br>TE: 146, 160, 174 |
| | 11.7.2 | Recognize and use a variety of language structures. | SE: 173, 174-177<br>TE: 146-151, 160-165, 174-177 |
| | 11.7.3 | Compare and use idiomatic, colloquial, and proverbial expressions in the target language. | SE: 145, 179<br>TE: 144 |
| | 11.7.5 | Compare systems of other cultures and the learner's own culture. | SE: 153, 169<br>TE: 137D, 152, 168 |
| | 11.7.6 | Compare and contrast elements that shape cultural identity in the learner's heritage and in the target cultures. | SE: 153, 169<br>TE: 152, 168 |

## Standard 8 COMMUNITIES:

| | | | |
|---|---|---|---|
| **Become an active global citizen by experiencing languages and cultures in multiple settings** *Learners use their knowledge of the target language and cultures both within and beyond the school setting for personal enrichment and civic engagement.* | 11.8.1 | Share experiences from the world language classroom with others. | TE: 178 |
| | 11.8.2 | Investigate and share with others the influences of the target language and cultures on the community. | SE: 153 |
| | 11.8.3 | Show evidence of becoming a life-long learner by using the target language and cultural knowledge for personal enrichment. | TE: 137C, 137D |

## Meeting the National Standards

### Communication
Comunicación, pp. 143, 145, 147, 149, 151, 157, 159, 161, 163, 165, 167

Game, p. 177

Situación, p. 179

### Cultures
Las fiestas, p. 137D

Practices and Perspectives, p. 142

Heritage Speakers, p. 143

Products and Perspectives, pp. 157, 172

Nota cultural, pp. 157, 161

Culture Project, p. 178

### Connections
Receta, p. 137D

Atlas Interactivo Mundial, p. 153

History Link, p. 153

Multiple Intelligences, p. 153

Advanced Learners, p. 155

Heritage Speakers, p. 169

Extension, p. 179

### Comparisons
Las fiestas, p. 137D

Nota cultural, pp. 143, 151

En inglés, pp. 146, 150, 162

Language to Language, p. 147

Comparing and Contrasting, pp. 151, 158

Comparaciones, p. 152

Language Note, pp. 156, 157

Post-Reading Activities, p. 169

### Communities
Una desgustación de comida caribeña, p. 137C

Community Link, p. 143

## Learning Tips
As students learn new vocabulary about the family, have them determine how the new terms correspond to their own family members. For example, they might make a list that includes **cuñada** → **Luisa.** This connection will help them remember the vocabulary more easily.

# Capítulo 4

# Entre familia

## OBJETIVOS
**In this chapter you will learn to**
- ask about the latest news
- react to news
- comment on food
- explain and give excuses

**And you will use**
- present progressive
- present perfect indicative
- present perfect subjunctive
- preterite
- **se** + indirect object pronouns
- past progressive

### ¿Qué ves en la foto?
- ¿A qué miembros de la familia ves?
- ¿Qué ves en su sala de estar?
- ¿Qué tienen en común con tu familia?

| Suggested pacing: | Traditional Schedule | Block Schedule |
|---|---|---|
| Vocabulario 1/Gramática 1 | 5 1/2 days | 2 1/2 blocks |
| Cultura | 1/2 day | 1/2 block |
| Vocabulario 2/Gramática 2 | 5 1/2 days | 2 1/2 blocks |
| Novela | 1/2 day | 1/4 block |
| Lectura cultural | 1/2 day | 1/2 block |
| Leamos y escribamos | 1 day | 1/2 block |
| Prepárate para el examen | 1/2 day | 1/4 block |
| Chapter Test | 1 day | 1/2 block |
| Integración | 1 day | 1/2 block |

Una familia dominicana en casa

# Chapter Opener

## Holt Grammar Logic
### CHAPTER 4

- *To ask about the latest news, and to react to news,* students must review the present progressive as well as the present perfect in the indicative. They will also need to use the present perfect subjunctive.
- *To comment on food, and to explain and give excuses,* students will need to review verbs with irregular stems in the preterite and verbs that change meaning in the preterite. Students will also need to use **se** + *indirect object pronoun* + *verb,* and the past progressive, including its use with the preterite.

## Using the Photo

Explain to students that it is not uncommon to have members of an extended family living in the same home in Latin America. Have them guess what family event this Dominican family is celebrating.

## DVD VIDEO OPTIONS

- **VideoCultura**
- **VideoNovela**
- **Variedades**
- **GramaVisión**

## LISTENING PRACTICE — Language Lab and Classroom Activities

**Vocabulario**
Activity 1, p. 142, CD 4, Tr. 1
Activity 7, p. 145, CD 4, Tr. 2
Activity 21, p. 156, CD 4, Tr. 9
Activity 27, p. 159, CD 4, Tr. 10

**Gramática**
Activity 9, p. 106, CD 4, Tr. 3
Activity 13, p. 108, CD 4, Tr. 4
Activity 17, p. 118, CD 4, Tr. 5

**Cultura**
**Comparaciones,** pp. 152–153, CD 4, Tr. 6–8

**Novela**
**Novela en video,** Escuchemos, p. 166

**Lectura cultural**
pp. 168–169, CD 4, Tr. 11

**Leamos**
pp. 170–171, CD 4, Tr. 12
**Escuchemos,** p. 170

**Repaso**
Activity 1, p. 174, CD 4, Tr. 13
Activity 6, p. 175, CD 4, Tr. 14
**Variedades,** Lab Book, p. 66

**Assessment Program**
CD 4, Tr. 15–18

**Additional Listening**
Pre-AP CD 1, Trs. 13–16

## Resources

**Planning:**

Lesson Planner, pp. 49–50, 210–211

One-Stop Planner

**Presentation:**

Teaching Transparencies
**Vocabulario** 4.1, 4.2

**Practice:**

Cuaderno de vocabulario y gramática, pp. 37–39

Activities for Communication, pp. 13–14

Teaching Transparencies
Bell Work 4.1
**Vocabulario y gramática** answers, pp. 37–39

Interactive Tutor, Disc 1

### Bell Work

Use Bell Work 4.1 in the *Teaching Transparencies*, or write this activity on the board.

**Completa las siguientes oraciones.**

1. Si yo fuera rico(a)…
2. Si tú tuvieras tiempo…
3. Si yo pudiera viajar a cualquier país…
4. Si tú fueras mi hermano,…
5. Si yo pudiera volver a hacer el examen…

1.2, 1.3

**Objetivos**
- Asking about the latest news
- Reacting to news

# Vocabulario en acción 1

## En Santo Domingo

## A reunirse con la familia

Me llamo Carlos y quiero presentarles a mi familia. Mi familia es grande y me encanta pasar tiempo con ellos. ¡Vamos a conocerlos a todos!

Ésta es una foto familiar de hace diez años. Aquí estoy sentado con mis papás y mis hermanas. Hace cinco años mis papás decidieron **separarse** y luego **se divorciaron.**

Ésta es mi mamá. El año pasado, mi mamá se casó con Jorge. Jorge es mi **padrastro** y su hijo Miguel es mi **hermanastro.**

Mi papá **se casó con** Laura, mi **madrastra,** después del **divorcio.** Ella era **divorciada** y tenía una hija, Elisa. Elisa es mi **hermanastra.** Este año, Laura **dio a luz** a un niño, Alejandro, mi **medio hermano.**

**Más vocabulario...**

| | |
|---|---|
| **la cuñada** | *sister-in-law* |
| **el funeral** | *funeral* |
| **la medio hermana** | *half sister* |
| **separado(a)** | *separated* |
| **la suegra** | *mother-in-law* |
| **el suegro** | *father-in-law* |

**También se puede decir...**

You may hear some **la sortija de compromiso** instead of **el anillo de compromiso.** Some Spanish speakers say **parir** for **dar a luz.**

### Pre-AP Practice

**AP Benchmark:** Communicate via formal and informal written communication.

**Focus:** Talking about the latest news

- SE p. 143, Act. 4
- TE p. 143, Communities: Community Link
- Assessment Program, p. 400, **Vocabulario 1/Gramática 1,** Written Assessment

## Core Instruction

### TEACHING VOCABULARIO

1. Use transparencies 4.1 and 4.2 to present the vocabulary. Model pronunciation and point to target vocabulary as you read each photo caption. **(2 min.)**
2. Present the words from **Más vocabulario** and check students' comprehension. **(2 min.)**
3. Practice vocabulary with students by asking **¿Alguien tiene un hermanastro?** Continue with other vocabulary words. **(3 min.)**
4. Have volunteers describe their own families using new and known vocabulary. **(3 min.)**

### TEACHING ¡EXPRÉSATE!

1. For review, ask students to identify family relationships. **El papá de mi esposa es mi ______.** **(1 min.)**
2. Act out both sides of a conversation as you model the expressions. For example, ask **¿Qué sabes del hermano de Ana?** Play the part of the second person and respond with: **Fíjate que se ha divorciado.** Use your tone of voice to express surprise. **(2 min.)**
3. Have pairs of students ask and answer questions about the latest news using **¡Exprésate!** expressions. **(2 min.)**

Visit Holt Online
go.hrw.com
KEYWORD: EXP3 CH4
Vocabulario 1 practice

Mi hermana Gabriela **está casada** con Alberto. Efraín, el hermano de Alberto, es **el cuñado** de Gabriela y es un buen amigo de la familia.

El año pasado **nació** Benjamín, el primer hijo de Gabriela y Alberto. Benjamín es mi sobrino.

Tengo otra hermana, Cristina. Ella y su novio Pablo **se comprometieron** justo después de **graduarse** de la universidad. Pablo le dio **un anillo de compromiso** muy bonito.

A mis parientes les encanta estar juntos. Nos reunimos todos para las bodas, los bautizos, los cumpleaños, la Nochebuena y ¡hasta buscamos pretextos para hacer una **reunión familiar!**



## ¡Exprésate!

| To ask about the latest news | To respond |
|---|---|
| **¿Qué sabes de...?** *What do you know about . . .?* | **Pues, sigue trabajando...** *Well, he's/she's still working . . .* |
| **¿Qué me cuentas de...?** *What can you tell me about . . .?* | **Según tengo entendido,...** *From what I understand, . . .* |
| **¿Qué anda haciendo...?** *What's . . . up to?* | **Fíjate que se ha casado.** *Get this: he/she got married.* |

Interactive TUTOR

Vocabulario y gramática, pp. 37–39 Online workbooks

▶ Vocabulario adicional — La familia, p. R16

### TPR

#### Total Physical Response

Have students create paper-doll cutouts and then form make-believe families, based on your commands. First, have students create dolls for two families, one with a father (Pepe), a mother (Ana), and two daughters (María and Lisa), and another with a father (David), a mother (Sara), and a son (Marcos). Then, have them move the dolls as you direct them.

**Marcos, te comprometiste con María. Ponte al lado de tu novia.**

**María, saluda a tu suegra.**

**Marcos, señala a tu cuñada.**

**Pepe y Ana, ustedes se divorciaron. Caminen en direcciones opuestas.**

1.2

### Common Error Alert

¡OJO!

Students may think they have to change the ending of **medio** in **medio hermano** and **medio hermana** so that the words agree in gender. Remind them that the ending of **medio** in this case does not change.

### También se puede decir...

Students may hear the term **parir** for **dar a luz.** Tell them that in some Spanish-speaking countries this term is not used to refer to people.

### Circumlocution

Have students describe the family relationships from **Vocabulario 1** without using the vocabulary words. For example, they might say: **Es la hija de mi padrastro y mi mamá. (medio hermana)** 1.1

## Differentiated Instruction

### Slower Pace Learners

**Additional Practice** Help identify the members of the family in the photographs on pages 140 and 141. Display the **Vocabulario** transparencies that show the photographs of the family. Have students scan the text for the names of family members, and write each name on the board. Then read the text aloud with students and have them tell who each person in the photo is. Write each person's name beside his or her photo on the transparency.

### Special Learning Needs

**Students with Learning Disabilities** Some students may not understand all of the family relationships described in this chapter. Have students refer to the vocabulary list from **Vocabulario adicional.** Review basic family terms such as **padre, madre, hermano, hermana, abuelo, abuela, primo, prima, nieto, nieta,** that students learned in Levels 1 and 2. In pairs, have students create an imaginary family tree using photographs cut out from magazines. Have pairs present their trees to the class, describing the family relationships in each.

**Differentiated Instruction** See the Differentiated Instruction CD-ROM.

## Resources

**Planning:**

Lesson Planner, pp. 49–50, 210–211

One-Stop Planner

**Presentation:**

Teaching Transparencies
**Vocabulario** 4.1, 4.2

**Practice:**

Cuaderno de vocabulario y gramática, pp. 37–39

Activities for Communication, pp. 13–14

Lab Book, pp. 25–28

Teaching Transparencies
**Vocabulario y gramática** answers, pp. 37–39

Audio CD 4, Tr. 1

Interactive Tutor, Disc 1

### 1 Script

¿Qué tal? Me llamo Alfonso y les presento a mi familia. Primero les presento a mi papá. Se llama Enrique. Vivo con él, con mi madrastra Paulina y mi medio hermana Érica en Santo Domingo. Érica y yo estudiamos en el mismo colegio. Mis abuelos viven en el mismo vecindario que nosotros. Mi abuelo se llama Eduardo y mi abuela se llama Roberta pero mi papá siempre les dice «suegro» y «suegra». Me alegra cuando nos visitan.

### Cultures

**Practices and Perspectives**

In the Dominican Republic, people tend to spend more time outside the house than indoors. When getting together with friends, groups will often meet somewhere rather than inviting friends into their home. How does this compare with practices in your community? What factors might contribute to spending more or less time in the home? 2.1, 4.2

CD 4, Tr. 1

### 1 ¡Una gran familia! 1.2

**Escuchemos** Escucha mientras Alfonso habla de su familia y completa el diagrama con el parentesco *(relationship)* entre las personas mencionadas.

el suegro
**Eduardo** ____ de Enrique

la suegra
**Roberta** ____ de Enrique

**Enrique**

la madrastra
**Paulina** ____ de Alfonso

**Alfonso**

la medio hermana
**Érica** ____ de Alfonso

### 2 ¿Qué significa? 1.2

**Leamos** Lee las siguientes definiciones y escoge la palabra del cuadro que va con su definición.

| | | |
|---|---|---|
| divorciarse | dar a luz | un funeral |
| graduarse | casarse | comprometerse |
| una reunión familiar | un anillo de compromiso | |

1. Una fiesta donde toda la familia está junta en un lugar.
2. Algo que se le da a una mujer para proponerle matrimonio.
3. El acto de completar los estudios de un colegio.
4. El acto de contraer matrimonio.
5. El acto de tener un bebé.
6. Una ceremonia después de la muerte de una persona.
7. El acto de proponerle matrimonio a otra persona.
8. El acto de terminar un matrimonio.

1. una reunión familiar
2. un anillo de compromiso
3. graduarse
4. casarse
5. dar a luz
6. un funeral
7. comprometerse
8. divorciarse

## Core Instruction

### VOCABULARY IN CONTEXT

Divide the class into groups of 6 or 8. Have each group form a family unit made up of any of the family members listed in **Vocabulario 1.** Each group will present themselves to the class, giving only the basic information the class needs to know about who each person is **(papá, mamá, hijos, esposo(a)…)**. Then the group will ask the class to tell the relationship of one of the family members to another. For example: **Sara y Eduardo son los papás de Silvia, y Pablo y Lisa son los papás de Jorge. Jorge y Silvia son casados. ¿Cuál es la relación entre Jorge y Sara? (Sara es la suegra de Jorge.)** Continue until each group has had a chance to present themselves to the class, and to ask questions.

See answers on p. 144.

**6 ¿Qué fue lo que contó?** 1.2

**Leamos/Escribamos** Basándote en el diálogo entre Marcela y su abuela, determina si cada oración es **cierta** o **falsa.** Corrige las falsas. Luego coloca las oraciones en el orden en que se mencionaron.

1. Héctor fue a Montana a trabajar de banquero.
2. Liliana no aceptó el anillo de compromiso.
3. El tío José renunció a su trabajo como banquero.
4. La abuela no pudo creer las noticias acerca de Rubén.
5. Rubén y su esposa se separaron.
6. Marcela fue a Nueva York a visitar a sus tíos.
7. La abuela sintió mucha pena cuando supo lo de Liliana y Héctor.

Tiendas con letreros en español en el barrio de Washington Heights, Nueva York

CD 4, Tr. 2 See script on p. 137E.

**7 ¡No me digas!** 1.2

**Escuchemos** Escucha las conversaciones en que una persona le da noticias a la otra. Indica si la persona
a) está sorprendida o
b) no está sorprendida con las noticias.

**1.** b **2.** a **3.** b **4.** a **5.** a **6.** b

## Comunicación

HOLT SoundBooth ONLINE RECORDING

**8 Novedades familiares** 1.1, 1.2

**Hablemos** En grupos de tres, dramaticen una conversación basándose en las fotos. Túrnense para dar noticias nuevas y reaccionar. Sean creativos y usen las expresiones de **Exprésate.**

**MODELO** —**Fíjate que Rodrigo le propuso matrimonio a mi hermana Marta.**
—**¡No me digas! ¡Qué emoción!**

1
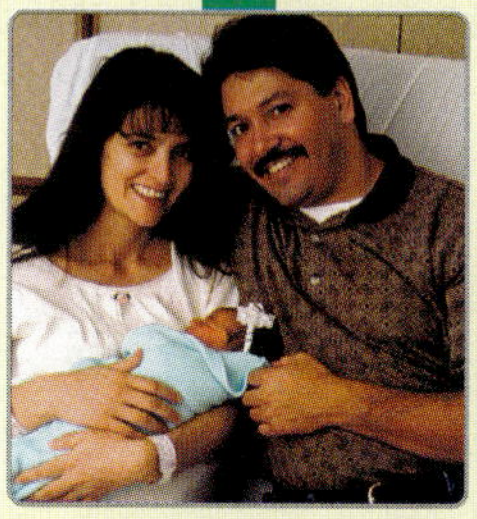
2

3

4

## Teacher to Teacher

**Kim Peters**
Mooresville High School
Mooresville, IN

To play **Alrededor del mundo,** divide the class into teams and have one student stand next to a row of seated students. Show a flash card. (You can create your own cards or use the Clip Art from the *One-Stop Planner.*) The first student to give the Spanish translation continues by moving to the next desk/student. A student is declared the winner when he or she goes through one row. The last student to lose to the winner then stands up to try to win against the next row. This can work with verb conjugations as well. 1.2

## Comunicación

### Class Activity: Interpersonal

Have students cut out several interesting articles about Hispanic actors or celebrities from a magazine such as *People en Español.* Have each student tell his or her partner the news from the article. The partner should react using expressions from **¡Exprésate!** 1.1

## Differentiated Instruction

### ADVANCED LEARNERS

**7 Extension** After students have completed Activity 7, play the audio script for them again. Have them write down the key expressions that let them know whether or not the person was surprised. Have them work with a partner to share news and practice these expressions. 1.2

### SPECIAL LEARNING NEEDS

**7 Students with Auditory Impairments** If you have students with auditory impairments, you can make photocopies of the script for Activity 7 that appears in the *Teacher's Edition.* Have students read the conversation and answer the Activity 7 questions. 1.2

### Assess

**Assessment Program**
**Prueba: Vocabulario 1,** pp. 61–62
Alternative Assessment, pp. 376, 388, 400

**Online Assessment**
**my.hrw.com**

**Test Generator**

## Resources

**Planning:**

Lesson Planner, pp. 51–53, 212–215

One-Stop Planner

**Presentation:**

Video Program **GramaVisión**

**Practice:**

Grammar Tutor for Students of Spanish, Chapter 4

Cuaderno de vocabulario y gramática, pp. 40–42

Cuaderno de actividades, pp. 31–33

Activities for Communication, pp. 13–14

Lab Book, pp. 25–28

Teaching Transparencies

Bell Work 4.2

**Vocabulario y gramática** answers, pp. 40–42

Audio CD 4, Tr. 3

Interactive Tutor, Disc 1

### Bell Work

Use Bell Work 4.2 in the *Teaching Transparencies*, or write this activity on the board.

**Usa las expresiones de ¡Exprésate! para reaccionar a las siguientes noticias que te dice tu amigo(a).**

1. **—Tu actriz favorita dio a luz a una niña ayer.**
2. **—Tu mejor amigo(a) se casó hoy.**
3. **—Un primo tuyo se divorció el mes pasado.**
4. **—Una chica de 15 años se graduó de la universidad.** 1.2

**Objetivos**
- Present progressive
- Present perfect indicative
- Present perfect subjunctive

# Gramática en acción 1

GramaVisión

Interactive TUTOR

### En inglés

**In English,** it's common to hear *I am going* or *I am coming.*

**In Spanish, ser, ir,** and **venir** are never used in the present progressive with **estar** or **andar** to express this idea. Use the simple present: **soy, voy, vengo.**

**¿Vienes** conmigo?
No, **voy** con Laura.

Think of one common English verb that is not used in the present progressive. 4.1

The verb *to know* is not used in the present progressive: **I am knowing.*

## Repaso Present progressive

**1** The **present progressive** is used to describe actions that are in progress at the present time. It is formed by using **estar** with the present participle of the verb, which is formed by removing **-ar, -er,** or **-ir** from the infinitive, and adding **-ando** or **-iendo.**

**2** Some verbs have spelling changes in their present participles, especially stem-changing verbs.

| | | | |
|---|---|---|---|
| **caer** → | **cayendo** | **mentir** → | **mintiendo** |
| **decir** → | **diciendo** | **morir** → | **muriendo** |
| **dormir** → | **durmiendo** | **pedir** → | **pidiendo** |
| **leer** → | **leyendo** | **traer** → | **trayendo** |

**3** When an **object pronoun** is used with the **present progressive,** place it before the first verb, or after and attached to the participle. When the **object pronoun** is attached to the participle, an accent mark is added.

Alicia **lo está escuchando.** — *Alicia is listening to it.*
Juan **está leyéndolo.** — *Juan is reading it.*

**4** The **present progressive** can also be used with the verbs **andar** and **seguir. Andar + present participle** give the impression that someone goes around doing something continuously, sometimes with a slightly negative connotation.

Él **anda pidiendo** favores. — *He goes around asking for favors.*

**Seguir + present participle** is used to say that someone keeps on doing something, or is still doing something.

**Sigo viviendo** en París. — *I'm still living in Paris.*

Vocabulario y gramática, pp. 40–42
Actividades, pp. 31–33
Online workbooks

CD 4, Tr. 3 See script on p. 137E.

**9** **¿Sigue pasando?** 1.2

**Escuchemos** Escucha las conversaciones y decide si la actividad o situación que menciona la primera persona continúa o **sigue pasando,** o **no.** **1.** no; **2.** sigue pasando; **3.** sigue pasando; **4.** sigue pasando; **5.** no; **6.** sigue pasando

## Core Instruction

### TEACHING GRAMÁTICA

1. Review the present progressive conjugation of verbs like **trabajar, comer, servir (i),** and **dormir (u).** **(2 min.)**
2. Go over point 2 and act out some of the irregular verbs. For example, pretend that you are reading and ask: **¿Qué estoy haciendo?** Students answer: **Está leyendo. (2 min.)**
3. Go over point 3. Use props to have students practice the present progressive with object pronouns. For example, pass your book to a student. **¿Quién está leyendo mi libro? Ana lo está leyendo. (2 min.)**
4. Go over point 4. Have students ask each other questions about themselves and family members using **andar** or **seguir** + present participle. **¿Qué anda haciendo tu tío? ¿Sigues tocando el piano? (2 min.)**
5. Go over **En inglés.** Act out both parts of a conversation in English and in Spanish: *Samuel, are you coming? Yes, I'm coming!* **Samuel, ¿vienes? ¡Sí, voy! (2 min.)**

### GramaVisión

For a video presentation of the present progressive, use GramaVisión.

GramaVisión

Visit Holt Online
**go.hrw.com**
KEYWORD: EXP3 CH4
Gramática 1 practice

**10 ¡A la defensa!** 1.2

**Leamos/Escribamos** Completa el párrafo con la forma correcta de **estar, andar** o **seguir** y el participio presente del segundo verbo.

Algunos parientes __1__ (andar) __2__ (decir) que mi primo Luis es un estudiante perezoso, pero no es cierto. Él __3__ (seguir) __4__ (ser) muy aplicado, como siempre. Este semestre, __5__ (estar) __6__ (tomar) clases extra para avanzar más rápido. Y además, Luis __7__ (seguir) __8__ (trabajar) en la tienda familiar con su tío. Yo __9__ (seguir) __10__ (pensar) que ha cambiado, y que por fin __11__ (estar) __12__ (hacer) algo con su vida. Las personas que __13__ (andar) __14__ (criticarlo) deben prestar más atención, porque ellos no __15__ (estar) __16__ (verlo) como realmente es.

1. andan
2. diciendo
3. sigue
4. siendo
5. está
6. tomando
7. sigue
8. trabajando
9. sigo
10. pensando
11. está
12. haciendo
13. andan
14. criticándolo
15. están
16. viéndolo

**11 Una excursión familiar** 1.2

**Escribamos** Describe en ocho oraciones la reunión familiar del dibujo. Usa **estar, andar, seguir** y el participio presente.

**MODELO** **Como siempre, la tía Gloria anda sacando fotos de todo el mundo.**

## Comunicación

HOLT SoundBooth ONLINE RECORDING

**12 Una reunión escolar** 1.1, 1.2

**Hablemos** En parejas, dramaticen una reunión escolar que va a ocurrir dentro de diez años. Mencionen tres noticias usando el presente progresivo, y respondan a las de su compañero(a).

**MODELO** **—¿Qué anda haciendo Inés?**
**—Está trabajando de modelo en Nueva York.**
**—¡No me digas!**

### Heritage Speakers

Have heritage speakers share a typical conversation that might be heard at one of their family reunions. 1.3

### Comparisons

#### Language to Language

Some students may have trouble deciding when to use the present tense versus the present progressive. Tell them that the present progressive is virtually the same in Spanish and English. The Spanish **-ando/-iendo** endings correspond to the English **-ing** ending. Tell them that in both cases, the present progressive indicates an action that is occurring right now, or a state or condition that is unfolding. Have them discuss the difference in meaning between *I walk to school.* **(Camino al colegio.)** and *I am walking to school.* **(Estoy caminando al colegio.)** 4.1

### Comunicación

#### Group Activity: Presentational

Have students work in groups of five or six to prepare a presentation for the class. They should act out a family reunion like the one shown in Activity 11, and create a conversation to go with it, asking and answering questions about what each family member is doing. Have groups take turns acting out their presentations for the class. 1.1, 1.3

## Differentiated Instruction

### SLOWER PACE LEARNERS

**11 Variation** Some students may have trouble creating different kinds of sentences to describe what is happening in the illustration in Activity 11. You may want to work as a class to describe the scene. If students are using only the **estar** + participle construction, ask questions to prompt them to include descriptions with **andar** or **seguir** + participle. For example, you might say: **¿Alejandra sigue contando chistes?** 1.2

### MULTIPLE INTELLIGENCES

**Kinesthetic** Have students pantomime an action for the class. The class has to then answer the question **¿Qué está haciendo?** using the present progressive. The student who guesses correctly pantomimes the next action. 1.2

**Differentiated Instruction** See the Differentiated Instruction CD-ROM.

## Resources

**Planning:**

Lesson Planner, pp. 51–53, 212–215

One-Stop Planner

**Presentation:**

Video Program **GramaVisión**

**Practice:**

Grammar Tutor for Students of Spanish, Chapter 4

Cuaderno de vocabulario y gramática, pp. 40–42

Cuaderno de actividades, pp. 31–33

Activities for Communication, pp. 13–14

Lab Book, pp. 25–28

Teaching Transparencies

Bell Work 4.3

**Vocabulario y gramática** answers, pp. 40–42

Audio CD 4, Tr. 4

Interactive Tutor, Disc 1

### Bell Work

Use Bell Work 4.3 in the *Teaching Transparencies*, or write this activity on the board.

**Completa las oraciones con la forma correcta del verbo en paréntesis.**

1. Miguel está _____ (hablar) con los miembros de la familia en una reunión.
2. Su cuñada anda _____ (buscar) trabajo.
3. Mi suegra sigue _____ (traerme) flores todos los días.
4. Sus hermanos están _____ (dormir) en la sala.
5. Su mamá anda _____ (servir) comida. 1.2

### 13 Script

See script on page 137E.

## Repaso Present perfect indicative

Interactive TUTOR

**1** To form the **present perfect indicative**, use the present tense of the helping verb **haber** followed by the **past participle** of the main verb.

| | | | |
|---|---|---|---|
| yo | **he hablado** | nosotros | **hemos hablado** |
| tú | **has hablado** | vosotros | **habéis hablado** |
| Ud., él, ella | **ha hablado** | Uds., ellos, ellas | **han hablado** |

If the stem of an **-er** or **-ir** verb ends in a vowel other than **u**, place an accent on the **i** in **-ido**.

**leer** → **leído** **traer** → **traído**

**2** The **present perfect indicative** is used to say what has or hasn't happened in a period of time up to the present or to talk about something that happened very recently. Use the **present perfect indicative** in Spanish when you would use the auxiliary verb "have" in English.

No **he hablado** con tu suegra todavía.
*I haven't spoken with your mother-in-law yet.*

Use the **preterite** for past actions that are viewed as over and not connected to the present.

**Hablé** con tu suegra ayer.
*I spoke with your mother-in-law yesterday.*

**3** When an **object pronoun** is used with the **present perfect indicative**, it should always go before the conjugated form of **haber**. Unlike the present progressive, a pronoun *cannot* be attached to the participle.

Florencia **nos ha contado** las buenas noticias.
**Me han invitado** a la boda.

Vocabulario y gramática, pp. 40–42
Actividades, pp. 31–33
Online workbooks

### ¿Te acuerdas?

Remember that the past participles of these verbs are irregular.

**abrir** → **abierto**
**cubrir** → **cubierto**
**decir** → **dicho**
**escribir** → **escrito**
**hacer** → **hecho**
**morir** → **muerto**
**poner** → **puesto**
**romper** → **roto**
**ver** → **visto**
**volver** → **vuelto**

Compound forms of these verbs are also irregular; for example:
**descubrir** → **descubierto**

CD 4, Tr. 4

### 13 Los mejores planes 1.2

**Escuchemos** Escucha mientras Luisa habla de los planes para una reunión familiar. Determina si habla de
a) algo que sucedió recientemente o está conectado al presente o de
b) algo que está sucediendo.

**1.** a **2.** b **3.** a **4.** a **5.** b **6.** a **7.** b **8.** b

## Core Instruction

### TEACHING GRAMÁTICA

1. Review **¿Te acuerdas?** Have volunteers use these verbs in sentences. **(2 min.)**
2. Go over point 1 with students. Ask questions to practice the present perfect indicative. **¿Has ido a una reunión familiar? ¿Tus amigos han visitado tu casa? (2 min.)**
3. Go over point 2. Tell students various facts using the preterite and the present perfect indicative to help them understand the difference. **Me levanté a las ocho pero todavía no he desayunado. He visto varias películas muy buenas. Ayer vi una película de acción.** Then ask students questions using the preterite and past perfect. **(3 min.)**
4. Go over point 3. Have students ask each other questions using pronouns with the present perfect indicative. **(3 min.)**

### GramaVisión

For a video presentation of the present perfect indicative, use GramaVisión.

GramaVisión

### 14 ¡Cuéntame qué pasa! 1.2

**Hablemos/Escribamos** Estás hablando por teléfono con tu primo durante una boda y le dices lo que ha pasado. Completa tus observaciones usando las frases de abajo.

**MODELO** **La tía Rosa/llorar mucho esta tarde**
**La tía Rosa ha llorado mucho esta tarde.**

1. Sonia/llegar con su novio
2. El fotógrafo/sacarnos un montón de fotos
3. El primo Nicolás/hacer travesuras
4. Mamá/reírse con los chistes del tío Román
5. Abuelo/bailar con la novia
6. Nosotros/ver a muchos parientes

### 15 Preparaciones para la fiesta 1.2

**Escribamos** Hay una gran lista de tareas que hacer para la fiesta. Explica cuáles se han hecho, basándote en las fotos que siguen.

**MODELO** **Yo he traído la música.**

yo/traer

1. yo/preparar

2. Mamá y papá/colgar

3. mis hermanos/poner

4. el pastelero/decorar

## Comunicación

HOLT SoundBooth ONLINE RECORDING

### 16 La encuesta 1.1, 1.2

**Hablemos** Trabaja en grupos pequeños. Busca a alguien de tu grupo que pueda responder "sí" a cada pregunta.

**MODELO** **ir a Egipto alguna vez**
**—¿Has ido a Egipto alguna vez?**

1. ver a su abuelo(a) este año
2. asistir a una reunión familiar alguna vez
3. ir a una boda recientemente
4. visitar a algún pariente en otro estado
5. decirle algo tonto a un amigo
6. comprar ropa nueva esta semana

### 14 Answers

1. Sonia ha llegado con su novio.
2. El fotógrafo nos ha sacado un montón de fotos.
3. El primo Nicolás ha hecho travesuras.
4. Mamá se ha reído con los chistes del tío Román.
5. Abuelo ha bailado con la novia.
6. Nosotros hemos visto a muchos parientes.

### 15 Answers

1. Yo he preparado los sándwiches.
2. Mamá y papá han colgado las decoraciones.
3. Mis hermanos han puesto la mesa.
4. El pastelero ha decorado el pastel.

### Language Note

Tell students that **todavía no** *(not yet)*, **ya** *(already)*, and **alguna vez** *(ever)* assume the present moment as a point of reference just as in English. These adverbs are used to talk about what has or has not happened up to the present moment of speech. *(He has not studied yet. He has already studied. Has he ever studied?)* These words will often be used with the present perfect tense. **Todavía no ha estudiado. Ya ha estudiado. ¿Ha estudiado alguna vez?**

## Comunicación

### Pair Activity: Interpersonal

Have students take turns interviewing a partner about things he has done. Each student should prepare at least five questions using the present perfect and take notes as she conducts the interview. Then have students summarize their partners' answers for the class. 1.1

## Differentiated Instruction

### SLOWER PACE LEARNERS

13 Before students do Activity 13, review the present progressive. Remind students that the present progressive is used to talk about actions in progress. Tell students to listen for verb forms that indicate an action in progress: **está comiendo, sigue hablando, anda haciendo.** Then have them listen for verbs that indicate completed actions: **he comido, ha dicho, hemos hecho.** Play the sentences one by one and let studentswrite down the verb before answering. 1.2

### SPECIAL LEARNING NEEDS

15 **Students with Learning Disabilities** For students who have trouble forming complete sentences in Spanish, modify Activity 15 by asking them whether each action has already been done: **¿Has preparado los bocadillos?** Students can imitate the sentence structure of your question and simply change the conjugation of the verb: **He preparado los bocadillos.** Have students answer aloud before writing sentences in their notebooks. Once you have finished, check their work. 1.2

**Differentiated Instruction** See the Differentiated Instruction CD-ROM.

## Resources

**Planning:**

Lesson Planner, pp. 51–53, 212–215

One-Stop Planner

**Presentation:**

Video Program **GramaVisión**

**Practice:**

Grammar Tutor for Students of Spanish, Chapter 4

Cuaderno de vocabulario y gramática, pp. 40–42

Cuaderno de actividades, pp. 31–33

Activities for Communication, pp. 13–14

Lab Book, pp. 25–28

Teaching Transparencies
Bell Work 4.4
**Vocabulario y gramática** answers, pp. 40–42

Audio CD 4, Tr. 5

Interactive Tutor, Disc 1

### Bell Work

Use Bell Work 4.4 in the *Teaching Transparencies,* or write this activity on the board.

**Contesta las siguientes preguntas.**

1. ¿Has peleado con un amigo alguna vez?
2. ¿Tus papás te han regalado algo especial?
3. ¿Adónde has viajado?
4. ¿Cuál es la mejor película que has visto?
5. ¿Qué programas de computadora has usado? 1.2

### 17 Script

See script on page 137F.

## Present perfect subjunctive

Interactive TUTOR

### En inglés

**In English,** the words *would* or *should* can imply the same idea as the Spanish subjunctive mood.

I'm surprised that he *would* do such a thing.

It's funny that you *should* say that.

**In Spanish,** the subjunctive mood is used instead.

Me sorprende que él *haga* tal cosa.

Es curioso que *digas* eso.

In addition to the present subjunctive, what other two Spanish verb forms can correspond to the English verb *would*? 4.1

Both the imperfect and the conditional in Spanish can correspond to the verb *would.*

**1** Remember that the **subjunctive** is used with expressions that **convey feelings.**

**Me alegra que vengan** mis amigos a nuestra fiesta.
**Temo que** mi novia **vaya** a romper conmigo.

**2** The **subjunctive** is also used with expressions that **convey judgments** about something.

**Es natural que estés** enojado con la decisión.
*It's natural that you're angry about the decision.*

**Me sorprende que** Gilberto **se comporte** tan raro.
*It surprises me that Gilberto behaves so strangely.*

**3** Use the **present perfect subjunctive (el presente perfecto del subjuntivo)** to express an emotion, judgment, doubt, or hope about something that has happened. It's formed with the subjunctive of **haber** and the past participle of the main verb.

| | | | |
|---|---|---|---|
| yo | **haya comido** | nosotros | **hayamos comido** |
| tú | **hayas comido** | vosotros | **hayáis comido** |
| Ud., él, ella | **haya comido** | Uds., ellos, ellas | **hayan comido** |

**Me choca que** ellos **hayan salido** tan de prisa.
**Es una lástima que** nuestro equipo **haya perdido** otro juego.

Vocabulario y gramática, pp. 40–42
Actividades, pp. 31–33
Online workbooks

**Some expressions that convey judgments or feelings**

| | | |
|---|---|---|
| es bueno que | es natural que | me enoja que |
| es curioso que | es normal que | me gusta que |
| es horrible que | es triste que | me molesta que |
| es lógico que | me alegra que | me parece bien que |
| es maravilloso que | me choca que | me sorprende que |

Una tienda para novias en la República Dominicana

CD 4, Tr. 5

**17 ¿Le gusta o no?** 1.2

**Escuchemos** Escucha cómo reaccionan estas personas ante una noticia y decide si su reacción es **positiva** o **negativa.**

1. positiva
2. negativa
3. positiva
4. negativa
5. positiva
6. negativa
7. positiva
8. positiva

## Core Instruction

### TEACHING GRAMÁTICA

1. Go over **En inglés** with students. **(1 min.)**
2. Go over points 1 and 2 and read the examples. Place special emphasis on the expressions that convey judgments. **(2 min.)**
3. Have students write a sentence using the present or future tense and read them aloud. React to their statements using expressions that convey judgments and the subjunctive. **Voy a viajar a Perú y bailar. / Es maravilloso que bailes en Perú. (3 min.)**
4. Go over point 3. Then have each student prepare a sentence using the present perfect. React to their statements using expressions that convey judgments and the present perfect subjunctive. **(3 min.)**
5. Have volunteers give statements in either the preterite or the present perfect and allow their classmates to react using expressions that convey judgment. **(2 min.)**

### GramaVisión

For a video presentation of the present perfect subjunctive, use **GramaVisión.**

GramaVisión

## 18 Me sorprende que... 1.2

**Leamos/Escribamos** Completa las oraciones con el presente perfecto del subjuntivo del verbo entre paréntesis.

1. Me sorprende que el profesor ___ (dar) el examen tan pronto. haya dado
2. Al profesor no le gusta que los estudiantes no ___ (estudiar) para el examen. hayan estudiado
3. Me da gusto que los estudiantes ___ (hablar) con el director. hayan hablado
4. Me alegra que mis amigos ___ (hacer) la tarea de historia. hayan hecho
5. A mis amigos les enoja que el entrenador ___ (cancelar) el partido de béisbol. haya cancelado
6. Es una lástima que mis compañeros no ___ (poder) terminar su trabajo. hayan podido

## 19 ¿Cómo reaccionarías? 1.2

**Leamos/Escribamos** Lee cada situación y escribe una oración sobre cómo reaccionarías o qué dirías. Usa el presente perfecto del subjuntivo.

**MODELO** **Tu mejor amigo, que vive en otra ciudad, te ha visitado este verano.**
**—Me alegra mucho que hayas venido a visitarme.**

1. Tus padres no te han permitido salir con tus amigos.
2. Un grupo de amigos te ha hecho una fiesta sorpresa.
3. Tu tía ha venido a visitarte y ha traído un postre delicioso.
4. Tu amigo(a) te ha invitado al cine pero no tienes dinero.
5. Tu hermano te ha pedido ayuda con la música para su boda.
6. Algunos parientes no han llegado a la ceremonia a tiempo.

### Nota cultural

En muchos países latinoamericanos, los novios tienen dos ceremonias de boda: una ceremonia civil y otra ceremonia religiosa. Durante la ceremonia civil, los novios firman los documentos legales en presencia de un juez y los testigos. Esta ceremonia es la que reconoce la ley pero la ceremonia religiosa es por lo general más importante para los novios.

¿Cómo son las bodas donde tú vives? 4.2

Novios argentinos, Buenos Aires

## Comunicación

HOLT SoundBooth ONLINE RECORDING

## 20 A dramatizar 1.1, 1.2

**Hablemos** Dramatiza con un(a) compañero(a) tres de las situaciones de la Actividad 19. Usen las expresiones de **Gramática.**

**MODELO** **Un grupo de amigos te ha hecho una fiesta sorpresa.**
**—Me sorprende mucho que me hayan hecho una fiesta.**
**—Pues, me alegra que haya sido una sorpresa de verdad.**



### Comparisons

**Comparing and Contrasting**

Have students read the **Nota cultural** on page 151 and compare a typical Latin American wedding with the weddings they have attended. Do the couples usually have two ceremonies? What part of the ceremony do they consider the most important? 2.1, 4.2

### Comunicación

**Class Activity: Presentational**

Have students change partners and prepare a conversation using another scenario from Activity 19 or one that they come up with on their own. Pairs take turns presenting their conversations to the class. 1.1, 1.3

### Differentiated Instruction

**ADVANCED LEARNERS**

**19 Personalization** After doing Activity 19, have students think about real situations from their lives. Have them write a paragraph explaining their reactions to one or several of these situations. Encourage them to use the **Gramática** expressions that convey judgments. When they have completed the paragraphs, have students exchange papers to check each other's work. Tell them to underline the verbs in the subjunctive. 1.3

**SPECIAL LEARNING NEEDS**

**17 Students with AD(H)D** Some students may have trouble focusing on whether the sentences in Activity 17 are positive or negative. Before playing the audio script, have them list the expressions that convey judgment in two categories, positive and negative. Then play the audio items, pausing after each one. Have them use their notes as they listen specifically for the expressions that convey judgment. 1.2

### Assess

**Assessment Program**

**Prueba: Gramática 1,** pp. 63–64

**Prueba: Aplicación 1,** pp. 65–66

Audio CD 1, Tr. 15

Alternative Assessment, pp. 376, 388, 400

**Online Assessment** my.hrw.com

**Test Generator**

## Resources

**Planning:**
Lesson Planner, pp. 54, 214–215
One-Stop Planner

**Presentation:**
Audio CD 4, Tr. 6–8
Video Program,
Videocassette 2
DVD Program
**VideoCultura**

**Practice:**
Cuaderno de actividades, p. 34
Video Guide, pp. 24–25
Lab Book, p. 66
Interactive Tutor, Disc 1

### Multicultural Link

Have students compare the need for bilingual workers and Spanish language materials in a multilingual city like Miami with other U.S. cities.

### Thinking Critically

Ask students if they have friends from the Caribbean. Do these friends live far from their family? Then ask students if they live far away from their family members. Ask them what it would be like to live separated from their family. Would this be difficult? How would they keep in touch?

# Cultura

Video/DVD
VideoCultura

## Comparaciones

Interactive TUTOR
CD 4, Tr. 6-8

Tíos, primos y abuelos se reúnen para cenar.

### A casa de tu tía, mas no cada día 1.3, 4.2

En los países hispanohablantes, la vida en familia es muy importante, tanto en la familia inmediata como con los tíos, primos, y abuelos. Muchos de los hermanos acaban viviendo en la misma ciudad que sus padres, y forman sus familias que se reúnen en casa de los abuelos muy a menudo. Los niños suelen conocer bien a sus primos y tíos. ¿Se parece esto a la situación de tu familia? ¿En qué se diferencian? ¿Crees que tener mucho contacto tiene más ventajas o desventajas?

### Inés
**Santo Domingo, República Dominicana**

***¿Tienes parientes que vivan en otras ciudades u otros países?***
Sí, en Zaragoza, España.

***¿Quiénes son?***
Mi padre, mis tíos, mis primos, y mis abuelos.

***¿Cómo se mantienen en contacto?***
Por el teléfono, por el correo, y por el Internet.

***¿Con qué frecuencia se ven?***
Los veo todos los veranos.

***Para ti, ¿por qué es importante que los parientes se mantengan en contacto aunque vivan lejos?***
Es importante compartir los asuntos de la familia.

## Pre-AP Practice

**AP Language Examination:** Have students first listen to the interviews with books closed to help prepare them for Section I, Part A: **Listening—Short Dialogues and Narratives.** Point out that Nelson, like many Spanish speakers from the Caribbean, may drop **b, d, g, v** between vowels, (**vi<u>v</u>e, Cu<u>b</u>a, lo <u>v</u>eo**).

## Core Instruction

### TEACHING CULTURA

1. Read and discuss the introductory paragraph as a class. **(2 min.)**
2. Have students read the interviews on their own. When they have finished, give them time to ask questions about parts they did not understand. Allow them to discuss their reactions to the interviews as a class. **(4 min.)**
3. Have students answer the questions in **Para comprender** and have them discuss the ideas in **Para pensar y hablar. (4 min.)**

### VideoCultura

For a video presentation of the interviews as well as an additional interview for this chapter, see Chapter 4 **VideoCultura** on Videocassette or on DVD.

Video/DVD
VideoCultura

## Nelson
**Miami, Florida**

***¿Tú tienes parientes que vivan en otros países?***

Sí, tengo parientes que viven en otros países, en Cuba particularmente.

***¿Quiénes son?***

Son mis tíos, mis primos, mis hermanos, mis abuelos.

***¿Cómo se mantienen en contacto?***

Bueno nos mantenemos en contacto por teléfono, por el Internet. Hablamos así de vez en cuando.

***¿Con qué frecuencia se ven?***

Nos vemos cada dos años. Ellos nos visitan. Nosotros los visitamos.

***Para ti, ¿es importante que los parientes se mantengan en contacto aunque vivan aparte?***

Sí. Es muy importante ya que la familia es algo muy importante para mí. Me gusta mantener una buena relación con la familia. Y uno siempre tiene que contar con la familia. Por eso es que lo veo importante.

Cultura

### Para comprender 1.2

1. ¿Quiénes de la familia de Inés viven en España?
2. ¿Con qué frecuencia ve Inés a su familia?
3. ¿En dónde tiene Nelson familia?
4. ¿Tiene Nelson una buena relación con su familia de Cuba?
5. Para Inés y Nelson, ¿por qué son importantes los lazos familares? Explica.

### Para pensar y hablar 1.3

¿Estás de acuerdo con Inés y Nelson en que la familia se debe mantener en contacto? ¿Por qué? ¿Cuáles son dos ventajas y dos desventajas de tener familiares en otros países? ¿Qué pasa si se pierde el contacto con un pariente lejano?

## Comunidad y oficio 2.2

### Alimentos importados

En Estados Unidos se encuentra una gran variedad de comestibles de países hispanohablantes: chorizos, azafrán y mariscos enlatados de España, frutas de Chile, frutas tropicales congeladas del Caribe y chiles de México. Diversas entidades participan en la importación de estos productos alimenticios, como las compañías distribuidoras, las empresas de transporte y los bancos. En tu supermercado, busca un producto de un país hispanohablante e investiga la compañía que lo distribuye. ¿De qué países hispanohablantes importa comestibles? ¿Con qué otras compañías trabaja? Haz un cartel que explique la ruta que ha seguido el producto que escogiste, desde su país de origen hasta tu comunidad.

**La Familia Grocery y otras tiendas en un barrio hispánico de la ciudad de Nueva York**

## Differentiated Instruction

### ADVANCED LEARNERS

**Extension** Have students read the interviews and answer the questions in **Para comprender** on their own. Then have them work in small groups to discuss the **Para pensar y hablar** questions. Have them discuss what they know about the various Caribbean countries and their relationship to the United States and how this affects the ability for immigrants from these countries to maintain family ties. Allow them to do some research on the Internet and present their findings to the class. 1.1, 1.2

### MULTIPLE INTELLIGENCES

**Logical/Mathematical** Have students use a Venn diagram to compare and contrast the responses given by Inés and Nelson in their interviews. Have them present their diagrams to the class in order to begin a discussion about the interviews. 3.2

## Atlas INTERACTIVO MUNDIAL

Have students use the interactive atlas at **go.hrw.com**.

**Map Activities**

1. Have students find the Dominican Republic and Florida, using the interactive atlas or map transparencies.
2. Ask them to comment on the relationship between Florida and the Caribbean countries.

3.1

### Answers

1. El padre, los tíos, los primos y los abuelos de Inés viven en España.
2. Inés y su familia se ven todos los veranos.
3. Nelson tiene familia en Cuba.
4. Sí, Nelson tiene una buena relación con su familia en Cuba. Se mantienen en contacto por teléfono y por Internet, y se ven cada dos años.
5. Answers will vary.

### Connections

**History Link**

After reading the interview with Nelson, have students investigate the history of the relationship between the United States and Cuba, and think about how this relationship has affected citizens of both countries. You may want to have a class discussion or ask students to write on this topic as a journal entry.

3.2

**Career Path**

Ask students to discuss career paths that interest them, for which knowledge of Spanish would be useful. How would knowing more than one language help them to function more effectively in these careers, particularly in multilingual communities?

**Resources**

**Planning:**

Lesson Planner, pp. 55–56, 216–217

One-Stop Planner

**Presentation:**

Teaching Transparencies
**Vocabulario** 4.3, 4.4

**Practice:**

Cuaderno de vocabulario y gramática, pp. 43–45

Activities for Communication, pp. 15–16

Teaching Transparencies
Bell Work 4.5
**Vocabulario y gramática** answers, pp. 43–45

Interactive Tutor, Disc 1

**Bell Work**

Use Bell Work 4.5 in the *Teaching Transparencies*, or write this activity on the board.

**Completa las oraciones con la forma correcta del verbo en paréntesis.**

1. Me sorprende que mis tíos no _____ (haber) llegado.
2. Creo que ellos _____ (ir) a cenar con nosotros.
3. Es bueno que mis primos _____ (estar) aquí.
4. Pero me molesta que mi suegra no _____ (querer) venir.
5. De todos modos, nosotros _____ (ir) a pasarlo bien. 1.2

**Objetivos**
- Commenting on food
- Explaining and giving excuses

# Vocabulario en acción 2

## En Santo Domingo La comida casera

Mi mamá sabe cocinar muy bien. Hoy hizo **pollo frito** con **frijoles** negros y arroz, y **coliflor** con queso. ¡Está muy rica la comida!

Uno de mis platos favoritos es la ensalada de frutas. Una buena ensalada de frutas debe llevar **sandía,** naranja, un poco de **toronja,** melón y uvas frescas.

También me gustan mucho los postres. Me encantan **el dulce de coco** y **el bizcocho de chocolate.** Y, bueno, si quiero bajar de peso, **¡el yogur** con **cerezas!**

**Más vocabulario...**

| | |
|---|---|
| el apio | *celery* |
| la crema (agria) | *(sour) cream* |
| la lima | *lime* |
| el limón | *lemon* |
| las pasas | *raisins* |
| el pavo (con relleno) | *turkey (with stuffing)* |
| la salchicha | *sausage* |

## Core Instruction

### TEACHING VOCABULARIO

1. Use transparencies 4.3 and 4.4 to present the vocabulary. Check students' understanding of the terms by asking whether they like certain things. Have volunteers describe each item. **¿Te gusta la coliflor? ¿Cómo es?** **(5 min.)**
2. Have volunteers talk about their favorite foods: **¿Cuál es tu plato favorito?** **(2 min.)**
3. Present the **Más vocabulario** food items and ask students questions about each one. **¿Cuándo comes el pavo con relleno?** **(3 min.)**

### TEACHING ¡EXPRÉSATE!

1. Introduce **¡Exprésate!**, modeling the pronunciation of each new expression. **(3 min.)**
2. Imagine you are at a restaurant. Have volunteers use words from **Vocabulario** to ask you how you like specific items. Respond using expressions from **¡Exprésate!** Use body language to convey the meaning of each expression. **¿Cómo está la langosta? Está para chuparse los dedos.** **(4 min.)**
3. Have volunteers use the **¡Exprésate!** expressions to comment on their favorite or least favorite foods. **(3 min.)**

Visit Holt Online
**go.hrw.com**
KEYWORD: EXP3 CH4
Vocabulario 2 practice

En ocasiones especiales servimos **langosta** y **camarones.**

Aunque me gustan los mariscos, mi plato preferido es el **puerco asado** con arroz y **frijoles** negros.

A veces mi mamá sirve **calabacín** o **chícharos** con un poco de sal y mantequilla.

En el verano solemos hacer refrescantes ensaladas con **pepino** y **aguacate.**

**También se puede decir...**

Instead of **la sandía,** you may hear **el melón** or **la patilla.** Central Americans may say **el guajalote** for **el pavo.** Some Spanish speakers use **cochino asado, cerdo asado,** or **lechón asado** instead of **puerco asado. Las arvejas** is another word for **los chícharos,** but in the Dominican Republic, the French term ***petit-pois*** is used.

## ¡Exprésate!

**To comment on food**

Interactive TUTOR

| | |
|---|---|
| **Está para chuparse los dedos.**<br>*It's good enough to lick your fingers.* | **Al (A la)... le falta sabor, pero no sé qué le falta.**<br>*The . . . lacks flavor, but I don't know what's missing.* |
| **Se me hace la boca agua.**<br>*It makes my mouth water.* | **Está pasada la leche.**<br>*The milk has gone bad.* |
| **Sabe delicioso(a).**<br>*It tastes delicious.* | **¡Qué asco!**<br>*That's disgusting!* |

Vocabulario y gramática, pp. 43–45 Online workbooks

Vocabulario 2

## TPR
### Total Physical Response

Cut out pictures of the food items in **Vocabulario 2** and bring them to class. Also include items students already know such as butter, salt, and pepper. Have students sit in a circle and place the pictures on the floor. Have individual students respond to the following commands, acting them out and using the food items as props.

**Pásame una salchicha, por favor.**

**Añade un poco de sal al pavo.**

1.2

## Language Note

Review **También se puede decir** with students. Ask them why they think a French term is used for *peas* in the Dominican Republic. Explain that the Spanish-speaking Dominican Republic shares the island with Haiti, whose population speaks French and French Creole. Both were initially Spanish colonies, but Haiti spent over a century under French rule. The French occupied the Dominican Republic briefly, but the most contact the Dominicans have had with the French language has been through a 22-year occupation by Haiti (1822–1842) and through the constant immigration of Haitians across the Haitian-Dominican border. Have students research other French terms that are used in the Dominican Republic. Point out that even though **chícharos** is the Spanish term, it would be more socially appropriate to say ***petit-pois*** when visiting the Dominican Republic.

## Heritage Speakers

Have heritage speakers share other food terms that are different in their native country.

## Differentiated Instruction

### ADVANCED LEARNERS

**Challenge** Have students work in pairs to create a menu for their ideal restaurant. They should have three appetizers, four main dishes, and three desserts. For the main dishes, have them write detailed descriptions telling what is included and how it is prepared. Have students present their menus to the class and ask students to decide which dishes sound the most appetizing. 3.1

### SPECIAL LEARNING NEEDS

**Students with AD(H)D/Learning Disabilities** Some students may have trouble deciding which terms in the caption go with each part of the photo. Review known food vocabulary with students. Have students cut out photos of the food items from magazines and glue them to index cards. Have them write the name of the item in Spanish on the card. Allow students to work in groups to quiz each other on the vocabulary words using the flash cards. 1.2

**Differentiated Instruction** See the Differentiated Instruction CD-ROM.

**Resources**

**Planning:**

Lesson Planner, pp. 55–56, 216–217

One-Stop Planner

**Presentation:**

Teaching Transparencies
**Vocabulario** 4.3, 4.4

**Practice:**

Cuaderno de vocabulario y gramática, pp. 43–45

Activities for Communication, pp. 15–16

Lab Book, pp. 25–28

Teaching Transparencies
**Vocabulario y gramática** answers, pp. 43–45

Audio CD 4, Tr. 9

Interactive Tutor, Disc 1

**21 Script**
For script, see page 137F.

**Comparisons**

**Language Note**

Ask students to reflect on what these two phrases have in common: **Está para chuparse los dedos. Se me hace la boca agua.** Both evoke a physical memory in the body, of something tasty enough to lick one's fingers and of eating something that makes one's mouth water. Point out that these expressions are idiomatic in both languages, in part because of this physical association with taste. Ask them if they can think of other idiomatic expressions in English that evoke body memory, and to research their Spanish equivalent to see if it does, as well.

4.1

1. e; no
2. d; sí
3. b; sí
4. a; no
5. f; no
6. c; sí

CD 4, Tr. 9 See script on p. 137F.

## 21 ¡Vamos a comer! 1.2

**Escuchemos** Escucha las conversaciones. Escoge la conversación que corresponde a cada foto. Luego, escribe **sí** o **no** para indicar si a la persona le gusta la comida o no.

a.

b.

c.

d.

e.

f.

## 22 Veamos el menú 1.2

**Leamos** Lee lo que le gusta o no a cada persona y decide qué puede pedir de comer. Algunas personas pueden tener más de una opción.

| ENTRADAS | PLATOS PRINCIPALES | POSTRES |
|---|---|---|
| Ensalada de aguacate | Langosta con calabacín | Sandía |
| Caldo de pollo | Puerco asado con papas fritas | Yogur con o sin cerezas |
| Salchichas | Pavo relleno y chícharos | Dulce de coco |

1. A Héctor le encantan los platos con carne, pero no le gustan las papas. ¿Qué puede pedir de plato principal?
2. Sofía prefiere no comer nada caliente para la cena. ¿Qué puede pedir?
3. A Patricia no le gustan las verduras. ¿Qué puede pedir de entrada y de plato principal?
4. Juan quiere postre, pero no puede comer productos lácteos *(dairy)*. ¿Qué puede pedir?
5. A Mónica no le gusta la fruta. ¿Qué puede pedir de postre?
6. Rosana no come carne. ¿Qué puede pedir de entrada y de plato principal?

1. pavo relleno y chícharos
2. ensalada de aguacate
3. salchichas, puerco asado con papas fritas
4. sandía
5. yogur sin cerezas
6. ensalada de aguacate, langosta con calabacín

## Core Instruction

### VOCABULARY IN CONTEXT

To review the vocabulary, bring in magazines and have students work in groups to find and cut out pictures of the food items. Ask them to paste the pictures to index cards and write the name in Spanish on the back of the card. Divide the class into teams. Hold up a flashcard showing the pictures and ask students to call out the vocabulary word. The first team to call out the word receives a point. Play until one team has five points.

As an alternative, you might want to write the name of a vocabulary food item in Spanish on a piece of construction paper. Write a number on each piece of paper on which students pasted pictures of food items. Display the pictures of food items, making sure the numbers are visible. Divide the class into two teams. Call out the name of a food item in Spanish. Students then give the number of the picture the food item corresponds to. Play until one team has five points.

**23** **Mis comidas favoritas** 1.2

**Leamos/Escribamos** Completa las oraciones según tus propios gustos.

1. Mi comida favorita es ___.
2. No me gusta ___. ¡Qué asco!
3. El plato de ___ está para chuparse los dedos.
4. A veces en casa preparamos ___. ¡Sabe delicioso!
5. Mi abuela siempre sirve ___ de postre. ¡Qué rico!
6. En el verano, suelo comer frutas como ___.
7. A mí me gusta preparar ___ a mediodía.
8. Mi postre favorito es ___ con ___.

**24** **¿Qué dices?** 1.2

**Leamos/Hablemos** Usa las palabras de **Vocabulario** y las expresiones de **Exprésate** para responder a cada situación.

**MODELO** **Sacas la leche del refrigerador y huele horrible.**
**—La leche está pasada. ¡Qué asco!**

1. La comida que preparó tu familia te encanta.
2. Tu novio(a) preparó el mejor bizcocho que has probado.
3. Tu hermano preparó un puerco asado y no tiene sabor.
4. En la cocina de tu abuela ves un pollo frito y un plato de papas fritas, tu comida favorita.
5. Unos amigos prepararon una cena y quieres decirles que es excepcional.
6. La sopa de verduras no te gustó para nada.
7. Preparaste una ensalada pero está muy salada.
8. Tu hermana preparó arroz con pollo, pero le falta algo.

### Nota cultural

No es de extrañar que el pescado sea una parte importante en la dieta de las islas caribeñas. El pescado servido con moro de gandules con coco es un plato típico de Samaná, en República Dominicana. El chillo, un tipo de pescado frito o al horno servido generalmente con una salsa llamada mojo, es un plato típico de Puerto Rico. El ceviche es otro plato popular, hecho a base de pescado crudo en un adobo de limón, cebolla picada, sal y ají.

¿Por qué crees que el pescado es importante en el Caribe? 2.1, 2.2

**Un ceviche de la República Dominicana**

## Comunicación

HOLT SoundBooth ONLINE RECORDING

**25** **La cena de la clase** 1.1, 1.3

**Hablemos/Escribamos** En parejas, organicen una cena para una reunión familiar. Túrnense para entrevistarse sobre qué quieren servir de entrada, plato principal, verduras y bebidas. Pónganse de acuerdo y escriban un plan para presentarlo a la clase.

**MODELO** **—¿Qué quieren preparar de entrada?**
**—¿Qué tal si preparamos un ceviche y unas verduras?**

## Differentiated Instruction

### SLOWER PACE LEARNERS

**24** If students have trouble doing Activity 24, write a possible answer for each item on the board, but not in order. Ask students to match each situation with an expression that makes sense. Once they have matched all of the expressions and situations, have volunteers suggest other expressions that could also be used in each situation. 1.2

### SPECIAL LEARNING NEEDS

**22** **Students with Learning Disabilities** Before students do Activity 22, review the food vocabulary that they should already know, especially the words presented in the menu (**entrada, plato principal, postre, caldo, ensalada, papas fritas**) and the words presented in the numbered items (**verduras, carne**). Go through the menu item by item, asking students whether the person should order each dish. Then have them explain why or why not. 1.2

### Cultures

**Products and Perspectives**

Ask students if they have tried any of the food items from **Vocabulario 2.** Have volunteers tell where they tried the food and whether or not they liked it. Then have students comment on other Latin American dishes they have tried. Where can they find food items imported from Latin America? Are the Latin American dishes served in the United States authentic? Have heritage speakers contribute their opinions. 2.2

### Comparisons

**Language Note**

Remind students that some negative expressions like **¡Qué asco!** would never be used in a formal situation or to comment on a host's cooking. Ask students what polite phrases would be used in English to comment on a host's cooking. Are these similar to the phrases they learned in Spanish? 4.1

### Comunicación

**Pair Activity: Interpersonal**

Have pairs exchange the menus they created in Activity 25 with another group. Then have the pairs imagine they are eating the dinner described in their menu. Ask them to comment on the food using expressions from **¡Exprésate!**

**MODELO**
**—¿Te gusta el puerco asado?**
**—Le falta sabor, pero no sé qué ingrediente le falta.** 1.1

**Differentiated Instruction** See the Differentiated Instruction CD-ROM.

## Resources

**Planning:**

Lesson Planner, pp. 55–56, 216–217

One-Stop Planner

**Presentation:**

Teaching Transparencies **Vocabulario** 4.3, 4.4

**Practice:**

Cuaderno de vocabulario y gramática, pp. 43–45

Activities for Communication, pp. 15–16

Lab Book, pp. 25–28

Teaching Transparencies **Vocabulario y gramática** answers, pp. 43–45

Audio CD 4, Tr. 10

Interactive Tutor, Disc 1

## Comparisons

### Comparing and Contrasting

Remind students that in Spain and many Latin American countries, the main meal is eaten around 2:00 in the afternoon. Families tend to eat dinner late, around 9:00 or 10:00, but it is a smaller meal. How does this compare with eating schedules in the United States? How might this eating schedule affect other daily routines?

2.1, 4.2

### 26 Answers

1. A Rafael se le fue la mano con la sal. Es la primera vez que hace arroz.
2. La ensalada de pepino.
3. Le falta ajo.
4. No; dice «¡Qué asco!»
5. No; dice que le gusta sin ajo.
6. A Rafael se le fue la mano con el azúcar.

Una cena en casa, Santo Domingo

## ¿Qué tal quedó la cena?

MAMÁ Pásenme sus platos, voy a servir la comida. Rafael preparó la cena esta noche. Vamos a ver cómo le quedó.
PAPÁ Pues, me imagino que está para chuparse los dedos.
HERMANO Oye, Rafa, el arroz está un poco salado, ¿no crees?
RAFAEL Ya lo sé, se me fue la mano con la sal. Es la primera vez que hago arroz.
MAMÁ Está bien, hijo, sabe delicioso.
PAPÁ Y al puerco asado le falta sabor, pero no sé qué le falta.
RAFAEL Lo siento, papá, es que se me olvidó ponerle ajo.
HERMANA A mí me gusta sin ajo.
PAPÁ Pero la ensalada de pepino te quedó exquisita, hijo. Se me hace la boca agua sólo de verla.
HERMANA Ay, ¿cómo pueden comer ensalada? ¡Qué asco!
*(Luego...)*
MAMÁ Me parece que el bizcocho está demasiado dulce.
RAFAEL ¡Lo sabía! Es que se me fue la mano con el azúcar.

### ¡Exprésate!

| To comment on food | To explain and give excuses |
|---|---|
| **El/La... está salado(a)/picante.** *The . . . is salty/spicy.* | **Se me fue la mano con...** *I got carried away with . . .* |
| **El/La... no sabe a nada.** *The . . . doesn't taste like anything.* | **Es que se me olvidó ponerle...** *It's just that I forgot to add . . .* |
| **El/La... está seco(a)/no está muy dulce.** *The . . . is dry/isn't very sweet.* | **Es que se me acabó...** *It's just that I ran out of . . .* |

Interactive TUTOR

Vocabulario y gramática, pp. 43–45 Online workbooks

## Core Instruction

### TEACHING ¡EXPRÉSATE!

1. Read the conversation aloud with the class. **(4 min.)**
2. Review the vocabulary that students might want to use to comment on food by asking them questions about what they like and dislike. **¿Te gusta la comida picante? ¿No te gusta el café con azúcar? (2 min.)**
3. Model both sides of a conversation using the expressions from **¡Exprésate!** to show what you might say to comment on food and how someone might respond to explain or to give an excuse. **(2 min.)**
4. Then imagine your students have prepared a dinner and have volunteers respond as you comment on the food. Use the following prompts: **La sopa está muy picante. Los camarones no saben a nada. El bizcocho está seco. (2 min.)**

See answers on p. 158.

## 26 La cena de Rafael 1.2

**Leamos/Escribamos** Contesta las preguntas basándote en el diálogo.

1. ¿Por qué está el arroz un poco salado?
2. ¿Cuál de los platos le hace la boca agua al papá?
3. ¿Por qué al puerco asado le falta sabor?
4. ¿A la hermana le gusta la ensalada? ¿Cómo lo sabes?
5. ¿Cree la hermana que le falta sabor al puerco? Explica.
6. ¿Por qué está el bizcocho demasiado dulce?

CD 4, Tr. 10

## 27 ¿Qué pasó en la cocina? 1.2

**Escuchemos** Escucha lo que le pasó a cada persona en la cocina e identifica el ingrediente que causó el problema.

a.

b.

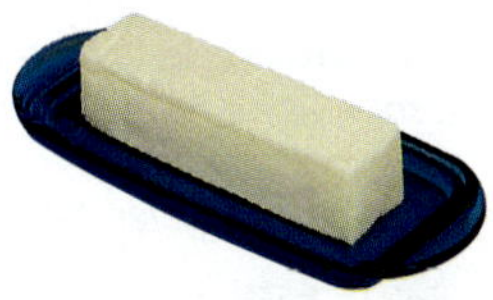
c.

d.

e.

f.

**1.** d **3.** c **5.** e
**2.** a **4.** b **6.** f

## Comunicación

HOLT SoundBooth ONLINE RECORDING

## 28 Una cena especial 1.1, 1.3

**Hablemos** Un(a) amigo(a) te preparó una cena para tu cumpleaños. Algunos platos salieron bien y otros mal. Preparen una conversación en la que Uds. comenten la comida. Tú debes hacer comentarios sobre los platos y tu amigo(a) te explica qué pasó.

MODELO **—El bizcocho no está muy dulce.**
**—Perdón, es que se me acabó el azúcar.**

Vocabulario 2

### 27 Script

1. —Me parece que al pollo le falta algo pero no sé qué le falta.
   —Ya lo sé. Se me olvidó ponerle pimienta.
2. —Esta sopa está demasiada salada. No me la puedo comer.
   —Tienes razón. Es que se me fue la mano con la sal.
3. —El bizcocho está un poco seco, ¿no crees?
   —Sí, está seco. Lo que pasa es que se me acabó la mantequilla.
4. —La ensalada de pepinos no tiene mucho sabor.
   —Perdón, es que se me olvidó ponerle limón.
5 —Este sándwich está muy seco. ¿Qué pasó?
   —Es que se me acabó la mayonesa y no tuve tiempo de ir al supermercado.
6. —El flan está muy dulce.
   —Lo siento, es que se me fue la mano con el azúcar.

### Comunicación

**Class Activity: Interpretive**
Have students think of a specific dish that they like. They should imagine they have made the dish but something is not quite right. Have them tell the class the ingredients they used without giving away the name of the dish. Then they should comment on what is wrong with it and explain why. The rest of the class will try to guess what the dish is. 1.2, 1.3

## Differentiated Instruction

### ADVANCED LEARNERS

**27 Extension** Once students have done Activity 27, have them answer true or false questions about the conversations to check comprehension. Play the audio recording again if necessary. Use the following examples or create new ones: **1. No le puso pimienta al pollo.** (cierto) **2. La sopa está muy dulce.** (falso) **3. Añadió demasiado mantequilla.** (falso) **4. A los pepinos les falta algo.** (cierto) **5. El sándwich no tiene mayonesa.** (falso) **6. El flan tiene demasiado azúcar.** (cierto) 1.2

### MULTIPLE INTELLIGENCES

**26 Kinesthetic** Before students answer the questions in Activity 26, read the questions aloud. Then have volunteers play the parts of **mamá, papá, hermano, hermana,** and Rafael. Ask them to act out the conversation for the class. Tell students to listen and watch for answers to the questions as their classmates present the conversation. Then answer the questions as a class. 1.1

### Assess

**Assessment Program**
**Prueba: Vocabulario 2,** pp. 67–68
Alternative Assessment, pp. 376, 388, 400

**Online Assessment**
**my.hrw.com**

**Test Generator**

**Assess** **Differentiated Instruction** See the Differentiated Instruction CD-ROM.

## Resources

**Planning:**

Lesson Planner, pp. 57–60, 218–221

One-Stop Planner

**Presentation:**

Video Program **GramaVisión**

**Practice:**

Grammar Tutor for Students of Spanish, Chapter 4

Cuaderno de vocabulario y gramática, pp. 46–48

Cuaderno de actividades, pp. 35–37

Activities for Communication, pp. 15–16

Teaching Transparencies
Bell Work 4.6
**Vocabulario y gramática** answers, pp. 46–48

Interactive Tutor, Disc 1

### Bell Work

Use Bell Work 4.6 in the *Teaching Transparencies,* or write this activity on the board.

**Preparaste la cena y tus amigos hacen estos comentarios. ¿Cómo respondes?**

1. Al pollo frito le falta sabor.
2. Los frijoles están muy picantes.
3. El puerco asado está para chuparse los dedos.
4. El bizcocho de chocolate está un poco seco.
5. La leche está pasada.

1.2

**Objetivos**
- Preterite
- *Se* + indirect object pronouns
- Past progressive

# Gramática en acción 2

Interactive TUTOR

## Repaso Preterite

**1** Use the **preterite** to show that actions were begun or completed at specific times in the past. Time markers such as **ayer, anoche, este fin de semana,** and **el verano pasado** are often used with the preterite.

Eduardo **habló** con Ana **anoche.**

**2** The **preterite** is used with **al** + **infinitive** or **en cuanto,** which mark the beginning of an event or situation.

**Al oír** las noticias, se **puso** a llorar.
*Upon hearing the news, she started crying.*

**En cuanto supo** la verdad, **hizo** las maletas y se **fue.**
*As soon as he found out the truth, he packed his bags and left.*

**3** These verbs have irregular stems in the **preterite.**

| | | | | | |
|---|---|---|---|---|---|
| estar | **estuv-** | saber | **sup-** | traer | **traj-** |
| poder | **pud-** | tener | **tuv-** | decir | **dij-** |
| poner | **pus-** | venir | **vin-** | querer | **quis-** |

The verbs **ir** and **ser** have the same irregular preterite forms: **fui, fuiste, fue, fuimos, fuisteis, fueron.**

**4** The meaning of some verbs can change in the **preterite.**

| | present | | preterite |
|---|---|---|---|
| conocer: | *know(s)* | → | *met, first saw* |
| saber: | *know(s)* | → | *found out, realized* |
| querer: | *want(s)* | → | *tried to, meant to* |
| no querer: | *do not (doesn't) want* | → | *wouldn't, didn't mean to* |

Vocabulario y gramática, pp. 46–48
Actividades, pp. 35–37
Online workbooks

### ¿Te acuerdas?

The verbs **estar, querer, poder, poner, saber, tener,** and **venir** have the following preterite endings:

| | |
|---|---|
| estuv**e** | estuv**imos** |
| estuv**iste** | estuv**isteis** |
| estuv**o** | estuv**ieron** |

The verbs **decir** and **traer** have the following preterite endings:

| | |
|---|---|
| dij**e** | dij**imos** |
| dij**iste** | dij**isteis** |
| dij**o** | dij**eron** |

### 29 En el restaurante... 1.2

1. fue
2. dijo
3. decidimos
4. fui
5. llegó
6. gritamos

**Leamos** Completa el párrafo con el pretérito de los verbos.

Ayer __1__ (ser) el cumpleaños de mi mamá. La semana pasada, ella __2__ (decir) que le gustaba la comida mexicana. Por eso, nosotros __3__ (decidir) ir a un restaurante mexicano. Yo __4__ (ir) temprano con mis hermanas. Cuando mi mamá __5__ (llegar), nosotros __6__ (gritar) "¡Feliz cumpleaños!"

## Core Instruction

### TEACHING GRAMÁTICA

1. Go over points 1 and 2. Ask students: **¿Qué comiste anoche? ¿Quién preparó la cena? ¿Qué hiciste luego? (4 min.)**
2. Go over point 3. Use each irregular verb in a sentence. **Anoche mis papás vinieron a casa. Ellos trajeron la comida. Yo puse la mesa. (2 min.)**
3. Go over point 4. Use each verb in the present tense and then in the preterite. **Yo conozco a tu mamá. La conocí en una reunión el año pasado./¿Sabes que Ana se casó con Paco? Supe la noticia ayer. (2 min.)**
4. Go over **¿Te acuerdas?** Have pairs of students practice the past tense by telling about the last time they had a family gathering. They should talk about who was present, what they ate, and what they did. **(2 min.)**

### GramaVisión

For a video presentation of the preterite, use **GramaVisión.**

Visit Holt Online
**go.hrw.com**
KEYWORD: EXP3 CH4
Gramática 2 practice

## 30 Todos tienen una opinión 1.2

**Leamos/Escribamos** Completa las oraciones con la forma correcta del verbo entre paréntesis.

**MODELO** **En cuanto (ver) el menú, mis padres (querer) irse.**
**En cuanto vieron el menú, mis padres quisieron irse.**

1. La última vez que mis amigos ____ (ir) a este restaurante, ellos ____ (conocer) al cocinero. fueron, conocieron
2. En cuanto te ____ (ver) llegar, Arturo nos ____ (poner) a cantar. vio, puso
3. Alejo ____ (venir) también, y le ____ (decir) a Arturo que el puerco asado estaba para chuparse los dedos. vino, dijo
4. Elvira ____ (traer) salsa picante y, a escondidas, les ____ (poner) un poquito a los tacos. trajo, puso

## 31 Un restaurante cubano 1.2

**Leamos/Hablemos** Lee la reseña *(review)* del restaurante y contesta las preguntas usando el pretérito.

> Anoche com en e l restaurante cubano "Buen Provecho". De entrada, pedí camarones en salsa roja, ¡pero el mesero me trajo una ensalada! Quise cambiarla, pero el mesero me dijo: "Se me olvidó decirle que hoy no tenemos camarones". Así que probé la ensalada ¡y me encantó! Luego llegó el plato principal: puerco asado con frijoles negros, arroz y chícharos. Eso me molestó porque había pedido calabacín en vez de chícharos.
>
> *— reseña de Paco Ortiz*

1. ¿Dónde cenó Paco?
2. ¿Qué pidió de entrada? ¿Qué pasó?
3. ¿Pudo cambiar la entrada? ¿Por qué?
4. ¿Por qué no le dijo el mesero que no tenían camarones?
5. ¿Qué hizo Paco con la ensalada?
6. ¿Qué pasó cuando llegó el plato principal?

### Nota cultural

El plato nacional de la República Dominicana es el **sancocho**, un estofado *(stew)* de carne y verduras que puede tener de todo: desde puerco y mariscos hasta ñame *(yam)* y yuca *(yucca)*. El sancocho prieto es un estofado de color oscuro hecho de siete tipos de carne. Pero el plato más popular del país es el arroz con pollo.

¿Cómo se refleja la mezcla de ingredientes americanos y europeos en estos platos dominicanos?

Un sancocho dominicano

## Comunicación

HOLT SoundBooth ONLINE RECORDING

## 32 Una cena terrible 1.1, 1.3

**Hablemos** Fuiste a un restaurante y todo salió mal. Explícale a tu compañero(a) cuatro cosas que no salieron bien.

### 31 Answers

1. Paco cenó en el restaurante cubano "Buen Provecho".
2. Pidió camarones en salsa roja de entrada. El mesero le trajo una ensalada.
3. No pudo cambiar la entrada porque no tenían camarones.
4. Al mesero se le olvidó decirle que no tenían camarones.
5. La probó y le gustó.
6. Paco se molestó porque el mesero trajo chícharos en vez de calabacín.

## Comunicación

### Class Activity: Interpretive

Have students work in groups to prepare a conversation set in a restaurant. One person should be the waiter and the others should be customers. They could present a situation where everything goes wrong; they don't receive what they ordered and don't like the food. Or, they could present a situation where everyone is happy with the food. After each group presents their conversation, the rest of the class will use the past tense to tell what happened. 1.1, 1.2

## Differentiated Instruction

### ADVANCED LEARNERS

**31 Extension** After completing Activity 31, have students write their own restaurant reviews. Suggest that they review a restaurant with Spanish or Latin American food. They can make it up or write about an actual experience. The review can be positive or negative, but should include details about the food and the service. Have students exchange reviews and then summarize their partners' experience for the class. 1.3

### SPECIAL LEARNING NEEDS

**31 Students with Visual Impairments** For students with visual impairments, read the restaurant review for Activity 31 aloud. Then answer the questions as a class. You may want to reread the passage after students have listened to all of the questions.

**30 Students with AD(H)D** To complete the sentences in Activity 30, have students refer to the preterite review in **Gramática** and the imperfect review in **¿Te acuerdas?** Have students explain their answers based on the grammar explanations on page 160. 1.2

**Differentiated Instruction** See the Differentiated Instruction CD-ROM.

## Resources

**Planning:**

Lesson Planner, pp. 57–60, 218–221

One-Stop Planner

**Presentation:**

Video Program **GramaVisión**

**Practice:**

Grammar Tutor for Students of Spanish, Chapter 4

Cuaderno de vocabulario y gramática, pp. 46–48

Cuaderno de actividades, pp. 35–37

Activities for Communication, pp. 15–16

Teaching Transparencies

Bell Work 4.7

**Vocabulario y gramática** answers, pp. 46–48

Interactive Tutor, Disc 1

### Bell Work

Use Bell Work 4.7 in the *Teaching Transparencies*, or write this activity on the board.

**Escribe cinco oraciones para describir lo que hiciste anoche.** 1.3

Interactive TUTOR

### En inglés

**In English,** to express unintentional events people might say:

The pizza (got) burned. (instead of *I burned the pizza.*)

**In Spanish**, people say:

Se me quemó la pizza. (instead of *Quemé la pizza.*)

**In English,** the possessive adjective is often used.

**My** books fell.

**In Spanish**, the definite article is used.

Se me cayeron **los** libros.

In what other situations does Spanish use the definite article where English uses the possessive adjective? 4.1

When using reflexive pronouns with parts of the body: *Me lavé las manos. I washed my hands.*

## Se + indirect object pronouns

**1** Use **se** + **indirect object pronoun** + **verb** to talk about unintentional events.

| | |
|---|---|
| A Julia **se le olvidaron** las bebidas. | *Julia forgot the drinks.* |
| A José **se le cayó** el libro. | *José dropped the book.* |

The **indirect object pronoun** refers to the person the event happened to. The **verb** agrees with the object(s) involved, and is always in the third person singular or plural.

*refers to* *agrees*
A ti **se te olvidó** la ensalada.
*You forgot the salad.*

*refers to* *agrees*
A nosotros **se nos olvidaron** los refrescos.
*We forgot the soft drinks.*

**2** Common verbs used in this construction are **quedar, quemar, perder, olvidar, caer, romper,** and **acabar.**

| | |
|---|---|
| **Se me rompieron** los vasos. | *I broke the glasses.* |

Vocabulario y gramática, pp. 46–48
Actividades, pp. 35–37 **Online** workbooks

### 33 ¿Fue un accidente? 1.2

**Leamos** Lee las oraciones y decide si la persona hizo cada cosa **a**) a propósito *(on purpose)* o si fue **b**) un accidente.

1. Se me olvidó hacer la tarea anoche. b
2. Esta mañana salí de mi casa a las siete. a
3. Se me quedó la mochila en el salón de clases. b
4. Llevé mis libros en las manos. a
5. En la entrada del colegio, se me cayeron todos los libros. b
6. Durante el examen, se me rompió el lápiz. b

### 34 No tengo la culpa 1.2

**Leamos/Escribamos** Completa las oraciones con la forma correcta de **se + pronombre + verbo.**

1. A Lourdes ═══ las llaves en casa. (olvidar)
2. No sé qué vamos a cenar porque ═══ las pizzas. (quemar)
3. Tengo que tomar jugo porque ═══ la leche. (acabar)
4. Comparto mi comida contigo si ═══ el almuerzo en casa. (quedar)
5. A Javier ═══ un plato mientras ponía la mesa. (caer)
6. Mamá se enojó cuando a Toni y Ana ═══ los vasos de la abuela. (romper)

1. se le olvidaron
2. se nos quemaron OR se me quemaron
3. se me acabó OR se nos acabó
4. se te quedó
5. se le cayó
6. se les rompieron

## Core Instruction

### TEACHING GRAMÁTICA

1. Go over the first part of point 1 with students and read the examples. **(2 min.)**
2. Go over the second part of point 1. Explain that the arrows indicate to whom the indirect object pronoun refers, and with which noun the verb must agree. **(2 min.)**
3. Go over point 2. Ask students questions using the verbs listed. **¿Se te rompió el plato? ¿Se te quemaron las papas? (3 min.)**
4. Go over **En inglés.** Ask students to note the difference between saying **Quemé la pizza.** and **Se me quemó la pizza.** Then go back to the examples in the grammar box and ask students how they would communicate the same information without using **se** + indirect object pronoun. Which they think is a more accurate description of an unintentional event? **(3 min.)**

### GramaVisión

For a video presentation of **se** + indirect object pronouns, use **GramaVisión.**

GramaVisión

## 35 ¿Qué les pasó? 1.2

**Escribamos** Mira las fotos y escribe una oración para explicar qué le pasó a cada persona.

1. Fabián y tú/quemar

2. Blanca/caer

3. Tina/olvidar

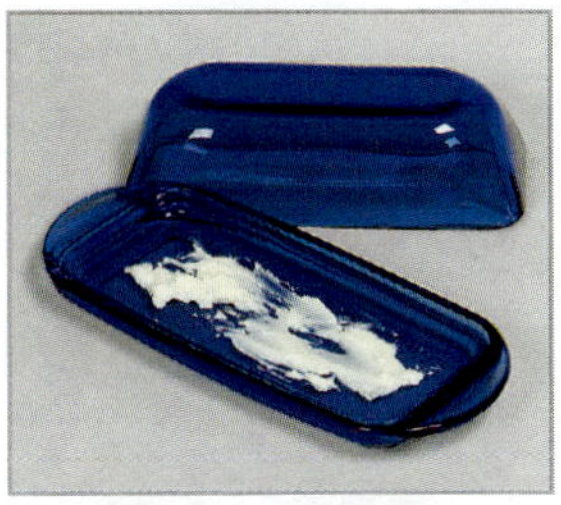
4. Diego/acabar

5. Lisa y yo/romper

6. Carla/caer

## Comunicación

HOLT SoundBooth ONLINE RECORDING

### 36 ¡Se le complica todo! 1.1, 1.2

**Hablemos** En parejas, cuenten la historia de lo que ven en los dibujos. Usen las palabras de **Vocabulario** y las expresiones de **Gramática.**

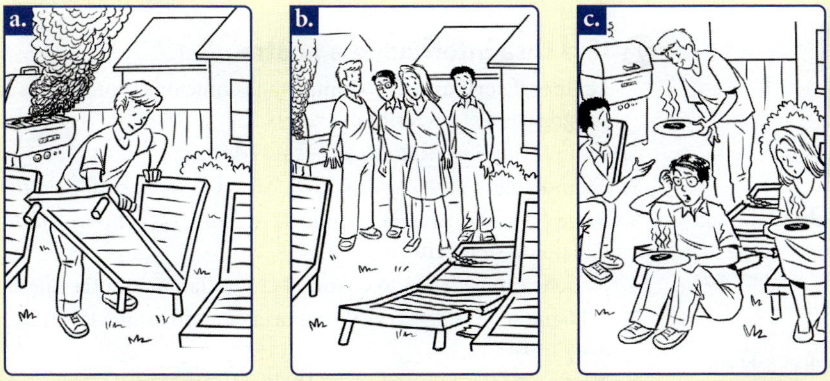


Gramática 2

### 35 Answers

1. A Fabián y a ti se les quemó el pan tostado.
2. A Blanca se le cayó la leche.
3. A Tina se le olvidó la bolsa.
4. A Diego se le acabó la mantequilla.
5. A nosotros se nos rompieron los vasos.
6. A Carla se le cayeron los platos.

Use the Chapter 4 *Picture Sequences Transparency.*

### 36 Sample Answer

**Mientras Pedro ponía las sillas en el jardín y hacía preparativos para la cena, se le olvidó la comida. Cuando llegaron los invitados uno no pudo sentarse porque se le rompió una silla. Y tampoco pudieron comer porque a Pedro también se le quemó la carne. ¡Pobre Pedro!**

### Comunicación

**Group Activity: Interpersonal**

Have students prepare short conversations using **se** + indirect object pronoun. Then have them take turns presenting their conversations to the class.

**MODELO**

**—¡Date prisa! ¡Vamos a llegar tarde al cine!**

**—Espera. ¡Se me perdieron las entradas!**

1.1

## Differentiated Instruction

### SLOWER PACE LEARNERS

**Additional Practice** Cut a transparency into color-coded strips and write on those marked RED: **a mí, a ti, a Ud., a él, a ella, a nosotros, a nosotras, a Uds., a ellos, a ellas;** GREEN: **se;** RED: the indirect object pronouns; ORANGE: the verb stems of **olvidar, caer, quedar, quemar, perder;** YELLOW: **la sal, los platos, el relleno, la crema, las limas, el puerco asado, los camarones.** Then create sentences that are complete except for the indirect object pronoun and the verb ending: **A mí se ______ acab______ la sal.** Ask students to complete the sentences. 1.2

### MULTIPLE INTELLIGENCES

**Bodily/Kinesthetic** Have groups of students imagine they are preparing a special family dinner and everything is going wrong. Have them create a conversation to present to the class. Ask them to use at least four **se** + indirect object pronoun constructions in their conversations. 1.1

**Differentiated Instruction** See the Differentiated Instruction CD-ROM.

## Resources

**Planning:**

Lesson Planner, pp. 57–60, 218–221

One-Stop Planner

**Presentation:**

Video Program **GramaVisión**

**Practice:**

Grammar Tutor for Students of Spanish, Chapter 4

Cuaderno de vocabulario y gramática, pp. 46–48

Cuaderno de actividades, pp. 35–37

Activities for Communication, pp. 15–16

Teaching Transparencies

Bell Work 4.8

**Vocabulario y gramática** answers, pp. 46–48

Interactive Tutor, Disc 1

### Bell Work

Use Bell Work 4.8 in the *Teaching Transparencies,* or write this activity on the board.

**Completa las oraciones con la palabra correcta.**

1. A papá se (le/les) cayeron los libros.
2. ¿A ti se (te/le) olvidó tu mochila otra vez?
3. Se me (rompió/rompieron) el lápiz.
4. Se nos (quemamos/quemaron) los camarones.
5. A ellas se les (quedó/quedaron) la tarea en casa.

1.2

## Past progressive

Interactive TUTOR

**1** The **past progressive (pasado progresivo)** is used to describe past actions in progress. It is formed with the **imperfect of estar** + the **present participle** of the main verb.

Nosotros **estábamos hablando.**

**2** When the **past progressive** and the **preterite** are used in the same sentence, the **past progressive** describes an action in progress, and the **preterite** describes completed actions or interrupting events within that setting.

*action in progress* — *interrupting event*

**Estábamos comiendo** cuando **llegó** Cristina.

**3** As with the present progressive, the **past progressive** refers to actions in progress. Past actions, conditions, or states that were ongoing or habitual, rather than in progress, referred to with the **imperfect.**

**Estaba lloviendo** cuando **salí** de casa.

**Llovía** mucho en el pueblo donde **vivían** mis abuelos.

Vocabulario y gramática, pp. 46–48
Actividades, pp. 35–37
Online workbooks

### ¿Te acuerdas?

1. The imperfect endings for **estar** are:

| | |
|---|---|
| est**aba** | est**ábamos** |
| est**abas** | est**abais** |
| est**aba** | est**aban** |

2. **Object pronouns** go before the verb or are attached to the participle and an accent is added.

**Me** estaba bañando.
Estaba bañándo**me**.

**Lo** estaba leyendo cuando **me** llamaste.

### 37 ¿Qué estaban haciendo? 1.2

**Leamos/Escribamos** Completa las oraciones.

1. Anoche yo estaba ____ cuando ____.
2. Ayer mis amigos y yo estábamos ____ cuando ____.
3. Esta mañana (yo) estaba ____ cuando ____.
4. Al mediodía mi amigo estaba ____ cuando ____.
5. Mi profesor(a) de español estaba ____ cuando ____.

### 38 Una cosa interrumpe a la otra 1.2

**Leamos/Escribamos** Completa las oraciones con el pasado progresivo o el pretérito del verbo.

1. Cuando sonó el teléfono yo ____ (dormir).
2. Cuando ellos ____ (llegar) a la casa de Elena, estaba lloviendo.
3. Jorge ____ (estudiar) cuando de repente escuchó un ruido debajo de su escritorio.
4. Anoche estaba leyendo cuando ____ (llamar) mi tía Clara.
5. A Diana se le ____ (caer) una taza cuando estaba lavando los platos.
6. No nos vieron porque ____ (hablar) con Manuel.

1. estaba durmiendo
2. llegaron
3. estaba estudiando
4. llamó
5. cayó
6. estaban hablando

## Core Instruction

### TEACHING GRAMÁTICA

1. Go over point 1. Ask students: **¿Qué estabas haciendo antes de esta clase? (2 min.)**
2. Go over points 2 and 3. Ask questions to check comprehension: **¿Qué estaban haciendo los estudiantes cuando llegaste al colegio? (2 min.)**
3. Read **¿Te acuerdas?** aloud. Give several examples of sentences with verbs that are used reflexively. In your examples, place the pronoun before the verb. Have students repeat the sentences, attaching the pronoun to the participle. **Me estoy bañando./Estoy bañándome. (4 min.)**
4. Have pairs of students practice the past progressive by asking each other questions about what they and members of their families were doing when certain events occured. **¿Qué estaba haciendo tu hermano cuando te levantaste hoy? (2 min.)**

### GramaVisión

For a video presentation of the past progressive, use **GramaVisión.**

GramaVisión

## 39 ¡Qué desastre! 1.2

**Escribamos** Para cada uno de los dibujos, escribe qué estaba haciendo cada persona cuando sucedió algo más.

1.

2.

3.

4.

### Nota cultural

Los platos típicos cubanos incluyen **el congrí**, una combinación de arroz y frijoles negros; **la ropa vieja**, un plato de carne de res deshebrada *(shredded beef)*; **el sofrito**, una salsa para sazonar *(season)* la comida; **la yuca**, un vegetal parecido a la papa; y **los plátanos**, un tipo de banano que se come frito o hervido.

¿Has probado alguno de estos platos? 1.3

### Comunicación

HOLT SoundBooth ONLINE RECORDING

## 40 Iba a hacerlo cuando... 1.1, 1.3

**Hablemos** En parejas, dramaticen una conversación donde el papá o la mamá le pregunte a su hijo(a) por qué no hizo sus quehaceres. El hijo (o la hija) le da una explicación.

**MODELO** **—¿Y el carro? ¿No lo ibas a lavar?**
**—Estaba saliendo a lavarlo cuando…**

Gramática 2

### 39 Answers

Answers will vary. Possible answers:

1. La estudiante estaba corriendo a clase cuando se dio un golpe con el profesor.
2. El chico estaba hablando por teléfono cuando se le quemó la comida.
3. El hijo estaba mirando televisión cuando volvieron los padres.
4. La chica estaba trayendo el pastel cuando se le cayó por culpa del perro.

### Más práctica

Have students work in groups to draw and caption a comic strip. They should include actions in progress and interrupting events. Their descriptions will use the past progressive and the preterite. 1.2

### Comunicación

#### Class Activity: Interpretive

Have groups of students present an action in progress and an interrupting event or completed action within a setting. For example, they may pretend to be having dinner and a person walks in. The rest of the class uses the present progressive and the preterite to describe the scene. **Estaban comiendo cuando llegó David.** Continue until each group has had the chance to present their scene for the class. 1.2

## Differentiated Instruction

### SLOWER PACE LEARNERS

**37 Variation** Some students may have difficulty thinking of verbs to complete the sentences in Activity 37. You might want to provide verbs by asking a question to prompt the responses outlined in each item. For example, for item one you could ask: **¿Qué estabas estudiando cuando empezó la tormenta anoche?** Students can then use the sentence frames to answer the questions. 1.2

### MULTIPLE INTELLIGENCES

**Mathematical** After presenting the grammar, use symbols to practice the past progressive with students. Create a symbol, such as a star *, for a completed action in the past and another symbol, such as an arrow ←, for a past action in progress. Give written or spoken examples using the preterite or past progressive and ask students to draw the appropriate symbol. Then present the symbol and an infinitive and ask students to form sentences.

### Assess

**Assessment Program**

**Prueba: Gramática 2,** pp. 69–70

**Prueba: Aplicación 2,** pp. 71–72

Audio CD 4, Tr. 16

Alternative Assessment, pp. 376, 388, 400

**Online Assessment**
**my.hrw.com**

**Test Generator**

**Assess** **Differentiated Instruction** See the Differentiated Instruction CD-ROM.

## Resources

**Planning:**

Lesson Planner, pp. 60, 220–221

One-Stop Planner

**Presentation:**

Video Program, Videocassette 2

DVD Program

**VideoNovela**

**Practice:**

Video Guide, pp. 26–28

Lab Book, pp. 67–68

## Visual Learners

Have students create a graphic organizer containing questions to fill in as the story unfolds.

**El profesor Luna**

↓

¿Quién es? ____________

↓

¿Qué información tiene el profesor? ____________

↓

¿Quiénes lo están siguiendo? ____________

1.2

## Gestures

Have students note the gestures used by the speakers to convey meaning. Do students think the gestures are the same or different from the ones they would use?

## Novela en video

# Clara perspectiva

## Episodio 4

**ESTRATEGIA** 1.2

**Connecting the dots** As a story unfolds, you get information in bits and pieces. You try to connect the dots in the most logical way possible. Write down everything you know up to now about Professor Luna's situation. See whether any information you gather in **Episodio 4** helps you to connect the dots. Who is following the professor? What information do they want? What is their stake in it? What is Professor Luna's role in their search?

### En la casa de los de la Rosa

**Clara** ¡Octavio! Hola. ¡Qué sorpresa! ¿Qué me cuentas? ¿A qué se debe el honor de tu presencia?
**Octavio** Hola Clara. Mira. Vine a devolverte esto. Se te quedó en la oficina.
**Clara** Ay, ya. Se me quedó en la oficina. ¡Qué bruta! Bueno, muchas gracias. Bueno Octavio, pasa no más. Quiero que conozcas a mi familia.

1

2

**Clara** Papá, mamá, quiero que conozcan a mi colega Octavio Medina. Trabaja conmigo en la revista.
**Papá** Mucho gusto, Octavio.
**Octavio** Mucho gusto Señor de la Rosa, Señora de la Rosa.
**Mamá** Octavio, encantada de conocerte. Estás en tu casa.

**Pablo** ¡Prima! ¿Cómo has estado?
**Clara** Muy bien, Pablo. ¿Qué me cuentas de tu media hermana y su pololo, Alberto? ¿Siguen saliendo?
**Pablo** Fíjate que se han comprometido.
**Clara** ¿En serio? ¡Qué sorpresa que se hayan comprometido tan pronto!

3

4

**Mamá** Hija, Octavio, yo creo, debe estar muerto de hambre. ¿Por qué no le preparas un plato?
**Pablo** Sí, Clara. La carne está deliciosa. Y las empanadas están para chuparse los dedos.
**Mamá** Bueno, creo que se me fue la mano con la sal.
**Clara** Ay, mamá, por favor. Ella es la mejor cocinera del mundo, así que no le hagas caso.
**Octavio** Se me hace agua la boca.

## Pre-AP Practice

**AP Benchmark:** Identify and summarize the main points and details and make inferences and predictions from a spoken source on a topic.

**Focus:** Summarizing the main points, and making inferences and predictions

- SE, p. 166, **Estrategia**
- TE, p. 167, **Comunicación**
- Video Guide, p. 28, Act. 5

## Core Instruction

### TEACHING NOVELA EN VIDEO

1. Ask students what questions they have about Profesor Luna. Then have students scan the **Novela en video** text. **(2 min.)**
2. Play the video, stopping periodically to ask comprehension questions. **(15 min.)**
3. Play the video a second time, then have groups of students practice the parts of the characters. **(10 min.)**
4. Answer the questions on page 167 as a class. **(3 min.)**

### Escuchemos

On the board write the following: **1. Clara, se te ____ esto en la oficina. 2. Qué sorpresa que se hayan ____. 3. Se ____ fue la mano con la sal.** As students watch the **Novela,** have them fill in the blanks based on what they hear. (**quedó, comprometido, me**)

**Novela en video**

Visit Holt Online
go.hrw.com
KEYWORD: EXP3 CH4
Online Edition

Novela en video

5

**Clara** Papá, parece que el profesor Luna tiene un problema grave. Alguien lo está amenazando.
**Papá** Mira, Clara, ¿estás segura que hay un problema?
**Clara** No papá, pero tengo la obligación de dejarme llevar por mis intuiciones. Mencionaron la región de Magallanes.
**Papá** Tienes que hablar con tu tío Arnoldo. Tú sabes que él tiene propiedades en esa región. Si algo está pasando en Magallanes, tu tío sabrá qué es.

**Tío Arnoldo** ¡Clarita! ¿Cómo estás? ¡Siempre agradable verte, hija!
**Clara** Tío, le presento a mi amigo Octavio.
**Tío Arnoldo** Octavio, hombre, o tratas bien a mi sobrina, o tienes problemas conmigo, ¿me explico?
**Clara** Ay, tío, por favor.

6

7

**Clara** Tío, ¿usted todavía tiene esa propiedad en Magallanes?
**Tío Arnoldo** Sí, pero el otro día recibí una oferta agradable para esa propiedad. Hablé con el señor Reyes Rodríguez de la empresa MaderaCorp. El problema es que los ecologistas están tratando de convencer al Congreso que esas propiedades no se deben desarrollar.

## En la oficina del profesor Luna

**Ecologista 2** ¿Tú ves los documentos del archivo?
**Ecologista 1** No, no los veo.
**Ecologista 2** ¿Por qué no te metes a buscar?
**Ecologista 1** ¿Yo? ¿Qué soy yo? ¿un hacker? Hazlo tú.

8

9

**Hombre 1** No puedo conseguir los archivos.
**Hombre 2** No importa. Mañana regresamos con un hacker.

### ¿COMPRENDES?

1. ¿Por qué vino Octavio a la casa de Clara? ¿A quiénes les presenta Clara a Octavio?
2. ¿Quién es Pablo? ¿Qué le pregunta Clara? ¿Qué le dice Pablo?
3. ¿Qué recibió el tío Arnoldo sobre su propiedad en Magallanes?
4. ¿Quién le hizo la oferta al tío Arnoldo? ¿Qué problema hay con las propiedades?
5. ¿Qué hacen los ecologistas en la oficina del profesor Luna? ¿Y los hombres de traje oscuro? ¿Consiguen lo que buscan?
6. ¿Qué eventos de la trama puedes relacionar? ¿Cómo se conectan?

1.2

**Próximo episodio**
*Clara y Octavio van a una exposición de arte chileno y se encuentran con alguien muy interesante. ¿Con quiénes crees que se van a encontrar?*
PÁGINAS 214–215

### Clara perspectiva, Episodio 4

In **Episodio 4,** Octavio meets some of Clara's family. Clara seeks her father's advice on how to handle the situation with the professor. He reminds her that her uncle, Arnoldo, has property in that area. Arnoldo tells them that he recently received a generous offer for the property from Reyes Rodríguez of MaderaCorp. Back at the university, the two young people seen with the professor in **Episodio 1** have managed to sneak into the professor's office but are unable to find the study they're looking for. Later, the two men seen with the professor in **Episodio 2** have broken into the professor's office.

### Language Note

Tell students that in Chile, the word **pololo** is slang for *boyfriend.*

### ¿Comprendes? Answers

1. para devolverle algo que ella había dejado en la oficina; a sus papás
2. el primo de Clara; si su medio hermana sigue saliendo con su pololo; le dice que se han comprometido
3. una oferta generosa
4. el señor Reyes Rodríguez, de la empresa MaderaCorp; los ecologistas están tratando de convencer al Congreso que esas propiedades no se deben desarrollar
5. Están buscando los documentos de un estudio; Los hombres de traje oscuro están buscando lo mismo; No consiguen lo que buscan.
6. Los ecologistas tienen algo que ver con la propiedad del tío Arnoldo, y unos ecologistas también están buscando algo que tiene el profesor Luna.

### Comunicación

### Pair Work: Interpersonal

After students have read the **Novela en video,** have them work in pairs to imagine what might happen in the next scene of the **Novela.** Ask them to think about the mysterious events and to imagine what the ecologists and the men in dark suits might be looking for. Have them create a conversation between two of the characters in the **Novela,** providing more information about the events. Encourage them to use **¡Exprésate!** expressions from **Vocabulario 1** and **Vocabulario 2** whenever possible.

1.1

**Resources**

**Planning:**

Lesson Planner, pp. 61, 222–223

One-Stop Planner

**Presentation:**

Audio CD 4, Tr. 11

**Practice:**

Cuaderno de actividades, p. 38

Reading Strategies and Skills Handbook, Chapter 4

Interactive Advanced Reader

**Pre-Reading Activity**

Have students describe their favorite desserts. Then, ask if anyone has tried any typical Latin American dishes: Tell students they are going to read about these popular Latin American desserts: **flan, dulce de leche, dulce de papaya,** and **tamales dulces.** Have them look at the photos and tell whether or not the desserts look like something they would like to try. Suggest that students pay special attention to how these dishes are made as they read the selection.

# Lectura cultural

CD 4, Tr. 11

## Los postres

*Cada postre, desde el flan hasta el tamal dulce tiene un sabor regional que hay que probar.*

Aunque la mayor parte del azúcar del mundo se produce en las Américas, los postres de Latinoamérica no son tan azucarados (ni tan complicados) como los de Estados Unidos. Sin embargo, parece que cada país tiene una variedad de postres regionales. ¡Todos son tan sabrosos como para chuparse los dedos!

el flan

**El flan**

El flan es tal vez el postre más común de toda Latinoamérica, aunque su origen es europeo. Es un postre muy sencillo que se hace con huevos, leche y azúcar, pero se puede añadir otros sabores. También se hace el flan con frutas (coco, manzana), pasta de arroz, nueces molidas, ¡o hasta con cebollas licuadas!

**El dulce de leche**

Mientras que el flan es originalmente europeo, el dulce de leche es un auténtico postre latinoamericano. Se originó en Argentina, pero se come en varios países. El dulce de leche es aún más sencillo que el flan; se hace sólo con leche y azúcar. A los argentinos les gusta comerlo con panqueques o arepas (que son parecidas a las tortillas), pero también se come con pan o sobre una galleta. Hay otro tipo de dulce de leche que se vende en forma de bolas pequeñas; éstas se comen solas o sobre una galleta.

el dulce de leche

**Pre-AP Practice**

**AP Language Examination:** **Lectura cultural** helps students prepare for Section I, Part B: **Reading Comprehension.** The audio recording helps them prepare for Part A: **Listening—Short Narratives.**

**Core Instruction**

**TEACHING LECTURA CULTURAL**

1. Read and discuss the first two paragraphs as a class. Ask students to name the ingredients that can be used to make flan. If they are uncertain of the meaning of any of the words, suggest that they look them up in the Glossary or in a dictionary and write the definitions on a separate piece of paper. Tell them they can use this list as a reference as they read the rest of the selection. **(5 min.)**
2. Have students read the rest of the selection to themselves and then have volunteers summarize the content. Ask them if they have changed their minds about which desserts they would like to try. **(10 min.)**
3. Have students answer the first set of **Comprensión** questions. Then go over the **¿Qué aprendiste?** questions as a class. **(10 min.)**

el dulce de papaya

**El dulce de papaya**

La papaya, también conocida como fruta bomba, es común en Cuba, donde se come este postre. El dulce de papaya se hace pelando[1] la papaya y quitándole las semillas. La fruta se corta en mitad, y se pone en agua durante medio día. Luego se hierve y se le agrega azúcar para formar un almíbar[2]. Este postre se sirve frío y se come con queso.

**Los tamales dulces**

Los tamales dulces son un postre muy mexicano. Estos tamales son populares en la región sureña de México. Los tamales se hacen con una masa de maíz molido[3] y se envuelven en hojas de maíz para cocinarlos al vapor[4]. A la masa de los tamales dulces se le añade azúcar o chocolate y a veces se rellenan con mermelada[5]. Por lo general, en México se come este postre acompañado con un café de olla[6].

1 peeling
2 syrup
3 ground corn
4 steam
5 they are filled with jam
6 coffee spiced with cinnamon and anise or cloves



## Comprensión

**A ¿Sí o no?** 1.2

1. El flan es un postre europeo. sí
2. Hay muchas variedades de flan. sí
3. El dulce de leche es un postre de Cuba. no
4. El dulce de leche es difícil de hacer. no
5. La papaya y la fruta bomba son dos frutas diferentes. no
6. El dulce de papaya se come en Cuba. sí
7. Los tamales dulces no tienen azúcar. no
8. Los tamales se envuelven en una hoja de maíz. sí

**B ¿Qué aprendiste?** 1.2

Contesta las preguntas basándote en lo que leíste.

1. ¿Dónde se come el flan hoy en día?
2. ¿Cuáles son los ingredientes del flan?
3. ¿Con qué se come el dulce de leche?
4. ¿Dónde se originó el dulce de leche?
5. ¿Qué hay que hacer con las papayas antes de cortarlas en mitad?
6. ¿En qué región de México son populares los tamales dulces?

## Actividad 1.3

**Tu postre favorito** Haz una lista de los ingredientes de tu postre favorito, o escribe una receta para prepararlo. Compara la lista o la receta con los postres latinoamericanos que ya conoces.



# Lectura cultural

### B Answers

1. en España y en muchas partes de Latinoamérica
2. huevos, leche y azúcar; también se puede hacer con frutas (coco, manzana), pasta de arroz, nueces molidas, o cebollas licuadas
3. con panqueques, arepas, pan o sobre una galleta
4. se originó en Argentina
5. pelar la papaya y quitarle las semillas
6. en la región sureña de México

### Heritage Speakers

Have heritage speakers choose a typical dessert from their country and write the recipe for the class. They should copy their recipe onto a transparency so the rest of the class can refer to it as students describe how to make each dessert. Ask heritage speakers to explain when the dessert is served. Is it only for special occasions? 1.3, 3.1

### Post-Reading Activities

Give students time to complete the **Actividad** and then have them share their recipes with the class. Have students compare their recipes with the desserts they read about in the **Lectura**. Suggest that students find recipes for those desserts or for other Latin American desserts. Plan a day for students to prepare the desserts at home and then bring them to school to share with the class. 1.3, 4.2

## Differentiated Instruction

### SLOWER PACE LEARNERS

For students who have trouble with reading comprehension in Spanish, have them skim the selection for food terms. Ask them to write the terms in their notebooks and look up any that they do not know. Have them use the list for reference as they read the selection.

### SPECIAL LEARNING NEEDS

**Students with Learning Disabilities/AD(H)D**

You may want to have volunteers read the selection aloud. Pause between each section and ask students what ingredients are used for the dessert. Write the name of the dessert and the ingredients on the board as students name them. Then ask if there are any ingredients with which students are not familiar. Provide definitions or translations as needed. Students can copy the notes from the board into their notebooks and use them as reference for answering the comprehension questions. 1.2

### Assess

**Assessment Program**

**Prueba: Lectura,** p. 73

**Online Assessment**

**my.hrw.com**

**Test Generator**

**Assess** **Differentiated Instruction** See the Differentiated Instruction CD-ROM.

# Leamos y escribamos

## Resources

**Planning**

Lesson Planner, pp. 61–62, 222–223

One-Stop Planner

**Presentation:**

Audio CD 4, Tr. 12

**Practice:**

Cuaderno de actividades, p. 38

Reading Strategies and Skills Handbook, Chapter 4

Interactive Advanced Reader

### AP Reading Suggestion

Have students analyze the poem from a cultural point of view. Ask them to research five of the foods mentioned in the poem and investigate their origins. Have them prepare a short presentation for the class about where the dish came from, how it is prepared, and on what occasions it is served. 2.2, 3.2

### Applying the Strategies

For more practice with using context clues, you might have students use the "Think Aloud" strategy from the *Reading Strategies and Skills Handbook.*

### Escuchemos

As students listen to the poem with their books closed, have them write down at least three foods they hear.

### Pre-AP Practice

**AP Language Examination:** **Leamos** helps students prepare for Section I, Part B: **Reading Comprehension.** The audio recording helps them prepare for Part A: **Listening—Short Narratives.**

# Leamos y escribamos

**ESTRATEGIA**

**para leer** If you see words you don't understand in a text, try to guess their meanings by looking at their context—the other words and sentences surrounding the unknown word. This will allow you to guess what the unknown word could mean. Then look up the word in the dictionary to see if you were right.

CD 4, Tr. 12

**Antes de leer** 1.2

**A** El poeta cubano Nicolás Guillén nació en Camagüey, Cuba en 1902. Escribió el siguiente poema durante una estancia en Europa, para dos amigas cubanas que estaban en España. En el poema, Guillén habla de varias comidas de su isla nativa.

Lee las primeras diez líneas del poema y haz una lista de las palabras desconocidas. Trata de adivinar el significado de cada palabra por medio de las otras palabras en la misma oración o verso. Luego busca las palabras en un diccionario para verificar sus significados.

## de Epístola

*de Nicolás Guillén*

*A dos amigas cubanas que invernaban en Palma de Mallorca*

Perdonad° al poeta
convertido en gastrónomo... Mas quiero
que me digáis si allá (junto al puchero°,
la fabada° tal vez o la munyeta°),
lograsteis decorar vuestros manteles
con blanco arroz y oscuro picadillo°,
orondos huevos fritos con tomate,
el solemne aguacate
y el rubicundo plátano amarillo.
¿O por ser más sencillo,
el chicharrón de puerco° con su masa,
dándole el brazo al siboney° casabe
la mesa presidió de vuestra casa?
Y del bronco lechón el frágil cuero

**1** Pardon **3** soup with pork **4** meat stew with beans **4** seasoned bean paste **6** dish of ground beef and vegetables **11** pork rinds **12** pre-Hispanic Caribbean people

## Core Instruction

### TEACHING LEAMOS

1. Read the **Estrategia para leer** with students. Remind them that photos and illustrations can also serve as context clues. **(2 min.)**
2. Read **Antes de leer** with students. Then point out the text in italics below the title and the author's name. Ask students if they know where Palma de Mallorca is. Point it out on a map. **(3 min.)**
3. Have students read the first ten lines of the poem, following the instructions for using context clues in **Antes de leer.** Ask how many words students were able to guess using context clues. Then have students read through the rest of the poem using the same strategy. Ask students to share the words they still could not figure out to see if a classmate might have guessed the answer. **(15 min.)**
4. Have students answer the **Comprensión** questions. **(5 min.)**

Visit Holt Online
go.hrw.com
KEYWORD: EXP3 CH4
Online Edition

dorado en púa° ¿no alumbró algún día
bajo esos puros cielos españoles
el amable ostracismo°? ¿Hallar pudisteis,
tal vez al cabo de mortal porfía,
en olas navegando
en rubias olas de cerveza fría,
nuestros negros frijoles,
para los cuales toda gula° es poca,
gordo tasajo° y cristalina yuca°,
de esa que llaman en Brasil mandioca°?
El maíz, oro fino
en sagradas pepitas,
quizás vuestros ayunos°
a perturbar con su riqueza vino.
El quimbombó° africano,
cuya baba° el limón corta y detiene,
¿no os suscitó el cubano
guiso de camarones,
o la tibia ensalada,
ante la cual espárragos ebúrneos°,
según doctos varones,
según doctos varones en cocina,
según doctos varones no son nada?
Veo el arroz con pollo,
que es a la vez hispánico y criollo°,
del cual es prima hermana
la famosa paella valenciana.
No me llaméis bellaco
si os hablo del ajiaco°,
del cilíndrico ñame° poderoso,
del boniato° pastoso,
o de la calabaza femenina
y el fufú° montañoso.
¡Basta! Os recuerdo el postre. Para eso
no más que el blanco queso,
el blanco queso que el montuno alaba°,
en pareja con cascos de guayaba.
Y al final, buen remate° a tanto diente,
una taza pequeña
de café carretero bien caliente.
Así pues, primas mías,
esperaré unos días,
para saber por carta detallada
si esto que pido aquí debe tacharse
de ser una demanda exagerada,
o es que puede encontrarse
al doblar una esquina
en la primera casa mallorquina°.
Si lo hay, voy volando,
mejor dicho, corriendo,
que es como siempre ando.
Pero si no, pues seguiré soñando...
Y cuando al fin os vea
vueltas las dos de España
a París, esta aldea°,
os sentaré a mi costa
frente a una eximia° y principal langosta
rociada° con champaña.

**15** rotisserie spit **17** banishment **22** gluttony **23** salted meat **23** yucca (also called manioc) **24** manioc, edible tubular root **27** fasts **29** okra **30** slime found in okra **34** (poetic) ivory-like **39** native to America **43** stew with tubular roots and spices **44** yam **45** sweet potato **47** mashed plantain with garlic and oil **50** praised by people in mountains **52** the end **62** from Mallorca **69** village, hamlet **71** most excellent **72** basted

## Differentiated Instruction

### ADVANCED LEARNERS

**Challenge** Have students research other poems by Nicolás Guillén. Ask them to pick out one that they like and study it. Have them keep a list of the words they do not know. Encourage them to try to figure out the meaning of each word using context clues. Then have them check their conclusions using a dictionary. 1.2

### MULTIPLE INTELLIGENCES

**Musical/Rhythmic** Some students may find it easier to grasp the concepts in the poem by listening to the rhythm. You might want to have them close their books as you read the poem aloud, emphasizing the musical rhythm of the verses. Once you have read it aloud once, have students open their books and follow along as you read it a second time. This time, pause every five verses or so to check comprehension. 1.2

# Leamos y escribamos

## Active Reading Questions

1. **¿Cuál es el tema del poema?**
2. **¿Cómo describe Guillén el aguacate en el verso 8?**
3. **¿El autor cree que la comida española es tan buena como la cubana?**
4. **¿Qué alimentos ves en las fotos?** 1.2, 3.2

## Using Context Clues

As students read the poem, remind them to keep a list of the words they do not recognize. Tell them to use context to determine the meanings of the words. Ask them to write down what they think each word means, and then discuss the words together as a class. Have students explain how the context helped them figure out the meaning of each word.

## Teaching Suggestion

Nicolás Guillén (1902-1987) was born in Cuba to an Afro-Cuban family. Guillén began writing at an early age and published his first poems in the 1920's in Cuban newspapers. Guillén was a writer, but was also interested in social issues, especially in the way Africans were treated in his native Cuba and around the world. In the 1930's, Guillén published a collection of poetry inspired by **son**, a popular form of Afro-Cuban music, thereby establishing Afro-Cuban music as part of mainstream Cuban literature. Have students investigate African-American musicians from the 1920's and 1930's. Ask students how African culture influenced music in the United States during this period.

**B Answers**

1. mandioca
2. oro fino
3. de África; como baba
4. Es a la vez hispánico y criollo.
5. Se parecen: tienen casi los mismos ingredientes.
6. No, está en París. Dice que va a ver a sus dos amigas cuando vuelvan a París, donde está él.

### Teaching Suggestion

Have students analyze the poem from a cultural point of view. Ask them to research five of the foods mentioned in the poem and investigate their origins. Have them prepare a short presentation for the class about where the dish came from, how it is prepared, and on what occasions it is served. 2.2

### Cultures

#### Products and Perspectives

Remind students that Nicolás Guillén wrote this poem while he was away from Cuba. He mentioned several foods from his native Cuba that he missed. He mentioned foods like **picadillo,** yucca, rice, black beans, roast pork, okra, and so on, in his poem. Have students imagine that they are living outside their country. What foods from home would they miss? Have students make a list of these foods and compare their lists with the foods that Guillén mentioned in his poem. Ask students if they have any of the foods mentioned in the poem on their lists. 2.2, 4.2

### Post-Reading Strategy

Have students discuss the parts that stood out for them in the poem, and why. What foods do they remember? Why do they think the author wrote this poem? Ask volunteers to give a brief synopsis of the poem. 1.2

## Comprensión 1.2

**B** Contesta las preguntas basándote en lo que leíste.

1. ¿Cómo se llama la yuca en Brasil?
2. ¿Con qué se compara el maíz en el poema?
3. ¿De dónde vendrá el quimbombó? Según el contexto, ¿cómo es?
4. ¿Cómo describe el autor el arroz con pollo?
5. ¿Qué quiere decir el autor con "prima hermana" al referirse a "la famosa paella valenciana"?
6. ¿Crees que el autor está en su país natal? ¿Cómo lo sabes?

**C** Busca en el poema el adjetivo que usó el autor para describir las siguientes cosas.

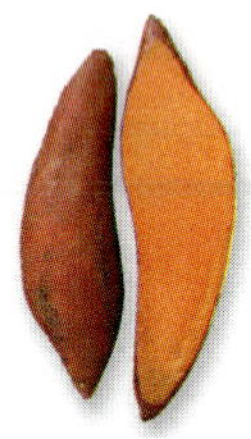
1. ñame

2. boniato

3. calabaza

4. yuca

5. picadillo

6. aguacate

1. poderoso
2. pastoso
3. femenina
4. cristalina
5. oscuro
6. solemne

## Después de leer 1.2

**D** ¿Cuántas palabras nuevas aprendiste? ¿Cuántos significados adivinaste según el contexto? Recuerda verificar el significado de las palabras en el diccionario. Es recomendable escribir las palabras nuevas en un cuaderno con sus significados.

## Core Instruction

### TEACHING ESCRIBAMOS

1. Discuss **Estrategia para escribir.** Then create a four-line verse as a class. First pick out two sets of rhyming words such as **sopa, ropa; lata, patata.** Have students help you form verses using one of the patterns outlined in **Estrategia para escribir.** The verses can be silly or nonsensical; the idea is to show students how to form verses in rhyme. **(1 min.)**
2. Have students do step 1 and organize their words in a graphic organizer like the one shown. **(5 min.)**
3. Have students do steps 2, 3, and 4 to complete their poems. Circulate around the class to assist students who are having difficulty writing the poem. Or, have students complete the poem for homework. **(15 min.)**

# Taller del escritor 1.3, 3.1

**ESTRATEGIA**

**para escribir** There are many types of rhyme you can use in a poem. For this activity you will use four-line verses. You can make lines 1 and 2 rhyme, then lines 3 and 4. You can also make line 1 rhyme with line 4 and line 2 rhyme with line 3, or alternate patterns between verses. Experiment and see what works best.

## Tu comida favorita

Vas a describir tu comida favorita en un poema. Puedes usar metáforas y otras figuras retóricas, como el símil o la hipérbole, para describir tu comida favorita. Por ejemplo, compara tu comida favorita con con otros objetos u otras comidas para crear una imagen.

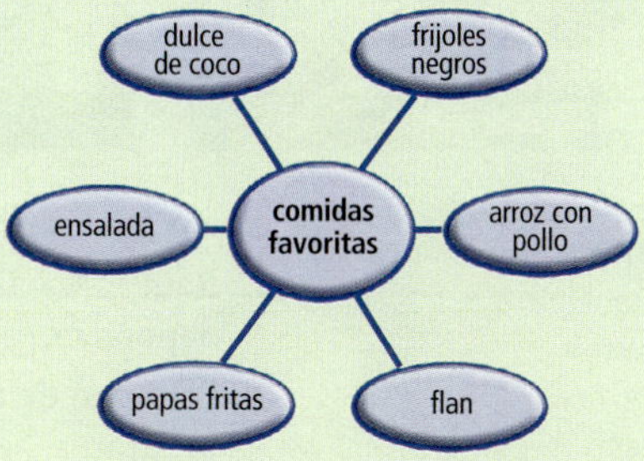


**1 Antes de escribir**

Escoge la(s) comida(s) favorita(s) que quieres describir en tu poema. Después puedes hacer varias listas de palabras relacionadas y escoger de estas listas las palabras que riman. Decide cómo quieres que rime tu poema y empieza a escribir.

**2 Escribir un borrador**

Empareja las palabras que riman de tus listas de palabras. Úsalas para escribir tus versos. Puedes cambiar el patrón *(pattern)* de la rima en cada verso.

**3 Revisar**

Lee tu poema en voz alta para ver cómo suena. Si es necesario, puedes ajustar la rima un poco. Corrige los errores de ortografía o de puntuación.

**4 Publicar**

Con un(a) compañero(a), túrnense para leer sus poemas en voz alta. Compara su comida favorita con la tuya. Puedes compartir tu poema con tus compañeros de clase para ver si otros escribieron acerca de la misma comida.

## Differentiated Instruction

### SLOWER PACE LEARNERS

Some students may have trouble coming up with rhyming words on their own. Tell them that a dictionary on CD is useful for finding rhyming words because they can search for words by ending. Remind them that they can always use the infinitives of verbs with the same ending when they cannot think of other rhyming words.

### MULTIPLE INTELLIGENCES

**Naturalist** Have students cut out pictures of the food they are going to write about or have them draw the food. They might want to include pictures of the basic ingredients. For example, for flan they could include photographs of eggs, milk, or sugar. These images will help them expand the types of words they come up with as they brainstorm rhyming words for the poem.

## Leamos y escribamos

### Process Writing

Explain to students that they should focus on the last syllables of a word to come up with rhyming words. An easy syllable to use for rhyme is **-ito(a)** because it can be added to many words to create the diminutive: **poquito, chiquito, etc.** Another easy way to rhyme is to use the infinitive endings **-ar, -er, -ir.** Practice finding rhyming words by writing several common final syllables on the board **(-aba, -oso, -ita, -ar, -isa)** and filling out a list for each.

### Writing Assessment

To assess the **Taller del escritor,** you can use the following rubric. For additional rubrics, see the *Alternative Assessment Guide.*

| Writing Rubric | 4 | 3 | 2 | 1 |
|---|---|---|---|---|
| **Content** (Complete—Incomplete) | | | | |
| **Comprehensibility** (Comprehensible—Seldom comprehensible) | | | | |
| **Accuracy** (Accurate—Seldom accurate) | | | | |
| **Organization** (Well-organized—Poorly organized) | | | | |
| **Effort** (Excellent effort—Minimal effort) | | | | |

18–20: A 14–15: C Under
16–17: B 12–13: D 12: F

### Pre-AP Practice

**AP Language Examination: Leamos and Escribamos** help students prepare for Section I, Part B: **Reading Comprehension** and Section II, Part A: **Informal Writing.**

### Assess

**Assessment Program**

**Prueba: Lectura,** p. 73

**Prueba: Escritura,** p. 74

**Online Assessment**

**my.hrw.com**

**Test Generator**

**Assess Differentiated Instruction** See the Differentiated Instruction CD-ROM.

## Resources

**Planning:**
Lesson Planner, pp. 62–63, 222–225
One-Stop Planner

**Presentation:**
Video Program, Videocassette 2
DVD Program
**Variedades**

**Practice:**
Activities for Communication, pp. 46, 61–62
Video Guide, pp. 24–25
Lab Book, pp. 4, 25–28, 66
Audio CD 4, Tr. 13–14
Pre-AP Instructional Resources
Pre-AP Audio CD 1, Trs. 13–16
Interactive Tutor, Disc 1
Teaching Transparencies
**Situación, Capítulo 4**
Picture Sequences, Chapter 4

## Teacher to Teacher

**Kristine Conlon**
Muscateen High School
Muscateen, IA

As a chapter project, I have the students make commercials like the ones in the video. They can use the Internet or magazine ads to find real Spanish or Latin American products and useful vocabulary. I tell them they only get fifteen minutes with the camera, so they have to be efficient. To add variety, I sometimes allow a group to imitate a **Comparaciones** cultural segment, followed by two or three commercials, using the format the regular video uses. 1.3, 3.2

Capítulo 4
Repaso

# Prepárate para el examen

Interactive TUTOR

CD 4, Tr. 13 See script on p. 137F. 1.2

**1** Escucha los diálogos y escoge la foto que corresponde a cada uno. **1.** B **2.** A **3.** C

A

B

C

**1 Vocabulario 1**
- asking about the latest news
- reacting to news

**pp. 140–145**

**2 Gramática 1**
- present progressive
- present perfect indicative
- present perfect subjunctive

**pp. 146–151**

**3 Vocabulario 2**
- commenting on food
- explaining and giving excuses

**pp. 154–159**

**2** Completa las oraciones con la forma correcta del verbo. 1.2

1. Raúl ____ (estar) ____ (organizar) la reunión del club deportivo. **1.** está, organizando
2. El amigo de Raúl ____ (seguir) ____ (trabajar) en el programa. **2.** sigue, trabajando
3. Raúl ya ____ (haber) ____ (reservar) un salón para la reunión. **3.** ha, reservado
4. Todos ____ (andar) ____ (decir) que mucha gente irá a la reunión. **4.** andan, diciendo
5. Yo ____ (estar) ____ (pensar) en no asistir a la reunión. **5.** estoy, pensando
6. Es bueno que mucha gente ____ (haber) ____ (decir) que quería ir. **6.** haya, dicho

**3** Lee las oraciones y escoge la frase del cuadro que mejor completa cada oración. 1.2

| | | |
|---|---|---|
| **se me olvidó** | **les falta algo** | **chuparse los dedos** |
| **se le fue la mano** | **se me acabó** | |

1. Marisol hizo un bizcocho de chocolate pero ____ con el azúcar y quedó muy dulce.
2. A los camarones ____ pero no sabemos qué les falta.
3. La sopa no tiene sabor porque ____ ponerle limón.
4. Las papas fritas están para ____. ¡Qué ricas!
5. El arroz no sabe a nada porque ____ la mantequilla.

**1.** se le fue la mano
**2.** les falta algo
**3.** se me olvidó
**4.** chuparse los dedos
**5.** se me acabó

## Oral Assessment

### Speaking Rubric

To assess the speaking activities in this section, you might use the following rubric. For additional speaking rubrics, see the Alternative Assessment section of the *Assessment Program.*

| Speaking Rubric | 4 | 3 | 2 | 1 |
|---|---|---|---|---|
| **Content** (Complete—Incomplete) | | | | |
| **Comprehension** (Total—Little) | | | | |
| **Comprehensibility** (Comprehensible—Incomprehensible) | | | | |
| **Accuracy** (Accurate—Seldom Accurate) | | | | |
| **Fluency** (Fluent—Not Fluent) | | | | |

18–20: A 16–17: B 14–15: C 12–13: D Under 12: F

**4** Completa las oraciones con la forma correcta del verbo. 1.2

Anoche yo __1__ (estar) __2__ (trabajar) en mi proyecto final cuando __3__ (llamar) mi amigo Rodrigo. Rodrigo __4__ (hablar) por media hora sin parar y __5__ (olvidar) terminar mi proyecto. Luego, me __6__ (dar) cuenta de la hora que era y __7__ (empezar) a trabajar. La computadora __8__ (estar) __9__ (grabar) mi archivo cuando se fue la luz. Le dije al profesor que __10__ (perder) el archivo.

**1.** estaba **2.** trabajando **3.** llamó **4.** habló **5.** se me olvidó **6.** di **7.** empecé **8.** estaba **9.** grabando **10.** se me perdió

**5** Contesta las preguntas. 1.2

1. Nombra un país latinoamericano donde se come el dulce de leche. Argentina
2. ¿Qué es una fruta bomba? La papaya
3. ¿Qué es el ceviche y cómo se prepara? **3.** Es un plato hecho con pescado crudo, limón, cebolla, sal y ají.
4. ¿Dónde se produce la mayor parte del azúcar? **4.** La mayor parte del azúcar se produce en las Américas.

CD 4, Tr. 14

**6** Escucha la conversación y escribe los cinco platos que se mencionan en una lista. 1.2 caldo de camarones, pollo frito, arroz con frijoles, ensalada de calabacín, salchichas con queso

Visit Holt Online
**go.hrw.com**
KEYWORD: EXP3 CH4
Chapter Self-test

**4 Gramática 2**
- preterite
- **se** + indirect object pronouns
- past progressive

**pp. 160–165**

**5 Cultura**
- **Comparaciones** **pp. 152–153**
- **Lectura cultural** **pp. 168–169**
- **Notas culturales** **pp. 143, 151, 157, 161, 165**

## Conversación

HOLT SoundBooth ONLINE RECORDING

**7** Role-play the following conversation with a partner. Partner A and Partner B are former classmates, getting caught up at a reunion. 1.1, 1.2

Partner A: Greet your partner and ask how the first year of college went.

Partner B: Respond, then ask your partner what he or she is up to.

Partner A: Respond, then tell your partner about what some other classmates have done lately.

Partner B: React with surprise. Then ask where Lupe is.

Partner A: Explain that she was planning on coming when her boss called her. She had to work and couldn't come.

Partner B: Express your disappointment. Ask if your partner wants to go get something to eat.

Partner A: Explain why you don't like the food at the reunion. Suggest that you both go out to eat later.

Partner B: Agree with your partner's suggestion, suggest a restaurant, and describe a dish you like there.

### 6 Script

—¿Ya preparaste el plato que vas a llevar a la muestra de comida internacional?
—Sí, el plato que preparé sabe delicioso. Preparé un caldo de camarones. Traté de preparar un pollo frito pero se me quemó.
—¡Qué horror! Pues, fíjate que yo también tuve algunos problemas. Iba a llevar un plato de arroz con frijoles pero se me fue la mano con la sal y la comida salió demasiado salada.
—¿Ah, sí?
—Sí. Y luego preparé una ensalada de calabacín, con pepino, lechuga y coliflor. Me salió muy bien la ensalada pero cuando fui a meterla en el refrigerador, se me fue el plato de la mano y se cayó al piso.
—¡No me digas!
—Entonces tuve que hacer algo rápido porque no tenía mucho tiempo. Así que preparé unas salchichas con queso.

### 7 Answers

Below is a sample student conversation.

(A) —Hola, Adriana, ¿cómo has estado? ¿Cómo te fue el primer año en la universidad?
(B) —Hola, Damián, mucho gusto en verte. Pues, todo bien. Me gustó mucho el primer año y he decidido seguir estudiando ciencias. ¿Y tú? ¿Qué andas haciendo en estos días?
(A) —Estoy tomando unos cursos en la universidad. Para el verano voy a estar trabajando con mi padre en la tienda. Oye, ayer vi a Lourdes y Miguel. ¿Sabes que se han casado?
(B) —¡No me digas! Pensaba que Miguel salía con Lupe. ¿Qué sabes de Lupe?
(A) —Lupe está bien, tiene un trabajo estupendo. Ella iba a venir, pero la llamó su jefe. Tuvo que trabajar esta noche.
(B) —¡Qué pena! Bueno... ¿tienes hambre? ¿Quieres comer algo?
(A) —Pues, la verdad es que la comida aquí no me gusta. A los sándwiches le faltan sabor y el bizcocho está muy seco. ¿Por qué no salimos a comer después de la reunión?
(B) —De acuerdo. Podemos ir al nuevo restaurante caribeño, si quieres. Sirven un puerco asado que está para chuparse los dedos.

## Conversación

### Additional Speaking Practice

For additional speaking practice, use the *Picture Sequences Transparency* for Chapter 4. Use the Speaking Rubric on the preceding page to evaluate their performance. You may also wish to use the Interviews and Role-Plays in the *Activities for Communication* book

### Pre-AP Practice

**7** In the Level 3 *Pre-AP Instructional Resources* you will find an alternative version of Activity 7. The following resources in that book will help you prepare students for the AP Language Exam:

- Blackline masters, pp. 30, 40, 50
- Pre-AP Audio CD 1, Trs. 13–16
- Scripts and answers, pp. 57–75

# Prepárate para el examen

## Grammar Review

For more practice with the grammar topics in this chapter, see the *Grammar Tutor,* the *Interactive Tutor,* or the *Cuaderno de vocabulario y gramática.*

GramaVisión

## Heritage Speakers

Remind your heritage speakers that the perfect tenses in Spanish and English share some similarities. Whereas we use the verb *to have* as the helping verb in English, we use forms of the verb **haber** as the helping verb in Spanish. In both instances, the auxiliary verb begins with the letter *h.*

## Teacher to Teacher

**Maritza and Robert Furillo**
Franklin Middle School
Columbus, OH

Have small groups of students create a board game by combining all the vocabulary and grammar from the chapter. The game can resemble Monopoly®, Life®, or any other game with which the students are familiar. The rules should be simple and easy to follow. Words on the game board, any game cards, and the rules should all be written in Spanish. The only part of this project that can be done in English is the explanation of how the group came up with the ideas for creating the game board and the basic object of the game. 1.2

**Gramática 1**
- present progressive
  **pp. 146–147**
- present perfect indicative
  **pp. 148–149**
- present perfect subjunctive
  **pp. 150–151**

## Repaso de Gramática 1

The **present progressive** is used to describe actions that are in progress at the present time. It is most often used with **estar + present participle** but can also be used with **andar** and **seguir.**

| | |
|---|---|
| Carmen **está leyendo** un libro. | *Carmen is reading a book.* |
| **Sigo jugando** al fútbol. | *I'm still playing soccer.* |

The **present perfect indicative** is used to say what has or hasn't happened in a period of time up to the present or to talk about something that happened very recently.

| | |
|---|---|
| No **he hablado** con Ana. | *I haven't spoken with Ana.* |

An **object pronoun** always goes before the form of **haber** in the **present perfect.**

| | |
|---|---|
| El entrenador **nos ha puesto** a correr todos los días. | *The coach has made us run every day.* |

Use the **present perfect subjunctive** to express an emotion, judgement, doubt, or hope about something that has happened. It is formed with the subjunctive of **haber + past participle.**

| | |
|---|---|
| Me alegra que los Tigres **hayan ganado** el partido. | *I'm glad that the Tigers have won the game.* |

**Gramática 2**
- preterite
  **pp. 160–161**
- **se** + indirect object pronouns
  **pp. 162–163**
- past progressive
  **pp. 164–165**

## Repaso de Gramática 2

The **preterite** is used to show that actions happened at specific points in the past. Some phrases (**al + infinitive, en cuanto**) mark the beginning of an event. Verbs like **conocer, saber, (no) querer** have different uses in the preterite.

Use **se + indirect object pronoun + verb** to talk about unintentional events. The **indirect object pronoun** refers to the person the event happened to. The **verb** agrees with the object(s) involved, and is always in the third person singular or plural.

| | |
|---|---|
| **Se me quedaron** los libros en casa. | *I left my books at home.* |

The **past progressive** describes past actions in progress. It is formed with the imperfect of **estar** + the present participle of the main verb. The **preterite** is used with the past progressive to describe an interrupting or completed event within that setting.

| | |
|---|---|
| Paulina **estaba durmiendo** cuando **sonó** el teléfono. | *Paulina was sleeping when the telephone rang.* |

## Chapter Review

**Teacher Management System**
To access, launch the program, type "admin" in the password area, and press RETURN. For more details, log on to www.hrw.com/CDROMTUTOR.

Create a variety of puzzles to review chapter vocabulary.

**DVD Program**

**Interactive Tutor**

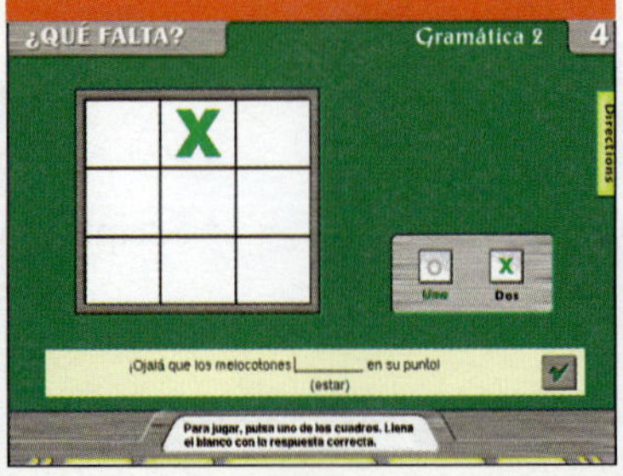


**PuzzlePro**

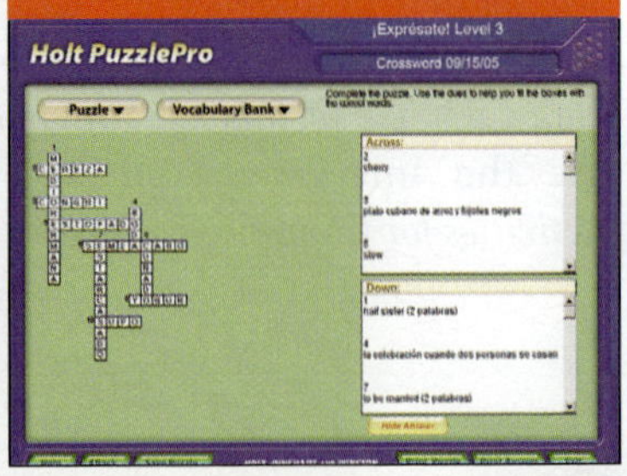

HOLT SoundBooth ONLINE RECORDING

## Repaso de Vocabulario 1

### Asking about the latest news

| | |
|---|---|
| el (anillo de) compromiso | *engagement (ring)* |
| casarse (con) | *to marry* |
| comprometerse | *to get engaged* |
| la cuñada | *sister-in-law* |
| el cuñado | *brother-in-law* |
| dar a luz | *to give birth* |
| divorciado(a)(s) | *divorced* |
| divorciarse (de) | *to divorce* |
| el divorcio | *divorce* |
| estar casado(a)(s) | *to be married* |
| Fíjate que se ha casado. | *Get this: he/she got married.* |
| el funeral | *funeral* |
| graduarse (de) | *to graduate (from)* |
| la hermanastra | *stepsister* |
| el hermanastro | *stepbrother* |
| la madrastra | *stepmother* |
| la medio hermana | *half sister* |
| el medio hermano | *half brother* |
| nacer | *to be born* |
| el padrastro | *stepfather* |
| Pues, sigue trabajando... | *Well, he's/she's still working . . .* |
| ¿Qué anda haciendo...? | *What's . . . up to?* |
| ¿Qué me cuentas de...? | *What can you tell me about . . . ?* |
| ¿Qué sabes de...? | *What do you know about . . . ?* |
| la reunión familiar | *family reunion* |
| Según tengo entendido, ... | *From what I understand, . . .* |
| separado(a) | *separated* |
| separarse (de) | *to separate* |
| la suegra | *mother-in-law* |
| el suegro | *father-in-law* |

### Reacting to news

| | |
|---|---|
| Me has dejado boquiabierto(a). | *You've left me speechless.* |
| ¡No me digas! | *You don't say!* |
| ¡No me lo puedo creer! | *I can't believe it!* |
| Qué pena que se hayan... | *What a shame that they have . . .* |
| ¡Qué sorpresa que se hayan...! | *What a surprise that they have . . . !* |

## Repaso de Vocabulario 2

### Commenting on food

| | |
|---|---|
| el aguacate | *avocado* |
| Al (A la)... le falta sabor, pero no sé qué le falta. | *The . . . lacks flavor, but I don't know what's missing.* |
| el apio | *celery* |
| el bizcocho de chocolate | *chocolate cake* |
| el calabacín | *zucchini* |
| el camarón, los camarones | *shrimp* |
| la cereza | *cherry* |
| los chícharos | *peas* |
| el coliflor | *cauliflower* |
| la crema (agria) | *(sour) cream* |
| el dulce de coco | *coconut candy* |
| Está para chuparse los dedos. | *It's good enough to lick your fingers.* |
| Está pasada la leche. | *The milk has gone bad.* |
| los frijoles | *beans* |
| la langosta | *lobster* |
| la lima | *lime* |
| el limón | *lemon* |
| las pasas | *raisins* |
| el pavo (con relleno) | *turkey (with stuffing)* |
| el pepino | *cucumber* |
| el pollo frito | *fried chicken* |
| el puerco asado | *roast pork* |
| ¡Qué asco! | *That's disgusting!* |
| Sabe delicioso(a). | *It tastes delicious.* |
| Se me hace la boca agua. | *It makes my mouth water.* |
| la salchicha | *sausage* |
| la sandía | *watermelon* |
| la toronja | *grapefruit* |
| el yogur | *yogurt* |

### Explaining and giving excuses

| | |
|---|---|
| El/La... no sabe a nada. | *The . . . doesn't taste like anything.* |
| El/La... está salado(a)/picante. | *The . . . is salty/spicy.* |
| El/La... está seco(a)/no está muy dulce. | *The . . . is dry/isn't very sweet.* |
| Es que se me acabó... | *It's just that I ran out of . . .* |
| Es que se me olvidó ponerle... | *It's just that I forgot to add . . .* |
| Se me fue la mano con... | *I got carried away with . . .* |

Prepárate para el examen

Capítulo 4

# Prepárate para el examen

### Vocabulary Review

For more practice with the vocabulary in this chapter, see the *Interactive Tutor* or the *Cuaderno de vocabulario y gramática.*

### Online Edition

Students might use the online textbook to hear the **Vocabulario** items.

### Game

**Riesgo** In this game you provide the answer **(Es una plato de frijoles y arroz, típico de Cuba.)** and students must come up with the appropriate question. **(¿Qué es el congrí?)** On the board, label the columns of a three-by-three grid with categories **(cultura, comida, familia).** For each category, prepare five answer cards. Write the answer on one side of the card and an assigned point value (25, 50, 75) on the other. Tape the cards in the grid squares, number side up. Divide the class into teams. Teams take turns selecting a grid square. Remove the card and read the answer. If the team formulates a reasonable question within a set time limit, they earn the points. The team with the highest score wins.

1.2

### Online Edition

### Transparency: Vocabulario

### Transparency: Situación

### Assess

**Assessment Program**

**Examen: Capítulo 4,** pp. 241–246

Audio CD 3, Trs. 17–18

**Examen oral:** p. 252

Alternative Assessment, pp. 376, 388, 400

**Online Assessment**

**my.hrw.com**

**Test Generator**

**Assess** **Differentiated Instruction** See the Differentiated Instruction CD-ROM.

## Resources

**Planning:**

Lesson Planner, pp. 63, 224–225

One-Stop Planner

**Presentation:**

Teaching Transparencies
Fine Art, Chapter 4

**Practice:**

Cuaderno de actividades, pp. 39–40

Lab Book, p. 4

## Más práctica

After students do Activity 2, have them write a letter about their family like the one Martín wrote. Tell them to include information about each family member, their courses at school, favorite activities, and favorite foods. Encourage them to look at the **Repaso de Vocabulario** and the **Repaso de Gramática** from Chapters 1–4 and to include as many vocabulary words from each chapter as they can. 1.3

Repaso cumulativo

# Integración
## capítulos 1–4

**1** Explica cómo prepararías estos platos y qué ingredientes usarías. 1.3

1.

2.

3.

4.

**2** Esto es parte de un ensayo que Martín escribió acerca de su familia para la clase de español. Lee su ensayo y contesta **cierto** o **falso** a las siguientes preguntas. 1.2

> Tengo dos hermanastros. El mayor, Luis, estudia en la universidad y no vive en casa. Carlos es de mi edad; de hecho, él nació dos d as antes que yo. Vamos al mismo colegio y tomamos una clase de geografa juntos. Es mi hermanastro pero también es mi mejor amigo. Cuando tengo problemas, me da consejos y siempre puedo confiar en él. Es más, somos fanáticos de los deportes y jugamos al fútbol los sábados. Nos encanta jugar a los videojuegos también. A veces nos peleamos como todos los hermanos, pero por lo general lo pasamos muy bien.

1. Luis trabaja en la universidad como profesor. falso
2. Martín nació dos días después de Carlos. cierto
3. Martín y Carlos van a la misma clase de geometría. falso
4. Martín y Carlos son hermanastros. cierto
5. Martín siente que se puede confiar en Carlos. cierto
6. A Martín y a Carlos les gusta jugar al fútbol y a los videojuegos. cierto
7. Martín y Carlos se la pasan peleando. falso

## Culture Project

Have students create a Caribbean cookbook. Ask them to find five recipes from each Caribbean country. They should copy the recipes and try to find a photo of each dish to include on the page. Have them arrange the recipes by country and put them together in a book. Then have students compare the recipes they found for each country. What are the similarities and differences? Are there specific ingredients that are used in many of the recipes? What are they? Have students investigate whether the ingredients used in Caribbean dishes are native to the region and which ingredients were introduced to the region from Spain. You might also want students to mention if these dishes are eaten during holidays or special occasions. Ask students to share their cookbooks with the class. 2.2

# Repaso cumulativo



**3** En grupos de tres, hablen acerca de lo que les gusta hacer con sus amigos los fines de semana. Digan adónde les gusta ir, qué hacen, qué comen, etc. Luego, consideren qué hacen los jóvenes en los países latinoamericanos que han estudiado ustedes. Imaginen que viven en un país latinoamericano. ¿Qué harían ustedes con sus amigos en ese país? Expliquen. **1.1, 4.2**

**4** Observa la pintura y escribe por lo menos ocho oraciones sobre lo que ves. En tus oraciones debes contestar las siguientes preguntas: ¿Dónde está la familia? ¿Qué crees que hacen? ¿Qué te sugiere el título de esta obra? **1.3**

Baile en la playa, 2003 by Julio Marcano, 45" × 35.5", acrylic on canvas. © Julio Marcano/Courtesy of Galería Fosil Arte

***Baile en la playa*** **de Julio Marcano**

**5** Imagina que acabas de regresar a casa de una visita a la República Dominicana, donde visitaste a un(a) amigo(a) y conociste a su familia. Escribe un párrafo sobre los platos que probaste y cómo se hacen. **1.3**

**6** **Situación** Conviertan el salón de clases en un restaurante. Escojan a dos o tres personas para ser meseros y una persona para ser cocinero. Con el vocabulario y la gramática que han aprendido, túrnense para pedir la comida y decirles a los meseros si les gustó la comida o no. **1.1, 1.2**

## Fine Art Connection

This painting by Julio Marcano is titled ***Baile en la playa.*** Marcano is a landscape painter from Puerto Rico. He graduated from the **Escuela Central de Artes Visuales** and participated in the annual exposition in the **Escuela Central** for six consecutive years. Today his art is displayed in various distinguished art galleries on the island. In his paintings, he tries to capture the personality of the Puerto Rican people using vivid colors to recreate the refreshing sensation created by typical landscapes of the island.

### Analyzing

Ask students how they would describe the personality of the island as depicted in **Baile en la playa.** Have them describe the atmosphere of the scene.

1. **¿Qué están haciendo las personas en la pintura?**
2. **¿Cómo están vestidas las personas?**
3. **¿Cómo es el clima en este lugar?**
4. **¿Cómo son las casas que ves en la pintura?**
5. **¿Qué instrumentos ves en la pintura?** **1.2**

### Extension

Have students research some of Marcano's landscape paintings. Ask them to write a one-paragraph analysis of one of the paintings. **3.1**

## ACTFL Performance Standards

The activities in Chapter 4 target the different communicative modes as described in the Standards.

| | | |
|---|---|---|
| **Interpersonal** | Two-way communication using receptive skills and productive skills | **Comunicación (SE),** pp. 143, 145, 147, 149, 151, 157, 159, 161, 163, 165<br>**Comunicación (TE),** pp. 143, 145, 149, 157, 163, 167<br>**Conversación,** p. 175<br>**Situación,** p. 179 |
| **Interpretive** | One-way communication using receptive skills | **Comunicación (SE),** pp. 145, 147, 149, 151, 163<br>**Comunicación (TE),** pp. 159, 161, 165<br>**Novela en video**, pp. 166–167<br>**Leamos,** pp. 170–172<br>**Conversación,** p. 175 |
| **Presentational** | One-way communication using productive skills | **Comunicación (SE),** pp. 143, 151, 157, 159, 161, 165<br>**Comunicación (TE),** pp. 147, 151 |

## Resources

**Planning:**

Lesson Planner, p. xv

One-Stop Planner

**Presentation:**

Teaching Transparencies **Mapa 5, Mapa 6**

Video Program, Videocassette 3
DVD Program **GeoVisión**

**Practice:**

Video Guide, pp. 29–30

Lab Book, pp. 5, 69

Interactive Tutor, Disc 1

## VIDEO OPTIONS

- **VideoCultura**
- **VideoNovela**
- **Variedades**
- **GramaVisión**

## Pre-AP Practice

**AP Benchmark:** Recognize cultural elements implicit in oral and written texts.

**Focus:** Cultural Products (**arquitectura**)

- SE, p. 182, **Época precolombina**
- TE, p. 183, **La arquitectura,** History Link
- TE, p. 185, Cultures: Products and Perspectives

GeoVisión

**Capítulos 5 y 6**

▲ **Las montañas Chisos,** en el Parque Nacional Big Bend en Texas, son la única cordillera que se encuentra en su totalidad dentro de un parque nacional en Estados Unidos.

# Geocultura
## El Suroeste y el Norte de México

◄ **Ellen Ochoa** (1958–) de California es doctora en ingeniería eléctrica y fue la primera mujer latina que llegó a ser astronauta y a navegar en el espacio.

◄ **La Fiesta Internacional de Globos** en Albuquerque, Nuevo México, atrae a aficionados de todo el mundo cada octubre.

### Almanaque

**Área del suroeste**
Partes de California, Arizona, Utah, Nevada, Nuevo México, Texas y el norte de México

**Idiomas principales**
inglés, español

**Industrias importantes**
agricultura, tecnología, turismo, recursos naturales

### ¿Sabías que...?

**Promesas de ciudades doradas trajeron al explorador español Francisco Vásquez de Coronado al territorio del suroeste en 1540. Coronado nunca encontró ni oro ni plata. Esto resultó en que los españoles abandonaran la región por casi cuarenta años. En 1583 el español Antonio de Espejo tomó posesión del territorio de los hopi en nombre de Felipe II, el rey de España.**

## Background Information

### History

The Spanish claimed what is now the western United States down to Central America as part of **Nueva España**. In the late 16th century, Spanish priests established the first **misiones** to teach the Catholic religion and Spanish culture. These territories remained under colonial control until 1821. Anglo settlers established a formal colony in Texas soon after. Texas declared independence in 1835 and was annexed by the U.S. in 1845. In 1846, war broke out between Mexico and the U.S., and Mexico lost half of its national territory in 1848.

### Geography

**The Southwest and Northern Mexico** is an enormous area of land containing a wide variety of ecosystems. There are coastal, forest, desert, and mountain ecosystems in this region. The largest desert in this region is the Sonora Desert, which includes a part of California, southern Arizona, and most of the Mexican state of Sonora. Northern Mexico is mountainous, with two major mountain chains: the **Sierra Madre Oriental,** which runs through the eastern part of the country into west Texas, and the **Sierra Madre Occidental** in the west, which extends to Arizona and California.

# El Suroeste

▼ **Eloy Rodríguez** (1947–), un tejano de herencia mexicana, es un investigador científico reconocido por haber inventado un campo de estudios completamente nuevo, la zoofarmacognosía. Él investiga la manera en que las plantas y los animales se curan cuando no están saludables.

▲ **El Río Grande** nace en las montañas de Colorado, pasa por Nuevo México, Texas y México y desemboca en el Golfo de México. Trece millones de personas viven en la cuenca del río y dependen de sus aguas.

◄ Científicos de todo el mundo trabajaron en el **Laboratorio Nacional de Los Álamos** en Nuevo México para crear la primera bomba nuclear del mundo.

► El **desierto de Sonora** tiene una extensión de 310.800 kilómetros cuadrados, desde Sonora, México, hasta Arizona y el sur de California. El cactus Saguaro, una especie única de este desierto, puede llegar hasta 50 pies de altura y alberga muchos animales desérticos. Tarda 75 años en echar su primer brazo.

Miles de personas cruzan **la frontera** entre Estados Unidos y México cada día, algunos para trabajar y otros para hacer turismo. Tijuana, México, con San Diego, California, y Juárez, México, con El Paso, Texas, son las zonas metropolitanas más grandes en la frontera de México y Estados Unidos.

## Atlas INTERACTIVO MUNDIAL

Have students use the interactive atlas at **go.hrw.com.**

**Map Activities**

1. Have students look at the map of the U.S. Southwest and Northern Mexico and name the U.S. states in this region. **(California, Nevada, Arizona, New Mexico, Colorado, Texas)**
2. Have students locate and name the deserts and rivers on the map. **(Desierto de Sonora, Desierto de Chihuahua, Río Grande/Río Bravo del Norte)**
3. Have students locate and name the major U.S. and Mexico border cities. **(San Diego, Tijuana, El Paso, Ciudad Juárez)**

3.1

## Comparisons

### Language to Language

The English language has adopted several words from Spanish, and many are commonly used today. One example is **rodeo,** which comes from **rodear** *(to surround).* These rodeos took place each year, and herds of cattle were rounded up and branded. The lasso, used to rope cattle, comes from the Spanish word **lazo.** Other words commonly used in U.S. English are **rancho, piñata, fiesta, taco, siesta, tortilla.** Have students think of other Spanish words used in English in their communities.

4.1

## ¿Sabías que... ?

Students might be interested in knowing the following facts about the U. S. Southwest and Northern Mexico.

- The San Ysidro-Tijuana border crossing near San Diego is twenty-four lanes wide.
- Grand Canyon National Park has a total of 1,217,403 acres and about 4 million people visit each year.
- The Rio Grande is 1,885 miles (3,033 km) long and covers an area of 180,000 square miles.
- Ciudad Juárez and El Paso have a combined population of about 2 million people, making it second in size to Tijuana and San Diego in this region.

## Preguntas

1. **¿Qué estudió Ellen Ochoa? (ingeniería eléctrica)**
2. **¿En dónde se hace la Fiesta Internacional de Globos? (en Albuquerque)**
3. **¿Qué estudio nuevo inventó Eloy Rodríguez? (la zoofarmacognosía)**
4. **¿Dónde desemboca el Río Grande? (en el Golfo de México)**
5. **¿Qué pasó en el laboratorio de los Álamos? (la creación de la bomba nuclear)**
6. **¿Cuántos años tarda el cactus Saguaro en que nazca su primer brazo? (75 años)**

1.2, 3.1

# La historia del Suroeste y del Norte de México

ÉPOCA PRECOLOMBINA | 1500 | 1750 | 1800

## Teaching Suggestion

Tell students that the Pueblo people of New Mexico had lived in the Southwest for centuries before Europeans came to the area. The indigenous tribes were given the name **Pueblo** by Spanish explorers who saw the adobe homes of the indigenous tribes clustered together in groups along the northern Rio Grande and were reminded of their own **pueblos.** The Spanish named each Pueblo settlement they came upon in honor of a Catholic saint. The Pueblo people are not one tribe, but 19 separate cultural groups, each with their own government and religion. A common link that they share is language. One of five Pueblo languages is spoken in each community. On the map, have students locate pueblos with saints' names.

## Answers

**Época precolombina:** Answers will vary.
**1532–1536:** Answers will vary. Possible answer: A lo mejor sintió extraño por las diferencias entre su cultura europea y la cultura nueva de los indígenas.
**1769:** Answers will vary.
**1810–1821:** Answers will vary.
**1836–1845:** La entrada a la unión estadounidense ayudó a garantizar su soberanía.
**1846–1848:** El tratado del 10 de diciembre de 1898 cuando España cedió Cuba, Puerto Rico y las Islas Filipinas a Estados Unidos
**1909:** El gobierno estadounidense obligó a la nación Apache a vivir en una reservación.
**1962–presente:** Answers will vary.

### Época precolombina

Los grupos indígenas de la región de Santa Fé y Taos vivían en estructuras de adobe, o *pueblos.* **El Pueblo de Taos** ha cambiado poco desde la fecha en que lo descubrieron los españoles en 1540. **Investiga cómo viven los habitantes del Pueblo de Taos hoy. ¿En qué se diferencia su vida de la de sus antepasados?** 3.1

### 1769 1.3, 2.2

Durante los siglos XVIII y XIX los españoles construyeron misiones y presidios en el suroeste. **La Misión de San Diego de Alcalá** fue establecida en 1769 en San Diego, California. **¿Has visitado una misión o un presidio fundado por los españoles? ¿Cómo es?**

### 1.3 1532–1536

**Álvar Núñez Cabeza de Vaca** fue uno de los primeros exploradores europeos de la región de Texas. Vivió varios años entre los grupos indígenas de esta región y describió sus experiencias en un libro. En este cuadro, saca la punta de una flecha del pecho de un indígena. **¿Qué crees que sintió Cabeza de Vaca al vivir con los indígenas por primera vez?**

### 1.3 1810–1821

Con el **Grito de Dolores,** *¡Viva México!,* el padre **Miguel Hidalgo** montó la primera rebelión contra los españoles en la madrugada del 16 de septiembre de 1810. México ganó su independencia de España en 1821. Hoy día se celebra **el día de la independencia en México** con una representación del Grito de Dolores, actuado por el presidente de la república desde su balcón del palacio nacional. **¿Has visto una representación pública de un evento histórico? ¿Qué representaba?**

## Core Instruction

### TEACHING LA HISTORIA

1. Point out the timeline at the top of the page. **(1 min.)**
2. Go over each point on the timeline with students. **(5 min.)**
3. Have students read captions individually or as a group. Help students with any unfamiliar vocabulary. **(8 min.)**
4. Call on volunteers to read the questions at the end of each caption to the class. **(3 min.)**
5. Have students answer the questions for each caption as a class. Help students as needed. **(10 min.)**

**¿Sabías que...?**
Con el tratado de Guadalupe Hidalgo en 1848 cerca de 77.000 mexicanos se convirtieron en estadounidenses de la noche a la mañana.

**Visit Holt Online**
**go.hrw.com**
KEYWORD: EXP3 CH5
Photo Tour

1850 1900 1950 2000

© North Wind Picture Archives

**1846–1848** 3.1
En 1846 las tropas estadounidenses llegaron al río Bravo del Norte para defender su nuevo estado de Texas. México todavía disputaba la frontera con Texas lo cual resultó en la **Guerra entre Estados Unidos y México**. En 1848 México se rindió y firmó el **tratado de Guadalupe Hidalgo,** cediendo los territorios de California, Nuevo México, Arizona y partes de Colorado, Nevada y Utah a Estados Unidos. **Investiga en la biblioteca o en Internet si hubo otros tratados en que Estados Unidos ganó territorio de otro país. Describe uno.**

**1909** 3.1
**Gerónimo,** de la nación Apache, fue el último líder indígena en rendirse al gobierno estadounidense después de enfrentarse contra una tropa de más de 5000 hombres en 1886. Murió prisionero de guerra, después de 23 años de encarcelamiento. **Investiga en Internet qué le pasó a la nación Apache de Gerónimo.**

1.3
**1962–presente**
**César Chávez** (1927–1993) y **Dolores Huerta** (1930–) fundaron la Asociación Nacional de Campesinos (más tarde conocida como Los Campesinos Unidos) en 1962. Promovieron la identidad chicana para llamar a acción a otros grupos de hispanohablantes. **¿Qué significa *chicano* para ti, hoy día?**

**1836–1845** 3.1
En marzo de 1836 las tropas mexicanas del general Santa Anna derrotaron completamente a los rebeldes tejanos en **la batalla del Álamo**. Un mes después de la derrota, los tejanos sorprendieron a las tropas de Santa Anna en **San Jacinto** y ganaron la batalla. Con esta victoria la República de Texas logró su independencia de México. En 1845 Texas fue anexado a Estados Unidos. **Investiga qué ventajas ganó Texas al unirse con Estados Unidos.**

## Interdisciplinary Links

### La arquitectura

**History Link** In the early 1700's, the Spanish built five missions along the San Antonio River in Texas. San Antonio de Valero, now known as the Alamo, was built in 1718. The Alamo is now a museum. The missions of San José, San Juan, Concepción, and Espada were built soon after. Except for the Alamo, these missions are still in use and open to the public. Have students investigate how Spanish culture influenced the U.S. Southwest. What other cultures have influenced regions in the U.S.? 3.1

### El arte

**Art Link** Mexican independence is a theme many Mexican artists have portrayed in their works. For example, Diego Rivera painted Mexican heroes from the war of independence such as Miguel Hidalgo y Costilla, and José María Morelos y Pavón. The scenes depicted in his murals give us a good idea of what life was like during the Mexican fight for independence. Why are these works still important today as symbols of national identity? How can they teach future generations the history of their country? 2.2

## Cultures

### Products and Perspectives

**Food** Southwestern cuisine is a blend of Hispanic and Native American cultures. Most Southwestern dishes include corn tortillas, pinto beans, cheese, and **chile** peppers. A spicy southwestern dish, **carne adovada,** is baked strips of pork marinated in red chile. **Chorizo,** or spicy pork sausage, is also common in this region. *Piki* bread is an extra flat pancake made from boiling finely-ground corn dough. The bread is typically eaten with stew. Have students create a menu for a meal of Southwestern cuisine. 2.2

### ¿Comprendes?

You can use the following questions to check students' comprehension of the **Geocultura.**

1. **¿De qué están hechas las estructuras de Taos? (de adobe)**
2. **¿Qué partes del suroeste exploró Cabeza de Vaca? (Texas, Nuevo México y Arizona)**
3. **¿En qué año se estableció la Misión de San Diego de Alcalá? (en 1769)**
4. **¿En qué fecha se celebra el día de la independencia de México hoy día? (el 16 de septiembre)**
5. **¿En dónde le sorprendieron a Santa Anna las tropas tejanas? (en San Jacinto)**
6. **¿Cómo se llama el tratado que puso fin a la guerra entre México y Estados Unidos ? (el tratado de Guadalupe Hidalgo)**
7. **¿Qué promovió César Chávez? (la identidad chicana)** 1.2, 3.1

# El arte del Suroeste y del Norte de México

ÉPOCA PRECOLOMBINA — 1800 — 1850

**1.500 A.C.–700 D.C.**
Estas figuras, de Galisteo, Nuevo México, fueron pintadas hace miles de años por los Anasazi, uno de **los primeros grupos indígenas de la región.** Figuras como éstas se encuentran en las piedras y los cañones del suroeste. **¿En qué se diferencian estas figuras de las imágenes encontradas** 3.1 **en Altamira, España?**

2.2, 3.1 **1797**
Los españoles dejaron sus huellas en la arquitectura del suroeste. **La Misión San Xavier del Bac,** construida en 1797 en Tucson, Arizona, es un ejemplo del estilo barroco del siglo XVIII. **Compara el estilo de esta misión con otras misiones que hayas visto.**

2.2, 3.1 **Siglos XVIII–XIX**
La palabra *adobe* se refiere a ladrillos de arcilla secados al sol o a estructuras construidas de este material. **La arquitectura de adobe** del suroeste y del norte de México es una síntesis de formas indígenas y españolas y de métodos de construcción usados durante el período colonial. **¿Por qué crees que utilizan el adobe en la arquitectura del suroeste?**

1.3 **1887–198**
En 1929 la pintora **Georgia O'Keeffe** viajó a Taos, Nuev México, y quedó enamorada de la región. O'Keeffe continu pintando en el suroeste, revelando las bellezas de la región **Describe a Georgia O'Keeffe en esta foto y busca un de sus obras en la biblioteca o en Internet**

## Comparisons

### Comparing and Contrasting

In modern Pueblo society, women have the tasks of making pottery and helping with the construction of homes, and the men are weavers. Women have an important role in both Eastern and Western Pueblo societies. In Western Pueblo culture, the women own the houses and the land. Family clans and religious figures are important for both Eastern and Western Pueblo societies. The Spanish introduced the concept of elected government officials to the Pueblo people. Today, the Pueblo elect tribal councils for tribal affairs. Ask students to brainstorm the benefits of electing a tribal council to rule the people. Do they think age plays an important role in electing officials? Have students compare this form of government with their local government.
4.2

## Answers

**1.500 A.C.–700 D.C.:** Estas pinturas son de personas y las de Altamira, España, son de animales.
**1797:** Answers will vary.
**XVIII–XIX:** Utilizan el adobe en la construcción en el suroeste porque la arcilla para hacer los ladrillos es abundante. El clima es otro factor en el uso de adobe.
**1887–1986:** Answers will vary.
**1970:** Answers will vary.
**1986:** El arte narrativo cuenta una historia. Un ejemplo es que el papá está partiendo la sandía para los niños.
**1998:** Answers will vary.
**Presente:** Una alfombra hecha a máquina es uniforme y no tiene mucha variedad.

## Presentation

### TEACHING EL ARTE

1. Have students look at the rock paintings in Galisteo. Tell students that A.C. stands for **Antes de Cristo,** and D.C. stands for **Después de Cristo.** **(2 min.)**
2. Have students look at the adobe construction and the Spanish mission. Have them look for any similarities between the two. **(2 min.)**
3. Have students look at each piece of artwork while you read the captions. **(5 min.)**
4. Have students look at ***Sandía*** on page 185. Have them describe as a class what they see. **(5 min.)**
5. Have students look at the sculptures and the mural on page 185. What similarities can students see? **(3 min.)**
6. Read the questions following each caption. Call on volunteers to answer the questions. **(10 min.)**

**¿Sabías que...?**
Se puede llevar casi todo un año para tejer una gran alfombra tradicional návajo.

**Visit Holt Online**
**go.hrw.com**
KEYWORD: EXP3 CH5
Photo Tour

1900 — 1950 — 2000

**3.1 1970**
Desde 1970, el muralista **David Tineo** contribuye sus talentos a la comunidad de Tucson, Arizona. El mural *Para los niños,* como muchas de sus obras, fue pintado con la colaboración de jóvenes de la comunidad. **¿Hay murales en tu ciudad? ¿Cuentan una historia o representan algo simbólico?**

**3.1 1986**
***Sandía*** fue pintado en 1986 por **Carmen Lomas Garza** (1948–). El arte narrativo de Lomas Garza refleja la niñez de la artista en Kingsville, Texas, con su familia mexicoamericana. Garza retrata los recuerdos alegres de la vida cotidiana. **¿Qué significa arte narrativo? ¿Puedes dar un ejemplo de lo narrativo en este cuadro?**

**Presente** 1.3
Hoy día los **artistas návajos del suroeste** tejen alfombras tradicionales con las mismas técnicas de sus antepasados. La artista convierte la lana en hilo que usará para tejer una preciosa alfombra. **¿En qué se diferencian las alfombras tradicionales de las que son hechas a máquina?**

**3.1 1998**
**Mario Torero,** de San Diego, California, es un activista y artista que crea murales, cuadros y esculturas, como *Voladores,* que reflejan el espíritu mexicoamericano contemporáneo. El arte de Torero tiene influencia del surrealismo. **¿Qué efecto crees que puede tener el arte en revitalizar un barrio?**

## Cultures

### Products and Perspectives

**Homes** Some homes in the U.S. Southwest have Spanish and Mexican influence. The roofing tiles commonly used in homes, called **tejados,** are curved, and made with clay or brick material. This type of roofing is common in Spain and Latin America. Some homes are painted pink, light yellow, blue, and other colors common in Mexican homes. Other homes may have fences or brick walls around them, which is also common in Mexico. Why do students think that there is Mexican influence in the U.S. Southwest? Have students find a photo or illustration of a home in the U.S. Southwest with Spanish or Mexican influence and describe it to a partner. 2.2

### ¿Comprendes?

1. **¿Quiénes pintaron las figuras en las piedras y los cañones? (los anasazi)**
2. **¿Cuál es el estilo de La Misión San Xavier del Bac? (barroco)**
3. **¿Cómo se hacen los ladrillos de adobe? (secar la arcilla al sol)**
4. **¿Cuándo llegó Georgia O'Keeffe al suroeste? (en 1929)**
5. **¿De qué trata *Sandía?* (los recuerdos alegres de la vida cotidiana)**
6. **¿Con qué se hacen las alfombras de los artistas navajos? (con hilo hecho de lana)** 1.2, 3.1

## Interdisciplinary Links

### La historia

**History Link** The image on the Mexican flag dates to Aztec times. According to Aztec legend, the **Mexica** tribe set out from an unknown location to build its capital city in a place where they found an eagle perched on a cactus eating a serpent. They built their capital, Tenochtitlán in 1325, which was later destroyed by the Spanish in 1521. Have students investigate the history of the Aztec. 3.1

### La música

**Music Link** Scholars believe that the modern form of the **corrido** was born in the U.S.-Mexico border region. The **corrido** is a song that tells a story, and was derived from Spanish romance songs introduced in the sixteenth century. In the twentieth century, the lyrics began to examine the experience of the Latino in the U.S. Southwest. Have students investigate the **corrido** and the issues they address. 2.2, 3.1

### Assess

**Assessment Program**
**Prueba: Geocultura,** pp. 95–96, 115–116

**Online Assessment**
**my.hrw.com**

**Test Generator**

Capítulo 5

# Planning Guide

## El arte y la música

| Chapter Section | | Print Resources |
|---|---|---|
| **Geocultura**<br>• **El Suroeste y el Norte de México** | pp. 180–185 | Video Guide, pp. 29–30/Lab Book, p. 69 |
| **Vocabulario 1**<br>• Art and architecture<br>**Gramática 1**<br>• Repaso: Comparatives of equality and superlatives<br>• Passive **se**<br>• Passive voice with **ser** | pp. 188–193<br><br>pp. 194–199 | Vocabulario 5.1, 5.2; Bell Work 5.1, 5.2, 5.3, 5.4<br>Cuaderno de vocabulario y gramática, pp. 49–54<br>Cuaderno de actividades, pp. 41–43<br>Activities for Communication, pp. 17–18<br>Grammar Tutor for Students of Spanish, pp. 143–146 |
| **Cultura: Comparaciones**<br>**Cultura: Comunidad** | p. 200<br>p. 201 | Video Guide, pp. 32–33/Lab Book, p. 70 |
| **Vocabulario 2**<br>• Music and theater arts<br>**Gramática 2**<br>• Repaso: Subjunctive with hopes and wishes<br>• More on subjunctive with hopes and wishes<br>• Past perfect | pp. 202–207<br><br>pp. 208–213 | Vocabulario 5.3, 5.4; Bell Work 5.5, 5.6, 5.7, 5.8<br>Cuaderno de vocabulario y gramática, pp. 55–60<br>Cuaderno de actividades, pp. 45–47<br>Activities for Communication, pp. 19–20<br>Grammar Tutor for Students of Spanish, pp. 147–148 |
| **Novela en video**<br>**Lectura cultural**<br>• **Diego Rivera**<br>**Leamos**<br>• **Danza negra**<br>**Escribamos**<br>• **¡A escribir una canción!** | pp. 214–215<br>pp. 216–217<br><br>pp. 218–220<br><br>p. 221 | Cuaderno de actividades, p. 48<br>Reading Strategies and Skills Handbook<br>Interactive Advanced Reader<br>Video Guide, pp. 34–36/Lab Book, pp. 71–72 |
| **Prepárate para el examen**<br>• **Repaso de vocabulario y gramática** | pp. 222–225 | Picture Sequences, Situación, Ch. 5<br>Activities for Communication, pp. 47, 63–64 |
| **Integración**<br>• **Repaso cumulativo** | pp. 226–227 | Fine Art, Ch. 5<br>Cuaderno de actividades, pp. 49–50<br>Reading Strategies and Skills Handbook<br>Interactive Advanced Reader |

Visit Holt Online
go.hrw.com
KEYWORD: EXP3 CH5
Online Edition

For correlations to national standards, see point-of-use references throughout the chapter.

## Pacing Suggestions

| | Essential | Recommended | Optional |
|---|---|---|---|
| **Vocabulario 1**<br>• Art and architecture<br>• **Nota cultural** | ✔ | | |
| **Gramática 1**<br>• Repaso: Comparatives of equality and superlatives<br>• Passive **se**<br>• Passive voice with **ser**<br>• **Nota cultural** | ✔ | | |
| **Cultura: Comparaciones** | | ✔ | |
| **Cultura: Comunidad** | | | ✔ |
| **Vocabulario 2**<br>• Music and theater arts<br>• **Nota cultural** | ✔ | | |
| **Gramática 2**<br>• Repaso: Subjunctive with hopes and wishes<br>• More on subjunctive with hopes and wishes<br>• Past perfect<br>• **Nota cultural** | ✔ | | |
| **Novela en video**<br>• Episodio 5: **Clara perspectiva** | | ✔ | |
| **Lectura cultural**<br>• **Diego Rivera** | | | ✔ |
| **Leamos**<br>• **Danza negra**<br>**Escribamos**<br>• **¡A escribir una canción!** | | ✔ | |
| **Prepárate para el examen** | | ✔ | |
| **Integración** | | | ✔ |

## Technology Resources

### ¡Exprésate! Online
- Student Edition with multi-media
- SoundBooth recording tool
- Interactive activities with feedback
- Self-tests with feedback
- Cuaderno de actividades (interactive workbook)
- Cuaderno de vocabulario y gramática (interactive workbook)
- Live Ink™ Reading Help
- Holt Online Assessment

### DVD Tutor, Disc 1
- GeoVisión
- GramaVisión
- VideoNovela
- Cultura
- Variedades

### Interactive Tutor
- Interactive practice games
- Writing and recording workshops

### Audio Program
- Textbook listening activities
- Assessment listening activities
- Songs

### One-Stop Planner
- Complete media and print resources
- ExamView® Pro Test Generator
- Holt Calendar Planner

### PuzzlePro
- Customizable word games

## Assessment

**Geocultura**
**Vocabulario 1 / Gramática 1**
**Vocabulario 2 / Gramática 2**
**Leamos**
**Escribamos**
**Prepárate para el examen**

### Assessment Program
**Prueba: Geocultura,** pp. 95–96
**Pruebas,** pp. 81–82, 83–84, 85–86
**Pruebas,** pp. 87–88, 89–90, 91–92
**Prueba,** p. 93
**Prueba,** p. 94
**Examen: Capítulo 5,** pp. 253–260
**Examen oral: Capítulo 5,** p. 264
**Alternative Assessment,** pp. 377, 389, 401
**Examen parcial:** pp. 265–279

### Online Assessment
**my.hrw.com**

### Test Generator
**ExamView® Pro Test Generator**

Planning Guide

Capítulo 5

# Projects

## El arte y la música

### Los artistas

In this project, students select one of the artists mentioned in the chapter and research biographical information about him or her. Students then work in groups to create their own murals or paintings imitating the artist's style and depicting an historical event that occurred during the artist's life, or period of their choice. You may want to give students at least one week to complete the project.

**SUGGESTED SEQUENCE**

1. Divide the class into groups of three.
2. Group members select an artist mentioned in the chapter that they would like to learn more about.
3. Group members research information and any remarkable characteristics about the artist's work.
4. Students write one page of information with details about the artist's work.
5. Groups decide what historical event they wish to depict and choose visual images to convey their message.
6. Students work in groups to create their mural or painting. Their artwork can be done on an 11″ × 17″ sheet of paper.
7. Groups present an oral report about the artist and his or her artwork. Each student in the group is responsible for a portion of the presentation. 1.3

### Partner Class Project

Students choose a form of art, architecture, or music, and research prominent Spanish or Latin American artists in that area. Have them create a survey to find out what students know about these artists. Then have them create a poster outlining the information that classmates did not know. 2.2

### e-community

**e-mail forum:**

Post the following question on the classroom e-mail forum:

**¿Quién es tu artista, cantante o escritor preferido?**

All students will contribute to the list and then share the items. 1.2

### Grading the projects

Suggested point distribution (100 points total)

| | |
|---|---|
| Language use | 30 |
| Oral presentation | 30 |
| Originality | 30 |
| Appearance | 10 |

**Game Bank**

For game ideas, see pages T64–T67.

Projects

# El arte y la música

## Música

The word **mariachi** can refer to a specific type of Mexican music or to the group of musicians themselves. The traditional costume of the **mariachi** is that of the Mexican cowboy, or **charro:** tight pants with shiny buttons down the legs, a short tight jacket, a tie, and a large **sombrero;** female singers often wear a long skirt. **Mariachi** traditions developed hundreds of years ago from a blend of native musical customs and newly-arrived Spanish instruments, which now include the **guitarrón** (a large, fat-bellied, six-string bass guitar), the **vihuela** (a nylon-string guitar), violins, trumpets, and occasionally a harp. **Mariachi** groups sing in restaurants and plazas throughout Mexico and the U.S., and at special occasions like **bodas** and **quinceañeras.** Have students interview native speakers of Mexican origin or do Internet research to find out which **Mariachi conjuntos** are currently popular. 2.1, 5.1

## Receta

Corn, the sacred plant of the Aztecs, has always been a staple of the Mexican diet. Sometimes the Aztecs ground corn into meal with a **molcajete** (a stone mortar and pestle), which required a great deal of work. Therefore, the Aztecs heated the kernels in a solution of lime until the hulls came off. When this mixture **(nixtamal)** was boiled in water, the kernels swelled up and became soft like cooked pasta. This gruel or thick soup was called **pozole** and was one of the many indigenous methods of preparing corn. **Pozole,** also known as hominy, is traditionally made with pork. This recipe can be prepared with chicken, pork, or both. Have students research additional pre-European ingredients that are staples of Mexican cuisine.

### Pozole

**para 4–6 personas**

1 libra de puerco (como para asar)

1 libra de pechugas de pollo

1/2 cucharadita de comino en polvo

1 cucharadita de orégano en polvo

1/2 taza de cebolla picada

2 cubitos de caldo de pollo

2 latas de pozole *(golden hominy),* sin agua

Ponga el puerco en una olla y añada agua hasta cubrir el puerco. Cocine por una hora. Agregue las pechugas de pollo y cocine unos 30 minutos más, hasta que la carne esté blanda. Saque la carne de la olla, déjela enfriar, quitando cualquier grasa que tenga, y desmenúcela. Deje enfriar también el caldo, quitándole la grasa. Agregue agua hasta tener diez tazas de caldo. Añada los cubitos de caldo, las especias, la carne desmenuzada y la cebolla picada. Cuando vuelva a hervir, agregue el pozole, baje el fuego y cocine a fuego lento unos 15 ó 20 minutos. Sirva la sopa con tortillas de maíz frescas o con tostadas.

2.2, 3.1

# Listening Activity Scripts

## El arte y la música



### Vocabulario en acción 1

**1** p. 190, CD 5, Track 1

For script and answers, see *Teacher's Edition,* p. 190.

**8** p. 193, CD 5, Track 2

OCTAVIO Oye Natalia, ¿sabes algo sobre Enrique Echeverría?

NATALIA Sí, claro, es uno de mis artistas favoritos. Ha hecho unos dibujos muy imaginativos. Creo que su estilo es realista.

OCTAVIO ¿Es español?

NATALIA No, es mexicano pero vivió en Europa durante un tiempo.

OCTAVIO Hablando de artistas mexicanos, ¿conoces la obra de Yvonne Domenge?

NATALIA Sí, conozco bien su obra. Hace esculturas abstractas.

OCTAVIO A propósito, el arte chicano es muy original también. Además, es moderno.

NATALIA ¿Conoces a algún artista chicano?

OCTAVIO Sí, Frank Romero ha creado unas obras muy creativas. Es de Los Ángeles.

NATALIA Oye, cambiando de tema, ¿cuándo empieza la clase de literatura?

OCTAVIO ¡Ay, la clase! ¡Se me olvidó por completo!

NATALIA ¡Vámonos!

**Answer to Activity 8**

Cambian de tema tres veces.

### Gramática en acción 1

**11** p. 194, CD 5, Track 3

For script, see *Teacher's Edition,* p. 195.

**15** p. 196, CD 5, Track 4

1. El alcalde anunció hace un mes que quiere construir un nuevo centro de arte para nuestra ciudad.
2. Se formó un comité de artistas para organizar el proyecto.
3. El comité organizó un concierto de música clásica en el parque.
4. Se construyó un lugar especial en el parque para el concierto.
5. Se vendieron todos los boletos antes del concierto.
6. Muchos pintores asistieron al concierto.
7. Los artistas vendieron refrescos durante la función.
8. Los músicos tocaron canciones famosas.
9. Se pudo comprar todo lo necesario para construir el nuevo centro de arte.

**Answers to Activity 15**

| | | |
|---|---|---|
| 1. a | 4. b | 7. a |
| 2. b | 5. b | 8. a |
| 3. a | 6. a | 9. b |

**19** p. 198, CD 5, Track 5

En la década de 1940, la casa de una familia rica de El Paso fue legada a la ciudad para fundar un museo de arte. El museo fue inaugurado en el año 1947, bajo el nombre Museo Internacional de El Paso. La colección de arte más famosa del museo fue donada por la familia Kress. Esta colección incluye varias obras hechas por artistas clásicos. Como condición para recibir esta colección, el museo tuvo que convertirse en una institución pública en los años 50. Al final de esa década, el nombre del museo fue cambiado a Museo de Arte de El Paso, y en el año 1960, la casa fue renovada y se construyeron varias galerías para poder exhibir más obras. Treinta años más tarde, en vez de construir más galerías, se decidió cambiarlo de lugar, y en 1998 el museo fue mudado a un edificio más grande en el distrito de artes culturales. Hoy en día tiene más de 5,000 obras de arte y es visitado por miles de personas cada año.

**Answers to Activity 19**

1. cierto
2. cierto
3. cierto
4. falso, en 1960
5. falso, a un edificio comercial
6. cierto

### Vocabulario en acción 2

**23** p. 204, CD 5, Track 9

For script, see *Teacher's Edition,* p. 205.

**Answers to Activity 23**

| | | |
|---|---|---|
| 1. a/le gustó | 3. f/no le gustó | 5. b/le gustó |
| 2. c/le gustó | 4. d/no le gustó | 6. e/no le gustó |

For Student Response Forms, see the *Lab Book*, pp. 29–32.

**30** p. 207, CD 5, Track 10

1. —Voy a ver una exposición de pintores realistas hoy por la tarde, ¿me acompañas?
   —Gracias por la invitación, pero ya la he visto. Fui a verla ayer precisamente.
2. —¿Por qué no vamos a ver este concierto la semana que viene?
   —Me parece muy buena idea. Mañana iremos a comprar los boletos.
3. —El sábado es el estreno de un drama español. ¿Qué te parece? ¿Quieres ir?
   —¡Claro! Me encantan las obras de teatro. Gracias por invitarme.
4. —¿Me acompañas a la presentación de baile moderno en el Centro de Artes? Dicen que es formidable.
   —Hoy no, gracias. ¿Por qué no lo dejamos para otro día?
5. —¿Te interesa ir a un festival de la cinematografía contemporánea de México?
   —¡Qué pena! Me gustaría ir, pero ya tengo otro compromiso.
6. —Mañana por fin estrenan la nueva película que quiero ver. ¿Qué dices? ¿Te interesa acompañarme?
   —¡Por supuesto! A mí también me llama la atención.
7. —¿Por qué no vamos a escuchar la orquesta en el parque? La música es hermosa.
   —Perdóname, pero tengo muchas cosas que hacer. Iré contigo la próxima vez que esté aquí.

**Answers to Activity 30**

1. no acepta
2. acepta
3. acepta
4. no acepta
5. no acepta
6. acepta
7. no acepta

## Gramática en acción 2

**33** p. 208, CD 5, Track 11

1. —Tengo ganas de escuchar música. ¿Qué me recomiendas?
   —Te recomiendo que vayas al museo de arte a ver la exposición de pintura moderna.
2. —Me gustaría salir a ver una película pero mi novia quiere ver una obra de teatro. Hoy es su cumpleaños. ¿Qué debo hacer?
   —Pues, como hoy es el cumpleaños de ella, es mejor que vayan al teatro. Pueden ir al cine otro día.
3. —Ya no puedo soportar más esta música tan estridente que pone mi vecino todos los días, a todas horas. ¡Me duele la cabeza de tanto ruido!
   —Te sugiero que bailes con tu vecino si pone esa música de nuevo.
4. —Me encantaría ir al ballet pero ya no hay entradas. ¿Qué me sugieres?
   —Te recomiendo que salgas conmigo esta noche. ¡Tengo entradas para el ballet!
5. —Mis padres quieren que tome clases de violín, pero no me interesa estudiar música. Quiero ser artista. ¿Qué me aconsejas?
   —Te aconsejo que tomes clases de piano tres veces a la semana.

**Answers to Activity 33**

1. no 2. sí 3. no 4. sí 5. no

**41** p. 212, CD 5, Track 12

1. Cuando llegamos al teatro, la obra todavía no había empezado.
2. Raúl ya había pedido refrescos cuando lo vimos.
3. Cuando fuimos a buscar los asientos, ya se habían apagado las luces.
4. Cuando encontré mi asiento los actores ya habían salido al escenario.
5. Todavía no me había sentado cuando empezó la música.
6. Cuando terminó la segunda escena, Raúl ya se había dormido.
7. Aún no había terminado la obra cuando salimos.
8. Cuando llegamos al carro la gente ya había empezado a salir.

**Answers to Activity 41**

1. llegar al teatro
2. pedir refrescos Raúl
3. apagarse las luces
4. salir al escenario los actores
5. empezar la música
6. dormirse Raúl
7. salir
8. empezar a salir la gente

## Prepárate para el examen capítulo 5

**6** p. 223, CD 5, Track 15

For script, see *Teacher's Edition*, p. 223.

**Answers to Activity 6**

Se recomienda la obra de teatro y la feria. No se recomienda la película ni la exposición.

## Integración capítulos 1–5

**1** p. 226, CD 5, Track 16

For script, see *Teacher's Edition*, p. 226.

**Answers to Activity 1**

1. D 2. B 3. C 4. A

# 50-Minute Lesson Plans

# El arte y la música

For more customized Lesson Plans, see the *Lesson Planner with Differentiated Instruction.*



## Day 1

### Objective
*Asking for an opinion*

### Core Instruction
**Chapter Opener**, pp. 186–187
**10 min.**
- See Chapter Objectives, p. 186.
- See Using the Photo, p. 187.

**Vocabulario en acción 1,** pp. 188–193
- See Teaching **Vocabulario,** p. 188. **10 min.**
- See Teaching **¡Exprésate!,** p. 188. **5 min.**
- Play Audio CD 5, Tr. 1 for Activity 1, p. 190. **5 min.**
- Have students do Activities 2–6, pp. 190–191. **20 min.**

### Optional Resources
- Slower Pace Learners, p. 189 ◆
- Multiple Intelligences, p. 189
- Slower Pace Learners, p. 191 ◆
- Multiple Intelligences, p. 191
- **Comunicación,** p. 191
- Heritage Speakers, p. 191 ■

### Homework Suggestions
Cuaderno de vocabulario y gramática, pp. 49–51
❀ 1.1, 1.2

## Day 2

### Objective
*Introducing and changing a topic of conversation*

### Core Instruction
**Vocabulario en acción 1,** pp. 188–193
- See Teaching **¡Exprésate!,** p. 192. **10 min.**
- Have students do Activity 7, p. 193. **10 min.**
- Play Audio CD 5, Tr. 2 for Activiy 8, p. 193. **10 min.**
- Have students do Activities 9–10, p. 193. **20 min.**

### Optional Resources
- **Comunicación,** p. 193
- Slower Pace Learners, p. 193 ◆
- Special Learning Needs, p. 193 ●

### Homework Suggestions
Study for **Prueba: Vocabulario 1**
❀ 1.1, 1.2

## Day 3

### Objective
*Comparisons of equality and superlatives*

### Core Instruction
**Vocabulario en acción 1,** pp. 188–193
- Review **Vocabulario en acción 1,** pp. 188–193. **5 min.**
- Give **Prueba: Vocabulario 1. 20 min.**

**Gramática en acción 1,** pp. 194–199
- Have students do Bell Work, p. 194. **5 min.**
- See Teaching **Gramática,** p. 194. **10 min.**
- Play Audio CD 5, Tr. 3 for Activity 11, p. 194. **5 min.**
- Have students do Activity 12, p. 195. **5 min.**

### Optional Resources
- **Comunicación,** p. 195
- Advanced Learners, p. 195 ▲
- Special Learning Needs, p. 195 ●

### Homework Suggestions
Cuaderno de vocabulario y gramática, pp. 52–54
Cuaderno de actividades, pp. 41–43
❀ 1.2

## Day 4

### Objective
*Passive **se***

### Core Instruction
**Gramática en acción 1,** pp. 194–199
- Have students do Activities 13–14, p. 195. **10 min.**
- Have students do Bell Work, p. 196. **5 min.**
- See Teaching **Gramática,** p. 196. **10 min.**
- Play Audio CD 5, Tr. 4 for Activity 15, p. 196. **5 min.**
- Have students do Activities 16–18, p. 197. **20 min.**

### Optional Resources
- **Comunicación,** p. 197
- Heritage Speakers, p. 197 ■
- Career Path, p. 197
- Slower Pace Learners, p. 197 ◆
- Special Learning Needs, p. 197 ●

### Homework Suggestions
Cuaderno de vocabulario y gramática, pp. 52–54
Cuaderno de actividades, pp. 41–43
❀ 1.1, 1.2

## Day 5

### Objective
*Passive voice with **ser***

### Core Instruction
**Gramática en acción 1,** pp. 194–199
- Have students do Bell Work, p. 198. **5 min.**
- See Teaching **Gramática,** p. 198. **15 min.**
- Play Audio CD 5, Tr. 5 for Activity 19, p. 198. **5 min.**
- Have students do Activities 20–22, p. 199. **25 min.**

### Optional Resources
- **Comunicación,** p. 199
- Advanced Learners, p. 199 ▲
- Special Learning Needs, p. 199 ●

### Homework Suggestions
Study for **Prueba: Gramática 1**
Cuaderno de vocabulario y gramática, pp. 52–54
Cuaderno de actividades, pp. 41–43
❀ 1.1, 1.2

## Day 6

### Objective
*Interviews from around the Spanish-speaking world*

### Core Instruction
**Gramática en acción 1,** pp. 194–199
- Review **Gramática en acción 1,** pp. 194–199. **5 min.**
- Give **Prueba: Gramática 1. 20 min.**

**Cultura,** pp. 200–201
- See Teaching **Cultura,** p. 200. **10 min.**
- Play Audio CD 5, Tr. 6–8, or show **VideoCultura. 15 min.**

### Optional Resources
- Art Link, p. 201
- Advanced Learners, p. 201 ▲
- Multiple Intelligences, p. 201

### Homework Suggestions
Cuaderno de actividades, p. 44
Online Practice (**go.hrw.com,** Keyword: EXP3 CH5)
❀ 1.2, 1.3, 2.2, 3.1, 4.2

## Day 7

### Objective
*Making suggestions and recommendations*

### Core Instruction
**Vocabulario en acción 2,** pp. 202–207
- See Teaching **Vocabulario,** p. 202. **10 min.**
- See Teaching **¡Exprésate!,** p. 202. **5 min.**
- Play Audio CD 5, Tr. 9 for Activity 23, p. 204. **5 min.**
- Have students do Activities 24–28, pp. 204–205. **30 min.**

### Optional Resources
- Slower Pace Learners, p. 203 ◆
- Multiple Intelligences, p. 203
- **Comunicación,** p. 205
- Advanced Learners, p. 205 ▲
- Multiple Intelligences, p. 205

### Homework Suggestions
Cuaderno de vocabulario y gramática, pp. 55–57
❀ 1.1, 1.2, 1.3

## Day 8

### Objective
*Apologizing*

### Core Instruction
**Vocabulario en acción 2,** pp. 202–207
- See Teaching **¡Exprésate!,** p. 206. **10 min.**
- Have students do Activity 29, p. 207. **5 min.**
- Play Audio CD 5, Tr. 10 for Activity 30, p. 207. **10 min.**
- Have students do Activities 31–32, p. 207. **25 min.**

### Optional Resources
- Teacher to Teacher, p. 207
- **Comunicación,** p. 207
- Advanced Learners, p. 207 ▲
- Multiple Intelligences, p. 207

### Homework Suggestions
Study for **Prueba: Vocabulario 2**
Cuaderno de vocabulario y gramática, pp. 55–57
❀ 1.1, 1.2

- For information on the **Geocultura** pages, see the *Lesson Planner with Differentiated Instruction.*
- For more detailed information on benchmarks, see point-of-use correlations on each page.
- To edit and create your own lesson plans, see the **One-Stop** Planner® CD-ROM

**KEY**
- ▲ Advanced Learners
- ◆ Slower Pace Learners
- ● Special Learning Needs
- ■ Heritage Speakers

## Day 9

### Objective
*Subjunctive with hopes and wishes*

### Core Instruction
**Vocabulario en acción 2,** pp. 202–207
- Review **Vocabulario en acción 2,** pp. 202–207. **10 min**
- Give **Prueba: Vocabulario 2. 20 min**

**Gramática en acción 2,** pp. 208–213
- See Teaching **Gramática,** p. 208. **10 min.**
- Play Audio CD 5, Track 11 for Activity 33, p. 208. **5 min.**
- Have students do Activity 34, p. 209. **5 min.**

### Optional Resources
- Advanced Learners, p. 209 ◆
- Multiple Intelligences, p. 209

### Homework Suggestions
Cuaderno de vocabulario y gramática, pp. 58–60
Cuaderno de actividades, pp. 45–47
1.2

## Day 10

### Objective
*More on subjunctive with hopes and wishes*

### Core Instruction
**Gramática en acción 2,** pp. 208–213
- Have students do Activities 35–36, p. 209. **15 min.**
- Have students do Bell Work, p. 210. **5 min.**
- See Teaching **Gramática,** p. 210. **10 min.**
- Have students do Activities 37–40, pp. 210–211. **20 min.**

### Optional Resources
- Advanced Learners, p. 211 ▲
- Special Learning Needs, p. 211 ●

### Homework Suggestions
Cuaderno de vocabulario y gramática, pp. 58–60
Cuaderno de actividades, pp. 45–47
1.1, 1.2, 1.3

## Day 11

### Objective
*Past progressive*

### Core Instruction
**Gramática en acción 2,** pp. 208–213
- Have students do Bell Work, p. 212. **5 min.**
- See Teaching **Gramática,** p. 212. **15 min.**
- Play Audio CD 5, Track 12 for Activity 41, p. 212. **5 min.**
- Have students do Activities 42–44, p. 213. **25 min.**

### Optional Resources
- **Comunicación,** p. 213
- Slower Pace Learners, p. 213 ◆
- Multiple Intelligences, p. 213

### Homework Suggestions
Study for **Prueba: Gramática 2**
Cuaderno de vocabulario y gramática, pp. 58–60
Cuaderno de actividades, pp. 45–47
1.1, 1.2

## Day 12

### Objective
*Developing listening and reading skills*

### Core Instruction
**Gramática en acción 2,** pp. 208–213
- Review **Gramática en acción 2,** pp. 208–213. **10 min.**
- Give **Prueba: Gramática 2. 20 min.**

**Novela en video,** pp. 214–215
- Show **VideoNovela.** See Teaching **Novela en video,** p. 214. **20 min.**

### Optional Resources
- Cultures, p. 215

**Assessment Program**
- Skills Quiz: **Vocabulario y gramática en acción 2**

### Homework Suggestions
Cuaderno de vocabulario y gramática, pp. 58–60

## Day 13

### Objective
*Developing listening and reading skills*

### Core Instruction
**Lectura cultural,** pp. 216–217
- See Teaching **Lectura cultural,** p. 216. **40 min.**

**Leamos y escribamos,** pp. 218–221
- See Teaching **Leamos,** points 1–2 p. 218. **10 min.**

### Optional Resources
- Slower Pace Learners, p. 217 ◆
- Special Learning Needs, p. 217 ●

### Homework Suggestions
Cuaderno de actividades, p. 48
1.2, 1.3, 3.1

## Day 14

### Objective
*Developing reading and writing skills*

### Core Instruction
**Leamos y escribamos,** pp. 218–221
- See Teaching **Leamos,** points 3–4, p. 218 **25 min.**
- See Teaching **Escribamos,** p. 220 **25 min.**

### Optional Resources
- Advanced Learners, p. 219 ▲
- Special Learning Needs, p. 219 ●
- Slower Pace Learners, p. 221 ◆
- Multiple Intelligences, p. 221

### Homework Suggestions
**Taller del escritor,** p. 221
1.3, 3.1

## Day 15

### Objective
*Chapter review*

### Core Instruction
**Prepárate para el examen,** pp. 222–225
- Have students do Activities 1–5, pp. 222–223. **10 min.**
- Play Audio CD 5, Tr. 15 for Activity 6, p. 223. **5 min.**
- Have students do Activity 7, p. 223. **5 min.**

**Integración,** pp. 226–227
- Play Audio CD 5, Tr. 16 for Activity 1, p. 226. **5 min.**
- Have students do Activities 2–6, pp. 226–227. **25 min.**

### Optional Resources
- Play Pre-AP Audio CD 1, Tr. 17, for Pre-AP Practice, p. 223
- Game, p. 225
- Fine Art Connection, p. 227

### Homework Suggestions
Study for Chapter Test
1.1, 1.2, 1.3, 2.2

## Day 16/Test

### Core Instruction
**Chapter Test 50 min.**

### Optional Resources
**Assessment Program**
- **Prueba: Lectura**
- **Prueba: Escritura**
- Test Generator

### Homework Suggestions
Cuaderno de actividades, pp. 49–50

# Indiana
## The Hoosier State

### Chapter 5

The following chart presents *¡Exprésate!* Chapter 5 correlations to the Indiana Academic Standards for World Languages, Grade 11. The correlations here are to the *Student Edition* (SE) and *Teacher's Edition* (TE) only. For additional teaching resources, see pages 185A-185B

| INDIANA ACADEMIC STANDARDS | | | CHAPTER 5 SE/TE CORRELATIONS |
|---|---|---|---|
| **Standard 1 COMMUNICATION:** | | | |
| **Write and speak in a language other than English** | 11.1.1 | Initiate, sustain, and close conversations in limited yet varied situations. | SE: 192, 206, 213, 227<br>TE: 202, 206 |
| | 11.1.2 | Exchange detailed information and opinions orally on a variety of topics. | SE: 192, 201, 206, 213<br>TE: 192, 200, 206 |
| | 11.1.3 | Exchange detailed information and opinions in written form on a variety of topics. | SE: 221<br>TE: 195, 209 |
| | 11.1.4 | Make requests and ask different types of questions in a variety of social situations. | SE: 195, 199<br>TE: 188, 192 |
| | 11.1.5 | Recognize and use situation-appropriate non-verbal communication. | SE: 197, 205, 209<br>TE: 205, 211, 214 |
| | 11.1.6 | Use speaking and listening strategies to facilitate communication. | SE: 195, 197, 199 |
| **Standard 2 COMMUNICATION:** | | | |
| **Interpret information in a language other than English** *Learners interpret written and spoken language on a variety of topics. (Interpretive)* | 11.2.1 | Respond to everyday requests, commands, and directions. | SE: 207<br>TE: 189, 203 |
| | 11.2.2 | Demonstrate comprehension of both authentic and non-authentic written and spoken language through developmentally appropriate tasks. | SE: 215, 217, 220<br>TE: 181, 183, 185, 200, 214, 216, 218 |
| | 11.2.3 | Make educated guesses about meaning in unfamiliar written and spoken contexts. | SE: 214, 218<br>TE: 214, 218 |
| **Standard 3 COMMUNICATION:** | | | |
| **Present information in a language other than English** *Learners present to an audience of listeners or readers on a variety of topics. (Presentational)* | 11.3.1 | Recite rhymes, proverbs, and poetry or sing songs of the target language and cultures. | SE: 221<br>TE: 226 |
| | 11.3.2 | Produce and present creative material on a variety of topics. | TE: 185C, 191, 201, 205, 207, 226 |
| | 11.3.3 | Read passages aloud to demonstrate improving intonation and pronunciation. | TE: 192, 214, 216, 219 |
| | 11.3.4 | Compose cohesive written information using appropriate formats and more varied vocabulary and structures. | SE: 221<br>TE: 185C, 220, 221 |
| **Standard 4 CULTURES:** | | | |
| **Develop awareness of other cultures.** *Learners examine, experience, and reflect on the relationships among the practices, products, and perspectives of the cultures studied.* | 11.4.1 | Analyze and reflect on cultural practices of the target cultures. | SE: 201, 217, 220<br>TE: 181, 183, 185, 185D, 200, 216, 218 |
| | 11.4.2 | Describe products, perspectives, and symbols of the target cultures. | SE: 184, 185, 201, 217, 220<br>TE: 181, 183, 185, 200, 216, 218, 226 |
| | 11.4.3 | Discuss factors that influence practices, products, and perspectives. | SE: 201, 217<br>TE: 181, 183, 185, 200, 216, 218, 226 |

| | | | |
|---|---|---|---|
| | 11.4.4 | Recognize the interrelations among the practices, products, and perspectives of the target cultures. | **SE:** 182-185, 201, 217, 220<br>**TE:** 185, 200, 216, 218, 226 |
| | 11.4.5 | Explain contributions from other cultures. | **SE:** 201, 217<br>**TE:** 185C, 185, 216, 218, 226 |
| | 11.4.6 | Identify significant events unique to the target cultures. | **SE:** 182, 183<br>**TE:** 183 |

## Standard 5 CONNECTIONS:

| | | | |
|---|---|---|---|
| **Make connections to other content areas** *Learners use the target language to expand their knowledge of and make connections among multiple content areas.* | 11.5.1 | Make connections with other content areas through resources intended for native speakers. | **TE:** 181, 185C, 226 |
| | 11.5.2 | Design and share activities and materials that integrate the target language and cultures with concepts and skills from other content areas. | **TE:** 185C, 225 |

## Standard 6 CONNECTIONS:

| | | | |
|---|---|---|---|
| **Access and connect information through various media** *Learners strengthen language proficiency and cultural knowledge by using current digital media and authentic resources.* | 11.6.1 | Use digital media and culturally authentic resources to build vocabulary, improve reading ability, and encourage cultural awareness. | **SE:** 218, 226<br>**TE:** 185E, 185F |
| | 11.6.2 | Use digital media and culturally authentic resources to study target cultures. | **SE:** 180, 200, 214<br>**TE:** 181, 203, 205 |
| | 11.6.3 | Identify and evaluate resources intended for native speakers. | **SE:** 180, 200, 214, 220<br>**TE:** 181, 203, 205, 219 |

## Standard 7 COMPARISONS:

| | | | |
|---|---|---|---|
| **Investigate the nature of language and culture** *Learners understand the nature of language and culture through comparisons of the languages and cultures studied and their own.* | 11.7.1 | Use elements of word formation to expand vocabulary and derive meaning. | **SE:** 195, 213<br>**TE:** 194, 208, 222 |
| | 11.7.2 | Recognize and use a variety of language structures. | **SE:** 208-213, 221, 222-225, 227<br>**TE:** 194-199 |
| | 11.7.3 | Compare and use idiomatic, colloquial, and proverbial expressions in the target language. | **SE:** 193, 227<br>**TE:** 192 |
| | 11.7.5 | Compare systems of other cultures and the learner's own culture. | **SE:** 183, 201, 216-217<br>**TE:** 180-185, 200, 216-217, 220 |
| | 11.7.6 | Compare and contrast elements that shape cultural identity in the learner's heritage and in the target cultures. | **SE:** 183, 201, 216-217<br>**TE:** 180-185, 200, 216-217, 220 |

## Standard 8 COMMUNITIES:

| | | | |
|---|---|---|---|
| **Become an active global citizen by experiencing languages and cultures in multiple settings** *Learners use their knowledge of the target language and cultures both within and beyond the school setting for personal enrichment and civic engagement.* | 11.8.1 | Share experiences from the world language classroom with others. | **TE:** 226 |
| | 11.8.2 | Investigate and share with others the influences of the target language and cultures on the community. | **SE:** 227<br>**TE:** 185D, 226 |
| | 11.8.3 | Show evidence of becoming a life-long learner by using the target language and cultural knowledge for personal enrichment. | **TE:** 185D, 203, 226 |

## Meeting the National Standards

**Communication**
Comunicación, pp. 191, 193, 195, 197, 199, 205, 207, 209, 211, 213, 215
Game, p. 225
Situación, p. 227

**Cultures**
El arte, p. 183
Products and Perspectives, pp. 183, 185, 192, 206
Música, p. 185D
Nota cultural, pp. 191, 207, 210
Comunidad y oficio, p. 201
Practices and Perspectives, pp. 205, 215
Culture Project, p. 226

**Connections**
Atlas Interactivo Mundial, pp. 181, 201
Interdisciplinary Links, pp. 183, 185
Receta, p. 185D
Art Link, p. 191
History Link, pp. 216, 220
Language Arts Link, p. 219
Community Link, p. 224

**Comparisons**
Language to Language, p. 181
Comparing and Contrasting, p. 184
Comparaciones, p. 200
Nota cultural, p. 207
En inglés, p. 208

**Communities**
Música, p. 185D
Career Path, p. 197

## Learning Tips

Tell students that when listening to spoken Spanish or completing a listening activity in Spanish, they might not always recognize every word. Remind them that they will usually be able to understand the main idea, even if they do not know all of the words.

# Capítulo 5

# El arte y la música

### OBJETIVOS

**In this chapter you will learn to**
- ask for and give opinions
- introduce and change a topic of conversation
- make suggestions and recommendations
- turn down an invitation

**And you will use**
- comparisons of equality and superlatives
- passive voice
- subjunctive for hopes and wishes
- past perfect

### ¿Qué ves en la foto?

- ¿Dónde están estos chicos?
- ¿Qué están haciendo?
- ¿Qué es lo que más te llama la atención de este mural?

| Suggested pacing: | Traditional Schedule | Block Schedule |
|---|---|---|
| Vocabulario 1/Gramática 1 | 5 1/2 days | 2 1/2 blocks |
| Cultura | 1/2 day | 1/2 block |
| Vocabulario 2/Gramática 2 | 5 1/2 days | 2 1/2 blocks |
| Novela | 1/2 day | 1/2 block |
| Lectura cultural | 1/2 day | 1/2 block |
| Leamos y escribamos | 1 day | 1/2 block |
| Prepárate para el examen | 1 day | 1/4 block |
| Chapter Test | 1 day | 1/2 block |
| Integración | 1/2 day | 1/4 block |

Mural del Mercado de Mayapán, El Paso, Texas

# Chapter Opener

## Holt Grammar Logic
### CHAPTER 5

- *To ask for and give opinions, and to introduce and change a topic of conversation,* students will need to review comparatives of equality and superlatives, and passive **se.** They will also need to use the passive voice with **ser.**
- *To make suggestions and recommendations, and to turn down an invitation,* students must review the subjunctive with hopes and wishes. They will also use the past perfect.

## Using the Photo
This photo shows a mural in the Mercado Mayapán in El Paso, Texas. The Mercado Mayapán is an effort to promote the economic revitalization of south-central El Paso. Explain that murals are works of art painted on walls or ceilings. Muralism was revived in the 20th century by Mexican muralists Diego Rivera, José Clemente Orozco, and David Alfaro Siqueiros, among others. Have students read the caption and answer the questions about the photo on page 186.

## Más vocabulario
**el mural** *mural*
**las mercancías** *merchandise*
**recoger** *to gather*

## LISTENING PRACTICE — Language Lab and Classroom Activities

**Vocabulario**
Activity 1, p. 190, CD 5, Tr. 1
Activity 8, p. 193, CD 5, Tr. 2
Activity 23, p. 204, CD 5, Tr. 9
Activity 30, p. 207, CD 5, Tr. 10

**Gramática**
Activity 11, p. 194, CD 5, Tr. 3
Activity 15, p. 196, CD 5, Tr. 4
Activity 19, p. 198, CD 5, Tr. 5
Activity 33, p. 208, CD 5, Tr. 11
Activity 41, p. 212, CD 5, Tr. 12

**Cultura**
**Comparaciones,** pp. 200–201, CD 5, Tr. 6–8

**Novela**
**Novela en video,** Escuchemos, p. 214

**Lectura cultural**
pp. 216–217, CD 5, Tr. 13

**Leamos**
pp. 218–219, CD 5, Tr. 14
**Escuchemos,** p. 218

**Repaso**
Activity 6, p. 223, CD 5, Tr. 15
**Variedades,** Lab Book, p. 70

**Integración**
Activity 1, p. 226, CD 5, Tr. 16

**Assessment Program**
CD 5, Tr. 17–22

**Additional Listening**
Pre-AP CD 1, Trs. 17–20

## Resources

**Planning:**

Lesson Planner, pp. 65–66, 226–227

One-Stop Planner

**Presentation:**

Teaching Transparencies
**Vocabulario** 5.1, 5.2

**Practice:**

Cuaderno de vocabulario y gramática, pp. 49–51

Activities for Communication, pp. 17–18

Teaching Transparencies
Bell Work 5.1
**Vocabulario y gramática** answers, pp. 49–51

Interactive Tutor, Disc 1

### Bell Work

Use Bell Work 5.1 in the *Teaching Transparencies*, or write this activity on the board.

**Completa las oraciones con el pasado progresivo del verbo.**

1. **Alejo ______ (comer) cuando llegué.**
2. **Cuando Vera entró, sus compañeros ______ (estudiar).**
3. **______ (llover) cuando salí de la casa.**
4. **¿Tú ______ (dormir) cuando llamé?**
5. **Rosa ______ (cantar) cuando sonó el teléfono.**

**1.2**

### Pre-AP Practice

**AP Benchmark:** Use information from sources provided to present a synthesis and express an opinion.

**Focus:** Asking for and giving an opinion

- SE, p. 191, Act. 6
- TE, p. 191, **Comunicación**
- Assessment Program, p. 377, Picture Sequences

**Objetivos**
- Asking for and giving opinions
- Introducing and changing a topic of conversation

# Vocabulario en acción 1

## Las artes plásticas y la arquitectura

A mí me **llaman la atención** los murales. Algunos son muy **modernos** e **imaginativos.**

La Ciudad de México es **impresionante.** Hay una mezcla de **arquitectura antigua** y **contemporánea.**

Hay **galerías** y museos de arte con pinturas típicas del Suroeste, pinturas **realistas** y otras de estilo **clásico.**

## Core Instruction

### TEACHING VOCABULARIO

1. Use transparencies **Vocabulario 5.1** and **5.2** to introduce vocabulary to students. Read each caption, placing emphasis on the targeted vocabulary words. **(5 min.)**
2. Ask students questions to monitor comprehension. **¿Hay una galería de arte cerca de aquí? ¿Cómo se llama? (2 min.)**
3. Use an art book as a prop and ask students questions about the photographs. For example, point to a sculpture and ask: **¿Es una pintura?** Students should respond: **No, es una escultura. (3 min.)**

### TEACHING ¡EXPRÉSATE!

1. Model both sides of a conversation using the **¡Exprésate!** expressions. Complete each sentence with either a positive or negative opinion, using facial expressions to convey meaning. **(2 min.)**
2. Using an art book, point to various pictures. Model the **¡Exprésate!** expressions as you give your opinion of each piece of art. **(1 min.)**
3. Ask volunteers to point to pictures of art in the book and to ask their classmates' opinions of each piece. **(2 min.)**

Cuando hay **una exposición** de pintura, me gusta ir a ver las obras. Me fascinan **las acuarelas.**

A mi hermano le gusta mucho **la fotografía.** Tomó una foto de **la estatua** fuera del museo.

Me gusta **la escultura.** Para poder **esculpir,** hay que aprender a usar las herramientas necesarias, pero sólo un artista puede crear una obra **maravillosa.**

Visit Holt Online
go.hrw.com
KEYWORD: EXP3 CH5
Vocabulario 1 practice

### Más vocabulario...

| | |
|---|---|
| la cinematografía | *cinematography* |
| el dibujo | *drawing* |
| original | *original* |
| el puente | *bridge* |
| tallar en madera | *to carve wood* |
| la torre | *tower* |

## ¡Exprésate!

| To ask for an opinion | To respond |
|---|---|
| **Este retrato fue pintado por... ¿Qué te parece?** *This portrait was painted by . . . What do you think of it?* | **A decir verdad, me parece...** *To tell the truth, it strikes me as . . .* |
| **¿Cuál de estas pinturas te gusta más, la de... o la de...?** *Which of these paintings do you like better, the one of (by) . . . or the one of (by) . . . ?* | **En realidad, admiro...** *Actually, I admire . . .* |
| **¿Qué opinas de...?** *What do you think of . . . ?* | **Lo/La encuentro muy...** *I find it to be very . . .* |

Interactive TUTOR

Vocabulario y gramática, pp. 49–51 Online workbooks

▶ Vocabulario adicional — Las artes y la arquitectura, p. R17

Vocabulario 1

## TPR
### Total Physical Response

Bring to class the following items, or photographs of the items: a wood carving, a sculpture, a painting, an example of modern and of ancient architecture, a photograph, and a drawing. Have individual students respond to the following commands.

**Señala algo tallado en madera.**

**Muestra una fotografía a la clase.**

**Toca la escultura.**

**Pásame una pintura.**

**Busca un ejemplo de la arquitectura antigua.**

**Señala un dibujo moderno.**

1.2

### Common Error Alert
### ¡OJO!

Students often misspell **arquitectura** using "ch". Remind them that the letters "qui" are used for the /ki/ sound in Spanish. Another common error is using the masculine article **el** with the word **foto.** Point out that the complete word, **fotografía,** is feminine, and therefore the correct article is **la foto.**

### También se puede decir...

When talking about a work of art, such as a painting, Spanish speakers often use the phrase **obra de arte.**

## Differentiated Instruction

### Slower Pace Learners

**Additional Practice** Since most of the vocabulary terms from this chapter are visual, you might suggest that students work in groups to find examples of each art form in magazines. Have them cut out the examples, paste them on construction paper, and write the Spanish term in large letters below. Allow students to hang the posters around the classroom as you cover this chapter.

### Multiple Intelligences

**Interpersonal** Provide various themes to students and ask them what art form they would use to represent each and why. For example, give them the theme **amor.** A student might respond: **Usaría una escultura para representar el amor. Esculpiría a una madre abrazando a su hijo.** Try the following themes or come up with your own: **la música, un paisaje bonito, la tristeza, la familia, la comida, la historia.** 1.2

## Resources

**Planning:**

Lesson Planner, pp. 65–66, 226–227

One-Stop Planner

**Presentation:**

Teaching Transparencies
**Vocabulario** 5.1, 5.2

**Practice:**

Cuaderno de vocabulario y gramática, pp. 49–51

Activities for Communication, pp. 17–18

Lab Book, pp. 29–32

Teaching Transparencies
**Vocabulario y gramática** answers, pp. 49–51

Audio CD 5, Tr. 1

Interactive Tutor, Disc 1

### 1 Script

1. —¿Qué piensas de esta figura tallada en madera? Es muy bonita, ¿verdad?
—Sí, la encuentro muy original.
2. —Aquí dice que este retrato fue pintado en 1788. ¿Te gusta?
—Sí, admiro mucho su estilo clásico.
3. —Esta estatua de mármol es de Italia y es muy antigua. ¿Qué te parece?
—La encuentro muy imaginativa.
4. —Se dice que éste es el edificio más viejo del pueblo.
—Lo creo. Es muy impresionante.
5. —Esta acuarela del campo es maravillosa. ¿Qué opinas?
—A decir verdad, no hay nada que me llame la atención.
6. —Mira este dibujo a lápiz. Qué interesante, ¿no?
—La verdad es que prefiero los dibujos de muchos colores.

CD 5, Tr. 1

### 1 Críticos de arte 1.2

**Escuchemos** Escucha las conversaciones e identifica la obra que describen. **1.** b **2.** e **3.** a **4.** f **5.** c **6.** d

A

B

C

D

E

F

Escultura de piedra en el Museo de Antropología, México

### 2 ¿Cómo se define? 1.2

**Leamos** Escoge la palabra del cuadro que va con cada definición.

| | | |
|---|---|---|
| un museo | tallar en madera | una fotografía |
| un puente | una escultura | una torre |

1. Una obra de arte que se puede hacer con piedra. **1.** una escultura
2. Una construcción sobre un río o una carretera. **2.** un puente
3. Un edificio de varios pisos o un monumento. **3.** una torre
4. Un lugar donde hay exposiciones de arte. **4.** un museo
5. Forma de trabajar una escultura de madera. **5.** tallar en madera
6. Forma de arte que requiere el uso de una cámara. **6.** la fotografía

### 3 Una no es del grupo 1.2

**Leamos** Lee cada serie de tres palabras. Indica la palabra que no se relaciona lógicamente con las otras dos y explica por qué.

| | | | |
|---|---|---|---|
| 1. | antiguo | contemporáneo | moderno |
| 2. | tallar en madera | esculpir | puente |
| 3. | torre | puente | clásico |
| 4. | escultura | estatua | dibujo |
| 5. | galería | arquitectura | exposición |
| 6. | clásico | cinematografía | fotografía |

## Core Instruction

### VOCABULARY IN CONTEXT

Divide the class into three teams. Call on volunteers from each team to draw a vocabulary word from a bag. When you say "Go!", the volunteers create a drawing or series of drawings to illustrate their word. The first team to guess its volunteer's word earns a point. A different volunteer should draw each new word. The team to earn the most points wins. You may wish to play this game as a description activity. Instead of drawing a picture to illustrate the word, have students describe the word in Spanish without naming it. The first team to guess the word being described wins a point.

### 4 ¿Cuál es tu opinión? 1.2

**Leamos/Escribamos** Escribe una opinión sobre cada comentario según la información entre paréntesis. Sigue el modelo.

MODELO **—Este retrato es maravilloso, ¿no crees? (no estás de acuerdo)**
**—A decir verdad, lo encuentro poco original.**

1. ¿Qué te parece la última novela de Carlos Fuentes? Yo la encuentro muy imaginativa. (no estás de acuerdo)
2. ¿Qué opinas de esta pintura realista? Es muy original, ¿no? (estás de acuerdo)
3. Me dejan frío las exposiciones de arte. (no estás de acuerdo)
4. El arte moderno es imaginativo, ¿no crees? (estás de acuerdo)
5. Esta torre es impresionante. Es toda una obra de arte. (estás de acuerdo)
6. La fotografía no es nada interesante. (no estás de acuerdo)

### Nota cultural

La influencia española en la arquitectura del norte de México es evidente. En el siglo XVII los españoles construyeron casas y algunas iglesias de adobe, el cual era muy abundante en el clima árido del norte de México. En la ciudad de Guanajuato, México, todavía se pueden apreciar varias iglesias construidas de adobe.
¿Hay estructuras de adobe donde tú vives? 2.2

### 5 Mi arte preferido 1.2

**Escribamos/Hablemos** Da tu opinión sobre los siguientes temas utilizando las expresiones de **Exprésate.**

1. tu música preferida
2. tu novela favorita
3. una galería de arte
4. un edificio que te gusta mucho
5. tu canción preferida
6. un(a) artista a quien admiras mucho

## Comunicación

HOLT SoundBooth ONLINE RECORDING

### 6 Comentemos el arte 1.1, 1.2

**Hablemos** Con un(a) compañero(a), túrnense para dar sus opiniones sobre las siguientes obras. Usen las expresiones de **Exprésate.**

una pirámide maya

una pintura abstracta

una escultura azteca

### Heritage Speakers

Have heritage speakers bring in, or report on, a work of art or an artist representative of their country of origin. Ask them to to describe the work of art for the class. As they talk, you might want to write on the board any unfamiliar words they use. 1.3

### Connections

**Art Link**

Ask students to share what they know about Spanish or Latin American artists. Have them research and report on Latin American or Spanish contributions to painting, sculpture, and architecture. 2.2, 3.1

### Comunicación

**Class Activity: Presentational**

Have students bring in photographs of their favorite pieces of art. Ask them to talk briefly about the art piece and then ask their classmates' opinions. Allow volunteers to respond. 1.3

## Differentiated Instruction

### SLOWER PACE LEARNERS

**3 Variation** Some students may have trouble deciding which words do not belong in Activity 3. Before you complete this activity, you might want to go over the sets of words and have students define each word. 1.2

### MULTIPLE INTELLIGENCES

**Kinesthetic** Have students bring in prints, posters, or magazine pictures. Display the art to create a museum atmosphere. Have students role-play a trip to the museum. Roles can include: art critic, curator, guard, guide, and visitors. 1.1

**Differentiated Instruction** See the Differentiated Instruction CD-ROM.

## Resources

**Planning:**

Lesson Planner, pp. 65–66, 226–227

One-Stop Planner

**Presentation:**

Teaching Transparencies
**Vocabulario** 5.1, 5.2

**Practice:**

Cuaderno de vocabulario y gramática, pp. 49–51

Activities for Communication, pp. 17–18

Lab Book, pp. 29–32

Teaching Transparencies
**Vocabulario y gramática** answers, pp. 49–51

Audio CD 5, Tr. 2

Interactive Tutor, Disc 1

## Cultures

### Products and Perspectives

Tell students that Rufino Tamayo (1899–1991), a Zapotec from Oaxaca, was one of many artists who attracted international attention to Mexican art. Tamayo's colorful work demonstrates pre-Hispanic and Mexican folk influence. He eventually left Mexico for New York, where he taught at the Dalton School and founded the Tamayo Workshop at the Art School of The Brooklyn Museum. Ask students if they know of other Mexican artists who have had an important impact in the United States and have students bring examples of their artwork to class.

2.2

En el parque de Chapultepec, México

# El viaje de Kevin y Emily a la Ciudad de México

EDUARDO ¡Hola, Kevin! ¡Hola, Emily! ¿Cómo están? ¿Qué les parece la Ciudad de México hasta ahora?

KEVIN ¡Es una ciudad impresionante! Tiene muchas cosas que me llaman la atención. Hay ruinas antiguas y arquitectura moderna en la misma ciudad.

EMILY Sí, es una mezcla de lo clásico con lo contemporáneo. Aquí hay edificios que me hacen pensar que estoy en otra época y hay otros que son muy modernos.

EDUARDO ¡Qué bien! Y hablando de arquitectura antigua, ¿qué opinan del Templo Mayor y de la catedral en el Zócalo?

EMILY Son edificios de verdad maravillosos.

KEVIN ¡Y el Palacio Nacional es gigantesco!

EDUARDO Cambiando de tema, muchachos, ¿qué más han visto de la ciudad?

EMILY Fuimos al Palacio de Bellas Artes y vimos una exposición de la cinematografía mexicana, además de muchas esculturas, dibujos y pinturas en acuarela.

KEVIN Luego, visitamos el Ángel de la Independencia. Me parece la estatua más bella de la ciudad. ¡La encontré fascinante!

EDUARDO Estoy de acuerdo. A propósito, ¿no pasaron por el Museo de Antropología? Está cerca del bosque de Chapultepec. Si quieren, los llevo.

KEVIN Sí, gracias, Eduardo.

EMILY De acuerdo, ¡vámonos!

## ¡Exprésate!

### To introduce and change a topic of conversation

Interactive TUTOR

**Eso me hace pensar en...**
*That makes me think about . . .*

**Cambiando de tema, ¿qué me dices de...?**
*Changing the subject, what do you have to say about . . . ?*

**A propósito, ¿qué has oído de el/la...?**
*By the way, what have you heard about the . . . ?*

**Hablando de arte, ¿qué me cuentas de...?**
*Speaking of art, what can you tell me about . . . ?*

Vocabulario y gramática, pp. 49–51 Online workbooks

## Core Instruction

### TEACHING ¡EXPRÉSATE!

1. Have volunteers read the conversation between Eduardo, Kevin, and Emily. **(3 min.)**
2. Ask students to look over the text and tell how many times the subject was changed during the conversation. **(2 min.)**
3. Model the **¡Exprésate!** functions for students. **(2 min.)**
4. Have volunteers use vocabulary terms to tell you something about art (an exposition they saw, a painting they have, an artist they like.) Use the **¡Exprésate!** sentences to respond and change the subject. **(3 min.)**

**7 ¿Quién lo dijo?** 1.2

**Leamos** Lee cada oración y decide si la dijo **Eduardo, Kevin** o **Emily.**

1. Me alegra que estén disfrutando la Ciudad de México. Eduardo
2. ¡Me fascinó la estatua del Ángel de la Independencia! vin
3. Les recomiendo el Museo de Antropología. Eduardo
4. El Palacio Nacional es el edificio más grande que hemos visto. Kevin
5. Algunos edificios me hacen pensar que estoy en otra época. Emily
6. A mí me encantaron las exposiciones del Palacio de Bellas Artes. Emily

La entrada del Museo Nacional de Antropología en la Ciudad de México

CD 5, Tr. 2

**8 Hablando de arte** 1.2

**Escuchemos** Escucha mientras Natalia y Octavio hablan de artistas y sus obras e indica cuántas veces cambian de tema. Cambian de tema tres veces.

**9 Novedades de la exposición** 1.2

**Leamos/Escribamos** Completa la conversación con las palabras de **Exprésate.**

CARMEN Oye, Saúl, ¿qué te __1__ la exposición de ayer? Estuvo buenísima, ¿verdad? **1.** pareció

SAÚL Sí, los cuadros realistas me gustaron mucho. ¿Te gustaron?

CARMEN La verdad, los __2__ muy aburridos. Lo que me llamó la atención fue la escultura zapoteca. **2.** encontré

SAÚL __3__ de escultura, ¿qué __4__ de las esculturas modernas que vimos? **3.** Hablando **4.** opinas

CARMEN En realidad, me impresionaron mucho.

SAÚL A __5__, ¿qué me __6__ de la próxima exposición? **5.** propósito

CARMEN Tengo entendido que es una exposición de fotografía. **6.** dices *or* cuentas

## Comunicación

HOLT SoundBooth ONLINE RECORDING

**10 Hablemos de otra cosa** 1.1, 1.2

**Hablemos** Estás hablando con unos compañeros de clase acerca de la pintura y terminan hablando de la clase de arte. Dramaticen una conversación que abarque *(includes)* los siguientes temas. Usen las expresiones de **Exprésate** para cambiar de tema.

1. la pintura
2. varios tipos de pintura
3. la nueva galería de arte
4. la clase de arte

**8 Script**

See script on page 185E.

## Comunicación

**Pair Activity: Interpersonal**

Tell students they have five mintues to find out as much as they can about what is going on around school and with classmates. Have them ask each other questions and use the **¡Exprésate!** functions several times as they change topics. When the five minutes are up, have pairs report on how many topics they covered and have them summarize what they found out about their partners. 1.1

## Differentiated Instruction

**SLOWER PACE LEARNERS**

**9 Additional Practice** Once students have done Activity 9, have them go back and write the expressions that were used to change the topic of conversation on a separate sheet of paper. Then have volunteers read the complete conversation aloud, placing emphasis on the phrases used to change the subject. 1.2

**SPECIAL LEARNING NEEDS**

**8 Students with Auditory Impairments** If you have students with auditory impairments, you can make photocopies of the conversation for Activity 8 that appears in the *Annotated Teacher's Edition* on page 185E. Have students read the conversation and answer the questions. 1.2

**Assess**

**Assessment Program**

**Prueba: Vocabulario 1,** pp. 81–82

Alternative Assessment, pp. 377, 389, 401

**Online Assessment**

**my.hrw.com**

**Test Generator**

## Resources

**Planning:**

Lesson Planner, pp. 67–69, 228–231

One-Stop Planner

**Presentation:**

Video Program
**GramaVisión**

**Practice:**

Grammar Tutor for Students of Spanish, Chapter 5

Cuaderno de vocabulario y gramática, pp. 52–54

Cuaderno de actividades, pp. 41–43

Activities for Communication, pp. 17–18

Lab Book, pp. 29–32

Teaching Transparencies
Bell Work 5.2
**Vocabulario y gramática** answers, pp. 52–54

Audio CD 5, Tr. 3

Interactive Tutor, Disc 1

### Bell Work

Use Bell Work 5.2 in the *Teaching Transparencies*, or write this activity on the board.

**Completa las siguientes conversaciones.**

1. —Me encanta la arquitectura moderna.
—Eso me hace pensar en…
2. —El arte de Diego Rivera es impresionante.
—Hablando de arte, ¿qué me cuentas de…? 1.2

**Objetivos**
- Comparisons of equality and superlatives
- Passive **se**
- Passive voice with **ser**

# Gramática en acción 1

GramaVisión

Interactive TUTOR

## Repaso — Comparisons of equality and superlatives

**1** Use **tan** + **adjective** + **como** to compare people and things. The adjective you use must agree in gender and number with the person or thing you compare.

Esta estatua es **tan bonita como** la otra.

Estos dibujos son **tan antiguos como** los que vimos ayer.

**2** In the second part of your comparison, you can use an **article** + **adjective** phrase or a **pronoun** to avoid repetition.

Este retrato es tan original como **aquél.**

Las películas de acción no son tan divertidas como **las cómicas.**

**3** There are two kinds of superlatives. One kind uses **el/la/los/las** + **más/menos** + **adjective** + **de** to mean *the most* or *the least.*

La torre Eiffel es **la más alta de** todas las que he visto.

Aquellos dibujos son **los menos creativos del** museo.

Adding **-ísimo/a/os/as** to the end of the adjective forms a superlative that intensifies the meaning of the adjective.

La exposición de arte contemporáneo es **buenísima.**
*The contemporary art exhibition is great (very good).*

Vocabulario y gramática, pp. 52–54
Actividades, pp. 41–43
Online workbooks

### ¿Te acuerdas?

To demonstrate which object is being spoken about, use demonstrative adjectives.

¿No te gustó **esa** exposición?

Me encantó **aquella** pintura de la rosa.

To talk about "this one" or "that one", use demonstrative pronouns.

¿Prefieres esta pintura o **ésa**?

Me gusta más **ésta.**

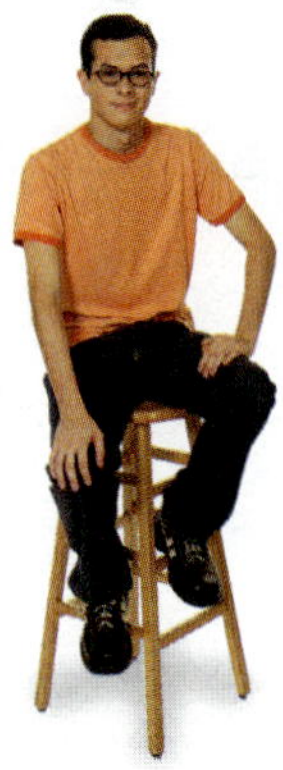

1. negativa
2. positiva
3. positiva
4. negativa
5. negativa
6. negativa
7. negativa
8. positiva

CD 5, Tr. 3 See script on p. 195.

### 11 ¿Cuál te gusta? 1.2

**Escuchemos** Escucha las siguientes conversaciones. Indica si la opinión que da la persona es **positiva** o **negativa.**

Sección de un mural, Centro Cultural Pueblo, Albuquerque

## Core Instruction

### TEACHING GRAMÁTICA

1. Go over point 1, placing emphasis on the endings that show gender agreement. **(1 min.)**
2. Reread each example, changing the number or gender of the noun to demonstrate how each adjective will change. **(2 min.)**
3. Go over **¿Te acuerdas?** and point 2. Point out the demonstrative pronoun accent. Write more examples, underlining the pronouns. Ask students to tell what each pronoun or article + adjective stands for. **El arte moderno no me impresiona tanto como** el clásico. (arte) **(4 min.)**
4. Go over point 3. Provide sentences using the construction **el/la/los/las** + **más/menos** + **adjective** + **de** and have students change the meaning of each sentence by adding **-ísimo/a/os/as** to the adjective. **(3 min.)**

### GramaVisión

For a video presentation of equality and superlatives, use **GramaVisión.**

GramaVisión

Visit Holt Online
**go.hrw.com**
KEYWORD: EXP3 CH5
Gramática 1 practice

## 12 Grandísimas en comparación 1.2

**Leamos/Escribamos** Completa las oraciones con las dos formas del superlativo o con el adjetivo según corresponda.

1. Los jardines de Chapultepec son ______. Son los jardines más ______ ______ México. (grande) grandísimos, grandes de
2. La Torre Sears en Chicago es ______. Es la torre más ______ ______ Estados Unidos. (alto) altísima, alta de
3. Fernando Botero es un pintor ______. Es tal vez el pintor más ______ ______ Colombia. (conocido) conocidísimo, conocido de
4. En mi opinión, las esculturas antiguas son ______. Para mí, son las más ______ ______ todas. (extraño) extrañísimas, extrañas de
5. La Gran Muralla de China es ______. Es la muralla más ______ ______ mundo. (largo) larguísima, larga del
6. Las comedias de Shakespeare son ______. Para mí son las más ______ ______ todas las obras de teatro. (divertido) divertidísimas, divertidas de

## 13 ¿Cómo lo ves? 1.2

**Escribamos** Escribe por lo menos dos oraciones con tu opinión sobre lo que ves en las fotos. Usa las dos formas del superlativo. Sigue el modelo.

**MODELO** **Este puente es larguísimo.**
**Creo que es el más largo que he visto.**

1

2

3

4

## Comunicación

HOLT SoundBooth ONLINE RECORDING

## 14 ¡Buenísima idea! 1.1, 1.2

**Hablemos** Dramatiza con un(a) compañero(a) una conversación en la que decidan qué hacer este fin de semana. Sugieran por lo menos tres ideas antes de llegar a un acuerdo y usen el superlativo. Sigan el modelo. *¿Se te olvidó?* **Nosotros** commands, p. 60

**MODELO** **—¿Por qué no vemos la nueva película?**
**—Ay, no. Pasar tres horas sentado en el cine me parece la cosa más aburrida del mundo. Hagamos una fiesta, mejor.**

## 11 Scripts

1. Las obras de esta galería no me parecen tan interesantes como otras que hemos visto, ¿sabes? ¿Por qué no vamos a otro sitio?
2. ¡Mira esa torre! ¡Es altísima y hermosísima! Me gustaría subirla para tener una vista de la ciudad.
3. ¡Este museo es buenísimo! Es el mejor que he visto.
4. No me gusta tanto este cuadro en acuarela; no es tan llamativo como los otros.
5. Esta escultura es feísima; creo que es la más fea de todo el museo.
6. Las pinturas de esta sala no son tan sofisticadas ni tan interesantes como las esculturas que vimos antes.
7. No puedo creer la actitud de esa artista, es creidísima. Además, sus dibujos son los más feos que he visto en mi vida.
8. Este mural es el más imaginativo que he pintado. No he visto otro tan colorido ni tan llamativo como éste.

## Comunicación

### Class Activity: Interpersonal

Have students bring in photographs of artwork and prepare five questions to ask opinions about the piece. In pairs, students ask their partners the questions. Remind students to use the **-ísimo** superlative if they strongly like or dislike one of the pieces. Have the rest of the class gauge how strongly the interviewee feels about the art by rating each response from 1 (strongly dislike) to 10 (strongly like). Ask volunteers to share their ratings and ask the interviewee whether the ratings are correct. 1.1

## Differentiated Instruction

### ADVANCED LEARNERS

**Challenge** Have students write a paragraph describing a piece of art that they have strong feelings about. Ask them to describe the piece of art and why it made such an impression on them. Have students exchange paragraphs with a partner and give them time to discuss them. 1.1, 1.3

### SPECIAL LEARNING NEEDS

**13 Students with Visual Impairments** If you have students with visual impairments, you may want to use photographs that can be shown on a transparency. You might also want to mention the names of the items shown.
MODELO: el puente Golden Gate
PHOTO A: la Torre Eiffel
PHOTO B: una estatua romana
PHOTO C: las pirámides de Teotihuacán
PHOTO D: "Personaje lanzando una piedra a un pájaro," por Joan Miró

## Resources

**Planning:**

Lesson Planner, pp. 67–69, 228–231

One-Stop Planner

**Presentation:**

Video Program
**GramaVisión**

**Practice:**

Grammar Tutor for Students of Spanish, Chapter 5

Cuaderno de vocabulario y gramática, pp. 52–54

Cuaderno de actividades, pp. 41–43

Activities for Communication, pp. 17–18

Lab Book, pp. 29–32

Teaching Transparencies
Bell Work 5.3
**Vocabulario y gramática** answers, pp. 52–54

Audio CD 5, Tr. 4

Interactive Tutor, Disc 1

### Bell Work

Use Bell Work 5.3 in the *Teaching Transparencies,* or write this activity on the board.

**Cambia cada adjetivo subrayado a la forma superlativa.**

1. Esta pintura es grande.
2. La película fue aburrida.
3. Frida Kahlo es una artista famosa. 1.2

### 15 Script

See script on page 185E.

Interactive TUTOR

## Repaso Passive se

**1** The **passive voice with se** is used to state that something *is done or has been done* without mentioning the agent, the person or thing causing the action.

**Se encontró** la pintura robada.
*The stolen painting was found.*

**Se vendieron** muchos boletos.
*Many tickets were sold.*

In contrast, the **active voice** takes the agent(s) into consideration even though the agent is not always clearly identified.

**Encontraron** los artefactos robados.
*(They) found the stolen artifacts.*

**Vendieron** muchos boletos.
*(They) sold many tickets.*

**2** You can express the **passive voice with se (se pasiva)** with the pronoun **se** plus a verb in the third person singular or plural. The verb agrees in number with the **recipient** of the action.

*agrees*
**Se presenta un concierto** gratuito en el parque este domingo.
*A free concert is being given at the park this Sunday.*

*agrees*
**Se ofrecen clases** de baile en el Centro de Bellas Artes.
*Dance classes are offered at the Centro de Bellas Artes.*

**3** Unlike **se pasiva, se impersonal** is always used with a verb in the third person singular. Like **se pasiva, se impersonal** constructions do not mention the agent. The agent is often translated as an anonymous *one, you,* or *people.*

**Se camina** mucho en esta ciudad.
*One walks a lot in this city.*

Vocabulario y gramática, pp. 52–54
Actividades, pp. 41–43
Online workbooks

En El Paso, se encuentran artefactos que parecen ser creados por el mismo desierto.

CD 5, Tr. 4

### 15 ¿Quién lo hizo? 1.2

**Escuchemos** Escucha las oraciones. Para cada una indica
**a**) si se menciona el agente o
**b**) si no se menciona.

**1.** a **2.** b **3.** a **4.** b **5.** b **6.** a **7.** a **8.** a **9.** b

## Core Instruction

### TEACHING GRAMÁTICA

1. Go over point 1 with students. Tell students that the passive voice is not used as often in Spanish as it is in English. **(2 min.)**
2. Go over point 2 with students. Read the examples, emphasizing the endings that show number agreement. **(2 min.)**
3. Create sentences in the passive voice with **se** and have students name the subject and verb in each sentence. **(vender/obras de arte; aceptar/tarjetas de crédito) (3 min.)**
4. Remind students that they have already learned to use impersonal **se.** Have students read point 3 and compare passive **se** and impersonal **se.** Tell them that their uses often overlap. **(3 min.)**

### GramaVisión

For a video presentation of passive **se,** use **GramaVisión.**

GramaVisión

**16** **¿Qué se hace en tu colegio?** 1.2

**Leamos/Escribamos** Lee las siguientes oraciones acerca del colegio de Mónica. Escribe **cierto** si lo que dice la oración es cierto en tu colegio. Si no, escribe **falso** y corrige la oración.

1. En mi colegio, no se ofrecen clases de artes plásticas.
2. Todos los años se presenta una exposición de arte estudiantil.
3. En mi colegio se enseñan clases de español, francés y ruso.
4. En la orquesta estudiantil se interpreta música variada.
5. El himno del colegio se toca todos los días por la mañana.
6. En mi colegio, se ofrece una clase de fotografía.
7. Todos los años se hacen varias excursiones.
8. Se han pintado murales por los pasillos y en la cafetería.

**17** **Donde yo vivo** 1.2

**Escribamos/Hablemos** Completa cada oración usando una frase con **se impersonal** y los verbos entre paréntesis.

MODELO **En mi casa... (comer, ver)**
**En mi casa se come a las seis y media.**
**Se ve televisión casi todas las noches.**

1. En la clase de escultura... (esculpir, observar)
2. En la clase de español... (leer, practicar)
3. En los partidos de fútbol... (gritar, correr)
4. En mi restaurante favorito... (preparar, pagar)
5. En el museo de arte... (ver, presentar)
6. En el centro comercial... (comprar, gastar)

Aficionados mexicanos asisten a un partido de la Copa Mundial en Dallas, Texas.

## Comunicación

HOLT SoundBooth ONLINE RECORDING

**18** **¿Cómo es en tu país?** 1.1, 1.2

**Hablemos** En parejas, dramaticen una conversación entre un estudiante de Estados Unidos y un estudiante de intercambio de otro país. Túrnense para hacerle preguntas al estudiante de intercambio acerca de su país. Sigan el modelo y usen las palabras dadas como guía.

MODELO **—En tu país, ¿se comen las mismas cosas que aquí?**
**—No, para nada. En mi país se comen cosas distintas.**

| | | | |
|---|---|---|---|
| comida | ropa | deportes | música |
| clases | pasatiempos | costumbres | televisión |

### Heritage Speakers

Ask heritage speakers to use the passive **se** to tell about things that are done differently in their country of origin. 1.3

### Communities

**Career Path**

Have students brainstorm careers related to the arts. Ask how the knowledge of a second language might be useful. For example, would it be important to know other languages as an art museum guide or director? Why? How might students prepare for a career in the art world? Suggest that students interested in this field research want ads in Spanish language newspapers online. 3.2, 5.1

### Language Note

Tell students that many Spanish speakers do not distinguish passive **se** from impersonal **se.** Both constructions express passive and impersonal meanings by suppressing the agent.

### Comunicación

**Class Activity: Presentational**

Have students think of something they know how to do well. Ask them to take turns using the passive **se** to tell the class how the activity is done. 1.3

## Differentiated Instruction

### SLOWER PACE LEARNERS

**Additional Practice** To review the use of the impersonal **se** as well as this chapter's vocabulary, present some true and false statements in Spanish about art. (**La escultura se hace en un lienzo.**) Have students tell whether the statements are true or false, and correct the false statements. Then have volunteers provide their own true or false statements for their classmates to respond to. 1.2

### SPECIAL LEARNING NEEDS

**Students with Learning Disabilities** You may wish to simplify the concept of passive **se** by forming simple sentences as a class. Provide the verb and the noun, for example: **construir/un edificio.** Ask students first whether the noun is singular or plural. Then have them conjugate the verb for the appropriate number, in this case singular: **construyó (construye).** Finally, add the **se** to form the sentence: **Se construyó un edificio.** Encourage students to follow this process when doing the activities. 1.2

**Differentiated Instruction** See the Differentiated Instruction CD-ROM.

**Resources**

**Planning:**

Lesson Planner, pp. 67–69, 228–231

One-Stop Planner

**Presentation:**

Video Program **GramaVisión**

**Practice:**

Grammar Tutor for Students of Spanish, Chapter 5

Cuaderno de vocabulario y gramática, pp. 52–54

Cuaderno de actividades, pp. 41–43

Activities for Communication, pp. 17–18

Lab Book, pp. 29–32

Teaching Transparencies
Bell Work 5.4
**Vocabulario y gramática** answers, pp. 52–54

Audio CD 5, Tr. 5

Interactive Tutor, Disc 1

**Bell Work**

Use Bell Work 5.4 in the *Teaching Transparencies*, or write this activity on the board.

**Completa las oraciones con el *se* pasivo.**

1. ______ (decir) que el arte es muy importante.
2. Ayer ______ (abrir) una exposición de pintura.
3. ______ (pintar) unos murales en la plaza de la ciudad.
4. ______ (arreglar) unos edificios antiguos.
5. ______ (cerrar) el puente más grande de la ciudad.

1.2

**19 Script**

See script on page 185E.

Interactive TUTOR

## ¡Te acuerdas?

The past participle of **-ar** verbs is formed by dropping the **-ar** and adding **-ado**, and the past participle of **-er** and **-ir** verbs is formed by dropping the **-er** or **-ir** and adding **-ido**.

habl**ar** → habl**ado**
com**er** → com**ido**
serv**ir** → serv**ido**

See p. 148 for irregular past participles.

## Passive voice with ser

**1** Another way to express a passive action is by using **ser + past participle.** This construction is similar to the **active voice** in that an agent can be specified. The **agent** is introduced by **por.**

| | |
|---|---|
| **Diego Rivera pintó** el mural. | El mural **fue pintado por Diego Rivera.** |
| *Diego Rivera painted the mural.* | *The mural was painted by Diego Rivera.* |

**2** Sentences in the **passive voice** with **ser** are formed by combining the recipient of the action + **ser + past participle** + **por** + **agent.** The participle must agree in number and gender with the recipient.

*agrees*
El mural **fue pintado** por **Diego Rivera.**

*agrees*
Los murales **fueron pintados** por **Diego Rivera.**

*agrees*
Una escultura **será presentada** por **mi profesor de arte.**

*agrees*
Varias esculturas **serán presentadas** por **los estudiantes.**

Vocabulario y gramática, pp. 52–54
Actividades, pp. 41–43
Online workbooks

CD 5, Tr. 5

### 19 El Museo de Arte de El Paso 1.2

**Escuchemos/Leamos** Escucha el pasaje acerca del Museo de Arte de El Paso. Luego, lee las oraciones que siguen y contesta **cierto** o **falso** basándote en lo que escuchaste. Si una oración es falsa, corrige la oración con la información correcta.

1. El museo fue abierto en 1947. **1.** cierto
2. El Museo de Arte de El Paso originalmente fue nombrado Museo Internacional de El Paso. **2.** cierto
3. El museo fue convertido en *(turned into)* una institución pública en los años 50. **3.** cierto
4. Las galerías adicionales fueron construidas en el año 1998. **4.** falso, en 1960
5. El museo fue mudado a una casa renovada en el distrito de artes culturales. **5.** falso, a un edificio comercial
6. El museo es visitado por miles de personas cada año. **6.** cierto

## Core Instruction

### TEACHING GRAMÁTICA

1. Review the information in **¿Te acuerdas?** with students. **(2 min.)**
2. Ask students if they remember any irregular past participles. If not, have them turn to page 148 to review them. **(3 min.)**
3. Go over point 1. Discuss how the passive voice with **ser** is similar to the active voice, and to the passive with **se** (compare the English translations). **(2 min.)**
4. Tell students that **ser** + past participle is commonly used to express the passive voice in Spanish. Go over point 2. **(3 min.)**
5. Write sample sentences using the passive voice on the board, and have volunteers underline the verb and circle the recipient of the action. Then have them tell whether each noun is singular or plural. **(5 min.)**

**GramaVisión**

For a video presentation of the passive voice with **ser**, use **GramaVisión.**

GramaVisión

## 20 Hecho por... 1.2

**Escribamos** Combina las frases para formar oraciones en voz pasiva. Sigue el modelo.

**MODELO** **el cuadro del museo/pintar/un artista conocido**
**El cuadro del museo fue pintado por un artista conocido.**

1. la sinfonía/interpretar/la orquesta juvenil
2. la obra de teatro/escribir/el club de drama
3. la torre de vidrio/diseñar/un arquitecto japonés
4. la ciudad de Machu Picchu/construir/los incas
5. el mural/pintar/unos artistas mexicanos
6. la estatua/tallar en madera/un estudiante de arte.

## 21 ¡De vacaciones! 1.2

**Leamos/Escribamos** Cambia cada oración de voz activa a voz pasiva. *¿Se te olvidó?* Past participle, p. 148

**MODELO** **Un arquitecto famoso diseñó el museo.**
**El museo fue diseñado por un arquitecto famoso.**

1. Los turistas visitaron el museo de arte.
2. El guía describió los dibujos más famosos.
3. El museo compró los cuadros hace cinco años.
4. El museo construyó una nueva sala de exposición.
5. El guía llevó a los turistas a la torre del castillo.
6. Mi hermano sacó varias fotos de la torre.
7. Alguien diseñó el castillo hace más de seiscientos años.
8. Un terremoto destruyó parte del castillo hace veinte años.

Exterior del Museo de Arte de El Paso

1. El museo de arte fue visitado por los turistas.
2. Los dibujos más famosos fueron descritos por el guía.
3. Los cuadros fueron comprados por el museo hace cinco años.
4. Una nueva sala de exposición fue construida por el museo.
5. Los turistas fueron llevados a la torre del castillo por el guía.
6. Varias fotos de la torre fueron sacadas por mi hermano.
7. El castillo fue diseñado por alguien hace más de seiscientos años.
8. Parte del castillo fue destruida por un terremoto hace veinte años.

## Comunicación

HOLT SoundBooth ONLINE RECORDING

## 22 Los gustos del arte 1.1, 1.2

**Hablemos** En grupos de tres, piensen en su canción, obra de teatro, novela y obra de arte favorita. Luego, túrnense para mencionar algo de su obra favorita. Sus compañeros(as) tienen que adivinarla *(guess it)*. Usen **ser + participio pasado** en sus oraciones. Sigan el modelo.

**MODELO** **canción favorita**
**—Mi canción favorita es contemporánea. Fue escrita por el grupo El Gran Silencio.**
**—¿Es "Dormir soñando"?**

### 20 Answers

1. La sinfonía fue interpretada por la orquesta juvenil.
2. La obra de teatro fue escrita por el club de drama.
3. La torre de vidrio fue diseñada por un arquitecto japonés.
4. La ciudad de Machu Picchu fue construida por los Incas.
5. El mural fue pintado por unos artistas mexicanos.
6. La estatua fue tallada en madera por un estudiante de arte.

### Circumlocution

Have students describe a piece of art without saying what it is and ask the rest of the class to guess what genre of art they are describing **(pintura, escultura, tallado en madera, arquitectura).** 1.1

## Comunicación

### Class Activity: Interpretive

Have students research a piece of artwork that interests them. Ask them to bring a photograph of the piece to class, with the artist's name written on the back. Write the names of the artists on the board, and hang the photographs around the classroom. Point to one and ask students to name the artist, using the passive voice with **ser. (Ese edificio fue diseñado por Antonio Gaudí.)** 1.2

## Differentiated Instruction

### ADVANCED LEARNERS

**Challenge** Have students find a short paragraph in Spanish from one of their readings. Ask them to rewrite the paragraph using the passive voice. Ask students how the paragraph is different when it is written in the passive voice. Have students share their paragraphs and discuss their findings as a class. 1.2

### SPECIAL LEARNING NEEDS

**Students with Dyslexia** For students with dyslexia, you may want to do Activity 21 as a class. Read each item aloud. Have students help you rewrite each sentence by asking these questions. **¿Qué visitaron los turistas? (el museo de arte contemporáneo)** Write **El museo…** on the board. **¿Es singular o plural? (singular)** Add **fue. ¿Cuál es el verbo? (visitar) ¿Cuál es el participio pasado de visitar? (visitado)** Add **visitado. ¿Por quién fue visitado? (los turistas).** Complete the sentence: **El museo de arte contemporáneo fue visitado por los turistas.** 1.2

### Assess

**Assessment Program**

**Prueba: Gramática 1,** pp. 83–84

**Prueba: Aplicación 1,** pp. 85–86

Audio CD 5, Tr. 17

Alternative Assessment, pp. 377, 389, 401

**Online Assessment**
**my.hrw.com**

**Test Generator**

# Cultura

VideoCultura

## Resources

**Planning:**

Lesson Planner, pp. 70, 230–231

One-Stop Planner

**Presentation:**

Audio CD 5, Trs. 6–8

Video Program, Videocassette 3

DVD Program

**VideoCultura**

**Practice:**

Cuaderno de actividades, p. 44

Video Guide, pp. 32–33

Lab Book, p. 70

Interactive Tutor, Disc 1

## Language Note

Tell students that **"una nueva onda"** means "a new wave". The materials artists are using in the new wave of art described by Lorena are aluminum **(aluminio)** and exposed concrete **(concreto expuesto).**

## Comparaciones

Interactive TUTOR

CD 5, Tr. 6-8

*De la conquista a 1930* de Diego Rivera

### Lo hermoso, a todos da gozo 1.3, 4.2

En los pueblos y ciudades de España y América Latina, siempre hay algún edificio antiguo o moderno que da gusto a sus habitantes y a los visitantes. Algunas ciudades son monumentales. Tienen rascacielos, parlamentos, iglesias, palacios, museos, plazas o esculturas que atraen a muchos turistas a ver su arte y su arquitectura. Esto da trabajo a muchas personas que hacen de guías turísticos. Imagina que tú eres guía de tu ciudad o región. ¿Qué edificios son los sobresalientes? ¿Cómo es su arquitectura?

### Mario
**Ciudad de México, México**

***¿Qué me puedes decir sobre el arte o la arquitectura de México?***

México ha sido siempre un país muy rico en artistas plásticos y arquitectos, donde el mundo ha encontrado inspiración.

***¿Quiénes son algunos artistas o arquitectos conocidos de México?***

Pues, de los más famosos, tenemos Frida Kahlo, Diego Rivera, arquitectos como Barragán, Arazúa.

***De ellos, ¿a quién prefieres y por qué?***

Uno de mis artistas preferidos es Diego Rivera, no sólo por su trabajo artístico sino también social.

***¿Cómo es su arte?***

Su arte tiene mucho que ver con los movimientos sociales que han pasado aquí en México, desde los aztecas hasta la conquista, la revolución industrial, la expropiación de petróleo, los movimientos sindicalistas, etcétera.

## Pre-AP Practice

**AP Language Examination:** Have students first listen to the interviews with books closed to help prepare them for Section I, Part A: **Listening—Short Dialogues and Narratives.** Point out that Loriana, like many Spanish speakers from Costa Rica, uses the alternate second person pronoun **vos** instead of **tú** and pronounces syllable final **r** much like the American *r* in *car.* **(moderno)**

## Core Instruction

### TEACHING CULTURA

1. Before teaching **Cultura,** find photographs of some of the architecture mentioned by Lorena in her interview (**el Teatro Nacional, el Melico Salazar**).
2. Play the audio for the introductory paragraph and have students discuss the questions. **(2 min.)**
3. Ask students to observe the photograph of the mural and to describe what they see. Tell them they will learn more about Diego Rivera later in this chapter. **(2 min.)**
4. Have volunteers read the interviews with Mario and Lorena. Show any photographs you are able to find of the architecture mentioned by Lorena. **(6 min.)**
5. Have students answer the **Para comprender** questions and then discuss the **Para pensar y hablar** questions in small groups.

### VideoCultura

For a video presentation of the interviews as well as for additional interviews, see Chapter 5 **VideoCultura** on Videocassette or on DVD.

Visit Holt Online
**go.hrw.com**
KEYWORD: EXP3 CH5
Online Edition

## Loriana
**San José, Costa Rica**

***¿Qué me cuentas del arte o de la arquitectura de Costa Rica?***

Bueno, tenemos muchos tipos. En ellos podemos destacar la arquitectura más antigua como el Teatro Nacional, el Melico Salazar o las casas antiguas del Barrio Amón, que son más que todo coloniales. Y para casas más modernas podemos mencionar lo que es el edificio de Arquitectos Ingenieros de Costa Rica.

***¿Quiénes son algunos artistas o arquitectos conocidos de esta región?***

Podemos mencionar a Jaime Rouillón, a Franz Beer, a Víctor Cañas, y también podemos mencionar a Bruno Stagno.

***¿De ellos, a quién prefieres?***

De ellos, me gusta Víctor Cañas.

***¿Cómo es su arte?***

Es un arte modernista. Es una nueva onda que se está usando en el país, que trata más que todo usar materiales como el aluminio y el concreto expuesto.

### Para comprender 1.2

1. ¿Quiénes son dos artistas que menciona Mario?
2. ¿Cómo es el arte de Diego Rivera?
3. ¿Quiénes son dos artistas costarricenses?
4. ¿Cómo es el arte de Víctor Cañas?
5. ¿Qué crees que indican las preferencias artísticas de Mario y Loriana sobre los gustos o personalidades de ellos?

### Para pensar y hablar 1.3, 3.1

¿Cómo pueden afectar los eventos políticos o culturales el arte de una comunidad? ¿En tu comunidad, la gente usa el arte como medio de expresión? Da unos ejemplos.

# Comunidad y oficio

## Arte hispano en Estados Unidos 2.2, 3.1

En Estados Unidos hay muchas oportunidades de disfrutar de arte hispano. Se pueden apreciar obras de artistas hispanos en museos por todo el país. De igual manera, se organizan anualmente festivales de arte hispano, en los que se presenta una diversidad de obras teatrales, películas, música y bailes. En grupos de cuatro, escojan un género artístico que les interese. Investiguen qué museos, teatros y otros establecimientos de su región presentan obras o exposiciones o patrocinan festivales de ese género, enfocándose en los artistas hispanos. Con la información que encuentren hagan una guía artística para la comunidad hispana de su región.

**En la Galería Mexic-Arte, Austin, Texas**

## Differentiated Instruction

### ADVANCED LEARNERS

**Challenge** Have students research one of the artists mentioned in the interview with Lorena. Ask them to write a paragraph with background information about the artist and information about his or her work. Encourage them to find some examples of the art to share with the class. Have each student give a five-minute presentation on the artist. 1.3

### MULTIPLE INTELLIGENCES

**Spatial** Have students choose a mural by Diego Rivera and research the historical context of the painting. Ask them to use the painting as a guide to describe to the class the social issues that Rivera depicts in his mural. 1.3

## Atlas INTERACTIVO MUNDIAL

Have students use the interactive atlas at **go.hrw.com**.

### Map Activities

1. Have students locate Mexico on the map on page R2, and ask them to find Mexico City. Then have them locate Costa Rica and ask them to find the city of San José on the map on page R7. Ask them what San José and Mexico City have in common. (They are the capital cities.)
2. Ask students whether they think Mexico City and San José would be important centers for art and culture. Have them explain their answers.
3. Have students research the architecture of Mexico City. 3.1

## Answers

1. Frida Kahlo, Diego Rivera
2. Tiene que ver con los movimientos sociales.
3. Jamie Rouillo, Franz Beer, Víctor Cañas, Bruno Estagno
4. modernista; usa materiales como el aluminio y el concreto expuesto
5. Answers will vary.

## Connections

### Art Link

Ask students if they have ever seen photographs of the **Palacio de Bellas Artes** (Palace of Fine Arts) in Mexico City. Construction of the **Palacio** began in 1904 under Italian architect Adamo Boari, but stopped when the heavy marble began to sink into the soil. In the 1930's, the interior was finished by architect Federico Mariscal. Have students research the murals in the **Palacio de Bellas Artes** and present their findings to the class. 3.1

## Resources

**Planning:**

Lesson Planner, pp. 71–72, 232–233

One-Stop Planner

**Presentation:**

Teaching Transparencies
**Vocabulario** 5.3, 5.4

**Practice:**

Cuaderno de vocabulario y gramática, pp. 55–57

Activities for Communication, pp. 19–20

Teaching Transparencies
Bell Work 5.5
**Vocabulario y gramática** answers, pp. 55–57

Interactive Tutor, Disc 1

### Bell Work

Use Bell Work 5.5 in the *Teaching Transparencies,* or write this activity on the board.

**Vuelve a escribir cada oración usando la voz pasiva.**

1. **Un escultor mexicano hizo esta escultura.**
2. **Diego Rivera pintó el mural en el Palacio Nacional.**
3. **Gaudí diseñó este edificio.**
4. **Un fotógrafo famoso sacó esta fotografía.**
5. **Mi amiga dibujó este puente.** 1.2

### Pre-AP Practice

**AP Benchmark:** Use language that is semantically and grammatically accurate according to a given context.

**Focus:** Making suggestions and recommendations

- SE, p. 205, Act. 28
- TE, p. 205, **Comunicación**
- **Cuaderno de vocabulario y gramática,** p. 55, Act. 17

**Objetivos**
- Making suggestions and recommendations
- Turning down an invitation

# Vocabulario en acción 2

## En la Ciudad de México

## La música y las artes dramáticas

La música y **las artes dramáticas** son **formidables.** Vamos a aprender un poco más de las expresiones **artísticas.**

Me encantan **las obras de teatro**, sobre todo **las comedias** porque son muy **entretenidas** y **creativas.**

Requiere mucho talento escribir una canción. Hay que escribir **la letra** y encontrar **el ritmo** adecuado además de **crear una melodía** bonita.

**Más vocabulario...**

| | |
|---|---|
| **el ballet** | *ballet* |
| **de buen/mal gusto** | *in good/bad taste* |
| **estridente** | *shrill* |
| **incomprensible** | *incomprehensible* |
| **pésimo(a)** | *terrible* |
| **la reseña** | *(critical) review* |
| **superficial** | *superficial* |
| **la tragedia** | *tragedy* |

## Core Instruction

### TEACHING VOCABULARIO

1. Use the **Vocabulario** transparencies to present the vocabulary. Tell students to use the photo and the context to determine the meaning of the vocabulary words in the captions. **(3 min.)**
2. Ask students which words they do not understand. Provide a definition and use the word in context. For example, if a student does not understand **formidable,** you might say: **Significa "de calidad extraordinaria". Me encanta esta obra. ¡Es formidable! (4 min.)**
3. Go over the words in **Más vocabulario** and use each in a sentence. **(3 min.)**

### TEACHING ¡EXPRÉSATE!

1. Read the sentences in **¡Exprésate!** aloud to model pronunciation. **(2 min.)**
2. Have students tell you what they would like to do this weekend, or ask your advice. Respond, using sentences from **¡Exprésate!** For example, if a student says: **Quiero ir al cine,** you might respond: **Es mejor que vayas al teatro. Los actores de la nueva comedia son excelentes. (3 min.)**

Visit Holt Online
**go.hrw.com**
KEYWORD: EXP3 CH5
Vocabulario 2 practice

Ésta es una clase de **drama.** Durante **una función** los actores **desempeñan sus papeles** para el **público.**

Es relajante escuchar **la orquesta** cuando toca una canción **hermosa** y **melodiosa.**

Los actores ensayan en **el escenario** antes de **presentar** la obra.

**También se puede decir...**

In some Spanish-speaking countries, people say **la danza** instead of **el baile.** You may also hear **desempeñar un papel** for **actuar,** and **la crítica** for **la reseña.**

## ¡Exprésate!

**To make suggestions and recommendations**

Interactive TUTOR

**Te aconsejo que vayas a la presentación de baile folclórico. Es muy...**
*I recommend that you go to the folk dance performance. It's very . . .*

**No te olvides de ir al ensayo de la banda.**
*Don't forget to go to band practice.*

**Es mejor que veas la ópera. Es formidable.**
*It's better for you to see the opera. It's great.*

**Sería buena idea ir al concierto de la sinfónica.**
*It would be a good idea to go to the symphony.*

Vocabulario y gramática, pp. 55–57 Online workbooks

### TPR
**Total Physical Response**

Bring in a diagram of a theater, clearly showing the stage, the audience, and the orchestra. Have students respond to the following commands.

**Señala el escenario.**

**Señala el público.**

**Señala la orquesta.**

Then have students imagine they are at the theater and have them respond to these commands.

**La música es estridente. Tápate los oídos.**

**La tragedia fue muy triste. Pásame un pañuelo de papel.** 1.2

### También se puede decir...

Instead of **el concierto de la sinfónica,** some Spanish speakers might say **la sinfonía** to refer to the symphony concert.

### Language Notes

- Tell students that in Spanish the term **comedia** can also be used to refer to a play, not just a comedy.
- The word **ensayo** can have a similar meaning to the English word *essay,* but it is usually used in Spanish to mean *rehearsal.*

### Common Error Alert ¡OJO!

Students often use the term **audiencia** instead of **público,** because they are thinking of the English term *audience*. Explain that in Spanish the term **audiencia** is most often used in the context of granting someone an audience. **El presidente concedió una audiencia a los trabajadores.** For the audience of a play, the term **público** is used.

## Differentiated Instruction

### Slower Pace Learners

**Additional Practice** Divide the class into small groups. Give each group an entertainment section of an online Spanish newspaper. Tell them to have one member start by finding an artistic or cultural event they would like to attend. Then have them pass the paper to the next student, and that student will recommend something else. Ask them to continue on until everyone has had a chance to make two recommendations. Then have them decide as a group which event to attend. 1.1

### Multiple Intelligences

**Spatial** Have small groups of students work together to create a floor plan for a center for the arts in their community. Tell them to include space for music practice, dance studios, photography labs, sculpture studios, and any other activities they think should be included. Have them label the floor plans with words from **Vocabulario 1** and **Vocabulario 2.** Allow groups to present their floor plans to the class. 3.1

**Differentiated Instruction** See the Differentiated Instruction CD-ROM.

Capítulo 5

# Vocabulario 2

## Resources

**Planning:**

Lesson Planner, pp. 71–72, 232–233

One-Stop Planner

**Presentation:**

Teaching Transparencies
**Vocabulario** 5.3, 5.4

**Practice:**

Cuaderno de vocabulario y gramática, pp. 55–57

Activities for Communication, pp. 19–20

Lab Book, pp. 29–32

Teaching Transparencies
**Vocabulario y gramática** answers, pp. 55–57

Audio CD 5, Tr. 9

Interactive Tutor, Disc 1

### 23 Script

**1.** —¿Adónde fuiste el sábado?
—El sábado fuimos a ver el grupo de baile folclórico de México. ¡Fue formidable!

**2.** —¿Fueron a ver la función de la ópera?
—Sí, fuimos anoche a verla. La cantante tiene una voz hermosa.

**3.** —¿Qué tal estuvo el ensayo de la banda?
—Uy, nos fue muy mal. Perdimos el ritmo mientras caminábamos.

**4.** —Dicen que la nueva comedia es muy entretenida.
—Ni vayas a verla. La vi el martes; estuvo bastante extraña y de muy mal gusto.

**5.** —Cuéntame, ¿cómo estuvo el concierto?
—Estuvo buenísimo. El público se puso de pie y estuvo cantando la letra de las canciones.

**6.** —¿Te gustó la presentación de la orquesta sinfónica?
—Uy, ¡qué horror! La música fue incomprensible y estridente. Salí con un dolor de cabeza enorme.

CD 5, Tr. 9

### 23 ¡Estuvo muy entretenido! 1.2

**Escuchemos** Escucha los comentarios, escoge la foto que corresponde al evento e indica si a la persona **le gustó** o **no le gustó**.

A

**1.** a; le gustó

B

**2.** c; le gustó

C

**3.** f; no le gustó

D

**4.** d; no le gustó

E

**5.** b; le gustó

F

**6.** e; no le gustó

### 24 Tus gustos 1.2

**Hablemos** Da un ejemplo para cada uno de los temas.

1. un programa de mal gusto
2. una canción incomprensible
3. una comedia muy entretenida
4. un(a) cantante pésimo(a)
5. una persona muy creativa
6. una novela dramática

### 25 El crítico lo dice todo 1.2

**Leamos/Escribamos** Completa la reseña con las palabras del cuadro.

| | | | |
|---|---|---|---|
| aconsejo | concierto | función | sería buena idea |
| comedia | entretenida | es mejor | te olvides |

Si quieres ver una obra de teatro, te ___1___ que vayas a ver "El chisme silencioso", una nueva ___2___ en el Teatro Nacional. Créeme, ¡te vas a morir de la risa! Pero si quieres conseguir un boleto para la ___3___, no ___4___ de llamar al teatro por lo menos un día antes. A quienes no les guste el teatro, ___5___ que vean la presentación de baile contemporáneo en el Centro de Cultura. Además de ser muy ___6___, su valor artístico es impresionante. Finalmente, ___7___ que los aficionados a la música clásica fueran al ___8___ de la sinfónica este sábado.

**1.** aconsejo
**2.** comedia
**3.** función
**4.** te olvides
**5.** es mejor
**6.** entretenida
**7.** sería buena idea
**8.** concierto

## Core Instruction

### VOCABULARY IN CONTEXT

Students use the words from **Vocabulario 2** to write a review of a concert. They can write a review of a show they have seen or make one up. Have students take turns reading their reviews aloud for the class. As the rest of the students listen, have them take notes on the vocabulary words they hear. The class will have to decide whether the review was good or bad, and list the words that led them to that conclusion.

**26** **¿Qué le dices?** 1.2

**Leamos/Hablemos** Lee las oraciones y decide qué decirle a tu amigo(a) en las siguientes situaciones. Usa las frases del cuadro.

| | |
|---|---|
| Es mejor que... | Te aconsejo que... |
| No te olvides de... | Sería buena idea |

**MODELO** **Tu amigo(a) no sabe qué museo visitar.**
**Te aconsejo que vayas al museo de arte contemporáneo.**

1. Un(a) amigo(a) no sabe qué película ir a ver este fin de semana.
2. Quieres recomendarle un buen libro a tu amigo(a).
3. Un(a) amigo(a) piensa ir a un concierto que ya viste y que estuvo pésimo.
4. Tu amigo(a) quiere ver una presentación de baile pero no sabe adónde ir.
5. Escuchaste una canción muy buena y quieres recomendarle el CD a tu amigo(a).
6. Quieres recordarle a tu amigo(a) que vaya a la clase de teatro.

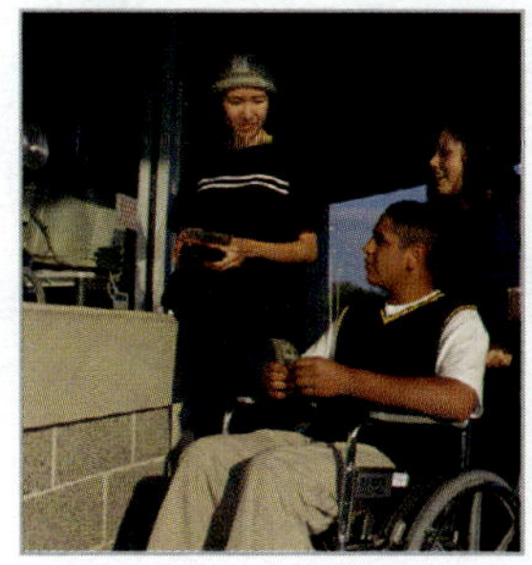
Unos amigos compran boletos para el cine.

**27** **En tus palabras** 1.2

**Escribamos** Escribe una reseña de ocho o diez oraciones acerca de un evento artístico muy bueno o de uno pésimo que hayas visto este año. Usa las palabras del cuadro en tu reseña.

| | | |
|---|---|---|
| de buen/mal gusto | Sería buena idea... | estridente |
| Te aconsejo que... | el escenario | impresionante |
| pésimo | Es mejor que... | entretenido |

## Comunicación

HOLT SoundBooth ONLINE RECORDING

**28** **Una buena recomendación** 1.1, 1.3

**Hablemos** Con un(a) compañero(a), dramaticen una conversación en que un estudiante de intercambio quiere saber a qué eventos culturales debe asistir durante su año de intercambio, y tú le das consejos y opiniones sobre varias actividades.

**MODELO** **—¿Puedes recomendarme un museo por aquí?**
**—Claro. Te aconsejo que vayas a...**

## Cultures

### Practices and Perspectives

Tell students that in Mexico, each state has its own particular dance and folkloric style. Most dances performed by the **Ballet Folclórico** are **bailes regionales,** (regional dances). Have students research the regional dances of one of the Mexican states and prepare a one-page report. 2.1

## Comunicación

### Group Work: Interpersonal

Bring in various Spanish-language entertainment guides. You might want to print out Madrid's **Guía del ocio** from the Internet, or other similar events listings from Mexico, Texas, or other Spanish-speaking countries. Have small groups of students set up a tourist information center. Students take turns being the information center employee. The other group members will tell what kinds of cultural events they are interested in, and the employee will use the guide to make suggestions. Have them switch guides with another group as the next person takes a turn as the information center employee. 1.1

## Differentiated Instruction

### ADVANCED LEARNERS

**Additional Practice** Have students find a review of a musical or theatrical performance from the entertainment section of a Spanish language newspaper. Ask them to read the review and underline the adjectives that describe the performance. Have them copy the adjectives in a notebook and try to guess their meaning though context. Then allow them to use a dictionary to check their work. Once they have all of the correct definitions, ask them to share their lists with the class. 1.2

### MULTIPLE INTELLIGENCES

**Rhythmic/Musical** Bring in Spanish music and play it for the students. (If possible, find music by well-known musicians.) Ask students to describe the rhythm and melody of the music and to tell whether they were able to pick up any of the words. Have them share their opinions of the music.

**Differentiated Instruction** See the Differentiated Instruction CD-ROM.

## Resources

**Planning:**

Lesson Planner, pp. 71–72, 232–233

One-Stop Planner

**Presentation:**

Teaching Transparencies
**Vocabulario** 5.3, 5.4

**Practice:**

Cuaderno de vocabulario y gramática, pp. 55–57

Activities for Communication, pp. 19–20

Lab Book, pp. 29–32

Teaching Transparencies
**Vocabulario y gramática** answers, pp. 55–57

Audio CD 5, Tr. 10

Interactive Tutor, Disc 1

## Cultures

### Products and Perspectives

Tell students that the famed golden age of Mexican film occurred during the 30s and 40s. At the peak of this "golden age," cinema became Mexico's third largest export and Mexican movie stars such as Pedro Infante and María Félix were known around the world. Ask students if they have seen or heard of Mexican films. Have them research the history of Mexican film and its relationship to the political situation in the country. Ask students if they can name any popular Mexican actors. Are they well-known in the United States?

2.2

### 29 Answers

1. Hablan de qué hacer este fin de semana.
2. Tiene otro compromiso.
3. Sugiere que vayan al teatro.
4. Dice que estuvo padrísima.
5. No dice por qué.
6. Quiere ir al Museo Metropolitano.

Estudiantes de la Ciudad de México

## Cada quien tiene su gusto

SOFÍA Oigan, ¿no quieren ir a ver el estreno de "Invasores del universo II" este viernes?

ROQUE No, el viernes no puedo. Tengo otro compromiso.

SOFÍA ¿Y tú, Celeste? ¿Qué dices?

CELESTE A decir verdad, no quiero ver esa película. Ramón me dijo que la primera parte estuvo pésima. ¿Por qué no vamos al teatro el sábado? Dicen que presentan una obra entretenida. ¿Les interesa ir a verla?

ROQUE ¿No será "El baile de los elefantes"? Ya la he visto y la obra estuvo padrísima. Es una comedia y el público no dejó de reírse. A mí me gustaría ir a verla de nuevo. ¿A qué hora empieza la función?

SOFÍA No sé, pero el sábado no puedo. Además, el título me da la impresión de que es una obra de muy mal gusto. Tengo otra idea. ¿Qué hacen el domingo? ¿Me acompañan al Museo Metropolitano? Hay una exposición de arte.

ROQUE Pues, fíjate que sería buena idea. No es tan divertido como el teatro, pero sí, iré contigo. ¿Y tú, Celeste?

CELESTE A mí me parece buena idea. Vamos al museo el domingo entonces.

### ¡Exprésate!

| To invite someone to do something | To turn down an invitation |
|---|---|
| **¿Quieres ir a ver...?** *Do you want to go see . . . ?* | **Gracias por invitarme, pero ya lo/la he visto.** *Thanks for inviting me, but I've already seen it.* |
| **¿Te interesa ir a...?** *Are you interested in going to . . . ?* | **Lo siento, pero ya tengo otros planes/otro compromiso.** *I'm sorry, but I already have other plans/another engagement.* |
| **¿Me acompañas a...?** *Do you want to come to . . . with me?* | **Gracias, pero tengo mucho que hacer. La próxima vez iré.** *Thanks, but I have a lot to do. I'll go next time.* |
| **¿Por qué no vamos a...?** *Why don't we go to . . . ?* | **Hoy no, gracias. ¿Por qué no lo dejamos para la próxima semana?** *Not today, thanks. Why don't we wait and do it next week?* |

Interactive TUTOR

Vocabulario y gramática, pp. 55–57 Online workbooks

## Core Instruction

### TEACHING ¡EXPRÉSATE!

1. Have volunteers read the conversation between Sofía, Roque, and Celeste. Ask students to summarize the conversation. **(3 min.)**
2. Use the sentences from **¡Exprésate!** to model both sides of a conversation, inviting someone to do something and turning down an invitation. **(2 min.)**
3. Ask volunteers to name activities they would like to do (**ir al cine**). Use the **¡Exprésate!** functions to invite one of the students to the activity. (**¿Me acompañas al cine esta tarde?**) Have the student give an excuse (**Tengo tarea.**), then use an **¡Exprésate!** sentence to model how to use the excuse to turn down the invitation. (**Gracias por invitarme, pero tengo mucha tarea hoy.**) **(5 min.)**

See answers on p. 206.

## 29 ¿Cómo fue? 1.2

**Leamos/Escribamos** Contesta las preguntas con base en el diálogo en la página 206.

1. ¿De qué hablan los tres amigos?
2. ¿Por qué no puede Roque ir a ver la película?
3. ¿Qué sugiere Celeste?
4. ¿Qué opina Roque de la obra que menciona Celeste?
5. ¿Por qué no puede ir Sofía al teatro?
6. ¿A dónde quiere ir Sofía el domingo?

CD 5, Tr. 10 See script on p. 185F.

## 30 Me gustaría pero... 1.2

**Escuchemos** Escucha las conversaciones e indica si la persona **acepta** o **no acepta** la invitación.

## 31 Te invito... 1.2

**Hablemos/Escribamos** Invita a cada persona al evento indicado.

1. tu mamá/un museo de arte
2. tu amigo(a)/una exposición de arte
3. tu novio(a)/una obra de teatro
4. tus compañeros de clase/una película
5. tu primo(a)/un concierto
6. tus abuelos/un restaurante

### Nota cultural

La música más popular del norte de México es la música norteña, la cual tiene sus orígenes en las polkas de Europa y refleja la influencia alemana en el uso del acordeón. Algunos grupos norteños exitosos son Pesado, Los Tigres del Norte, y Los Tucanes de Tijuana. Otros géneros populares en el norte de México incluyen la banda, el grupero y la cumbia. ¿Cómo se compara la música del norte de México con la del suroeste de Estados Unidos? 2.2, 4.2

## Comunicación

HOLT SoundBooth ONLINE RECORDING

## 32 Tengo muchas cosas que hacer 1.1, 1.2

**Leamos/Hablemos** Tu amigo(a) te invita a salir, pero tienes mucho que hacer. Consulta tu agenda y acepta o rechaza (*refuse*) las invitaciones según tus actividades. Usa las expresiones de **Exprésate.**

| 21 lunes | 22 martes | 23 miércoles | 24 jueves | 25 viernes | 26 sábado | 27 domingo |
|---|---|---|---|---|---|---|
| • clase de pintura 4:00<br>• ensayo de coro 6:00<br>• estudiar para el examen de inglés 7:30 | • cine con Ruth 6:00<br>• estudiar para el examen de inglés 8:30 | • examen de inglés 10:00 a.m.<br>• clase de pintura 4:00<br>• museo con Gabriel 6:00 | • almuerzo con Juan Luis 1:30<br>• ensayo de coro 4:30<br>• trabajar en la galería 6:00–8:00 | • tarea con Sonia 4:00<br>• ensayo de coro 5:00<br>• concierto de coro 7:00 | • cena con la familia 5:00<br>• trabajar en la galería 6:00–8:00<br>• cine con mis amigos 8:30 | • teatro con abuela 4:30<br>• limpiar mi cuarto 6:30<br>• hacer tarea de ciencias 8:00 |



### 30 Script, Answers

See script and answers on page 185F.

### Teacher to Teacher

**Aura Cole**
Parkway Central Middle School
Chesterfield, MO

Students choose a partner, then extend and accept invitations through e-mail. They first greet each other, then each asks how the other is doing. One extends an invitation, and the other responds by saying he or she doesn't like that activity, and suggests another. The invitation is accepted. I have them print the correspondence, and then act it out as if it were a phone call. 1.1

### Comunicación

**Pair Activity: Interpersonal**

Pass out Spanish-language entertainment guides to pairs of students. Have partners take turns inviting each other to events listed in the guides. The partner should turn down several invitations, making an excuse before agreeing to attend an event. 1.1

## Differentiated Instruction

### ADVANCED LEARNERS

**Challenge** Have students research instruments used in Latin American music. They might want to look for information on instruments such as **la quena, el charango, el banjo,** or **el güiro.** Have them make a short presentation on the instruments, what countries they are used in, and for what kind of music. 2.2

### MULTIPLE INTELLIGENCES

**Linguistic** Have students brainstorm words they might use when inviting someone to do something or turning down an invitation. Write two heads on the board, **Invitar** and **Rechazar la invitación.** Encourage students to use terms from **Vocabulario 1** and **Vocabulario 2** as well as other known words, and write them under the appropriate heads as students provide them. Have students use the words to add variety to their sentences as they practice inviting and turning down invitations. 1.2

### Assess

**Assessment Program**
**Prueba: Vocabulario 2,** pp. 87–88
Alternative Assessment, pp. 377, 389, 401

**Online Assessment**
**my.hrw.com**

**Test Generator**

**Assess** **Differentiated Instruction** See the Differentiated Instruction CD-ROM.

## Resources

**Planning:**

Lesson Planner, pp. 73–75, 234–237

One-Stop Planner

**Presentation:**

Video Program
**GramaVisión**

**Practice:**

Grammar Tutor for Students of Spanish, Chapter 5

Cuaderno de vocabulario y gramática, pp. 58–60

Cuaderno de actividades, pp. 45–47

Activities for Communication, pp. 19–20

Lab Book, pp. 29–32

Teaching Transparencies
Bell Work 5.6
**Vocabulario y gramática** answers, pp. 58–60

Audio CD 5, Tr. 11

Interactive Tutor, Disc 1

### Bell Work

Use Bell Work 5.7 in the *Teaching Transparencies*, or write this activity on the board.

**Completa las oraciones con la forma correcta del verbo.**

1. Sugiero que ustedes ______ (ir) al concierto de la sinfónica.
2. Mi profesor quiere que nosotros ______ (sacar) buenas notas.
3. ¿Quieres que Alberto te ______ (ayudar) con la escultura?
4. El actor espera que el público ______ (divertirse).
5. Es mejor que mis papás ______ (llegar) al cine primero.

1.2

**Objetivos**
- Subjunctive for hopes and wishes
- Past perfect

# Gramática en acción 2

GramaVisión

Interactive TUTOR

## Repaso: Subjunctive for hopes and wishes

**1** After verbs for hopes or wishes you can use a second verb in the **infinitive**. The subject of the infinitive or infinitive phrase is the same as that of the conjugated verb.

*infinitive phrase; Ana is subject*

Ana espera **ir** al museo.

**2** If the subject of the second verb is different from that of the first verb, then add the word **que** and conjugate the second verb. The phrase formed using **que** is called a subordinate clause.

*main clause* — *subordinate clause, indicative*

Ana **cree** **que** María Elena **va** al museo.

*change of subject*

**3** If the verb in the main clause expresses **a wish, suggestion,** or **recommendation** AND if there is a change of subject, use the **subjunctive mood** in the subordinate clause.

*expresses hope* — *subordinate clause, subjunctive*

Ana **espera** **que** María Elena **vaya** al museo.

*change of subject*

**More expressions of wish, suggestion and recommendation**

| | | | |
|---|---|---|---|
| **aconsejar que** | *to advise* | **recomendar (ie) que** | *to recomme* |
| **es mejor que...** | *it's better . . .* | **sugerir (ie) que** | *to suggest* |
| **querer (ie) que** | *to want* | | |

Vocabulario y gramática, pp. 58–60
Actividades, pp. 45–47
Online workbooks

### En inglés

**In English,** some verbs can take an infinitive even if there is change of subject. The word *for* sometimes comes before the second subject.

Ana wants (for) Lili to go...

Other verbs take *that* + a verb in the **indicative** or **subjunctive**.

Ana says that Lili goes...

Ana prefers that Lili go...

Look at the verbs in the box. Which English verbs take an infinitive and which take *that* + a conjugated verb?

4.1

*To want* takes an infinitive, *to recommend* and *to suggest* take the subjunctive, and *to advise* takes both.

CD 5, Tr. 11 See script on p. 185F.

**33 Consejos lógicos** 1.2

**1.** no **2.** sí **3.** no **4.** sí **5.** no

**Escuchemos** Escucha las conversaciones y decide si la segunda persona da consejos lógicos o no. Indica **sí** o **no.**

## Core Instruction

### TEACHING GRAMÁTICA

1. Go over **En inglés** with students. **(2 min.)**
2. Remind students that they have already learned to use the subjunctive with hopes and wishes. Go over point 1. **(2 min.)**
3. Go over point 2. Write more examples on the board and have students identify the main and subordinate clauses. Have volunteers go to the board and underline the verb in the subjunctive. **Quiero que mis amigos vengan a la fiesta. El profesor recomienda que leamos este libro. (3 min.)**
4. Go over point 3 with students. After reading the example, modify the sentence so that there is a change in subject to emphasize the difference: **Yo quiero que ella tome una clase de arte. (3 min.)**

### GramaVisión

For a video presentation of the subjunctive with hopes and wishes, use **GramaVisión.**

GramaVisión

Visit Holt Online
**go.hrw.com**
KEYWORD: EXP3 CH5
Gramática 2 practice

## 34 ¿Qué quieren hacer? 1.2

**Escribamos** Combina las frases y describe lo que cada persona quiere hacer este fin de semana.

1. Enrique/querer/que todos/ir a un concierto
2. Yo/preferir/que nosotros/ver una película
3. Ana/esperar/que alguien/querer ir al partido
4. Alex/recomendar/que los chicos/practicar ciclismo
5. Tú/aconsejarnos/que todos/hacer algo juntos
6. Mamá/sugerir/que yo/estudiar el sábado

## 35 Querida Paquita... 1.3

**Leamos/Escribamos** Imagina que eres "Querida Paquita" y responde a cada carta con uno o dos consejos y recomendaciones.

*¿Se te olvidó?* Subjunctive mood, p. 18

Querida Paquita:
Tengo un problema. Me encantan las artes, especialmente el baile. Mis amigas me dicen que bailo muy bien y quiero tomar clases de baile, pero mis padres no pueden pagármelas. ¿Qué debo hacer?

Inés

Querida Paquita:
Me interesa mucho estar en el coro de mi colegio, pero me da miedo hacer una audición frente a tantas personas. Creo que canto mejor en grupos. ¿Qué me aconsejas?

David

## Comunicación

HOLT SoundBooth ONLINE RECORDING

## 36 ¿Qué hago? 1.1, 1.3

**Hablemos** Dramaticen una escena entre dos amigos o amigas. Tú quieres salir con un(a) chico(a), y sabes que a él (ella) le gusta el arte y la cinematografía, pero no sabes adónde ir. Pídele consejos a tu amigo(a). Tu amigo(a) debe responder con algunas recomendaciones.

**MODELO** **—Oye, Tomás, ¿crees que debo llevar a Sonia al cine?**
**—Pues, te sugiero que vayan al museo. Hay una nueva exposición allí que es bellísima.**

Gramática 2

### 34 Answers

1. Enrique quiere que todos vayan a un concierto.
2. (Yo) prefiero que (nosotros) vayamos a una película.
3. Ana espera que alguien quiera ir al partido.
4. Alex recomienda que los chicos practiquen ciclismo.
5. (Tú) nos aconsejas que todos hagan algo juntos.
6. Mamá sugiere que yo estudie el sábado.

### 35 Answers

Answers will vary. Possible answers:
Querida Inés,
Te recomiendo que hables con los maestros y el director del estudio de danza. Muchas veces permiten que alguien con talento tome clases de danza gratis en cambio por horas voluntarias; por ejemplo, es posible que trabajes en la oficina vendiendo boletos.
Buena suerte, Paquita

Querido David,
Te aconsejo que hables con tus amigos de la clase de música para que te acompañen a la audición. Con tus amigos entre las caras que mires durante la audición, te dará más confianza.
¡Suerte! Paquita

## Comunicación

### Class Activity: Interpersonal

Tell students to imagine that they are going to create an art center for their school. Have them work in small groups to come up with ideas for the center. Remind them to use expressions of hopes and wishes.

**MODELO**
**—Propongo que creemos una sala para exposiciones de arte.**
**—Es mejor que tengamos un lugar para pintar y esculpir.**
1.1

## Differentiated Instruction

### ADVANCED LEARNERS

**35 Additional Practice** Have students write their own **Querida Paquita** letters and exchange them with a partner. Ask them to write at least three sentences of advice for their partners. When they have finished, have them exchange letters with one more partner and then compare the advice they receive from each person. 1.1

### MULTIPLE INTELLIGENCES

**Interpersonal** Have students imagine they are the principal of the school. Have them write a short paragraph descibing what they wish for the student body this year. Have volunteers share their paragraphs with the class. 1.3

**Differentiated Instruction** See the Differentiated Instruction CD-ROM.

## Resources

**Planning:**

Lesson Planner, pp. 73–76, 234–237

One-Stop Planner

**Presentation:**

Video Program
**GramaVisión**

**Practice:**

Grammar Tutor for Students of Spanish, Chapter 5

Cuaderno de vocabulario y gramática, pp. 58–60

Cuaderno de actividades, pp. 45–47

Activities for Communication, pp. 19–20

Teaching Transparencies
Bell Work 5.7
**Vocabulario y gramática** answers, pp. 58–60

Interactive Tutor, Disc 1

### Bell Work

Use Bell Work 5.7 in the *Teaching Transparencies,* or write this activity on the board.

**Completa las oraciones con la forma correcta del verbo.**

1. **Sugiero que ustedes ______ (ir) al concierto de la sinfónica.**
2. **Mi profesor quiere que nosotros ______ (sacar) buenas notas.**
3. **¿Quieres que Alberto te ______ (ayudar) con la escultura?**
4. **El actor espera que el público ______ (divertirse).**
5. **Es mejor que mis papás ______ (llegar) al cine primero.** 1.2

### Language Note

The word **ensayo** can have a similar meaning to the English word *essay,* but it is usually used in Spanish to mean *rehearsal.*

Interactive TUTOR

## More on subjunctive for hopes and wishes

**1** You know that the **subjunctive** is used in sentences that express a **wish, suggestion,** or **recommendation** for another person or group of people. Other expressions used with the subjunctive are:

**Propongo** que **hagamos** las dos cosas.
*I propose we do both things.*

Nos **dicen** que **compremos** los boletos.
*They're telling us to buy the tickets.*

**Necesito** que **me ayudes.**
*I need you to help me.*

**Hace falta** que **practiques** más.
*You have to practice more.*

Vocabulario y gramática, pp. 58–60
Actividades, pp. 45–47
Online workbooks

**More expressions of wish, suggestion and recommendation**

| | | | |
|---|---|---|---|
| **es importante que...** | *it's important . . .* | **ojalá (que)...** | *let's hope . .* |
| **es necesario que...** | *it's necessary . . .* | **pedir (i) que** | *to ask for* |

### Nota cultural

Frida Kahlo es una de las artistas más conocidas de México. Lo popular, lo religioso y los símbolos mexicanos son parte del estilo de sus obras. Ella se casó con el famoso pintor Diego Rivera en 1929. Fue Diego quien le sugirió a Frida que usara ropa tradicional mexicana. Ella siguió su consejo y por eso se conoce por sus vestidos largos de colores brillantes (al estilo tradicional mexicano) y sus joyas exóticas.

Investiga una obra de esta artista y explica algunos de los símbolos mexicanos que encuentres en ella. 2.2, 3.1

Photo by Nickolas Muray © Nicolas Murray Photo Archives/Courtesy George Eastman House

### 37 ¿Estás de acuerdo? 1.2

**Leamos/Hablemos** Lee las oraciones y di si **estás de acuerdo** o **no** con cada una. Si no estás de acuerdo, da tu propia opinión.

1. Propongo que veamos tu concierto favorito en televisión.
2. Para estudiar arte, es importante que seas muy creativo.
3. Para graduarte, es necesario que sepas hablar otro idioma.
4. Hace falta que el público esté callado durante la ópera.
5. Es necesario que una orquesta interprete música variada.
6. Te recomiendo que vayas al teatro si te gustan los dramas.

### 38 El ensayo 1.2

**Leamos/Escribamos** Completa el diálogo con la forma correcta de los verbos entre paréntesis.

PAULINA Quiero (participar) __1__ en la orquesta, pero mis amigos me dicen que no lo (hacer) __2__. *participar* *haga*

PROFESORA Es importante que tú misma (tomar) __3__ la decisión; no es bueno que tus amigos (decidir) __4__ por ti. *tom* *decidan*

PAULINA Espero que ellos no me (poder) __5__ convencer, porque me encanta la música. Creo que sólo desean (pasar) __6__ más tiempo conmigo. *puedan* *pasar*

PROFESORA Ya veo. Los profesores y yo esperamos (empezar) __7__ los ensayos pronto, y hace falta que tú (practicar) __8__. *empe* *prac*

## Core Instruction

### TEACHING GRAMÁTICA

1. Go over point 1 with students and read the examples. Remind students that they already know some expressions of hopes and wishes that take the subjunctive. **(2 min.)**
2. Go over point 2. Provide examples: **Necesito que compres el periódico para ver el horario. Necesito comprar el periódico para ver el horario. (2 min.)**
3. Give students sample sentences in which there is no change in subject between the main and subordinate clause, and have them change the sentence to include a change in subject. Remind them to use the subjunctive. **(3 min.)**

### GramaVisión

For a video presentation of the subjunctive with hopes and wishes, use **GramaVisión.**

GramaVisión

## 39 A Opiniones ❀ 1.2

**Leamos/Escribamos** Haz una recomendación para las siguientes oraciones, usando las expresiones del cuadro.

| | | |
|---|---|---|
| Es importante que | Hace falta que | Les aconsejo que |
| Les recomiendo que | Es mejor que | Ojalá que |

1. La presentación de bailes folclóricos estuvo formidable.
2. El escenario me pareció impresionante.
3. Recuerden que sólo hay una función diaria.
4. En cambio, la obra de teatro fue pésima.
5. Los actores no eran muy originales.
6. En realidad, toda la obra me pareció de mal gusto.

## 39 B Oraciones revueltas ❀ 1.2

**Escribamos** Forma cinco oraciones con una palabra o frase de cada columna. Usa el subjuntivo.

| | | | |
|---|---|---|---|
| los artistas | querer | que | el público... |
| el público | proponer | | los alumnos... |
| el director del museo | recomendar | | el colegio... |
| la profesora de arte | preferir | | yo... |
| yo | decir | | los críticos... |

## Comunicación

HOLT SoundBooth ONLINE RECORDING

## 40 Una entrevista de trabajo ❀ 1.1, 1.3

**Hablemos** Con un(a) compañero(a), dramaticen una conversación en la que una persona explica lo que le pasó en la entrevista y la otra le da consejos para mejorar en la próxima entrevista.

## Answers

Use the Chapter 5 *Picture Sequences Transparency.*

**43 Sample Answer**

—Ay José, ayer llegué tarde a la entrevista en el museo. Y también se me cayó el café de la directora del museo. Ella se puso furiosa. Luego, me hizo muchas preguntas sobre el arte y yo no supe las respuestas.

—Pues Pablo, te recomiendo que llegues veinte minutos temprano a las entrevistas. Es importante que estés tranquilo cuando llegues. También te sugiero que busques trabajo en otro lugar. Pienso que la directora no te va a entrevistar de nuevo.

## Comunicación

### Group Activity: Interpersonal

Ask students to imagine that they are artists trying to find a gallery to exhibit their art. Have them work in pairs and take turns playing the parts of gallery director and artist. The artist should tell about his or her artwork and express a wish to exhibit the art. The director will then tell the artist what he or she needs to do in order to do so. Suggest that students use phrases such as **propongo que, es importante que, necesito que, ojalá, hace falta que, es necesario que.** ❀ 1.1

## Differentiated Instruction

### ADVANCED LEARNERS

**38 Personalization** Have students work in pairs to discuss a problem a friend is having, like the one in Activity 38. They should take turns sharing their problems and giving advice. ❀ 1.1

### SPECIAL LEARNING NEEDS

**38 Students with AD(H)D** Before students do Activity 38, have them scan the text and underline the phrases that express hopes and wishes. Remind them that when the subject does not change, **que** is omitted and the infinitive is used. Have them circle the word **que** whenever it appears after an expression of hopes and wishes. Go over each item together, and have volunteers write the answers on the board. Ask the rest of the class to copy the answers in their notebooks. Then read the completed conversation as a class. ❀ 1.2

**Differentiated Instruction** See the Differentiated Instruction CD-ROM.

## Resources

**Planning:**

Lesson Planner, pp. 73–75, 234–237

One-Stop Planner

**Presentation:**

Video Program
**GramaVisión**

**Practice:**

Grammar Tutor for Students of Spanish, Chapter 5

Cuaderno de vocabulario y gramática, pp. 58–60

Cuaderno de actividades, pp. 45–47

Activities for Communication, pp. 19–20

Lab Book, pp. 29–32

Teaching Transparencies
Bell Work 5.8

**Vocabulario y gramática** answers, pp. 58–60

Audio CD 5, Tr. 12

Interactive Tutor, Disc 1

### Bell Work

Use Bell Work 5.8 in the *Teaching Transparencies,* or write this activity on the board.

**Completa las oraciones.**

1. Mis papás quieren que yo...
2. El profesor recomienda que nosotros...
3. Yo quiero...
4. Es necesario...
5. Sugiero que ustedes....

1.2

### 41 Script

See script and answers on page 185F.

Interactive TUTOR

## Past perfect

**1** To narrate a sequence of events in the past, use the **past perfect (pluscuamperfecto)** for the event that happened first, and the **preterite** or **imperfect** for the event that happened later.

| 3:00 → | 3:45 → | 6:45 → | 7:00 |
|---|---|---|---|
| estábamos en casa | salimos de casa | Luis llegó al teatro | llegamos al teatro |

Luis nos **llamó** a las cuatro, pero ya **habíamos salido.**
*Luis called us at four, but we had already left.*

**Llegamos** al teatro a las siete. Luis ya **había llegado.**
*We got to the theater at seven. Luis had already arrived.*

**2** The past perfect is formed by combining the **imperfect of haber** with the **past participle** of the main verb.

| | | | |
|---|---|---|---|
| **había** | **habíamos** | | |
| **habías** | **habíais** | + | **past participle** |
| **había** | **habían** | | |

**3** The past perfect is frequently used with **cuando, ya, aún no,** or **todavía no.**

Cuando **llegué** al teatro, **aún no había visto** a Luis.
*When I arrived at the theater, I still hadn't seen Luis.*

**Entró** tarde pero **todavía no había empezado** la obra.
*He went in late but the play had not yet started.*

### ¡Te acuerdas?

The following verbs have irregular past participles:

abrir: **abierto**
decir: **dicho**
describir: **descrito**
descubrir: **descubierto**
escribir: **escrito**
freír: **frito**
hacer: **hecho**
morir: **muerto**
poner: **puesto**
resolver: **resuelto**
romper: **roto**
satisfacer: **satisfecho**
ver: **visto**
volver: **vuelto**

Vocabulario y gramática, pp. 45–47
Actividades, pp. 58–60
Online workbooks

CD 5, Tr. 12

### 41 ¿Qué pasó primero? 1.2

**Escuchemos** Escucha las oraciones que siguen y di cuál de las dos acciones ocurrió primero, basándote en lo que oyes.

1. llegar al teatro/empezar la obra
2. pedir refrescos Raúl/ver a Raúl
3. buscar los asientos/apagarse las luces
4. encontrar el asiento/salir al escenario los actores
5. sentarme/empezar la música
6. terminar la segunda escena/dormirse Raúl
7. salir/terminar la obra
8. llegar al carro/empezar a salir la gente

## Core Instruction

### TEACHING GRAMÁTICA

1. Go over point 1 with students. Read the first example. Ask **¿A qué hora salieron de casa?** (3:45) **¿A qué hora llamó Luis?** (4:00). **(3 min.)**
2. Read the second example. Check comprehension. **¿Quién llegó primero, Luis o sus amigos?** (Luis) **(3 min.)**
3. Go over point 2 with examples: **Tú habías comido. Ellos habían hablado. Yo había salido. (2 min.)**
4. Go over point 3. Ask students to review the past participles in **¿Te acuerdas? (2 min.)**
5. Draw a timeline on the board with four events such as: **1:00 comí; 1:45 vi las noticias; 2:30 me llamó Lisa; 3:45 salí de la casa.** Ask students questions about the timeline using the past perfect. **Cuando Lisa me llamó, ¿ya había comido? (5 min.)**

### GramaVisión

For a video presentation of the past perfect, use **GramaVisión.**

GramaVisión

## 42 Preparativos 1.2

**Escribamos** Combina las frases y describe los preparativos que se habían hecho antes del comienzo de la feria de arte del colegio. Usa el pluscuamperfecto.

**MODELO** **yo/mandar invitaciones a todos los padres**
**Yo había mandado invitaciones a todos los padres.**

1. la profesora de arte/colgar las obras en el gimnasio
2. varios alumnos/llevar las esculturas a la cafetería
3. los estudiantes de arte/ponerles títulos a todas las obras
4. el director del colegio/escribir un anuncio para el periódico
5. el profesor de música/leer el anuncio en la radio
6. unos chicos creativos/hacer carteles para anunciar la feria

## 43 Mal planeado 1.2

**Hablemos** Mira los dibujos y describe las escenas usando el pluscuamperfecto. *¿Se te olvidó?* Preterite, p. 160

**MODELO** **Cuando llegamos al cine para comprar las entradas, ya habían cerrado.**

1.

2.

3.

4.

## Comunicación



## 44 Hablemos del pasado 1.1, 1.2

**Hablemos** Usa la siguiente información para entrevistar a un(a) compañero(a) de clase. Sigue el modelo.

**MODELO** **10 años/tomar clases de piano**
**—¿Ya habías tomado clases de piano cuando tenías 10 años?**

1. 5 años/leer un libro entero
2. 10 años/aprender a dibujar
3. 15 años/visitar un museo
4. 5 años/sacar una foto
5. 10 años/ver una película en el cine
6. 15 años/ver una obra de teatro

## Gramática 2

### 42 Answers

1. La profesora de arte había colgado las obras en el gimnasio.
2. Varios alumnos habían llevado las esculturas a la cafetería.
3. Los estudiantes de arte les habían puesto títulos a todas las obras.
4. El director del colegio había escrito un anuncio para el periódico.
5. El profesor de música había oído el anuncio en la radio.
6. Unos chicos creativos habían hecho carteles para anunciar la feria.

### Más práctica

Have students complete the following sentences with the past perfect of the verb in parentheses.

1. **Cuando llegamos al cine aún no _____ (empezar) la película.**
2. **Julia ya _____ (ver) esa película.**
3. **Yo todavía no _____ (comprar) las entradas.**
4. **Nosotros no _____ (cenar).**
5. **Nuestros amigos todavía no _____ (llegar).** 1.2

### Comunicación

#### Class Activity: Interpretive

Have students work in small groups to present one of the timelines from one of the **Geocultura** spreads. Ask them to use the past perfect to discuss what had already happened when certain events occurred. Allow the rest of the class to ask questions. 1.2

## Differentiated Instruction

### SLOWER PACE LEARNERS

**41 Personalization** After students have done Activity 41, have them write down a series of activities they did during the weekend. Then have them tell a partner about what happened this weekend, using the past perfect to indicate what happened prior to each action. (**Cuando me levanté el sábado, todo el mundo ya se había levantado.**) 1.2

### MULTIPLE INTELLIGENCES

**Linguistic** Have students work in pairs to describe the events of a favorite movie to a partner. Encourage them to use the past perfect to emphasize when certain actions occurred. (**Cuando llegó la mujer, su novio ya se había ido.**) 1.1

### Assess

**Assessment Program**

**Prueba: Gramática 2,** pp. 89–90

**Prueba: Aplicación 2,** pp. 91–92

Audio CD 3, Tr. 18

Alternative Assessment, pp. 377, 389, 401

**Online Assessment** my.hrw.com

**Test Generator**

**Assess** **Differentiated Instruction** See the Differentiated Instruction CD-ROM.

## Resources

**Planning:**

Lesson Planner, pp. 76, 236–237

One-Stop Planner

**Presentation:**

Video Program, Videocassette 3

DVD Program

**VideoNovela**

**Practice:**

Video Guide, pp. 34–36

Lab Book, pp. 71–72

### Visual Learners

Have students prepare a chart with their list of deductions from **Episodio 3** and their list of connections from **Episodio 4.** Have them calculate how many of the items on their list were confirmed. 1.2

| Deductions: EPISODIO 3 | Confirmed | Not Confirmed |
|---|---|---|
| | | |
| Connections: EPISODIO 4 | | |
| | | |

### Gestures

Have students observe the gestures used throughout this episode. Are there any points where the characters exaggerate their gestures? Why? How do the gestures used by the characters change with the context of the **Novela?**

Novela en video

# Clara perspectiva

## Episodio 5

**ESTRATEGIA**

**Getting confirmation** As a story unfolds, it is important to decide whether the deductions and the connections you have made are correct. This allows you to move forward in the story. Take your list of deductions from **Episodio 3** and your connections from **Episodio 4**, and place a check mark by the ones that are confirmed in this episode. If they are not confirmed, decide whether they might still turn out to be true, or whether you think you can discard them. 1.2

### En la oficina del señor Ortega

1

**Sr. Ortega** Espero que no tengan nada que hacer esta tarde. Se abre al público una exposición de artistas chilenos en el Museo de Artes Visuales. Es la exposición más esperada del año.

**Clara** No, Señor Ortega, por mi parte, estoy a su disposición.

**Octavio** Yo también.

2

**Clara** La compañía *MaderaCorp* es la patrocinadora de la exposición. Un porcentaje de las ganancias se va a donar al grupo *EcoChile,* el grupo ecologista de mayor influencia en Chile.

**Sr. Ortega** Aunque interesante, Clara, eso no tiene importancia para nuestro artículo. El artículo se va a concentrar en la reacción del público a la exposición. ¿Qué dice la gente sobre el arte moderno de Chile? ¿Es realista, o imaginativo?; ¿Es artístico, o incomprensible?; ¿Es de buen gusto, o pésimo? Éstas son las preguntas que queremos hacerle al público.

### En el Museo de Artes Visuales

MUSEO DE ARTES VISUALES
COLECCIÓN SANTA CRUZ · YACONI

3

4

## Core Instruction

### TEACHING NOVELA EN VIDEO

1. Have students scan the **Novela en video** text for the settings included in this episode. **(1 min.)**
2. Play the video, stopping periodically to ask comprehension questions. **(5 min.)**
3. Have volunteers play the parts of the characters and read the video text aloud. Encourage them to be expressive and use gestures as they read. **(5 min.)**
4. Answer the questions on page 215 as a class. **(5 min.)**

### Escuchemos

As students watch the **Novela,** have them listen for two people giving their opinion about the art exhibit. Are the opinions favorable or not?

Novela en video

Visit Holt Online
**go.hrw.com**
KEYWORD: EXP3 CH5
Online Edition

5

6

7

8

9

**En un bosque de Chile**

***El profesor Luna trabaja en los bosques de Pirque, cerca de Santiago.***

## ¿COMPRENDES?

1. ¿Adónde tienen que ir Clara y Octavio para su nueva tarea? ¿De qué se tratan las entrevistas?
2. ¿A quién ve Clara?
3. ¿Quién da un discurso? ¿Sobre qué? ¿Quién va a recibir alguna parte de las ganancias de la exposición?
4. ¿Quién mencionó al señor Reyes en el Episodio 4?
5. ¿Quiénes interrumpen la exposición? ¿Qué confirman sus acciones?
6. ¿Qué les parece raro a Octavio y a Clara?

1.2

**Próximo episodio**
***Clara lee más en el periódico sobre el problema entre MaderaCorp y los ecologistas. ¿Quién crees que está al centro del debate?***
PÁGINAS 256–257

Novela en video

## ¿Comprendes? Answers

1. al museo de artes visuales; la reacción del público a la exposición
2. al hombre que había grabado hablando con el profesor
3. el presidente de MaderaCorp; la exposición "El arte del Chile de hoy"; las organizaciones que quieren salvar los bosques de Chile
4. Tío Arnoldo
5. los ecologistas; MaderaCorp no quiere perservar los bosques de Chile.
6. MaderaCorp y los ecologistas no están de acuerdo.

## Cultures

### Practices and Perspectives

On the weekends, people head from Santiago to the Río Maipo for camping, hiking, climbing, whitewater rafting, skiing, or cycling. The quiet, laid-back village of Pirque is one of the canyon's gateways, and attracts crowds with its weekend craft market and **Viña Concha y Toro** wine tours. In the Natural Reserve of Pirque, visitors can find a variety of plant life, crystal lakes, birds, and other animals. Have students research Web sites in Spanish on the Natural Reserve of Pirque **(Reserva Nacional Río Clarillo)** to find out the regulations on commercial development in the area.

2.1

## Clara perspectiva, Episodio 5

In **Episodio 5,** Señor Ortega asks Clara and Octavio to go to an art exhibit and interview attendees on their opinions of the works. Clara points out that *MaderaCorp* is sponsoring the event in conjunction with *EcoChile.* Señor Ortega snaps back that **Chile en la Mira** is not interested in that aspect of the exhibit. At the museum, Octavio and Clara rehearse their interviews. The president of *MaderaCorp* steps up to a podium, accompanied by two bodyguards. Clara recognizes the men as the same two who threatened the professor in **Episodio 2.** As the president of *MaderaCorp* gives his speech, a group of protestors storms in shouting pro-environmental, anti-*MaderaCorp* slogans. Clara is confused because she understood that *MaderaCorp* supported the environmental agenda of *EcoChile.* Later we see Professor Luna gathering samples at Pirque, a forest near Santiago.

## Comunicación

### Pair Activity: Interpersonal

Have students work in pairs to discuss their unconfirmed deductions about the **Novela.** Do they still think the deductions are true or can they discard them?

1.1

# Lectura cultural

## Resources

**Planning:**

Lesson Planner, pp. 77, 238–239

One-Stop Planner

**Presentation:**

Audio CD 5, Tr. 13

**Practice:**

Cuaderno de actividades, p. 48

Reading Strategies and Skills Handbook, Chapter 5

Interactive Advanced Reader

## Pre-Reading Activity

Have students talk about a painting, mural, or sculpture they have seen recently. What did it depict? Were there any social or political issues portrayed in the work? Ask students if they are familiar with Mexican art. Which Mexican artists have they heard of? Have students look at the photographs and read the captions. What do they know about Diego Rivera?

## Connections

### History Link

Have students find some photographs of Diego Rivera's murals on the Internet or in the library. Students will select their favorite mural and analyze it. Have them identify at least one famous person or important historical event of the time portrayed in the mural and explain why they think it was included.

2.2, 3.1

## Pre-AP Practice

**AP Language Examination: Lectura cultural** helps students prepare for Section I, Part B: **Reading Comprehension.** The audio recording helps them prepare for Part A: **Listening—Short Narratives.**

# Lectura cultural

Los murales de Diego Rivera son conocidos a nivel internacional.

Diego Rivera

CD 5, Tr. 13

## Diego Rivera

Diego Rivera, considerado el pintor mexicano más importante del siglo XX, tuvo una profunda influencia en el mundo artístico internacional. Rivera nació en Guanajuato, México en 1886. Empezó a estudiar pintura desde joven y en 1907 se fue a Europa. Vivió mucho tiempo en París, donde estudió las obras de artistas importantes como Cézanne, Gauguin, Renoir, y Matisse. Estaba buscando una nueva forma de pintar, una manera de expresar sus complejas ideas y a la vez hacerlas llegar al público. No fue hasta que vio los frescos de Italia que encontró lo que buscaba. Con una visión del futuro, regresó a México.

**Los frescos**

Los frescos son pinturas en murales hechas sobre yeso. Rivera creyó que el tamaño de los frescos era el lienzo perfecto para comunicar sus ideas sobre la historia y el futuro. Hizo su primer mural, "La Creación", en 1922, para el anfiteatro Simón Bolívar de la Escuela Nacional Preparatoria. Allí conoció a Frida Kahlo, con quién se casó el 21 de agosto de 1929. Rivera estaba particularmente interesado en la tecnología y el progreso y trató mucho el tema de los trabajadores de los años treinta y sus luchas contra la industria y la sociedad. Mucha gente de Estados Unidos estaba fascinada con el arte de Rivera, por lo que recibió el encargo de hacer grandes murales en San Francisco, en el Instituto de Arte de Detroit y en el Rockefeller Center de Nueva York. Este último mural fue muy criticado por la figura de Lenin que Rivera había pintado en él, y fue destruido por el Rockefeller Center. Luego, Rivera lo reprodujo en el Palacio de Bellas Artes de México.

**Los últimos años**

En sus últimas pinturas, Rivera desarrolló un estilo indigenista y social de gran atractivo popular. Por esa época empezó su proyecto más ambicioso, un mural épico sobre la historia de México, para el Palacio Nacional. Pero Rivera murió el 25 de noviembre de 1957, antes de terminar su gran proyecto.

## Core Instruction

### TEACHING LECTURA CULTURAL

1. Have a volunteer read the introductory caption. Ask students why they think Diego Rivera is known around the world. **(2 min.)**
2. Read the first paragraph to students. Call students' attention to the year that Diego Rivera went to Europe, and what artists he studied. Lead a discussion about why artists might go to Europe for inspiration. **(3 min.)**
3. Ask a volunteer to read the first sentence of the second paragraph. Have students think about how a mural can communicate ideas or send a message. After students have read the rest of the selection, ask them for examples. **(10 min.)**
4. Have students complete the **Comprensión** activities in pairs. **(10 min.)**
5. Have students complete the **Actividad** and share their paragraphs with the class. **(15 min.)**

Visit Holt Online
go.hrw.com
KEYWORD: EXP3 CH5
Online Edition

El estudio de Diego Rivera en México

**El proyecto del Mural de Diego Rivera**
Una de las obras más importantes de Diego Rivera es el mural en el City College de San Francisco, California. Es una visión inspirada en la unidad panamericana con su síntesis de arte, religión, historia, política y tecnología del continente americano. El Proyecto del Mural de Diego Rivera tiene el propósito de acercar de nuevo al público a esta obra de arte que es tan válida hoy como lo fue en 1940 cuando miles de personas fueron a ver su inauguración. Entre otras cosas, los organizadores del proyecto quieren lograr tener un guía bilingüe que presente el mural al público, un folleto informativo y una presentación en multimedia que explique los temas, los personajes y el contenido histórico del mural.

## Comprensión

**A Los hechos** Basándote en lo que leíste, contesta las preguntas. 1.2

1. ¿De dónde es Diego Rivera?
2. ¿Por qué es famoso?
3. ¿Cuándo vivió?
4. ¿Qué tipo de pinturas hizo?
5. ¿Adónde viajó para buscar su nueva forma de pintar? ¿Dónde la encontró?
6. ¿Qué temas toca Rivera en sus pinturas?

**B ¿Qué piensas?** Basándote en lo que leíste, contesta las preguntas. 1.2

1. ¿Crees que Rivera tenía miedo de expresar sus ideas políticas?
2. ¿Por qué fue destruido el mural de Rivera en el Rockefeller Center de Nueva York?
3. ¿En qué otras partes de Estados Unidos se encuentran murales de Rivera?
4. ¿Qué es el Proyecto del Mural de Diego Rivera?
5. ¿Qué quieren lograr los organizadores de este proyecto?

### Actividad 1.3, 3.1

**Los murales** Escribe un párrafo sobre un mural que hayas visto. ¿Cómo es? ¿En qué te hace pensar y cómo te hace sentir? Comparte tu párrafo con la clase.

Lectura cultural

# Lectura cultural

### A Answers

1. Guanajuato, México
2. Pintaba frescos con estilo propio que trataban temas sociales.
3. Vivió de 1886 a 1957.
4. Hizo frescos.
5. Viajó a París. Encontró su estilo en Italia.
6. Toca los temas sociales e indigenistas.

### B Answers

1. No, porque hizo algunas pinturas controvertidas.
2. Fue destruido porque incluyó la figura de Lenin.
3. Se encuentran en San Francisco, Detroit, Nueva York.
4. Es una exposición de la obra de Diego Rivera de City College.
5. Quieren desarrollar un guía bilingüe para proveer información y crear una presentación acerca de la obra.

### Post-Reading Activities

Have students think about why Diego Rivera's art was important not only in Mexico, but also in the United States and around the world. Remind students that the Mexican Revolution was underway early in Rivera's career and that many new social changes were taking place in his country. Have students select their favorite Rivera mural and analyze it. They should identify at least one famous person or important historical event of the time portrayed in the mural and explain why they think it was included. The United States was also facing social issues during Rivera's career. Have students compare some important social issues both in Mexico and the United States during Diego Rivera's career.
2.2, 3.1

## Differentiated Instruction

### SLOWER PACE LEARNERS

**Building on Previous Skills** Have students make a list of some of the current events they have seen recently in the news. They may focus on political, sports, music, or art-related events. Once they have a list completed, have students think about which events they could include in a mural that would best depict the world today. Discuss their ideas as a class.

### SPECIAL LEARNING NEEDS

**Students with Learning Disabilities** These students may have a difficult time grasping the content of the reading. You may want to print out some of the Rivera murals from the Internet mentioned in the reading, so students have a visual reference of these works. Having a visual connection to what is being discussed in the reading may aid students' understanding of the text.

### Assess

**Assessment Program**
**Prueba: Lectura,** p. 93
**Online Assessment**
my.hrw.com
**Test Generator**

**Assess** **Differentiated Instruction** See the Differentiated Instruction CD-ROM.

# Leamos y escribamos

**ESTRATEGIA**

**para leer** Drawing inferences about a poem or a story is useful when you don't understand every word. You can read the title of the work or the first paragraph and make an inference of what the work might be about. Context clues can also help.

CD 5, Tr. 14

### Antes de leer 1.2

**A** Luis Palés Matos nació en Puerto Rico en 1898. En sus obras, trata los temas de la gente de origen africano en Cuba y en Puerto Rico. Utiliza el habla local combinada con palabras inventadas para captar la musicalidad y el ritmo típicos de los africanos.

Lee el verso del poema: "El cerdo en el fango gruñe…" Es probable que no conozcas todas las palabras en este verso pero al usar las que sí conoces, puedes adivinar el significado de las palabras desconocidas. Por ejemplo, si conoces "cerdo" y no conoces "fango" puedes pensar en el lugar favorito de un cerdo, el lodo *(mud)*, que es otra manera de decir "fango". Usa este método mientras lees el poema como ayuda con las palabras que no conoces.

# Danza negra

*de Luis Palés Matos*

Calabó y bambú.
Bambú y calabó.
El Gran Cocoroco° dice: tu–cu–tú.
La Gran Cocoroca dice: to–co–tó.
Es el sol de hierro que arde en Tombuctú°.
Es la danza negra de Fernando Póo°.

**3** chief of some African tribes **5** city in the Republic of Mali **6** island in the Gulf of Guinea

## Leamos y escribamos

### Resources

**Planning:**

Lesson Planner, pp. 77–78, 238–239

One-Stop Planner

**Presentation:**

Audio CD 5, Tr. 14

**Practice:**

Cuaderno de actividades, p. 48

Reading Strategies and Skills Handbook, Chapter 5

Interactive Advanced Reader

### Pre-Reading Activity

Remind students that African influence is strong in the Caribbean. Have students identify musical instruments or styles that were introduced to the Caribbean by African cultures. Have them research the instruments to verify their guesses 2.1, 2.2

### Applying the Strategies

For more practice with paraphrasing, have students use the "Retellings" strategy from the *Reading Strategies and Skills Handbook.*

### Escuchemos

As students listen to the poem with their books closed, have them write down any words they recognize.

### Pre-AP Practice

**AP Language Examination: Leamos** helps students prepare for Section I, Part B: **Reading Comprehension.** The audio recording helps them prepare for Part A: **Listening—Short Narratives.**

## Core Instruction

### TEACHING LEAMOS

1. Have students look at the illustrations of the dancers and the instruments. Ask students where they think a dance like the one in the illustration may be performed. **(5 min.)**
2. Read the **Estrategia para leer** with students. Remind them that as they read they should stop at an unfamiliar word and infer its meaning from the context. Give an example if necessary. **(5 min.)**
3. Have students read the poem individually, assisting students who need help. **(10 min.)**
4. Have students answer the **Comprensión** activities on p. 220 in pairs or small groups. **(15 min.)**

Visit Holt Online
go.hrw.com
KEYWORD: EXP3 CH5
Online Edition

El cerdo° en el fango° gruñe: pru–pru–prú.
El sapo° en la charca° sueña: cro–cro–cró.
Calabó y bambú
Bambú y calabó.
Rompen los junjunes° en furiosa ú.
Los gongos° trepidan° con profunda ó.
Es la raza negra que ondulando va
en el ritmo gordo del mariyandá°.
Llegan los botucos° a la fiesta ya.
Danza que te danza la negra se da.

Calabó y bambú.
Bambú y calabó.
El Gran Cocoroco dice: tu–cu–tú.
La Gran Cocoroca dice: to–co–tó.

Pasan tierras rojas, islas de betún°:
Haití, Martinica, Congo, Camerún,
las papiamentosas° antillas° del ron°
y las patualesas° islas del volcán,
que en el grave son
del canto se dan.

Calabó y bambú.
Bambú y calabó.
Es el sol de hierro que arde en Tombuctú.
Es la danza negra de Fernando Póo.
El alma africana que vibrando está
en el ritmo gordo del mariyandá.

Calabó y bambú.
Bambú y calabó.
El Gran Cocoroco dice: tu–cu–tú.
La Gran Cocoroca dice: to–co–tó.

**7** pig **7** mud **8** toad **8** puddle **11** violin-type musical instrument used by some African tribes **12** percussion instruments **12** shake, vibrate **14** dance of Africans in Puerto Rico **15** chiefs of the black tribes of Fernando Póo **21** pine tar, pitch **23** full of gibberish, slang **23** Antilles (West Indies) **23** rum **24** speaking **patualés**, a French dialect of the French Antilles



# Leamos y escribamos

## AP Reading Suggestion

Have students read the poem aloud and listen to the sounds they hear. Ask them to compare these sounds to a musical instrument and to identify the African influences in this poem. 3.1

## Active Reading Questions

1. **¿Qué te parece el ritmo de "Danza Negra"?**
2. **¿Por qué crees que se usan sonidos de los animales en el poema?**
3. **¿Qué propósitos tienen los sonidos en este poema?**
4. **Aparte del Caribe, ¿en qué otras partes crees que existe este tipo de música?** 1.2, 3.2

## Drawing Inferences

Have students use the title and context words to draw conclusions about the theme of the poem. Ask them to cite passages to support their inferences. 3.1, 3.2

## Connections

### Language Arts Link

Luis Palés Matos reintroduced Africanism in Puerto Rican poetry and is well-known for his use of onomatopoeia. Ask students to research information about Matos' life and his other publications. 3.1

## Differentiated Instruction

### ADVANCED LEARNERS

**Challenge** For advanced learners, you may want to find a tongue twister in Spanish and have students practice reading it. Have them identify the sound that the tongue twister is targeting. How is the tongue twister they are practicing similar to the reading? 1.2

### SPECIAL LEARNING NEEDS

**Students with Dyslexia** Students may have trouble reading words with many short and repetitious consonant-vowel combinations. Read a stanza aloud to students, modeling the pronunciation. Read the stanza a second time together with students, monitoring their pronunciation.

## Heritage Speakers

Ask your heritage speakers to read **"Danza negra"** as a group. If possible, have them practice the group reading outside. The idea is for them to simulate the sounds of the drums with their voices. When they are ready, they can perform the poem in front of the class.

## Connections

### History Link

Tell students that at the time of **"Danza Negra",** Fernando Póo was part of what was then called Spanish Guinea. Today it is known as Bioko Island (population 63,000), a small island off the west coast of Africa. It is part of the African republic of Equatorial Guinea and is home to that nation's capital, Malabo. The official language today is still Spanish, a result of its being mostly a Spanish possession from 1778 until its independence in 1968. Have students research other African regions that were under Spanish control during the 18th and 19th centuries and investigate how both African and Spanish influences are present in the continent today.

3.1

## Post-Reading Activity

Have students explain why a dance like this would be fun. Ask students if they would learn a dance like this if they had the opportunity. What types of instruments would they pick for a song similar to **"Danza negra"?**

## Pre-AP Practice

**AP Language Examination:** **Leamos and Escribamos** help students prepare for Section I, Part B: **Reading Comprehension** and Section II, Part A: **Informal Writing.**

### Comprensión 1.2

**B** Contesta las preguntas.

1. ¿Cuáles son los sonidos o las letras que aparecen con más frecuencia en este poema? la *o* y la *u*
2. ¿Quiénes son el Gran Cocoroco y la Gran Cocoroca? Son los jefes.
3. ¿Tiene ritmo este poema? Sí
4. ¿Crees que hay influencia africana en Haití y Martinica? ¿Por qué? Sí, porque todo el poema trata el tema de la cultura africana.
5. ¿Te parece interesante que un hombre que no es de origen africano escriba poesía como "Danza negra"? Explica.

**C** Basándote en lo que leíste, determina si cada oración es **cierta** o **falsa.**

1. Este poema trata de una tribu africana del Congo. falsa
2. El cerdo y el sapo están bailando. falsa
3. La danza negra es de Fernando Póo. cierta
4. El mariyandá es un baile de Puerto Rico. cierta
5. Las tierras rojas que menciona el autor están en Estados Unidos. falsa
6. Es el alma africana que vibra en esta danza. cierta

### Después de leer 1.3, 3.1

**D** ¿Te gustaría aprender un baile como la "Danza negra"? Imagina que vas a crear la música para este poema. ¿Qué instrumentos musicales usarías? ¿Seguirías un ritmo similar al del poema? ¿Qué cambiarías?

## Core Instruction

### TEACHING ESCRIBAMOS

1. Explain the **Estrategia para escribir** to the class **(2 min.)**
2. Have students complete Pre-writing Activity 1 by making a list of words that rhyme. Provide students with a short sample list on the board or on a transparency if necessary. **(3 min.)**
3. Have students write and revise their short songs individually (Activities 2 and 3). **(15 min.)**
4. Collect all songs and select volunteers to read a few at random. Have students select the song they think is the most striking. Encourage positive feedback. **(5 min.)**

# Taller del escritor

1.3, 3.1

**ESTRATEGIA**

**para escribir** It's best to have a plan before you begin writing. Your plan will be different depending on what you're writing. You should always include things such as a list of ideas for your theme, a list of words or phrases you can use, and an outline.

## ¡A escribir una canción!

¿Cómo se escribe una canción? Aquí tendrás la oportunidad de escribir tu propia canción. Puedes elegir el tema de tu canción, pero ten en cuenta que necesita rimar. Puedes buscar ideas en "Danza negra" para empezar.

### 1 Antes de escribir

Para empezar, piensa en el tema de tu canción y en las ideas que quieres desarrollar. Luego haz una lista de las palabras que quieres usar, recordando que algunas de ellas deben rimar. Usa un diccionario si es necesario.

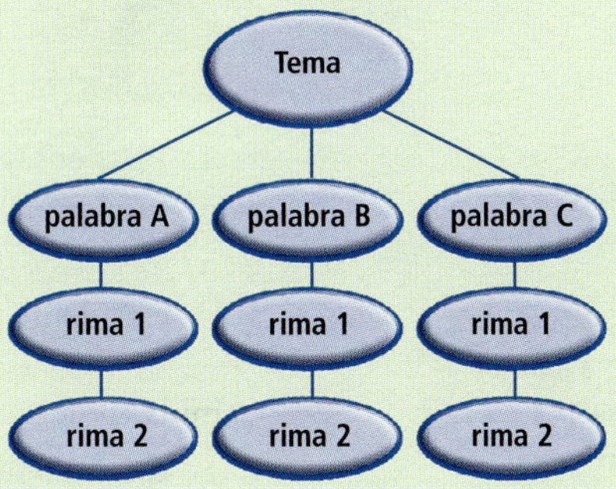


### 2 Escribir un borrador

Haz un borrador de tu canción. Desarrolla tus ideas y asegúrate de combinar las palabras que riman para que tu canción llame la atención.

### 3 Revisar

Revisa lo que escribiste. Haz las correcciones necesarias y luego lee tu canción en voz alta para ver si la rima fluye como imaginaste.

### 4 Publicar

Graba tu canción o preséntala en vivo. La clase tendrá un concurso y votará por la mejor canción. ¡Suerte!

## Process Writing

Ask students to think about how they want their song to sound. Then have them think about the story they would like to tell with their song. Have them brainstorm the theme of their story and some related words to the theme. From the list of words students create, they can find synonyms in the dictionary that rhyme. Have students refer to the graphic organizer if they need ideas.

## Writing Assessment

To assess the **Taller del escritor,** use the following rubric.

| Writing Rubric | 4 | 3 | 2 | 1 |
|---|---|---|---|---|
| **Content** (Complete—Incomplete) | | | | |
| **Comprehensibility** (Comprehensible—Seldom comprehensible) | | | | |
| **Accuracy** (Accurate—Seldom accurate) | | | | |
| **Organization** (Well-organized—Poorly organized) | | | | |
| **Effort** (Excellent effort—Minimal effort) | | | | |

18–20: A 16–17: B 14–15: C 12–13: D Under 12: F

## Differentiated Instruction

### SLOWER PACE LEARNERS

Allow students to complete the writing activities in groups. Assign roles to each group member. For example, one member of the group should contribute ideas for a possible topic. Other members should then brainstorm a list of words that rhyme. One student in the group could be assigned to help find synonyms in a thesaurus. 1.2

### MULTIPLE INTELLIGENCES

**Musical/Rhythmic** Have students create a beat to their songs using materials in the classroom such as pencils. Students may adjust the speed of the tempo depending on the tone they believe their song has.

## Assess

**Assessment Program**

**Prueba: Lectura,** p. 93

**Prueba: Escritura,** p. 94

**Online Assessment**
**my.hrw.com**

**Test Generator**

**Assess** **Differentiated Instruction** See the Differentiated Instruction CD-ROM.

## Resources

**Planning:**

Lesson Planner, pp. 79, 240–241

One-Stop Planner

**Presentation:**

Video Program, Videocassette 3

DVD Program

**Variedades**

**Practice:**

Activities for Communication, pp. 47, 63–64

Video Guide, pp. 32–33

Lab Book, pp. 5, 29–32, 70

Audio CD 5, Tr. 15

Pre-AP Instructional Resources

Pre-AP Audio CD 1, Trs. 17–20

Interactive Tutor, Disc 1

Teaching Transparencies

**Situación, Capítulo 5**

Picture Sequences, Chapter 5

### 2 Answers

1. La obra fue aplaudida.
2. Se descubrió un templo durante la excavación.
3. Unas acuarelas fueron mostradas en la exposición.
4. Esa estatua fue esculpida en 1972.
5. Se vendieron todas las figuras de madera.
6. Se construyeron unas casas muy modernas.

### Heritage Speakers

Have your heritage speakers work in groups of four to come up with popular compliments, or **piropos,** in Spanish. Remind them of the importance of decorum in the classroom. They can use polite phrases they have heard or used themselves. For example, **Mi corazón es una batidora cada vez que te veo.** What would be an appropriate response for a girl who hears these lines? The students can then share their **piropos** and responses with the whole class. 1.3

Capítulo 5
Repaso

# Prepárate para el examen

Interactive TUTOR

**1** Mira las fotos y lee las oraciones. Escoge la foto que corresponde a cada oración. 1.2

1

2

3

**1 Vocabulario 1**
- asking for and giving opinions
- introducing and changing a topic of conversation

**pp. 188–193**

1. Pilar ensaya mucho para desempeñar su papel.
2. Prefiero la pintura, pero Víctor admira las estatuas.
3. Te aconsejo que no vayas al concierto. La música es muy estridente.

**1.** c **2.** a **3.** b

**2 Gramática 1**
- comparatives of equality and superlatives
- passive **se**
- passive voice with **ser**

**pp. 194–199**

**2** Cambia cada oración a otra forma de la voz pasiva. 1.2

1. Se aplaudió la obra.
2. Un templo fue descubierto durante la excavación.
3. Se mostraron unas acuarelas en la exposición.
4. Se esculpió esa estatua en 1972.
5. Todas las figuras de madera fueron vendidas.
6. Unas casas muy modernas fueron construidas.

**3 Vocabulario 2**
- making suggestions and recommendations
- turning down an invitation

**pp. 202–207**

**3** Lee las oraciones y escoge la palabra del cuadro que mejor completa cada oración. 1.2

| | | |
|---|---|---|
| **la comedia** | **el concierto de la sinfónica** | **creativo** |
| **de mal gusto** | **la letra** | **la orquesta** |

1. Te recomiendo que veas ____ porque estuvo divertida. la comedia
2. Enrique es muy ____. Sabe pintar, esculpir y cantar bien. creativo
3. Lupe toca el violín en ____ del colegio. la orquesta
4. Magda nos contó un chiste ____. de mal gusto
5. Cristóbal quería cantar pero se le olvidó ____ de la canción. la letra
6. Siento haberme perdido ____. Me dijeron que fue hermoso. el concierto de la sinfónica

## Oral Assessment

### Speaking Rubric

To assess the speaking activities in this section, you might use this rubric. For additional speaking rubrics, see the Alternative Assessment section of the *Assessment Program.*

| Speaking Rubric | 4 | 3 | 2 | 1 |
|---|---|---|---|---|
| **Content** (Complete—Incomplete) | | | | |
| **Comprehension** (Total—Little) | | | | |
| **Comprehensibility** (Comprehensible—Incomprehensible) | | | | |
| **Accuracy** (Accurate—Seldom Accurate) | | | | |
| **Fluency** (Fluent—Not Fluent) | | | | |

18–20: A 16–17: B 14–15: C 12–13: D Under 12: F

Visit Holt Online
go.hrw.com
KEYWORD: EXP3 CH5
Chapter Self-test

**4** Completa las oraciones con el presente del subjuntivo o el pluscuamperfecto del verbo entre paréntesis. 1.2

1. Diego me sugirió ir al museo, pero yo ya ____ (hacer) otros planes. había hecho
2. Quiero que Esteban ____ (ir) conmigo al baile. vaya
3. Llamé a Luis a las seis, pero él ya ____ (irse) a las cinco. se había ido
4. Cristina me recomienda que ____ (invitar) a David. invite
5. Espero que él ____ (querer) ir. quiera
6. Cuando hablé con él, todavía no ____ (terminar) la tarea. había terminado

**5** Contesta las preguntas. 1.2, 2.2

1. ¿Qué tipo de pintura hacía Diego Rivera?
2. ¿Qué temas trató Rivera en sus pinturas?
3. ¿Cuáles son los orígenes de la música norteña?
4. ¿Cómo se vestía Frida Kahlo?

CD 5, Tr. 15

**6** Escucha la conversación y escribe dos listas: una lista con dos cosas que se recomiendan y otra con dos cosas que no se recomiendan. 1.2

**4 Gramática 2**
- subjunctive for hopes and wishes
- past perfect

pp. 208–213

**5 Cultura**
- Comparaciones pp. 200–201
- Lectura cultural pp. 216–217
- Notas culturales pp. 191, 207, 210

## Conversación

HOLT SoundBooth ONLINE RECORDING

**7** Role-play the following conversation with a partner. Partner A and Partner B are friends, talking about going out. 1.1, 1.2

| | |
|---|---|
| Partner A: | Ask your partner to see a movie with you this evening. |
| Partner B: | Explain that you have to go to band practice. Suggest your partner invite Ana. |
| Partner A: | Say that you called Ana earlier, but she had already left for a dance lesson. |
| Partner B: | Say speaking of Ana, has your partner heard that her folk dance group will be at the festival this weekend? |
| Partner A: | Give your opinion of folk dancing. Say you hope Ana has fun and that a lot of people go to the festival. |
| Partner B: | Suggest you both go to the festival, then to the movies. |
| Partner A: | Agree. Ask if your partner prefers to see the new science fiction movie or the horror movie. |
| Partner B: | Say you prefer the science fiction movie; you've heard the horror movie is awful. End the conversation. |

## Conversación

### Additional Speaking Practice

For additional speaking practice, use the *Picture Sequences Transparency* for Chapter 5. Use the Speaking Rubric on the preceding page to evaluate their performance. You may also wish to use the Interviews and Role-Plays in the *Activities for Communication* book.

### Pre-AP Practice

**7** In the Level 3 *Pre-AP Instructional Resources* you will find an alternative version of Activity 7. The following resources in that book will help you prepare students for the AP Language Exam:

- Blackline masters, pp. 31, 41, 51
- Pre-AP Audio CD 1, Trs. 17–20
- Scripts and answers, pp. 57–75

### 5 Answers

**1.** murales **2.** temas sociales e históricos **3.** Frida Kahlo **4.** las polkas de Europa, con influencia alemana en el uso del acordeón **5.** con ropa tradicional mexicana

### 6 Script

—Fernando sugiere que vayamos a la obra de teatro. Dice que es estupenda.

—Bueno, yo quería ver la nueva película pero Sandra me dijo que era pésima. Mejor veamos la obra de teatro.

—De acuerdo. ¿Qué me dices de esa exposición en el museo de arte moderno?

—No pierdas el tiempo. Ya fui a verla y estuvo aburridísima.

—Entonces, propongo que pasemos por la feria de escultura en el centro cultural. Luis me acaba de aconsejar que la veamos.

—¡Buena idea! Yo quería ir la semana pasada pero tenía otro compromiso. ¡Vamos!

### 6 Answers

Se recomienda la obra de teatro y la feria. No se recomienda ni la película ni la exposición.

### 7 Answers

Below is a sample conversation.

(A) —Oye, ¿quieres ir conmigo a ver una película esta noche?

(B) —Gracias, pero esta noche tengo que ir a un ensayo de banda. ¿Por qué no llamas a Ana?

(A) —Sí, llamé a Ana esta tarde, pero ella ya había salido para una clase de baile.

(B) —Hablando de Ana, y de baile, ¿has oído que el grupo de baile folclórico de Ana va a estar en el festival de arte este fin de semana?

(A) —Sí, me lo dijo ella. A decir verdad, a mí el baile folclórico no me interesa mucho. Pero espero que Ana se divierta y que mucha gente vaya al festival.

(B) —Bueno, tengo una idea. ¿Por qué no me acompañas al festival el sábado? Y después, podemos ir con Ana al cine.

(A) —Muy bien. ¿Prefieres ver la nueva película de ciencia ficción o la de horror?

(B) —Sugiero que vayamos a ver la de ciencia ficción. Leí una reseña de la otra, y dicen que es pésima. Bueno, ¡entonces nos vemos el sábado!

# Prepárate para el examen

## Grammar Review

For more practice with the grammar topics in this chapter, see the *Grammar Tutor,* the *Interactive Tutor,* or the *Cuaderno de vocabulario y gramática.*

GramaVisión

## Connections

### Community Link

Have students check the arts section in a Spanish-language newspaper from a nearby city to see what types of international arts programs are taking place in the near future. Have students report their findings to the class. As an alternative, students might check the arts section of an online newspaper from Spain or Latin America.

3.2

### Más práctica

Write the following items on the board and have students rewrite them using the past perfect. Remind students that the other verb will have to be changed to the imperfect or preterite as well.

1. **Matías trata de comprar una acuarela, pero ya se han vendido todas.**
2. **Yo quiero comprar la estatua que no se ha vendido aún.**
3. **Manuel es actor, pero no ha conseguido un papel durante mucho tiempo.**
4. **Verónica llega al museo, pero ya ha cerrado.**
5. **Lorena prefiere ir al teatro pero su hermano ya ha ido tres veces esta semana.**
6. **¿Todavía tienen entradas para la obra, o se han agotado?**

1.2

**Gramática 1**
- comparisons of equality and superlatives **pp. 194–195**
- passive **se** **pp. 196–197**
- passive voice with **ser** **pp. 198–199**

## Repaso de Gramática 1

Use **tan + adjective + como** to compare people or things. You can follow **como** with an **article + adjective** or a **pronoun** to avoid repetition.

Esta pintura es **tan creativa como las de Goya.**

There are two kinds of superlatives: **el/la/los/las + más/menos + adjective + de; -ísimo/a/os/as** added to the end of the adjective.

Es **la más bella de** todas las pinturas. Es **hermosísima.**

The **passive voice with se (se pasiva)** is used to state that something *is done or has been done* without mentioning the agent. It is expressed with the pronoun **se** plus a verb in the third person singular or plural. The recipient of the action must agree in number with the verb.

**Se construyeron dos edificios** modernos.

In the **passive voice with ser** the agent may or may not be indicated. When mentioned, it is introduced by **por.** The **passive voice with ser** is formed with **ser + past participle + (por) + (agent). Ser** must agree in number, and the participle must agree in gender and number, with the recipient of the action.

Las fotografías **fueron tomadas por** un fotógrafo profesional.

La ópera **fue escrita** en 1778.

**Gramática 2**
- subjunctive for hopes and wishes **pp. 208–211**
- past perfect **pp. 212–213**

## Repaso de Gramática 2

Use the **subjunctive** when the main clause in a sentence expresses a **wish, suggestion,** or **recommendation,** the subject changes between clauses, and the clauses are joined by **que.**

Dámaso **recomienda que practiquemos** todos los días.

When there is no change in subject between the main and subordinate clause in a sentence, omit **que** and use the **infinitive.**

**Quiero cantar** en el coro.

The **past perfect (pluscuamperfecto)** is used to express a sequence of events in the past. Use the **past perfect** for the event that happens first. It's formed by using the **imperfect of haber** with the **past participle** of the main verb.

El público quería más, pero la banda **se había ido** del teatro.

The **past perfect** is frequently used with words such as **cuando, ya, aún no,** or **todavía no.**

## Chapter Review

### Teacher Management System

To access, launch the program, type "admin" in the password area, and press RETURN. For more details, log on to www.hrw.com/CDROMTUTOR.

Create a variety of puzzles to review chapter vocabulary.

**DVD Program**

**Interactive Tutor**

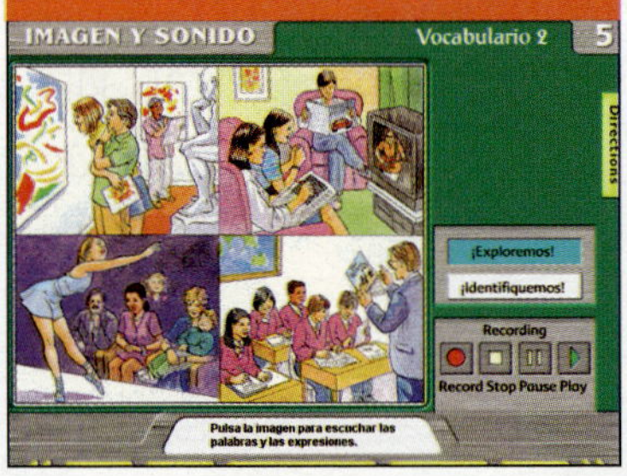


**PuzzlePro**

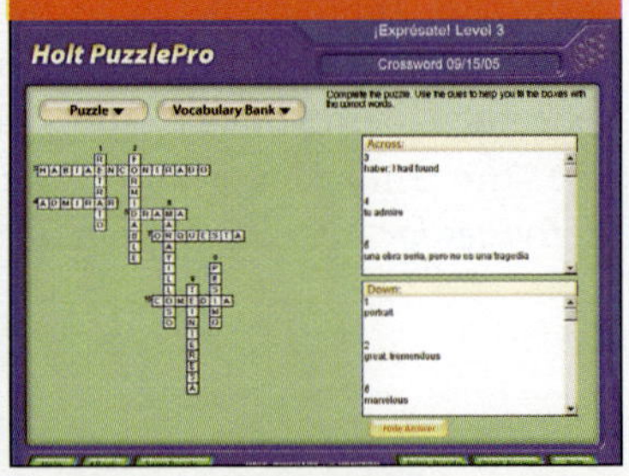

HOLT SoundBooth ONLINE RECORDING

## Repaso de Vocabulario 1

**Asking for and giving opinions**

| | |
|---|---|
| **A decir verdad, me parece...** | *To tell the truth, it strikes me as . . .* |
| **la acuarela** | *watercolor* |
| **antiguo(a)** | *antique* |
| **la arquitectura** | *architecture* |
| **las artes plásticas** | *plastic arts (sculpture, painting, architecture)* |
| **la cinematografía** | *cinematography* |
| **clásico(a)** | *classic* |
| **contemporáneo(a)** | *contemporary* |
| **¿Cuál de estas pinturas te gusta más, la de... o la de...?** | *Which of these paintings do you like better, the one of (by) . . . or the one of (by) . . . ?* |
| **el dibujo** | *drawing* |
| **esculpir** | *to sculpt* |
| **la escultura** | *sculpture* |
| **la estatua** | *statue* |
| **Este retrato fue pintado por...** | *This portrait was painted by . . .* |
| **la exposición** | *exhibit* |
| **la fotografía** | *photography* |
| **la galería** | *gallery* |
| **imaginativo(a)** | *imaginative* |
| **impresionante** | *impressive* |
| **llamar la atención** | *to attract one's attention* |
| **Lo/La encuentro muy...** | *I find it to be very . . .* |
| **maravilloso(a)** | *marvelous* |
| **moderno(a)** | *modern* |
| **original** | *original* |
| **el puente** | *bridge* |
| **¿Qué opinas de...?** | *What do you think of . . .?* |
| **¿Qué te parece?** | *What do you think of it?* |
| **En realidad, admiro...** | *Actually, I admire . . .* |
| **realista** | *realistic* |
| **tallar en madera** | *to carve wood* |
| **la torre** | *tower* |

**Introducing and changing a topic of conversation** . . . . . . . . . . . .*See p. 192.*

## Repaso de Vocabulario 2

**Making suggestions and recommendations**

| | |
|---|---|
| **las artes dramáticas** | *dramatic arts* |
| **artístico(a)** | *artistic* |
| **el ballet** | *ballet* |
| **la comedia** | *comedy or play* |
| **crear** | *to create* |
| **creativo(a)** | *creative* |
| **de buen/mal gusto** | *in good/bad taste* |
| **desempeñar (el papel de...)** | *to play (the role of . . .)* |
| **el drama** | *drama* |
| **entretenido(a)** | *entertaining* |
| **Es mejor que veas la ópera. Es formidable.** | *It's better for you to see the opera. It's great.* |
| **el escenario** | *stage/scenery* |
| **estridente** | *shrill* |
| **formidable** | *great, tremendous* |
| **la función** | *performance* |
| **hermoso(a)** | *beautiful* |
| **incomprensible** | *incomprehensible* |
| **la letra** | *lyrics* |
| **la melodía** | *melody* |
| **melodioso(a)** | *melodic* |
| **No te olvides de ir al ensayo de la banda.** | *Don't forget to go to band practice.* |
| **la obra (de teatro)** | *play* |
| **la orquesta** | *orchestra, band* |
| **pésimo(a)** | *terrible* |
| **presentar** | *to present* |
| **el público** | *audience* |
| **la reseña** | *(critical) review* |
| **el ritmo** | *rhythm* |
| **Sería buena idea ir al concierto de la sinfónica.** | *It would be a good idea to go to the symphony.* |
| **superficial** | *superficial* |
| **Te aconsejo que vayas a la presentación de baile folclórico. Es muy...** | *I recommend that you go to the folk dance performance. It's very . . .* |
| **la tragedia** | *tragedy* |

**Inviting someone to do something and turning down an invitation** . . . . . .*See p. 206.*



Capítulo 5

# Prepárate para el examen

### Vocabulary Review

For more practice with the vocabulary in this chapter, see the *Interactive Tutor* or the *Cuaderno de vocabulario y gramática.*

### Online Edition

Use the online textbook to hear the **Vocabulario** items.

### Game

Prepare a game grid with enough squares to represent each member of the class. Ask students to write two things about themselves that are not common knowledge. Select one item per student and write it on the grid in Spanish. Make a copy of the grid for each student. Make an answer key by writing each student's name in the appropriate box.

Students ask each other questions in Spanish to find out the identity of the person described in each square and write that person's initials in the appropriate square on the grid. Students ask a follow-up question relating to the attribute or opinion and jot down the response next to the initials. The first student to obtain initials and responses in boxes forming a straight horizontal, vertical, or diagonal line wins the game. 1.2

**Online Edition**

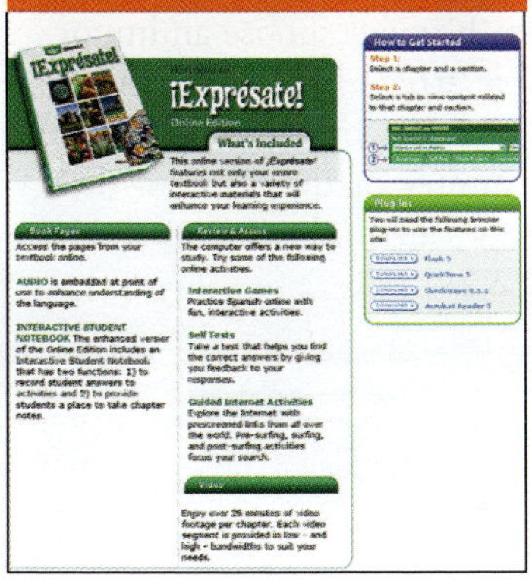


**Transparency: Vocabulario**

**Transparency: Situación**

### Assess

**Assessment Program**

**Examen: Capítulo 5,** pp. 253–258

Audio CD 5, Trs. 19–20, 21–22

**Examen oral: Capítulo 5,** p. 264

**Examen parcial:** pp. 265–272

Alternative Assessment, pp. 377, 389, 401

**Online Assessment**
**my.hrw.com**

**Test Generator**

**Assess** **Differentiated Instruction** See the Differentiated Instruction CD-ROM.

## Resources

**Planning:**

Lesson Planner pp. 79, 240–241

One-Stop Planner

**Presentation:**

Teaching Transparencies
Fine Art, Chapter 5

**Practice:**

Cuaderno de actividades, pp. 49–50

Lab Book, pp. 5, 29–32

Audio CD 5, Tr. 16

Interactive Tutor, Disc 1

### 1 Script

1. —Mira todas esas esculturas. Son geniales. ¿Qué te parece la escultura que tiene forma abstracta?
   —Pues, a mí no me llama mucho la atención. No me parece muy original.
2. —A mí me encanta esta música. La melodía es impresionante. ¿Y a ti Efraín, te gusta?
   —No, para nada. Yo la encuentro muy estridente. Me gusta otro tipo de música, como la música clásica.
3. —Vamos a bailar Luis, ¿quieres?
   —No, gracias. No quiero.
   —Vamos, ¡no seas tan aburrido!
4. —Qué horror. Esa película estuvo fatal.
   —¡Qué va! Al contrario, estuvo buenísima.

### 2 Answers

1. Le gustó.
2. Tocó obras de Brahms, Mozart y Beethoven.
3. Fueron interpretadas dramáticamente.
4. Aplaudió largo rato.
5. Quedaron impresionados.
6. No se pierdan el concierto.

## Repaso cumulativo

# Integración
## capítulos 1–5

CD 5, Tr. 16

**1** Escucha las conversaciones y escoge la foto que corresponde. 1.2
**1.** D **2.** B **3.** C **4.** A

A

B

C

D

**2** Elisa escribió esta reseña de un concierto de la sinfónica. Léela y contesta las preguntas. 1.2

Anoche fui con mi mamá a un concierto de la sinfónica. Cuando llegamos, el teatro estaba lleno y casi no había asientos. Mucha gente se quedó fuera del teatro. La orquesta interpretó algunas obras de Brahms, Mozart y Beethoven. Todas fueron interpretadas dramáticamente y el director de la orquesta estuvo formidable. Es un compositor de fama internacional. El público disfrutó mucho de todas las obras y aplaudió largo rato al final de cada una. Tanto mi mamá como yo quedamos muy impresionadas. Les aconsejo que no se pierdan ese concierto y que vayan temprano.

1. ¿A Elisa le gustó o no el concierto de la sinfónica?
2. ¿Qué música tocó la orquesta?
3. ¿Cómo fue la interpretación de la orquesta?
4. ¿Cuál fue la reacción del público?
5. ¿Cuál fue la reacción de Elisa y su mamá?
6. ¿Cuál es el consejo de Elisa?

**3** En grupos de tres, hablen de la última exposición de arte, el último concierto, la última película o la última obra de teatro que vieron. Basándose en los comentarios, den sus recomendaciones al resto de la clase. 1.1, 1.3

### Culture Project

Tell students they are going to combine the elements of art, history, music, and theater. Have them work in small groups to research the life of a famous Latin American artist. They will prepare a presentation with brief background information about the artist and samples of his or her work. Then they will choose an important moment in the artist's life and dramatize the scene for the class. Encourage them to use music from the country of the artist in their presentation if they can find samples in the library. 2.1, 2.2

**Repaso cumulativo**

4 Observa la pintura y escribe tus reacciones en ocho oraciones. ¿Qué opinas de la obra? ¿Qué ves en la escena? ¿Qué pasa o qué va a pasar? 1.3

Panel 1 de *Unidad panamericana* de Diego Rivera

5 Imagina que eres director(a) de una escuela de arte. Escribe un anuncio en el que expliques los cursos que se ofrecen, las destrezas que se aprenden, y menciona algunos graduados famosos. ¡Sé creativo(a) y exagera si quieres! 1.3

6 **Situación** En grupos de cuatro, hagan una guía de actividades para el periódico escolar. La guía debe incluir información sobre películas, museos, restaurantes y otros eventos o centros culturales de su comunidad. Incluyan sus recomendaciones sobre qué hacer cada noche de la próxima semana. 1.1, 1.3

## Fine Art Connection

Tell students that the mural ***Unidad panamericana*** was painted by the famous Mexican muralist Diego Rivera. The organ izers of the 1940 Golden Gate International Exposition commissioned Rivera to paint a large-scale fresco for an exhibit where fairgoers could watch artists at work. After the fair, it was supposed to be placed in the new library of San Francisco Junior College. World War II interrupted the plans, and the library was never built. The mural was eventually installed in the the Theater of the City College of San Francisco, now known as the Diego Rivera Theater.

### Analyzing

Ask students what the title of the painting means to them. Have them tell what they notice about the age, ethnic background, and nationality of the people in the mural. Are they working? playing? Do they seem to be doing their activities in harmony? What do the students think Diego Rivera was trying to communicate with this mural? 3.1

### Extension

Have students research a mural by Diego Rivera not shown in this chapter. Ask them to prepare a short presentation for the class in which they show a photograph of the mural, tell the social or historical issue depicted in the mural, and explain the elements in detail. Tell them to give their own opinions of the mural and how they think it is relevant today. 1.3, 3.1

## ACTFL Performance Standards

The activities in Chapter 5 target the different communicative modes as described in the Standards.

| | | |
|---|---|---|
| **Interpersonal** | Two-way communication using receptive skills and productive skills | **Comunicación (SE),** pp. 191, 193, 195, 197, 199, 205, 207, 209, 211, 213<br>**Comunicación (TE),** pp. 193, 195, 205, 207, 209, 211, 215<br>**Conversación,** p. 223 |
| | One-way communication using receptive skills | **Comunicación (SE),** pp. 191, 193, 195, 197, 199, 207, 213<br>**Comunicación (TE),** pp. 199, 213<br>**Novela en video,** pp. 214–215<br>**Leamos,** pp. 218–220<br>**Conversación,** p. 223 |
| **Presentational** | One-way communication using productive skills | **Comunicación (SE),** pp. 205, 209, 211<br>**Comunicación (TE),** pp. 191, 197, 199, 213<br>**Taller del escritor,** p. 221<br>**Situación,** p. 227 |

Capítulo 6

# Planning Guide

## ¡Ponte al día!

| Chapter Section | | Print Resources |
|---|---|---|
| **Geocultura**<br>• **El Suroeste** | pp. 180–185 | Video Guide, pp. 29–30/Lab Book, p. 69 |
| **Vocabulario 1**<br>• Electronic media<br>**Gramática 1**<br>• Indicative after expressions of certainty<br>• Subjunctive after expressions of doubt and disbelief<br>• Uses of **haber** | pp. 230–235<br><br>pp. 236–241 | Vocabulario 6.1, 6.2; Bell Work 6.1, 6.2, 6.3, 6.4<br>Cuaderno de vocabulario y gramática, pp. 61–66<br>Cuaderno de actividades, pp. 51–53<br>Activities for Communication, pp. 21–22<br>Grammar Tutor for Students of Spanish, pp. 149–150 |
| **Cultura: Comparaciones**<br>**Cultura: Comunidad** | p. 242<br>p. 243 | Video Guide, pp. 38–39/Lab Book, p. 73 |
| **Vocabulario 2**<br>• Print media<br>**Gramática 2**<br>• Review of indefinite expressions<br>• Gender of nouns<br>• Indicative in compound sentences | pp. 244–249<br><br>pp. 250–255 | Vocabulario 6.3, 6.4; Bell Work 6.5, 6.6, 6.7, 6.8<br>Cuaderno de vocabulario y gramática, pp. 67–72<br>Cuaderno de actividades, pp. 55–57<br>Activities for Communication, pp. 23–24 |
| **Novela en video**<br>**Lectura informativa**<br>• **Recuperar la tierra**<br>**Leamos**<br>• **del Popol Vuh**<br>**Escribamos**<br>• **Una historia con fluidez** | pp. 256–257<br>pp. 258–259<br><br>pp. 260–262<br><br>p. 263 | Cuaderno de actividades, p. 58<br>Reading Strategies and Skills Handbook<br>Interactive Advanced Reader<br>Video Guide, pp. 40–42/Lab Book, pp. 74–75 |
| **Prepárate para el examen**<br>• **Repaso de vocabulario y gramática** | pp. 264–267 | Picture Sequences, **Situación,** Ch. 6<br>Activities for Communication, pp. 48, 65–66 |
| **Integración**<br>• **Repaso cumulativo** | pp. 268–269 | Fine Art, Ch. 6<br>Cuaderno de actividades, pp. 59–60<br>Reading Strategies and Skills Handbook<br>Interactive Advanced Reader |

For correlations to national standards, see point-of-use references throughout the chapter.

Visit Holt Online
**go.hrw.com**
KEYWORD: EXP3 CH6
Online Edition

## Pacing Suggestions

| | Essential | Recommended | Optional |
|---|---|---|---|
| **Vocabulario 1** • Electronic media • **Nota cultural** | ✔ | | |
| **Gramática 1** • Indicative after expressions of certainty • Subjunctive after expressions of doubt and disbelief • Uses of **haber** • **Nota cultural** | ✔ | | |
| **Cultura: Comparaciones** | | ✔ | |
| **Cultura: Comunidad** | | | ✔ |
| **Vocabulario 2** • Print media • **Nota cultural** | ✔ | | |
| **Gramática 2** • Review of indefinite expressions • Gender of nouns • Indicative in compound sentences • **Nota cultural** | ✔ | | |
| **Novela en video** • Episodio 6: **Clara perspectiva** | | ✔ | |
| **Lectura informativa** • **Recuperar la tierra** | | | ✔ |
| **Leamos** • **del Popol Vuh** **Escribamos** • **Una historia con fluidez** | | ✔ | |
| **Prepárate para el examen** | | ✔ | |
| **Integración** | | | ✔ |

## Technology Resources

### ¡Exprésate! Online
- Student Edition with multi-media
- SoundBooth recording tool
- Interactive activities with feedback
- Self-tests with feedback
- Cuaderno de actividades (interactive workbook)
- Cuaderno de vocabulario y gramática (interactive workbook)
- Live Ink™ Reading Help
- Holt Online Assessment

### DVD Tutor, Disc 2
- GeoVisión
- GramaVisión
- VideoNovela
- Cultura
- Variedades

### Interactive Tutor
- Interactive practice games
- Writing and recording workshops

### Audio Program
- Textbook listening activities
- Assessment listening activities
- Songs

### One-Stop Planner
- Complete media and print resources
- ExamView® Pro Test Generator
- Holt Calendar Planner

### PuzzlePro
- Customizable word games

## Assessment

**Geocultura**
**Vocabulario 1 / Gramática 1**
**Vocabulario 2 / Gramática 2**
**Leamos**
**Escribamos**
**Prepárate para el examen**

### Assessment Program
**Prueba: Geocultura,** pp. 115–116
**Pruebas,** pp. 101–102, 103–104, 105–106
**Pruebas,** pp. 107–108, 109–110, 111–112
**Prueba,** p. 113
**Prueba,** p. 114
**Examen: Capítulo 6,** pp. 281–286
**Examen oral: Capítulo 6,** p. 292
**Alternative Assessment,** pp. 378, 390, 402

### Online Assessment
**my.hrw.com**

### Test Generator
**ExamView® Pro Test Generator**

Planning Guide

# Projects

## ¡Ponte al día!

### En la ciudad de...

In this project, students work in groups of three or four to research a city in a Spanish-speaking area and write a short newscast reporting on the challenges faced by that city. You may want to allow a week for groups to collect information in Spanish on the city they choose.

**SUGGESTED SEQUENCE**

1. Divide the class into groups of three or four students and have them choose a city to research. Allow them library time to research the addresses of and write letters in Spanish to the Chamber of Commerce or the Tourist Bureau of their chosen city. Have students also collect as much information from the Internet as possible.
2. After students have gathered their information, they may begin preparing their written newscast. They should be encouraged to report on the city's current events, cultural resources, recent problems and solutions, and outlook for the near future.
3. Students prepare several broadcast screen inserts (icons or pictures that appear behind the shoulder of the newscaster as he or she is introducing the upcoming story). Encourage students to be creative in their representations and to choose an image that depicts the main idea of their reports.
4. Students present their news broadcasts to the class. You may want to record groups' projects on videocassette. 1.3, 3.2

### Grading the projects

Suggested point distribution (100 points total)

| | |
|---|---|
| Use of Spanish | 30 |
| Vocabulary | 30 |
| Creativity of visuals | 20 |
| Presentation | 20 |

### Partner Class Project

Have students work in pairs to analyze the content and format of two different Spanish-language online newspapers. Students should compare the format of each newspaper and the topics that are highlighted in each. What is included in the editorial section? What is the focus of the international news? What articles are shown on the home page? Have students prepare a short presentation for the class, comparing and contrasting the two news sites. 3.2

### Game Bank

For game ideas, see pages T64–T67.

### e-community

**e-mail forum:**

Post the following questions on the classroom e-mail forum:

**¿Qué secciones del periódico sueles leer? ¿Prefieres las noticias en línea, en la televisión o en el periódico? ¿Por qué?¿Qué secciones del periódico sueles leer? ¿Prefieres las noticias en línea, en la televisión o en el periódico? ¿Por qué?**

All students will contribute to the list and then share the items. 1.3

# ¡Ponte al día!

## Las pirámides

Pyramids were built in Mexico as ceremonial centers to worship the gods or as astronomical observatories. The first pyramid was built by the Olmecs around 1500 B.C. There are hundreds of archaeological sites with pyramids in Mesoamerica. In Teotihuacán, there are two incredible pyramids: the Pyramid of the Sun and the Pyramid of the Moon. In southern Mexico, Monte Albán and Tajín were two beautiful cities with pyramids and platforms. Other important centers are the Mayan cities of Palenque, Uxmal, and Chichén Itzá, with their distinctive pyramids and palaces. Have students research the architecture and history of the Aztec, Toltec, Zapotec, and Mayan ceremonial centers. You might have groups create plaster-of-Paris molds or clay replicas of specific sites. 2.2, 3.1

## Receta

You might have students make the following recipe as a class project or for extra credit.

### Chilaquiles

**para 4–6 personas**

8 tortillas de maíz
aceite para freír
1 ó 2 chiles serranos o jalapeños (al gusto)
1 diente de ajo picado
2 tomates cocinados (se puede usar tomates enlatados)
1/2 cucharadita de orégano
1/2 taza de agua
sal al gusto
1/2 taza de cebolla picada
1/2 taza de queso *Monterey Jack,* rallado
1/2 taza de crema agria

Corte las tortillas en pedazos de 1″ × 1″. Licúe los tomates, el orégano, los chiles, el ajo picado y el agua en una licuadora. En una sartén grande, ponga una cucharada de aceite y añada la salsa de tomate, sazone con sal y cocine a fuego moderado, revolviéndola de vez en cuando, por unos cinco minutos. Retírela del fuego, y manténgala caliente. En otra sartén, fría las tortillas a fuego un poco alto hasta que estén doradas. Escúrralas sobre toallas de papel. Cuando estén fritas todas las tortillas, saque el aceite de la sartén dejando sólo 1/2 taza. Ponga las tortillas y la cebolla en la sartén y cocine hasta que la cebolla esté transparente. Añada la salsa de tomate y cocine, dándole vueltas, por unos tres minutos. Sírvalas inmediatamente con el queso y la crema encima.

2.2, 3.1

# Listening Activity Scripts

## ¡Ponte al día!



### Vocabulario en acción 1

**3** p. 233, CD 6, Track 1

For script, see *Teacher's Edition* p. 233.

**Answers to Activity 3**

1. negativo
2. positivo
3. negativo
4. positivo
5. positivo
6. negativo

### Gramática en acción 1

**10** p. 236, CD 6, Track 2

1. —¿Viste el reportaje en el periódico de hoy sobre la crisis ambiental en el Golfo de México? Me pareció excelente.
   —Está claro que la reportera hizo un gran esfuerzo para escribir ese artículo. Me parece que ella sabe investigar las cosas muy a fondo.
2. —Ya son las seis. ¿Está bien si pongo el noticiero? Quiero saber si van a dar más información sobre las elecciones.
   —Insistes en ver el noticiero en la tele todas las noches, pero estoy convencida de que los sitios de noticias en Internet son más informativos.
3. —Me gusta mucho el reportero de esta emisora porque es muy cómico. ¿A ti te gusta?
   —No estoy segura de que sea fiable. Dudo que sepa mucho de política.
4. —¿Has visto el concurso que ponen a las diez en el canal once? Es mi favorito.
   —Claro que sí. No cabe duda que el concurso de las diez es el más divertido de todos.
5. —No me gusta hablar de política con Alejo. Sus opiniones no están basadas en la realidad.
   —Es obvio que Alejo no está bien informado. Pasa demasiado tiempo viendo las telenovelas y no está al tanto de lo que pasa en el mundo.
6. —Acabo de comprar el libro que Pablo Aquino reseñó en el periódico. ¿Viste el artículo? Dice que es el mejor libro del año.
   —No estoy convencido de que el señor Aquino reseñe los libros de modo imparcial.

**Answers to Activity 10**

1. a 2. a 3. b 4. a 5. a 6. b

**14** p. 238, CD 6, Track 3

1. —¿Sabías que Alberto está trabajando para la revista "Gente"?
   —No es cierto que Alberto trabaje para esa revista. Él es un mentiroso.
2. —Creo que el equipo de volibol de nuestro colegio va a salir en el noticiero de las nueve.
   —Sin duda va a salir. Yo vi al reportero hoy durante el partido.
3. —Celia dice que podemos leer en Internet su artículo sobre los nuevos concursos en la televisión.
   —Es imposible que hayan publicado ese artículo en Internet. Es pésimo.
4. —En el noticiero de las nueve, no dijeron nada sobre la crisis económica.
   —No pienso que hayan pasado por alto un tema tan importante.
5. —Leí un reportaje en línea sobre la crisis ambiental en la Ciudad de México que es muy informativo.
   —Dudo que sea más educativo que el documental que vi en la televisión anoche. Trataron el tema a fondo.
6. —El periódico en nuestro colegio es mucho más interesante que el de otros colegios.
   —No cabe duda que nuestro periódico es el mejor de todos.

**Answers to Activity 14**

1. b 2. a 3. b 4. b 5. b 6. a

**18** p. 240, CD 6, Track 4

Cuando estaba en el primer año del colegio, no había sala de computadoras pero ahora sí. Es una sala grande con muchas computadoras pero no hay ni una impresora en la sala. Tenemos que usar la impresora de los profesores. Suelo usar la computadora para leer las noticias en línea por las mañanas. Hay un televisor en una de las salas también para ver las noticias, pero la sala siempre está llena de estudiantes. Antes había un video, pero algunos estudiantes veían películas durante las clases así que lo quitaron. Hay un periódico, pero es del colegio y no tiene noticias locales o internacionales. Escucharía la radio porque me gusta el locutor de la emisora local, pero no hay radio en mi colegio. Menos mal que puedo ponerme al tanto por Internet.

**Answers to Activity 18**

| Hay | No hay |
|---|---|
| sala de computadoras | periódico local |
| periódico del colegio | radio |
| televisor | impresora |
| | vídeo |

### Vocabulario en acción 2

**23** p. 246, CD 6, Track 8

For script, see *Teacher's Edition* p. 247.

**Answers to Activity 23**

1. a 2. c 3. b 4. a 5. a 6. c

For Student Response Forms, see the *Lab Book,* pp. 33–36.

## Gramática en acción 2

### 31 p. 250, CD 6, Track 9

1. —¡Alguien reseñó el documental que hicimos sobre México y dijo que era pésimo!
   —Es imposible que alguien haya dicho algo así.
2. —Este periódico es buenísimo. Creo que vale la pena suscribirse porque los periodistas son los más fiables.
   —Estoy de acuerdo y estoy convencida de que los fotógrafos son los mejores también.
3. —Creo que algunos estudiantes quieren participar en el concurso para jóvenes.
   —Lo dudo. Hablé con muchos de ellos y nadie quiere participar.
4. —Que yo sepa, no tenemos ningún artículo en el periódico del colegio sobre la nueva piscina.
   —Es cierto y además no conozco a ningún estudiante que quiera escribir el artículo.
5. —Tienes que escribir un artículo o sobre el partido de tenis o sobre el debate político.
   —Es imposible. No estoy al tanto ni de los deportes ni de la política.
6. —Si no lees el periódico, no puedes estar al tanto de las noticias. ¿No te importa estar bien informado?
   —¿Qué dices? Yo estoy bien informado. No leo el periódico, pero siempre leo las noticias en línea y por la noche veo los noticieros en la televisión.

**Answers to Activity 31**

1. niega 2. afirma 3. niega 4. afirma 5. niega 6. niega

### 34 p. 252, CD 6, Track 10

1. —Esta ciudad es el centro de gobierno del país y es donde se hacen las leyes.
2. —Compré un aparato nuevo para escuchar mis canciones favoritas.
3. —Por fin los científicos descubrieron el remedio para esta enfermedad.
4. —Queremos publicar un periódico en el colegio, pero no tenemos el dinero para poder empezar.
5. —Este cuarto está muy limpio. Veo que todo está muy organizado.

**Answers to Activity 34**

1. la capital 3. la cura 5. el orden
2. la radio 4. el capital

### 39 p. 255, CD 6, Track 11

1. Los reporteros afirman que dos mujeres acaban de cruzar el Mar de Cortés nadando.
2. El presidente anuncia que va a visitar el suroeste de Estados Unidos.
3. Los arqueólogos mexicanos dudan que la cerámica encontrada en Guadalajara sea de los mayas.
4. Los expertos dudan que la lluvia sea gran problema para el festival de El Paso.
5. Los colegios de Tucson buscan profesores de matemáticas.
6. Un biólogo afirma que ha visto un oso pardo en la Sierra Madre.

**Answers to Activity 39**

1. a 2. a 3. b 4. b 5. a 6. a

## Prepárate para el examen capítulo 6

### 1 p. 264, CD 6, Track 14

1. —¿Oye, supiste lo de la crisis ambiental a causa del petróleo en el mar?
   —No, para nada. ¿Y tú? ¿Cómo te enteraste?
   —Lo acabo de ver aquí en las noticias en línea.
2. —¿Viste el noticiero anoche?
   —Sí. ¿Y te diste cuenta de lo mal informado que estaba el reportero?
   —Deberían investigar los temas más a fondo, ¿no crees?
3. —No puedo creer que no haya podido ver el partido anoche. Estuvo buenísmo porque ganó mi equipo uno a cero contra el Cruz Azul.
   —Oye, ¿cómo lo sabes?
   —Porque acabo de leer la reseña del partido en la sección deportiva.
4. —Parece mentira que ese candidato haya ganado el concurso. De los cinco, él fue el peor.
   —Es cierto, pero a mí todos parecen iguales.
5. —Qué bueno que por fin nos suscribamos al periódico. Ahora puedo estar al tanto de todo lo que pasa en el mundo.
   —Oye, ¿me prestas los editoriales?
   —Con mucho gusto.
6. —¿Qué estación de radio escuchas?
   —Escucho la ciento punto tres. Estoy loca por la música que ponen.
   —Fíjate que a mí también me gusta.

**Answers to Activity 1**

1. e 2. b 3. a 4. d 5. f 6. c

### 6 p. 265, CD 6, Track 15

For script, see *Teacher's Edition* p. 265.

**Answers to Activity 6**

1. c 2. a 3. b 4. c 5. b 6. a

## Integración capítulos 1–6

### 1 p. 268, CD 6, Track 16

For script, see *Teacher's Edition* p. 268.

**Answers to Activity 1**

1. B 2. D 3. A 4. C

# 50-Minute Lesson Plans

For more customized Lesson Plans, see the *Lesson Planner with Differentiated Instruction.*

## ¡Ponte al día!

### Day 1

**Objective**
*Expressing certainty*

**Core Instruction**
**Chapter Opener**, pp. 228–229 **10 min.**
- See Chapter Objectives and Using the Photo, p. 228.

**Vocabulario en acción 1**, pp. 230–235
- Have students do Bell Work, p. 230.
- See Teaching **Vocabulario**, p. 230. **10 min.**
- See Teaching **¡Exprésate!**, p. 230. **10 min.**
- Have students do Activities 1–2, p. 232. **10 min.**
- Play Audio CD 6, Tr. 1 for Activity 3, p. 233. **5 min.**
- Have students do Activities 4–6, p. 233. **5 min.**

**Optional Resources**
- Advanced Learners, p. 231 ▲
- Multiple Intelligences, p. 231
- Slower Pace Learners, p. 233 ◆
- Multiple Intelligences, p. 233

**Homework Suggestions**
Cuaderno de vocabulario y gramática, pp. 61–63
❀ 1.1, 1.2

### Day 2

**Objective**
*Expressing doubt and disbelief*

**Core Instruction**
**Vocabulario en acción 1**, pp. 230–235
- See Teaching **¡Exprésate!**, p. 234. **10 min.**
- Have students do Activities 7–9, p. 235. **25 min.**
- See **Comunicación** suggestion p. 235. **15 min.**

**Optional Resources**
- Slower Pace Learners, p. 235 ◆
- Special Learning Needs, p. 235 ●

**Homework Suggestions**
Study for **Prueba: Vocabulario 1**
Cuaderno de vocabulario y gramatica, pp. 61–63
❀ 1.1, 1.2, 1.3

### Day 3

**Objective**
*Indicative after expressions of certainty*

**Core Instruction**
**Vocabulario en acción 1**, pp. 230–235
- Review **Vocabulario en acción 1**, pp. 230–235. **5 min.**
- Give **Prueba: Vocabulario 1. 20 min.**

**Gramática en acción 1**, pp. 236–241
- Have students do Bell Work, p. 236. **5 min.**
- See Teaching **Gramática**, p. 236. **10 min.**
- Play Audio CD 6, Tr. 2 for Activity 10, p. 236. **5 min.**
- Have students do Activity 11, p. 236. **5 min.**

**Optional Resources**
- **Comunicación**, p. 237
- Advanced Learners, p. 237 ▲
- Multiple Intelligences, p. 237

**Homework Suggestions**
Cuaderno de vocabulario y gramática, p. 64–66
Cuaderno de actividades, pp. 51–53
❀ 1.2

### Day 4

**Objective**
*Subjunctive after expressions of doubt and disbelief*

**Core Instruction**
**Gramática en acción 1**, pp. 236–241
- Have students do Activities 12–13, p. 237. **15 min.**
- Have students do Bell Work, p. 238. **5 min.**
- See Teaching **Gramática**, p. 238. **10 min.**
- Play Audio CD 6, Tr. 3 for Activity 14, p. 238. **5 min.**
- Have students do Activities 15–17, pp. 238–239 **15 min.**

**Optional Resources**
- **Comunicación**, p. 239
- Advanced Learners, p. 239 ▲
- Special Learning Needs, p. 239 ●

**Homework Suggestions**
Cuaderno de vocabulario y gramática, pp. 64–66
Cuaderno de actividades, pp. 51–53
❀ 1.1, 1.2

### Day 5

**Objective**
*Uses of* ***haber***

**Core Instruction**
**Gramática en acción 1**, pp. 236–241
- See Teaching **Gramática**, p. 240. **10 min.**
- Play Audio CD 6, Tr. 4 for Activity 18, p. 240. **5 min.**
- Have students do Activities 19–22, pp. 240–241. **30 min.**

**Optional Resources**
- **Comunicación**, p. 241
- Advanced Learners, p. 241 ▲
- Special Learning Needs, p. 241 ●

**Homework Suggestions**
Study for **Prueba: Gramática 1**
Cuaderno de vocabulario y gramática, pp. 64–66
Cuaderno de actividades, pp. 51–53
❀ 1.1, 1.2

### Day 6

**Objective**
*Interviews from around the Spanish-speaking world*

**Core Instruction**
**Gramática en acción 1**, pp. 236–241
- Review **Gramática en acción 1**, pp. 236–241 **5 min.**
- Give **Prueba: Gramática 1. 20 min.**

**Cultura**, pp. 242–243
- See Teaching **Cultura**, p. 242. **10 min.**
- Play Audio CD 6, Tr. 5–7, or show **VideoCultura. 15 min.**

**Optional Resources**
- Advanced Learners, p. 243 ▲
- Special Learning Needs, p. 243 ●

**Homework Suggestions**
Cuaderno de actividades, p. 54
Online Practice (**go.hrw.com**, Keyword: EXP3 CH6)
❀ 1.2, 1.3, 3.1, 5.1

### Day 7

**Objective**
*Asking about information and explaining where you found it*

**Core Instruction**
**Vocabulario en acción 2**, pp. 244–249
- Present **Vocabulario**, pp. 244–245. See Teaching **Vocabulario**, p. 244. **10 min.**
- See Teaching **¡Exprésate!**, p. 244. **10 min.**
- Play Audio CD 6, Tr. 8 for Activity 23, p. 246. **10 min.**
- Have students do Activities 24–26, pp. 246–247. **20 min.**

**Optional Resources**
- Advanced Learners, p. 245 ▲
- Multiple Intelligences, p. 245
- Vocabulary in Context, p. 246

**Homework Suggestions**
Cuaderno de vocabulario y gramática, pp. 67–69
❀ 1.2

### Day 8

**Objective**
*Talking about what you know and don't know*

**Core Instruction**
**Vocabulario en acción 2**, pp. 244–249
- Have students do Activity 27, p. 247. **5 min.**
- See **Comunicación** suggestion, p. 247 **10 min.**
- See Teaching **¡Exprésate!**, p. 248. **10 min.**
- Have students do Activities 28–30, p. 249. **25 min.**

**Optional Resources**
- **Comunicación**, p. 249
- Advanced Learners, p. 249 ▲
- Special Learning Needs, p. 249 ●

**Homework Suggestions**
Study for **Prueba: Vocabulario 2**
Cuaderno de vocabulario y gramática, pp. 67–69
❀ 1.1, 1.2, 1.3

- For information on the **Geocultura** pages, see the *Lesson Planner with Differentiated Instruction.*
- For more detailed information on benchmarks, see point-of-use correlations on each page.
- To edit and create your own lesson plans, see the **One-Stop** Planner® CD-ROM

**KEY**
▲ Advanced Learners
◆ Slower Pace Learners
● Special Learning Needs
■ Heritage Speakers

## Day 9

### Objective
*Indefinite expressions*

### Core Instruction
**Vocabulario en acción 2,** pp. 244–249
- Review **Vocabulario en acción 2,** pp. 244–249. **10 min.**
- Give **Prueba: Vocabulario 2. 20 min.**

**Gramática en acción 2,** pp. 250–255
- See Teaching **Gramática,** p. 250. **10 min.**
- Play Audio CD 6, Tr. 9 for Activity 31, p. 250. **10 min.**

### Optional Resources
- **Comunicación,** p. 251
- Advanced Learners, p. 251 ▲
- Special Learning Needs, p. 251 ●

### Homework Suggestions
Cuaderno de vocabulario y gramática, pp. 70–72
Cuaderno de actividades, pp. 55–57
1.2

## Day 10

### Objective
*Gender of nouns*

### Core Instruction
**Gramática en acción 2,** pp. 250–255
- Have students do Bell Work, p. 252. **5 min.**
- Have students do Activities 32–33, p. 251. **15 min.**
- See Teaching **Gramática,** p. 252. **10 min.**
- Play Audio CD 6, Tr. 10 for Activity 34, p. 252. **5 min.**
- Have students do Activities 35–37, p. 253. **15 min.**

### Optional Resources
- **Comunicación,** p. 253
- Slower Pace Learners, p. 253 ◆
- Special Learning Needs, p. 253 ●

### Homework Suggestions
Cuaderno de vocabulario y gramática, pp. 70–72
Cuaderno de actividades, pp. 55–57
1.1, 1.2

## Day 11

### Objective
*Indicative in compound sentences*

### Core Instruction
**Gramática en acción 2,** pp. 250–255
- Have students do Bell Work, p. 254. **5 min.**
- See Teaching **Gramática,** p. 254. **10 min.**
- Have students do Activity 38, p. 254. **10 min.**
- Play Audio CD 6, Tr. 11 for Activity 39, p. 255. **10 min.**
- Have students do Activities 40–41, p. 255. **15 min.**

### Optional Resources
- **Comunicación,** p. 255
- Advanced Learners, p. 255 ▲
- Special Learning Needs, p. 255 ●

### Homework Suggestions
Study for **Prueba: Gramática 2**
Cuaderno de vocabulario y gramática, pp. 70–72
Cuaderno de actividades, pp. 55–57
1.1, 1.2

## Day 12

### Objective
*Indicative in compound sentences*

### Core Instruction
**Gramática en acción 2,** pp. 250–255
- Review **Gramática en acción 2,** pp. 250–255. **15 min.**
- Give **Prueba: Gramática 2. 20 min.**

**Novela en video,** pp. 256–257
- Show **VideoNovela.** See Teaching **Novela en video,** p. 256. **15 min.**

### Optional Resources
- **Comunicación,** p. 257 ▲
- Visual Learners, p. 257 ●

### Homework Suggestions
Cuaderno de vocabulario y gramática, pp. 70–72
1.2, 1.3, 3.1

## Day 13

### Objective
*Developing listening and reading skills*

### Core Instruction
**Lectura informativa,** pp. 258–259
- See Teaching **Lectura informativa,** p. 258. **35 min.**

**Leamos y escribamos,** pp. 260–263
- See Teaching **Leamos,** points 1–3, p. 260. **15 min.**

### Optional Resources
- Advanced Learners, p. 259 ▲
- Multiple Intelligences, p. 259
- Advanced Learners, p. 261 ▲
- Multiple Intelligences, p. 261

### Homework Suggestions
Cuaderno de actividades, p. 58
1.2, 1.3

## Day 14

### Objective
*Developing reading and writing skills*

### Core Instruction
**Leamos y escribamos,** pp. 260–263
- See Teaching **Leamos,** point 4, p. 260. **10 min.**
- See Teaching **Escribamos,** points 1–3, p. 262. **10 min.**

**Prepárate para el examen,** pp. 264–267
- Play Audio CD 6, Tr. 14 for Activity 1, p. 264. **5 min.**
- Have students do Activities 2–5, pp. 264–265. **25 min.**

### Optional Resources
- Slower Pace Learners, p. 263 ◆
- Multiple Intelligences, p. 263

### Homework Suggestions
**Taller del escritor,** p. 263
1.2, 1.3, 3.1

## Day 15

### Objective
*Chapter review*

### Core Instruction
**Prepárate para el examen,** pp. 264–267
- Play Audio CD 6, Tr. 15 for Activity 6, p. 265. **5 min.**
- Have students do Activity 7, p. 265. **5 min.**

**Integración,** pp. 268–269
- Play Audio CD 6, Tr. 16 for Activity 1, p. 268. **10 min.**
- Have students do Activities 2–6, pp. 268–269. **30 min.**

### Optional Resources
- Play Pre-AP Audio CD 2, Tr. 1, for Pre-AP Practice, p. 265
- Game, p. 267
- Fine Art Connection, p. 269

### Homework Suggestions
Study for Chapter Test
1.1, 1.2, 1.3

## Day 16/Test

### Core Instruction
**Chapter Test 50 min.**

### Optional Resources
**Assessment Program**
- **Prueba: Lectura**
- **Prueba: Escritura**
- Test Generator

### Homework Suggestions
Cuaderno de actividades, pp. 59–60

# Indiana
## The Hoosier State

Indianapolis

Autumn in Northern Indiana

State capitol building at dusk

### Chapter 6

The following chart presents *¡Exprésate!* Chapter 6 correlations to the Indiana Academic Standards for World Languages, Grade 11. The correlations here are to the *Student Edition* (SE) and *Teacher's Edition* (TE) only. For additional teaching resources, see pages 227A-227B

| INDIANA ACADEMIC STANDARDS | | | CHAPTER 6 SE/TE CORRELATIONS |
|---|---|---|---|
| **Standard 1 COMMUNICATION:** | | | |
| **Write and speak in a language other than English** | 11.1.1 | Initiate, sustain, and close conversations in limited yet varied situations. | SE: 235, 248, 267<br>TE: 230, 234, 244 |
| | 11.1.2 | Exchange detailed information and opinions orally on a variety of topics. | SE: 234, 237, 239, 243, 247, 267<br>TE: 234, 242, 248, 267 |
| | 11.1.3 | Exchange detailed information and opinions in written form on a variety of topics. | SE: 263<br>TE: 249, 255 |
| | 11.1.4 | Make requests and ask different types of questions in a variety of social situations. | SE: 235, 247, 249 |
| | 11.1.5 | Recognize and use situation-appropriate non-verbal communication. | TE: 256 |
| | 11.1.6 | Use speaking and listening strategies to facilitate communication. | SE: 237, 239, 241 |
| **Standard 2 COMMUNICATION:** | | | |
| **Interpret information in a language other than English** *Learners interpret written and spoken language on a variety of topics. (Interpretive)* | 11.2.1 | Respond to everyday requests, commands, and directions. | TE: 231 |
| | 11.2.2 | Demonstrate comprehension of both authentic and non-authentic written and spoken language through developmentally appropriate tasks. | SE: 257, 259, 262<br>TE: 242, 256, 258, 260 |
| | 11.2.3 | Make educated guesses about meaning in unfamiliar written and spoken contexts. | SE: 256, 260<br>TE: 256, 260 |
| **Standard 3 COMMUNICATION:** | | | |
| **Present information in a language other than English** *Learners present to an audience of listeners or readers on a variety of topics. (Presentational)* | 11.3.2 | Produce and present creative material on a variety of topics. | TE: 227C, 261, 268 |
| | 11.3.3 | Read passages aloud to demonstrate improving intonation and pronunciation. | SE: 263<br>TE: 256, 262 |
| | 11.3.4 | Compose cohesive written information using appropriate formats and more varied vocabulary and structures. | SE: 263<br>TE: 227C, 262, 263 |
| **Standard 4 CULTURES:** | | | |
| **Develop awareness of other cultures.** *Learners examine, experience, and reflect on the relationships among the practices, products, and perspectives of the cultures studied.* | 11.4.1 | Analyze and reflect on cultural practices of the target cultures. | SE: 243, 259, 262, 269<br>TE: 258, 260, 269 |
| | 11.4.2 | Describe products, perspectives, and symbols of the target cultures. | SE: 243, 259, 262, 269<br>TE: 227D, 242, 258, 260, 269 |
| | 11.4.3 | Discuss factors that influence practices, products, and perspectives. | SE: 243, 259, 262, 269<br>TE: 242, 258, 260, 269 |

| | | | |
|---|---|---|---|
| | 11.4.4 | Recognize the interrelations among the practices, products, and perspectives of the target cultures. | SE: 243, 259<br>TE: 242, 258, 260, 269 |
| | 11.4.5 | Explain contributions from other cultures. | SE: 259, 262, 264, 269<br>TE: 258, 260, 263, 269 |
| | 11.4.6 | Identify significant events unique to the target cultures. | SE: 259 |

## Standard 5 CONNECTIONS:

| | | | |
|---|---|---|---|
| **Make connections to other content areas** *Learners use the target language to expand their knowledge of and make connections among multiple content areas.* | 11.5.1 | Make connections with other content areas through resources intended for native speakers. | SE: 259<br>TE: 227C, 268 |
| | 11.5.2 | Design and share activities and materials that integrate the target language and cultures with concepts and skills from other content areas. | TE: 227C, 267 |

## Standard 6 CONNECTIONS:

| | | | |
|---|---|---|---|
| **Access and connect information through various media** *Learners strengthen language proficiency and cultural knowledge by using current digital media and authentic resources.* | 11.6.1 | Use digital media and culturally authentic resources to build vocabulary, improve reading ability, and encourage cultural awareness. | TE: 227E, 227F |
| | 11.6.2 | Use digital media and culturally authentic resources to study target cultures. | SE: 242, 256<br>TE: 245, 249 |
| | 11.6.3 | Identify and evaluate resources intended for native speakers. | SE: 256<br>TE: 245, 249 |

## Standard 7 COMPARISONS:

| | | | |
|---|---|---|---|
| **Investigate the nature of language and culture** *Learners understand the nature of language and culture through comparisons of the languages and cultures studied and their own.* | 11.7.1 | Use elements of word formation to expand vocabulary and derive meaning. | SE: 241, 253, 264, 267<br>TE: 236, 252, 264, 267 |
| | 11.7.2 | Recognize and use a variety of language structures. | SE: 264, 268, 269<br>TE: 236-241, 250-255, 267 |
| | 11.7.3 | Compare and use idiomatic, colloquial, and proverbial expressions in the target language. | SE: 235, 269<br>TE: 234, 282 |
| | 11.7.5 | Compare systems of other cultures and the learner's own culture. | SE: 243, 259<br>TE: 242, 259 |
| | 11.7.6 | Compare and contrast elements that shape cultural identity in the learner's heritage and in the target cultures. | SE: 243, 259<br>TE: 242, 259 |

## Standard 8 COMMUNITIES:

| | | | |
|---|---|---|---|
| **Become an active global citizen by experiencing languages and cultures in multiple settings** *Learners use their knowledge of the target language and cultures both within and beyond the school setting for personal enrichment and civic engagement.* | 11.8.1 | Share experiences from the world language classroom with others. | SE: 243<br>TE: 268 |
| | 11.8.2 | Investigate and share with others the influences of the target language and cultures on the community. | SE: 243<br>TE: 268 |
| | 11.8.3 | Show evidence of becoming a life-long learner by using the target language and cultural knowledge for personal enrichment. | SE: 243, 252<br>TE: 227D, 251 |

# Chapter Opener

## Meeting the National Standards

**Communication**
Comunicación, pp. 233, 235, 237, 239, 247, 249, 251, 253, 255, 257
Game, p. 267
Situación, p. 269

**Cultures**
Receta, p. 227D
Las pirámides, p. 227D
Products and Perspectives, p. 249

**Connections**
Las pirámides, p. 227D
Atlas Interactivo Mundial, p. 243
Community Link, p. 251
Nota cultural, pp. 241, 252
Social Studies Link, p. 259
History Link, p. 261

**Comparisons**
Comparing and Contrasting, p. 245
En inglés, p. 250
Language to Language, p. 266

**Communities**
Community Link, pp. 237, 248
Comunidad y oficio, p. 243

## Using the Photo

In this photograph we see El Paso, the fourth largest city in Texas, and Ciudad Juárez, Mexico, in the background. El Paso sits in the westernmost corner of Texas, where Texas, New Mexico, and Mexico meet. El Paso has been linked culturally and economically with Juárez since its founding. The cities are separated by the Río Grande. El Paso has a rich cultural life, with contributions from many ethnic groups.

## Más vocabulario

Students may want to use some of these words to discuss the photo.

**la cámara de video** *video camera*
**el micrófono** *microphone*
**rodar** *to film*
**la toma** *shot*

# Capítulo 6

# ¡Ponte al día!

**OBJETIVOS**

**In this chapter you will learn to**
- express certainty
- express doubt and disbelief
- ask about and explain where you found information
- talk about what you know and don't know

**And you will use**
- indicative after expressions of certainty
- subjunctive after expressions of doubt and disbelief
- **haber**
- indefinite expressions
- gender of nouns
- indicative in compound sentences

**¿Qué ves en la foto?**
- **¿Qué están haciendo estos chicos?**
- **¿Sobre qué asunto crees que está informando la chica?**
- **¿Con qué frecuencia ves tú el noticiero?**

| Suggested pacing: | Traditional Schedule | Block Schedule |
|---|---|---|
| Vocabulario 1/Gramática 1 | 5 1/2 days | 2 1/2 blocks |
| Cultura | 1/2 day | 1/2 block |
| Vocabulario 2/Gramática 2 | 5 1/2 days | 2 1/2 blocks |
| Novela | 1/2 day | 1/2 block |
| Lectura cultural | 1 day | 1/2 block |
| Leamos y escribamos | 1 day | 1/2 block |
| Prepárate para el examen | 1/2 day | 1/4 block |
| Chapter Test | 1 day | 1/2 block |
| Integración | 1/2 day | 1/4 block |

Noticiero estudiantil en El Paso

# Chapter Opener

## Holt Grammar Logic

### CHAPTER 6

- *To express certainty, and to express doubt and disbelief,* students will need to use the indicative after expressions of certainty and the subjunctive after expressions of doubt and disbelief. They will also need to review and further their knowledge of the forms and uses of the impersonal form of **haber.**
- *To talk about a source of information,* and to talk about what they know and don't know, students will need to review affirmative and negative indefinite expressions, learn more about the gender of nouns, and review the use of the indicative mood in compound sentences.
- In this chapter students practice the various forms of **haber,** including **había** and **hubo.**

## DVD VIDEO OPTIONS

- **VideoCultura**
- **VideoNovela**
- **Variedades**

- **GramaVisión**

## LISTENING PRACTICE — Language Lab and Classroom Activities

**Vocabulario**
Activity 3, p. 233, CD 6, Tr. 1
Activity 23, p. 246, CD 6, Tr. 8

**Gramática**
Activity 10, p. 236, CD 6, Tr. 2
Activity 14, p. 238, CD 6, Tr. 3
Activity 18, p. 240, CD 6, Tr. 4
Activity 31, p. 250, CD 6, Tr. 9
Activity 34, p. 252, CD 6, Tr. 10
Activity 39, p. 255, CD 6, Tr. 11

**Cultura**
**Comparaciones**, pp. 242–243, CD 6, Tr. 5–7

**Novela**
**Novela en video**, Escuchemos, p. 256

**Lectura informativa**
pp. 258–259, CD 6, Tr. 12

**Leamos**
pp. 260–263, CD 6, Tr. 13
Escuchemos, p. 260

**Repaso**
Activity 1, p. 264, CD 6, Tr. 14
Activity 6, p. 265, CD 6, Tr. 15
**Variedades,** Lab Book, p. 73

**Integración**
Activity 1, p. 268, CD 6, Tr. 16

**Assessment Program**
CD 6, Tr. 17–20

**Additional Listening**
Pre-AP CD 2, Tr. 1–4

## Resources

**Planning:**

Lesson Planner, pp. 81–82, 242–243

One-Stop Planner

**Presentation:**

Teaching Transparencies **Vocabulario** 6.1, 6.2

**Practice:**

Cuaderno de vocabulario y gramática, pp. 61–63

Activities for Communication, pp. 21–22

Teaching Transparencies Bell Work 6.1

**Vocabulario y gramática** answers, pp. 61–63

Interactive Tutor, Disc 2

### Bell Work

Use Bell Work 6.1 in the *Teaching Transparencies,* or write this activity on the board.

**Completa las oraciones con el pluscuamperfecto del verbo.**

1. **Cuando hablé con Marta, ella todavía no (escuchar) la noticia.**
2. **Aún no (hablar) mi locutor favorito cuando encendí la televisión.**
3. **Cuando encontré el canal, ya (terminar) el reportaje.**
4. **Ya (irse) la gente cuando llegó el reportero.**

1.2

### Pre-AP Practice

**AP Benchmark:** Describe, narrate, and present information and/or arguments in a presentation of two or three minutes.

**Focus:** Talking about current events

- SE, p. 235, Act. 9
- TE, p. 235, **Comunicación**
- TE, p. 235, Slower Pace Learners

**Objetivos**
- Expressing certainty
- Expressing doubt and disbelief

# Vocabulario en acción 1

## Los medios electrónicos

Me gusta **estar al tanto** de las noticias. Siempre leo el periódico y veo **los noticieros** en la televisión.

Leo a menudo **las noticias en línea.** Estoy convencida de que los que navegamos mucho por Internet **estamos bien informados.**

Este **reportero** nunca está bien informado. No **trata los temas muy a fondo.** El año pasado, por ejemplo, **investigó la crisis ambiental** y **el reportaje** que hizo fue muy superficial. **Pasó por alto** muchos detalles importantes.

En cambio, **la locutora** del **canal** 13 es mi favorita. Sus reportajes son **detallados** e **informativos.** Siempre presenta las noticias **de modo** muy **imparcial,** sobre todo los asuntos **controvertidos.** Por eso **me inspira confianza.**

Este señor **reseña** las últimas películas. Es evidente que sabe muchísimo de cinematografía.

## Core Instruction

### TEACHING VOCABULARIO

1. Introduce the vocabulary using transparencies **Vocabulario 6.1** and **6.2.** Model pronunciation and point to vocabulary as you read the photo captions. **(3 min.)**
2. Present **Más vocabulario,** making sure students understand the meaning of each word. **(2 min.)**
3. Practice vocabulary by asking **¿Cuál es tu noticiero favorito?,** and so on. **(2 min.)**
4. Talk about something you saw on the news, using new and known words. **(3 min.)**

### TEACHING ¡EXPRÉSATE!

1. Ask students what they are learning this week in their History or Social Studies classes. **¿Sobre qué tema están aprendiendo esta semana? (3 min.)**
2. Act out the expressions of certainty using body language; for example, look confident and gesture for emphasis when you model **Estoy convencido(a) de que… (4 min.)**
3. Ask volunteers to make a statement about a history or social studies topic on which they have a strong opinion, using an expression of certainty. **(3 min.)**

Visit Holt Online
go.hrw.com
KEYWORD: EXP3 CH6
Vocabulario 1 practice

Mis programas preferidos son **los concursos** y **las telenovelas,** aunque también me interesan los programas **educativos** como los **documentales.**

Me encanta escuchar **la radio.** En mi **emisora** favorita ponen música pop en español y **alguna que otra** canción en inglés.

**Más vocabulario...**

| | |
|---|---|
| **estar mal informado(a)** | *to be poorly informed* |
| **informar** | *to report* |
| **parcial** | *biased* |
| **(poco) fiable** | *(un)trustworthy* |
| **el programa de radio (a micrófono abierto)** | *(call-in) radio show* |

**¡Exprésate!**

**To express certainty**

Interactive TUTOR

**Estoy convencido(a) de que...**
*I'm convinced that . . .*

**Estoy seguro(a) (de) que...**
*I'm positive that . . .*

**Es evidente que...**
*It's evident that . . .*

Vocabulario y gramática, pp. 61–63 Online workbooks

Vocabulario 1

## TPR
### TOTAL PHYSICAL RESPONSE

Bring to class a radio, a television, a newspaper, and a computer. Have individual students use the props to respond to the following commands.

**Señala el medio de comunicación que más usas para estar informado.**

**Busca una reseña de una película en el periódico.**

**Encuentra un sitio Web con noticias en línea.**

**Muéstranos el nombre del reportero de un artículo.**

**Enciende la radio.**

**Pon tu emisora favorita.**

**Enciende la televisión.**

**Pon un canal que esté dando una telenovela.**

1.2

### COMMON ERROR ALERT
¡OJO!

Students often use the article **el** with **radio** in Spanish because it ends in *-o* and therefore appears to be masculine. Explain that **radio** is masculine when it refers to the apparatus **(¿Dónde está el radio que tenía en mi cuarto?),** but is feminine when it refers to radio waves **(Tina va a hablar por la radio.).**

### También se puede decir...

Students might hear people say **de una manera...** instead of **de modo...** They might also hear **con mucho detalle** for **a fondo.**

## Differentiated Instruction

### ADVANCED LEARNERS

**Challenge** Have advanced students work in pairs to choose a news topic and research it in depth. Based on the information gathered, have them write ten detailed questions they would ask an expert on that topic. Once they have written their questions, students can exchange them and interview each other on what they have learned about each topic.
1.1

### MULTIPLE INTELLIGENCES

**Spatial** Have students think about the visual construction of a news program feature. Ask them to draw a 10-square "story board" or outline of the video, consisting of a series of squares with the different scenes to be shot depicted in the chronological order of the story. Have students present their story boards to the class, telling who will be the reporter and describing the report. Is it a controversial topic? Is the reporter reliable? Will the report include many details? 1.3

## Resources

**Planning:**

Lesson Planner, pp. 81–82, 242–243

One-Stop Planner

**Presentation:**

Teaching Transparencies **Vocabulario** 6.1, 6.2

**Practice:**

Cuaderno de vocabulario y gramática, pp. 61–63

Activities for Communication, pp. 21–22

Lab Book, pp. 33–36

Teaching Transparencies **Vocabulario y gramática** answers, pp. 61–63

Audio CD 6, Tr. 1

Interactive Tutor, Disc 2

## Language Note

Have students read through the list of programs in Activity 2. Tell them that **en vivo (Béisbol en vivo)** means *live.*

## Heritage Speakers

Ask heritage speakers if their family watches any programs on the Spanish channel. Have them tell what programs each member of the family watches. Ask them to give the class some information on each program.

Varios documentales sobre la naturaleza investigan las crisis ambientales, como la falta de agua.

### 1 Estamos al tanto 1.2

**Leamos** Completa las oraciones con la(s) palabra(s) correcta(s).

1. En mis clases _____ diferentes temas por medio de Internet y los periódicos. a
   **a.** investigamos **b.** nos consideramos
2. Es muy importante _____ lo que está pasando en el mundo. b
   **a.** pasar por alto **b.** estar al tanto de
3. Para saber algo sobre la política, mi profesor sugiere que veamos _____. b
   **a.** las telenovelas **b.** los noticieros
4. Voy a escuchar la radio esta noche porque mi _____ favorita va a transmitir un programa sobre la situación económica. a
   **a.** emisora **b.** telenovela
5. El locutor de este programa es muy justo; siempre explica los dos lados de cualquier tema de modo _____. a
   **a.** imparcial **b.** parcial
6. Algunos locutores solamente explican un lado del tema por lo que me parecen _____. b
   **a.** imparciales **b.** poco fiables

### 2 ¿Qué programa sugieres? 1.2

**Leamos/Hablemos** Lee lo que a los miembros de la familia Montoya les gusta ver en la televisión y decide qué puede ver cada persona.

CANAL 5 **¡Tenemos algo para todos!**

| | |
|---|---|
| 4 p.m. | Dibujos animados: "El rey león" |
| 5 p.m. | Concurso: "A millón" |
| 6 p.m. | Béisbol en vivo: Los Rangers contra los Yankees |
| 7 p.m. | Reportaje especial: "La crisis económica" |
| 8 p.m. | Documental: "Animales de la selva tropical" |
| 9 p.m. | Telenovela: "El sueño del amor" |
| 10 p.m. | Noticiero: "Noticias internacionales" |

1. Ernesto está loco por los deportes.
2. A la mamá le interesan las últimas noticias económicas.
3. A Inés le gustan los programas románticos.
4. Pepe tiene solamente siete años.
5. Al señor Montoya le fascina la naturaleza.
6. A Alejandra le gusta estar al tanto de las noticias de todo el mundo.
7. A la abuela le encantan los programas en los cuales se puede ganar dinero.

1. Béisbol en vivo: Los Rangers contra los Yankees
2. Reportaje especial: "La crisis económica"
3. Telenovela: "El sueño del amor"
4. Dibujos animados: "El rey león"
5. Documental: "Descubre los animales del bosque lluvioso"
6. Noticiero: "Noticias internacionales"
7. Concurso: "A millón"

## Core Instruction

### VOCABULARY IN CONTEXT

Give each student two or three words from **Vocabulario 1** to teach the class. Students should present their words using illustrations, pantomine, or circumlocution and make flashcards for each word. After every third student has made a presentation, collect the flashcards and review the new vocabulary with the students. Have students define the words in Spanish, give an English equivalent, and then, as a challenge, ask them to use the word or expression in an original sentence. Continue in this manner until all the words in **Vocabulario 1** have been presented and practiced. Next, divide students randomly into groups of four to create a story using all their vocabulary words. Have students present their stories to the class.

CD 6, Tr. 1

## 3 ¿Positivo o negativo? 1.2

**Escuchemos** Escucha los comentarios y determina si cada uno es **positivo** o **negativo.** 1. negativo 2. positivo 3. negativo 4. positivo 5. positivo 6. negativo

## 4 ¿Es cierto? 1.2

**Leamos/Escribamos** Lee las oraciones. Si en tu caso una oración no es cierta, cámbiala.

1. Me encantan las telenovelas.
2. De vez en cuando veo concursos en la televisión.
3. Mi emisora favorita pone música en español.
4. Creo que hay demasiados programas violentos en la tele.
5. Antes de ver una película, me gusta leer las reseñas sobre ella.
6. Creo que estoy bien informado(a) de lo que pasa en el mundo.
7. No me gusta hablar de temas controvertidos.

En este quiosco mexicano se pueden comprar periódicos locales y nacionales y una variedad de revistas.

## 5 En mi experiencia... 1.2

**Escribamos** Usa una palabra o expresión de cada columna y escribe por lo menos seis oraciones sobre los medios de comunicación en tu área.

**MODELO** **El periódico de mi ciudad reseña las últimas películas.**

| | | |
|---|---|---|
| El periódico de mi ciudad | informar | temas superficiales |
| Mi emisora favorita | estar al tanto | las noticias |
| Las noticias en línea | reseñar | las crisis ambientales |
| Los reporteros del canal... | investigar | los asuntos controvertidos |
| Una revista popular | tratar a fondo | las últimas películas |
| Los programas de radio | presentar | las noticias políticas |

## Comunicación

HOLT SoundBooth ONLINE RECORDING

## 6 ¿Estás bien informado(a)? 1.1, 1.2

**Escribamos/Hablemos** En grupos pequeños, túrnense para hablar sobre los medios de comunicación. Usen las expresiones del cuadro y de **Exprésate** para hacer y contestar cinco preguntas.

- ¿Con qué frecuencia lees...?
- En tu opinión, ¿son parciales o imparciales...?
- ¿Qué tipo de programas...?
- ¿Te consideras...?
- ¿Te interesan...?

### 3 Script

1. Este sitio de Internet me parece poco fiable, ¿sabes? Presentan las noticias de un modo muy parcial y superficial.
2. ¡Date prisa! Ya empieza el concurso en la tele. No me lo quiero perder; me encantan los temas que los participantes van a debatir.
3. Estoy convencida de que Roberto Salazar es el peor reportero del mundo. ¿Cómo es posible que siga trabajando para ese canal? ¡Es tan parcial y siempre está tan mal informado!
4. Es cierto que este documental sobre el medio ambiente trata el tema de la contaminación muy a fondo. Es muy informativo y estoy aprendiendo muchísimo.
5. Los locutores que comentan los partidos de fútbol en vivo explican todo en detalle y con mucho entusiasmo. ¡Parece que estamos allá viendo el partido!
6. Es evidente que los locutores de esta emisora no saben nada de música porque dijeron que Jennifer López es una cantante de ópera.

### Comunicación

**Pair Activity: Interpersonal**

Have students work in pairs to discuss the news they have read or seen on television lately, especially the current events that interest them most. Have them share their opinions of different news sources. 1.1

## Differentiated Instruction

### SLOWER PACE LEARNERS

**5 Variation** You may want to modify Activity 5 if students have trouble forming complete sentences with the fragments provided. Instead, combine the fragments yourself in the form of questions. For example, you might ask **¿Los reporteros del canal 5 investigan temas superficiales?** Complete the activity aloud as a class and have students write an answer to each question in their notebooks. Circulate around the classroom to check answers. 1.2

### MULTIPLE INTELLIGENCES

**Musical** Have students watch a Spanish language TV station and then tell the class about songs that are memorable to them. How do commercial songs on Spanish TV compare to those heard on English TV in the U.S.? They might want to hum or sing the songs for the class. Have them suggest what kind of message the music seems to be conveying, or whether it is effective in establishing a certain mood. Encourage them to take note of the music used in news reports and documentaries. 3.2, 4.2

**Differentiated Instruction** See the Differentiated Instruction CD-ROM.

## Resources

**Planning:**

Lesson Planner, pp. 81–82, 242–243

One-Stop Planner

**Presentation:**

Teaching Transparencies **Vocabulario** 6.1, 6.2

**Practice:**

Cuaderno de vocabulario y gramática, pp. 61–63

Activities for Communication, pp. 21–22

Teaching Transparencies **Vocabulario y gramática** answers, pp. 61–63

Interactive Tutor, Disc 2

## Heritage Speakers

Have heritage speakers work with a partner to come up with ways to express doubt and disbelief other than the ones presented in **¡Exprésate!** Can they substitute the expressions they came up with for those in the box? 1.1

## Teacher to Teacher

**Linda Hale**
Sonoma Valley High School
Sonoma, CA

For this unit, I have students write and practice a TV broadcast. In pairs, students make maps and practice a weather report, or they write interview questions for a famous person or another student and practice them out loud. Another pair of students in the group tells about upcoming events or sports. Then we videotape their shows. Students love to see themselves on television, and really practice to sound authentic. 1.3

## ¡Un concierto a todo dar!

En un café Internet, Costa Rica

SEBASTIÁN Hola, Carolina. ¿Estás leyendo las noticias en línea?

CAROLINA Claro, me gusta estar bien informada. Oye, ¿has leído sobre el concierto de rock de esta noche?

SEBASTIÁN Sí, me imagino que va a haber poca gente.

CAROLINA ¿Poca gente? Según Guillermo Torres, el reportero que reseña películas y conciertos, va a haber miles de personas.

SEBASTIÁN ¡Qué va! No creo que eso sea verdad. Nadie va a ver un grupo como "Los de abajo". ¡Son pésimos! Estoy convencido de que Guillermo Torres es poco fiable en sus opiniones sobre los conciertos. Sólo un aburrido iría a ese concierto.

CAROLINA Pues, él no exagera, Sebastián. Ya se vendieron todos los boletos.

SEBASTIÁN ¿Y cómo lo sabes?

CAROLINA ¡Porque esta "aburrida" compró el último!

### ¡Exprésate!

**To express doubt and disbelief**

Interactive TUTOR

| | |
|---|---|
| **Dudo que estés bien informado(a) sobre.../que sepas...** *I doubt that you're well informed about . . ./that you know . . .* | **Parece mentira que haya.../que digan...** *It's hard to believe that there are . . ./that they say . . .* |
| **No creo que los periodistas/los noticieros sean...** *I don't think that journalists/newcasts are . . .* | **No estoy seguro(a) (de) que tengas razón sobre...** *I'm not sure that you're right about . . .* |

Vocabulario y gramática, pp. 61–63 Online workbooks

## Core Instruction

### TEACHING ¡EXPRÉSATE!

1. Ask volunteers to tell you about issues reported in their local radio or television newscasts about which they might have doubts or which they found completely unbelievable. **—¿Has escuchado o leído una noticia que te parece increíble?—Sí. ¡El nuevo equipo de béisbol ha ganado el campeonato!** **(4 min.)**
2. Act out both sides of a conversation as you model the expressions of doubt and disbelief from **¡Exprésate!** Use gestures and body language to convey the meaning of the expressions. For example, raise your eyebrows and open your eyes wide when expressing disbelief. **(3 min.)**
3. Make up a list with a mix of doubtful and of completely unbelievable statements. Have volunteers respond to each statement using expressions from **¡Exprésate!** (**Parece mentira que un equipo nuevo pueda ganar el campeonato.**) **(3 min.)**

3. falso; Sebastián cree que son pésimos.
4. falso; Sebastián está convencido de que Guillermo Torres es poco fiable.

**7 ¿Quién está al tanto?** 1.2

**Leamos/Escribamos** Basándote en el diálogo, contesta **cierto** o **falso.** Corrige las oraciones falsas.

1. Carolina no está al tanto de las noticias. falso; Carolina está bien informada.
2. Ella cree que las noticias en línea no son informativas. cierto
3. Sebastián está loco por el grupo "Los de abajo".
4. Él cree que Guillermo Torres está al tanto de la música.
5. Sebastián duda que mucha gente vaya al concierto. cierto
6. Carolina está segura de que ya se vendieron todos los boletos. cierto

**8 ¿Qué dirías?** 1.2

**Leamos/Hablemos** Usa las expresiones de **Exprésate** de las páginas 231 y 234 para responder a las siguientes situaciones.

**MODELO** **Tu amigo(a) nunca gana en los concursos que hacen las emisoras.**
**—Estoy seguro(a) de que vas a ganar la próxima vez.**

1. Tu hermano(a) te acaba de decir que el presidente va a visitar tu colegio.
2. Un(a) amigo(a) te pregunta si un reportero sabe mucho de un tema, pero no has visto sus informes.
3. Tu papá no cree que se pueda ver el partido de básquetbol en la televisión. Viste las noticias y sabes que van a televisar el partido en vivo.
4. Te sorprende que un locutor haya presentado un tema controvertido de modo imparcial.
5. El reportero del canal 8 dice que va a nevar hoy. Hace sol y la temperatura está muy alta.
6. Un(a) amigo(a) dice que las noticias del canal cinco son las más informativas. Estás de acuerdo.

### Nota cultural

Los primeros programas en español transmitidos en Estados Unidos fueron producidos fuera del país (la mayoría venían de México) y comprados por compañías estadounidenses para usarlos en sus canales en español. Ahora, muchas empresas están invirtiendo dinero en desarrollar sus propias producciones en español, o por lo menos están intentando incorporar programas en español a su programación.

¿Qué programas en español conoces? 1.3

## Comunicación

HOLT SoundBooth ONLINE RECORDING

**9 ¿Es cierta la noticia?** 1.1, 1.3

**Escribamos/Hablemos** Nombra dos eventos de tu vida que van a suceder o que sucedieron de verdad y dos inventados. En parejas, túrnense para compartir sus noticias, reaccionar a las noticias y decidir si son de verdad.

**MODELO** **—Este año voy a China con mis padres.**
**—Dudo mucho que vayas a China. ¿Lo dices en serio?**
**—Sí, es verdad. Vamos a visitar a mis abuelos.**

Vocabulario 1

**COMMON ERROR ALERT**
**¡OJO!**

Students tend to use the indicative with the expressions listed in **¡Exprésate!.** Point out that the verbs in the **¡Exprésate!** sentences are in the subjunctive. Tell students they will learn more about the subjunctive with expressions of doubt and disbelief in **Gramática 2.**

### Teaching Suggestion

Read the **Nota cultural** with students. Have them comment on the Spanish language programming available in their communities. What kinds of shows have they seen on their Spanish channels? What is their opinion of these shows?

## Comunicación

### Class Activity: Interpersonal

Ask for six volunteers, and have them form pairs. Each pair in turn will model a conversation in front of the class in which they each discuss one wish they have that they doubt they can achieve, and why. Have them use the expressions of doubt learned in class. **Dudo que pueda viajar a México porque tengo que ir al colegio.** 1.1

## Differentiated Instruction

### SLOWER PACE LEARNERS

**Personalization** Ask students that have difficulties grasping the complexities of current events to prepare a conversation with a partner titled **Un día típico de mi vida.** They can make up a conversation with a reporter who is asking them about their life, or a conversation with a family member or anyone else with whom they come into contact on a regular basis. 1.1

### SPECIAL LEARNING NEEDS

**Students with Visual Impairments** Have students go to the Web site of a Spanish news network and download and listen to two news reports they are interested in. Have them list the sounds they hear throughout the report. For example, a report about an environmental crisis might have the following: 1. sounds of birds singing interrupted by the sound of bulldozers, 2. a voice talking about urban sprawl ruining bird habitats, 3. slogans being chanted at a rally, 4. the sound of a cement truck. 3.2

### Assess

**Assessment Program**
**Prueba: Vocabulario 1,** pp. 101–102
Alternative Assessment, pp. 378, 390, 402

**Online Assessment**
**my.hrw.com**

**Test Generator**

## Resources

**Planning:**

Lesson Planner, pp. 83–85, 244–247

One-Stop Planner

**Presentation:**

Video Program **GramaVisión**

**Practice:**

Grammar Tutor for Students of Spanish, Chapter 6

Cuaderno de vocabulario y gramática, pp. 64–66

Cuaderno de actividades, pp. 51–53

Activities for Communication, pp. 21–22

Lab Book, pp. 33–36

Teaching Transparencies

Bell Work 6.2

**Vocabulario y gramática** answers, pp. 64–66

Audio CD 6, Tr. 2

Interactive Tutor, Disc 2

### Bell Work

Use Bell Work 6.2 in the *Teaching Transparencies*, or write this activity on the board.

**Completa las oraciones con una palabra de Vocabulario.**

1. El reportaje es muy ______; cuenta sólo un punto de vista.
2. Hay que ______ a la comunidad sobre la crisis ambiental.
3. El informe es muy ______; tiene mucha información.
4. Puedes confiar en este canal, los locutores son muy ______.
5. Mi ______ de radio favorita toca música folklórica internacional.

1.2

**Objetivos**
- Indicative after expressions of certainty
- Subjunctive after expressions of doubt and disbelief
- Haber

# Gramática en acción 1

GramaVisión

Interactive TUTOR

## Indicative after expressions of certainty

**1** **Expressions of certainty (expresiones de certeza)** are followed by a verb in the **indicative mood.** Expressions of certainty indicate that in the speaker's mind, the event described is a fact.

*expressions of certainty followed by indicative*

**Es cierto** que José **está** bien informado.
*It's true that José is well-informed.*

**2** Remember to use the **subjunctive** when the main clause in a sentence expresses negation or denial.

*expressions of negation/denial followed by subjunctive*

**No es verdad** que esa reportera **sea** imparcial.

**Some common expressions of certainty**

| | |
|---|---|
| claro que | estar seguro(a) (de) que |
| es cierto que | me/te/le/nos/les parece que |
| es evidente que | no cabe duda (de) que |
| es obvio que | por supuesto que |
| está claro que | sin duda alguna |
| estar convencido(a) de que | todo el mundo sabe que |

Vocabulario y gramática, pp. 64–66
Actividades, pp. 51–53
Online workbooks

En una tienda de libros en Guadalajara, México

CD 6, Tr. 2 See script on p. 227E.

**10** **¿Está seguro(a)?** 1.2

**Escuchemos** Escucha las conversaciones y determina si la segunda persona **a)** está segura de lo que dice o **b)** no está segura de lo que dice. **1.** a **2.** a **3.** b **4.** a **5.** a **6.** b

**11** **Por supuesto** 1.2

**Escribamos** Contesta las siguientes preguntas usando una expresión de certeza.

MODELO **¿Ha cambiado la tecnología nuestras vidas?**
**No cabe duda de que ha cambiado nuestras vidas.**

1. ¿Navega más por Internet ahora la gente?
2. ¿Tienen muchas universidades sus propios sitios Web?
3. ¿Los estudiantes pueden investigar en Internet?
4. ¿Hay sitios de Internet con contenido no apropiado para niños?
5. Hoy en día, ¿saben muchos jóvenes crear páginas Web?

## Core Instruction

### TEACHING GRAMÁTICA

1. Go over point 1 with students. **(2 min.)**
2. Have students write down all the indicative forms of the verbs **ir, venir, estar,** and **sentir. (2 min.)**
3. Write sample sentences on the board using the expressions of certainty from point 2 with the indicative forms of the verbs students just wrote down. **Claro que el profesor viene hoy. No cabe duda que el locutor está bien informado. (3 min.)**
4. Call on students to point to the expressions of certainty. **(2 min.)**
5. Write more examples using other expressions of certainty. **Sin duda alguna, voy a comprar el periódico hoy. Todo el mundo sabe que esa reportera no es fiable.** Ask volunteers to underline the indicative form of the verb in each sentence. **(1 min.)**

### GramaVisión

For a video presentation of the indicative after expressions of certainty, use **GramaVisión.**

GramaVisión

Visit Holt Online
**go.hrw.com**
KEYWORD: EXP3 CH6
Gramática 1 practice

## 12 ¿Qué diría el autor? 1.2

**Leamos** Lee el artículo y decide si el doctor Centerwall estaría de acuerdo con los siguientes comentarios.

### Claves para ver mejor la televisión

El doctor Brandon Centerwall de la Escuela de Salud Pública de Seattle ha afirmado que "ver la televisión a menudo no debería ser dañino si los niños aprenden a interpretar lo que ven". Según él, restringir el acceso a ciertos programas es una solución eficaz pero pasajera *(temporary)*. "Lo más importante es enseñar al televidente desde pequeño a controlar la televisión. Esto significa explicar a los niños cómo funciona la tecnología audiovisual, quién diseña los programas, cómo se miden las audiencias y qué significa cada pieza del lenguaje televisivo".

1. No cabe la menor duda de que ver televisión les hace daño a los niños. no
2. Estoy convencido de que los adultos deben controlar el acceso de los niños a ciertos programas. no
3. Es evidente que restringir el acceso a la televisión es una solución permanente. no
4. Está claro que debemos enseñarles a los niños cómo interpretar lo que ven en la televisión. sí
5. Sin duda alguna, los niños deben saber cómo funciona la tecnología audiovisual. sí
6. Me parece que no hace falta entender qué significa cada pieza del lenguaje televisivo. no

Esta joven trabaja con una amiga en un "laboratorio migrante" en el colegio López de Brownsville, Texas.

## Comunicación

HOLT SoundBooth ONLINE RECORDING

## 13 Sin duda 1.1, 1.2

**Escribamos/Hablemos** Escribe tus opiniones sobre cada uno de estos temas: los profesores, las clases, la tarea, la comida en la cafetería y los equipos deportivos. En parejas, túrnense para compartir sus opiniones y afirmar o contradecir *(contradict)* las de su compañero(a). *¿Se te olvidó?* Subjunctive with negation or denial, pp. 108–109

MODELO **—Nunca como en la cafetería. Es obvio que la comida es mala.**
**—¡Sin duda alguna! Todo el mundo sabe que es horrible.**
**(—No, no es cierto que sea mala. A mí me gusta mucho.)**

## Differentiated Instruction

### ADVANCED LEARNERS

**11 Challenge** Have students work in pairs. Ask them to write and then share with each other five questions about a future event. Have each student respond to his or her partner's questions, using expressions of certainty where appropriate. 1.1

### MULTIPLE INTELLIGENCES

**Naturalist** Have students bring in charts or photos of different kinds of birds of prey, ferns, and rocks. Have them use expressions of certainty followed by the indicative to talk about different elements in the charts. For example: **Es obvio que esta planta vive en el desierto.** 1.1

## Communities

### Community Link

Have students get together to brainstorm and research ways to enhance their learning of Spanish as a second language. If they come up with a good, viable idea, encourage them to contact school administrators for help in carrying it out. For example, they could meet once a week with Spanish-speaking ESL students so that they could tutor the ESL students in English, and the Spanish-speaking students could tutor them in Spanish, focusing on speaking skills. They could initiate the tutoring program with an article in the school newspaper. 5.1

## Comunicación

### Pair Activity: Interpersonal

Have pairs of students make up sentences having to do with current events. Ask them to use expressions of certainty to talk about the news and current events.

### Group Activity: Interpersonal

Ask students to discuss whether politicians tend to be sure of themselves when they are interviewed in the news. Have students work in groups of three or four to prepare a presentation for the class. Have them create a fictional conversation between a politician and reporters in which the politician uses many expressions of certainty to respond to the reporters' questions. Have groups take turns acting out their presentations for the class. 1.1

## Resources

**Planning:**

Lesson Planner, pp. 83–85, 244–247

One-Stop Planner

**Presentation:**

Video Program **GramaVisión**

**Practice:**

Grammar Tutor for Students of Spanish, Chapter 6

Cuaderno de vocabulario y gramática, pp. 64–66

Cuaderno de actividades, pp. 51–53

Activities for Communication, pp. 21–22

Lab Book, pp. 33–36

Teaching Transparencies
Bell Work 6.3
**Vocabulario y gramática** answers, pp. 64–66

Audio CD 6, Tr. 3

Interactive Tutor, Disc 2

### Bell Work

Use Bell Work 6.3 in the *Teaching Transparencies,* or write this activity on the board.

**Completa las oraciones con la forma correcta del verbo.**

1. Me parece que en este canal se ______ (investigar) los temas a fondo.
2. No cabe la menor duda de que el ejercicio ______ (ser) bueno.
3. Sin duda alguna mi madre ______ (hacer) el mejor bizcocho de chocolate.
4. Estoy convencida de que este reportero no ______ (saber) nada.

1.2

### Más práctica

Once students have done Activity 15, have them rewrite each sentence using an expression of certainty and the indicative. Ask volunteers to share their sentences with the class. 1.2

## Subjunctive after expressions of doubt and disbelief

Interactive TUTOR

### ¡Te acuerdas?

To form the **present perfect subjunctive,** use the subjunctive forms of **haber** followed by the past participle of the main verb.

| | | |
|---|---|---|
| haya | hayamos | + past participle |
| hayas | hayáis | |
| haya | hayan | |

Parece mentira que Tina **haya comprado** esa revista.

No es cierto que los vendedores **hayan bajado** los precios.

1. When an **expression of doubt or disbelief** is used in the main clause of a sentence, the **subjunctive mood** is used in the subordinate clause.

*expressions of doubt/disbelief followed by subjunctive*

**Dudo** que mi prima **esté** al tanto.

2. The **present subjunctive** and **present perfect subjunctive** can both be used with expressions of doubt and disbelief.

**Parece mentira** que no **tengan** acceso a Internet en todos los colegios.

**Es increíble** que **hayan publicado** ese artículo tan parcial en el periódico.

**Some common expressions of doubt and disbelief**

| | |
|---|---|
| dudar que | no es cierto que |
| es dudoso que | no estar seguro(a) (de) que |
| es increíble que | no está claro que |
| es imposible que | no (poder) creer que |
| no pensar que | parece mentira que |

Vocabulario y gramática, pp. 64–66
Actividades, pp. 51–53
Online workbooks

CD 6, Tr. 3 See script on p. 227E.

### 14 ¿Están de acuerdo? 1.2

**Escuchemos** Escucha las conversaciones e indica si la segunda persona **1.** b **2.** a **3.** b **4.** b **5.** b **6.** a
**a)** está de acuerdo o
**b)** no está de acuerdo
con lo que dice la primera persona.

### 15 ¡No lo creo! 1.2

**Escribamos** Mariel no cree en nada de lo que lee en el periódico sobre los políticos *(politicians).* Forma oraciones completas para expresar lo que opina Mariel.

1. No puedo creer/el presidente/reseñar películas para ganar dinero
2. Es increíble/la senadora/participar en los concursos de televisión
3. Parece mentira/la esposa del presidente/ver telenovelas todo el día
4. Dudo/los políticos/tomar tres meses de vacaciones al año
5. No creo/el vicepresidente/ser miembro de un equipo de fútbol americano
6. Es imposible/la secretaria del presidente/haber robado un banco

**1.** No puedo creer que el presidente reseñe películas para ganar dinero.
**2.** Es increíble que la senadora participe en los concursos de la televisión.
**3.** Parece mentira que la esposa del presidente vea telenovelas todo el día.
**4.** Dudo que los políticos tomen tres meses de vacaciones al año.
**5.** No creo que el vicepresidente sea miembro de un equipo de fútbol americano.
**6.** Es imposible que la secretaria del presidente haya robado un banco.

## Core Instruction

### TEACHING GRAMÁTICA

1. Go over point 1. Ask questions to practice the subjunctive mood after expressions of doubt and disbelief. **¿A los gatos les gusta ir al veterinario? Es dudoso que a los gatos les guste ir al veterinario. (2 min.)**
2. Go over point 2 by modeling an expression of doubt and disbelief using first the present subjunctive and then the present perfect subjunctive. **No es cierto que este locutor mienta. No es cierto que este locutor haya mentido. (2 min.)**
3. Go over point 3. Write sentences using expressions of doubt with the present subjunctive and expressions of certainty with the present indicative. Have students tell whether each sentence includes an expression of doubt or of certainty, and then discuss the corresponding verb forms. **(5 min.)**

### GramaVisión

For a video presentation of the subjunctive after expressions of doubt and disbelief, use **GramaVisión.**

GramaVisión

Gramática 1

**16** **¿Podría ser?** 1.2

**Leamos/Hablemos** Estás leyendo los titulares *(headlines)* de un periódico sensacionalista *(tabloid)*. Usa las expresiones de duda o incredulidad y el presente perfecto del subjuntivo para dar tu opinión sobre cada uno.

*¿Se te olvidó?* Present perfect subjunctive, p. 150

**MODELO** **Encuentran una nave espacial en España**
**No es cierto que hayan encontrado una nave espacial en España.**

1. **Dos leones se escapan del zoológico y se esconden en un banco**
2. Nio de diez años gana el maratón de Boston
3. **Bebé recién nacido aprende a leer y hablar**
4. **Vendedor de carros inventa un carro que puede volar**
5. Dos hombres dicen que llevan cinco años viviendo en la Luna
6. **Perro va en busca de su dueño desde Utah hasta Ohio**

CRONICA MADRID
Los candidatos se juegan su futuro
CONSTRUIMOS SUEÑOS. PARA TODOS
AROCASA

Un artículo de política en *Crónica de Madrid*, un periódico de Madrid

## Comunicación

HOLT SoundBooth ONLINE RECORDING

**17** **¡Increíble!** 1.1, 1.2

**Escribamos/Hablemos** En parejas, preparen cinco titulares absurdos. Luego cambien de pareja y túrnense para leer sus titulares y dar su opinión usando expresiones de duda o incertidumbre.

**MODELO** **—Un chico de catorce años se gradúa de médico de la Universidad Nacional.**
**—Es imposible que un chico de catorce años se haya graduado de médico.**

## Heritage Speakers

Heritage speakers may have problems with the subjunctive expressions below. If they learn the following chart with the verb **ser,** they can transfer the concept to any other verb. Students should repeat each phrase until they learn it, and then play a game where one student says the phrase in the first column and a partner provides the corresponding indicative or subjunctive form. This is a fun activity if students are allowed to be fast and loud. 1.2

| | |
|---|---|
| Yo creo que | es |
| Yo estoy seguro que | es |
| Es cierto que | es |
| Es evidente que | es |
| Es verdad que | es |
| No dudo que | es |
| No niego que | es |
| No es dudoso que | es |
| | |
| Yo no creo que | sea |
| Yo no estoy seguro que | sea |
| No es cierto que | sea |
| No es evidente que | sea |
| No es verdad que | sea |
| Dudo que | sea |
| Niego que | sea |
| Es dudoso que | sea |

## Comunicación

### Pair Activity: Interpersonal

Following Activity 17, have students form new pairs and write five more absurd sentences about their school. The other partner can respond with an expression of doubt followed by a dependent clause, using either the present subjunctive or the present perfect subjunctive.

**MODELO**
**—El director dijo que vamos a tener cinco meses de vacaciones.**
**—Dudo que haya dicho eso.**
1.1

## Differentiated Instruction

### ADVANCED LEARNERS

**15** **Extension** Have students read the news online and write sentences expressing doubt or disbelief about six articles. Invite them to share their sentences with the class. Encourage students to contradict their classmates' statements, using expressions of certainty. 1.1

### SPECIAL LEARNING NEEDS

**14** **Students with AD(H)D** Write the letters **a** and **b** on the board. Under **a,** write the expressions of certainty that students have learned, and under **b,** those of doubt and disbelief. Next, have students copy the two groups of expressions into their notebooks. Play each conversation twice. The first time, have students mark the expression the second speaker uses. The second time, have them check the expression and then answer **a** or **b.** Go over the answers together after each question. 1.2

## Resources

**Planning:**

Lesson Planner, pp. 83–85, 244–247

One-Stop Planner

**Presentation:**

Video Program **GramaVisión**

**Practice:**

Grammar Tutor for Students of Spanish, Chapter 6

Cuaderno de vocabulario y gramática, pp. 64–66

Cuaderno de actividades, pp. 51–53

Activities for Communication, pp. 21–22

Lab Book, pp. 33–36

Teaching Transparencies Bell Work 6.4

**Vocabulario y gramática** answers, pp. 64–66

Audio CD 6, Tr. 4

Interactive Tutor, Disc 2

### Bell Work

Use Bell Work 6.4 in the *Teaching Transparencies,* or write this activity on the board.

**Indica si cada oración usa una frase de duda o de certeza.**

1. **Es increíble que las montañas nevadas no se vean desde aquí.**
2. **Es cierto que hay una crisis ambiental.**
3. **Es imposible que hayan dicho tantas mentiras.**
4. **No está claro que no haya sido fiable.**
5. **Creo que el concurso empieza a las siete.**

1.2

### 18 Script

See script on page 227E.

## Uses of haber

Interactive TUTOR

**1** The impersonal form of **haber** is always used in the third person singular. The present tense form is **hay** *(there is, there are).*

Creo que **hay** tiempo para ver la tele.

**Hay** muchas revistas en la mesa.

**2** The impersonal form of **haber** in the preterite tense is **hubo.** The impersonal form of **haber** in the imperfect tense is **había.** Both forms mean *there was* or *there were.*

**Hubo** un documental en la tele anoche.

Ayer **hubo** dos reuniones.

Todos los días **había** un reportaje especial sobre la crisis.

**Había** dos periodistas en la sala cuando entré.

**3** The impersonal form of **haber** in the present subjunctive is **haya.**

Dudo que **haya** un periódico aquí.
*I doubt there is a newspaper here.*

No creo que **haya** telenovelas buenas.
*I don't believe there are good soap operas.*

**4** The future tense form **habrá** can be used to say or to predict what there will be, or to wonder or make a conjecture about what there is.

En el futuro **habrá** menos concursos en la tele.

### ¿Te acuerdas?

The **preterite** tense is used to show that actions in the past had a specific beginning or end.

**Hubo** un reportaje ayer sobre el robo.

The **imperfect** tense is used to express habitual or ongoing actions in the past or to describe the setting in the past.

Cuando era niño, **había** concursos en la tele todas las noches.

CD 6, Tr. 4

### 18 ¿Qué hay? 1.2

**Escuchemos** Escucha mientras Débora describe lo que hay en su colegio. Escribe una lista de las cosas que **hay** en su colegio y otra de las cosas que **no hay.**

### 19 ¿Cierto o falso? 1.2

**Leamos** Lee cada oración y decide si es **cierta** o **falsa** para ti.

1. Este fin de semana habrá un baile en nuestro colegio.
2. El mes pasado hubo un huracán en mi estado.
3. Es dudoso que haya una fiesta en la clase de español mañana.
4. El año pasado hubo un examen en la clase de ciencias todos los viernes.
5. Hay un parque muy bonito en el centro de mi ciudad.
6. Hubo un incendio en el bosque cerca de mi ciudad el verano pasado.

## Core Instruction

### TEACHING GRAMÁTICA

1. Go over point 1. **(2 min.)**
2. Go over point 2 and remind students that the indicative mood denotes certainty. Read the examples and then go over **¿Te acuerdas?** Have volunteers think of sentences using **haber** in the imperfect or in the preterite. **(3 min.)**
3. Go over point 3. Then substitute an expression of certainty for each expression of doubt and write the new sentences on the board. **Es cierto que hay un periódico aquí. Creo que hay telenovelas buenas.** Have volunteers tell what form of **haber** is used in these examples and why. **(3 min.)**
4. Go over point 4. Ask volunteers to make more predictions using **habrá. (2 min.)**

### GramaVisión

For a video presentation of the uses of **haber,** use **GramaVisión.**

GramaVisión

## 20 ¿Qué hubo? 1.2

**Escribamos** Combina las frases para escribir una oración con **hubo.**

**MODELO** **huracán/Golfo de México/el 2005**
**Hubo varios huracanes en el Golfo de México en el 2005.**

1. varios terremotos/suroeste de los Estados Unidos/el 2004
2. documental sobre México/canal cinco/anoche
3. descubrimiento importante/norte de México/el año pasado
4. carrera *(race)* de caballos/Chihuahua/el verano pasado
5. muchos tornados/Oklahoma/el 2003
6. festival cultural/Reynosa/la semana pasada

## 21 Los colegios: antes y ahora 1.2

**Leamos/Escribamos** Guillermo está comparando los colegios que hay ahora en su ciudad con los que había hace diez años. Usa la información de la tabla y escribe cinco oraciones comparando los colegios. *¿Se te olvidó?* Time constructions, pp. 32–33

**MODELO** **Ahora hay seis colegios bilingües. Hace 10 años, sólo había uno.**

| Colegios | Ahora | Hace 10 años |
|---|---|---|
| ...bilingües | 6 | 1 |
| 1. ...con acceso a Internet | 8 | 2 |
| 2. ...que ofrecen clases por Internet | 4 | 1 |
| 3. ...con salas de computadoras | 10 | 3 |
| 4. ...que ofrecen clases de español | 10 | 5 |
| 5. ...con programas de intercambio | 7 | 2 |

### Nota cultural

En 1983, un profesor de la Universidad de Nuevo México descubrió que con una radio de onda corta *(shortwave)* se podía escuchar los noticieros de emisoras de Latinoamérica. En esa época, no existían los medios de comunicación que tenemos ahora. El profesor sabía que tener acceso a estos noticieros sería muy útil para la gente que estudiaba Latinoamérica. Ahora gracias a Internet existen varios boletines de noticias en línea sobre Latinoamérica, que se conocen como *The Latin America Data Base.*

¿Cómo te enteras de las noticias de Latinoamérica? 3.1

## Comunicación

HOLT SoundBooth ONLINE RECORDING

## 22 ¡Noticias! 1.1, 1.2

**Hablemos/Escribamos** En grupos de tres, decidan qué noticias publicar en el periódico del colegio. Comenten lo que pasó, lo que pasa esta semana y lo que va a pasar en su colegio, usando el verbo **haber.** Después, escojan las tres noticias más importantes y escriban una oración para resumir cada una.

**MODELO** **—Hay una competencia de atletismo esta tarde.**
**—Anoche hubo una reunión del club de español.**

### 20 Answers

1. Hubo varios terremotos en el suroeste de los E.U. en el 2004.
2. Hubo un documental sobre México en el canal cinco anoche.
3. Hubo un descubrimiento importante en el norte de México el año pasado.
4. Hubo una carrera de caballos en Chihuahua el verano pasado.
5. Hubo muchos tornados en Oklahoma en el 2003.
6. Hubo un festival en Reynosa la semana pasada.

### 21 Answers

1. Ahora hay ocho colegios con acceso a Internet. Hace 10 años, sólo había dos.
2. Ahora hay cuatro colegios que ofrecen clases por Internet. Hace 10 años, sólo había uno.
3. Ahora hay diez colegios con salas de computadoras. Hace 10 años, sólo había tres.
4. Ahora hay diez colegios que ofrecen clases de español. Hace 10 años, sólo había cinco.
5. Ahora hay siete colegios con programas de intercambio. Hace 10 años, sólo había dos.

### Comunicación

**Group Activity: Interpersonal**

As an extension of Activity 22, ask students to talk in groups about events outside of school that they would like to see covered, or to receive additional coverage by the media, and why. 1.1

## Differentiated Instruction

### ADVANCED LEARNERS

**22 Extension** After doing Activity 22, have students write the first paragraph for each news story idea they had for the school newspaper. Have them use the verb **haber** at least once in each paragraph. 1.3

### SPECIAL LEARNING NEEDS

**21 Students with AD(H)D** Some students may have trouble grasping the details in the table. You might want to copy the table onto a transparency and display it. Go over the **Modelo** with students, pointing to the *6* in the first column as you read the first sentence and then pointing to the *1* as you read the second sentence. Do the activity as a class, pointing to the corresponding row as you ask: **¿Cuántos colegios hay con acceso a Internet? ¿Cuántos había hace 10 años?** Have students write the answers. 1.2

### Assess

**Assessment Program**

**Prueba: Gramática 1,** pp. 103–104

**Prueba: Aplicación 1,** pp. 105–106

Audio CD 6, Tr. 17

Alternative Assessment, pp. 378, 390, 402

**Online Assessment**
**my.hrw.com**

**Test Generator**

## Resources

**Planning:**

Lesson Planner, pp. 86, 246–247

One-Stop Planner

**Presentation:**

Audio CD 6, Trs. 5–7

Video Program, Videocassette 3
DVD Program
**VideoCultura**

**Practice:**

Cuaderno de actividades, p. 54

Video Guide, pp. 38–39

Lab Book, p. 73

Interactive Tutor, Disc 2

## Teaching Suggestion

Have students ask their parents and grandparents about the media and means of communication that were most widely used when they were teenagers. Students should ask them what advantages or disadvantages they see in modern media. Do they find that there are more violent images in the media today? How do they think these images affect society? Do they feel that journalists are trustworthy? How do they compare with the journalists from their childhood?

# Cultura

Video/DVD
**VideoCultura**

## Comparaciones

Interactive TUTOR

CD 6, Tr. 5-7

Un quiosco en el centro de la Ciudad de México

### A la cama no te irás sin saber una cosa más 1.3

Hoy en día, la radio y la televisión llegan hasta el último rincón de América Latina. Las grandes ciudades tienen una gran oferta de medios de comunicación, como televisión por cable y por satélite, que sin embargo son servicios algo caros. Los noticieros incluyen noticias del país, y también bastantes noticias internacionales. También cada vez más, la gente se informa por medio de Internet. ¿Ves tú los noticieros de la televisión? ¿Te gustaría poder ver canales de otros países por televisión? ¿Has visto las páginas Web de algún periódico extranjero?

### Sumitsuki

**El Paso, Texas**

***Vamos a hablar sobre los medios de comunicación de El Paso, Texas. ¿Estás bien informada sobre los eventos de tu país?***

Sí, estoy muy bien informada.

***¿Cómo te pones al tanto?***

Yo veo las noticias, escucho el radio, y leo el periódico.

***¿Cuántas veces por semana ves las noticias?***

Cinco veces.

## Pre-AP Practice

**AP Language Examination:** Have students first listen to the interviews with books closed to help prepare them for Section I, Part A: **Listening—Short Dialogues and Narratives.** Point out that Octavio, like many Spanish speakers, may pronounce the vowel combination **ea** as the diphthong **ia (peleando, recreándolo).**

## Core Instruction

### TEACHING CULTURA

1. Read and discuss the introductory paragraph as a class. **(2 min.)**
2. Read the interview questions and have volunteers read Sumisuki's and Octavio's responses. **(4 min.)**
3. Have students answer the questions in **Para comprender** and then have them work in pairs to discuss **Para pensar y hablar. (4 min.)**

### VideoCultura

For a video presentation of the interviews as well as for additional interviews for this chapter, see Chapter 6 **VideoCultura** on Videocassette or on DVD.

Video/DVD
**VideoCultura**

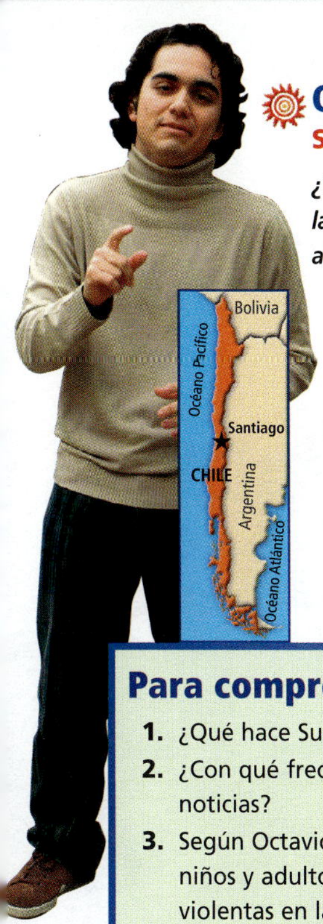


## Octavio
**Santiago, Chile**

***¿Tú crees que las imágenes violentas en la televisión, el cine o las noticias nos afectan de modo negativo y por qué?***

Yo creo que sí nos afectan, deberían no afectarnos, pero la mentalidad de los hombres, parece que no está preparada para recibir imágenes tan fuertes. Yo creo que el ejemplo claro está en los niños. Cuando un niño ve [a] dos hombres peleando, van con su amigo y lo repiten, lo recrean. Yo creo que todos tenemos algo de niño y todo lo hacemos recreándolo.

***¿Tú crees que es verdad que los periodistas siempre tratan de dar informes de un modo imparcial? ¿Por qué sí or por qué no?***

No, yo creo que es imposible que un periodista tenga una visión imparcial por muy profesional que sea, porque es humano y siente y se apasiona y tal como siente y se apasiona, se apasiona con ciertos temas. Es imposible que una persona que crea esto diga imparcialmente lo contrario.

Cultura

### Para comprender 1.2

1. ¿Qué hace Sumitsuki para estar al tanto?
2. ¿Con qué frecuencia ve Sumitsuki las noticias?
3. Según Octavio, ¿cómo reaccionan los niños y adultos después de ver imágenes violentas en la televisión?
4. ¿Por qué no cree Octavio que los periodistas traten siempre los temas de un modo imparcial?

### Para pensar y hablar 1.3, 3.1

En tu opinión, ¿hay una relación entre la violencia y los medios de comunicación y de entretenimiento? ¿Crees que las imágenes que se ven en la televisión, el cine o los periódicos deben ser controladas por la comunidad o el gobierno? ¿Por qué sí o por qué no?

## Comunidad y oficio

### Los medios de comunicación en español 5.1

En este país, hay varias emisoras que ofrecen programación en español. Haz una investigación sobre una emisora de radio o de televisión en tu comunidad o en otra parte del país que tenga programación en español. Habla con alguien que trabaje allí y pregúntale sobre la importancia de ofrecer esos servicios a los hispanohablantes de la zona y sobre cómo escogen la programación. También investiga la demanda de programación en español en tu comunidad.

**Jorge Ramos es un locutor de noticias en Univisión.**

## Differentiated Instruction

### ADVANCED LEARNERS

**Extension** Have students work in pairs to interview each other using the questions from the **Cultura** interviews or making up their own. Ask students to share the information they learned about their partners with the rest of the class. 1.1

### SPECIAL LEARNING NEEDS

**Students with Learning Disabilities** Students with learning disabilities may not be able to understand Octavio's long responses to the interview questions. After reading his first response with the class, summarize it in simple Spanish: **Sí, Octavio cree que las imágenes violentas nos afectan de modo negativo. Él cree que la gente repite lo que ve.** Do the same with his second response: **Octavio cree que es imposible dar un informe de modo imparcial. Es natural que uno tenga opiniones y es difícil no communicarlas.**

### Atlas INTERACTIVO MUNDIAL

Have students use the interactive atlas at **go.hrw.com**.

**Map Activities**

Use transparencies **Mapa 4** and **6.**

1. Have students say why they think there is a large Spanish-speaking population in Texas. Then have them find Texas on a map and name the bordering country. Ask them to talk about the size of Texas compared to that of other states in the U.S.
2. Have students locate Chile. What is unique about this country? What landscapes can be found on its eastern and western borders? 3.1

### Para comprender Answers

1. Ve las noticias, escucha la radio y lee el periódico.
2. cinco veces por semana
3. Recrean lo que ven.
4. Es imposible porque los humanos se apasionan con ciertos temas.

### Career Path

On the board or on a transparency, list fields related to communications (advertising, journalism, radio, television, film). Ask students to think about careers in each of these fields (advertising graphic designer, foreign correspondent, disc jockey, broadcast journalist, film director, script writer, speech pathologist). How might Spanish be useful in these careers? What role does technology play in these careers? Do they know of any Spanish-speaking people in their community that have the careers listed above?

**Resources**

**Planning:**

Lesson Planner, pp. 87–88, 248–249

One-Stop Planner

**Presentation:**

Teaching Transparencies
**Vocabulario** 6.3, 6.4

**Practice:**

Cuaderno de vocabulario y gramática, pp. 67–69

Activities for Communication, pp. 23–24

Teaching Transparencies
Bell Work 6.5
**Vocabulario y gramática** answers, pp. 67–69

Interactive Tutor, Disc 2

**Bell Work**

Use Bell Work 6.5 in the *Teaching Transparencies*, or write this activity on the board.

**Completa las oraciones con la forma correcta de *haber*.**

1. Hoy en día ______ muchos medios de comunicación.
2. Dudo que ______ muchos libros sobre el periodismo en la biblioteca.
3. El fin de semana pasado ______ dos artículos en el periódico sobre mi colegio.
4. ¿______ algunas copias de los artículos en mi oficina?
5. ______ un documental sobre la historia de los medios de comunicación anoche.

1.2

**Objetivos**
- Asking about and explaining where you found information
- Talking about what you know and don't know

# Vocabulario en acción 2

## Los medios de comunicación impresos

**Más vocabulario...**

| | |
|---|---|
| **los anuncios clasificados** | *classified ads* |
| **la censura** | *censorship* |
| **el comentario** | *commentary* |
| **la prensa** | *the press* |
| **la sección financiera** | *financial section* |

## Core Instruction

### TEACHING VOCABULARIO

1. Show transparencies **6.3** and **6.4.** Have students tell which words are shown in the photos. Check understanding by asking how students feel about sections of the paper and why. **¿Te gustan las tiras cómicas? ¿Cuál es tu favorita? (4 min.)**
2. Have volunteers talk about newspapers they read. **(3 min.)**
3. Present words from **Más vocabulario** and ask volunteers to answer questions on each one. For example, **¿Cuál es el efecto de la censura en un país? (3 min.)**

### TEACHING ¡EXPRÉSATE!

1. Introduce **¡Exprésate!** by modeling both sides of the conversation given, then make up some exchanges of your own. **(3 min.)**
2. Ask questions with **¿Cómo supiste...?** and **¿Cómo te enteraste de...?** Have students say in which newspaper section they found what you are asking about. **(3 min.)**
3. Break the class into pairs and have them alternate making up two **¿Cómo supiste...?** and **¿Cómo te enteraste de...?** questions. Their partners will answer. **(4 min.)**

A mi hermanita le gusta leer **la sección de moda** para saber de los nuevos estilos de ropa.

A mi mamá también le gusta leer **la sección de cocina** para ver las recetas y para tener más ideas sobre qué platos servir cuando tenemos invitados.

Mi papá lee **la sección de ocio** para enterarse de las exposiciones de arte, los conciertos y las películas. Le gusta cuando **entrevistan** a algún artista o director de cine.

A ella también le gusta **la sección de sociedad** para saber quién se casó y quiénes asistieron a las fiestas de gala.

Mi abuela lee **los obituarios** para saber de los funerales.

Visit Holt Online
**go.hrw.com**
KEYWORD: EXP3 CH6
Vocabulario 2 practice

**También se puede decir...**

You may also hear **los muñequitos** for **las tiras cómicas**, **la sección de entretenimiento** for **la sección de ocio**, and **las defunciones** instead of **los obituarios**.

## ¡Exprésate!

| To ask about information | To explain where you found it |
|---|---|
| **¿Cómo supiste el resultado?** *How did you find out the score?* | **Lo leí en la sección deportiva.** *I read it in the sports section.* |
| **¿Cómo te enteraste de...?** *How did you find out about . . . ?* | **Estaba en primera plana.** *It was on the front page.* |

Interactive TUTOR

Vocabulario y gramática, pp. 67–69 — Online workbooks

▶ Vocabulario adicional — En las noticias, p. R17

Vocabulario 2

## TPR
### Total Physical Response

Go to the Web site of a major daily newspaper from a Spanish-speaking country and print out the first page of each section in that day's paper or, if possible, bring in a Spanish newspaper. Spread out the newspaper sections on a table in the front of the classroom, and have individual volunteers respond to the following commands.

**Busca la sección deportiva.**

**Señala la sección donde hay noticias internacionales.**

**Pásame la sección de moda.**

**Busca la sección donde se puede leer las opiniones de los editores.**

**Señala un artículo de los anuncios clasificados.**

**Abre la sección de sociedad.** 1.2

## Más práctica

For additional practice, you may want to either use the printed-out newspaper pages from above, or have students close their textbooks. Read various headlines from the newspaper or from the textbook, and then prompt students to guess in which section they might read that particular article. 1.2

## Differentiated Instruction

### ADVANCED LEARNERS

**Challenge** Have students look through the front pages for any given day of at least three major daily newspapers from Mexico, printed from online sources. Have them compare and contrast the stories, noticing if the subject matter is repeated in the different papers or not, and write down why they think the editor chose certain stories over others. 3.2

### MULTIPLE INTELLIGENCES

**Logical/Mathematical** Have students look through the editorials of at least three major daily newspapers from Mexico. Have them make a chart in which they record how many editorials, opposing editorials, and letters to the editor are printed on each. Then ask them to categorize the articles by topic and calculate the totals for each topic. Have them share the results with the class. 3.2

## Comparisons

### Comparing and Contrasting

Have students research an international issue in a U.S. newspaper and an online newspaper from Mexico or another country in Latin America. Are there differences in the way the issue is presented in each newspaper? What might account for these differences? Ask students to discuss their ideas. 3.2, 4.2

**Differentiated Instruction** See the Differentiated Instruction CD-ROM.

## Resources

**Planning:**

Lesson Planner pp. 87–88, 248–249

One-Stop Planner

**Presentation:**

Teaching Transparencies
**Vocabulario** 6.3, 6.4

**Practice:**

Cuaderno de vocabulario y gramática, pp. 67–69

Activities for Communication, pp. 23–24

Lab Book, pp. 33–36

Teaching Transparencies
**Vocabulario y gramática** answers, pp. 67–69

Audio CD 6, Tr. 8

Interactive Tutor, Disc 2

## Teacher to Teacher

**Wayne Calhoon**
Hirschi High School
Wichita Falls, TX

**News Conference** I divide students into groups of four. At the end of each week, a different group gives a 10-minute news conference in Spanish about current events from that week. The current events can be local, state, national, world, or even school events. Students must work together outside of class on their presentation. They primarily use newspapers, TV, and the Internet to collect news stories. This is an ongoing project that can last all year. 1.1, 1.3

El equipo mexicano celebra un gol durante la Copa Mundial.

CD 6, Tr. 8 See script on p. 247.

### 23 ¿Cómo lo supiste? 1.2

**Escuchemos** Escucha las conversaciones. Indica si cada persona supo la noticia a través de **a**) el periódico, **b**) la televisión o **c**) otra persona. **1.** a **2.** c **3.** b **4.** a **5.** a **6.** c

### 24 ¿Dónde lo leíste? 1.2

**Leamos/Hablemos** ¿En qué sección del periódico puedes leer algo sobre los siguientes temas?

1. las noticias mundiales más importantes la sección de noticias internacionales
2. la crisis económica en Argentina la sección financiera
3. la última moda francesa e italiana la sección de moda
4. una reseña de una película mexicana la sección de ocio
5. una receta para una cena típica tex-mex la sección de cocina
6. el resultado de un partido de fútbol la sección deportiva
7. la boda de una vecina la sección de noticias locales
8. las opiniones de los editores sobre las elecciones los editoriales

### 25 Las noticias del día 1.2

**Leamos/Escribamos** Completa el diálogo con las palabras del cuadro.

| | | | |
|---|---|---|---|
| suscribí | deportiva | enfoque local | supiste |
| titular | ocio | editoriales | anuncios clasificados |

PAPÁ Oye, hijo, pásame la sección __1__. Quiero saber el resultado del partido de fútbol de anoche. deportiva

FELIPE Ganó Cruz Azul, 5 a 2.

PAPÁ ¿Cómo __2__ el resultado? supiste

FELIPE Lo leí en las noticias en línea. Ahora estaba leyendo los __3__ para saber la opinión de un comentarista sobre las peleas en los partidos de fútbol. editoriales

PAPÁ Cambiando de tema, ¿has leído el artículo sobre el incendio en el cine del centro? El __4__ estaba en la primera plana, pero todavía no he leído el artículo en el __5__ para saber los detalles. **4.** titular **5.** enfoque local

FELIPE Ahora entiendo por qué no habían anunciado ninguna película en el cine del centro en la sección de __6__. ocio

PAPÁ Bueno, Felipe, tengo que salir y me voy a llevar el periódico. Te dejo los __7__ para que busques un apartamento. ¡Ya llevas dos meses aquí! anuncios clasificados

FELIPE Gracias, Papá. Me __8__ a un boletín en Internet y me mandan una lista de apartamentos todos los días. suscribí

## Core Instruction

### VOCABULARY IN CONTEXT

**Cooperative Learning** Divide the class into groups of three. Write the vocabulary words that name a section of the newspaper on index cards, and give each group a card. Have each group come up with three titles of articles that might appear in that section. Their titles should be short sentences of three to five words. Then have groups read their titles to the class. The class must guess which section of the newspaper each group has.

**26** **¿Qué leen?** 1.2

**Escribamos** Escribe una oración para explicar qué sección del periódico leen tus parientes y amigos, con qué frecuencia y por qué.

**MODELO** **Mi papá lee sólo la primera plana porque tiene prisa en las mañanas.**

la primera plana

1

2

3

4

5

6

7

8

## Comunicación

HOLT SoundBooth ONLINE RECORDING

**27** **El periódico del colegio** 1.1, 1.3

**Hablemos** Uds. son reporteros del periódico de su colegio. En grupos de tres, escojan qué secciones y temas quieren incluir en el periódico esta semana. Cada persona será responsable de sugerir ideas y titulares para los artículos de dos secciones. Luego, los grupos se turnarán para presentar sus ideas a la clase.

**MODELO** **—Necesitamos hacer una sección deportiva esta semana, porque hay un partido de básquetbol muy importante.**
**—¡Sí! ¿Y te enteraste del viaje que van a hacer los estudiantes de francés? Debemos incluir un artículo sobre eso en la primera plana.**

Vocabulario 2

### 23 Script

1. —Leí en los obituarios que murió José Izaguirre, el escritor de Nuevo México. ¡Qué triste! Me gustan mucho sus cuentos.
2. —Oye, me enteré de que tu hermano Sebastián se va a casar con una muchacha de México.
   —Sí, así es... pero ¿cómo lo supiste? Todavía no ha salido el anuncio en el periódico.
   —No, me lo dijo tu mamá.
3. —Pedro, ¿estás bien? Me dio mucho miedo cuando escuché que hubo un incendio en tu casa.
   —Todos estamos bien, gracias. Pero, ¿cómo lo supiste?
   —Lo vi en el noticiero de las once.
4. —Buenos días, señor Fajardo. ¿Está contento? ¡Ganó Monterrey el partido de fútbol!
   —¡No puede ser! ¿Cómo lo supo Ud.?
   —Estaba en la sección deportiva esta mañana.
5. —¿Sabías que hay una crisis ambiental en nuestro estado?
   —¡No me digas! ¿En qué parte? ¿Qué pasó?
   —Pensé que tú lo sabrías. Yo solamente leí la primera plana cuando estaba en el supermercado.
6. —¡Qué triste! ¡Van a cancelar el Festival de Jazz de Nueva Orleans este año!
   —Es imposible que cancelen el Festival. ¿Lo viste en el noticiero?
   —No, mi hermana me lo dijo.
   —Pues, dudo que ella sea muy fiable.

## Differentiated Instruction

### SLOWER PACE LEARNERS

**27** **Additional Practice** If students had a hard time coming up with suggestions for stories in this activity, provide them with copies of their favorite two sections of the newspaper. Have them review the sections and then come up with two topics to cover in each section that week.

### SPECIAL LEARNING NEEDS

**Students with Visual Impairments** Have students go to an online news source that has audio reports. Have them choose stories from their three favorite sections and say why they find those more interesting. 1.2

## Comunicación

**Pair Activity: Interpersonal**

Have pairs of students imagine that their student newspaper staff received a grant this year to travel to a foreign country and report on schools in a specific town or city. Have them discuss which country they would choose, and what questions they would ask their counterparts abroad.

1.1

**Differentiated Instruction** See the Differentiated Instruction CD-ROM.

**Resources**

**Planning:**

Lesson Planner pp. 87–88, 248–249

One-Stop Planner

**Presentation:**

Teaching Transparencies **Vocabulario** 6.3, 6.4

**Practice:**

Cuaderno de vocabulario y gramática, pp. 67–69

Activities for Communication, pp. 23–24

Teaching Transparencies **Vocabulario y gramática** answers, pp. 67–69

Interactive Tutor, Disc 2

**Circumlocution**

Have volunteers say which topics they know little or nothing about because they never read a certain section of the newspaper. Tell the volunteers not to mention the section they are thinking of. For example, the student might say: **No sé nada de lo que está pasando en otros países.** The rest of the class must identify the section of the newspaper that the student is not reading. 1.1

**Communities**

**Community Link**

Explain to the class that federal law allows for cable franchising authorities in different communities to create public, educational, and governmental (PEG) access channels on cable television. These stations offer classes and use of their equipment and facilities free of charge to community members in exchange for volunteer work, or for a nominal fee. Have students write a short news feature in Spanish for broadcast at a local cable access station or to present to the class. 1.3, 5.1

## Hay que estar al tanto de todo

MIGUEL Últimamente no he tenido mucho tiempo para leer el periódico.

CARMEN Pobre de ti, porque la profesora de ciencias sociales quiere que estemos al tanto de las noticias. Es más, pasado mañana tenemos un examen sobre las noticias de esta semana.

MIGUEL ¡Se me había olvidado! Oye, ¿me ayudas a estudiar? Sólo pude leer una que otra sección del periódico esta semana.

CARMEN Cómo no. ¿Ya supiste que se casa la hija del presidente?

MIGUEL No tenía la menor idea que se casaba, nunca leo la sección de sociedad.

CARMEN ¡Pero esa noticia estaba en primera plana!

MIGUEL No sé cómo me la perdí. Y espero que la profesora no nos pregunte sobre asuntos financieros porque yo no sé ni jota de economía.

CARMEN Bueno, yo entiendo poco de economía pero sé que hubo problemas financieros. ¿Ya te enteraste de quién ganó las elecciones en Guatemala?

MIGUEL Que yo sepa, empataron, ¿no?

CARMEN No, empataron el partido de béisbol. En las elecciones ganó una mujer. Ay, Miguel, ¡me tienes desesperada!

**¡Exprésate!**

**To talk about what you know and don't know**

Interactive TUTOR

**Entiendo algo de..., pero nada de...**
*I understand a little about . . ., but nothing about . . .*

**No tengo la menor idea si...**
*I don't have the slightest idea if . . .*

**Que yo sepa, (no) hay...**
*That I know of, there is/are (isn't/aren't). . .*

**¿Qué sé yo de...? No entiendo ni jota de...**
*What do I know about . . .? I don't understand a thing about . . .*

Vocabulario y gramática, pp. 67–69 Online workbooks

**Core Instruction**

**TEACHING ¡EXPRÉSATE!**

1. Model each expression in **¡Exprésate!,** then call on volunteers to do the same with their own examples. **(2 min.)**
2. Point out that no one knows everything, and that to ask the right questions is often as much a sign of intelligence as to have the right answers. In that spirit, call on volunteers to talk about what they know compared with that which they do not know. For example: **Entiendo algo de fútbol, pero nada de básquetbol. (3 min.)**
3. Have the students form pairs and continue this discussion, taking turns expressing what they know and what they do not know. **(3 min.)**

**28** **¿Quién lo diría?** 1.2

**Leamos** Basándote en el diálogo, decide quién diría las siguientes oraciones, **Miguel** o **Carmen.**

1. No tengo la menor idea de lo que está pasando en el mundo. Miguel
2. ¿Qué sé yo de economía? Miguel
3. Estoy al tanto de las elecciones en Guatemala. Carmen
4. Supe de los problemas financieros porque leí la sección financiera. Carmen
5. No me enteré de la boda de la hija del presidente. Miguel
6. Leí todas las secciones del periódico esta semana. Carmen

**29** **Una entrevista** 1.2

**Leamos/Hablemos** Eres el (la) presidente(a) de la clase y un(a) compañero(a) te está entrevistando para el periódico del colegio. Usa las expresiones de **Exprésate** para responderle.

**MODELO** —**¿Qué sabes de la crisis económica en los colegios?**
—**Sé algo del problema, pero no conozco muchos detalles.**

1. La directora dijo que necesitamos comprar nuevas computadoras para todas las clases. ¿Qué nos cuentas de eso?
2. ¿Hay planes de ofrecer clases durante el verano?
3. Algunos estudiantes piensan establecer una emisora estudiantil. ¿Qué nos puedes decir sobre eso?
4. Los profesores discutieron la censura de ciertos sitios de Internet en las computadoras del colegio. ¿Es verdad?
5. El club de español quiere empezar un programa de intercambio con un colegio de otro país. ¿Sabes qué país eligieron y cómo lo van a hacer?

Una emisora estudiantil en la Universidad de Veracruz, México

## Comunicación

HOLT SoundBooth ONLINE RECORDING

**30** **Un concurso** 1.1, 1.2

**Hablemos** Imaginen que participan en un concurso de conocimientos generales. En grupos pequeños, túrnense para hacerles preguntas a sus compañeros. Un(a) participante elige un tema del cuadro, y el (la) locutor(a) le hace una pregunta sobre el tema. Los participantes deben usar las expresiones de **Exprésate** para contestarlas.

- deportes
- ciencias
- programas de televisión
- artes
- palabras en español
- actores famosos

**MODELO** —**¿Quién ganó la última Copa Mundial?**
—**No sé. Yo no entiendo ni jota de deportes.**

## Cultures

### Products and Perspectives

Have students bring in local newspapers. Then assign a country in Latin America to pairs of students and have them look for an online newspaper from their country. Ask them to compare the sections they find in each newspaper and the types of articles within each section. Have pairs of students prepare a short presentation for the class telling what they found and explaining what factors they think might account for the differences. 2.2, 4.2

## Comunicación

### Pair Activity: Interpersonal

Have pairs of students conduct an interview, taking turns playing the role of either a school newspaper reporter or the president of a school club of their choice. Each writes two questions, and then does the interview. The interviewee should either answer the question or use an expression from **¡Exprésate!** to explain that they do not know the answer. 1.1

## Differentiated Instruction

### ADVANCED LEARNERS

**Challenge** Have students read an opinion column by a local or syndicated writer. Have them make a list of the main points in the article, and write a two-paragraph response to the column. 1.2

### SPECIAL LEARNING NEEDS

**28 Students with Learning Disabilities** Before students do Activity 28, summarize the conversation as a class. Ask questions to guide students towards the information they will need to answer the questions. **¿Miguel sabe lo que está pasando en el mundo? ¿Carmen lee el periódico? ¿Miguel sabe quién ganó las elecciones en Guatemala?** Have volunteers answer the questions and read the section of the conversation where they found the answer. 1.2

## Assess

**Assessment Program**

**Prueba: Vocabulario 2,** pp. 107–108

Alternative Assessment, pp. 378, 390, 402

**Online Assessment** my.hrw.com

**Test Generator**

## Resources

**Planning:**

Lesson Planner, pp. 89–92, 250–253

One-Stop Planner

**Presentation:**

Video Program **GramaVisión**

**Practice:**

Grammar Tutor for Students of Spanish, Chapter 6

Cuaderno de vocabulario y gramática, pp. 70–72

Cuaderno de actividades, pp. 55–57

Activities for Communication, pp. 23–24

Lab Book, pp. 33–36

Teaching Transparencies

Bell Work 6.6

**Vocabulario y gramática** answers, pp. 70–72

Audio CD 6, Tr. 9

Interactive Tutor, Disc 2

### Bell Work

Use Bell Work 6.6 in the *Teaching Transparencies*, or write this activity on the board.

**Indica en qué sección del periódico se podría encontrar los siguientes titulares.**

1. Accidente ocurre en supermercado local
2. ¡Fabuloso concierto de la sinfónica!
3. Líderes de varios países se reúnen en España
4. Chicago gana el partido de béisbol
5. Óscar de la Renta lanza su nueva colección de ropa en París
6. Actriz italiana gana premio importante

1.2

**Objetivos**
- Indefinite expressions
- Gender of nouns
- Indicative in compound sentences

# Gramática en acción 2

GramaVisión

Interactive TUTOR

## Repaso Indefinite expressions

**1** Indefinite words can be used in **affirmative** or **negative** expressions. You will often see **no** paired with a negative expression.

| Affirmative | | Negative | |
|---|---|---|---|
| **algo** | *some* | **nada** | *nothing, not . . . anything* |
| **alguien** | *someone* | **nadie** | *no one, not . . . anyone* |
| **algún, alguna** | *some, any* | **ningún, ninguna** | *none, (not . . .) any* |
| **alguno(a), algunos(as)** | *some, any* | **ninguno(a), ningunos(as)** | *none, (not . . .) any* |
| **también** | *also* | **tampoco** | *not . . . either* |
| **siempre** | *always* | **nunca, jamás** | *never* |
| **o** | *or* | **ni** | *nor* |

**2** The words **o** *(or)* and **ni** *(nor)* can be used in pairs to express *either . . . or* and *neither . . . nor.*

**O** me pasas esa sección **o** me voy.

Esta locutora **no** es **ni** fiable **ni** imparcial.

**3** Indefinite adjectives and pronouns must agree with the nouns they modify or represent. When a negative word precedes the verb, **no** is left out. **Alguno** and **ninguno** shorten to **algún** and **ningún** before a masculine singular noun. Plural forms are not used in the negative.

¿Tienes **algunas** ideas?

**No** tengo **ninguna** idea.

¿**No** sabe **nadie** la respuesta?

**Ningún** estudiante sabe la respuesta.

Vocabulario y gramática, pp. 70–72
Actividades, pp. 55–57
Online workbooks

### En inglés

**In English,** only one negative word is used in negative expressions.

I **don't** know **anything** about politics.

**Nobody** wants to read **any** articles.

In English, what can two negative expressions do in a sentence?

**In Spanish,** double negatives are often used in negative expressions.

**No** sé **nada** de política.

**Nadie** quiere leer **ningún** artículo.

4.1

They can cancel each other out and be understood as an affirmative: *I didn't do it for nothing.*

CD 6, Tr. 9 See script on p. 227F.

**31** **¿Afirma o niega?** 1.2

**Escuchemos** Escucha las conversaciones e indica si la segunda persona **afirma** *(affirms)* o **niega** *(denies)* lo que dice la primera persona. **1.** niega **2.** afirma **3.** niega **4.** afirma **5.** niega **6.** niega

## Core Instruction

### TEACHING GRAMÁTICA

1. Go over point 1. **(3 min.)**
2. Model sentences with indefinite expressions stating whether certain items are in the classroom. (**Hay algunos libros en la mesa.**) Students answer **cierto** or **falso,** correcting false sentences. (**No hay ningún libro en la mesa.**) **(4 min.)**
3. Go over point 2. Students make sentences with **o** and **ni** using cues you provide. (Call out **ir a la playa, ir al parque,** and a student answers: **O voy a la playa o voy al parque. No voy ni a la playa ni al parque, sino a casa.**) Explain that **o** and **ni** can be used in pairs for emphasis, but can also be used alone. (**¿Quieres ir al cine o al museo?**) **(4 min.)**
4. Go over point 3. Call on students to find the indefinite adjective or pronoun in each example, and state the gender and number of the noun it modifies. **(4 min.)**

### GramaVisión

For a video presentation of indefinite expressions, use **GramaVisión.**

GramaVisión

Visit Holt Online
**go.hrw.com**
KEYWORD: EXP3 CH6
Gramática 2 practice

**32 ¿Hay algo para mí?** 1.2

**Leamos/Hablemos** Usa las palabras de **Gramática** para contestar las preguntas.

| | |
|---|---|
| Recetas mexicanas: enchiladas, arroz con leche, chiles rellenos | **Sección de cocina** |
| Jugador de tenis gana dos campeonatos | **Sección de deportes** |
| Cantantes famosos asisten a una fiesta de gala en Nueva York | **Sección de sociedad** |
| Opiniones: la crisis ambiental, los viajes del presidente | **Editoriales** |
| Miles de mujeres italianas compran nuevo estilo de zapatos | **Sección de moda** |
| Cine y teatro | **Sección de ocio** |

1. ¿Hay algún artículo aquí que te interese? ¿Cuál es?
2. ¿Hay algún artículo sobre la moda? ¿Cómo se llama?
3. ¿Puedes encontrar algún artículo sobre deportes?
4. ¿Hay algún artículo sobre gente famosa?
5. ¿Alguien escribió algún editorial sobre la crisis política?
6. ¿Hay alguna receta que te apetezca?

## Comunicación

HOLT SoundBooth ONLINE RECORDING

**33 ¿Sabes algo?** 1.1, 1.2

**Hablemos** Haz una pregunta sobre cada tema del cuadro para averiguar cuánto saben tus compañeros del tema. En parejas, túrnense para hacer las preguntas y contestarlas.

**MODELO** —**¿Sabes algo de...?**
—**Pues, la verdad es que no sé nada de...**
(—**Claro que sí. Entiendo que...**)

| | |
|---|---|
| el medio ambiente | las playas de Baja California |
| la política en México | la arquitectura maya |
| la música norteña | los escritores de Nuevo México |

El Templo de Kukulcán, México

# Gramática 2

## Connections

### Community Link

Have students find out what foreign language newspapers are available in their community or surrounding communities. Are they published locally or shipped from somewhere else? If Spanish-language newspapers are available, where are they sold? What sorts of goods or services are advertised there? What audience do they seem to target? Have students do an analysis of the articles: how many deal with local issues? national or international issues? Which Spanish-speaking countries are covered the most? Have students report their findings to the class.
1.2, 3.2

## Comunicación

### Class Activity: Presentational

As an extension of Activity 33, call on volunteers to come to the front of class and add to the list in the chart by writing on the board two topics, one about which they know something and one about which they know nothing. They should then say **Sé algo de...** or **No sé nada de...**
1.3

## Differentiated Instruction

### ADVANCED LEARNERS

**32 Challenge** As an extension, pass out different newspaper sections to students. Then ask questions such as the following and have individual students respond using indefinite expressions whenever possible. **¿Alguien tiene la sección deportiva? ¿Hay algún artículo sobre las películas? ¿Has leído esa sección alguna vez? ¿Alguien tiene los editoriales? ¿Siempre hay editoriales en el periódico?**
1.1

### SPECIAL LEARNING NEEDS

**31 Students with Auditory Impairments** For students with hearing impairments, you might want to pass out a copy of the script. Or, if students are able to hear better when working with a partner rather than a recording, hand out half of the script to one student and the other half to his or her partner. Students take turns reading their items aloud while their partners decide whether the speaker affirms or denies what was said. Then have them look at the script together to check their answers.
1.1

**Differentiated Instruction** See the Differentiated Instruction CD-ROM.

## Resources

**Planning:**

Lesson Planner, pp. 89–92, 250–253

One-Stop Planner

**Presentation:**

Video Program **GramaVisión**

**Practice:**

Grammar Tutor for Students of Spanish, Chapter 6

Cuaderno de vocabulario y gramática, pp. 70–72

Cuaderno de actividades, pp. 55–57

Activities for Communication, pp. 23–24

Lab Book, pp. 33–36

Teaching Transparencies
Bell Work 6.7
**Vocabulario y gramática** answers, pp. 70–72

Audio CD 6, Tr. 10

Interactive Tutor, Disc 2

### Bell Work

Use Bell Work 6.7 in the *Teaching Transparencies,* or write this activity on the board.

**Completa las oraciones con una palabra de Gramática de la página 250.**

1. No sé ______ sobre la historia de México.
2. ¿Cónoces ______ restaurante en la Ciudad de México?
3. ______ debes pasar por alto el Museo Frida Kahlo en Coyoacán.
4. A ella le encantan las pirámides y a mí ______.
5. Mi mamá ______ va al cine los viernes. Le fascina.
6. Sara no ha ido a ______ museo pero quiere ir.

1.2

## Gender of nouns

Interactive TUTOR

**1** These general rules will help you distinguish between **masculine** and **feminine** nouns that don't end in **-o** or **-a**. Remember, however, that there are always exceptions to these rules.

- Nouns ending in **-dad**, **-ión**, **-z**, **-is**, **-ie**, and **-umbre** are typically **feminine.**
  **la verdad, la nación, la voz, la crisis, la serie, la costumbre**
- Nouns ending in **-aje**, **-al**, **-és**, **-ín**, and **-ma** are typically **masculine.**
  **el paisaje, el corral, el inglés, el boletín, el problema**
- Compound nouns are usually **masculine.**
  **el lavaplatos** **el abrelatas** **el tocadiscos**
- Nouns ending in **-l**, **-n**, and **-r** can be **masculine** or **feminine.**
  **el árbol** **el plan** **el sur**
  **la piel** **la razón** **la labor**

**2** Many nouns referring to people have **masculine** and **feminine** forms. The article changes depending on the gender of the person, but the form of the noun does not change.

**el/la estudiante** **el/la periodista** **el/la testigo**
**el/la gerente** **el/la artista** **el/la modelo**

**3** The article used can change the meaning of some nouns.

| | | | |
|---|---|---|---|
| **la radio** | *radio as a medium* | **el radio** | *radio apparatus, radius, radium* |
| **la cura** | *cure* | **el cura** | *priest* |
| **la capital** | *government capital* | **el capital** | *money* |
| **la mañana** | *morning* | **el mañana** | *future* |
| **la orden** | *command* | **el orden** | *order, organization* |

**4** **Feminine** nouns beginning with a stressed **a-** or **ha-** take **el** in the singular. In these cases, the article does not indicate the gender of the noun.

**el arte, las artes** **el hacha, las hachas** **el ala, las alas**

Vocabulario y gramática, pp. 70–72
Actividades, pp. 55–57
Online workbooks

### Nota cultural

Algunos concursos populares en español son *El gran juego de la oca,* basado en un juego de mesa, y *Dando y dando.* Varios canales han adaptado programas en inglés de Estados Unidos y creado nuevas versiones en español. Por ejemplo, Univisión tuvo su propia versión del concurso *Who Wants to Be a Millionaire?* que se llamaba *A millón.* Televisa adaptó el concurso *Family Feud* para crear su programa *Cien mexicanos dijeron.*

¿Qué concursos en español puedes ver en tu comunidad? ¿En qué se parecen a los concursos en inglés? 3.1

*El Bus,* un concurso español

1. la capital
2. la radio
3. la cura
4. el capital
5. el orden

CD 6, Tr. 10 See script on p. 253.

**34** **¿Cuál es?** 1.2

**Escuchemos** Escucha las oraciones y escribe la palabra que se define en cada oración.

## Core Instruction

### TEACHING GRAMÁTICA

1. Review point 1 and model the pronunciation of listed nouns. **(2 min.)**
2. Call on students to name more nouns that fit into the categories in point 1. **(1 min.)**
3. Use each word in point 2 in a sentence. Ask students to identify the masculine or feminine form in each sentence. **(2 min.)**
4. Make up sentences with the nouns in point 3 to show how the article changes the meaning of the nouns. **(3 min.)**
5. For point 4, model the pronunciation of the singular form of the nouns with both **el** and **la** to show students that using **la** before nouns beginning with a stressed **a-** or **ha-** sounds awkward. Check that students do not think these nouns are masculine when singular, and feminine when plural; and have them model similar nouns with articles. (**el agua, el águila**) **(2 min.)**

### GramaVisión

For a video presentation of the gender of nouns, use **GramaVisión.**

GramaVisión

## 35 Más de un artículo 1.2

**Leamos** Completa las oraciones con las palabras correctas.

1. Esta mañana en (el/la) capital se anunció que dos científicos han descubierto (el/la) cura para el cáncer.
2. El gobierno de (el/la) comunidad creó (un/una) plan para mantener (el/la) orden durante (el/la) festival.
3. (El/La) presidente de (el/la) organización dice que va a visitar los estados que están en (el/la) sur del país.
4. Los estudiantes le mandan (un/una) mensaje (al/a la) artista Juan Gómez para darle las gracias por su visita.
5. (El/La) plan que propone el candidato no soluciona (el/la) problema.
6. El congreso de (la/el) nación se preocupa por (el/la) crisis ambiental.
7. (El/La) periodista Ignacio Rey escribió un artículo sobre (el/la) testigo Mónica López.

El Congreso mexicano se reúne en el Palacio Nacional, México.

## 36 Defínelo 1.2

**Leamos/Escribamos** Escribe la palabra para cada definición y su artículo correspondiente.

1. Un territorio que tiene un solo gobierno. una nación
2. Una persona que va al colegio y toma clases. un(a) estudiante
3. Otra palabra para referirse al "trabajo". la labor
4. De esta planta que crece en el bosque obtenemos la madera. el árbol
5. Esta palabra describe un problema muy grande o serio. la crisis
6. Algo que se puede usar para escuchar discos. el tocadiscos

## Comunicación

HOLT SoundBooth ONLINE RECORDING

## 37 Un boletín 1.1, 1.2

**Escribamos/Hablemos** En parejas, preparen un boletín de noticias para el colegio usando las palabras del cuadro.

MODELO —**El presidente de Chile hablará en la ceremonia de graduación sobre el tema «La crisis del mañana».**
—**Mañana habrá una serie de presentaciones sobre nuevos programas de estudio.**

| | | | |
|---|---|---|---|
| presidente | verdad | graduación | serie |
| problema | crisis | mañana | acción |
| artistas | arte | plan | radio |

### 34 Script

1. —Esta ciudad del país es el centro del gobierno y es donde se hacen las leyes.
2. —Compré un aparato nuevo para escuchar mis canciones favoritas.
3. —Por fin los científicos descubrieron el remedio para esta enfermedad.
4. —Queremos publicar un periódico en el colegio, pero no tenemos el dinero para poder empezar.
5. —Este cuarto está muy limpio. Veo que todo está muy organizado.

### Heritage Speakers

On page 252, students learned that **compound nouns** are usually masculine and they are provided with three examples. Ask your heritage speakers to come up with other such compound nouns. They should pay attention to words that normally end in the letter *s* even though they are singular. Have students work in pairs or in groups of four. After they check word spelling in the dictionary, ask for volunteers to report their findings to the rest of the class. 1.1

### Comunicación

### Group Activity: Interpretive

Assign a section of the newspaper to pairs of students. Have them work together to write ten beginning sentences for invented articles for their newspaper section. Then have them exchange sentences with another pair to check the use of masculine and feminine articles. As a challenge, ask students to guess for which section of the newspaper the other pair was writing. 1.2

## Differentiated Instruction

### SLOWER PACE LEARNERS

**Additional Practice** Have students work in groups to come up with more nouns that would fit into each category in point 1 of **Gramática**. Have each group write their words on index cards, with the correct article on the back. Ask groups to take turns holding up cards. The group that provides the correct article first gets a point. Continue until all cards have been used or until a group has gotten 10 points. 1.2

### SPECIAL LEARNING NEEDS

**Students with Dyslexia** If you have students with difficulties reading or spelling correctly, remind them that in Spanish, the sound of a given vowel is always the same, and that there are a few easily recognizable exceptions when it comes to consonants. The latter are governed by predictable rules; for example, **c** sounds like an **s** before **i** or **e,** and like a **k** before **a, o,** and **u.** Dictate nouns and have volunteers write them on the board: **el águila, la crisis, el árbol, la piel, el sur.** Ask the class to check the spelling. 1.2

**Differentiated Instruction** See the Differentiated Instruction CD-ROM.

## Resources

**Planning:**

Lesson Planner pp. 89–92, 250–253

One-Stop Planner

**Presentation:**

Video Program **GramaVisión**

**Practice:**

Grammar Tutor for Students of Spanish, Chapter 6

Cuaderno de vocabulario y gramática, pp. 70–72

Cuaderno de actividades, pp. 55–57

Activities for Communication, pp. 23–24

Lab Book, pp. 33–36

Teaching Transparencies Bell Work 6.8

**Vocabulario y gramática** answers, pp. 70–72

Audio CD 6, Tr. 11

Interactive Tutor, Disc 2

### Bell Work

Use Bell Work 6.8 in the *Teaching Transparencies,* or write this activity on the board.

**Completa las oraciones con el artículo correcto.**

1. Siempre me ha parecido curioso ______ arte surrealista.
2. Es importante aprender sobre ______ filosofía de Unamuno.
3. Hay que luchar por combatir ______ hambre.
4. Para contar historias hay que ejercer ______ imaginación.
5. Los científicos siguen buscando ______ cura para el SIDA. 1.2

### 38 Script

See script on page 227F.

## Repaso — Indicative in compound sentences

Interactive TUTOR

### ¿Te acuerdas?

**Decir** is often used in the **preterite** to report what someone said.

Agustín **dijo** que el documental fue muy educativo.

1. As you know, compound sentences have two parts or clauses: a main clause and a subordinate clause. A subordinate clause often begins with **que.**

   main clause / subordinate clause
   Me parece / que el periódico de nuestra ciudad es malo.

2. If the main clause indicates *doubt, denial, disbelief,* or *uncertainty,* among others, the verb in the subordinate clause is in the **subjunctive mood.**

   main clause / subordinate clause
   Ignacio no cree / que ese locutor **sea** fiable.

3. If the main clause indicates *certainty* or *truth* in the speaker's mind, the verb in the subordinate clause is in the **indicative mood.**

   main clause / subordinate clause
   Cristina dice / que Nora **tiene** la sección de moda.

4. Verbs typically followed by the **indicative** in the subordinate clause are: **decir, informar, anunciar, afirmar, contar, enterarse.**

   La reportera **informó** que el comité **iba** a reunirse hoy.

   Todos **afirman** que el periodista **sabe** mucho.

5. Verbs like **decir** and **pedir** are followed by the **subjunctive** in the subordinate clause when they mean *to order* or *to ask (someone to do something).*

   Mis padres me **dicen** que **escuche** el reportaje.

Vocabulario y gramática, pp. 70–72
Actividades, pp. 55–57
**Online** workbooks

### 38 La crisis económica 1.2

**Leamos** Completa el párrafo con la forma correcta de los verbos.

Hoy el gobierno anunció que la crisis económica __1__ (siga/sigue) siendo grave. Según dijo un experto, es probable que los precios __2__ (suban/suben). El presidente dice que la crisis __3__ (va/vaya) a durar poco tiempo, especialmente si todos mantenemos la calma. Los economistas afirman que __4__ (sea/es) muy importante estar bien informado en este momento. Dicen que __5__ (escuchemos/escuchamos) los noticieros todos los días. Hoy los locutores informaron también que los bancos __6__ (están/estén) cerrados, pero no creen que __7__ (cierren/cierran) mañana.

## Core Instruction

### TEACHING GRAMÁTICA

1. Review compound sentences by reading the example in point 1 aloud and pointing out the main and subordinate clauses. **(2 min.)**
2. Go over points 2 and 3. Emphasize the difference between the subjunctive and indicative moods in compound sentences and model the examples given for each. **(3 min.)**
3. After covering point 4, write sentences on the board with the verbs **informar, anunciar,** and **contar** in the main clause and a subordinate clause with an indicative verb. Have volunteers identify the main and subordinate clauses, and the verb in the subordinate clause. **El profesor nos informó que vamos a tener un examen. Mi primo anunció que se casa en mayo. (3 min.)**
4. Go over the use of **decir que** in **¿Te acuerdas?** and compare it to the use of **decir que** and **pedir que** in point 5. **(3 min.)**

### GramaVisión

For a video presentation of the indicative and subjunctive in compound sentences, use **GramaVisión.**

GramaVisión

CD 6, Tr. 11 See script on p. 227F.

## 39 ¿Hecho o posibilidad? 1.2

**Escuchemos** Escucha los comentarios del locutor. Indica si el locutor está comentando **a)** un hecho o **b)** una posibilidad.

*¿Se te olvidó?* Subjunctive with negation or denial, pp. 108–109

1. a 2. a 3. b 4. b 5. a 6. a

## 40 ¿Subjuntivo o indicativo? 1.2

**Escribamos** Combina una palabra o expresión de cada columna y añade tus propias ideas para formar oraciones completas. Según el verbo, la segunda parte de la oración puede estar en el subjuntivo o el indicativo.

**MODELO** **El reportero informó que los problemas en los colegios son graves.**

| | | |
|---|---|---|
| el (la) profesor(a) | decir que | yo... |
| el (la) presidente | anunciar que | los estudiantes... |
| mis padres | esperar que | el gobernador... |
| el (la) reportero(a) | informar que | mis amigos... |
| mi amigo(a) | contar que | el gobierno... |
| el (la) director(a) | pedir que | el problema... |

# Comunicación

HOLT SoundBooth ONLINE RECORDING

## 41 ¿Te enteraste? 1.1, 1.2

**Hablemos** En parejas, dramaticen un diálogo basándose en los dibujos. Usen las expresiones de **Gramática** para reportar las noticias. *¿Se te olvidó? To react to news, p. 144*

## Answers

Use the Chapter 6 Picture Sequences Transparency.

41 Sample answer:

—Oye, me enteré por la tele que cancelaron las clases. ¿Quieres salir a jugar en la nieve?

—Pues, prefiero quedarme en casa. El gobernador dice que no salgamos de casa.

—Mira, mamá, el periodista reportó que los bomberos encontraron a tres chicos atrapados en la nieve.

—Ojalá que estén bien.

# Comunicación

## Class Activity: Presentational

Have students form groups of four and imagine they are radio news reporters making announcements. Have them use the main clause verbs found in point 4 of **Gramática** on p. 254 to create compound sentences with indicative verbs in the subordinate clauses. 1.3

# Differentiated Instruction

## ADVANCED LEARNERS

**Challenge** Have students research a current events topic of their choice. Ask them to write a short news report using several compound sentences. At least half of their compound sentences should have the indicative in the subordinate clause, with the remainder in the subjunctive. 1.3

## SPECIAL LEARNING NEEDS

**40 Students with Learning Disabilities** Some students may not be able to make complete sentences using the fragments in the boxes. Form the sentences for students. Write each on the board, leaving a blank for the verb. As a class, decide whether the verb will be in the indicative or the subjunctive, and have volunteers explain why. Ask students to write the correct verb form in their notebooks. Circulate around the classroom to check their work. 1.2

## Assess

**Assessment Program**

**Prueba: Gramática 2,** pp. 109–110

**Prueba: Aplicación 2,** pp. 111–112

Audio CD 6, Tr. 18

Alternative Assessment, pp. 378, 390, 402

**Online Assessment**
**my.hrw.com**

**Test Generator**

## Resources

**Planning:**
Lesson Planner, pp. 92, 252–253
One-Stop Planner

**Presentation:**
Video Program, Videocassette 3
DVD Program
**VideoNovela**

**Practice:**
Video Guide, pp. 40–42
Lab Book, pp. 74–75

### Gestures

Ask students to make note of the gestures Clara and her father use as they discuss the article. Have volunteers read the first section and mimic the gestures. Have students talk about situations in which they would use the same gestures. Then ask them if Clara and Professor Luna use gestures in their phone conversation. Is the phone conversation harder or easier to understand?

Novela en video

# Clara perspectiva

## Episodio 6

**ESTRATEGIA** 1.3, 3.1

**Analyzing viewpoints** Every story has two sides. The two sides in this story are the ecologists' and the corporation's. In order to better understand the conflict between these two groups, analyze their viewpoints. Based on what you know so far about the land in **Magallanes,** list three things the ecologists might want for the property, and three things that the corporation might want. Argue both sides. After you watch the episode, compare your lists and your arguments with what Clara learns from the newspaper article.

### En la casa de los de la Rosa

1

**Clara** Buenos días, papá. ¿Me prestas las noticias locales, por favor? Quiero saber si aparece algo sobre la exposición de artistas de ayer.
**Papá** Está bien, hija, toma. Yo sólo quiero la sección deportiva.

2

**Clara** ¡Mira! ¡El reportaje sobre la exposición está en la primera plana!
**Papá** Sí, hija, ya veo. ¿Qué dice?
**Clara** Ayer en la exposición de artistas chilenos en el Museo de Artes Visuales, el debate entre la empresa maderera *MaderaCorp* y un grupo de ecologistas culminó en un intercambio dramático entre el presidente de la empresa y dos ecologistas.

3

**Clara** La empresa maderera *MaderaCorp* quiere comprar 250 mil hectáreas de bosque nativo en la región de Magallanes. Según *MaderaCorp,* el proyecto estimularía la economía de la región generando empleos y otras actividades económicas.
**Papá** No cabe duda que la gente en esa región está a favor de mayores empleos… ¿cuál es el problema?

4

**Clara** Los ecologistas afirmaron que con el desarrollo del ecoturismo en la región se podrían obtener mayores utilidades en el uso del bosque.
**Papá** No estoy seguro que los ecologistas tengan la razón. Estoy convencido que es posible combinar la ecología con los negocios, ¿no crees, Clara?

## Pre-AP Practice

**AP Benchmark:** Identify and summarize the main points and details and make inferences and predictions from a spoken source on a topic.

**Focus:** Comprehending and interpreting main ideas
- SE, p. 256, **Estrategia**
- SE, p. 257, **¿Comprendes?**
- Video Guide, p. 42, Act. 5

## Core Instruction

### TEACHING NOVELA EN VIDEO

1. Have volunteers summarize what has happened so far in **Clara perspectiva. (2 min.)**
2. Play the video. Ask students to pay attention to the viewpoints of Clara and her father regarding MaderaCorp. **(5 min.)**
3. Have volunteers read the parts of Professor Luna and Clara in the section **En los bosques de Pirque. (5 min.)**
4. Answer the questions on page 257 as a class. If students have trouble answering any of the questions, reread the appropriate sections. **(3 min.)**

### Escuchemos

Novela en video

As students watch the **Novela,** have them listen for the word Clara uses for *newspaper.* (**el diario**) What two sections of the newspaper do she and her father mention? (**la sección deportiva, la primera plana**)

**Clara** Armando Luna, profesor de estudios ambientales en la Pontificia Universidad Católica de Chile, es el encargado de realizar estudios de impacto ambiental.
**Papá** ¿Ése es tu profesor, no? Uy, no quisiera estar en sus zapatos. Está en una situación muy difícil. Sus estudios de impacto ambiental podrían afectar a muchas personas.

## En los bosques de Pirque

**Profesor Luna** ¿Quién habla?
**Clara** Clara de la Rosa, Profesor.
**Profesor Luna** ¿Qué pasa, Clara? No es un momento oportuno para hablar de tus estudios…
**Clara** No, Profesor…

**Profesor Luna** Clara, ¿recuerdas esa recomendación que me pediste? Ve a mi oficina e imprime todos los archivos bajo el título "Recomendaciones". Imprímelos, ¿me entiendes? No trates de copiarlos, imprímelos. Pídele la contraseña a Mercedes. Ella te la dará si le dices el apellido de soltera de mi madre: Contreras.
**Ecologista 1** Termine la conversación, Profesor Luna. Tenemos que hablar.

## ¿COMPRENDES?

1. ¿Qué le pide Clara a su padre? ¿Qué encuentra ella ahí?
2. Según el artículo, ¿qué quiere la empresa *MaderaCorp?* ¿Qué quieren los ecologistas?
3. ¿Quién está en el centro del debate? ¿Por qué?
4. ¿Qué información del artículo te ayuda a analizar el punto de vista de los ecologistas? ¿y el de la empresa *MaderaCorp?*
5. ¿Qué le pide el profesor a Clara? ¿Qué le dice que no haga?
6. ¿Qué tiene que saber ella para poder abrir los archivos? ¿Qué es? 1.2

**Próximo episodio**
*Clara va a la oficina del profesor Luna para imprimir los archivos. ¿Crees que le va a resultar fácil hacerlo? ¿Por qué sí o por qué no?*
PÁGINAS 304–305

Novela en video

### Visual Learners

Have students make a graphic organizer listing the three things the ecologists want and those the corporation wants. Once they have watched the episode, students add the information from the article to the third column. They can them compare their original arguments with what Clara learns from the article.

| Los ecologistas | La corporación | El artículo |
|---|---|---|
| 1. | 1. | 1. |
| 2. | 2. | 2. |
| 3. | 3. | 3. |

1.2

### ¿Comprendes? Answers

1. las noticias nacionales; un reportaje sobre la exposición
2. comprar 250 mil hectáreas de bosque nativo en la región de Magallanes; desarrollar el ecoturismo
3. el profesor Luna; está haciendo los estudios de impacto ambiental
4. Los ecologistas afirmaron que con el desarrollo del ecoturismo en la región se podrían obtener mayores utilidades en el uso del bosque. Según *MaderaCorp*, el proyecto estimularía la economía de la región generando empleos y otra actividad económica.
5. imprimir todos los archivos bajo el título "Recomendaciones"; no tratar de copiarlos
6. su contraseña: el apellido de soltera de su madre

## Clara perspectiva, Episodio 6

In **Episodio 6,** Clara and her father are having breakfast at home. Clara asks her father for the national news section. She reads that *MaderaCorp* is a development firm seeking to buy and develop land in the region of Magallanes and that *EcoChile* is opposed to *MaderaCorp's* plans. She realizes who the men she saw threatening her professor were. She calls her professor. During their conversation, the two men seen with the professor in **Episodio 1** approach him and coerce him into their van. Before hanging up, the professor gives Clara a code word that she can use to convince his secretary, Mercedes, to allow her to enter his office and print out the studies.

## Comunicación

### Pair Work: Interpersonal

Have students work in pairs to debate the issue of how to use the region of Magallanes. One student will argue the side of *MaderaCorp* and the other will argue the side of the ecologists. Tell them they can use the arguments discussed in **Novela** or they can come up with their own.

1.1

# Lectura informativa

## Resources

**Planning:**

Lesson Planner, pp. 93, 254–255

One-Stop Planner

**Presentation:**

Audio CD 6, Tr. 12

**Practice:**

Cuaderno de actividades, p. 58

Reading Strategies and Skills Handbook, Chapter 6

Interactive Advanced Reader

## Teaching Suggestion

In the editorial **"Recuperar la tierra",** Atiénzar says that one of the problems with the Kyoto Protocol is that some of the countries whose practices are harming the environment will not sign the agreement. Ask students to research information about the countries that have not signed the agreement. What activities would the countries have to change if they signed the agreement? Would it be an expensive change? How would it affect the people of the country? Ask students to discuss why they think these countries have refused to sign the agreement.

# Lectura informativa

CD 6, Tr. 12

## Recuperar la tierra

*Este editorial lo escribió María José Atiénzar en el periódico* El Sol de Texas. *En el artículo, la autora comenta algunos problemas con las leyes que hay sobre el medio ambiente.*

"Nunca en la historia de la humanidad se ha hecho tanto, en tan corto tiempo, para destruir el maravilloso ecosistema que nos brinda sustento[1]". Con estas palabras, Kofi Annan, Secretario General de la Organización de las Naciones Unidas (ONU), comunica que las acciones destructivas sobre el medio ambiente van a afectar las generaciones futuras de modo que puede tomar miles de años corregir.

Kofi Annan pronuncia un discurso en la ONU.

Hay muchos desafíos pendientes: la preservación de la capa de ozono, la lucha contra la desertificación, la protección de la diversidad biológica, la escasez[2] de agua y tantos otros.

El barco *Prestige,* que cargaba millones de barriles de petróleo, se hundió en la costa de Galicia en noviembre del 2002.

En el Protocolo de Kioto se ha tratado de regular algunos de esos temas. La dificultad está en que algunos de los países que cometen muchas de las ofensas ambientales no han firmado[3] el acuerdo.

Otro de los "agujeros"[4] del Protocolo de Kioto es la exclusión de las emisiones ocasionadas por el transporte aéreo y marítimo. La aviación representa el 4% de las

1. sustains us 2. shortage 3. signed 4. loopholes

## Core Instruction

**TEACHING LECTURA INFORMATIVA**

1. Read and discuss the introductory paragraph as a class. Ask volunteers to say how they feel about Annan's statement. **(5 min.)**
2. Lead a short discussion about the material after you read each paragraph as a class. **(20 min.)**
3. Have students answer the **Comprensión** questions with a partner. Ask volunteers for their thoughts on the questions in **Tu opinión.** Use the opinions expressed as a springboard for a wider class discussion. **(10 min.)**

## Pre-AP Practice

**AP Language Examination: Lectura informativa** helps students prepare for Section I, Part B: **Reading Comprehension.** The audio recording helps them prepare for Part A: **Listening—Short Narratives.**

Docenas de soldados españoles llevaron cubos de petróleo crudo durante la limpieza. Duró varios meses y limpiaron cientos de millas de la costa de España y Francia.

emisiones de gases de invernadero[5]. En el mar, el accidente del barco *Prestige*[6] en la costa de Galicia es un ejemplo del peligro y daño irrecuperable de estas áreas. Por eso, el transporte aéreo y marítimo deberían estar incluidos.

Hacen falta mayores esfuerzos y voluntad para tomar acciones concretas. Son necesarios más control, la educación ambiental, la participación de las comunidades locales y la aplicación de tecnologías sostenibles.

5. greenhouse gases
6. The boat, carrying millions of barrels of oil, sank in November of 2002.



## Comprensión

**A** **¿Sí o no?** 1.2

1. La ONU no está preocupada por la situación del medio ambiente. no
2. Todos los países del mundo firmaron el Protocolo de Kioto. no
3. Las acciones de un país afectan el clima o el ecosistema de otros países. sí
4. La aviación es responsable, en parte, de las emisiones de gases dañinos. sí
5. La autora del editorial piensa que el Protocolo de Kioto es muy completo y protege el medio ambiente. no

**B** **¿Qué aprendiste?** 1.2

1. Nombra tres problemas ambientales que tenemos, según el artículo.
2. ¿Cuál es el propósito del Protocolo de Kioto?
3. ¿Qué es necesario hacer para mejorar el medio ambiente?

**C** **Tu opinión** ¿Cuál de los problemas del medio ambiente solucionarías primero? ¿Por qué? ¿Cómo lo harías? 1.3

### Actividad 1.1, 3.1

**Investigación** Con un(a) compañero(a), investiguen un desastre que haya afectado el medio ambiente, como el accidente del barco *Prestige* que se menciona en el artículo. Resuman lo que pasó y hablen de las leyes que aprobarían *(you would pass)* para que no vuelva a suceder.



# Lectura informativa

## Pre-Reading Activity

Have students go to the United Nations web site (www.un.org), download, and read the English and Spanish versions of the preamble and Chapter 1 of the U.N. Charter, as well as the Universal Declaration of Human Rights. Ask them to think about how taking care of the Earth is intertwined with protecting human rights. Ask students what they know about the Kyoto Protocol and tell them that the selection they are about to read will give them more information on the United Nations Framework Convention on climate change. 3.1

### B Answers

1. Tres de estos problemas: la preservación de la capa de ozono, la lucha contra la desertificación, la protección de la diversidad biológica, la escasez de agua
2. regular los temas del medio ambiente
3. más control, la educación ambiental, la participación de las comunidades locales, la aplicación de tecnologías sostenibles

## Connections

### Social Studies Link

Have students research the history of the United Nations and list all the reasons that led to its formation. Have them find out about its current activities and then describe one or two of these in which a Spanish-speaking country is participating. 3.1

## Differentiated Instruction

### ADVANCED LEARNERS

**Challenge** Have students search for articles about the environment in online newspapers from Latin America. What topics get the most coverage? Then have them look for articles about the environment in U.S. newspapers. Are the topics similar? What differences do they find? 3.2, 4.2

### MULTIPLE INTELLIGENCES

**Naturalist** Ask students to think of an environmental issue that is of particular concern to them. Have them prepare a short presentation for the class in which they present the issue and talk about ways that students such as themselves might be able to make a difference in resolving the issue. 1.3

### Assess

**Assessment Program**
**Prueba: Lectura,** p. 113

**Online Assessment**
**my.hrw.com**

**Test Generator**

**Resources**

**Planning:**

Lesson Planner pp. 93–94, 254–255

One-Stop Planner

**Presentation:**

Audio CD 6, Tr. 13

**Practice:**

Cuaderno de actividades, p. 58

Reading Strategies and Skills Handbook, Chapter 6

Interactive Advanced Reader

### Analyzing Chronological Order

As students read the story, have them think about the important events. When they have finished reading, ask volunteers to give an important event from the story. Write each event on the board. Have students help you put the items in chronological order. Have them use order words such as **primero, segundo, luego, después,** and **finalmente.** Ask volunteers to summarize the story using the numbered list as a guide to the order of events. Then ask students to discuss how analyzing the chronological order helps them to understand the story better. 1.2, 3.1

### Escuchemos

Play the recording of the reading, and have students listen with their books closed. Then have them complete the following sentence: **Parece mentira que Junajpú e Xbalamqué....** Have them explain their answers.

### Pre-AP Practice

**AP Language Examination:** **Leamos** helps students prepare for Section I, Part B: **Reading Comprehension.** The audio recording helps them prepare for Part A: **Listening—Short Narratives.**

# Leamos y escribamos

**ESTRATEGIA**

**para leer** When you read a story like the *Popol Vuh,* it's important to know the order in which the events happened. The best way to follow and understand a story is to make a list of events in chronological order. This will help you keep track of events from the beginning to the end of the story.

CD 6, Tr. 13

**Antes de leer** 1.2

**A** El *Popol Vuh* es el libro sagrado maya que explica la creación del mundo y el desarrollo de la naturaleza y de los seres humanos. La selección que vas a leer trata de los hermanos Xbalamqué y Junajpú, que con la ayuda de la naturaleza y de poderes sobrehumanos, logran vencer el mal. Los hermanos llamaron la atención de los Señores del Infierno *(hell)* con su juego de pelota *(ball)* y por eso tuvieron que someterse a desafíos *(challenges)* imposibles. Mientras lees, escribe en orden cronológico los desafíos que enfrentaron los hermanos y las otras cosas que hicieron los Señores para hacerles daño, y cuáles fueron los resultados.

## del Popol Vuh

Los muchachos dijeron a los Señores del Infierno, los Ajawab de Xibalbá:

—A los dos primeros no los saludamos porque son muñecos[1] hechos de madera y trapos[2], pero a vosotros sí: Jun Camé, y Wukub Camé, Xiquiripat y Cuchumaquic, Ajalpuj y Ajalk'aná, Ajalmez y Ajaltok'ob, Chamiabac y Chamiajolom, Quicxic y Patán, Quicré y Quicrixcac[3]. Y tú, Jolomán, que estás sentado en un banco.

Nada gustaron de esto[4] los Ajawab y los invitaron a sentarse.

—Eso no, dijeron los muchachos, ese asiento es piedra que está quemando; no nos sentamos en ella.

—Ea, pues, dijeron los Señores, vayan a descansar a la posada[5].

Por orden de los Señores fueron conducidos[6] a la Casa Oscura, donde les llevaron dos ocotes[7] y dos cigarros y les advirtieron[8] que, ardiendo[9] toda la noche, los habían de devolver[10] enteros por la mañana. Ellos tomaron dos plumas[11] de la cola de la guacamaya y las pusieron en el ocote y en las puntas de los cigarros pusieron dos luciérnagas[12]. Así estuvieron haciendo como[13] que ardían toda la noche.

Los señores quedaron muy admirados de ver los cigarros y los ocotes enteros e invitaron a los muchachos a jugar a la pelota. Primero jugaron con una cabeza de puma y después con la pelota de hule[14] de Junajpú e Xbalamqué.

Otra noche los metieron[15] en la Casa del Fuego, pero éste no les hizo daño alguno sino salieron muy hermosos por la mañana.

1 figures, dolls 2 rags, cloth 3 *names of the lords of hell* 4 didn't like that at all 5 guest house 6 were taken/led 7 sliver of ocote pine 8 warned, advised 9 (keeping them) burning 10 they were to return them 11 feathers 12 glow worms, fireflies 13 pretending 14 rubber ball 15 put them

## Core Instruction

### TEACHING LEAMOS

1. Have students look at the illustrations and read the background information in **Antes de leer.** Ask them what roles a ball game might have in a story about a struggle between the protagonists and their enemies. **(2 min.)**
2. Read the **Estrategia para leer** with students. Provide them with a list of the events on page 260 in scrambled order. Tell them to read the part of the story on page 260 and to put the events in chronological order. **Los muchachos fueron a la Casa Oscura. Los señores y los muchachos jugaron a la pelota. Los muchachos saludaron a los señores. Los muchachos pasaron la noche en la Casa del Fuego. (5 min.)**
3. Have students continue with the rest of the story, stopping to monitor comprehension and to go over their list of events in chronological order. **(10 min.)**
4. Have students complete the **Comprensión** activities on page 262. **(8 min.)**

A la noche siguiente llevaron a los muchachos a la Casa de los Murciélagos[16], donde había infinidad de ellos.

Junajpú e Xbalamqué se metieron dentro de sus cerbatanas a dormir, y aunque los murciélagos revoloteaban a su alrededor, no pudieron morderlos[17]. Junajpú quiso ver si ya había amanecido[18] y al sacar[19] la cabeza para certificarlo se la cortó[20] Camazotz, el Murciélago, quedando[21] sólo el cuerpo.

Los murciélagos fueron a poner la cabeza de Junajpú al atrio donde se jugaba a la pelota.

Xbalamqué llamó al pizote[22], al puerco y a todos los grandes y pequeños animales, para que lo ayudaran a remendar[23] a Junajpú y todos acudieron[24].

A lo último vino Coc, la Tortuga, balanceándose y dando vueltas a un lado y otro para caminar. Tomóla Xbalamqué[25] y labró de ella[26] la cabeza de Junajpú, la cual salió perfecta después de hacerle boca y ojos.

Esto fue hecho con mucha sabiduría[27] porque así lo dispuso Uc'ux Caj, el Corazón del Cielo.

Al terminar la cabeza se la pusieron al cuerpo de Junajpú y éste pudo hablar.

Puesta la cabeza de Junajpú en el atrio, los Señores fueron a celebrar el vencimiento[28] de los muchachos y se pusieron a jugar a la pelota.

Xbalamqué rebatió fuertemente la pelota que fue a caer junto a un tomatal[29] donde estaba un conejo, aconsejado por Xbalamqué, que salió corriendo y los Señores detrás de él creyendo que era la pelota.

Quedó solo todo el atrio e Xbalamqué tomó la cabeza de Junajpú y se la puso al cuerpo cambiándola por la cabeza de tortuga, la que colocó[30] en su lugar en el atrio.

Los Señores estaban admirados de ver el prodigio[31] que sucedía con Junajpú.

16 bats 17 bite them 18 if the sun had come up 19 upon sticking out 20 (the bat) cut it off 21 leaving behind 22 coati, a raccoon-like animal 23 to fix, to mend 24 came to help 25 Xbalamqué took her 26 made out of her 27 wisdom 28 defeat 29 tomato patch 30 put 31 *prodigio* wonder, miracle

## Active Reading Questions

1. **Explica todo lo que le hicieron los murciélagos a la cabeza de Junajpú.**
2. **Describe en orden cronológico los acontecimientos que ocurrieron en la transformación de la tortuga en la cabeza de Junajpú.**
3. **¿Qué hizo el conejo para engañar a los Señores de Xibalbá?**
4. **¿Qué crees que opinan los señores de los muchachos?** 1.2

## Connections

### History Link

Have students research what is known about the **juego de pelota** and Mayan ball courts. Then have them discuss the importance of this story in the context of Mayan history. (Although several ball courts have been discovered throughout Mayan territory, no official rules or guidelines for playing it have ever been found. All of the information known today is based on carvings and artwork found in Mayan ruins, and texts such as the ***Popol Vuh.***) 3.1

## Applying the Strategies

For more practice with the ordering of events, you might have students use the "Probable Passage" strategy from the *Reading Strategies and Skills Handbook.*

## Differentiated Instruction

### ADVANCED LEARNERS

**Challenge** Have students work in groups to present the ***Popol Vuh*** selection as a presentation for the class. Allow them to bring in props and costumes. Suggest that one student play the role of the narrator as the others play characters in the story. Have students vote for the best presentation. 1.1

### MULTIPLE INTELLIGENCES

**Linguistic** Have students work in small groups to make up a short chapter detailing the ingenuity of Xbalamqué and Junajpú in the ongoing battles against the Señores de Xibalbá. Once groups have come up with a story, ask them to practice their oral storytelling skills by telling the class what happens in their invented chapters. 1.3

## Connections

### Social Studies Link

Explain to students that the symbols on page 260 and 262 are examples of Mayan glyphs. The Mayan language was made up of these symbols that represented words or syllables depending on the arrangement of their various parts. Each glyph typically contained three to four symbols, which are roughly equivalent to syllables. Ask students to research Mayan glyphs online and try to write their names phonetically, using the information they find. Ask students if they know of other languages (modern or historical) that use symbols to represent words or syllables. 3.1

### Post-Reading Strategy

Have students discuss the main idea of the story. How did the Señores de Xibalbá try to defeat the boys? How were the boys able to triumph over evil? What were their strengths? Ask the students to talk about the symbolism of various elements of the text. What form does evil take? Then have them talk about other myths with which they are familiar and have them tell what form evil takes in each myth. 1.2

Junajpú e Xbalamqué pasaron por todos estos castigos[32] y en ninguno de ellos murieron, hasta que por fin los Ajawab de Xibalbá, los Señores del Infierno, hicieron una gran hoguera[33] en un hoyo[34] y llamaron a Junajpú y a Xbalamqué. Estos se pusieron uno frente al otro y, extendiendo los brazos, se dejaron ir sobre el fuego[35].

Molieron[36] sus huesos y hechos polvo[37] los arrojaron a[38] la corriente del río; pero el agua no se los llevó sino que, yéndose al fondo[39], se convirtieron en dos hermosos muchachos.

---

32 hardships, punishments 33 bonfire 34 hole, pit 35 fire 36 They ground 37 (having been made into) dust 38 hurled them into 39 sinking to the bottom

### Comprensión 1.2

1. f 2. d 3. c 4. a 5. b 6. e

**B** Coloca los hechos en orden cronológico.

1. ____ 
2. ____ 
3. ____ 
4. ____ 
5. ____ 
6. ____ 

**a.** Xbalamqué le hizo una cabeza a Junajpú.
**b.** Los Señores de Xibalbá pensaron que un conejo era la pelota.
**c.** Xbalamqué les pidió ayuda a los animales.
**d.** Un murciélago le cortó la cabeza a Junajpú.
**e.** Junajpú sacó la cabeza de Junajpú del atrio y se la puso al cuerpo.
**f.** Xbalamqué y Junajpú pasaron la noche en la Casa Oscura.

### Pasó así 1.2

**C** Indica si cada oración es **cierta** o **falsa.** Corrige las falsas.

1. Los Señores de Xibalbá querían castigar a los muchachos Junajpú e Xbalamqué. cierto
2. Los Señores eran poco fiables. cierto
3. Los muchachos pudieron descansar en las posadas. cierto
4. Junajpú usó la cabeza del conejo para hablar. falso
5. El conejo ayudó a engañar *(trick)* a los Señores. cierto
6. Los murciélagos ayudaron a los muchachos. falso
7. Los muchachos murieron en el juego de pelota. falso

### Después de leer 1.3

**D** ¿Qué aprendiste de esta historia? ¿Por qué crees que los mayas escribieron una historia de dos muchachos que juegan a la pelota?

## Core Instruction

### TEACHING ESCRIBAMOS

1. Explain to students that there are many ways to tell stories. For instance, you can concentrate on important people or on events. **(1 min.)**
2. Discuss the **Estrategia para escribir** as a class. **(1 min.)**
3. Have students do prewriting Activity 1 in small groups. Members work together to come up with a sequence of at least five chronological elements they want to include in a story about their town or city. **(8 min.)**
4. Have students do Activity 2 for homework.
5. Have students do Activity 3 individually, and pair up with someone else to do Activity 4. **(15 min.)**
6. Have volunteers read their stories aloud. **(10 min.)**

## Pre-AP Practice

**AP Language Examination: Leamos and Escribamos** help students prepare for Section I, Part B: **Reading Comprehension** and Section II, Part A: **Informal Writing.**

Visit Holt Online
**go.hrw.com**
KEYWORD: EXP3 CH6
Online Edition

# Taller del escritor
1.3, 3.1

**ESTRATEGIA**

**para escribir** When writing a story of various chapters or parts, it's important to keep track of the chronological ordering of your story. If you include events that are out of place or repeated, you can confuse the reader. It's best to brainstorm a chain of events for your story first and then decide which way to order them.

## Una historia con fluidez

Imagínate que eres historiador(a) y quieres escribir una historia de tu pueblo o ciudad. ¿Qué incluirías en tu historia y cómo la escribirías en un orden fácil de seguir?

### 1 Antes de escribir

Antes de empezar tu historia, piensa en los eventos más importantes que quieres mencionar. Después pon esos eventos en orden y organízalos en un plan de escritura para que tu historia fluya *(flows)*.

### 2 Escribir un borrador

Empieza a escribir tu historia con la lista que hiciste. Asegúrate de incluir los eventos en orden cronológico.

### 3 Revisar

Revisa tu borrador y corrige errores de gramática y ortografía, si los hay. Lee tu borrador para verificar que los eventos de la historia estén en orden.

### 4 Publicar

Intercambia tu historia con un(a) compañero(a). Determinen Uds. si las historias tienen todos los elementos en el orden correcto. Pueden compartir sus historias con la clase para aprender la historia de los pueblos o ciudades de otros compañeros.

Leamos y escribamos

## Leamos y escribamos

### Process Writing

Explain to students that it is important to convey chronological order in their stories. Have them use a graphic organizer like the one on page 263 to put the events of their story in order before they begin to write. Tell them that a good way to help readers follow the order of events is to use order words such as **primero, luego, antes, después, al final, finalmente.** Have students brainstorm other order words that would be useful as they write their stories. Write the words on the board.

### Writing Assessment

To assess the **Taller del escritor,** you can use the following rubric.

| Writing Rubric | 4 | 3 | 2 | 1 |
|---|---|---|---|---|
| **Content** (Complete—Incomplete) | | | | |
| **Comprehensibility** (Comprehensible—Seldom comprehensible) | | | | |
| **Accuracy** (Accurate—Seldom accurate) | | | | |
| **Organization** (Well-organized—Poorly organized) | | | | |
| **Effort** (Excellent effort—Minimal effort) | | | | |

18–20: A 14–15: C Under
16–17: B 12–13: D 12: F

## Differentiated Instruction

### SLOWER PACE LEARNERS

3 Have students who need more time and assistance do two rounds of Activity 3. Take the time to help them with the first draft before they begin work on their second draft.

### MULTIPLE INTELLIGENCES

**Spatial** Have students include elements of their town or city's urban planning history. Ask them to assess whether their town was planned well or whether development seemed to occur unsystematically. You might suggest that they make a basic map of their town to include in the essay.

### Assess

**Assessment Program**
**Prueba: Lectura,** p. 113
**Prueba: Escritura,** p. 114
**Online Assessment**
my.hrw.com
**Test Generator**

**Assess** **Differentiated Instruction** See the Differentiated Instruction CD-ROM.

## Resources

**Planning:**

Lesson Planner pp. 94–95, 254–257

One-Stop Planner

**Presentation:**

Video Program, Videocassette 3

DVD Program

**Variedades**

**Practice:**

Activities for Communication, pp. 48, 65–66

Video Guide, pp. 38–39

Lab Book, pp. 6, 33–36, 73

Audio CD 6, Trs. 14–15

Pre-AP Instructional Resources

Pre-AP Audio CD 2, Trs. 1–4

Interactive Tutor, Disc 2

Teaching Transparencies

**Situación, Capítulo 6**

Picture Sequences, Chapter 6

### 1 Script

See script on p. 227F.

### 2 Answers

1. Yo no creo que haya un partido de fútbol esta noche. 2. Ayer hubo un reportaje sobre las elecciones. 3. Ya no había periódicos cuando llegué. 4. Hoy en la tarde habrá un documental en el canal seis. 5. No es posible que haya tantos exámenes hoy. 6. Dudo que haya programas educativos en la televisión.

### 3 Answers

1. las tiras cómicas
2. la sección de cocina
3. la sección financiera
4. la sección de sociedad
5. la sección de ocio
6. los anuncios clasificados

### 5 Answers

1. Están creando nuevas versiones en español. 2. Se hundió y gotó petróleo crudo al mar. 3. De fuera de E.U.; la mayoría venían de México. 4. En Internet, son boletines de noticias en línea sobre Latinoamérica.

Capítulo 6
Repaso

# Prepárate para el examen

Interactive TUTOR

CD 6, Tr. 14

**1** Escucha las conversaciones y escoge la foto que corresponde a cada una. 1.2 **1.** e **2.** b **3.** a **4.** d **5.** f **6.** c

A

B

C

D

E

F

**1 Vocabulario 1**
- expressing certainty
- expressing doubt and disbelief

**pp. 230–235**

**2 Gramática 1**
- indicative after expressions of certainty
- subjunctive after expressions of doubt and disbelief
- uses of **haber**

**pp. 236–241**

**3 Vocabulario 2**
- asking about and explaining where you found information
- talking about what you know and don't know

**pp. 244–249**

**2** Escribe oraciones con **haber.** 1.2

**MODELO** **la semana pasada/un concierto en el colegio**
**La semana pasada hubo un concierto en el colegio.**

1. no creo que/haber/un partido de fútbol esta noche
2. ayer/haber/un reportaje sobre las elecciones
3. ya no/haber/periódicos cuando llegué
4. hoy en la tarde/haber/un documental en el canal seis
5. no es posible que/haber/tantos exámenes hoy
6. dudo que/haber/programas educativos en la televisión

**3** Indica la sección del periódico que busca cada persona. 1.2

1. Miguelito quiere divertirse con los cuentos sobre sus personajes favoritos.
2. La señora Ortiz quiere encontrar una receta para la cena.
3. Gustavo quiere saber cómo va la economía.
4. Mariana quiere información sobre sus actores favoritos.
5. Paulina está buscando una lista de películas.
6. El señor Flores quiere comprar una computadora usada.

## Oral Assessment

### Speaking Rubric

To assess the speaking activities in this section, you might use the following rubric. For additional speaking rubrics, see the Alternative Assessment section of the *Assessment Program.*

| Speaking Rubric | 4 | 3 | 2 | 1 |
|---|---|---|---|---|
| **Content** (Complete—Incomplete) | | | | |
| **Comprehension** (Total—Little) | | | | |
| **Comprehensibility** (Comprehensible—Incomprehensible) | | | | |
| **Accuracy** (Accurate—Seldom Accurate) | | | | |
| **Fluency** (Fluent—Not Fluent) | | | | |

18–20: A 16–17: B 14–15: C 12–13: D Under 12: F

4 Completa las oraciones con la palabra correcta. 1.2

1. Escuchamos (el/la) radio para mantenernos informados sobre la crisis.
2. El reportero dice que el presidente (vaya/va) a hablar.
3. Vi un documental sobre (el/la) paisaje del desierto.
4. Quiero leer (algún/ningún) artículo de la sección de sociedad.
5. Esta emisora afirma que la princesa se (casa/case).
6. Leemos todas las noticias en (el/la) boletín del colegio.

5 Contesta las preguntas. 1.2

1. ¿Qué adaptaciones de concursos estadounidenses han hecho algunos canales latinoamericanos?
2. ¿Qué le pasó al barco *Prestige* en la costa gallega en 2002?
3. ¿De dónde venían los primeros programas en español?
4. ¿Qué es el *Latin America Data Base?*

CD 6, Tr. 15 1.2

6 Escucha las conversaciones y determina si las personas se enteraron de las noticias que mencionan por **a)** la radio, **b)** la televisión o **c)** el periódico. **1.** c **2.** a **3.** b **4.** c **5.** b **6.** a



**4 Gramática 2**
- indefinite expressions
- gender of nouns
- indicative in compound sentences

**pp. 250–255**

**5 Cultura**
- **Comparaciones** **pp. 242–243**
- **Lectura informativa** **pp. 258–259**
- **Notas culturales** **pp. 235, 241, 252**

## Conversación

HOLT SoundBooth ONLINE RECORDING

7 Role-play the following conversation with a partner. Partner A and Partner B are friends, talking about news around school. 1.1, 1.2

| | |
|---|---|
| Partner A: | Ask if your partner has seen the latest news on the school Web site yet. |
| Partner B: | Say no, and ask what the news is. |
| Partner A: | Tell your partner about a surprising event reported on the site. |
| Partner B: | Express your doubts. Say the reporters for the site are biased and not well-informed. |
| Partner A: | Disagree, and explain why you like the Web site. |
| Partner B: | Change the subject, and ask if your partner knows when (your favorite music group's) concert is going to be. |
| Partner A: | Say you heard that it was going to be next Thursday and that it was going to be great. |
| Partner B: | Say what you read about it in the entertainment section of the paper. Make plans to go with your partner. |

### 6 Script

**1.** —Los Tigres ganaron el partido.
—¡No es cierto!
—Si no me crees, aquí está la sección deportiva.

**2.** —¿Hay un incendio cerca de aquí?
—Sí, ¿no escuchaste la noticia en la radio?

**3.** —No sabía que el dinero se hacía con papel especial.
—Ni yo. ¿Cómo lo sabes?
—Lo vi anoche en un documental sobre los bancos.

**4.** —Se alquila un departamento en la calle Suárez.
—¿Ah, sí?
—Sí, te paso los anuncios clasificados.

**5.** —Me encanta el noticiero de las diez. Siempre me mantiene al tanto de todo.
—Sí, sus reportajes son muy informativos.

**6.** —Oye, ¿cómo va el partido?
—Estoy escuchándolo ahora. El locutor piensa que van a ganar los Pumas.

### 7 Answers

Below is a sample student conversation.

(A) —¿Leíste el sitio Web "El Mundo de Hoy"?
(B) —No, todavía no. ¿Qué pasó?
(A) —Pues, leí que investigaron la crisis ambiental del Golfo de México. A causa del huracán, muchos animales han muerto.
(B) —Dudo que eso sea cierto. Los reporteros de "El Mundo de Hoy" son muy parciales y no están bien informados.
(A) —No estoy de acuerdo. Me gusta el sitio porque siempre ponen artículos y reportajes detallados e informativos.
(B) —Cambiando de tema, ¿sabes cuándo es el concierto de Tacuba?
(A) —Oí que iba a ser el viernes próximo y que iba a ser fantástico.
(B) —Es cierto. Leí en la sección del ocio que van a tocar alguna que otra canción en inglés.

## Conversación

### Additional Speaking Practice

For additional speaking practice, use the *Picture Sequences Transparency* for Chapter 6. Use the Speaking Rubric on the preceding page to evaluate their performance. You may also wish to use the Interviews and Role-Plays in the *Activities for Communication* book.

### Pre-AP Practice

7 In the Level 3 *Pre-AP Instructional Resources* you will find an alternative version of Activity 7. The following resources in that book will help you prepare students for the AP Language Exam:

- Blackline masters, pp. 32, 42, 52
- Pre-AP Audio CD 2, Trs. 1–4
- Scripts and answers, pp. 57–75

Capítulo 6

# Prepárate para el examen

## Grammar Review

For more practice with the grammar topics in this chapter, see the *Grammar Tutor,* the *Interactive Tutor,* or the *Cuaderno de vocabulario y gramática.*

GramaVisión

## Más práctica

Have pairs of students take opposing viewpoints on the following statements, one responding with expressions of certainty and the other with expressions of doubt.

1. **Tener clases los sábados es una buena idea.**
2. **El documental sobre el Amazonas resulta muy interesante.**
3. **La crisis ambiental no nos afecta en Estados Unidos.**
4. **Las noticias en línea parecen más fiables que los periódicos.**
5. **Debemos discutir la política más en esta clase.**
6. **Los periodistas escriben artículos bastante imparciales.** 1.1

## Comparisons

### Language to Language

Remind students that double negatives are often used in Spanish. Write these sentences on the board and have volunteers underline the negative words in each. **Elena no conoce a nadie aquí.** (Elena doesn't know anyone here.) **Pedro no ha ido nunca a España.** (Pedro has never gone to Spain.) As a class, discuss the differences in translation between English and Spanish. 1.2, 4.1

**Gramática 1**

- indicative after expressions of certainty **pp. 236–237**
- subjunctive after expressions of doubt and disbelief **pp. 238–239**
- uses of **haber** **pp. 240–241**

## Repaso de Gramática 1

**Expressions of certainty** are followed by a verb in the **indicative mood.**

**Me parece que** hoy **va** a llover.

Other expressions of certainty are: **claro que, creo que, es cierto que, estoy convencido(a) de que, es obvio que, es evidente que,** etc.

When an **expression of doubt or disbelief** is used in a sentence, the **subjunctive mood** is used in the subordinate clause.

**No creo que llueva** hoy.

The **present perfect subjunctive** can also be used with these expressions.

**No creo que hayan hecho** un gran trabajo.

The impersonal forms of **haber** in the present, preterite, imperfect, present subjunctive, and future are: **hay, hubo, había, haya, habrá.**

**Gramática 2**

- indefinite expressions **pp. 250–251**
- gender of nouns **pp. 252–253**
- indicative in compound sentences **pp. 254–255**

## Repaso de Gramática 2

There are **affirmative** and **negative** forms of indefinite expressions.

No sé **nada** de política, pero hay **alguien** que te puede ayudar.

Indefinite adjectives and pronouns agree in gender and number with nouns.

Tienen **algunas** idea**s** para solucionar el problema.

Nouns that refer to people can be **masculine** or **feminine.**

**el/la** testigo **el/la** modelo

Some nouns have a different meaning depending on the article used.

**la orden** *command* **el orden** *order, organization*

Use the article **el** with the singular of feminine nouns beginning with a stressed **a-** or **ha-.**

**el** águila **las** águilas

A subordinate clause often begins with **que.**

Use the **subjunctive** when the main clause expresses uncertainty, denial, or doubt, and the **indicative** when it indicates certainty or truth in the speaker's mind.

No creo que **sea** muy informativo el programa.

Daniel dice que el programa **es** bastante completo.

## Chapter Review

### Teacher Management System

To access, launch the program, type "admin" in the password area, and press RETURN. For more details, log on to www.hrw.com/CDROMTUTOR.

Create a variety of puzzles to review chapter vocabulary.

**DVD Program**

**Interactive Tutor**

**PuzzlePro**

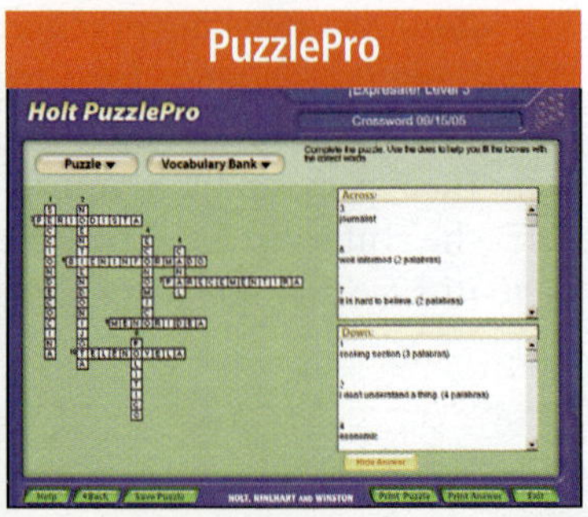

HOLT SoundBooth ONLINE RECORDING

## Repaso de Vocabulario 1

**To express certainty**

| | |
|---|---|
| alguno(a) que otro(a) (cosa) | *the occasional (thing)* |
| el canal | *channel* |
| el concurso | *game show* |
| considerarse | *to consider oneself* |
| controvertido(a) | *controversial* |
| la crisis ambiental/económica/política | *environmental/economic/political crisis* |
| detallado(a) | *detailed* |
| el documental | *documentary* |
| de modo... | *in a . . . way* |
| educativo(a) | *educational* |
| la emisora | *radio/TV station* |
| Es evidente que... | *It's evident that . . .* |
| estar al tanto | *to be up-to-date* |
| estar bien/mal informado(a) | *to be well/poorly informed* |
| Estoy convencido(a) de que... | *I'm convinced that . . .* |
| Estoy seguro(a) (de) que... | *I'm positive that . . .* |
| imparcial | *unbiased, objective* |
| informar | *to inform* |
| informativo(a) | *informative* |
| inspirarle confianza | *to inspire trust in (someone)* |
| investigar | *to research* |
| el (la) locutor(a) | *announcer, newscaster* |
| el programa de radio (a micrófono abierto) | *(call-in) radio show* |
| las noticias (en línea) | *(online) news* |
| el noticiero | *newscast* |
| parcial | *biased* |
| pasar por alto | *to overlook* |
| (poco) fiable | *(un)trustworthy* |
| la radio | *radio (as a medium)* |
| el reportaje | *news report* |
| el (la) reportero(a) | *reporter* |
| reseñar | *to review, critique* |
| la telenovela | *soap opera* |
| tratar un tema a fondo | *to cover a topic in depth* |

**To express doubt and disbelief**

| | |
|---|---|
| Dudo que estés bien informado(a) sobre.../que sepas... | *I doubt that you're well informed about . . ./that you know . . .* |
| No creo que los periodistas/los noticieros sean... | *I don't think that journalists/newscasts are . . .* |
| No estoy seguro(a) (de) que tengas razón sobre... | *I'm not sure that you're right about . . .* |
| Parece mentira que haya.../que digan... | *It's hard to believe that there are . . ./that they say . . .* |

## Repaso de Vocabulario 2

**To ask about and explain where you found information**

| | |
|---|---|
| los anuncios clasificados | *classified ads* |
| el artículo | *article* |
| la censura | *censorship* |
| el comentario | *commentary* |
| ¿Cómo supiste el resultado? | *How did you find out the score?* |
| ¿Cómo te enteraste de...? | *How did you find out about . . .?* |
| los editoriales | *editorial section* |
| el enfoque local/nacional/mundial | *local/national/world perspective* |
| entrevistar | *to interview* |
| Estaba en primera plana. | *It was on the front page.* |
| Lo leí en la sección deportiva. | *I read it in the sports section.* |
| los obituarios | *obituaries* |
| opinar | *to think, to be of the opinion* |
| el (la) periodista | *journalist* |
| la prensa | *the press* |
| la primera plana | *front page* |
| la sección de cocina | *cooking section* |
| la sección deportiva | *sports section* |
| la sección financiera | *financial section* |
| la sección de moda | *fashion section* |
| la sección de ocio | *entertainment section* |
| la sección de sociedad | *society section* |
| suscribirse a | *to subscribe to* |
| las tiras cómicas | *comic strips* |
| los titulares | *headlines* |

**To talk about what you know and don't know**

| | |
|---|---|
| Entiendo algo de..., pero nada de... | *I understand a little about . . ., but nothing about . . .* |
| ¿Qué sé yo de...? No entiendo ni jota de... | *What do I know about . . .? I don't understand a thing about . . .* |
| No tengo la menor idea si... | *I don't have the slightest idea if . . .* |
| Que yo sepa, (no) hay... | *That I know of, there is/are (isn't/aren't) . . .* |

Prepárate para el examen

Capítulo 6

# Prepárate para el examen

### Vocabulary Review

For more practice with the vocabulary in this chapter, see the *Interactive Tutor* or the *Cuaderno de vocabulario y gramática.*

### Online Edition

Students might use the online textbook to hear the **Vocabulario** items.

### Game

**Fuera de lugar** Give an index card to each student and ask students to write four words or phrases on the card. Three words should belong to a group based on meaning or part of speech; one should not belong (nouns: **el artículo, la primera plana, el periódico, investigar**). Collect the cards and shuffle them.

Divide the class into two teams and give each person on both teams a card. The first person on Team A asks the first person on Team B **¿Qué palabra está fuera de lugar?** and then reads the four words on his or her card. If the person on Team B answers correctly, he or she scores a point. Teams alternate asking the questions until all cards have been read. The team with the most points wins.

1.1

**Online Edition**

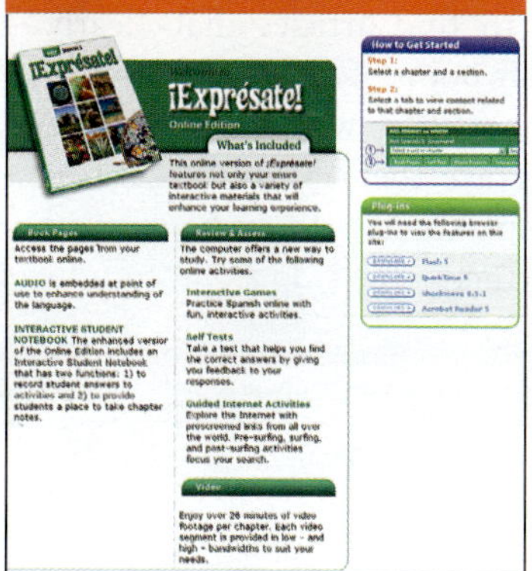


**Transparency: Vocabulario**

**Transparency: Situación**

## Assess

**Assessment Program**

**Examen: Capítulo 6,** pp. 281–286

Audio CD 6, Trs. 19–20

**Examen oral: Capítulo 6,** p. 292

Alternative Assessment, pp. 378, 390, 402

**Online Assessment**

**my.hrw.com**

**Test Generator**

## Resources

**Planning:**

Lesson Planner, pp. 95, 256–257

One-Stop Planner

**Presentation:**

Teaching Transparencies Fine Art, Chapter 6

**Practice:**

Cuaderno de actividades, pp. 59–60

Lab Book, pp. 6, 33–36

Audio CD 6, Tr. 16

### 1 Script

1. Un hombre lleva cinco días practicando ciclismo sin parar. Quiere cruzar todo el país. ¡Es un fanático!
2. Cocinero famoso dice que quiere preparar una cena para el ganador del concurso. ¡Seguramente estará para chuparse los dedos!
3. Artista esculpe una estatua moderna para la plaza del centro de la ciudad. Todo el mundo dice que es maravillosa.
4. La obra de teatro "Sueño de una noche de verano" es incomprensible. Sé que la escribió Shakespeare, pero yo no entendí ni jota.

## Communities

### Community Link

This group activity may be conducted in small groups or as an all-class activity. Help the class identify appropriate online Spanish-language newspapers. Students first search for three entertainment reviews written by the same person. Students read the chosen reviews, summarize the author's opinion on each performance, state whether or not the author liked the performances, and why. Have a volunteer write the reviewer about the class's consensus about the three performances, and ask the reviewer about his qualifications and how he became a reviewer. 3.2, 5.2

Repaso cumulativo

# Integración

## capítulos 1–6

CD 6, Tr. 16

**1** Escucha las noticias e indica a qué persona se refiere cada una. 1.2 **1.** B **2.** D **3.** A **4.** C

A
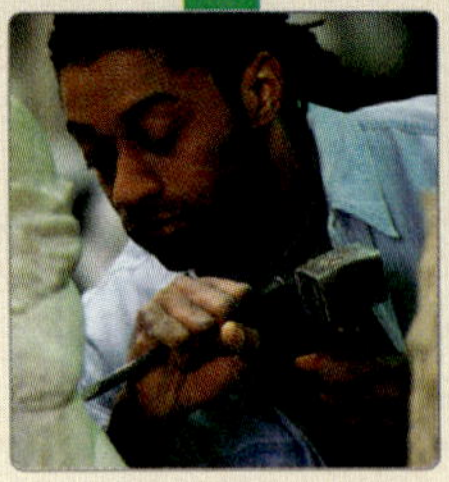
B

C

D

**2** Ésta es parte de un editorial que una periodista escribió sobre los equipos de deportes en los colegios. Lee el artículo y determina si la periodista **a)** estaría de acuerdo con los siguientes comentarios o **b)** si no estaría de acuerdo. 1.2

Muchos directores han decidido que no quieren tener equipos deportivos en sus colegios porque creen que los estudiantes sacan malas notas a causa de los deportes. Personalmente, estoy muy decepcionada con su actitud hacia los deportes. Parece mentira que puedan tener una impresión tan equivocada. Los equipos deportivos son como el grupo de teatro y la banda. ¡El colegio no sería lo mismo sin estos grupos! Son pasatiempos importantes para los estudiantes y son una fuente de orgullo para ellos. Estoy convencida de que los estudiantes necesitan tiempo para descansar y pasarlo bien y tienen que hacer ejercicio. No creo que vayan a resolver el problema así.

1. No creo que sea importante tener equipos deportivos en los colegios. b
2. Estoy segura de que los deportes no son la causa de las malas notas. a
3. Me choca la actitud de los directores hacia los deportes. a
4. Estoy convencida de que los ensayos de banda no valen la pena. b
5. A mi parecer, los colegios deben ofrecer actividades para los estudiantes. a

## Culture Project

Have students find an article that they disagree with from an online Spanish-language newspaper. Encourage them to use a newspaper from a country in Latin America, and to find an article about an issue particular to that country. They may wish to look in the opinion section in order to find articles that clearly express a particular point of view. Ask them to write a paragraph telling why they disagree with the article. Have them bring the article and their paragraph to class to exchange and discuss with a partner. 1.3, 3.2

Visit Holt Online
**go.hrw.com**
KEYWORD: EXP3 CH6
Cumulative Self-test

## Repaso cumulativo

**3** En grupos de tres, reseñen una película que hayan visto. Túrnense para responder a lo que dicen sus compañeros sobre los actores, la música, el tema, los acontecimientos y los detalles importantes de la película. 1.1, 1.3

**4** Describe lo que ves en esta parte del Códice Mendoza e imagina que tienes que leer el mensaje. Escribe ocho oraciones explicando qué crees que significa. 1.3

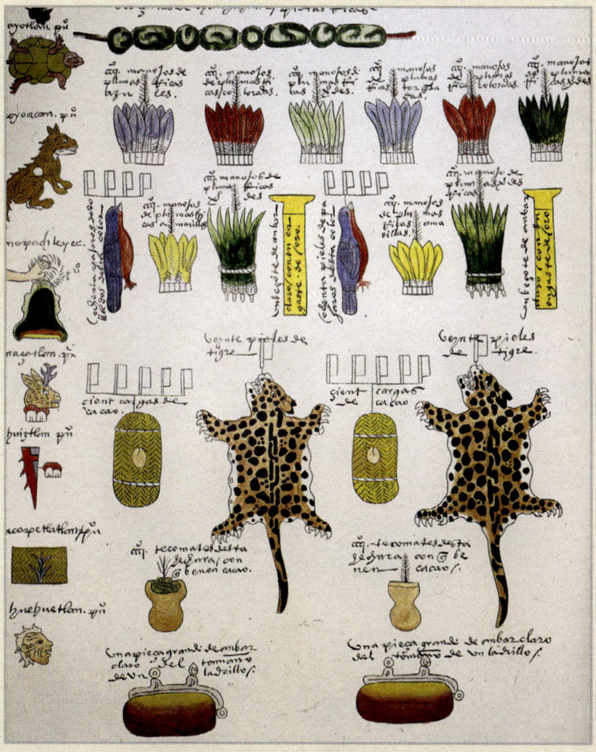



Del *Códice Mendocino*, parte II (registro de tributos)

**5** Tienes que escribir un editorial para el periódico de tu colegio explicando tu opinión sobre la comida en la cafetería. Describe las comidas que a los estudiantes les gustaría comer y por qué. 1.3

**6** **Situación**

En grupos de cuatro, preparen un noticiero de diez minutos con los siguientes temas: 1.1, 1.3

1. el enfoque local
2. una reseña de arte
3. un reportaje sobre el medio ambiente
4. las noticias mundiales

### Fine Art Connection

Organized societies have always required tribute or taxation of their citizens and conquered subjects, either in the form of currency or valuable articles. The Aztec empire was no different. The illustration dates to the time of the reign of Lord Montezuma, between 1502 and 1520. It shows the tributes that peoples conquered by the Aztecs had to pay every six months.

### Analyzing

**1.** Ask students to describe what they see in the left-hand column. Explain: **En la columna de la izquierda están los símbolos para los pueblos que debían pagar tributo a los aztecas.**
**2. ¿Qué representan los símbolos de cada uno de estos pueblos? (un cactus, una tortuga, un perro, una mano encima de una cabeza con pelo, la cabeza de un venado, un escudo, una manta bordada con la figura de una planta, la cabeza de un guerrero)**
**3. ¿Cuáles son los cinco tipos de artículos pagados en tributo que se encuentran en esta representación pictográfica? (piedras preciosas, plumas de varios colores y tamaños, pieles de pájaros y animales, cacao y envases para beber)** 3.1

### Extension

Have students research the economic organization of the Aztec empire throughout its history, including currency and tribute. Alternatively, students could research the history of cacao and chocolate. 3.1

### ACTFL Performance Standards

The activities in Chapter 6 target the different communicative modes as described in the Standards.

| | | |
|---|---|---|
| **Interpersonal** | Two-way communication using receptive skills and productive skills | **Comunicación (SE),** pp. 233, 235, 237, 239, 241, 247, 249, 251, 253, 255<br>**Comunicación (TE),** pp. 233, 235, 237, 239, 241, 247, 249, 257<br>**Conversación,** p. 265<br>**Situación,** p. 269 |
| **Interpretive** | One-way communication using receptive skills | **Comunicación (SE),** pp. 233, 237, 239, 241, 249, 251, 253, 255<br>**Comunicación (TE),** p. 253<br>**Novela en video,** pp. 256–257<br>**Leamos,** pp. 260–262<br>**Conversación,** p. 265 |
| **Presentational** | One-way communication using productive skills | **Comunicación (SE),** pp. 235, 247, 253<br>**Comunicación (TE),** pp. 251,255<br>**Taller del escritor,** p. 263 |

## Resources

**Planning:**

Lesson Planner, p. xv

One-Stop Planner

**Presentation:**

Teaching Transparencies **Mapa 3**

Video Program, Videocassette 4

DVD Program **GeoVisión**

**Practice:**

Video Guide, pp. 43–44

Lab Book, pp. 7, 76

Interactive Tutor, Disc 2

## VIDEO OPTIONS

- **VideoCultura**
- **VideoNovela**
- **Variedades**
- **GramaVisión**

## Pre-AP Practice

**AP Benchmark:** Recognize cultural elements implicit in oral and written texts.

**Focus:** Cultural Products (**los textiles**)

- SE, p. 275, **Miguel Andrango**
- TE, p. 271, Cultures
- TE, p. 275, Cultures

GeoVisión

Capítulos 7 y 8

▲ **El Huascarán** es la montaña más alta de Perú. Mide 6.768 metros de altura. En 1975 el Parque Nacional Huascarán se fundó para proteger las especies indígenas de la región. 2

# Geocultura
## *Los Andes*
### Ecuador, Perú y Bolivia

▶ **El Lago Titicaca,** a 3.810 metros sobre el nivel del mar, es el lago navegable más alto del mundo. Hay más de 40 islas en el lago, cada cual con sus propias costumbres. 1

### Almanaque

**Países, poblaciones y capitales de los Andes centrales**
Ecuador, 13.363.593 (Quito)
Perú, 27.925.628 (Lima)
Bolivia, 8.857.870 (Sucre, oficial), (La Paz, sede del gobierno)

**Idiomas principales**
español, quechua, aymara

**Industrias importantes**
agricultura, productos de madera, alimentos procesados, metales, textiles

### ¿Sabías que...?

**La Cordillera de los Andes, con picos que alcanzan alturas hasta cerca de 7.000 metros, se estrecha por unos 8.000 kilómetros desde el punto más sureño de Sudamérica hasta la costa del Mar Caribe en el extremo norte del continente.**

▶ **Los trajes folklóricos** del altiplano peruano tienen sus raíces en tradiciones españolas e incaicas.

## Background Information

### History

The Inca empire rivaled that of the Romans in size and sophistication and flourished in this region, centuries before the arrival of Francisco Pizarro in 1532. It included parts of southern Colombia and stretched nearly the entire length of the Andes into Chile. The Inca empire came to an end in 1533 with the capture and execution of Atahualpa. The newly conquered territories formed part of the Viceroyalty of Peru. Simón Bolívar and his army liberated the country in 1823.

### Geography

**The Andes** mountain range in this region is divided into two parallel ranges called the **Cordillera Negra** and the **Cordillera Blanca.** In Peru, the Andes are divided into five climate regions: **yunga, quechua, suni, puna,** and the **selva alta** in the eastern foothills.

**Lake Titicaca** is the highest navigable lake in the world and forms part of the border between Peru and Bolivia. Lake Titicaca covers 8,300 km$^2$ and is the second largest lake in South America, after Lake Maracaibo in Venezuela.

**Quito** is surrounded by major volcanoes. The most active volcano in the area is Cotopaxi.

# Los Andes

▲ **Machu Picchu,** escondido del mundo hasta 1911, hoy atrae a miles de turistas a Perú. Probablemente la ciudad fue construida alrededor del año 1450 y abandonada unos 100 años después. 3

▲ **El cañón del Colca** en Perú es el cañón más profundo del mundo, con 3.182 metros de profundidad. En la Cruz del Cóndor los visitantes pueden observar el ave voladora más grande del mundo, el cóndor. 4

► **La papa y el maíz** son las comidas principales en el altiplano andino. Los españoles llevaron los dos productos a Europa en el siglo XVI. Hoy día se comen papas en todo el mundo.

▲ **La Paz** es la ciudad andina de origen aymara más importante y es la sede del gobierno nacional de Bolivia. A una altura de 3.610 metros es la sede de gobierno más alta del mundo.

► **El Cinturón de Fuego del Pacífico** es una línea de volcanes que se extiende por la costa occidental de Sudamérica y por las costas orientales de Asia. El volcán Cotopaxi en Ecuador es el volcán activo más alto del mundo. 5

## Atlas INTERACTIVO MUNDIAL

Have students use the interactive atlas at **go.hrw.com**.

### Map Activities

1. Have students look at the map of South America on page R8. Have students find and name the countries in the Andes region. **(Ecuador, Perú, Bolivia)**
2. Have students locate and name the capital cities of the Andean countries. **(Quito, Lima, La Paz y Sucre)**
3. Have students identify and name oceans, rivers, and lakes in the region. **(Río Amazonas, Océano Pacífico, Lago Titicaca)**

3.1

## Cultures

### Products and Perspectives

**Clothing** The climate in the Andes region is cold at high elevations. Therefore, warm clothes are a necessity. Unlike people in other areas, the people in the Andes region do not have large animals available to use for their skins. The people of the Andes also have no major cotton industry. Since pre-Hispanic times, the people in this region have depended on the wool from the llama and the alpaca to make their clothing. This is because these animals are plentiful in the region and their wool is of excellent quality. Ask students what else they believe the llama and the alpaca may be used for in this region.

2.2

## ¿Sabías que... ?

Students might be interested in knowing the following facts about the Andes region.

- One of the largest herbs in the world, the *Puya raimondii*, grows in the Andes region and can survive at elevations of 13,000 feet (4,000 m). This plant can live for up to 100 years.
- The greatest recorded depth in lake Titicaca is 920 ft. (280 m), near the island of Soto.
- *Acamama* or *Aqha-mama* was the ancient name for the city of *Qosqo* or "Cuzco." *Qosqo* means *navel* in Quechua and was the center of the Inca empire.

## Preguntas 1.2, 3.1

1. **¿Cuántas islas hay en el lago Titicaca? (más de 30)**
2. **¿En qué año se descubrió Machu Picchu? (en 1911)**
3. **¿Cuáles son las comidas principales del altiplano andino? (el maíz y la papa)**
4. **¿Cuál es el volcán activo más alto del mundo? (Cotopaxi)**
5. **¿Qué profundidad tiene el Cañón del Colca? (3.182 metros)**
6. **¿Qué origen tiene la ciudad de La Paz? (aymara)**

## Language Note

Quechua is the language of the Inca. In Peru alone, there are twelve regional Quechua and Aymara dialects spoken in over sixty Andean communities. The three largest groups are the **Jíbaro** in the north, the **Pano** in the central region, and the **Arahuaca** in the south.

## Cultures

### Practices and Perspectives

**Inti Raymi** is celebrated on June 24th each year in Cuzco. This celebration dates back to Inca times when a high priest declared this day **Inti Raymi** *(new year)*. The Inca celebrated the winter solstice on June 24th because Incan astronomers had calculated that the winter solstice began on this date. Today, **Inti Raymi** is still celebrated in Cuzco at the *Sascayhuamán*, or the Incan house of the Sun. The celebrations include live music at the **Plaza de Armas** and dance performances. There are also historical reenactments, which culminate with a speech in Quechua, given by an actor playing the **Sapa Inca** honoring the Sun. Ask students why they think this celebration is still important today. Why is the winter solstice in June in Peru? Is **Inti Raymi** similar to any celebrations where you live? 2.1, 4.2

### Answers

**Siglo XIII–1532:** Cuzco era la capital del Imperio inca.
**1532–1533:** Atahualpa pensaba que los españoles no eran un peligro.
**1569–1821:** el feudalismo en Europa, la esclavitud en las Américas
**1821:** Simón Bolívar era de Venezuela y José de San Martín era de Argentina.
**1879–1883:** Quería tener acceso a los recursos minerales del Atacama.
**1979:** Argentina, Chile, Paraguay, Brasil, Perú, México, Cuba, entre otros
**1998:** parte de la frontera entre Colombia y Venezuela, las islas Malvinas en Argentina, la franja de Gaza, Cachemira, entre otros

# La historia de los Andes—Ecuador, Perú y Bolivia

1500 | 1550 | 1800

1.2 **Siglo XIII–1532**
**Cuzco, la capital del Imperio inca** se estableció en el siglo XIII. El imperio se extendió desde el sur de Colombia hasta el norte de Chile. Atahualpa, el último emperador inca, cayó en manos de los españoles en 1532. **¿Cuál era la capital del Imperio inca?**

**1569–1821** 3.1
**Durante la época colonial** los españoles instituyeron el sistema de *la encomienda*, en el cual los indígenas tenían que trabajar los campos para los españoles. **¿Conoces sistemas similares que se usaban en otras partes del mundo?**

**1821** 1.2
El venezolano **Simón Bolívar** y el argentino **José de San Martín** encabezaron la lucha por la independencia en Sudamérica. En 1822 se encontraron en Guayaquil, Ecuador, y anunciaron la formación de la Gran Colombia, que incluía Ecuador, Venezuela y Colombia. **¿De dónde eran Simón Bolívar y José de San Martín?**

**1532–1533** 3.1
**Francisco Pizarro** marchó a Cajamarca, Perú, con menos de 200 soldados para tender una emboscada a los incas. Después de capturar al emperador Atahualpa, los españoles pidieron 24 toneladas de oro y plata por su rescate. Pizarro traicionó a los incas y mató a Atahualpa en la plaza principal en 1533. **¿Cómo crees que Pizarro consiguió conquistar un imperio con sólo 200 hombres?**

## Core Instruction

### TEACHING LA HISTORIA

1. Have students look at the timeline at the top of the page and at the photos and illustrations. Compare the styles of the drawings on page 272. **(3 min.)**
2. Point out the dates in the colonial period. Remind students that the colonial period lasted for nearly 300 years. Ask volunteers why they think the colonial period lasted so long. **(5 min.)**
3. Have students read captions individually or as a group. Help students with any unfamiliar vocabulary. **(8 min.)**
4. Call on volunteers to read the questions at the end of each caption to the class. **(3 min.)**
5. Have students answer the questions for each caption as a class. Help students as needed. **(10 min.)**

## ¿Sabías que...?

Los incas se comunicaban por medio de mensajeros, o *chasquis*, que corrían unos 2.400 kilómetros por la carretera imperial que se extendía desde Quito, Ecuador, a Cuzco, Perú, en sólo cinco días.



50 | 1900 | 1950 | 2000

### 1879–1883 (1.2)

**La Guerra del Pacífico** entre Chile, Perú y Bolivia empezó en 1879. Se quería tomar posesión de la provincia de Tarapacá, en el terreno del desierto de Atacama, el cual contenía valiosos minerales. En la **Batalla de Iquique,** Perú perdió su nave más moderna, la *Independencia,* cediendo control de la costa a Chile, que ganó la guerra en 1883. **¿Qué quería ganar Chile en la guerra?**

### (3.1) 1979

En 1979, después de muchos años de dictaduras militares y civiles, hubo elecciones en **Ecuador. Jaime Roldós** (1940–1981) fue el primer líder elegido por el voto popular después de la dictadura de **José María Velasco Ibarra.** Se estableció un nuevo gobierno y se implementó una nueva constitución. **Investiga en qué otros países latinoamericanos ha habido dictaduras.**

### (3.1) 1998

**Perú y Ecuador** se levantaron en armas tres veces sobre territorio disputado en sus fronteras (1941, 1981 y 1995). En 1998 el presidente ecuatoriano, Jamil Mahuad, y el presidente peruano, Alberto Fujimori, firmaron **el tratado de paz final,** estableciendo fronteras definitivas entre los dos países por primera vez en medio siglo. **En el mundo actual, ¿dónde hay territorios disputados?**

## Thinking Critically

The Inca built an extensive road network and infrastructure to move information and goods. Incan messengers, called **chasquis,** relayed messages to other **chasquis** stationed at checkpoints along the road. They would pass the message on to the next messenger until it was relayed to the rulers in Cuzco. Because of the mountainous terrain, goods were carried on the backs of llamas and alpacas. Ask students if they believe the Incan road system was a valuable asset to the Incan empire. What advantages did it bring to the Incan people?

## ¿Comprendes?

You can use the following questions to check students' comprehension of the **Geocultura.**

1. **¿Cuál era la extensión del Imperio inca? (desde el sur de Colombia hasta el norte de Chile)**
2. **¿Cuál era el precio del rescate de Atahualpa? (24 toneladas de oro y plata)**
3. **¿Dónde se anunció la formación de la Gran Colombia? (en Guayaquil, Ecuador)**
4. **¿Qué país ganó La Guerra del Pacífico? (Chile)**
5. **¿Quién fue el primer líder elegido por voto popular en Ecuador? (Jaime Roldós)**
6. **¿Quiénes firmaron el tratado de paz final entre Ecuador y Perú? (Jamil Mahuad y Alberto Fujimori)** (1.2, 3.1)

## Interdisciplinary Links

### Las matemáticas

**Math Link** The Inca managed a large empire without a written number system. Instead, they relied on the **quipu,** which means *knot* in Quechua. The **quipu** is a set of multicolored strings with a series of knots tied at different points. The message depended on the color of each string, the number of knots tied into the **quipu,** and the distance between each one. It was used to take the census, to count goods, and for record keeping in the Incan government. Ask students if they believe the **quipu** was an efficient record-keeping tool.

### La historia

**History Link** Simón Bolívar planned a large, unified South American country. His vision was **Gran Colombia,** and it was completed with the liberation of Ecuador in 1822. However, while Bolívar was fighting in wars to liberate Peru and Bolivia from Spanish rule, there were regional struggles for power going on in **Gran Colombia.** Venezuela and Ecuador declared their independence from **Gran Colombia** in 1830. Ask students why they think there were problems with **Gran Colombia.** What differences or similarities do they see in U.S. history?

# *El arte* de los Andes—Ecuador, Perú y Bolivia

ÉPOCA PRECOLOMBINA | 1500 | 1800 | 1850

### 3.1 Época precolombina

**La cultura Chimú** reinó en partes de Perú hasta su conquista por los incas en 1476. Los chimúes trabajaron el oro, la plata y el cobre empleando técnicas muy avanzadas, más tarde adoptadas por los incas. **Investiga cómo usaban los chimúes este cuchillo.**

### 3.1 1534

**La construcción de la Iglesia de San Francisco** en Quito, Ecuador, comenzó en 1534, pocos días después de la fundación de la ciudad. La fachada es una reproducción arquitectónica del palacio de El Escorial de España. **En Internet o en la biblioteca busca una foto de El Escorial y compáralo con la Iglesia de San Francisco.**

### Siglo XVII–XVIII 3.1

Para decorar las iglesias y catedrales los **pintores indígenas** pintaron cuadros en la tradición europea del arte barroco. Desarrollaron un estilo propio añadiendo símbolos, seres e imágenes indígenas. Este cuadro, *Piscis,* de la **Escuela Cuzqueña,** pintado por Diego Quispe Tito, se encuentra en la Catedral de Cuzco. **¿Qué otro cuadro de la Escuela Cuzqueña conoces?**

### 1.2 1888–1956

**José Sabogal** (1888–1956) es uno de los pintores más reconocidos de Perú y uno de los fundadores del **estilo indigenista,** arte que tiene como meta hacer resaltar al indígena. Su obra *La Santusa* (1932) ejemplifica el estilo indigenista. **¿Qué es el arte indigenista?**

## Comparisons

### Comparing and Contrasting

Bolivia has one of the largest indigenous populations in South America. Sixty percent of the population in Bolivia is either of Quechua or Aymara descent. More than fifty percent of the population maintains its traditional dress, values, and beliefs. Indigenous textile production has also changed little over 3,000 years. Ask students to compare the values and traditions that their community has maintained with those maintained by indigenous Bolivian communities.

2.1, 4.2

## Answers

**Época precolombina:** Lo usaban en ceremonias.
**1534:** Answers will vary.
**Siglo XVII–XVIII:** Answers will vary.
**1888–1956:** Es arte que resalta al indígena.
**Siglo XX:** Answers will vary.
**1975:** Answers will vary.
**2000:** las casas, la ropa, entre otros
**2003:** Answers will vary.

## Comparisons

### Comparing and Contrasting

Have students research the cultural origins of **el Día de Todos Santos** in the Andes and compare it to Halloween's origin in the Celtic festival of **Samhain.** (In both cases, Catholic holidays were superimposed upon pre-existing nature celebrations held by native populations.)

2.1, 4.2

## Core Instruction

### TEACHING EL ARTE

1. Have students look at the photograph of the gold knife. Tell students that the Andes region was rich in gold and civilizations predating the Incas were skilled at crafting gold. **(2 min.)**
2. Have students look at the paintings on p. 274. What similarities or differences do they see? **(3 min.)**
3. Have students look at the ceramics on p. 275. Ask students what patterns they see. Tell them that geometrical designs in pottery date to early pre-Hispanic times. **(3 min.)**
4. Have students look at each piece of artwork while you read the captions. **(5 min.)**
5. Read the questions following each caption. Call on volunteers to answer the questions. **(10 min.)**

## ¿Sabías que...?

**Oswaldo Guayasamín siempre se metía en problemas con las profesoras del colegio por las caricaturas que dibujaba.**

Visit Holt Online
**go.hrw.com**
KEYWORD: EXP3 CH7
Photo Tour

1900 — 1950 — 2000

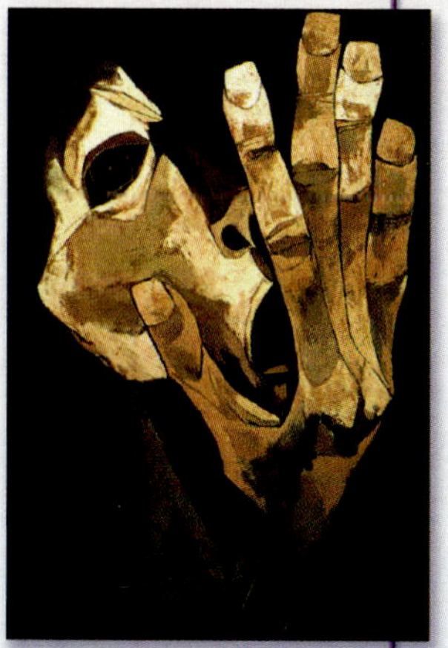

**1.2 Siglo XX**

**Oswaldo Guayasamín** (1919–1999), de Ecuador, es reconocido como uno de los artistas más importantes de Sudamérica. Su colección *La edad de la ira* refleja el dolor, la miseria y la injusticia sufrida por la humanidad en el siglo XX. El cuadro *El Grito* (1983) es muestra de esta etapa artística. **Inventa otro título para esta obra.**

**1.3 1975**

**Miguel Andrango** fundó la Escuela de Tejidos de Tahuantinsuyo en Otavalo, Ecuador, con el propósito de conservar las tradiciones textiles de la región. El artista viaja por todo el mundo dando clases, demostrando su técnica y asistiendo a festivales. **¿Hay un juego, un cuento, una canción o una artesanía que tus padres te hayan enseñado y que tú pienses continuar?**

**2003 1.2**

**La antigua Estación de Desamparados,** en Lima, Perú, se usa hoy como museo de arte. La cerámica *Tinaja con cara 2 niveles* y el tallado en madera *Shipibos en madera* del artista Pablo Yuimachi se exponen en una exhibición especial. Las dos piezas se basan en diseños indígenas. **Al visitar un museo de arte, ¿qué tipo de arte esperas ver?**

**1.2 2000**

**Juan de la Cruz Machicado** es un pintor peruano que se dedicó a pintar su ciudad adoptiva, Cuzco. Estudió arte en la Escuela Regional de Arte «Diego Quispe Tito» en Cuzco. Esta obra, óleo sobre lienzo, se llama *Familia cuzqueña en San Blas.* **En este cuadro, ¿qué te parece típico de la vida en Cuzco?**

## Cultures

### Products and Perspectives

Textile production continues in the Andes today much like it did more than a thousand years ago. Modern weavers use nearly the same techniques as their ancestors did, creating colorful geometric patterns in their textiles. There are regional variations, each using colors and patterns which vary from village to village. Ask students why they think that there are variations in the textiles. How are Andean textiles different from others that students have seen? 2.2, 4.2

### ¿Comprendes?

You can use the following questions to check students' comprehension of the **Geocultura.**

1. **¿En qué año fueron conquistados los chimú por los incas? (1476)**
2. **¿Qué añadieron los pintores indígenas al estilo barroco? (símbolos, figuras de seres e imágenes indígenas)**
3. **¿Quién fue uno de los fundadores del estilo indigenista? (José Sabogal)**
4. **¿Qué refleja la colección *La edad de la ira?* (el dolor, la miseria y la injusticia del siglo XX)**
5. **¿Cuál es el propósito de la Escuela de Tejidos de Tahuantinsuyo? (conservar las tradiciones textiles)** 1.2, 3.1

## Interdisciplinary Links

### El arte

**Art Link** Elements of indigenous religion and culture have influenced art in the Andes region. The mixing of indigenous icons and symbols into the European baroque style created a new style of art unique to this region. Have students compare the indigenous features seen in works from the **Escuela Cuzqueña** and those in some of Diego Rivera's works. How do the works show the culture of each region? 2.2

### La agricultura

**Science Link** Farming is difficult in the Andes region due to the steep, mountainous terrain. The Incas built terraces into the steep hillsides out of stone and filled them with layers of gravel, sand, clay, and topsoil. The terraces prevented erosion and were irrigated by a series of canals. Have students look at a photo of **Machu Picchu** and identify the advantages of building farming terraces at this site. 2.1

## Assess

**Assessment Program**
**Prueba: Geocultura,** pp. 135–136, 155–156

**Online Assessment**
**my.hrw.com**

**Test Generator**

**Assess** **Differentiated Instruction** See the Differentiated Instruction CD-ROM.

Capítulo 7

# Planning Guide

## Mis aspiraciones

| Chapter Section | | Print Resources |
|---|---|---|
| **Geocultura**<br>• **Los Andes Centrales** | pp. 270–275 | Video Guide, pp. 43–44/Lab Book, p. 76 |
| **Vocabulario 1**<br>• Challenges and accomplishments<br>**Gramática 1**<br>• Preterite and imperfect of stative verbs<br>• Grammatical reflexives<br>• **Lo** and **lo que** | pp. 278–283<br>pp. 284–289 | Vocabulario 7.1, 7.2; Bell Work 7.1, 7.2, 7.3, 7.4<br>Cuaderno de vocabulario y gramática, pp. 73–78<br>Cuaderno de actividades, pp. 61–63<br>Activities for Communication, pp. 25–26<br>Grammar Tutor for Students of Spanish, pp. 151–156 |
| **Cultura: Comparaciones**<br>**Cultura: Comunidad** | p. 290<br>p. 291 | Video Guide, pp. 46–47/Lab Book, p. 77 |
| **Vocabulario 2**<br>• Plans for the future<br>**Gramática 2**<br>• Subjunctive after adverbial conjunctions<br>• Subjunctive with future actions<br>• Indicative with habitual or past actions | pp. 292–297<br>pp. 298–303 | Vocabulario 7.3, 7.4; Bell Work 7.5, 7.6, 7.7, 7.8<br>Cuaderno de vocabulario y gramática, pp. 79–84<br>Cuaderno de actividades, pp. 65–67<br>Activities for Communication, pp. 27–28 |
| **Novela en video**<br>**Lectura informativa**<br>• **Los grupos étnicos de Perú**<br>**Leamos**<br>• **Oda al presente**<br>**Escribamos**<br>• **Un escrito que haga pensar** | pp. 304–305<br>pp. 306–307<br>pp. 308–310<br>p. 311 | Cuaderno de actividades, p. 68<br>Reading Strategies and Skills Handbook<br>Interactive Advanced Reader<br>Video Guide, pp. 48–50/Lab Book, pp. 78–79 |
| **Prepárate para el examen**<br>• **Repaso de vocabulario y gramática** | pp. 312–315 | Picture Sequences, Situación, Ch. 7<br>Activities for Communication, pp. 49, 67–68 |
| **Integración**<br>• **Repaso cumulativo** | pp. 316–317 | Fine Art, Ch. 7<br>Cuaderno de actividades, pp. 69–70<br>Reading Strategies and Skills Handbook<br>Interactive Advanced Reader |

For correlations to national standards, see point-of-use references throughout the chapter.

Visit Holt Online
**go.hrw.com**
KEYWORD: EXP3 CH7
Online Edition

## Pacing Suggestions

| | Essential | Recommended | Optional |
|---|---|---|---|
| **Vocabulario 1**<br>• Challenges and accomplishments<br>• **Nota cultural** | ✔ | | |
| **Gramática 1**<br>• Preterite and imperfect of stative verbs<br>• Grammatical reflexives<br>• **Lo** and **lo que**<br>• **Nota cultural** | ✔ | | |
| **Cultura: Comparaciones** | | ✔ | |
| **Cultura: Comunidad** | | | ✔ |
| **Vocabulario 2**<br>• Plans for the future<br>• **Nota cultural** | ✔ | | |
| **Gramática 2**<br>• Subjunctive after adverbial conjunctions<br>• Subjunctive with future actions<br>• Indicative with habitual or past actions<br>• **Nota cultural** | ✔ | | |
| **Novela en video**<br>• Episodio 7: **Clara perspectiva** | | ✔ | |
| **Lectura informativa**<br>• **Los grupos étnicos de Perú** | | | ✔ |
| **Leamos**<br>• **Oda al presente**<br>**Escribamos**<br>• **Un escrito que haga pensar** | | ✔ | |
| **Prepárate para el examen** | | ✔ | |
| **Integración** | | | ✔ |

## Technology Resources

### ¡Exprésate! Online
- Student Edition with multi-media
- SoundBooth recording tool
- Interactive activities with feedback
- Self-tests with feedback
- Cuaderno de actividades (interactive workbook)
- Cuaderno de vocabulario y gramática (interactive workbook)
- Live Ink™ Reading Help
- Holt Online Assessment

### DVD Tutor, Disc 2
- GeoVisión
- GramaVisión
- VideoNovela
- Cultura
- Variedades

### Interactive Tutor
- Interactive practice games
- Writing and recording workshops

### Audio Program
- Textbook listening activities
- Assessment listening activities
- Songs

### One-Stop Planner
- Complete media and print resources
- ExamView® Pro Test Generator
- Holt Calendar Planner

### PuzzlePro
- Customizable word games

## Assessment

| | Assessment Program |
|---|---|
| Geocultura | **Prueba: Geocultura,** pp. 135–136 |
| Vocabulario 1 / Gramática 1 | **Pruebas,** pp. 121–122, 123–124, 125–126 |
| Vocabulario 2 / Gramática 2 | **Pruebas,** pp. 127–128, 129–130, 131–132 |
| Leamos | **Prueba,** p. 133 |
| Escribamos | **Prueba,** p. 134 |
| Prepárate para el examen | **Examen: Capítulo 7,** pp. 293–300 |
| | **Examen oral: Capítulo 7,** p. 304 |
| | **Alternative Assessment,** pp. 379, 391, 403 |

### Online Assessment
**my.hrw.com**

### Test Generator
**ExamView® Pro Test Generator**

Planning Guide

# Projects

## Mis aspiraciones

### La feria del empleo

In this project, students explore the careers they would like to pursue by preparing a presentation and display for a job fair. This is an individual project, although students with similar aspirations might coordinate their research efforts. They will need to emphasize the reasons careers in their particular field are interesting and rewarding. Encourage them to tell how knowledge of Spanish might be useful in their career.

**SUGGESTED SEQUENCE**

1. Students choose a career or field that interests them.
2. They gather as much information as possible about their career or field on the Internet, in the library, or from their guidance counselor. Students contact a person in a Spanish-speaking culture who is in their chosen field and ask questions about it.
3. Students write a report in which they explain the nature of the work, why that career or field interests them, and the goals they would pursue through their work.
4. They clip appropriate pictures from magazines or create their own artwork to assemble an appealing visual presentation that will interest their classmates in pursuing a career in that field.
5. Students post their displays and make their oral presentations to the class. 1.1, 1.3

### Grading the projects

Suggested point distribution (100 points total)

| | |
|---|---|
| Language use | 40 |
| Oral presentation | 30 |
| Originality | 20 |
| Appearance | 10 |

### Partner Class Project

Students should research information about a famous Hispanic person in the United States. They might find interviews from magazines or newspapers on the Internet. Have them find out how the person they chose achieved his or her goals and overcame any obstacles. What can they learn from this person? Have them prepare a short presentation for the class. 1.3

### Game Bank

For game ideas, see pages T64–T67.

### e-community

**e-mail forum:**

Post the following question on the classroom e-mail forum:

**¿Cuáles son tus aspiraciones?**

All students will contribute to the list and then share the items. 1.3

# Traditions

## Mis aspiraciones

### La agricultura

Due to the extreme diversity of the landscape, contemporary Andean farmers use innovative agricultural techniques that were developed by pre-conquest Incan farmers. In the narrow coastal regions, fruits, tomatoes, and peanuts are grown. On steep mountain terraces, corn, beans, and a variety of squashes are raised. On the highest plots, potatoes and **quínoa** (sometimes called "mother grain" in English), which is high in protein, are grown. Unique irrigation and food preservation techniques that were developed by pre-conquest Incan farmers are still in use today. The Incas were the first to freeze-dry food: they cut up potatoes, dried them in the sun, left them out at night to freeze, then stomped out the moisture before storage—a process still used today. Have students find South American recipes that contain some of these native foods and report to the class. 2.1, 3.1

### Receta

**Locro** is a potato soup typical of Andean Ecuador. Potatoes originated in the Andes, and come in an astonishing variety of sizes, shapes, and colors, including red, gold, blue, and black. This recipe uses **achiote** (small red seeds) adding color and flavor, but paprika can be used if **achiote** is unavailable. **Locro** is served with a slice of avocado. You might have students make the following recipe as a class project or for extra credit.

#### Locro

**para 4 personas**

8 papas medianas (de piel roja), cortadas en cuadros

1 cebolla pequeña, picada

1/3 de taza de queso *cheddar* o *muenster,* rallado

1/4 taza de leche

1 cucharada de aceite

1 cucharadita de achiote, o pimentón dulce

sal y pimienta al gusto

una pizca de ajo en polvo

Caliente el aceite, agregue el achiote y cocine unos segundos sin que hierva. Saque los achiotes y tírelos. El aceite habrá quedado colorado. Fría la cebolla en el aceite hasta que esté transparente, agregue las papas y añada agua hasta cubrirlas. Añada la sal, la pimienta y el ajo en polvo. Luego cocínelo, moviéndolo de vez en cuando, hasta que las papas estén cocidas y se vayan deshaciendo. Agregue el queso y la leche. Hierva unos minutos y sírvalo. 2.2, 3.1

# Listening Activity Scripts

## Mis aspiraciones



### Vocabulario en acción 1

**1 p. 280, CD 7, Track 1**

1. Mi familia y yo vinimos a este país el año pasado. Todavía es difícil expresarme en inglés, y por eso estoy frustrada a veces.
2. Soy la primera persona de mi familia que asiste a la universidad. Mis padres hicieron muchos sacrificios para poder pagar los estudios, pero por fin lo lograron.
3. Cuando llegué aquí hice un gran esfuerzo y encontré trabajo. Ahora puedo hacer mi aporte a la sociedad y también ayudar a mi familia.
4. Todos los días enfrento muchos obstáculos en este país. Algunas personas en el colegio discriminan a la gente que no habla inglés y tienen muchos prejuicios.
5. Todos los grupos étnicos tienen su propio modo de ser y me cuesta trabajo asimilar las costumbres de los norteamericanos.
6. Tuve que hacer un gran esfuerzo, pero por fin siento que pertenezco a este país.

**Answers to Activity 1**

1. a 3. b 5. a
2. b 4. a 6. b

### Gramática en acción 1

**10 p. 284, CD 7, Track 2**

1. Cuando el profesor nos puso el examen sorpresa ese día, me sentía muy mal. Por eso saqué mala nota.
2. Yo tenía mucho sueño cuando mi hermano me pidió ayuda, y por eso le dije que no. Es que no había dormido lo suficiente la noche anterior.
3. Cuando la mujer no entendió lo que yo trataba de decirle, tuve ganas de llorar. Tengo que aprender a expresarme mejor en inglés.
4. Mi amigo y yo caminábamos por el centro y cuando olimos el olor del pan horneado quisimos entrar a la panadería.
5. Mis amigos y yo estábamos muy entusiasmados cuando fuimos a hablar con el profesor sobre nuestra idea para un club de intercambio.
6. El director estuvo decepcionado largo rato cuando la profesora le dijo que ningún estudiante había hecho la tarea hoy.

**Answers to Activity 10**

1. b 2. a 3. b 4. a 5. a 6. b

**14 p. 286, CD 7, Track 3**

1. La mayoría de las personas en este país se casan a los quince años.
2. Normalmente los padres se molestan cuando los hijos sacan malas notas.
3. La gente nunca se acostumbra a una nueva casa o apartamento.
4. Si alguien sabe expresarse bien en otro idioma, entonces podrá comunicarse fácilmente con la gente que habla ese idioma.
5. Algunos estudiantes se quedan en el colegio después de las clases para participar en actividades como deportes.
6. Nadie se muda de casa antes de los cuarenta años.

**Answers to Activity 14**

1. falsa 3. falsa 5. cierta
2. cierta 4. cierta 6. falsa

**20 p. 289, CD 7, Track 4**

ALBERTO Fátima, ¿qué es lo que te costó más trabajo cuando llegaste a este país?

FÁTIMA Bueno, para mí fue mantener las costumbres de nuestra cultura.

ALBERTO ¿De veras? Para mí eso fue lo más fácil. No quise adaptarme al modo de ser de la gente aquí.

FÁTIMA Pero Alberto, ¡eso es lo más importante! Asimilé el nuevo estilo de vida enseguida porque sentí que alguna gente discrimina a los que no encajan en el grupo. No entiendo la discriminación.

ALBERTO No la entiendo tampoco. Pero es terrible perder tus tradiciones. Debes estar orgullosa de tu herencia cultural. Me molesta mucho cuando la gente olvida sus raíces.

FÁTIMA Bueno, Alberto, tenemos puntos de vista diferentes. Pero lo que nunca olvidaré es todo lo que han hecho mis papás por mí.

ALBERTO Por lo menos estamos de acuerdo en algo. También les estoy muy agradecido a mis papás.

**Answers to Activity 20**

1. Fátima 3. ambos 5. ambos
2. Fátima 4. Alberto 6. ambos

### Vocabulario en acción 2

**24 p. 294, CD 7, Track 8**

1. Sueño con tomar clases de kárate. Sé que algún día llegaré a ser muy buena.
2. Tengo que esforzarme mucho si quiero pasar el examen de la semana que viene. Mi meta es sacar la nota más alta de la clase.

For Student Response Forms, see the *Lab Book*, pp. 37–40.

3. Quiero llegar a ser profesora en cuanto termine los estudios universitarios. Sé que tengo que luchar por esa meta, y no me daré por vencida.
4. Quiero registrarme para votar. Es una oportunidad maravillosa de aportar algo a la comunidad.

**Answers to Activity 24**

1. D  2. B  3. A  4. C

## Gramática en acción 2

### 38 p. 301, CD 7, Track 9

LEO Oye, Pati, debemos hacer una fiesta e invitar a toda la clase.

PATI Sería genial. Pero tenemos que hacerla después de que nos graduemos.

LEO Pero Pati, mucha gente normalmente sale de viaje en cuanto terminan las clases.

PATI Pues, yo no puedo hacer una fiesta en mi casa tan pronto.

LEO Está bien. Mis papás se van de viaje antes de que empecemos los exámenes y me dijeron que podíamos hacerla en mi casa.

PATI ¡Perfecto! Mañana les mandaré un correo electrónico a todos en cuanto vuelva a casa.

LEO De acuerdo. No haré la lista de compras hasta que sepamos cuántas personas vendrán.

**Answers to Activity 38**

1. falsa; Pati quiere hacer la fiesta después de que se gradúen.
2. cierta
3. falsa; Los papás de Leo se van de vacaciones antes de que empiecen los exámenes
4. falsa; Pati va a mandar un correo electrónico en cuanto vuelva a casa.
5. cierta

### 41 p. 302, CD 7, Track 10

1. Me llamo Mariana y soy de Perú. Un año después de que llegué a este país, aprendí a expresarme bien en inglés.
2. Mi amigo se llama Pedro. En cuanto se establezca en su nueva ciudad, va a buscar trabajo.
3. Mi abuelo se llama José. Él enfrentó muchos obstáculos cuando emigró de su país, pero no se dio por vencido hasta que alcanzó sus metas.
4. Yo soy Teresa. Todos los días voy a la biblioteca a estudiar antes de ir a trabajar.
5. Me llamo Lisa y quiero ser actriz. Voy a trabajar muy duro hasta que llegue a ser famosa.
6. Mi mamá se llama Sara. Tan pronto como ella tomó la iniciativa, encontró trabajo como profesora.

**Answers to Activity 41**

1. del pasado
2. del futuro
3. del pasado
4. habitual
5. del futuro
6. del pasado

## Prepárate para el examen capítulo 7

### 1 p. 312, CD 7 Track 12

1. Me acuerdo del día en que logré graduarme. ¡Me sentí tan orgullosa cuando me dieron el diploma!
2. Yo soy de ascendencia japonesa. En casa, tratamos de mantener las costumbres de nuestra cultura. Lo que más me gusta es la comida japonesa.
3. Tengo muchas aspiraciones. Voy a esforzarme mucho hasta que se realicen mis sueños. Quiero llegar a ser médico cuando sea mayor.
4. En el colegio, jugaba al boliche con el equipo. Mi éxito en el boliche se debe a que lo practico todos los días. Este año tuve buena suerte en el campeonato.

**Answers to Activity 1**

1. C  2. A  3. D  4. B

### 6 p. 313, CD 7, Track 13

For script and answers, see *Teacher's Edition*, p. 313.

## Integración capítulos 1–7

### 1 p. 316, CD 7 Track 14

1. Supe de la boda ayer porque tuve una carta de mi hermanastra.
2. Tengo fama de ser perezosa pero no es cierto. Mis buenas notas se deben a las horas que paso estudiando.
3. Es cierto que veo muchas telenovelas. ¡Son geniales!
4. Me la paso viendo exposiciones de arte. La escultura clásica me parece maravillosa.

**Answers to Activity 1**

1. B  2. D  3. A  4. C

# 50-Minute Lesson Plans

# Mis aspiraciones

For more customized Lesson Plans, see the *Lesson Planner with Differentiated Instruction.*



## Day 1

### Objective
*Talking about challenges*

### Core Instruction
**Chapter Opener,** pp. 276–277 **10 min.**
- See Chapter Objectives and Using the Photo, p. 276.

**Vocabulario en acción 1,** pp. 278–283
- Have students do Bell Work, p. 278.
- See Teaching **Vocabulario,** p. 278. **10 min.**
- See Teaching **¡Exprésate!,** p. 278. **5 min.**
- Play Audio CD 7, Tr. 1 for Activity 1, p. 280. **5 min.**
- Have students do Activities 2–5, pp. 280–281. **20 min.**

### Optional Resources
- Slower Pace Learners, p. 279 ◆
- Multiple Intelligences, p. 279
- **Comunicación,** p. 281
- Heritage Speakers, p. 281 ■
- Advanced Learners, p. 281 ▲
- Multiple Intelligences, p. 281

### Homework Suggestions
Cuaderno de vocabulario y gramática, pp. 73–75

❀ 1.2, 3.2

## Day 2

### Objective
*Talking about accomplishments*

### Core Instruction
**Vocabulario en acción 1,** pp. 278–283
- Have students do Activity 6, p. 281. **10 min.**
- See Teaching **¡Exprésate!,** p. 282. **10 min.**
- Have students do Activities 7–9, p. 283. **30 min.**

### Optional Resources
- Circumlocution, p. 283
- **Comunicación,** p. 283
- Slower Pace Learners, p. 283 ◆
- Special Learning Needs, p. 283 ●

### Homework Suggestions
Study for **Prueba: Vocabulario 1**

❀ 1.1, 1.2, 1.3

## Day 3

### Objective
*Verbs that change meaning in preterite and imperfect*

### Core Instruction
- Review **Vocabulario en acción 1,** pp. 278–283. **5 min.**
- Give **Prueba: Vocabulario 1. 20 min.**

**Gramática en acción 1,** pp. 284–289
- See Teaching **Gramática,** p. 284. **10 min.**
- Play Audio CD 7, Tr. 2 for Activity 10, p. 284. **5 min.**
- Have students do Activities 11–13, p. 285. **15 min.**

### Optional Resources
- Teacher to Teacher, p. 285
- Slower Pace Learners, p. 285 ◆
- Special Learning Needs, p. 285 ●

### Homework Suggestions
Cuaderno de vocabulario y gramática, pp. 76–78
Cuaderno de actividades, pp. 61–63

❀ 1.1, 1.2

## Day 4

### Objective
*Grammatical reflexives*

### Core Instruction
**Gramática en acción 1,** p. 284–289
- See Teaching **Gramática,** p. 286. **10 min.**
- Play Audio CD 7, Tr. 3 for Activity 14, p. 286. **5 min.**
- Have students do Activities 15–18, pp. 286–287. **35 min.**

### Optional Resources
- **Comunicación,** p. 287
- Heritage Speakers, p. 287 ■
- Advanced Learners, p. 287 ▲
- Special Learning Needs, p. 287 ●

### Homework Suggestions
Cuaderno de vocabulario y gramática, pp. 76–78
Cuaderno de actividades, pp. 61–63

❀ 1.1, 1.2

## Day 5

### Objective
***Lo** and **lo que***

### Core Instruction
**Gramática en acción 1,** pp. 284–289
- See Teaching **Gramática,** p. 288. **10 min.**
- Have students do Activity 19, p. 288. **5 min.**
- Play Audio CD 7, Tr. 4 for Activity 20, p. 289. **10 min.**
- Have students do Activities 21–23, p. 289. **25 min.**

### Optional Resources
- **Comunicación,** p. 289
- Advanced Learners, p. 289 ▲
- Special Learning Needs, p. 289 ●

### Homework Suggestions
Study for **Prueba: Gramática 1**
Cuaderno de vocabulario y gramática, pp. 76–78
Cuaderno de actividades, pp. 61–63

❀ 1.1, 1.2, 1.3

## Day 6

### Objective
*Interviews from around the Spanish-speaking world*

### Core Instruction
**Gramática en acción 1,** pp. 284–289
- Review **Gramática en acción 1,** pp. 284–289. **5 min.**
- Give **Prueba: Gramática 1. 20 min.**

**Cultura,** pp. 290–291
- See Teaching **Cultura,** p. 290. **10 min.**
- Play Audio CD 7, Tr. 5–7, or show **VideoCultura. 15 min.**

### Optional Resources
- Advanced Learners, p. 291 ▲
- Multiple Intelligences, p. 291

### Homework Suggestions
Cuaderno de actividades, p. 64
Online Practice (**go.hrw.com,** Keyword: EXP3 CH7)

❀ 1.2, 1.3, 3.1, 4.2, 5.1

## Day 7

### Objective
*Talking about future plans*

### Core Instruction
**Vocabulario en acción 2,** pp. 292–297
- See Teaching **Vocabulario,** p. 292. **15 min.**
- See Teaching **¡Exprésate!,** p. 292. **10 min.**
- Play Audio CD 7, Tr. 8 for Activity 24, p. 294. **5 min.**
- Have students do Activities 25–29, pp. 294–295. **20 min.**

### Optional Resources
- Slower Pace Learners, p. 293 ◆
- Multiple Intelligences, p. 293
- **Comunicación,** p. 295
- Advanced Learners, p. 295 ▲
- Special Learning Needs, p. 295 ●

### Homework Suggestions
Cuaderno de vocabulario y gramática, pp. 79–81

❀ 1.1, 1.2

## Day 8

### Objective
*Expressing cause and effect*

### Core Instruction
**Vocabulario en acción 2,** pp. 292–297
- See Teaching **¡Exprésate!,** p. 296. **10 min.**
- Have students do Activities 30–32, p. 297. **30 min.**
- Review **Vocabulario en acción 2,** pp. 292–297. **10 min.**

### Optional Resources
- **Comunicación,** p. 297
- Slower Pace Learners, p. 297 ◆
- Multiple Intelligences, p. 297

### Homework Suggestions
Study for **Prueba: Vocabulario 2**
Cuaderno de vocabulario y gramática, pp. 79–81

❀ 1.1, 1.2, 1.3

- For information on the **Geocultura** pages, see the *Lesson Planner with Differentiated Instruction.*
- For more detailed information on benchmarks, see point-of-use correlations on each page.
- To edit and create your own lesson plans, see the **One-Stop** Planner® CD-ROM

**KEY**
- ▲ Advanced Learners
- ◆ Slower Pace Learners
- ● Special Learning Needs
- ■ Heritage Speakers

## Day 9

### Objective
*Subjunctive after adverbial conjunctions*

### Core Instruction
**Vocabulario en acción 2,** pp. 292–297
- Give **Prueba: Vocabulario 2.** **20 min**

**Gramática en acción 2,** pp. 298–303
- See Teaching **Gramática,** p. 298. **10 min.**
- Have students do Activities 33–36, pp. 298–299. **20 min.**

### Optional Resources
- **Comunicación,** p. 299
- Slower Pace Learners, p. 299 ◆
- Special Learning Needs, p. 299 ●

### Homework Suggestions
Cuaderno de vocabulario y gramática, pp. 82–84
Cuaderno de actividades, pp. 65–67

1.1, 1.2

## Day 10

### Objective
*Subjunctive with future actions*

### Core Instruction
**Gramática en acción 2,** pp. 298–303
- See Teaching **Gramática,** p. 300. **10 min.**
- Have students do Activity 37, p. 300. **5 min.**
- Play Audio CD 7, Tr. 9 for Activity 38, p. 301. **5 min.**
- Have students do Activities 39–40, p. 301. **20 min.**
- See Teaching **Gramática,** p. 302. **10 min.**

### Optional Resources
- **Comunicación,** p. 301
- Advanced Learners, p. 301 ▲
- Multiple Intelligences, p. 301

### Homework Suggestions
Cuaderno de vocabulario y gramática, pp. 82–84
Cuaderno de actividades, pp. 65–67

1.1, 1.2

## Day 11

### Objective
*Indicative with habitual or past actions*

### Core Instruction
**Gramática en acción 2,** pp. 298–303
- Play Audio CD 7, Tr. 10 for Activity 41, p. 302. **10 min.**
- Have students do Activities 42–44, pp. 302–303. **30 min.**
- Review **Gramática en acción 2,** pp. 298–303. **10 min.**

### Optional Resources
- **Comunicación,** p. 303
- Slower Pace Learners, p. 303 ◆
- Special Learning Needs, p. 303 ●

### Homework Suggestions
Study for **Prueba: Gramática 2**
Cuaderno de vocabulario y gramática, pp. 82–84
Cuaderno de actividades, pp. 65–67

1.1, 1.2

## Day 12

### Objective
*Developing listening and reading skills*

### Core Instruction
**Gramática en acción 2,** pp. 298–303
- Give **Prueba: Gramática 2.** **20 min.**

**Novela en video,** pp. 304–305
- Show **VideoNovela.** See Teaching **Novela en video,** p. 304. **30 min.**

### Optional Resources
- **Comunicación,** p. 305

**Assessment Program:**
- Skills Quiz: **Vocabulario y gramática 2**

### Homework Suggestions
Cuaderno de vocabulario y gramática, pp. 82–84

1.2, 1.3

## Day 13

### Objective
*Developing reading and writing skills*

### Core Instruction
**Lectura informativa,** pp. 306–307
- See Teaching **Lectura informativa,** p. 306. **20 min.**

**Leamos y escribamos,** pp. 308–311
- See Teaching **Leamos,** p. 308. **30 min.**

### Optional Resources
- Advanced Learners, p. 307 ▲
- Multiple Intelligences, p. 307
- Special Learning Needs, p. 309 ●
- Multiple Intelligences, p. 309

### Homework Suggestions
Cuaderno de actividades, p. 68

1.2, 1.3, 3.1

## Day 14

### Objective
*Developing reading and writing skills*

### Core Instruction
**Leamos y escribamos,** pp. 308–311
- See Teaching **Escribamos,** p. 310. **30 min.**

**Prepárate para el examen,** pp. 312–315
- Play Audio CD 7, Tr. 12 for Activity 1, p. 312. **5 min.**
- Have students do Activities 2–5, pp. 312–313. **15 min.**

### Optional Resources
- Slower Pace Learners, p. 311 ◆
- Multiple Intelligences, p. 311

### Homework Suggestions
**Taller del escritor,** p. 311

1.2

## Day 15

### Objective
*Chapter review*

### Core Instruction
**Prepárate para el examen,** pp. 312–315
- Play Audio CD 7, Tr. 13 for Activity 6, p. 313. **5 min.**
- Have students do Activity 7, p. 313. **5 min.**

**Integración,** pp. 316–317
- Play Audio CD 7, Tr. 14 for Activity 1, p. 316. **5 min.**
- Have students do Activities 2–6, pp. 316–317. **35 min.**

### Optional Resources
- Play Pre-AP Audio CD 2, Tr. 5, for Pre-AP Practice, p. 313
- Game, p. 315
- Fine Art Connection, p. 317

### Homework Suggestions
Study for Chapter Test

1.1, 1.2, 1.3, 3.1

## Day 16/Test

### Core Instruction
**Chapter Test** **50 min.**

### Optional Resources
**Assessment Program**
- Alternative Assessment
- **Prueba: Lectura**
- **Prueba: Escritura**
- Test Generator

### Homework Suggestions
Cuaderno de actividades, pp. 69–70

# Indiana
## The Hoosier State

Suspension bridge, Columbus

State capitol, Indianapolis

Indiana covered bridge

## Chapter 7

The following chart presents *¡Exprésate!* Chapter 7 correlations to the Indiana Academic Standards for World Languages, Grade 11. The correlations here are to the *Student Edition* (SE) and *Teacher's Edition* (TE) only. For additional teaching resources, see pages 275A-275B

| INDIANA ACADEMIC STANDARDS | | | CHAPTER 7 SE/TE CORRELATIONS |
|---|---|---|---|
| **Standard 1 COMMUNICATION:** | | | |
| **Write and speak in a language other than English** | 11.1.1 | Initiate, sustain, and close conversations in limited yet varied situations. | SE: 283, 297, 299, 317<br>TE: 278, 282, 292, 296 |
| | 11.1.2 | Exchange detailed information and opinions orally on a variety of topics. | SE: 282, 296, 299, 317<br>TE: 282, 290, 296, 299, 316 |
| | 11.1.3 | Exchange detailed information and opinions in written form on a variety of topics. | SE: 311<br>TE: 287, 289, 295, 301 |
| | 11.1.5 | Recognize and use situation-appropriate non-verbal communication. | SE: 303<br>TE: 304, 305 |
| | 11.1.6 | Use speaking and listening strategies to facilitate communication. | SE: 285, 287, 289<br>TE: 298 |
| **Standard 2 COMMUNICATION:** | | | |
| **Interpret information in a language other than English**<br>*Learners interpret written and spoken language on a variety of topics. (Interpretive)* | 11.2.1 | Respond to everyday requests, commands, and directions. | TE: 279, 293 |
| | 11.2.2 | Demonstrate comprehension of both authentic and non-authentic written and spoken language through developmentally appropriate tasks. | SE: 305, 307<br>TE: 271, 273, 275, 290, 304, 308 |
| | 11.2.3 | Make educated guesses about meaning in unfamiliar written and spoken contexts. | SE: 304, 308<br>TE: 304, 308 |
| **Standard 3 COMMUNICATION:** | | | |
| **Present information in a language other than English**<br>*Learners present to an audience of listeners or readers on a variety of topics. (Presentational)* | 11.3.2 | Produce and present creative material on a variety of topics. | TE: 275C, 287, 307, 316 |
| | 11.3.3 | Read passages aloud to demonstrate improving intonation and pronunciation. | TE: 290 |
| | 11.3.4 | Compose cohesive written information using appropriate formats and more varied vocabulary and structures. | SE: 311<br>TE: 275C, 311-312 |
| **Standard 4 CULTURES:** | | | |
| **Develop awareness of other cultures.**<br>*Learners examine, experience, and reflect on the relationships among the practices, products, and perspectives of the cultures studied.* | 11.4.1 | Analyze and reflect on cultural practices of the target cultures. | SE: 274, 291<br>TE: 271, 273, 275, 290, 306, 316 |
| | 11.4.2 | Describe products, perspectives, and symbols of the target cultures. | SE: 291, 307<br>TE: 271, 273, 275, 290, 306, 316 |
| | 11.4.3 | Discuss factors that influence practices, products, and perspectives. | SE: 291, 307<br>TE: 271, 273, 275, 290, 306, 316 |
| | 11.4.4 | Recognize the interrelations among the practices, products, and perspectives of the target cultures. | SE: 291, 307<br>TE: 271, 273, 275, 306, 316 |

| | | | |
|---|---|---|---|
| | **11.4.5** | Explain contributions from other cultures. | **SE:** 307<br>**TE:** 271, 273, 275, 306, 316 |
| | **11.4.6** | Identify significant events unique to the target cultures. | **SE:** 272, 273<br>**TE:** 275 |
| **Standard 5 CONNECTIONS:** | | | |
| **Make connections to other content areas** *Learners use the target language to expand their knowledge of and make connections among multiple content areas.* | **11.5.1** | Make connections with other content areas through resources intended for native speakers. | **TE:** 271, 316 |
| | **11.5.2** | Design and share activities and materials that integrate the target language and cultures with concepts and skills from other content areas. | **TE:** 275C, 315 |
| **Standard 6 CONNECTIONS:** | | | |
| **Access and connect information through various media** *Learners strengthen language proficiency and cultural knowledge by using current digital media and authentic resources.* | **11.6.1** | Use digital media and culturally authentic resources to build vocabulary and improve receptive and productive language skills. | **SE:** 270, 280, 286, 302, 303<br>**TE:** 227E, 227F |
| | **11.6.2** | Use digital media and culturally authentic resources to study target cultures. | **SE:** 290, 304<br>**TE:** 271 |
| | **11.6.3** | Identify and evaluate resources intended for native speakers. | **SE:** 290, 304, 310<br>**TE:** 271, 309 |
| **Standard 7 COMPARISONS:** | | | |
| **Investigate the nature of language and culture** *Learners understand the nature of language and culture through comparisons of the languages and cultures studied and their own.* | **11.7.1** | Use elements of word formation to expand vocabulary and derive meaning. | **SE:** 286, 303<br>**TE:** 284, 298, 312 |
| | **11.7.2** | Recognize and use a variety of language structures. | **SE:** 298-303, 311, 317<br>**TE:** 284-289, 312-315 |
| | **11.7.3** | Compare and use idiomatic, colloquial, and proverbial expressions in the target language. | **SE:** 283, 317 |
| | **11.7.5** | Compare systems of other cultures and the learner's own culture. | **SE:** 272, 291<br>**TE:** 275, 290, 306, 316 |
| | **11.7.6** | Compare and contrast elements that shape cultural identity in the learner's heritage and in the target cultures. | **SE:** 272, 291<br>**TE:** 275, 290, 306 |
| **Standard 8 COMMUNITIES:** | | | |
| **Become an active global citizen by experiencing languages and cultures in multiple settings** *Learners use their knowledge of the target language and cultures both within and beyond the school setting for personal enrichment and civic engagement.* | **11.8.1** | Share experiences from the world language classroom with others. | **TE:** 316 |
| | **11.8.2** | Investigate and share with others the influences of the target language and cultures on the community. | **TE:** 316 |
| | **11.8.3** | Show evidence of becoming a life-long learner by using the target language and cultural knowledge for personal enrichment. | **SE:** 281<br>**TE:** 275D, 281, 283 |

# Capítulo 7

# Mis aspiraciones

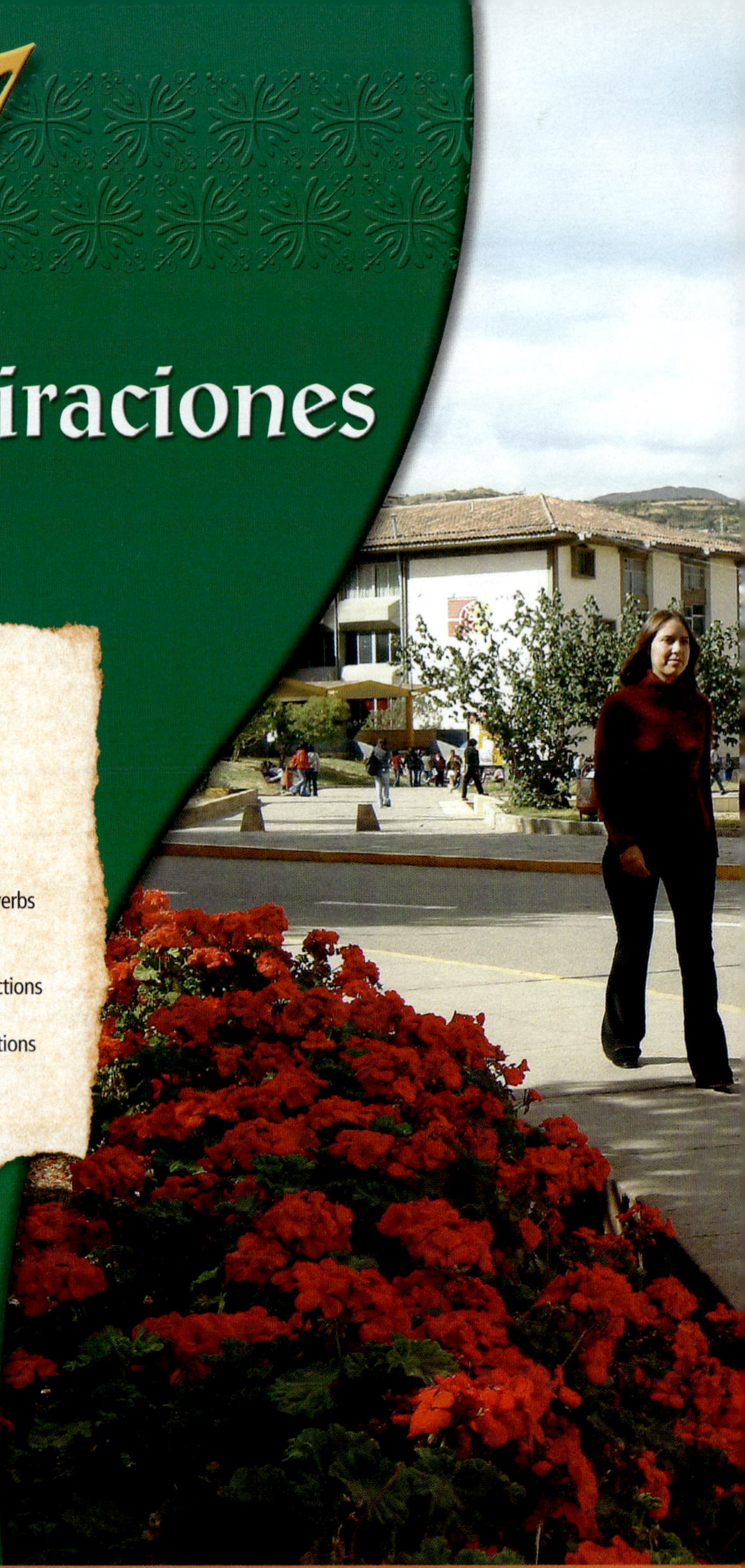

**OBJETIVOS**

**In this chapter you will learn to**

- talk about challenges
- talk about accomplishments
- talk about future plans
- express cause and effect

**And you will use**

- preterite and imperfect of stative verbs
- grammatical reflexives
- **lo** and **lo que**
- subjunctive after adverbial conjunctions
- subjunctive with future actions
- indicative with habitual or past actions

**¿Qué ves en la foto?**

- **¿Quiénes son estas personas?**
- **¿Cómo crees que se siente el estudiante en el centro? ¿Por qué?**
- **¿Te gustaría asistir a una universidad en otro país? ¿Por qué?**

## Meeting the National Standards

### Communication
Comunicación, pp. 281, 283, 285, 287, 289, 295, 297, 299, 301, 303, 305
Game, p. 315
Situación, p. 317

### Cultures
Products and Perspectives, pp. 271, 275, 282, 289
Practices and Perspectives, pp. 272, 291, 297, 307
El arte, p. 275
La agricultura, pp. 275, 275D
Receta, p. 275D
Culture Project, p. 316

### Connections
Atlas Interactivo Mundial, pp. 271, 291
Nota cultural, pp. 286, 289, 297, 302
Social Studies Link, p. 295
Economics Link, p. 305

### Comparisons
Comparing and Contrasting, p. 274
Comparaciones, p. 290
Language to Language, pp. 306, 314
Culture Project, p. 316

### Communities
Comunidad, p. 291
Community Link, p. 310
Teacher to Teacher, p. 316

## Using the Photo

Tell students that the Universidad Nacional San Antonio Abad del Cusco was founded in 1692 by Pope Inocencio XII and authorized to grant the degrees of **Bachiller** (Associate's degree), **Licenciado** (Bachelor's degree), **Maestro** (Master's degree) y **Doctorado** (Doctoral degree). Today over 14,000 students are enrolled at the University. Have students look at the official website for the Universidad Nacional San Antonio to find out how the university system works in Peru. 3.2

| Suggested pacing: | Traditional Schedule | Block Schedule |
|---|---|---|
| Vocabulario 1/Gramática 1 | 5 1/2 days | 2 1/2 blocks |
| Cultura | 1/2 day | 1/2 block |
| Vocabulario 2/Gramática 2 | 5 1/2 days | 2 1/2 blocks |
| Novela | 1/2 day | 1/2 block |
| Lectura informativa | 1/2 day | 1/2 block |
| Leamos y escribamos | 1 day | 1/2 block |
| Prepárate para el examen | 1 day | 1/4 block |
| Chapter Test | 1 day | 1/2 block |
| Integración | 1/2 day | 1/4 block |

Un graduado de la Universidad Nacional San Antonio Abad del Cusco, Perú

# Chapter Opener

## Holt Grammar Logic

### CHAPTER 7

- *To talk about challenges, and to talk about accomplishments,* students will need to review preterite and imperfect stative verbs (**estar, ser,** and **tener**). They will also need to learn about grammatical reflexives (such as **quedarse** or **enojarse**) and to use the expressions **lo** + *adjective* and **lo que** + *verb.*
- *To talk about future plans, and to express cause and effect,* students must use subjunctive after adverbial conjunctions, including those that express future time. They will also need to use the indicative with habitual or past actions.
- In this chapter, students learn about the use of the imperfect to express a state of being and the preterite for the beginning or ending of a state.

## Más vocabulario

Students may want to use some of these words to discuss the photo.

| | |
|---|---|
| **el birrete** | *cap* |
| **la toga** | *gown* |
| **(en artes/en ciencias)** | *(of arts/of sciences)* |
| **la ceremonia** | *ceremony* |

## LISTENING PRACTICE — Language Lab and Classroom Activities

**Vocabulario**
Activity 1, p. 280, CD 7, Tr. 1
Activity 24, p. 294, CD 7, Tr. 8

**Gramática**
Activity 10, p. 284, CD 7, Tr. 2
Activity 14, p. 286, CD 7, Tr. 3
Activity 20, p. 289, CD 7, Tr. 4
Activity 38, p. 301, CD 7, Tr. 9
Activity 41, p. 302, CD 7, Tr. 10

**Cultura**
**Comparaciones**, pp. 290–291, CD 7, Tr. 5–7

**Novela**
**Novela en video**, Escuchemos, p. 304

**Lectura informativa**
pp. 306–307, CD 7, Tr. 11

**Leamos**
Escuchemos, p. 308

**Repaso**
Activity 1, p. 312, CD 7, Tr. 12
Activity 6, p. 313, CD 7, Tr. 13
**Variedades,** Lab Book, p. 77

**Integración**
Activity 1, p. 316, CD 7, Tr. 14

**Assessment Program**
CD 7, Tr. 15–18

**Additional Listening**
Pre-AP CD 2, Tr. 5–8

**Resources**

**Planning:**

Lesson Planner, pp. 97–98, 258–259

One-Stop Planner

**Presentation:**

Teaching Transparencies
**Vocabulario** 7.1, 7.2

**Practice:**

Cuaderno de vocabulario y gramática, pp. 73–75

Activities for Communication, pp. 25–26

Teaching Transparencies
Bell Work 7.1
**Vocabulario y gramática** answers, pp. 73–75

Interactive Tutor, Disc 2

**Bell Work**

Use Bell Work 7.1 in the *Teaching Transparencies*, or write this activity on the board.

**Completa las oraciones con la forma correcta de los verbos entre paréntesis.**

1. El profesor anunció que nosotros (ir) a tener un examen hoy.
2. Me frustra que él (dar) tantos exámenes.
3. Es imposible que él ya (terminar) el examen.
4. Creo que yo (poder) aprobarlo.
5. La profesora dijo que el examen (ser) largo y difícil.

1.2

**Objetivos**
- Talking about challenges
- Talking about accomplishments

# Vocabulario en acción 1

## En Perú
## Los desafíos

En Perú existen muchos **grupos étnicos.** Cada grupo tiene su propio **modo de ser** y cada uno hace su **aporte** a la sociedad. Todos **contribuyen** con sus ideas, experiencias, **costumbres** y talentos a la rica y variada cultura de Perú.

Cuando llegaron a este país, el sueño de mis abuelos era abrir un restaurante, y por fin lo **alcanzaron.** Mi **herencia** es **un orgullo** para mí, y con el restaurante podemos **mantener** algunas de **las tradiciones** de nuestro país de **origen.**

**Soy de ascendencia** quechua. Mis **antepasados** vivían en los Andes pero mis padres vinieron a la ciudad cuando yo era pequeña. **Estoy muy agradecida por** todos **los sacrificios** que hicieron al dejar su hogar y quiero **aprovechar** las oportunidades que tengo aquí.

**Más vocabulario...**

| | |
|---|---|
| **apoyar** | *to support* |
| **el apoyo** | *support* |
| **el compromiso** | *commitment, obligation* |
| **las raíces** | *roots* |
| **tener éxito** | *to be successful* |

## Core Instruction

### TEACHING VOCABULARIO

1. Have students look at the photos as you read the captions. After reading each caption, ask questions to monitor comprehension. For example, for the first photo you might ask: **¿Toda la gente de Perú es igual?** **(5 min.)**
2. Go over the words in **Más vocabulario** and use each in a sentence. **(2 min.)**
3. Model the vocabulary in sentences as you talk about your experiences. **(3 min.)**

### TEACHING ¡EXPRÉSATE!

1. Model the sentences from **¡Exprésate!** using vocabulary words to complete each one. **(2 min.)**
2. Model the expressions by talking about your own family, your students, or your community. **(3 min.)**
3. Continue to model the expressions by telling a story about the life of a famous person. Have students raise their hands when they hear one of the **¡Exprésate!** phrases. **(3 min.)**

**Me crié en** un pueblo de los Andes. Cuando tenía doce años, mi padre tuvo que buscar trabajo en la ciudad y nos mudamos a Lima. Fue difícil **asimilar el estilo de vida** de la ciudad y a veces sentía que no **encajaba en** ningún grupo. Pero ahora tengo nuevos amigos en la universidad y siento que **pertenezco al** grupo.

Vivo en un pueblo de los Andes y hablo quechua. Cuando venía a la ciudad para vender mis productos, era difícil al principio **expresarme** en español. A veces la gente **discrimina** a los diferentes grupos étnicos porque no los entiende.

**También se puede decir...**

You may hear some Spanish speakers use **el reto** for **el desafío,** as well as **la forma de ser** or **la manera de ser** instead of **el modo de ser.**

## ¡Exprésate!

**To talk about challenges**

Interactive TUTOR

| | |
|---|---|
| **Había muchos desafíos en...** *There were many challenges in . . .* | **Poco a poco se adaptaron a...** *Little by little they adapted to . . .* |
| **Mis... enfrentaron obstáculos cuando...** *My . . . faced obstacles when . . .* | **Tuvimos que hacer un gran esfuerzo para...** *We had to make a big effort to . . .* |
| **Nos costó trabajo acostumbrarnos a...** *It took work for us to get used to . . .* | |

Vocabulario y gramática, pp. 73–75 Online workbooks

### TPR
### Total Physical Response

Hang a map of the world on the wall and have individual students respond to the following commands.

**Señala el pais de origen de tus antepasados.**

**Señala el lugar donde te criaste.**

**Señala un lugar en Perú donde todavía se mantienen vivas las costumbres quechuas.** 1.2

### Common Error Alert ¡OJO!

Students often use **el compromiso** to mean *compromise.* Remind them that **el compromiso** is used to mean *a commitment* or *obligation.*

### También se puede decir...

Tell students they can also use the verb **agradecer** for **estoy agradecido(a) por: Agradezco mucho lo que hicieron./Estoy muy agradecido(a) por lo que hicieron.**

## Differentiated Instruction

### Slower Pace Learners

**Additional Practice** Go over the vocabulary words one by one and have volunteers give examples of each. For example, you might say **grupos étnicos.** Students respond: **los peruanos, los japoneses, los españoles.** For **antepasados** students might respond: **abuelos, bisabuelos.** 1.2

### Multiple Intelligences

**Interpersonal** Have students form small groups to talk about the difficulties immigrants to the United States might have to overcome. Tell them to imagine that they are politicians or social workers trying to come up with ways to make the transition to a new culture easier. Ask them to come up with several ideas to discuss with the class. 1.1

## Resources

**Planning:**

Lesson Planner, pp. 97–98, 258–259

One-Stop Planner

**Presentation:**

Teaching Transparencies **Vocabulario** 7.1, 7.2

**Practice:**

Cuaderno de vocabulario y gramática, pp. 73–75

Activities for Communication, pp. 25–26

Lab Book, pp. 37–40

Teaching Transparencies **Vocabulario y gramática** answers, pp. 73–75

Audio CD 7, Tr. 1

Interactive Tutor, Disc 2

### 1 Script

1. Mi familia y yo vinimos a este país el año pasado. Todavía es difícil expresarme en inglés, y por eso estoy frustrada a veces.
2. Soy la primera persona de mi familia que asiste a la universidad. Mis padres hicieron muchos sacrificios para poder pagar el colegio, pero por fin lo lograron.
3. Cuando llegué aquí hice un gran esfuerzo y encontré trabajo. Ahora puedo hacer mi aporte a la sociedad y también ayudar a mi familia.
4. Todos los días enfrento muchos obstáculos en este país. Algunas personas en el colegio discriminan a la gente que no habla inglés y tienen muchos prejuicios.
5. Todos los grupos étnicos tienen su propio modo de ser y me cuesta trabajo asimilar las costumbres de los norteamericanos.
6. Tuve que hacer un gran esfuerzo, pero por fin siento que pertenezco a este país.

### 3 Answers

1. de Perú
2. orgulloso
3. trabaja como profesor
4. Sentía que no encajaba en ningún grupo.
5. el consejero del colegio; La animó a inscribirse en el club de teatro.
6. contenta; Tiene amigos en el club de drama.

1. desafío
2. éxito
3. éxito
4. desafío
5. desafío
6. éxito

CD 7, Tr. 1 1.2

### 1 ¿Desafío o éxito?

**Escuchemos** Escucha los comentarios y decide si la persona está hablando de **a)** un desafío o **b)** un éxito.

### 2 Grupos de palabras 1.2

**Leamos/Hablemos** Determina qué palabra o frase no pertenece al grupo. Explica por qué no pertenece.

**MODELO** **discriminar** **acostumbrarse** **asimilar**
***Discriminar*** **no pertenece porque** ***acostumbrarse*** **y** ***asimilar*** **describen cómo una persona se adapta a un lugar.**

| | | |
|---|---|---|
| **1.** el desafío | el origen | las raíces |
| **2.** alcanzar metas | tener éxito | criarse en |
| **3.** el aporte | contribuir | discriminar |
| **4.** la ascendencia | el sacrificio | los antepasados |
| **5.** el estilo de vida | el modo de ser | el grupo étnico |
| **6.** encajar en | estar agradecido por | pertenecer a |

### 3 ¿Qué alcanzaron? 1.2

**Leamos/Escribamos** Lee los comentarios y contesta las preguntas.

**Javier Bravo**
Soy de ascendencia peruana. Estoy muy orgulloso de mi herencia cultural y me gusta compartir las tradiciones y costumbres de mi familia. Estoy muy agradecido por los sacrificios de mis padres y quiero hacer un aporte a la sociedad también. Por eso encontré trabajo como profesor.

**Susana Vera**
Para mí, fue un gran desafío cambiar de colegio en el último año. No conocía a nadie y sentía que no encajaba en ningún grupo. Hablé con el consejero del colegio y él me ayudó mucho. Por ejemplo, me animó a inscribirme en el club de teatro porque me encanta el drama. Ahora siento que pertenezco a un grupo.

1. ¿De dónde son los antepasados de Javier?
2. ¿Cómo se siente Javier acerca de su herencia cultural?
3. ¿Qué hace Javier para contribuir a la sociedad?
4. ¿Por qué fue difícil para Susana adaptarse al nuevo colegio?
5. ¿Quién ayudó a Susana? ¿Qué hizo?
6. ¿Cómo se siente Susana ahora? ¿Por qué?

## Core Instruction

### VOCABULARY IN CONTEXT

Have students use cluster diagrams to categorize vocabulary words and expressions. Once they have created their diagrams, have volunteers share them with the class. Allow students to tell whether or not they agree with their classmates' categories and why. Then have students choose one category and create a word web of other related words. For example, for a cluster diagram with **antepasados, raíces, origen, costumbres, tradiciones, herencia,** they might add the words **familia, abuelos, fiestas, comidas, reunión familiar,** or they might personalize it with specific words that show what the words in the cluster mean to them: **tortilla española, flamenco, España, abuela María.**

## 4 Consejos 1.2

**Escribamos** Escribe una carta de 5 a 7 oraciones para responderle a una de las personas de la Actividad 3. En la carta puedes ofrecer consejos o comparar la experiencia de la persona con tus propias experiencias. Usa las expresiones del cuadro.

| | | |
|---|---|---|
| enfrentar obstáculos | me costó trabajo | poco a poco |
| hacer un gran esfuerzo | con el tiempo | acostumbrarse |
| superar | alcanzar mis metas | gracias al apoyo de |

## 5 Poco a poco... 1.2

**Escribamos** Cuenta la historia de esta familia usando las palabras de **Vocabulario** y las expresiones de **Exprésate.**

1. 2. 3. 4.

## Comunicación

HOLT SoundBooth ONLINE RECORDING

## 6 ¿Qué opinas? 1.1, 1.2

**Hablemos** Indica si estás de acuerdo o no con las siguientes oraciones. Compara tus opiniones con las de tus compañeros. Usa las palabras de **Vocabulario.**

1. En nuestro país, la gente discrimina a los diferentes grupos étnicos.
2. Para tener éxito en nuestra sociedad, hay que ser rico.
3. Todas las personas que viven en Estados Unidos deben saber expresarse en inglés.
4. Los padres siempre deben apoyar a sus hijos y hacer sacrificios por ellos.
5. Es responsabilidad de los hijos adultos mantener a sus padres.
6. Es difícil ser amigo(a) de alguien que no es de mi grupo étnico.

### COMMON ERROR ALERT ¡OJO!

Students often confuse the verb **superar** with **superarse.** Tell them that **superar** is used to mean *to overcome.* **(Superé los obstáculos.) Superarse** means *to better oneself.* **(Siempre intento superarme.)**

### Heritage Speakers

Ask heritage speakers to talk about the obstacles their ancestors had to overcome when they came to this country. Ask them to share other expressions, in addition to those in **¡Exprésate!,** that they might use to talk about challenges. 1.3

### Comunicación

### Group Activity: Presentational

Have groups of students talk about challenges that they have faced in their lives and what they have had to do to overcome obstacles. Ask students to choose one of the challenges and to role-play the situation for the class. Then have the rest of the class describe what happened in each presentation. 1.1, 1.3

## Differentiated Instruction

### ADVANCED LEARNERS

**2 Extension** Once students have done Activity 2, have them list the six words that do not belong. Ask them to write a sentence using each word. Call on volunteers to write a sentence on the board or on a transparency, leaving the vocabulary word blank. Have the rest of the class guess the missing word.
1.2

### MULTIPLE INTELLIGENCES

**Intrapersonal** Have students reread the paragraphs by Javier Bravo and Susana Vera. Then ask them to write their own testimony about a challenge they've overcome. Encourage them to describe in detail what they had to do and how they felt about it. Ask volunteers to share their paragraphs with the class.
1.3

**Differentiated Instruction** See the Differentiated Instruction CD-ROM.

**Resources**

**Planning:**

Lesson Planner, pp. 97–98, 258–259

One-Stop Planner

**Presentation:**

Teaching Transparencies **Vocabulario** 7.1, 7.2

**Practice:**

Cuaderno de vocabulario y gramática, pp. 73–75

Activities for Communication, pp. 25–26

Teaching Transparencies **Vocabulario y gramática** answers, pp. 73–75

Interactive Tutor, Disc 2

**Cultures**

**Products and Perspectives**

The city of Cuzco is filled with Inca-built stone walls and the majority of the citizens are indigenous and speak Quechua. Impressive ruins of the Incan empire are scattered throughout the city. The Coricancha ruins in the eastern part of the city were once covered with gold; only the stonework remains today. Have students investigate other ruins near Cuzco such as **Sacsayhuamán, Qenko, Puca Pucara** or **Tambo Machay,** to find out the role of each site in the Incan empire.

2.2, 3.1

Escenas de Cuzco y Lima

# Logros y sacrificios

Querida Mayta:

¡Qué bueno que vengas a vivir a Cuzco! Me preguntas por qué vine y cómo logré tener éxito aquí. Pues, te contaré mi historia.

En mi pueblo natal, había desafíos. Era difícil encontrar empleo y no había muchas oportunidades para mis hermanos y para mí. Por eso, mis padres decidieron mudarse (*move*) a Cuzco, pero no fue fácil. Nos costó trabajo adaptarnos. Cuando llegué aquí, no sabía expresarme en español porque en mi pueblo se hablaba solamente quechua. Mi papá no tenía empleo y mi mamá no estaba acostumbrada a un pequeño apartamento.

Pero poco a poco nos adaptamos al nuevo hogar. Mi papá alcanzó su sueño de trabajar como profesor y mi mamá encontró trabajo en un restaurante. Trabajaron duro y por fin lograron comprar una casa más grande. Con el tiempo, pude aprender español y saqué buenas notas en la universidad. Me acuerdo de aquel día en que logré graduarme. Estoy muy agradecido por el apoyo de mis padres y de mis profesores.

Ahora trabajo como abogado. Mi familia ha hecho muchos sacrificios, pero hemos podido superar todos los obstáculos. Estoy seguro de que tú también podrás asimilar el estilo de vida aquí. Tienes que hacer un gran esfuerzo y te apoyaré en todo.

Con cariño,

Felipe

## ¡Exprésate!

**To talk about accomplishments**

Interactive TUTOR

**Con el tiempo pude asimilar...**
*With time I was able to assimilate . . .*

**Gracias al apoyo de..., he podido superar...**
*Thanks to the support of . . . , I have been able to overcome . . .*

**Nos esforzamos en...**
*We made a big effort to . . .*

**Por fin, logré...**
*Finally, I managed to . . .*

**Trabajo duro... y por eso...**
*I work hard . . . and for that reason . . .*

Vocabulario y gramática, pp. 73–75 Online workbooks

## Core Instruction

### TEACHING ¡EXPRÉSATE!

1. Read the letter as a class and ask students to note the expressions that are used to talk about accomplishments. **(4 min.)**
2. Model the sentences in **¡Exprésate!**, inserting examples to complete each sentence. **Con el tiempo pude asimilar el estilo de vida del pueblo y entender sus costumbres. Gracias al apoyo de mis viejos amigos…** **(2 min.)**
3. Ask students to use the expressions to talk about the accomplishments of Felipe´s family. **(3 min.)**
4. Model sentences about the accomplishments of someone in your community or in your school using expressions from **¡Exprésate!** to tell how they accomplished their goals. **(3 min.)**

**7 ¿Qué pasó primero?** 1.2

**Leamos** Coloca los eventos de la vida de Felipe en orden cronológico. 3, 7, 5, 4, 6, 1, 2

1. Felipe logra graduarse de la universidad.
2. Felipe trabaja como abogado.
3. La familia de Felipe enfrenta dificultades en su pueblo natal.
4. El papá de Felipe logra encontrar trabajo como maestro.
5. Felipe no sabe expresarse en español.
6. La familia se muda a una casa más grande.
7. La familia de Felipe se muda a Cuzco.

La iglesia de la Compañía de Jesús en la Plaza Mayor de Cuzco es conocida por su bella fachada colonial.

**8 Me costó trabajo...** 1.3

**Escribamos** Escoge cinco temas del cuadro y describe, en una o dos oraciones, los desafíos de cada uno. Puedes mencionar tu experiencia propia o puedes describir los desafíos que una persona enfrentaría en cada situación.

MODELO **Al principio fue muy difícil para mí nadar con el equipo de natación de mi colegio. Me costó trabajo...**

nadar con el equipo de natación
hacer una pintura en la clase de arte
sacar fotos para el anuario *(yearbook)*
resolver un problema con un(a) amigo(a)
sacar una A en la clase de matemáticas
participar en una obra de teatro
empezar un club de español
ser presidente de la clase

## Comunicación

HOLT SoundBooth ONLINE RECORDING

**9 Lo que hemos logrado** 1.1, 1.3

**Hablemos** En parejas, preparen un discurso *(speech)* corto sobre los desafíos que los estudiantes y su colegio han enfrentado y los éxitos que han tenido. Las parejas se turnarán para presentar sus discursos a la clase.

MODELO **Este año, hemos tenido que superar varios obstáculos. Por ejemplo, hubo un huracán en septiembre que...**

### Circumlocution

Write the words **desafío, éxito, sacrificio, costumbre,** and **apoyo** on index cards and hand them out to students. Each student must come up with a sentence that corresponds to the vocabulary word on his or her card. For example, for the word **desafío** a student might say: **Me va a costar mucho trabajo aprender a hablar el chino.** Students would have to guess that this sentence describes **un desafío.** 1.1

## Comunicación

### Pair Activity: Interpersonal

Have pairs of students talk about the challenges they think they and their classmates might face ten years from now. What do they hope to accomplish in the next ten years? How will they overcome obstacles? Ask pairs to share their ideas with the class. 1.1, 1.3

## Differentiated Instruction

### SLOWER PACE LEARNERS

**8 Personalization** Some students may have trouble imagining the challenges associated with the activities listed in Activity 8. You might suggest that students choose activities or situations from their own personal experience. Have them work in pairs to talk about the challenges they faced. 1.1

### SPECIAL LEARNING NEEDS

**7 Students with Dyslexia** If you have students with dyslexia, you may wish to read the letter on page 282 aloud a second time while students put the items for Activity 7 in order. First have them read the items. Then have them put the events in order as you read the letter. Once they have put the events in order, read the letter a third time so they can check their answers. 1.2

### Assess

**Assessment Program**
**Prueba: Vocabulario 1,** pp. 121–122
Alternative Assessment, pp. 379, 391, 403

**Online Assessment**
**my.hrw.com**

**Test Generator**

## Resources

**Planning:**

Lesson Planner, pp. 99–101, 260–263

One-Stop Planner

**Presentation:**

Video Program **GramaVisión**

**Practice:**

Grammar Tutor for Students of Spanish, Chapter 7

Cuaderno de vocabulario y gramática, pp. 76–78

Cuaderno de actividades, pp. 61–63

Activities for Communication, pp. 25–26

Lab Book, pp. 37–40

Teaching Transparencies Bell Work 7.2

**Vocabulario y gramática** answers, pp. 76–78

Audio CD 7, Tr. 2

Interactive Tutor, Disc 2

### Bell Work

Use Bell Work 7.2 in the *Teaching Transparencies*, or write this activity on the board.

**Completa las siguientes oraciones.**

1. Gracias al apoyo de mis amigos, he podido...
2. Me esforcé en...
3. Con el tiempo pude...
4. Por fin logré...
5. Trabajo duro y por eso...

1.2

**Objetivos**
- Preterite and imperfect of stative verbs
- Grammatical reflexives
- **Lo** and **lo que**

# Gramática en acción 1

GramaVisión

interactive TUTOR

## Preterite and imperfect of stative verbs

**1** **Stative verbs** express *situations* or *states of being* rather than actions. The **imperfect** is typically used to describe past situations or states. When the **preterite** is used, the change *into* or *out of* a state resembles an action and can require a different translation in English. The **preterite** is also used to express *the duration* of past situations or states.

| | IMPERFECT | PRETERITE |
|---|---|---|
| **estar** | *was (for an unspecified period of time)* | *was (for a specified period of time)* |
| **ser** | *was (for an unspecified period of time)* | *was (sums up a situation or event that ended)* |
| **tener** | *had* | *got* |
| **tener que** | *had to (but did not necessarily do it)* | *had to (and did)* |

Quería verte, pero no **estabas.**
*I wanted to see you, but you weren't there.*

**Estuve** en Perú en mayo.
*I was in Perú in May.*

Mis padres **eran** muy trabajadores.
*My parents were very hardworking.*

Su apoyo **fue** muy importante.
*Their support was very important.*

Isa y yo **teníamos** la misma idea para el proyecto.
*Isa and I had the same idea for the project.*

Leo **tuvo** una gran idea.
*Leo got a great idea.*

Yo **tenía que** hacer la tarea pero lo dejé para mañana.
*I had to do my homework but I left it for tomorrow.*

Como **tuve que** hacer la tarea, no salí.
*Since I had to do homework, I didn't go out.*

Vocabulario y gramática, pp. 76–78
Actividades, pp. 61–63
Online workbooks

### ¿Te acuerdas?

The verbs **conocer, saber, querer** and **poder** have different uses in the **preterite** and **imperfect** tenses.

**Conocí** al cantante.
*I met the singer.*

**Conocía** al cantante.
*I knew the singer.*

**Supe** la respuesta.
*I found out the answer.*

**Sabía** la respuesta.
*I knew the answer.*

Pepe no **quiso** ensayar.
*Pepe refused to practice.*

Pepe no **quería** ensayar.
*Pepe didn't want to practice.*

**Pude** lograr mi sueño.
*I was able to achieve my dream.*

Sabía que **podía** lograrlo.
*I knew I could achieve it.*

CD 7, Tr. 2 See script on p. 275E.

**10** **¿Una reacción?** 1.2

**1.** a **2.** a **3.** b **4.** b **5.** a **6.** b

**Escuchemos** Escucha lo que dice cada persona y determina si habla de **a**) cómo se sentía cuando ocurrió algo o **b**) su reacción ante algo que ocurrió.

## Core Instruction

### TEACHING GRAMÁTICA

1. Go over **¿Te acuerdas?** Ask students questions to review the meaning of the verbs. **¿Cómo supiste del incendio? ¿Conociste a mi hermana? (2 min.)**
2. Go over point 1. Illustrate a change into or out of a state with facial expressions and gestures, or with a diagram (time line) and drawings on the board. **(2 min.)**
3. One by one, read the preterite and imperfect meanings for each verb, and then read the corresponding examples. Allow students to discuss the differences and to ask questions. **(2 min.)**
4. Write sentences on the board with **estar, ser, tener,** and **tener que,** but do not fill in the correct form of the verb. Have students state whether the verb should be in the preterite or imperfect and explain why. **(4 min.)**

### GramaVisión

For a video presentation of the preterite and imperfect of stative verbs, use **GramaVisión.**

GramaVisión

Visit Holt Online
**go.hrw.com**
KEYWORD: EXP3 CH7
Gramática 1 practice



### 11 El sueño de Eduardo 1.2

**Leamos/Escribamos** Completa el párrafo con las formas correctas de los verbos en paréntesis.

Eduardo quería ser periodista. Así que se mudó a Lima. No (sabía/supo) ___1___ si allí (podía/pudo) ___2___ encontrar trabajo para un periódico o no. Primero consiguió trabajo repartiendo periódicos. Cuando (tenía/tuvo) ___3___ tiempo, escribía. Una noche, (conocía/conoció) ___4___ al director del periódico en una fiesta y le dio uno de sus escritos. Al día siguiente, (tenía/tuvo) ___5___ noticias del director. Le ofreció trabajo como periodista. Por fin Eduardo (podía/pudo) ___6___ realizar su sueño.

### 12 ¿Qué pasó? 1.2

**Escribamos** Completa las oraciones. Usa el pretérito o el imperfecto. *¿Se te olvidó?* Preterite and imperfect, pp. 160–161

1. Mis antepasados (tener que)...
2. Enfrenté muchos obstáculos cuando (estar)...
3. Mis papás (querer) alcanzar...
4. Cuando yo era niño(a), (conocer) a...
5. Mi mamá (estar)... cuando (saber)...
6. Mi mejor amigo(a) (poder)...

Estos bailadores con máscaras celebran el festival de la Virgen del Carmen en Paucartambo, Perú.

## Comunicación

HOLT SoundBooth ONLINE RECORDING

### 13 ¿Qué no quiso hacer? 1.1, 1.2

**Hablemos** En parejas, hagan una historia de lo que ven en los dibujos. Usen las formas correctas de los verbos **tener (que), estar, poder, saber** y **querer** en su historia.

## Teacher to Teacher

**Marsha Meegan**
South Windsor High School
South Windsor, CT

For additional practice with **querer** and **poder,** students must write a scene in which they discuss what they wanted to do and the reason why they were unable to. Then, in groups, they must act out (in an overly dramatic way) a very brief ***telenovela*** scene, which is filmed in class. This activity provides needed practice as well as much laughter. Prizes might be awarded for creativity and acting ability. 1.1

## Answers

Use the Chapter 7 *Picture Sequences Transparency.*

**13 Sample Answer**

**Paula tenía que estudiar mucho para el examen de historia y por eso no pudo salir con sus amigos. Quería ver la televisión con su familia, pero no pudo porque tenía que estudiar para su examen. Ella trabajó duro y al final tuvo éxito. Supo todas las respuestas en el examen.**

## Differentiated Instruction

### SLOWER PACE LEARNERS

**12** Some students may have trouble completing the sentences in Activity 12. You may want to modify the activity by asking questions to prompt specific answers from students. For example, for item 1 you might ask: **¿Tus antepasados tuvieron que hacer muchos sacrificios?** Ask students to answer in complete sentences and then copy the answers in their notebooks. 1.2

### SPECIAL LEARNING NEEDS

**10 Students with Auditory Impairments**
If you have students with auditory impairments, you might want to provide them with headphones so that they can control the volume and speed of the listening track for Activity 10. An alternative would be to provide them with the written script.

## Comunicación

### Pair Activity: Interpretive

Have students work with a partner to come up with pairs of sentences for each verb listed on page 284 in the preterite and imperfect. Ask them to read their sentences for the class and the rest of the class should describe the difference in meaning between the two sentences. 1.2

**Differentiated Instruction** See the Differentiated Instruction CD-ROM.

## Resources

**Planning:**

Lesson Planner, pp. 99–101, 260–263

One-Stop Planner

**Presentation:**

Video Program **GramaVisión**

**Practice:**

Grammar Tutor for Students of Spanish, Chapter 7

Cuaderno de vocabulario y gramática, pp. 76–78

Cuaderno de actividades, pp. 61–63

Activities for Communication, pp. 25–26

Lab Book, pp. 37–40

Teaching Transparencies

Bell Work 7.3

**Vocabulario y gramática** answers, pp. 76–78

Audio CD 7, Tr. 3

Interactive Tutor, Disc 2

### Bell Work

Use Bell Work 7.3 in the *Teaching Transparencies*, or write this activity on the board.

**Escribe tres oraciones en el pretérito con los verbos *estar, poder,* y *tener*.**

1.3

### 14 Script

See script on page 275E.

Interactive TUTOR

### Nota cultural

Muchas palabras de los idiomas indígenas se han incorporado al español de la gente de los Andes. Tanto es así que mucha gente lo llama el español andino. Por ejemplo, las palabras **choclo** *(corn)*, **soroche** *(altitude sickness)*, **guagua** *(baby)*, **porotos** *(beans)* y **yapa** *(a small amount given in addition)* vienen del quechua. El idioma aymara ha prestado algunas palabras al español también, como **aguayo** *(multicolored cloth; mainly used in Bolivia)*.

¿Por qué crees que el español andino ha incorporado palabras quechuas y aymaras?

3.1

Madre e hijos, Cuzco, Perú

**1.** me crié **2.** se mudó **3.** se expresaba **4.** nos comunicábamos **5.** nos acostumbramos **6.** me preocupaba **7.** gustaba **8.** asimilamos **9.** me gradué **10.** se casó

## Grammatical reflexives

**1** When a verb is used reflexively, the action is directed back on the subject and a **reflexive pronoun,** referring to the subject of the verb, is used.

| | |
|---|---|
| Yo **me** peiné. | *I combed (my hair).* |
| Tú **te** bañaste. | *You bathed (yourself).* |
| Él **se** lavó los dientes. | *He brushed his teeth.* |

**2** Some verbs, known as grammatical reflexives, take a reflexive pronoun, but their action is not directed back on the subject. Three such verbs are **criarse**, **comunicarse**, and **casarse**.

**3** These verbs often express a process or change in state.

| | |
|---|---|
| **Nos criamos** en el campo. | *We grew up in the country.* |
| **Me comunico** con mis padres por teléfono. | *I communicate with my parents by telephone.* |
| ¿**Te casaste** con Raúl? | *Did you marry Raúl?* |

Vocabulario y gramática, pp. 76–78
Actividades, pp. 61–63
Online workbooks

**More grammatical reflexives**

| | | | |
|---|---|---|---|
| **acostumbrarse** | *to get used to* | **graduarse** | *to graduate* |
| **burlarse** | *to make fun of* | **mudarse** | *to move* |
| **enojarse** | *to get angry* | **preocuparse** | *to worry* |
| **esforzarse** | *to make an effort* | **quedarse** | *to stay, to end up* |
| **expresarse** | *to express oneself* | **quejarse** | *to complain* |

CD 7, Tr. 3

### 14 ¿Cierto o falso? 1.2

**Escuchemos** Escucha las oraciones y determina si cada una es **cierta** o **falsa.**

**1.** falsa **2.** cierta **3.** falsa **4.** cierta **5.** cierta **6.** falsa

### 15 La vida en la ciudad 1.2

**Leamos/Escribamos** Completa el párrafo con las formas correctas de los verbos en paréntesis. Usa el pretérito o el imperfecto.

Yo __1__ (criarse) en el campo, pero mi familia __2__ (mudarse) a la ciudad cuando yo tenía doce años. Hablábamos aymara en mi pueblo, y mi mamá no __3__ (expresarse) bien en español. Mis hermanos y yo __4__ (comunicarse) sin problema porque habíamos estudiado español en el colegio. Con dificultad nosotros __5__ (acostumbrarse) al estilo de vida. Yo __6__ (preocuparse) por todo. No me __7__ (gustar) el ruido de los carros. Pero poco a poco, nostros __8__ (asimilar) el modo de ser de la gente de la cuidad. Yo __9__ (graduarse) de la universidad hace poco, mi hermano mayor ahora es arquitecto, y mi hermano menor __10__ (casarse) el mes pasado.

## Core Instruction

### TEACHING GRAMÁTICA

**1.** Go over point 1, having students give other examples of verbs used reflexively. **(2 min.)**

**2.** Go over point 2. Remind students that they already know several grammatical reflexives, such as **graduarse, expresarse,** and **criarse.** **(2 min.)**

**3.** Have students practice conjugating the verbs listed in point 2. First have them conjugate in the present tense. Give a subject and verb: **yo, graduarse,** and students will respond **Me gradúo.** Then practice conjugation in the preterite. For example, **nosotros, comunicarse,** will prompt the response: **Nos comunicamos. (3 min.)**

**4.** Go over point 3. Have students explain why these verbs express a process or change in state. **(3 min.)**

### GramaVisión

For a video presentation of the grammatical reflexives, use **GramaVisión**.

GramaVisión

## 16 Cómo cambian las cosas... 1.2

**Escribamos** Usa una palabra o expresión de cada columna para escribir seis oraciones.

**MODELO** **Mi abuelo se comunicaba bien en español.**

| | | |
|---|---|---|
| Mis antepasados | quejarse | las costumbres |
| Mis amigos y yo | enojarse | el modo de ser |
| Tú | burlarse | la gente que discrimina |
| Los inmigrantes | graduarse | el estilo de vida |
| Yo | comunicarse | la universidad |
| Mi familia | acostumbrarse | las tradiciones |
| Mi abuelo | preocuparse | en inglés/en español |

## 17 Descríbelo 1.2

**Escribamos** Describe en una oración lo que pasa o lo que ha pasado en cada foto. Usa el verbo indicado.

1. Raúl/graduarse
2. Carolina/criarse
3. Leo/mudarse
4. Ricardo y Yolanda/casarse

## Comunicación

HOLT SoundBooth ONLINE RECORDING

## 18 El futuro 1.1, 1.2

**Hablemos** Imagina que estás veinte años en el futuro. En parejas, túrnense para explicar lo que lograron durante esos años y los obstáculos que superaron. Hablen también de lo que hicieron sus familias y sus amigos. Usen algunos de los verbos del cuadro.

| | | | | |
|---|---|---|---|---|
| criarse | expresarse | graduarse | preocuparse | casarse |
| comunicarse | acostumbrarse | enojarse | mudarse | quedarse |

### Heritage Speakers

Have heritage speakers talk about the traditions their family maintains. What traditions do they want to continue as they get older? Which ones are hard to maintain? Are there any American customs that they have adopted? 1.3, 2.1

### Comunicación

**Class Activity: Presentational**

Have students imagine they are famous actors or actresses. Ask them to work in pairs to come up with a conversation they can present to the class. Have them talk about the challenges they had to face to get where they are today. Encourage students to use as many grammatical reflexives and words they learned in **Vocabulario 1** as possible. Tell them not to say who they are, and see if the class can guess from their conversations. 1.2, 1.3

## Differentiated Instruction

### ADVANCED LEARNERS

**Challenge** Have students invent a character that moves to Peru from the United States. Ask them to write a paragraph about the challenges the character faces and things he or she is able to achieve. Tell them to use at least three of the grammatical reflexives from the presentation box on page 286. Encourage them to use the information they have learned about Peru to make the story realistic. Have them share their paragraphs with the class. 1.3

### SPECIAL LEARNING NEEDS

**17 Students with Visual Impairments** If you have students with visual impairments, you might want to add a step to Activity 17. For each photo, have volunteers describe what they see. Then read the captions aloud and have students write their sentences. As an alternative, you might have students work with a partner who gives a description of each illustration.

**Differentiated Instruction** See the Differentiated Instruction CD-ROM.

## Resources

**Planning:**

Lesson Planner, pp. 99–101, 260–263

One-Stop Planner

**Presentation:**

Video Program **GramaVisión**

**Practice:**

Grammar Tutor for Students of Spanish, Chapter 7

Cuaderno de vocabulario y gramática, pp. 76–78

Cuaderno de actividades, pp. 61–63

Activities for Communication, pp. 25–26

Lab Book, pp. 37–40

Teaching Transparencies
Bell Work 7.4
**Vocabulario y gramática** answers, pp. 76–78

Audio CD 7, Tr. 4

Interactive Tutor, Disc 2

### Bell Work

Use Bell Work 7.4 in the *Teaching Transparencies,* or write this activity on the board.

**Completa las oraciones con la forma correcta de los verbos entre paréntesis.**

1. **Elena ______ (quejarse) mucho después de su operación el mes pasado.**
2. **Es cierto que Lisa y Roberto ______ (casarse) el año que viene.**
3. **Todavía nosotros no ______ (acostumbrarse) a la casa nueva.**
4. **Los estudiantes nuevos ______ (adaptarse) muy pronto a nuestro colegio.**

1.2

### 20 Script

See script on p. 275E.

## Lo and lo que

Interactive TUTOR

**1** The expression **lo** + **adjective** is used to express an abstract idea *(the . . . thing).*

**Lo bueno** es que tuvimos éxito.
*The good thing is that we were successful.*

**Lo malo** es que gastamos mucho dinero.
*The bad thing is that we spent a lot of money.*

**2** The expression **lo que** + **verb** is also used to express an idea *(the thing that, what),* such as what was said or done, that will be defined in the same sentence.

Ahora, **lo que necesitamos** hacer es entrenar.
*Now what we need to do is train.*

Hablemos de **lo que** me **contaste** ayer.
*Let's talk about what you told me yesterday.*

**Lo que** me **dijo** Ana fue increíble.
*What Ana told me was incredible.*

Eso no es **lo que hicimos** la vez pasada.
*That is not what we did the last time.*

Vocabulario y gramática, pp. 76–78
Actividades, pp. 61–63
Online workbooks

### 19 Lo que pasa... 1.2

**Leamos** Decide qué oración corresponde a cada foto.

1

2

3

4

1. Lo que le cuesta trabajo a Antonio es recordar las palabras en español. 4
2. Lo bueno del trabajo de Pedro es que puede comer allí mismo. 3
3. Lo que tiene que aprender Gustavo es cómo usar este programa. 1
4. Lo malo es que no hay viento hoy. 2

## Core Instruction

### TEACHING GRAMÁTICA

1. Go over point 1. Tell students some adjectives that can easily be used with this construction are **bueno, malo, difícil, fácil, impresionante,** and **importante.** Provide examples. **(2 min.)**
2. Have students read point 2 and its examples aloud. **(2 min.)**
3. Provide several sentences for students and then rephrase each sentence using **lo que** so they get a better understanding of how it is used. **Susana hizo algo tonto. Lo que hizo Susana fue tonto. (3 min.)**
4. Provide more sentences and have students rewrite them on their own using **lo que. (3 min.)**

### GramaVisión

For a video presentation of **lo** and **lo que,** use **GramaVisión.**

GramaVisión

CD 7, Tr. 4

**20 Dos opiniones** 1.2

**Escuchemos/Leamos** Escucha la conversación entre Alberto y Fátima sobre las dificultades de mudarse a otro país e indica cuál de los dos estaría de acuerdo con las siguientes ideas: **Alberto, Fátima** o **ambos.**

1. Lo difícil es mantener las tradiciones de la familia. Fátima
2. Lo más importante es asimilar el estilo de vida de la gente de este país. Fátima
3. Lo que nunca olvidaré son los sacrificios de mis papás. ambos
4. Lo malo es que muchas personas pierden sus costumbres y no están orgullosas de su herencia cultural. Alberto
5. Lo que no entiendo es por qué la gente discrimina a los grupos étnicos. ambos
6. Debemos estar agradecidos por lo que hicieron nuestros papás. ambos

**21 El mercado en Otavalo** 1.2

**Leamos/Escribamos** Completa cada oración con **lo** o **lo que.**

1. ___ venden los otavaleños son artesanías hechas a mano. Lo que
2. Los artistas quieren ganarse la vida con ___ pueden hacer ellos mismos. lo que
3. ___ impresionante es que cada artículo es diferente. Lo
4. ___ noto es que todo el mundo contribuye algo al negocio. Lo que
5. Ellos dicen que ___ importante es aprovechar las oportunidades que tienen. lo
6. Me parece increíble ___ han logrado en este mercado. lo que

**22 Lo que lograste** 1.2

**Escribamos** Escribe seis oraciones sobre los obstáculos que has enfrentado. Usa **lo** o **lo que** en cada oración. Puedes usar las expresiones del cuadro.

| | | |
|---|---|---|
| lo bueno... | lo malo... | lo más difícil... |
| lo que me costó trabajo... | lo que alcancé... | lo que logré... |

## Comunicación

HOLT SoundBooth ONLINE RECORDING

**23 Lo bueno y lo malo** 1.1, 1.3

**Hablemos/Escribamos** En parejas, comenten lo bueno y lo malo de mudarse a otro país. Hagan una lista para compartir con la clase.

### Nota cultural

Otavalo es un pueblo del altiplano andino de Ecuador. Es famoso por su mercado de artesanías (abajo) donde se venden suéteres de lana, sombreros típicos, hamacas, tapices *(tapestries)* y bolsas. Aunque tienen un negocio de mucho éxito, los otavaleños todavía mantienen su identidad y sus costumbres. Muchos otavaleños todavía hablan el quechua y usan ropa tradicional. Están muy orgullosos de haber creado su mercado sin la ayuda de organizaciones y negocios comercializados.

¿Por qué crees que mantener su identidad sería difícil para un grupo indígena en el mundo actual? 3.1

Gramática 1

## Cultures

### Products and Perspectives

Tell students that some of the most popular goods that can be found at the Otavalo marketplace are made of alpaca wool. The alpaca is a domesticated South American mammal, related to the llama, that lives high in the Andes and has fine, long wool. The **otavaleños** make sweaters, rugs, and scarves of the silky wool that is often called "The Gold of the Andes." Have students research the materials used in other products of Otavalo and share their findings with the class. 1.3, 2.2

## Comunicación

### Group Activity: Interpersonal

Have students refer back to **Geocultura,** pp. 270–275. Ask them to get together in groups to comment on the information, using **lo** and **lo que** as much as possible in their conversations. For example, have them comment on what they found interesting or surprising in **Geocultura. (Lo más interesante es que...; Lo que me sorprendió fue...)** 1.1

## Differentiated Instruction

### ADVANCED LEARNERS

**20 Extension** As an extension of Activity 20, have students tell whether they agree with each of the items listed. Ask them to choose one item and explain their own opinion in a short paragraph. Have students exchange paragraphs and discuss them with their partners. 1.2, 1.3

### SPECIAL LEARNING NEEDS

**21 Students with AD(H)D** Before students do Activity 21, you might want to have them focus specifically on the word following the blank in each item. Ask students to copy the sentences in their notebooks and then circle the word after the blank if it is a verb, and underline it if it is an adjective. Then remind them that **lo que** is followed by a verb and **lo** is followed by an adjective. Have them use this information to fill in the blanks. Then have volunteers read the completed sentences aloud. 1.2

## Assess

**Assessment Program**

**Prueba: Gramática 1,** pp. 123–124

**Prueba: Aplicación 1,** pp. 125–126

Audio CD 7, Tr. 15

Alternative Assessment, pp. 379, 391, 403

**Online Assessment** my.hrw.com

**Test Generator**

**Resources**

**Planning:**

Lesson Planner, pp. 102, 262–263

One-Stop Planner

**Presentation:**

Audio CD 7, Trs. 5–7

Video Program, Videocassette 4
DVD Program
**VideoCultura**

**Practice:**

Cuaderno de actividades, p. 64

Video Guide, pp. 46–47

Lab Book, p. 77

Interactive Tutor, Disc 2

# Cultura

VideoCultura

## Comparaciones

CD 7, Tr. 5-7

3.1, 4.2

### El que persevera, triunfa

En los países hispanos hay por lo general menos universidades que en Estados Unidos. Existen grandes universidades a nivel regional con miles de alumnos, y también algunas universidades privadas, tanto grandes como pequeñas. Sin embargo, no existen las pequeñas escuelas profesionales del tipo *community college,* y la educación para adultos no está tan desarrollada. Por otro lado, muchas veces ir a una universidad pública no es muy caro. ¿Cómo se compara este sistema con el sistema universitario estadounidense?

La Universidad Católica Boliviana, La Paz, Bolivia

### Dana

**Lima, Perú**

***¿En qué año del colegio estás?***
Ya terminé el colegio el año pasado.

***¿Tienes planes para el próximo año?***
Sí, quisiera estudiar en la Universidad de Lima.

***¿A qué te piensas dedicar algún día?***
Quisiera estudiar comunicaciones y ser una cineasta.

***Y para el futuro inmediato, ¿qué te gustaría hacer?***
Me gustaría viajar a Estados Unidos y así poder aprender más inglés.

**Pre-AP Practice**

**AP Language Examination:** Have students first listen to the interviews with books closed to help prepare them for Section I, Part A: **Listening—Short Dialogues and Narratives.** Point out that Matías, like many Spanish speakers, may drop **b, d, g** between vowels, especially in words ending in **-ado (adecuado, de nada).**

**AP Benchmark:** Identify and summarize the main points and details and predict outcomes from a conversation from a familiar topic.

**Focus:** Talking about school and the future
- SE, p. 291, **Para comprender**
- SE, p. 291, **Para pensar y hablar**
- TE, p. 291, Advanced Learners

**Core Instruction**

**TEACHING CULTURA**

1. Read and discuss the introductory paragraph as a class. **(3 min.)**
2. Have volunteers read aloud the interview with Dana. Ask students if they know any young people with goals like Dana's. **(4 min.)**
3. Have volunteers read aloud the interview with Matías. Ask them to compare his plans with Dana's. **(4 min.)**
4. Answer the questions in **Para comprender** as a class. Then have students discuss the question in **Para pensar y hablar**. **(4 min.)**

**VideoCultura**

For a video presentation of the interviews as well as an additional interview, see Chapter 7 **VideoCultura** on Videocassette or on DVD.

VideoCultura

## Matías

**Santiago, Chile**

***¿En qué nivel estás en el colegio?***
Ya egresé del colegio.

***¿Tienes planes para el próximo año?***
Sí, quizás estudiar. Aún no lo sé, no lo tengo muy claro.

***¿Piensas asistir a la universidad?***
Sí, me gustaría entrar a la Universidad de Chile... sería lo adecuado.

***¿A qué te piensas dedicar algún día?***
Pintor sería una de las cosas que me gustaría ser.

***Y para el futuro inmediato, ¿qué te gustaría hacer?***
Aún no lo sé pero me gustaría quizás viajar, estudiar, algo por el estilo.

Cultura

### Para comprender 1.2

1. ¿Qué quiere hacer Dana el año que viene? ¿A qué piensa dedicarse en el futuro?
2. ¿Por qué le gustaría viajar a Estados Unidos?
3. ¿A qué universidad le gustaría entrar a Matías? ¿A qué piensa dedicarse?
4. ¿Qué quiere hacer Matías para el futuro inmediato?
5. ¿Te parece que Dana y Matías tienen muy claros sus planes para el futuro? ¿Por qué?

### Para pensar y hablar 1.3

En tu opinión, ¿por qué puede ser difícil seguir adelante con tus sueños y realizar las cosas que piensas hacer? ¿Qué es lo difícil de decidir lo que quieres hacer en el futuro?

## Comunidad

### Los hispanos en Estados Unidos 5.1

La presencia de la comunidad hispana en este país empezó hace más de quinientos años con los primeros españoles que pasaron por el sur de lo que hoy es Estados Unidos. Ahora los hispanos son uno de los grupos minoritarios de mayor crecimiento en nuestro país. En el año 2004, se calculó que 41.3 millones de latinos vivían en Estados Unidos. Los hispanos han contribuido como astronautas, diputados, científicos, músicos, políticos, profesores, escritores y atletas. Investiga a un hispano que haya sido importante en tu comunidad o estado. Comparte tus hallazgos con la clase. ¿Cuál ha sido el impacto de los hispanos en tu comunidad hasta el presente?

**Bill Richardson, mexicoamericano, actualmente gobernador de Nuevo México y ex-embajador ante las Naciones Unidas, ha servido en varias funciones políticas.**

## Atlas INTERACTIVO MUNDIAL

Have students use the interactive atlas at **go.hrw.com**.

**Map Activities**
Use transparency **Mapa 6**.

1. Have students find Lima, Peru on the map and tell what they know about it. What do they observe about its location?
2. Have students locate Santiago, Chile, and compare its location to Lima's.

3.1

### Para comprender Answers

1. estudiar en la Universidad de Lima; a comunicaciones y ser cineasta
2. para aprender más inglés
3. la Universidad de Chile; a la pintura
4. viajar, estudiar
5. Dana tiene más claro sus planes. Matías aún no sabe exactamente qué quiere hacer.

### Cultures

#### Practices and Perspectives

Tell students that the University of Lima has a study abroad program with connections at several prestigious universities around the world. The goal of the program is to promote international contact and cultural exchange in the university community. Have students research specific study abroad programs at U.S. universities.

2.1

### Career Path

Have students think about how they could use Spanish for a career in education. Ask them to brainstorm in small groups positions in which Spanish would be useful. Have groups share their ideas with the class. 1.3

## Differentiated Instruction

### ADVANCED LEARNERS

**Challenge** Have students interview students in different classes using the questions from the **Cultura** interview. Whenever possible, have them conduct the interview in Spanish. Ask them to present their findings to the class. For their presentations, have them consider the following questions: Were students' answers similar to those of Dana and Matías? Do they think students in different countries would have very different answers? Were older students more certain of their future plans? 1.1, 1.3

### MULTIPLE INTELLIGENCES

**Interpersonal** Have students work in groups to create a questionnaire to advise fellow classmates on their future plans. The questions should help them identify the interviewee's interests, talents, strengths, weaknesses, and experiences. Based on the answers, students will suggest where to study or travel and what area of work to go into. Once they have had five classmates complete the questionnaire and they have given them advice based on the answers, have the interviewees tell the class whether they felt they were given good advice. 1.1

**Resources**

**Planning:**

Lesson Planner, pp. 103–104, 264–265

One-Stop Planner

**Presentation:**

Teaching Transparencies
**Vocabulario** 7.3, 7.4

**Practice:**

Cuaderno de vocabulario y gramática, pp. 79–81

Activities for Communication, pp. 27–28

Teaching Transparencies
Bell Work 7.5
**Vocabulario y gramática** answers, pp. 79–81

Interactive Tutor, Disc 2

**Bell Work**

Use Bell Work 7.5 in the *Teaching Transparencies,* or write this activity on the board.

**Completa las oraciones con *lo* o *lo que*.**

1. ______ malo es que tenemos un examen.
2. Vamos a repasar ______ aprendimos ayer.
3. Me preocupa ______ me dijo Silvia.
4. Creo que ______ importante es que todos estudiemos mucho.
5. ______ más difícil es tomar notas.

1.2

**Objetivos**
- Talking about future plans
- Expressing cause and effect

# Vocabulario en acción 2

## En Perú
## Las aspiraciones

Mis antepasados llegaron a Perú hace años. Tuvieron que **acostumbrarse** a una nueva vida y **luchar por** alcanzar sus **metas.**

La vida puede ser difícil en un país nuevo, pero tenemos que **seguir adelante** y no perder de vista nuestros **objetivos.**

Tenemos que **tomar la iniciativa** para poder **realizar** nuestros sueños.

**Más vocabulario...**

| | |
|---|---|
| enfocarse en | *to focus on* |
| triunfar | *to triumph* |

## Core Instruction

### TEACHING VOCABULARIO

1. Introduce vocabulary using transparencies **Vocabulario 7.3** and **7.4.** Read each photo caption and model the pronunciation of each vocabulary word. **(4 min.)**
2. Have students answer **sí** or **no** as you ask them questions. **¿Es importante luchar por alcanzar tus metas? (3 min.)**
3. Model each word in **Más vocabulario. (2 min.)**
4. Ask students questions using a targeted word: **Nombra algunas metas que alguien podría tener cuando se muda a otro país. (2 min.)**

### TEACHING ¡EXPRÉSATE!

1. Model the expressions for students by completing each sentence with terms from **Vocabulario. (2 min.)**
2. Ask students questions and then repeat their answers using **¡Exprésate!** functions. For example, **¿Qué te gustaría ser cuando seas mayor?** If the student responds **médico,** repeat the sentence using a phrase from **¡Exprésate!: Cuando seas mayor, te gustaría ser médico. (2 min.)**

Visit Holt Online
**go.hrw.com**
KEYWORD: EXP3 CH7
Vocabulario 2 practice

**Nos empeñamos en** trabajar duro en nuestro negocio y **nos esforzamos por** realizar nuestras **aspiraciones.**

**Sueño con** ir a la universidad y **llegar a ser** profesora cuando sea mayor.

Sé que algún día **lograré** obtener un empleo en una gran compañía. **No me daré por vencido** hasta encontrarlo y **establecerme** en el mundo de los negocios.

## ¡Exprésate!

**To talk about future plans**

| | |
|---|---|
| **Antes de que empiecen las clases, quiero...** *Before classes start, I want to . . .* | **Voy a... con la idea de...** *I'm going to . . . with the intention of . . .* |
| **Cuando sea mayor, me gustaría...** *When I'm older, I'd like to . . .* | **Tan pronto como... pienso...** *As soon as . . . I plan on . . .* |
| **En cuanto cumpla los... años, voy a...** *As soon as I turn . . . years old, I'm going to . . .* | **Tengo la intención de...** *I intend to . . .* |

Interactive TUTOR

Vocabulario y gramática, pp. 79–81 — Online workbooks

Vocabulario 2

## TPR

### Total Physical Response

Bring to class a college application, a first aid kit, a textbook, and a diploma. Have individual students respond to the following commands using these props or other classroom items.

**Señala lo que necesitas si sueñas con ir a la universidad.**

**Pásame lo que usarás si llegas a ser médico.**

**Busca un libro que debes usar si tu meta es aprender el español.**

**Señala lo que te darán si logras graduarte.** 1.2

### También se puede decir...

Let students know that the verb **efectuar** might be used for **realizar.** Many Spanish speakers might also use **adaptarse** for **acostumbrarse.**

### Language Note

Tell students that when the verb **realizar** is used reflexively **(realizarse),** it means to be fulfilled or to feel satisfied by having achieved one's goals.

## Differentiated Instruction

### SLOWER PACE LEARNERS

**Additional Practice** Divide the class into groups and ask students to interview each other: **¿Qué tipo de trabajo quieres tener? ¿Vas a ir a la universidad? ¿Quieres vivir en este país?** After the interviews, ask someone from each group to describe a group member without revealing his or her name. Other groups guess who is being described. 1.1

### MULTIPLE INTELLIGENCES

**Logical/Mathematical** Have students create a timeline with their plans for the next ten years. They should write their plans in the appropriate sections and then prepare a short presentation for the class. Have them include the age they will be for each year. Ask them to use the timeline as a guide as they present their future plans to the class. 1.3

## Resources

**Planning:**

Lesson Planner, pp. 103–104, 264–265

One-Stop Planner

**Presentation:**

Teaching Transparencies **Vocabulario** 7.3, 7.4

**Practice:**

Cuaderno de vocabulario y gramática, pp. 79–81

Activities for Communication, pp. 27–28

Lab Book, pp. 37–40

Teaching Transparencies **Vocabulario y gramática** answers, pp. 79–81

Audio CD 7, Tr. 8

Interactive Tutor, Disc 2

### 24 Script

1. Sueño con tomar clases de kárate. Sé que un día puedo llegar a ser muy buena.
2. Tengo que esforzarme mucho si quiero pasar el examen de la semana que viene. Mi meta es sacar la nota más alta de la clase.
3. Quiero llegar a ser profesora en cuanto termine los estudios universitarios. Sé que tengo que luchar por esa meta, y no me daré por vencida.
4. Quiero registrarme para votar. Es una oportunidad maravillosa de aportar algo a la comunidad.

### Heritage Speakers

Ask your heritage speakers about their personal aspirations. What do they expect to do in the future? How can they prepare to achieve their dreams? What do they need to do now? In one year? In five years? How can their knowledge of Spanish help them? They can discuss this in a small group, then write two or three paragraphs about it. Encourage students to use the vocabulary on pages 292–293. This can then be turned in for a grade and/or shared with the rest of the class. 1.3

CD 7, Tr. 8

### 24 Metas y aspiraciones 1.2

**Escuchemos** Escucha los siguientes comentarios y escoge la foto que corresponde a cada uno. **1.** D **2.** B **3.** A **4.** C

A

B

C

D

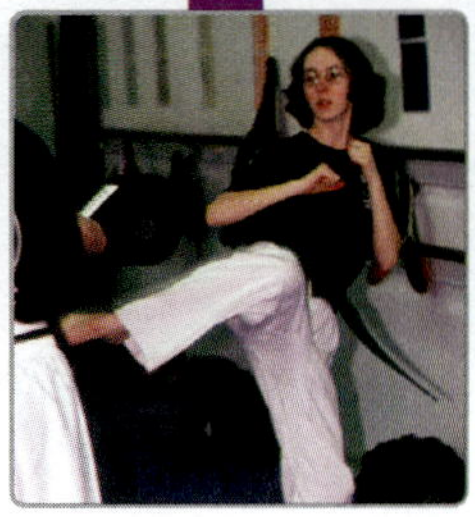

### 25 Lo que queremos hacer 1.2

**Leamos/Escribamos** Completa las siguientes oraciones con las palabras del cuadro.

| | | |
|---|---|---|
| aspiraciones | empeñarnos | seguir adelante |
| luchar por | se enfoca | oportunidad |

1. Mis amigos tienen muchas ═══ de ir a la universidad. aspiraciones
2. Ellos tienen que ═══ alcanzar su objetivo. luchar por
3. Paula ═══ mucho en sus estudios porque quiere ser abogada. se enfoca
4. Joaquín tiene la ═══ de trabajar en otro país porque habla dos idiomas. oportunidad
5. Para poder alcanzar nuestros sueños, tenemos que ═══ en el trabajo. empeñarnos
6. Cuando enfrentamos un obstáculo, tenemos que ═══ y superarlo. seguir adelante

### 26 Un discurso 1.2

**Escribamos** Gustavo no puede terminar las oraciones de su discurso *(speech)*. Ayúdalo a terminarlas con las palabras de **Vocabulario** y **Exprésate.**

1. Nadie puede darse por vencido antes de realizar un sueño porque...
2. Hay que tener muchas aspiraciones en la vida porque...
3. Para lograr una meta, hay que...
4. Es bueno tener la oportunidad de...
5. A veces no es fácil acostumbrarse a algo nuevo porque...
6. Hay que luchar por nuestros objetivos porque...

## Core Instruction

### VOCABULARY IN CONTEXT

**Group Work** Divide the class into four or five teams to play a word association game. Write each vocabulary word on an index card ahead of time. Shuffle the cards. Draw a card and read it aloud. Have each team write down as many things as they can think of that are associated with that word. Sometimes there may be only one association to make, while at other times there will be more than one. Teams earn a point for each accurate association they make.

**27** **Un lugar nuevo** 1.2

**Leamos/Escribamos** Eduardo le envió un correo electrónico a su amigo en el que le cuenta sus experiencias en un nuevo lugar. Completa su mensaje con las palabras del cuadro.

| | | | |
|---|---|---|---|
| des por vencido | establecerme | acostumbrarme | realizar |
| seguir adelante | esforzarme | llegar a ser | la oportunidad |

Hola amigo:

Te escribo desde mi nueva casa. Cuando llegué aquí, pensé que no tendría __1__ de participar en un club de ciclismo, pero fíjate que el nuevo colegio tiene uno. Quiero __2__ en el club y algún día, __3__ una parte importante del equipo. Ya sabes que no me es fácil __4__ al nuevo colegio pero el club me ayudará a __5__. Voy a __6__ mucho por __7__ mis metas este año. Según lo que me cuentas, tú también tienes muchas aspiraciones. Bueno amigo, no te __8__. ¡Buena suerte!

–Eduardo

1. la oportunidad
2. establecerme
3. llegar a ser
4. acostumbrarme
5. seguir adelante
6. esforzarme
7. realizar
8. des por vencido

**28** **¿Serán sus metas?** 1.2

**Escribamos** Usa una palabra o expresión de cada columna para escribir seis oraciones. Usa el futuro.

| | | |
|---|---|---|
| mis amigos | acostumbrarse | los problemas del país |
| yo | llegar a ser | mujer/hombre de negocios |
| tú | registrarse para | votar |
| el presidente | tomar la iniciativa | sacar buenas notas |
| los profesores | enfocarse en | ver televisión |

## Comunicación

HOLT SoundBooth ONLINE RECORDING

**29** **¡Hablen de sus planes!** 1.1, 1.2

**Hablemos** Con un(a) compañero(a), hablen de sus planes para el futuro. Pueden hablar de sus planes verdaderos o pueden inventar algo. Sean creativos y usen las palabras de **Vocabulario** y las expresiones de **Exprésate.**

MODELO **—En cuanto me gradúe de la universidad...**
**—¿Ah, sí? Pues, yo tengo la intención de...**

## Connections

### Social Studies Link

Ellen Ochoa, the first Hispanic woman in space, is a role model for all students to inspire them to do the best they can do to achieve their goals. The Hispanic community contributes to every aspect of United States society; Ellen Ochoa is just one example. Have students research the biography of Ellen Ochoa or another Hispanic man or woman who has made an important contribution to society. Encourage them to use terms from **Vocabulario 1** to tell the class about the person. They should describe the individual's aspirations and what that person did to achieve his or her goals. 1.3, 3.1

### Community Link

Tell students that using the language in a real context outside of the classroom is an excellent way to practice their language skills. Point out that e-mail has made communication with people around the world quick and easy. Have them research ways to find e-mail buddies from Latin American schools. They might also be able to find language exchange groups in the community.

## Comunicación

### Group Work: Interpersonal

Have students work in groups to create a survey about fellow classmates' future plans. Have them circulate around the classroom to conduct the survey and remind them to take notes on the answers. Ask the groups to prepare a chart to show their findings. For example, **el 30% quiere casarse, el 60% piensa ir a la universidad, el 20% piensa viajar, el 10% empezará a trabajar y el 20% no sabe.** 1.1

## Differentiated Instruction

### ADVANCED LEARNERS

**27 Extension** As an extension of Activity 27, have students respond to Eduardo's e-mail. Ask them to comment on what Eduardo wrote and then to write about their own aspirations. You might want to have students write actual e-mail messages and exchange them with a partner. 1.1

### SPECIAL LEARNING NEEDS

**Students with Learning Disabilities** You might want to have students work in groups to practice vocabulary. Ask groups to imagine they have been given the opportunity to begin a new club in school. Have them brainstorm ideas about what they want to accomplish with their club, and come up with three specific goals. Have a spokesperson from the group share the information with the rest of the class. 1.1, 1.3

**Differentiated Instruction** See the Differentiated Instruction CD-ROM.

## Resources

**Planning:**

Lesson Planner, pp. 103–104, 264–265

One-Stop Planner

**Presentation:**

Teaching Transparencies **Vocabulario** 7.3, 7.4

**Practice:**

Cuaderno de vocabulario y gramática, pp. 79–81

Activities for Communication, pp. 27–28

Teaching Transparencies **Vocabulario y gramática** answers, pp. 79–81

Interactive Tutor, Disc 2

## Heritage Speakers

Review the vocabulary on pages 292–293 and tie it to the **¡Exprésate!** feature on cause and effect. Then ask your heritage speakers to examine their daily activities. What are the consequences of their typical activities? How will these consequences fit in with their personal aspirations? Students usually are more honest if they know an adult is not judgmental. Just ask them to write about it and turn it in to you. The focus here is on self examination and correct language use. 1.3

## Más práctica

Have students work in pairs. Ask them to use expressions from **¡Exprésate!** to share the effect of their actions this month. **(Anoche salí con mis amigos; por lo tanto estoy muy cansado(a) hoy. No estudié para el examen de matemáticas, así que saqué una mala nota.)** Then have them modify the activity. They should tell their partner about one of their actions and see if the partner can guess the effect. 1.1

Unos estudiantes de Cuzco

## Una entrevista con Felipe

ALEJANDRA Hola, Felipe. Gracias por venir. Me llamo Alejandra. Soy reportera del periódico de nuestro colegio y me gustaría hacerte algunas preguntas acerca de tus experiencias en la ciudad. ¿Qué me puedes decir?

FELIPE Bueno, mi familia vino a la ciudad porque mis padres tenían aspiraciones de montar *(set up)* un negocio. Por lo tanto se establecieron aquí para realizar su sueño.

ALEJANDRA ¿Tuvieron Uds. problemas en acostumbrarse a otro estilo de vida?

FELIPE Bueno, sí. Imagínate, la vida en el campo es distinta a la de la ciudad; por consiguiente, tuvimos problemas en ajustarnos. Pero seguimos adelante, y todo lo que hemos logrado se debe al trabajo de toda la familia.

ALEJANDRA ¿Y qué planes tienes ahora que te vas a graduar del colegio?

FELIPE Tengo la intención de estudiar administración de empresas. En cuanto termine la carrera, voy a trabajar de tiempo completo en el negocio familiar. ¡Quiero que el negocio llegue a ser muy próspero!

ALEJANDRA Muy bien, veo que tienes todo planeado para el futuro.

### ¡Exprésate!

**To express cause and effect** Interactive TUTOR

| | |
|---|---|
| **Hablamos del tema; por consiguiente...** *We discussed the issue; consequently, . . .* | **No estudié, así que...** *I didn't study, so . . .* |
| **Mi éxito en... se debe a...** *My success in . . . is due to . . .* | **Soy bilingüe; por lo tanto, tengo muchas oportunidades...** *I'm bilingual; therefore, I have many opportunities . . .* |

Vocabulario y gramática, pp. 79–81 Online workbooks

## Core Instruction

### TEACHING ¡EXPRÉSATE!

1. Have volunteers role-play the parts of Alejandra and Felipe. Ask students to discuss which parts of the conversation show cause and effect. **(3 min.)**
2. Model the **¡Exprésate!** functions for students. **(1 min.)**
3. Use some of the functional expressions to talk about Alejandra and Felipe. Have students respond **cierto** or **falso.** For example, say: **La familia de Felipe tenía aspiraciones de montar un negocio, así que se mudaron a la ciudad.** (cierto) **(3 min.)**
4. Model other sentences using the **¡Exprésate!** expressions and have students say whether each sentence is logical. For example: **Estudié mucho; por consiguiente no aprobé el examen.** (no) **(3 min.)**

**30 ¿Así lo dijo?** 1.2

**Leamos** Basándote en el diálogo, indica si cada oración es **cierta** o **falsa.**

1. Alejandra trabaja para una revista de negocios. falsa
2. Los papás de Felipe montaron un negocio en la ciudad. cierta
3. La familia de Felipe se acostumbró a la ciudad sin problemas. falsa
4. La vida en el campo es diferente a la vida en la ciudad. cierta
5. La familia de Felipe ha trabajado mucho para lograr sus objetivos. cierta
6. Felipe no quiere estudiar en la universidad. falsa
7. Felipe va a trabajar de tiempo completo en el negocio familiar en el futuro. cierta
8. Felipe piensa que a lo mejor el negocio no tendrá éxito. falsa

**31 Consejos para todos** 1.2

**Leamos/Escribamos** Lee lo que varias personas dicen de sus aspiraciones. Para cada una, escribe un consejo.

MODELO **Me gustaría ser doctor cuando sea grande.**
**Lo puedes lograr si trabajas muy duro.**

1. Tengo la intención de montar un negocio.
2. Mi mayor aspiración es ser pintor.
3. No sé cómo lograr mi objetivo de jugar al béisbol profesional.
4. Me gustaría ir a la universidad y estudiar geografía.
5. Quiero acostumbrarme a vivir en esta ciudad pero no es fácil.
6. Mi meta es establecerme en mi nuevo país tan pronto como pueda.

### Nota cultural

En las riberas del Lago Titicaca, el lago navegable más alto del mundo, se pueden encontrar varios artefactos de los antepasados de la población andina. Cerca de la ciudad de Puno, por ejemplo, hay pinturas antiguas en las cuevas y puntas de lanza *(spearheads)* en el suelo. Los Uros son un grupo de 40 islas en el lago formadas por totora *(large reeds).* A los indígenas que habitan las islas también se les llama uros; su cultura es una de las más antiguas del continente.

¿Qué más sabes de los uros y de otras culturas indígenas de los Andes? 3.1

Dos habitantes del lago Titicaca con su balsa fabricada de totora

## Comunicación

HOLT SoundBooth ONLINE RECORDING

**32 Una cosa resulta de la otra** 1.1, 1.3

**Hablemos** En grupos de tres o cuatro, hablen de algo que pasó a consecuencia de otro evento. Pueden mencionar, por ejemplo, tener reuniones de un club, aprobar un examen, ganar un trofeo o presentar una obra de teatro. Mencionen por lo menos cuatro consecuencias en su conversación y usen las frases de **Exprésate.**

MODELO **—Conseguimos un salón para el club de español, por lo tanto podemos tener reuniones cada semana.**
**—¡Excelente! Así que podemos reunirnos mañana.**

### Cultures

#### Practices and Perspectives

Tell students that Puno is a commercial border town across the lake from Bolivia. It is the capital of the *altiplano* region and the folkloric center of Peru. Festivals take place throughout the year, and the streets are filled with music and dancing. During the first week of November, the town of Puno celebrates its founding. A lavish procession takes place on November 4 and 5 as masked dancers commemorate the beginning of the Inca Empire when Manco Cápac and Mamá Ocllo were sent to Earth by the Sun and rose forth from Lake Titicaca. Have students research the legend of Manco Cápac and Mamá Ocllo. 2.1

### Comunicación

#### Pair Activity: Interpretive

Have students bring in headlines that tell either the cause or the effect of an event. For each headline that describes a cause, have the class discuss what they think may have been the effect, and vice versa. If possible, have students print out headlines from online Spanish-language newspapers to use in the activity. 1.2

## Differentiated Instruction

### SLOWER PACE LEARNERS

31 You may wish to have students brainstorm ideas for each item in Activity 31. Write the ideas on the board and then have students work in pairs to write the sentences. Have students exchange papers with another pair to peer-edit. 1.1

### MULTIPLE INTELLIGENCES

**Intrapersonal** Ask each student to tell a partner the effect of at least two of his or her actions this week. (**Me esforcé mucho en el partido; por consiguiente logré meter un gol. No llamé a mi novio en toda la semana, así que él dejó de hablar conmigo.**) 1.1

### Assess

**Assessment Program**
**Prueba: Vocabulario 2,** pp. 127–128
Alternative Assessment, pp. 379, 391, 403

**Online Assessment**
**my.hrw.com**

**Test Generator**

## Resources

**Planning:**

Lesson Planner, pp. 105–107, 266–269

One-Stop Planner

**Presentation:**

Video Program **GramaVisión**

**Practice:**

Grammar Tutor for Students of Spanish, Chapter 7

Cuaderno de vocabulario y gramática, pp. 82–84

Cuaderno de actividades, pp. 65–67

Activities for Communication, pp. 27–28

Teaching Transparencies Bell Work 7.6

**Vocabulario y gramática** answers, pp. 82–84

Interactive Tutor, Disc 2

### Bell Work

Use Bell Work 7.6 in the *Teaching Transparencies*, or write this activity on the board.

**Usa las expresiones de ¡Exprésate! para describir un posible efecto de cada acción.**

1. **Le mentiste a tu amigo(a).**
2. **Estudiaste mucho para un examen.**
3. **Te criaste en otro país.**
4. **Olvidaste tu libro de matemáticas en casa.**
5. **Le dijiste a tu amigo(a) que le quedaba mal la camisa que llevaba.**

1.2

**Objetivos**
- Subjunctive after adverbial conjunctions
- Subjunctive with future actions
- Indicative with habitual or past actions

# Gramática en acción 2

GramaVisión

Interactive TUTOR

## Subjunctive after adverbial conjunctions

**1** The **subjunctive** is always used following these expressions, called **adverbial conjunctions:**

| | |
|---|---|
| **a menos (de) que** *unless* | **antes de que** *before* |
| **con tal (de) que** *provided that* | **en caso de que** *in case* |
| **para que** *in order that, so that* | **sin que** *without* |

No iré al cine **a menos de que** Juan me **llame**.
*I won't go to the movies unless Juan calls me.*

Ayudo a mis padres **sin que** me **pidan** ayuda.
*I help my parents without them asking for help.*

Llegaremos temprano al cine **antes de que se acaben** las entradas.
*We'll get to the movies early before the tickets run out.*

Tomás, estudia **para que puedas** aprobar el examen.
*Tomás, study so that you can pass the exam.*

Les repito la información **en caso de que** no **hayan entendido**.
*I'll repeat the information in case you haven't understood.*

Van a la reunión **con tal de que tengan** tiempo.
*They're going to the meeting provided they have time.*

Vocabulario y gramática, pp. 82–84
Actividades, pp. 65–67
Online workbooks

Las ruinas de Machu Picchu quedan cerca de Cuzco. Aquí se ven desde el sendero Inca.

### 33 Una encuesta 1.2

**Leamos** Tus compañeros del colegio prepararon una encuesta. Para cada oración de la encuesta, indica **cierto** o **falso** según tu propio caso.

1. Me esfuerzo más cada día para que mi trabajo salga bien.
2. Siempre ayudo a mis padres con tal de que me lo paguen.
3. No me daré por vencido a menos de que sea muy difícil realizar mis sueños.
4. Trato de ayudar a mis amigos sin que me lo pidan.
5. Hay que tomar la iniciativa antes de que alguien más lo haga.
6. En caso de que no me gradúe, siempre puedo trabajar para mis padres.

## Core Instruction

### TEACHING GRAMÁTICA

1. Go over point 1 with students. Ask them with which adverbial conjunctions they are familiar. **(2 min.)**
2. Read the examples. Go back over each example and then model new sentences by adding new verbs in the subjunctive. For example: **A menos de que Juan me haya llamado, no iré al cine. (A menos de que Juan pueda ir, no iré al cine.) (3 min.)**
3. Provide students with the first part of a sentence using an adverbial conjunction and a verb in the subjunctive, and have them complete the sentences with a logical ending. You might say: **Antes de que lleguen mis papás... (Antes de que lleguen mis papás, voy a limpiar la casa.) (5 min.)**

### GramaVisión

For a video presentation of the subjunctive after adverbial conjunctions, use **GramaVisión**.

GramaVisión

Visit Holt Online
**go.hrw.com**
KEYWORD: EXP3 CH7
Gramática 2 practice

## 34 Todo tiene propósito 1.2

**Leamos/Escribamos** Completa el párrafo con la forma correcta del presente del subjuntivo. *¿Se te olvidó?* Present subjunctive, pp. 59–60

Hay que practicar mucho para que el equipo __1__ (ganar) el partido. Queremos ganarlo sin que nos __2__ (costar) demasiado esfuerzo. Raúl va a hablar con el entrenador antes de que __3__ (empezar) las clases, con tal de que __4__ (tener) tiempo. Quedó en ver al entrenador a las ocho a menos que los dos __5__(llegar) tarde. Yo también pasaré por la oficina del entrenador a las diez en caso de que no __6__ (estar) allí antes.

1. gane
2. cueste
3. empiecen
4. tenga
5. lleguen
6. esté

## 35 Una entrevista 1.2

**Leamos/Hablemos** A Jorge lo están entrevistando para entrar a la universidad. Completa sus oraciones.

1. Quiero tomar más clases de español para que...
2. Me gustaría estudiar en el extranjero a menos de que...
3. Tengo la intención de participar en los deportes sin que...
4. Deseo conocer al entrenador de tenis antes de que...
5. Voy a traer mi propia computadora con tal de que...
6. Quiero llegar a ser médico para que...
7. Tengo mi solicitud aquí en caso de que...
8. ¿Puedo dar un paseo por el campus antes de que...?

## Comunicación

HOLT SoundBooth ONLINE RECORDING

## 36 Por si acaso 1.1, 1.2

**Hablemos** En parejas, túrnense para describir lo que dirían las personas en los dibujos. Usen las expresiones de **Exprésate.** ¿Cuántas expresiones pueden usar para cada dibujo?

**MODELO** **Vamos a casa antes de que empiece a llover.**

1. 2. 3.

### Más práctica

Review the structure of the subjunctive. Then write these incomplete sentences on the board or on a transparency.

1. **A menos de que..., no podré visitar a mi amiga.**
2. **Voy a graduarme este año a menos de que...**
3. **En caso de que..., voy a llevar un paraguas.**
4. **Con tal de que... aprobaré el curso.**

Ask students to fill in the missing verb or grammatical expression. 1.2

### Comunicación

**Pair Activity: Interpersonal**

Have students interview each other about their future goals. Encourage them to use the adverbial conjunctions from **Gramática** to explain their responses.
**(¿Cuándo quieres ir a la universidad? Quiero ir a la universidad antes de que vaya mi hermano menor.)** 1.1

## Differentiated Instruction

### SLOWER PACE LEARNERS

**Additional Practice** Write ten sentences on the board or on a transparency using the conjunctions, and have groups of four copy the sentences on paper so that each group has all the sentences. Have students cut the sentences into strips, then cut the strips in half after the conjunctions. Then have students exchange their sentence strips with another group. Ask the groups to put the sentences back together, check their work with the sentence on the board, and continue exchanging sentence strips until each group has arranged all the sentences. 1.2

### SPECIAL LEARNING NEEDS

**34 Students with Learning Disabilities** You might want to review with students the conjugations of verbs in the subjunctive. Using three of the verbs from Activity 34, go over the complete conjugation of each and write the forms on the board. Tell students to use these verbs as references as they do the activity.

**Differentiated Instruction** See the Differentiated Instruction CD-ROM.

**Resources**

**Planning:**

Lesson Planner, pp. 105–107, 266–269

One-Stop Planner

**Presentation:**

Video Program **GramaVisión**

**Practice:**

Grammar Tutor for Students of Spanish, Chapter 7

Cuaderno de vocabulario y gramática, pp. 82–84

Cuaderno de actividades, pp. 65–67

Activities for Communication, pp. 27–28

Lab Book, pp. 37–40

Teaching Transparencies

Bell Work 7.7

**Vocabulario y gramática** answers, pp. 82–84

Audio CD 7, Tr. 9

Interactive Tutor, Disc 2

**Bell Work**

Use Bell Work 7.7 in the *Teaching Transparencies*, or write this activity on the board.

**Completa las siguientes oraciones.**

1. Voy a trabajar con tal de que…
2. Estudiaré en caso de que…
3. No llamaré a Sara a menos de que…
4. Quiero llegar antes de que…
5. Yo pago mi entrada con tal de que... 1.2

## Subjunctive with future actions

Interactive TUTOR

**1** The following **adverbial conjunctions** express time. Adverbial conjunctions join a dependent clause and an independent clause in the same sentence.

| | |
|---|---|
| **cuando** *when* | **hasta que** *until* |
| **después de que** *after* | **tan pronto como** *as soon as* |
| **en cuanto** *as soon as* | |

**2** Use the **subjunctive** with conjunctions that express time when the verb refers to an action that hasn't happened yet.

Voy a comprar un carro **en cuanto tenga** el dinero.
*I'm going to buy a car as soon as I have the money.*

**Después de que** Rosa **salga** de clases, iremos al parque.
*After Rosa gets out of class, we'll go to the park.*

Voy a esperar **hasta que lleguen** mis amigos.
*I'm going to wait until my friends get here.*

**Tan pronto como** Luis **termine** su tarea irá a su clase de natación.
*As soon as Luis finishes his homework he'll go to his swimming class.*

Vamos a salir con ellos **cuando pasen** por nosotros.
*We're going to go out with them when they come for us.*

**3** The **indicative** can also be used with conjunctions of time when talking about habitual or past actions. You will see examples of this in the next grammar section.

Vocabulario y gramática, pp. 82–84
Actividades, pp. 65–67
Online workbooks

Estos ciclistas entrenan para una carrera cerca de Portoviejo, Ecuador.

### 37 El verano en Ecuador 1.2

**Leamos/Escribamos** Completa cada oración con las formas correctas de los verbos en paréntesis.

1. Voy a buscar trabajo en cuanto ___ (terminar) las clases. terminen
2. Vamos a viajar a Portoviejo después de que mi hermano ___ (graduarse). se gradúe
3. Tan pronto como los estudiantes ___ (irse), vamos a descansar. se vayan
4. Cuando ___ (llegar) mi amiga de Ecuador, practicaré español con ella. llegue
5. No podemos pasear por Portoviejo hasta que Mario nos ___ (traer) el mapa. traiga
6. ¿Celia va a cuidar a tus animales cuando ___ (salir) de viaje? salgas

## Core Instruction

### TEACHING GRAMÁTICA

1. Have students look over the conjunctions of time in point 1. **(1 min.)**
2. Go over point 2. After each example, clarify that the action has not yet happened. (**Voy a comprar un carro en cuanto tenga el dinero. Todavía no tengo el dinero.**) **(4 min.)**
3. Provide more examples for each conjunction and ask whether each action has already occurred. **Tan pronto como empiece la película, voy a quedarme dormida. ¿Ha empezado la película?** (no) **(4 min.)**
4. Go over point 3 with students and explain that in this section they will be focusing on the use of the subjunctive with conjunctions of time. **(1 min.)**

### GramaVisión

For a video presentation of the subjunctive with future actions, use **GramaVisión**.

GramaVisión

CD 7, Tr. 9

## 38 Una fiesta 1.2

**Escuchemos/Leamos** Decide si cada oración es **cierta** o **falsa**, basándote en la conversación entre Pati y Leo. Corrige las oraciones falsas.

1. Pati quiere hacer la fiesta antes de que se gradúen.
2. Muchos estudiantes salen de viaje tan pronto como terminan las clases. cierta
3. Los papás de Leo se van de vacaciones en cuanto empiecen los exámenes.
4. Pati va a mandar un correo electrónico en cuanto llegue al colegio.
5. Leo va a hacer la lista de compras después de que sepa cuántas personas vendrán. cierta

**1.** falsa; Pati quiere hacer la fiesta después de que se gradúen.
**3.** falsa; Los papás de Leo se van de vacaciones antes de que empiecen los exámenes.
**4.** falsa; Pati va a mandar un correo en cuanto vuelva a casa.

## 39 Cuando sea mayor... 1.2

**Escribamos** Describe en dos oraciones lo que las personas de los dibujos quieren hacer. Usa las expresiones de **Gramática.**

## Comunicación

HOLT SoundBooth ONLINE RECORDING

## 40 Hay mucho que hacer 1.1, 1.2

**Hablemos** Imagina que acabas de llegar a este país y tienes muchos planes. En parejas, túrnense para entrevistarse sobre sus planes. Usen expresiones como las del cuadro.

| | |
|---|---|
| ¿Cuándo vas a...? | ¿En qué momento irás...? |
| ¿Qué planes tienes para...? | Pienso... antes de que... |
| Empezaré a trabajar en cuanto... | Después de que... voy a... |
| Me gustaría... tan pronto como... | No haré... hasta que... |

Gramática 2

### 38 Script

Leo Oye, Pati, debemos hacer una fiesta e invitar a toda la clase.
Pati Sería genial. Pero tenemos que hacerla después de que nos graduemos.
Leo Pero Pati, mucha gente normalmente sale de viaje en cuanto terminan las clases.
Pati Pues, yo no puedo hacer una fiesta en mi casa tan pronto.
Leo Está bien. Mis papás se van de viaje antes de que empecemos los exámenes, y me dijeron que podíamos hacerla en mi casa.
Pati ¡Perfecto! Mañana les mandaré un correo electrónico a todos en cuanto vuelva a casa.
Leo De acuerdo. No haré la lista de compras hasta que sepamos cuántas personas vendrán.

## Comunicación

### Pair Activity: Interpersonal

Have students prepare a list of five things they would like to accomplish in the next ten years. Ask them to exchange lists with a partner. Have them take turns using conjunctions that express time to say when they think their partners will do each activity.

**MODELO**

**—Tan pronto como te gradúes del colegio, irás a la universidad.**

**—En cuanto tengas el dinero, comprarás una casa.**

1.1

## Differentiated Instruction

### ADVANCED LEARNERS

**Challenge** Have students write a paragraph describing their plans for the summer. Ask them to use at least four conjunctions that express time. Have them exchange paragraphs with a partner. The partner should underline the time conjunctions and circle the verbs in the subjunctive. 1.2, 1.3

### MULTIPLE INTELLIGENCES

**Naturalist** Ask students to write five sentences to tell about a park or natural landscape they would like to visit. Have them describe what they would like to do and when. **Tan pronto como empiecen las vacaciones, quiero ir al parque de Yellowstone con mis amigos. Después de que un guía nos dé un mapa, vamos a hacer senderismo.** 1.3

**Differentiated Instruction** See the Differentiated Instruction CD-ROM.

## Resources

**Planning:**

Lesson Planner, pp. 105–107, 266–269

One-Stop Planner

**Presentation:**

Video Program **GramaVisión**

**Practice:**

Grammar Tutor for Students of Spanish, Chapter 7

Cuaderno de vocabulario y gramática, pp. 82–84

Cuaderno de actividades, pp. 65–67

Activities for Communication, pp. 27–28

Lab Book, pp. 37–40

Teaching Transparencies

Bell Work 7.8

**Vocabulario y gramática** answers, pp. 82–84

Audio CD 7, Tr. 10

Interactive Tutor, Disc 2

### Bell Work

Use Bell Work 7.8 in the *Teaching Transparencies*, or write this activity on the board.

**Completa las oraciones con la forma correcta del verbo.**

1. Tan pronto como Ignacio ______ (terminar) la tarea, va a salir.
2. Cuando ______ (llegar) mis amigos, veremos la película.
3. No voy a salir hasta que ______ (dejar) de llover.
4. Uds. pueden quedarse hasta que ______ (regresar) mis papás. 1.2

### 41 Script

See script on p. 275F.

Interactive TUTOR

### Nota cultural

Los Andes, las montañas que atraviesan toda América del Sur, son el hogar de los incas, famosos por sus logros en la agricultura, la arquitectura y la ingeniería. Los incas construyeron un sistema de carreteras que va desde Quito, Ecuador, hasta Cuzco, Perú. Lo hicieron tan bien que partes de estas carreteras todavía se usan hoy.

Da unos ejemplos de carreteras u otras estructuras, construidas por civilizaciones antiguas, todavía en pie hoy. 3.1

Sección de una carretera incaica

## Indicative with habitual or past actions

**1** Use the **indicative** with **en cuanto, cuando, después de que, hasta que,** and **tan pronto como** when the verb refers to a habitual action.

**Cuando visitábamos** a mis parientes mis primos y yo siempre jugábamos.
*When we'd visit my relatives my cousins and I would always play.*

**Tan pronto como termino** un examen me gusta escuchar música.
*As soon as I finish an exam I like to listen to music.*

**2** The **indicative** is also used when describing completed actions in the past.

**En cuanto llegamos** a la clase, empezó el examen.
*As soon as we arrived in class, the exam started.*

No me interesaba la historia **hasta que fui** a Perú.
*I wasn't interested in history until I went to Peru.*

**Después de que** Alicia me **contó** lo que pasó, me sentí mejor.
*After Alicia told me what happened, I felt better.*

**3** Compare the use of the **indicative** to the **subjunctive** with **adverbial conjunctions of time.**

*completed in the past*
**Tan pronto como llegué,** todo el mundo se fue.

*hasn't happened yet*
**Tan pronto como llegue,** vamos a preparar la cena.

Vocabulario y gramática, pp. 82–84
Actividades, pp. 65–67
Online workbooks

CD 7, Tr. 10

### 41 ¿Pasado o futuro? 1.2

**Escuchemos** Escucha los comentarios y determina si cada acción es **a)** del pasado, **b)** del futuro o **c)** habitual.

**1.** del pasado **2.** del futuro **3.** del pasado **4.** habitual **5.** del futuro **6.** del pasado

### 42 El viaje de Miguel 1.2

**Leamos/Escribamos** Completa el párrafo con las formas correctas de los verbos en paréntesis.

Estaba muy animado cuando __1__ (llegar) a Ecuador. Tan pronto como __2__ (bajarse) del avión, busqué un restaurante. En el restaurante pensé: "Después de que nosotros __3__ (terminar) de comer, buscaré un mapa. Quiero ir a Otavalo, pero antes de que nosotros __4__ (ir), aprovecharé para visitar los museos de Quito". Luego tomé un autobús a Otavalo. En cuanto __5__ (ver) las artesanías, quise comprar algo. Caminé por todo el mercado hasta que __6__ (encontrar) un suéter de lana para mi mamá.

**1.** llegué
**2.** me bajé
**3.** terminemos
**4.** vayamos
**5.** vi
**6.** encontré

## Core Instruction

### TEACHING GRAMÁTICA

1. Remind students to pay attention to the context of the sentence in order to decide which verb tense and mood to use with time conjunctions. Go over point 1. **(2 min.)**
2. Point out that often words such as **siempre, todos los años,** and **cada día** signal habitual actions. Also, when the sentence refers to a habitual action, the verb in the main clause is in the present tense. **(2 min.)**
3. Go over point 2. Point out that for completed actions in the past, the preterite is used in the main clause. **(3 min.)**
4. Go over point 3. Provide more examples and have students decide whether each describes a habitual action, a completed action in the past, or a future action. **(3 min.)**

### GramaVisión

For a video presentation of the indicative with habitual or past actions, use **GramaVisión.**

GramaVisión

## 43 Un intercambio en Lima 1.2

**Leamos/Escribamos** Lee esta parte de una conversación entre un profesor de español y un estudiante de intercambio. Completa las oraciones con las formas correctas de los verbos en paréntesis.

1. Cuando tú ═══ (llegar) a Lima, ¿fuiste a la casa de un estudiante peruano? llegaste
2. ¿Viviste con una familia peruana hasta que ═══ (terminar) el viaje? terminó
3. Hablábamos solamente en español después de que ═══ (salir) de Estados Unidos. salimos
4. No sabíamos cuántas clases íbamos a tomar hasta que ═══ (hablar) con la directora. hablamos
5. Después de que yo ═══ (descansar) un poco, tuvimos tiempo para conocer la ciudad. descansé
6. Fuimos a los museos tan pronto como ═══ (encontrar) un mapa. encontramos
7. Tendrás muchas experiencias para contarles a tus niños cuando ═══ (ser) mayor. seas
8. Siempre traigo regalos para mi familia cuando ═══ (volver) a casa. vuelvo

Plaza de Armas, Lima, Perú

## Comunicación

HOLT SoundBooth ONLINE RECORDING

## 44 Prepárate para la entrevista 1.1, 1.2

**Hablemos** En parejas, dramaticen la siguiente situación. Un(a) amigo(a) tiene su primera entrevista de trabajo y te pide consejos. Explícale qué sueles hacer para una entrevista y qué crees que él o ella debe hacer. Pueden usar las frases del cuadro.

**MODELO** **—Siempre me pongo ropa formal cuando voy a una entrevista.**

**—Debes llegar al lugar diez minutos antes de que comience la entrevista.**

> Tan pronto como tú...
> Después de que ustedes...
> Antes de que (irse), siempre...
> No digas nada sobre...hasta que el jefe (la jefa)...
> Suelo tomar la iniciativa antes de que...

### Más práctica

On the board or on a transparency, write the first half of ten sentences using the time conjunctions with a variety of tenses. **(No vamos a salir hasta que..., Me levanté tan pronto como...)** Have students complete each sentence with a verb in the appropriate tense. Then ask volunteers to restate the entire sentence in a different tense. **(Ayer no salimos hasta que salió el sol.)** 1.2

### Comunicación

**Pair Activity: Interpersonal**

After students have done Activity 44, have them pair up with different partners to tell about what happened in their imaginary interviews. Remind them that this time they will be talking about completed actions, which take the indicative after conjunctions of time. 1.1

## Differentiated Instruction

### SLOWER PACE LEARNERS

43 Before students do Activity 43, have them copy the sentences and underline the verb in the main clause. They should also circle clue phrases such as **siempre** or **todos los días**, which indicate that they should use the indicative. Remind them that if the verb in the main clause is in the past tense, the verb following the time conjunction will be in the indicative, and if the verb in the main clause is in the future, the verb following the time conjunction will be in the subjunctive. 1.2

### SPECIAL LEARNING NEEDS

43 **Students with Dyslexia** If you have students with dyslexia, you might want to do Activity 43 as a listening activity. Write the targeted verb for each item on the board. Read each sentence aloud and have students listen for context clues such as verb tense and words that indicate habitual actions. Then read the sentence again and have volunteers conjugate the verb. Write the answers on the board as students provide them, and have them copy the words in their notebooks. 1.2

### Assess

**Assessment Program**

**Prueba: Gramática 2,** pp. 129–130

**Prueba: Aplicación 2,** pp. 131–132

Audio CD 7, Tr. 16

Alternative Assessment, pp. 379, 391, 403

**Online Assessment**

**my.hrw.com**

**Test Generator**

## Resources

**Planning:**

Lesson Planner, pp. 108, 268–269

One-Stop Planner

**Presentation:**

Video Program, Videocassette 4

DVD Program

**VideoNovela**

**Practice:**

Video Guide, pp. 48–50

Lab Book, p. 78–79

### Visual Learners

To help students separate the essential from the non-essential, have them prepare a graphic organizer with the following heads: **Esencial, No esencial.** As they watch the episode, have them note the information in the appropriate columns. 1.2

| Esencial | No esencial |
|---|---|
| 1. | 1. |
| 2. | 2. |
| 3. | 3. |
| 4. | 4. |

### Gestures

Ask students to notice what gestures Clara uses to communicate the urgency of her task. Do her gestures help the students understand the meaning of her words?

Novela en video

# Clara perspectiva

## Episodio 7

**ESTRATEGIA**

**Separating the essential from the non-essential** A story often provides essential information as well as non-essential information. In **Episodio 7**, Clara must convince Mercedes, Professor Luna's secretary, to let her have access to his computer. What essential information does Clara have to use to persuade her? What essential information does Mercedes give Clara in her mission? What non-essential information does she give Clara? Write down the essential and the non-essential information that Mercedes gives Clara. Does the list give you any clues into Mercedes's character? 1.2

1

### En los bosques de Pirque

**Ecologista 2** Profesor, si nos hace el favor.

**Profesor Luna** Parece que no tengo otra opción.

**Ecologista 1** No lo tome a mal, profesor, sólo queremos hablar un rato con usted.

### En la oficina del profesor Luna

**Clara** Buenos días, Mercedes.

**Mercedes** Buenos días. No hay clases y el profesor Luna no se encuentra ahora.

**Clara** Ya sé, Mercedes, pero…

2

3

**Clara** Mercedes, por favor, ¡es urgente! Necesito imprimir unos archivos del profesor Luna. Hablé con él hoy en la mañana. Por alguna razón, me pidió que imprimiera todos los archivos en su computadora bajo el título "Recomendaciones". No tenemos mucho tiempo. Parecía urgente hacerlo inmediatamente.

**Mercedes** No, el profesor Luna no permite que cualquier estudiante entre a su oficina a usar su computadora.

4

## Core Instruction

### TEACHING NOVELA EN VIDEO

1. Have students scan the **Novela en video** text and look at the photos from the episode. **(1 min.)**
2. Play the video, stopping periodically to ask comprehension questions. If students have trouble understanding any portion of the video, you might want to use the captioned version of the episode. **(5 min.)**
3. Play the video a second time, and have students take notes in a chart on essential and non-essential information. **(5 min.)**
4. Have students work in pairs to answer the questions on page 305. When they have finished, go over the answers together. **(5 min.)**

### Escuchemos

As students watch the **Novela,** have them listen for the expressions Mercedes uses to talk about her life and the challenges she has faced. Have them write down two accomplishments she mentions.

Novela en video

Visit Holt Online
go.hrw.com
KEYWORD: EXP3 CH7
Online Edition

Novela en video

**Clara** No entiendo por qué el profesor quería que imprimiera los archivos en vez de copiarlos. No tengo mucho tiempo. Quizás no estaba pensando bien. Voy a copiarlos.

**Mercedes** ¡No! Si haces una copia de los archivos, ¡se autodestruyen! No sé cómo copiarlos sin que se autodestruyan. Hay mucha gente que está interesada en copiar los trabajos del profesor. Por eso el profesor creó un sistema tan complicado.

5

**Mercedes** ¿Sabías que no soy chilena? Soy de ascendencia ecuatoriana... Me crié en Quito. En mi país, había muchos problemas económicos. Por eso mis padres decidieron mudarse a Santiago. Al principio, nos costó trabajo adaptarnos. Todo aquí era distinto, la forma de ser, el estilo de vida, las tradiciones, las costumbres... Pero poco a poco nos fuimos acostumbrando y nos adaptamos a nuestro nuevo hogar. Hubo algunos obstáculos, pero nada que no pudiéramos superar... sólo tuvimos que hacer el esfuerzo.

6

7

**Mercedes** Estoy tan agradecida de la bienvenida que nos dieron los chilenos. No sentimos ninguna discriminación. Todos en mi familia, mis padres, mis hermanos, mis hermanas y yo tomamos la iniciativa de triunfar en nuestro nuevo país. Fue un desafío. Aprovechamos todas las oportunidades que se nos dieron. Yo, por ejemplo, tomé clases en inglés. Y ahora, soy bilingüe. Por lo tanto, tengo más oportunidades en el trabajo.

8

## ¿COMPRENDES?

1. ¿Qué quieren los ecologistas? ¿Quiere irse con ellos el profesor Luna? ¿Cómo lo sabes?
2. ¿Qué le dice Clara a Mercedes que tiene que hacer?
3. Al principio, ¿cree Mercedes a Clara? ¿Qué le convence?
4. ¿Es Mercedes chilena? ¿De dónde es? ¿Es esencial esta información? ¿Cómo lo sabes?
5. Mientras imprimen los documentos, ¿qué historia le cuenta Mercedes a Clara? Escribe una breve descripción de su historia. ¿Es esencial esta información? ¿Cómo lo sabes?

1.2, 1.3

**Próximo episodio**

***Clara sigue con su investigación mientras Octavio tiene que defender su ausencia en la revista. ¿Y dónde crees que está el profesor?***

PÁGINAS 346–347

### ¿Comprendes? Answers

1. hablar con el profesor; no; dice que parece que no tiene otra opción
2. imprimir unos archivos del profesor
3. no; Clara sabe su contraseña
4. no; Ecuador; no; no tiene nada que ver con la acción principal
5. la historia de su mudanza a Chile; descriptions will vary; no es esencial porque no afecta la acción del cuento

### Connections

#### Economics Link

Have students discuss what Mercedes tells Clara about her move from Ecuador to Chile. Tell them that the effects of natural disasters and the depressed oil market of the late 90's hurt Ecuador's economy. These events, combined with the collapse of the banking sector, led to a very unstable economy. Chile, on the other hand, became a role model for economic reform in the 1990's. Chile has a reputation for strong financial institutions and sound economic policies. Have students do research on the Internet or in the library to compare the Chilean and Ecuadorean economies.

3.1

### Clara perspectiva, Episodio 7

In **Episodio 7,** at Pirque, the two men who we now know to be ecologists with *EcoChile* are taking the professor someplace where they can talk. Clara, while trying to get into the professor's office, is confronted by Mercedes. After some conversation, she remembers the code word the professor gave her, which makes it clear to Mercedes that the professor is in trouble and that Clara should be allowed into the professor's office to print out the documents. While they wait, Mercedes tells Clara her life story and how she and her family moved to Chile from Ecuador. After the documents are through printing, Clara collects them and leaves.

### Comunicación

#### Group Activity: Interpersonal

After students have read the **Novela en video,** have them work in pairs to discuss what it would be like to move to a different country. Ask them to talk about some of the reasons people might make such a move.

1.1

# Lectura informativa

**Resources**

**Planning:**

Lesson Planner, pp. 109, 270–271

One-Stop Planner

**Presentation:**

Audio CD 7, Tr. 11

**Practice:**

Cuaderno de actividades, p. 68

Reading Strategies and Skills Handbook, Chapter 7

Interactive Advanced Reader

**Pre-Reading Activity**

Ask students what they have learned so far in this chapter about the people of Peru. Remind them that Peru has a varied population of different ethnic groups. Have them share any information they know about Peru's history. Remind them that ancient Peru was the seat of several prominent Andean civilizations, most notably that of the Incas whose empire was destroyed by the Spanish conquistadors in 1533.

**Comparisons**

**Language to Language**

Tell students that other Quechua words used in English include **llama, puma,** and **jerky.** Why do they think we use these words in English? Ask them what Spanish words are used in English and vice versa. 4.1

**Pre-AP Practice**

**AP Language Examination:** **Lectura informativa** helps students prepare for Section I, Part B: **Reading Comprehension.** The audio recording helps them prepare for Part A: **Listening—Short Narratives.**

# *Lectura informativa*

CD 7, Tr. 11

## Los grupos étnicos de Perú

Varios grupos étnicos viven en Perú. El grupo más grande son los indígenas (45%), luego los mestizos (37%), los de ascendencia europea (15%) y los africanos, japoneses y chinos (3%). El español y el quechua son los idiomas oficiales del país. Aproximadamente el 75% de los peruanos hablan español. Y además del quechua, hablado por casi 25% de los peruanos, el aymara es otro idioma indígena hablado en Perú con más de 200.000 hablantes. Se hablan más de 103 idiomas indígenas en Perú, pero solamente se hablan entre pequeños grupos étnicos del altiplano y las amazonas.

**Los quechuas**

Hoy en día hay más de 60 grupos distintos de indígenas peruanos. El grupo más grande son los quechuas, que son descendientes de los incas. Los incas no hablaban el idioma quechua originalmente; lo adoptaron al establecerse en la región. Los quechuas se refieren a sí mismos con la palabra *runa* (la gente). En América del Sur, hay más de 10 millones de quechuas en siete países, y el quechua es el idioma amerindio más hablado del mundo. Hay varias palabras en inglés y en español que vienen del quechua, como *cóndor, puma* y *lima* (la legumbre).

**El aporte de los japoneses**

La emigración de los japoneses a Perú empezó el 3 de abril de 1899 cuando un grupo de 790 japoneses llegó a Perú para trabajar en los campos de caña de azúcar. Luego el número de inmigrantes creció

Esta mujer japonés-peruana prepara brochetas de pollo, Lima, Perú.

**Core Instruction**

**TEACHING LECTURA INFORMATIVA**

1. Read the first paragraph as a class. Ask students if they were surprised to learn that Peru has two official languages. **(5 min.)**
2. Have students read the second paragraph and then ask: **¿Quiénes son los quechuas?** Ask them to name some Spanish words that come from the Quechua language. **(5 min.)**
3. Have students read the third paragraph. Ask them what they know about Alberto Fujimori. **(5 min.)**
4. Have students work in pairs to answer the **Comprensión** questions. **(5 min.)**

Una mujer afro-hispana vende vegetales locales en un mercado al aire libre.

Estas estudiantes mestizas asisten a la Universidad de San Marcos, la más grande de Perú.

a casi 20.000, y hoy en día hay alrededor de 100.000 habitantes de origen japonés en el país. Aunque vinieron para trabajar en la agricultura, la mayoría de los inmigrantes abandonaron el cultivo de la caña de azúcar y se mudaron a las ciudades. Poco a poco, los japoneses se integraron a la sociedad peruana, y en 1990 los peruanos eligieron al primer presidente de origen japonés, Alberto Fujimori.

Visit Holt Online
go.hrw.com
KEYWORD: EXP3 CH7
Online Edition

## Comprensión

**A ¡Defínelo!** Indica la palabra que va con la definición correcta. 1.2

1. aymara 3. quechua 5. altiplano
2. Fujimori 4. mestizos

a. la región donde se habla la mayoría de los idiomas indígenas
b. el primer presidente de origen japonés en Perú
c. un idioma indígena con más de 200.000 hablantes que no es un idioma oficial de Perú
d. el segundo grupo étnico más grande de Perú
e. uno de los idiomas oficiales de Perú

**B Datos de Perú** Basándote en lo que leíste, contesta las preguntas. 1.2

1. ¿Cuántos idiomas se hablan en Perú? ¿Cuáles son los idiomas oficiales del país?
2. ¿Cuál es el grupo étnico más grande de Perú?
3. ¿Por qué emigraron los japoneses a Perú?
4. ¿Cuántos habitantes de origen japonés viven actualmente en Perú?

## Actividad 1.3

**Otra cultura** ¿Has vivido en o viajado a un país donde hayas tenido que adaptarte a la cultura? ¿Conoces a otras personas que hayan tenido que adaptarse a otra cultura? Escribe un párrafo sobre tu experiencia o la experiencia de alguien que conozcas.



# Lectura informativa

**A Answers**
1. c
2. b
3. e
4. d
5. a

**B Answers**
1. más de 103; español, quechua
2. los indígenas
3. para trabajar en los campos de caña de azúcar
4. alrededor de 100,000

### Cultures

**Practices and Perspectives**

The great cultural history of the Aymara can be seen at Tiahuanaco, an ancient native ruin south of Lake Titicaca, near the Peruvian border. It was probably the center of a pre-Incan empire and many believe it was built by the Aymara. Have students research the historic and contemporary status of the Aymara. (Though they were subjugated by the Incas in the fifteenth century, the Aymara still dominate the region and have retained their pastoral and agricultural culture.) 2.1

### Post-Reading Activities

Ask students to find information about where the different ethnic groups in Peru live. Tell them, for example, that the city of Cuzco is mostly indigenous. Once they have done the research, ask them to share the information with the class. 1.3

## Differentiated Instruction

### ADVANCED LEARNERS

**Challenge** Have students look back at the three parts of the selection. Ask them to decide which part they would like to learn more about, and have them research information online. Suggest that they look for newspaper articles, especially if they would like to learn more about recent developments. Divide the class into three groups, based on the part of the selection they researched. Have the groups discuss what they learned and then have groups take turns presenting their findings to the class. 3.1, 3.2

### MULTIPLE INTELLIGENCES

**Naturalist** Have students research information about what kinds of crops are grown in Peru. Are the crops grown for export? What is farming like in the Andes? Ask them to prepare a short presentation. 1.3, 2.2

### Assess

**Assessment Program**
**Prueba: Lectura,** p. 133
Standardized Assessment Tutor, pp. 29–32
**Online Assessment**
**my.hrw.com**
**Test Generator**

**Resources**

**Planning:**

Lesson Planner, pp. 109–110, 270–271

One-Stop Planner

**Practice:**

Cuaderno de actividades, p. 68

Reading Strategies and Skills Handbook, Chapter 7

Interactive Advanced Reader

**Applying the Strategies**

For more practice with making inferences, you might have students use the "Read, Rate, Reread" strategy from the *Reading Strategies and Skills Handbook.*

**Escuchemos**

Play the recording of the reading, and have students tally the number of times they hear the adverbial conjunction **hasta que.** (twice)

**Pre-AP Practice**

**AP Language Examination:** **Leamos** helps students prepare for Section I, Part B: **Reading Comprehension.** To help prepare students for Part A: **Listening—Short Narratives,** have students analyze the poem by listening to the rhythm and the sounds. Ask for volunteers to take turns reading the poem aloud, with the class listening for repeated sounds. Do the lines rhyme? What is the effect of the repeated sounds in the poem?

**AP Benchmark:** Write an analytical or persuasive essay.

**Focus:** Making inferences

- SE, p. 311, **Taller del escritor**
- TE, p. 311, Slower Pace Learners
- TE, p. 311, Multiple Intelligences

# Leamos y escribamos

**ESTRATEGIA**

**para leer** When you read a poem or a short story, sometimes you might have to make inferences. This means that you will be able to make an informed guess or an interpretation of what you think the author is trying to say using the information from the reading. Some authors intentionally leave their writing open to these types of interpretations.



## Antes de leer 1.3, 3.1

**A** El poema que vas a leer, "Oda al presente" *(Ode to the present)* es de Pablo Neruda. Neruda nació en Chile en 1904 y su nombre legal era Ricardo Neftalí Reyes Basoalto. En 1946 adoptó Pablo Neruda como su nombre legal. Además de ser escritor, también fue funcionario público y diplomático. Fue elegido al senado de Chile en 1945 y en 1970 fue embajador de Chile en París. Neruda ganó el Premio Nobel de literatura en 1971. El poeta murió en Chile el 23 de septiembre de 1973. Antes de leer el poema entero, lee las primeras diez líneas, y trata de adivinar de qué va a hablar. ¿Cómo será el poema?

# Oda al presente

*de Pablo Neruda*

Este
presente
liso°
como una tabla,
fresco°,
esta hora,
este día
limpio
como una copa nueva
—del pasado
no hay una
telaraña°—,
tocamos
con los dedos
el presente,
cortamos
su medida,
dirigimos°
su brote°,
está viviente,

3 smooth 5 fresh 12 cobweb 18 we direct 19 bloom

## Core Instruction

### TEACHING LEAMOS

1. Read the **Estrategia para leer** with students. **(1 min.)**
2. Ask students if they have read any poems by Pablo Neruda. Have them read **Antes de leer**. **(2 min.)**
3. Read the poem aloud. Then have students read it to themselves, using the suggested strategy. **(10 min.)**
4. Remind students that even if they did not understand the entire poem, they should be able to get a general idea of what the author is trying to say. Ask volunteers to tell the main idea of the poem. **(3 min.)**
5. Answer the questions in Activity B as a class, and have students do Activities C and D for homework. **(4 min.)**
6. Have students work in small groups to answer the questions in **Después de leer.** **(5 min.)**

vivo,
nada tiene
de ayer irremediable°,
de pasado perdido,
es nuestra
criatura,
está creciendo
en este
momento, está llevando
arena, está comiendo
en nuestras manos,
cógelo°,
que no resbale,
que no se pierda en sueños
ni palabras,
agárralo,
sujétalo
y ordénalo
hasta que te obedezca,
hazlo camino,
campana,
máquina,
beso, libro,
caricia°,
corta su deliciosa
fragancia de madera
y de ella
hazte una silla,
trenza°
su respaldo°,
pruébala,
o bien
escalera!

Sí,
escalera,
sube
en el presente,
peldaño°
tras peldaño,
firmes
los pies en la madera
del presente,
hacia arriba,
hacia arriba,
no muy alto,
tan sólo
hasta que puedas
reparar
las goteras°
del techo,
no muy alto,
no te vayas al cielo,
alcanza
las manzanas,
no las nubes,
ésas
déjalas
ir por el cielo, irse
hacia el pasado.
Tú
eres
tu presente,
tu manzana:
tómala
de tu árbol,
levántala
en tu
mano,
brilla
como una estrella,
tócala,
híncale el diente° y ándate
silbando° en el camino.

23 without remedy 32 grab it 44 caress 49 braid, weave 50 back (chair) 58 step (of staircase) 69 leaks
92 sink your teeth into it 93 whistling



## Leamos y escribamos

### Active Reading Questions

1. **¿En qué imágenes piensas mientras lees este poema?**
2. **¿Qué imágenes asocia el autor con el pasado? ¿Cómo son?**
3. **¿Estás de acuerdo con la actitud del autor hacia el presente y el pasado?**
4. **¿Crees que el autor diría que debemos tomar la iniciativa para alcanzar nuestros sueños?** 1.2

### Drawing Inferences

Have students draw conclusions about what the author is trying to say in this poem. Have them cite passages from the text to support their inferences. Remind them that often poems can have many different interpretations. As long as they can support their inferences with examples from the poem, there is no right or wrong answer. 1.2, 3.1

### Language Note

Point out to students that **lo** can stand for abstract things like the past and the present. Ask students to analyze the meanings of **lo** in lines 26 and 32. (In line 32, **lo** stands for the abstract present; although it also refers to the metaphor for the present, **criatura,** in line 26.) 1.2

## Differentiated Instruction

### SPECIAL LEARNING NEEDS

**Students with AD(H)D** If you have students with AD(H)D in your class, you might want to suggest that they write a one-line summary after every five to ten lines, in order to maintain focus on the poem. 1.2

### MULTIPLE INTELLIGENCES

**Musical/Rhythmic** Have volunteers read the poem aloud as the rest of the students close their eyes. Ask students to focus on the rhythm and sound of the poem. Do they hear harsh sounds? soft sounds? How do the rhythm and sound of the poem help convey meaning? If they were to put this poem to music, what instruments would they use?

### B Sample Answers

1. liso, fresco, limpio, vivo
2. una tabla, una copa nueva, una criatura
3. agarrarlo, sujetarlo, ordenarlo
4. hasta poder reparar las goteras del techo, hasta las manzanas; para quedarse en el presente
5. algo malo que no nos deja disfrutar del presente; dejarlas ir por el cielo hacia el pasado
6. tomarlo del árbol, levantarlo en la mano y comerlo

### Communities

**Community Link**

The objective of the **Fundación Pablo Neruda** is to cultivate and promote the arts, which was one of Neruda's aspirations. Just before his fiftieth birthday, the poet donated his library to the University of Chile. He wanted to create a foundation for the study of poetry. But the military coup in September of 1973 impeded his plans. After his death, the **Fundación Pablo Neruda** was finally created. The foundation has conserved the contents of his home, including his art and his writings, for the public to view and enjoy. The organization also has its own publications, offers poetry workshops to inspire young writers, promotes art and literature in high schools and other community groups through printed materials and videos, and organizes cultural events. Ask students what organizations exist in their communities to promote the arts. Are there any that promote Spanish arts and literature? If so, encourage them to attend the events. 3.1, 5.2

**Post-Reading Strategy**

Have students share what they think is the main idea of the poem. Ask them to tell what inferences they made in their interpretation of the poem. 1.3

## Comprensión 1.2

**B** Contesta las siguientes preguntas basándote en el poema.

1. ¿Cómo es el presente, según el poema?
2. ¿Con qué se compara el presente?
3. Según el poema, ¿qué debemos hacer con el presente?
4. ¿Hasta qué punto se debe subir la escalera del verso 53? ¿Por qué?
5. ¿Qué son las nubes del verso 75? ¿Qué debemos hacer con ellas?
6. Al final del poema, ¿qué hay que hacer con el presente?

**C** Lee los siguientes fragmentos del poema y escribe con tus propias palabras lo que cada fragmento significa para ti.

1. «liso como una tabla, fresco, esta hora, este día»
2. «tocamos con los dedos el presente, cortamos su medida»
3. «es nuestra criatura, está creciendo en este momento»
4. «escalera, sube en el presente, peldaño tras peldaño»
5. «no te vayas al cielo, alcanza las manzanas, no las nubes»
6. «tu presente, tu manzana: tómala de tu árbol»

**D** Lee las palabras de la lista a la izquierda. Para cada palabra, indica qué expresión se usa en el poema para referirse a esa palabra.

| | |
|---|---|
| 1. manzana c | a. perdido |
| 2. fragancia de madera e | b. liso |
| 3. ayer d | c. brilla como una estrella |
| 4. tabla b | d. irremediable |
| 5. este día f | e. deliciosa |
| 6. pasado a | f. limpio como copa nueva |

## Después de leer 1.3

**E** Al leer este poema, ¿qué inferencias hiciste sobre los términos usados por el poeta? ¿Qué significa este poema para ti? ¿Piensas que el narrador tiene una actitud positiva hacia el presente? ¿Cómo lo sabes? ¿Estás de acuerdo con el narrador cuando dice que el pasado está perdido? Explica.

## Core Instruction

### TEACHING ESCRIBAMOS

1. Read the **Estrategia para escribir** and the introductory paragraph with students. **(1 min.)**
2. Have students use a word web like the one on page 311 as they complete item 1. **(5 min.)**
3. Have students complete items 2 and 3. Circulate around the classroom to help any students that are having difficulty with their writing. **(20 min.)**
4. Have students exchange their descriptions with a partner to complete item 4. **(5 min.)**

# Taller del escritor

1.3

ESTRATEGIA

**para escribir** In order to lead readers to make correct inferences, the author must be careful about what he or she reveals. The author needs to lead readers in the right direction in order for them to understand the intended meaning, without saying too much.

## Un escrito que haga pensar

Para que el lector infiera el significado de algo que no está escrito en un texto, es necesario darle suficiente información por medio de palabras, ideas parecidas o comparaciones. Piensa en algo y sin mencionar su nombre, descríbelo de manera que el lector entienda de qué estás hablando.

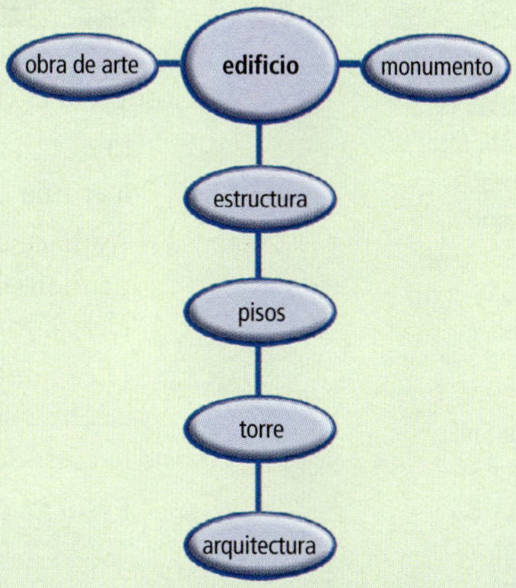


### 1 Antes de escribir

Escoge la palabra o concepto que el lector debe inferir y haz una lista de palabras relacionadas. Luego, piensa en una comparación que puedas hacer para que el lector pueda inferir correctamente la palabra que seleccionaste.

### 2 Escribir un borrador

Describe tu concepto en un párrafo usando las palabras y comparaciones de tu lista. Incluye suficiente información, pero no demasiada, para que el lector no vaya a confundirse.

### 3 Revisar

Revisa tu borrador y corrige los errores de gramática y ortografía. Verifica que las palabras y comparaciones que usaste para definir tu concepto sean claras.

### 4 Publicar

Intercambien sus párrafos en grupos de cuatro estudiantes y traten de inferir la palabra o concepto que cada uno tenía en mente. ¿Cuántos hicieron las inferencias correctamente?

## Differentiated Instruction

### SLOWER PACE LEARNERS

While students are doing item 1, you might want to discuss their topics with them individually. Look over the lists they made in item 1, and help them brainstorm other words to use. Show them examples of comparisons they might use to add life to their descriptions.

### MULTIPLE INTELLIGENCES

**Kinesthetic** Have students read their description to the class. Then have them reread the description, using their tone of voice, expressions, and gestures to convey meaning. Ask students to discuss how the second reading helped them make inferences about what they heard.

## Leamos y escribamos

### Process Writing

Remind students that they must include all key information in their writing. Explain that not all information must be directly stated. For example, they might use a comparison to convey information about what something looks like, or they might use sounds to communicate a certain atmosphere.

### Writing Assessment

To assess the **Taller del escritor,** you can use the following rubric. For additional rubrics, see the *Alternative Assessment Guide.*

| Writing Rubric | 4 | 3 | 2 | 1 |
|---|---|---|---|---|
| **Content** (Complete—Incomplete) | | | | |
| **Comprehensibility** (Comprehensible—Seldom comprehensible) | | | | |
| **Accuracy** (Accurate—Seldom accurate) | | | | |
| **Organization** (Well-organized—Poorly organized) | | | | |
| **Effort** (Excellent effort—Minimal effort) | | | | |

18–20: A 14–15: C Under
16–17: B 12–13: D 12: F

### Pre-AP Practice

**AP Language Examination: Leamos and Escribamos** help students prepare for Section I, Part B: **Reading Comprehension** and Section II, Part A: **Informal Writing.**

### Assess

**Assessment Program**
**Prueba: Lectura,** p. 133
**Prueba: Escritura,** p. 134
**Online Assessment**
**my.hrw.com**
**Test Generator**

# Prepárate para el examen

## Resources

**Planning:**

Lesson Planner, pp. 110–111, 270–273

One-Stop Planner

**Presentation:**

Video Program, Videocassette 4

DVD Program

**Variedades**

**Practice:**

Activities for Communication, pp. 49, 67–68

Video Guide, pp. 46–47

Lab Book, pp. 7, 37–40, 77

Audio CD 7, Trs. 12–13

Pre-AP Instructional Resources

Pre-AP Audio CD 2, Trs. 5–8

Interactive Tutor, Disc 2

Teaching Transparencies

**Situación, Capítulo 7**

Picture Sequences, Chapter 7

### 1 Script

1. Me acuerdo del día en que logré graduarme. ¡Me sentí tan orgullosa cuando me dieron el diploma!
2. Yo soy de ascendencia japonesa. En casa, tratamos de mantener las costumbres de nuestra cultura. Lo que más me gusta es la comida japonesa.
3. Tengo muchas aspiraciones. Voy a esforzarme mucho hasta que se realicen mis sueños. Quiero llegar a ser médico cuando sea mayor.
4. En el colegio, jugaba al boliche con el equipo. Mi éxito en el boliche se debe a que lo practico todos los días. Este año tuve buena suerte en el campeonato.

### 5 Answers

**1.** Es el español que se habla en los Andes; se ha incorporado muchas palabras de los idiomas indígenas. **2.** los quechuas **3.** Son conocidos por mantener su identidad y sus costumbres; el pueblo de Otavalo es famoso por su mercado. **4.** Son habitantes indígenas que viven en las islas Uros en el Lago Titicaca.

Capítulo 7
Repaso

# Prepárate para el examen

Interactive TUTOR

CD 7, Tr. 12

**1** Escucha los comentarios y escoge la foto que corresponde a cada uno. 1.2 **1.** c **2.** a **3.** d **4.** b

A

B

C

D

**1 Vocabulario 1**
- talking about challenges
- talking about accomplishments

pp. 278–283

**2 Gramática 1**
- preterite and imperfect of stative verbs
- grammatical reflexives
- **lo** and **lo que**

pp. 284–289

**3 Vocabulario 2**
- talking about future plans
- expressing cause and effect

pp. 292–297

**2** Completa el diálogo con las formas correctas de los verbos. 1.2

RITA Oye, Carlos, ayer yo __1__ (tenía/tuve) la oportunidad de leer una carta de Rosa.

CARLOS Ay, hace tiempo que no hablo con ella. __2__ (Lo que/Lo) primero que voy a hacer es llamarla cuando llegue a casa. Por cierto, ¿qué te cuenta?

RITA Dice que fue difícil mudarse a otro país, pues ya sabes que __3__ (crió/se crió) aquí. __4__ (Lo/Lo que) más trabajo le costó fue acostumbrarse al estilo de vida.

CARLOS Escuché que ella trató de obtener un puesto político pero no __5__ (podía/pudo). ¿Qué va a hacer?

RITA Pues, ella no se dará por vencida hasta que logre __6__ (lo/lo que) quiere.

**3** Completa cada oración con una palabra o frase del cuadro. 1.2

| | | |
|---|---|---|
| sueña con | tan pronto como | luchar por |
| llegar a ser | aspiraciones | acostumbrarme |

1. Para mí, fue muy difícil ═══ a un nuevo país. acostumbrarme
2. luchar por Creo que es muy importante ═══ alcanzar nuestras metas.
3. Mi hermano ═══ ir a la universidad. sueña con
4. Yo quiero ═══ una actriz famosa. llegar a ser
5. aspiraciones Tenemos muchas ═══ y nos esforzamos por alcanzarlas.
6. Tan pronto como ═══ me gradúe, voy a buscar trabajo en Hollywood.

## Oral Assessment

### Speaking Rubric

To assess the speaking activities in this section, you might use the following rubric. For additional speaking rubrics, see the Alternative Assessment section of the *Assessment Program.*

| Speaking Rubric | 4 | 3 | 2 | 1 |
|---|---|---|---|---|
| **Content** (Complete—Incomplete) | | | | |
| **Comprehension** (Total—Little) | | | | |
| **Comprehensibility** (Comprehensible—Incomprehensible) | | | | |
| **Accuracy** (Accurate—Seldom Accurate) | | | | |
| **Fluency** (Fluent—Not Fluent) | | | | |

18–20: A 16–17: B 14–15: C 12–13: D Under 12: F

4 Completa las oraciones con las formas correctas del verbo. 1.2

1. El entrenador siempre habla con el equipo antes de que (nosotros) ___ (empezar) a jugar. empecemos
2. ¡Hoy nadie quiere salir de aquí hasta que ellos nos ___ (haber) dado el trofeo! hayan
3. El año pasado todos se pusieron tristes cuando otro equipo lo ___ (recibir). recibió
4. Siempre como en cuanto ___ (terminar) un partido. termina
5. Después de que (nosotros) ___ (comer) hoy, nos acostaremos. comamos

5 Contesta las preguntas. 1.2

1. ¿Qué es el español andino?
2. ¿Cuál es el grupo étnico más grande de Perú?
3. ¿Por qué son conocidos los otavaleños y el pueblo de Otavalo?
4. ¿Quiénes son los uros y dónde viven?

CD 7, Tr. 13

6 Escucha mientras Fernando y Dora hablan de sus aspiraciones. Luego, escribe dos cosas que cada persona quiere hacer y cuándo quiere hacerlo. 1.2

Visit Holt Online
**go.hrw.com**
KEYWORD: EXP3 CH7
Chapter Self-test

**4 Gramática 2**
- subjunctive after adverbial conjunctions
- subjunctive with future actions
- indicative with habitual or past actions

**pp. 298–303**

**5 Cultura**
- Comparaciones **pp. 290–291**
- Lectura informativa **pp. 306–307**
- Notas culturales **pp. 286, 289, 297, 302**

## Conversación

HOLT SoundBooth ONLINE RECORDING

7 Role-play the following conversation with a partner. Partner A is the younger sibling of Partner B, a college student back from a semester in Peru. 1.1, 1.2

| | |
|---|---|
| Partner A: | Ask your partner how the semester in Peru went. |
| Partner B: | Say you faced some challenges in the beginning, and it took a lot of work for you to get used to it. |
| Partner A: | Ask what the biggest challenge or obstacle was. |
| Partner B: | Explain what was different about life in Lima. Say that little by little, you were able to adapt to the way of life. |
| Partner A: | Say when you go to college, you'd like to study in Latin America also. |
| Partner B: | Ask your partner about his or her plans for college. |
| Partner A: | Explain what you intend to study and what kind of business you'd like to start after you graduate. |
| Partner B: | Say if your partner focuses on his or her objectives, he or she will accomplish those goals. |

## Conversación

### Additional Speaking Practice

For additional speaking practice, use the *Picture Sequences Transparency* for Chapter 7. Use the Speaking Rubric on the preceding page to evaluate their performance. You may also wish to use the Interviews and Role-Plays in the *Activities for Communication* book.

### Pre-AP Practice

7 In the Level 3 *Pre-AP Instructional Resources* you will find an alternative version of Activity 7. The following resources in that book will help you prepare students for the AP Language Exam:

- Blackline masters, pp. 33, 43, 53
- Pre-AP Audio CD 2, Trs. 5–8
- Scripts and answers, pp. 57–75





### 6 Script

—Dora, vamos a graduarnos el próximo año. ¿Hay algo que quieras hacer antes de que nos graduemos?
—Pues, sí, Fernando, quiero participar en el club de teatro después de que termine este semestre. Es un sueño que siempre he tenido.
—¡Qué bien! Yo también participé en el club y me encantó. Lo que yo quiero hacer antes de que nos graduemos es viajar a Perú con el club de intercambio.
—¡Debes apuntarte rápido en caso de que haya pocos espacios!
—Sí, voy a apuntarme tan pronto como llegue el profesor de español.
—Quiero viajar a Latinoamérica también en cuanto tenga el dinero.
—¿Cuándo piensas ir?
—No sé, probablemente después de graduarme de la universidad.
—Mis papás me obligan a trabajar ahora con tal de que pueda viajar después de la graduación. Oye, tú debes buscar un trabajo también. El mío es genial.

### 6 Answers

Fernando quiere viajar a Perú con el club de intercambio antes de que se gradúen. Quiere apuntarse tan pronto como llegue el profesor de español.

Dora quiere participar en el club de teatro después de que termine este semestre. Quiere viajar a Latinoamérica en cuanto tenga el dinero.

### 7 Answers

Below is a sample student conversation.
(A) —¿Cómo te fue este semestre en Perú?
(B) —Bueno, hubo muchos desafíos, pero puse todo mi esfuerzo en asimilarme.
(A) —¿Cuál fue el mayor obstáculo?
(B) —Es que las personas en ciudades grandes como Lima tienen costumbres diferentes, pero poco a poco me adapté al estilo de vida.
(A) —Cuando yo termine mis estudios, quiero ir a Latinoamérica también.
(B) —¿Qué otros planes tienes para la universidad?
(A) —Pienso estudiar comercio internacional y buscar un trabajo con un banco internacional.
(B) —Si te enfocas en tus objetivos, tendrás éxito.

# Prepárate para el examen

### Grammar Review

For more practice with the grammar topics in this chapter, see the *Grammar Tutor,* the *Interactive Tutor,* or the *Cuaderno de vocabulario y gramática.*

GramaVisión

### Comparisons

#### Language to Language

Remind students that **lo que** means *what* when *what* implies *the thing that,* but not when it is used as a question word. Provide some English equivalents to show students the difference. For example, in the following sentence *what* means *the thing that:* Did you hear what dad said this morning? **(¿Escuchaste lo que dijo papá esta mañana?)** However, in this sentence *what* is a question word: What do you want to do today? **(¿Qué quieres hacer hoy?)** Have students provide other sentences using *what* in English, and ask volunteers to translate them using **que** or **lo que.**

1.2, 4.1

**Gramática 1**

- Preterite and imperfect of stative verbs **pp. 284–285**
- grammatical reflexives **pp. 286–287**
- **lo** and **lo que** **pp. 288–289**

## Repaso de Gramática 1

**Estar, tener (que),** and **ser** are stative verbs that have different uses in the **imperfect** and the **preterite** tenses.

| | |
|---|---|
| Yo **tenía** que ir a clase. | *I had to go to class.* |
| Ayer **tuvimos** una reunión. | *We had (held) a meeting yesterday.* |

Some verbs that take a reflexive pronoun, but whose action is not directed back on the subject, are: **criarse, expresarse, graduarse, preocuparse, casarse comunicarse, acostumbrarse, esforzarse, mudarse, enojarse, quejarse, burlarse, quedarse.**

These verbs express a process or a change in state.

**Me crié** en otro país.

Mi primo **se casó** el verano pasado.

**Lo** + **adjective** expresses an abstract idea *(the . . . thing).*

Tenemos que ver **lo bueno** de la situación.

**Lo malo** es que no tenemos otra idea.

**Lo que** + **verb** is also to express an abstract idea *(the thing that, what).*

**Lo que** más **me preocupa** es el examen de geografía.

**Gramática 2**

- subjunctive after adverbial conjunctions **pp. 298–299**
- subjunctive with future actions **pp. 300–301**
- indicative with habitual or past actions **pp. 302–303**

## Repaso de Gramática 2

Always use the **subjunctive** after these **adverbial conjunctions: a menos (de) que, antes de que, con tal (de) que, en caso de que, para que,** and **sin que.**

Julio quiere viajar a Europa **sin que le cueste** mucho dinero.

Verónica no viene con nosotros **a menos que** la **hayas invitado.**

Tenemos que leer este capítulo **antes de que empiece** la clase.

These conjunctions express time: **en cuanto, hasta que, cuando, tan pronto como,** and **después de que.**

The **subjunctive** is used with these conjunctions when it refers to an action that hasn't happened yet.

**En cuanto termine** la película te llamaré. *(future)*

Use the **indicative** with these conjunctions when referring to habitual or past actions.

**Cuando voy** a la playa me gusta tomar el sol. *(habitual)*

**Tan pronto como llegaron,** empezó la función. *(past)*

### Chapter Review

**Teacher Management System**

To access, launch the program, type "admin" in the password area, and press RETURN. For more details, log on to www.hrw.com/CDROMTUTOR.

Create a variety of puzzles to review chapter vocabulary.

**DVD Program**

**Interactive Tutor**

**PuzzlePro**

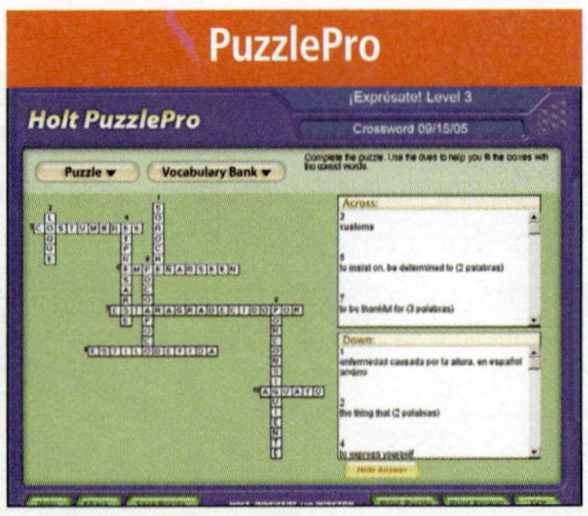

HOLT SoundBooth ONLINE RECORDING

Capítulo 7

# Prepárate para el examen

## Repaso de Vocabulario 1

### Talking about challenges

| | |
|---|---|
| alcanzar | *to reach* |
| los antepasados | *ancestors* |
| el aporte | *contribution* |
| apoyar | *to support* |
| el apoyo | *support* |
| aprovechar | *to take advantage of* |
| asimilar | *to assimilate* |
| el compromiso | *commitment, obligation* |
| contribuir | *to contribute* |
| las costumbres | *customs* |
| criarse (en) | *to grow up (in)* |
| el desafío | *challenge* |
| discriminar | *to discriminate* |
| encajar (en) | *to fit in* |
| el estilo de vida | *lifestyle* |
| estar agradecido(a) por | *to be thankful for* |
| expresarse | *to express (yourself)* |
| el grupo étnico | *ethnic group* |
| Había muchos desafíos en... | *There were many challenges in . . .* |
| la herencia | *heritage* |
| mantener | *to maintain* |
| Mis... enfrentaron obstáculos cuando... | *My . . . faced obstacles when . . .* |
| el modo de ser | *way of being* |
| Nos costó trabajo acostumbrarnos a... | *It took a lot of work for us to get used to . . .* |
| el orgullo | *pride* |
| el origen | *origin* |
| pertenecer a | *to belong to* |
| Poco a poco se adaptaron a... | *Little by little they adapted to . . .* |
| las raíces | *roots* |
| el sacrificio | *sacrifice* |
| ser de ascendencia... | *to be of . . . descent* |
| la tradición | *tradition* |
| tener éxito | *to be successful* |
| Tuvimos que hacer un gran esfuerzo para... | *We had to make a big effort to . . .* |

### Talking about accomplishments

| | |
|---|---|
| Con el tiempo pude asimilar... | *With time I was able to assimilate . . .* |
| Gracias al apoyo de..., he podido superar... | *Thanks to the support of . . . I have been able to overcome . . .* |
| Nos esforzamos en... | *We made a big effort to . . .* |
| Por fin, logré... | *Finally, I managed to . . .* |
| Trabajo duro... y por eso... | *I work hard . . . and for that reason . . .* |

## Repaso de Vocabulario 2

### Talking about future plans

| | |
|---|---|
| acostumbrarse | *to get accustomed to* |
| Antes de que empiecen las clases, quiero... | *Before classes start, I want to . . .* |
| las aspiraciones | *aspirations* |
| Cuando sea mayor, me gustaría... | *When I'm older, I'd like to . . .* |
| (no) darse por vencido(a) | *to (not) give up* |
| empeñarse en | *to insist on, be determined to* |
| En cuanto cumpla los... años, voy a... | *As soon as I turn . . . years old, I'm going to . . .* |
| enfocarse en | *to focus on* |
| esforzarse (ue) por | *to make an effort to* |
| establecerse | *to get established* |
| llegar a ser | *to become* |
| lograr | *to achieve, to manage (to do something)* |
| luchar por | *to fight for* |
| la meta | *goal* |
| el objetivo | *objective* |
| realizar (un sueño) | *to fulfill (a dream)* |
| seguir adelante | *to move forward* |
| soñar (ue) con | *to dream of* |
| Tan pronto como... pienso... | *As soon as . . . I plan on . . .* |
| Tengo la intención de... | *I intend to . . .* |
| tomar la iniciativa | *to take the initiative* |
| triunfar | *to triumph* |
| Voy a... con la idea de... | *I'm going to . . . with the intention of . . .* |

### Expressing cause and effect

| | |
|---|---|
| Hablamos del tema; por consiguiente... | *We discussed the issue; consequently . . .* |
| Mi éxito en... se debe a... | *My success in . . . is due to . . .* |
| No estudié, así que... | *I didn't study, so . . .* |
| Soy bilingüe; por lo tanto, tengo muchas oportunidades... | *I'm bilingual; therefore, I have many opportunities . . .* |

Prepárate para el examen

### Vocabulary Review

For more practice with the vocabulary in this chapter, see the *Interactive Tutor* or the *Cuaderno de vocabulario y gramática.*

### Online Edition

Students might use the online textbook to hear the **Vocabulario** items.

### Game

Ask students to write one sentence based on each **Gramática** presentation in the chapter. Make enough copies so that each team of four or five students will have a complete set. Cut the sentences into strips and then cut the strips in half. Place each set of sentences into a separate envelope. Divide the students into teams. Give each team a set of sentences. Teams take turns drawing and reading a sentence fragment aloud. The listening teams race to complete the sentence logically. The first team to do so earns a point. There may be more than one logical completion to a given fragment. Play continues until all cards have been read. The team with the most points wins. 1.1, 1.2

**Online Edition**

**Transparency: Vocabulario**

**Transparency: Situación**

### Assess

**Assessment Program**

**Examen: Capítulo 7,** pp. 293–298

Audio CD 7, Trs. 17–18

**Examen oral: Capítulo 7,** p. 304

Alternative Assessment, pp. 379, 391, 403

**Online Assessment**

**my.hrw.com**

**Test Generator**

**Assess** **Differentiated Instruction** See the Differentiated Instruction CD-ROM.

# Capítulo 7
## Integración

**Resources**

**Planning:**

Lesson Planner, pp. 111, 272–273

One-Stop Planner

**Presentation:**

Teaching Transparencies

Fine Art, Chapter 7

**Practice:**

Cuaderno de actividades, pp. 69–70

Lab Book, pp. 7, 37–40

Audio CD 7, Tr. 14

**Teacher to Teacher**

**Gudrun U. Martyny**
Timber Creek High School
Orlando, FL

My Level 3 students have a mentoring relationship with a Level 2 class. Every two weeks they write each other a postcard. For example, the Level 2 students may tell the Level 3 students about their favorite sport or food, and the Level 3 students may tell of their visit to the Dalí Museum in St. Petersburg. Themes may be connected to holidays. They can decorate the front of the card at home, but the text is written in class. The Level 3 students review and process Level 2 content, while the Level 2 students benefit from the challenge of communicating with an upper classman in Spanish. 1.3, 5.1

**Repaso cumulativo**

# Integración
## capítulos 1–7

CD 7, Tr. 14 For script, see p. 275F.

**1** Mira las fotos, escucha las descripciones e indica a qué persona se refiere cada una. 1.2

1. B 2. D 3. A 4. C

A

B

C

D

**2** El profesor ha dejado instrucciones para el día del examen. Pon en orden los pasos que tus compañeros de clase y tú deben seguir. 1.2

No empiecen el examen hasta que hayan le do todo el cuento. Lean las preguntas antes de leer el cuento para que sepan en qué detalles enfocarse. Cuando hayan terminado de leer el cuento y contestar las preguntas, escriban un resumen corto. En cuanto terminen el resumen, entreguen la primera parte del examen y el asistente les dará el tema para el ensayo. Después de que hagan un esquema, escriban el ensayo. Cuando lo hayan revisado, pueden entregar la segunda parte del examen.

1. b
2. c
3. f
4. d
5. h
6. e
7. a
8. g

**a.** escribir el ensayo
**b.** leer las preguntas
**c.** leer el cuento
**d.** escribir un resumen
**e.** escribir un esquema
**f.** contestar las preguntas
**g.** revisar el ensayo
**h.** entregar la primera parte del examen

**Culture Project**

Ask students to work in small groups to research the employment/labor laws of a Spanish speaking country. You might suggest that they first do some research on the employment/labor laws of the United States so that they have a point of comparison. Tell them it is important to understand the historical context within which laws were established. Have them create a visual guide such as a chart, comparing the laws of the United States and the country they investigated. Have them report their findings to the class. 2.1, 4.2

Visit Holt Online
**go.hrw.com**
KEYWORD: EXP3 CH7
Cumulative Self-test

3 En grupos de tres, hablen de dos éxitos de los que estén orgullosos(as) y dos cosas que no hayan podido lograr. Expliquen la causa y el efecto de cada cosa. 1.1, 1.3

4 Describe lo que ves en esta pintura. Imagina que eres uno de los personajes en la escena y escribe seis oraciones sobre tu herencia, tus costumbres y tus aspiraciones en este momento. 1.3, 3.1

Benito's Village, 10" x 13" by Benito Huillcahuaman. © Benito Huillcahuaman/Equator Gallery

***Benito's Village*** **de Benito Huillcahuaman**

5 Acabas de graduarte de la universidad. Tu prima comienza el colegio este año y sueña con ir a la misma universidad. Escríbele una carta dándole consejos sobre lo que debe hacer para lograr su sueño. Si quieres, puedes usar algunas de las frases del cuadro. 1.3

| | | |
|---|---|---|
| **yo que tú** | **tomar la iniciativa** | **los objetivos** |
| **aprovechar** | **aprobar** | **sugiero que** |

6 **Situación** Junto con un(a) compañero(a), imaginen que Uds. son capitanes del equipo de básquetbol de su colegio. Piensen en las metas del equipo este año y cómo van a lograr estas metas. Luego, presenten las ideas a la clase. 1.1, 1.3

## Fine Art Connection

Tell students that this painting, *Benito's Village,* is by Benito Huillcahuaman. Huillcahuaman is a Peruvian painter whose brightly colored watercolors feature the countryside and people of Peru. The painter studied at the Regional School of the Arts in Cuzco, as well as the School of Fine Art and the Educational Institute of Diverse Arts in Lima. He has had shows in Peru and Spain.

### Analyzing

Have students talk about the setting of the painting. Where are the people depicted in the painting? Ask students to describe the village and the people shown. 3.1

### Extension

Have students make up a short story about the people in the painting. Encourage them to use real facts about Peru as they create their story. Ask volunteers to share their stories with the class. 1.3

## ACTFL Performance Standards

The activities in Chapter 4 target the different communicative modes as described in the Standards.

| | | |
|---|---|---|
| **Interpersonal** | Two-way communication using receptive skills and productive skills | **Comunicación (SE),** pp. 281, 283, 285, 287, 289, 295, 297, 299, 301, 303<br>**Comunicación (TE),** pp. 283, 289, 295, 299, 301, 303, 305<br>**Conversación,** p. 313<br>**Situación,** p. 317 |
| **Interpretive** | One-way communication using receptive skills | **Comunicación (SE),** pp. 281, 285, 287, 295, 299, 301, 303<br>**Comunicación (TE),** pp. 285, 297<br>**Leamos,** pp. 308–310<br>**Novela en video,** pp. 304–305<br>**Conversación,** p. 313 |
| **Presentational** | One-way communication using productive skills | **Comunicación (SE),** pp. 283, 285, 289, 297<br>**Comunicación (TE),** pp. 281, 287<br>**Taller del escritor,** p. 311 |

Capítulo 8

# Planning Guide

## ¿A qué te dedicas?

| Chapter Section | | Print Resources |
|---|---|---|
| **Geocultura**<br>• **Los Andes** | pp. 270–275 | Video Guide, pp. 43–44/Lab Book, p. 76 |
| **Vocabulario 1**<br>• Technology<br>**Gramática 1**<br>• Verbs with indirect object pronouns<br>• Verbs that express "to become"<br>• Uses of **se** | pp. 320–325<br><br>pp. 326–331 | Vocabulario 8.1, 8.2; Bell Work 8.1, 8.2, 8.3, 8.4<br>Cuaderno de vocabulario y gramática, pp. 85–90<br>Cuaderno de actividades, pp. 71–73<br>Activities for Communication, pp. 29–30<br>Grammar Tutor for Students of Spanish, pp. 157–158 |
| **Cultura: Comparaciones**<br>**Cultura: Comunidad** | p. 332<br>p. 333 | Video Guide, pp. 52–53/Lab Book, p. 80 |
| **Vocabulario 2**<br>• The workplace<br>**Gramática 2**<br>• Repaso: Conditional<br>• Past subjunctive with hypothetical statements<br>• More on past subjunctive | pp. 334–339<br><br>pp. 340–345 | Vocabulario 8.3, 8.4; Bell Work 8.5, 8.6, 8.7, 8.8<br>Cuaderno de vocabulario y gramática, pp. 91–96<br>Cuaderno de actividades, pp. 75–77<br>Activities for Communication, pp. 31–32 |
| **Novela en video**<br>**Lectura cultural**<br>• **El trabajo en Latinoamérica**<br>**Leamos**<br>• **de Senderos fronterizos**<br>**Escribamos**<br>• **Personajes con vida propia** | pp. 346–347<br>pp. 348–349<br><br>pp. 350–352<br><br>p. 353 | Cuaderno de actividades, p. 87<br>Reading Strategies and Skills Handbook<br>Interactive Advanced Reader<br>Video Guide, pp. 69–70/Lab Book, pp. 55–56 |
| **Prepárate para el examen**<br>• **Repaso de vocabulario y gramática** | pp. 354–357 | Picture Sequences, Situación, Ch. 8<br>Activities for Communication, pp. 78, 50–51 |
| **Integración**<br>• **Repaso cumulativo** | pp. 358–359 | Fine Art, Ch. 8<br>Cuaderno de actividades, pp. 79–80<br>Reading Strategies and Skills Handbook<br>Interactive Advanced Reader |

Planning Guide

For correlations to national standards, see point-of-use references throughout the chapter.

Visit Holt Online
**go.hrw.com**
KEYWORD: EXP3 CH8
Online Edition

## Pacing Suggestions

| | Essential | Recommended | Optional |
|---|---|---|---|
| **Vocabulario 1** • Technology • **Nota cultural** | ✔ | | |
| **Gramática 1** • Verbs with indirect object pronouns • Verbs that express "to become" • Uses of **se** • **Nota cultural** | ✔ | | |
| **Cultura: Comparaciones** | | ✔ | |
| **Cultura: Comunidad** | | | ✔ |
| **Vocabulario 2** • The workplace • **Nota cultural** | ✔ | | |
| **Gramática 2** • **Repaso:** Conditional • Past subjunctive with hypothetical statements • More on past subjunctive • **Nota cultural** | ✔ | | |
| **Novela en video** • Episodio 8: **Clara perspectiva** | | ✔ | |
| **Lectura cultural** • **El trabajo en Latinoamérica** | | | ✔ |
| **Leamos** • **de Senderos fronterizos** **Escribamos** • **Personajes con vida propia** | | ✔ | |
| **Prepárate para el examen** | | ✔ | |
| **Integración** | | | ✔ |

## Technology Resources

### ¡Exprésate! Online
- Student Edition with multi-media
- SoundBooth recording tool
- Interactive activities with feedback
- Self-tests with feedback
- Cuaderno de actividades (interactive workbook)
- Cuaderno de vocabulario y gramática (interactive workbook)
- Live Ink™ Reading Help
- Holt Online Assessment

### DVD Tutor, Disc 2
- GeoVisión
- GramaVisión
- VideoNovela
- Cultura
- Variedades

### Interactive Tutor
- Interactive practice games
- Writing and recording workshops

### Audio Program
- Textbook listening activities
- Assessment listening activities
- Songs

### One-Stop Planner
- Complete media and print resources
- ExamView® Pro Test Generator
- Holt Calendar Planner

### PuzzlePro
- Customizable word games

## Assessment

**Geocultura**
**Vocabulario 1 / Gramática 1**
**Vocabulario 2 / Gramática 2**
**Leamos**
**Escribamos**
**Prepárate para el examen**

### Assessment Program

**Prueba: Geocultura,** pp. 155–156
**Pruebas,** pp. 141–142, 143–144, 145–146
**Pruebas,** pp. 147–148, 149–150, 151–152
**Prueba,** p. 153
**Prueba,** p. 154
**Examen: Capítulo 8,** pp. 305–312
**Examen oral: Capítulo 8,** p. 316
**Alternative Assessment,** pp. 380, 392, 404

### Online Assessment

**my.hrw.com**

### Test Generator

**ExamView® Pro Test Generator**

Planning Guide

# Projects

## ¿A qué te dedicas?

### La entrevista

In this project, the class role-plays both sides of a job interview to practice talking about former jobs, future plans, and goals.

**SUGGESTED SEQUENCE**

1. Have students write a description in Spanish of the business or organization they would like to run later in life.
2. They then describe the type of entry-level position they would expect to take in that business to enable them to reach the top.
3. Pair up students and have them exchange descriptions with their partners. Students read their partner's descriptions, and think about what the head of such a business would look for in a candidate for that entry-level position. They then create a job application, which will elicit that information from an applicant.
4. Students exchange job applications, fill them out, and return them to their partner.
5. Schedule a day for interviews. On that day, students come to class dressed as they would for a job interview.
6. Taking turns, students play the role of the head of the business or organization described by their partner, and interview him or her for the entry-level position, using the job application for reference.
7. Students hand in their job descriptions and applications for grading.
8. You might videotape the interviews and then show them to the class so that students can critique each other's performance and offer suggestions. 1.1, 1.3

### Grading the projects

Suggested point distribution (100 points total)

| | |
|---|---|
| Written work | 35 |
| Oral presentation | 35 |
| Originality | 20 |
| Appearance | 10 |

### Partner Class Project

Have students look through the want ads online for jobs requiring Spanish. Each student should print out an ad and exchange with a partner. The partner must analyze the job description and then write a letter to apply for the job. Have students exchange letters and ask each one to write a response, either inviting the applicant for an interview or explaining why he or she does not qualify. 1.1

### Game Bank

For game ideas, see pages T64–T67.

### e-community

**e-mail forum:**

Post the following question on the classroom e-mail forum:

**¿En qué trabajos sería una ventaja hablar español?**

All students will contribute to the list and then share the items. 1.3

# ¿A qué te dedicas?

## Otavalo

Otavalo, a town about 70 miles north of Quito, is world-renowned for its colorful and high-quality textiles. The Quechua-speaking indigenous peoples of this region, called **otavaleños,** have been using the loom to weave intricately-designed clothing for over 3,000 years. These beautiful textiles have made them one of the wealthiest indigenous groups in Latin America. The **otavaleños** display their expertly-woven ponchos, scarves, sweaters, blankets, and tapestries (**tapices**) at the Plaza de Ponchos market in Otavalo. Have students research Ecuadorean weaving designs and patterns to create a **tapiz** on poster board representing their school's colors and mascot. You might set up an imaginary market in which students take turns bargaining to buy their **tapices.** Then arrange to display students' work publicly in an appropriate area of the school. 2.1, 2.2

## Receta

This coconut candy comes from Bolivia. The tropical climate of Bolivia's Amazonian plains produces fruits and vegetables, such as coconuts, which are markedly different from those grown in the colder climate of Bolivia's Andean region. You might have students make the following recipe as a class project or for extra credit.

### Cocadas

**para 8 personas**

2 2/3 tazas de coco rallado

1 huevo

3/4 de taza de leche condensada

1/4 de cucharadita de extracto de almendras

En un recipiente hondo, combine el coco, el huevo, la leche condensada y el extracto de almendras hasta que todo se quede bien mezclado. Déjelo reposar dos o tres minutos. Unte una bandeja para hornear galletas con un poco de mantequilla. Usando dos cucharaditas, ponga cantidades pequeñas de la mezcla en la bandeja. Hornéelas a 325°F unos 25 minutos o hasta que estén doradas, secas y lisas. Hace 24 cocadas.

2.2, 3.1

Capítulo 8

# Listening Activity Scripts

## ¿A qué te dedicas?

### Vocabulario en acción 1

**1** p. 322, CD 8, Track 1

For script and answers, see *Teacher's Edition,* p. 322.

### Gramática en acción 1

**10** p. 326, CD 8, Track 2

—María, me gusta mucho tu agenda electrónica.

—Gracias, Clara. El problema es que me resulta difícil usarla.

—¿Por qué? Ángel tiene una y dice que le es muy fácil usarla.

—Sí, Ángel me enseñó a usarla, pero todavía no la entiendo bien. Me frustra que me resulte tan difícil, aunque mi amiga Gabriela tiene el mismo problema. Trató de usar una agenda electrónica y todo le salió mal. ¡Fue a la peluquera cuando tenía que ir al dentista y fue al médico en vez de ir a mi fiesta!

—¡No me cabe en la cabeza que ustedes no logren entender una tecnología tan sencilla!

—Clara, no seas así. Yo sé que te es imposible entender tu teléfono celular. ¡Nunca contestas mis llamadas porque no sabes escuchar tus mensajes!

**Answers to Activity 10**

1. falsa 2. cierta 3. cierta 4. falsa 5. falsa 6. cierta

**14** p. 328, CD 8, Track 3

1. ¡Hola, Anita! ¿Cómo estás? ¡Estás tan bonita como siempre!
2. ¿Te acuerdas del profesor Paz? Pues, se ha convertido en un monstruo.
3. Oye, Roberto, dice Claudia que sigues trabajando como voluntario. ¡Ya veo que te gusta esa clase de trabajo!
4. ¡Vaya, Rosa, te has puesto delgadita! ¿Cómo lo lograste?
5. Me alegra mucho que hayas llegado a tener tanto éxito, Jorge. Antes no te esforzabas por alcanzar tus metas, pero ahora has trabajado muy duro, y te lo mereces.
6. ¿Te acuerdas de la profesora Montesinos? Pues, la pobre casi se volvió loca con las presiones del colegio y ya no trabaja aquí.

**Answers to Activity 14**

1. b 2. a 3. b 4. a 5. a 6. a

### Vocabulario en acción 2

**22** p. 336, CD 8, Track 7

—Buenos días, Srta. Garza. Soy el señor Maldonado, gerente de la oficina.

—Encantada de conocerlo, Sr. Maldonado.

—Veo en su currículum que usted tiene mucha experiencia como programadora de computadoras. ¿Ha supervisado a sus compañeros de trabajo?

—Pues, no. Pero sí he dirigido grandes proyectos.

—Es que tenemos un puesto a tiempo completo para un supervisor, y un puesto a medio tiempo para un programador.

—¿Puede Ud. explicarme un poco los requisitos para cada puesto?

—Bueno, el jefe va a darle más detalles. Yo le voy a explicar los beneficios y los horarios. Ofrecemos el seguro médico después de tres meses en empresa. También tendrá dos semanas de vacaciones el primer año.

—Me parece perfecto.

—Aquí viene el señor Benavides, el jefe. Él le hará la entrevista y luego si usted tiene cualquier pregunta, no dude en llamarme.

**Answers to Activity 22**

1. falsa; Es gerente de la oficina.
2. cierta
3. falsa; Solicitó un puesto de programadora.
4. falsa; Recibirá seguro médico después de tres meses.
5. cierta
6. falsa; Tienen dos puestos abiertos.

For Student Response Forms, see the *Lab Book*, pp. 41–44.

**28** **p. 339, CD 8, Track 8**

CONSEJERO Bueno, Juana, hiciste una cita porque quieres hablarme de tus planes para el futuro, ¿verdad?

JUANA Sí. Tengo muchas ideas pero no puedo enfocarme bien. Estoy preparando mi solicitud para la universidad, pero tengo que decidir qué quiero hacer para saber adónde mandarla.

CONSEJERO Pues, ¿qué es lo que te gustaría estudiar en la universidad?

JUANA Me gustaría estudiar literatura.

CONSEJERO A mí me encanta la literatura también. ¿Pero qué te gustaría hacer en tu carrera?

JUANA Es que no estoy segura. Me interesaría ser profesora, pero no quiero solamente una carrera. ¡Quiero tener varias! Además, quiero viajar.

CONSEJERO Bueno, vamos por partes. Te gusta viajar, ¿eh? Si tuvieras la oportunidad de estudiar en otro país, ¿adónde irías?

JUANA Si pudiera, iría a Perú. Siempre he querido visitar las ruinas de Machu Picchu.

CONSEJERO Pues, la ventaja de trabajar como profesora es que tienes los veranos libres para viajar. Pero no tienes que decidirte ahora. Sabes lo que te interesaría estudiar y que te gustaría hacer en un programa de intercambio. Esto nos ayudará a elegir las universidades que cumplan con tus requisitos.

For answers, see *Teacher's Edition,* p. 339.

## Gramática en acción 2

**31** **p. 340, CD 8, Track 9**

MARCELA Mamá, creo que tengo casi todo listo para la entrevista. Leí la página Web de la empresa y escribí una lista de preguntas.

MAMÁ ¿Pusiste una copia de tu currículum en la carpeta?

MARCELA Sí, aquí está.

MAMÁ ¿Está actualizada esta copia?

MARCELA La actualizaría, pero no está funcionando la computadora.

MAMÁ ¿Y tus referencias? Creo que requieren tres referencias.

MARCELA Requieren solamente dos. Quiero pedírselas a mi profesor de química y al jefe que tenía el año pasado. Los llamaría ahora, pero ya es tarde. Creo que puedo mandar las referencias después de la entrevista.

MAMÁ Está bien. Oye, acuérdate de planchar tu vestido.

MARCELA ¡Ya lo planché, mamá!

**Answers to Activity 31**

1. a 2. a 3. a 4. b 5. a 6. a

## Prepárate para el examen capítulo 8

**1** **p. 354, CD 8, Track 12**

For script and answers, see *Teacher's Edition,* p. 354.

**6** **p. 355, CD 8, Track 13**

For script, see *Teacher's Edition,* p. 355. Answers will vary.

## Integración capítulos 1–8

**1** **p. 358, CD 8, Track 14**

1. —Siempre está trabajando como voluntaria. Es una persona muy generosa y este trabajo la hace feliz.
   —Sí, ha ayudado a los animales y a la gente en los hospitales.
   —Sería perfecto si consiguiera un empleo a medio tiempo para que pudiera donar tiempo a una causa.
2. —Está loca por la tecnología. Ha creado sus propios juegos de computadora.
   —Le resulta fácil programar en la computadora. Estoy impresionada porque yo no entiendo ni jota de computadoras.
   —Si tuviera el tiempo, podría empezar su propio negocio por Internet.
3. —¿Sigue buscando trabajo Fernando?
   —Fíjate que consiguió un empleo a medio tiempo. Es cocinero en un restaurante cerca de su casa.
4. —¿Supiste que Mario ya encontró un empleo a tiempo completo?
   —No, no lo sabía. ¿A qué se dedica?
   —Trabaja como carpintero y según tengo entendido, la empresa le da muchos beneficios.

**Answers to Activity 1**

1. b 2. d 3. c 4. a

# 50-Minute Lesson Plans

For more customized Lesson Plans, see the *Lesson Planner with Differentiated Instruction.*

## ¿A qué te dedicas?



### Day 1

**Objective**
*Saying what you can and cannot do*

**Core Instruction**
**Chapter Opener**, pp. 318–319 **10 min.**
- See Chapter Objectives and Using the Photo, p. 318.

**Vocabulario en acción 1,** pp. 320–325
- Have students do Bell Work, p. 320.
- See Teaching **Vocabulario,** p. 320. **10 min.**
- See Teaching **¡Exprésate!,** p. 320. **5 min.**
- Play Audio CD 8, Tr. 1 for Activity 1, p. 322. **5 min.**
- Have students do Activities 2–4, pp. 322–323. **20 min.**

**Optional Resources**
- Advanced Learners, p. 321 ▲
- Multiple Intelligences, p. 321
- **Comunicación,** p. 323
- Slower Pace Learners, p. 323 ◆
- Special Learning Needs, p. 323 ●

**Homework Suggestions**
Cuaderno de vocabulario y gramática, pp. 85–87
1.2, 1.3

### Day 2

**Objective**
*Talking about what you do and do not understand*

**Core Instruction**
**Vocabulario en acción 1,** pp. 320–325
- Have students do Activities 5–6, p. 323. **15 min.**
- See Teaching **¡Exprésate!,** p. 324. **10 min.**
- Have students do Activities 7–9, p. 325. **25 min.**

**Optional Resources**
- **Comunicación,** p. 325
- Advanced Learners, p. 325 ▲
- Multiple Intelligences, p. 325

**Homework Suggestions**
Study for **Prueba: Vocabulario 1**
Cuaderno de vocabulario y gramática, pp. 85–87
1.1, 1.2

### Day 3

**Objective**
*Verbs with indirect object pronouns*

**Core Instruction**
**Vocabulario en acción 1,** pp. 320–325
- Review **Vocabulario en acción 1,** pp. 320–325. **10 min.**
- Give **Prueba: Vocabulario 1. 20 min.**

**Gramática en acción 1,** pp. 326–331
- See Teaching **Gramática,** p. 326. **10 min.**
- Play Audio CD 8, Tr. 2 for Activity 10, p. 326. **5 min.**
- Have students do Activity 11, p. 327. **5 min.**

**Optional Resources**
- **Comunicación,** p. 327
- Slower Pace Learners, p. 327 ◆
- Multiple Intelligences, p. 327 ●

**Homework Suggestions**
Cuaderno de vocabulario y gramática, pp. 88–90
Cuaderno de actividades, pp. 71–73
1.2

### Day 4

**Objective**
*Verbs that express "to become"*

**Core Instruction**
**Gramática en acción 1,** pp. 326–331
- Have students do Activities 12–13, p. 327. **10 min.**
- See Teaching **Gramática,** p. 328. **15 min.**
- Play Audio CD 8, Tr. 3 for Activity 14, p. 328. **5 min.**
- Have students do Activities 15–17, p. 329. **20 min.**

**Optional Resources**
- **Comunicación,** p. 329
- Heritage Speakers, p. 329 ■
- Advanced Learners, p. 329 ▲
- Multiple Intelligences, p. 329

**Homework Suggestions**
Cuaderno de vocabulario y gramática, pp. 88–90
Cuaderno de actividades, pp. 71–73
1.1, 1.2

### Day 5

**Objective**
*Uses of se*

**Core Instruction**
**Gramática en acción 1,** pp. 326–331
- See Teaching **Gramática,** p. 330. **10 min.**
- Have students do Activities 18–21, pp. 330–331. **30 min.**
- Review **Gramática en acción 1,** pp. 326–331. **10 min.**

**Optional Resources**
**Comunicación,** p. 331
- Slower Pace Learners, p. 331 ◆
- Multiple Intelligences, p. 331

**Homework Suggestions**
Cuaderno de vocabulario y gramática, pp. 88–90
Cuaderno de actividades, pp. 71–73
1.1, 1.2, 1.3

### Day 6

**Objective**
*Interviews from around the Spanish-speaking world*

**Core Instruction**
**Gramática en acción 1,** pp. 326–331
- Give **Prueba: Gramática en acción 1. 20 min.**

**Cultura,** pp. 332–333
- See Teaching **Cultura,** p. 332. **15 min.**
- Play Audio CD 8, Tr. 4–6, or show **VideoCultura. 15 min.**

**Optional Resources**
- Advanced Learners, p. 333 ▲
- Multiple Intelligences, p. 333

**Homework Suggestions**
Cuaderno de actividades, p. 74
Online Practice (**go.hrw.com,** Keyword: EXP3 CH8)
1.2, 1.3, 5.1

### Day 7

**Objective**
*Writing a formal letter*

**Core Instruction**
**Vocabulario en acción 2,** pp. 334–339
- See Teaching **Vocabulario,** p. 334. **10 min.**
- See Teaching **¡Exprésate!,** p. 334. **10 min.**
- Play Audio CD 8, Tr. 7 for Activity 22, p. 336. **5 min.**
- Have students do Activities 23–25, pp. 336–337. **25 min.**

**Optional Resources**
- Slower Pace Learners, p. 335 ◆
- Multiple Intelligences, p. 335

**Homework Suggestions**
Cuaderno de vocabulario y gramática, pp. 91–93
1.2

### Day 8

**Objective**
*Talking about your plans*

**Core Instruction**
**Vocabulario en acción 2,** pp. 334–339
- Have students do Activity 26, p. 337. **10 min.**
- See Teaching **¡Exprésate!,** p. 338. **10 min.**
- Have students do Activity 27, p. 339. **5 min.**
- Play Audio CD 8, Tr. 8 for Activity 28, p. 339. **5 min.**
- Have students do Activities 29–30, p. 339. **20 min.**

**Optional Resources**
- **Comunicación,** p. 339
- Advanced Learners, p. 339 ▲
- Multiple Intelligences, p. 339

**Homework Suggestions**
Study for **Prueba: Vocabulario 2**
1.1, 1.2, 1.3

- For information on the **Geocultura** pages, see the *Lesson Planner with Differentiated Instruction.*
- For more detailed information on benchmarks, see point-of-use correlations on each page.
- To edit and create your own lesson plans, see the **One-Stop** Planner® CD-ROM

**KEY**
- ▲ Advanced Learners
- ◆ Slower Pace Learners
- ● Special Learning Needs
- ■ Heritage Speakers

## Day 9

### Objective
*Conditional*

### Core Instruction
**Vocabulario en acción 2,** pp. 334–339
- Review **Vocabulario en acción 2,** pp. 334–339. **10 min.**
- Give **Prueba: Vocabulario 2. 20 min.**

**Gramática en acción 2,** pp. 340–345
- See Teaching **Gramática,** p. 340. **10 min.**
- Play Audio CD 8, Tr. 9 for Activity 31, p. 340. **10 min.**

### Optional Resources
- **Comunicación,** p. 341
- Slower Pace Learners, p. 341 ◆
- Multiple Intelligences, p. 341

### Homework Suggestions
Cuaderno de vocabulario y gramática, pp. 94–96
Cuaderno de actividades, pp. 75–77
1.2

## Day 10

### Objective
*Past subjunctive with hypothetical statements*

### Core Instruction
**Gramática en acción 2,** pp. 340–345
- Have students do Activities 32–34, p. 341. **15 min.**
- See Teaching **Gramática,** p. 342. **10 min.**
- Have students do Activities 35–37, pp. 342–343. **25 min.**

### Optional Resources
- **Comunicación,** p. 343
- Advanced Learners, p. 343 ▲
- Multiple Intelligences, p. 343

### Homework Suggestions
Cuaderno de vocabulario y gramática, pp. 94–96
Cuaderno de actividades, pp. 75–77
1.1, 1.2, 1.3

## Day 11

### Objective
*More past subjunctive*

### Core Instruction
**Gramática en acción 2,** pp. 340–345
- Have students do Activity 38, p. 343. **5 min.**
- See Teaching **Gramática,** p. 344. **10 min.**
- Have students do Activities 39–43, pp. 344–345. **35 min.**

### Optional Resources
- **Comunicación,** p. 345
- Advanced Learners, p. 345 ▲
- Multiple Intelligences, p. 345

### Homework Suggestions
Cuaderno de vocabulario y gramática, pp. 94–96
Cuaderno de actividades, pp. 75–77
1.1, 1.2, 1.3

## Day 12

### Objective
*Developing listening and reading skills*

### Core Instruction
**Gramática en acción 2,** pp. 340–345
- Review **Gramática en acción 2,** pp. 340–345. **5 min.**
- Give **Prueba: Gramática 2. 20 min.**

**Novela en video,** pp. 346–347
- Show **VideoNovela.** See Teaching **Novela en video,** p. 346. **25 min.**

### Optional Resources
- **Comunicación,** p. 347

**Assessment Program:**
- Skills Quiz: **Vocabulario y gramática 2**

### Homework Suggestions
Cuaderno de vocabulario y gramática, pp. 94–96
1.2, 1.3

## Day 13

### Objective
*Developing listening and reading skills*

### Core Instruction
**Lectura cultural,** pp. 348–349
- See Teaching **Lectura cultural,** p. 348. **25 min.**

**Leamos y escribamos,** pp. 350–353
- See Teaching **Leamos,** p. 350. **25 min.**

### Optional Resources
- Slower Pace Learners, p. 351 ◆
- Special Learning Needs, p. 351 ●

### Homework Suggestions
Cuaderno de actividades, p. 78
1.2, 1.3

## Day 14

### Objective
*Developing reading and writing skills*

### Core Instruction
**Leamos y escribamos,** pp. 350–353
- See Teaching **Escribamos,** points 1–3, p. 352. **30 min.**

**Prepárate para el examen,** pp. 354–357
- Play Audio CD 8, Tr. 12 for Activity 1, p. 354. **5 min.**
- Have students do Activities 2–4, pp. 354–355. **15 min.**

### Optional Resources
- Slower Pace Learners, p. 353 ◆
- Multiple Intelligences, p. 353

### Homework Suggestions
**Taller del escritor,** p. 353
1.2

## Day 15

### Objective
*Chapter review*

### Core Instruction
**Prepárate para el examen,** pp. 354–357
- Have students do Activity 5, p. 355. **5 min.**
- Play Audio CD 8, Tr. 13 for Activity 6, p. 355. **5 min.**
- Have students do Activity 7, p. 355. **5 min.**

**Integración,** pp. 358–359
- Play Audio CD 8, Tr. 14 for Activity 1, p. 358. **5 min.**
- Have students do Activities 2–6, pp. 358–359. **35 min.**

### Optional Resources
- Play Pre-AP Audio CD 2, Tr. 9, for Pre-AP Practice, p. 355
- Game, p. 357
- Fine Art Connection, p. 359

### Homework Suggestions
Study for Chapter Test
1.1, 1.2, 1.3

## Day 16/Test

### Core Instruction
**Chapter Test 50 min.**

### Optional Resources
**Assessment Program**
- **Prueba: Lectura**
- **Prueba: Escritura**
- Test Generator

### Homework Suggestions
Cuaderno de actividades, pp. 79–80

# Indiana
## The Hoosier State

## Chapter 8

The following chart presents *¡Exprésate!* Chapter 8 correlations to the Indiana Academic Standards for World Languages, Grade 11. The correlations here are to the *Student Edition* (SE) and *Teacher's Edition* (TE) only. For additional teaching resources, see pages 317A-317B

| INDIANA ACADEMIC STANDARDS | | | CHAPTER 8 SE/TE CORRELATIONS |
|---|---|---|---|
| **Standard 1 COMMUNICATION:** | | | |
| **Write and speak in a language other than English** | 11.1.1 | Initiate, sustain, and close conversations in limited yet varied situations. | SE: 323, 327, 345, 359<br>TE: 320, 324, 327, 334, 336, 338, 345, 359 |
| | 11.1.2 | Exchange detailed information and opinions orally on a variety of topics. | SE: 323, 327, 331, 333, 359<br>TE: 323, 327, 332, 358 |
| | 11.1.3 | Exchange detailed information and opinions in written form on a variety of topics. | SE: 353<br>TE: 351, 354 |
| | 11.1.4 | Make requests and ask different types of questions in a variety of social situations. | SE: 339<br>TE: 338 |
| | 11.1.5 | Recognize and use situation-appropriate non-verbal communication. | TE: 304, 305, 327, 346 |
| | 11.1.6 | Use speaking and listening strategies to facilitate communication. | SE: 323, 327, 345, 359<br>TE: 340 |
| **Standard 2 COMMUNICATION:** | | | |
| **Interpret information in a language other than English** *Learners interpret written and spoken language on a variety of topics. (Interpretive)* | 11.2.1 | Respond accurately to everyday requests, commands, and directions. | TE: 321, 335 |
| | 11.2.2 | Demonstrate comprehension of both authentic and non-authentic written and spoken language through developmentally appropriate tasks. | SE: 347, 349, 352<br>TE: 350, 351 |
| | 11.2.3 | Make educated guesses about meaning in unfamiliar written and spoken contexts. | SE: 346, 350<br>TE: 346, 350 |
| **Standard 3 COMMUNICATION:** | | | |
| **Present information in a language other than English** *Learners present to an audience of listeners or readers on a variety of topics. (Presentational)* | 11.3.2 | Produce and present creative material on a variety of topics. | TE: 317C, 325, 339, 358 |
| | 11.3.3 | Read passages aloud to demonstrate improving intonation and pronunciation. | TE: 332 |
| | 11.3.4 | Compose cohesive written information using appropriate formats and more varied vocabulary and structures. | SE: 353<br>TE: 317C, 352, 353 |
| **Standard 4 CULTURES:** | | | |
| **Develop awareness of other cultures.** *Learners examine, experience, and reflect on the relationships among the practices, products, and perspectives of the cultures studied.* | 11.4.1 | Analyze and reflect on cultural practices of the target cultures. | SE: 333, 349<br>TE: 332, 348, 358 |
| | 11.4.2 | Describe products, perspectives, and symbols of the target cultures. | SE: 333, 349<br>TE: 332, 348, 358 |
| | 11.4.3 | Discuss factors that influence practices, products, and perspectives. | SE: 333, 349<br>TE: 332, 348, 358 |

| | | | |
|---|---|---|---|
| | **11.4.4** | Recognize the interrelations among the practices, products, and perspectives of the target cultures. | **SE:** 333, 349<br>**TE:** 332, 348, 358 |
| | **11.4.5** | Explain contributions from other cultures. | **SE:** 349<br>**TE:** 348, 358 |

## Standard 5 CONNECTIONS:

| | | | |
|---|---|---|---|
| **Make connections to other content areas** *Learners use the target language to expand their knowledge of and make connections among multiple content areas.* | **11.5.1** | Make connections with other content areas through resources intended for native speakers. | **TE:** 358 |
| | **11.5.2** | Design and share activities and materials that integrate the target language and cultures with concepts and skills from other content areas. | **SE:** 343, 359<br>**TE:** 317C, 317D, 357 |

## Standard 6 CONNECTIONS:

| | | | |
|---|---|---|---|
| **Access and connect information through various media** *Learners strengthen language proficiency and cultural knowledge by using current digital media and authentic resources.* | **11.6.1** | Use digital media and culturally authentic resources to build vocabulary and improve receptive and productive language skills. | **SE:** 324, 354<br>**TE:** 317E, 317F |
| | **11.6.2** | Use digital media and culturally authentic resources to study target cultures. | **SE:** 332, 346 |
| | **11.6.3** | Identify and evaluate resources intended for native speakers. | **SE:** 332, 346, 352<br>**TE:** 351 |

## Standard 7 COMPARISONS:

| | | | |
|---|---|---|---|
| **Investigate the nature of language and culture** *Learners understand the nature of language and culture through comparisons of the languages and cultures studied and their own.* | **11.7.1** | Use elements of word formation to expand vocabulary and derive meaning. | **SE:** 327, 343<br>**TE:** 326, 340, 354 |
| | **11.7.2** | Recognize and use a variety of language structures. | **SE:** 326-331, 353, 354-357, 359<br>**TE:** 340-347 |
| | **11.7.3** | Compare and use idiomatic, colloquial, and proverbial expressions in the target language. | **SE:** 325, 359<br>**TE:** 324 |
| | **11.7.4** | Compare and use authentic forms of address in familiar and unfamiliar social situations. | **SE:** 336, 337<br>**TE:** 317C, 348, 349 |
| | **11.7.5** | Compare systems of other cultures and the learner's own culture. | **SE:** 333, 349<br>**TE:** 332, 348-349 |
| | **11.7.6** | Compare and contrast elements that shape cultural identity in the learner's heritage and in the target cultures. | **SE:** 333, 349<br>**TE:** 332, 348-349 |

## Standard 8 COMMUNITIES:

| | | | |
|---|---|---|---|
| **Become an active global citizen by experiencing languages and cultures in multiple settings** *Learners use their knowledge of the target language and cultures both within and beyond the school setting for personal enrichment and civic engagement.* | **11.8.1** | Share experiences from the world language classroom with others. | **SE:** 333 |
| | **11.8.2** | Investigate and share with others the influences of the target language and cultures on the community. | **SE:** 333<br>**TE:** 358 |
| | **11.8.3** | Show evidence of becoming a life-long learner by using the target language and cultural knowledge for personal enrichment. | **SE:** 349<br>**TE:** 317C, 317D, 349 |

# Chapter Opener

## Meeting the National Standards

**Communication**
Comunicación, pp. 323, 325, 327, 329, 331, 337, 339, 341, 343, 345, 347
Game, p. 357
Situación, p. 359

**Cultures**
Nota cultural, p. 336
Practices and Perspectives, p. 347
Hertitage Speakers, p. 348
Culture Project, p. 358

**Connections**
Science Link, p. 326
Nota cultural, pp. 328, 329
Atlas Interactivo Mundial, p. 333
Social Studies Link, p. 349
Languages Arts Link, p. 351

**Comparisons**
Language to Language, p. 324
Nota cultural, p. 336
En inglés, p. 342

**Communities**
Comunidad y oficio, p. 333
Community Link, p. 337
Career Path, p. 344

## Learning Tips

Have students look up volunteer or work activities in which Spanish is required. Ask them to find one that interests them and write a list of terms associated with that field. Have them look up the terms they do not know in Spanish and write them in a notebook to use as reference. 1.2

## Using the Photo

Tell students this photo was taken in the **Plaza San Francisco** in Cuzco, Peru, the hub of the Incan empire. In this plaza is the **Iglesia de San Francisco,** a church that was built over an ancient Incan temple. Discuss the questions on p. 318 as a class. Ask if they have ever planted trees or flowers.

# Capítulo 8

# ¿A qué te dedicas?

## OBJETIVOS

**In this chapter you will learn to**
- say what you can and cannot do
- talk about what you do and do not understand
- write a formal letter
- talk about your plans

**And you will use**
- verbs with indirect object pronouns
- verbs that express "to become"
- uses of **se**
- conditional
- past subjunctive with hypothetical statements
- more past subjunctive

## ¿Qué ves en la foto?

- **¿Quiénes son estas personas y qué hacen?**
- **¿Cómo ayuda este trabajo a la comunidad?**
- **¿Qué haces tú para ayudar a tu comunidad?**

| Suggested pacing: | Traditional Schedule | Block Schedule |
|---|---|---|
| Vocabulario 1/Gramática 1 | 5 1/2 days | 2 1/2 blocks |
| Cultura | 1/2 day | 1/2 block |
| Vocabulario 2/Gramática 2 | 5 1/2 days | 2 1/2 blocks |
| Novela | 1/2 day | 1/2 block |
| Lectura cultural | 1/2 day | 1/2 block |
| Leamos y escribamos | 1 day | 1/2 block |
| Prepárate para el examen | 1 day | 1/4 block |
| Chapter Test | 1 day | 1/2 block |
| Integración | 1/2 day | 1/4 block |

Visit Holt Online
**go.hrw.com**
KEYWORD: EXP3 CH8
Online Edition

Un grupo de estudiantes siembra árboles en la Plaza San Francisco, Cuzco, Perú.

# Chapter Opener

## Holt Grammar Logic

### CHAPTER 8

- *To say what they can and cannot do, and to talk about what they do and do not understand,* students will need to review and learn more about contexts that require the use of indirect object pronouns. They will also learn the various ways to express "to become," and will review the uses of the pronoun **se.**
- *To write a formal letter, and to talk about their plans,* students will need to review the conditional, and they will also need to learn about the past subjunctive with hypothetical statements and in subordinate clauses (i.e. after **que**).

## DVD VIDEO OPTIONS

- **VideoCultura**
- **VideoNovela**
- **Variedades**
- **GramaVisión**

## LISTENING PRACTICE — Language Lab and Classroom Activities

**Vocabulario**
Activity 1, p. 322, CD 8, Tr. 1
Activity 22, p. 336, CD 8, Tr. 7
Activity 28, p. 339, CD 8, Tr. 8

**Gramática**
Activity 10, p. 326, CD 8, Tr. 2
Activity 14, p. 328, CD 8, Tr. 3
Activity 31, p. 340, CD 8, Tr. 9

**Cultura**
**Comparaciones**,pp. 332–333, CD 8, Tr. 4–6

**Novela**
**Novela en video**, Escuchemos, p. 346

**Lectura cultural**
pp. 348–349, CD 8, Tr. 10

**Leamos**
pp. 350–353, CD 8, Tr. 11
Escuchemos, p. 350

**Repaso**
Activity 1, p. 354, CD 8, Tr. 12
Activity 6, p. 355, CD 8, Tr. 13
**Variedades,** Lab Book, p. 80

**Integración**
Activity 1, p. 358, CD 8, Tr. 14

**Assessment Program**
CD 8, Tr. 15-18

**Additional Listening**
Pre-AP CD 2, Tr. 9–12

## Resources

**Planning:**

Lesson Planner, pp. 113–114, 274–275

One-Stop Planner

**Presentation:**

Teaching Transparencies **Vocabulario** 8.1, 8.2

**Practice:**

Cuaderno de vocabulario y gramática, pp. 85–87

Activities for Communication, pp. 29–30

Teaching Transparencies Bell Work 8.1

**Vocabulario y gramática** answers, pp. 85–87

Interactive Tutor, Disc 2

### Bell Work

Use Bell Work 8.1 in the *Teaching Transparencies.*

**Objetivos**
- Saying what you can and cannot do
- Talking about what you do and do not understand

# Vocabulario en acción 1

## Unos jóvenes peruanos ¡Manos a la obra!

Tengo **talento** para diseñar páginas Web. Me encanta **utilizar** los programas de diseño y entiendo las nuevas **tecnologías** fácilmente.

Yo **me decidiría a** trabajar con mi padre **en un santiamén.** Es un **hombre de negocios** que trabaja para una compañía internacional.

Quiero hacerme médica para ayudar a **mejorar** la calidad de vida de la gente. Con **los adelantos** de la medicina, podría curar a personas.

Me gusta trabajar como **voluntario.** Quiero ayudar a **cambiar** la vida de las personas. **Trataré de** unirme a algún grupo voluntario **inmediatamente** después de graduarme, porque quiero empezar a trabajar **enseguida.**

**Más vocabulario...**

| | |
|---|---|
| la agenda electrónica | *electronic planner* |
| el (la) auxiliar administrativo(a)/médico(a)/de laboratorio | *administrative/medical/laboratory assistant* |
| el contestador automático | *answering machine* |
| la fotocopiadora | *photocopier* |
| la mujer de negocios | *businesswoman* |
| sembrar | *to plant* |

## Core Instruction

### TEACHING VOCABULARIO

1. Introduce the vocabulary using transparencies **8.1** and **8.2.** Model the pronunciation of each word. Then call on volunteers to read the captions next to the photos in the textbook. **(5 min.)**
2. Go over **Más vocabulario** and model pronunciation. **(3 min.)**
3. Ask students questions to prompt them to use vocabulary words in full but simple sentences. **¿Qué puedes usar para organizar tu horario? ¿En qué máquina se deja un mensaje por teléfono? (2 min.)**

### TEACHING ¡EXPRÉSATE!

1. Model the **¡Exprésate!** sentences for students. **(1 min.)**
2. Have students respond to your questions using the expressions listed about what they can and cannot do. **¿Te resulta fácil usar una fotocopiadora? ¿Te cuesta trabajo usar las nuevas tecnologías? (2 min.)**
3. Name different school subjects and have volunteers use the **¡Exprésate!** sentences to tell which subjects they find difficult and which subjects are easy for them. **(3 min.)**

### Pre-AP Practice

**AP Benchmark:** Initiate, maintain, and close a conversation on a familiar topic.

**Focus:** Talking about what you can and cannot do
- SE, p. 323, Act. 6
- TE, p. 323, **Comunicación**
- Activities for Communication, p. 29, Act. 1A–1B

Visit Holt Online
go.hrw.com
KEYWORD: EXP3 CH8
Vocabulario 1 practice

**También se puede decir...**

You may hear **el (la) negociante** or **el (la) empresario(a)** instead of **el hombre/la mujer de negocios.** Some Spanish speakers also say **la grabadora** instead of **el contestador automático,** and **el asistente administrativo** rather than **el auxiliar administrativo.**

## ¡Exprésate!

### To say what you can and cannot do

Interactive TUTOR

| | |
|---|---|
| **Está fuera de/a mi alcance.** *It's outside/within my reach.* | **Soy capaz de (hacer)...** *I'm capable of (doing) . . .* |
| **Eso me resulta fácil/bastante difícil.** *That's easy/pretty difficult for me.* | **Lo puedo hacer.** *I can do it.* |
| **No me es nada difícil.** *It's not hard for me at all.* | **Me cuesta trabajo (hacer)...** *It takes a lot of work for me (to do) . . .* |

Vocabulario y gramática, pp. 85–87 Online workbooks

▶ Vocabulario adicional — La tecnología, p. R18

## TPR
### Total Physical Response

Bring to class a toy or real microscope, a picture of a robot, a flyer announcing you are selling a bicycle, a textbook, and an electronic planner. Have individual students respond to the following commands.

**Señala un instrumento que se usa para mejorar la vida con adelantos médicos.**

**Señala algo que puedes utilizar si eres un hombre o una mujer de negocios.**

**Muéstrame lo que debes usar más si quieres mejorar tus notas.**

**Haz una pantomima de la máquina que facilitará todo en la vida diaria.**

1.2

### Common Error Alert ¡OJO!

Students often have trouble deciding which article to use with new vocabulary words. Tell students that technological fields of study always take the feminine article: **la ingeniería, la robótica, la fotocomposición.**

### También se puede decir...

Along with **sembrar,** students may also hear **plantar** and **cultivar** for *to plant.*

## Differentiated Instruction

### Advanced Learners

**Extension** Have students do extra research on Spanish vocabulary words in a historical (e.g. **la imprenta**), modern (e.g. **la informática**), or futuristic (e.g. **la nanotecnología**) technological field of their choice. They can look for English/Spanish glossaries on the Internet and also set their search engines to look for only Spanish Web sites on their chosen fields. 3.2

### Multiple Intelligences

**Naturalist** Ask students to research two pesticides that occur in nature that are suitable for growing crops organically. Have them write two paragraphs in Spanish and then share their findings with the class. 1.3

**Differentiated Instruction** See the Differentiated Instruction CD-ROM.

Capítulo 8

# Vocabulario 1

## Resources

**Planning:**

Lesson Planner, pp. 113–114, 274–275

One-Stop Planner

**Presentation:**

Teaching Transparencies
**Vocabulario** 8.1, 8.2

**Practice:**

Cuaderno de vocabulario y gramática, pp. 85–87

Activities for Communication, pp. 29–30

Lab Book, pp. 41–44

Teaching Transparencies
**Vocabulario y gramática** answers, pp. 85–87

Audio CD 8, Tr. 1

Interactive Tutor, Disc 2

### 1 Script

1. Cuando mi papá tenía mi edad, era imposible viajar y a la vez mantener contacto con la oficina. Pero ahora puedo hablar con mi jefe desde cualquier lugar, y eso me facilita mucho el trabajo.
2. Mi empleada trabaja desde su casa y siempre está muy ocupada, así que casi nunca contesta el teléfono. Pero le dejo un mensaje y ella me vuelve a llamar enseguida.
3. Trabajo como voluntario en un hospital para niños. Me encanta escribir cuentos para ellos, pero lo que pasa es que tengo una sola copia del cuento para muchos niños. Así que hago muchas copias de mis cuentos con una máquina.
4. La tecnología es increíble. Antes yo solo tenía que hacer todo en la oficina. ¡Ahora tengo un auxiliar que no necesita comer ni dormir y hace de todo! Me lleva un café en las mañanas, hace las citas y hasta limpia la oficina en la noche cuando no estoy.

CD 8, Tr. 1

### 1 Gracias a la tecnología... 1.2

**Escuchemos** Escucha los siguientes comentarios y determina a qué adelanto tecnológico se refiere cada uno. 1. c 2. a 3. c 4. b

1. **a.** el robot **b.** la agenda electrónica **c.** el teléfono celular
2. **a.** el contestador automático **b.** la fotocopiadora **c.** el robot
3. **a.** la agenda electrónica **b.** el teléfono celular **c.** la fotocopiadora
4. **a.** la fotocopiadora **b.** el robot **c.** el teléfono celular

Un grupo de voluntarios ayuda a mantener limpia la ciudad de Buenos Aires, Argentina.

### 2 El club de voluntarios 1.2

**Leamos** Lee lo que dice la presidenta del club de voluntarios y completa su discurso con las palabras del cuadro.

| sembrar | talentos | mejorar | alcance | tratar de | decidirse | a la vez |
|---|---|---|---|---|---|---|

Muchas gracias por __1__ a ser miembros de nuestro club. Todos pueden contribuir con sus ideas y sus __2__ especiales. Esta semana, queremos __3__ cómo se ve nuestra comunidad. Vamos a __4__ árboles en las aceras y en los parques. __5__ que sembremos, vamos a poner basureros en estos lugares. Tenemos que __6__ ayudar a mantener limpia la ciudad. Es un poco difícil, pero está a nuestro __7__.

1. decidirse 2. talentos 3. mejorar 4. sembrar 5. A la vez 6. tratar de 7. alcance

### 3 El mundo de los negocios 1.2

**Leamos** Basándote en lo que dice Teresa, indica si cada una de las siguientes oraciones es **cierta** o **falsa.**

*Me llamo Teresa y soy la auxiliar administrativa de un hombre de negocios. No me es nada difícil hacer tres cosas a la vez, y cuando mi jefe pide algo se lo hago en un santiamén. Pero sueño con hacerme una mujer de negocios y sé que está a mi alcance. Sólo me falta tomar unas clases en la universidad por la noche. Estoy segura de que en cuanto me gradúe, encontraré trabajo enseguida porque tengo mucha experiencia y mi jefe me dará una recomendación muy buena. Además, con mi conocimiento de la tecnología, creo que sería capaz de empezar mi propio negocio algún día.*

1. Teresa hace trabajo voluntario en un hospital. falsa
2. Cuando su jefe le pide algo, ella siempre se lo hace inmediatamente. cierta
3. Teresa no puede hacer más de una cosa a la vez. falsa
4. A Teresa le resulta difícil usar las nuevas tecnologías. falsa
5. Ella cree que no está a su alcance ser mujer de negocios. falsa
6. Teresa es una mujer muy competente. cierta

## Core Instruction

### VOCABULARY IN CONTEXT

Divide the class into groups of three to create vocabulary notebooks. Students will have the following roles: **investigador(a), traductor(a),** and **escritor(a).** The **investigador(a)** looks up each vocabulary word in a monolingual Spanish dictionary and reads its definition to the group. The **traductor(a)** looks up the vocabulary words in a Spanish-English dictionary and reads the English translation to the group. The **escritor(a)** writes the Spanish definition and English translation in the group's notebook. All group members then work together to compose a sentence using the vocabulary word in context. Once the notebook is completed, each group will make copies so that all members have their own notebook.

**4 Ventajas y desventajas** 1.3

**Escribamos/Hablemos** Describe las ventajas y las desventajas de los adelantos tecnológicos en las fotos.

1 
2 
3 
4 

**5 ¿Puedes hacerlo?** 1.2

**Leamos/Escribamos** Usa las expresiones de **Exprésate** para indicar si puedes hacer cada actividad o no.

MODELO **diseñar páginas Web**
**Soy capaz de diseñar páginas Web.**

1. ser hombre (mujer) de negocios
2. usar las nuevas tecnologías
3. organizar las citas en una agenda electrónica
4. utilizar un contestador automático
5. hacer dos cosas a la vez
6. trabajar como auxiliar médico(a)

## Comunicación

HOLT SoundBooth ONLINE RECORDING

**6 ¿Está a tu alcance?** 1.1, 1.2

**Hablemos** En grupos pequeños, hablen de estos temas y expliquen sus puntos de vista. ¿Creen que serán capaces de hacer estas cosas en el futuro? ¿Por qué?

MODELO **—En el futuro no podremos trabajar sin computadora.**
**—Pues no estoy de acuerdo. Yo no necesito computadora.**

1. trabajar sin computadora
2. vivir sin teléfono celular
3. usar un robot en la vida diaria
4. hacer trabajo voluntario
5. trabajar para una empresa internacional
6. mejorar la calidad de vida de la gente

Vocabulario 1

### 4 Answers

Answers will vary. Possible answers:

1. El teléfono celular nos permite comunicar con otros en cualquier momento, pero puede ser descortés usarlo en frente de otras personas.
2. Las computadoras facilitan la vida diaria, pero pasar mucho tiempo frente a ellas nos hace perezosos.
3. El correo electrónico nos da noticias inmediatamente, pero la desventaja es que pocas personas escriben cartas a mano hoy en día.
4. Un robot para cortar el césped sería una gran ventaja porque nos daría más tiempo libre. La desventaja es que los robots rompen fácilmente.

### Teaching Suggestion

Have students describe their interaction with technological devices on a typical day, from the moment they wake up to the moment they go to sleep. Have them think about which ones they could do without, or could use less of. For example, could they survive watching less TV? Also have them think of how a technological device they do not currently have could make their lives better. 1.3

## Comunicación

### Pair Activity: Interpersonal

Have students discuss in pairs a dream job, either paid or voluntary, they would each like to have the following summer, and how they would use some of the technological items identified in the vocabulary. Have them talk about jobs that they might have already done or jobs that their relatives might have, which use different forms of modern technology. 1.1

## Differentiated Instruction

### SLOWER PACE LEARNERS

**Variation** Have students work in pairs to write four sentences using the vocabulary learned in the lesson. Have them use specifically the adverbs **a la vez** and **enseguida,** the verbs **decidirse a** and **mejorar,** and the nouns **la ventaja** and **el talento.** Have them use the adjective **competente** in at least two of the sentences. 1.2

### SPECIAL LEARNING NEEDS

**Students with Visual Impairments** Have students describe how technology enhances or could further enhance learning for all students. For example, voice recognition software might help students with visual impairments. Have them use their imagination to suggest technology that might not exist or that is not widely implemented in both private and public places that could facilitate learning for students with special needs.

**Differentiated Instruction** See the Differentiated Instruction CD-ROM.

## Resources

**Planning:**

Lesson Planner, pp. 113–114, 274–275

One-Stop Planner

**Presentation:**

Teaching Transparencies
**Vocabulario** 8.1, 8.2

**Practice:**

Cuaderno de vocabulario y gramática, pp. 85–87

Activities for Communication, pp. 29–30

Teaching Transparencies
**Vocabulario y gramática** answers, pp. 85–87

Interactive Tutor, Disc 2

## Comparisons

### Language to Language

Point out that the English translations for some of the **¡Exprésate!** sentences are not literal translations. Explain that many of the expressions are idiomatic, and do not have direct equivalents in English. Ask students to think of other idiomatic expressions they have learned that cannot be directly translated into English and vice versa.

4.1

### 7 Answers

1. Trata de entenderla pero piensa que es muy difícil.
2. Martín le sugiere que vuelva a la primera página para estudiar los ejemplos.
3. Dice que la tarea le cuesta trabajo.
4. Cree que Martín tiene ventaja porque tiene los apuntes de su hermano mayor.
5. Answers will vary. Possible answer: Creo que a Martín le resulta fácil hacer la tarea porque él está ayudándole al amigo.
6. A Ricardo se le escapa entender su propia letra en los apuntes.

## ¡No entiendo!

En un colegio de Lima

MARTÍN Eres capaz de hacer esta tarea, Ricardo. Sólo tienes que concentrarte y lo captarás enseguida.

RICARDO Trato de entenderla una y otra vez, pero no me cabe en la cabeza.

MARTÍN No te preocupes; esto sí está a tu alcance. Mira, vuelve a la primera página y estudia los ejemplos.

RICARDO A ver... creo que puedo hacer estos problemas... ¡Sí! Pues, el primer paso no me resultó tan difícil.

MARTÍN ¿Está más claro ahora?

RICARDO Un poco, pero sí me cuesta trabajo. Me parece que tú tienes ventaja, porque tu hermano mayor ya tomó este curso.

MARTÍN Sí, tengo sus apuntes, pero me resulta casi imposible leer lo que escribió porque tiene muy mala letra.

RICARDO Ya veo. Mira, ahora que lo dices, hay algo en mi tarea que se me escapa.

MARTÍN ¿Qué es?

RICARDO Mi propia letra. ¡No logro entenderla!

### ¡Exprésate!

**To talk about what you do and do not understand**

Interactive TUTOR

| | |
|---|---|
| **Hay algo que se me escapa.** *There's something that I can't quite grasp.* | **No me cabe en la cabeza.** *I don't get it.* |
| **No logro entender...** *I can't seem to understand . . .* | **¡Vaya! Por fin capto la idea.** *Aha! I finally get the idea.* |
| **¡Ya caigo! Está más claro ahora.** *I get it! It's clearer now.* | |

Vocabulario y gramática, pp. 85–87 Online workbooks

## Core Instruction

### TEACHING ¡EXPRÉSATE!

1. Read the conversation aloud with students. **(2 min.)**
2. Ask students to tell you about the last time they asked a fellow student for help with their Spanish homework. How was it similar or different from what is represented in this conversation? **(3 min.)**
3. Model the **¡Exprésate!** sentences for students, then role-play both sides of a conversation using the sentences.

**—No logro entender la geometría. ¿Y tú?**
**—Sí, por fin capto la idea.** **(3 min.)**

4. Have volunteers help you create a conversation about using computer programs. Begin by telling what you do not understand, and have volunteers respond by agreeing or by saying that they get the idea. **(2 min.)**

See answers on p. 324.

**7 ¿Lograste entenderlo?** 1.2

**Leamos/Escribamos** Basándote en el diálogo entre Ricardo y Martín, contesta las preguntas.

1. ¿Cuál es la opinión de Ricardo sobre su habilidad para hacer la tarea?
2. ¿Qué le sugiere Martín a Ricardo para que logre entender la tarea?
3. Aunque el primer paso no le resultó tan difícil, ¿qué dice Ricardo del trabajo?
4. ¿Por qué cree Ricardo que Martín tiene ventaja?
5. ¿Crees que a Martín le resulta fácil hacer la tarea? ¿Por qué?
6. ¿Qué se le escapa a Ricardo al final?

**8 El mundo tecnológico** 1.2

**Leamos/Escribamos** Completa las oraciones con las palabras del cuadro.

| caigo | logro | alcance | cabe | ventajas | captó |
|---|---|---|---|---|---|

1. No ═══ entender las nuevas tecnologías. logro
2. Las nuevas tecnologías tienen muchas ═══. ventajas
3. Me han enseñado a usar la computadora pero no me ═══ en la cabeza. cabe
4. Aprender a usar las nuevas tecnologías está al ═══ de todos. alcance
5. Le expliqué a una amiga cómo mandar un correo electrónico y al fin ═══ la idea. captó
6. ¡Ya ═══! No sabía que había que hacerlo así. caigo

Una planta hidroeléctrica cerca de Baños, Ecuador

## Comunicación

HOLT SoundBooth ONLINE RECORDING

**9 ¡No me cuesta nada!** 1.1, 1.2

**Hablemos** En parejas, comenten los siguientes temas. Túrnense para explicar si es algo que saben hacer bien o algo que les cuesta trabajo. Usen las expresiones de las páginas 321 y 324.

MODELO —**No logro entender los nuevos programas de computación.**
—**A mí me pasa lo mismo. Siempre hay algo que se me escapa.**

1. las matemáticas
2. las ciencias
3. la tecnología
4. los deportes
5. los idiomas
6. el teatro
7. la música y el arte
8. trabajar y ser estudiante a la vez

Vocabulario 1

## Connections

### Science Link

Explain to students that Ecuador is highly dependent upon hydroelectric power. Over half of the country's electrical energy is generated by plants like the one shown on this page. The largest power plant is at the Paute dam, which can account for over 40% of the country's electrical power. When there is a shortage of rainfall, however, Ecuador has to rely more on its thermoelectric plants, which burn oil and are not as environmentally friendly. Have students research alternative power sources that Ecuador and other Andean countries are exploring to supplement their traditional power sources. 3.1, 3.2

## Comunicación

### Class Activity: Interpersonal

As an extension of Activity 9, have students call on each other using the **¡Exprésate!** expressions and slight variations on the examples they are given on the exercise.

MODELO

— **¡Vaya! Por fin capto la idea de los ejercicios de álgebra. ¿Y tú, Miguel?**

— **Yo todavía no los puedo entender.**

1.1

## Differentiated Instruction

### ADVANCED LEARNERS

**Additional Practice** Have students work in pairs to do advanced searches in Spanish on the Internet on a technological topic of their choice. Ask each pair to prepare a presentation for the class. They should include some visual material in their presentations. 1.3, 3.2

### MULTIPLE INTELLIGENCES

**Spatial** Have students design and draw the ideal technologically-equipped classroom/laboratory. Have them label in Spanish machines they have learned about, and look up the Spanish words that they have not yet learned for other machines. Tell them to include in their design all the traditional classroom items such as desks and blackboards, labeling them in Spanish as well. 1.3

## Assess

**Assessment Program**

**Prueba: Vocabulario 1,** pp. 141–142

Alternative Assessment, pp. 380, 392, 404

**Online Assessment**
**my.hrw.com**

**Test Generator**

**Assess** **Differentiated Instruction** See the Differentiated Instruction CD-ROM.

## Resources

**Planning:**

Lesson Planner, pp. 115–117, 276–279

One-Stop Planner

**Presentation:**

Video Program **GramaVisión**

**Practice:**

Grammar Tutor for Students of Spanish, Chapter 8

Cuaderno de vocabulario y gramática, pp. 88–90

Cuaderno de actividades, pp. 71–73

Activities for Communication, pp. 29–30

Lab Book, pp. 41–44

Teaching Transparencies

Bell Work 8.2

**Vocabulario y gramática** answers, pp. 88–90

Audio CD 8, Tr. 2

Interactive Tutor, Disc 2

### Bell Work

Use Bell Work 8.2 in the *Teaching Transparencies*, or write this activity on the board.

**Escribe cinco oraciones para describir lo que entiendes o lo que no entiendes de tus clases de español, matemáticas, estudios sociales y ciencias. Usa las expresiones de ¡Exprésate! de la página 324.** 1.3

**Objetivos**
- Verbs with indirect object pronouns
- Verbs that express "to become"
- Uses of se

# Gramática en acción 1

GramaVisión

Interactive TUTOR

## Repaso: Verbs with indirect object pronouns

**1** An **indirect object pronoun** is used with some verbs to indicate *to whom* or *for whom* an action occurs. The verbs below are often used with indirect object pronouns.

¿**Te molesta** hacer dos cosas a la vez?
*Does it bother you to do two things at once?*

**Me resulta** fácil usar este programa.
*It is easy for me to use this program.*

No **me cabe** en la cabeza.
*I can't get it into my head.*

¿**Le pusiste** tu número en su agenda electrónica?
*Did you put your number in his electronic planner?*

A Sara no **le es** fácil la geografía.
*Geography is not easy for Sara.*

A ellos **les cuesta** trabajo hacer la tarea.
*It takes a lot of work for them to do the homework.*

**2** The **indirect object pronoun** indicates *to whom* or *for whom* the action occurs. The **verb** must agree with the subject.

*for whom* — *agrees with subject*

¿A Uds. **les resultó** fácil el examen?

**3** If the subject is an **infinitive,** the verb must be in the third person singular.

*agrees with subject*

**Me cuesta** trabajo **entender** este cuento.

Vocabulario y gramática, pp. 88–90
Actividades, pp. 71–73
Online workbooks

### ¿Te acuerdas?

The direct object pronouns **me, te, lo, la, nos, os, los, las** stand for people or things that directly receive the action of the verb. Verbs like **gustar** and **molestar** do not take a direct object pronoun but rather an indirect object pronoun that stands for the person experiencing the action.

CD 8, Tr. 2

**10 La tecnología** 1.2 See script on p. 327.

**Escuchemos** Escucha la conversación entre Clara y María y determina si las siguientes oraciones son **ciertas** o **falsas.**

1. Clara dice que no le gusta la agenda de María. falsa
2. A María le resulta difícil usar su agenda electrónica. cierta
3. Gabriela tampoco sabe usar su agenda electrónica. cierta
4. Todo le salió bien a Gabriela cuando usó su agenda electrónica. falsa
5. Clara entiende por qué sus amigas no logran entender la tecnología. falsa
6. Clara no sabe usar su teléfono celular. cierta

## Core Instruction

### TEACHING GRAMÁTICA

1. Go over **¿Te acuerdas?** with students. **(1 min.)**
2. Write the sentences in point 1 on the board. Go over point 1, reading aloud the sentences in Spanish and English. After finishing each sentence, ask **¿a quién?** or **¿para quién?** (*to whom* or *for whom?*) (answers: **a ti; a mí; a mí; a él/ella; a Sara; a ellos**) **(3 min.)**
3. Go over point 2. Students go to the board and draw arrows between the verbs and the subjects in the sentences in point 1. Have them write in the subject if it is left out. **(3 min.)**
4. Go over point 3 and provide more examples of sentences with infinitive subjects. Have students point out the infinitive subjects. **Les resulta difícil levantarse temprano. (3 min.)**

### GramaVisión

For a video presentation of verbs with indirect object pronouns, use **GramaVisión.**

GramaVisión

Visit Holt Online
**go.hrw.com**
KEYWORD: EXP3 CH8
Gramática 1 practice

## 11 En el trabajo 1.2

**Leamos/Escribamos** Completa las oraciones con la palabra correcta en paréntesis.

1. A Samuel ==== (le/les) parece excelente el trabajo de Martín, su auxiliar administrativo.
2. Me ==== (llamo/llama) la atención el talento de Martín.
3. A Samuel ==== (se/ le) es imposible trabajar sin él.
4. A todos los empleados aquí, ==== (le/les) resulta difícil hacer más de una cosa a la vez.
5. A Samuel y a Martín no les ==== (importan/importa) trabajar hasta muy tarde.
6. A nosotros ==== (nos/les) cuesta trabajo entender cómo ellos logran hacer tantas cosas.
7. Pero nos ==== (gusta/gustan) observarlos.
8. Queremos dar==== (les/nos) las gracias por su ayuda.

En una oficina de Lima

## 12 ¡A escribir! 1.2

**Escribamos/Hablemos** Combina las frases de las columnas para escribir seis oraciones. Usa los pronombres del complemento indirecto correctos.

| | | |
|---|---|---|
| A mí | gustar | usar las nuevas tecnologías |
| A mis padres | caber en la cabeza | usar una agenda electrónica |
| A mi abuelo | resultar fácil/difícil | tratar de hacer dos cosas a la vez |
| A ti | ser complicado | utilizar la nueva computadora |
| A mis amigos y a mí | costar trabajo | programar el contestador automático |
| A mi jefe | salir mal | cambiar su auxiliar por un robot |

## Comunicación

HOLT SoundBooth ONLINE RECORDING

## 13 La tecnología cambia la vida 1.1, 1.2

**Hablemos** En parejas, hablen de cómo los siguientes adelantos tecnológicos cambiarían sus vidas en la casa o en el colegio. *¿Se te olvidó?* Conditional, pp. 120–121

**MODELO** **acceso a la tarea por Internet**
**—Nos sería más fácil hacer la tarea por Internet.**
**—Estoy de acuerdo. Me molesta llevar los libros a casa.**

1. un programa tecnológico interactivo para ayudar en las tareas
2. un robot para hacer los quehaceres
3. computadoras con acceso a Internet en todos los salones de clase
4. una agenda electrónica que habla

### 10 Script

—María, me gusta mucho tu agenda electrónica.
—Gracias, Clara. El problema es que me resulta difícil usarla.
—¿Por qué? Ángel tiene una y dice que le es muy fácil usarla.
—Sí, Ángel me enseñó a usarla, pero todavía no la entiendo bien. Me frustra que me resulte tan difícil, aunque mi amiga Gabriela tiene el mismo problema. Trató de usar una agenda electrónica y todo le salió mal. ¡Fue a la peluquera cuando tenía que ir al dentista y fue al médico en vez de ir a mi fiesta!
—¡No me cabe en la cabeza que Uds. no logren entender una tecnología tan sencilla!
—Clara, no seas así. Yo sé que te es imposible entender tu teléfono celular. ¡Nunca contestas mis llamadas porque no sabes escuchar tus mensajes!

### Más práctica

Have students create a four-line conversation with a friend in which they discuss using a technological device. Have them use indirect object pronouns with verbs that indicate *to whom* or *for whom* in every sentence. 1.1

### Comunicación

**Class Activity: Presentational**

Call on volunteers to go to the front of the class and dramatize using a technological device. Have them tell about the devices using indirect object pronouns. For example, a student can act out talking on a cell phone from his or her pocket, dialing it, putting it next to the ear, and then saying: **Me encantan los teléfonos celulares.** 1.3

## Differentiated Instruction

### SLOWER PACE LEARNERS

**Variation** Have students formulate sentences at their own pace, using the verbs listed in the **Gramática** presentation. Then have them work with a partner to think of other verbs that might take indirect objects. Ask them to write sentences together using each verb they come up with. Have pairs share their sentences with the class. 1.2

### MULTIPLE INTELLIGENCES

**12 Spatial** You may wish to give students strips of paper with the eighteen phrases from Activity 12 so that they can rearrange the sentence parts themselves and write the required six sentences. 1.2

**Differentiated Instruction** See the Differentiated Instruction CD-ROM.

## Resources

**Planning:**

Lesson Planner, pp. 115–117, 276–279

One-Stop Planner

**Presentation:**

Video Program
**GramaVisión**

**Practice:**

Grammar Tutor for Students of Spanish, Chapter 8

Cuaderno de vocabulario y gramática, pp. 88–90

Cuaderno de actividades, pp. 71–73

Activities for Communication, pp. 29–30

Lab Book, pp. 41–44

Teaching Transparencies
Bell Work 8.3

**Vocabulario y gramática** answers, pp. 88–90

Audio CD 8, Tr. 3

Interactive Tutor, Disc 2

### Bell Work

Use Bell Work 8.3 in the *Teaching Transparencies,* or write this activity on the board.

**Completa las oraciones.**

1. A Pablo (les/le) resulta fácil usar las nuevas tecnologías.
2. Me (parece/parezco) que no estás haciendo bien el trabajo.
3. ¿A ti (me/te) molesta llegar al trabajo temprano?
4. Qué bien que a ustedes les (salió/salieron) bien el proyecto.
5. A mi hermano no (me/le) cabe en la cabeza que yo saqué buenas notas este semestre. 1.2

### 14 Script

See script on p. 317E.

Interactive TUTOR

### Nota cultural

Tradicionalmente en Latinoamérica y España, las horas de trabajo han sido desde las nueve de la mañana hasta las dos, y otra vez desde las cuatro o cinco hasta las ocho. Entre las dos y las cuatro, la gente volvía a casa para comer con la familia y dormir la "siesta". Pero hoy en día esta tradición está cambiando. Ahora muchos empleados en estos países tienen un horario parecido al horario típico de trabajo de Estados Unidos.

¿Cuales serían las ventajas y desventajas de seguir las horas de trabajo tradicionales de España y Latinoamérica? 3.1

Un café Internet en la República Dominicana

## Verbs that express "to become"

**1** You can use the verbs **hacerse, volverse, ponerse, convertirse en, quedarse,** and **llegar a ser** to convey a change in state (*to get* or *to become*). The preterite is often used to talk about a particular change or reaction in the past.

**2** **Hacerse** + **adjective** or **noun** describes *a change where a personal effort is involved.*

Juan **se hizo** **abogado.**
*Juan became a lawyer.*

**3** **Ponerse** + **adjective** describes *a sudden physical or mental change.*

Ana **se puso** **triste** cuando no pudo ir al concierto.
*Ana became sad when she couldn't go to the concert.*

**4** **Volverse** + **adjective** can describe a more gradual change.

**Me estoy volviendo** **loca** con esta computadora.
*I'm going crazy with this computer.*

**5** **Convertirse en** + **noun** expresses *to change into or to turn into.*

La tienda familiar **se convirtió en** un **almacén** grande.
*The family store turned into a big department store.*

**6** Use **quedarse** + **adjective** in some idiomatic expressions and with certain adjectives such as **ciego(a), sordo(a),** and **calvo(a)** to express *to be left, to wind up* a certain way.

**Me quedé** **boquiabierta.**
*I was left speechless.*

**7** Use **llegar a ser** + **adjective** or **noun** to express *to become or to get to be after a series of events or after a long time.*

Por fin **llegaron a ser** buenas **amigas.**
*They finally got to be good friends.*

Era pobre, pero **llegó a ser** **rico.**
*He was poor but he became rich.*

Vocabulario y gramática, pp. 88–90
Actividades, pp. 71–73
Online workbooks

CD 8, Tr. 3

### 14 Los mejores planes 1.2

**Escuchemos** Algunos estudiantes regresan a Cuzco, donde hicieron un programa de intercambio. Escucha cada comentario y determina si la persona **1.** b **2.** a **3.** b **4.** a **5.** a **6.** a

**a)** ha cambiado o

**b)** no ha cambiado.

## Core Instruction

### TEACHING GRAMÁTICA

1. Review point 1 and the different verbal expressions meaning *to become.* **(2 min.)**
2. Go over points 2 through 4 by reviewing the combinations listed and modeling each sentence. Write the example on the board, underlining the adjective. Invite students to come up with other adjectives to replace the underlined word. **(4 min.)**
3. Go over point 5. Write other nouns that might be used with **convertirse en** to express *to turn into.* **(2 min.)**
4. Go over points 6 and 7. **(3 min.)**
5. Write sample sentences on the board leaving out the verb that expresses *to become,* and have volunteers tell which verb to use for each sentence. **(4 min.)**

### GramaVisión

For a video presentation of verbs that express *to become,* use **GramaVisión.**

GramaVisión

## 15 ¿Cómo cambiaron? 1.2

**Leamos** Completa cada oración con la forma correcta del verbo.

1. Ellos ═══ furiosos por la mala noticia. a
   **a.** se pusieron **b.** se volvieron **c.** se hicieron
2. El señor ═══ terco con el paso de los años. c
   **a.** se convirtió en **b.** se hizo **c.** se volvió
3. Carlos y Memo ═══ ricos con su negocio por Internet. b
   **a.** se convirtieron **b.** se hicieron **c.** se pusieron
4. Su hermano ═══ feliz cuando le cuentas un chiste. c
   **a.** se vuelve **b.** se hace **c.** se pone
5. Este niño ═══ un problema. a
   **a.** se ha convertido en **b.** se ha puesto **c.** se ha hecho

### Nota cultural

El precio de acceso a Internet ha bajado mucho en Perú en los últimos años. El gobierno peruano está tratando de mejorar el sistema de telecomunicaciones y crear un ambiente favorable para el desarrollo del comercio electrónico.

¿Por qué crees que sería importante tener un buen sistema de telecomunicaciones y acceso a Internet en un país andino? 3.1

## 16 Antes y después 1.2

**Leamos/Escribamos** Escribe oraciones completas usando las siguientes frases. Utiliza el presente o el presente perfecto.

*¿Se te olvidó?* Present perfect, pp. 148–149

1. yo/volverse/muy estudiosa porque ahora tengo clases por Internet
2. mi abuela/hacerse/mujer de negocios y vende cosas por Internet
3. mi papá/llegar a ser/muy competente con las nuevas tecnologías
4. mis hermanos/volverse/locos por los juegos de computadora
5. la tecnología/convertirse en/el centro de nuestra vida diaria

1. ...me he vuelto...
2. ...se ha hecho...
3. ...ha llegado a ser...
4. ...se vuelven...
5. ...se ha convertido en...

## Comunicación

HOLT SoundBooth ONLINE RECORDING

## 17 ¿Qué le pasó a Guillermo? 1.1, 1.2

**Hablemos** En parejas, cuenten lo que le pasó a Guillermo en los siguientes dibujos. Usen los verbos de **Gramática.**

Gramática 1

### Heritage Speakers

Have heritage speakers look at the pictures in the **Comunicación** activity and think of words or phrases they have said or have heard relatives say when trying to encourage individual athletes or sports teams in spectator sports. For example, **¡Sí se puede!**

### Answers

Use the Chapter 8 *Picture Sequences Transparency.*

**17 Sample Answer**

**Guillermo se puso triste cuando fue a entrenarse y no pudo levantar las pesas. Decidió cambiar su rutina. Después de entrenarse mucho, le resultó fácil levantar pesas. Su entrenador se quedó boquiabierto. Guillermo se hizo tan fuerte que llegó a ser entrenador.**

### Comunicación

### Pair Activity: Interpersonal

As an extension of Activity 17, have students pair up and, using the verbs learned in **Gramática,** talk about how they felt when they first used a technological device with which they were clumsy, but with which they are now very comfortable. Ask them to create a conversation in which they take turns helping each other learn how to use the device. 1.1

## Differentiated Instruction

### ADVANCED LEARNERS

**Challenge** Have students do research in Spanish on a technology-related issue of their choice, and make up a series of sentences describing the investigation process for them using verbs that express *to become.* For example: **Me puse muy contenta al saber que tenía suficiente memoria en mi computadora para instalar un programa de música.** 3.2

### MULTIPLE INTELLIGENCES

**Intrapersonal** Have students write five sentences describing in detail how technological devices affect their moods, enable them to accomplish personal goals, or enhance the quality of their lives. Then have them write five more sentences about technological devices that they feel affect their lives negatively. Ask students to share their sentences with the class and allow their classmates to comment on each one. 1.3

**Differentiated Instruction** See the Differentiated Instruction CD-ROM.

## Resources

**Planning:**

Lesson Planner, pp. 115–117, 276–279

One-Stop Planner

**Presentation:**

Video Program **GramaVisión**

**Practice:**

Grammar Tutor for Students of Spanish, Chapter 8

Cuaderno de vocabulario y gramática, pp. 88–90

Cuaderno de actividades, pp. 71–73

Activities for Communication, pp. 29–30

Teaching Transparencies Bell Work 8.4

**Vocabulario y gramática** answers, pp. 88–90

Interactive Tutor, Disc 2

### Bell Work

Use Bell Work 8.4 in the *Teaching Transparencies,* or write this activity on the board.

**Escribe seis oraciones con *hacerse, ponerse, volverse, convertirse en, quedarse* y *llegar a ser.*** 1.3

### Más práctica

You might offer more practice for students by having them rewrite the following sentences, using **se** properly.

1. Muchas cartas de solicitud fueron recibidas.
2. Después de cuatro años, Luisa recibió su diploma de la universidad.
3. El robot le trajo la limonada a mamá.
4. Diego abraza a Ángela, y Ángela abraza a Diego.
5. Sin querer, yo dejé caer el vaso al suelo.
6. Con mucho esfuerzo, Nando llegó a ser el mejor estudiante de su clase. 1.2

Interactive TUTOR

## Repaso Uses of se

The pronoun **se** has many uses.

**1** It is used with verbs that are used reflexively **(acción reflexiva).**

Caterina **se** compró un contestador automático.

**2** It can indicate unintentional events **(acto no intencional).**

**Se** me olvidó la reunión.

**3** It replaces **le** or **les** before the direct object pronouns **lo, los, la,** and **las.**

*reemplaza le o les*

—¿**Le** dijiste que no fuera? —**Se** lo dije mil veces.

**4** It is used in impersonal sentences **(acción impersonal).**

**Se** dice que ha habido muchos adelantos en la medicina.

**5** It is used to express the passive voice **(acción pasiva).**

**Se** oyeron muchas opiniones sobre las ventajas del programa.

**6** It is used with certain "process" verbs to show a change in status or in physical or emotional state **(un cambio).**

Carmela **se** graduó de la universidad.

Manolo **se** hizo hombre de negocios.

Vocabulario y gramática, pp. 88–90
Actividades, pp. 71–73
Online workbooks

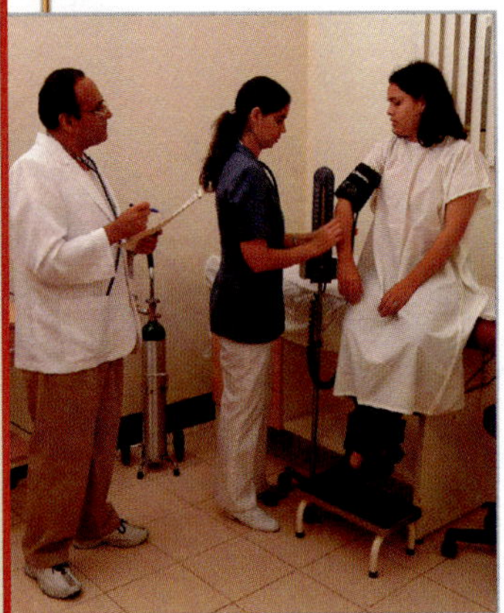

Un doctor y una enfermera atienden a una paciente en Perú.

### 18 ¿Por qué se usa? 1.2

**Leamos** Lee las siguientes oraciones y determina qué indica el **se: a)** una acción reflexiva, **b)** un acto no intencional, **c)** una sustitución para *le* o *les,* **d)** una acción impersonal, **e)** una acción pasiva o **f)** un cambio.

1. Miguel se puso furioso cuando supo la noticia. f
2. Se cancelaron las clases a causa de la nieve. e
3. Francisco se baña dos veces al día. a
4. Se lo mandé por correo ayer. c
5. Se cree que la situación ha mejorado. d
6. Se me rompió el vaso. b
7. Pamela se acostumbró a la vida diaria después de unas semanas. f

## Core Instruction

### TEACHING GRAMÁTICA

1. Tell students that **se** is a very versatile personal pronoun. It is easy to distinguish from **sé,** the indicative present of **saber,** because the latter takes an accent. **(1 min.)**
2. Go over points 1 through 7, explaining each use of **se** and modeling the sample sentences. **(2 min.)**
3. Go back through the seven points by having students complete the first part of the sentences with different endings of their own. For example, you say **Caterina se compró...** and a volunteer might answer **una agenda electrónica. (4 min.)**
4. Provide sentences with the different uses of **se** listed in the presentation. Students tell which use of **se** corresponds to each example sentence by stating the number from the presentation. **(3 min.)**

### GramaVisión

For a video presentation of the uses of **se,** use **GramaVisión.**

GramaVisión

**19 Oraciones con "se"** 1.2

**Leamos/Escribamos** Vuelve a escribir estas oraciones con **se.**

1. Todos dicen que la compañía tiene una crisis económica. Se dice que la compañía tiene una crisis económica.
2. En esta compañía, la gente generalmente empieza a trabajar a las nueve. En esta compañía, generalmente se empieza a trabajar a las nueve.
3. Me olvidé de ir a la reunión. Se me olvidó ir a la la reunión.
4. Las fotocopias fueron encontradas en la sala de conferencias.
5. Marisol llegó a ser directora de la empresa.
6. Le di la información a la jefa ayer. Se la di a la jefa ayer.

**4.** Se encontraron las fotocopias en la sala de conferencias.
**5.** Marisol se hizo directora de la empresa.

**20 ¿Qué pasa?** 1.2

**Hablemos** Observa las fotos y expresa lo que pasa o lo que ha pasado en cada una, usando **se.**

1

2

3

4

5

6

## Comunicación

HOLT SoundBooth ONLINE RECORDING

**21 Se dice que...** 1.1, 1.3

**Hablemos** En parejas, hablen sobre la tecnología. Comenten los siguientes temas, tratando de usar oraciones con **se.**

1. ¿Qué dice la gente sobre la tecnología?
2. ¿Cómo reacciona la gente cuando la tecnología no funciona bien?
3. ¿Has tenido algún problema con tu computadora alguna vez?

### 20 Answers

Answers will vary. Possible answers:

1. La chica se peina/se está peinando.
2. Al señor se le rompió un vaso/se le ha roto un vaso.
3. Se dice que el desastre en Alaska ha causado una crisis ambiental.
4. Se cayó la ropa/se ha caído la ropa.
5. Se gradúa/se graduó/se va a graduar.
6. Al chico se le olvidó poner el despertador y por eso se despertó tarde.

## Comunicación

### Pair Activity: Interpersonal

Have pairs of students take turns telling their partners about their week. Ask them to include at least four different uses of **se** in their conversations. Allow them a few minutes to prepare before starting their conversations.

1.1

## Differentiated Instruction

### SLOWER PACE LEARNERS

**Variation** Some students may have difficulty coming up with sentences using all of the variations of **se.** You might have students work in pairs to write down five simple sentences using **se.** For example, **Alicia se bañó.** Circulate around the classroom to check students' work. If pairs are having difficulty with a particular use of **se,** give them an example as a model. 1.2

### MULTIPLE INTELLIGENCES

**Bodily/Kinesthetic** Have students work in pairs to write five sentences with **se** that could be acted out. For example: **Juan se puso a brincar. María se cepilla los dientes.** Ask them to take turns acting out sentences as the rest of the class tries to guess the activity. 1.2

### Assess

**Assessment Program**

**Prueba: Gramática 1,** pp. 143–144

**Prueba: Aplicación 1,** pp. 145–146

Audio CD 8, Tr. 15

Alternative Assessment, pp. 380, 392, 404

**Online Assessment**
**my.hrw.com**

**Test Generator**

## Resources

**Planning:**

Lesson Planner, pp. 118, 278–279

One-Stop Planner

**Presentation:**

Audio CD 8, Tr. 4–6

Video Program, Videocassette 4

DVD Program **VideoCultura**

**Practice:**

Cuaderno de actividades, p. 74

Video Guide, pp. 52–53

Lab Book, p. 80

Interactive Tutor, Disc 2

## Language Note

Point out to students that when Ulises mentions the "mini-Palm" he is referring to a brand of **agenda electrónica** called the Palm Pilot®. His usage of the verb **chatear** comes from the English "to chat" in electronic forums. **Chatear** is used by Spanish speakers in the Internet domain, but has not been formally accepted into modern Spanish.

# Cultura

VideoCultura

## Comparaciones

Interactive TUTOR

CD 8, Tr. 4-6

Unos jóvenes navegan por Internet en San José, Costa Rica.

### Vale más una imagen que mil palabras 1.3

El acceso de los ciudadanos a la tecnología moderna es uno de los retos que tienen los países hispanos. En general, es caro comprar una computadora, pero a los jóvenes les interesa mucho la tecnología. En algunos países como Perú, México y muchos otros, hay muchos cibercafés, donde se puede alquilar computadoras para Internet, y también para videojuegos, y resulta bastante barato. También, mucha gente usa el teléfono móvil. ¿Crees que la tecnología será más importante aún en el futuro? ¿Cómo cambiará nuestra vida, y la de otros países?

### Omar
**Cuzco, Perú**

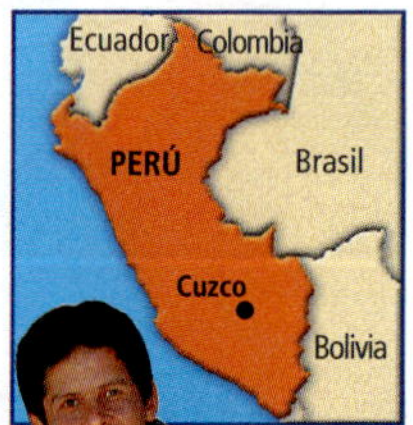

***Vamos a hablar sobre la tecnología. ¿A qué tipo de tecnología tienes acceso?***

Tengo acceso a la telefonía celular, a la televisión por cable y al Internet.

***¿Te resulta fácil usar una computadora?***

Me resulta fácil usar el Internet porque los sistemas cada vez son más amigables.

***¿Cuáles son las ventajas y desventajas de depender tanto de la tecnología?***

La principal ventaja de la tecnología es de que me permite acceder a mucha información, conocer otros idiomas por ejemplo, así como muchas personas. Como desventaja, es de que a veces existe mucha saturación en mensajes publicitarios.

***¿Crees que la tecnología te facilita la vida?***

La tecnología me ayuda bastante porque me mantiene comunicado en cualquier momento y lugar, así puedo comunicarme con mis amigos y mis clientes.

## Pre-AP Practice

**AP Language Examination:** Have students first listen to the interviews with books closed to help prepare them for Section I, Part A: **Listening—Short Dialogues and Narratives.** Point out that Ulises, like many Spanish speakers from Mexico, uses the diminutive form of the adverb **ahora (ahorita),** which is commonly used to mean *right now.*

## Core Instruction

### TEACHING CULTURA

1. Read the introductory paragraph as a class. Ask students whether they have ever been to a cybercafe and whether they prefer to surf the Web or play videogames there, at home, or at a friend's house. **(2 min.)**
2. Have volunteers play the roles of the interviewer and Omar, and another two, the interviewer and Ulises, and listen for the technology items with which they are familiar or use on a regular basis. **(8 min.)**
3. Have students answer the questions in **Para comprender** with a partner. Discuss **Para pensar y hablar** with the class. **(5 min.)**

### VideoCultura

For a video presentation of the interviews as well as for an additional interview for this chapter, see Chapter 8 **VideoCultura** on Videocassette or on DVD.

Cultura

## Ulises
**Ciudad de México, México**

***Vamos a hablar sobre la tecnología. ¿A qué tipo de tecnología tienes acceso?***

A celular, a Internet, a mi mini-Palm, juegos de video.

***¿Te resulta fácil usar tu celular?***

Sí, muy sencillo. Bueno, últimamente, es... ya, de moda.

***¿Cuáles son las ventajas y desventajas de depender tanto de la tecnología?***

Bueno, las ventajas es que te ahorra tiempo, distancias y, por eso es muy práctico. Y desventajas, que estás un poco más flojo porque dependes mucho de eso y tú, como persona, ya no haces muchas cosas.

***¿Crees que la tecnología te facilita la vida?***

Sí, me facilita mucho porque ahorita últimamente, sin un celular o sin computadora, sería todavía mandar cartitas y ya no podría chatear. Entonces sí sería muy difícil.

### Para comprender 1.2

1. ¿Qué tecnología usa Omar?
2. ¿Cómo le facilita la tecnología la vida a Omar?
3. ¿Qué dice Ulises sobre su celular y su uso?
4. Según Ulises, ¿cómo sería el no tener acceso al celular o a la computadora?
5. ¿Cómo se comparan Omar y Ulises en su uso de la tecnología? ¿Son parecidos o diferentes?

### Para pensar y hablar 1.3

¿Cuál es la tecnología más imprescindible *(indispensable)* para ti? ¿Te puedes imaginar la vida sin ella? ¿Cómo sería? ¿Cuáles son las ventajas y desventajas de vivir con esta tecnología?

## Comunidad y oficio

### El español y el mundo de negocios 5.1

Hoy en día es una gran ventaja hablar más de un idioma a la hora de buscar trabajo. Las personas bilingües tienen amplias oportunidades de avanzar en sus trabajos. Son cada vez más numerosas las empresas que hacen negocios en Latinoamérica o que hacen campañas de publicidad y mercadeo dirigidas a la población hispanohablante en Estados Unidos. Busca una empresa o una agencia de publicidad en tu comunidad que tenga necesidad de personal bilingüe en su negocio. Habla con el (la) representante de la empresa y pregúntale por qué es importante tener empleados bilingües y la ventaja que eso le da a la empresa.

**En las oficinas de Renault, en Buenos Aires, Argentina**

## Atlas INTERACTIVO MUNDIAL

Have students use the interactive atlas at **go.hrw.com**.

**Map Activities**

Transparency **Mapa 1**

1. Have students locate Peru on a modern map of the entire American continent, and then name the capital and other major cities.
2. Then have them locate a pre-Hispanic map of the area of modern-day Peru that shows the names of the most important Incan settlements.
3. Ask them to research the contribution of the Incas to modern-day technologies. 3.1

## Para comprender Answers

1. la telefonía celular, la televisión por cable y el Internet
2. Le permite acceder a mucha información y conocer otros idiomas y personas.
3. que le resulta sencillo, que está de moda, que se ahorra tiempo, pero que uno depende mucho de él
4. "...sería todavía mandar cartitas y ya no podría chatear."
5. Son similares en cuanto a las ventajas, pero en cuanto a las desventajas, Omar se concentra en un elemento externo a sí (los anuncios publicitarios), y Ulises se concentra en cómo la tecnología le afecta a él como ser humano (que se pone muy dependiente).

## Differentiated Instruction

### ADVANCED LEARNERS

**Challenge** Have students research Spanish Web sites to learn how land-based cellular communication technology differs from satellite cell technology. Have them list at least one advantage and disadvantage of each. Ask them to share their findings with the class. 3.2

### MULTIPLE INTELLIGENCES

**Interpersonal** Have students write answers to the interview questions based on their own experiences. Ask them to take turns asking and answering the inteview questions with a partner. Then have them report to the class whether they had similar experiences. 1.1, 1.3

**Resources**

**Planning:**

Lesson Planner, pp. 119–120, 280–281

One-Stop Planner

**Presentation:**

Teaching Transparencies **Vocabulario** 8.3, 8.4

**Practice:**

Cuaderno de vocabulario y gramática, pp. 91–93

Activities for Communication, pp. 31–32

Teaching Transparencies Bell Work 8.5

**Vocabulario y gramática** answers, pp. 91–93

Interactive Tutor, Disc 2

**Bell Work**

Use Bell Work 8.5 in the *Teaching Transparencies*, or write this activity on the board.

**Escribe cinco oraciones con el *se* reflexivo.** 1.3

**Objetivos**

- Writing a formal letter
- Talking about your plans

# Vocabulario en acción 2

## En Lima
## ¿A qué se dedican tus padres?

Mi papá **supervisa** edificios en construcción. Su trabajo es comprobar que **el ambiente de trabajo** sea seguro para todos los trabajadores. Es un trabajo que **requiere** mucha responsabilidad.

Mi padre lee **las solicitudes** de las personas que quieren **una entrevista** de empleo. También les explica **los salarios** y **beneficios** que ofrece **la empresa,** como **el seguro médico**.

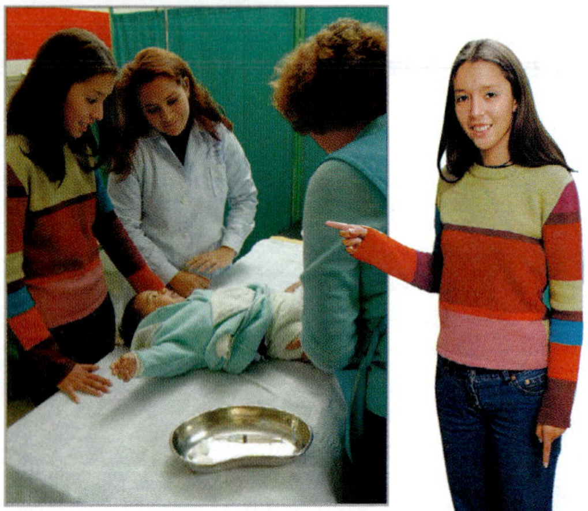

A mi madre le gusta **donar tiempo a una causa.** Actualmente está encargada de **dirigir** a todos los voluntarios de esta clínica. Le encantan sus **compañeros de trabajo.**

**Más vocabulario...**

| | |
|---|---|
| el empleo a tiempo completo | *full-time job* |
| el jefe | *boss* |

**También se puede decir...**

In some Spanish-speaking countries, you may hear **el sueldo** instead of **el salario** and **las prestaciones** instead of **los beneficios.**

**Pre-AP Practice**

**AP Benchmark:** Communicate via formal and informal written correspondence.

**Focus:** Writing a letter and an ad

- TE, p. 335, Multiple Intelligences
- TE, p. 337, Advanced Learners
- Assessment Program, p. 392, Written Activity

## Core Instruction

### TEACHING VOCABULARIO

1. Introduce the vocabulary using transparencies **8.3** and **8.4,** modeling the pronunciation of each vocabulary word. Call on volunteers to read the different captions accompanying the pictures in their textbook. **(4 min.)**
2. Illustrate the meaning of the vocabulary words by making up sentences of your own. For example, **El director del colegio me supervisa. (3 min.)**
3. Go over **Más vocabulario** and **También se puede decir,** using sentences to illustrate the meaning of the words. **(3 min.)**

### TEACHING ¡EXPRÉSATE!

1. Model the **¡Exprésate!** phrases. **(1 min.)**
2. Have students assist you as you write a formal letter on the board or on a transparency. Ask, for example, **¿Cómo empiezo una carta al señor González? (Muy estimado Sr. González:)** Prompt them to provide **¡Exprésate!** phrases as you write the letter. **¿Cómo le digo que voy a incluir un currículum vitae? (Le adjunto un currículum vitae.) (5 min.)**
3. Have volunteers read your letter aloud to practice the expressions. **(4 min.)**

Visit Holt Online
**go.hrw.com**
KEYWORD: EXP3 CH8
Vocabulario 2 practice

Hace un mes, mi papá decidió cambiar de **carrera.** Ahora está tomando clases para **conseguir** otro título académico y también tiene **un empleo a medio tiempo** en un restaurante. Cuando termine sus estudios, va a poder **actualizar** su **currículum vitae.**

Mi mamá tiene **el puesto** más alto de su compañía: ¡es **la jefa!** Ella **solicita** las opiniones de todos sus empleados antes de tomar decisiones.

Mi papá es **gerente** de nuestro almacén familiar. Él habla con todos **los empleados** y les explica **los requisitos** y **el horario** de trabajo.

## ¡Exprésate!

**To write a formal letter**

Interactive TUTOR

| | |
|---|---|
| **Muy estimado(a) Sr./Sra./Srta.:** *Dear Sir/Madam/Miss:* | **Reciba un cordial saludo,** *Kind regards,* |
| **Por medio de la presente...** *The purpose of this letter is . . .* | **Muy atentamente,** *Most sincerely,* |
| **Le/Les adjunto un(a)...** *I'm enclosing a . . .* | |

Vocabulario y gramática, pp. 91–93 Online workbooks

Vocabulario 2

## TPR
### Total Physical Response

Put four stacks of papers on your desk and put one of the following labels next to each: **Solicitudes de empleo a tiempo completo, Solicitudes de empleo a tiempo parcial, Solicitudes para donar tiempo, Solicitudes para conseguir un nuevo título académico.** Then call on four volunteers to stand up in front of the class after taking one of the following name tags: **Gerente, Empleado(a), Director(a), Estudiante.** Finally, command different volunteers to do the following.

**Toma una solicitud de empleo a tiempo parcial y dásela al gerente.**

**Toma una solicitud para conseguir un nuevo título académico y dásela al estudiante.**

**Toma una solicitud para donar tiempo y dásela al director de voluntarios.**

**Toma una solicitud de empleo a tiempo completo y dásela al gerente.** 1.2

### Common Error Alert
**¡OJO!**

Students often end letters with a direct translation from English: **Sinceramente.** Tell them that **Atentamente** is the preferred ending in Spanish.

## Differentiated Instruction

### Slower Pace Learners

**Personalization** Have students invent their own companies. Who would be the boss? Who would be the manager? What kinds of employees would they look for, and what would the work schedule be like? Is there anything special they would do to create a good work atmosphere? Ask students to take notes and then share their ideas with the class. 1.3

### Multiple Intelligences

**Linguistic** Have students research volunteer work they would like to do that involves Spanish. They should write a short application letter in Spanish to the volunteer coordinator for the type of work they choose. Tell students to explain in their letters why they want to donate time, how many hours they could give, and any special skills they could contribute. They can write to a government agency, a non-profit organization, or a private company, depending on their interests. 1.3

### Heritage Speakers

Have heritage speakers give other expressions they might use in a formal letter. Write their examples on the board or on a transparency and ask students to copy them in their notebooks.

**Differentiated Instruction** See the Differentiated Instruction CD-ROM.

## Resources

**Planning:**

Lesson Planner, pp. 119–120, 280–281

One-Stop Planner

**Presentation:**

Teaching Transparencies **Vocabulario** 8.3, 8.4

**Practice:**

Cuaderno de vocabulario y gramática, pp. 91–93

Activities for Communication, pp. 31–32

Lab Book, pp. 41–44

Teaching Transparencies **Vocabulario y gramática** answers, pp. 91–93

Audio CD 8, Tr. 7

Interactive Tutor, Disc 2

### 22 Script

See script on p. 317E.

### 22 Answers

1. falsa; Es gerente de la oficina.
2. cierta
3. falsa; Solicitó un puesto de programadora.
4. falsa; Recibirá seguro médico después de tres meses.
5. cierta
6. falsa; Tienen dos puestos abiertos.

### Career Path

Encourage students who are interested in eventually taking on the responsibility of supervising to visit a large company, factory, or big farm. Tell them to call ahead of time so they may set up an interview with the supervisor or anyone in a supervisory role. Have them search for jobs where knowledge of Spanish would be an advantage.

### Nota cultural

En partes de Latinoamérica, la **licenciatura** es el título que se recibe al graduarse de la universidad. Para recibir la licenciatura, el estudiante a veces tiene que aprobar un examen sobre todo lo que ha estudiado durante su carrera universitaria. En algunas universidades latinoamericanas, el estudiante tiene que hacer una tesis además de presentar el examen. A una persona que se ha graduado de la universidad y que ha cumplido con los requisitos, se le llama **licenciado(a)**.

¿Como se compara el proceso que hay que seguir para sacar la licenciatura en Latinoamérica con los requisitos universitarios de Estados Unidos?

2.1, 4.2

Anfiteatro de la Universidad de los Andes, Santiago

CD 8, Tr. 7

### 22 La entrevista 1.2

**Escuchemos/Escribamos** Escucha la entrevista y determina si cada oración es **cierta** o **falsa.** Corrige las oraciones falsas.

1. El señor Maldonado es el jefe de la empresa.
2. El señor Maldonado ha visto el currículum de la señorita Garza.
3. La señorita Garza ha solicitado empleo en un restaurante.
4. Si ella consigue el puesto, recibirá seguro médico enseguida.
5. La señorita Garza ha dirigido grandes proyectos.
6. La empresa tiene sólo un puesto vacante y es a medio tiempo.

### 23 Anuncios clasificados 1.2

**Leamos/Hablemos** Lee estos anuncios de trabajo y decide si el candidato **a)** cumple con los requisitos o **b)** no cumple con los requisitos. Si no cumple, explica por qué.

**CANDIDATOS**

1. Soy un estudiante recién graduado de la universidad y busco trabajo como auxiliar administrativo en una empresa internacional. Tengo títulos en tecnología y francés.
2. Soy ingeniera y quiero cambiar de carrera. Solicito trabajo como profesora de ciencias o de matemáticas a cualquier nivel. Título universitario.
3. Soy carpintero y quiero donar tiempo a una causa. Deseo usar mi talento para mejorar nuestra comunidad. Puedo trabajar por las noches. No requiero salario ni beneficios.
4. Soy artista y solicito trabajo a medio tiempo. Doy clases de pintura a adultos por las tardes y busco trabajo por las mañanas.
5. Tengo 10 años de experiencia supervisando oficinas de empresas grandes. Solicito un trabajo de cuarenta horas a la semana con beneficios.

**ANUNCIOS**

Empresa comercial busca empleado para contestar el teléfono y actualizar el sistema de computadoras. Requisitos: saber otro idioma y tener título en computación.

Colegio busca profesor(a) de química para estudiantes del tercer año. Requisitos: tres años de experiencia como profesor(a).

Oficina de trabajo social busca voluntario para construir residencias. Requisitos: que sepa construir y que desee mejorar la vida de personas sin hogar.

Museo de arte busca a alguien que pueda presentar exposiciones de arte de las 4 hasta las 6 de la tarde. Requisitos: conocimiento de la pintura.

Banco busca gerente de oficina para trabajar a tiempo completo en oficina central. Vacaciones y seguro médico. Requisitos: más de cinco años de experiencia como supervisor.

1. a
2. b; no tiene experiencia como profesora
3. a
4. b; no puede trabajar por la tarde
5. a

## Core Instruction

### VOCABULARY IN CONTEXT

Collect several photographs showing scenes of different work environments. Have students work in groups to practice **Vocabulario** by describing each scene. Tell them to imagine who the people in the pictures are. For example, is the boss present? What are the employees doing? What is the atmosphere like? What kind of organization is shown? Then have one member of each group describe what they saw in the photo. Are the responses similar?

### 24 Una carta de solicitud ❀ 1.2

**Leamos/Escribamos** Completa la siguiente carta de solicitud con las palabras del cuadro.

| | | | | |
|---|---|---|---|---|
| adjunto | estimada | carrera | medio | empresa |
| entrevista | conseguir | gerente | saludo | capaz |

Muy ___1___ Sra. Casas:

Por ___2___ de la presente, quisiera solicitar el puesto a medio tiempo como auxiliar del gerente de diseño. Actualmente estoy estudiando la ___3___ de diseño gráfico en la universidad. Me gustaría ___4___ un empleo relacionado con el diseño. He leído su página Web y estoy muy impresionado con los servicios que ofrece su ___5___. Soy ___6___ de hacer muchas tareas a la vez y sin duda podría facilitarle el trabajo al ___7___.

Le ___8___ mi currículum vitae con esta carta. Puedo reunirme con Ud. para una ___9___ a la hora que le sea conveniente.

Reciba un cordial ___10___ de,

Pablo Duque

1. estimada
2. medio
3. carrera
4. conseguir
5. empresa
6. capaz
7. gerente
8. adjunto
9. entrevista
10. saludo

### 25 Mi trabajo ideal ❀ 1.2

**Leamos/Escribamos** Completa las oraciones para describir tu trabajo ideal. *¿Se te olvidó?* Subjunctive with unknown or nonexistent, pp. 72–73

1. Busco un ambiente de trabajo que sea...
2. Me gustaría conseguir un puesto de...
3. Yo donaría tiempo a una causa como...
4. Es muy importante tener compañeros de trabajo que...
5. Prefiero un jefe (una jefa) que...
6. Requiero un empleo que ofrezca beneficios como...
7. Quiero un salario mínimo de...
8. En mi trabajo, quiero dirigir...

Los futuros dueños de esta casa colaboran con Hábitat para la Humanidad en su construcción en Tacna, Perú.

## Comunicación

HOLT SoundBooth ONLINE RECORDING

### 26 Solicito el puesto ❀ 1.1, 1.3

**Hablemos** En parejas, escojan uno de los anuncios de trabajo de la Actividad 23. Dramaticen una entrevista entre la persona que solicita el puesto y el (la) gerente. Luego presenten la entrevista a la clase.

MODELO **—Veo que acabas de graduarte de la universidad.**
**—Sí, y estoy muy interesado en el puesto de gerente de oficina que vi en su anuncio de trabajo.**

### Circumlocution

Have students form pairs. Each student should choose one of the vocabulary words and describe it for the other to guess.

MODELO
**—Sara habla con todos los empleados de la empresa y describe lo que tienen que hacer. ¿Cuál es su puesto?**
**—La gerente.** ❀ 1.1

## Communities

### Community Link

Tell students that Habitat for Humanity is only one of many non-governmental organizations that are active in South America. Habitat for Humanity volunteers help people in need to build homes. There are many other organizations, such as **La Federación de Organizaciones Indígenas de las Faldas del Chimborazo** in Ecuador, which supports families of the province of Chimborazo in Mt. Chimborazo's National Park. Ask students to use Spanish resources in the library or on the Internet to research other non-governmental organizations and find out what services they provide. Have them discuss how they might be able to use their Spanish skills to volunteer in these organizations at home or abroad. ❀ 5.1

## Differentiated Instruction

### ADVANCED LEARNERS

**Variation** Have students write three newspaper ads seeking employees and/or volunteers for different positions. Have them be creative in the benefits offered to entice applicants. ❀ 1.3

### SPECIAL LEARNING NEEDS

**Students with AD(H)D** Have students work with partners to brainstorm strengths they could bring to a job. Each student should tell his or her partner what strengths they think the partner could bring to a workplace. For example, a student might say: **Tú te llevarías bien con los compañeros de trabajo.** ❀ 1.1

## Comunicación

### Pair Activity: Interpersonal

As an extension of Activity 26, have students continue role-playing interviews but have each partner make up the ad they are responding to. Encourage them to make up ads for jobs that are different from those discussed in Activity 26. ❀ 1.1

**Resources**

**Planning:**

Lesson Planner, pp. 119–120, 280–281

One-Stop Planner

**Presentation:**

Teaching Transparencies **Vocabulario** 8.3, 8.4

**Practice:**

Cuaderno de vocabulario y gramática, pp. 91–93

Activities for Communication, pp. 31–32

Lab Book, pp. 41–44

Teaching Transparencies **Vocabulario y gramática** answers, pp. 91–93

Audio CD 8, Tr. 8

Interactive Tutor, Disc 2

**Career Path**

Have students imagine they are business people in Latin America. Tell them to write a formal letter to a partner. Students' letters may be business-related or a cover letter for a position in a company. Students may use **¡Exprésate!** expressions or other vocabulary for formal letter writing. After exchanging letters with their partner, students will answer their partner's letter. 1.1, 1.3

## Una solicitud de trabajo

Muy estimado Sr. Prieto:

Me dirijo a Uds. para solicitar un puesto en su compañía. Entiendo que su empresa tiene una vacante en el departamento de seguros. Tengo mucha experiencia en este campo, porque llevo cinco años en un puesto similar. He asistido a varias reuniones y conferencias para actualizar mis conocimientos y creo cumplir con los requisitos que Uds. buscan.

Le adjunto mi solicitud de trabajo y el currículum vitae. Les agradecería que se comunicaran conmigo sobre las posibilidades de empleo en su empresa.

Muy atentamente,
Federico Villarreal

Estimado Sr. Villarreal:

Acusamos recibo de su atenta carta, y tengo el gusto de invitarlo a una entrevista el jueves próximo, 24 de marzo, a las 4:00 de la tarde. Después de la entrevista, que durará unos 30 minutos, me he permitido organizar una breve reunión con nuestro departamento de beneficios, para que Ud. tenga la oportunidad de informarse sobre el sueldo y los beneficios. Le ruego que traiga consigo una carta de recomendación de su jefe actual. Agradeciéndole el interés en nuestra empresa,

Reciba un cordial saludo de,

Alberto Prieto

### ¡Exprésate!

| To ask about someone's plans | To talk about your plans |
| --- | --- |
| **¿Qué te gustaría hacer?**<br>*What would you like to do?* | **Me gustaría ser un(a)...**<br>*I would like to be a . . .*<br>**Me interesaría estudiar para ser un(a)...**<br>*I would be interested in studying to be a . . .*<br>**Siempre he querido ser un(a)...**<br>*I have always wanted to be a . . .* |
| **Si tuvieras la oportunidad, ¿adónde irías?**<br>*If you had the chance, where would you go?* | **Si pudiera, iría a... a estudiar...**<br>*If I could, I would go to . . . to study . . .* |

Interactive TUTOR

Vocabulario y gramática, pp. 91–93 Online workbooks

## Core Instruction

### TEACHING ¡EXPRÉSATE!

1. Tell students to imagine you are playing the roles of two different students as you model both sides of the conversation using the questions and responses in **¡Exprésate!** **(3 min.)**
2. Then ask the questions on the left column and have volunteers answer using the expressions on the right and completing them to make sentences. **(3 min.)**
3. Using just the last two expressions, demonstrate a variation. Model the expression on the left, and have volunteers answer with all the words in the expression on the right except **estudiar,** which they can now substitute with any verb in the infinitive such as **trabajar, donar tiempo, aprender a cuidar caballos,** and so on. **(4 min.)**

## 27 La carta de Federico 1.2

**Leamos/Escribamos** Contesta las preguntas basándote en las cartas de la página anterior.

1. ¿Cuál es el puesto que Federico solicita? un puesto en el departamento de seguros
2. ¿Cómo ha actualizado sus conocimientos? ha asistido a reuniones y conferencias
3. ¿Cumple él con los requisitos que busca la empresa? sí, es invitado a una entrevista
4. ¿Qué manda Federico con la carta? su solicitud de trabajo y su curriculum vitae
5. ¿Qué información le van a dar a Federico después de la entrevista? información sobre el sueldo y los beneficios
6. ¿Quién tiene que escribirle una carta de recomendación a Federico? su jefe actual

CD 8, Tr. 8

## 28 Me gustaría... 1.2

**Escuchemos/Escribamos** Escucha la conversación entre Juana y el consejero de su colegio y contesta las preguntas.

1. ¿Cuál es el problema de Juana?
2. ¿Qué le interesaría estudiar a Juana?
3. Si pudiera estudiar en otro país, ¿adónde iría?
4. Según Juana, ¿cuál es la desventaja de una carrera como profesora?
5. Según el consejero, ¿cuál es la ventaja de ser profesora?

## 29 La carrera ideal 1.2

**Hablemos** ¿Qué diría cada una de estas personas sobre sus planes para el futuro? Usa las expresiones de **Exprésate.**

1.

2.

3.

## Comunicación

HOLT SoundBooth ONLINE RECORDING

## 30 Mis planes para el futuro 1.1, 1.3

**Hablemos** En parejas, túrnense para entrevistar a su compañero(a) sobre qué carrera le gustaría seguir en el futuro.

# Vocabulario 2

### 28 Script

See script on p. 317F.

### 28 Answers

1. Tiene muchas ideas pero no puede decidir qué quiere hacer.
2. Literatura
3. A Perú
4. Quiere tener varias carreras.
5. Tendría los veranos libres, para viajar.

### Más práctica

Have students imagine they are being interviewed by a possible employer about a position in a company. Tell them to create a conversation where students describe their ideal job, workplace, career, and so on.

**MODELO**

**—¿Qué buscas en un trabajo?**
**—Busco un ambiente de trabajo formal y un horario de trabajo flexible.** 1.1

### Comunicación

### Class Activity: Presentational

Call on volunteers to come to the front of the class and talk about a career they dream about. Have them begin with one of the **¡Exprésate!** phrases and use the vocabulary learned in this chapter. Have each volunteer answer a question or two from their classmates about the content of their presentation. 1.1, 1.3

## Differentiated Instruction

### ADVANCED LEARNERS

**Extension** Have students research on the Internet a career in which they are interested. Have them work with partners to make an oral presentation about that career. The partners should interview each other about the education or training needed, the advantages and disadvantages of the job, and so on. 1.1, 1.3

### MULTIPLE INTELLIGENCES

**Logical/Mathematical** Have students use the library or Internet to research universities where they might want to pursue university studies. They should then create a chart with the names of the universities in the left vertical column, and a row at the top with four factors that are important to them such as **Fama de la universidad, Lugar geográfico, Precio de la matrícula, Número de estudiantes.** They should rank each university according to their factors to see which one rates highest among their choices. 1.3

### Assess

**Assessment Program**

**Prueba: Vocabulario 2,** pp. 147–148

Alternative Assessment, pp. 380, 392, 404

**Online Assessment** my.hrw.com

**Test Generator**

## Resources

**Planning:**

Lesson Planner, pp. 121–123, 282–285

One-Stop Planner

**Presentation:**

Video Program **GramaVisión**

**Practice:**

Grammar Tutor for Students of Spanish, Chapter 8

Cuaderno de vocabulario y gramática, pp. 94–96

Cuaderno de actividades, pp. 75–77

Activities for Communication, pp. 31–32

Lab Book, pp. 41–44

Teaching Transparencies
Bell Work 8.6

**Vocabulario y gramática** answers, pp. 94–96

Audio CD 8, Tr. 9

Interactive Tutor, Disc 2

### Bell Work

Use Bell Work 8.6 in the *Teaching Transparencies*, or write this activity on the board.

**Escribe cinco oraciones sobre tus planes de trabajo para el futuro.**
1.3

**Objetivos**
- Conditional
- Past subjunctive with hypothetical statements
- More past subjunctive

# Gramática en acción 2

GramaVisión

Interactive TUTOR

## Repaso Conditional

**1** As you know, the **conditional** is used to tell what *would happen* or what someone *would do* in a given set of circumstances, and to say what someone *would* or *would not like.*

Yo **conseguiría** un trabajo.

Me **gustaría** trabajar en un hospital.

**2** The regular **conditional** endings, added to the infinitive form of **-ar, -er,** and **-ir** verbs, are:

| | | | |
|---|---|---|---|
| yo | dirigir**ía** | nosotros(as) | dirigir**íamos** |
| tú | dirigir**ías** | vosotros(as) | dirigir**íais** |
| Ud., él, ella | dirigir**ía** | Uds., ellos, ellas | dirigir**ían** |

**3** The **conditional** is also used with the preterite of **decir** to express what someone said he or she *would or would not do.*

Dijeron que **vendrían** a visitarme.
*They said that they would come to visit me.*

**4** The **conditional** can also be used to express the *probability* that something happened in the past.

**Serían** las nueve cuando llegaron.
*It was probably nine when they arrived.*

### ¿Te acuerdas?

Verbs that have irregular stems in the future tense also have irregular stems in the conditional.

| | |
|---|---|
| caber: **cabr-** | querer: **querr-** |
| decir: **dir-** | saber: **sabr-** |
| haber: **habr-** | salir: **saldr-** |
| hacer: **har-** | tener: **tendr-** |
| poder: **podr-** | valer: **valdr-** |
| poner: **pondr-** | venir: **vendr-** |

Vocabulario y gramática, pp. 94–96
Actividades, pp. 75–77
Online workbooks

CD 8, Tr. 9 See script on p. 317F.

**31 ¿Estás preparada?** 1.2

**Escuchemos** Escucha la conversación entre Marcela y su mamá. Para las siguientes actividades indica si Marcela dijo que **a**) ya lo hizo o **b**) lo haría.

1. leer la página Web a
2. escribir una lista de preguntas a
3. poner una copia del currículum en la carpeta a
4. actualizar el currículum b
5. llamar a sus referencias b
6. planchar el vestido a

## Core Instruction

### TEACHING GRAMÁTICA

**1.** Go over points 1 and 2. Have volunteers suggest an **-ar** and **-er** verb, and the class conjugate its conditional forms as you write them on the board. **(4 min.)**

**2.** Write the conditional forms of two of the verbs with irregular stems in **¿Te acuerdas?** and use each in a sentence. **(2 min.)**

**3.** Go over point 3. Call on volunteers to make up sentences starting with **Dijeron que** followed by the conditional. **(2 min.)**

**4.** Go over point 4. Give students other examples of cases where they might use the conditional of probability. For example, when you think you know who someone is: **Sería la mamá de Pablo la que le regaló el suéter.** Tell them the conditional of probability is often used with the verb **ser. (2 min.)**

### GramaVisión

For a video presentation of the conditional, use **GramaVisión.**

GramaVisión

Visit Holt Online
**go.hrw.com**
KEYWORD: EXP3 CH8
Gramática 2 practice

## 32 El ambiente de trabajo 1.2

**Leamos/Escribamos** Completa el diálogo con la forma correcta de los verbos en paréntesis. Usa el condicional.

NICOLÁS No me gusta el ambiente de trabajo aquí. __1__ (Tratar) de cambiarlo, pero no sé qué hacer. Trataría

ANDRÉS La primera cosa que yo __2__ (hacer) es hablar con los compañeros. ¿Cuál es el problema? haría

NICOLÁS Es que todo el mundo se queja de los beneficios. Todos dicen que __3__ (pedir) más días de vacaciones, pero le tienen miedo al jefe. pedirían

ANDRÉS ¿El único problema es el de las vacaciones? ¿__4__ (Poder) hablar con el jefe tú solo? Podrías

NICOLÁS Bueno, también nos __5__ (gustar) pedir seguro médico. gustaría

ANDRÉS En tu lugar, yo __6__ (hablar) con el jefe inmediatamente para resolver estos problemas. hablaría

## 33 ¿Qué dijeron que harían? 1.2

**Escribamos** Imagina qué dijeron todas estas personas sobre lo que harían durante el verano. Usa los verbos del cuadro en el condicional.

**MODELO** **Mi mejor amigo...**
**Mi mejor amigo dijo que viajaría a España.**

| | | | |
|---|---|---|---|
| viajar | visitar | comprar | salir |
| trabajar | conseguir | dirigir | ir a |

1. Mis compañeros de clase...
2. Mi profesor(a) de español...
3. Los vecinos...
4. El director del colegio...
5. Mi familia...
6. Mis amigos y yo...
7. Mi mejor amigo(a)...

La Universidad Nacional de San Marcos, Lima

## Comunicación

HOLT SoundBooth ONLINE RECORDING

## 34 Mis sueños 1.1, 1.3

**Hablemos** Explícale a tu compañero(a) qué harías si pudieras realizar tus sueños. Recuerda lo que dice tu compañero(a) para poder contárselo luego a la clase. *¿Se te olvidó?* Contrary-to-fact situations, pp. 122–123

**MODELO** **—Si yo pudiera, trabajaría para una empresa internacional.**
**—¿Sí? Pues yo trabajaría en un hospital.**



### Más práctica

Have students pick four of the verbs listed in the box in Activity 33 and write sentences with each about the following people:

**1. Mi mejor amigo(a)...**
**2. Mi tío/a...**
**3. La biblioteca del colegio...**
**4. Uno(a) de los/las cocineros(as) del colegio...**
1.2

### Heritage Speakers

Have heritage speakers describe what they know about work schedules in Spain and Latin America. Have them explain the importance of this custom and whether it is still practiced in their country of origin. 1.3

### Comunicación

**Pair Activity: Interpersonal**

Have pairs of students discuss the **Nota cultural.** Have them talk about whether they would enjoy having a long lunch break, if they think they could get used to the different rhythm of the days, and whether they prefer the work hours kept in the U.S. 1.1

## Differentiated Instruction

### SLOWER PACE LEARNERS

**Building on Previous Skills** Have students go back to **¿Te acuerdas?** and choose two verbs that have not been conjugated in class before. Ask students to conjugate them in the conditional, and then make short sentences using each conjugation. 1.2

### MULTIPLE INTELLIGENCES

**Interpersonal** Have students imagine they are guidance counselors at the school. Tell them to write down "recommendations" to fellow students that they know best, about the possible course of study they should pursue. For example: **Tomás, me parece que tú serías muy buen diseñador de software. Deberías considerar la posibilidad de estudiar programación en la Universidad X o la Universidad Y.** 1.3

## Resources

**Planning:**

Lesson Planner, pp. 121–123, 282–285

One-Stop Planner

**Presentation:**

Video Program **GramaVisión**

**Practice:**

Grammar Tutor for Students of Spanish, Chapter 8

Cuaderno de vocabulario y gramática, pp. 94–96

Cuaderno de actividades, pp. 75–77

Activities for Communication, pp. 31–32

Teaching Transparencies

Bell Work 8.7

**Vocabulario y gramática** answers, pp. 94–96

Interactive Tutor, Disc 2

## Bell Work

Use Bell Work 8.7 in the *Teaching Transparencies,* or write this activity on the board.

**Completa las oraciones con la forma correcta del condicional de los verbos entre paréntesis.**

1. Me ______ (gustar) ser gerente de una empresa.
2. En mi lugar, ¿tú ______ (hablar) con los empleados?
3. Nosotros ______ (poder) hablar con el jefe si nos dieran tiempo libre.
4. Ella nunca ______ (pedir) más días de vacaciones.
5. No sé si ______ (ser) fácil o no conseguir un trabajo en esta época.

1.2

## Past subjunctive with hypothetical statements

Interactive TUTOR

**1** You have learned some expressions with **fuera(s), tuviera(s),** and **pudiera(s).** These verbs are in the **past subjunctive.**

Si yo **fuera** el jefe, contrataría a más personas.

Si yo **tuviera** la oportunidad, iría a España.

Si **pudieras,** ¿estudiarías periodismo?

**2** The **past subjunctive** is formed by removing the **-on** from the third person plural form of the preterite and adding the following endings. Note that an accent is added to the **nosotros** form of the verb. Any irregularities in the third person plural preterite are also reflected in the past subjunctive forms.

pedir → pidier~~on~~ → pidier-

| | | | |
|---|---|---|---|
| yo | pidier**a** | nosotros(as) | pidiér**amos** |
| tú | pidier**as** | vosotros(as) | pidier**ais** |
| Ud., él, ella | pidier**a** | Uds., ellos, ellas | pidier**an** |

**3** The **past subjunctive** is used after **si** *(if)* in hypothetical sentences *(oraciones hipotéticas)* that are contrary to fact or unlikely to happen. The **conditional** is used in the other clause.

Si yo **pudiera, trabajaría** en un banco.
*If I could, I would work in a bank.*

**Viajaríamos** a México si **tuviéramos** más tiempo.
*We would travel to Mexico if we had more time.*

Vocabulario y gramática, pp. 94–96
Actividades, pp. 75–77
Online workbooks

### En inglés

**In English,** in hypothetical statements, the past subjunctive has the same form as the simple past for all verbs except *to be.*

If I **knew** the answer, I'd tell you.

For *to be*, the past subjunctive forms for all persons is *were*.

If Paul **were** angry, you would know it.

In English, what helping verb do you use in the clause that follows the past subjunctive?

**In Spanish,** the past subjunctive has a form different from other tenses and moods.

Si **supiera** la respuesta, te la diría.

Si Pablo **estuviera** enojado, lo sabrías.

4.1

You use the helping verb *would*.

### 35 El mundo de los negocios 1.2

**Leamos/Escribamos** Completa las siguientes oraciones con los verbos correctos del cuadro.

**cumpliera hablara hicieras supiéramos tuviera mandaran**

1. Si yo ══ mejor el español, buscaría un trabajo en Ecuador. hablara
2. Sara y Benito conseguirían más entrevistas si ══ más cartas de solicitud. mandaran
3. El gerente entrevistaría a esta mujer si ══ con los requisitos. cumpliera
4. Si ══ mejor tu trabajo, el jefe te ofrecería un salario mejor. hicieras
5. Si Felipe ══ más tiempo, donaría un poco a una causa. tuviera
6. Nosotros trataríamos de escribir un artículo si ══ algo del tema. supiéramos

## Core Instruction

### TEACHING GRAMÁTICA

1. Review point 1. Then reread each example, changing the subject to **tú** or **yo.** **(2 min.)**
2. Model other sentences with **si pudiera, si tuviera,** and **si fuera** followed by the conditional. **(3 min.)**
3. Go over point 2. After you have finished reviewing the conjugation of **pedir,** conjugate the past subjunctive of **querer** on the board to illustrate how the irregularities in the third person plural preterite are carried over into the past subjunctive form: **quisieron** → **yo quisiera, tú quisieras.** **(5 min.)**
4. After reviewing point 3, present more hypothetical sentences using the subjects **él, nosotros,** and **ustedes.** **(3 min.)**

### GramaVisión

For a video presentation of the past subjunctive with hypothetical statements, use **GramaVisión.**

GramaVisión

## 36 Si pudiera... ❀ 1.2

**Hablemos** Usa el pasado del subjuntivo y el condicional para decir lo que están pensando las siguientes personas.

**MODELO** **Si tuviera tiempo, jugaría al tenis todos los días.**

yo/tener tiempo/jugar

1. Ana/poder/viajar

2. tú/tener dinero/comprar

3. nosotros/estar en forma/competir

4. mis amigos/vivir en el campo/tener

## 37 En la oficina... ❀ 1.2

**Leamos/Escribamos** Cambia cada oración para formar una oración hipotética.

**MODELO** **Si consigo el puesto, voy a trabajar muy duro.**
**Si consiguiera el puesto, trabajaría muy duro.**

1. Si encuentras un trabajo a medio tiempo, podrás donar tiempo a una causa.
2. Va a facilitar el proceso si Teresa supervisa a los empleados.
3. Si Uds. cambian el horario, voy a poder trabajar a tiempo completo.
4. Vamos a comprar nuevas computadoras si podemos conseguir el dinero.
5. Si me dan el puesto de gerente, voy a tener más responsabilidad.
6. Si los compañeros de trabajo toman una actitud negativa, va a empeorarse el ambiente de trabajo.

1. Si encontraras un trabajo a medio tiempo, podrías donar tiempo a una causa.
2. Facilitaría el proceso si Teresa supervisara a los empleados.
3. Si Uds. cambiaran el horario, podría trabajar a tiempo completo.
4. Compraríamos nuevas computadoras si pudiéramos conseguir el dinero.
5. Si me dieran el puesto de gerente, tendría más responsabilidad.
6. Si los compañeros de trabajo tomaran una actitud negativa, se empeoraría el ambiente de trabajo.

### Comunicación

HOLT SoundBooth ONLINE RECORDING

## 38 Mi propio negocio ❀ 1.1, 1.3

**Hablemos** En parejas, túrnense para comentar cómo sería su negocio si tuvieran la oportunidad de abrir una oficina.

**MODELO** **—Si pudiera elegir a los empleados, les daría todos los puestos a mis amigos.**
**—Yo también, y si tuviera el dinero les daría nuevas computadoras.**

### 36 Answers

1. Si pudiera, Ana viajaría a Perú.
2. Si tuvieras dinero, comprarías una televisión nueva.
3. Si nosotros estuviéramos en forma, competiríamos en una carrera de bicicletas.
4. Si mis amigos vivieran en el campo, tendrían un perro.

### Más práctica

Have students cut three or four photos from a magazine showing something students would be interested in doing. Have them glue the photos onto a piece of construction paper. Under each photo, have students write a sentence in the conditional like those in Activity 36. ❀ 1.2

### Comunicación

#### Pair Activity: Interpersonal

Have students research the life of an author from one of the Andean countries, such as Pablo Neruda, Mario Vargas Llosa, or Alberto Fuguet. Then have pairs of students use the verbs in the past subjunctive to create an interview.

**MODELO**
**—¿Qué harías si fueras...?**
**—Si yo fuera Pablo Neruda, escribiría un poema sobre mi colegio.**
**—Si yo fuera Mario Vargas Llosa, contaría un cuento sobre el colegio.**
**—Si yo fuera Alberto Fuguet, haría una película sobre el colegio.**
❀ 1.1

## Differentiated Instruction

### ADVANCED LEARNERS

**Challenge** Have students consult Spanish-language reference materials to find topographical data as well as information on professions and regional economies. Then have them create four hypothetical sentences in which they express the desire to work in those countries.
**Si fuera arqueólogo, me mudaría a Cuzco para investigar las ruinas incaicas. Si pudiera, sería un(a) guía de senderismo en la Patagonia chilena.** ❀ 3.2

### MULTIPLE INTELLIGENCES

**Spatial** Have students locate a map showing the Incan network of roads built in the Americas and a map showing the network of roads built by the Romans in Europe and compare them to see if they were equally vast and intricate. If they prefer, they may research any other public systems such as aqueducts, sewers, or canals for transporting goods on barges. Have students look up the information on Spanish-language Web sites, putting together a Spanish/English glossary of terms they might not know. ❀ 2.2, 3.2

**Differentiated Instruction** See the Differentiated Instruction CD-ROM.

## Resources

**Planning:**

Lesson Planner, pp. 121–123, 282–285

One-Stop Planner

**Presentation:**

Video Program **GramaVisión**

**Practice:**

Grammar Tutor for Students of Spanish, Chapter 8

Cuaderno de vocabulario y gramática, pp. 94–96

Cuaderno de actividades, pp. 75–77

Activities for Communication, pp. 31–32

Teaching Transparencies

Bell Work 8.8

**Vocabulario y gramática** answers, pp. 94–96

Interactive Tutor, Disc 2

### Bell Work

Use Bell Work 8.8 in the *Teaching Transparencies*, or write this activity on the board.

**Responde a las siguientes preguntas.**

1. **¿Adónde viajarías si pudieras ir a cualquier lugar?**
2. **Si tus amigos tuvieran un millón de dólares, ¿qué comprarían?**
3. **¿Qué haría tu mamá si fuera la directora del colegio?**
4. **Si pudieras elegir un trabajo, ¿cuál elegirías?**

1.2, 1.3

### Career Path

For students interested in a career in journalism, suggest that they find a Spanish-language newspaper or magazine that interests them. Many publications have a section for letters to the editor. Ask them to write a letter or an article and send it to the editor for publication in the magazine or newspaper. 3.2, 5.1

## More past subjunctive

Interactive TUTOR

**1** When the verb in the main clause of a sentence requiring the subjunctive is in a **past tense**, the **past subjunctive** is used in the subordinate clause.

*past tense requires past subjunctive*

Mis padres **preferían** que **estudiara** medicina.
*My parents preferred that I study medicine.*

*past tense requires past subjunctive*

**Insistí** en que Rita **fuera** conmigo a la entrevista.
*I insisted that Rita go with me to the interview.*

Vocabulario y gramática, pp. 94–96
Actividades, pp. 75–77
Online workbooks

### ¿Te acuerdas?

Expressions that require the subjunctive include:

1. Expressions of doubt or disbelief
   Ellos dudaron que Adán **consiguiera** un puesto.
2. Expressions of emotion
   A mamá le alegró que la **ayudáramos** en la casa.
3. Expressions of will or wish
   Yo esperaba que mis amigos **llegaran** a tiempo.
4. Impersonal expressions
   Era importante que **donaras** tiempo a una causa.
5. Expressions with certain adverbial clauses
   Íbamos a salir para que **pudieras** dormir.

### 39 ¿Cuándo ocurrió? 1.2

**Leamos** Lee las oraciones y decide si describen algo del **pasado** o del **presente.**

1. Quiero encontrar un puesto de trabajo antes de que empiecen las vacaciones. presente
2. Le pedí a Felipe que le entregara mi currículum al jefe. pasado
3. Él dudaba que yo consiguiera un puesto en su compañía. pasado
4. No creo que él tenga razón. presente
5. Le hice muchos cambios al currículum para que el jefe se impresionara. pasado
6. Espero que me llame hoy para una entrevista. presente

### 40 Un día de trabajo 1.2

**Leamos/Escribamos** Adela está contándole a su amiga lo que pasó en el trabajo ayer. Completa sus oraciones con la forma correcta del verbo en paréntesis. *¿Se te olvidó?* Preterite, pp. 160–161

1. Era muy importante que nosotros ____ (tener) un buen artículo para la revista. tuviéramos
2. El jefe quería que nosotros ____ (preparar) una foto para la primera plana. preparáramos
3. Yo esperaba que los compañeros de trabajo ____ (escoger) mi foto. escogieran
4. Miguel dudaba que a los editores les ____ (gustar) mi idea. gustara
5. ¡A todos les sorprendió que el jefe ____ (decidir) usarla! decidiera
6. Mis compañeros de trabajo estuvieron muy felices de que yo ____ (poder) dirigir el proyecto. pudiera

## Core Instruction

### TEACHING GRAMÁTICA

1. Go over point 1 with students, modeling the pronunciation of the two sentences. **(3 min.)**
2. Model sentences in which the main clause is in the past, thus requiring a past subjunctive in the second clause, and write them on the board. Leave a blank for the verb in the second clause and have volunteers help you complete each sentence. **(2 min.)**
3. Review **¿Te acuerdas?,** modeling all the sentences. Have volunteers substitute the verb in each sentence with a new verb that you provide. **(4 min.)**

### GramaVisión

For a video presentation of the past subjunctive, use **GramaVisión.**

GramaVisión

See answers on p. 344.

## 41 Roberto solicita un trabajo 1.2

**Leamos/Escribamos** Usa las siguientes frases para escribir oraciones completas en el pasado.

1. Yo/dudar que/Roberto/conseguir el trabajo
2. Roberto/estar cansado de que/yo/no apoyarle
3. Los jefes/requerir que/los empleados/tener experiencia
4. Mis papás y yo/preferir que/Roberto/solicitar otro puesto
5. Tú/no creer que/nosotros/tener razón
6. Yo/querer que/alguien/aconsejarle a Roberto
7. Todos/estar sorprendidos de que/el jefe/darle el puesto a Roberto

**Zona comercial Las Amazonas de Quito, Ecuador**

## 42 El primer empleo 1.2

**Leamos/Hablemos** Lee la página del diario que Alejandra escribió cuando se graduó de la universidad. Luego vuelve a contar, en el pasado, lo que sucedió cuando buscaba trabajo.

**MODELO** **Alejandra tenía una entrevista de trabajo con el periódico. Necesitaba que su profesor de periodismo le ayudara a actualizar su currículum vitae.**

El miércoles tengo una entrevista de trabajo en el periódico. Necesito que mi profesor de periodismo me ayude a actualizar mi currículum vitae. Dudo que me ofrezcan un puesto a tiempo completo, porque no tengo experiencia. Pero espero que por lo menos me den algo a medio tiempo. Es importante que trabaje por lo menos veinte horas a la semana. Mis padres insisten en que solicite puesto en varios lugares.

Alejandra tenía una entrevista de trabajo con el periódico. Necesitaba que su profesor de periodismo le ayudara a actualizar su currículum vitae. Dudaba que le ofrecieran un puesto a tiempo completo, porque no tenía experiencia. Pero esperaba que por lo menos le dieran algo a medio tiempo. Era importante que trabajara por lo menos veinte horas a la semana. Sus padres insistieron en que solicitara puesto en varios lugares.

## Comunicación

HOLT SoundBooth ONLINE RECORDING

### 43 Mi juventud 1.1, 1.2

**Hablemos** En parejas, túrnense para contarle a su compañero(a) algunas cosas sobre su niñez. Usen las expresiones del cuadro.

**Cuando era niño, esperaba que...**
**Me molestaba que...**
**Mi familia no pensaba que...**
**Era muy importante que...**
**(No) me gustaba que...**
**Mis padres preferían que...**

### 41 Answers

1. Yo dudaba que Roberto consiguiera el trabajo.
2. Roberto estaba cansado de que yo no le apoyara.
3. Los jefes requerían que los empleados tuvieran experiencia.
4. Mis papás y yo preferían que Roberto solicitara otro puesto.
5. Tú no creías que nosotros tuviéramos razón.
6. Yo quería que alguien le aconsejara a Roberto.
7. Todos estábamos sorprendidos de que el jefe le diera el puesto a Roberto.

## Comunicación

**Class Activity: Presentational**

Call on volunteers to talk about a past job using the past subjunctive. If they have not had a job before, have them talk about a complicated errand they have had to run or a household chore they have had to do. 1.3

## Differentiated Instruction

### ADVANCED LEARNERS

**41 Challenge** Have students interview classmates who work for the school newspaper about their work experiences in the past. Then have them work with partners in Spanish class and talk about the student newspaper writers using the past subjunctive. 1.1

### MULTIPLE INTELLIGENCES

**Linguistic** Ask students to choose an experience in their past that impacted them greatly, and have them tell the class about it. Have them use the past subjunctive to describe feelings they experienced. 1.3

### Assess

**Assessment Program**
**Prueba: Gramática 2,** pp. 149–150
**Prueba: Aplicación 2,** pp. 151–152
Audio CD 8, Tr. 16
Alternative Assessment, pp. 380, 392, 404

**Online Assessment**
**my.hrw.com**

**Test Generator**

## Resources

**Planning:**

Lesson Planner, pp. 124, 284–285

One-Stop Planner

**Presentation:**

Video Program, Videocassette 4

DVD Program

**VideoNovela**

**Practice:**

Video Guide, pp. 54–56

Lab Book, pp. 81–82

## Visual Learners

To help students evaluate Clara's choices, have them write down each choice and then categorize each in a separate list under the headers **Inteligentes, Tontas,** and **Peligrosas.** Have them use their lists to discuss with the class what they might have done differently in Clara's situation.

| Las decisiones de Clara | | |
|---|---|---|
| Inteligentes | Tontas | Peligrosas |
| | | |

1.2

## Gestures

Ask students to note the gestures used by different characters in this episode. What kinds of gestures does Señor Ortega use to show he is annoyed with Clara? Does Octavio use any specific gestures as he defends Clara? Ask students if they would use the same gestures.

Novela en video

# Clara perspectiva

## Episodio 8

**ESTRATEGIA** 1.2, 1.3

**Evaluating choices** Clara has had to make a lot of tough choices in her quest to help her professor. Think back and write down all the choices she has made thus far. As you go through **Episodio 8**, add in the choices she makes here. Then decide which choices were smart, which ones were foolish, and which ones were dangerous. Where would you have made a different choice? Why? Do Clara's choices tell you something about her?

### En la oficina del señor Ortega

**Sr. Ortega** Señor Medina, ¿me puede explicar qué sucede con su colega? ¿No se da cuenta que tiene responsabilidades? ¿que este empleo no es un voluntariado? ¿que tiene que cumplir con sus obligaciones?

**Octavio** Por favor, Señor Ortega, tiene que haber un problema muy serio... Clara no es la clase de persona que evita sus responsabilidades.

1

2

**Sr. Ortega** Este trabajo tiene muchas obligaciones, y la más importante es que uno tiene que presentarse todos los días, sin falta. Clara nunca se hará periodista si no toma sus responsabilidades en serio. Como su jefe, es mi responsabilidad supervisarla. Soy capaz de despedirla. Clara nunca va a tener una carrera en periodismo si no aparece en un santiamén.

**Octavio** Si yo pudiera, la traería aquí en seguida, Señor Ortega.

### En un quiosco de Santiago

El profesor Armando Luna, profesor de estudios ambientales en la Universidad Pontificia Católica de Chile, no se ha visto en dos días. Su auto fue encontrado abandonado cerca del pueblo de Pirque y por eso, algunos están convencidos que ha sido secuestrado. Todo el mundo sabe que el profesor está programado para presentar una serie de estudios de impacto ambiental al Congreso la semana que viene. Al centro de los estudios está el proyecto controvertido de la empresa maderera *MaderaCorp.*

3

4

## Core Instruction

### TEACHING NOVELA EN VIDEO

1. Have students scan the **Novela en video** text. **(1 min.)**
2. Play the video and have students take notes on what kinds of choices Clara makes throughout the episode. **(15 min.)**
3. Have students summarize what happens in each scene. **(5 min.)**
4. Have students read the text on their own and then answer the questions on page 347. **(5 min.)**

### Escuchemos

Have students watch the **Novela.** Then have them complete the following sentences: **El señor Ortega no logra entender por qué....** and **Si Octavio pudiera, él....**

Novela en video

5

### En una bodega

**Profesor Luna** La propuesta de la empresa *MaderaCorp* no es tan mala, tenemos que llegar a un acuerdo.
**Ecologista 2** No se puede negociar con el enemigo. Nada de lo que ellos hagan puede ser ventajoso para el bosque, ni para la gente que vive en los alrededores.

**Hombre 1** Profesor Luna. Espero que ahora esté feliz de vernos.
**Profesor Luna** No, en realidad no. ¿Qué quieren?
**Hombre 2** Lo de siempre. El estudio de impacto ambiental.
**Ecologista 1** No hay por qué dárselo a ustedes. Nosotros somos los jefes aquí.

6

7

**Profesor Luna** Tenemos que tener una reunión entre ustedes y el presidente de *MaderaCorp*.
**Hombre 1** Esperen, voy a contactarlo... Sí, en sus oficinas... dentro de dos horas. Estaremos allí.

### En la comisaría

**Detective** ¿Qué es esto?
**Clara** Son documentos. El profesor Luna me pidió que los imprimiera.
**Sargento** ¿Usted habló con el profesor Luna? ¿Usted sabe algo de su desaparición?

8

### ¿COMPRENDES?

1. ¿Qué piensa el señor Ortega sobre la ausencia de Clara? ¿Qué piensa Octavio?
2. ¿De qué se da cuenta Clara al escuchar el reportaje de la radio?
3. ¿Qué cree Graciela que debe hacer Clara? ¿Está de acuerdo Clara?
4. ¿Qué decide hacer Clara con la información que tiene? ¿Es buena decisión? ¿Por qué sí o por qué no?
5. ¿Qué quiere el profesor Luna? ¿Están de acuerdo los ecologistas?
6. ¿Adónde van a tener que ir los ecologistas y el profesor con los hombres? ¿Es buena decisión? ¿Por qué sí o por qué no? 1.2, 1.3

**Próximo episodio**
***Una reunión importante ocurre en las oficinas de MaderaCorp. ¿Crees que puede resolver Clara el misterio de la desaparición del profesor?***

PÁGINAS 394–395

### Clara perspectiva, Episodio 8

In **Episodio 8,** at *Chile en la Mira,* Octavio and Señor Ortega are waiting for Clara to arrive. Meanwhile, Clara stops at a kiosk and hears a radio news report that Professor Luna has disappeared. She calls her friend Graciela for advice. They conclude that she must go to the police and tell them what she knows. At an unknown location, in a warehouse, the two ecologists are arguing with the professor over the results of the environmental impact studies and *MaderaCorp*'s development plans. The two bodyguards, who have been following the ecologists and the professor, arrive at the scene. They all conclude that they must have a meeting with the president of *MaderaCorp.* At the police station, Clara tells the authorities about the professor's disappearance.

### ¿Comprendes? Answers

1. está molesto; cree que debe tener buena razón por no estar
2. El profesor Luna ha desaparecido.
3. presentarse a las autoridades; sí
4. entregar los documentos a las autoridades; Answers will vary.
5. llegar a un acuerdo con *MaderaCorp;* no
6. a buscar el estudio de impacto ambiental; Answers will vary.

### Cultures

#### Practices and Perspectives

Have students discuss the way Octavio interacts with Señor Ortega. Do you think it is appropriate for him to defend Clara's absence? Does Señor Ortega seem like a typical boss that students might encounter in their community? Is Clara a typical employee?

2.1

### Comunicación

#### Group Activity: Interpersonal

After students have read the **Novela en video,** have them work in groups to discuss the decisions they would have made in Clara's position. Have groups share their ideas with the rest of the class, and then discuss how the story might have changed if Clara had made different decisions.

1.1

# Lectura cultural

**Resources**

**Planning:**
Lesson Planner, pp. 125, 286–287
One-Stop Planner

**Presentation:**
Audio CD 8, Tr. 10

**Practice:**
Cuaderno de actividades, p. 78
Reading Strategies and Skills Handbook, Chapter 8
Interactive Advanced Reader

**Pre-Reading Activity**
Have students talk about their impressions of the typical work atmosphere in the United States. Is it formal? Does it vary by job? Do they think the atmosphere would be similar in Latin American countries? Have students look at the photographs and read the captions. What is the impression they get from the photos? 2.1, 4.2

**Heritage Speakers**
Ask heritage speakers if they have been, and whether they continue to be, in situations where they have had to address anyone formally in Spanish. Have them share the terms they use. 2.1

**Pre-AP Practice**
**AP Language Examination:** **Lectura cultural** helps students prepare for Section I, Part B: **Reading Comprehension.** The audio recording helps them prepare for Part A: **Listening—Short Narratives.**

# Lectura cultural

CD 8, Tr. 10

## El trabajo en Latinoamérica

*El ambiente de trabajo es diferente en Latinoamérica. El uso de títulos, la manera de vestir y los beneficios son algunas de las diferencias más marcadas.*

**El ambiente de trabajo**
En muchos países de Latinoamérica, el ambiente de trabajo es más formal que en Estados Unidos. Los empleados no tratan al jefe o a la jefa de *tú*, sino de *Ud.* Además, mucha gente usa títulos como *doctor(a)* o *licenciado(a)*, o simplemente un título de respeto como Sr. Vázquez, don Antonio o doña Cecilia. La manera de vestir para ir al trabajo también suele ser más conservadora. Las empresas estadounidenses que hacen negocios en Latinoamérica tienen que seguir estas normas culturales para tener éxito.

Las oficinas de noche en Quito, Ecuador

Un grupo de políticos participa en una reunión formal.

**Core Instruction**

**TEACHING LECTURA CULTURAL**

1. Call on a volunteer to read the introductory paragraph aloud and ask students what they think about using titles as a sign of respect. **(2 min.)**
2. Have another volunteer read the second paragraph aloud. Then lead a discussion about the advantages and disadvantages of more and less vacation time. **(3 min.)**
3. Ask a third volunteer to read the third paragraph aloud. Tell them that in the U.S. it is illegal under national and state laws to fire someone for being pregnant or for taking an unpaid leave for maternity. **(5 min.)**
4. Have students complete the **Comprensión** activities. Ask them to complete Activity A on their own and Activity B with a partner. **(10 min.)**
5. Have students complete the **Comparaciones** activity and share their answers with the class. **(5 min.)**

Una mujer de negocios trabaja con un compañero.

**Las vacaciones**
Las empresas de España y Latinoamérica suelen ofrecer más días de vacaciones que las empresas estadounidenses. Además, cuando un día festivo cae durante la semana, todo el mundo aprovecha para tomar vacaciones los otros días entre el día festivo y el fin de semana. Estas vacaciones se llaman el "puente festivo". Pero esta tradición, al igual que la famosa "siesta", está desapareciendo poco a poco mientras las empresas tratan de competir con las industrias internacionales.

**Los beneficios**
En algunos países de Latinoamérica, a las mujeres se les da más tiempo de licencia de maternidad que en Estados Unidos. En Chile, por ejemplo, las mujeres reciben 18 semanas pagadas por el estado, seis semanas antes de dar a luz y doce semanas después. En Estados Unidos los empleados del gobierno federal y de empresas grandes reciben 12 semanas de licencia de maternidad.

## Comprensión 1.2

**A ¿Cierto o falso?** Contesta **cierto** o **falso.**

1. El ambiente de trabajo de los países latinoamericanos suele ser muy informal. falso
2. Los empleados de una empresa latinoamericana tratarían a su jefe de *tú*. falso
3. Es común escuchar a una persona usar el título "licenciado" cuando está hablando con su jefe o con un(a) compañero(a) de trabajo. cierto
4. En Chile, las empresas ofrecen dieciocho semanas de licencia de maternidad. cierto
5. En Estados Unidos no existe una política nacional sobre la licencia de maternidad. cierto

**B ¿Comprendiste?** Contesta las preguntas.

1. ¿Cómo suelen vestir los empleados para ir al trabajo en Latinoamérica?
2. ¿Cómo pueden las empresas estadounidenses tener más éxito en Latinoamérica?
3. ¿Qué es el "puente festivo"? ¿Te parece buena idea?
4. ¿Qué está pasando con las tradiciones de la siesta y el puente festivo?

## Actividad 1.3

**Comparaciones** ¿Cuál es tu opinión sobre el ambiente de trabajo y los beneficios en Latinoamérica? Si pudieras trabajar en un país de Latinoamérica, ¿lo harías? ¿Qué país escogerías? ¿Qué otras diferencias crees que encontrarías?

## Lectura cultural

### B Answers

1. Suelen vestirse formalmente.
2. Asegurándose que sus empleados se vistan formalmente, usen títulos de respeto y ofrezcan horas de trabajo y beneficios comparables a las empresas locales.
3. Tomar días de vacaciones alrededor de días festivos que caen a mitad de semana.
4. Están desapareciendo poco a poco porque las empresas tratan de competir con las industrias internacionales.

### Connections

**Social Studies Link**
Have students research and chart the number and percentage of women in the workforce in the U.S. and the number in the Andean countries. They can ask the school librarian for help if they are having trouble locating the information on the Internet. 3.1, 4.2

### Post-Reading Activities

Ask students to think of situations where they have had to address someone formally, such as their teachers, their parents, or bosses. Ask them for the term in English and then translate it into Spanish. Also, have students list other types of benefits that employers offer, which might differ when comparing the U.S. work environment to that in Latin America. 4.1, 4.2

## Differentiated Instruction

### ADVANCED LEARNERS

**Extension** Have students do a search for employment ads in the online version of daily newspapers of the Latin American country they might choose to live in, according to what they answered in the **Actividad** on page 349. Have them pick out their three favorite job postings and tell a partner what attracts them about the jobs. 3.2

### MULTIPLE INTELLIGENCES

**Logical/Mathematical** Have students continue the Social Studies Link activity by researching labor statistics in each Andean country and comparing them with the statistics for the U.S. They can choose which categories and characteristics to compare, such as educational achievement statistics in various professions and trades. 3.1, 4.2

### Assess

**Assessment Program**
**Prueba: Lectura,** p. 153

**Online Assessment**
my.hrw.com

**Test Generator**

# Leamos y escribamos

## Resources

**Planning:**

Lesson Planner, pp. 125–126, 286–287

One-Stop Planner

**Presentation:**

Audio CD 8, Tr. 11

**Practice:**

Cuaderno de actividades, p. 78

Reading Strategies and Skills Handbook, Chapter 8

Interactive Advanced Reader

## Pre-Reading Activity

Ask students what they know about recent Mexican immigrants in the U.S. Ask students whether they have encountered immigrants in school, at the stores, or anywhere else in their community. Also ask students to think about what might lead a family to immigrate to the U.S.

## Escuchemos

On the board write the following: **1. Mike Nevel ____ darle trabajo a un ayudante. 2. Mike le ____ más de un dólar la hora. 3. ¿Qué tal le ____ sustituirle a Mike?** As students watch the **Novela,** have them fill in the blanks based on what they hear. **(podría, pagaría, parecería)**

## Pre-AP Practice

**AP Language Examination: Leamos** helps students prepare for Section I, Part B: **Reading Comprehension.** The audio recording helps them prepare for Part A: **Listening—Short Narratives.**

# Leamos y escribamos

**ESTRATEGIA**

**para leer** It's often important to ask yourself what motivated the author to write the story you're going to read. As you read, think of some reasons why the author wrote the story. You may want to find out more about Jiménez's experiences growing up. This will help you better understand an autobiographical work such as this one.

CD 8, Tr. 11

**Antes de leer** 1.2, 1.3

**A** La historia que vas a leer es verdadera. Es de *Senderos fronterizos,* una novela de Francisco Jiménez en la que cuenta sus experiencias como hijo de inmigrantes mexicanos en California. La historia se narra desde la perspectiva del autor y nos cuenta los sacrificios que hizo la familia Jiménez y los problemas que enfrentó en Estados Unidos. Antes de leer, piensa en algunos temas que posiblemente encontrarás en esta lectura y en lo que le llevó al autor a escribir sobre su vida. Si tuvieras que narrar tu vida, ¿qué sucesos incluirías?

## de Senderos fronterizos

*de Francisco Jiménez*

Como era de costumbre, al final del día escolar, Roberto y yo nos encontramos en el estacionamiento y nos dirigimos hacia Main Street Elementary School. Íbamos en el carro por Broadway, pasando al lado de estudiantes que llenaban las aceras[1] como vistosas hormigas en un desfile. Cuando dábamos la vuelta en la esquina hacia Main Street, Roberto dio un giro cerrado[2] y se estacionó junto a una camioneta[3] vieja y amarilla que tenía en sus costados un letrero que decía *Santa María Window Cleaners.* —Yo he visto antes a ese tipo, —dijo Roberto, señalando a un hombre que recién terminaba de lavar las ventanas exteriores de *Kress,* la tienda de cinco y diez centavos. El hombre metió el enjugador de goma[4] y el paño en el bolsillo posterior de su pantalón, recogió el balde[5] y la escoba y se dirigió hacia la camioneta.

—Hola — dijo mi hermano nerviosamente, mientras el hombre cargaba su equipo en la parte trasera de la camioneta —. Mi nombre es Roberto.

—Yo me llamo Mike Nevel — dijo el hombre con una voz ronca[6] y profunda.

1 sidewalks 2 *giro...* tight turn 3 pick-up truck 4 squeegee 5 bucket 6 hoarse

## Core Instruction

### TEACHING LEAMOS

1. Ask students to look at the pictures to predict the subject matter of the story. Have them describe the three characters depicted and what the situation seems to be. Ask students to tell whether they have ever washed windows for pay or in their own homes. **(2 min.)**
2. Read **Estrategia para leer** with students. Have them read the first paragraph and apply the strategy to help them understand what they read. Have pairs present their conclusions about what is happening in the story and the elements of style that might make it pleasant to read, such as the comment about how the students look walking on the sidewalk. **(3 min.)**
3. Have them continue with the rest of the story, stopping to monitor comprehension as needed. **(15 min.)**
4. Have students complete the **Comprensión** activities on page 352. **(5 min.)**

—Quisiera saber si... ¿no necesita usted algún ayudante?
—preguntó Roberto.

—¿Quieres decir que si yo quiero contratar[7] a alguien?

—Sí —respondió Roberto.

—Podría darle trabajo a un ayudante de tiempo parcial. ¿Tienes alguna experiencia?

—Oh, no es para mí —contestó Roberto—. Es para mi papá. Él necesita un empleo.

—¿Ha hecho alguna vez trabajo de limpieza?

—No, pero él es un buen trabajador.

—Bueno, tendría que verlo y conversar con él.

—Él no habla inglés —dije yo. —Sólo español.

—No me sirve. En este negocio necesito a alguien que sepa hablar inglés y que tenga experiencia. ¿No quieres ser tú?

—Mi hermano ya tiene un empleo —dije—. Yo tengo experiencia. He estado ayudándole a él a limpiar Main Street Elementary School.

—Tú estás muy pequeño, —dijo él, mirándome de arriba abajo y riéndose maliciosamente. Se volteó hacia Roberto y continuó: —Así que tienes experiencia en Main Street Elementary School...

—Soy conserje[8] de tiempo parcial ahí —dijo Roberto.

—¿Y los fines de semana? ¿Trabajas ahí los fines de semana?

—No, sólo de lunes a viernes.

—¿Qué te parecería trabajar para mí los fines de semana? Te pagaría un dólar y veinticinco centavos la hora.

—Bien —respondió Roberto inmediatamente.

—¿Y yo qué? —pregunté—. Yo puedo trabajar con él.

—Puedes ayudarle si quieres, pero a ti no puedo pagarte. Cuando vio nuestras expresiones de abatimiento[9], agregó rápidamente. —Muy bien, si él da buen resultado yo le pagaré. Pero sólo si da buen resultado.

—No hay duda. Lo logré —dije lleno de confianza.

Durante las siguientes cuatro semanas, Roberto y yo trabajamos con Mike Nevel, limpiando oficinas y lavando ventanas. El primer día, Mike trabajó muy de cerca con nosotros, mostrándonos qué cosa íbamos a limpiar y observando cómo trabajábamos. Eventualmente, Mike Nevel dejó que Roberto y yo hiciéramos el trabajo sin su ayuda.

**7** to hire **8** janitor **9** discouragement



# Leamos y escribamos

## Active Reading Questions

1. **¿Piensas que Roberto y Francisco son valientes por acercarse a Mike Nevel y pedirle trabajo?**
2. **¿Qué tal te parece la idea de trabajar los fines de semana?**
3. **¿Qué indica la cortesía de Mike al invitar a Roberto y a Francisco a pasar por su casa para presentarles a su esposa?**
4. **¿Por qué va a estar orgulloso el papá de los muchachos?** 1.2

## Connections

### Language Arts Link

Have students analyze the reading by looking at the character traits of each person. What character traits helped the boys get the job? How would they describe each character in the story? 3.1, 3.2

### Author's Credibility

Have students think about the author's credibility and what motivated the author to write this story. Have students find passages from the story and give their opinion about why the author included it. Have them think about how the passages make the author's story more credible. There is no right or wrong answer as long as students explain their point of view. 3.1, 3.2

### Applying the Strategies

For more practice with analyzing the author's purpose, you might have students use the "Probable Passage" strategy from the *Reading Strategies and Skills Handbook.*

## Differentiated Instruction

### SLOWER PACE LEARNERS

**Additional Practice** Have students reread the parts of the story with which they had trouble. Tell them they can read at their own pace, ask you questions, and write down summaries of each paragraph or portion of conversations. 1.2

### SPECIAL LEARNING NEEDS

**Students with Dyslexia** Before covering the story in class, have pairs of students read the story aloud to each other. Having heard the story and being familiarized with the words, students can concentrate more on comprehension.

## Connections

### Literature Link

Francisco Jiménez came to the U.S. with his family when he was a child. The story of ***Senderos fronterizos*** is the second part in a series in which Jiménez describes his experiences as a Mexican immigrant in southern California. Jiménez overcame great challenges in this country and is currently a university professor. Have students find the personal accounts of other Hispanic authors on their experiences in the United States. Have students compare them with what they read in ***Senderos fronterizos*** and explain the similarities and differences. 3.1

### Heritage Speakers

Ask heritage speakers if they have been, and whether they continue to be, in situations where they have had to address anyone formally in Spanish. Have them share the terms they use. 2.1

### Post-Reading Activity

Have students think about why it is illegal in the U.S. for young children to get paid for working. Would poor families be more likely to keep children out of school and have them work instead to contribute to the family's earnings?

Cada sábado y domingo, mi hermano y yo íbamos en carro a la casa de Mike Nevel en West Donovan para recoger las llaves de la camioneta.

Un sábado por la noche, cuando llegamos a devolver[10] la camioneta, Mike Nevel nos invitó a entrar a su casa. Nos presentó a su esposa. Roberto y yo nos sentamos en un sofá grande frente a Mike, quien se sentó en una silla reclinable[11].

—¿Cómo van las cosas? —preguntó Mike.

—Bien —respondimos nosotros al mismo tiempo. Roberto se metió la mano en la bolsa y sacó un aro[12] lleno de llaves y se las entregó a Mike.

—No, guárdetelas tú —dijo Mike—. Tengo un juego extra. Roberto y yo nos miramos mutuamente y sonreíamos. Mike me dijo: —Me estoy poniendo demasiado viejo y estoy cansado de trabajar por las noches durante la semana. ¿Qué tal te parecería sustituirme?

—¡Seguro que sí! —respondí emocionado.

—Limpiarás unos cuantos de los lugares que tú y Roberto han estado limpiando los fines de semana.

Roberto y yo le dimos las gracias y regresamos a casa emocionados. "Papá va a estar orgulloso de nosotros", pensé.

10 return 11 recliner 12 key ring

### Comprensión 1.2

**B** Contesta las preguntas.

1. ¿Dónde trabajan Francisco y Roberto? **1.** Trabajan en Main Street Elementary School.
2. ¿A quién conocieron Francisco y Roberto en el estacionamiento? **2.** Conocieron a Mike Nevel.
3. ¿Quién está buscando trabajo en la familia Jiménez? **3.** El papá de Francisco y Roberto está buscando trabajo.
4. ¿Qué tipo de empleado está buscando Mike Nevel? **4.** Está buscando a alguien que sepa hablar inglés y que tenga experiencia en limpieza.
5. ¿Por qué dice Mike Nevel que no le va a pagar a Francisco? **5.** Porque piensa que es muy pequeño y no va a dar resultado.
6. ¿Cómo reaccionó Francisco cuando Mike Nevel le preguntó si quería sustituirlo? **6.** Francisco se puso feliz.

### Pasó así 1.2

**C** Coloca las siguientes oraciones en orden cronológico. e, c, b, a, f, d

a. Roberto y Francisco empezaron a trabajar con Mike Nevel.
b. Mike Nevel contrató a Roberto y a Francisco para ayudarle.
c. Roberto le preguntó al señor de la camioneta si necesitaba un ayudante.
d. Mike Nevel le preguntó a Francisco si quería sustituirlo.
e. Francisco vio a su hermano en el estacionamiento.
f. Mike Nevel invitó a Roberto y a Francisco a entrar en su casa.

### Después de leer 1.3

**D** Al leer esta historia, ¿qué aprendiste sobre la vida de Francisco? ¿Cómo era su vida? ¿Por qué tuvo que trabajar de niño? ¿Por qué crees que el autor decidió contar la historia de su familia? ¿Crees que hay otras familias que hayan tenido la misma experiencia en Estados Unidos?

## Pre-AP Practice

**AP Language Examination:** **Leamos and Escribamos** help students prepare for Section I, Part B: **Reading Comprehension** and Section II, Part A: **Informal Writing.**

## Core Instruction

### TEACHING ESCRIBAMOS

1. Discuss **Estrategia para escribir** as a class. **(2 min.)**
2. Have students complete pre-writing Activity 1 by writing down what they think are the characteristics of their best friend and themselves. **(2 min.)**
3. Have students write and revise their conversations individually (Activities 2 and 3). **(20 min.)**
4. Ask students to exchange their completed conversations with a classmate and complete Activity 4. **(6 min.)**

# Taller del escritor 1.3

**ESTRATEGIA**

**para escribir** A good way to bring your stories to life is through dialogue. Natural-sounding dialogues make your characters seem realistic. Dialogues can be used in a real-life story to tell what people said, or they can be used in fiction to help develop a character.

## Personajes con vida propia

Los personajes en *Senderos fronterizos* se desarrollan a través del diálogo. Imagina que tú y tu mejor amigo acaban de conocerse por primera vez. Escribe un diálogo entre ustedes dos de por lo menos diez líneas. Tu diálogo debe darle al lector una idea de cómo son ustedes.

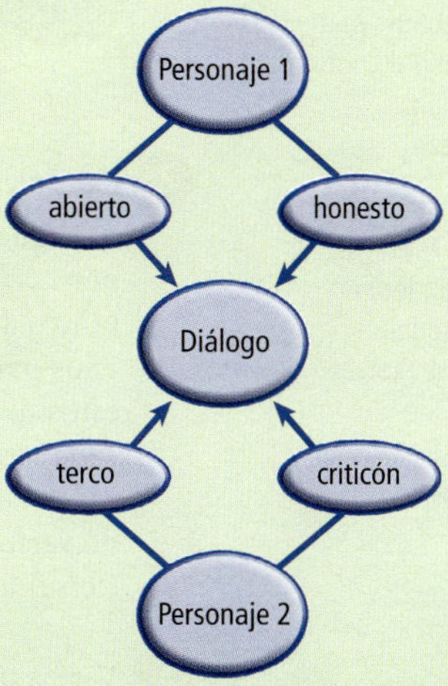


### 1 Antes de escribir

Haz una lista de características de los personajes que vas a incluir en tu diálogo. Después piensa en lo que podrían decir para que el lector sepa cómo son. Por ejemplo, si un personaje es terco y el otro es abierto, eso se puede reflejar en su conversación.

### 2 Escribir un borrador

Ahora que tienes definidos los personajes, empieza tu borrador. Usa la lista que hiciste como guía.

### 3 Revisar

Revisa tu borrador y corrige los errores de gramática y ortografía, si los hay. Lee tu borrador para verificar que lo que dicen los personajes refleje cómo son. Identifica qué cambios hay que hacer para que los personajes sean más vivos.

### 4 Publicar

Intercambia tu diálogo con un(a) compañero(a). Lee el diálogo de tu compañero(a) y haz una lista de las características de los personajes. Tu compañero(a) hará lo mismo y te entregará su lista. Compara esta lista con la que hiciste antes de escribir tu diálogo para ver si tu compañero(a) identificó las mismas características.

## Leamos y escribamos

### Process Writing

Ask students to think ahead about the subject matter and the situation their characters are going to be discussing. They should try to come up with themes and circumstances that will help highlight and define the traits of their characters. For example, if one of them is particularly opinionated, they could be having a conversation after seeing a film or a play.

### Writing Assessment

To assess **Taller del escritor,** you can use the following rubric.

| Writing Rubric | 4 | 3 | 2 | 1 |
|---|---|---|---|---|
| **Content** (Complete—Incomplete) | | | | |
| **Comprehensibility** (Comprehensible—Seldom comprehensible) | | | | |
| **Accuracy** (Accurate—Seldom accurate) | | | | |
| **Organization** (Well-organized—Poorly organized) | | | | |
| **Effort** (Excellent effort—Minimal effort) | | | | |

18–20: A
16–17: B
14–15: C
12–13: D
Under 12: F

## Differentiated Instruction

### SLOWER PACE LEARNERS

Allow students to complete their conversations after class. They must, however, write at least six lines of dialogue in the 10 minutes allotted, and exchange their conversations with classmates to complete Activity 4. 1.1

### MULTIPLE INTELLIGENCES

**Linguistic** Allow students to add more lines of dialogue if they wish. They can add characters to their dialogue, or illustrate multiple characteristics in two characters. Encourage them to make their conversations as creative as possible. 1.1

### Assess

**Assessment Program**
**Prueba: Lectura,** p. 153
**Prueba: Escritura,** p. 154
**Online Assessment**
**my.hrw.com**
**Test Generator**

Capítulo 8

# Prepárate para el examen

## Resources

**Planning:**

Lesson Planner, pp. 126–127, 286–289

One-Stop Planner

**Presentation:**

Video Program, Videocassette 4

DVD Program

**Variedades**

**Practice:**

Activities for Communication, pp. 50, 69–70

Video Guide, pp. 52–53

Lab Book, pp. 8, 41–44, 80

Audio CD 8, Tr. 12–13

Pre-AP Instructional Resources

Pre-AP Audio CD 2, Trs. 9–12

Interactive Tutor, Disc 2

Teaching Transparencies

**Situación, Capítulo 8**

Picture Sequences, Chapter 8

### 1 Script

1. Necesito diez copias de esta hoja. Por favor, sácamelas en colores.
2. Oye, no te olvides de la reunión. Es el martes a las once de la mañana.
3. Mira, tu nuevo compañero de trabajo no es una persona. Es un hombre electrónico. Puedes programarlo para hacer varias tareas.
4. Por favor, vaya a mi oficina y escuche mis mensajes. Dígame si alguien importante me ha llamado.

### 5 Answers

1. la licenciatura
2. Tradicionalmente ha sido desde las 9 am hasta las 2 pm y desde las 4 o 5 hasta las 8 pm. Pero hoy en día está cambiando a un horario parecido al horario típico de trabaje en EE.UU.
3. Ha creado un ambiente favorable para el desarrollo del comercio electrónico.
4. La tradición de la siesta está desapareciendo porque mucha gente está trabajando durante estas horas de la tarde.

Capítulo 8
Repaso

**1 Vocabulario 1**
- saying what you can and cannot do
- talking about what you do and do not understand

**pp. 320–325**

**2 Gramática 1**
- verbs with indirect object pronouns
- verbs that express "to become"
- uses of **se**

**pp. 326–331**

**3 Vocabulario 2**
- writing a formal letter
- talking about your plans

**pp. 334–339**

# Prepárate para el examen

Interactive TUTOR

CD 8, Tr. 12

**1** El jefe le pide varias cosas a su auxiliar. Escucha los comentarios y escoge la foto que corresponde a lo que debe usar el auxiliar para cumplir cada tarea. 1.2 **1.** b **2.** a **3.** d **4.** c

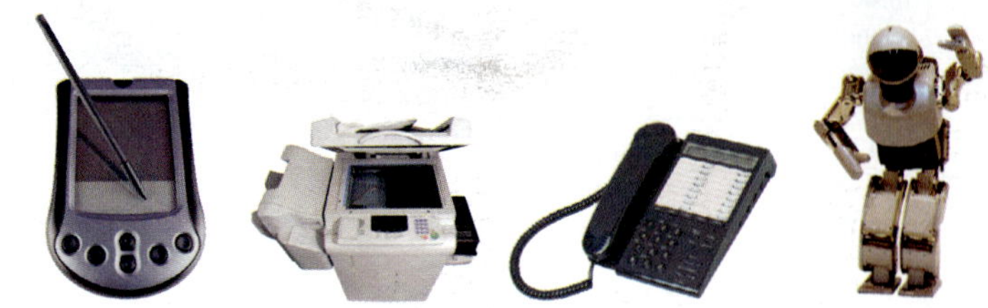

a. b. c. d.

**2** Completa el párrafo con la palabra correcta en paréntesis. 1.2

Ana quería cambiar de trabajo. Era una mujer muy competente, pero __1__ (le/se) resultaba difícil trabajar en una oficina con tantos adelantos tecnológicos. __2__ (Le/Se) era fácil crear diseños para los anuncios, pero no entendía cómo implementar estos diseños en la computadora. Trató de hacerlo mil veces y cada vez que __3__ (le/se) salía mal, __4__ (le/se) frustraba más. Así que decidió que __5__ (le/se) haría pintora. Después de varios años, llegó a ser famosa. Era su propia jefa, y __6__ (le/se) levantaba cada día a la hora que quería. Estaba feliz.

**3** Varias personas están comentando sobre sus trabajos. Completa las oraciones con la palabra correcta del cuadro. 1.2

| solicitud | beneficios | medio | puesto | donar | superviso |
|---|---|---|---|---|---|

1. Estoy buscando empleo a ═══ tiempo porque tomo clases por las mañanas. medio
2. Prefiero un ═══ en una oficina grande. puesto
3. Trabajo como voluntario porque me gusta ═══ tiempo a los niños enfermos. donar
4. En mi empresa tengo ═══ como seguro médico y vacaciones. beneficios
5. Soy el jefe y ═══ a los empleados. superviso
6. No tengo trabajo, pero voy a mandar unas cartas de ═══. solicitud

## Oral Assessment

### Speaking Rubric

To assess the speaking activities in this section, you might use the following rubric. For additional speaking rubrics, see the Alternative Assessment section of the *Assessment Program.*

| Speaking Rubric | 4 | 3 | 2 | 1 |
|---|---|---|---|---|
| **Content** (Complete—Incomplete) | | | | |
| **Comprehension** (Total—Little) | | | | |
| **Comprehensibility** (Comprehensible—Incomprehensible) | | | | |
| **Accuracy** (Accurate—Seldom Accurate) | | | | |
| **Fluency** (Fluent—Not Fluent) | | | | |

18–20: A 16–17: B 14–15: C 12–13: D Under 12: F

Visit Holt Online
**go.hrw.com**
KEYWORD: EXP3 CH8
Chapter Self-test

**4** Completa el párrafo con las formas correctas de los verbos. 1.2

Yo les pedí a mis papás que me __1__ (pagar) un curso de francés. Pero mis papás querían que __2__ (estudiar) español. Si pudiera, __3__ (aprender) los dos idiomas. Pero mis profesores me sugirieron que me __4__ (enfocar) en el español ahora. __5__ (Ir) a España si __6__ (tener) el dinero, porque así podría trabajar en una empresa donde se hablara solamente español. Pero por ahora, buscaré trabajo aquí.

**1.** pagaran **2.** estudiara **3.** aprendería **4.** enfocara **5.** Iría **6.** tuviera

**4 Gramática 2**
- conditional
- past subjunctive with hypothetical statements
- more past subjunctive

**pp. 340–345**

**5** Contesta las preguntas. 1.2 See answers on p. 354.

1. ¿Cómo se llama el título que se recibe en Latinoamérica cuando uno se gradúa de la universidad?
2. ¿Cómo es el horario de trabajo en Latinoamérica y en España?
3. ¿Qué efecto tiene el bajo precio de acceso a Internet en Perú?
4. ¿Por qué está desapareciendo la tradición de la siesta?

**5 Cultura**
- Comparaciones **pp. 332–333**
- Lectura cultural **pp. 348–349**
- Notas culturales **pp. 328, 329, 336**

CD 8, Tr. 13

**6** Escucha la entrevista con Rosalía Bogantes. Basándote en la conversación, escribe en cinco oraciones lo que le gustaría hacer en la empresa y las ventajas que tiene. 1.3

## Conversación

HOLT SoundBooth ONLINE RECORDING

**7** Role-play the following conversation with a partner. Partner A is interviewing Partner B for a summer job at a travel agency. 1.1, 1.2

| | |
|---|---|
| Partner A: | Greet your partner. Say you've read his or her resumé and cover letter. Ask why he or she left a previous job. |
| Partner B: | Respond. Explain why you want this job and what makes you the perfect candidate. |
| Partner A: | Ask about your partner's experience working in an office with other people and lots of stress. |
| Partner B: | Describe a similar job you've had. |
| Partner A: | Ask if your partner knows one of the skills needed for the job. |
| Partner B: | Say yes. Then name a skill you don't have, but want to learn more about. |
| Partner A: | Describe the job schedule, benefits, and salary. |
| Partner B: | Respond positively, and say when you could start. Thank your partner for the interview. |

## Conversación

### Additional Speaking Practice

For additional speaking practice, use the *Picture Sequences Transparency* for Chapter 8. Use the Speaking Rubric on the preceding page to evaluate their performance. You may also wish to use the Interviews and Role-Plays in the *Activities for Communication* book.

### Pre-AP Practice

**7** In the Level 3 *Pre-AP Instructional Resources* you will find an alternative version of Activity 7. The following resources in that book will help you prepare students for the AP Language Exam:

- Blackline masters, pp. 34, 44, 54
- Pre-AP Audio CD 2, Trs. 9–12
- Scripts and answers, pp. 57–75

### 6 Script

—Buenos días, Srta. Bogantes. Soy el jefe de la empresa, Pedro Morales.
—Encantada. Gracias por recibirme.
—Dígame, Srta. Bogantes, si tuviera la oportunidad de trabajar con nuestra empresa, ¿qué es lo que le gustaría hacer?
—Pues, la verdad es que me interesaría trabajar como auxiliar administrativa. Soy capaz de mejorar su sistema usando las nuevas tecnologías para organizar los documentos.
—Eso sería fabuloso porque aquí nos resulta difícil entender las nuevas tecnologías. Nos volvemos locos con estas computadoras. Estamos muy desorganizados. ¿Ha trabajado como auxiliar administrativa antes?
—Hice trabajo voluntario para una empresa y actualicé todos sus sistemas. Querían que les enseñara a conectar sus agendas electrónicas a las computadoras y a ser más eficientes, y lo pude hacer. Quedaron muy satisfechos con mi trabajo.
—Y en qué posición se ve en cinco años?
—Sin duda, quiero llegar a ser gerente de un departamento de tecnología. Una vez que conozca el sistema aquí, estará a mi alcance dirigir un equipo.

### 7 Answers

Below is a sample conversation.
(A) —Buenas tardes. Ya he leído su currículum vitae y solicitud. ¿Por qué dejó usted su puesto anterior?
(B) —No me quisieron ofrecer empleo a tiempo completo. Me gustaría trabajar en una empresa grande. Tengo mucha experiencia como agente de viajes.
(A) —Cuénteme algo acerca de su experiencia trabajando en una oficina con mucha gente y mucho estrés.
(B) —Hace dos años trabajé en una oficina con muchos clientes y mucho estrés.
(A) —Uno de los requisitos para este puesto es saber inglés o francés. ¿Sabe usted otro idioma?
(B) —Sí, el inglés. No sé francés pero me gustaría aprenderlo.
(A) —Bueno, el puesto es de tiempo completo, de las nueve de la mañana a las cinco de la tarde. El salario es…
(B) —Muy bien. Puedo empezar inmediatamente. Muchas gracias por la entrevista.

# Prepárate para el examen

## Grammar Review

For more practice with the grammar topics in this chapter, see the *Grammar Tutor,* the *Interactive Tutor,* or the *Cuaderno de vocabulario y gramática.*

GramaVisión

## Teacher to Teacher

**Kimberly Bromley**
Warren Township
Gurnee, IL

After dividing students into pairs or groups of four, I write six verbs from the **Vocabulario** and number them 1–6 on the board or on a transparency. I give each group two dice. One die represents the six infinitive verbs, while the other die represents the six forms of a conjugated verb (1 for first person singular, 2 for second person singular, and so on). Students roll the dice and the first person or group to conjugate the correct verb in the correct form puts an X or O on his or her Tic-Tac-Toe board. The students peer-correct their answers. 1.2

**Gramática 1**
- verbs with indirect object pronouns
  pp. 326–327
- verbs that express "to become"
  pp. 328–329
- uses of **se**
  pp. 330–331

## Repaso de Gramática 1

An **indirect object pronoun** is used with some verbs to indicate *to whom* or *for whom* an action occurs.

¿**Te resulta** difícil usar esta agenda?
A Toni **le cuesta** trabajo entender el problema.

The verbs **hacerse, volverse, ponerse, convertirse en, quedarse,** and **llegar a ser** can be used to express a change in state *(to get, to become).* See page 328 for rules on when to use which verb.

A form of the pronoun **se** is used:
- with verbs that are used reflexively: **Se** lavó los dientes.
- to indicate unintentional events: ¿**Se** te perdió el libro?
- to replace **le** or **les** when they appear together with the direct object **lo, los, la,** and **las: Se** lo presté ayer.
- in impersonal sentences: **Se** dice que hubo un robo.
- to express the passive voice: **Se** hizo tarde.
- with certain "process" verbs: **Se** mudó a la ciudad.
- with verbs that express "to become": **Se** hizo abogado.

**Gramática 2**
- conditional
  pp. 340–341
- past subjunctive with hypothetical statements
  pp. 342–343
- more past subjunctive
  pp. 344–345

## Repaso de Gramática 2

The **conditional** is used to tell what *would happen* or what someone *would do.* It is also used to express what someone *would* or *would not like,* or the probability that something happened in the past.

Pablo **trabajaría** en un colegio.
Me **gustaría** ir de viaje.
**Serían** las ocho cuando llamó mi mamá.

The conditional endings, which are added to the infinitive, are: **-ía, -ías, -ía, -íamos, -íais, -ían.**

The **past subjunctive** is used after **si** *(if)* in hypothetical sentences that are contrary to fact or unlikely to happen. The **conditional** is used in the other clause.

Si **fuera** rico, **compraría** un carro.

The past subjunctive endings, added to the third person plural form of the preterite after removing the **-on,** are: **-a, -as, -a, -amos, -ais, -an.**

When the verb in the main clause of a sentence that requires the subjunctive is in a **past tense,** the **past subjunctive** is used in the subordinate clause.

Yo **temía** que él **se enojara.**

## Chapter Review

**Teacher Management System**
To access, launch the program, type "admin" in the password area, and press RETURN. For more details, log on to www.hrw.com/CDROMTUTOR.

Create a variety of puzzles to review chapter vocabulary.

**DVD Program**

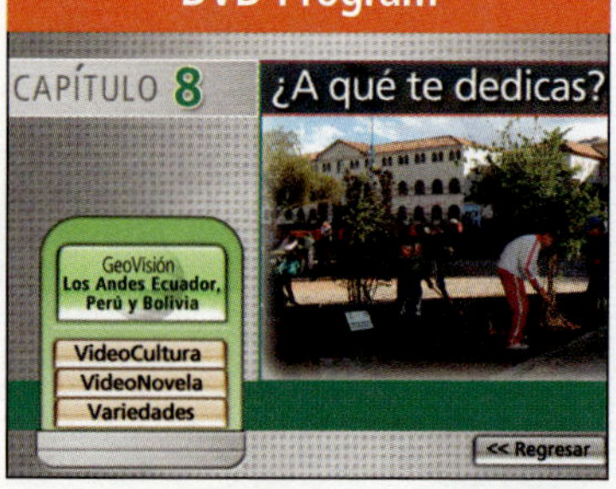


**Interactive Tutor**

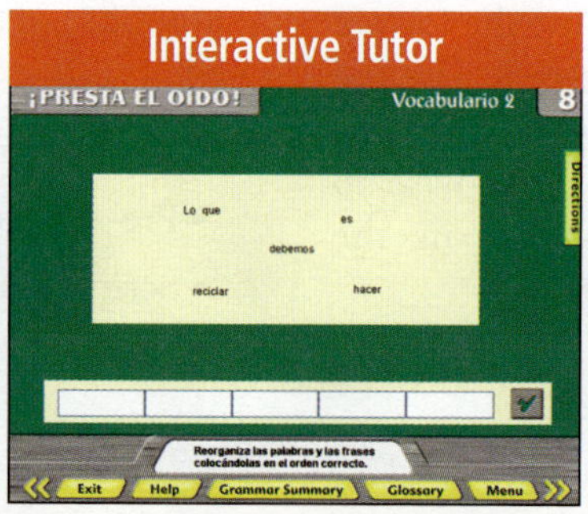


**PuzzlePro**

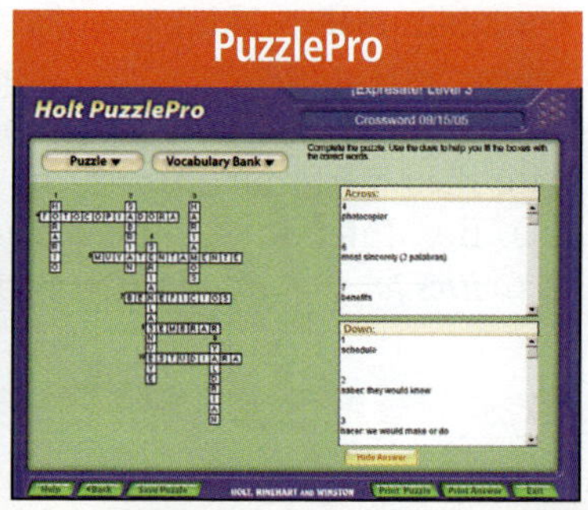

# Prepárate para el examen

## Repaso de Vocabulario 1

### Saying what you can and cannot do

| | |
|---|---|
| a la vez | *at the same time* |
| los adelantos | *advances* |
| la agenda electrónica | *electronic planner* |
| el (la) auxiliar administrativo(a)/médico(a)/de laboratorio | *administrative/medical/laboratory assistant* |
| cambiar | *to change* |
| competente | *competent* |
| el contestador automático | *answering machine* |
| decidirse a + *infinitive* | *to decide to* |
| la desventaja | *disadvantage* |
| empeorar | *to make worse* |
| enseguida | *right away* |
| en un santiamén | *instantly* |
| Eso me resulta fácil/bastante difícil. | *That's easy/pretty difficult for me.* |
| Está fuera de/a mi alcance. | *It's outside/within my reach.* |
| facilitar | *to facilitate* |
| la fotocopiadora | *photocopier* |
| el hombre/la mujer de negocios | *businessman/businesswoman* |
| hoy (en) día | *these days* |
| inmediatamente | *immediately* |
| Lo puedo hacer. | *I can do it.* |
| Me cuesta trabajo (hacer)... | *It takes a lot of work for me (to do) . . .* |
| mejorar | *to improve* |
| No me es nada difícil. | *It's not hard for me at all.* |
| el robot | *robot* |
| sembrar | *to plant* |
| Soy capaz de (hacer)... | *I am capable of (doing) . . .* |
| tratar de + *infinitive* | *to try to* |
| el talento | *talent* |
| la tecnología | *technology* |
| utilizar | *to utilize* |
| la ventaja | *advantage* |
| la vida diaria | *daily life* |
| el (la) voluntario(a) | *volunteer* |

### Talking about what you do and do not understand

| | |
|---|---|
| Está más claro ahora. | *It's clearer now.* |
| Hay algo que se me escapa. | *There's something I can't quite grasp.* |
| No logro entender... | *I can't seem to understand . . .* |
| No me cabe en la cabeza. | *I don't get it.* |
| ¡Vaya! Por fin capto la idea. | *Aha! I finally get the idea.* |
| ¡Ya caigo! | *I get it!* |

## Repaso de Vocabulario 2

### Writing a formal letter

| | |
|---|---|
| actualizar | *to update* |
| el ambiente de trabajo | *work environment* |
| los beneficios | *benefits* |
| la carrera | *career* |
| los compañeros de trabajo | *colleagues* |
| conseguir | *to obtain* |
| el currículum (vitae) | *resumé* |
| dirigir | *to direct* |
| donar tiempo a una causa | *to donate time to a cause* |
| el (la) empleado(a) | *employee* |
| el empleo a tiempo completo/medio tiempo | *full-time/part-time job* |
| la empresa | *company* |
| la entrevista | *interview* |
| Muy estimado(a) Sr./Sra./Srta.: | *Dear Sir/Madam/Miss:* |
| el (la) gerente | *manager* |
| el horario | *schedule* |
| el jefe, la jefa | *boss* |
| Le/Les adjunto un(a)... | *I'm enclosing a . . .* |
| Muy atentamente, | *Most sincerely,* |
| Por medio de la presente... | *The purpose of this letter is . . .* |
| el puesto (de trabajo) | *position (for work)* |
| Reciba un cordial saludo, | *Kind regards,* |
| requerir (ie) | *to require* |
| los requisitos | *requirements* |
| el salario | *salary* |
| el seguro (médico) | *(medical) insurance* |
| solicitar | *to apply, to ask for* |
| la solicitud | *application* |
| supervisar | *to supervise* |

### Talking about your plans

| | |
|---|---|
| Me gustaría ser un(a)... | *I would like to be a . . .* |
| Me interesaría estudiar para ser un(a)... | *I would be interested in studying to be a . . .* |
| ¿Qué te gustaría hacer? | *What would you like to do?* |
| Si pudiera, iría a... a estudiar.... | *If I could, I would go to . . . to study . . .* |
| Si tuvieras la oportunidad, ¿adónde irías? | *If you had the chance, where would you go?* |
| Siempre he querido ser un(a)... | *I have always wanted to be a . . .* |



## Vocabulary Review

For more practice with the vocabulary in this chapter, see the *Interactive Tutor* or the *Cuaderno de vocabulario y gramática.*

## Online Edition

Students might use the online textbook to hear the **Vocabulario** items.

## Game

**El crucigrama** Students will need at least two sheets of graph paper each. Have each student create a crossword puzzle for a classmate to solve. They should fit about twenty vocabulary words or phrases into the grid going across and down. The words should be numbered and a clue in both English and Spanish should be given for each word. Definitions, equivalent words, fill-in-the-blank sentences, or other clues can be used. Have each student create the final puzzle on another sheet of graph paper with just the numbers, blank squares, and clues. The games are then exchanged and solved by other students. 1.2

### Online Edition

### Transparency: Vocabulario

### Transparency: Situación

## Assess

**Assessment Program**

**Examen: Capítulo 8,** pp. 305–310

Audio CD 8, Tr. 17–18

**Examen oral: Capítulo 8,** p. 316

Alternative Assessment, pp. 380, 392, 404

**Online Assessment**

**my.hrw.com**

**Test Generator**

**Assess** **Differentiated Instruction** See the Differentiated Instruction CD-ROM.

## Resources

**Planning:**

Lesson Planner, pp. 127, 288–289

One-Stop Planner

**Presentation:**

Teaching Transparencies
Fine Art, Chapter 8

**Practice:**

Cuaderno de actividades, pp. 79–80

Lab Book, pp. 8, 41–44

Audio CD 8, Tr. 14

### 1 Script

1. —Siempre está trabajando como voluntaria. Es una persona muy generosa y este trabajo la hace feliz.
—Sí, ha ayudado a los animales y a la gente en los hospitales.
—Sería perfecto si consiguiera un empleo a medio tiempo para que pudiera donar tiempo a una causa.
2. —Está loca por la tecnología. Ha creado sus propios juegos de computadora.
—Le resulta fácil programar en la computadora. Estoy impresionada porque yo no entiendo ni jota de computadoras.
—Si tuviera el tiempo, podría empezar su propio negocio por Internet.
3. —¿Sigue buscando trabajo Fernando?
—Fíjate que consiguió un empleo a medio tiempo. Es cocinero en un restaurante cerca de su casa.
4. —¿Supiste que Mario ya encontró un empleo a tiempo completo?
—No, no lo sabía. ¿A qué se dedica?
—Trabaja como carpintero y según tengo entendido, la empresa le da muchos beneficios.

### 2 Answers

1. directora del departamento de español
2. necesita 5 años de experiencia y quieren que haya vivido en un país hispanohablante; no
3. sí
4. auxiliar de dirección
5. sí; porque dice que le parece que sería una auxiliar excelente

# Repaso cumulativo

# Integración
## capítulos 1–8

CD 8, Tr. 14

**1** Escucha las conversaciones y determina de quién hablan. 1.2
1. b 2. d 3. c 4. a

A

B

C

D

1.2

**2** Mónica Corrales le mandó una carta de solicitud a un colegio y recibió esta respuesta. Lee la respuesta y contesta las preguntas.

**COLEGIO CENTRAL**

**Estimada Srta. Corrales:**

**Muchas gracias por su carta de solicitud. Desafortunadamente, Ud. no cumple con los requisitos para el puesto de directora del departamento de español. Buscamos a alguien con por lo menos cinco años de experiencia y que además haya vivido en un país hispanohablante.**

**De todos modos, nos gustaría invitarla a una entrevista para hablar del puesto de auxiliar de dirección. El puesto es a medio tiempo y consiste en dar clases de conversación a los estudiantes dos veces a la semana. Además, tendría la oportunidad de dirigir el programa de intercambio que tenemos en Ecuador.**

**Es evidente que Ud. conoce muy bien el idioma y me parece que sería una auxiliar excelente.**

**Reciba un cordial saludo de,**
**Manolo Pérez**
**Director**

1. ¿Cuál es el puesto que solicitó Mónica?
2. ¿Cuáles son los requisitos del puesto? ¿Cumple Mónica con los requisitos?
3. ¿Al director le interesa hablar con Mónica?
4. ¿Cuál es el puesto que el director le menciona a Mónica?
5. ¿Crees que el director le daría este puesto a Mónica si a ella le interesara? ¿Por qué?

## Culture Project

Have students research the main industries of Peru. Ask them to find statistics on the labor force, unemployment, income, imports, and exports. What percentage of the population speaks English? Are there job opportunities for bilingual workers? Encourage them to find out the average pay and requirements for a job in their field of interest. Ask them to prepare a presentation on their findings. You might want to extend the culture project by having students take notes during the class presentations on job opportunities in Peru. Have groups of three or four students compile their notes and create a company based on that information. Teams will then make a list of job positions they have open at their company and write ads for a newspaper listing the job requirements. 1.3, 2.2

Visit Holt Online
**go.hrw.com**
KEYWORD: EXP3 CH8
Cumulative Self-test

3 En grupos de cuatro, hablen de su futuro. ¿Qué carrera les interesaría? ¿Dónde les gustaría vivir? Si pudieran vivir en otro país, ¿dónde vivirían? Luego, cada estudiante le explicará a la clase los sueños de un miembro del grupo. 1.1, 1.3

4 Observa la pintura llamada "A woman at a fruit stall, Mollendo, Peru" de A.S. Forrest y escribe ocho oraciones sobre lo que ves. En tus oraciones debes contestar las siguientes preguntas: ¿Cómo es la vida diaria de esta persona? ¿La afecta a su vida la tecnología? Si pudieras hablar con ella, ¿qué le preguntarías? 1.3

***A woman at a fruit stall, Mollendo, Peru*** **de A. S. Forrest**

5 Piensa en el lugar donde trabaja alguien de tu familia. Escribe un párrafo sobre el ambiente de trabajo allí, qué hacen los empleados y qué tecnología usan. 1.3

6 **Situación** Imagina que tú y tus compañeros son profesores del colegio. Hablen de los problemas que ven y propongan soluciones. Decidan qué harían si tuvieran suficiente dinero y el apoyo del director. Hablen de cómo mejorarían el colegio para los estudiantes y también cómo mejorarían el ambiente de trabajo para los profesores. 1.1, 1.3

## Fine Art Connection

Tell students that this painting, "A woman at fruit stall, Mollendo, Peru" is an illustration by A.S. Forrest for a book. Forrest illustrated a number of works, mainly books about foreign countries including *The West Indies, Through Portugal,* and *Morocco.* He also illustrated the 1934 edition of *Westward Ho!* He both wrote and illustrated the books *Pictures for Little Englanders, A Tour through Old Provence,* and *A Tour through South America.*

### Analyzing

Have students talk about the woman in the painting. What is she doing? What do they notice about the way she is dressed? In what kind of story do they think they might find such an illustration? 3.1

### Extension

Have students find out where in Peru the town of Mollendo is located. Ask them to prepare a short report about the town. Have students share their reports with the class. 1.3

## ACTFL Performance Standards

The activities in Chapter 8 target the different communicative modes as described in the Standards.

| | | |
|---|---|---|
| **Interpersonal** | Two-way communication using receptive skills and productive skills | **Comunicación (SE),** pp. 323, 325, 327, 329, 331, 337, 339, 341, 343, 345<br>**Comunicación (TE),** pp. 323, 325, 329, 331, 337, 339, 341, 343, 347<br>**Conversación,** p. 355<br>**Situación,** p. 359 |
| **Interpretive** | One-way communication using receptive skills | **Comunicación (SE),** pp. 323, 325, 327, 329, 345<br>**Novela en video**, pp. 346–347<br>**Leamos,** pp. 350–352<br>**Conversación,** p. 355 |
| **Presentational** | One-way communication using productive skills | **Comunicación (SE),** pp. 331, 337, 339, 341, 343<br>**Comunicación (TE),** pp. 327, 339, 345<br>**Taller del escritor,** p. 353 |

**Resources**

**Planning:**
Lesson Planner, p. xv
One-Stop Planner

**Presentation:**
Teaching Transparencies **Mapa 3**
Video Program, Videocassette 5
DVD Program
**GeoVisión**

**Practice:**
Video Guide, pp. 57–58
Lab Book, pp. 9, 83
Interactive Tutor, Disc 2

**VIDEO OPTIONS**
- **VideoCultura**
- **VideoNovela**
- **Variedades**
- **GramaVisión**

GeoVisión

Capítulos 9 y 10

# Geocultura
## El Cono Sur

▲ **El desierto de Atacama,** en el norte de Chile, es conocido como uno de los lugares más secos del mundo. Hay partes en las que nunca ha llovido. Artefactos arqueológicos, preservados por el clima árido, prueban que el desierto sostuvo varias civilizaciones durante miles de años. Actualmente está poblado por los trabajadores de las minas de plata, oro, hierro y cobre. 3

► **Con cerca de 6.000 kilómetros de costa,** ningún lugar de Chile está lejos del mar. Gracias a las muchas especies de peces en la costa y a los criadores de salmón, Chile es uno de los mayores exportadores de pescado en el mundo. Valparaíso es uno de los mayores puertos de Chile. 2

### Almanaque

**Países, poblaciones y capitales del Cono Sur**
Chile, 15.980.912 (Santiago)
Argentina, 39.537.943 (Buenos Aires)
Uruguay, 3.415.920 (Montevideo)
Paraguay, 6.347.884 (Asunción)

**Idioma principal**
español

**Industrias importantes**
agricultura, ganadería, pesca, minería

▼ **Músicos de la tuna universitaria de la Universidad de Concepción,** en Concepción, Chile, cantan y tocan la pandera, la guitarra y el laúd durante uno de sus viajes por su país. La tradición de las tunas universitarias se remonta hasta el siglo XIII. 1

### ¿Sabías que...?
**Chile es tan largo de norte a sur que si fuera parte de Norteamérica, se extendería desde el sur de Alaska hasta el sur de México.**

## Background Information

### History
The Southern cone region was the last of the South American territories to be claimed by Spain. Present day Argentina, Bolivia, and Paraguay were part of the territory that was never fully conquered by the Spanish due to the fierce resistance of the Araucano Indians. Between 1809 and 1811, these countries declared their independence from Spain. With the help of Bernardo O'Higgins, José de San Martín, and their armies, the newly formed republics won their independence.

### Geography
**La cordillera de los Andes** forms a natural border between Chile and Argentina. The snow-capped peaks of the Andes have isolated the two countries throughout history.

**La Patagonia** in Argentina covers a large section of the southern interior. There are flat grasslands in northern Patagonia and glaciers in the south.

**El Río de la Plata** is a large river estuary formed by the convergence of the Paraná and Uruguay rivers. It forms the border between Argentina and Uruguay. It is one of the most urbanized areas of South America.

### Pre-AP Practice

**AP Benchmark:** Recognize cultural elements implicit in oral and written texts.

**Focus:** Cultural Practices (**la naturaleza**)
- SE, p. 361, **El cerro Aconcagua**
- SE, p. 361, **El Gran Chaco**
- TE, p. 361, Connections

# El Cono Sur

▲ La mayoría de **la población del Cono Sur** se halla en las grandes ciudades. En Buenos Aires, la capital de Argentina, reside más del 30% de la población del país. Con avenidas anchas, monumentos históricos, museos y parques, Buenos Aires es una ciudad moderna y cosmopolita.

▶ Dos científicos argentinos **Bernardo Alberto Houssay** y **Luis Federico Leloir** han recibido un premio Nobel. Houssay ganó el premio de Fisiología y Medicina en 1947. Leloir en 1970 fue el ganador del premio Nobel de Química.

▶ **Montevideo,** la capital de Uruguay, está ubicado en la embocadura del Río de la Plata. El viaje en barca de Buenos Aires a Montevideo tarda cerca de tres horas.

▼ **El Gran Chaco** es una gran llanura que cubre el 60% de Paraguay, partes del norte de Argentina y áreas de Brasil y Bolivia. Los veranos son muy calientes pero después de las lluvias las llanuras se convierten en un paraíso para los pájaros. 4

▼ **El cerro Aconcagua,** en la cordillera de los Andes en Argentina, es la montaña más alta de las Américas. Mide 6.960 metros y constituye un desafío aun para los alpinistas más expertos. 5

## Atlas
### INTERACTIVO MUNDIAL

Have students use the interactive atlas at **go.hrw.com**.

**Map Activities**

1. Have students look at the map of South America and name the countries in the Southern cone. **(Argentina, Chile, Paraguay, Uruguay)**
2. Ask students to find and name all countries that border Argentina. **(Bolivia, Brasil, Chile, Paraguay, Uruguay)**
3. Have students locate the largest river in the region on the map and name it. **(Paraná)**

3.1

## Connections

### Science Link

The **Gran Chaco** region of Paraguay has great potential for eco-tourism. Adventurous tourists enjoy the nearly untouched wilderness. The **Gran Chaco** covers the majority of the country and is home to many species of hardwood trees and medicinal plants. It is also home to many birds like the South American ostrich, and to jaguars, ocelots, pumas, and brown wolves. Ask students their opinions on why it would be important to conserve a place like this. Have students research other popular eco-tourism destinations in the Southern cone region.

3.1

## ¿Sabías que... ?

Students might be interested in knowing the following facts about the Southern cone region.

- Chile is the most European country in South America. Ninety-five percent of the population is of European and mestizo descent.
- Italians are the largest immigrant group in Argentina.
- The **Gran Chaco** covers approximately 280,000 square miles (725,000km$^2$) in four different countries.

## Preguntas 1.2, 3.1

1. **¿Quiénes viven en el desierto de Atacama actualmente?** (los trabajadores de las minas)
2. **¿Chile es uno de los mayores exportadores de qué producto?** (el pescado)
3. **¿Hasta qué siglo se remonta la tradición de la tuna universitaria?** (el siglo XIII)
4. **¿Qué porcentaje de la población argentina vive en Buenos Aires?** (el 30%)
5. **¿Cuánto se tarda en viajar desde Buenos Aires a Montevideo en barco?** (tres horas)
6. **¿Dónde está el Gran Chaco?** (en Bolivia, Paraguay, Brasil y Argentina)

## Cultures

### Practices and Perspectives

**La semana criolla** in Uruguay is the week in which **gaucho** culture is celebrated. **Gauchos,** or cowboys, from all over the country come to Montevideo for this occasion. The activities include livestock shows and **jineteadas,** similar to bronco-busting competitions. Traditional **gaucho** dishes, folk music, and dance are also part of the festivities. Typical **gaucho** dress is worn for the competitions. The dress consists of riding pants called **bombachas,** a white shirt, a handkerchief worn around the neck, riding boots, and a wide belt called a **rastra.** The **payada** competitions are also a part of the celebration. Two singers compete by improvising verses in rhyme to the music of a guitar. The tradition began with the first **gauchos.** Ask students if they know of a similar celebration in their community. What is the history behind the celebration?

2.1, 4.2

### Answers

**Siglo XV:** Es difícil conquistar un pueblo sin una autoridad central.
**1541:** Answers will vary.
**1813–1818:** Answers will vary.
**1829–1852:** Tenían poder porque tenían muchos terrenos y dinero. Contrataban pequeños ejércitos para defender sus terrenos.
**1946–1974:** Answers will vary.
**1973–1985:** Chile, Cuba, La República Dominicana, Nicaragua
**1973–1990:** Ricardo Lagos
**1982:** Las Islas Malvinas pertenecen a Gran Bretaña.

# La historia del Cono Sur

1450 · 1500 · 1800 · 1850

1.3, 3.1 **Siglo XV**
**Los araucanos, o mapuches,** organizados en clanes familiares descentralizados, poblaron gran parte de Chile antes de la llegada de los incas y, más tarde, los españoles. Pararon la conquista de los incas y resistieron la dominación hispánica hasta 1883. **¿Cómo crees que la organización descentralizada les ayudó a resistir la colonización?**

**1541**
En 1541 el conquistador **Pedro de Valdivia** fundó la ciudad de Santiago. Doce años después Valdivia murió en la guerra contra los araucanos. Chile, por su falta de grandes vetas de oro o plata, fue de poco interés para el gobierno español. **¿Crees que era una ventaja o una desventaja para el desarrollo de Chile, el no tener riquezas de oro o plata?** 1.3, 3.1 **¿Por qué?**

© The Granger Collection

1.3, 3.1 **1813–1818**
**Chile** ya había declarado su independencia, cuando en 1813 el virrey de Perú invadió a Chile para recuperar la colonia para España. En 1814, el líder revolucionario de Chile, **Bernardo O'Higgins,** huyó a Argentina para juntarse con **José de San Martín,** hoy conocido como el libertador de Chile, Argentina y Perú. O'Higgins y San Martín cruzaron los Andes a Chile en 1817 y ayudaron a lograr la independencia de Chile en 1818. **¿Cómo se comparan los hechos de O'Higgins y San Martín con los de algunos líderes estadounidenses?**

1.3, 3.1 **1829–1852**
**En Argentina** la lucha por el poder en las provincias dominó la política durante el siglo XIX. Los caudillos, poderosos terratenientes, controlaban regiones enteras llamadas republiquetas. En 1829 el **caudillo** más famoso, **Juan Manuel de Rosas,** fue elegido gobernador de Buenos Aires y en 1835 logró el control del resto del país. La dictadura de Rosas duró hasta 1852. **¿Por qué crees que tenían los caudillos tanto poder?**

## Core Instruction

### TEACHING LA HISTORIA

1. Have students look at the photographs and illustrations. Ask volunteers to describe what they see in the photos. **(2 min.)**
2. Have students read the captions individually or as a group. Help students with any unfamiliar vocabulary. **(8 min.)**
3. Call on volunteers to read the questions at the end of each caption. **(5 min.)**
4. Work with students to answer the questions for each caption as a class. **(10 min.)**

## ¿Sabías que...?

El Cono Sur, especialmente sus capitales cosmopolitas, se considera la parte más europea de Sudamérica debido a la extensa inmigración de italianos, españoles, alemanes y otros europeos durante los siglos XIX y XX.

Visit Holt Online
go.hrw.com
KEYWORD: EXP3 CH9
Photo Tour

1900 | 1950 | 2000

3.1 **1946–1974**
En Argentina **Juan Perón** triunfó en las elecciones presidenciales de 1946, 1951 y 1973. Su doctrina del «Justicialismo» concedió beneficios sociales a la clase obrera y marcó el curso de la industrialización argentina. Perón se casó con Eva Duarte, conocida como **Evita,** una actriz, quien se hizo famosa por ser la voz del público en muchos asuntos sociales. **Investiga qué es lo que hizo Evita por el pueblo argentino.**

**1982** 3.1
En 1982, el dictador argentino Leopoldo Galtieri montó una campaña para apoderarse de las **Islas Malvinas,** que habían pertenecido a Gran Bretaña desde 1833. **La guerra entre Argentina y Gran Bretaña** sólo duró 74 días y ocasionó el fin del gobierno militar en Argentina. Argentina volvió a celebrar elecciones democráticas en 1983. **Investiga a qué país pertenecen hoy las Islas Malvinas.**

3.1 **1973–1985**
**En Uruguay,** después de años de prosperidad gracias a la exportación de lana y carne, **una crisis económica** causó que un gobierno militar asumiera el poder en 1973. En 1985 un gobierno civil se estableció. **Investiga qué otros países del mundo hispano tuvieron una dictadura militar en el siglo XX.**

**1973–1990** 3.1
En 1973 las fuerzas militares chilenas atacaron el Palacio de la Moneda en Santiago para derrocar al presidente **Salvador Allende.** Allende murió en el asalto y el **General Augusto Pinochet** tomó el poder. Su dictadura duró hasta 1990, cuando cedió la presidencia. **Investiga quién es el presidente de Chile hoy.**

## Cultures

### Practices and Perspectives

Sports fans in Argentina are passionate about soccer. Argentina has been successful in the World Cup competitions, winning the championship in 1978 and 1986. The most famous soccer player in Argentina was Diego Maradona. Have students research the soccer tradition in Latin America and discuss the differences and similarities with soccer in the U.S. Have volunteers name the Latin American soccer players they know.
2.1, 4.2

## ¿Comprendes?

You can use the following questions to check students' comprehension of the **Geocultura.**

1. **¿Cómo estaban organizados los araucanos? (en clanes familiares descentralizados)**
2. **¿Por qué fue Chile de poco interés para el gobierno español? (por la falta de oro y plata)**
3. **¿Quiénes ayudaron a lograr la independencia de Chile? (Bernardo O'Higgins y José de San Martín)**
4. **¿Quiénes eran los caudillos? (poderosos terratenientes que controlaban territorios grandes)**
5. **¿Qué era Evita antes de casarse con Juan Perón? (Era actriz.)**
6. **¿Cuánto tiempo duró la guerra entre Argentina y Gran Bretaña? (72 días)** 1.2, 3.1

## Interdisciplinary Links

### La historia

**History Link** **El Palacio de la Moneda** was designed by Italian architect Joaquín Toesca y Ricci to house Chile's national mint. Construction began in 1784 and the palace was officially opened in 1805. It was the largest building erected by the Spanish government in the 18th century. In 1922, all mint operations were moved and the entire palace was used for government ministries and the official residence. Have students investigate the history of the White House and compare it with that of **El Palacio de la Moneda.** 3.1

### La naturaleza

**Science Link** The Andes are located directly above where the Nazca and South American plates come together. An earthquake of 6.9 hit the north central region of Chile in 2003 and was felt as far away as Buenos Aires. In 1997 an earthquake in Ovalle, Chile, killed a dozen people, injured 300, and destroyed 10,000 homes. Have students investigate other large earthquakes in the Southern cone region. Ask students if they know of an area in the U.S. that is prone to earthquakes or other natural disasters and compare the two regions. 3.1

## Comparisons

### Comparing and Contrasting

Pollution is a problem in Santiago de Chile because of the number of cars and traffic jams in downtown streets. As a way to reduce the traffic jams and pollution, large arteries in downtown Santiago switch directions for the morning or afternoon commutes. For example, a large avenue that usually has two directions of traffic would be switched to just one direction during hours of heavy congestion. Ask students what they think about measures like these to fight pollution in cities. Ask students to investigate what has been done in their communities to reduce traffic and automobile pollution. How do these measures compare with pollution-reduction measures in Chile?

2.1, 4.2

### Answers

**Siglo 1000–1400:** Los geoglifos se hicieron con piedras y con el raspado de tierra.
**Siglo XVI–presente:** Answers will vary.
**1865:** Answers will vary.
**1902:** Se respetan las formas naturales del cuerpo humano y los objetos en la obra.
**Siglo XX:** Roberto Matta es de Chile.
**1968:** Answers will vary.
**1995:** Es una forma espontánea de arte.

# El arte del Cono Sur

ÉPOCA PRECOLOMBINA — 1500 — 1800 — 1850

1.2 **1000–1400**
**Los geoglifos del Cerro Unitas,** al norte de la ciudad de Iquique, Chile, son un conjunto de 21 figuras hechas mediante la acumulación de piedras y el raspado del terreno. *El Gigante de Atacama* mide 86 metros de altura y fue elaborado entre los años 1000 y 1400 d.C. **¿Cómo fueron creados los geoglifos del Cerro Unitas?**

3.1 **1858**
**La Catedral Basílica de Salta,** Argentina, se construyó en 1858. La fachada es de estilo italiano clásico con columnas y arcos. **Busca la ciudad de Salta en un mapa de Argentina.**

1.3 **Siglo XVI–presente**
Apropiándose de las técnicas traídas por los españoles, **la cultura mapuche** comenzó a desarrollar su fina artesanía de plata en el siglo XVI. Los mapuches continúan elaborando y luciendo orgullosamente sus joyas. **¿Has visto joyas indígenas donde vives tú? ¿De qué material son?**

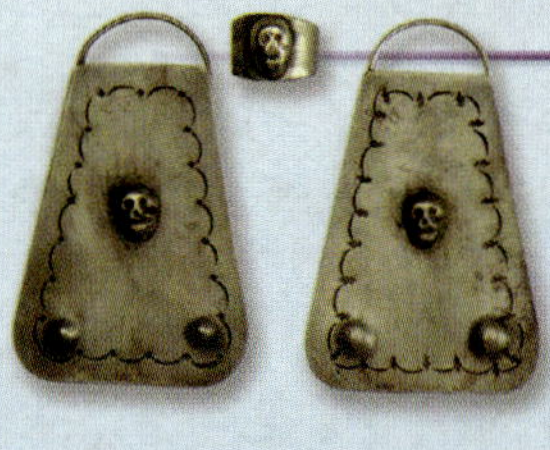

1.3 **1865**
Uno de los primeros artistas de Argentina fue el soldado **Cándido López** (1840–1902), quien participó en la guerra de Paraguay (1864–1870). A pesar de perder su brazo derecho en la guerra, López aprendió a pintar con su brazo izquierdo y dejó una representación visual de más de 50 óleos de escenas de guerra. **¿Por qué crees que López pintó imágenes de la guerra?**

## Core Instruction

### TEACHING EL ARTE

1. Have students look at the geoglyphs and describe to the class the forms they see. **(2 min.)**
2. Point out the Cándido López painting. Call on volunteers to describe what the soldiers are doing. **(4 min.)**
3. Ask students to compare the paintings on p. 365. Have groups describe how the paintings are different or which they like best. **(5 min.)**
4. Read the first caption to the class. Call on volunteers to read the remaining captions. **(5 min.)**
5. Read the questions following each caption. As a class, have students answer the questions. **(10 min.)**

**¿Sabías que...?**
Pedro Lira organizó clases especiales de anatomía para que los artistas entendieran mejor el cuerpo humano.

Visit Holt Online
**go.hrw.com**
KEYWORD: EXP3 CH9
Photo Tour

1900 — 1950 — 2000

**1902** 1.3, 3.1
**Pedro Lira** (1845–1912) es considerado el primer gran maestro del arte chileno. Se dedicó exclusivamente al arte, organizando exposiciones y fundando la Unión Artística en 1884. Su cuadro *El niño enfermo* (1902) pertenece a la etapa naturalista del pintor. **¿Por qué crees que el estilo de este cuadro se llama «naturalismo»?**

**1995** 1.3, 3.1
**Carlos Federico Reyes** (nacido en 1909), artista paraguayo, recrea en sus retratos de estilo naïf escenas de su niñez en las campiñas de Bejarano, Asunción. Un ejemplo es *La Primera Comunión*. **¿Qué crees que significa «estilo naïf»?**

3.1 **Siglo XX**
Uno de los artistas predominantes del movimiento surrealista, **Roberto Matta** (1911–2002) contribuyó mucho al desarrollo del arte universal contemporáneo. **Investiga de qué país es Matta.**

**1968** 1.3, 3.1
El pintor chileno **Mario Toral** (1934–) es conocido por su estilo abstracto. Su obra *Torre de Babel II* (1968) muestra formas abstractas y colores vivos. Se encuentra en el Museo Nacional de Bellas Artes de Santiago, Chile. **En tu opinión, ¿qué significa «abstracto» en cuanto a la pintura?**

## Cultures

### Products and Perspectives

**Máscaras Chané** are made by the indigenous **chané** people of Argentina for use in the **carnaval** celebrations. The masks are made of wood and are painted to look like animals or other creatures. The wood **chané** masks are attracting more attention from art fans in Argentina for their indigenous motifs. Have students name other places and occasions where masks are used and why. What does the mask represent in these contexts? 2.2

### ¿Comprendes?

You can use the following questions to check students' comprehension of the **Geocultura.**

1. **¿De dónde vienen las técnicas que usan los mapuche para elaborar sus joyas? (de España)**
2. **¿Qué tipo de escenas pintó Cándido López? (Pintó escenas de guerra.)**
3. **¿En qué año se fundó la Unión Artística en Chile? (en 1884)**
4. **¿Qué estilo usa Mario Toral en sus obras? (el abstracto)**
5. **¿Qué refleja Carlos Federico Reyes en sus obras? (su niñez)**

1.2, 3.1

## Interdisciplinary Links

### La música

**Music Link** The **gaucho** is an important cultural icon in the Southern cone region. **Gauchos** were skilled in handling horses and livestock and were also known for their music. **Gaucho** songs are about their work and their solitary lives. The songs were accompanied by a guitar and the verses were often improvised. Have students compare the cultural status of the cowboy in the U.S. with the South American **gaucho.** How are they similar? Did the American cowboy also play music? How does music help to preserve traditions? 2.1, 4.2

### La historia

**Art link** The War of the Triple Alliance (1864–1870) was the bloodiest war in South American history. Paraguayan dictator Francisco López and his army fought against Argentine, Brazilian, and Uruguayan forces. Cándido López, an Argentine self-taught painter and a soldier in the conflict, created more than 30 paintings capturing scenes from the war. Have students find some of Lopez's works on the Internet and ask them how they think his paintings show what the war was like. 3.1

## Assess

**Assessment Program**
**Prueba: Geocultura,** pp. 175–176, 195–196

**Online Assessment**
**my.hrw.com**

**Test Generator**

**Assess Differentiated Assesment** See the Differentiated Assessment CD-ROM.

Capítulo 9

# Planning Guide

## Huellas del pasado

| Chapter Section | | Print Resources |
|---|---|---|
| **Geocultura**<br>• **El Cono Sur** | pp. 360–365 | Video Guide, pp. 57–58/Lab Book, p. 83 |
| **Vocabulario 1**<br>• Legends and stories<br>**Gramática 1**<br>• Repaso: Preterite and imperfect in storytelling<br>• Repaso: Preterite and imperfect contrasted<br>• Repaso: **Por** and **para** | pp. 368–373<br><br>pp. 374–379 | Vocabulario 9.1, 9.2; Bell Work 9.1, 9.2, 9.3, 9.4<br>Cuaderno de vocabulario y gramática, pp. 97–102<br>Cuaderno de actividades, pp. 81–83<br>Activities for Communication, pp. 33–34<br>Grammar Tutor for Students of Spanish, pp. 159–162 |
| **Cultura: Comparaciones**<br>**Cultura: Comunidad** | p. 380<br>p. 381 | Video Guide, pp. 60–61/Lab Book, p. 84 |
| **Vocabulario 2**<br>• Historic events<br>**Gramática 2**<br>• Repaso: Uses of subjunctive<br>• Sequence of tenses<br>• More on sequence of tenses | pp. 382–387<br><br>pp. 388–393 | Vocabulario 9.3, 9.4; Bell Work 9.5, 9.6, 9.7, 9.8<br>Cuaderno de vocabulario y gramática, pp. 103–108<br>Cuaderno de actividades, pp. 85–87<br>Activities for Communication, pp. 35–36<br>Grammar Tutor for Students of Spanish, pp. 163–164 |
| **Novela en video**<br>**Lectura informativa**<br>• **Un territorio con historia**<br>**Leamos**<br>• **El Caleuche**<br>**Escribamos**<br>• **Una buena descripción** | pp. 394–395<br>pp. 396–397<br><br>pp. 398–400<br><br>p. 401 | Cuaderno de actividades, p. 88<br>Reading Strategies and Skills Handbook<br>Interactive Advanced Reader<br>Video Guide, pp. 62–64/Lab Book, pp. 85–86 |
| **Prepárate para el examen**<br>• **Repaso de vocabulario y gramática** | pp. 402–405 | Picture Sequences, **Situación,** Ch. 9<br>Activities for Communication, pp. 51, 71–72 |
| **Integración**<br>• **Repaso cumulativo** | pp. 406–407 | Fine Art, Ch. 9<br>Cuaderno de actividades, pp. 89–90<br>Reading Strategies and Skills Handbook<br>Interactive Advanced Reader |

For correlations to national standards, see point-of-use references throughout the chapter.

Visit Holt Online
**go.hrw.com**
KEYWORD: EXP3 CH9
Online Edition

## Pacing Suggestions

| | Essential | Recommended | Optional |
|---|---|---|---|
| **Vocabulario 1**<br>• Legends and stories<br>• **Nota cultural** | ✔ | | |
| **Gramática 1**<br>• **Repaso:** Preterite and imperfect in storytelling<br>• **Repaso:** Preterite and imperfect contrasted<br>• **Repaso: Por** and **para**<br>• **Nota cultural** | ✔ | | |
| **Cultura: Comparaciones** | | ✔ | |
| **Cultura: Comunidad** | | | ✔ |
| **Vocabulario 2**<br>• Historic events<br>• **Nota cultural** | ✔ | | |
| **Gramática 2**<br>• **Repaso:** Uses of subjunctive<br>• Sequence of tenses<br>• More on sequence of tenses<br>• **Nota cultural** | ✔ | | |
| **Novela en video**<br>• Episodio 9: **Clara perspectiva** | | ✔ | |
| **Lectura informativa**<br>• **Un territorio con historia** | | | ✔ |
| **Leamos**<br>• **El Caleuche**<br>**Escribamos**<br>• **Una buena descripción** | | ✔ | |
| **Prepárate para el examen** | | ✔ | |
| **Integración** | | | ✔ |

## Technology Resources

### ¡Exprésate! Online
- Student Edition with multi-media
- SoundBooth recording tool
- Interactive activities with feedback
- Self-tests with feedback
- Cuaderno de actividades (interactive workbook)
- Cuaderno de vocabulario y gramática (interactive workbook)
- Live Ink™ Reading Help
- Holt Online Assessment

### DVD Tutor, Disc 2
- GeoVisión
- GramaVisión
- VideoNovela
- Cultura
- Variedades

### Interactive Tutor
- Interactive practice games
- Writing and recording workshops

### Audio Program
- Textbook listening activities
- Assessment listening activities
- Songs

### One-Stop Planner
- Complete media and print resources
- ExamView® Pro Test Generator
- Holt Calendar Planner

### PuzzlePro
- Customizable word games

## Assessment

**Geocultura**
**Vocabulario 1 / Gramática 1**
**Vocabulario 2 / Gramática 2**
**Leamos**
**Escribamos**
**Prepárate para el examen**

### Assessment Program

**Prueba: Geocultura,** pp. 175–176
**Pruebas,** pp. 161–162, 163–164, 165–166
**Pruebas,** pp. 167–168, 169–170, 171–172
**Prueba,** p. 173
**Prueba,** p. 174
**Examen: Capítulo 9,** pp. 317–324
**Examen oral: Capítulo 9,** p. 328
**Alternative Assessment,** pp. 381, 393, 405

### Online Assessment

**my.hrw.com**

### Test Generator

**ExamView® Pro Test Generator**

# Projects

## Huellas del pasado

### Un cuento de hadas

Groups of four to five students create a puppet show of a legend or fairy tale. They use what they have learned about storytelling: setting the scene, moving the action along, and ending a story. Students then create puppets and perform for the class. Alternatively, you might have students make props and costumes and act out their story.

**SUGGESTED SEQUENCE**

1. Students decide on a legend or fairy tale. They write an outline of the story, breaking it down into scenes.
2. Assign students leadership roles: Organizer, Editor, Designer, Notetaker, and so on.
3. The group assigns an equal number of scenes to be written by each member. Scenes should be proofread by two other members.
4. The Editor and Notetaker compile the script. Other group members design the set, gather materials, and make their puppets and stage.
5. Groups rehearse and memorize their lines. Everyone should have approximately the same amount of speaking time.
6. The final script is turned in to you and the puppet show is performed for the class. You might have audience members review the performance. 1.3

### Partner Class Project

Have students work in pairs to analyze the content and format of two different Spanish-language travel websites about Argentina or Chile. Students should compare the format of each site and the topics that are highlighted in each. How well does each site present the history of the country and its current situation? How well does each convey the logistics of travel in the country (general safety, quality and cost of public transportation, restaurants)? How well does it cover the attractions? Have students prepare a short presentation for the class, comparing and contrasting the two websites. 1.3, 5.1

### e-community

**e-mail forum:**

Post the following questions on the classroom e-mail forum:

**¿Qué tipo de turismo prefieres: aventuras ecológicas, viajes culturales o una combinación? ¿Alguna vez has visitado un museo histó-rico (de histo-ria natural, industrial o cualquier otro tipo)? Si has visitado alguno, ¿qué te gustó más y por qué?**

All students will contribute to the list and then share the items. 1.3

### Grading the projects

Suggested point distribution (100 points total)

Group grade (written product) ............50

Individual grade (performance) ...............50

(5 points each for vocabulary, grammar, clarity, usage, and creativity, and 25 points for comprehensibility and natural speech)

### Game Bank

For game ideas, see pages T64–T67.

# Huellas del pasado

## El tango

The origins of the tango are as complicated as its dance steps. Music historians believe that it is derived from the music of African slaves and a combination of indigenous rhythms and early Spanish colonial music. The tango emerged in the mid-nineteenth century in the poorer neighborhoods of Buenos Aires; its moods and rhythms seem to reflect the character of the city's people, called **porteños.** The music's most characteristic sound comes from the **bandoneón,** an accordion-like instrument with buttons instead of keys. The dance itself is improvised: the man chooses the steps and timing, depending on the music, the partner, and the space. The woman, in turn, adds her own embellishments. Since this is done with a complex series of body signals, the tango is sometimes called a "conversation without words." Have students listen to tango music and describe the emotional tone (nostalgic, sad, passionate). With what other style of music would students compare the tango's feel and themes? (Some might see a parallel with country music or blues, which reflect the everyday concerns of people.) 2.1

## Receta

Rice was brought to Latin America by the Spanish and is grown in coastal regions. Latin Americans love rice, which has become a staple of their diet. Rice can be used as a main dish with beans or chicken, in soups and stews, and even in making drinks, such as **horchata.** One of the most popular dishes throughout Latin America is **arroz con leche.** It is a refreshing dessert that is served cold. You might have students make the following recipe as a class project or for extra credit.

### Arroz con leche

**para 5 personas**

- 1 taza de arroz
- 2 tazas de agua
- 7 tazas de leche
- cáscara rallada de limón
- 2 palitos de canela
- canela en polvo
- 2 tazas de azúcar
- 1/2 cucharadita de sal

Cocine el arroz en el agua y hiérvalo unos siete minutos hasta que se ablande un poco y hasta que el agua casi se haya evaporado. Agregue la leche, los palitos de canela y la cáscara de limón. Cocine durante unos cinco o seis minutos más, revolviendo con una cuchara de madera, hasta que el arroz esté blando. Agregue el azúcar y cocine todo 30 minutos más a fuego lento, revolviendo frecuentemente. Agregue la sal y cocine durante uno o dos minutos más. Retire la mezcla del fuego y póngala en un recipiente hondo. Espolvorée el arroz con leche con la canela en polvo y coloque el recipiente en el refrigerador. Se sirve frío en platitos individuales.

2.2, 3.1

# Listening Activity Scripts

## Huellas del pasado



### Vocabulario en acción 1

**1** p. 370, CD 9, Track 1

1. Él es el hijo del rey. Se enamora de una mujer bonita que está en poder de un malvado.
2. Él le da consejos al príncipe sobre cómo ganarle al malvado. Es muy inteligente y vale la pena seguir sus consejos.
3. Él tiene poderes mágicos y los puede usar para bien o para mal. Puede hacer que el príncipe se convierta en gato o puede hacer que desaparezca.
4. Él era amigo del príncipe. Pero un día decidió traicionar a su amigo y ayudar al malvado.
5. Ella tiene poder sobre todos. Está casada con el rey.
6. Esta persona creó el mundo pero no vive en la tierra. La gente de la tierra construye templos en su honor.

**Answers to Activity 1**

1. b 2. a 3. b 4. b 5. b 6. a

### Gramática en acción 1

**15** p. 377, CD 9, Track 2

En una leyenda sobre la Luna, se cuenta que el Sol y la Luna eran muy buenos amigos. Pero después de un tiempo, el Sol se enamoró de la Luna. Quería casarse con ella, pero ella era muy independiente y quería mantener su libertad. Pero no sabía qué decirle al Sol. Entonces le dijo que si el Sol encontrara un bonito vestido para ella, entonces ella se casaría con él. El Sol la miró bien para saber el tamaño correcto y fue a buscar el vestido. Regresó con un vestido de estrellas, pero la Luna se había puesto delgadita, y ya no le servía. Frustrado, el Sol se fue otra vez a buscar un vestido. Pero esta vez la Luna había engordado. Después de varios intentos, el Sol decidió que no podía encontrarle el vestido perfecto. Y a partir de entonces, la Luna vivió sola y fue feliz.

**Answers to Activity 15**

1. Eran muy buenos amigos.
2. El Sol se enamoró de la Luna.
3. Tenía miedo de perder su libertad.
4. Le pidió que buscara un vestido bonito.
5. No le servía ningún vestido porque ella siempre cambiaba de tamaño.
6. Decidió que no podía encontrarle el vestido perfecto.

### Vocabulario en acción 2

**21** p. 384, CD 9, Track 6

1. —¿Viste que el candidato del partido laboral ganó las elecciones para la presidencia?
   —Sí, ¡estoy tan feliz! ¿Y viste cómo la gente se regocijaba en la plaza?
2. —Vi en la televisión una reunión muy importante de líderes mundiales. ¿De qué se trata?
   —¿No te enteraste? Hoy acordaron la paz para poner fin al conflicto.
3. —Hoy se conmemora el Día de la Independencia de nuestro país.
   —Así es. Vamos a ver el monumento antes de que empiece la ceremonia.
4. —¿Te imaginas cómo era la vida hace tres siglos? La gente exploraba continentes y mares desconocidos. Ahora no hay ningún lugar que explorar.
   —No es cierto. Al contrario, hay muchos lugares. Hoy en día, los exploradores van desde el fondo del mar hasta el espacio para explorar nuevos mundos desconocidos.

**Answers to Activity 21**

1. D 2. A 3. B 4. C

### Gramática en acción 2

**34** pp. 390, CD 9, Track 7

1. Elena y Carmen dicen que quieren ver el campo de batalla.
2. Les dije que yo iría con ellas.
3. Han dicho que fue una batalla muy grande.
4. Las tropas pensaban que no iban a ganar la batalla.
5. Pues, yo diría que las tropas fueron muy valientes ese día.
6. Sugiero que vayamos a ver el campo de batalla ahora.

**Answers to Activity 34**

1. presente 2. futuro 3. pasado 4. pasado 5. pasado 6. presente

For Student Response Forms, see the *Lab Book,* pp. 45–48.

# Prepárate para el examen capítulo 9

**6** p. 403, CD 9, Track 10

1. Hace mucho tiempo, vivía una princesa triste y sola. Le gustaba jugar en el jardín del palacio.
2. El castillo de la princesa encantada es muy grande, con más de cien torres mágicas.
3. El rey poderoso castigará al malvado por haberlo traicionado en la guerra, y todos se van a regocijar.
4. Todos en el reino esperan que el príncipe se case con una princesa valiente y bonita.
5. Por causa de las acciones del hechicero, el castillo de la reina malvada desaparecerá para siempre, y todos vivirán felices después.
6. El rey fue un hombre poderoso, fuerte y muy querido por todos. Todos lamentaron su muerte.

**Answers to Activity 6**

1. pasado 2. presente 3. futuro 4. presente, futuro 5. futuro 6. pasado

# 50-Minute Lesson Plans

## Huellas del pasado

For more customized Lesson Plans, see the *Lesson Planner with Differentiated Instruction.*

### Day 1

**Objective**
*Setting the scene for a story*

**Core Instruction**
**Chapter Opener**, pp. 366–367 **10 min.**
- See Chapter Objectives and Using the Photo, p. 366.

**Vocabulario en acción 1,** pp. 368–373
- Have students do Bell Work, p. 368.
- See Teaching **Vocabulario,** p. 368. **10 min.**
- See Teaching **¡Exprésate!,** p. 368. **5 min.**
- Play Audio CD 9, Tr. 1 for Activity 1, p. 370. **10 min.**
- Have students do Activities 2–3, p. 370. **15 min.**

**Optional Resources**
- Advanced Learners, p. 369 ▲
- Multiple Intelligences, p. 369
- Heritage Speakers, p. 371 ■
- Slower Pace Learners, p. 371 ◆
- Multiple Intelligences, p. 371

**Homework Suggestions**
Cuaderno de vocabulario y gramática, pp. 97–99

1.2, 1.3, 2.1, 4.2

### Day 2

**Objective**
*Continuing and ending a story*

**Core Instruction**
**Vocabulario en acción 1,** pp. 368–373
- Have students do Activities 4–5, p. 371. **10 min.**
- See Teaching **¡Exprésate!,** p. 372. **15 min.**
- Have students do Activities 6–8, p. 373. **25 min.**

**Optional Resources**
- **Comunicación**, p. 373
- Advanced Learners, p. 373 ▲
- Multiple Intelligences, p. 373

**Homework Suggestions**
Study for **Prueba: Vocabulario 1**

1.1, 1.2, 1.3

### Day 3

**Objective**
*Preterite and imperfect in storytelling*

**Core Instruction**
**Vocabulario en acción 1,** pp. 368–373
- Review **Vocabulario en acción 1,** pp. 368–373. **5 min.**
- Give **Prueba: Vocabulario 1. 20 min.**

**Gramática en acción 1,** pp. 374–379
- See Teaching **Gramática,** p. 374. **10 min.**
- Have students do Activities 9–12, pp. 374–375. **15 min.**

**Optional Resources**
- **Comunicación**, p. 375
- Advanced Learners, p. 375 ▲
- Multiple Intelligences, p. 375

**Homework Suggestions**
Cuaderno de vocabulario y gramática, pp. 100–102
Cuaderno de actividades, pp. 81–83

1.1, 1.2

### Day 4

**Objective**
*Preterite and imperfect contrasted*

**Core Instruction**
**Gramática en acción 1,** pp. 374–379
- Have students do Bell Work, p. 376. **5 min.**
- See Teaching **Gramática,** p. 376. **10 min.**
- Have students do Activities 13–14, pp. 376–377. **15 min.**
- Play Audio CD 9, Tr.2 for Activity 15, p. 377. **5 min.**
- Have students do Activity 16, p. 377. **15 min.**

**Optional Resources**
- **Comunicación**, p. 377
- Advanced Learners, p. 377 ▲
- Multiple Intelligences, p. 377

**Homework Suggestions**
Cuaderno de vocabulario y gramática, pp. 100–102
Cuaderno de actividades, pp. 81–83

1.1, 1.2, 1.3

### Day 5

**Objective**
*Por and para*

**Core Instruction**
**Gramática en acción 1,** pp. 374–379
- Have students do Bell Work, p. 378. **5 min.**
- See Teaching **Gramática,** p. 378. **15 min.**
- Have students do Activities 17–20, pp. 378–379. **30 min.**

**Optional Resources**
- **Comunicación**, p. 379
- Slower Pace Learners, p. 379 ◆
- Multiple Intelligences, p. 379

**Homework Suggestions**
Study for **Prueba: Gramática 1**
Cuaderno de vocabulario y gramática, pp. 100–102
Cuaderno de actividades, pp. 81–83

1.1, 1.2, 1.3

### Day 6

**Objective**
*Interviews from around the Spanish-speaking world*

**Core Instruction**
**Gramática en acción 1,** pp. 374–379
- Review **Gramática en acción 1,** pp. 374–379. **5 min.**
- Give **Prueba: Gramática 1. 20 min.**

**Cultura,** pp. 380–381
- See Teaching **Cultura**, p. 380. **10 min.**
- Play Audio CD 9, Tr. 3–5, or show **VideoCultura**. **15 min.**

**Optional Resources**
- Advanced Learners, p. 381 ▲
- Multiple Intelligences, p. 381

**Homework Suggestions**
Cuaderno de actividades, p. 84
Online Practice (**go.hrw.com,** Keyword: EXP3 CH9)

1.2, 1.3, 3.1

### Day 7

**Objective**
*Talking about your hopes and wishes*

**Core Instruction**
**Vocabulario en acción 2,** pp. 382–387
- See Teaching **Vocabulario,** p. 382. **10 min.**
- See Teaching **¡Exprésate!,** p. 382. **10 min.**
- Play Audio CD 9, Tr. 6 for Activity 21, p. 384. **5 min.**
- Have students do Activities 22–25, pp. 384–385. **25 min.**

**Optional Resources**
- Advanced Learners, p. 383 ▲
- Multiple Intelligences, p. 383
- **Comunicación**, p. 385
- Slower Pace Learners, p. 385 ◆
- Special Learning Needs, p. 385 ●

**Homework Suggestions**
Cuaderno de vocabulario y gramática, pp. 103–105

1.2

### Day 8

**Objective**
*Expressing regret and gratitude*

**Core Instruction**
**Vocabulario en acción 2,** pp. 382–387
- Have students do Activity 26, p. 385. **10 min.**
- See Teaching **¡Exprésate!,** p. 386. **10 min.**
- Have students do Activities 27–29, p. 387. **30 min.**

**Optional Resources**
- **Comunicación**, p. 387
- Advanced Learners, p. 387 ▲
- Special Learning Needs, p. 387 ●

**Homework Suggestions**
Study for **Prueba: Vocabulario 2**
Cuaderno de vocabulario y gramática, pp. 103–105

1.1, 1.2, 1.3

- For information on the **Geocultura** pages, see the *Lesson Planner with Differentiated Instruction.*
- For more detailed information on benchmarks, see point-of-use correlations on each page.
- To edit and create your own lesson plans, see the **One-Stop Planner® CD-ROM**

**KEY**
- ▲ Advanced Learners
- ◆ Slower Pace Learners
- ● Special Learning Needs
- ■ Heritage Speakers

## Day 9

**Objective**
*Uses of subjunctive*

**Core Instruction**
**Vocabulario en acción 2,** pp. 382–387
- Review **Vocabulario en acción 2,** pp. 382–387. **10 min.**
- Give **Prueba: Vocabulario 2. 20 min.**

**Gramática en acción 2**, pp. 388–393
- See Teaching **Gramática,** p. 388. **10 min.**
- Have students do Activities 30–31, pp. 388–389. **10 min.**

**Optional Resources**
- **Comunicación**, p. 389
- Advanced Learners, p. 389 ▲
- Special Learning Needs, p. 389 ●

**Homework Suggestions**
Cuaderno de vocabulario y gramática, pp. 106–108
Cuaderno de actividades, pp. 85–87
1.2

## Day 10

**Objective**
*Sequence of tenses*

**Core Instruction**
**Gramática en acción 2,** pp. 388–393
- Have students do Activities 32–33, p. 389. **15 min.**
- Have students do Bell Work. See Bell Work suggestion, p. 390. **5 min.**
- See Teaching **Gramática,** p. 390. **10 min.**
- Play Audio CD 9, Tr. 7, for Activity 34, p. 390. **5 min.**
- Have students do Activities 35–38, p. 391. **15 min.**

**Optional Resources**
- **Comunicación**, p. 391
- Slower Pace Learners, p. 391 ◆
- Multiple Intelligences, p. 391

**Homework Suggestions**
Cuaderno de vocabulario y gramática, pp. 106–108
Cuaderno de actividades, pp. 85–87
1.1, 1.2, 1.3

## Day 11

**Objective**
*Sequence of tenses*

**Core Instruction**
**Gramática en acción 2,** pp. 388–393
- Have students do Bell Work. See Bell Work suggestion, p. 392. **5 min.**
- See Teaching **Gramática,** p. 392. **10 min.**
- Have students do Activities 39–42, pp. 392–393. **35 min.**

**Optional Resources**
- **Comunicación**, p. 393
- Advanced Learners, p. 393 ▲
- Special Learning Needs, p. 393 ●

**Homework Suggestions**
Study for **Prueba: Gramática 2**
Cuaderno de vocabulario y gramática, pp. 106–108
Cuaderno de actividades, pp. 85–87
1.1, 1.2

## Day 12

**Objective**
*Devloping listening and reading skills*

**Core Instruction**
**Gramática en acción 2,** pp. 388–393
- Review **Gramática en acción 2,** pp. 388–393. **10 min.**
- Give **Prueba: Gramática 2. 20 min.**

**Novela en video,** pp. 394–395
- Show **VideoNovela.** See Teaching **Novela en video,** p. 394. **20 min.**

**Assessment Program:**
- Skills Quiz: **Vocabulario y gramática 2**

**Homework Suggestions**
Cuaderno de vocabulario y gramática, pp. 106–108
1.2

## Day 13

**Objective**
*Developing reading and writing skills*

**Core Instruction**
**Lectura informativa,** pp. 396–397
- See Teaching **Lectura informativa,** p. 396. **35 min.**

**Leamos y escribamos,** pp. 398–401
- See Teaching **Leamos,** points 1–3, p. 398. **15 min.**

**Optional Resources**
- Advanced Learners, p. 397 ▲
- Multiple Intelligences, p. 397

**Homework Suggestions**
Cuaderno de actividades, p. 88
1.2, 1.3

## Day 14

**Objective**
*Developing reading and writing skills*

**Core Instruction**
**Leamos y escribamos,** pp. 398–401
- See Teaching **Leamos,** point 4, p. 398. **10 min.**
- See Teaching **Escribamos,** points 1–3, p. 400. **10 min.**

**Prepárate para el examen,** pp. 402–405
- Have students do Activities 1–5, pp. 402–403. **25 min.**
- Play Audio CD 9, Tr. 10 for Activity 6, p. 403. **5 min.**

**Optional Resources**
- Advanced Learners, p. 399 ▲
- Multiple Intelligences, p. 399
- Slower Pace Learners, p. 401 ◆
- Multiple Intelligences, p. 401

**Homework Suggestions**
**Taller del escritor,** p. 401
1.2

## Day 15

**Objective**
*Chapter review*

**Core Instruction**
**Prepárate para el examen,** pp. 402–405
- Have students do Activity 7, p. 403. **5 min.**

**Integración,** pp. 406–407
- Have students do Activities 1–6, pp. 406–407. **45 min.**

**Optional Resources**
- Play Pre-AP Audio CD 2, Tr. 13, for Pre-AP Practice, p. 403
- Game, p. 405
- Fine Art Connection, p. 407

**Homework Suggestions**
Study for Chapter Test
1.1, 1.2, 1.3

## Day 16/Test

**Core Instruction**
**Chapter Test 50 min.**

**Optional Resources**
**Assessment Program**
- **Prueba: Lectura**
- **Prueba: Escritura**
- Test Generator

**Homework Suggestions**
Cuaderno de actividades, pp. 89–90

50-Minute Lesson Plans

# Indiana
## The Hoosier State

Rocky Hollow Turkey Run State Park

Sim Smith's Bridge

Indianapolis at night

### Chapter 9

The following chart presents *¡Exprésate!* Chapter 9 correlations to the Indiana Academic Standards for World Languages, Grade 11. The correlations here are to the *Student Edition* (SE) and *Teacher's Edition* (TE) only. For additional teaching resources, see pages 365A-365B

| INDIANA ACADEMIC STANDARDS | | | CHAPTER 9 SE/TE CORRELATIONS |
|---|---|---|---|
| **Standard 1 COMMUNICATION:** | | | |
| **Write and speak in a language other than English** | 11.1.1 | Initiate, sustain, and close conversations in limited yet varied situations. | SE: 371, 373, 375, 387, 407<br>TE: 372, 386, 407 |
| | 11.1.2 | Exchange detailed information and opinions orally on a variety of topics. | SE: 371, 373, 381, 386, 407<br>TE: 372, 380, 386, 406 |
| | 11.1.3 | Exchange detailed information and opinions in written form on a variety of topics. | SE: 401<br>TE: 385 |
| | 11.1.5 | Recognize and use situation-appropriate non-verbal communication. | SE: 379<br>TE: 394 |
| | 11.1.6 | Use speaking and listening strategies to facilitate communication. | SE: 375, 389<br>TE: 388 |
| **Standard 2 COMMUNICATION:** | | | |
| **Interpret information in a language other than English** *Learners interpret written and spoken language on a variety of topics. (Interpretive)* | 11.2.1 | Respond accurately to everyday requests, commands, and directions. | TE: 369, 383 |
| | 11.2.2 | Demonstrate comprehension of both authentic and non-authentic written and spoken language through developmentally appropriate tasks. | SE: 371, 395, 397, 400<br>TE: 380, 394, 396, 398 |
| | 11.2.3 | Make educated guesses about meaning in unfamiliar written and spoken contexts. | SE: 394, 398<br>TE: 394, 398 |
| **Standard 3 COMMUNICATION:** | | | |
| **Present information in a language other than English** *Learners present to an audience of listeners or readers on a variety of topics. (Presentational)* | 11.3.1 | Recite rhymes, proverbs, and poetry or sing songs of the target language and cultures. | TE: 397 |
| | 11.3.2 | Produce and present creative material on a variety of topics. | SE: 373, 377, 379, 387, 393, 407<br>TE: 365C, 393, 406 |
| | 11.3.4 | Compose cohesive written information using appropriate formats and more varied vocabulary and structures. | SE: 401<br>TE: 365C, 400, 401 |
| **Standard 4 CULTURES:** | | | |
| **Develop awareness of other cultures.** *Learners examine, experience, and reflect on the relationships among the practices, products, and perspectives of the cultures studied.* | 11.4.1 | Analyze and reflect on cultural practices of the target cultures. | SE: 381, 397, 407<br>TE: 361, 363, 380, 396, 407 |
| | 11.4.2 | Describe products, perspectives, and symbols of the target cultures. | SE: 381, 397, 407<br>TE: 361, 363, 365, 380, 396, 407 |
| | 11.4.3 | Discuss factors that influence practices, products, and perspectives. | SE: 362, 363, 381, 397, 407<br>TE: 361, 363, 365, 380, 396, 407 |

| | | | |
|---|---|---|---|
| | **11.4.4** | Recognize the interrelations among the practices, products, and perspectives of the target cultures. | **SE:** 362, 363, 381, 397, 407<br>**TE:** 361, 363, 365, 380, 396 |
| | **11.4.5** | Explain contributions from other cultures. | **SE:** 397, 407<br>**TE:** 361, 363, 365, 396, 407 |
| | **11.4.6** | Identify significant events unique to the target cultures. | **SE:** 362, 363, 396-397<br>**TE:** 363, 396 |

## Standard 5 CONNECTIONS:

| | | | |
|---|---|---|---|
| **Make connections to other content areas** *Learners use the target language to expand their knowledge of and make connections among multiple content areas.* | **11.5.1** | Make connections with other content areas through resources intended for native speakers. | **TE:** 361, 365C, 406 |
| | **11.5.2** | Design and share activities and materials that integrate the target language and cultures with concepts and skills from other content areas. | **SE:** 387, 391<br>**TE:** 365C, 405 |

## Standard 6 CONNECTIONS:

| | | | |
|---|---|---|---|
| **Access and connect information through various media** *Learners strengthen language proficiency and cultural knowledge by using current digital media and authentic resources.* | **11.6.1** | Use digital media and culturally authentic resources to build vocabulary and improve receptive and productive language skills. | **SE:** 360, 402, 406<br>**TE:** 365E, 365F |
| | **11.6.2** | Use digital media and culturally authentic resources to study target cultures. | **SE:** 380, 394<br>**TE:** 361, 387 |
| | **11.6.3** | Identify and evaluate resources intended for native speakers. | **SE:** 380, 394, 400<br>**TE:** 361, 387, 399 |

## Standard 7 COMPARISONS:

| | | | |
|---|---|---|---|
| **Investigate the nature of language and culture** *Learners understand the nature of language and culture through comparisons of the languages and cultures studied and their own.* | **11.7.1** | Use elements of word formation to expand vocabulary and derive meaning. | **SE:** 374-389, 402<br>**TE:** 374, 388, 402 |
| | **11.7.2** | Recognize and use a variety of language structures. | **SE:** 401, 407<br>**TE:** 374-379, 402-405 |
| | **11.7.3** | Compare and use idiomatic, colloquial, and proverbial expressions in the target language. | **SE:** 407<br>**TE:** 386 |
| | **11.7.5** | Compare systems of other cultures and the learner's own culture. | **SE:** 364, 381, 396-397<br>**TE:** 362, 363, 365, 380, 381, 396-397 |
| | **11.7.6** | Compare and contrast elements that shape cultural identity in the learner's heritage and in the target cultures. | **SE:** 364, 381, 396-397<br>**TE:** 362, 363, 365, 380, 381, 396-397 |

## Standard 8 COMMUNITIES:

| | | | |
|---|---|---|---|
| **Become an active global citizen by experiencing languages and cultures in multiple settings** *Learners use their knowledge of the target language and cultures both within and beyond the school setting for personal enrichment and civic engagement.* | **11.8.2** | Investigate and share with others the influences of the target language and cultures on the community. | **TE:** 406 |
| | **11.8.3** | Show evidence of becoming a life-long learner by using the target language and cultural knowledge for personal enrichment. | **TE:** 365D |

## Chapter Opener

### Meeting the National Standards

**Communication**
Comunicación, pp. 371, 373, 375. 377, 379, 385, 387, 389, 391, 393, 395
Game, p. 405
Situación, p. 407

**Cultures**
Practices and Perspectives, pp. 362, 363, 385
Products and Perspectives, pp. 365, 399
Culture Project, p. 406

**Connections**
Atlas Interactivo Mundial, pp. 361, 381
Science Link, p. 361
Math Link, p. 370
Nota cultural, pp. 370, 384, 391
Language Arts Link, pp. 373, 375, 397, 404
History Link, pp. 385, 387
Social Studies Link, p. 391
Literature Link, p. 400

**Comparisons**
Comparing and Contrasting, p. 364
En inglés, p. 374
Language Arts Link, p. 404

**Communities**
Family Link, p. 372
Language Arts Link, p. 373
Career Path, p. 380

### Using the Photo

Tell students that this is a picture of **huasos,** Chilean cowboys, taken at the **Fiesta de la Chilenidad** at the **Parque Intercomunal** in Santiago, Chile. Their typical dress includes the wide-brimmed **cordobés** hats and the **chamanto,** a colorful woven poncho. Have students research and compare this fiesta to **rodeos** in the U.S. 2.1, 4.2

### Más vocabulario

**el corral** *pen*
**las riendas** *reins*
**la silla de montar** *saddle*

# Capítulo 9

# Huellas del pasado

## OBJETIVOS

**In this chapter you will learn to**
- set the scene for a story
- continue and end a story
- talk about your hopes and wishes
- express regret and gratitude

**And you will use**
- preterite and imperfect
- **por** and **para**
- subjunctive
- sequence of tenses

**¿Qué ves en la foto?**
- **¿Qué crees que están haciendo estas personas?**
- **¿Qué tipo de ropa usan?**
- **¿Has visto un evento similar a éste alguna vez?**

| Suggested pacing: | Traditional Schedule | Block Schedule |
|---|---|---|
| Vocabulario 1/Gramática 1 | 5 1/2 days | 2 1/2 blocks |
| Cultura | 1/2 day | 1/2 block |
| Vocabulario 2/Gramática 2 | 5 1/2 days | 2 1/2 blocks |
| Novela | 1/2 day | 1/2 block |
| Lectura cultural | 1/2 day | 1/2 block |
| Leamos y escribamos | 1 day | 1/2 block |
| Prepárate para el examen | 1 day | 1/4 block |
| Chapter Test | 1 day | 1/2 block |
| Integración | 1/2 day | 1/4 block |

Fiesta de la Chilenidad, Parque Intercomunal, Santiago, Chile

# Chapter Opener

## Holt Grammar Logic
### CHAPTER 9

- *To set the scene for a story, and to continue and end a story,* students must review the preterite and imperfect in storytelling, and they must contrast the uses of the two aspects. They will also need to review and contrast the uses of **por** and **para.**
- *To talk about their hopes and wishes, and to express regret and gratitude,* students must review the uses of the subjunctive. They will also learn about sequence of tenses.
- In this chapter, students get a comprehensive review of preterite and imperfect.

## Learning Tips

Have students look up information about the **huasos** on Chilean web sites. Have them find out about their history, clothing, and current lifestyle, as well as **huaso** music and dance. Ask students to compare notes, and practice the new words they learn from their research. 2.1

## LISTENING PRACTICE — Language Lab and Classroom Activities

**Vocabulario**
Activity 1, p. 370, CD 9, Tr. 1
Activity 21, p. 384, CD 9, Tr. 6

**Gramática**
Activity 15, p. 377, CD 9, Tr. 2
Activity 34, p. 390, CD 9, Tr. 7

**Cultura**
**Comparaciones**, pp. 380–381, CD 9, Tr. 3–5

**Novela**
**Novela en video,** Escuchemos, p. 394

**Lectura informativa**
pp. 396–397, CD 9, Tr. 8

**Leamos**
pp. 398–401, CD 9, Tr. 9
Escuchemos, p. 398

**Repaso**
Activity 6, p. 403, CD 9, Tr. 10
**Variedades,** Lab Book, p. 84

**Assessment Program**
CD 9, Tr. 11–14

**Additional Listening**
Pre-AP CD 2, Tr. 13–16

## Resources

**Planning:**

Lesson Planner, pp. 129–130, 290–291

One-Stop Planner

**Presentation:**

Teaching Transparencies
**Vocabulario** 9.1, 9.2

**Practice:**

Cuaderno de vocabulario y gramática, pp. 97–99

Activities for Communication, pp. 33–34

Teaching Transparencies
Bell Work 9.1
**Vocabulario y gramática** answers, pp. 97–99

Interactive Tutor, Disc 2

### Bell Work

Use Bell Work 9.1 in the *Teaching Transparencies,* or write this activity on the board.

**Completa las oraciones con la forma correcta del verbo.**

1. **Yo quería que mi abuela nos _____ (leer) un libro.**
2. **Mi hermano prefería que nosotros _____ (ver) una película.**
3. **Mis papás esperaban que tú _____ (llegar) temprano.**
4. **Tú dudabas que yo _____ (entender) el cuento.**
5. **Era importante que yo _____ (acabar) el proyecto.**

1.2

**Objetivos**
- **Setting the scene for a story**
- **Continuing and ending a story**

# Vocabulario 1 *en acción*

## Las leyendas

Las civilizaciones del presente y del pasado tienen sus **leyendas** y **mitos** para contar sus historias o para explicar algún fenómeno. En Latinoamérica hay tradiciones de las culturas indígenas, africanas y europeas. Aquí en Chile hay tradiciones y leyendas de los mapuches, también conocidos como los araucanos, y de la cultura europea, sobre todo la española.

Los aztecas en México, los incas en los Andes y los mapuches en Chile tenían **dioses** y **diosas.** Estas civilizaciones construyeron **templos** dedicados a sus dioses. **Aunque** estas civilizaciones **han desaparecido,** sus construcciones y mitos todavía existen.

**Más vocabulario...**

| | |
|---|---|
| **ahora bien** | *well, nevertheless* |
| **castigar** | *to punish* |
| **el castigo** | *punishment* |
| **la creación** | *creation* |
| **traicionar** | *to betray* |
| **el (la) traidor(a)** | *traitor* |

## Core Instruction

### TEACHING VOCABULARIO

1. Introduce the vocabulary using transparencies **Vocabulario 9.1** and **9.2.** Model the pronunciation of the expressions and point to target vocabulary as you read the caption for each illustration. **(3 min.)**
2. Present the words from **Más vocabulario** and model the meaning of each word in a sentence. **(2 min.)**
3. Model vocabulary by describing the icons on the map. **Esta pirámide es el Templo del Sol de México. Parece que este príncipe está enamorado de una princesa.**

### TEACHING ¡EXPRÉSATE!

1. Model the **¡Exprésate!** functions for students. **(2 min.)**
2. Use the **¡Exprésate!** functions in sentences that describe fairy tales with which the students are familiar. **Érase una vez, en un lugar muy lejano, vivía una mujer con un espejo encantado.** See if students recognize the fairy tale. (Snow White/**Blancanieves**) **(3 min.)**

Visit Holt Online
**go.hrw.com**
KEYWORD: EXP3 CH9
Vocabulario 1 Practice

**Los cuentos de hadas** vienen de Europa y en ellos los personajes a menudo **se enamoran**. En general, estos cuentos ocurren en lugares **encantados.** Muchas veces hay un personaje **desconocido** y **misterioso** o **un fantasma.**

**Los hechos** de los mitos pueden ser muy variados, al igual que sus personajes. En muchos mitos hay **un sabio** que aconseja a los demás, o **un hechicero** con **poderes mágicos.**

En muchas leyendas, **el rey** vive en **un palacio** que comparte con su esposa, **la reina,** y sus hijos, **el príncipe** y **la princesa.**

**También se puede decir...**

Some Spanish speakers use **el acontecimiento** or **el suceso** instead of **el hecho.** You may also hear **Había una vez** in addition to **Érase una vez**.

## ¡Exprésate!

**To set the scene for a story**

| | |
|---|---|
| **Érase una vez, en un lugar muy lejano...** *Once upon a time, in a faraway place, there was . . .* | **Hace muchos años,...** *Many years ago, . . .* |
| **Según nos dicen, el malvado...** *From what they tell us, the villain . . .* | **Se cuenta que de pronto...** *The story goes that all of a sudden . . .* |

interactive TUTOR

Vocabulario y gramática, pp. 97–99 · Online workbooks

Vocabulario 1

## TPR

### Total Physical Response

Bring to class illustrations from myths and fairy tales and display them in the classroom. Illustrations should include a prince, princess, king, queen, wizard, palace, and temple. Have individual students respond to the following commands.

**Señala a la princesa.**
**Señala al rey.**
**Señala al hechicero.**
**Señala el palacio.** 1.2

### También se puede decir...

Students might read stories of legends and myths that begin with **Hubo una vez** or **Había una vez** instead of **Érase una vez.** The latter is considered antiquated and no longer used in regular conversational language.

### Connections

**Art Link**

Have students research artistic representations of ancient mythical figures of the pre-Columbian indigenous peoples from the Southern Cone, such as the Incas, Mapuches, and Patagones. Have them write the names of the figures, describe their role in particular myths, and provide as much information about the art piece as possible (date, location, materials used). 3.1

## Differentiated Instruction

### ADVANCED LEARNERS

**Challenge** Have students find a legend or myth from Argentina, Chile, Uruguay, or Paraguay. Ask them to read it aloud for the class and then have volunteers summarize what they heard. As an alternative, you may wish to divide the class into small groups and have students summarize their legend or myth for the group. 1.2

### MULTIPLE INTELLIGENCES

**Linguistic** Have students take turns using the new terms from **Vocabulario 1** and the sentences from **¡Exprésate!** to summarize well-known legends and myths. Tell them to be sure to include the important details that will help their classmates recognize each story. Have the rest of the class guess the myth or legend that is being described. 1.2

**Differentiated Instruction** See the Differentiated Instruction CD-ROM.

## Resources

**Planning:**

Lesson Planner, pp. 129–130, 290–291

One-Stop Planner

**Presentation:**

Teaching Transparencies **Vocabulario** 9.1, 9.2

**Practice:**

Cuaderno de vocabulario y gramática, pp. 97–99

Activities for Communication, pp. 33–34

Lab Book, pp. 45–48

Teaching Transparencies **Vocabulario y gramática** answers, pp. 97–99

Audio CD 9, Tr. 1

Interactive Tutor, Disc 2

**1 Script**

See script on page 365E.

## Connections

### Math Link

The Incas had a computing method similar to an abacus called the **quipu.** It consisted of a chord with other braided chords tied onto it indicating a number value. The Incas also used the decimal system for their calculations of the population. Have students look into the different uses of the **quipu** using the decimal system.

3.1

### Nota cultural

Antes de la llegada de los europeos, existían en Argentina dos grupos principales de indígenas. En la parte noroeste, cerca de Bolivia y los Andes, vivían los diaguitas, y al sureste vivían los guaraníes. Los dos grupos desarrollaron el cultivo del maíz y se les recuerda porque tuvieron éxito en evitar la expansión del imperio inca en el resto de Argentina.

¿Qué más sabes de las civilizaciones precolombinas del Cono Sur?

3.1

**En Paraguay, este señor talla máscaras de madera para una ceremonia guaraní.**

**Answers to Activity 2**

1. palacio
2. príncipe
3. desconocido
4. poderes
5. se enamorara
6. malvado
7. desapareció
8. Ahora bien
9. Aunque
10. castigo

CD 9, Tr. 1

### 1 ¿Quién es? 1.2

**Escuchemos** Escucha las descripciones de los personajes y determina de quién están hablando.

1. **a.** el dios **b.** el príncipe b
2. **a.** el sabio **b.** la reina a
3. **a.** el traidor **b.** el hechicero b
4. **a.** el rey **b.** el traidor b
5. **a.** el fantasma **b.** la reina b
6. **a.** el dios **b.** el malvado a

### 2 El príncipe y la reina 1.2

**Leamos/Escribamos** Completa el párrafo con las palabras del cuadro.

| | | | |
|---|---|---|---|
| príncipe | desapareció | poderes | aunque |
| desconocido | se enamorara | castigo | ahora bien |
| malvado | palacio | | |

Hace muchos años vivía una reina en un enorme __1__. Ella les había dicho a sus hijos que no quería que nadie entrara. Pero el __2__ desobedeció a su madre e invitó a un hombre __3__ al palacio. Lo dejó entrar porque este hombre, a quien nadie había visto nunca, le dijo que usaría sus __4__ mágicos para que la mujer más bonita del mundo __5__ de él. Pero realmente era un __6__ que quería apoderarse del palacio. Entró y de pronto __7__. ¡El príncipe no sabía dónde estaba! __8__, como la reina era muy inteligente, se dio cuenta de lo que estaba pasando y atrapó al malvado. __9__ no quiso castigar a su hijo, al malvado le dio un duro __10__. Según nos dicen, lo convirtió en una serpiente.

### 3 Mi cuento de hadas 1.3

**Escribamos** Completa las oraciones para crear tu propio cuento de hadas.

1. Érase una vez, en un lugar muy lejano...
2. Se cuenta que el príncipe se enamoró de...
3. De pronto un hechicero convirtió a la mujer en...
4. El sabio tenía una varita mágica *(magic wand)* que...
5. El príncipe castigó a...
6. Según la leyenda, el príncipe llegó a ser...
7. Ahora bien, la mujer...
8. Según nos dicen, al final...

## Core Instruction

### VOCABULARY IN CONTEXT

Bring in a short fairy tale in Spanish and read it aloud. You might want to choose a classic that students already know, such as Snow White **(Blancanieves).** Since students already know the story, they will be able to focus on the language used. Ask comprehension questions about the story, using words from **Vobabulario 1.** Questions should require students to either use the vocabulary contextually in their answers or ask them to define the words within the context of the selection. For example, **¿El espejo de la reina era encantado? Explica. ¿Qué hizo la reina para castigar a Blancanieves? ¿Qué hizo el príncipe cuando vio a Blancanieves?**

### 4 Leyendas de Argentina y Chile 1.2

**Leamos/Escribamos** Lee los resúmenes de las leyendas y contesta las preguntas.

**Según una leyenda chilena, los mapuches creían que sus antepasados vivían en el cielo. Cada estrella era uno de sus abuelos. Éstos vivían protegidos por los dioses el Sol y la Luna. Los llamaban Padre y Madre.**

**En un mito argentino, se cuenta que hubo un tiempo en que las hojas de los árboles eran siempre verdes. Pero Kamshout encontró un bosque mágico donde las hojas cambiaban de color en el otoño. Como nadie creyó su historia, él se convirtió en loro y volvió a su tierra para teñir las hojas. Desde entonces las hojas cambian de color cada otoño.**

**Los selknam de Tierra del Fuego estaban divididos en varios grupos. El hijo del jefe de un grupo se enamoró de una joven de ojos negros, pero el papá de ella era enemigo del jefe. Según nos dicen, un hechicero los descubrió y para castigarlos convirtió a la joven en una planta peligrosa para que el joven no pudiera tocarla.**

1. ¿Quiénes eran los dioses de los mapuches? sus antepasados
2. ¿De dónde viene el mito sobre Kamshout? de Argentina
3. ¿Por qué era mágico el bosque que descubrió Kamshout? porque las hojas cambiaban de color en otoño
4. ¿De quién se enamoró el joven selknam? de una joven de ojos negros, hija de un jefe enemigo
5. ¿Cuál fue el castigo de los jóvenes enamorados? La joven fue convertida en una planta peligrosa que el joven no podía tocar.
6. ¿Quién castigó a la joven? un hechicero

## Comunicación

HOLT SoundBooth ONLINE RECORDING

### 5 Mis leyendas favoritas 1.1, 1.3

**Hablemos** En parejas, túrnense para resumir una leyenda o un cuento de hadas conocido, para ver si su compañero(a) puede adivinar cuál es. Cada persona debe resumir dos leyendas o cuentos.

**MODELO** **—Érase una vez una princesa hermosa que...**

## Differentiated Instruction

### SLOWER PACE LEARNERS

**5 Variation** You may want to modify Activity 5 if students have trouble summarizing known legends. Instead, have them make up stories of their own and have their partners ask questions using the vocabulary words and expressions to prompt them to the next stage of the story. For example: **¿Y ese lugar era muy lejano? ¿Quién era el traidor?** 1.1

### MULTIPLE INTELLIGENCES

**Musical** Have students watch a Spanish-language film production of a fairy tale, legend, or non-fiction program about the myths of different cultures. Have them note the different auditory cues that they get from the score about the action and the characters. For example: **Cada vez que entra el monstruo malvado, se oyen los mismos sonidos.** If possible, have them make simple recordings of these sounds or songs so they can share them with the class. 3.2

### Heritage Speakers

Ask heritage speakers to tell the class about the legends and fairy tales they heard as children. Were some of them Spanish versions of the same fairy tales their classmates grew up with? 1.3

### Teacher to Teacher

**Meruchy Haedo**
Eastside High School
Gainesville, FL

To practice writing stories and legends, I pair students and give each pair the body of a fairy tale or indigenous legend. Partners complete the story by writing an original beginning and ending. Have them read their completed story to the class. As a variation, create a class book. First select a theme of stories to assign, such as fairy tales, legends, or folklore. Assign a different story to each pair. Pairs complete their story as above and include illustrations to complement it. Compile class stories into a book, each pair writing their own "chapter." If you wish to implement technology, have students use PowerPoint™ to present their stories. 1.2

## Comunicación

### Pair Activity: Interpersonal

Have students form pairs. Ask them to discuss the fairy tales or legends they read or were told when they were children, and whether they still enjoy them. Have them look up the titles of the more famous ones in Spanish on the Internet by searching for bilingual editions. 1.1

**Differentiated Instruction** See the Differentiated Instruction CD-ROM.

# Vocabulario 1

## Resources

**Planning:**

Lesson Planner, pp. 129–130, 290–291

One-Stop Planner

**Presentation:**

Teaching Transparencies **Vocabulario** 9.1, 9.2

**Practice:**

Cuaderno de vocabulario y gramática, pp. 97–99

Activities for Communication, pp. 33–34

Teaching Transparencies **Vocabulario y gramática** answers, pp. 97–99

Interactive Tutor, Disc 2

## Communities

### Family Link

Have students ask a Spanish-speaking older person or family member: **¿Qué cuentos de hadas te contaron de pequeño(a)? ¿Quiénes te los contaron?** Have students compare and contrast answers with their own experience and that of the class. 5.2

### Heritage Speakers

Have heritage speakers share other common expressions for continuing and ending a story. Ask them to use the expressions to tell parts of a well-known legend or myth so students can hear the phrases in context. 1.3

En un parque de Santiago

## La mujer con poderes mágicos

DON PABLO ¿Quieren escuchar una leyenda de mi pueblo?

TODOS ¡Sí!

DON PABLO Se cuenta que esta leyenda está basada en hechos reales. ¡No se vayan a asustar!

FABIOLA ¡Cuéntenos!

DON PABLO Bueno, hace mucho tiempo, en mi pueblo, vivía una mujer con muchos poderes misteriosos para curar a la gente. Según nos dicen, era una mujer que parecía una diosa; no les miento, era como en un cuento de hadas. Bueno, hace muchos años vino esa mujer desconocida a mi pueblo. Y tan pronto como llegó, todos comenzaron a hablar mal de ella. Algunos dijeron que era una hechicera y que seguramente los castigaría con sus poderes. De hecho, resultó que era muy sabia y podía curar las enfermedades. Se cuenta que una vez salvó a un niño de la muerte. Pero con los cuentos de la gente chismosa, la mujer se ofendió y se fue. A partir de entonces, mucha gente del pueblo empezó a enfermarse. A causa de esto, muchos se asustaron y abandonaron el pueblo. Al final, los del pueblo se dieron cuenta de la importancia de tratar bien a la gente; porque si no, se puede recibir un castigo. Y ésa, muchachos, es la leyenda de mi pueblo.

## ¡Exprésate!

### To continue and end a story

Interactive TUTOR

| | |
|---|---|
| **Hace tiempo, vino un desconocido...** *Some time ago, a stranger came . . .* | **Al final, nos dimos cuenta de...** *In the end, we realized . . .* |
| **Tan pronto como llegó...** *As soon as he/she arrived . . .* | **A partir de entonces, vivieron siempre felices.** *From then on, they lived happily ever after.* |
| **A causa de esto...** *Because of this . . .* | |

Vocabulario y gramática, pp. 97–99 Online workbooks

## Core Instruction

### TEACHING ¡EXPRÉSATE!

1. Have volunteers read **La mujer con poderes mágicos.** Model the **¡Exprésate!** functions for continuing and ending a story by pronouncing them and then pointing out how they are used in the story. **(10 min.)**
2. Model the different functions from **¡Exprésate!** creating your own endings so that students can see how they are used in other ways. **(2 min.)**
3. As you model more expressions, have students tell whether you are modeling an ending or continuing a story. **(3 min.)**

## 6 ¿Qué pasó primero? 1.2

**Leamos** Basándote en la leyenda de Don Pablo, pon los hechos en el orden correcto. 1. c 2. e 3. a 4. f 5. b 6. d

a. La mujer salvó a un niño de la muerte.
b. La gente empezó a enfermarse.
c. La mujer desconocida llegó al pueblo.
d. Todos se dieron cuenta de la importancia de tratar bien a la gente.
e. La gente comenzó a hablar mal de la mujer.
f. La mujer se fue del pueblo.

## 7 Haz el cuento 1.2

**Escribamos** Basándote en los dibujos, escribe un cuento de hadas. Usa las expresiones del cuadro.

| | | |
|---|---|---|
| Había una vez... | Se cuenta que... | Tan pronto como... |
| A causa de esto... | A partir de entonces... | Al final, nos dimos cuenta de... |

## Comunicación

HOLT SoundBooth ONLINE RECORDING

## 8 Un cuento del grupo 1.1, 1.3

**Hablemos** En grupos pequeños, inventen un cuento de hadas. La primera persona dice la primera oración y empieza la segunda. La segunda persona termina la oración y empieza otra. Sigan así hasta terminar el cuento. Usen las expresiones de **Exprésate.** Luego, un miembro del grupo tratará de resumir el cuento para la clase.

MODELO —**Érase una vez, en un lugar muy lejano, un rey que vivía en un enorme castillo. Según nos dicen,...**

—**...el rey tenía dos hijos. El príncipe mayor...**

## Vocabulario 1

### Connections

**Language Arts Links**

- Have students research modern fables written by two authors from Chile and/or Argentina. Have them note a few details about at least one narrative by each author, such as whether the fables are original or adaptations of older fables, and the main plot events, magical elements, and the moral of the story.
- Have students contact a student from a Spanish-speaking country to ask what stories or fairy tales he or she listened to as a child. Alternately, have students interview native Spanish-speakers in their own community on the same topic. Students should write out the narrated fairy tale, have a classmate peer-correct it, and then present the story to the class.

3.2, 5.2

### Comunicación

**Class Activity: Presentational**

As a follow up to Activity 8, ask the small groups to present to the class the fairy tales they made up using the **¡Exprésate!** functions. Have the rest of the class give feedback, including suggestions for additional developments to the stories.

1.3

## Differentiated Instruction

### ADVANCED LEARNERS

**8 Challenge** To show students how legends are altered as they are passed down from one generation to another, ask the students to write out the stories they created in small groups for Activity 8. Then have them take turns reading their stories to their group. Ask them to discuss the differences in the stories. What parts of the story changed? What parts remained the same? Why do they think legends change over time? 1.2

### MULTIPLE INTELLIGENCES

**Logical/Mathematical** Choose a short fable, reproduce the text, and distribute it to students. Ask them to make up charts in which they number the characters, the sections of the story, and spell out and draw arrows between events and their consequences. Have each student arrange the material in the way that is most useful to them, as long as they organize it into columns and rows. Have them use their charts to tell the fable to their classmates.

### Assess

**Assessment Program**

**Prueba: Vocabulario 1,** pp. 161–162

Alternative Assessment, pp. 381, 393, 405

**Online Assessment**
**my.hrw.com**

**Test Generator**

**Assess Differentiated Assessment** See the Differentiated Assessment CD-ROM.

## Resources

**Planning:**

Lesson Planner, pp. 131–133, 292–295

One-Stop Planner

**Presentation:**

Video Program **GramaVisión**

**Practice:**

Grammar Tutor for Students of Spanish, Chapter 9

Cuaderno de vocabulario y gramática, pp. 100–102

Cuaderno de actividades, pp. 81–83

Activities for Communication, pp. 33–34

Teaching Transparencies Bell Work 9.2

**Vocabulario y gramática** answers, pp. 100–102

Interactive Tutor, Disc 2

### Bell Work

Use Bell Work 9.2 in the *Teaching Transparencies*, or write this activity on the board.

**Escribe dos oraciones con dos de las siguientes palabras o frases: los mitos, la creación, ahora bien, misterioso, los poderes mágicos.** 1.3

**Objetivos**
- Preterite and imperfect in storytelling
- Preterite and imperfect contrasted
- **Por** and **para**

# Gramática en acción 1

GramaVisión

Interactive TUTOR

## Repaso: Preterite and imperfect in storytelling

1. When telling a story, the **imperfect** is used to describe the setting or the background of the story.

   Una vez, **había** un rey con poderes mágicos.

   Se cuenta que **estaba** nublado aquel día.

2. The **preterite** is used to show that an event or situation in the story had a specific beginning or end.

   A causa de esto el rey **castigó** al malvado.

   A partir de entonces, nunca **volvió** al castillo.

3. The **preterite** and the **imperfect** often occur in the same sentence. The **imperfect** describes what was going on and the **preterite** indicates completed actions within that setting. The same occurs with the **past progressive (pasado progresivo)** and the **preterite.**

   **Había** mucha gente en el palacio cuando **habló** el rey.

   La reina **estaba** en el campo cuando el hechicero la **traicionó.**

   **Estaba leyendo** un cuento de hadas cuando **se fue** la luz.

Vocabulario y gramática, pp. 100–102
Actividades, pp. 81–83
Online workbooks

### En inglés

**In English,** the simple past tense doesn't tell whether or not an action has ended.

John said that there was a game today, and he still wants to go.

John said that there was a game today, but our team lost.

**In Spanish,** the imperfect means that something may or may not have ended. The preterite means it already ended.

How would you express the two sentences above in Spanish? 4.1

Juan dijo que había un partido hoy y que todavía quiere ir.
Juan dijo que hubo un partido hoy, pero que nuestro equipo perdió.

### 9 Un pájaro misterioso 1.2

**Leamos** Completa las oraciones con las formas correctas de los verbos en paréntesis.

1. Hace mucho tiempo vivía un joven que (tuvo/tenía) poderes mágicos.
2. Un día el joven (estaba/estuvo) caminando por el bosque cuando (veía/vio ) un pájaro.
3. El pájaro (era/fue) muy colorido y misterioso.
4. De pronto, el pájaro le (decía/dijo) al joven que una princesa se había perdido cerca del lago.
5. (Estaba/Estuvo) oscuro cuando el joven (llegó/llegaba) al lago.
6. El joven (se enamoraba/se enamoró) enseguida de la princesa.
7. Los enamorados (se casaron/se casaban) poco después.
8. A partir de entonces, (fueron/iban) todos los días al bosque a hablar con el pájaro.

### Pre-AP Practice

**AP Benchmark:** Describe, narrate, and present information and/or arguments in a presentation of two or three minutes.

**Focus:** Preterite and imperfect in storytelling
- SE, p. 375, Act. 12
- TE, p. 375, Connections
- TE, p. 375, Multiple Intelligences

## Core Instruction

### TEACHING GRAMÁTICA

1. Go over point 1. Explain that the first sentence gives background information. The second sentence describes the setting. Provide other examples: **hacía sol, había mucha gente, era una princesa bonita. (2 min.)**
2. In point 2, explain that these verbs show a specific beginning, end or duration. **(2 min.)**
3. Go over point 3, pointing out that the first two sentences use the imperfect and the preterite, whereas the third uses the past progressive and the preterite. Explain that the completed action in the preterite is often introduced by the word **cuando. (3 min.)**
4. Have students think of verbs that would often be used to set the scene (**ser, estar, haber**) and verbs that would often be used to describe completed actions (**castigar, traicionar, salir**). **(2 min.)**

### GramaVisión

For a video presentation of the preterite and imperfect in storytelling, use **GramaVisión.**

GramaVisión

Visit Holt Online
**go.hrw.com**
KEYWORD: EXP3 CH9
Gramática 1 Practice

**10 Iasá y Tupá** 1.2

**Leamos/Escribamos** Completa el párrafo con el imperfecto o el pretérito de los verbos en paréntesis.

Hace mucho tiempo __1__ (vivir) Iasá, una joven tan bonita que todos los que la __2__ (ver) __3__ (enamorarse) de ella. Pero Iasá solamente __4__ (amar) a Tupá, el hijo de un dios muy poderoso. Un día un malvado __5__ (decidir) hablar con la mamá de Iasá mientras ella __6__ (estar) en el campo. El malvado __7__ (convencer) a la mamá de que él debía casarse con su hija. Cuando Iasá __8__ (saber) la decisión de su mamá, ella __9__ (empezar) a llorar sin parar. A partir de entonces, no __10__ (querer) hablar con nadie.

1. vivía
2. veían
3. se enamoraban
4. amaba
5. decidió
6. estaba
7. convenció
8. supo
9. empezó
10. quiso

**11 La boda** 1.2

**Escribamos** Combina los fragmentos para escribir oraciones. Usa las formas correctas del pretérito y del imperfecto o del pasado progresivo. *¿Se te olvidó?* Past progressive, pp. 164–165

**MODELO** **el príncipe/tener veinte años/enamorarse de una princesa**
**El príncipe tenía veinte años cuando se enamoró de una princesa.**

1. el príncipe/ver a la princesa por primera vez/ella/estar bailando en una fiesta
2. los invitados/estar saliendo/el príncipe/hablar con ella
3. las estrellas/brillar en el cielo/el príncipe/pedir la mano de la princesa
4. el príncipe/esperar de rodillas/la princesa/dar su respuesta
5. el rey/estar en el palacio/la reina/darle la noticia
6. hacer buen tiempo/los enamorados/casarse

## Comunicación

HOLT SoundBooth ONLINE RECORDING

**12 ¡Cuéntame!** 1.1, 1.2

**Hablemos** En grupos de cuatro, inventen un cuento de hadas moderno. Usen el imperfecto para describir la escena y el pretérito para narrar lo que pasó. Cada miembro del grupo debe contribuir con tres oraciones. Luego compartan el cuento con la clase.

### 11 Answers

1. El príncipe vio a la princesa por primera vez cuando ella estaba bailando en una fiesta.
2. Los invitados estaban saliendo cuando el príncipe habló con ella.
3. Las estrellas brillaban en el cielo cuando el príncipe pidió la mano de la princesa.
4. El príncipe esperaba de rodillas cuando la princesa le dio su respuesta.
5. El rey estaba en el palacio cuando la reina le dio la noticia.
6. Hacía muy buen tiempo cuando los enamorados se casaron.

### Connections

**Language Arts Link**

Tell students that the legend of Iasá y Tupá comes from the Cashinahua people, an indigenous group with a strong oral tradition, who live in Brazil and parts of Peru. Ask students to find the complete legend at the library or on the Internet. Have them read the story and summarize it for the class. Then have them discuss any legends they know that are similar to this one. 3.1

### Comunicación

**Pair Activity: Interpersonal**

Have pairs of students tell each other about an event they have experienced in the last year. Have them use the imperfect to describe the scene and the preterite to tell what happened. 1.1

## Differentiated Instruction

**ADVANCED LEARNERS**

**Challenge** Have students research famous couples throughout world history and literature (Anthony and Cleopatra, Tristan and Iseult, Calixto and Melibea, Romeo and Juliet) and write a paragraph about the couple. Tell students to include the imperfect, the preterite, and the past progressive in their descriptions. 1.3

**MULTIPLE INTELLIGENCES**

**Interpersonal** Have students research birds that have magical powers in different cultures, such as the quetzal for the Mayas. Ask them to choose one of the birds and research the culture in which it has magical powers. Tell them to use what they learn about the culture to determine why the particular bird may have been singled out as special.

**Differentiated Instruction** See the Differentiated Instruction CD-ROM.

## Resources

**Planning:**

Lesson Planner, pp. 131–133, 292–295

One-Stop Planner

**Presentation:**

Video Program **GramaVisión**

**Practice:**

Grammar Tutor for Students of Spanish, Chapter 9

Cuaderno de vocabulario y gramática, pp. 100–102

Cuaderno de actividades, pp. 81–83

Activities for Communication, pp. 33–34

Lab Book, pp. 45–48

Teaching Transparencies

Bell Work 9.3

**Vocabulario y gramática** answers, pp. 100–102

Audio CD 9, Tr. 2

Interactive Tutor, Disc 2

### Bell Work

Use Bell Work 9.3 in the *Teaching Transparencies*, or write this activity on the board.

**Escribe una oración con las siguientes combinaciones de verbos en el imperfecto y el pretérito.**

1. haber/salir
2. estar/castigar
3. ser/llegar

1.3

## Repaso Preterite and imperfect contrasted

Interactive TUTOR

**1** The **preterite** is used:

- to show that an event or situation had a clear beginning or end

  La niña **vio** un fantasma y **empezó** a llorar.

- to give special meanings to verbs like **saber** and **conocer** that usually refer to mental states without a particular beginning or end

  La reina **supo** la noticia ayer.

**2** The **imperfect** is used:

- to describe habitual, ongoing past actions

  Los aztecas siempre **iban** al templo.

- to describe mental or physical states in the past without expressing their beginning or end

  La princesa **era** alta y morena.

- to indicate time or age in the past

  **Eran** las diez y media.

  El príncipe **tenía** ocho años.

Vocabulario y gramática, pp. 100–102
Actividades, pp. 81–83
Online workbooks

### ¿Te acuerdas?

The verbs **saber, querer, conocer, tener, poder,** and **estar** all have special meanings in the **preterite.**

Nunca **supimos** lo que pasó.
*We never found out what happened.*

La princesa no **quiso** casarse con el malvado.
*The princess refused to marry the villain.*

### 13 La vida de la princesa 1.2

**Leamos/Escribamos** Completa las oraciones con las formas correctas de los verbos en paréntesis.

1. De niña, la princesa _____ (fue/era) muy tímida.
2. Cuando ella _____ (tuvo/tenía) cinco años, _____ (empezó/empezaba) a estudiar con el sabio.
3. Cuando la princesa _____ (conoció/conocía) al sabio, ella supo que él la ayudaría.
4. El sabio le _____ (enseñó/enseñaba) a ser valiente y la _____ (ayudó/ayudaba) a ser fuerte.
5. Un día ella quiso buscar al malvado y lo _____ (hizo/hacía) sin miedo.
6. _____ (Fueron/Eran) las diez de la noche cuando ella _____ (regresó/regresaba) al palacio.
7. Su mamá se _____ (puso/ponía) muy feliz cuando ella _____ (llegó/llegaba).
8. A partir de entonces la princesa siempre _____ (enfrentó/enfrentaba) cualquier reto.

## Core Instruction

### TEACHING GRAMÁTICA

1. Go over points 1 and 2. **(2 min.)**
2. Review **¿Te acuerdas?** after discussing the second usage of the preterite. Discuss the difference in meaning between **supo** *(found out, knew from that point on)* and **sabía** *(knew)*. Then use **conocer, tener, poder,** and **estar** in sentences in both moods to demonstrate the difference in meaning. **(3 min.)**
3. Describe the uses of the imperfect by going over point 3 with students. **(1 min.)**
4. Model more sentences using the imperfect, and have students tell whether each sentence describes a habitual or ongoing past action, a mental or physical state, time, or age. **(5 min.)**

### GramaVisión

For a video presentation contrasting the preterite and imperfect, use **GramaVisión.**

GramaVisión

## 14 Las pirámides 1.2

**Leamos/Escribamos** Completa el párrafo con la forma correcta del verbo en paréntesis.

Hace mucho tiempo __1__ (haber) varias civilizaciones indígenas en México. Todos los grupos __2__ (tener) varios dioses. Los miembros de uno de los grupos __3__ (decidir) crear un lugar especial en la ciudad de Teotihuacán para honrar a sus dioses. Así que les __4__ (construir) algunos templos. Este grupo __5__ (saber) mucho sobre la arquitectura y por eso __6__ (hacer) los templos dentro de unas pirámides muy fuertes.

1. había 2. tenían 3. decidieron 4. construyeron 5. sabía 6. hizo

CD 9, Tr. 2

## 15 El Sol y la Luna 1.2

**Escuchemos** Escucha el mito y contesta las preguntas.

1. ¿Cómo eran el Sol y la Luna? ¿Cómo era su relación?
2. ¿Qué pasó que hizo cambiar su amistad?
3. ¿De qué tenía miedo la Luna?
4. ¿Qué le pidió al Sol?
5. ¿Por qué no le servía el vestido?
6. ¿Qué decidió el Sol al final de la historia?

Durante los equinoccios, el reflejo del Sol en esta pirámide de Chichén-Itzá produce una sombra de serpiente en las escaleras.

# Comunicación

HOLT SoundBooth ONLINE RECORDING

## 16 ¿Qué hizo el hechicero? 1.1, 1.2

**Hablemos** En parejas, inventen un cuento basándose en los dibujos. Usen el pretérito y el imperfecto.

### 15 Script

See script on p. 365E.

### 15 Answers

1. Eran muy buenos amigos.
2. El Sol se enamoró de la Luna.
3. Tenía miedo de perder su libertad.
4. Le pidió que buscara un vestido bonito.
5. No le servía porque ella siempre cambiaba de tamaño.
6. Decidió que no podía encontrarle el vestido perfecto.

Use the Chapter 9 *Picture Sequences Transparency.*

### 16 Sample Answer

**Había un rey que era un hombre muy antipático, y Merlín, el hechicero del palacio, quería castigarlo. Merlín usó sus poderes mágicos y de repente el rey y el hechicero desaparecieron. Merlín apareció en el lugar del rey, y el rey se convirtió en gato. Al final, el hechicero y la reina se rieron mucho.**

# Comunicación

### Pair Activity: Interpersonal

As an extension of Activity 16, have students work in pairs and imagine they are magicians like the one depicted that turned the king into a cat. Ask them to tell their partners two spells they have cast and why, using the preterite and the imperfect. 1.1

## Differentiated Instruction

### ADVANCED LEARNERS

**15 Challenge** Have students research myths about the Sun and the Moon from other cultures. Ask them to find at least two myths and to talk about the time to which they date, the culture to which they belong, and how important each was to the different peoples. 1.3

### MULTIPLE INTELLIGENCES

**14 Kinesthetic** Distribute the script of the audio story about the Sun and the Moon to groups of three and have them create a short conversation to act out the legend for the class. One student will play the Sun, one will play the Moon, and the third student will narrate. 1.1

**Differentiated Instruction** See the Differentiated Instruction CD-ROM.

## Resources

**Planning:**

Lesson Planner, pp. 131–133, 292–295

One-Stop Planner

**Presentation:**

Video Program **GramaVisión**

**Practice:**

Grammar Tutor for Students of Spanish, Chapter 9

Cuaderno de vocabulario y gramática, pp. 100–102

Cuaderno de actividades, pp. 81–83

Activities for Communication, pp. 33–34

Teaching Transparencies Bell Work 9.4

**Vocabulario y gramática** answers, pp. 100–102

Interactive Tutor, Disc 2

### Bell Work

*Use Bell Work 9.4 in the Teaching Transparencies, or write this activity on the board.*

**Indica si los siguientes verbos están en el pretérito o el imperfecto y usa cada uno en una oración.**

| | |
|---|---|
| **1. pudo** | **4. tejió** |
| **2. llovía** | **5. hacía** |
| **3. sacaba** | |

1.2

### COMMON ERROR ALERT ¡OJO!

Students often think that the words **por** and **para** are always translated as *for* in English. Have them read the sample sentences in the **Gramática** presentation, and then tell how they would say each sentence in English. Point out that **por** and **para** can be used to mean *for, through, by, in, per,* and *to.*

4.1

## Repaso Por and para

Interactive TUTOR

**1 Por** can be used to express

| | |
|---|---|
| • *through* or *by:* | El sabio pasó **por** el bosque. |
| • by, by means of: | Mandaron los libros **por** avión. |
| • a period of time: | La princesa durmió **por** cien años. |
| • a time of day: | El rey desapareció **por** la mañana. |
| • in exchange for: | Le pagó en oro **por** el secreto. |
| • *per*: | Tenemos que leer un cuento **por** día. |
| • the agent of action, *by*: | Fue construido **por** los aztecas. |

**2 Para** can be used to express

| | |
|---|---|
| • purpose or intention: | Vino **para** buscar al rey. |
| • a recipient: | El templo es **para** el dios del sol. |
| • destination: | Salieron **para** un lugar lejano. |
| • employment: | El malvado trabaja **para** el hechicero. |
| • a deadline: | La tarea es **para** mañana. |
| • an opinion: | **Para** mí, la leyenda es muy interesante. |

Vocabulario y gramática, pp. 100–102
Actividades, pp. 81–83
Online workbooks

### ¿Te acuerdas?

**Por** is also used in idiomatic expressions such as:

| | |
|---|---|
| **por ahora** | *for now* |
| **por cierto** | *by the way* |
| **por consiguiente** | *consequently* |
| **por favor** | *please* |
| **por fin** | *finally* |
| **por lo tanto** | *as a result* |
| **por supuesto** | *of course* |
| **por todas partes** | *everywhere* |

**Para** is also used in idiomatic expressions such as:

| | |
|---|---|
| **para nada** | *not at all* |
| **para siempre** | *forever* |

### 17 Un nuevo libro 1.2

**Leamos** Completa las oraciones con **por** o **para.**

1. Diego compró un libro de mitos y leyendas ═══ su hija, Ángela. para
2. Sólo pagó cinco dólares ═══ el libro porque estaba en oferta. 2. por
3. Ángela quería el libro ═══ saber más sobre sus leyendas favoritas. para
4. A ella le fascinaba el libro porque tenía dos dibujos ═══ página. por
5. Ángela miró los dibujos de los templos ═══ mucho tiempo. por
6. Diego le explicó que estos templos fueron construidos ═══ los mayas. por
7. El libro dice que también construyeron palacios ═══ los reyes. 7. para
8. Ángela quería escuchar los cuentos ═══ aprender más sobre los mayas. para
9. ═══ Ángela, lo más interesante fue la descripción de los dioses. 9. Para
10. Ella quería leer más, pero Diego dijo que dejarían un poco ═══ el día siguiente. para

## Core Instruction

### TEACHING GRAMÁTICA

1. Go over the seven listed uses of **por** and read the sample sentences in point 1. Write seven additional sentences with each usage on the board in scrambled order. Have students say in which way **por** is used in each sentence. **(5 min.)**
2. Go over the six listed uses of **para** and read the sample sentences in point 2. Write six additional sentences with each usage on the board in scrambled order. Have students say in which way **para** is used in each sentence. **(5 min.)**
3. Go over **¿Te acuerdas?** creating sentences that use each of the idiomatic expressions with **por** and **para,** so as to better illustrate them. **(5 min.)**

### GramaVisión

For a video presentation of **por** and **para,** use **GramaVisión.**

GramaVisión

## 18 Vamos al parque 1.2

**Leamos** Completa el diálogo con **por** o **para.**

CLARA Hice comida __1__ el picnic. ¿Puedes traer bebidas, __2__ favor? 1. para 2. por

IGNACIO __3__ supuesto. ¿Tal vez unos refrescos? 3. Por

CLARA Ay, no. No me gustan __4__ nada. 4. para

IGNACIO Pero no quiero pagar $5 __5__ un jugo natural. 5. por

CLARA __6__ cierto, ¿a qué hora vamos a salir __7__ la Patagonia? 6. Por 7. para

IGNACIO Pasaré __8__ ti a las once. 8. por

CLARA Estaremos esperándote __9__ mucho tiempo si vienes a las once. ¿Por qué no vienes más temprano? 9. por

IGNACIO Es que tengo que trabajar __10__ la mañana. 10. por

## 19 Preparaciones para el viaje 1.2

**Leamos/Escribamos** Estás planeando un viaje con tu familia a las cataratas del Iguazú. Pregunta quién puede hacer cada tarea, reemplazando las frases subrayadas con **por** o **para.**

**MODELO** **pasar a recoger los boletos**
**¿Quién puede pasar por los boletos?**

1. llenar los papeles que necesitamos entregar mañana
2. comprarle un regalo a nuestro guía
3. comprar un boleto que cuesta menos de $500
4. averiguar si se puede ir en autobús o en tren?
5. pasar a buscar a Elena el día del viaje
6. averiguar el costo de acampar en el parque durante una semana

### Nota cultural

El Parque Nacional Iguazú de Argentina es un lugar espectacular. Se llama Iguazú por las famosas cataratas que están en la frontera entre Argentina y Brasil. La palabra **iguazú** significa *great waters* en guaraní. Hay varias leyendas de los guaraníes sobre una serpiente monstruosa que vivía en las cataratas del Iguazú.

¿Sabes de otras leyendas basadas en fenómenos naturales? 1.3

Vista de las cataratas, Parque Nacional Iguazú

### Comunicación

HOLT SoundBooth ONLINE RECORDING

## 20 Un intercambio 1.1, 1.3

**Hablemos** En parejas, dramaticen una conversación entre un(a) profesor(a) de español y un(a) estudiante de intercambio de otro país. Usen las preguntas del cuadro.

> ¿Por qué quisiste ser estudiante de intercambio?
> Para ti, ¿qué significa hacer amigos de otro país?
> ¿Por cuánto tiempo vas a estar en el país?
> ¿Qué consejos tienes para otros estudiantes de intercambio?
> ¿Qué piensas hacer para conocer mejor este país?

### 19 Answers

1. ¿Quién puede llenar los papeles para mañana?
2. ¿Quién puede comprar un regalo para nuestro guía?
3. ¿Quién puede comprar un boleto por menos de $500?
4. ¿Quién puede averiguar si se puede ir por autobús o por tren?
5. ¿Quién puede pasar por Elena el día del viaje?
6. ¿Quién puede averiguar el costo de acampar en el parque por una semana?

### Comunicación

**Pair Activity: Interpersonal**

Have students imagine they are going to visit the **Parque Provincial Aconcagua** in Argentina, where the highest peak in all of the Americas is located (6,960 meters). Tell them that climbing the mountain is a challenging endeavor, but that there are several short hikes at low altitudes appropriate for all, such as the one leading to **Laguna Los Horcones.** The students should use **por** and **para** to discuss several things they have to do before they visit the park. They have to get permits in Mendoza, they have to decide what transportation to use, and what food and clothing to bring. 1.1

## Differentiated Instruction

### SLOWER PACE LEARNERS

**18 Additional Practice** Have students work in pairs to review **¿Te acuerdas?** on page 378. Have them make up a conversation using the idiomatic expressions listed, alternating between those with **por** and **para.** 1.1

### MULTIPLE INTELLIGENCES

**Naturalist** Have students research more information about the **Iguazú** park in Argentina. They may wish to find out more about the interesting animals of the region such as tapirs, giant anteaters, howler monkeys, ocelots, jaguars and caimans. Or they may prefer to focus on plant life, or activities for tourists. Have students present a summary of their findings to the class. 3.1

### Assess

**Assessment Program**

**Prueba: Gramática 1,** pp. 163–164

**Prueba: Aplicación 1,** pp. 165–16

Audio CD 9, Tr. 11

Alternative Assessment, pp. 381, 393, 405

**Online Assessment**
**my.hrw.com**

**Test Generator**

**Assess** **Differentiated Assessment** See the Differentiated Assessment CD-ROM.

# Cultura

VideoCultura

## Resources

**Planning:**

Lesson Planner, pp. 134, 294–295

One-Stop Planner

**Presentation:**

Audio CD 9, Tr. 3–5

Video Program, Videocassette 5
DVD Program
**VideoCultura**

**Practice:**

Cuaderno de actividades, p. 84

Video Guide, pp. 60–61

Lab Book, p. 84

Interactive Tutor, Disc 2

## Communities

### Career Path

Have students research companies that lead expeditions to remote parts of South America, such as the Galápagos Islands, Machu Picchu, or Patagonia. Ask them to contact one of the guides at one of these companies to find out their personal story of how they got the job, what their qualifications are, and what qualities make for an excellent guide.

5.1

## Pre-AP Practice

**AP Language Examination:** Have students first listen to the interviews with books closed to help prepare them for Section I, Part A: **Listening—Short Dialogues and Narratives.** Point out that Héctor, like many Spanish speakers from Chile, may pronounce **je** as **jie (mujer)** and pronounces **ch** more with the tip of the tongue toward the teeth instead of the blade of the tongue on the palate **(Chile, Chiloé).**

## Comparaciones

Interactive TUTOR

CD 9, Tr. 3-5

Las muchas leyendas que existen entre los pescadores chilenos son, en algunos casos, la fuente de los nombres y símbolos para sus botes.

### Ahora que tenemos tiempo, cuéntame un cuento 1.3

En muchas partes de Hispanoamérica hay leyendas de los pueblos indígenas (incas, aztecas, mayas) que explican el origen de la vida y del hombre. También hay leyendas que se refieren a elementos naturales, como montañas, ríos, valles, la luna o el sol. Y muchos cuentos populares hablan de animales y les dan características humanas, como la astucia (el zorro) o la valentía (el puma). También se pueden referir a personajes de la historia, como bandidos o exploradores, o imaginarios, como fantasmas. ¿Sabes tú de alguna leyenda de tu región? ¿algún "cuento de viejas" al que no le hayas hecho nunca caso?

### Héctor
**Santiago, Chile**

***Vamos a hablar sobre las leyendas de Chile. ¿Te sabes una leyenda de aquí?***

Sí, claro. Ésta es la leyenda, es una leyenda del sur de Chile, de la isla de Chiloé. Habla sobre una mujer, mitad pez, mitad hembra, la Pincoya. Dice la leyenda que esta mujer, cuando se encuentra mirando hacia el mar, la pesca estará buena. Pero en cambio, cuando se encuentra mirando hacia la tierra, quiere decir que la pesca estará mala, incluso peligrosa, para las embarcaciones y para los pescadores.

## Core Instruction

### TEACHING CULTURA

1. Read and discuss the introductory paragraph as a class. **(2 min.)**
2. Read the interview questions and have volunteers read Héctor and Miguel's responses. **(4 min.)**
3. Have students answer the questions in **Para comprender** and then have them work in pairs to discuss **Para pensar y hablar. (4 min.)**

### VideoCultura

For a video presentation of the interviews as well as for an additional interview for this chapter, see Chapter 9 **VideoCultura** on Videocassette or on DVD.

VideoCultura

Visit Holt Online
go.hrw.com
KEYWORD: EXP3 CH9
Online Edition

Cultura

**Miguel**
**Lima, Perú**

***¿Te sabes alguna leyenda de aquí?***

Sí, me sé una, la de Manco Cápac y Mama Ocllo.

***¿Nos la puedes contar?***

Sí. Cuenta la historia que hace mucho tiempo, el dios sol y la diosa luna mandaron [a] dos hijos, los cuales iban a formar un imperio. Ellos se llamaban Manco Cápac y Mama Ocllo. Ellos poseían una barra de oro, la cual donde se hundiese, ahí iban a formar [el] imperio incaico. Viajaron mucho, mucho tiempo en unas nubes. Cierto día, la barra de oro se hundió en una inmensa roca. Y ahí supieron que era el lugar indicado. Formaron el imperio incaico, el cual lo llamaron Cuzco, el ombligo del mundo. Es la historia del imperio incaico.

## Para comprender 1.2

1. ¿Dónde se encuentra y cómo se llama la isla donde se originó la leyenda que cuenta Héctor? ¿Quién es la Pincoya?
2. ¿Qué dice la leyenda que pasará si la Pincoya se encuentra mirando hacia el mar?
3. ¿De qué imperio habla la leyenda de Perú? ¿Quiénes enviaron a sus hijos y qué les mandaron hacer?
4. ¿Quiénes son Manco Cápac y Mama Ocllo?
5. ¿Cómo supieron los hijos que era el lugar que buscaban? ¿Cómo llamaron el lugar?

## Para pensar y hablar 1.3

¿Por qué son importantes las leyendas? ¿Qué crees que enseñan estas dos leyendas? ¿Qué otras lecciones puede enseñar una leyenda?

# Comunidad y oficio

## Los exploradores dejan sus nombres en América

Cuando los exploradores españoles llegaron a América del Sur, les dieron nombres a diferentes ciudades, países y regiones. Por ejemplo, el pueblo de Amarillo, Texas, fue nombrado por el color de la tierra cerca de un río del área. ¿Hay alguna ciudad en tu región que tenga un nombre español? Si no, ¿a qué regiones en Estados Unidos les pusieron nombres los exploradores españoles? Busca un pueblo o ciudad en Estados Unidos con un nombre español e investiga cómo recibió su nombre. 3.1

**Hernando de Soto, explorador español**

## Atlas INTERACTIVO MUNDIAL

See atlas at **go.hrw.com**.

**Map Activities**

Transparency **Mapa 6**

1. Have students click on the map for the South Atlantic Ocean. This map shows that the world underneath ocean waters in many ways resembles the one above: there are ridges, plateaus, plains, and trenches.
2. Have students click on the map of South America and name the countries along the Atlantic coast. **(Venezuela, Guyana, Surinam, Guayana Francesa, Brasil, Uruguay, Argentina)** Which countries are enclosed by land on all sides? **(Paraguay, Bolivia)** 3.1

## Answers

1. Se llama Chiloé; es una criatura mítica, mitad mujer, mitad pez.
2. Dice que si La Pincoya está mirando hacia el mar, la pesca estará buena.
3. Habla del imperio de los Incas. El dios Sol y la diosa Luna mandaron a sus hijos a formar un imperio.
4. Son los hijos de los dioses Sol y Luna.
5. Supieron que era el lugar porque su barra de oro se hundió en una inmensa roca. Lo llamaron Cuzco, lo cual significa *el ombligo del mundo.*

## Differentiated Instruction

### ADVANCED LEARNERS

**Challenge** Have students do a special project on the island of Chiloé. Have them print five maps of the area at different scales, starting with the one covering the whole country to the zoomed in version that fits only the archipelago. Have them identify different points on the map to distinguish cities, towns, and topographical formations. Ask them to look up all map terminology in the dictionary and create an English-Spanish glossary of those terms. 3.1

### MULTIPLE INTELLIGENCES

**Linguistic** Have students research and write about the mythology of the Chiloé Archipelago. Ask them to elaborate on why this spot in Chile might have such a developed mythological universe, and to find out more information on **la Pincoya.** 3.1, 3.2

## Connections

### Thinking Critically

Have students research the writings of Fray Bartolomé de las Casas and compare them to Alexander von Humboldt's publications. De las Casas advocated recognizing the dignity of indigenous people, and von Humboldt favored the abolition of enslavement. What is similar and different about the world views and styles of these two chroniclers from different centuries? 3.1

**Resources**

**Planning:**

Lesson Planner, pp. 135–136, 296–297

One-Stop Planner

**Presentation:**

Teaching Transparencies
**Vocabulario** 9.3, 9.4

**Practice:**

Cuaderno de vocabulario y gramática, pp. 103–105

Activities for Communication, pp. 35–36

Teaching Transparencies
Bell Work 9.5
**Vocabulario y gramática** answers, pp. 103–105

Interactive Tutor, Disc 2

**Bell Work**

Use Bell Work 9.5 in the *Teaching Transparencies,* or write this activity on the board.

**Completa las oraciones con *por* o *para.***

1. **Llamé ______ pedirte algo.**
2. **Te doy un dólar ______ el libro.**
3. **Mi papá trabaja ______ el señor Aquino.**
4. **La mujer caminó ______ el jardín.**
5. **Tengo que hacer el proyecto ______ mañana.**

1.2

**Objetivos**
- Talking about your hopes and wishes
- Expressing regret and gratitude

# Vocabulario en acción 2

## Los eventos históricos

Hace más de quinientos años, llegaron **los exploradores** españoles a América y establecieron **un imperio.**

Después de trescientos años de un gobierno colonial, Argentina, como todos los países de Latinoamérica, decidió luchar por **la independencia** y **declaró la guerra** para **liberar** el país. En las guerras, siempre hay **víctimas.**

## Core Instruction

### TEACHING VOCABULARIO

1. Introduce the vocabulary using transparencies **9.3** and **9.4.** Read the captions aloud. Check students' understanding by asking yes or no questions. **¿Las víctimas son las que sufren?** (sí) **¿Cuando se acuerda la paz, sigue la guerra?** (no) **(4 min.)**
2. On the board write two column headings: **sustantivos** and **verbos.** Have students tell you in which column each item should be placed. **(3 min.)**
3. Present words from **Más vocabulario** and use each in a sentence. **(3 min.)**

### TEACHING ¡EXPRÉSATE!

1. Introduce the **¡Exprésate!** functions used to talk about hopes and wishes. **(3 min.)**
2. Model the expressions using vocabulary words to complete each one. **(3 min.)**
3. Use the expressions in more sentences and have students tell you whether each sentence is logical or illogical. **Es de esperar que perdamos la guerra.** (illogical) **Ojalá que los soldados sean valientes.** (logical) **(4 min.)**

Visit Holt Online
**go.hrw.com**
KEYWORD: EXP3 CH9
Vocabulario 2 Practice

Estos **valientes soldados** esperaban ver **la derrota** de sus **enemigos** en **la batalla.** Fueron al **campo de batalla** para luchar por su **libertad.**

Después de **la victoria** de **las tropas** argentinas contra los españoles, el gran libertador José de San Martín **acordó la paz** con España. Todo el país **se regocijó** y a San Martín lo declararon **un héroe.**

Claro, hubo problemas después de la independencia. Algunos países latinoamericanos tuvieron **dictadores** que no respetaban **la justicia.** A veces fueron removidos del poder por **una revolución.**

**Más vocabulario...**

| | | | |
|---|---|---|---|
| **la bandera** | *flag* | **lamentar** | *to regret* |
| **cobarde** | *cowardly* | **la mujer soldado** | *female soldier* |
| **la heroína** | *heroine* | **sufrir** | *to suffer* |
| **honrar** | *to honor* | **vencer** | *to defeat* |

## ¡Exprésate!

**To talk about your hopes and wishes**

Interactive TUTOR

**El sueño de mi vida es vencer a...**
*My life-long dream is to overcome (defeat) . . .*

**Es de esperar que...**
*Hopefully . . .*

**Ojalá que los países aún en guerra lleguen a un acuerdo.**
*I hope that the countries still at war can reach an agreement.*

**Tenía muchas esperanzas de...**
*I had many hopes of . . .*

Vocabulario y gramática, pp. 103–105 Online workbooks

▶ **Vocabulario adicional** — Eventos históricos, p. R19

Vocabulario 2

## TPR
**Total Physical Response**

Bring to class illustrations of the following: soldiers, explorers, a statue of a hero, a well-known dictator. Ask individual students to respond to the following commands.

**Señala al dictador.**

**Señala a los exploradores.**

**Señala la estatua de un héroe.**

**Señala a los soldados.**

1.2

## Circumlocution

Have students guess the vocabulary word you are referring to with the following two clues: **(a) nación que logra gobernarse a sí misma ha obtenido ______; (b) una mujer que logra distinguirse en algún tipo de batalla se considera una ______.** 1.1

## Language Note

Arabic, spoken by the Moors who occupied parts of Spain for nearly eight hundred years, has influenced Spanish with thousands of words. **¡Ojalá!** (I hope!) comes from the Arabic phrase *wa-sha Allah* (God willing). Have students research other words in the Spanish language that come from Arabic.

## Differentiated Instruction

### ADVANCED LEARNERS

**Challenge** Remind students that important national historical figures are not just those that fight battles, but include those who distinguish themselves as diplomats and lawmakers. Have students research the life of Hernán Santa Cruz, a Chilean who participated in the committee that drafted the 1948, UN Universal Declaration of Human Rights. Have them focus on the contributions that he made to the final document. 3.1

### MULTIPLE INTELLIGENCES

**Kinesthetic** Have students take turns pantomiming different words from **Vocabulario 2.** The rest of the class must guess what word is being pantomimed. As an extension, you may wish to divide the class into small groups. Have groups act out complete scenes based on vocabulary words. The other groups will come up with a few sentences to describe what happened. A volunteer from each group will read their summary and the actors will decide which group had the best summary. 1.2

**Differentiated Instruction** See the Differentiated Instruction CD-ROM.

## Resources

**Planning:**

Lesson Planner, pp. 135–136, 296–297

One-Stop Planner

**Presentation:**

Teaching Transparencies
**Vocabulario** 9.3, 9.4

**Practice:**

Cuaderno de vocabulario y gramática, pp. 103–105

Activities for Communication, pp. 35–36

Lab Book, pp. 45–48

Teaching Transparencies
Bell Work 9.5
**Vocabulario y gramática** answers, pp. 103–105

Audio CD 9, Tr. 6

Interactive Tutor, Disc 2

### 21 Script

1. —¿Viste que el candidato del partido laboral ganó las elecciones para la presidencia?
—Sí, ¡estoy tan feliz! ¿Y viste cómo la gente se regocijaba en la plaza?
2. —Vi en la televisión una reunión muy importante de líderes mundiales. ¿De qué se trata?
—¿No te enteraste? Hoy acordaron la paz para poner fin al conflicto.
3. —Hoy se conmemora el Día de la Independencia de nuestro país.
—Así es. Vamos a ver el monumento antes de que empiece la ceremonia.
4. —¿Te imaginas cómo era la vida hace tres siglos? La gente exploraba continentes y mares desconocidos. Ahora no hay ningún lugar que explorar.
—No es cierto. Al contrario, hay muchos lugares. Hoy en día, los exploradores van desde el fondo del mar hasta el espacio para explorar nuevos mundos desconocidos.

CD 9, Tr. 6

### 21 Los eventos importantes 1.2

**Escuchemos** Escucha las conversaciones y escoge la foto que corresponde a cada una. **1.** D **2.** A **3.** B **4.** C

A

B

C

D

### Nota cultural

La derrota del gobierno de Salvador Allende en Chile ocurrió en 1973 cuando el dictador Augusto Pinochet tomó el poder. Pinochet gobernó el país hasta 1990 pero por fin cedió el poder a Patricio Aylwin Azócar (abajo), el presidente que había sido elegido por el pueblo. Desde entonces, Chile ha mantenido un gobierno democrático.

¿Qué sabes de la política actual de los otros países del Cono Sur? 3.1

### 22 La palabra definida 1.2

**Leamos/Hablemos** Lee las definiciones y escoge la palabra del cuadro que corresponde a cada una.

| | | |
|---|---|---|
| los exploradores | valiente | la libertad |
| acordar la paz | el imperio | la bandera |

1. Es rectangular y tiene símbolos que representan una nación. la bandera
2. Cuando una persona tiene derecho a hacer o a decir lo que quiere. la libertad
3. Lo contrario de cobarde. valiente
4. Un territorio extenso gobernado por un rey o un emperador. el imperio
5. Las personas que viajan a lugares desconocidos. los exploradores
6. Una manera de terminar una guerra entre dos naciones. acordar la paz

### 23 Los héroes 1.2

**Leamos** Completa las oraciones con la palabra correcta.

1. Fuimos al monumento para ═══ (honrar/liberar) a los que participaron en la batalla.
2. Lamentablemente hubo muchas ═══ (banderas/víctimas) en la guerra.
3. Todos los años, ═══ (conmemoramos/nos regocijamos) las fechas importantes de nuestra historia.
4. También recordamos a los ═══ (héroes/dictadores) de nuestro país.
5. Los héroes son personas muy ═══ (valientes/cobardes).
6. Nuestra ═══ (libertad/revolución) se la debemos a los soldados que lucharon por nosotros.

## Core Instruction

### VOCABULARY IN CONTEXT

Divide the vocabulary words among four groups of students. Students are to make one set of note cards with a synonym, definition, or drawing for each word assigned to their group. They are to make another set of note cards with the vocabulary words written on them. Groups shuffle their cards, then pass them to another group. Give students three minutes to match the new sets of cards. The original group then checks that the second group has matched the cards correctly. Cards are shuffled again and passed to a third group. Play continues in this manner until all vocabulary words have been practiced by each group. Finally, have students create sentences using their group's original set of words to demonstrate usage in context.

## 24 Algo de historia 1.2

**Escribamos** Usa las frases para escribir oraciones completas sobre algunos eventos históricos. Sigue el modelo.

MODELO **los soldados/llevar/la bandera a la batalla.**
**Los soldados llevaron la bandera a la batalla.**

1. los exploradores/llegar/América en 1492
2. los países de Latinoamérica/comenzar/la guerra de la independencia
3. los españoles/vencer/los incas
4. San Martín/ser/héroe de la guerra de independencia
5. la gente/regocijarse de/la victoria
6. los líderes/conmemorar/la fecha de la batalla
7. los soldados/luchar/por la libertad
8. los ciudadanos/honrar/la heroína

Esta estatua en Quito conmemora a José de San Martín, el libertador de Argentina, Chile y Perú.

## 25 Eventos históricos 1.2

**Escribamos/Hablemos** Usa una palabra o expresión de cada columna para escribir seis oraciones sobre los eventos históricos. Añade tus propios detalles y sé creativo.

MODELO **Los exploradores descubrieron una isla muy grande y en ella establecieron su imperio.**

| | | |
|---|---|---|
| los soldados | acordarse (ue) | la victoria |
| el héroe/la heroína | descubrir | la batalla |
| el dictador | vencer | las víctimas |
| el enemigo | honrar | la paz |
| los exploradores | liberar | el imperio |
| la gente | declarar la guerra | la independencia |

## Comunicación

HOLT SoundBooth ONLINE RECORDING

## 26 Hablando de la historia 1.1, 1.2

**Hablemos** Con un(a) compañero(a), creen un diálogo sobre algunos eventos históricos que conozcan. Usen las expresiones de **Exprésate** y las palabras de **Vocabulario.** Sigan el modelo.

MODELO **—Lamento que hubiera tantas víctimas en la Segunda Guerra Mundial.**
**—Ojalá que no haya otra guerra igual en el futuro.**

► Vocabulario adicional — Eventos históricos, p. R19

Vocabulario 2

### 24 Answers

1. Los exploradores llegaron a América en 1492.
2. Los países de Latinoamérica comenzaron la guerra de la independencia.
3. Los españoles vencieron a los incas.
4. San Martín fue el héroe de la guerra de independencia.
5. La gente se regocijó de la victoria.
6. Los líderes conmemoraron la fecha de la batalla.
7. Los soldados lucharon por la libertad.
8. Los ciudadanos honraron a la heroína.

### Connections

**History Link**

Tell students that many Latin American countries have lived under the oppression of a dictator in the past. Have them investigate one dictator and write a short summary of the impact he had on the country. Ask students to share the information with the class. 1.3, 3.1

### Cultures

**Practices and Perspectives**

Discuss holidays in the United States that commemorate important events in the country's history. You might want to talk about holidays such as Flag Day. What is its significance? How is it similar to holidays like Mexico's **Cinco de Mayo?** Have students research Latin American holidays that commemorate important historical events. 2.1, 4.2

### Comunicación

**Pair Activity: Presentational**

Have students imagine they are world leaders making a speech at the United Nations **(Naciones Unidas).** They are to speak on any topic related to the vocabulary. 1.3

## Differentiated Instruction

### SLOWER PACE LEARNERS

**Additional Practice** If students had a hard time coming up with suggestions for the conversations in Activity 26 and the pair activity above, have them review Activity 25. Ask them to organize sentences using elements from two out of the three columns, and create an original sentence ending. 1.2

### SPECIAL LEARNING NEEDS

**Students with Visual Impairments** Have students go to the library and listen to an audio tape of any historical text or to the narration of a historical film. Have them write a summary in Spanish of what they heard to present to a classmate. Have them use as many vocabulary words as possible. Have them note any special production qualities such as sound effects for battles, or actors playing the parts of historical characters in dialogues. 1.2

**Differentiated Instruction** See the Differentiated Instruction CD-ROM.

## Resources

**Planning:**

Lesson Planner, pp. 135–136, 296–297

One-Stop Planner

**Presentation:**

Teaching Transparencies
**Vocabulario** 9.3, 9.4

**Practice:**

Cuaderno de vocabulario y gramática, pp. 103–105

Activities for Communication, pp. 35–36

Teaching Transparencies
Bell Work 9.5
**Vocabulario y gramática** answers, pp. 103–105

Interactive Tutor, Disc 2

## Career Path

Ask students what fields of study focus on groups of people—their legends, social structure, and so on. (anthropology, archaeology, sociology, political science, linguistics, folklore) Other fields can aid this work: mathematics, geology, geography, and physics. How can Spanish help anthropologists or archaeologists? (They can travel to sites in the Spanish-speaking world; they can gain access to research that has not been translated into English; they can communicate with local people.) Where might Spanish be most useful for doing this type of research? (Spain, Latin America, the southwestern United States)

# Un editorial sobre la guerra

## La cara fea de la guerra

A través de la historia de la civilización humana, ha habido guerras. Cuando un pas está en gue rra con otro, alguna gente sólo quiere ver su cara bonita, o sea la victoria. Pero la guerra no es nada bonita, en realidad es una de las peores pesadillas que podemos sufrir. En pocas palabras: es lamentable que los líderes mundiales piensen a veces que no tienen otra opción. Ojalá que no sea así siempre. Hay varias razones o pretextos para mandar tropas al campo de batalla; puede ser para defender la patria, para lograr la derrota de un dictador, por la independencia o por la justicia. Las víctimas civiles son la cara fea de la guerra y es lógico que la gente se regocije cuando por fin se acuerda la paz. Luego, la gente conmemora el fin de la guerra y honra a los soldados que perdieron sus vidas en el conflicto. Generaciones de valientes del mundo entero se han sacrificado en defensa de sus países, pero ojalá que un día podamos lograr la paz sin sacrificar ni una sola vida.

### ¡Exprésate!

**To express regret and gratitude**

Interactive TUTOR

**Se arrepiente de que...**
*He/she regrets that . . .*

**Es lamentable que...**
*It's too bad that . . .*

**Les agradecieron a...**
*They thanked . . .*

Vocabulario y gramática, pp. 103–105 Online workbooks

## Core Instruction

### TEACHING ¡EXPRÉSATE!

1. Read the editorial aloud with students. Ask them to note any expressions used to express regret or gratitude. Have volunteers read the expressions. **(2 min.)**
2. Model each **¡Exprésate!** function used to express regret or gratitude. **(2 min.)**
3. Use the **¡Exprésate!** functions in complete sentences to talk about current events. **(3 min.)**
4. Have students provide historical topics and comment on each topic using an expression from **¡Exprésate! (3 min.)**

**27** **¿Qué opina la autora?** 1.2

**Leamos** Basándote en el editorial, decide si cada oración es **cierta** o **falsa.** Corrige las falsas.

1. Ha habido muchas guerras en el pasado. cierta
2. La gente sólo quiere ver los aspectos positivos de la guerra. cierta
3. La periodista piensa que la guerra es una pesadilla. cierta
4. Los líderes mundiales piensan que la guerra no es necesaria. falsa
5. Una razón para mandar tropas a la guerra es defender la patria. cierta
6. No hay víctimas civiles en la guerra. falsa
7. La gente se regocija cuando se acuerda la paz. cierta
8. La periodista piensa que no se puede lograr la paz sin la guerra. falsa

**28** **Los eventos en imágenes** 1.2

**Escribamos** Mira las imágenes y escribe una oración sobre lo que está ocurriendo. Usa las palabras de **Vocabulario** y las expresiones de **Exprésate** en tus oraciones.

## Comunicación

HOLT SoundBooth ONLINE RECORDING

**29** **A crear una nación** 1.1, 1.3

**Hablemos** En grupos de tres, preparen una historia de un país ficticio. Por ejemplo, pueden hablar de los exploradores que descubrieron el país y lo que pasó después. Usen las palabras de **Vocabulario** y ¡sean creativos!

*¿Se te olvidó?* Preterite and imperfect in storytelling, pp. 374–375

MODELO —**Verdelandia fue descubierto por exploradores de otro mundo. La gente de Verdelandia tenía muchas esperanzas de...**

Vocabulario 2

**28** **Answers**

Answers will vary. Possible answers:

1. Los exploradores llegaron a América y establecieron un imperio.
2. Todo el mundo tiene una bandera de la república.
3. Las valientes tropas chilenas luchan por la libertad.
4. Se regocijan la victoria en una celebración de la independencia.

## Connections

### History Link

Have students research the names of Latin American laureates of the Nobel Peace Prize, conferred every year since 1901 by the Committee created by Sweden's Alfred Nobel. Have them write short presentations that they could give to the class on each prize recipient, using the vocabulary words learned. 3.1

## Comunicación

### Pair Activity: Interpersonal

As an extension of Activity 29, have students create a conversation between citizens of a fictitious country. This country is distinctive in that it has never known war. Have them talk about their feelings about the rest of the world. 1.1

## Differentiated Instruction

### ADVANCED LEARNERS

**Challenge** Have students research at least three Spanish-language publications online to find opinion columns from the last six months having to do with war and peace. Have them make a list of the main points in the articles, and write short responses to them. 3.2

### SPECIAL LEARNING NEEDS

**Students with Learning Disabilities** Provide students with a copy of the editorial on page 386 in an outline form so they can better understand how it is constructed. Separate the sentences from each other and number the reasons listed for sending troops into battle.

## Assess

**Assessment Program**

**Prueba: Geocultura,** pp. 167–168

Alternative Assessment, pp. 381, 393, 405

**Online Assessment** my.hrw.com

**Test Generator**

**Assess** **Differentiated Assessment** See the Differentiated Assessment CD-ROM.

## Resources

**Planning:**

Lesson Planner, pp. 137–140, 298–301

One-Stop Planner

**Presentation:**

Video Program
**GramaVisión**

**Practice:**

Grammar Tutor for Students of Spanish, Chapter 9

Cuaderno de vocabulario y gramática, pp. 106–108

Cuaderno de actividades, pp. 85–87

Activities for Communication, pp. 35–36

Teaching Transparencies
Bell Work 9.6
**Vocabulario y gramática** answers, pp. 106–108

Interactive Tutor, Disc 2

### Bell Work

Use Bell Work 9.6 in the *Teaching Transparencies*, or write this activity on the board.

**Escribe oraciones con las siguientes palabras o frases.**

1. soldados
2. acordar la paz
3. explorar
4. honrar

1.3

### Teaching Suggestion

Have students research the history of their community. Were any historical battles fought where they live? Are there statues in their community to honor those who have made contributions? How has their community changed over the past 100 years? Have things changed for the better? Are there events they regret?

**Objetivos**
- Subjunctive
- Sequence of tenses

# Gramática en acción 2

GramaVisión

## Repaso Uses of subjunctive

Interactive TUTOR

**1** You've used verbs in both the **indicative mood** and the **subjunctive mood,** and you've learned that the **subjunctive mood** is used in the subordinate clause:

- with expressions of hope, wish, or recommendation
  Te sugiero que no **creas** ni una palabra de sus cuentos.
- with expressions of feelings, emotions, or judgment
  Me sorprende que no **conozcas** esa leyenda.
- with descriptions of people, places, or things that are not personally known to the speaker (unknown) or that do not exist according to the speaker (nonexistent)
  No hay guerra que no **tenga** víctimas.
- with expressions of doubt or denial
  Los exploradores dudan que la zona **sea** segura para entrar.

**2** Use the **subjunctive** after certain adverbial conjunctions such as **a menos (de) que, antes de que, con tal (de) que, en caso de que, para que,** and **sin que;** also with **en cuanto, cuando, después de que, hasta que,** and **tan pronto como** when they indicate future events.

Tenemos que ser valientes **cuando empiece** la batalla.

Vocabulario y gramática, pp. 106–108
Actividades, pp. 85–87
**Online** workbooks

### ¡Te acuerdas?

Impersonal expressions (formed with **ser** + *adjective* + **que**) take the subjunctive when they convey feelings or emotions **(es lamentable que),** judgment **(es importante que),** doubt or denial **(es imposible que).** When the impersonal expression conveys facts or something that the speaker considers to be true, the indicative is used.

**Es importante que** acuerden la paz.

**Es cierto que** fue un héroe.

### 30 El discurso 1.2

**Leamos** Completa las oraciones con el verbo correcto.

1. Quiero decirles que (tengo/tenga) muy buenas noticias.
2. Liberaron a los soldados después de que (vencimos/venzamos) al enemigo.
3. Cuando (llega/llegue) una ocasión como ésta, hay que celebrar.
4. Es dudoso que pronto (se resuelvan/se resuelvan) los problemas.
5. Por eso es importante que (nos esforzamos/nos esforcemos) siempre para mejorar la vida.
6. Y sobre todo, ojalá que (podemos/podamos) conseguir la paz.

## Core Instruction

### TEACHING GRAMÁTICA

1. Review the different uses of the subjunctive, as listed in point 1 and model the sample sentences. Provide an additional sample sentence for each usage and call on volunteers to identify the subjunctive expressions. **(3 min.)**
2. Go over point 2 and model additional examples with the subjunctive. Then ask volunteers to come up with similar sentences using the indicative to refer to past or habitual events. **(3 min.)**
3. Review the different impersonal expressions that take the subjunctive and the ones that take the indicative, which are listed in **¿Te acuerdas?** Model the sample sentences. **(4 min.)**

### GramaVisión

For a video presentation of the uses of the subjunctive, use **GramaVisión**.

GramaVisión

**31 Batalla de opiniones** 1.2

**Leamos/Escribamos** Completa el diálogo con la forma correcta de los verbos en paréntesis.

— No me gusta este videojuego. Quiero que mi personaje __1__ (ser) malo, pero sólo juega como héroe. sea

— Pues yo prefiero que mi personaje __2__ (luchar) por la justicia, así que debemos cambiar. luche

— Tu soldado no __3__ (poder) lograr la victoria a menos que __4__ (haber) un traidor entre mis tropas. **3.** puede **4.** haya

— Estás equivocado. No vamos a terminar el juego hasta que el héroe __5__ (sufrir) la derrota a manos del malvado. sufra

— Es triste que tú siempre __6__ (perder) cuando juegas conmigo. pierdas

— Sé que casi siempre ganas cuando juegas conmigo, pero dudo que __7__ (ganar) esta vez. ganes

**32 Una batalla** 1.3

**Leamos/Escribamos** Maribel está leyendo una historia sobre una batalla. Completa sus reacciones basándote en los dibujos.

1. Estoy triste porque...
2. Un soldado cobarde teme que...
3. Van a liberar a los soldados tan pronto como...
4. Todos se regocijaron después de que...

## Comunicación

HOLT SoundBooth ONLINE RECORDING

**33 En el futuro...** 1.1, 1.3

**Hablemos** En parejas, expresen sus opiniones sobre algunos problemas en su colegio o en su comunidad. Hablen de lo que ha ocurrido en el pasado y lo que esperan que ocurra en el futuro.

MODELO **—Cuando llegué aquí, no había ningún club de español.**
**—Espero que ahora podamos empezar un club.**

### COMMON ERROR ALERT ¡OJO!

Students often memorize the adverbial conjunctions listed in the grammar presentation and then always use the subjunctive with those conjunctions. Make sure to emphasize the fact that some of these conjunctions do not take the subjunctive when they indicate past or habitual events.

### Art Link

Have students view a Hollywood film depicting battle scenes, either in modern or past times. Encourage them to look for films set in Latin America. They should choose a favorite scene or two and write sentences about what happens in the plot with expressions that take the subjunctive. 1.3

### Comunicación

**Class Activity: Presentational**

As an extension of Activity 31, have students work in pairs to write a short debate on a historical event in which they use expressions that take the subjunctive. After they are satisfied with their debate, the groups can present it to the entire class. 1.3

## Differentiated Instruction

### ADVANCED LEARNERS

**32 Challenge** Have students refer to the battle scenes from Activity 32 and make up two new plot twists that they might have suggested to the script writer. Ask them to write the additions with expressions that take the subjunctive. They can discuss their work with a classmate for feedback. 1.2

### SPECIAL LEARNING NEEDS

**33 Students with Auditory Impairments** Have students complete Activity 33 as a written conversation with a partner. Ask them to write everything down on the same sheet of paper so as to create a coherent written exchange. As an alternative, you might allow them to have a conversation in instant message format so they can save the text on the computer. 1.1

**Differentiated Instruction** See the Differentiated Instruction CD-ROM.

## Resources

**Planning:**

Lesson Planner, pp. 137–140, 298–301

One-Stop Planner

**Presentation:**

Video program **GramaVisión**

**Practice:**

Grammar Tutor for Students of Spanish, Chapter 9

Cuaderno de vocabulario y gramática, pp. 106–108

Cuaderno de actividades, pp. 85 87

Activities for Communication, pp. 35–36

Lab Book, pp. 45–48

Teaching Transparencies
Bell Work 9.7
**Vocabulario y gramática** answers, pp. 106–108

Audio CD 9, Tr. 7

Interactive Tutor, Disc 2

### Bell Work

Use Bell Work 9.7 in the *Teaching Transparencies*, or write this activity on the board.

**Completa las oraciones con la expresión correcta.**

1. (Con tal que/Es cierto que) los ingleses fueron derrotados por los franceses bajo el mando de Juana de Arco.
2. (Me sorprende que/En cuanto) no sepas nada de la guerra civil.
3. (Es importante que/Para que) estudiemos la historia del mundo para evitar guerras en el futuro. 1.2

### 34 Script

See script on p. 365E.

Interactive TUTOR

## Sequence of tenses

**1** The phrase **sequence of tenses** describes the agreement between the verb in the **main clause** and the verb in the **subordinate clause.** The verb tense in the **subordinate clause** is determined by the verb tense in the **main clause.**

| | |
|---|---|
| **Ana dice que quiere ir.** | **Ana dijo que quería ir.** |
| **Ana dice que irá.** | **Ana dijo que iría.** |
| **Ana dice que ya ha ido.** | **Ana dijo que ya había ido.** |
| **Ana dice que vayas tú.** | **Ana dijo que fueras tú.** |
| **Ana irá en cuanto llegues.** | **Ana iba a ir en cuanto llegaras.** |
| **Ana duda que haya ido.** | **Ana dudaba que hubiera ido.** |

Este póster de Chile anuncia una película clásica del cine chileno.

**2** If the main clause is in the **present, present perfect, future,** or is a **command,** and if there is no expression requiring the subjunctive, the subordinate clause will be in the **indicative,** and can be in the past, present, or future.

| Main clause | | Subordinate clause |
|---|---|---|
| Dice | que | **va** al cine. |
| Ha dicho | | **irá** al cine mañana. |
| Dirá | | **había** mucha gente. |
| Dile | | **ha ido** al cine ya. |
| | | **fue** al cine ayer. |

**3** If the main clause is in the **present, present perfect, future,** or is a **command,** and contains an expression requiring the subjunctive, the subordinate clause may also be in the **present subjunctive.**

| Main clause | | Subordinate clause |
|---|---|---|
| Quiere | que | **vayan** ellos también. |
| Diles | | |
| Les he dicho | | |

Vocabulario y gramática, pp. 106–108
Actividades, pp. 85–87
Online workbooks

CD 9, Tr. 7

### 34 ¿Pasado, presente o futuro? 1.2

**Escuchemos** Escucha los comentarios y decide si la cláusula subordinada está en el **pasado, presente** o **futuro.**

**1.** presente **2.** futuro **3.** pasado **4.** pasado **5.** pasado **6.** presente

## Core Instruction

### TEACHING GRAMÁTICA

1. Go over point 1. Emphasize that just as a subordinate clause is always dependent on a main clase, so is the tense of the verb contained in each one. **(2 min.)**
2. Ask students to identify the tense of the verbs in each sentence. Then have them plot the event or state for each clause on a timeline. **(4 min.)**
3. Go over point 2. Demonstrate the flexibility of combining certain verbs in the main and subordinate clauses. **(2 min.)**
4. Go over point 3. Ask students what kinds of present tense verbs in the main clause might be followed by the present subjunctive (**esperar, dudar, sugerir,** and so on). **(2 min.)**

### GramaVisión

For a video presentation of sequence of tenses, use **GramaVisión.**

GramaVisión

## 35 La heroína 1.2

**Leamos** Completa las oraciones con el verbo correcto.

1. La mujer soldado cree que la guerra no (va/vaya) a terminar nunca.
2. Le sorprenderá que (ha/haya) terminado ya.
3. Los líderes dijeron que (acordaron/acordarán) la paz ayer.
4. Dile a la mujer soldado que (venga/viene) al palacio.
5. Es cierto que ella (fue/sea) muy valiente.
6. Será importante que la (honramos/honremos) como heroína.

## 36 Tiempos de valor 1.2

**Leamos/Escribamos** Completa el párrafo con las formas correctas de los verbos en paréntesis.

El soldado sube la montaña. Dice que __1__ (colocar) una bandera chilena en la cima *(top)* esta tarde. Quiere que todo el mundo __2__ (recordar) a las víctimas de la guerra. Sabe que el dictador __3__ (escaparse) anoche. Todo el mundo espera que no __4__ (regresar). El soldado piensa que la guerra __5__ (ser) necesaria a veces, pero lamenta que tantas personas __6__ (sufrir).

**1.** colocará **2.** recuerde **3.** se escapó **4.** regrese **5.** es **6.** hayan sufrido, sufran

## 37 Mis opiniones sobre la historia 1.3

**Leamos/Escribamos** Completa las oraciones basándote en lo que has aprendido sobre los exploradores.

1. He aprendido que los exploradores...
2. Mis profesores dicen que Pizarro...
3. No he estudiado ningún imperio que...
4. Me sorprende que muchos grupos indígenas...
5. Nunca he dudado que los exploradores...
6. Cristóbal Colón es recordado porque...
7. Nos han enseñado que en el Nuevo Mundo...
8. Mañana nos dirán que otras civilizaciones...

### Nota cultural

La bandera chilena fue izada *(raised)* por primera vez en público el 12 de febrero de 1818, durante la proclamación de la Independencia del país. Diseñada por el militar español Antonio Arcos, la bandera (abajo) tiene los colores rojo, azul y blanco que representan la sangre derramada *(spilled)* durante la guerra de independencia, el color del cielo chileno y las puntas nevadas de la cordillera de los Andes. Se dice que la estrella de cinco puntas simboliza los poderes del Estado, que sirve de guía en el camino al progreso y que honra la valentía de los mapuches.

¿Cómo se comparan los símbolos en la bandera chilena con los que llevan la bandera estadounidense? 3.1

## Comunicación

HOLT SoundBooth ONLINE RECORDING

## 38 Mis sueños para mi país 1.1, 1.3

**Hablemos** Imagina que tú y tu compañero(a) son políticos. Túrnense para explicar lo que quieren para su país ahora y lo que les dirán a sus hijos sobre su país.

MODELO **—Quiero que dejemos de tener guerras.**
**—Les diré que nuestro país ha logrado mucho.**

### Connections

**Social Studies Link**

Tell students that mountaineering and alpine back-country skiing are big industries in Chile and Argentina because of the magnificent opportunities offered by the Andes. Businesses offering guide services for tours and ascents employ professionals that not only know how to practice sports, but also know the terrain intimately and are extensively trained in first aid and other emergency management techniques. Have students research information on the mountains of Chile and Argentina. 3.1

### Comunicación

**Pair Activity: Interpersonal**

Have students work with a partner to discuss things they are going to do next weekend. Then have them pretend the weekend has arrived and discuss the same things in the present tense. Finally, ask them to imagine that the weekend has passed and have them discuss the things they already did using the past tense. 1.1

## Differentiated Instruction

### SLOWER PACE LEARNERS

**34 Additional Practice** Have students listen to the script for Activity 34 a second time. Also provide them with a transcript so that this time they can see the verbs spelled out as they listen to the script. After identifying all the verbs correctly, the students can conjugate them in the subordinate clauses with one of the other two tenses. 1.2

### MULTIPLE INTELLIGENCES

**37 Linguistic** As an extension of Activity 37, have students make up new sentences by adding subordinate clauses to four or five of the main clauses listed. Have them choose the sentences carefully so as to be able to form a coherent historical narrative between them as a whole. 1.2

**Differentiated Instruction** See the Differentiated Instruction CD-ROM.

## Resources

**Planning:**

Lesson Planner, pp. 137–140, 298–301

One-Stop Planner

**Presentation:**

Video program **GramaVisión**

**Practice:**

Grammar Tutor for Students of Spanish, Chapter 9

Cuaderno de vocabulario y gramática, pp. 106–108

Cuaderno de actividades, pp. 85–87

Activities for Communication, pp. 35–36

Teaching Transparencies Bell Work 9.8

**Vocabulario y gramática** answers, pp. 106–108

Interactive Tutor, Disc 2

### Bell Work

Use Bell Work 9.8 in the *Teaching Transparencies,* or write this activity on the board.

**Escribe oraciones con las siguientes combinaciones de verbos. Usa el primer verbo en la cláusula principal y el segundo en la subordinada.**

**1. pensó/participaría**
**2. declarará/prefiere**
**3. sorprende/vaya**

### Heritage Speakers

Ask your heritage speakers, particularly those from Chile, what else they know about Salvador Allende and Augusto Pinochet: What were Allende's political ideas? Why was he removed from power? How is he believed to have died? What role did the United States play in the coup d'etat? What repercussions have resulted from that involvement? What kind of president was Pinochet? What was he accused of? You might want to show them the movie "Missing." It deals with part of that history.

1.3

## More on sequence of tenses

Interactive TUTOR

**1** As you know, **sequence of tenses** describes the agreement between the verb in the **main clause** and the verb in the **subordinate clause.** The verb tense in the **subordinate clause** is determined by the verb in the **main clause.**

**Sé que quieres ir.** **Sabía que querías ir.**

**2** If the main clause is in the **preterite, imperfect, past perfect,** or **conditional,** and if there is no expression requiring the subjunctive, the subordinate clause will be in the **indicative**, and generally in the past.

| Main clause | | Subordinate clause |
|---|---|---|
| Dijo | que | **fue** al cine. |
| Decía | | **iba** al cine mañana. |
| Había dicho | | **iría** al día siguiente. |
| Diría | | **había ido** a pie. |

**3** In some cases, if the main clause is in the past or conditional and contains an expression requiring the subjunctive, the subordinate clause will be in the **past subjunctive.**

| Main clause | | Subordinate clause |
|---|---|---|
| Quería | que | **fuéramos** al cine hoy. |
| Le gustaría | | |

Vocabulario y gramática, pp. 106–108
Actividades, pp. 85–87
**Online** workbooks

### 39 Un nuevo mundo 1.2

**Leamos** Completa cada oración con el verbo correcto.

1. Cristóbal Colón decidió que (buscaría/buscara) una nueva ruta a las Indias.
2. Él ya le había pedido al rey de Portugal que (pagó/ pagara) su viaje.
3. El rey no creía que (fuera/fue) una buena idea.
4. Pero la reina Isabel de Castilla dijo que le (ayudaría/ayudó) con el viaje si le diera más información sobre sus exploraciones.
5. Sería bueno que todos (fuimos/fuéramos) a ver el monumento a Colón en Barcelona.
6. Mi papá me enseñó fotos del monumento para que (pudiera/pueda) reconocerlo.
7. Me dijo que él (fuera/había ido) solamente una vez a Barcelona.
8. Me gustaría que (viéramos/veamos) la nueva película sobre Colón.

## Core Instruction

### TEACHING GRAMÁTICA

1. Read point 1 aloud to remind students that sequence of tenses describes the agreement between the verbs in the main and subordinate clauses. Model the sample sentences. **(3 min.)**
2. Go over point 2 and model different combinations of the main and subordinate clauses listed in the chart. **(4 min.)**
3. Go over point 3, modeling the sentence listed. Provide other examples: **Ella dudaba que yo llegara a tiempo. Esperaban que terminara pronto la guerra. (3 min.)**

### GramaVisión

For a video presentation of sequence of tenses, use **GramaVisión.**

GramaVisión

## 40 Una lección de historia 1.2

**Leamos/Escribamos** Completa las oraciones con la forma correcta del verbo en paréntesis.

1. El profesor de historia sugirió que nosotros ═══ (estudiar) la revolución para el examen. estudiáramos
2. También nos había pedido que ═══ (entrevistar) a alguien de esa época. entrevistáramos
3. El profesor me recomendó que ═══ (visitar) un campo de batalla. visitara
4. A mí me interesó mucho lo que mi abuelo me ═══ (contar) de la revolución. contó
5. Él siempre decía que la revolución ═══ (ser) importante para nuestro país. fue
6. Me sorprendió que mi abuelo ═══ (recordar) todos los detalles como si fuera ayer. recordara

Jóvenes chilenos hablan de las películas que han visto.

## 41 Del presente al pasado 1.2

**Leamos/Escribamos** Vuelve a escribir cada oración en el pasado y reemplaza el verbo subrayado con el verbo en paréntesis.

**MODELO** **Ellos piensan que la película es buena. (pensaron)**
**Ellos pensaron que la película era buena.**

1. Marisa prefiere que vayamos a una película de fantasía. (prefería) 1. Marisa prefería que fuéramos a una película de fantasía.
2. Blanca dice que ya la ha visto. (dijo) 2. Blanca dijo que ya la había visto.
3. Creo que ha salido la nueva película. (Creía) 3. Creía que había salido la nueva película.
4. El profesor ha pedido que veamos esta película. (había pedido) 4. El profesor había pedido que viéramos esta película.
5. Me extraña que Blanca la quiera ver. (extrañó) 5. Me extrañó que Blanca la quisiera ver.
6. Marisa nos recomienda que hagamos otra actividad. (había recomendado) 6. Marisa nos había recomendado que hiciéramos otra actividad.

## Comunicación

HOLT SoundBooth ONLINE RECORDING

## 42 Un cuento de encuentros 1.1, 1.2

**Hablemos** Con un(a) compañero(a), cuenten una historia sobre lo que pasa. Primero, cuéntenla en el presente y luego vuelvan a contarla en el pasado.

### Más práctica

For more practice, you might have students write the following sentences using the correct sequence of tenses. Have students underline the main clause once and the subordinate clause twice in each sentence and label them **cláusula principal** and **cláusula subordinada.**

1. **Ernesto (querer) que nosotros (ver) el estreno de una película.**
2. **Él (decir) que la película (tratar) de una mujer soldado.**
3. **La gente (decir) que la mujer soldado (ser) una heroína.**
4. **Carla y Félix ya me (decir) que ellos (ir) conmigo a verla el sábado.**

1.2

### Comunicación

### Group Activity: Presentational

Have students form groups of three and imagine that they are radio news reporters making short announcements. Have them use sentences with main and subordinate clauses to talk about current events or other issues of interest to students.

1.3

## Differentiated Instruction

### ADVANCED LEARNERS

**Challenge** Have students research the influence of nationalities other than the Spanish on Chile and Argentina. For example, there are large English, German, and Italian populations in both countries, each arriving roughly in that order chronologically. Ask them to write a short paragraph about one of the groups. Have them peer-edit each other's paragraphs to check for the correct sequence of tenses. 1.3

### SPECIAL LEARNING NEEDS

**41 Students with AD(H)D** Before students do Activity 41, have them copy each sentence and put a star next to those in the subjunctive mood. Then have them circle the verb in the subordinate clause of each sentence. Have them underline the verb in the main clause and then replace the underlined verb with the verb in parenthesis. Finally, they should leave a blank for the second verb. They now have a fill-in-the-blank activity and can focus on choosing the correct verb tense for the subordinate clause. 1.2

### Assess

**Assessment Program**

**Prueba: Gramática 2,** pp. 169–170

**Prueba: Aplicación 2,** pp. 171–172

Audio CD 9, Tr. 12

Alternative Assessment, pp. 381, 393, 405

**Online Assessment** **my.hrw.com**

**Test Generator**

**Assess** **Differentiated Assessment** See the Differentiated Assessment CD-ROM.

**Resources**

**Planning:**

Lesson Planner, pp. 140, 300–301

One-Stop Planner

**Presentation:**

Video Program, Videocassette 5

DVD Program

**VideoNovela**

**Practice:**

Video Guide, pp. 62–64

Lab Book, pp. 85–86

## Visual Learners

Have students write in circles: **Clara, El profesor Luna, El presidente de *MaderaCorp*, Los ecologistas,** then draw lines to the events from the episode that relate to each character. Below, they hypothesize how the story might end. 1.2

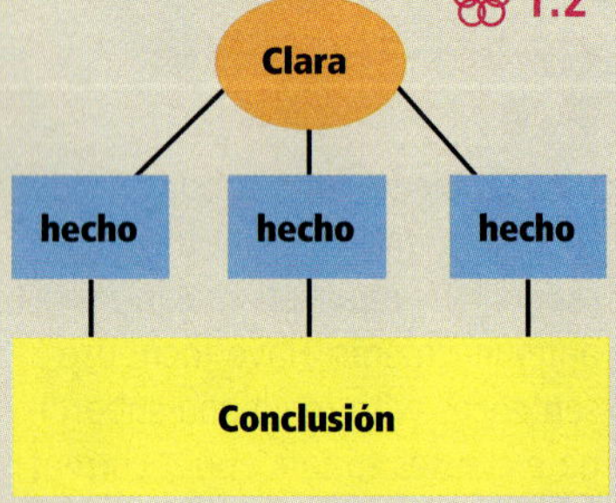


Novela en video

# Clara perspectiva

## Episodio 9

**ESTRATEGIA**

**Predicting** As you near the end of a story, you naturally start making predictions about what is going to happen. Based on what you know, make a prediction about the following people regarding each of their situations: 1) Clara and her job at ***Chile en la Mira;*** 2) Clara and her search for the professor; 3) the professor and his environmental studies; 4) the professor and his safety; 5) the president of ***MaderaCorp*** and his bid to buy the land in **Magallanes**; 6) the ecologists and their attempt to stop ***MaderaCorp.*** 1.2

### En la oficina del señor Ortega

**Sr. Ortega** Señor Medina, como su colega todavía no se ha presentado, usted va a estar a cargo de una investigación que necesitamos hacer para un artículo sobre la Isla de Pascua. Hay muchos mitos y leyendas asociados con la isla.

**Octavio** Sí, Rapa Nui.

**Sr. Ortega** Sí, es su nombre polinésico.

1

2

**Octavio** ¿De qué se trata el artículo?

**Sr. Ortega** Queremos explicar la historia de la isla y cómo llegó a ser gobernada por Chile. Según tengo entendido, los primeros habitantes llegaron a la isla entre los años 400–600 después de Cristo.

**Octavio** ¿Y se sabe de dónde eran?

**Sr. Ortega** Hay muchas teorías—la más aceptada es que vinieron de Polinesia. Pero también hay los que creen que es posible que hayan venido de Perú.

**Octavio** Muy bien. Pero el enfoque se debe quedar ¿sobre qué?

**Sr. Ortega** La Isla de Pascua tiene una historia larga y llena de tragedia, de guerras civiles, de explotación de las tierras, de culturas intentando sobrevivir. También hay una leyenda muy interesante sobre los hombres pájaros.

**Octavio** Y los gigantescos monumentos, los moais, ¿vamos a escribir algo sobre el misterio de su existencia?

**Sr. Ortega** Sí, los moais. Se cuenta que los moais representaban a los dioses sagrados. Lo que no se sabe es cómo pudieron las enormes esculturas llegar a situarse en donde hoy se encuentran.

3

4

**Sr. Ortega** Quiero que leas todo lo que puedas, libros, artículos y también lo que puedas encontrar en Internet. Queremos resolver el misterio de la Isla de Pascua, aquí en las páginas de *Chile en la Mira.*

**Octavio** Sí, Señor Ortega. Manos a la obra.

**Sr. Ortega** Y si te encuentras con la señorita de la Rosa, por favor, mándale mis saludos.

## Core Instruction

### TEACHING NOVELA EN VIDEO

1. Have volunteers summarize what has happened so far in **Clara perspectiva. (2 min.)**
2. Play the video. Ask students to pay attention to the different places where the action takes place. **(5 min.)**
3. Have volunteers read the exchange between Clara and the sergeant in the section **En la comisaría. (5 min.)**
4. Answer the questions on page 395 as a class. If students have trouble answering any of the questions, have them reread the appropriate sections. **(3 min.)**

### Escuchemos

As students watch the **Novela,** have them listen with their books closed, and then answer **cierto** or **falso** to the following statements: **1. Los moais representaban a los hombres pájaros. 2. Muchos creen que los primeros habitantes de la Isla de Pascua vinieron de Polinesia. 3. Un almirante holandés descubrió la isla en el día de Navidad. (f, c, f)**

Novela en video

## En *MaderaCorp*

**Profesor Luna** Señor Reyes, si examina la propuesta de los ecologistas, verá que contiene ideas que no serían difíciles de implementar.
**Señor Reyes** Bueno, tendré que pensarlo. Y claro es imprescindible que consulte con los inversionistas.
**Ecologista 2** ¿Qué te dije? Nunca van a aceptar nuestras condiciones.
**Ecologista 1** Tranquila, Sarita, déjalo leer primero.

5



## En la comisaría

**Clara** Al final, me di cuenta que los documentos que imprimí eran los estudios de impacto ambiental que el profesor Luna iba a presentar.
**Sargento** Pero, ¿por qué quería que usted los imprimiera?
**Clara** No sé. Quizás pensaba que alguien los iba a destruir. Y quería tener una copia antes de que eso pasara.

6

7

**Sargento** ¿El profesor estará recibiendo dinero?
**Clara** No, imposible. Nunca trataría de abusar de su posición.
**Sargento** No podemos especular. Tenemos que encontrarlo.
**Detective** ¿Por dónde empezamos?
**Clara** En las oficinas de *MaderaCorp.* Es lógico, ¿no?
**Sargento** Muy bien. Vamos.
**Detective** Un auto… sí… y dos carabineros. No sabemos qué vamos a encontrar.

## En *MaderaCorp*

**Clara** ¡Profesor Luna! ¡Está bien!
**Profesor Luna** ¡Clara! ¿Qué estás haciendo acá?
**Sargento** Profesor Luna, ¿no ha visto las noticias? Pensábamos que estaba secuestrado.
**Profesor Luna** Por Dios. Estaba tan involucrado en la situación, que olvidé llamar a Mercedes.
**Señor Reyes** Bienvenidos. Pasen. Estamos a punto de resolver nuestras diferencias.

8

## ¿COMPRENDES?

1. ¿Qué cosas sobre la historia de Rapa Nui tiene que investigar Octavio? ¿Dónde tiene que buscar?
2. ¿Qué leyenda le interesa al señor Ortega? ¿Qué cosas misteriosas le interesan a Octavio?
3. ¿Está enojado el señor Ortega con Clara? ¿Qué puedes predecir sobre el futuro de Clara en *Chile en la Mira?*
4. ¿Dónde deciden empezar a buscar al profesor? ¿Es lógico empezar ahí?  ¿Por qué sí o por qué no?
5. ¿Está interesado el presidente de *MaderaCorp* en la propuesta de los ecologistas? ¿A quiénes tiene que consultar? ¿Qué puedes predecir sobre el acuerdo entre los ecologistas y MaderaCorp? 1.2

**Próximo episodio**
*¿Sobre qué crees que se va a tratar el próximo artículo de Clara y Octavio? ¿Por qué crees eso?*
PÁGINAS 436–437

Novela en video

### Gestures

Ask students to note the gestures that Señor Ortega and Octavio use as they discuss Octavio's new assignment about Easter Island. Have volunteers read the first section and mimic the gestures. Have students talk about situations in which they would use the same gestures.

### ¿Comprendes? Answers

1. todo lo que sea posible sobre Rapa Nui, pero especialmente su variada historia; en todo lo que pueda: libros, artículos e Internet
2. la leyenda de los hombres-pájaros; los gigantescos monumentos
3. Aunque el Sr. Ortega esté enojado con Clara, lo más seguro es que ya no lo esté cuando ella logre tener una posición exclusiva desde la cual podría contar la historia de los sucesos de las negociaciones entre los ecologistas y MaderaCorp.
4. en las oficinas de MaderaCorp; Sí, es lógico porque Clara había visto a los guardaespaldas de la compañía amenazar al profesor.
5. Sí; a los inversionistas; que ambas partes lograrán negociar un poco porque les conviene llegar a un acuerdo en el que puedan coexistir pacíficamente

### Comunicación

#### Group Activity: Presentational

Have students work in teams of three or four. First, students should put a list of their predictions together as to how the **MaderaCorp** executives and the ecologists are going to settle their differences. When the list is complete, students will select a scenario, write the dialog, and act it out.

1.3

## Clara perspectiva, Episodio 9

In **Episodio 9,** back at *Chile en la Mira,* Octavio and Señor Ortega have concluded that Clara will not be coming to work. Señor Ortega assigns Octavio to research the history of Easter Island for an article. At *MaderaCorp,* the meeting with the ecologists, *MaderaCorp,* and the professor has begun. The president of *MaderaCorp* reviews the conditions and limitations that the ecologists want to impose on their development plans. Meanwhile, Clara and the authorities storm the meeting to find the professor, the president of *MaderaCorp,* and the ecologists resolving their differences. Professor Luna realizes that he had neglected to inform anyone of his whereabouts.

## Resources

**Planning:**

Lesson Planner, pp. 141, 302–303

One-Stop Planner

**Presentation:**

Audio CD 9, Tr. 8

**Practice:**

Cuaderno de actividades, p. 88

Reading Strategies and Skills Handbook, Chapter 9

Interactive Advanced Reader

### Pre-Reading Activity

Have students find out about the topography of the Falklands/Malvinas, and in what economic activity its residents have engaged throughout history.

# Lectura informativa

CD 9, Tr. 8

# Un territorio con historia

*La historia de las Islas Malvinas*

Las Islas Malvinas, ubicadas en el océano Atlántico al este de la costa de Argentina, tienen una larga historia colonial. Aunque las Islas Malvinas están cerca de Argentina, son gobernadas por Inglaterra. Algunos historiadores creen que las islas fueron descubiertas por el español Esteban Gómez en 1520. Otros afirman que el explorador John Davis las descubrió en 1592. Las islas han sido ocupadas por España, Francia, Inglaterra y Argentina en diferentes momentos de su historia.

Las Islas Malvinas están al este de la costa de Argentina.

**Países europeos reclaman las islas**

España fue el primer país en reclamar las Malvinas para su imperio, poco después de su descubrimiento. En 1764 llegaron los franceses y ocuparon una parte de las islas donde establecieron un puerto. Ellos le dieron el nombre de *Malouines* a las islas. Poco después los españoles tomaron control de las islas y convirtieron el nombre francés en *Malvinas.* En 1765 llegó una expedición inglesa a las islas y las nombró *Falkland Islands,* que hoy es el nombre reconocido por el gobierno de Inglaterra. España sacó a los ingleses en 1770 y mantuvo control sobre las islas hasta que Argentina consiguió su independencia en 1816.

## Core Instruction

**TEACHING LECTURA INFORMATIVA**

As a pre-reading activity, you may wish to have students find out about the topography of the Falklands/Malvinas, and in what economic activity its residents have engaged throughout history.

1. Read and discuss the introductory paragraph as a class. Ask volunteers why they think that the Falklands/Malvinas have been occupied by four different countries since they were first explored by Europeans. **(5 min.)**
2. Lead an ongoing discussion about the material after you read each paragraph as a class. **(25 min.)**
3. Have students answer the **Comprensión** questions with a partner. Discuss **Actividad** with the class. **(5 min.)**

### Pre-AP Practice

**AP Language Examination: Lectura informativa** helps students prepare for Section I, Part B: **Reading Comprehension.** The audio recording helps them prepare for Part A: **Listening—Short Narratives.**

Visit Holt Online
**go.hrw.com**
KEYWORD: EXP3 CH9
Online Edition

# Lectura informativa

1. falsa; Posiblemente fueron descubiertas en 1520 por Esteban Gómez, o en 1592 por John Davis.

Hoy en día Inglaterra gobierna las Islas Malvinas.

**El debate de las Malvinas sigue**

La nueva nación de Argentina dio permiso a Luis Vernet en 1828 para establecer una colonia y mandó a cien gauchos e indígenas para desarrollar la cría de ganado[1]. En 1833, el gobierno de Inglaterra expulsó[2] a las autoridades argentinas y tomó el control de las islas. En 1982, más de cien años después, el gobierno de Argentina tomó las islas por la fuerza y las ocupó durante 10 semanas. Los ingleses enviaron sus tropas y expulsaron a los argentinos de las islas en una guerra sangrienta[3]. El debate sobre quién debe gobernar las Islas Malvinas sigue hoy en día. Los gobiernos de Argentina e Inglaterra han establecido relaciones diplomáticas de nuevo y las dos naciones quieren llegar a un acuerdo. Sin embargo, los dos países se mantienen firmes en sus posiciones en cuanto a las Islas Malvinas. El gobierno de Gran Bretaña no quiere retirarse[4] de las islas y Argentina afirma que tiene soberanía[5] sobre las Malvinas. ■

1 livestock 2 expelled 3 bloody 4 withdraw 5 sovereignty

## Comprensión

**A Detalles de la historia** Indica si cada oración es **cierta** o **falsa**. Corrige las oraciones falsas. 1.2

1. Cristóbal Colón descubrió las Islas Malvinas en 1500.
2. Los franceses dieron el nombre *Malouines* a estas islas. cierta
3. Los ingleses llegaron a las islas en 1765 y las llamaron "Islas Malvinas". falsa; Las llamaron *Falkland Islands.*
4. El gobierno de Inglaterra expulsó a las autoridades argentinas y tomó las islas en 1833. cierta
5. Hoy en día las Islas Malvinas son gobernadas por Argentina. falsa; Hoy en día las Malvinas son gobernadas por Inglaterra.

**B ¿Comprendiste?** Contesta las preguntas. 1.2

1. ¿Dónde están las Islas Malvinas?
2. ¿Cuántos países han ocupado las islas?
3. ¿Qué hizo el gobierno de Argentina para desarrollar la cría de ganado en las islas?
4. ¿Durante cuánto tiempo ocuparon las islas las tropas argentinas?
5. ¿Cuál es la posición de Inglaterra y de Argentina en cuanto a las Malvinas?

## Actividad 1.3

**Tu opinión** ¿Cuál es tu opinión sobre la historia de las Islas Malvinas? Si fueras diplomático *(diplomat)*, ¿qué sugerirías para resolver el conflicto?

Lectura informativa

### B Answers

1. en el océano Atlántico, al este del extremo sur de Argentina
2. Cuatro países: España, Francia, Argentina e Inglaterra
3. Estableció una colonia. Mandó a cien gauchos e indígenas para desarrollar la cría del ganado.
4. Las tropas argentinas ocuparon las islas por 10 semanas.
5. El gobierno de Inglaterra no quiere retirarse, y el gobierno de Argentina afirma que tiene soberanía sobre las Malvinas.

### Connections

**Language Arts Link**

Despite having gone to war with Britain over the Falklands/Malvinas in 1982, many Argentines have a positive view of the English. One of the most renowned writers of the twentieth century was Argentine Jorge Luis Borges, whose masterful stories often display this admiration towards the English in his choice of settings, characters, and style. Have students read a poem by Borges and share their impressions with the class. 3.1

**Post-Reading Activities**

Visit the web sites for the Argentine dailies *Clarín* and *La Nación,* and the British dailies *The London Times* and *The Guardian.* Do a search in the Argentine papers for "Malvinas" and for "Falklands" in the British papers. See how recently there has been any coverage of the issue, and also visit the archives to read old stories dating back to the war in 1982. 3.1, 3.2

### Differentiated Instruction

**ADVANCED LEARNERS**

**Challenge** Have students research the Malvinas/Falkland Islands war in depth, focusing on the motivations of the two nations at that particular historical time. Why did the Argentines initiate hostilities after the islands had been under British rule for almost 150 years? Why would the British care so much about a group of islands thousands of miles away where, by some counts, sheep outnumber human inhabitants? 3.1

**MULTIPLE INTELLIGENCES**

**Musical** Try to locate recordings on tape, CD, or the Internet of typical Chilean and Argentine music from different regions and different times, reminding students that the "top 40" in the U.S. are also heard on popular radio stations in Latin America. Distribute the music among different students and have them research basic aspects of it such as its origins, the instruments used, the content of the lyrics, and so on. Encourage those who know how to play instruments to learn to play some of the songs and perform them in class. 2.2, 3.1

### Assess

**Assessment Program**
**Prueba: Lectura,** p. 173
**Online Assessment**
my.hrw.com
**Test Generator**

**Assess Differentiated Assessment** See the Differentiated Assessment CD-ROM.

# Leamos y escribamos

**Resources**

**Planning:**

Lesson Planner, pp. 141–142, 302–303

One-Stop Planner

**Presentation:**

Audio CD 9, Tr. 9

**Practice:**

Cuaderno de actividades, p. 88

Reading Strategies and Skills Handbook, Chapter 9

Interactive Advanced Reader

**Applying the Strategies**

For more practice with determining the main idea, you might have students use the "Retellings" strategy from the *Reading Strategies and Skills Handbook.*

**Escuchemos**

Play the recording of the reading, and have students listen with their books closed. Then have them complete one of the following sentences: **Es lamentable que....** or **Don Segundo les agradeció a personas bondadosas por....**

**Pre-AP Practice**

**AP Language Examination:** **Leamos** helps students prepare for Section I, Part B: **Reading Comprehension.** The audio recording helps them prepare for Part A: **Listening—Short Narratives.**

**AP Benchmark:** Identify and summarize the main points and details and make inferences and predictions from a written text.

**Focus:** Identifying the main idea and relevant details

- SE, p. 398, Act. A
- SE, p. 400, Act. B
- TE, p. 400, Post-Reading Activity

# Leamos y escribamos

**ESTRATEGIA**

**para leer** In order to understand a text, it's best to try and determine the main idea first. To do this, focus on the first sentence in each paragraph as you read. Don't worry about unknown words the first time you read the text. Take notes on information you find in each paragraph. When finished, look over your notes and determine the main idea.

CD 9, Tr. 9

### Antes de leer 1.2

**A** *El Caleuche* es una leyenda chilena que trata de un barco fantasma que navega los mares entre las islas de la costa chilena. Los marineros le tienen mucho miedo al barco fantasma porque piensan que si lo ven, morirán en circunstancias misteriosas. Antes de leer esta leyenda, prepara una hoja de papel con el título de la leyenda. Escribe *Párrafo 1* en la hoja. Deja un espacio para cada párrafo hasta el 24. Mientras lees, vas a llenar los espacios con los detalles de la leyenda, para así determinar la idea principal.

# EL CALEUCHE

*Adaptación de Carlos Ducci Claro*

No era un pueblo, no podía serlo, se trataba sólo de un pequeño número de casas agrupadas a la orilla del mar, como si quisieran protegerse del clima tormentoso, de la lluvia constante y de las acechanzas[1] que pudieran venir de la tierra o del mar.

En la pieza[2] grande de la casa de don Pedro se habían reunido casi todos los hombres del caserío. El tema de su charla era la próxima faena[3]. Saldrían a pescar de anochecida y sería una tarea larga y de riesgo; pensaban llegar lejos, quizá hasta la isla Chulín, en busca de jurel, róbalo y corvina[4].

Deseaban salir porque la pesca sería buena. Durante la noche anterior estaban seguros de haber visto a la bella Pincoya[5] que, saliendo de las aguas con su maravilloso traje de algas, había bailado frenéticamente en la playa mirando hacia el mar. Todo esto presagiaba una pesca abundante y los hombres estaban contentos.

No todos saldrían, porque, como siempre, don Segundo, el hombre mayor, se quedaría en tierra.

Uno de los jóvenes le preguntó: "Usted, don Segundo, ¿por qué no se embarca[6]? Usted conoce más que cualquiera las variaciones del tiempo, el ritmo de las mareas[7], los cambios del viento y, sin embargo, permanece siempre en tierra sin adentrarse en el mar". Se hizo un silencio, todos miraron al joven, extrañados de su insolencia, y el mismo joven abismado de su osadía[8], inclinó silencioso la cabeza sin explicarse por qué se había atrevido a preguntar.

1 ambushes 2 room 3 task (in this case, a fishing expedition) 4 *jurel...* saurel, sea bass, and corbina (types of fish)
5 a mythical mermaid 6 go aboard 7 tides 8 *abismado...* absorbed in his boldness

## Core Instruction

**TEACHING LEAMOS**

1. Have students look at the illustrations and format of the text. Have them predict what the story might be about (a Chilean maritime tale involving a mysterious ship). **(2 min.)**
2. Read **Estrategia para leer** with students. Have them read the first paragraph and apply the strategy to help them understand what they read. Have pairs present their conclusions about what is happening in the story. **(5 min.)**
3. Have them continue with the rest of the story, stopping to monitor comprehension as needed. **(8 min.)**
4. Have students complete the **Comprensión** activities on page 400. **(10 min.)**

Don Segundo, sin embargo, parecía perdido en un ensueño[9] y contestó automáticamente: "Porque yo he visto el Caleuche".

Dicho esto pareció salir de su ensueño y, ante la mirada interrogante de todos exclamó: "Algún día les contestaré".

Meses después estaban todos reunidos en la misma pieza. Era de noche, y nadie había podido salir a pescar, llovía en forma feroz, como si toda el agua del mundo cayera sobre aquella casa, el viento huracanado parecía arrancar las tejuelas[10] del techo y las paredes y el mar no eran un ruido lejano y armonioso, sino un bramido[11] sordo y amenazador.

Don Segundo habló de improviso y dijo: "Ahora les contaré...". Su relato contenido durante muchos años cobró una realidad mágica para los que le escuchaban curiosos y atemorizados[12].

Hace mucho tiempo había salido navegando desde Ancud con el propósito de llegar hasta Quellón. No se trataba de una embarcación pequeña, sino de una lancha grande de alto bordo[13] y sin embargo fácil de conducir, con dos velas[14] que permitían aprovechar al máximo un viento favorable. Era una lancha buena para el mar y que había desafiado con éxito muchas tempestades[15].

La tripulaban[16] cinco hombres, además de don Segundo, y el capitán era un chilote recio[17], bajo y musculoso, que conocía todas las islas y canales del archipiélago, y de quien se decía que había navegado hasta los estrechos del sur y había cruzado el Paso del Indio y el Canal Messier.

La segunda noche de navegación se desató la tempestad. "Peor que la de ahora", dijo don Segundo. Era una noche negra en que el cielo y el mar se confundían, en que el viento huracanado levantaba el mar y en que los marineros aterrorizados usaban los remos para tratar de dirigir la lancha y embestir[18] de frente a las olas enfurecidas.

Habían perdido la noción del tiempo y empapados y rendidos encomendaban[19] su alma, seguros de morir.

No obstante, la tormenta pareció calmarse y divisaron[20] a lo lejos una luz que avanzaba sobre las aguas. Fue acercándose y la luz se transformó en un barco, un hermoso y gran velero[21], curiosamente iluminado, del que salían cantos y

9 daydream 10 shingles 11 howling 12 terrified 13 *lancha*...large vessel 14 sails 15 storms 16 *La*... It was manned by 17 big, strong Chilean 18 attack 19 *empapados*... drenched and exhausted, they entrusted 20 they saw 21 sailing vessel

## Leamos y escribamos

### Active Reading Questions

1. **Señala en qué momento don Segundo comienza a narrar su historia. ¿Qué sucesos cuenta hasta el final de la página?**
2. **¿Qué datos sobre el barco y la tripulación presenta don Segundo para establecer la acción?**
3. **¿Qué dice don Segundo sobre el tiempo?** 1.2

### Identifying Main Idea

Have students identify the main idea and use important details to summarize the story. 3.1

### AP Reading Suggestion

Have students research other maritime myths from around the world about beautiful, luminous apparitions, which actually spell disaster, or are merely mirages for the weary.

### Cultures

#### Products and Perspectives

**El Caleuche** is just one of many myths from the Southern Cone region. An example of a well-known Chilean maritime myth is that of a mysterious mermaid called **Pincoya.** It is said that a sighting of **Pincoya** will bring good fortune to fishermen and that she will come to the rescue of a shipwrecked crew. Have students find more information about **Pincoya** and ask them if there is more than one version of the myth. Ask students if they know of a maritime myth from the U.S. and compare it with **Pincoya.**

2.2, 4.2

## Differentiated Instruction

### ADVANCED LEARNERS

**Extension** As an extension of the **Después de leer** activity on page 400, have students do research on legends depicted in pirate movies. They can think of legends in films they have seen, or look at detailed plot summaries to find more. Ask them to write the information in Spanish. 3.1

### MULTIPLE INTELLIGENCES

**Linguistic** Ask students to make up a legend about a mysterious sea creature in which one of the characters tells a story within a story, like Don Segundo does. Have them edit it in such a way that it is told in installments so as to increase the suspense. 1.3

**B Answers**

1. Hablaban de sus planes a salir a pescar de noche.
2. La pregunta por qué no los acompaña en la pesca.
3. No va porque había visto el Caleuche antes de ser naufragado.
4. Seis, contando don Segundo y el capitán.
5. La lancha volcó.
6. lo encontraron unas personas bondadosas y extrañas. No se sabe, pero se supone que se ahogaron en el mar aquella noche.

## Connections

### Literature Link

Many fiction stories have been written about maritime mythical figures. Novels like *Moby Dick* or *20,000 Leagues Under The Sea* are based on giant sea creatures that terrify the characters in the story. Have students search the library or the Internet for books from around the world about a mythical creature. Ask students to include details about the mythical creature and where the book was written. Ask students if they believe culture plays a role in the creation of myths. 3.1

### Post-Reading Activity

Have students discuss the **Después de leer** questions in pairs. In answering the second and third questions, tell students that if they do not know of any legends, they can make some up. 1.1

### Pre-AP Practice

**AP Language Examination: Leamos and Escribamos** help students prepare for Section I, Part B: **Reading Comprehension** and Section II, Part A: **Informal Writing.**

voces. Irradiaba una extraña luminosidad en medio de la noche, lo que permitía que se destacaran[22] su casco[23] y velas oscuras. Si no fuera por su velamen[24], si no fuera por los cantos, habríase dicho un inmenso monstruo marino.

Al verlo acercarse los marinos gritaron alborozados[25], pues, no obstante lo irreal de su presencia, parecía un refugio tangible frente a la cierta y constante amenaza del mar.

El capitán no participó de esa alegría. Lo vieron y mortalmente pálido exclamó: "¡¡No es la salvación, es el Caleuche!! Nuestros huesos, como los de todos los que lo han visto, estarán esta noche en el fondo del mar".

El Caleuche ya estaba casi encima de la lancha cuando repentinamente desapareció. Se fue la luz y volvió la densa sombra en que se confundían el cielo y el agua.

Al mismo tiempo, volvió la tempestad, tal vez con más fuerza, y la fatiga de los hombres les impidió dirigir la lancha en el embravecido mar, hasta que una ola gigantesca la volcó[26]. Algo debió golpearlo, porque su último recuerdo fue la gran ola negra en la oscuridad de la noche.

Despertó arrojado en una playa en que gentes bondadosas y extrañas trataban de reanimarlo. Dijo que había naufragado[27] y contó todo respecto del viaje y la tempestad, menos las circunstancias del naufragio y la visión del Caleuche. De sus compañeros no se supo más, y ésta es la primera vez en que la totalidad de la historia salía de sus labios.

---

22 highlighted 23 hull 24 ship sails 25 with joy 26 *la*... overturned it 27 shipwrecked

### Comprensión 1.2

**B** Basándote en lo que leíste, contesta las preguntas.

1. ¿De qué hablaban los pescadores en la casa de don Pedro?
2. ¿Qué le pregunta el joven a don Segundo?
3. ¿Por qué no va don Segundo a pescar con sus compañeros?
4. ¿Cuántas personas tripulaban la lancha en que iba don Segundo?
5. ¿Qué pasó después de que desapareció el Caleuche?
6. ¿Quién encontró a don Segundo? ¿Qué les pasó a sus compañeros?

### Pasó así 1.2

**C** Decide si cada oración es **cierta** o **falsa.**

1. Los protagonistas en la leyenda son pescadores. cierta
2. Don Segundo es un hombre joven y no sabe pescar. falsa
3. Don Segundo tiene mucho miedo de salir al mar. cierta
4. Un joven le pregunta a don Segundo por qué no quiere embarcarse. cierta
5. Don Segundo dice que el Caleuche es un monstruo. falsa
6. El Caleuche no deja que los hombres lo vean. falsa

### Después de leer 1.3

**D** ¿Qué significa el Caleuche para don Segundo? ¿Has escuchado alguna vez una leyenda parecida a ésta? ¿Hay alguna leyenda famosa en la región donde vives?

## Core Instruction

### TEACHING ESCRIBAMOS

1. Explain to students that there are many ways to tell stories. For instance, you can concentrate on events in the order in which they occur, or you can have narrations within narrations happening in different times and space, told by different characters. **(1 min.)**
2. Discuss **Estrategia para escribir** as a class. **(1 min.)**
3. Have students complete pre-writing Activity 1 in small groups. Members work together to create a sequence of at least five chronological elements they want to include in their legend. **(8 min.)**
4. Have students complete Activity 2 for homework.
5. Have students complete Activity 3 individually, and pair up with a partner to do Activity 4. **(15 min.)**
6. Have volunteers read their legends to the class. **(10 min.)**

# Taller del escritor

1.3

**ESTRATEGIA**

**para escribir** Legends can be a way to explain a natural event like the eruption of a volcano, or to tell the story of a person who may have done extraordinary things during his or her lifetime. Think of a mysterious person, event, or thing (real or fictitious) and write a legend about it, using detailed descriptions.

### Una buena descripción

Una manera de dar vida propia a tus escritos es incluir buenas descripciones. Hay que considerar varios elementos que hacen que una descripción sea completa. Por ejemplo, si describes un árbol, tienes que tomar en cuenta su color, su tamaño, etc. Al describir algo, decide qué le puede ayudar al lector a tener una imagen viva y precisa del objeto.

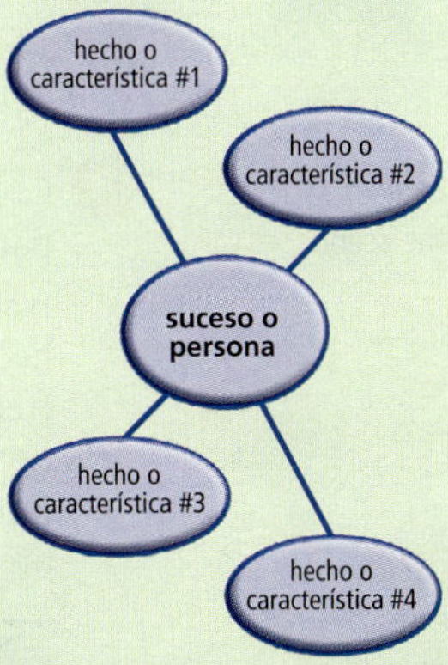


### 1 Antes de escribir

Haz una lista de personas, lugares, sucesos u objetos que quieres describir. De esta lista, escoge la cosa que más te interese y apunta las características y los hechos asociados con ese suceso o persona.

### 2 Escribir un borrador

Empieza tu borrador con la lista que hiciste. Puedes poner las características y los hechos en distintos párrafos. No nombres lo que decidiste describir en tu borrador.

### 3 Revisar

Revisa tu borrador y corrige los errores de gramática y ortografía, si los hay. Lee tu borrador para verificar que tu descripción sea precisa y completa. Considera otras características que te puedan ayudar a completar la imagen.

### 4 Publicar

Intercambia tu descripción con la de un(a) compañero(a) y trata de adivinar lo que él/ella describe. Luego, pueden juntar todas las descripciones de la clase y adivinar qué fue lo que describió cada persona.

## Leamos y escribamos

### Process Writing

Explain to students that in order to write a detailed description, they should use varied adjectives. They might want to use a word web to brainstorm topics for their legend. In the center of each word web they should write the topic, and around each topic they should write adjectives that could be used to describe the topic.

### Writing Assessment

To assess the **Taller del escritor,** you can use the following rubric.

| Writing Rubric | 4 | 3 | 2 | 1 |
|---|---|---|---|---|
| **Content** (Complete—Incomplete) | | | | |
| **Comprehensibility** (Comprehensible—Seldom comprehensible) | | | | |
| **Accuracy** (Accurate—Seldom accurate) | | | | |
| **Organization** (Well-organized—Poorly organized) | | | | |
| **Effort** (Excellent effort—Minimal effort) | | | | |

18–20: A 14–15: C Under
16–17: B 12–13: D 12: F

## Differentiated Instruction

### SLOWER PACE LEARNERS

Have students who need more time and assistance do two rounds of Activity 3. Take the time to assist them directly with the first draft before they work on their second draft.

### MULTIPLE INTELLIGENCES

**Bodily/Kinesthetic** After students finish their legends, have them read them to the class and vote on the best two to dramatize. Have students make simple costumes and props for the dramatic adaptations of their legends. 1.2, 1.3

### Assess

**Assessment Program**
**Prueba: Lectura,** p. 173
**Prueba: Escritura,** p. 174

**Online Assessment**
**my.hrw.com**

**Test Generator**

**Assess** **Differentiated Assessment** See the Differentiated Assessment CD-ROM.

Capítulo 9

# Prepárate para el examen

## Resources

**Planning:**

Lesson Planner, pp. 142–143, 302–305

One-Stop Planner

**Presentation:**

Video Program, Videocassette 5

DVD Program

**Variedades**

**Practice:**

Activities for Communication, pp. 51, 71–72

Video Guide, pp. 60–61

Lab Book, pp. 9, 45–48, 84

Audio CD 9, Tr. 10

Pre-AP Instructional Resources

Pre-AP Audio CD 2, Trs. 13–16

Interactive Tutor, Disc 2

Teaching Transparencies

**Situación, Capítulo 9**

Picture Sequences, Chapter 9

### 1 Answers

Possible answers:

1. La leyenda nos cuenta que hace muchos años el príncipe traicionó al rey.
2. Vivieron siempre felices en el palacio encantado.
3. Érase una vez, en un lugar lejano, un hechicero malvado que hizo desaparecer a la reina.
4. En el cuento de hadas, el rey se enamoró de la princesa.

### Heritage Speakers

Ask your heritage speakers what they know about the history of their parents' country of origin. Are they familiar with any specific historical events their family members personally observed? What do they know about important historical figures of that country? Give the students an opportunity to discuss this at home with their relatives or to look up the information in the Internet. They may choose to share the information they learn with the rest of the class. 1.3

Capítulo 9
Repaso

# Prepárate para el examen

Interactive TUTOR

**1** Mira los dibujos y usa palabras de **Vocabulario** para describir cada uno. 1.2

1

2

3

4

**1 Vocabulario 1**
- setting the scene for a story
- continuing and ending a story

**pp. 368–373**

**2 Gramática 1**
- preterite and imperfect in storytelling
- preterite and imperfect contrasted
- **por** and **para**

**pp. 374–379**

**3 Vocabulario 2**
- talking about your hopes and wishes
- expressing regret and gratitude

**pp. 382–387**

**2** 1.2 Completa el párrafo con la forma correcta del verbo en paréntesis. **1.** tenía **2.** conoció **3.** Eran **4.** tenía **5.** estaba **6.** apareció

Ivania __1__ (tener) once años cuando __2__ (conocer) al hechicero. __3__ (Ser) las tres de la tarde, y ella __4__ (tener) que estar en la casa a las tres y media. Ella __5__ (estar) caminando muy rápido cuando de pronto __6__ (aparecer) un hombre muy gracioso. __7__ (Llevar) un sombrero negro. Ivania __8__ (asustarse) y él también. Él le __9__ (preguntar) una dirección y __10__ (irse) corriendo. Pero se le __11__ (caer) su varita mágica. Ivania la guardó __12__ (por/para) regalársela a su mejor amiga.

**7.** Llevaba **8.** se asustó **9.** preguntó **10.** se fue **11.** cayó **12.** para

**3** Completa cada oración con las formas correctas de las palabras del cuadro. 1.2

| conmemorar | bandera | dictador | imperio | regocijarse | cobarde |
|---|---|---|---|---|---|

1. Cuando vencieron al enemigo, los soldados ____ en la calle. **1.** se regocijaron
2. Este traidor es un ____ que le tiene miedo a todo. cobarde
3. Cada año nosotros ____ la fecha en que ganamos la libertad. **3.** conmemoramos
4. El ____ gobernó sin justicia y nos quitó nuestra libertad. **4.** dictador
5. La ____ es un símbolo importante de cualquier país. bandera
6. Los incas tenían un gran ____. imperio

## Oral Assessment

### Speaking Rubric

To assess the speaking activities in this section, you might use the following rubric. For additional speaking rubrics, see the Alternative Assessment section of the *Assessment Program.*

| Speaking Rubric | 4 | 3 | 2 | 1 |
|---|---|---|---|---|
| **Content** (Complete—Incomplete) | | | | |
| **Comprehension** (Total—Little) | | | | |
| **Comprehensibility** (Comprehensible—Incomprehensible) | | | | |
| **Accuracy** (Accurate—Seldom Accurate) | | | | |
| **Fluency** (Fluent—Not Fluent) | | | | |

18–20: A 16–17: B 14–15: C 12–13: D Under 12: F

Visit Holt Online
**go.hrw.com**
KEYWORD: EXP3 CH9
Chapter Self-test

**4** Completa las oraciones con la forma correcta del verbo. 1.2

1. La profesora dijo que nosotros ═══ (ir) a estudiar las civilizaciones precolombinas. **1.** íbamos
2. Me gusta que nosotros ═══ (tener) la oportunidad de aprender más sobre ellas. **2.** tengamos
3. Es curioso que los expertos no ═══ (saber) qué les pasó a varias civilizaciones antiguas. **3.** sepan
4. Parece mentira que el imperio inca ═══ (haber) desaparecido.
5. Era imposible que los incas ═══ (continuar) su imperio.
6. Laura me dijo que ═══ (haber) un documental anoche sobre este tema. **4.** haya **5.** continuaran **6.** hubo

**4 Gramática 2**
- uses of subjunctive
- sequence of tenses

pp. 388–393

**5** Contesta las preguntas. 1.2

1. ¿Qué significan los tres colores de la bandera chilena?
2. ¿Qué país gobierna las Islas Malvinas?
3. ¿Quién fue el dictador de Chile desde 1973 hasta 1990?
4. ¿Dónde están las cataratas del Iguazú?

**5 Cultura**
- Comparaciones pp. 380–381
- Lectura informativa pp. 396–397
- Notas culturales pp. 370, 379, 384, 391

CD 9, Tr. 10 1.2

**6** Escucha los fragmentos de varios cuentos de hadas y determina si se refieren **al presente, al pasado** o **al futuro.**
**1.** pasado **2.** presente **3.** futuro **4.** presente, futuro **5.** futuro **6.** pasado

## Conversación

HOLT SoundBooth ONLINE RECORDING

**7** Role-play the following conversation with a partner. Partner A and Partner B are siblings, telling a story to a younger brother or sister. 1.1, 1.2

| | |
|---|---|
| Partner A: | Say you and your partner are going to tell a mysterious story. |
| Partner B: | Tell about a family who lived long ago in a faraway place. Describe the place and the family. |
| Partner A: | Explain what the family used to do every day. Then say the youngest child saw a strange animal one day. |
| Partner B: | Explain that this animal could talk. Tell what it did. |
| Partner A: | Say how the child felt, and what he or she did. Then tell what the animal did. |
| Partner B: | Tell what the animal said to the child. |
| Partner A: | Explain what the child did next. |
| Partner B: | End the story by explaining what the family did afterwards. |

## Conversación

### Additional Speaking Practice

For additional speaking practice, use the *Picture Sequences Transparency* for Chapter 9. Use the Speaking Rubric on the preceding page to evaluate their performance. You may also wish to use the Interviews and Role-Plays in the *Activities for Communication* book.

### Pre-AP Practice

**7** In the Level 3 *Pre-AP Instructional Resources* you will find an alternative version of Activity 7. The following resources in that book will help you prepare students for the AP Language Exam:

- Blackline masters, pp. 35, 45, 55
- Pre-AP Audio CD 2, Trs. 13–16
- Scripts and answers, pp. 57–75

**5 Answers**

1. El rojo significa la sangre derramada durante la guerra de independencia, el azul significa el cielo chileno, el blanco significa las puntas nevadas de la cordillera de los Andes.
2. Inglaterra
3. Augusto Pinochet
4. en la frontera entre Argentina y Brasil

**6 Script**

1. Hace mucho tiempo, vivía una princesa triste y sola. Le gustaba jugar en el jardín del palacio.
2. El castillo de la princesa encantada es muy grande, con más de cien torres mágicas.
3. El rey poderoso castigará al malvado por haberlo traicionado en la guerra, y todos se van a regocijar.
4. Todos en el reino esperan que el príncipe se case con una princesa valiente y bonita.
5. Por causa de las acciones del hechicero, el castillo de la reina malvada desaparecerá para siempre, y todos vivirán felices después.
6. El rey fue un hombre poderoso, fuerte y muy querido por todos. Todos lamentaron su muerte.

**7 Answers**

Below is a sample student conversation.

(A)—Te vamos a contar un cuento de misterio.
(B)—Érase una vez en una tierra lejana una familia de cinco personas: el padre, la madre, y tres hijos. Vivían en un bosque muy grande.
(A)—Todos los días, el padre salía a trabajar en un rancho. La madre cuidaba a los hijos en la casa. Un día, el hijo caminaba por el bosque cuando se encontró con un oso.
(B)—Miró al oso con mucho cuidado. ¿Y sabes qué? Mientras lo miraba, vio que el oso tenía un celular. Y lo que es más, el oso estaba hablando. El oso vio al muchacho y dejó de hablar.
(A)—El hijo no lo pudo creer. Le dio mucha risa ver a un oso que sabía hablar. Entonces, el oso colgó el teléfono.
(B)—Luego, el oso le habló al muchacho y le dio su número de teléfono.
(A)—Después, el hijo les contó lo del oso a su familia. Nadie se lo quiso creer.
(B) —Al final, los padres llamaron al número y se sorprendieron cuando el oso contestó.

Capítulo 9

# Prepárate para el examen

## Grammar Review

For more practice with the grammar topics in this chapter, see the *Grammar Tutor,* the *Interactive Tutor,* or the *Cuaderno de vocabulario y gramática.*

GramaVisión

## Más práctica

Have students write a five-sentence paragraph for the beginning of a fairy tale using the preterite and imperfect.

## Language Note

Remind students that along with the imperfect, the past progressive is often used in storytelling to describe the setting or the action in progress when another action occurred. **Hacía sol cuando se despertó la princesa. Estaba lloviendo cuando salió de la casa.**

## Connections

### Language Arts Link

Have students find a Spanish-language fairy tale online. Ask them to print out the fairy tale and read it to themselves. Then have them underline the verbs in the imperfect and circle the verbs in the preterite. Allow them to exchange fairy tales with a partner to check each other's work. Have them discuss what happened in their fairy tales. With the same partner, have students discuss the similarities and differences between comparable linguistic markers in Spanish and English.

**Gramática 1**

- preterite and imperfect in storytelling **pp. 374–375**
- preterite and imperfect contrasted **pp. 376–377**
- por and para **pp. 378–379**

## Repaso de Gramática 1

In storytelling, the **imperfect** is used to describe the setting or background of a story and the **preterite** is used to express the events that occurred at specific moments in the story's plot. For specific uses of the **imperfect** and the **preterite,** see page 374.

**Hacía** sol cuando **apareció** el sabio.

The **preterite** is used to refer to completed past actions with a clear beginning or end. It is also used to give special meanings to certain verbs. For more information on contrasting the **imperfect** and the **preterite,** see page 376.

El rey **salió** del palacio.

The **imperfect** is used to describe habitual, ongoing past actions, to describe ongoing past mental or physical states, to indicate time in the past, and to indicate age in the past.

La princesa siempre **caminaba** por el jardín.

For specific uses of **por** and **para,** see page 378.

**Gramática 2**

- uses of subjunctive **pp. 388–389**
- sequence of tenses **pp. 390–393**

## Repaso de Gramática 2

The **subjunctive mood** is used with expressions of:

| | |
|---|---|
| hope, wish, recommendation: | Ojalá que se **enamoren.** |
| feelings, emotions or judgment: | Me entristece que no pueda **trabajar.** |
| unknown or nonexistent people, places, or things: | Busco un soldado que **sea** valiente. |
| doubt or denial: | Dudo que **construyan** el templo. |

It is also used with certain adverbial conjunctions: **a menos (de) que, antes de que, con tal (de) que, en caso de que, para que,** and **sin que;** also with **en cuanto, cuando, después de que, hasta que,** and **tan pronto como** when they refer to the future.

The phrase **sequence of tenses** describes the agreement between the verb in the **main clause** and the verb in the **subordinate clause.** For more information on sequence of tenses, see page 390.

For specific uses of sequence of tenses, see page 392.

## Chapter Review

### Teacher Management System

To access, launch the program, type "admin" in the password area, and press RETURN. For more details, log on to www.hrw.com/CDROMTUTOR.

Create a variety of puzzles to review chapter vocabulary.

**DVD Program**

**Interactive Tutor**

**PuzzlePro**

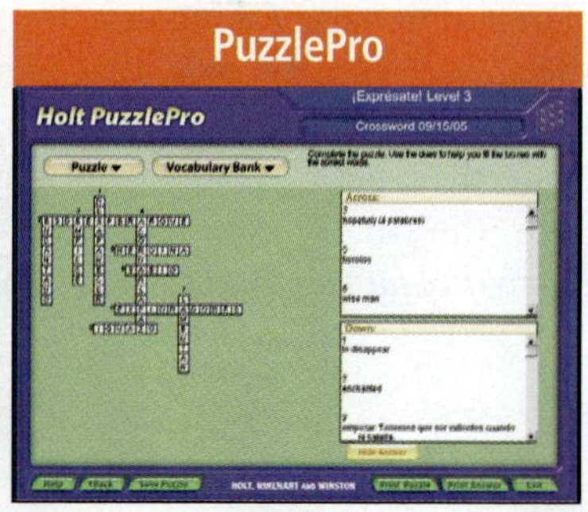

## Repaso de Vocabulario 1

**Setting the scene for a story**

| | |
|---|---|
| **ahora bien** | *well, nevertheless* |
| **aunque** | *although* |
| **castigar** | *to punish* |
| **el castigo** | *punishment* |
| **la creación** | *creation* |
| **el cuento (de hadas)** | *(fairy) tale* |
| **desaparecer** | *to disappear* |
| **desconocido(a)** | *unknown* |
| **el (la) dios(a)** | *god/goddess* |
| **enamorarse** | *to fall in love* |
| **encantado(a)** | *enchanted* |
| **Érase una vez, en un lugar muy lejano...** | *Once upon a time, in a faraway place, there was . . .* |
| **el fantasma** | *ghost* |
| **Hace muchos años,...** | *Many years ago, . . .* |
| **el (la) hechicero(a)** | *sorcerer, sorceress* |
| **el hecho** | *fact, event, deed* |
| **la leyenda** | *legend* |
| **mágico(a)** | *magic* |
| **el (la) malvado(a)** | *villain* |
| **misterioso(a)** | *mysterious* |
| **el mito** | *myth* |
| **el palacio** | *palace* |
| **los poderes** | *powers* |
| **la princesa** | *princess* |
| **el príncipe** | *prince* |
| **la reina** | *queen* |
| **el rey** | *king* |
| **el (la) sabio(a)** | *wise man, wise woman* |
| **Se cuenta que de pronto...** | *The story goes that all of a sudden . . .* |
| **Según nos dicen, el malvado...** | *From what they tell us, the villain . . .* |
| **el templo** | *temple* |
| **traicionar** | *to betray* |
| **el (la) traidor(a)** | *traitor* |

**Continuing and ending a story**

| | |
|---|---|
| **A causa de esto...** | *Because of this . . .* |
| **Al final, nos dimos cuenta de...** | *In the end, we realized . . .* |
| **A partir de entonces, vivieron siempre felices.** | *From then on, they lived happily ever after.* |
| **Hace tiempo, vino un desconocido...** | *Some time ago, a stranger came . . .* |
| **Tan pronto como llegó...** | *As soon as he/she arrived . . .* |

## Repaso de Vocabulario 2

**Talking about your hopes and wishes**

| | |
|---|---|
| **acordar (ue) la paz** | *to make peace* |
| **la bandera** | *flag* |
| **la batalla** | *battle* |
| **el campo de batalla** | *battlefield* |
| **cobarde** | *cowardly* |
| **declarar la guerra** | *to declare war* |
| **la derrota** | *defeat* |
| **el (la) dictador(a)** | *dictator* |
| **El sueño de mi vida es vencer a...** | *My life-long dream is to overcome (defeat) . . .* |
| **Es de esperar que...** | *Hopefully . . .* |
| **el (la) enemigo(a)** | *enemy* |
| **los exploradores** | *explorers* |
| **el héroe, la heroína** | *hero, heroine* |
| **honrar** | *to honor* |
| **el imperio** | *empire* |
| **la independencia** | *independence* |
| **la justicia** | *justice* |
| **lamentar** | *to lament* |
| **liberar** | *to liberate* |
| **la libertad** | *liberty* |
| **la mujer soldado** | *female soldier* |
| **Ojalá que los países aún en guerra lleguen a un acuerdo.** | *I hope that the countries still at war can reach an agreement.* |
| **regocijarse** | *to rejoice* |
| **la revolución** | *revolution* |
| **el soldado** | *soldier* |
| **sufrir** | *to suffer* |
| **Tenía muchas esperanzas de...** | *I had many hopes of . . .* |
| **las tropas** | *troops* |
| **valiente** | *brave* |
| **vencer** | *to defeat* |
| **la víctima** | *victim* |
| **la victoria** | *victory* |

**Expressing regret and gratitude**

| | |
|---|---|
| **Es lamentable que...** | *It's too bad that . . .* |
| **Les agradecieron a...** | *They thanked . . .* |
| **Se arrepiente de que...** | *He/She regrets that . . .* |





# Prepárate para el examen

### Vocabulary Review

For more practice with the vocabulary in this chapter, see the *Interactive Tutor* or the *Cuaderno de vocabulario y gramática.*

### Online Edition

Students might use the online textbook to hear the **Vocabulario** items.

### Game

**¡Construyan!** Write several sentences with main and subordinate clauses in large print on slips of paper. For each sentence, cut the strips one word at a time. You might want to add a few extra words to increase difficulty. Place each set of slips in an envelope. Distribute two or three envelopes per group. When you say **¡Construyan!,** students open one envelope and assemble the sentence. When a person or team completes a sentence, they call out **¡Construida!** All players must stop. If the completed sentence is correct, that player or team gets a point.

**Online Edition**

**Transparency: Vocabulario**

**Transparency: Situación**

**Assess**

**Assessment Program**

**Examen: Capítulo 9,** pp. 317–322

Audio CD 9, Trs. 13–14

**Examen oral: Capítulo 9,** p. 328

Alternative Assessment, pp. 381, 393, 405

**Online Assessment**

**my.hrw.com**

**Test Generator**

**Assess** **Differentiated Assessment** See the Differentiated Assessment CD-ROM.

## Resources

**Planning:**

Lesson Planner, pp. 143, 304–305

One-Stop Planner

**Presentation:**

Teaching Transparencies

Fine Art, Chapter 9

**Practice:**

Cuaderno de actividades, pp. 89–90

Lab Book, pp. 9, 45–48

Audio CD 9

### Más práctica

For more practice with the conditional tense, have students think of six things they are interested in doing. Have students write a sentence for each activity using the conditional with **fuera, pudiera, tuviera,** and so on. Once students have finished writing their sentences, have them find a partner and each student will read their partner's sentences using the **tú** form. 1.2

Repaso cumulativo

# Integración

## capítulos 1–9

1 Explica lo que haría cada persona si pudiera. 1.2

1

2

3

4

1.2

2 Lee el comentario de Celia sobre lo que aprendió en la clase de historia. Luego contesta **cierto** o **falso** a las siguientes preguntas.

Me fascina la leyenda de Quetzalcóatl. Aunque algunas partes de la leyenda están basadas en hechos reales, otras están basadas en mitos. Se dice que Quetzalcóatl era un hombre alto, rubio y blanco. Según nos dicen, después de su muerte, se convirtió en dios para muchos grupos ind genas. Ellos creían que él iba a regresar a México un día como rey. Un día un hombre alto y rubio llegó a México con sus soldados, y todos los indígenas pensaron que él era Quetzalcóatl. Pero no era cierto. ¡Era el explorador Hernán Cortés! Es lamentable que Cortés les mintiera a los indígenas, pero eso fue lo que hizo. La historia es muy interesante. Si yo pudiera, viajaría a México para ver las ruinas del templo dedicado a Quetzalcóatl. Este año no puedo ir pero en cuanto tenga el dinero, iré.

1. Ninguna parte de la leyenda de Quetzalcóatl está basada en hechos reales. falso
2. Se dice que Quetzalcóatl era un hombre rubio. cierto
3. Quetzalcóatl regresó a México con sus soldados. falso
4. Cortés era un hombre honesto y les dijo la verdad a los indígenas. falso
5. Hay un templo dedicado a Quetzalcóatl en Tenochtitlán. cierto
6. Celia va a viajar a Tenochtitlán este año. falso

### Culture Project

Cultures often share similar myths and legends. For example, the legend of Big Foot, a creature whose footprints are said to be seen in the forests of the western United States, has a counterpart in France (The Wolf of Gévaudan). Divide the class into groups. Have each group research the legends of three different Latin American countries to find cultures that share a similar legend. Have each group include details such as the name of the main characters in the myth, the origins of the myth, and the community it came from. Have each group write the legend in their own words and present it in class. Inform groups that they may illustrate the myths they researched if they would like. As an extension to the Culture Project, have students interview a native Spanish-speaking friend or relative about a legend, and report to the class if the legend is similar to one that they are familiar with, or if it is different. 1.1, 2.2

**Visit Holt Online**
**go.hrw.com**
KEYWORD: EXP3 CH9
Cumulative Self-test

**3** En grupos de tres, inventen una leyenda sobre un hecho que pasó en tu pueblo hace mucho tiempo. Imaginen que un reportero ha llegado para investigar el asunto. Cada persona en el grupo contará una parte de la leyenda y lo que espera que encuentre el reportero. 1.1, 1.3

**4** Describe lo que ves en esta pintura. Comenta el contraste entre los soldados y las otras personas. 1.3

*Soldiers at Attention* from the work *José de San Martín Reviewing His Troops at Rancagua*, 1820 (detail) by Juan Manuel Blanes. Location: Museo Histórico Nacional de Buenos Aires. ©Museo Histórico Nacional de Buenos Aires/Dagli Orti/Art Archive

***La revista de Rancagua*** de Juan Manuel Blanes

**5** Acabas de regresar de un viaje a un templo antiguo en México. Escribe una carta a un(a) amigo(a) para contarle algo interesante que te pasó en el viaje. Describe la escena y los acontecimientos en detalle. 1.3

**6** **Situación**

Tú y un(a) amigo(a) van a ver una obra de teatro sobre un mito. A tu amigo(a) no le gustan los mitos y tiene muchas ideas negativas sobre cómo será la obra. Tú no estás de acuerdo y expresas tus ideas positivas. 1.1, 1.3

## Repaso cumulativo

### Fine Art Connection

Tell students that the image in Activity 4 is a detail from the painting "La Revista de Rancagua" by Juan Manuel Blanes. Blanes was born on June 8, 1830, in Montevideo, Uruguay, and from a young age showed a special interest in drawing and painting. At age 20, he moved to Entre Ríos, where he was hired by General Urquiza to decorate his **Palacio de San José.** In 1861, he went to Italy to perfect his studies. He is well-known for his historical paintings of Uruguay. With his work, he helped transform the image of the **gaucho** from an outcast to an important root of Uruguayan history. Both Montevideo and Buenos Aires have a street named in his honor.

### Analyzing

Tell students that the term **revista** in the title means *inspection.* Explain that this painting depicts General San Martín's inspection of his troops in Chile. Ask students to think about the contrast of the soldiers who lined up ready for battle, to the women and children holding flowers behind them. Have them describe the atmosphere of the scene.
3.1

### Extension

Have students find another painting by Juan Manuel Blanes. Ask them to research information about the historical context of the painting. They should prepare a short presentation for the class.
1.3, 3.1

### ACTFL Performance Standards

The activities in Chapter 9 target the different communicative modes as described in the Standards.

| | | |
|---|---|---|
| **Interpersonal** | Two-way communication using receptive skills and productive skills | **Comunicación (SE),** pp. 371, 373, 375, 377, 379, 385, 387, 389, 391, 393<br>**Comunicación (TE),** pp. 371, 375, 377, 379, 387, 391<br>**Conversación,** p. 403<br>**Situación,** p. 407 |
| **Interpretive** | One-way communication using receptive skills | **Comunicación (SE),** pp. 375, 377, 385, 393<br>**Novela en video,** pp. 394–395<br>**Leamos,** pp. 398–400<br>**Conversación,** p. 403 |
| **Presentational** | One-way communication using productive skills | **Comunicación (SE),** pp. 371, 373, 377, 379, 387, 389, 391, 393<br>**Comunicación (TE),** pp. 373, 385, 389, 393, 395<br>**Taller del escritor,** p. 401 |

Capítulo 10

# Planning Guide

## El mundo en que vivimos

| Chapter Section | | Print Resources |
|---|---|---|
| **Geocultura**<br>• **El Cono Sur** | pp. 360–365 | Video Guide, pp. 57–58/Lab Book, p. 83 |
| **Vocabulario 1**<br>• Past events<br>**Gramática 1**<br>• Repaso: Present and past progressive<br>• Repaso: **haber**<br>• Repaso: Expressions of time | pp. 410–415<br>pp. 416–421 | Vocabulario 10.1, 10.2; Bell Work 10.1, 10.2, 10.3, 10.4<br>Cuaderno de vocabulario y gramática, pp. 109–114<br>Cuaderno de actividades, pp. 91–93<br>Activities for Communication, pp. 37–38 |
| **Cultura: Comparaciones**<br>**Cultura: Comunidad** | p. 422<br>p. 423 | Video Guide, pp. 66–67/Lab Book, p. 87 |
| **Vocabulario 2**<br>• Present problems and future solutions<br>**Gramática 2**<br>• Repaso: Future tense<br>• Repaso: Subjunctive with doubt, denial, and feelings<br>• Repaso: Subjunctive and indicative in adverbial clauses | pp. 424–429<br>pp. 430–435 | Vocabulario 10.3, 10.4; Bell Work 10.5, 10.6, 10.7, 10.8<br>Cuaderno de vocabulario y gramática, pp. 115–120<br>Cuaderno de actividades, pp. 95–97<br>Activities for Communication, pp. 39–40 |
| **Novela en video**<br>**Lectura informativa**<br>• **Chile y el medio ambiente**<br>**Leamos**<br>• **de El Gaucho Martín Fierro**<br>**Escribamos**<br>• **Un personaje folclórico** | pp. 436–437<br>pp. 438–439<br>pp. 440–442<br>p. 443 | Cuaderno de actividades, p. 98<br>Reading Strategies and Skills Handbook<br>Interactive Advanced Reader<br>Video Guide, pp. 68–70/Lab Book, pp. 88–89 |
| **Prepárate para el examen**<br>• **Repaso de vocabulario y gramática** | pp. 444–447 | Picture Sequences, **Situación,** Ch. 10<br>Activities for Communication, pp. 52, 73–74 |
| **Integración**<br>• **Repaso cumulativo** | pp. 448–449 | Fine Art, Ch. 10<br>Cuaderno de actividades, pp. 99–100<br>Reading Strategies and Skills Handbook<br>Interactive Advanced Reader |

For correlations to national standards, see point-of-use references throughout the chapter.

## Pacing Suggestions

| | Essential | Recommended | Optional |
|---|---|---|---|
| **Vocabulario 1**<br>• Past events<br>• **Nota cultural** | ✔ | | |
| **Gramática 1**<br>• Repaso: Present and past progressive<br>• Repaso: **haber**<br>• Repaso: Expressions of time<br>• **Nota cultural** | ✔ | | |
| **Cultura: Comparaciones** | | ✔ | |
| **Cultura: Comunidad** | | | ✔ |
| **Vocabulario 2**<br>• Present problems and future solutions<br>• **Nota cultural** | ✔ | | |
| **Gramática 2**<br>• Repaso: Future tense<br>• Repaso: Subjunctive with doubt, denial, and feelings<br>• Repaso: Subjunctive and indicative in adverbial clauses<br>• **Nota cultural** | ✔ | | |
| **Novela en video**<br>• Episodio 10: **Clara perspectiva** | | ✔ | |
| **Lectura informativa**<br>• **Chile y el medio ambiente** | | | ✔ |
| **Leamos**<br>• **de El Gaucho Martín Fierro**<br>**Escribamos**<br>• **Un personaje folclórico** | | ✔ | |
| **Prepárate para el examen** | | ✔ | |
| **Integración** | | | ✔ |

Visit Holt Online
**go.hrw.com**
KEYWORD: EXP3 CH10
Online Edition

## Technology Resources

### ¡Exprésate! Online
- Student Edition with multi-media
- SoundBooth recording tool
- Interactive activities with feedback
- Self-tests with feedback
- Cuaderno de actividades (interactive workbook)
- Cuaderno de vocabulario y gramática (interactive workbook)
- Live Ink™ Reading Help
- Holt Online Assessment

### DVD Tutor, Disc 2
- GeoVisión
- GramaVisión
- VideoNovela
- Cultura
- Variedades

### Interactive Tutor
- Interactive practice games
- Writing and recording workshops

### Audio Program
- Textbook listening activities
- Assessment listening activities
- Songs

### One-Stop Planner
- Complete media and print resources
- ExamView® Pro Test Generator
- Holt Calendar Planner

### PuzzlePro
- Customizable word games

## Assessment

**Geocultura**
**Vocabulario 1 / Gramática 1**
**Vocabulario 2 / Gramática 2**
**Leamos**
**Escribamos**
**Prepárate para el examen**

### Assessment Program
**Prueba: Geocultura,** pp. 195–196
**Pruebas,** pp. 181–182, 183–184, 185–186
**Pruebas,** pp. 187–188, 189–190, 191–192
**Prueba,** p. 193
**Prueba,** p. 194
**Examen: Capítulo 10,** pp. 329–336
**Examen oral: Capítulo 10,** p. 340
**Alternative Assessment,** pp. 382, 394, 406
**Examen final:** pp. 341–355

### Online Assessment
**my.hrw.com**

### Test Generator
**ExamView® Pro Test Generator**

Planning Guide

Capítulo 10

# Projects

## El mundo en que vivimos

### Mis objetivos futuros

In this project, students will illustrate some of their goals for the future in a collage.

**SUGGESTED SEQUENCE**

1. Give students the phrase **En cinco años...** Ask them to create a collage that represents some of the things they would like to be doing five years from now. Tell them they will present their collage to the class.
2. Discuss with students some of the things they might express in their collage. For example, they might learn to do something, acquire something, or travel.
3. Ask students to write a short paragraph that describes their goals.
4. Have students write a brief outline of how they plan to present their collage. Provide feedback and suggestions if necessary.
5. Students should then compile their materials and complete their project.
6. Ask students to make a short presentation to the class. After the collages have been presented, you might display them around the classroom. 1.3

### Partner Class Project

Assign pairs of students the following Argentine cultural topics to research for a presentation: tango, **yerba mate,** Boom writers, modern writers, filmmakers, **fútbol,** and **gauchos.** Allow them library and computer time to consult different sources. Students should include audio elements and visual props whenever possible, such as a recording by Carlos Gardel, a popular singer of tango music; a picture of a **mate** gourd and silver straw; pictures of authors Borges or Cortázar and readings of their works; clips of Luis Puenzo's *La historia oficial;* a chart of Argentine **fútbol** teams or reports about Gabriel Batistuta, a well-known soccer player from Argentina; a list of famous **novelas gauchescas,** and pictures of **gauchos** in typical dress. 1.3, 2.2

### e-community

**e-mail forum:**

Post the following question on the classroom e-mail forum:

**¿Cómo nos afectan hoy en día los eventos del pasado?**

All students will contribute to the list and then share the items. 1.3

### Grading the projects

Suggested point distribution (100 points total)

| | |
|---|---|
| Outline | 10 |
| Content | 40 |
| Presentation | 30 |
| Creativity | 20 |

**Game Bank**

For game ideas, see pages T64–T67.

# El mundo en que vivimos

## Los mapuches

Today, more than 900,000 **mapuches,** an indigenous people, live in Chile. Many live in the southern part of the country. This territory is part of the cultural and historic patrimony of the Mapuche people, who since colonial times have made a great effort to preserve their heritage. During the military regime, the indigenous communities not only lost their land, but also many of their rights. With the return of democracy, the **mapuches** have begun to launch political campaigns. Currently their goals include protecting the environment, restoring forests, and avoiding the construction of large dams in nature areas. Have students research a **mapuche** legend or tradition to share with the class. 2.2, 3.1

## Receta

### Dulce de leche con panqueques

**Dulce de leche** is Argentina's traditional dessert. The process of caramelizing sugar in milk can take a couple of hours. Often, **dulce de leche** is eaten wrapped in a crepe called a **panqueque.** You might have students make the following recipe as a class project or for extra credit.

### Dulce de leche

$12\frac{3}{4}$ tazas de leche

$3\frac{1}{2}$ tazas de azúcar

2 cucharadas grandes de vainilla

media cucharada de bicarbonato de sodio

Mezcle en la olla todos los ingredientes en este orden: leche, azúcar, vainilla y el bicarbonato. Ponga la olla a fuego lento. Bata la mezcla lentamente hasta que se ponga bien espesa y de color marrón. La preparación casera dura 2 horas en total.

### Panqueques

2 tazas de harina

3 tazas de leche

2 huevos

mantequilla

Mezcle la harina, la leche y los huevos en una licuadora. Caliente una sartén a fuego alto. Añada un poquito de mantequilla. Cubra la sartén con una capa fina de la mezcla. Cuando empieza a ponerse dorado, dele la vuelta y cocine por un minuto más. Saque el panqueque de la sartén y cúbralo con dulce de leche. Sírvalo caliente.

2.2, 3.1

# Listening Activity Scripts

## El mundo en que vivimos



### Vocabulario en acción 1

**1** p. 412, CD 10, Track 1

1. La nueva película argentina salió ayer. Una hora antes de empezar, había una cola de personas esperando. ¡Parece que esta película tendrá mucho éxito!
2. Pasó un grupo grande por la calle principal hoy y todos llevaban letreros a favor de la paz. Otro grupo estaba sentado frente a las oficinas del gobierno, y todavía está allí. Los participantes dicen que se quedarán hasta que se firme un acuerdo de paz.
3. Se cayeron dos hombres mientras hacían escalada deportiva en la región de la Patagonia cuando se les rompió una cuerda. Los dos fueron llevados al hospital y están bien. Dicen que no saben qué pasó.
4. La gente está preocupada por la falta de interés en el problema de las personas sin hogar. Los políticos y los trabajadores sociales no han hecho nada para resolver el problema.
5. A causa de la crisis económica, la gente está actuando sin pensar. Muchos tienen miedo de perder su dinero, y están sacando lo que pueden del banco.
6. ¡Una empresa en Nueva York ha creado un automóvil que funciona con agua en vez de gasolina! Este invento cambiará el mundo.

**Answers to Activity 1**

1. d 2. c 3. e 4. f 5. a 6. b

**8** p. 415, CD 10, Track 2

BÁRBARA Alejo, me parece que la vida moderna es muy complicada. ¿Qué opinas?

ALEJO Aunque estoy de acuerdo, creo que hoy en día hay más solidaridad entre los países.

BÁRBARA ¿Cómo puedes decir eso? Lo que yo noto es que hay muchas guerras en todas partes del mundo.

ALEJO Es cierto que hay guerras, pero por otro lado hay mucha cooperación entre los países para tratar de resolver los conflictos.

BÁRBARA No sé, creo que era mejor antes. Ahora, con los medios de comunicación y los medios de transporte, es casi imposible que un país actúe independientemente.

ALEJO Pero creo que vale la pena acordarse de la solidaridad que esto puede crear entre los países. No te olvides, Bárbara, de cómo se ayudan los países cuando hay un desastre.

BÁRBARA Sin embargo, ten en cuenta que la vida era más simple cuando había menos tecnología. Mira España, Alejo. Siempre tenía la costumbre de la hora de la siesta y ¡ahora tiene que adaptarse a los horarios de los otros países europeos!

ALEJO De todos modos, creo que los adelantos van a crear un mundo más unido. Aunque la vida era más sencilla sin la tecnología, no era mejor. Había conflictos de otro tipo.

**Answers to Activity 8**

1. c 2. b 3. a 4. a 5. b 6. a 7. b 8. b

### Gramática en acción 1

**10** p. 416, CD 10, Track 3

1. —¿Qué estabas haciendo cuando se fue la luz?
   —Estaba viendo el estreno de la nueva película cuando de pronto el cine se quedó en la oscuridad. ¡Fue aterrador!
2. —Siento mucha compasión por los refugiados yugoslavos que llegaron a Chile.
   —Yo también. Estoy trabajando con ellos para ayudarlos a adaptarse.
3. —Mamá, ¿fuiste al hospital con tía Elena cuando nació Ana María en 1983?
   —No, estaba celebrando el año nuevo en la Plaza de Mayo.
4. —¿Ya dejó de trabajar el senador?
   —¡Qué va! Está preparándose para las elecciones. ¡Quiere seguir trabajando!
5. —¿Sabes algo del accidente en la carretera?
   —Estamos leyendo el artículo ahora. Parece que todo el mundo está bien.
6. —Teresa, ¿viste el campeonato ayer? Fue muy emocionante.
   —No, tuve que cuidar a mi hermano. Pasamos toda la tarde en el parque.

**Answers to Activity 10**

1. a 2. b 3. a 4. b 5. b 6. a

**19** p. 420, CD 10, Track 4

DAVID Hace tres meses que el nuevo presidente está gobernando el país.

NORA Desde que él tomó el poder, hay muy poca cooperación entre los políticos.

For Student Response Forms, see the *Lab Book*, pp. 49–52.

DAVID Ten en cuenta que hace poco tiempo sucedió un acontecimiento trágico en la capital.

NORA Sí, hoy es la tercera vez que sale un mensaje en la televisión en que el presidente les pide solidaridad a los ciudadanos.

DAVID Hace diez años que vivo en este país y lo que noto es que la gente tiene mucha compasión.

NORA Estoy de acuerdo. Las personas ayudan a sus vecinos menos afortunados.

For answers, see *Teacher's Edition*, p. 420.

## Vocabulario en acción 2

### 24 p. 426, CD 10, Track 8

1. Tenemos que mejorar la calidad del agua de los mares y ríos porque ahora es peligroso comer pescado.
2. El gobierno va a implementar nuevos programas para combatir el problema de las drogas en los colegios.
3. La gente que va al trabajo en carro está muy frustrada porque hay demasiados carros en la carretera. Algunos se quejan porque tardan dos horas en llegar al trabajo.
4. Una alternativa a usar los recursos no renovables para calentar las casas es utilizar un recurso renovable: la energía que viene del sol.
5. Muchos agricultores han dejado de usar pesticidas y otros productos químicos al cultivar verduras y frutas, para evitar las enfermedades que éstos pueden causar.
6. El número de personas sin trabajo está aumentando.

**Answers to Activity 24**

a. 4 b. 2 c. 3 d. 5 e. 1 f. 6

## Gramática en acción 2

### 34 p. 430, CD 10, Track 9

JAIME El gobierno está promoviendo muchos programas que han mejorado nuestra comunidad.

RAQUEL Sí, aunque todavía hay mucha gente sin trabajo, se dice que la tasa de desempleo bajará.

JAIME Además, han desarrollado algunos programas muy buenos para combatir el problema de la drogadicción.

RAQUEL Y para ayudar a la gente sin hogar, pondrán más camas en los refugios. ¿Esto mejorará también el problema del hambre?

JAIME Pues, una vez que implementen el nuevo sistema para distribuir la comida, habrá menos gente con hambre en la ciudad.

RAQUEL Ya hemos visto resultados en otras cosas. Por ejemplo, ha habido menos crimen este año.

JAIME El presidente vendrá la próxima semana y hablará sobre todos los programas, cómo han ayudado en la comunidad y cómo van a ayudar en el futuro.

**Answers to Activity 34**

1. b 2. a 3. b 4. b 5. a 6. b

### 42 p. 435, CD 10, Track 10

SARA Pedro, ¿vas a votar por Laura Rodríguez?

PEDRO Sí, voy a apoyarla, con tal de que prometa hacer algo por el medio ambiente.

SARA Ella dijo que iba a implementar un programa de reciclaje en cuanto ganara las elecciones.

PEDRO Pero yo quiero saber si va a promover fuentes de energía alternativas.

SARA Pues, no lo va a hacer hasta que tenga más información.

PEDRO Cuando habló con los científicos, le dijeron que le darían la información tan pronto como terminaran el estudio.

SARA Bueno, yo decidiré por quién votar después de que veamos el debate.

PEDRO Buena idea. Yo también.

For answers, see *Teacher's Edition*, p. 435.

## Prepárate para el examen capítulo 10

### 1 p. 444, CD 10, Track 13

For script and answers, see *Teacher's Edition*, p. 444.

### 6 p. 445, CD 10, Track 14

For script and answers, see *Teacher's Edition*, p. 445.

## Integración capítulos 1–10

### 1 p. 448, CD 10, Track 15

For script and answers, see *Teacher's Edition* p. 448.

# 50-Minute Lesson Plans

## El mundo en que vivimos

For more customized Lesson Plans, see the *Lesson Planner with Differentiated Instruction.*



### Day 1

**Objective**
*Talking about a past event*

**Core Instruction**
**Chapter Opener**, pp. 408–409 **10 min.**
- See Chapter Objectives and Using the Photo, p. 408.

**Vocabulario en acción 1,** pp. 410–415
- Have students do Bell Work, p. 410.
- See Teaching **Vocabulario,** p. 410. **10 min.**
- See Teaching **¡Exprésate!,** p. 410. **10 min.**
- Play Audio CD 10, Tr. 1 for Activity 1, p. 412. **5 min.**
- Have students do Activities 2–3, p. 412. **15 min.**

**Optional Resources**
- Slower Pace Learners, p. 411 ◆
- Multiple Intelligences, p. 411
- **Comunicación,** p. 413
- Heritage Speakers, p. 413 ■
- Advanced Learners, p. 413 ▲
- Multiple Intelligences, p. 413

**Homework Suggestions**
Cuaderno de vocabulario y gramática, pp. 109–111
❀ 1.2

### Day 2

**Objective**
*Expressing and supporting a point of view*

**Core Instruction**
**Vocabulario en acción 1,** pp. 410–415
- Have students do Activities 4–6, p. 413. **20 min.**
- See Teaching **¡Exprésate!,** p. 414. **10 min.**
- Have students do Activity 7, p. 415. **10 min.**
- Play Audio CD 10, Tr. 2 for Activity 8, p. 415. **5 min.**
- Have students do Activity 9, p. 415. **5 min.**

**Optional Resources**
- **Comunicación,** p. 415
- Slower Pace Learners, p. 415 ◆
- Multiple Intelligences, p. 415

**Homework Suggestions**
Study for **Prueba: Vocabulario 1**
Cuaderno de vocabulario y gramática, pp. 109–111
❀ 1.1, 1.2, 1.3

### Day 3

**Objective**
*Present and past progressive*

**Core Instruction**
**Vocabulario en acción 1,** pp. 410–415
- Review **Vocabulario en acción 1,** pp. 410–415. **5 min.**
- Give **Prueba: Vocabulario 1. 20 min.**

**Gramática en acción 1,** pp. 416–421
- See Teaching **Gramática,** p. 416. **15 min.**
- Play Audio CD 10, Tr. 3 for Activity 10, p. 416. **5 min.**
- Have students do Activity 11, p. 417. **5 min.**

**Optional Resources**
- Advanced Learners, p. 417 ▲
- Special Learning Needs, p. 417 ●

**Homework Suggestions**
Cuaderno de vocabulario y gramática, pp. 112–114
Cuaderno de actividades, pp. 91–93
❀ 1.2, 1.3

### Day 4

**Objective**
**Haber**

**Core Instruction**
**Gramática en acción 1,** pp. 416–421
- Have students do Activities 12–13, p. 417. **10 min.**
- See Teaching **Gramática,** p. 418. **15 min.**
- Have students do Activities 14–18, pp. 418–419. **25 min.**

**Optional Resources**
- **Comunicación,** p. 419
- Heritage Speakers, p. 419 ■
- Advanced Learners, p. 419 ▲
- Multiple Intellegences, p. 419

**Homework Suggestions**
Cuaderno de vocabulario y gramática, pp. 112–114
Cuaderno de actividades, pp. 91–93
❀ 1.1, 1.2, 1.3

### Day 5

**Objective**
*Expressions of time*

**Core Instruction**
**Gramática en acción 1,** pp. 416–421
- See Teaching **Gramática,** p. 420. **10 min.**
- Play Audio CD 10, Tr. 4 for Activity 19, p. 420. **5 min.**
- Have students do Activities 20–23, pp. 420–421. **25 min.**
- Review **Gramática en acción 1,** pp. 416–421. **10 min.**

**Optional Resources**
- **Comunicación,** p. 421
- Slower Pace Learners, p. 421 ◆
- Multiple Intelligences, p. 421

**Homework Suggestions**
Study for **Prueba: Gramática 1**
Cuaderno de vocabulario y gramática, pp. 112–114
❀ 1.1, 1.2

### Day 6

**Objective**
*Interviews from around the Spanish-speaking world*

**Core Instruction**
**Gramática en acción 1,** pp. 416–421
- Give **Prueba: Gramática 1. 20 min.**

**Cultura,** pp. 422–423
- See Teaching **Cultura,** p. 422. **15 min.**
- Play Audio CD 10, Tr. 5–7, or show **VideoCultura. 15 min.**

**Optional Resources**
- Advanced Learners, p. 423 ▲
- Multiple Intelligences, p. 423

**Homework Suggestions**
Cuaderno de actividades, p. 94
Online Practice (**go.hrw.com,** Keyword: EXP CH10)
❀ 1.2, 1.3, 3.1

### Day 7

**Objective**
*Making predictions and giving warnings*

**Core Instruction**
**Vocabulario en acción 2,** pp. 424–429
- See Teaching **Vocabulario,** p. 424. **10 min.**
- See Teaching **¡Exprésate!,** p. 424. **10 min.**
- Play Audio CD 10, Tr. 8 for Activity 24, p. 426. **5 min.**
- Have students do Activities 25–28, pp. 426–427. **25 min.**

**Optional Resources**
- Advanced Learners, p. 425 ▲
- Multiple Intelligences, p. 425
- **Comunicación,** p. 427
- Slower Pace Learners, p. 427 ◆
- Special Learning Needs, p. 427 ●

**Homework Suggestions**
Cuaderno de vocabulario y gramática, pp. 115–117
❀ 1.2, 1.3

### Day 8

**Objective**
*Expressing assumptions*

**Core Instruction**
**Vocabulario en acción 2,** pp. 424–429
- Have students do Activity 29, p. 427. **5 min.**
- See Teaching **¡Exprésate!,** p. 428. **10 min.**
- Have students do Activities 30–33, p. 429. **35 min.**

**Optional Resources**
- **Comunicación,** p. 429
- Advanced Learners, p. 429 ▲
- Multiple Intelligences, p. 429

**Homework Suggestions**
Study for **Prueba: Vocabulario 2**
Cuaderno de vocabulario y gramática, pp. 115–117
❀ 1.1, 1.2, 1.3

- For information on the **Geocultura** pages, see the *Lesson Planner with Differentiated Instruction.*
- For more detailed information on benchmarks, see point-of-use correlations on each page.
- To edit and create your own lesson plans, see the **One-Stop** Planner® CD-ROM

**KEY**
- ▲ Advanced Learners
- ◆ Slower Pace Learners
- ● Special Learning Needs
- ■ Heritage Speakers

## Day 9

**Objective**
*Future tense*

**Core Instruction**
**Vocabulario en acción 2,** pp. 424–429
- Review **Vocabulario en acción 2,** pp. 424–429. **10 min.**
- Give **Prueba: Vocabulario 2. 20 min.**

**Gramática en acción 2,** pp. 430–435
- See Teaching **Gramática,** p. 430. **10 min.**
- Play Audio CD 10, Tr. 9 for Activity 34, p. 430. **5 min.**
- Have students do Activity 35, p. 431. **5 min.**

**Optional Resources**
- **Comunicación,** p. 431
- Slower Pace Learners, p. 431 ◆
- Multiple Intelligences, p. 431

**Homework Suggestions**
Cuaderno de vocabulario y gramática, pp. 118–120

1.2

## Day 10

**Objective**
*Subjunctive with doubt, denial, and feelings*

**Core Instruction**
**Gramática en acción 2,** pp. 430–435
- Have students do Activities 36–37, p. 431. **15 min.**
- See Teaching **Gramática,** p. 432. **10 min.**
- Have students do Activities 38–41, pp. 432–433. **25 min.**

**Optional Resources**
- **Comunicación,** p. 433
- Advanced Learners, p. 433 ▲
- Multiple Intelligences, p. 433

**Homework Suggestions**
Cuaderno de vocabulario y gramática, pp. 118–120
Cuaderno de actividades, pp. 95–97

1.1, 1.2, 1.3

## Day 11

**Objective**
*Subjunctive and indicative with adverbial clauses*

**Core Instruction**
**Gramática en acción 2,** pp. 430–435
- See Teaching **Gramática,** p. 434. **15 min.**
- Play Audio CD 10, Tr. 10 for Activity 42, p. 435. **10 min.**
- Have students do Activities 43–44, p. 435. **25 min.**

**Optional Resources**
- **Comunicación,** p. 435
- Slower Pace Learners, p. 435 ◆
- Special Learning Needs, p. 435 ●

**Homework Suggestions**
Study for **Prueba: Gramática 2**
Cuaderno de vocabulario y gramática, pp. 118–120
Cuaderno de actividades, pp. 95–97

1.1, 1.2, 1.3

## Day 12

**Objective**
*Developing listening and reading skills*

**Core Instruction**
**Gramática en acción 2,** pp. 430–435
- Review **Gramática en acción 2,** pp. 430–435. **5 min.**
- Give **Prueba: Gramática 2. 20 min.**

**Novela en video,** pp. 436–437
- Show **VideoNovela.** See Teaching **Novela en video,** p. 436. **25 min.**

**Optional Resources**
- **Comunicación,** p. 437

**Assessment Program**
- **Prueba: Vocabulario y gramática 2**

**Homework Suggestions**
Cuaderno de vocabulario y gramática, pp. 118–120

1.2, 1.3

## Day 13

**Objective**
*Developing listening and reading skills*

**Core Instruction**
**Lectura informativa,** pp. 438–439
- See Teaching **Lectura informativa,** p. 438. **25 min.**

**Leamos y escribamos,** pp. 440–443
- See Teaching **Leamos,** p. 440. **25 min.**

**Optional Resources**
- Multiple Intelligences, p. 439
- Special Learning Needs p. 441 ●
- Multiple Intelligences, p. 441

**Homework Suggestions**
Cuaderno de actividades, p. 98

1.1, 1.2, 1.3, 3.1

## Day 14

**Objective**
*Developing reading and writing skills*

**Core Instruction**
**Leamos y escribamos,** pp. 440–443
- See Teaching **Escribamos,** p. 442. **30 min.**

**Prepárate para el examen,** pp. 444–447
- Play Audio CD 10, Tr. 13 for Activity 1, p. 444. **5 min.**
- Have students do Activities 2–4, pp. 444–445. **15 min.**

**Optional Resources**
- Slower Pace Learners, p. 443 ◆
- Multiple Intelligences, p. 443

**Homework Suggestions**
**Taller del escritor,** p. 443

1.2

## Day 15

**Objective**
*Chapter review*

**Core Instruction**
**Prepárate para el examen,** pp. 444–447
- Have students do Activity 5, p. 445. **5 min.**
- Play Audio CD 10, Tr. 14 for Activity 6, p. 445. **5 min.**
- Have students do Activity 7, p. 445. **5 min.**

**Integración,** pp. 448–449
- Play Audio CD 10, Tr. 15 for Activity 1, p. 448. **5 min.**
- Have students do Activities 2–6, pp. 448–449. **30 min.**

**Optional Resources**
- Play Pre-AP Audio CD 2, Tr. 17, for Pre-AP Practice, p. 445
- Game, p. 447
- Fine Art Connection, p. 449

**Homework Suggestions**
Study for Chapter Test

1.1, 1.2, 1.3

## Day 16/Test

**Core Instruction**
**Chapter Test 50 min.**

**Optional Resources**
**Assessment Program**
- **Prueba: Lectura**
- **Prueba: Escritura**
- Test Generator

**Homework Suggestions**
Cuaderno de actividades, pp. 99–100

# Indiana
## The Hoosier State

State capitol, Indianapolis

Covered bridge, Kahorne

Indiana Dunes State Park

### Chapter 10

The following chart presents *¡Exprésate!* Chapter 10 correlations to the Indiana Academic Standards for World Languages, Grade 11. The correlations here are to the *Student Edition* (SE) and *Teacher's Edition* (TE) only. For additional teaching resources, see pages 407A-407B

| INDIANA ACADEMIC STANDARDS | | | CHAPTER 10 SE/TE CORRELATIONS |
|---|---|---|---|
| **Standard 1 COMMUNICATION:** | | | |
| **Write and speak in a language other than English** | **11.1.1** | Initiate, sustain, and close conversations in limited yet varied situations. | **SE:** 413, 415, 419, 427, 429, 431, 433, 439, 449<br>**TE:** 414, 424, 428, 439, 449 |
| | **11.1.2** | Exchange detailed information and opinions orally on a variety of topics. | **SE:** 415, 419, 423, 427, 429, 431, 433, 439, 449<br>**TE:** 414, 422, 427, 429, 431, 433, 439, 448 |
| | **11.1.3** | Exchange detailed information and opinions in written form on a variety of topics. | **SE:** 443 |
| | **11.1.4** | Make requests and ask different types of questions in a variety of social situations. | **SE:** 419, 431 |
| | **11.1.5** | Recognize and use situation-appropriate non-verbal communication. | **SE:** 449<br>**TE:** 436 |
| | **11.1.6** | Use speaking and listening strategies to facilitate communication. | **SE:** 417, 419, 421<br>**TE:** 415, 430 |
| **Standard 2 COMMUNICATION:** | | | |
| **Interpret information in a language other than English** *Learners interpret written and spoken language on a variety of topics. (Interpretive)* | **11.2.1** | Respond accurately to everyday requests, commands, and directions. | **TE:** 411 |
| | **11.2.2** | Demonstrate comprehension of both authentic and non-authentic written and spoken language through developmentally appropriate tasks. | **SE:** 439, 441<br>**TE:** 436, 438, 440 |
| | **11.2.3** | Make educated guesses about meaning in unfamiliar written and spoken contexts. | **SE:** 436, 440<br>**TE:** 436, 440 |
| **Standard 3 COMMUNICATION:** | | | |
| **Present information in a language other than English** *Learners present to an audience of listeners or readers on a variety of topics. (Presentational)* | **11.3.2** | Produce and present creative material on a variety of topics. | **TE:** 407C, 419, 431, 448 |
| | **11.3.3** | Read passages aloud to demonstrate improving intonation and pronunciation. | **TE:** 441 |
| | **11.3.4** | Compose cohesive written information using appropriate formats and more varied vocabulary and structures. | **SE:** 443<br>**TE:** 407C, 442, 443 |
| **Standard 4 CULTURES:** | | | |
| **Develop awareness of other cultures.** *Learners examine, experience, and reflect on the relationships among the practices, products, and perspectives of the cultures studied.* | **11.4.1** | Analyze and reflect on cultural practices of the target cultures. | **SE:** 423, 439<br>**TE:** 422, 438, 448 |
| | **11.4.2** | Describe products, perspectives, and symbols of the target cultures. | **SE:** 423, 439<br>**TE:** 422, 438, 448 |
| | **11.4.3** | Discuss factors that influence practices, products, and perspectives. | **SE:** 423, 439<br>**TE:** 422, 438, 448 |

| | | | SE | TE |
|---|---|---|---|---|
| | 11.4.4 | Recognize the interrelations among the practices, products, and perspectives of the target cultures. | 423, 439 | 407C, 422, 438, 448 |
| | 11.4.5 | Explain contributions from other cultures. | 439 | 438, 448 |
| | 11.4.6 | Identify significant events unique to the target cultures. | 422 | 422 |

## Standard 5 CONNECTIONS:

| | | | SE | TE |
|---|---|---|---|---|
| **Make connections to other content areas** *Learners use the target language to expand their knowledge of and make connections among multiple content areas.* | 11.5.1 | Make connections with other content areas through resources intended for native speakers. | | 448 |
| | 11.5.2 | Design and share activities and materials that integrate the target language and cultures with concepts and skills from other content areas. | 427, 429 | 407C, 447 |

## Standard 6 CONNECTIONS:

| | | | SE | TE |
|---|---|---|---|---|
| **Access and connect information through various media** *Learners strengthen language proficiency and cultural knowledge by using current digital media and authentic resources.* | 11.6.1 | Use digital media and culturally authentic resources to build vocabulary, improve reading ability, and encourage cultural awareness. | 434, 436, 438 | 407E, 407F |
| | 11.6.2 | Use digital media and culturally authentic resources to study target cultures. | 422, 436 | |
| | 11.6.3 | Identify and evaluate resources intended for native speakers. | 422, 436, 442 | 441 |

## Standard 7 COMPARISONS:

| | | | SE | TE |
|---|---|---|---|---|
| **Investigate the nature of language and culture** *Learners understand the nature of language and culture through comparisons of the languages and cultures studied and their own.* | 11.7.1 | Use elements of word formation to expand vocabulary and derive meaning. | 419, 444 | 416, 430, 444 |
| | 11.7.2 | Recognize and use a variety of language structures. | 416-421, 443, 449 | 430-435, 444-447 |
| | 11.7.3 | Compare and use idiomatic, colloquial, and proverbial expressions in the target language. | 415, 448 | 414 |
| | 11.7.5 | Compare systems of other cultures and the learner's own culture. | 423, 439 | 422, 438 |
| | 11.7.6 | Compare and contrast elements that shape cultural identity in the learner's heritage and in the target cultures. | 423, 439 | 422, 438 |

## Standard 8 COMMUNITIES:

| | | | SE | TE |
|---|---|---|---|---|
| **Become an active global citizen by experiencing languages and cultures in multiple settings** *Learners use their knowledge of the target language and cultures both within and beyond the school setting for personal enrichment and civic engagement.* | 11.8.2 | Investigate and share with others the influences of the target language and cultures on the community. | 449 | 406 |
| | 11.8.3 | Show evidence of becoming a life-long learner by using the target language and cultural knowledge for personal enrichment. | 413, 415, 419, 427, 429, 431, 433, 435, 439, 449 | 407D, 410, 419, 425, 426, 427, 431, 432, 433, 435, 438, 439, 448 |

## Meeting the National Standards

**Communication**
Comunicación, pp. 413, 415, 417, 419, 421, 427, 429, 431, 433, 435, 437
Game, p. 447
Situación, p. 449

**Cultures**
Los mapuches, p. 407D
Receta, p. 407D
Products and Perspectives, pp. 411

**Connections**
Receta, p. 407D
Social Studies Link, p. 413
Nota cultural, pp. 413, 415, 418, 426, 431, 432, 435
Atlas Interactivo Mundial, p. 423
Comunidad y oficio, p. 423
Language Arts Link, p. 431
Science Link, p. 433
History Link, p. 436

**Comparisons**
Comparing and Contrasting, pp. 414, 438
Language to Language, p. 446
Culture Project, p. 448

**Communities**
Career Path, pp. 423, 428
Community Link, p. 429

## Using the Photo

Argentina's capitol building is modeled after the one in Washington, D.C. **La Plaza de los Dos Congresos** honors the 1813 Assembly in Buenos Aires and the 1816 congress in Tucumán, which together led Argentina to independence on July 9, 1816, under the name of the United Provinces of the Río de la Plata. Have students research from which regime Argentina broke free. (Spain's Viceroyalty of the Río de la Plata)

## Más vocabulario

**las columnas** *columns*
**la cúpula** *dome*
**las palomas** *pigeons*
**las rejas** *railings*

# Capítulo 10

# El mundo en que vivimos

## OBJETIVOS

**In this chapter you will learn to**
- talk about past events
- express and support a point of view
- make predictions and give warnings
- express assumptions

**And you will use**
- present and past progressive
- **haber**
- expressions of time
- future tense
- subjunctive with doubt, denial, and feelings
- subjunctive and indicative with adverbial clauses

**¿Qué ves en la foto?**
- **¿Qué están haciendo estas personas?**
- **¿Cómo son los edificios que ves en la plaza?**
- **¿Has visto edificios similares a éstos alguna vez?**

| Suggested pacing: | Traditional Schedule | Block Schedule |
|---|---|---|
| Vocabulario 1/Gramática 1 | 5 1/2 days | 2 1/2 blocks |
| Cultura | 1/2 day | 1/2 block |
| Vocabulario 2/Gramática 2 | 5 1/2 days | 2 1/2 blocks |
| Novela | 1/2 day | 1/2 block |
| Lectura cultural | 1/2 day | 1/2 block |
| Leamos y escribamos | 1 day | 1/2 block |
| Prepárate para el examen | 1 day | 1/4 block |
| Chapter Test | 1 day | 1/2 block |
| Integración | 1/2 day | 1/4 block |

Visit Holt Online
**go.hrw.com**
KEYWORD: EXP3 CH10
Online Edition

En la Plaza de Los Dos Congresos, Buenos Aires, Argentina

# Chapter Opener

## Holt Grammar Logic
### CHAPTER 10

- *To talk about past events, and to express and support a point of view,* students will review the present and past progressive tenses. They will also need to review expressions of time as well as the forms and uses of **haber.**
- *To make predictions, to give warnings, and to express assumptions,* students must review the future tense. They will also review the uses of the subjunctive with doubt, denial, and feelings, and will contrast the use of the subjunctive and indicative in adverbial clauses.

## DVD VIDEO OPTIONS

- **VideoCultura**
- **VideoNovela**
- **Variedades**
- **GramaVisión**

## LISTENING PRACTICE — Language Lab and Classroom Activities

**Vocabulario**
Activity 1, p. 412, CD 10, Tr. 1
Activity 8, p. 415, CD 10, Tr. 2
Activity 24, p. 426, CD 10, Tr. 8

**Gramática**
Activity 10, p. 416, CD 10, Tr. 3
Activity 19, p. 420, CD 10, Tr. 4
Activity 34, p. 430, CD 10, Tr. 9
Activity 42, p. 435, CD 10, Tr. 10

**Cultura**
Comparaciones, pp. 422–423, CD 10, Tr. 5–7

**Novela**
**Novela en video,** Escuchemos, p. 436

**Lectura informativa**
pp. 438–439, CD 10, Tr. 11

**Leamos**
pp. 440–443, CD 10, Tr. 12
Escuchemos, p. 440

**Repaso**
Activity 1, p. 444, CD 10, Tr. 13
Activity 6, p. 445, CD 10, Tr. 14
**Variedades,** Lab Book, p. 87

**Integración**
Activity 1, p. 448, CD 10, Tr. 15

**Assessment Program**
CD 10, Tr. 16–19

**Additional Listening**
Pre-AP CD 2, Tr. 17–20

## Resources

**Planning:**

Lesson Planner, pp. 145–146, 306–307

One-Stop Planner

**Presentation:**

Teaching Transparencies **Vocabulario** 10.1, 10.2

**Practice:**

Cuaderno de vocabulario y gramática, pp. 109–111

Activities for Communication, pp. 37–38

Teaching Transparencies Bell Work 10.1

**Vocabulario y gramática** answers, pp. 109–111

Interactive Tutor, Disc 2

### Bell Work

Use Bell Work 10.1 in the *Teaching Transparencies.*

**Objetivos**
- Talking about past events
- Expressing and supporting a point of view

# Vocabulario en acción 1

## Del pasado al presente

Es necesario estudiar la historia de nuestro país, así como la del resto del mundo, para saber lo que sucedió en el pasado y cómo estos **acontecimientos** influyen en el presente.

Los exploradores **descubrieron** los restos de esta **nave hundida,** que se perdió en el mar hace años.

El gobierno demuestra **compasión** al recibir a **los refugiados** en tiempos difíciles.

**Las manifestaciones** de las madres de la Plaza de Mayo son muy **conmovedoras.** La gente se reúne allí para mostrar su **solidaridad** con las madres de hijos desaparecidos y para recordar los acontecimientos **trágicos** de la «guerra sucia».

La Copa Mundial es un **campeonato** de fútbol muy importante. En 1994 alguien amenazó con hacer **estallar una bomba** durante los partidos. **La cooperación** entre diferentes autoridades es necesaria para garantizar la seguridad en estos eventos.

### Pre-AP Practice

**AP Benchmark:** Use language that is semantically and grammatically accurate according to a given context.

**Focus:** Expressing and supporting a point of view
- SE, p. 415, Act. 9
- TE, p. 415, Slower Pace Learners
- **Cuaderno de vocabulario y gramática,** p. 111, Act. 7

## Core Instruction

### TEACHING VOCABULARIO

1. Introduce the vocabulary using transparencies **Vocabulario 10.1** and **10.2.** Have students look at the photos as you read the captions. To monitor comprehension, you might ask a question for each photo, such as: **¿Han visto manifestaciones pacíficas aquí en Estados Unidos?** **(6 min.)**
2. Discuss the words in **Más vocabulario** and model each in a sentence. **(4 min.)**

### TEACHING ¡EXPRÉSATE!

1. Model expressions in **¡Exprésate!** using words from **Vocabulario 1.** **(2 min.)**
2. Model the expressions by talking about public events in the recent past with which students should be familiar. For example, **—¿Te acuerdas cuando sucedieron 793 manifestaciones a favor de la paz alrededor del mundo el 15 de febrero de 2003? —Lo recuerdo como si fuera ayer.**

Visit Holt Online
go.hrw.com
KEYWORD: EXP3 CH10
Vocabulario 1 practice

**Un desastre** natural, como **la erupción de un volcán**, puede ser **aterrador** y causar mucha **destrucción.** La erupción de un volcán causa **pánico** entre la población.

**El descubrimiento de** momias antiguas en el desierto de Atacama, Chile fue una experiencia **emocionante** para los arqueólogos, ya que las momias son unas de las más antiguas del **planeta.**

No sabía que iban a **estrenar** la nueva película sobre la Plaza de Mayo esta semana. Mis amigos fueron al **estreno** anoche.

**Más vocabulario...**

| | |
|---|---|
| **el accidente** | *accident* |
| **las elecciones** | *elections* |
| **espantoso(a)** | *terrible, frightening* |
| **la indiferencia** | *indifference* |
| **los inmigrantes** | *immigrants* |
| **el invento** | *invention* |

## ¡Exprésate!

| To ask about a past event | To respond |
|---|---|
| **¿Te acuerdas (de) cuando sucedió...?** *Do you remember when . . . happened?* | **Lo recuerdo como si fuera ayer./ No, no me acuerdo para nada.** *I remember it like it was yesterday./ No, I don't remember at all.* |
| **¿Dónde estabas y qué estabas haciendo cuando...?** *Where were you and what were you doing when . . . ?* | **Estaba en casa cuando...** *I was at home when . . .* |

Interactive TUTOR

Vocabulario y gramática, pp. 109–111 Online workbooks

### TPR
**TOTAL PHYSICAL RESPONSE**

Bring to class photographs of the following items: a volcano, a political demonstration, a group of refugees, a planet, a destroyed building. As an alternative, you may wish to bring in articles that discuss each topic listed. Have individual volunteers respond to the following commands:

**Señala la foto que corresponde a la palabra erupción.**

**Pásame la foto del planeta.**

**Toca la foto que muestra destrucción.**

**Señala la foto de los refugiados.**

**Pásame la foto de las manifestaciones.** 1.2

### También se puede decir...

Tell students they can also use **evento** or **suceso** for the word **acontecimiento.**

### Cultures

#### Products and Perspectives

Tell students that the mummies found in the Atacama desert date back to 18,000 B.C. The mummies are displayed in the museum of San Miguel de Azapa in the Azapa Valley. The museum also has a collection of some 20,000 objects found in the desert. Another world-famous museum, the Museo Arqueológico Padre Gustavo Le Paige in San Pedro de Atacama, contains a collection of over 300,000 pieces which include pottery, woven fragments, and mummies discovered in the area. Have students research information about the pieces in one of these collections and find out what they tell us about the ancient civilization of Atacama.

2.2

## Differentiated Instruction

### SLOWER PACE LEARNERS

**Additional Practice** Have students complete fill-in-the-blank sentences using the new vocabulary. You might want to use content the students are very familiar with, such as: **El campeonato máximo del fútbol americano es el "Super Bowl."** 1.2

### MULTIPLE INTELLIGENCES

**Interpersonal** Have students form small groups to talk about the difficulties people have to confront when facing a natural disaster in their area. After choosing a type of disaster, have them think about the services provided by public officials, such as transportation, emergency food and shelter, and counseling. Ask them to come up with several ideas to discuss with the class. They should use vocabulary words and **¡Exprésate!** phrases, and they may look up unknown words in the dictionary. 1.1

**Differentiated Instruction** See the Differentiated Instruction CD-ROM.

# Vocabulario 1

## Resources

**Planning:**

Lesson Planner, pp. 145–146, 306–307

One-Stop Planner

**Presentation:**

Teaching Transparencies **Vocabulario** 10.1, 10.2

**Practice:**

Cuaderno de vocabulario y gramática, pp. 109–111

Activities for Communication, pp. 37–38

Lab Book, pp. 49–52

Teaching Transparencies **Vocabulario y gramática** answers, pp. 109–111

Audio CD 10, Tr. 1

Interactive Tutor, Disc 2

### 1 Script

1. La nueva película argentina salió ayer. Una hora antes de empezar, había una cola de personas esperando. ¡Parece que esta película tendrá mucho éxito!
2. Pasó un grupo grande por la calle principal hoy y todos llevaban letreros a favor de la paz. Otro grupo estaba sentado frente a las oficinas del gobierno, y todavía está allí. Los participantes dicen que se quedarán hasta que se firme un acuerdo de paz.
3. Se cayeron dos hombres mientras hacían escalada deportiva en la región de la Patagonia cuando se les rompió una cuerda. Los dos fueron llevados al hospital y están bien. Dicen que no saben qué pasó.
4. La gente está preocupada por la falta de interés en el problema de las personas sin hogar. Los políticos y los trabajadores sociales no han hecho nada para resolver el problema.
5. A causa de la crisis económica, la gente está actuando sin pensar. Muchos tienen miedo de perder su dinero, y están sacando lo que pueden del banco.
6. ¡Una empresa en Nueva York ha creado un automóvil que funciona con agua en vez de gasolina! Este invento cambiará el mundo.

CD 10, Tr. 1

### 1 Las noticias del día 1.2

**Escuchemos** Escucha el noticiero y escoge la palabra que corresponde a cada noticia.

1. d  **a.** el pánico
2. c  **b.** el invento
3. e  **c.** las manifestaciones
4. f  **d.** el estreno
5. a  **e.** un accidente
6. b  **f.** la indiferencia

### 2 Acontecimientos históricos 1.2

**Leamos** Indica qué oración corresponde a cada foto.

A

B

C

D

1. a
2. d
3. c
4. b

1. Los arqueólogos celebran el descubrimiento de artefactos *(artifacts)* en Argentina.
2. La erupción del volcán Villarica en Chile en 1971 causó mucha destrucción.
3. Argentina celebra su victoria en el campeonato de fútbol de 1978.
4. El descubrimiento de la nave hundida fue un momento emocionante.

Raúl Pateras de Pescara, un inventor argentino, pone a prueba su helicóptero en 1924.

### 3 Definiciones 1.2

**Leamos/Hablemos** Decide qué palabra de **Vocabulario** corresponde a cada definición.

1. Un producto que no existía antes. un invento
2. Las personas que buscan un lugar seguro. los refugiados
3. Las personas que se van de su país y se establecen en otro. los inmigrantes
4. El sentimiento de pena o lástima por alguien que sufre. la compasión
5. Un suceso involuntario que causa daño. un accidente
6. Una ruina o pérdida grande. la destrucción
7. El proceso de votar por la persona que va a ocupar un puesto importante. las elecciones
8. Presentar por primera vez. estrenar

## Core Instruction

### VOCABULARY IN CONTEXT

Have students use cluster diagrams to categorize vocabulary words and expressions. Once they have created their diagrams, have volunteers share them with the class. Then have students choose one category and create a word web of other related words. For example, for a cluster diagram with **desastre, erupción, destrucción, accidente,** they might add the words **tornado, huracán, devastación, terremoto,** or they might personalize it with specific words that show what the words in the cluster mean to them: **incendios forestales, el Monte St. Helens, edificio derrumbado, lastimarse la pierna.**

## 4 Hablando del pasado 1.2

**Leamos/Escribamos** Completa la conversación con las palabras del cuadro.

| | | |
|---|---|---|
| sucedió | aterradora | trágico |
| estalló | solidaridad | pánico |

—¿Te acuerdas cuando ___1___ una bomba en los Juegos Olímpicos? **1.** estalló

—Sí, lo recuerdo. Fue una explosión ___2___ y estaba muy asustado. **2.** aterradora

—¿Dónde estabas cuando ___3___? **3.** sucedió

—Estaba entrando al estadio cuando sentí algo como un terremoto y todo el mundo sintió ___4___. **4.** pánico

—Fue ___5___, pero me impresionó la ___6___ entre todos los países que se apoyaron para que continuaran los Juegos.

**5.** trágico **6.** solidaridad

## 5 Me acuerdo... 1.3

**Leamos/Escribamos** Completa las oraciones según tus experiencias. Da tantos detalles como puedas.

1. Fui al estreno de...
2. En las últimas elecciones...
3. Me acuerdo cuando sucedió...
4. Un acontecimiento trágico del año pasado fue...
5. Fue emocionante el descubrimiento de...
6. Muchos refugiados vinieron a Estados Unidos porque...

### Nota cultural

La década de los 90 fue marcada por crisis económicas en México, Asia y Brasil. Argentina fue también afectada por estos sucesos; los precios de los productos argentinos subieron, los productos de exportación bajaron, y a finales de los años 90, comenzó una crisis económica en Argentina. En 2001, las imágenes en la televisión eran escenas de caos y pánico en las ciudades de Argentina. El desempleo alcanzó niveles de más del 20%. ¿Por qué crees que una crisis económica en un país o región podría contribuir a crisis parecidas en otros países? 3.1

## Comunicación

HOLT SoundBooth ONLINE RECORDING

## 6 ¿Dónde estabas cuando...? 1.1, 1.2

**Hablemos** Con un(a) compañero(a), hablen de las cosas emocionantes que han pasado en el colegio este año. Pregúntense si recuerdan el acontecimiento y dónde estaban cuando sucedió. Usen las palabras de **Vocabulario** y las expresiones de **Exprésate.**

**MODELO** **—¿Te acuerdas cuando nuestro equipo de básquetbol ganó el campeonato?**

**—Lo recuerdo como si fuera ayer. ¡Qué emocionante!**

## Differentiated Instruction

### ADVANCED LEARNERS

**Challenge** After reading the **Nota cultural,** have students conduct research by going to the Web sites of **La Nación, Clarín,** *The Washington Post,* and *The New York Times* on the roles of the **Fondo Monetario Internacional** and the **Banco Mundial** in Argentina. The **FMI** and **Banco Mundial** have their own Web sites as well. Ask them to focus on the conditions imposed on the country for foreign debt repayment and privatization, and their effects on unemployment. 3.1, 3.2

### MULTIPLE INTELLIGENCES

**Intrapersonal** Have students think about how they would respond if they ever had to live through a natural disaster. How would they help others? Ask them to write a paragraph describing an imaginary, but conceivable disaster, and the role they would play. For example, the last of the sentences might read, **Ayudaría a los trabajadores a repartir provisiones de emergencia a los refugiados.** 1.3

Vocabulario 1

### Heritage Speakers

Ask heritage speakers to talk about how their ancestors came to this country. Were they **refugiados** or **inmigrantes?**

### Connections

#### Social Studies Link

As an extension of the information in the **Nota cultural,** tell students that Argentina's fragile economy has been combined with a fragile government that at one point saw five presidents in two weeks! Ask students to do research to find out what the Argentinean government and citizens are doing today to try to improve their economy and strengthen their government. What solutions do students suggest? 3.1

### Comunicación

#### Group Activity: Presentational

Have groups of students talk about how they relate to events of the past. Are events far in the past something they experience best when seeing a film, reading essays or fiction with people's thoughts and observations from another time, seeing pictures, or visiting a historical museum with many artifacts and people in period costumes? Are there other mediums that they prefer? Ask groups of students to role-play a scene for the class to demonstrate how each medium helps them relate to or understand the past. 1.3

**Differentiated Instruction** See the Differentiated Instruction CD-ROM.

## Resources

**Planning:**

Lesson Planner, pp. 145–146, 306–307

One-Stop Planner

**Presentation:**

Teaching Transparencies
**Vocabulario** 10.1, 10.2

**Practice:**

Cuaderno de vocabulario y gramática, pp. 109–111

Activities for Communication, pp. 37–38

Lab Book, pp. 49–52

Teaching Transparencies
**Vocabulario y gramática** answers, pp. 109–111

Audio CD 10, Tr. 2

Interactive Tutor, Disc 2

## Comparisons

### Comparing and Contrasting

Argentina's and Chile's governments both have a bicameral legislature consisting of a Senate and a Chamber of Representatives or **Cámara de Diputados.** Both countries have a constitution calling for an independent judiciary. Unlike parliamentary democracies, popularly-elected presidents serve six-year terms in Chile; this was recently amended to four-year terms in Argentina. Ask students to research the governmental structure in Chile and Argentina and compare each to the structure of the United States government. How are they similar to and different from the government in the U.S.?

3.1, 4.2

# Memorias de un acontecimiento trágico

En un parque de Buenos Aires

JOSÉ Abuelo, ¿te acuerdas cuando sucedió el accidente en la mina de cobre?

ABUELO Sí, lo recuerdo como si fuera ayer, a pesar de que han pasado muchos años. Fue algo aterrador que creó pánico entre los mineros, desesperados por salir.

JOSÉ ¿Dónde estabas cuando supiste lo del desastre?

ABUELO Precisamente estaba muy cerca trabajando en mi jardín cuando oí un ruido espantoso. Todos corrimos hacia la mina para ayudar. Fue conmovedor ver la solidaridad de la gente ante aquel trágico evento.

JOSÉ ¿Es cierto que la muerte de muchos mineros pudo haberse evitado?

ABUELO Quizás tengas razón, pero ten en cuenta que en aquella época no teníamos el equipo de rescate que existe actualmente.

JOSÉ Aunque estoy de acuerdo, yo creo que no pudo evitarse porque no había las medidas de seguridad necesarias.

ABUELO Claro, por eso creo que vale la pena analizar las causas que provocan este tipo de accidente para evitar que ocurran en el futuro.

## ¡Exprésate!

### To express and support a point of view

Interactive TUTOR

| | |
|---|---|
| **Me parece que...**<br>*It seems to me that . . .* | **Aunque estoy de acuerdo..., creo que...**<br>*Although I agree . . . , I think that . . .* |
| **Creo que vale la pena acordarse de...**<br>*I think it's worth remembering . . .* | **Lo que noto es que...**<br>*What I notice is that . . .* |
| **Ten en cuenta que...**<br>*Keep in mind that . . .* | **A pesar de que hubo..., por otro lado...**<br>*Although there was/were . . . , on the other hand . . .* |

Vocabulario y gramática, pp. 109–111 Online workbooks

## Core Instruction

### TEACHING ¡EXPRÉSATE!

1. As a class, read the conversation between José and his grandfather about the copper mine tragedy. Ask students to note the expressions that are used to talk about past events, and to express and support a point of view. **(3 min.)**
2. Model the sentences in **¡Exprésate!,** inserting examples to complete each sentence. **(2 min.)**
3. Write on the board and model sentences about the accomplishments of someone in your community or in your school using expressions from **¡Exprésate!** to tell how they accomplished their goals. **(3 min.)**
4. Have volunteers come to the board, underline an **Exprésate** expression and tell whether it is one used to a) talk about past events or b) express and support a point of view. **(2 min.)**

## 7 ¿Cierto o falso? 1.2

**Leamos/Escribamos** Decide si cada oración es **cierta** o **falsa.** Corrige las oraciones falsas. 1. falsa; Lo recuerda como si fuera ayer. 2. falsa; Reaccionaron con pánico. 3. falsa; Estaba cerca, trabajando en su jardín.

1. El abuelo no se acuerda del accidente en la mina de cobre.
2. Los mineros reaccionaron con indiferencia.
3. El abuelo estaba en la mina cuando ocurrió el derrumbe.
4. En aquella época no tenían el mismo equipo de rescate que existe hoy en día. cierta
5. El abuelo piensa que vale la pena analizar las causas de este tipo de accidente. cierta

CD 10, Tr. 2

## 8 Del pasado al presente 1.2

**Escuchemos/Leamos** Bárbara y Alejo están hablando de la vida moderna. Escucha su conversación y determina quién estará de acuerdo con las siguientes ideas: **Bárbara, Alejo** o **ambos.**

1. Creo que la vida moderna es muy complicada. ambos
2. Creo que ahora hay más solidaridad entre los países. Alejo
3. Me parece que los países no pueden ser independientes ahora. Bárbara
4. Lo que noto es que hay muchas guerras hoy en día. Bárbara
5. Vale la pena acordarse de los acontecimientos que muestran solidaridad entre los países. Alejo
6. La vida era mejor cuando había menos tecnología. Bárbara
7. Aunque había menos tecnología en el pasado, también había conflictos. Alejo
8. Los adelantos van a crear un mundo más unido. Alejo

### Nota cultural

A la gente de Buenos Aires se le conoce como *porteños.* Esta ciudad es el puerto principal de Argentina y uno de los puertos más importantes del mundo. Está ubicado en la orilla sur del estuario del Río de la Plata donde éste llega al Atlántico. Da otros ejemplos de ciudades principales en otros países que también sean puertos. 3.1

## Comunicación

HOLT SoundBooth ONLINE RECORDING

## 9 ¿Qué opinas? 1.1, 1.2

**Hablemos** En grupos, comenten sus puntos de vista sobre los siguientes temas. Expresen y apoyen sus opiniones usando las expresiones de **Exprésate.**

1. El campeonato mundial de golf es el evento deportivo más emocionante de todos.
2. Las manifestaciones políticas deberían ser ilegales.
3. El teléfono celular es el mejor invento del siglo XX.
4. Parece mentira que no descubrieran el *Titanic* hasta 1985.
5. No vale la pena ir al estreno de una película. Es mejor verla en video.

### 8 Script

See script on page 407E.

### Circumlocution

Write the words **trágico, solidaridad, elecciones, descubrimiento,** and **planeta** on index cards and hand them out to students. Each student is to write a sentence that illustrates the vocabulary word on his or her card. For example, for the word **trágico** a student might say: **Ese accidente de carro fue terrible.** Read the sentences to the class and have students guess which word was described.

### Comunicación

### Pair Activity: Interpersonal

Have pairs of students look over the information on the **Geocultura** pages about Chile and Argentina. Ask them to comment on the historical and cultural information provided there. Encourage them to express their opinions about specific events outlined on the pages. 1.1

## Differentiated Instruction

### SLOWER PACE LEARNERS

**9 Personalization** Some students may not have opinions about some of the topics in Activity 9. You might suggest that students choose events or issues from their own personal experience and express their points of view on each event. Have them work in pairs to discuss topics of their choosing. 1.1

### MULTIPLE INTELLIGENCES

**Spatial** Have students find city maps from Chile or Argentina on the Internet and identify the downtown area, noting how streets are laid out. They may wish to compare a Chilean or Argentine city with an American city of comparable size and outline similiarities and differences such as number and size of parks and city layout. Ask them to present their findings to the class. 1.3, 3.2

### Assess

**Assessment Program**

**Prueba: Vocabulario 1,** pp. 181–182

Alternative Assessment, pp. 382, 394, 406

**Online Assessment**

**my.hrw.com**

**Test Generator**

## Resources

**Planning:**

Lesson Planner, pp. 147–149, 308–311

One-Stop Planner

**Presentation:**

Video Program
**GramaVisión**

**Practice:**

Grammar Tutor for Students of Spanish, Chapter 10

Cuaderno de vocabulario y gramática, pp. 112–114

Cuaderno de actividades, pp. 91–93

Activities for Communication, pp. 37–38

Lab Book, pp. 49–52

Teaching Transparencies
Bell Work 10.2

**Vocabulario y gramática** answers, pp. 112–114

Audio CD 10, Tr. 3

Interactive Tutor, Disc 2

### Bell Work

Use Bell Work 10.2 in the *Teaching Transparencies*, or write this activity on the board.

**Completa las siguientes oraciones.**

**1.** Recuerdo _____ como si fuera ayer.
**2.** ¿Dónde estabas y qué hacías cuando _____?
**3.** Me acuerdo de cuando sucedió _____
**4.** Los desastres naturales pueden _____. 1.2

**Objetivos**
- Present and past progressive
- Haber
- Expressions of time

# Gramática en acción 1

GramaVisión

Interactive TUTOR

## Repaso Present and past progressive

**1** As you know, the **progressive tenses** indicate an action in progress.

**2** To indicate actions occurring right now, use the present progressive. This is formed with the **present tense of estar, andar,** or **seguir** + **present participle.**

**Estoy viendo** el noticiero.
José **anda haciendo** entrevistas.
**Siguen investigando** el asunto.

**3** To indicate actions that were in progress in the past, use the past progressive. This is formed with **imperfect tense of estar, andar,** or **seguir** + **present participle.**

**Estaba viendo** el noticiero.
*I was watching the news.*
José **andaba haciendo** entrevistas.
*José was (going around) doing interviews.*
Victoria **seguía llegando** tarde aunque al jefe no le gustaba.
*Victoria kept coming in late even though the boss didn't like it.*

**4** The past progressive is often used to tell what was happening in the past when an interrupting event occurred.

**Estaba viendo** el noticiero cuando me enteré del accidente.
*I was watching the news when I found out about the accident.*

Vocabulario y gramática, pp. 112–114
Actividades, pp. 91–93
Online workbooks

### ¿Te acuerdas?

The present participle is formed by dropping the ending and adding **-ando** for **-ar** verbs and **-iendo** for **-er** and **-ir** verbs.

estrenar → estrenando
hacer → haciendo
ocurrir → ocurriendo

CD 10, Tr. 3 See script on p. 407E.

### 10 ¿Cuándo pasó? 1.2

**Escuchemos** Escucha las siguientes conversaciones y di si se habla de algo que **a)** estaba ocurriendo en el pasado o **b)** está ocurriendo ahora.

1. ver el estreno a
2. trabajar con los refugiados b
3. celebrar en la Plaza de Mayo a
4. prepararse para las elecciones b
5. leer el artículo b
6. cuidar al hermano a

## Core Instruction

### TEACHING GRAMÁTICA

**1.** Go over **¿Te acuerdas?** Write a list of **-ar, -er,** and **-ir** verbs and conjugate them in the present progressive. **(3 min.)**

**2.** Read point 1 aloud. Then go over point 2. Read the sample sentences and then write three more examples on the board using **estar, andar, seguir,** and the present participle of the second verb. **(4 min.)**

**3.** Go over point 3. Go over the sample sentences and make up three new ones for emphasis. **(3 min.)**

**4.** Go over point 4 and model the sample sentence. Then write several fill-in-the-blank sentences, using verbs taught in this chapter. **Estaba nadando cuando _____ un pez interesante. (descubrí) (5 min.)**

### GramaVisión

For a video presentation of the present and past progressive tenses, use **GramaVisión.**

GramaVisión

Visit Holt Online
go.hrw.com
KEYWORD: EXP3 CH10
Gramática 1 practice

**11 Queremos ayudar** 1.3

**Escribamos** Contesta las siguientes preguntas según tus experiencias.

1. ¿Qué anda haciendo tu mejor amigo(a)?
2. ¿Qué estaba diciendo tu profesor(a) cuando entraste hoy?
3. ¿Sigues practicando los deportes que practicabas de niño(a)?
4. ¿Qué estaban desayunando todos en tu casa cuando te levantaste?
5. ¿Qué estás estudiando este año?

**12 ¿Qué estabas haciendo?** 1.2

**Escribamos/Hablemos** Mira las fotos y explica qué estaban haciendo todos cuando ocurrió el terremoto.

1. Carmen y Lola

2. Sebastián

3. Susana y yo

4. Melisa

Gramática 1

## Comunicación

HOLT SoundBooth ONLINE RECORDING

**13 ¿Qué estaba haciendo cuando...?** 1.1, 1.2

**Hablemos** Ana siempre se pierde los acontecimientos emocionantes, como los desfiles *(parades)*. Mira los dibujos y, con un(a) compañero(a), cuenta lo que estaba haciendo Ana cuando sucedieron las cosas hoy y lo que está haciendo ahora.

*¿Se te olvidó?* Preterite and imperfect contrasted, pp. 376–377

a. Esta mañana

b. Esta tarde

c. Ahora

### Language Note

In Argentina, the **lunfardo** slang, which originated in working class immigrant neighborhoods in the 1880s, is now used by everyone. Some **lunfardo** words and phrases are: **bondi** *(bus)*, **buena onda** *(good vibes)*, **che** *(hey)*, **guita** *(money)*, **pibe/piba** *(cool young person)*, and **una maza** *(something excellent or cool)*.

### Answers

Use the Chapter 10 *Picture Sequences Transparency*.

**13 Sample Answer**

Ana estaba leyendo esta mañana cuando pasó el desfile por la calle en frente de la ventana de la biblioteca. Estaba paseando al perro esta tarde cuando cayó un rayo en un árbol cerca de ellos. Y ahora está durmiendo mientras estallan los fuegos artificiales.

### Comunicación

**Group Activity: Interpersonal**

Have students bring in newspaper articles about recent events. Divide the class into small groups and ask them to look at the articles together. Have them discuss what they were doing when each event occurred. 1.1

## Differentiated Instruction

### ADVANCED LEARNERS

**Challenge** Have students research a history of European migration to Argentina in the nineteenth and twentieth centuries. What groups came and at what time? Why? After doing a general overview, they may focus on one group, such as the Irish and Basque sheep farmers that settled the Pampas in the 1850s, or the Spaniards who fled Spain when General Francisco Franco took power in 1939. Ask students to present a short summary of their research to the class. 1.3, 3.1

### SPECIAL LEARNING NEEDS

**10 Students with Auditory Impairments** You might want to provide students with auditory impariments with headphones so that they can control the volume and speed of the audio for Activity 10. An alternative would be to provide them with the written script.

**Differentiated Instruction** See the Differentiated Instruction CD-ROM.

## Resources

**Planning:**

Lesson Planner, pp. 147–149, 308–311

One-Stop Planner

**Presentation:**

Video Program **GramaVisión**

**Practice:**

Grammar Tutor for Students of Spanish, Chapter 10

Cuaderno de vocabulario y gramática, pp. 112–114

Cuaderno de actividades, pp. 91–93

Activities for Communication, pp. 37–38

Teaching Transparencies Bell Work 10.3

**Vocabulario y gramática** answers, pp. 112–114

Interactive Tutor, Disc 2

### Bell Work

Use Bell Work 10.3 in the *Teaching Transparencies,* or write this activity on the board.

**Escribe tres oraciones con los verbos *estar, andar* y *seguir,* y el participio presente de *descubrir, estallar, estrenar* o *suceder.*** 1.3

### 15 Answers

1. habrán llegado
2. habría ido
3. he podido
4. había visto
5. hayan tomado
6. ha sido

Interactive TUTOR

## Repaso Haber

**1** As you know, the verb **haber** in the third-person singular indicates existence or non-existence of something.

No **hubo** víctimas en el terremoto.

Creo que **habrá** otro terremoto muy pronto.

Los científicos negaron que **hubiera** señales del terremoto.

**2** To express the present perfect indicative or subjunctive, use the present indicative or present subjunctive forms of **haber** + **past participle.** To express past perfect indicative or subjunctive, use the imperfect or past subjunctive forms of **haber** + **past participle.** To express future or conditional perfect, use the future or conditional forms of **haber** + **past participle.**

| | |
|---|---|
| present perfect indicative | **He** hecho muchos sacrificios. |
| past perfect indicative | Mis papás **habían** hecho muchos sacrificios en el pasado. |
| present perfect subjunctive | Me alegro de que **hayan** ganado el campeonato. |
| future perfect | **Habré** hecho muchos sacrificios cuando llegue a su edad. |
| conditional perfect | **Habríamos** ido al estreno, pero se vendieron las entradas. |

Vocabulario y gramática, pp. 112–114
Actividades, pp. 91–93
Online workbooks

### Nota cultural

Chile enfrenta la amenaza constante de desastres naturales como terremotos, erupción de volcanes y maremotos *(tidal waves).* El terremoto más grande del siglo veinte ocurrió en Chile en 1960, con una magnitud de 9.5 en la escala de Richter. El terremoto causó maremotos que llegaron hasta Japón y las Filipinas. Causó también desprendimientos de tierras *(landslides)* en los Andes que dieron origen a un lago.

¿Qué relación hay entre la geografía de Chile, su ubicación y los desastres naturales que ocurren allí? 3.1

Edificios destruidos tras el terremoto de 1960, Valdivia, Chile

### 14 Una excursión 1.2

**Leamos/Escribamos** Completa el diálogo con la forma correcta de **haber.**

—¿Supiste que __1__ un accidente ayer en las montañas de Patagonia? hubo

—Sí, es terrible. Desafortunadamente, creo que __2__ más accidentes. A veces la gente hace senderismo sin el equipo necesario. habrá

—Me sorprende que no __3__ guías aquí ahora para ayudar a la gente. haya

—Usualmente __4__ muchos guías pero parece que ayer no __5__ nadie cuando empezaron la excursión. hay, había

—Me extraña que no __6__ nadie ayer. Eso nunca pasa. hubiera

—Pues, José, no __7__ nadie aquí ahora. Así que pasa a veces. hay

## Core Instruction

### TEACHING GRAMÁTICA

1. Go over point 1. Write three more sentences on the board using the preterite, future, and past subjunctive of **haber. (5 min.)**
2. Write several more sentences on the board and have students identify the tense of the verb. **(3 min.)**
3. Go over point 2, modeling the sample sentences for the five tenses of **haber** covered. After reading each sentence the first time, turn it into a question and call on students to answer **sí** or **no. ¿Has hecho muchos sacrificios? ¿Habrás conocido a alguien famoso a los 20 años? (3 min.)**
4. Write additional sample sentences for each tense of **haber** introduced in point 2. For variety, change the person to first, second, third, or impersonal. **(4 min.)**

### GramaVisión

For a video presentation of **haber,** use **GramaVisión.**

GramaVisión

## 15 Las playas más bonitas 1.2

**Leamos/Escribamos** Completa las oraciones con la forma correcta de **haber** y el verbo entre paréntesis.

1. En dos horas, mis amigos ═══ (llegar) a Las Grutas. habrán llegado
2. Yo ═══ (ir) con ellos pero tengo que trabajar. habría ido
3. Yo nunca ═══ (poder) ir a esas playas. he podido
4. Tomás me dijo que él nunca ═══ (ver) una arena tan blanca hasta que llegó a Las Grutas. había visto
5. Me alegra que ellos ═══ (tomar) sus vacaciones. hayan tomado
6. Este verano ═══ (ser) muy difícil para mí. ha sido

Las playas bonitas de Viña del Mar, Chile

## 16 Con el tiempo 1.2

**Hablemos/Escribamos** Imagina que estamos en junio. Escribe cinco oraciones sobre cuántos estrenos ha habido hasta ahora y cuántos habrá el resto del año.

**MODELO** **En marzo hubo seis estrenos.**

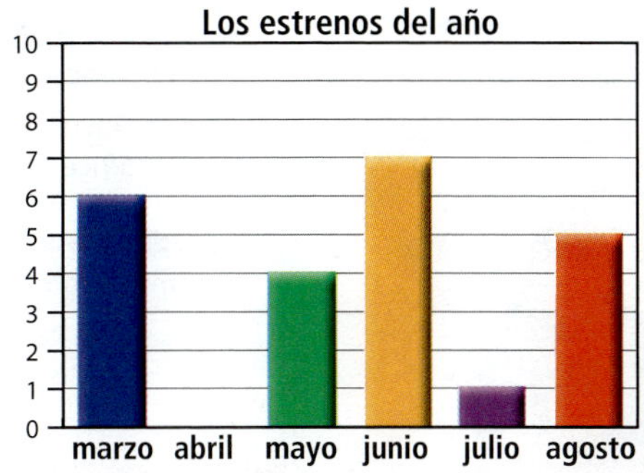


## 17 En el colegio 1.2

**Hablemos/Escribamos** Completa las oraciones.

*¿Se te olvidó?* Present perfect, pp. 148–149

1. Cuando empecé a asistir a este colegio, yo ya había...
2. El día que me gradúe, habrá...
3. En el club de teatro hubo...
4. Este año, mis amigos y yo hemos...
5. En mi colegio, hay mucha...
6. No estoy de acuerdo con que haya...

## Comunicación

HOLT SoundBooth ONLINE RECORDING

## 18 El futuro 1.1, 1.3

**Hablemos** Habla con un(a) compañero(a) de cómo ha cambiado tu comunidad en los últimos diez años. ¿Qué había antes que no hay ahora? ¿Qué cosas hay ahora? Comenten sobre cómo creen que habrá cambiado para el año 2040.

## Heritage Speakers

Have heritage speakers think about slang words they might have heard growing up or still use that are unique to their Spanish-speaking country of origin, similar to the **lunfardo** words and phrases from Argentina.

## COMMON ERROR ALERT ¡OJO!

Students often forget that when using **haber** to indicate existence, it is always conjugated in the third person singular. You may wish to emphasize this point by using **haber** to indicate existence of singular and then plural items. **Habrá un profesor en la reunión. Habrá varios profesores en la reunión.**

## Comunicación

### Class Activity: Presentational

As an extension of Activity 15, have students research different stretches of beaches in Chile and Argentina. Have them make a presentation on the unique aspects of one or two of the beaches. Some might be known for their resort facilities, some as good fishing areas, and some for their extraordinary beauty or unique wildlife. Put up a map of South America on the wall so they can locate the beaches for the class. Have students structure the presentation in a monologue form, using the different tenses of **haber.**

1.3

## Differentiated Instruction

### ADVANCED LEARNERS

**18 Extension** Have students concentrate on one specific aspect of their community that might change in the future, as they continue talking with a partner after doing Activity 18. For instance, they can discuss technology, politics, or architecture. Have them share some of their favorite projections with the class. 1.1

### MULTIPLE INTELLIGENCES

**Naturalist** Have students do research on three different species of mammals or birds from Patagonia. You may suggest the amusingly-maned South American sea lion *(Otaria Flavenscens),* the llama-like guanacos *(Lama Guanicoe),* or the scarlet-patched Chilean flamingo *(Phoenicopterus Chilensis).* Ask students to find the names of the species in Spanish and search Spanish reference sources for information. Ask them to make a presentation for the class using different forms of **haber.** 1.3, 3.1

**Differentiated Instruction** See the Differentiated Instruction CD-ROM.

## Resources

**Planning:**

Lesson Planner, pp. 147–149, 308–311

One-Stop Planner

**Presentation:**

Video Program
**GramaVisión**

**Practice:**

Grammar Tutor for Students of Spanish, Chapter 10

Cuaderno de vocabulario y gramática, pp. 112–114

Cuaderno de actividades, pp. 91–93

Activities for Communication, pp. 37–38

Lab Book, pp. 49–52

Teaching Transparencies
Bell Work 10.4
**Vocabulario y gramática** answers, pp. 112–114

Audio CD 10, Tr. 4

Interactive Tutor, Disc 2

### Bell Work

Use Bell Work 10.4 in the *Teaching Transparencies.*

### 19 Script

David: Hace tres meses que el nuevo presidente está gobernando el país.
Nora: Desde que él tomó el poder, hay muy poca cooperación entre los políticos.
David: Ten en cuenta que hace poco tiempo sucedió un acontecimiento trágico en la capital.
Nora: Sí, hoy es la tercera vez que sale un mensaje en la televisión en que el presidente les pide solidaridad a los ciudadanos.
David: Hace diez años que vivo en este país y lo que noto es que la gente tiene mucha compasión.
Nora: Estoy de acuerdo. Las personas ayudan a sus vecinos menos afortunados.

### 20 Answers

**1.** Hace **2.** Desde **3.** hace **4.** Desde **5.** Desde

## Repaso Expressions of time

Interactive TUTOR

**1** The construction **hace + amount of time + que** + verb in the **present tense** is used to tell *for how long* an action has been going on.

**Hace tres meses que vivimos** en este país.
*We have been living in this country for three months.*

**2** The construction **hace + amount of time + (que +)** verb in the **past tense** is used to tell *how long ago* something happened.

**Hace diez años, vivía** en Chile.
*Ten years ago, I lived in Chile.*

**Hace dos meses que vine** a Chile.
*I came to Chile two months ago.*

**3** The phrase **desde que** followed by a verb in the past tense expresses *(ever) since*.

**Desde que** ocurrió el accidente, somos más cuidadosos.
*Since the accident happened, we are more careful.*

**4** **Ordinal numbers** can be used with **vez** to explain how many times something has occurred.

Es la **tercera** vez que hemos ganado el campeonato.
*This is the third time we've won the championship.*

Vocabulario y gramática, pp. 112–114
Actividades, pp. 91–93
Online workbooks

### ¿Te acuerdas?

The **ordinal numbers** from one to ten are:

| | |
|---|---|
| **primero(a)** | **sexto(a)** |
| **segundo(a)** | **séptimo(a)** |
| **tercero(a)** | **octavo(a)** |
| **cuarto(a)** | **noveno(a)** |
| **quinto(a)** | **décimo(a)** |

CD 10, Tr. 4

### 19 Dos opiniones 1.2

**Escuchemos/Leamos** Escucha la conversación entre David y Nora y contesta las preguntas.

1. ¿Cuánto tiempo hace que el nuevo presidente está gobernando?
2. ¿Desde cuándo hay muy poca cooperación entre los políticos?
3. ¿Cuándo sucedió un acontecimiento trágico en la capital?
4. ¿Cuántas veces ha salido el presidente en la televisión? Tres
5. ¿Cuánto tiempo hace que David vive en este país? Diez años

**1.** Tres meses **2.** Desde que el presidente tomó el poder. **3.** Hace poco tiempo

La Plaza de Mayo, frente a La Casa Rosada, Buenos Aires

### 20 Las elecciones 1.2

**Leamos/Escribamos** Completa las oraciones con **hace** o **desde.**

—¿Te acuerdas de las últimas elecciones?
—Claro. __1__ tres años que tenemos un alcalde que me gusta.
—__2__ que ganó las elecciones, nuestra vida ha mejorado.
—Pero __3__ poco tiempo, descubrieron que él había mentido.
—__4__ que salió la noticia, todos creen que no es fiable.
—Y con razón. __5__ que lo supe, ya no confío en él.

## Core Instruction

### TEACHING GRAMÁTICA

**1.** Review point 1. Make up more sentences, keeping the same ending and substituting different amounts of time. **Hace cinco años que vinimos a este país. (3 min.)**

**2.** Go over point 2. Create sentences with the construction for how long ago something happened, using past tenses other than the imperfect. **Hace cinco días remé por el Río Serrano. (3 min.)**

**3.** Go over point 3. Have students make new sentences with **desde que. (2 min.)**

**4.** Go over point 4 and **¿Te acuerdas?** Prompt students with a list of activities that a person in love with the arts has done since December and include how many times. **Comprar boletos para el concierto de la sinfónica (sexta vez) → Era la sexta vez que compraba boletos para... (2 min.)**

### GramaVisión

For a video presentation of expressions of time, use **GramaVisión.**

GramaVisión

## 21 ¿Cuántas veces? ❀ 1.2

**Leamos/Escribamos** Usa las frases y números ordinales para formar oraciones completas.

**MODELO** **nueve veces/suceder un accidente en esta carretera**
**Es la novena vez que sucede un accidente en esta carretera.**

1. tres veces/nosotros/ganar el campeonato
2. cinco veces/yo/ver un estreno en este teatro
3. seis veces/tú/escribirle una carta al presidente
4. diez veces/los arqueólogos/descubrir algo tan antiguo
5. una vez/mis amigos/ver la erupción de un volcán
6. ocho veces/los refugiados/tratar de regresar a su país

1. Es la tercera vez que ganamos el campeonato.
2. Es la quinta vez que veo un estreno en este teatro.
3. Es la sexta vez que le escribo una carta al presidente.
4. Es la décima vez que los arqueólogos descubren algo tan antiguo.
5. Es la primera vez que mis amigos ven la erupción de un volcán.
6. Es la octava vez que los refugiados tratan de regresar a su país.

## 22 Antes y ahora ❀ 1.2

**Escribamos** Escribe seis oraciones para explicar cuánto tiempo hace que se hicieron cambios en este barrio.

**MODELO** **Hace diez años, no había árboles.**

## Comunicación

HOLT SoundBooth ONLINE RECORDING

## 23 Acontecimientos del pasado ❀ 1.1, 1.2

**Hablemos** Con un(a) compañero(a), comenta los siguientes acontecimientos. Para cada uno, digan cuánto tiempo hace que pasó.

1. las últimas elecciones presidenciales
2. el estreno de tu película favorita
3. el campeonato mundial de tu deporte preferido
4. el descubrimiento de algo increíble
5. el lanzamiento de un invento tecnológico



### Teaching Suggestion

Have students discuss ways in which they can get involved in their own communities to protect the environment. They might do research to find out what their community is doing to improve air quality. For example, some local Climate Action Networks have successfully lobbied their municipalities to purchase low or zero-emission public transportation buses and city or town vehicles. Ask students to find information about protecting the environment in Spanish. ❀ 3.1

### Comunicación

**Pair Activity: Interpersonal**

As an extension of Activity 23, have students pair up and discuss exciting events that they have personally experienced in the past. Have them take notes and then tell another pair of students how long ago their partners did each activity. ❀ 1.1

## Differentiated Instruction

### SLOWER PACE LEARNERS

**Additional Practice** Have students create a grid in which they use these headers for rows: *for how long, how long ago, since, ordinal numbers.* Then they can use varieties of the same sentence next to them.

| | |
|---|---|
| *for how long* | **Hace tres meses que pesco.** |
| *how long ago* | **Hace tres meses vi a mi tío.** |
| *since* | **Desde que vi a mi tío, he aprendido a conducir.** |
| *ordinal numbers* | **Es la tercera vez que he visitado a mi tío.** |

❀ 1.2

### MULTIPLE INTELLIGENCES

**Bodily/Kinesthetic** Have groups of three or four students make up a dance or physical routine of some kind in which they act out ten different steps or moves so as to illustrate ordinal numbers used as adjectives. **Modelo: Primero damos un pasito para adelante. Segundo, damos una vueltita para atrás.** Have the groups present their routines in front of the class. ❀ 1.3, 3.1

### Assess

**Assessment Program**

**Prueba: Gramática 1,** pp. 183–184
**Prueba: Aplicación 1,** pp. 185–186
Audio CD 10, Tr. 16
Alternative Assessment, pp. 382, 394, 406

**Online Assessment**
**my.hrw.com**

**Test Generator**

**Assess** **Differentiated Instruction** See the Differentiated Instruction CD-ROM.

**Resources**

**Planning:**

Lesson Planner, pp. 150, 310–311
One-Stop Planner

**Presentation:**

Audio CD 10, Trs. 5–7
Video Program, Videocassette 5
DVD Program
**VideoCultura**

**Practice:**

Cuaderno de actividades, p. 94
Video Guide, pp. 66–67
Lab Book, p. 87
Interactive Tutor, Disc 2

# Cultura

VideoCultura

## Comparaciones

interactive TUTOR

CD 10, Tr. 5-7

1.3

### Al mal tiempo, buena cara

El ataque en La Moneda, el palacio presidencial en Santiago, Chile, 11 de septiembre de 1973

Algunos eventos quedan grabados para siempre en la memoria de la gente. A veces es la fuerza destructora de la naturaleza: huracanes, terremotos, tornados, inundaciones, incendios. Otra vez es, por desgracia, la acción violenta del hombre: atentados, guerras, asesinatos. Pero en general, la gente reacciona a estos acontecimientos uniéndose más con sus vecinos, y estrechando relaciones con sus amigos y conocidos. ¿Recuerdas tú algún evento trágico en tu ciudad o región? ¿Cuál fue el efecto inmediato? ¿Cómo reaccionó la gente a largo plazo?

### Laura
**Santiago, Chile**

***¿Hay un evento grabado en tu memoria?***

Sí, el 11 de septiembre del 73, el golpe militar.

***¿Dónde estabas y qué estabas haciendo cuando pasó?***

Yo vivía al frente del colegio donde estudiaba. Entonces se empezaba a sentir como mucho ruido, mucha gente que hablaba, algo que estaba pasando extraño. Y cuando nos dejaron ir, los compañeros nos fuimos a mi casa. Entonces era una situación entre juego, cosas dramáticas.

***Para ti, ¿cuál fue el momento más conmovedor?***

Bueno después, llegó una tía con mis primos. Estaba muy afectada porque habían tomado su esposo, o sea mi tío. Lo habían tomado prisionero y no sabía qué hacer, no sabía si estaba vivo. Entonces fue como también tomar la opción de protegerla a ella, de dejarla en la casa como de asumir lo que estaba sucediendo con mi familia.

***¿Crees que vale la pena recordar los eventos del pasado?***

Creo que darle vueltas es un poco insano. Hay [que] sanar estos acontecimientos, sobre todo si han sido dolorosos o si han marcado tu vida en tu futuro.

**Pre-AP Practice**

**AP Language Examination:** Have students first listen to the interviews with books closed to help prepare them for Section I, Part A: **Listening—Short Dialogues and Narratives.** Point out that Héctor, like many Spanish speakers from South Texas and Northern Mexico, may pronounce **ch** much like the English *sh* **(mu<u>ch</u>os, mu<u>ch</u>as)**. You may also want to tell students that when Laura uses the phrase **darle vueltas** she means *to keep going over something in your mind.*

## Core Instruction

### TEACHING CULTURA

1. Read and discuss the introductory paragraph as a class. **(3 min.)**
2. Have volunteers read the interview with Laura aloud. **(4 min.)**
3. Have students read the interview with Héctor. Ask them to compare his experience with Laura's. **(4 min.)**
4. Answer the questions in **Para comprender** as a class. Then have students discuss the question in **Para pensar y hablar**. **(4 min.)**

### VideoCultura

VideoCultura

For a video presentation of the interviews as well as for an additional interview, see Chapter 10 **VideoCultura** on Videocassette or on DVD.

Visit Holt Online
**go.hrw.com**
KEYWORD: EXP3 CH10
Online Edition

## Héctor
**El Paso, Texas**

***¿Hay un evento grabado en tu memoria?***

Sí, hay muchos eventos que recordar, pero uno en específico tendría que ser el ataque terrorista del 11 de septiembre de 2001.

***¿Dónde estabas y qué estabas haciendo cuando te enteraste?***

Recuerdo que estaba en la clase, acababa de entrar en las clases, y los estudiantes me empezaron a comentar y los maestros prendieron el televisor.

***Para ti, ¿cuál fue el momento más conmovedor?***

Tendría que ser cuando las personas se estaban tirando de las torres gemelas. Fue algo muy trágico.

***¿Crees que vale la pena recordar los eventos trágicos del pasado?***

En este caso, sí. Muchas personas fallecieron y es bueno recordar a las personas.

Cultura

### Para comprender 1.2

1. ¿Qué pasó el 11 de septiembre de 1973 en Chile? ¿Cómo lo describe Laura?
2. ¿Dónde estaba Laura cuando sucedió? ¿Qué le pasó a su tío aquel día?
3. ¿De qué evento habla Héctor?
4. ¿Dónde estaba él cuando supo del evento? ¿Cómo describe el evento?
5. ¿Cómo respondieron los dos a la última pregunta? ¿Estás de acuerdo con las respuestas? ¿Por qué sí o por qué no? ¿Cómo responderías tú a la pregunta?

### Para pensar y hablar 1.3

Suceden tragedias por todo el mundo: guerras, desastres naturales, atentados, muertes inesperadas. ¿Crees que puede surgir algo bueno en la reacción de la gente ante sucesos trágicos? Explica.

# Comunidad y oficio

## Los pesticidas en Latinoamérica

¿Cómo nos afecta el uso de pesticidas en Latinoamérica? Estados Unidos importa miles de millones de dólares de frutas y verduras cada año, la mayoría de Latinoamérica. La próxima vez que vayas al supermercado, toma nota de dónde vienen las frutas y verduras que compras. Haz una investigación sobre una fruta o una verdura cultivada en Latinoamérica, como los plátanos de Honduras o Ecuador, o los aguacates de Chile o México. ¿Cómo se cultivan estos productos y qué tipos de pesticidas se usan? 1.2, 3.1

**Plátanos y bananas importados de Latinoamérica**

## Differentiated Instruction

### ADVANCED LEARNERS

**Challenge** Have students work in pairs to compare their answers to the questions from the **Cultura** interview to those of other students. Have them conduct more research about the historical moments cited by students for the third question by looking at newspaper, magazine, and Internet articles on the subject. Ask them to present their findings to the class. 1.1, 1.3

### MULTIPLE INTELLIGENCES

**Logical/Mathematical** Have students gather agricultural statistics for Chile and Argentina and compare them. They can look at the percentage of land under cultivation, the amounts and kinds of crops raised, the methods of cultivation, the land ownership structure, where the products are consumed, and so on. They may also wish to explore issues such as whether genetically modified crops are allowed and how extensive their cultivation is. 2.1, 2.2

### Atlas INTERACTIVO MUNDIAL

Have students use the interactive atlas at **go.hrw.com**.

**Map Activities**

1. Using the interactive atlas or Map transparencies, have students compare how far South America stretches south to the Antarctic continent compared with the southern tip of the African continent.
2. Have students estimate the length of the **Cordillera de los Andes.**

3.1

### Para comprender Answers

1. el golpe militar; una situación entre juego, cosas dramáticas
2. en clase; lo habían tomado prisionero
3. del ataque terrorista del 11 de septiembre de 2001
4. en clase, muy trágico
5. Answers will vary.

### Communities

**Career Path**

Ask students to research information about careers in ecology. What international organizations exist to deal with environmental issues? What positions require that employees know a second language? Are there organizations in the United States that help Latin American countries deal with environmental issues? How would knowing Spanish give students more opportunities to help in various communities?

5.1

### Language Note

Tell students that when Laura uses the phrase **darle vueltas** she means *to keep going over something in your mind.*

## Resources

**Planning:**

Lesson Planner, pp. 151–152, 312–313

One-Stop Planner

**Presentation:**

Teaching Transparencies **Vocabulario** 10.3, 10.4

**Practice:**

Cuaderno de vocabulario y gramática, pp. 115–117

Activities for Communication, pp. 39–40

Teaching Transparencies Bell Work 10.5 **Vocabulario y gramática** answers, pp. 115–117

Interactive Tutor, Disc 2

### Bell Work

Use Bell Work 10.5 in the *Teaching Transparencies,* or write this activity on the board.

**Contesta las siguientes preguntas.**

1. **¿Cuánto tiempo hace que estudias español?**
2. **¿Cuándo fueron las últimas elecciones presidenciales?**
3. **¿Cuánto tiempo hace que asistes a este colegio?**
4. **¿A qué hora llegaste a esta clase?**

**1.2**

**Objetivos**
- **Making predictions and giving warnings**
- **Expressing assumptions**

# Vocabulario en acción 2

## Del presente al futuro

Tenemos que dejar de **desperdiciar** nuestros recursos. Muchas veces, tiramos cosas al **basurero** que podemos **reciclar.**

Es cada vez más importante usar **los recursos naturales** con inteligencia. Algunos recursos como los bosques son **renovables** pero otros, como **los combustibles,** son **no renovables.**

## Core Instruction

### TEACHING VOCABULARIO

1. Read each caption and model the pronunciation of each word. Check comprehension with questions such as **¿Qué artículos podemos reciclar aquí en el colegio? (5 min.)**
2. Have students answer **sí** or **no** as you ask them questions using the new vocabulary words. **¿Es renovable el viento como combustible para generar energía? (3 min.)**
3. Go over the words in **Más vocabulario** and use each one in a sentence. **(2 min.)**

### TEACHING ¡EXPRÉSATE!

1. Model the expressions for students by completing each sentence with terms from **Vocabulario 2. (3 min.)**
2. Model more sentences for students, making predictions and giving warnings regarding some of the issues raised in the captions. **(3 min.)**
3. Make predictions and give warnings. Ask students whether they agree or not. **Ya verán que van a promover los carros híbridos. ¿Están de acuerdo? (4 min.)**

Visit Holt Online
**go.hrw.com**
KEYWORD: EXP3 CH10
Vocabulario 2 practice

### Más vocabulario...

| | |
|---|---|
| **el carro eléctrico/híbrido** | *electric/hybrid car* |
| **cometer (un crimen, un error)** | *to commit (a crime), to make (a mistake)* |
| **contaminado(a)** | *contaminated, polluted* |
| **innovador(a)** | *innovative* |
| **la ley (en contra/a favor de)** | *law (against/in favor of)* |
| **los programas (de)** | *programs (for)* |

Hay que **sembrar** productos **de cultivo biológico** en vez de usar **pesticidas,** que causan **la contaminación** del agua.

**La calidad del aire** es un tema importante. **La energía solar** es una **alternativa a las fuentes de energía** tradicionales, y es posible que **la fusión nuclear** lo sea algún día.

Hay mucho que podemos hacer hoy para que nuestros hijos **crezcan** saludables y para protegerlos contra **las enfermedades.**

### También se puede decir...

You may hear Caribbeans use **el latón de basura** or **el zafacón** instead of **el basurero**. Some Latin Americans may say **malgastar** instead of **desperdiciar**.

## ¡Exprésate!

### To make predictions and give warnings

Interactive TUTOR

| | |
|---|---|
| **A que no va a bajar la tasa de...** *I bet that the rate of . . . won't go down.* | **Es muy posible que el tráfico aumente con...** *It's quite possible that traffic will increase with . . .* |
| **Calculo que van a implementar...** *I predict that they are going to implement . . .* | **Te apuesto que...** *I bet you that . . .* |
| **Ya verás que van a promover...** *You'll see that they're going to promote . . .* | **Se advierte que...** *They warn/advise that . . .* |

Vocabulario y gramática, pp. 115–117 Online workbooks

▶ Vocabulario adicional — El medio ambiente, p. R19

Vocabulario 2

## TPR
### Total Physical Response

Bring to class the following items: white scrap paper, seeds, non-recyclable garbage, and photographs of a doctor and a forest.

**Señala algo que no se puede reciclar.**

**Pon la basura en el basurero.**

**Pásame algo que se puede sembrar.**

**Señala la foto de un recurso natural importante.**

**Toca la foto de alguien que combate las enfermedades.** 1.2

### Common Error Alert
### ¡OJO!

Sometimes students do not realize that **la taza,** which means *cup,* is spelled differently from **la tasa,** which is the index or rate of something, such as **la tasa de desempleo.**

### También se puede decir...

Tell students that the word **basurero** can also be used to mean *landfill,* along with the words **vertedero, estercolero,** or **albañal.**

### Language Note

Chilean slang expressions include **pasarlo chancho** *(to have a good time)* and —**¿Cachai?** —**Te cacho.** *(Did you get or understand that? I understand.)*

## Differentiated Instruction

### Advanced Learners

**Challenge** Look at various environmental government ministries and non-governmental groups in Chile and Argentina that have Web sites. Assign one entity to groups of students for research. Students' presentations should include the missions, activities, and campaigns of their object of research. Students should be sure to use the vocabulary and **¡Exprésate!** phrases they have learned. 1.3

### Multiple Intelligences

**Naturalist** Have students locate maps showing areas of South America covered by forests. Have them compare these types of maps to see where deforestation and reforestation might be happening. Also, have them find the names of at least three tree species common throughout the different regions of Chile and Argentina. 3.1

## Resources

**Planning:**

Lesson Planner, pp. 151–152, 312–313

One-Stop Planner

**Presentation:**

Teaching Transparencies **Vocabulario** 10.3, 10.4

**Practice:**

Cuaderno de vocabulario y gramática, pp. 115–117

Activities for Communication, pp. 39–40

Lab Book, pp. 49–52

Teaching Transparencies **Vocabulario y gramática** answers, pp. 115–117

Audio CD 10, Tr. 8

Interactive Tutor, Disc 2

## Teacher to Teacher

**Luisa Reina**
Parkway North High School
St. Louis, MO

I have students address an original postcard to their pen pals in a Spanish-speaking country. The postcard should depict an ecological problem they have found on the Internet or in a magazine, or have made up themselves. On the postcard students will describe the problem, talk about the consequences of not addressing the problem, talk about obligations and solutions, and express their agreement or disagreement with what is currently being done about the situation. I then post final student work on a bulletin board. 1.3

CD 10, Tr. 8

### 24 ¿Qué pasa en el mundo? 1.2

**Escuchemos/Leamos** Lee los siguientes titulares antes de escuchar los comentarios. Luego escoge el titular que corresponde a cada comentario.

**a.** La energía solar: una alternativa para conservar energía 4
**b.** Se desarrollan programas contra la drogadicción 2
**c.** Los trabajadores se quejan del tráfico 3
**d.** Los productos orgánicos son más saludables 5
**e.** La contaminación del agua causa problemas 1
**f.** Aumenta la tasa de desempleo 6

### 25 ¿Cómo protegemos el medio ambiente? 1.2

**Leamos** Completa las oraciones con una palabra del cuadro.

| | | | |
|---|---|---|---|
| innovador | desperdiciar | sembrar | conservar |
| fusión | promover | híbrido | combustible |

1. Tenemos que ═══ el medio ambiente para futuras generaciones. 1. conservar
2. No debemos ═══ recursos naturales como el agua. 2. desperdiciar
3. En el futuro, es posible que la ═══ nuclear sea una fuente de energía. 3. fusión
4. El carro ═══ combina elementos del carro tradicional y del carro eléctrico. 4. híbrido 5. innovador 6. combustible
5. Si los sistemas actuales no funcionan, necesitamos un programa ═══ para bajar los niveles de contaminación. 7. sembrar
6. El petróleo es un ═══ que puede empeorar la calidad del aire.
7. Debemos ═══ los árboles para proteger los bosques del planeta.
8. Es muy importante ═══ programas de reciclaje. 8. promover

### Nota cultural

Argentina tiene muchos recursos naturales. La mayoría de su riqueza natural se encuentra en la zona de las Pampas, donde la tierra es buena para cultivar granos y cereales. Sus recursos minerales incluyen depósitos de petróleo y de gas natural y, en cantidades más pequeñas, aluminio, cobre, hierro, oro, plata, plomo, uranio, zinc y mica. El nombre Argentina viene del latín *argentum,* que significa *plata,* porque el explorador Sebastian Cabot recibió regalos de plata de la gente indígena.

¿Sabes el origen del nombre de tu estado? 3.1

Artesanías de plata, Buenos Aires

### 26 Tu opinión del medio ambiente 1.2

**Leamos/Escribamos** Lee las oraciones y decide si estás de acuerdo o no. Si no estás de acuerdo, escribe otra oración con tu opinión.

1. Mucha gente piensa que los carros eléctricos contaminan el aire.
2. Todo el mundo debe reciclar porque esto ayuda a conservar los recursos naturales.
3. Las leyes contra la contaminación del medio ambiente no son necesarias.
4. No hay que buscar fuentes de energía alternativas porque el petróleo abunda.
5. Los productos orgánicos se cultivan sin pesticidas.
6. Todos los recursos naturales son renovables y no hace falta protegerlos.

## Core Instruction

### VOCABULARY IN CONTEXT

Give each student two or three words or expressions from **Vocabulario 2** to teach the class. Students should present their words using whatever method they see fit and make flashcards for each word or expression. After every third student has given a presentation, collect the flashcards and review the new vocabulary with students. Have students define the words in Spanish, give an English equivalent, and then, as a challenge, ask them to use the word or expression in an original sentence. Continue in this manner until all the words in **Vocabulario 2** have been presented. Next, divide students randomly into groups of four to create a story using all their vocabulary words. Have students present their stories to the class.

27 **¿Cuáles son los problemas?** 1.3

**Escribamos/Hablemos** Describe los problemas que ves en cada dibujo y sus posibles consecuencias.

A

B

C

D

28 **Mis predicciones** 1.2

**Leamos/Escribamos** Haz una predicción o una advertencia *(warning)* para el futuro sobre los siguientes temas. Usa las expresiones de **Exprésate.**

**MODELO** **Ya verás que los carros eléctricos serán muy importantes en el futuro.**

1. los productos de cultivo biológico
2. las alternativas a los combustibles
3. la contaminación del aire
4. el hambre
5. la energía solar
6. las leyes contra los pesticidas
7. el crimen

Contaminación de aire, Santiago, Chile

## Comunicación

HOLT SoundBooth ONLINE RECORDING

29 **¿Qué pasará?** 1.1, 1.3

**Hablemos** En parejas, hablen de por lo menos tres problemas que afectan a su comunidad. Hagan predicciones sobre lo que pasará en el futuro si no se resuelven esos problemas, y digan lo que harían Uds. para resolverlos.

**MODELO** **—Se advierte que habrá problemas con la calidad del aire.**
**—Tenemos que ayudar a conservar la calidad del aire.**

▶ Vocabulario adicional — El medio ambiente, p. R19

### 24 Script

1. Tenemos que mejorar la calidad del agua de los mares y ríos porque ahora es peligroso comer pescado.
2. El gobierno va a implementar nuevos programas para combatir el problema de las drogas en los colegios.
3. La gente que va al trabajo en carro está muy frustrada porque hay demasiados carros en la carretera. Algunos se quejan porque tardan dos horas en llegar al trabajo.
4. Una alternativa a usar los recursos no renovables para calentar las casas es utilizar un recurso renovable: la energía que viene del sol.
5. Muchos agricultores han dejado de usar pesticidas y otros productos químicos al cultivar verduras y frutas, para evitar las enfermedades que éstos pueden causar.
6. El número de personas sin trabajo está aumentando.

## Comunicación

### Pair Activity: Interpersonal

Have students talk in pairs about ways in which they could contribute to creating a better environment. For example, they could plan on purchasing a hybrid or hydrogen fuel cell car when they buy their first car, or they could work in trail maintenance or habitat restoration at a local park, or encourage their family to recycle. 1.1

## Differentiated Instruction

### SLOWER PACE LEARNERS

28 **Additional Practice** Have students work in pairs to make their own list of topics that they think will be important in the future. Have them use the sentences from **¡Exprésate!** to practice talking about the issues. 1.1

### SPECIAL LEARNING NEEDS

**Students with Learning Disabilities** You might want to have students work in groups to practice vocabulary. Ask groups to go back to all the captions on pages 424–425 and read them aloud. After finishing each one, have them make sentences using the highlighted words. 1.2

**Resources**

**Planning:**

Lesson Planner, pp. 151–152, 312–313

One-Stop Planner

**Presentation:**

Teaching Transparencies
**Vocabulario** 10.3, 10.4

**Practice:**

Cuaderno de vocabulario y gramática, pp. 115–117

Activities for Communication, pp. 39–40

Teaching Transparencies
**Vocabulario y gramática** answers, pp. 115–117

Interactive Tutor, Disc 2

**Communities**

**Career Path**

Have students interview a Spanish-speaking person who works for an environmental agency or non-profit organization. Ask them about how they got the job, what they had to study beforehand, and what their job involves. Also, have the person tell what other kinds of projects the organization is planning to take on in the future. Have students ask for materials like annual reports as well as the usual handouts for the public. Ask them to share the materials with the class. Were the materials available in Spanish? Have students discuss whether they think it would be a good idea for the organizations to provide materials in Spanish. 5.1

# El club de ecología

Grupo de voluntarios limpiando un parque de Buenos Aires

RAÚL ¡Hola, Diana! Como presidenta del club de ecología de nuestro colegio, seguro que nos puedes hablar sobre cómo conservar nuestros recursos naturales y proteger el medio ambiente.

DIANA Claro que sí, Raúl, con mucho gusto.

RAÚL Bueno, con tantos automóviles y fábricas que usan combustibles, ¿qué podemos hacer para mejorar la calidad del aire?

DIANA Podríamos utilizar alternativas a los combustibles, por ejemplo la energía solar y la fusión nuclear.

RAÚL Diana, háblame un poco sobre el programa de reciclaje que promueves en nuestro colegio.

DIANA Pues, noté que los estudiantes tiran muchas cosas a la basura que se pueden reciclar, y por eso me dediqué a desarrollar este programa. Hemos logrado bajar la tasa de desperdicios no sólo en el colegio sino en todo el vecindario.

RAÚL Y ahora cambiando de tema, ¿tú crees que el comer frutas y verduras de cultivo biológico puede ayudar a combatir la contaminación?

DIANA ¡Claro! Todo producto de cultivo biológico beneficia al medio ambiente porque no se usan pesticidas ni otros productos químicos en el cultivo de las frutas y verduras.

RAÚL ¿Cómo ves el futuro de nuestra comunidad en cuanto a la ecología?

DIANA Bueno, Raúl, es de suponer que el futuro será mejor que el presente. Así que, me imagino que para el año 2020 veremos mucho menos desperdicio, contaminación y enfermedades. En cuanto a la contaminación del aire, creo que nos va a ayudar mucho el carro eléctrico. Ya verás que van a promover este tipo de carro en el futuro. ¡A que sí se hará!

**¡Exprésate!**

**To express assumptions**

Interactive TUTOR

| | |
|---|---|
| **Es de suponer que...** *I suppose that . . .* | **Supongo que sí.** *I suppose so.* |
| **Me imagino que para el año... habrá...** *I imagine that by the year . . . there will be . . .* | **A lo mejor habrá...** *Maybe there will be . . .* |

Vocabulario y gramática, pp. 115–117 Online workbooks

**Core Instruction**

**TEACHING ¡EXPRÉSATE!**

1. Have volunteers role-play the parts of Raúl and Diana. Ask students to discuss which parts of the conversation express assumptions. **(3 min.)**
2. Model the **¡Exprésate!** phrases for students. **(1 min.)**
3. Use phrases from **¡Exprésate!** to talk about what Diana might have had to do in preparation for the outing pictured. For example: **Es de suponer que Diana tuvo que comprar bolsas de basura para repartir entre el grupo. (3 min.)**
4. Make up other sentences using the **¡Exprésate!** expressions and have students say whether each sentence says something which is **cierto** or **falso.** For example: **El cultivo biológico contamina el medio ambiente.** (falso) **(3 min.)**

**30** **La entrevista** ❀ 1.2

**Leamos** Basándote en la entrevista, decide si Diana **a**) estaría de acuerdo o **b**) no estaría de acuerdo con los siguientes comentarios. **1.** b **2.** a **3.** b **4.** a **5.** a

1. Prefiero las fuentes de energía tradicionales a la energía solar.
2. El programa de reciclaje ha ayudado a bajar la tasa de desperdicios.
3. Los productos de cultivo biológico no benefician al medio ambiente.
4. A lo mejor en el futuro veamos menos desperdicio.
5. Es de suponer que el carro eléctrico ayudará a bajar el nivel de contaminación.

Un carro eléctrico en un estacionamiento

**31** **¿Qué crees?** ❀ 1.2

**Escribamos** Usa una palabra o expresión de cada columna para formar seis oraciones sobre lo que puede pasar en el futuro.

| | | |
|---|---|---|
| Es posible que | aumentar | los recursos renovables |
| Me imagino que | bajar | el tráfico en las ciudades |
| Es de suponer que | sembrar | programas innovadores de reciclaje |
| A lo mejor | promover | árboles en las ciudades y en los bosques |
| Ya verás que | reciclar | los recursos naturales |

**32** **En veinte años** ❀ 1.2

**Leamos/Escribamos** En veinte años, ¿cómo será el mundo? Contesta las preguntas. Usa las expresiones de **Exprésate.**

1. ¿Habrá leyes contra el uso de productos que no sean de cultivo biológico?
2. ¿El gobierno promoverá el uso de la energía solar?
3. ¿Qué pasará con la tasa de desempleo?
4. ¿Bajará la cantidad de recursos naturales?
5. ¿Habrá tanto crimen como hoy en día?

## Comunicación

HOLT SoundBooth ONLINE RECORDING

**33** **El club de ecología** ❀ 1.1, 1.2

**Hablemos** Tus compañeros y tú van a empezar un club de ecología en su colegio. ¿Qué tipo de programas implementarán? ¿Cómo ayudarán a mejorar la comunidad? Usen las palabras de **Vocabulario** y las expresiones de **Exprésate.** Luego presenten sus ideas a la clase.

▶ **Vocabulario adicional** — El medio ambiente, p. R19

### Communities

**Community Link**

Ask students to find out what their school does to protect the environment. Have students create posters where they provide information about how the school protects the environment. Students can display the posters around the school, or as an alternative, the information can be posted to a school-sponsored Web site. You might want to assign the project for extra credit. ❀ 1.3, 5.1

### Comunicación

**Pair Activity: Interpretive**

Have students look through local Spanish-language newspaper and periodical stories about the environment in their community. Have students look through Chile's *El Mercurio* and Argentina's *Clarín* newspaper dailies online for regional environmental stories. Have them print them out and summarize them for their classmates. ❀ 1.2, 3.2

## Differentiated Instruction

### ADVANCED LEARNERS

**Challenge** Have students research one-week or two-week environmental programs and eco-tours in Spanish-speaking countries catering to both domestic and foreign high school students. Also have them research possible funding sources, such as grants or corporate sponsorships, which might enable the Ecology Club to go on one of these trips during spring break or the summer vacation.

### MULTIPLE INTELLIGENCES

**Intrapersonal** Ask each student to tell a partner the effect of at least two of his or her actions on the environment this week. (**Viajé en bicicleta o en transporte público en vez de en carro. Le escribí al (a la) senador(a) de mi estado para que votara a favor del proyecto de ley ambiental.**) ❀ 1.1

### Assess

**Assessment Program**

**Prueba: Vocabulario 2,** pp. 187–188

Alternative Assessment, pp. 382, 394, 406

**Online Assessment**
**my.hrw.com**

**Test Generator**

## Resources

**Planning:**

Lesson Planner, pp. 153–155, 314–317

One-Stop Planner

**Presentation:**

Video Program **GramaVisión**

**Practice:**

Grammar Tutor for Students of Spanish, Chapter 10

Cuaderno de vocabulario y gramática, pp. 118–120

Cuaderno de actividades, pp. 95–97

Activities for Communication, pp. 39–40

Lab Book, pp. 49–52

Teaching Transparencies Bell Work 10.6 **Vocabulario y gramática** answers, pp. 118–120

Audio CD 10, Tr. 9

Interactive Tutor, Disc 2

### Bell Work

Use Bell Work 10.6 in the *Teaching Transparencies*, or write this activity on the board.

**Completa las siguientes oraciones con la palabra de vocabulario correcta.**

1. Las turbinas de viento son (una fuente de energía alternativa/ combustibles fósiles).
2. El uso de pesticidas sintéticos provoca que los ríos estén (limpios/ contaminados).
3. Escribiste un informe para la revista de ecología sobre los programas de (energía solar/ música).

1.2

### 34 Script

See script on page 407E.

**Objetivos**
- Future tense
- Subjunctive with doubt, denial, and feelings
- Subjunctive and indicative with adverbial clauses

# Gramática en acción 2

GramaVisión

interactive TUTOR

## Repaso Future tense

**1** You have learned that **ir a** + **infinitive** is used to express future actions.

**Voy a reciclar** estas botellas.
*I am going to recycle these bottles.*

**Vamos a promover** el programa de reciclaje.
*We are going to promote the recycling program.*

**2** As you already know, the **future tense** is also used to talk about future events.

**Reciclaré** estas botellas mañana.
*I will recycle these bottles tomorrow.*

Este año, **promoveremos** el programa de reciclaje.
*This year, we will promote the recycling program.*

**3** You have also learned that the **future tense** is used to express probability of something happening or being true.

—¿Qué es eso? —**Será** el nuevo centro de reciclaje, supongo.

**4** The **future** endings are added to the infinitive form of regular verbs:

| | | | |
|---|---|---|---|
| yo | conservar**é** | nosotros | conservar**emos** |
| tú | conservar**ás** | vosotros | conservar**éis** |
| Ud., él, ella | conservar**á** | Uds., ellos, ellas | conservar**án** |

Vocabulario y gramática, pp. 118–120
Actividades, pp. 95–97
Online workbooks

### ¿Te acuerdas?

These verbs are irregular in the future:

| | |
|---|---|
| decir: **dir-** | saber: **sabr-** |
| haber: **habr-** | salir: **saldr-** |
| hacer: **har-** | tener: **tendr-** |
| poder: **podr-** | valer: **valdr-** |
| poner: **pondr-** | venir: **vendr-** |
| querer: **querr-** | |

CD 10, Tr. 9 See script on p. 407F.

### 34 Nuestra comunidad 1.2

**Escuchemos/Leamos** Escucha la conversación y di si cada acontecimiento o situación **a)** ya pasó o **b)** pasará en el futuro.

1. bajar la tasa de desempleo b
2. desarrollar programas para combatir la drogadicción a
3. poner más camas en los refugios b
4. haber menos gente con hambre en la ciudad b
5. haber menos crimen a
6. venir el presidente b

## Core Instruction

### TEACHING GRAMÁTICA

1. Go over point 1. **(2 min.)**
2. Remind students how to talk about future events as you review point 2. Model the sentences and create more with the future tenses of **conservar** and **sembrar. (2 min.)**
3. Go over point 3 with students. **(2 min.)**
4. Review point 4. After conjugating the future of **conservar,** model the forms of **desperdiciar** and **implementar. (2 min.)**
5. Go over **¿Te acuerdas?** Conjugate with students at least two of the irregular verbs listed. **(2 min.)**

### GramaVisión

For a video presentation of the future tense, use **GramaVisión.**

GramaVisión

Visit Holt Online
go.hrw.com
KEYWORD: EXP3 CH10
Gramática 2 practice

**35** **¿Qué van a hacer?** 1.2

**Escribamos** Forma oraciones para decir lo que harán las siguientes personas en el futuro.

1. Yo/hacer un esfuerzo para reciclar
2. Mis compañeros/estudiar las fuentes de energía alternativas
3. Mis papás/comprar un carro híbrido
4. Tú/comer más productos orgánicos
5. Mis amigos y yo/poner basureros en el parque
6. El gobierno/promover el uso de recursos renovables

**36** **¿Qué pasará?** 1.2

**Hablemos** Mira las fotos y di lo que estas personas harán para conservar el medio ambiente.

1

2

3

4

## Nota cultural

Aunque Argentina tiene los típicos problemas ambientales de una economía industrial, como la deforestación, la degradación del suelo *(soil)* y la contaminación del agua y del aire, sigue siendo un líder mundial en establecer controles voluntarios sobre los gases que causan el efecto invernadero *(greenhouse effect)*.

¿Qué problemas ambientales enfrentan los otros países del Cono Sur? 3.1

Puerto contaminado, Buenos Aires

## Comunicación

HOLT SoundBooth ONLINE RECORDING

**37** **Crearemos un programa** 1.1, 1.3

**Hablemos** Un(a) compañero(a) y tú van a desarrollar un programa de actividades para combatir los problemas de la drogadicción y el crimen. ¿Cómo será su programa? ¿Qué tipo de actividades tendrán? Comenten sus ideas y luego los grupos se turnarán para explicar a la clase qué van a hacer.

Gramática 2

### Connections

**Language Arts Link**

Have students read Julio Cortázar's short story **"El final del juego"** which is set in Buenos Aires. In pairs, have students do a character analysis of the three young sisters, Holanda, Leticia, and the narrator, and discuss whether they have ever played games like the one depicted in the story. Ask students if they think the title has a double meaning.

3.1

### Teacher to Teacher

**Jack A. Gaddess**
The Ellis School
Pittsburgh, PA

**Graduation Party** For the future tense, I divide students in pairs or groups of three and have them prepare a presentation of their anticipated high-school graduation party. What foods will be served? Who will be invited? What music will they play? I encourage students to either draw a scene of their party, or bring in props to help them explain. They really get into it and make it their own!

1.3

### Comunicación

**Pair Activity: Interpersonal**

Have students interview each other about their plans for the following summer. Encourage them to use words from **Vocabulario 1** and **Vocabulario 2.**

1.1

## Differentiated Instruction

### SLOWER PACE LEARNERS

**Additional Practice** As an extension of **¿Te acuerdas?** and Activity 35, give students new sentences with each irregular verb listed in the infinitive so they can conjugate it. For example, **(Ellos) Poder/salvar muchas aves si restauran sus hábitats; Podrán salvar muchas aves si restauran sus hábitats.**

1.2

### MULTIPLE INTELLIGENCES

**Naturalist** Have students research endangered species lists to try to determine which species are included from the **Cono Sur** countries. Make a list of the ones that are the most endangered and ask students to look for information on efforts by the governments or nongovernmental organizations to try to save them. 3.1

## Resources

**Planning:**

Lesson Planner, pp. 153–155, 314–317

One-Stop Planner

**Presentation:**

Video Program **GramaVisión**

**Practice:**

Grammar Tutor for Students of Spanish, Chapter 10

Cuaderno de vocabulario y gramática, pp. 118–120

Cuaderno de actividades, pp. 95–97

Activities for Communication, pp. 39–40

Teaching Transparencies Bell Work 10.7

**Vocabulario y gramática** answers, pp. 118–120

Interactive Tutor, Disc 2

### Bell Work

Use Bell Work 10.7 in the *Teaching Transparencies*, or write this activity on the board.

**Completa las oraciones con la forma correcta del verbo para expresar algo que ocurre en el futuro.**

1. **Nosotros (conservar) este terreno baldío para hacer un parque.**
2. **Yo (promover) el programa de energía solar en mi vecindario.**
3. **Tú (desarrollar) una gira ecoturística en el parque estatal.**
4. **Él (bajar) de la montaña después de haber alcanzado la cima.**

1.2

Interactive TUTOR

## Repaso: Subjunctive with doubt, denial, and feelings

**1** As you know, main clauses containing expressions of **doubt, denial,** or **feelings** require the **subjunctive** in the subordinate clause.

**Dudo que** el río **esté** contaminado.

**No es cierto que** la tasa de desempleo **haya** aumentado.

**Me alegra que recicles.**

**2** Expressions of **doubt** and **denial** you have learned include:

| | |
|---|---|
| **dudar que** | **no estar seguro(a) que** |
| **no creer que** | **no es verdad que** |
| **no es cierto que** | **negar que** |
| **no estar de acuerdo que** | **parece mentira que** |

**3** Expressions of **feelings** you have learned include:

| | |
|---|---|
| **es triste que** | **me (te, le...) gusta que** |
| **es una lástima que** | **me (te, le...) molesta que** |
| **me (te, le...) alegra que** | **me (te, le...) preocupa que** |
| **me (te, le...) frustra que** | **me (te, le...) sorprende que** |

Vocabulario y gramática, pp. 118–120
Actividades, pp. 95–97
Online workbooks

### Nota cultural

Argentina es el segundo país más grande de América del Sur, después de Brasil. La capital, Buenos Aires, es el centro económico y cultural del país. Se conoce como "la París de América del Sur" por sus anchos bulevares, grandes parques y edificios adornados en estilos barroco, rococó y neoclásico. La calle principal, la Avenida 9 de julio (abajo), se nombró en honor a la fecha en 1816 cuando Argentina declaró su independencia de España. Es una de las calles más anchas del mundo.

¿Cómo se comparan los edificios y calles de Buenos Aires con los de la capital de Estados Unidos?

3.1

### 38 Cada persona puede ayudar 1.2

**Leamos/Escribamos** Completa el diálogo con el presente del indicativo o del subjuntivo de los verbos en paréntesis.

—Me preocupa que la gente ___1___ (tirar) productos reciclables a la basura. tire

—Tienes razón, es una lástima que la gente en esta ciudad no ___2___ (reciclar) más pero, ¿qué podemos hacer? recicle

—Hay mucho que se puede hacer. Me sorprende que no ___3___ (haber) nadie preocupado por desarrollar un programa de reciclaje. haya

—Pues, dudo que alguien lo ___4___ ( hacer) pronto. haga

—Estoy de acuerdo. Con tantos problemas, no creo que el gobierno ___5___ (enfocarse) en esto ahora. se enfoque

—Pero al menos tú siempre ___6___ (reciclar) y compras productos orgánicos. reciclas

—Bueno, es cierto que ambas cosas ___7___ (ayudar). ayudan

## Core Instruction

### TEACHING GRAMÁTICA

1. Review the uses of the subjunctive listed in point 1, and model the sample sentences. **(2 min.)**
2. Go over the expressions of doubt reviewed in point 2 and read the examples. After each example, create a sentence to further illustrate the expression. **(4 min.)**
3. Go over the expressions of feelings listed in point 3. Ask questions with the expressions and have students answer **sí** or **no.** For example: **¿Es triste que la gente no utilice la energía solar? (sí) ¿Es una lástima que hayan encontrado una cura para la enfermedad? (no)** **(4 min.)**

### GramaVisión

For a video presentation of the subjunctive with doubt, denial, and feelings, use **GramaVisión.**

GramaVisión

**39** **¿Cómo te hace sentir?** 1.3

**Escribamos** Mira las fotos y escribe una oración con tu opinión sobre lo que ves.

1

2

3

4

5

6

**40** **No estoy de acuerdo** 1.2

**Leamos/Escribamos** Responde a cada comentario con una frase de duda o negación.

1. Nadie está a favor de la energía solar y los carros híbridos.
2. No es necesario conservar los recursos naturales.
3. El tráfico ayuda a combatir la contaminación.
4. Vamos a dejar de reciclar en el futuro.
5. Aumentará el uso de combustibles en los próximos años.
6. El hambre no es un problema en el mundo.

## Comunicación

HOLT SoundBooth ONLINE RECORDING

**41** **El futuro del planeta** 1.1, 1.3

**Hablemos** Con un(a) compañero(a), comenten lo que han escuchado sobre el medio ambiente y el futuro del planeta. Hablen de las predicciones en las que no creen y en las que sí creen. Luego, hablen de los problemas del medio ambiente que les afectan más y cómo les hacen sentir.

Gramática 2

## Connections

### Science Link

Ask students to describe what they see in photo 4 in Activity 39. Do they know how solar panels work? Have them find information from Spanish-language Web sites about the use of solar panels in Latin America. Ask them to take notes and use them to describe to the class how the solar panels work and where they are currently used.

3.1

## Comunicación

### Pair Activity: Interpersonal

Have students prepare a list of five things they would do or call for to combat hunger in their communities. Ask them to discuss their ideas, and to consider the following, as well as other options:

- **Conseguir que los restaurantes donen la comida que no usen**
- **Conseguir que las granjas provean comida a cambio de trabajo voluntario**
- **Procurar legislación para que las compañías agrícolas den parte de sus cosechas a la gente sin hogar**

1.1

## Differentiated Instruction

### ADVANCED LEARNERS

**Challenge** Have students research and write a short report on energy production in their area. They can contact their public utility company and try to tour the plant(s) where electricity is generated. Is it done by burning fossil fuels like oil or coal? Is it through harnessing hydro power? Are there any wind turbines? Are there individual homes, businesses, or public road signs lit by solar panels?
1.3, 3.1

### MULTIPLE INTELLIGENCES

**Spatial** Have students research train transportation in Chile and Argentina. Have them try to determine how extensive both the freight and passenger services are, both in terms of the layout of rails in the national map as well as the amount of cargo and passengers transported annually. Also, have students consider how the two countries compare. 2.1

**Differentiated Instruction** See the Differentiated Instruction CD-ROM.

## Resources

**Planning:**

Lesson Planner, pp. 153–155, 314–317

One-Stop Planner

**Presentation:**

Video Program
**GramaVisión**

**Practice:**

Grammar Tutor for Students of Spanish, Chapter 10

Cuaderno de vocabulario y gramática, pp. 118–120

Cuaderno de actividades, pp. 95–97

Activities for Communication, pp. 39–40

Lab Book, pp. 49–52

Teaching Transparencies
Bell Work 10.8
**Vocabulario y gramática** answers, pp. 118–120

Audio CD 10, Tr. 10

Interactive Tutor, Disc 2

### Bell Work

Use Bell Work 10.8 in the *Teaching Transparencies,* or write this activity on the board.

**Completa las oraciones con el subjuntivo del verbo en paréntesis.**

1. No creo que (aumentar) los precios de la gasolina.
2. No estoy de acuerdo en que nuestro país (desarrollar) más los combustibles fósiles.
3. Me alegra que (haber) abierto un sendero de bicicletas.
4. Me preocupa que las empresas no (estar) promoviendo los autos híbridos. 1.2

Interactive TUTOR

En una estación de metro, Santiago de Chile

## Repaso Subjunctive and indicative with adverbial clauses

**1** Adverbial clauses with **a menos (de) que, antes de que, con tal (de) que, en caso de que, para que,** and **sin que** always contain the **subjunctive.**

*followed by subjunctive*
Iré en carro **a menos (de) que haya** tráfico.

*followed by subjunctive*
Tengo que sembrar las flores **antes de que llueva.**

*followed by subjunctive*
Desarrollaré el programa **con tal de que** tú lo **implementes.**

**2** Adverbial clauses with **cuando, en cuanto, después de que, hasta que,** and **tan pronto como** contain the **subjunctive** when they refer to a future action. These clauses are followed by the **indicative** when they refer to a past action, or an action that occurs habitually or on a regular basis.

| future action | past or habitual action |
|---|---|
| Compraré un carro cuando **tenga** el dinero. *I'll buy a car when I have the money.* | Compré un carro cuando **tuve** el dinero. *I bought a car when I got the money.* |
| Voy a leer el periódico en cuanto **tenga** tiempo. *I'm going to read the paper as soon as I have time.* | Leo el periódico en cuanto **tengo** tiempo. *I read the paper as soon as I have time.* |
| Reciclaré esta botella después de que **termine** de usarla. *I will recycle this bottle after I finish using it.* | Reciclo las botellas después de que **termino** de usarlas. *I recycle the bottles after I finish using them.* |
| La calidad del aire no mejorará hasta que **dejemos** de contaminar. *Air quality won't improve until we stop polluting.* | La calidad del aire no mejoró hasta que **dejamos** de contaminar. *Air quality didn't improve until we stopped polluting.* |

Vocabulario y gramática, pp. 118–120
Actividades, pp. 95–97
Online workbooks

## Core Instruction

### TEACHING GRAMÁTICA

1. Go over point 1 and write the adverbial clause examples on the board or on a transparency, circling the subjunctive verb. Create new sentences by using different verbs with each adverbial phrase. For example: **Iré en carro a menos que tenga tiempo para caminar.** **(5 min.)**
2. Go over point 2 and model the examples for expressing future (subjunctive), past or habitual actions (indicative) with the adverbial clauses listed. **(5 min.)**
3. Write four additional sentences on the board for the left and for the right column, but scramble their order. Write the verbs in the infinitive that need to be in the subjunctive or indicative moods, and have volunteers conjugate them. **(5 min.)**

### GramaVisión

For a video presentation of the subjunctive and indicative with adverbial clauses, use **GramaVisión**.

GramaVisión

CD 10, Tr. 10

**42 ¿Cierta o falsa?** 1.2

**Escuchemos/Leamos** Escucha la conversación entre Sara y Pedro y decide si cada oración es **cierta** o **falsa.**

1. Pedro ya votó por Laura Rodríguez. falsa
2. Laura Rodríguez implementó un programa de reciclaje. falsa
3. Ella no va a promover las fuentes de energía alternativas hasta que tenga más información. cierta
4. Los científicos todavía no han terminado su estudio sobre las fuentes de energía alternativas. cierta
5. Sara va a decidir antes de que vea el debate. falsa
6. Pedro dijo que no le interesa ver el debate. falsa

**43 Los pesticidas** 1.2

**Leamos/Escribamos** Completa el párrafo con las formas correctas de los verbos.

Mi abuelo vive en Chile. Él nació antes de que los agricultores __1__ (empezar) a usar pesticidas. Empezaron a usarlos para que los cultivos de frutas __2__ (ser) más productivos. Sin embargo, leí que muchas mujeres chilenas sufrieron de enfermedades después de que __3__ (recoger) la cosecha. Por eso hay personas que sólo comen productos biológicos con tal de que no se __4__ (usar) pesticidas en los cultivos. De hecho, el gobierno de Canadá está trabajando con el de Chile para desarrollar nuevas técnicas de cultivo, pero los agricultores no adoptarán esas técnicas hasta que __5__ (aprender) a implementarlas. Ya veremos que bajará el uso de pesticidas tan pronto como los chilenos __6__ (tener) alternativas. **1.** empezaran **2.** fueran **3.** recogieron **4.** usen **5.** aprendan **6.** tengan

### Nota cultural

En junio de 2003, Chile y Estados Unidos firmaron un tratado de libre comercio. Chile es el primer país latinoamericano que se ha hecho socio comercial de Estados Unidos. Estados Unidos reconoció que Chile tiene una de las economías más liberales y competitivas de Latinoamérica y el acuerdo fue una señal del éxito económico del país.

Investiga qué productos exporta Chile a Estados Unidos. 3.1

Mina de sal, Chile

## Comunicación

HOLT SoundBooth ONLINE RECORDING

**44 Mis planes para el futuro** 1.1, 1.3

**Hablemos** Con un(a) compañero(a), hablen de qué han hecho para mejorar el medio ambiente y qué piensan hacer en el futuro.

MODELO —**Reciclo mucho para que no haya tanta contaminación.**
—**Todos tenemos que hacerlo antes de que le hagamos más daño al medio ambiente.**

**42 Script**

See script on page 407F.

### Más práctica

After completing Activity 44, have students work with different partners to think about even more ways in which they have helped or hope to help the environment. 1.1

## Comunicación

### Group Activity: Presentational

Have students form groups of three to research the terms of the U.S.-Chile free trade agreement mentioned in the **Nota cultural.** Then have them compare the terms to other agreements such as CAFTA, which was signed by the U.S. and four Central American countries on December 17, 2003, or NAFTA. Encourage them to use official Internet sites in their research, such as the Web site of the Office of the U.S. Trade Representative. Ask groups to present their research to the class. 1.3, 3.2

## Differentiated Instruction

### SLOWER PACE LEARNERS

**42** Before students do Activity 42, hand them a written script of the audio so they can follow along as they listen. Have them read over the sections with which they are having trouble, and encourage them to underline verbs and look up any words they do not know. 1.2

### MULTIPLE INTELLIGENCES

**43 Students with Dyslexia** You might want to do Activity 43 as a listening activity. Write the targeted verb for each item on the board or on a transparency. Read each sentence aloud and have students listen for context clues such as verb tense and words that indicate habitual actions. Then read the sentence again and have volunteers conjugate the verb. Write the answers as students provide them, and have them copy the words in their notebooks. 1.2

## Assess

**Assessment Program**

**Prueba: Gramática 2,** pp. 189–190

**Prueba: Aplicación 2,** pp. 191–192

Audio CD 10, Tr. 17

Alternative Assessment, pp. 382, 394, 406

**Online Assessment** my.hrw.com

**Test Generator**

## Resources

**Planning:**

Lesson Planner, pp. 156, 316–317

One-Stop Planner

**Presentation:**

Video Program, Videocassette 5

DVD Program

**VideoNovela**

**Practice:**

Video Guide, pp. 68–70

Lab Book, pp. 88–89

## Visual Learners

Have students create a graphic organizer with a box for each **Episodio** in which to write the important details as well as unanswered questions. As they read the final **Episodio,** have them connect the "puzzle pieces" with arrows and write conclusions at the bottom of the page. 1.2

| Episodio 10 |
|---|
| **Detalles importantes:** |
| **Preguntas:** |

## Connections

### History Link

Despite differences in language and geographic locations, what happened in the **Novela** could have happened anywhere where there is an economic and political democracy. Between 1973 and the election of Patricio Aylwin Azócar in 1989, Chile's democracy was taken away by the military. Have students research this time period and tell how the **Novela** might have ended had it taken place in those years. 3.1

Novela en video

# Clara perspectiva

## Episodio 10

### ESTRATEGIA

**Putting the pieces together** In the finale, all the pieces of the puzzle are put together. Pretend you are Octavio or Clara and must write a magazine article about what happened to Professor Luna. If you need to, go back to each episode and write down all the pertinent details of his story. Make sure you tie together all the events and that you draw a conclusion about Professor Luna's role in preserving the forests of **Magallanes**. Feel free to add or change the details in your article after you have watched the finale. Try to write a factual report that fairly describes the viewpoints of all sides. 1.2, 1.3

1

### En la oficina del profesor Luna

**Clara** ¡Profesor! ¡Explíquenos todo en detalle, desde el principio!

**Octavio** Sí. Quizás podamos escribir un artículo para la revista.

**Profesor Luna** Todo empezó cuando el Congreso me contrató para hacer unos estudios de impacto ambiental. Sólo tenía que averiguar si los bosques nativos de la región de Magallanes podrían soportar el desarrollo que quería intentar la empresa *MaderaCorp.*

Un día, un hombre vino a la universidad y me pidió que le diera una copia de los estudios. Claro que le dije que no.

2

3

Luego, dos personas, un hombre y una mujer, se me presentaron y me dieron un documento. No sabía quiénes eran, ni qué querían. Cuando por fin pude leer el documento que me habían entregado, me di cuenta que eran ecologistas tratando de preservar el bosque.

La situación se complicó. El primer hombre volvió con otro hombre. Me dijeron que iban a conseguir los estudios antes de que los finalizara, con o sin mi cooperación.

4

5

Luego, se me hizo claro que había varias personas tratando de infiltrar mi computadora para conseguir esos mismos estudios. Querían saber los resultados antes de que se los presentara al Congreso. Con esa información podrían tratar de influir en el voto o alterar los datos.

## Core Instruction

### TEACHING NOVELA EN VIDEO

1. Have students scan the **Novela en video** text and look at the photos from the episode. **(1 min.)**
2. Play the video, stopping periodically to ask comprehension questions. If students have trouble understanding any portion of the video, you might want to use the captioned version of the episode. **(15 min.)**
3. Have students take notes in a chart on essential and non-essential information. **(4 min.)**
4. Have students work in pairs to answer the questions on page 437. When they have finished, go over the answers together. **(5 min.)**

### Escuchemos

As students watch the **Novela,** have them listen for five current issues or problems that Octavio mentions. (**el medio ambiente, el crimen, la drogadicción, el desempleo, la fusión nuclear**)

Novela en video

Visit Holt Online
**go.hrw.com**
KEYWORD: EXP3 CH10
Online Edition

Novela en video

6 **Clara** Cuando vi el artículo, supe que usted estaba en peligro. Fue cuando lo llamé y me pidió que fuera a su oficina e imprimiera todos los documentos bajo el título "Recomendaciones". Luego fui a las autoridades.

7 **Profesor Luna** Sí, y yo estaba con los ecologistas y *MaderaCorp* tratando de llegar a un acuerdo.

Y, al final, ¿cuál fue el acuerdo al que llegaron?

*MaderaCorp* puede crear empleos para toda la comunidad. Además un 25% de los bosques se preservarían para una zona de biodiversidad inviolable. *MaderaCorp* promete no realizar talas rasas, no sustituir el bosque nativo por especies exóticas y no exportar astillas.

8

## En *Chile en la Mira*

**Octavio** Espero que le vaya a gustar el artículo al señor Ortega. Nunca he trabajado tan duro. El medio ambiente me interesa mucho más que el crimen, la drogadicción, el desempleo y la fusión nuclear.
**Clara** Yo creo que para el año 2030 viviremos en una Tierra que utiliza todos sus elementos sin abusar de ellos.

9

10

**Sr. Ortega** Han hecho un trabajo admirable.
**Clara** Gracias, Señor Ortega.
**Sr. Ortega** No se relaje tanto, Señorita de la Rosa, usted tiene mucho que compensar todavía.
**Octavio** Pero, Señor Ortega, ¿no cree que lo que hizo Clara fue muy valiente?
**Sr. Ortega** Vamos a hablar de eso otro día. Ahora tengo sus nuevas tareas.

## ¿COMPRENDES?

1. ¿Cómo empezó todo, según el profesor Luna?
2. ¿Quiénes vinieron a ver al profesor Luna? ¿cuántas personas en total? ¿Cómo se complicó la situación?
3. ¿Qué hizo Clara en un momento oportuno? ¿Por qué fue oportuno?
4. ¿Con quiénes estaba el profesor cuando Clara imprimía los documentos? Entonces, ¿qué pasó?
5. ¿Cuál fue el acuerdo que resolvió el problema?
6. ¿Está feliz el señor Ortega al ver a Clara? ¿Cree él que fue valiente lo que hizo ella? ¿Qué crees tú? 1.2

**Episodio final**
*¿Te sorprendió el final? ¿Por qué sí o por qué no?*

### Gestures

Ask students to notice whether the characters use any gestures that are unusual. Discuss these gestures as a group.

### ¿Comprendes? Answers

1. Empezó cuando el gobierno contrató al profesor Luna para hacer unos estudios de impacto ambiental.
2. Vino un hombre, y después otro hombre y una mujer, y después uno de los mismos hombres junto con otro. Cuatro personas vinieron en total. Le dijeron al profesor que iban a conseguir los estudios con o sin su cooperación.
3. Llamó al profesor tras haber leído el artículo en el diario. Fue oportuno porque Clara logró hacer una copia de los documentos originales antes de que alguien los alterara o destruyera.
4. Estaba con los ecologistas tratando de negociar un acuerdo. Los hombres de la empresa llegaron y trataron de controlar la situación.
5. *MaderaCorp* puede utilizar el bosque y crear empleos para toda la comunidad, y un 25% de los bosques se preservarían en una zona inviolable.
6. Sí. Sí, aunque no lo hace muy obvio. Answers will vary.

## Clara perspectiva, Episodio 10

In **Episodio 10,** at Professor Luna's office, the professor reveals that he was asked to perform an environmental impact study on the region of Magallanes. Representatives from *MaderaCorp* and *EcoChile* try to influence his report. Someone had also been trying to steal the files from his computer. Both parties issued threats before they all got together to find a solution. Later, as Clara and Octavio work on the article, they talk about their experience and the conditions in Magallanes. When the article is published, Señor Ortega congratulates them both but still admonishes Clara for some of her recent absences.

## Comunicación

### Pair Activity: Interpersonal

After students have read the **Novela en video,** have them work in pairs to invent an interview in which Clara asks Professor Luna additional questions with information not included in the **Novela** such as:
**—¿Cómo le afectó el sentirse amenazado?**
1.1

# Lectura informativa

**Resources**

**Planning:**

Lesson Planner, pp. 157, 318–319

One-Stop Planner

**Presentation:**

Audio CD 10, Tr. 11

**Practice:**

Cuaderno de actividades, p. 98

Reading Strategies and Skills Handbook, Chapter 10

Interactive Advanced Reader

**Comparisons**

**Comparing and Contrasting**

Have students go to the official Web site of the **Comisión Nacional del Medio Ambiente.** Ask them to work in small groups to outline the information they find on the site. Then have them do the same with the official site of the Environmental Protection Agency. Ask each group to present a summary of the similarities and differences they found.

3.2, 4.2

**Pre-AP Practice**

**AP Language Examination:** **Lectura informativa** helps students prepare for Section I, Part B: **Reading Comprehension.** The audio recording helps them prepare for Part A: **Listening—Short Narratives.**

**AP Benchmark:** Use information from sources provided to present a synthesis and express an opinion.

**Focus:** Talking about the environment
- SE, p. 439, **Actividad**
- TE, p. 439, Advanced Learners
- Assessment Program, p. 193, Acts. A–C

# lectura informativa

CD 10, Tr. 11

## Chile y el medio ambiente

*Un tema importante para CORFO hoy en día es el medio ambiente.*

**CORFO**

La Corporación de Fomento de la Producción (CORFO) fue creada en 1939 en Chile para mejorar la actividad productiva nacional. Un propósito[1] de la organización es generar más empleos y oportunidades para la modernización productiva. Una manera de lograr su meta es a través de la innovación y el desarrollo tecnológico. Hoy en día, un tema importante en sus proyectos es el medio ambiente.

**El reciclaje**

Como resultado de un acuerdo mediado por CORFO en 2002, empezó un esfuerzo nacional para aumentar el reciclaje y disminuir la cantidad de basura producida en Chile. Los ministerios de economía, salud y educación y la Comisión Nacional del Medio Ambiente (CONAMA) apoyaron el acuerdo, que es parte del programa de producción más limpia[2] de CORFO. La meta del programa es incorporar tecnologías más limpias a los procesos de producción para que haya menos basura.

Buscan métodos para usar energía solar del desierto

Chile paga el precio por sus productos exportados

¿Quién se hace cargo de la basura de Santiago?

**La energía solar**

En abril de 2003, un grupo de empresarios[3] chilenos, apoyados por CORFO, asistieron a una conferencia en Alemania sobre nuevas tecnologías para aprovechar[4] fuentes renovables de energía. Algunos de ellos creen que en el futuro cercano, se podrían utilizar paneles solares para "cosechar" la energía del sol en el desierto de Atacama en el norte de Chile. Creen que esta energía, que no se usa en el norte, se podría utilizar en el sur del país.

**Los pesticidas**

En la década de los noventa, con el aumento de los productos cultivados en Chile para la exportación, en especial las frutas,

1 purpose 2 cleaner production 3 businessmen 4 to utilize

## Core Instruction

**TEACHING LECTURA INFORMATIVA**

1. Read the first paragraph as a class. Ask students if they were surprised to learn that an economic development organization is still thriving after 60 years. **(4 min.)**
2. Have students read the second paragraph and then ask how they think recycling is a beneficial part of an economic program. **(4 min.)**
3. Have students read the third paragraph. Ask them if they knew that the technology exists to harvest enough solar energy to power not just individual buildings, but entire towns miles away. **(4 min.)**
4. Have students read the fourth paragraph and then ask when was the last time they ate fruit from Chile purchased at a local supermarket. **(4 min.)**
5. Have students read the fifth paragraph. Then tell them that there are also international treaties under the auspices of the U.N. and other organizations to which signatories agree to curb or eliminate the uses of certain chemicals. **(4 min.)**
6. Have students work in pairs to answer the **Comprensión** questions. **(5 min.)**

Paneles solares en el desierto

aumentó el uso de los pesticidas. Con la presión[5] de exportar grandes cantidades de uvas, manzanas, peras, kiwis, melocotones y ciruelas, Chile usaba pesticidas muy tóxicos y peligrosos que ya eran ilegales en otros países. CORFO está trabajando para establecer acuerdos de producción limpia con la agroindustria para que usen pesticidas que no dañen el medio ambiente.

**La colaboración con otros países**

El grupo CONAMA ha desarrollado una colaboración[6] con varios grupos prestigiosos de Estados Unidos como la Universidad de Harvard, la Universidad de California, el Departamento de la Gestión de Calidad del Aire del Sur de California y el Instituto Tecnológico de Massachusetts. Con el apoyo de estos grupos, Chile espera educar y capacitar[7] a profesionales ligados[8] a temas ambientales como la calidad del aire. Otro objetivo de esta cooperación es el establecimiento de un grupo que ayudará al gobierno chileno a implementar los proyectos y acuerdos de cooperación ambiental asociados al Tratado de Libre Comercio[9] con Estados Unidos y la alianza con la Unión Europea.

5 pressure 6 working relationship, collaboration
7 to train 8 connected to 9 Free Trade Agreement



## Comprensión

**A ¿Comprendiste?** Contesta las preguntas. 1.2

1. ¿Cómo quiere CORFO mejorar la actividad productiva nacional?
2. ¿Cuál es el programa de producción más limpio?
3. ¿Qué creen algunos empresarios chilenos que se puede "cosechar" en el desierto?
4. Menciona uno de los productos principales exportados por Chile.
5. ¿Cuál fue el resultado de la presión de tener que cultivar grandes cantidades de productos para la exportación?

**B ¿Cómo protegen el medio ambiente?** 1.2 Indica si cada oración es **cierta** o **falsa.** Corrige las oraciones falsas.

1. El reciclaje reducirá la cantidad de basura.
2. La Comisión Nacional del Medio Ambiente no está de acuerdo con el programa de producción más limpio.
3. Los chilenos asistieron a una conferencia sobre la energía solar.
4. CORFO quiere ayudar a la agroindustria a usar pesticidas que no hagan daño.

### Actividad 1.1, 1.3

**Tu opinión** Con un(a) compañero(a), comenten sus respuestas a las siguientes preguntas: ¿Estás de acuerdo con los programas de CORFO? ¿Qué otros temas son importantes para proteger el medio ambiente? ¿Tenemos organizaciones parecidas en este país? ¿Crees que la protección del medio ambiente es un tema global?



# Lectura informativa

### A Answers

1. Quiere generar más empleos y oportunidades para la modernización productiva.
2. Es un programa que incorpora tecnologías más limpias a los procesos de producción para que haya menos basura.
3. la energía solar
4. las frutas
5. Chile usaba pesticidas tóxicos.

### B Answers

1. cierta
2. falsa; Apoyaron el acuerdo, que es parte del programa de producción más limpia.
3. cierta
4. cierta

### Connections

**Social Studies Link**

Lauca National Park's landscape includes volcanos, lagoons, salt flats, tiny pre-Hispanic settlements, and a variety of wildlife. Chungara Lake is one of the highest lakes in the world, at the foot of the Payachata twin volcanoes. Have students work in small groups to find more information about the park and to plan an itinerary outlining their activities for a week-long trip. Have groups share their itineraries with the class. 3.1

### Post-Reading Activity

Ask students to research international environmental treaties dealing with agricultural practices. Have them present their findings to the class. 1.3, 3.1

## Differentiated Instruction

**ADVANCED LEARNERS**

**Challenge** Have students look back at the three parts of the selection. Ask them to decide which part they would like to learn more about, and have them research information online. Suggest that they look for newspaper articles, and that they go to the Web sites of CORFO and CONAMA. Divide the class into five groups, based on the part of the selection they researched. Have the groups discuss what they learned and then have groups take turns presenting their findings to the class. 1.1, 3.2

**MULTIPLE INTELLIGENCES**

**Naturalist** Have students research and take notes in Spanish on historical information about the farming methods of indigenous peoples in pre-Columbian times. They can look into the Aymara, the Atacameños, the Chango, the Diaguitas, the Mapuche, the Picunches, and the Cunco people. Encourage students to research whether some of the pre-Columbian agricultural practices survive to this day, and what modern agriculture might learn from them. 2.1

### Assess

**Assessment Program**

**Prueba: Lectura,** p. 193

Standardized Assessment Tutor, pp. 41–44

**Online Assessment**
**my.hrw.com**

**Test Generator**

## Resources

**Planning:**

Lesson Planner, pp. 157–158, 318–319

One-Stop Planner

**Presentation:**

Audio CD 10, Tr. 12

**Practice:**

Cuaderno de actividades, p. 98

Reading Strategies and Skills Handbook, Chapter 10

Interactive Advanced Reader

### Applying the Strategies

For more practice with deciphering words, you might have students use the "Story Impressions" strategy from the *Reading Strategies and Skills Handbook.*

### Escuchemos

As students listen to the poem with their books closed, have them raise their hand every time they hear a verb in the progressive **-ando** or **-iendo** form.

### Pre-AP Practice

**AP Language Examination: Leamos** helps students prepare for Section I, Part B: **Reading Comprehension.** The audio recording helps them prepare for Part A: **Listening—Short Narratives.**

# Leamos y escribamos

**ESTRATEGIA**

**para leer** Sometimes authors play with language in order to convey how characters speak and to give readers a better picture of character and setting. The author of this poem modified the spelling of some words to convey the speech of gauchos in mid-1800s Argentina. When you see words you don't recognize, think of words that are spelled similarly.

CD 10, Tr. 12

**Antes de leer** 1.2

**A** El poema *El Gaucho Martín Fierro* fue escrito por el argentino José Hernández en 1872. Martín Fierro es un gaucho que vive feliz con su familia hasta que las autoridades lo mandan a la frontera. Cuando vuelve a su casa, su rancho está en ruinas y su familia ha desaparecido. Mientras lees, busca las palabras que el autor ha modificado para darnos una idea de cómo hablaban los gauchos. Haz una lista de estas palabras y busca sus significados.

## de *El Gaucho Martín Fierro*

de José Hernández

Aquí me pongo a cantar
al compás° de la vigüela°,
que el hombre que lo desvela°
una pena extrordinaria,
como la ave solitaria
con el cantar se consuela.

Pido a los santos del Cielo
que ayuden mi pensamiento;
les pido en este momento
que voy a cantar mi historia
me refresquen la memoria
y aclaren mi entendimiento.

Vengan santos milagrosos,
vengan todos en mi ayuda,
que la lengua se me añuda°
y se me turba la vista°;
pido a mi Dios que me asista
en una ocasión tan ruda.

Yo he visto muchos cantores,
con famas bien obtenidas,
y que después de adquiridas
no las quieren sustentar°:
parece que sin largar
se cansaron en partidas.

Mas° ande otro criollo pasa
Martín Fierro ha de pasar:
nada lo hace recular°
ni los fantasmas lo espantan;
y dende° que todos cantan
yo también quiero cantar.

**2** to the rhythm of **2** type of guitar with six strings **3** keep awake **15** gets tied in knots **16** I can't see clearly **22** to support **25** but **27** to go back **29** *desde*

## Core Instruction

### TEACHING LEAMOS

1. Read **Estrategia para leer** with students. **(1 min.)**
2. Ask students if they have ever read any literature about the Argentine gauchos. Have them read **Antes de leer. (2 min.)**
3. Read the poem aloud. Then have students read it to themselves, using the suggested strategy. **(10 min.)**
4. Remind students that even if they did not understand the entire poem, they should be able to get a general idea of what the author is trying to say. Ask volunteers to tell the main idea of the poem. **(3 min.)**
5. Answer the questions in Activity B as a class and have students do Activities C and D for homework. **(4 min.)**
6. Have students work in small groups to answer the questions in **Después de leer. (5 min.)**

Cantando me he de morir,
cantando me han de enterrar,
y cantando he de llegar
al pie del Eterno padre:
dende el vientre° de mi madre
vine a este mundo a cantar.

Que no se trabe mi lengua
ni me falte la palabra:
el cantar mi gloria labra°
y poniéndome a cantar,
cantando me han de encontrar
aunque la tierra se abra.

Me siento en el plan de un bajo
a cantar un argumento;
como si soplara el viento
hago tiritar° los pastos°.
Con oros, copas y bastos°
juega allí mi pensamiento.

Yo no soy cantor letrao°,
mas si me pongo a cantar
no tengo cuándo acabar
y me envejezco cantando:
las coplas me van brotando°
como agua de manantial°.

Con la guitarra en la mano
ni las moscas se me arriman°,
naides° me pone el pie encima,
y cuando el pecho se entona°,
hago gemir° a la prima
y llorar a la bordona°.

Yo soy toro en mi rodeo
y torazo en rodeo ajeno;
siempre me tuve por güeno°
y si me quieren probar,
salgan otros a cantar y
veremos quién es menos.

No me hago al lao de la güeya°
aunque vengan degollando°,
con los blandos yo soy blando
y soy duro con los duros,
y ninguno en un apuro
me ha visto andar tutubiando°.

En el peligro, ¡qué Cristos!
el corazón se me enancha°,
pues toda la tierra es cancha°,
y de esto naides se asombre:
el que se tiene por hombre
donde quiera hace pata ancha.

Soy gaucho, y entiendaló°
como mi lengua lo esplica°:
para mí la tierra es chica
y pudiera ser mayor;
ni la víbora° me pica
ni quema mi frente el sol.

Nací como nace el peje°
en el fondo de la mar;
naides me puede quitar
aquello que Dios me dió:
lo que al mundo truje° yo
del mundo lo he de llevar.

Mi gloria es vivir tan libre
como el pájaro del cielo;
no hago nido en este suelo
ande hay tanto que sufrir,
y naides me ha de seguir
cuando yo remuento el vuelo°.

**35** womb **39** builds **46** shiver, shake **46** pastures **47** *oros,...* playing cards **49** learned **53** gushing forth **54** spring **56** come close **57** *nadie* **58** gets in tune **59** to wail **60** 6th guitar string **63** *bueno* **67** *huella* **68** to cut someone's throat **72** to shy away from **74** to enlarge **75** playing field, court **79** *entiéndalo* **80** *explica* **83** snake **85** fish **89** *traje* **96** when I begin to soar

## Differentiated Instruction

### SPECIAL LEARNING NEEDS

**Students with AD(H)D** If you have students with AD(H)D in your class, you might want to suggest that they write a one-line summary after every 5–10 lines or so, in order to maintain focus on the poem. 1.2

### MULTIPLE INTELLIGENCES

**Musical/Rhythmic** Have volunteers read the poem aloud as the rest of the students close their eyes. Ask students to focus on the steady rhythm and rhyme of the poem. How does the rhythm and sound of the poem help convey meaning? If at all possible, obtain a recording of this poem put to music. 1.2, 3.1

# Leamos y escribamos

## Pre-Reading Activity

Ask students to reflect on the genre of the "Old West" in the U.S. What images come to mind? Do they think that rural cowboys have a particular way of speaking? How does it differ from urban speech? Tell them that the poem they are about to read reflects the mythological cowboy of Argentina, the **gaucho.** As they read, they should be aware of similarities and differences from the parallel cowboy culture of the American West.

## Active Reading Questions

1. **¿En qué imágenes piensas cuando lees este poema?**
2. **En tu opinión, ¿por qué quiere el autor imitar el habla de las gauchos?**
3. **¿Qué tiene que ver este poema con los temas de compasión, libertad, justicia y sueños?**
4. **¿Crees que el autor diría que debemos darle a mal tiempo buena cara?**

2.2, 3.2

## Word Identification

Tell students that they can use context clues to figure out the meaning of the words with modified spellings in the poem. Ask them to cover the footnotes as they read the poem and try to figure out the words on their own. They should be able to figure out many of the words by thinking about words with similar spellings that fit in the context of the poem. When they have finished reading the poem and compiling a list, have them check their answers. 1.2

Yo no tengo en el amor
quien me venga con querellas°;
como esas aves tan bellas
que saltan de rama en rama,
yo hago en el trébol mi cama,
y me cubren las estrellas.

Y sepan cuantos escuchan
de mis penas el relato,
que nunca peleo ni mato
sino por necesidá°,
y que a tanta alversidá°
sólo me arrojó el mal trato°.

Y atiendan la relación
que hace un gaucho perseguido,
que padre y marido ha sido
empeñoso y diligente,
y sin embargo la gente
lo tiene por un bandido.

**98** complaints **106** *necesidad* **107** *adversidad* **108** *me arrojó...* treated me badly

## Comprensión 1.2

**B** Contesta las preguntas.

1. ¿Cómo se siente Martín Fierro al principio del poema?
2. ¿Qué hace para consolarse?
3. ¿Con qué compara su creación poética en la novena estrofa *(stanza)?*
4. ¿Qué es la gloria para el gaucho, según Martín Fierro?
5. ¿Qué quiere decir con «no hago nido»?
6. ¿Cree Martín Fierro que la gente tiene una impresión equivocada de los gauchos? Explica.

**C** El autor usa metáforas en sus descripciones. Completa las siguientes metáforas según las descripciones del autor.

| toro | manta | agua | ave | soplara |
|---|---|---|---|---|

1. El hombre se consuela con su música como un ═══ solitaria. ave
2. Las coplas salen de su boca como ═══ de manantial. agua
3. Las estrellas son la ═══ del gaucho. manta
4. Hace tiritar los pastos como si ═══ el viento. soplara
5. Él es ═══ en su rodeo. toro

## Después de leer 1.3

**D** El autor usa un dialecto rural para describir mejor al personaje del gaucho. ¿Cómo es el gaucho? ¿Qué tipo de personaje es? ¿Cómo es su vida? ¿Con quién se podría comparar en el folclor de Estados Unidos? Describe la imagen que te dio el poema.

### B Answers

1. triste y solo
2. cantar como el ave solitaria
3. con agua de manantial
4. vivir tan libre como un pájaro del cielo
5. que no tiene que quedarse en un lugar, en su casa; puede irse adondequiera y dormir afuera
6. Sí, la gente piensa que son bandidos, pero son empeñosos y diligentes.

### Teaching Suggestions

- Have students analyze the poem from a historical point of view. Ask them to research the history of the **gauchos** and use the information to describe what happens in the poem. 1.2, 3.1
- Tell students that **"Cantor y gaucho"** is only the first part of the poem ***El Gaucho Martín Fierro.*** If students liked the poem, you might recommend that they read more parts. You may wish to assign different sections to students and have each student summarize his or her section for the class. 1.2

### Post-Reading Activity

Have students share what they think is the main idea of the poem. Ask them to tell what inferences they made in their interpretation of the poem. 1.2

## Core Instruction

### TEACHING ESCRIBAMOS

1. Read **Estrategia para escribir** and the introductory paragraph with students. **(1 min.)**
2. Have students use a word web like the one on page 443 as they complete step 1. **(5 min.)**
3. Have students do steps 2 and 3. Circulate around the classroom to help any students that are having difficulty with their writing. **(20 min.)**
4. Have students exchange their descriptions with a partner to complete step 4. **(4 min.)**

### Pre-AP Practice

**AP Language Examination:** **Leamos and Escribamos** help students prepare for Section I, Part B: **Reading Comprehension** and Section II, Part A: **Informal Writing.**

# Taller del escritor ❀ 1.3, 3.1

**ESTRATEGIA**

**para escribir** An excellent way to create images in the minds of your readers is to use rhetorical devices such as metaphors and similes. These techniques are especially useful in poetry, which uses fewer words to convey ideas.

## Un personaje folclórico

Vas a describir a un personaje folclórico de tu país, como un famoso vaquero *(cowboy)* del oeste. Tienes que inventar al personaje y escribir un poema corto, al estilo del poema *Martín Fierro.* Escribe el poema desde el punto de vista del personaje que vas a inventar.

### 1 Antes de escribir

Escoge a un personaje y piensa en sus características. ¿Qué tipo de persona es? ¿Qué hace? ¿Cómo se siente? Haz una lista de palabras para describirlo.

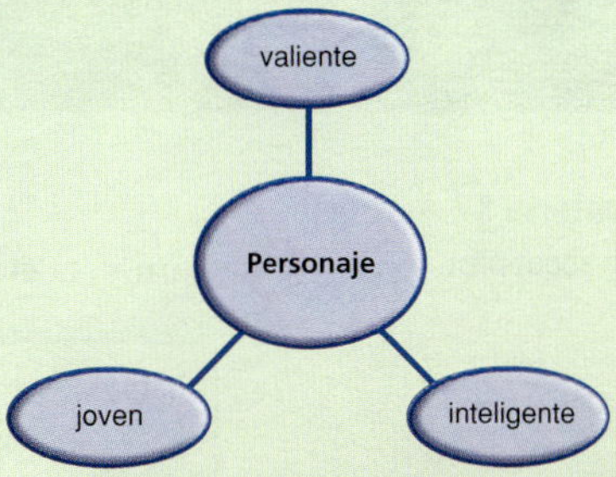


### 2 Escribir un borrador

Piensa en las características más importantes de tu personaje y con qué lo puedes comparar. Por ejemplo, si le gusta pelear, ¿es como un soldado? Si es independiente y fuerte, ¿es como un caballo salvaje? Haz una lista de cosas con las cuales se puede comparar al personaje o sus acciones. Usa la lista para escribir versos con metáforas o símiles.

### 3 Revisar

Lee tu borrador y decide si las figuras retóricas expresan lo que quieres comunicar. Si es necesario, añade versos para completar la descripción. Revisa tu poema para ver si contiene errores de ortografía y puntuación.

### 4 Publicar

Con un(a) compañero(a), túrnense para leer sus poemas en voz alta. Descríbanse las imágenes que les vienen a la mente al escuchar los poemas. ¿Son las imágenes que tenía en su mente el escritor? Juntos, piensen en otras comparaciones que también expresen las ideas que querían comunicar.

# Leamos y escribamos

## Process Writing

Remind students that they must include all key information in their writing. Explain that not all information must be directly stated. For example, they might use a comparison to convey information about what something looks like, or they might use sounds to communicate a certain atmosphere.

## Writing Assessment

To assess the **Taller del escritor,** you can use the following rubric.

| Writing Rubric | 4 | 3 | 2 | 1 |
|---|---|---|---|---|
| **Content** (Complete—Incomplete) | | | | |
| **Comprehensibility** (Comprehensible—Seldom comprehensible) | | | | |
| **Accuracy** (Accurate—Seldom accurate) | | | | |
| **Organization** (Well-organized—Poorly organized) | | | | |
| **Effort** (Excellent effort—Minimal effort) | | | | |

18–20: A
16–17: B
14–15: C
12–13: D
Under 12: F

## Differentiated Instruction

### SLOWER PACE LEARNERS

1 While students are doing step 1, you might want to discuss their topics with them individually. Look over the lists they made in step 1, and help them brainstorm other words to use. Show them examples of comparisons they might use to add life to their descriptions. Make sure students treat the natural landscape as a separate character.

### MULTIPLE INTELLIGENCES

**Linguistic** Have students go back to their list of words from *El Gaucho Martín Fierro* that were modified by José Hernández to give a sense of how the **gauchos** speak. Have them write a conversation using those words on a topic **gauchos** might discuss. ❀ 1.1

## Assess

**Assessment Program**

**Prueba: Lectura,** p. 193

**Prueba: Lectura,** p. 194

**Online Assessment**

**my.hrw.com**

**Test Generator**

## Resources

**Planning:**

Lesson Planner, pp. 158–159, 318–321
One-Stop Planner

**Presentation:**

Video Program, Videocassette 5
DVD Program
**Variedades**

**Practice:**

Activities for Communication, pp. 52, 73–74
Video Guide, pp. 66–67
Lab Book, pp. 10, 49–52, 87
Audio CD 10, Trs. 13–14
Pre-AP Instructional Resources
Pre-AP Audio CD 2, Trs. 17–20
Interactive Tutor, Disc 2
Teaching Transparencies
**Situación, Capítulo 10**
Picture Sequences, Chapter 10

### 1 Script

1. Los refugiados llegan a Chile desde muchas partes del mundo.
2. Hay manifestaciones muy a menudo en la Plaza de Mayo.
3. Chile va a competir en el campeonato de fútbol este año.
4. El descubrimiento de la nave hundida fue un momento emocionante.

### 5 Answers

1. El terremoto más grande del siglo veinte, con una magnitud de 9.5 en la escala Richter.
2. Quieren "cosechar" la energía solar del desierto de Atacama en el norte de Chile.
3. Hay recursos naturales en la zona de las Pampas.
4. Chile fue el primer país latinoamericano en convertirse en socio comercial de Estados Unidos.

Capítulo 10
Repaso

# Prepárate para el examen

Interactive TUTOR

CD 10, Tr. 13

**1** Escucha los comentarios y escoge la foto que corresponde a cada uno. 1.2 **1.** B **2.** D **3.** C **4.** A

A

B

C

D

**1 Vocabulario 1**
- talking about past events
- expressing and supporting a point of view

pp. 410–415

**2 Gramática 1**
- present and past progressive
- **haber**
- expressions of time

pp. 416–421

**2** Completa el párrafo con las palabras del cuadro. 1.2

| | | | |
|---|---|---|---|
| había | hay | estaba | hasta que |
| hace | primera | desde que | protestando |

La Plaza de Mayo de Buenos Aires se construyó __1__ más de tres siglos. En el pasado __2__ muchos mercados en la plaza, pero hoy en día no __3__ ni uno. En 1977, las madres de hijos desaparecidos que estaban __4__ en silencio se reunieron en la plaza por __5__ vez. La Plaza se ha convertido en un símbolo de justicia __6__ ellas empezaron a hacer sus manifestaciones allí. Por ejemplo, en 2001 mucha gente __7__ en La Plaza gritándole al presidente que renunciara. La gente no pensaba irse __8__ él lo hiciera.

1. hace
2. había
3. hay
4. protestando
5. primera
6. desde que
7. estaba
8. hasta que

**3 Vocabulario 2**
- making predictions and giving warnings
- expressing assumptions

pp. 424–429

**3** Empareja cada palabra con la definición correcta. 1.2

1. desperdiciar d
2. biológico a
3. implementar e
4. leyes c
5. reciclar f
6. innovador b

a. cultivado de forma natural
b. algo nuevo
c. las reglas del gobierno
d. no usar bien
e. poner en funcionamiento
f. usar otra vez

## Oral Assessment

### Speaking Rubric

To assess the speaking activities in this section, you might use the following rubric. For additional speaking rubrics, see the Alternative Assessment section of the *Assessment Program.*

| Speaking Rubric | 4 | 3 | 2 | 1 |
|---|---|---|---|---|
| **Content** (Complete—Incomplete) | | | | |
| **Comprehension** (Total—Little) | | | | |
| **Comprehensibility** (Comprehensible—Incomprehensible) | | | | |
| **Accuracy** (Accurate—Seldom Accurate) | | | | |
| **Fluency** (Fluent—Not Fluent) | | | | |

18–20: A 16–17: B 14–15: C 12–13: D Under 12: F

Visit Holt Online
go.hrw.com
KEYWORD: EXP3 CH10
Chapter Self-test

**4** Completa las oraciones con las formas correctas de los verbos. 1.2

1. Se están promoviendo fuentes de energía renovables para que la gente no ═══ (desperdiciar) los recursos naturales. desperdicie
2. Calculo que ═══ (venderse) más carros eléctricos en el futuro.
3. Dudo que el presidente ═══ (haber) implementado el programa de reciclaje. haya
4. Nosotros siempre comprábamos productos biológicos a menos que no los ═══ (encontrar) en el mercado. encontráramos
5. Buscaré trabajo en cuanto ═══ (bajar) la tasa de desempleo. baje
6. Hay que controlar el nivel de contaminación antes de que nosotros ═══ (destruir) el medio ambiente. destruyamos

2. se venderán

**4 Gramática 2**
- future tense
- subjunctive with doubt, denial, and feelings
- subjunctive and indicative with adverbial clauses

pp. 430–435

**5** Contesta las preguntas. 1.2

1. ¿Qué pasó en Chile en 1960?
2. ¿En qué parte de Chile quieren "cosechar" la energía solar?
3. ¿En qué parte de Argentina hay recursos naturales?

**5 Cultura**
- Comparaciones pp. 422–423
- Lectura informativa pp. 438–439
- Notas culturales pp. 413, 415, 418, 426, 431, 432, 435

CD 10, Tr. 14

**6** Escucha la conversación y haz una lista de los problemas que se mencionan. 1.2 el desempleo la contaminación la calidad del aire la calidad del agua el crimen el hambre

## Conversación

HOLT SoundBooth ONLINE RECORDING

**7** Role-play the following conversation with a partner. Partner A and Partner B live in a town where a natural disaster occurred recently. 1.1, 1.2

Partner A: Ask where your partner was and what he or she was doing when the disaster occurred.

Partner B: Respond. Ask what happened to your partner.

Partner A: Answer, then ask what your partner did immediately after the disaster.

Partner B: Respond. Describe what things were like or what you saw.

Partner A: Ask your partner's opinion about what the government did to help after the disaster.

Partner B: Respond, and support your opinion with examples.

Partner A: Disagree, and give examples to support your own point of view.

Partner B: End with a prediction about what will happen next, or what people will do to prepare for the next disaster.

**6 Script**

—Hola, Mónica. ¿Qué estás leyendo?
—Leo un artículo en el periódico sobre la tasa de desempleo. La semana pasada subió bastante.
—Sí, es un problema que tenemos que resolver antes de que se ponga peor. Según lo que he leído, el desempleo no es el único problema que hay en la ciudad. También hay problemas de contaminación, con la calidad del aire y del agua, además del crimen y el hambre.
—Hay varios problemas, pero por otro lado hay varias soluciones. Por ejemplo, hay varios productos que podemos reciclar en vez de tirarlos a la basura.
—Leí que el gobierno implementará un programa para reciclar el año que viene.
—¡Qué bueno! Es un buen comienzo, pero todavía hay mucho que hacer.

**7 Answers**

Below is a sample student conversation.

(A) —¿Te acuerdas de dónde estabas y qué estabas haciendo cuando ocurrió el terremoto?
(B) —Claro. Estaba en el autobús. Volvía a casa. ¿Dónde estabas tú?
(A) —Estaba en casa. Estaba preparando la cena cuando sentí el terremoto. ¿Qué pasó en el autobús? ¿Qué hicieron?
(B) —El conductor paró el autobús y todos nos bajamos. Vimos que hubo muchos accidentes en la calle y que muchos edificios se habían caído. Fue espantoso.
(A) —¿Qué piensas de la reacción del gobierno?
(B) —Estoy muy enojado. Las autoridades no estaban preparadas con servicios auxiliares para los heridos ni tenían un plan para los que perdieron sus casas, a pesar de que los terremotos en nuestra ciudad son normales.
(A) —Aunque estoy de acuerdo, me parece que no es posible prepararse para un desastre tan grande.
(B) —Si no construimos mejores edificios y si no estamos preparados con mejores servicios de emergencia, cuando ocurra el próximo terremoto grande, muchas más personas morirán.

## Conversación

### Additional Speaking Practice

For additional speaking practice, use the *Picture Sequences Transparency* for Chapter 10. Use the Speaking Rubric on the preceding page to evaluate their performance. You may also wish to use the Interviews and Role-Plays in the *Activities for Communication* book.

### Pre-AP Practice

**7** In the Level 3 *Pre-AP Instructional Resources* you will find an alternative version of Activity 7. The following resources in that book will help you prepare students for the AP Language Exam:

- Blackline masters, pp. 36, 46, 56
- Pre-AP Audio CD 2, Trs. 17–20
- Scripts and answers, pp. 57–75

# Prepárate para el examen

## Grammar Review

For more practice with the grammar topics in this chapter, see the *Grammar Tutor,* the *Interactive Tutor,* or the *Cuaderno de vocabulario y gramática.*

GramaVisión

## Comparisons

### Language to Language

Tell students that while the verb *to explode* can be translated as **explotar,** the verb **explotar** can also mean *to exploit, to cultivate or farm (land), to tap (resources), to commercialize, to operate (a factory).* You might point out that many of the vocabulary words in this chapter have English cognates. Have students work in groups to find the words with cognates.

4.1

**Gramática 1**
- present and past progressive
  **pp. 416–417**
- haber
  **pp. 418–419**
- expressions of time
  **pp. 420–421**

## Repaso de Gramática 1

The **progressive tenses** describe present and past actions in progress.

Marta **está desarrollando** un programa.

**Haber** in the third-person singular indicates existence. The construction **haber** + **past participle** is used to form the present and past perfect indicative or subjunctive tenses.

**Hay** mucho tráfico en la ciudad.

Útimamente, **hemos visto** más carros eléctricos.

For specific uses of **haber,** see page 418.

The construction **hace + amount of time + que** + **present tense** is used to tell *for how long* an action has been going on. The construction **hace + amount of time** + **past tense** is used to tell *how long ago* something happened. The phrase **desde que** is used to express *since.*

For more information on expressions of time, see page 420.

**Gramática 2**
- future tense
  **pp. 430–431**
- subjunctive with doubt, denial, and feelings
  **pp. 432–433**
- subjunctive and indicative with adverbial clauses
  **pp. 434–435**

## Repaso de Gramática 2

Future actions can be expressed by using the construction **ir a** + **infinitive** or the **future tense.**

**Voy a sembrar** unas flores. Las flores **crecerán** rápido.

Main clauses containing expressions of **doubt, denial,** or **feelings** require the **subjunctive** in the subordinate clause.

Dudo que **podamos** comprar frutas biológicas aquí.

For uses of the **subjunctive** with expressions of **doubt, denial,** or **feelings,** see page 432.

Adverbial clauses with **a menos (de) que, antes de que, con tal (de) que, en caso de que, para que,** and **sin que** always contain the **subjunctive.**

No tomaremos el agua **en caso de que** el lago **esté** contaminado.

Adverbial clauses with **cuando, en cuanto, después de que, hasta que,** and **tan pronto como** contain the **subjunctive** when referring to a future action and the **indicative** when referring to a past action or an action that occurs habitually or on a regular basis.

Voy a leer el periódico en cuanto **llegue** a casa.

For uses of the **subjunctive** and **indicative** with adverbial clauses, see page 434.

## Chapter Review

### Teacher Management System

To access, launch the program, type "admin" in the password area, and press RETURN. For more details, log on to www.hrw.com/CDROMTUTOR.

Create a variety of puzzles to review chapter vocabulary.

**DVD Program**

**Interactive Tutor**

**PuzzlePro**

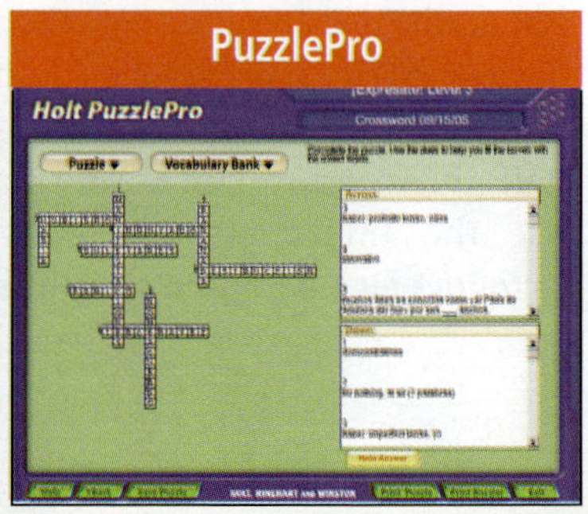

## Repaso de Vocabulario 1

### Talking about past events

| | |
|---|---|
| el accidente | *accident* |
| el acontecimiento | *event* |
| aterrador(a) | *terrifying* |
| la bomba | *bomb* |
| el campeonato | *championship* |
| la compasión | *compassion* |
| conmovedor(a) | *touching, moving* |
| la cooperación | *cooperation* |
| el desastre | *disaster* |
| el descubrimiento (de) | *discovery (of)* |
| descubrir | *to discover* |
| la destrucción | *destruction* |
| ¿Dónde estabas y qué estabas haciendo cuando...? | *Where were you and what were you doing when . . . ?* |
| las elecciones | *elections* |
| emocionante | *exciting, moving* |
| la erupción (de un volcán) | *eruption (of a volcano)* |
| espantoso(a) | *terrible, frightening* |
| Estaba en casa cuando... | *I was at home when . . .* |
| estallar | *to explode* |
| estrenar (una película) | *to open/premiere (a movie)* |
| el estreno | *opening/premiere* |
| la indiferencia | *indifference* |
| los inmigrantes | *immigrants* |
| el invento | *invention* |
| Lo recuerdo como si fuera ayer./No, no me acuerdo para nada. | *I remember it like it was yesterday./No, I don't remember at all.* |
| las manifestaciones | *demonstrations* |
| la nave hundida | *sunken ship* |
| el pánico | *panic* |
| el planeta | *planet* |
| los refugiados | *refugees* |
| la solidaridad | *solidarity* |
| ¿Te acuerdas (de) cuando sucedió...? | *Do you remember when . . . happened?* |
| trágico(a) | *tragic* |

### Expressing and supporting a point of view

| | |
|---|---|
| A pesar de que hubo..., por otro lado... | *Although there was/were . . . , on the other hand . . .* |
| Aunque estoy de acuerdo..., creo que... | *Although I agree . . . , I think that . . .* |
| Creo que vale la pena acordarse de... | *I think it's worth remembering . . .* |
| Lo que noto es que... | *What I notice is that . . .* |
| Me parece que... | *It seems to me that . . .* |
| Ten en cuenta que... | *Keep in mind that . . .* |

## Repaso de Vocabulario 2

### Making predictions and giving warnings

| | |
|---|---|
| A que no va a bajar la tasa de... | *I bet that the rate of . . . won't go down.* |
| las alternativas (a) | *alternatives (to)* |
| el basurero | *garbage can* |
| biológico(a) | *organic* |
| Calculo que van a implementar... | *I predict that they are going to implement . . .* |
| la calidad del aire/agua | *air/water quality* |
| el carro eléctrico/híbrido | *electric/hybrid car* |
| los combustibles | *fuels* |
| cometer (un crimen, un error) | *to commit (a crime), to make (a mistake)* |
| conservar | *to conserve* |
| la contaminación | *contamination/pollution* |
| contaminado(a) | *contaminated/polluted* |
| crecer (zc) | *to grow* |
| el crimen | *crime* |
| de cultivo biológico | *organic (products)* |
| desarrollar | *to develop* |
| el desempleo | *unemployment* |
| desperdiciar | *to waste* |
| la drogadicción | *drug addiction* |
| la energía solar | *solar energy* |
| la enfermedad | *sickness, disease* |
| Es muy posible que el tráfico aumente con... | *It's quite possible that traffic will increase with . . .* |
| las fuentes de energía | *sources of energy* |
| la fusión nuclear | *nuclear fusion* |
| el futuro | *future* |
| el hambre | *hunger* |
| innovador(a) | *innovative* |
| la ley (en contra/a favor de) | *law (against/in favor of)* |
| el medio ambiente | *environment* |
| los pesticidas | *pesticides* |
| los programas (de) | *programs (for)* |
| reciclar | *to recycle* |
| los recursos naturales | *natural resources* |
| renovable/no renovable | *renewable/non-renewable* |
| Se advierte que... | *They warn/advise that . . .* |
| sembrar | *to plant* |
| Te apuesto que... | *I bet you that . . .* |
| Ya verás que van a promover... | *You will see that they're going to promote . . .* |

**Expressing assumptions** . . . . . . . . . . *See p. 428.*





### Vocabulary Review

For more practice with the vocabulary in this chapter, see the *Interactive Tutor* or the *Cuaderno de vocabulario y gramática.*

### Online Edition

Students might use the online textbook to hear the **Vocabulario** items.

### Game

**Preguntas** This game reviews vocabulary and grammar. Ask students to create a large grid of four-by-four squares on a sheet of paper. In each square, they should write a question using the grammar and vocabulary from the chapter. Have students work their way around the room in search of a different classmate to answer each question. A student asks the question of a classmate, who, after answering, jots down his or her answer and signs the questioner's grid in the appropriate square. You may want to play rounds for different winners (e.g., the first to get four squares signed vertically, horizontally, diagonally, or to complete the whole grid). As a follow-up activity, have individuals report on their classmates' answers. 1.2

### Online Edition

### Transparency: Vocabulario

### Transparency: Situación

### Assess

**Assessment Program**

**Examen: Capítulo 10,** pp. 329–334

Audio CD 10, Trs. 18–19, 20–22

**Examen oral: Capítulo 10,** p. 340

**Examen final:** pp. 341–348

Alternative Assessment, pp. 382, 394, 406

**Online Assessment**

**my.hrw.com**

**Test Generator**

**Assess** **Differentiated Instruction** See the Differentiated Instruction CD-ROM.

**Resources**

**Planning:**

Lesson Planner, pp. 159, 320–321

One-Stop Planner

**Presentation:**

Teaching Transparencies
Fine Art, Chapter 10

**Practice:**

Cuaderno de actividades, pp. 99–100

Lab Book, pp. 10, 49–52

Audio CD 10, Tr. 15

Interactive Tutor, Disc 2

### 1 Script

1. —Oigan, ¡estos camarones están para chuparse los dedos! ¿No los probaron?
   —Bueno, no están malos, pero yo no diría que están así de buenos. Les falta algo pero no sé qué.
2. —La semana pasada hablé con el consejero del colegio para ver qué puedo hacer para mejorar mis notas de matemáticas.
   —¿Y qué te dijo?
   —Me recomendó que estudiara con mis compañeros de clase, pero todavía no logro entender lo que hacemos en clase.
3. —¿Andas buscando trabajo todavía?
   —Sí, estoy viendo los anuncios clasificados pero no he encontrado nada. No hay trabajo para un diseñador gráfico este verano.
4. —¿Quieres ver el estreno de la película francesa? Me han dicho que es muy entretenida.
   —Gracias, pero ya la he visto. ¿Por qué no vemos otra?
   —De acuerdo, veamos otra.

**Repaso cumulativo**

# Integración
## capítulos 1–10

CD 10, Tr. 15

**1** Escucha las conversaciones y escoge la foto que corresponde a cada una. 1.2 **1.** b **2.** a **3.** d **4.** c

A

B

C

D

**2** Lee el artículo que escribió Olga y decide si cada oración es **cierta** o **falsa**. Corrige las oraciones falsas. 1.2

## El futuro del medio ambiente

Quieren Uds. vivir en un mundo sucio y contaminado? Pues, yo no. Nosotros podemos actuar hoy para conservar el medio ambiente para el futuro. Podemos ayudar a bajar el nivel de desperdicios aquí mismo en nuestro colegio. Y empezaremos con el desarrollo de un programa de reciclaje. Recomiendo que coloquemos cajas para el reciclaje al lado de los basureros. En vez de echar papeles, botellas de vidrio y de plástico y demás productos a la basura, podríamos reciclarlos, y ¡hasta ahorraríamos dinero para el colegio! Piénsenlo un poco, podremos ahorrar dinero y combatir la contaminación al mismo tiempo.

1. Olga piensa que el mundo no está contaminado.
2. Los estudiantes pueden ayudar a conservar el medio ambiente.
3. Ella propone el desarrollo de un programa de reciclaje.
4. No hay basureros en el colegio.
5. Todos los productos que se tiran a la basura se pueden reciclar.
6. El colegio podría ahorrar dinero con el programa de reciclaje.

1. falsa; Ella cree que el mundo está contaminado.
2. cierta
3. cierta
4. falsa; Hay basureros pero no hay cajas de reciclaje.
5. falsa; Algunos productos que se tiran a la basura se pueden reciclar.
6. cierta

### Culture Project

Divide the class into groups. Ask each group to select a group of vocabulary words from page 447 for which they will research enviromental issues in **el cono sur.** Have the students include details about the environmental problems and the solutions in place to resolve each problem. Each group writes a report based on its research and presents it to the class. Tell students that they should consider certain questions when researching their environmental issue: How is this same environmental issue viewed differently in the United States? What types of measures are being taken to correct the problem? How do these measures differ from those in the United States? Do these solutions have anything to do with culture? Why or why not? 3.1, 4.2

Visit Holt Online
**go.hrw.com**
KEYWORD: EXP3 CH10
Cumulative Self-test

3 En grupos, piensen en algunos problemas del medio ambiente y para cada uno, digan cómo cambiaría el medio ambiente en el futuro si todos empezaran a cuidarlo. ¿Qué quieren hacer Uds. para ayudar? 1.1, 1.3

4 Mira la pintura y escribe por lo menos seis oraciones sobre lo que ves. ¿Qué inventos o avances tecnológicos ves en la pintura? ¿Qué crees que piensa la artista de ellos? Explica. 1.3

*Mirando un paracaídas II*, 1985 (Diptych) by Patricia Figueroa. Acrylic and pastel on paper, 160 × 240 cm. © Colección Museo Nacional de Bellas Artes, Chile/Museo Nacional de Bellas Artes, Chile

***Mirando un paracaídas II*** de Patricia Figueroa

5 Imagina que tienes que preparar un ensayo para los arqueólogos del futuro que explique cómo es el mundo hoy en día. Incluye algunos eventos históricos importantes y cómo han cambiado el mundo actual. También puedes incluir algunos avances tecnológicos y explicar cómo piensas que éstos cambiarán el mundo en el futuro. 1.3

6 Situación 1.1, 1.3

Conviertan el salón de clases en una exposición de nuevas tecnologías que ayuden a bajar los niveles de contaminación del medio ambiente. Uds. pueden trabajar en grupos para presentar sus ideas a la clase. Pueden elegir dos o tres personas para escoger las mejores ideas.

## Fine Art Connection

Tell students that the painting ***Mirando un paracaídas II*** is located in the **Museo Nacional de Bellas Artes** in Chile. It was painted by Patricia Figueroa in 1985. Figueroa was born in Santiago, Chile, in 1949. She studied Pedagogy in the Arts at the University of Chile, received her degree in 1978, and gave classes in drawing, painting, and engraving until 1981. She received a scholarship from **Amigos del Arte** in 1980 and 1981, and in 1987 she was chosen to represent Chile in the **XIX Bienal,** an international art fair, in Sao Paulo, Brazil. Her early paintings show an ecological vision in the series **Hombre-ciudad** and **Área verde.** In 1980, the themes of her paintings revolved around the bombings of Hiroshima and Nagasaki, and later they portrayed her preoccupation with America in the series **Buscando América** and **A Ixtlán.**

### Analyzing

Ask students how they would classify this painting. Is it abstract? classical? modern? Have them give their opinions of the painting. What does it make them think of? What mood does it evoke? 3.1

### Extension

Have students research information on the **Museo Nacional de Bellas Artes** in Chile. Ask them to choose a piece of artwork on display in the museum and write a short report about it for the class. 3.1

### ACTFL Performance Standards

The activities in Chapter 10 target the different communicative modes as described in the Standards.

| | | |
|---|---|---|
| **Interpersonal** | Two-way communication using receptive skills and productive skills | **Comunicación (SE),** pp. 413, 415, 417, 419, 421, 427, 429, 431, 433, 435<br>**Comunicación (TE),** pp. 415, 417, 421, 427, 431, 433, 437<br>**Conversación,** p. 445 |
| **Interpretive** | One-way communication using receptive skills | **Comunicación (SE),** pp. 413, 415, 421, 429<br>**Comunicación (TE),** p. 429<br>**Novela en video**, pp. 436–437<br>**Leamos,** pp. 440–442<br>**Conversación,** p. 445 |
| **Presentational** | One-way communication using productive skills | **Comunicación (SE),** pp. 419, 427, 431, 433, 435<br>**Comunicación (TE),** pp. 413, 419, 435<br>**Taller del escritor,** p. 443 |

# Páginas de referencia

# El mundo

OCÉANO ÁRTICO
ALASKA (EE.UU.)
GROENLANDIA (DINAMARCA)
CANADÁ
AMÉRICA DEL NORTE
Ottawa
Nueva York
Washington, D.C.
ESTADOS UNIDOS DE AMÉRICA
OCÉANO ATLÁNTICO
BERMUDA (R.U.)
BAHAMAS
ISLAS HAWAII (EE.UU.)
La Habana
CUBA
MÉXICO
Ciudad de México
JAMAICA
REP. DOMINICANA
PUERTO RICO (EE.UU.)
BELICE
HAITÍ
San Juan
HONDURAS
GUATEMALA
EL SALVADOR
NICARAGUA
COSTA RICA
PANAMÁ
Caracas
TRINIDAD Y TOBAGO
VENEZUELA
GUAYANA
SURINAM
GUAYANA FRANCESA
Bogotá
COLOMBIA
OCÉANO PACÍFICO
Ecuador
Islas Galápagos (Ecuador)
ECUADOR
KIRIBATI
AMÉRICA DEL SUR
BRASIL
PERÚ
Lima
BOLIVIA
PARAGUAY
Río de Janeiro
ARGENTINA
CHILE
Santiago
Buenos Aires
URUGUAY
Islas Malvinas (R.U.)
OCÉANO ATLÁNTICO
MARRUECOS
Islas Canarias (Esp.)
SAHARA OCCIDENTAL
MAURITANIA
MALÍ
CABO VERDE
SENEGAL
GAMBIA
GUINEA-BISSAU
GUINEA
BURKINO FASO
SIERRA LEONA
COSTA DE MARFIL
GHANA
TOGO
LIBERIA
GUINEA ECUATORIA
SANTO TOMÉ Y PRÍNCIPE
N
0 1.000 2.000 Kilómetros
0 1.000 2.000 Millas
A N

| | PAÍS | CAPITAL |
|---|---|---|
| 1 | REPÚBLICA CHECA | Praga |
| 2 | REPÚBLICA ESLOVACA | Bratislava |
| 3 | ESLOVENIA | Liubliana |
| 4 | CROACIA | Zagreb |
| 5 | BOSNIA Y HERZEGOVINA | Sarajevo |
| 6 | MACEDONIA | Skopje |
| 7 | YUGOSLAVIA | Belgrado |
| 8 | LITUANIA | Vilna |
| 9 | LETONIA | Riga |
| 10 | ESTONIA | Tallin |
| 11 | LIECHTENSTEIN | Vaduz |
| 12 | LUXEMBURGO | Luxemburgo |

# La Península Ibérica

# México

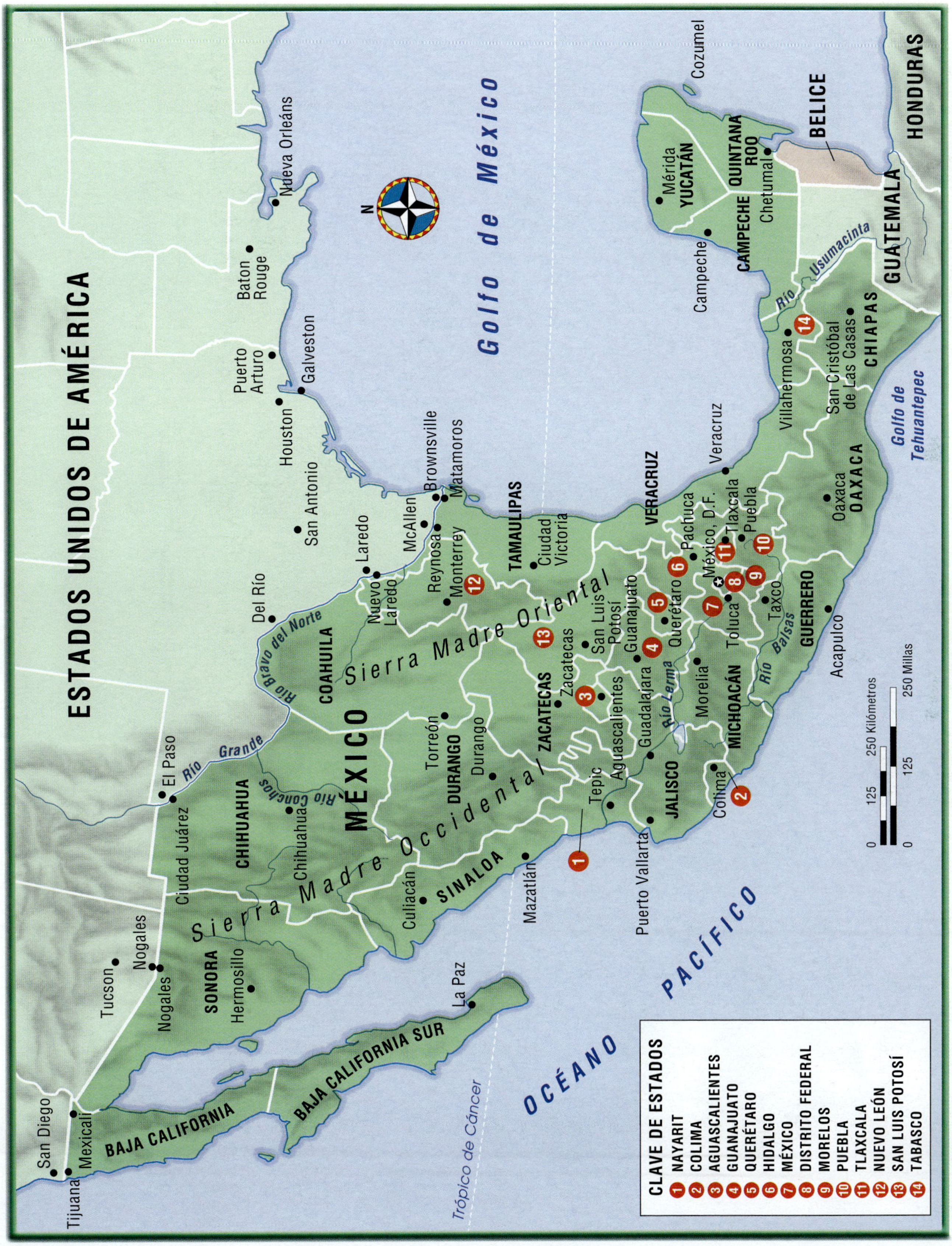
ESTADOS UNIDOS DE AMÉRICA
Golfo de México
OCÉANO PACÍFICO
MÉXICO
Sierra Madre Occidental
Sierra Madre Oriental
Trópico de Cáncer
Golfo de Tehuantepec
BELICE
GUATEMALA
HONDURAS
N
Río Grande
Río Bravo del Norte
Río Conchos
Río Lerma
Río Balsas
Río Usumacinta
BAJA CALIFORNIA
BAJA CALIFORNIA SUR
SONORA
CHIHUAHUA
COAHUILA
SINALOA
DURANGO
ZACATECAS
TAMAULIPAS
JALISCO
MICHOACÁN
GUERRERO
OAXACA
CHIAPAS
VERACRUZ
CAMPECHE
YUCATÁN
QUINTANA ROO
San Diego
Tijuana
Mexicali
Tucson
Nogales
Nogales
Hermosillo
El Paso
Ciudad Juárez
Chihuahua
Culiacán
Mazatlán
La Paz
Del Río
San Antonio
Houston
Galveston
Puerto Arturo
Baton Rouge
Nueva Orleáns
Laredo
Nuevo Laredo
McAllen
Reynosa
Brownsville
Matamoros
Monterrey
Ciudad Victoria
Torreón
Durango
Zacatecas
San Luis Potosí
Aguascalientes
Guanajuato
Querétaro
Tepic
Guadalajara
Puerto Vallarta
Colima
Morelia
Toluca
México, D.F.
Pachuca
Tlaxcala
Puebla
Taxco
Acapulco
Veracruz
Oaxaca
Villahermosa
San Cristóbal de Las Casas
Campeche
Mérida
Chetumal
Cozumel
0 125 250 Kilómetros
0 125 250 Millas
CLAVE DE ESTADOS
1 NAYARIT
2 COLIMA
3 AGUASCALIENTES
4 GUANAJUATO
5 QUERÉTARO
6 HIDALGO
7 MÉXICO
8 DISTRITO FEDERAL
9 MORELOS
10 PUEBLA
11 TLAXCALA
12 NUEVO LEÓN
13 SAN LUIS POTOSÍ
14 TABASCO

# Estados Unidos de América

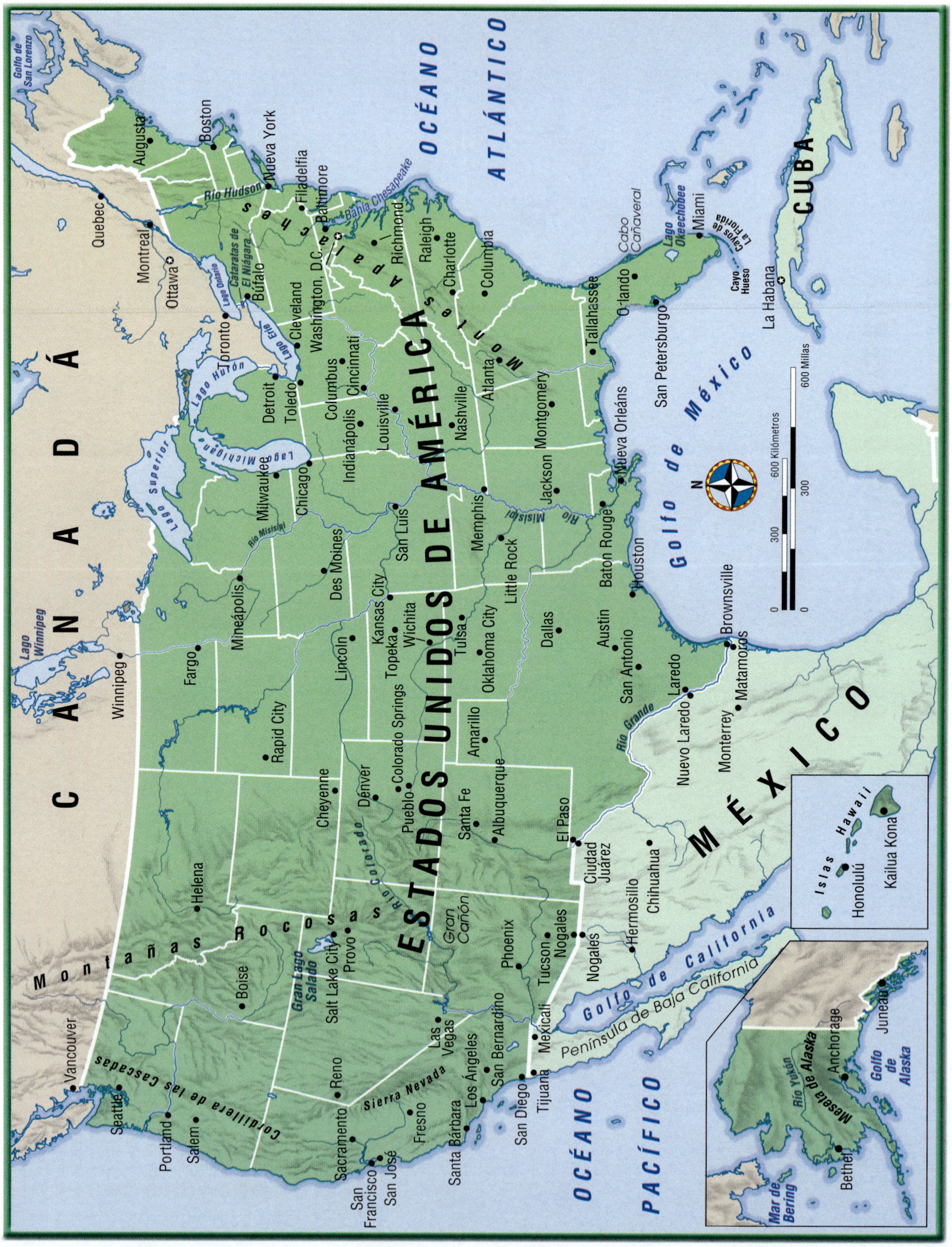

# América Central y las Antillas

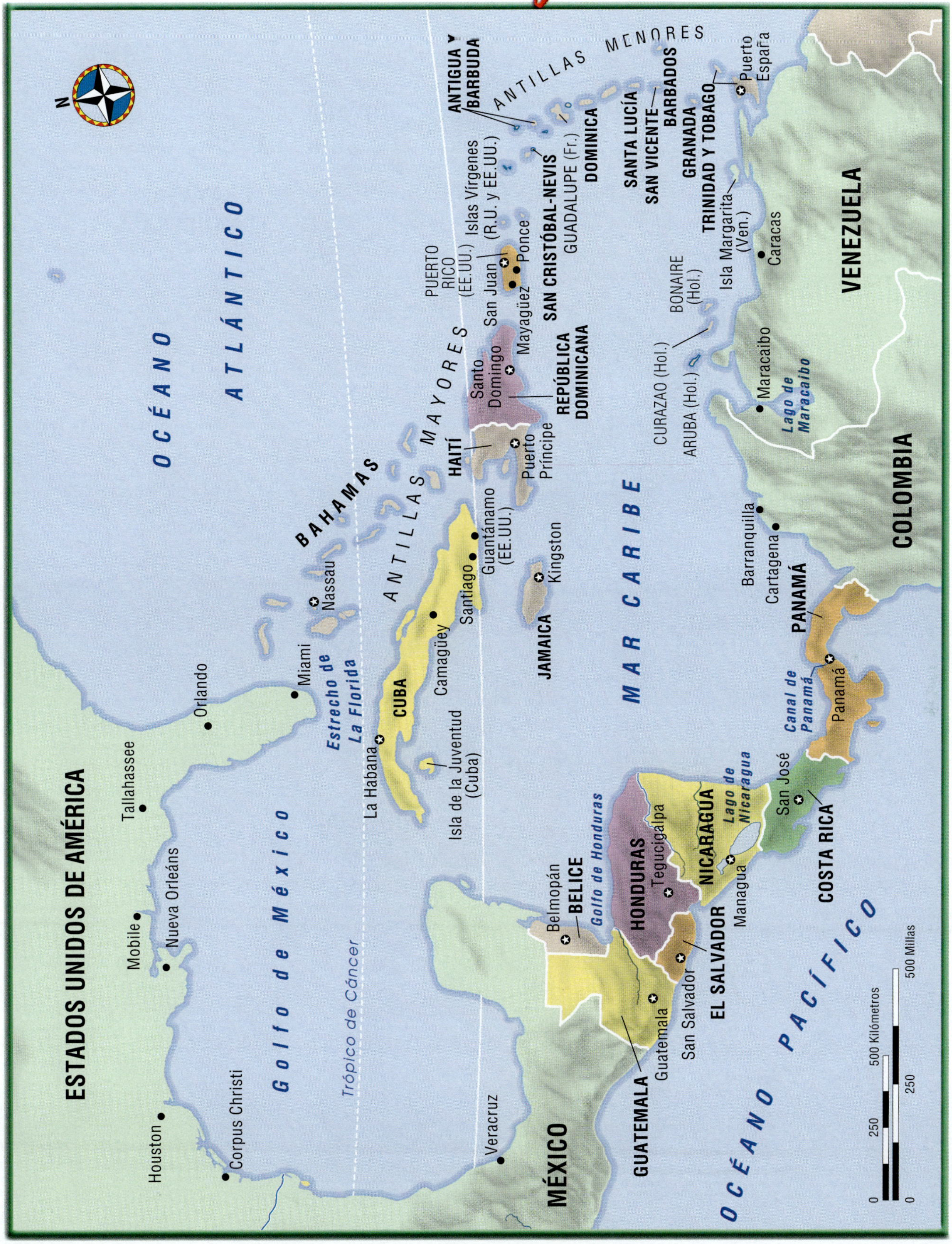

# América del Sur

# Repaso de vocabulario

This list includes words introduced in *¡Exprésate!* Level 2. If you can't find the words you need here, try the Spanish–English and English–Spanish vocabulary sections beginning on page R47.

## Descripciones (*Descriptions*)

| | |
|---|---|
| **activo(a)** | *active* |
| **alto(a)** | *tall* |
| **amable** | *friendly* |
| **atlético(a)** | *athletic* |
| **aventurero(a)** | *adventuresome* |
| **bajo(a)** | *short* |
| **bondadoso(a)** | *generous* |
| **bonito(a)** | *pretty* |
| **callado(a)** | *quiet* |
| **cariñoso(a)** | *affectionate* |
| **chismoso(a)** | *gossipy* |
| **chistoso(a)** | *funny* |
| **cómico(a)** | *funny* |
| **consentido(a)** | *spoiled* |
| **conversador(a)** | *talkative* |
| **curioso(a)** | *curious* |
| **egoísta** | *selfish* |
| **estricto(a)** | *strict* |
| **extrovertido(a)** | *outgoing* |
| **impaciente** | *impatient* |
| **juguetón/juguetona** | *playful* |
| **moreno(a)** | *dark-haired, dark-skinned* |
| **obediente** | *obedient* |
| **paciente** | *patient* |
| **rubio(a)** | *blond(e)* |
| **serio(a)** | *serious* |
| **simpático(a)** | *friendly* |
| **solitario(a)** | *solitary* |

## Los quehaceres (*Chores*)

| | |
|---|---|
| **barrer** | *to sweep* |
| **cortar el césped** | *to mow the lawn* |
| **darles de comer a los animales** | *to feed the animals* |
| **hacer diligencias** | *to run errands* |
| **limpiar el baño** | *to clean the bathroom* |
| **regar las plantas** | *to water the plants* |
| **sacar la basura** | *to take out the trash* |
| **sacudir los muebles** | *to dust the furniture* |

## Actividades (*Activities*)

| | |
|---|---|
| **andar** | *to walk* |
| **coleccionar estampillas (monedas, pósters)** | *to collect stamps (coins, posters)* |
| **conocer el centro** | *to get to know downtown* |
| **conversar** | *to talk, to have a conversation* |
| **cortarse el pelo** | *to get a haircut* |
| **coser** | *to sew* |
| **crear un álbum** | *to create an album, scrapbook* |
| **crear/grabar CDs** | *to burn CDs* |
| **cuidar a una mascota** | *to take care of a pet* |
| **dar una vuelta** | *to go for a walk* |
| **diseñar páginas Web** | *to design Web pages* |
| **disfrutar de** | *to enjoy* |
| **hacer crucigramas** | *to do crossword puzzles* |
| **hacer diseño por computadora** | *to do computer design* |
| **hacer ejercicios aeróbicos** | *to do aerobics* |
| **intercambiar** | *to exchange, to trade* |
| **ir al zoológico** | *to go to the zoo* |
| **ir de compras al mercado** | *to go shopping at the market* |
| **jugar (ue) naipes** | *to play cards* |
| **llamarle la atención (algo)** | *to interest* |
| **participar** | *to participate* |
| **pasear en bote** | *to go boating* |
| **pasear** | *to go for a walk* |
| **practicar las artes marciales** | *to do martial arts* |
| **tejer** | *to knit* |
| **tocar la guitarra (el violín)** | *to play the guitar (violin)* |
| **tomar clases de...** | *to take . . . lessons* |
| **trabajar en mecánica** | *to work on cars* |
| **trotar** | *to jog* |
| **visitar un museo** | *to visit a museum* |

## Los oficios *(Jobs)*

| | |
|---|---|
| **el (la) abogado(a)** | *lawyer* |
| **el (la) astronauta** | *astronaut* |
| **el (la) banquero(a) internacional** | *international banker* |
| **el (la) bombero(a)** | *firefighter* |
| **el (la) carpintero(a)** | *carpenter* |
| **el (la mujer) cartero** | *mail carrier* |
| **el (la) cocinero(a)** | *cook* |
| **el (la) comerciante** | *merchant* |
| **el (la) conductor(a)** | *driver* |
| **el (la) dentista** | *dentist* |
| **el (la) enfermero(a)** | *nurse* |
| **el (la) farmacéutico(a)** | *pharmacist* |
| **el (la) ingeniero(a)** | *engineer* |
| **el (la) mecánico** | *mechanic* |
| **el (la) médico(a)** | *doctor* |
| **el (la) peluquero(a)** | *hairstylist* |
| **el (la) periodista** | *journalist* |
| **el (la) policía** | *police officer* |
| **el (la) programador(a)** | *programmer* |
| **el (la) secretario(a)** | *secretary* |
| **el (la) trabajador(a) social** | *social worker* |

## En la casa *(At home)*

| | |
|---|---|
| **la alfombra** | *carpet, rug* |
| **la bañera** | *bathtub* |
| **la cómoda** | *chest of drawers, armoire* |
| **el cuadro** | *painting* |
| **la ducha** | *shower* |
| **el estante** | *bookcase* |
| **la estufa** | *stove* |
| **el fregadero** | *(kitchen) sink* |
| **el inodoro** | *toilet* |
| **la lámpara** | *lamp* |
| **el lavabo** | *(bathroom) sink* |
| **la lavadora** | *washing machine* |
| **el lavaplatos** | *dishwasher* |
| **la mesita de noche** | *bedside table* |
| **la pared** | *wall* |
| **el piso** | *floor* |
| **la secadora** | *dryer* |
| **el sillón** | *armchair* |
| **el techo** | *ceiling, roof* |
| **el televisor** | *TV set* |

## En el pueblo *(Around town)*

| | |
|---|---|
| **la acera** | *sidewalk* |
| **el acuario** | *aquarium* |
| **la avenida** | *avenue* |
| **la autopista** | *freeway, highway* |
| **el ayuntamiento** | *town hall* |
| **la banca** | *park bench* |
| **el banco** | *bank* |
| **la carnicería** | *butcher shop* |
| **la clínica** | *clinic* |
| **el café** | *café* |
| **la catedral** | *cathedral* |
| **la carretera** | *road* |
| **el cementerio** | *cemetery* |
| **el centro recreativo** | *recreation center* |
| **la comisaría** | *police department* |
| **el cruce** | *intersection* |
| **la cuadra** | *(city) block* |
| **la embajada** | *embassy* |
| **la esquina** | *corner* |
| **el estacionamiento** | *parking lot* |
| **la estación de autobuses** | *bus station* |
| **la estación de bomberos** | *fire station* |
| **la estación de tren** | *train station* |
| **la fábrica** | *factory* |
| **la floristería** | *flower shop* |
| **la frutería** | *fruit shop* |
| **la fuente** | *fountain* |
| **la heladería** | *ice cream shop* |
| **el hospital** | *hospital* |
| **el mercado** | *market* |
| **el monumento** | *monument* |
| **la mueblería** | *furniture store* |
| **la oficina** | *office* |
| **la panadería** | *bakery* |
| **la parada del metro** | *subway stop* |
| **la pastelería** | *pastry shop* |
| **la peluquería** | *hair salon* |
| **la pescadería** | *fish market* |
| **la plaza** | *town square, plaza* |
| **el puerto** | *port* |
| **el quiosco** | *stand, kiosk* |
| **la sala de emergencias** | *emergency room* |
| **seguir (i, i)** | *to keep going* |
| **seguir (i, i) adelante/derecho** | *to go straight* |
| **el semáforo** | *traffic light* |

| | |
|---|---|
| el supermercado | *supermarket* |
| la tienda de comestibles | *grocery store* |
| la zona peatonal | *pedestrian zone* |
| la zona verde | *green belt, park* |

## Después del colegio *(After school)*

| | |
|---|---|
| el (la) animador(a) | *cheerleader* |
| animar | *to cheer* |
| el atletismo | *track and field* |
| la banda escolar | *school band* |
| la competencia | *competition* |
| el debate | *debate* |
| empatar | *to tie a game* |
| el (la) entrenador(a) | *coach* |
| el equipo | *team* |
| la equitación | *horseback riding* |
| el esquí acuático | *water skiing* |
| el éxito | *success* |
| el fracaso | *failure* |
| ganar | *to win* |
| la gimnasia | *gymnastics* |
| el golf | *golf* |
| el (la) jugador(a) | *player* |
| la lucha libre | *wrestling* |
| montar a caballo | *to ride a horse* |
| la natación | *swimming* |
| la oratoria | *speech, public speaking* |
| el patinaje sobre hielo | *ice skating* |
| el patinaje en línea | *in-line skating* |
| perder (ie) | *to lose* |
| el puntaje | *score* |
| el trofeo | *trophy* |

## Reacciones *(Reactions)*

| | |
|---|---|
| la alegría | *happiness* |
| gritar | *to shout* |
| llorar | *to cry* |
| la rabia | *anger* |
| reaccionar | *to react* |
| reírse (i, i) | *to laugh* |
| la tristeza | *sadness* |
| la vergüenza | *embarrassment* |

## El cuerpo *(The body)*

| | |
|---|---|
| las cejas | *eyebrows* |
| el cerebro | *brain* |
| el codo | *elbow* |
| el corazón | *heart* |
| cortarse | *to cut oneself* |
| darse un golpe en... | *to bump one's . . .* |
| el dedo del pie | *toe* |
| enfermarse | *to get sick* |
| la enfermedad | *illness* |
| estar mal | *to be sick* |
| estar resfriado(a) | *to have a cold* |
| estornudar | *to sneeze* |
| hinchado(a) | *swollen* |
| el hueso | *bone* |
| los labios | *lips* |
| lastimarse | *to injure/hurt oneself* |
| la mejilla | *cheek* |
| la muñeca | *wrist* |
| el muslo | *thigh* |
| la oreja | *ear* |
| la piel | *skin* |
| los pulmones | *lungs* |
| quemarse | *to get a sunburn, to get burned* |
| resfriarse | *to catch a cold* |
| la rodilla | *knee* |
| romperse | *to break* |
| tener (ie) tos | *to have a cough* |
| tener (ie) un calambre | *to have a cramp* |
| el tobillo | *ankle* |
| torcerse (ue) | *to sprain* |
| la uña | *nail* |

## Por la mañana *(In the morning)*

| | |
|---|---|
| acabar de | *to have just* |
| acordarse (ue) de | *to remember* |
| agarrar | *to get, to hold* |
| apagar la luz (las luces) | *to turn off the light(s)* |
| arreglarse | *to get ready, to get dressed* |
| cepillarse | *to brush* |
| cerrar (ie) la puerta con llave | *to lock the door* |
| la crema | *cream* |
| darle de comer al perro | *to feed the dog* |
| darse prisa | *to hurry* |
| ducharse | *to take a shower* |
| el impermeable | *raincoat* |
| irse | *to leave* |

| | |
|---|---|
| **el lápiz labial** | *lipstick* |
| **los lentes de contacto** | *contact lenses* |
| **la llave** | *key* |
| **el paraguas** | *umbrella* |
| **peinarse** | *to comb one's hair* |
| **pintar** | *to paint* |
| **pintarse las uñas** | *to paint one's nails* |
| **ponerse** | *to put something on* |
| **recoger** | *to pick up* |
| **tardar** | *to take long, to be late* |
| **el teléfono celular** | *cell phone* |

## De pequeño *(As a child)*

| | |
|---|---|
| **los animales de peluche** | *stuffed animals* |
| **columpiarse** | *to swing (on a swing)* |
| **compartir los juguetes** | *to share toys* |
| **los dibujos animados** | *cartoons* |
| **echar carreras** | *to run races* |
| **hacer travesuras** | *to play tricks* |
| **jugar (ue) a la casita** | *to play house* |
| **jugar (ue) a las damas** | *to play checkers* |
| **jugar (ue) al escondite** | *to play hide and seek* |
| **jugar (ue) con bloques** | *to play with blocks* |
| **las láminas** | *sports cards* |
| **las muñecas** | *dolls* |
| **sacar buenas/malas notas** | *to get good/ bad grades* |
| **saltar a la cuerda** | *to jump rope* |
| **trepar a los árboles** | *to climb trees* |

## En el restaurante *(At the restaurant)*

| | |
|---|---|
| **el aceite de oliva** | *olive oil* |
| **el agua mineral** | *mineral water* |
| **aguado(a)** | *watery, weak* |
| **el ají** | *chili pepper* |
| **al gusto** | *to one's taste* |
| **la almendra** | *almond* |
| **añadir** | *to add* |
| **el azúcar** | *sugar* |
| **las bebidas** | *drinks* |
| **el bistec a la parrilla** | *grilled steak* |
| **el bistec encebollado** | *steak with onions* |
| **los bocadillos** | *finger food* |
| **el caldo de pollo** | *chicken soup* |
| **los carbohidratos** | *carbohydrates* |
| **la carne asada** | *roast meat* |
| **la cebolla** | *onion* |
| **las chuletas de cerdo con habichuelas** | *pork chops with beans* |
| **cocido(a)** | *cooked* |
| **la comida rápida** | *fast food* |
| **congelado(a)** | *frozen* |
| **crudo(a)** | *raw* |
| **cubrir** | *to cover* |
| **la cucharada** | *tablespoon* |
| **la cucharadita** | *teaspoon* |
| **dejar la propina** | *to leave the tip* |
| **derretido(a)** | *melted* |
| **derretir (i, i)** | *to melt* |
| **la dieta balanceada** | *balanced diet* |
| **echar** | *to put in, to add* |
| **la ensalada mixta** | *mixed salad* |
| **los entremeses** | *appetizers* |
| **las especias** | *spices* |
| **evitar** | *to avoid* |
| **el flan de vainilla** | *vanilla flan* |
| **freír (i, i)** | *to fry* |
| **las fresas con crema** | *strawberries and cream* |
| **frito(a)** | *fried* |
| **el gazpacho** | *cold tomato soup* |
| **hervir (ie, i)** | *to boil* |
| **hornear** | *to bake* |
| **los huevos revueltos** | *scrambled eggs* |
| **los ingredientes** | *ingredients* |
| **la lata de salsa de tomate** | *can of tomato sauce* |
| **la lechuga** | *lettuce* |
| **la mantequilla** | *butter* |
| **los mariscos** | *seafood* |
| **la mayonesa** | *mayonnaise* |
| **la mostaza** | *mustard* |
| **nutritivo(a)** | *nutritious* |
| **la pera** | *pear* |
| **picado(a)** | *diced* |
| **picar** | *to dice* |
| **la pimienta** | *black pepper* |
| **la piña** | *pineapple* |
| **el plátano** | *plantain, banana* |
| **el plato del día** | *daily special* |
| **el plato principal** | *main dish* |
| **el pollo asado con gandules** | *roasted chicken with peas* |
| **las proteínas** | *proteins* |
| **la receta** | *recipe* |

| | |
|---|---|
| **rico(a)** | *tasty, delicious* |
| **sabroso(a)** | *tasty* |
| **la sal** | *salt* |
| **la sopa de ajo (de fideos)** | *garlic (noodle) soup* |
| **el surtido de frutas frescas** | *assorted fresh fruit* |
| **la taza de medir** | *measuring cup* |
| **el té** | *tea* |
| **tostado(a)** | *toasted* |
| **el trozo** | *piece, chunk* |
| **los vegetales** | *vegetables* |
| **vegetariano(a)** | *vegetarian* |
| **el vinagre** | *vinegar* |
| **las vitaminas** | *vitamins* |

## La ropa *(Clothing)*

| | |
|---|---|
| **ancho(a)** | *wide* |
| **apretado(a)** | *tight* |
| **la bufanda** | *scarf* |
| **el cinturón** | *belt* |
| **la corbata** | *tie* |
| **el espejo** | *mirror* |
| **la etiqueta** | *price tag* |
| **la falda a media pierna** | *mid-length skirt* |
| **flojo(a)** | *baggy, loose* |
| **los guantes** | *gloves* |
| **hacer juego** | *to match, to go with* |
| **la minifalda** | *miniskirt* |
| **el probador** | *fitting room* |
| **probarse (ue)** | *to try on* |
| **el traje** | *suit* |
| **la venta de liquidación** | *clearance sale* |

## En el mercado *(At the market)*

| | |
|---|---|
| **el acero** | *steel* |
| **los adornos** | *decorations, ornaments* |
| **los artículos de cuero** | *leather goods* |
| **el barro** | *clay* |
| **la cadena** | *chain* |
| **la cerámica** | *ceramic* |
| **la cesta** | *basket* |
| **el collar** | *necklace* |
| **el encaje** | *lace* |
| **estar bordado(a)** | *to be embroidered* |
| **la figura tallada** | *carved figure* |
| **el gran surtido** | *wide assortment* |
| **la hamaca** | *hammock* |
| **hecho(a) a mano** | *handmade* |
| **las joyas** | *jewelry* |
| **la madera** | *wood* |
| **el mantel** | *tablecloth* |
| **la máscara** | *mask* |
| **el oro** | *gold* |
| **la paja** | *straw* |
| **las pinturas** | *paintings* |
| **el plástico** | *plastic* |
| **la plata** | *silver* |
| **el plato hondo** | *bowl* |
| **el puesto de mercado** | *market stand* |
| **rebajar** | *to lower* |
| **los tejidos** | *woven cloth, textiles* |
| **la última oferta** | *last offer* |
| **el vidrio** | *glass* |

## El mundo y el clima *(The world and the weather)*

| | |
|---|---|
| **árido(a)** | *arid, dry* |
| **el bosque** | *forest* |
| **la brisa** | *breeze* |
| **el clima** | *climate, weather* |
| **el desierto** | *desert* |
| **el granizo** | *hail* |
| **las hojas** | *leaves* |
| **húmedo(a)** | *humid* |
| **el huracán** | *hurricane* |
| **llover (ue) (a cántaros)** | *to rain (cats and dogs)* |
| **lloviznar** | *to drizzle* |
| **la montaña** | *mountain* |
| **la naturaleza** | *nature* |
| **nevar (ie)** | *to snow* |
| **la niebla** | *fog* |
| **la nieve** | *snow* |
| **la piedra** | *stone, rock* |
| **el relámpago** | *lightning* |
| **el río** | *river* |
| **seco(a)** | *dry* |
| **soleado(a)** | *sunny* |
| **la temperatura** | *temperature* |
| **el terremoto** | *earthquake* |
| **la tormenta** | *storm* |
| **el tornado** | *tornado* |
| **el trueno** | *thunder* |

## Durante el verano *(In the summer)*

| | |
|---|---|
| **las aguas termales** | *hot springs* |
| **la arena** | *sand* |
| **el balón de playa** | *beachball* |
| **bañarse en el mar** | *to swim in the sea* |
| **los binóculos** | *binoculars* |
| **bucear** | *to scuba dive* |
| **la caña de pescar** | *fishing rod* |
| **la catarata** | *waterfall* |
| **coleccionar caracoles** | *to collect seashells* |
| **la costa** | *coast* |
| **la crema protectora** | *sunblock* |
| **el desierto** | *desert* |
| **el ecoturismo** | *ecotourism* |
| **explorar cuevas** | *to explore caves, to go spelunking* |
| **explorar la selva** | *to explore the jungle* |
| **la fogata** | *campfire* |
| **las gafas de sol** | *sunglasses* |
| **hacer camping** | *to go camping* |
| **hacer senderismo** | *to go hiking* |
| **hacer un tour** | *to take a guided tour* |
| **hacer windsurf** | *to windsurf* |
| **la isla tropical** | *tropical island* |
| **el lago** | *lake* |
| **la linterna** | *lantern, flashlight* |
| **el mar** | *sea* |
| **la marea (baja/alta)** | *(low/high) tide* |
| **observar la naturaleza** | *to observe nature* |
| **la orilla del lago/ del río** | *lakeshore/riverbank* |

| | |
|---|---|
| **las olas** | *waves* |
| **remar** | *to row* |
| **la tienda de campaña** | *tent* |
| **tirarse al agua** | *to dive in the water* |
| **el viento** | *wind* |
| **volar (ue) con ala delta** | *to go hang gliding* |

## De viaje *(Traveling)*

| | |
|---|---|
| **el albergue juvenil** | *youth hostel* |
| **los aseos** | *public restrooms* |
| **el billete** | *bill, money* |
| **la cabina telefónica** | *phone booth* |
| **el castillo** | *castle* |
| **los cheques de viajero** | *travelers' checks* |
| **comprar recuerdos** | *to buy souvenirs* |
| **el efectivo** | *cash* |
| **firmar** | *to sign* |
| **la guía turística** | *guide book* |
| **hacer una llamada por cobrar** | *to make a collect call* |
| **hacer una reservación** | *to make a reservation* |
| **hacerse amigo(a) de alguien** | *to make friends with someone* |
| **hospedarse en...** | *to stay at . . .* |
| **ir a cafés** | *to go to cafés* |
| **ir a un cibercafé** | *to go to a cybercafé* |
| **la oficina de turismo** | *tourism office* |

| | |
|---|---|
| **el parque nacional** | *national park* |
| **pedir (i, i) información** | *to ask for information* |
| **la pensión** | *boarding house, inn* |
| **el plano de la ciudad** | *city map* |
| **quedarse con parientes** | *to stay with relatives* |
| **el (la) recepcionista** | *receptionist* |
| **recomendarle (ie) (a alguien)** | *to recommend (to someone)* |
| **el rollo de película** | *roll of film* |
| **saltar en paracaídas** | *to go skydiving* |
| **sugerirle (ie, i) (a alguien)** | *to recommend (for someone)* |
| **la tarjeta de crédito** | *credit card* |
| **el (la) taxista** | *taxi driver* |
| **tomar un taxi** | *to take a taxi* |
| **el (la) turista** | *tourist* |
| **el volcán** | *volcano* |

# Vocabulario adicional

This list includes additional vocabulary that you may want to use to personalize activities. If you can't find the words you need here, try the Spanish–English and English–Spanish vocabulary sections beginning on page R47.

## Los viajes

| | |
|---|---|
| **a tiempo** | *on time* |
| **el (la) aduanero(a)** | *customs agent* |
| **el andén** | *(train) platform* |
| **el asiento** | *seat* |
| **atrasado(a)** | *delayed* |
| **la azafata** | *flight attendant* |
| **la demora** | *delay* |
| **el equipaje** | *luggage* |
| **el folleto** | *brochure, pamphlet* |
| **hacer una parada** | *to make a stop* |
| **el pasillo** | *aisle, hallway* |
| **el recuerdo** | *souvenir* |
| **revelar** | *to develop (film)* |
| **el rollo (de película)** | *roll (of film)* |
| **tardar una hora/ dos días en...** | *to take an hour/ two days to...* |
| **la tarjeta postal** | *postcard* |
| **el viaje de ida y vuelta** | *round-trip voyage* |
| **el visado** | *visa* |

## Los deportes

| | |
|---|---|
| **andar en patineta** | *to skateboard* |
| **el (la) árbitro** | *umpire, referee* |
| **el bate** | *bat* |
| **el (la) bateador(a)** | *batter* |
| **el billar** | *pool, billiards* |
| **el (la) boxeador(a)** | *boxer* |
| **boxear** | *to box* |
| **la cancha** | *court* |
| **la carrera de autos** | *auto racing* |
| **el casco** | *helmet* |
| **el cesto** | *basket* |
| **el deporte extremo** | *extreme sport* |
| **disparar el balón (al gol)** | *to shoot/kick the ball (at the goal)* |

| | |
|---|---|
| **el hoyo** | *(golf) hole* |
| **ir de cacería** | *to go hunting* |
| **ir en balsa en aguas blancas** | *to go whitewater rafting* |
| **el jonrón** | *home run* |
| **el kayac** | *kayak* |

| | |
|---|---|
| **lanzar/tirar** | *to throw* |
| **la liga** | *league* |
| **el (la) luchador(a)** | *wrestler* |
| **el maratón** | *marathon* |
| **el palo** | *golf club* |
| **la patineta** | *skateboard* |
| **la pelota** | *ball* |
| **la pista** | *track, rink* |
| **la plancha de nieve** | *snowboard* |
| **la plataforma, la tabla** | *diving board* |
| **el (la) portero(a)** | *goalie* |
| **la raqueta** | *racket* |
| **rebotar** | *to bounce* |
| **la red** | *net* |
| **el salto con cuerda elástica** | *bungee jumping* |
| **servir (i, i)/sacar la pelota** | *to serve the ball* |
| **el surf sobre nieve** | *snowboarding* |
| **la telesilla** | *chairlift* |
| **el uniforme** | *uniform* |
| **el yoga** | *yoga* |
| **zambullirse** | *to dive* |

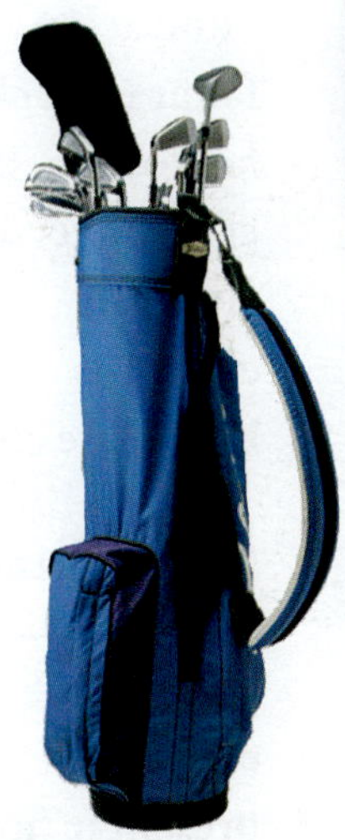

## Los estudios

| | |
|---|---|
| **la administración de empresas** | *business administration* |
| **la anatomía** | *anatomy* |
| **la antropología** | *anthropology* |
| **el árabe** | *Arabic* |
| **el chino** | *Chinese* |
| **la ciencia del hogar** | *home economics* |
| **dominar una materia** | *to master a subject* |
| **el examen de sorpresa** | *pop quiz* |
| **el examen de ubicación** | *placement test* |
| **faltar (una clase)** | *to miss (a class)* |
| **la filosofía** | *philosophy* |
| **el globo terráqueo** | *globe* |
| **el griego** | *Greek* |
| **el hebreo** | *Hebrew* |
| **la hora de entrada** | *(the time when) school begins* |
| **la hora de salida** | *(the time when) school ends* |
| **el japonés** | *Japanese* |
| **el latín** | *Latin* |
| **presentar (un examen)** | *to take (a test)* |
| **el (la) profesor(a) suplente** | *substitute teacher* |
| **el proyecto** | *project* |
| **el ruso** | *Russian* |
| **el taller** | *workshop* |
| **la tesis** | *thesis (paper)* |
| **tomar lista** | *to take attendance* |
| **la trigonometría** | *trigonometry* |

## La familia

| | |
|---|---|
| **la ahijada** | *goddaughter* |
| **el ahijado** | *godson* |
| **la bisabuela** | *great grandmother* |
| **el bisabuelo** | *great grandfather* |
| **la bisnieta** | *great granddaughter* |
| **el bisnieto** | *great grandson* |
| **la familia política** | *in-laws* |
| **la madrina** | *godmother* |
| **la tatarabuela** | *great-great grandmother* |
| **el tatarabuelo** | *great-great grandfather* |
| **la tataranieta** | *great-great granddaughter* |
| **el tataranieto** | *great-great grandson* |
| **la nuera** | *daughter-in-law* |
| **el padrino** | *godfather* |
| **el (la) primo(a) segundo(a)** | *second cousin* |
| **el yerno** | *son-in-law* |

## Las artes y la arquitectura

| | |
|---|---|
| **abstracto(a)** | *abstract* |
| **la arcilla** | *clay* |
| **el arco** | *arch* |
| **el atril** | *easel* |
| **el bosquejo** | *sketch* |
| **la cerámica** | *ceramics* |
| **el cianotipo** | *blueprint* |
| **el cincel** | *chisel* |
| **el enfoque** | *focus* |
| **garabatear** | *to scribble, doodle* |
| **gótico(a)** | *Gothic* |
| **impresionista** | *impressionist* |
| **el lienzo** | *canvas* |
| **el marco** | *frame* |
| **el mármol** | *marble* |
| **el martillo** | *hammer* |
| **montar (un cuadro)** | *to hang (a picture)* |
| **la naturaleza muerta** | *still life* |
| **la obra maestra** | *masterpiece* |
| **el óleo** | *oil (paint)* |
| **el paisaje** | *landscape* |
| **el pilar** | *pillar* |
| **el pincel** | *paint brush* |
| **raspar** | *to scrape* |
| **surrealista** | *surreal* |
| **tallar** | *to carve* |
| **el taller** | *workshop* |
| **el trasfondo** | *background* |
| **el yeso** | *plaster* |

## En las noticias

| | |
|---|---|
| **el boletín** | *bulletin* |
| **la bolsa (de valores)** | *stock market* |
| **la cadena** | *network* |
| **el canal** | *channel* |
| **el (la) comentarista** | *commentator* |
| **el (la) corresponsal** | *correspondent* |
| **el (la) crítico(a)** | *critic* |
| **el debate** | *debate* |
| **el déficit** | *deficit* |
| **los derechos civiles** | *civil rights* |
| **la difamación** | *libel* |
| **el discurso** | *speech* |
| **en directo/en vivo** | *live* |
| **el ejemplar** | *issue (of a newspaper/ magazine)* |
| **el escándalo** | *scandal* |
| **la huelga** | *(workers') strike* |
| **el partido político** | *political party* |
| **la polémica** | *controversy* |
| **el pronóstico (del clima)** | *(weather) forecast* |
| **las relaciones internacionales** | *international relations* |

## Empleos y carreras

| | |
|---|---|
| **el (la) agente de aduana** | *customs agent* |
| **el (la) agente de viajes** | *travel agent* |
| **el (la) agricultor(a)** | *farmer* |
| **el (la) albañil** | *mason, bricklayer* |
| **el ama de casa** | *homemaker* |
| **el (la) aprendiz** | *apprentice* |
| **el (la) camionero(a)** | *truck driver* |
| **el (la) chofer** | *driver* |
| **el (la) científico(a)** | *scientist* |

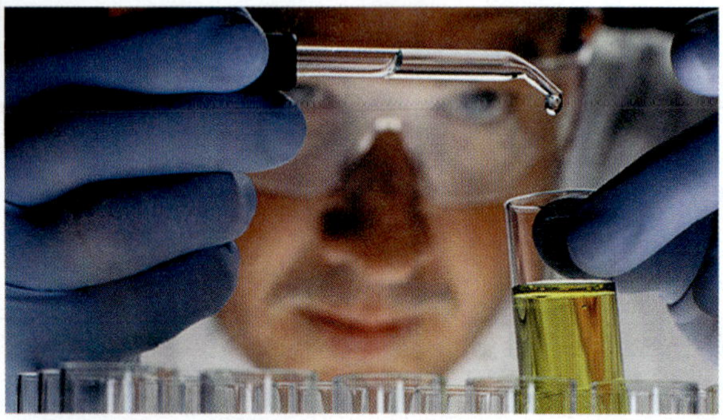

| | |
|---|---|
| **el (la) constructor(a)** | *construction worker, builder* |
| **el (la) contador(a)** | *accountant* |
| **el (la) corredor(a) de bolsa** | *stockbroker* |
| **la costurera** | *seamstress* |
| **el (la) dentista** | *dentist* |
| **el (la) economista** | *economist* |
| **el (la) electricista** | *electrician* |
| **el (la) físico** | *physicist* |
| **el (la) fisioterapeuta** | *physical therapist* |
| **el (la) intérprete** | *interpreter* |
| **el (la) investigador(a)** | *researcher* |
| **el (la) juez** | *judge* |
| **la modista** | *dressmaker, designer* |
| **el (la) piloto(a)** | *pilot* |
| **el (la) plomero(a)** | *plumber* |
| **el (la) político** | *politician* |
| **el (la) repostero(a)** | *baker* |
| **el sastre** | *tailor* |
| **el (la) senador(a)** | *senator* |
| **el (la) supervisor(a)** | *supervisor* |
| **el (la) técnico** | *technician* |
| **el (la) traductor(a)** | *translator* |
| **el (la) veterinario(a)** | *veterinarian* |

## La tecnología

| | |
|---|---|
| **el archivo** | *file* |
| **arrastrar y soltar (ue)** | *to drag and drop* |
| **los audífonos** | *headphones* |
| **bajar/subir archivos** | *to download/upload files* |
| **las bocinas** | *speakers* |
| **la búsqueda** | *search* |
| **el canal de chat** | *chat room* |
| **charlar** | *to chat* |
| **la computadora portátil** | *laptop computer* |
| **la conexión de banda ancha** | *broadband connection* |
| **la contraseña, el código** | *password* |
| **la copia de respaldo** | *backup* |
| **el correo de voz** | *voicemail* |
| **el cursor** | *cursor* |
| **el DVD** | *DVD* |
| **el diskette** | *floppy disk, diskette* |
| **el doble pulso** | *double click* |
| **las gráficas** | *graphics* |
| **la guía** | *prompt* |
| **el ícono** | *icon* |
| **la ingeniería genética** | *genetic engineering* |
| **la inteligencia artificial** | *artificial intelligence* |
| **el menú de cortina** | *pull-down menu* |
| **la página inicial** | *homepage* |
| **el procesamiento de textos** | *word processing* |

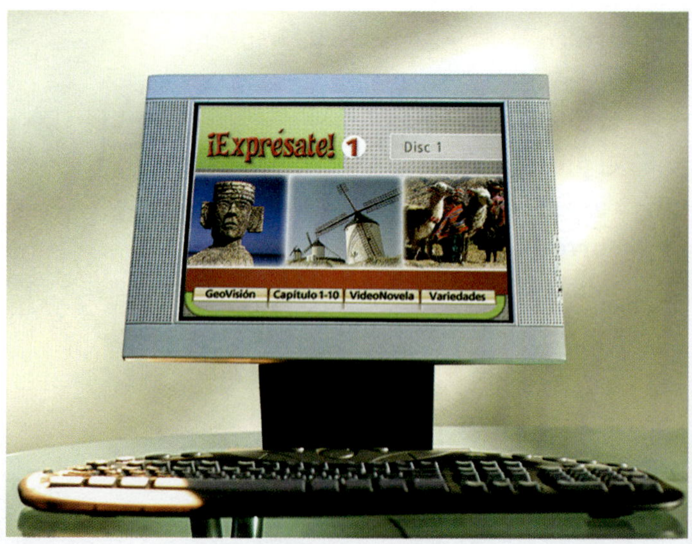

| | |
|---|---|
| **pulsar** | *to click* |
| **el puntero** | *pointer* |
| **el quemador (de CDs)** | *(CD) burner* |
| **el ratón** | *mouse* |
| **la realidad virtual** | *virtual reality* |
| **el reproductor de MP3** | *MP3 player* |
| **la robótica** | *robotics* |
| **subir archivos** | *to upload files* |
| **la tarjeta débito** | *debit card* |
| **la tecla de aceptación** | *return/enter key* |
| **la tecla de borrar** | *delete key* |
| **la tecla de mayúsculas** | *shift key* |
| **la ventana** | *window* |
| **el vínculo** | *link* |

## Eventos históricos

| | |
|---|---|
| **a.C.** | *antes de Cristo* |
| **el asesinato** | *assassination* |
| **la civilización** | *civilization* |
| **d.C.** | *después de Cristo* |
| **los derechos civiles** | *civil rights* |
| **el desarrollo** | *development* |
| **el dominio** | *rule, dominion* |
| **la Edad Media** | *Middle Ages* |
| **el ejército** | *army* |
| **En la época de...** | *In the time of...* |
| **la esclavitud** | *slavery* |
| **los esclavos** | *slaves* |
| **la exploración** | *exploration* |
| **la fuerza aérea** | *air force* |
| **las fuerzas armadas** | *armed forces* |
| **el golpe de estado** | *coup d'etat* |
| **el (la) historiador(a)** | *historian* |
| **la inauguración** | *inauguration* |
| **la invasión** | *invasion* |
| **la invención** | *invention (act of inventing)* |
| **la liberación femenina** | *women's liberation* |
| **la marina** | *navy* |
| **el milenio** | *millennium* |
| **el nacimiento** | *birth* |
| **el reino** | *kingdom* |
| **el siglo** | *century* |
| **el Siglo de las Luces** | *Age of Enlightenment* |

## El medio ambiente

| | |
|---|---|
| **la capa de ozono** | *ozone layer* |
| **los combustibles fósiles** | *fossil fuels* |
| **consumir** | *to consume* |
| **la deforestación** | *deforestation* |
| **deforestar** | *to deforest* |
| **el (la) ecólogo(a)** | *ecologist* |
| **el efecto invernadero** | *greenhouse effect* |
| **la erosión** | *erosion* |

| | |
|---|---|
| **extinto(a)** | *extinct* |
| **los fertilizantes orgánicos (químicos)** | *organic (chemical) fertilizers* |
| **industrializado(a)** | *industrialized* |
| **el insecticida** | *insecticide* |
| **malgastar los recursos naturales** | *to waste natural resources* |
| **minar** | *to mine* |
| **la superpoblación** | *overpopulation* |

Vocabulario adicional

# Expresiones de ¡Exprésate!

*Functions* are probably best defined as the ways in which you use a language for particular purposes. When you find yourself in specific situations, such as in a restaurant, in a grocery store, or at school, you will want to communicate with those around you. In order to do that, you have to "function" in Spanish: you place an order, make a purchase, or talk about your class schedule.

Here is a list of the functions presented in this book and the Spanish expressions you'll need to communicate in a wide range of situations. Following each function is the chapter and page number where it is introduced.

## Socializing

***Inviting someone to do something***
**Ch. 2, p. 54**

¿Te gustaría...? Yo te invito.
No, gracias. Iba a...
No vayamos... No aguanto...
Como quieras. Me da lo mismo.

***Turning down an invitation***
**Ch. 5, p. 206**

¿Quieres ir a ver...?
Gracias por invitarme, pero ya lo/la he visto.
¿Te interesa ir a...?
Lo siento, pero ya tengo otros planes/otro compromiso.
¿Me acompañas a...?
Gracias, pero tengo mucho que hacer. La próxima vez iré.
¿Por qué no vamos a...?
Hoy no, gracias. ¿Por qué no lo dejamos para la próxima semana?

## Exchanging Information

***Asking about someone's plans and talking about your own***
**Ch. 8, p. 338**

¿Qué te gustaría hacer?
Me gustaría ser un(a)...
Me interesaría estudiar para ser un(a)...
Siempre he querido ser un(a)...
Si tuvieras la oportunidad, ¿adónde irías?
Si pudiera, iría a... a estudiar...

***Setting the scene for a story***
**Ch. 9, p. 369**

Érase una vez, en un lugar muy lejano...
Hace muchos años...
Según nos dicen, el malvado...
Se cuenta que de pronto...

***Continuing and ending a story***
**Ch. 9, p. 372**

Hace tiempo, vino un desconocido...
Tan pronto como llegó...
A causa de esto...
Al final, nos dimos cuenta de...
A partir de entonces, vivieron siempre felices.

***Asking about a past event***
**Ch. 10, p. 411**

¿Te acuerdas (de) cuando sucedió...?
Lo recuerdo como si fuera ayer./No, no me acuerdo para nada.
¿Dónde estabas y qué estabas haciendo cuando...?
Estaba en casa cuando...

***Talking about the past***
**Ch. 1, p. 9**

¿Qué hiciste el verano pasado?
Viajé a España.
¿Qué tal lo pasaste?
Lo pasé de película/de maravilla.
¿Adónde fuiste?
Fui a las montañas.
¿Qué te pareció...?
Lo encontré muy interesante.

*Saying what you liked and used to do*
**Ch. 1, p. 12**
De niño(a), me gustaba…
Cuando era joven, solía…
De pequeño, me lo pasaba bomba…
Cuando tenía diez años, me encantaba…
Siempre disfrutaba de…
Lo encontraba genial…

*Talking about the future*
**Ch. 1, p. 26**
¿Qué vas a hacer…?
Voy a estudiar…
¿Adónde piensas ir…?
Pienso ir…
¿Cómo vas a mantenerte en forma?
Voy a practicar…
¿Qué cambios vas a hacer?
De hoy en adelante participaré en…

*Describing the ideal friend*
**Ch. 2, p. 65**
¿Cómo debe ser un(a) buen(a) amigo(a)?
Un buen amigo debe apoyarme y… No debe…
¿Qué buscas en un(a) novio(a)?
Busco a alguien a quien le guste(n)… y que sepa algo de…

*Getting the latest news*
**Ch. 4, p. 141**
¿Qué sabes de…?
Pues, sigue trabajando…
¿Qué me cuentas de…?
Según tengo entendido,…
¿Qué anda haciendo…?
Fíjate que se ha casado.

*Explaining and giving excuses*
**Ch. 4, p. 158**
Se me fue la mano con…
Es que se me olvidó ponerle…
Es que se me acabó…

*Introducing and changing a topic of conversation*
**Ch. 5, p. 192**
Eso me hace pensar en…
A propósito, ¿qué has oído del/de la…?
Cambiando de tema, ¿qué me dices de…?
Hablando de arte, ¿qué me cuentas de…?

*Asking about information and explaining where you found it*
**Ch. 6, p. 245**
¿Cómo supiste el resultado?
Lo leí en la sección deportiva.
¿Cómo te enteraste de…?
Estaba en primera plana.

*Talking about what you know and don't know*
**Ch. 6, p. 248**
Entiendo algo de…, pero nada de…
No tengo la menor idea si…
Que yo sepa, (no) hay…
¿Qué sé yo de…? No entiendo ni jota de…

*Talking about challenges*
**Ch. 7, p. 279**
Había muchos desafíos en…
Mis… enfrentaron obstáculos cuando…
Nos costó trabajo acostumbrarnos a…
Poco a poco se adaptaron a…
Tuvimos que hacer un gran esfuerzo para…

*Talking about accomplishments*
**Ch. 7, p. 282**
Con el tiempo pude asimilar…
Gracias al apoyo de… he podido superar…
Nos esforzamos en…
Por fin… logró…
Trabajo duro… y por eso…

*Talking about future plans*
**Ch. 7, p. 293**
Antes de que empiecen las clases, quiero…
Cuando sea mayor, me gustaría…
En cuanto cumpla los… años, voy a…
Tan pronto como… pienso…
Tengo la intención de…
Voy a… con la idea de…

*Expressing cause and effect*
**Ch. 7, p. 296**
Hablamos del tema; por consiguiente…
Mi éxito en… se debe a…
No estudié, así que…
Soy bilingüe; por lo tanto, tengo muchas oportunidades…

*Saying what you can and cannot do*
**Ch. 8, p. 321**
Está fuera de/a mi alcance.
Eso me resulta fácil/bastante difícil.
No me es nada difícil.
Soy capaz de (hacer)…
Lo puedo hacer.
Me cuesta trabajo (hacer)…

*Talking about what you do and do not understand*
**Ch. 8, p. 324**
Hay algo que se me escapa.
No logro entender…
No me cabe en la cabeza.
¡Vaya! Por fin capto la idea.
¡Ya caigo! Está más claro ahora.

*Writing a formal letter*
**Ch. 8, p. 335**
Muy estimado(a) Sr./Sra./Srta.:
Por medio de la presente…
Le/Les adjunto un(a)…
Reciba un cordial saludo,
Muy atentamente,

## Expressing Attitudes and Opinions

*Expressing interest and displeasure*
**Ch. 2, p. 51**
Soy un(a) gran aficionado(a) a… ¿Qué deporte te gusta a ti?
Pues, la verdad es que…
Eres muy bueno(a) para…, ¿verdad?
Sí, me la paso… Estoy loco(a) por…
Los/Las… me dejan frío(a).
¿Ah, sí? Pues, yo creo que son…

*Complaining*
**Ch. 3, p. 99**
Me choca la actitud de… hacia… ¡No aguanto más!
El (La) consejero(a) insiste en que tome… ¡No me gusta para nada!
¿Mañana vamos a tener otra prueba en…? ¡Esto es el colmo!

*Expressing an opinion and disagreeing*
**Ch. 3, p. 102**
A mi parecer, no hay igualdad entre…
¡Qué va! Eso no es cierto.
No me parece que sea justo.
¡Al contrario! No estoy de acuerdo.

*Commenting on food*
**Ch. 4, pp. 155, 158**
Está para chuparse los dedos.
Se me hace la boca agua.
Sabe delicioso(a).
Al (A la)… le falta sabor, pero no sé qué le falta.
Está pasada la leche.
¡Qué asco!
El/La… está salado(a)/picante.
El/La… no sabe a nada.
El/La… está seco(a)/no está muy dulce.

*Describing art and giving opinions*
**Ch. 5, p. 189**
Este retrato fue pintado por… ¿Qué te parece?
A decir verdad, me parece…
¿Cuál de estas pinturas te gusta más, la de… o la de…?
En realidad, admiro…
¿Qué opinas de…?
Lo/La encuentro muy…

*Expressing certainty*
**Ch. 6, p. 231**
Estoy convencido(a) de que…
Estoy seguro(a) (de) que…
Es evidente que…

*Expressing doubt and disbelief*
**Ch. 6, p. 234**
Dudo que estés bien informado(a) sobre…/que sepas…
No creo que los periodistas/los noticieros sean…
Parece mentira que haya…/que digan…
No estoy seguro(a) (de) que tengas razón sobre…

*Talking about your hopes and wishes*
**Ch. 9, p. 383**
Es de esperar que…
El sueño de mi vida es vencer a…
Ojalá que los países aún en guerra lleguen a un acuerdo.
Tenía muchas esperanzas de…

*Expressing and supporting a point of view*
**Ch. 10, p. 414**
Me parece que…
Creo que vale la pena acordarse de…
Ten en cuenta que…
Aunque estoy de acuerdo…, creo que…
Lo que noto es que…
A pesar de que hubo…, por otro lado…

*Making predictions and giving warnings*
**Ch. 10, p. 425**
A que no va a bajar la tasa de...
Calculo que van a implementar...
Ya verás que van a promover...
Es muy posible que el tráfico aumente con...
Te apuesto que...
Se advierte que...

*Expressing assumptions*
**Ch. 10, p. 428**
Es de suponer que...
Me imagino que para el año... habrá...
Supongo que sí.
A lo mejor habrá...

## Expressing Feelings and Emotions

*Expressing happiness and unhappiness*
**Ch. 2, p. 68**
¿Qué te pasa? ¿Estás dolido(a)?
Sí, estoy decepcionado(a) porque...
Me dan ganas de llorar.
Te veo de buen humor.
Sí, estoy entusiasmado(a) porque...

*Apologizing*
**Ch. 3, p. 116**
Te juro que no lo volveré a hacer.
Perdóname. No sé en qué estaba pensando.
Créeme que fue sin querer.
No lo hice a propósito.
No quise hacerte daño.
No quise ofenderte.

*Reacting to news*
**Ch. 4, p. 144**
¡Qué sorpresa que se hayan...!
Qué pena que se hayan...
¡No me lo puedo creer!
¡No me digas!
Me has dejado boquiabierto(a).

*Expressing regret and gratitude*
**Ch. 9, p. 386**
Se arrepiente de que...
Es lamentable que...
Les agradecieron a...

## Persuading

*Asking for and giving advice*
**Ch. 1, p. 23**
¿Qué consejos tienes?
Te aconsejo que...
¿Puedes darme algún consejo?
Hay que...
¿Qué debo hacer?
Debes...
¿Qué me recomiendas?
Te recomiendo que...

*Making suggestions*
**Ch. 3, p. 113**
No te olvides de...
¿Has pensado en...?
Sería una buena/mala idea romper con...
Sugiero que no hagas caso a los rumores.
No te conviene...
Date tiempo para pensarlo.

*Making suggestions and recommendations*
**Ch. 5, p. 203**
Te aconsejo que vayas a la presentación de baile folclórico. Es muy...
No te olvides de ir al ensayo de la banda.
Es mejor que veas la ópera. Es formidable.
Sería buena idea ir al concierto de la sinfónica.

# Síntesis gramatical



## NOUNS AND ARTICLES

### Gender of Nouns

In Spanish, nouns (words that name a person, place, or thing) are grouped into two classes or genders: masculine and feminine. All nouns, both persons and things, fall into one of these groups. Nouns that end in **-o, -aje, -al, -és, -ín,** and **-ma,** as well as compound nouns, are typically masculine, although some nouns ending in **-o** are feminine **(la mano).** Nouns that end in **-a, -ad, -ión, -z, -is, -ie,** and **-umbre** are typically feminine, although there are exceptions **(el mapa, el lápiz).** Nouns ending in **-l, -n,** and **-r** can be masculine or feminine, and many nouns referring to people **(el/la cliente, el/la artista, el/la modelo)** have one form that is used with both masculine and feminine articles. Some nouns have different meanings depending on the article used **(el/la orden, el/la radio).**

| Masculine Nouns | | Feminine Nouns | |
|---|---|---|---|
| libro | paisaje | mesa | libertad |
| corral | inglés | situación | actriz |
| botiquín | problema | crisis | serie |
| | | costumbre | |

**FORMATION OF PLURAL NOUNS**

| | Add **-s** to nouns that end in a vowel. | | Add **-es** to nouns that end in a consonant. | | With nouns that end in **-z,** the **-z** changes to a **-c.** | |
|---|---|---|---|---|---|---|
| **SINGULAR** | libro | casa | profesor | papel | vez | lápiz |
| **PLURAL** | libro**s** | casa**s** | profesor**es** | papel**es** | ve**ces** | lápi**ces** |

### Definite Articles

There are words that signal the gender of the noun. The *definite articles* are one such group. In English, there is one definite article: *the.* In Spanish, there are four: **el, la, los, las.**

**SUMMARY OF DEFINITE ARTICLES**

| | Masculine | Feminine |
|---|---|---|
| **SINGULAR** | **el** chico | **la** chica |
| **PLURAL** | **los** chicos | **las** chicas |

**CONTRACTIONS**

| | |
|---|---|
| a + el → | **al** |
| de + el → | **del** |

### Indefinite Articles

Another group of words used with nouns are the *indefinite articles:* **un, una,** (*a* or *an*) and **unos, unas** (*some* or *a few*).

| | Masculine | Feminine |
|---|---|---|
| **SINGULAR** | **un** chico | **una** chica |
| **PLURAL** | **unos** chicos | **unas** chicas |

## Pronouns

| Subject Pronouns | Direct Object Pronouns | Indirect Object Pronouns | Objects of Prepositions | Reflexive Pronouns |
|---|---|---|---|---|
| **yo** | **me** | **me** | **mí** | **me** |
| **tú** | **te** | **te** | **ti** | **te** |
| **usted, él, ella** | **lo, la** | **le** | **usted, él, ella** | **se** |
| **nosotros, nosotras** | **nos** | **nos** | **nosotros, nosotras** | **nos** |
| **vosotros, vosotras** | **os** | **os** | **vosotros, vosotras** | **os** |
| **ellos, ellas, ustedes** | **los, las** | **les** | **ellos, ellas, ustedes** | **se** |

### Double Object Pronouns

When used together, the indirect object pronoun always comes before the direct object pronoun: **¿Me la puedes traer?**

**Se** replaces **le** and **les** before the direct object pronouns **lo, la, los,** and **las.**

**Se lo di al director.**

### Demonstrative Pronouns

Demonstrative pronouns are used to say *this one, that one, these,* and *those.* They agree with the noun they stand for: **éste, éstos, ésta, éstas, ése, ésos, ésa, ésas, aquél, aquéllos, aquélla, aquéllas.**

### Reflexive Pronouns

Reflexive pronouns indicate that the subject both performs and receives the action of the verb: **Carlos se levantó temprano.**

Here are some verbs used with reflexive pronouns:

| | | | | |
|---|---|---|---|---|
| **acostarse** | **bañarse** | **despertarse** | **lavarse** | **peinarse** |
| **afeitarse** | **cepillarse** | **ducharse** | **levantarse** | **pintarse** |
| **arreglarse** | **darse prisa** | **estirarse** | **maquillarse** | **secarse** |

Some verbs take a reflexive pronoun but their action is not directed back on the subject. These include **criarse, expresarse, graduarse, preocuparse, casarse, comunicarse, acostumbrarse, esforzarse, mudarse, enojarse, quejarse, burlarse,** and **quedarse.**

The verbs **hacerse, volverse, ponerse, convertirse en, quedarse,** and **llegar a ser** can be used to imply a process *(to get, to become)* that results in a change in the subject's state or status.

**Voy a volverme loca con tanto trabajo.**

**Sergio se pone furioso cuando la gente no llega a tiempo.**

### The Pronoun *se*

A form of the pronoun **se** is used:

1. with verbs that are used reflexively or reciprocally (**Pepe se lava la cara. Ellos se saludan.**)
2. to indicate unintentional events (**Se me rompió el vaso.**)
3. to replace **le** or **les** when they appear together with the direct objects **lo, los, la,** or **las** (**Yo le doy los libros a Juan. Yo se los doy.**)
4. in impersonal sentences (**Se vive bien en esa ciudad.**)
5. to express the passive voice (**El edificio se construyó en 1857.**)
6. with certain "process" verbs (**Adela se graduó de la universidad.**)
7. with verbs that mean "to become" (**Julia se hizo doctora.**)

## Indefinite Pronouns

The indefinite pronoun **lo** can be used with an adjective to express the idea of the *(adjective) thing* or *that which is (adjective).*

**Tenemos que ver lo bueno de la situación.**

It can also be used with a verb to express the idea of *the thing that,* or *what.*

**Lo que más me preocupa es el examen de geografía.**

## Indefinite Expressions

Indefinite pronouns can be used in affirmative or negative expressions depending on whether an affirmative or negative adverb is used. You will often see **no** paired with a negative expression.

| Affirmative | Negative |
|---|---|
| **algo** | **nada** |
| **alguien** | **nadie** |
| **algún, alguna** | **ningún, ninguna** |
| **alguno(a), algunos(as)** | **ninguno(a), ningunos(as)** |
| **también** | **tampoco** |
| **siempre** | **nunca, jamás** |
| **o (o...o)** | **ni (ni...ni)** |

The words **o...o** and **ni...ni** mean *either...or* and *neither...nor,* respectively. The indefinite expressions **alguno(a), algunos(as), ninguno(a), ningunos(as)** must agree with the nouns they modify or represent. When a negative word precedes the verb, **no** is left out:

**No vino nadie.**

**Nadie vino.**

## Ordinal Numbers

Ordinal numbers are used to express ordered sequences. When used as adjectives, they agree in number and gender with the noun they modify. The ordinal numbers **primero** and **tercero** drop the final **o** before a singular, masculine noun. Ordinal numbers are seldom used after 10. Cardinal numbers are used instead: **Alfonso XIII, Alfonso Trece.**

| | | | | | | | | | |
|---|---|---|---|---|---|---|---|---|---|
| **1st** | **primero/a** | **3rd** | **tercero/a** | **5th** | **quinto/a** | **7th** | **séptimo/a** | **9th** | **noveno/a** |
| **2nd** | **segundo/a** | **4th** | **cuarto/a** | **6th** | **sexto/a** | **8th** | **octavo/a** | **10th** | **décimo/a** |

# ADJECTIVES

Adjectives are words that describe nouns. The adjective must agree in gender (masculine or feminine) and number (singular or plural) with the noun it modifies. Adjectives that end in **-e** or a consonant only agree in number.

| | | Masculine | Feminine |
|---|---|---|---|
| Adjectives that end in **-o** or **-a** | **SINGULAR** | el chico alt**o** | la chica alt**a** |
| | **PLURAL** | los chicos alt**os** | las chicas alt**as** |
| Adjectives that end in **-e** | **SINGULAR** | el chico inteligent**e** | la chica inteligent**e** |
| | **PLURAL** | los chicos inteligent**es** | las chicas inteligent**es** |
| Adjectives that end in a consonant | **SINGULAR** | el examen difícil | la clase difícil |
| | **PLURAL** | los exámenes difícil**es** | las clases difícil**es** |

## Demonstrative Adjectives

Demonstrative adjectives are used to point out things with their relationship to the speaker. They correspond to the English demonstrative adjectives *this, that, these,* and *those.*

| | Masculine | Feminine | | Masculine | Feminine |
|---|---|---|---|---|---|
| SINGULAR | **este** chico | **esta** chica | SINGULAR | **ese** chico | **esa** chica |
| PLURAL | **estos** chicos | **estas** chicas | PLURAL | **esos** chicos | **esas** chicas |

| | Masculine | Feminine |
|---|---|---|
| SINGULAR | **aquel** chico | **aquella** chica |
| PLURAL | **aquellos** chicos | **aquellas** chicas |

## Possessive Adjectives

These words also modify nouns and show ownership or relationship between people (*my* car, *his* book, *her* mother).

| Singular | | Plural | |
|---|---|---|---|
| Masculine | Feminine | Masculine | Feminine |
| **mi** libro | **mi** casa | **mis** libros | **mis** casas |
| **tu** libro | **tu** casa | **tus** libros | **tus** casas |
| **su** libro | **su** casa | **sus** libros | **sus** casas |
| **nuestro** libro | **nuestra** casa | **nuestros** libros | **nuestras** casas |
| **vuestro** libro | **vuestra** casa | **vuestros** libros | **vuestras** casas |

## Stressed Possessive Adjectives

Stressed possessive adjectives are used for emphasis and always follow the noun they modify: **Ellos son amigos míos.** Stressed possessive adjectives may be used as pronouns by using the definite article and the adjective and simply dropping the noun: **Tus zapatos son más caros que los míos.**

| Singular | | Plural | |
|---|---|---|---|
| Masculine | Feminine | Masculine | Feminine |
| **mío** | **mía** | **míos** | **mías** |
| **tuyo** | **tuya** | **tuyos** | **tuyas** |
| **suyo** | **suya** | **suyos** | **suyas** |
| **nuestro** | **nuestra** | **nuestros** | **nuestras** |
| **vuestro** | **vuestra** | **vuestros** | **vuestras** |
| **suyo** | **suya** | **suyos** | **suyas** |

## Comparisons

Comparisons are used to compare people or things. With comparisons of inequality, the same structure is used with adjectives, adverbs, or nouns. With comparisons of equality, **tan** is used with adjectives and adverbs, and **tanto/a/os/as** with nouns.

**COMPARISONS OF INEQUALITY**

| | | | |
|---|---|---|---|
| **más** / **menos** + | adjective / adverb / noun | + **que** | **más** / **menos** + **de** + number |

**COMPARISONS OF EQUALITY**

**tan** + adjective or adverb + **como**
**tanto/a/os/as** + noun + **como**

These adjectives have irregular comparative forms.

| | | | |
|---|---|---|---|
| bueno(a) *good* | malo(a) *bad* | joven *young* | viejo(a) *old* |
| **mejor(es)** *better* | **peor(es)** *worse* | **menor(es)** *younger* | **mayor(es)** *older* |

## Superlatives

To single something out as *the most* or *the least,* use **el/la/los/las** + (noun) + **más/menos** + adjective (+ **de**): **Es la película más divertida del año.**

The suffix **-ísimo** added to the stem of the adjective is a way to say *very* or *extremely* in Spanish: **grande: grandísimo, guapa: guapísima.**

## Interrogative Words

| | | | |
|---|---|---|---|
| **¿Adónde?** | **¿Cuándo?** | **¿De dónde?** | **¿Qué?** |
| **¿Cómo?** | **¿Cuánto?** | **¿Dónde?** | **¿Quién(es)?** |
| **¿Cuál(es)?** | **¿Cuánto(a)(s)?** | **¿Por qué?** | |

## Adverbs

Adverbs make the meaning of a verb, an adjective, or another adverb more definite. Adverbs do not show agreement.

| | | | |
|---|---|---|---|
| **siempre** | *always* | **a veces** | *sometimes* |
| **nunca** | *never* | **muy** | *very* |
| **todos los días** | *every day* | **mucho** | *a lot* |
| **casi nunca** | *almost never* | **poco** | *a little* |

Síntesis gramatical

Other adverbs can be formed by adding **-mente** to the feminine singular form of adjectives. This is the equivalent of adding *-ly* to an adjective in English.

| | |
|---|---|
| Adjectives ending with an **-o** change **o** to **a** and add **-mente:** | **claro: claramente** |
| Adjectives ending with an **-a,** an **-e,** or with a consonant, just add **-mente:** | **general: generalmente**<br>**horrible: horriblemente**<br>**feliz: felizmente** |

## Prepositions

Prepositions are words or groups of words that show the relationship of a noun or pronoun to another word. These are common prepositions in Spanish, many of which are used with adverbs.

| | | | | | |
|---|---|---|---|---|---|
| **a** | *to* | **desde** | *from* | **entre** | *between* |
| **al lado de** | *next to* | **después de** | *after* | **hacia** | *toward* |
| **antes de** | *before* | **detrás de** | *behind* | **hasta** | *until* |
| **con** | *with* | **en** | *in, on* | **para** | *for, in order to* |
| **de** | *of, from* | **encima de** | *over, on top of* | **por** | *for, by* |
| **debajo de** | *under* | **enfrente de** | *in front of, facing* | **sin** | *without* |
| **delante de** | *in front of* | | | | |

## *Por* vs. *Para*

Even though the English preposition *for* translates into Spanish as both **por** and **para,** they cannot be used interchangeably:

| PARA | POR |
|---|---|
| Expresses purpose:<br>**Estudio para aprender.** | Expresses *through* or *by:*<br>**Caminamos por el parque.** |
| Indicates a recipient:<br>**El regalo es para papá.** | Expresses mode of transportation:<br>**Carlos fue por autobús.** |
| Indicates destination:<br>**Salieron para Perú.** | Indicates a period of time:<br>**Estudié por tres horas.** |
| Indicates employment:<br>**Trabaja para el señor López.** | Expresses *in exchange for:*<br>**Pagué $20.000 por mi carro.** |
| Indicates a deadline:<br>**Completen la tarea para mañana.** | Expresses *per:*<br>**La gasolina cuesta $2,45 por galón.** |
| Indicates a person's opinion:<br>**Para mí, esa novela es excelente.** | Indicates the agent of an action:<br>**Fue construido por los romanos.** |

# COMMON EXPRESSIONS

## Expressions with *tener*

| | | | |
|---|---|---|---|
| **tener... años** | *to be . . . years old* | **tener (mucha) prisa** | *to be in a (big) hurry* |
| **tener (mucho) calor** | *to be (very) hot* | **tener que...** | *to have to . . .* |
| **tener ganas de...** | *to feel like . . .* | **tener (la) razón** | *to be right* |
| **tener (mucho) frío** | *to be (very) cold* | **tener (mucha) sed** | *to be (very) thirsty* |
| **tener (mucha) hambre** | *to be (very) hungry* | **tener (mucho) sueño** | *to be (very) sleepy* |
| **tener (mucho) miedo** | *to be (very) afraid* | **tener (mucha) suerte** | *to be (very) lucky* |

## Weather Expressions

| | |
|---|---|
| **Hace muy buen tiempo.** | *The weather is very nice.* |
| **Hace mucho calor.** | *It's very hot.* |
| **Hace fresco.** | *It's cool.* |
| **Hace mucho frío.** | *It's very cold.* |
| **Hace muy mal tiempo.** | *The weather is very bad.* |
| **Hace mucho sol.** | *It's very sunny.* |
| **Hace mucho viento.** | *It's very windy.* |
| But: | |
| **Está lloviendo mucho.** | *It's raining a lot.* |
| **Hay mucha neblina.** | *It's very foggy.* |
| **Está nevando.** | *It's snowing.* |
| **Está nublado.** | *It's overcast.* |

## Expressions of Time

To ask how long someone has been doing something, use:
**¿Cuánto tiempo hace que** + present tense?

To say how long someone has been doing something, use:
**Hace** + quantity of time + **que** + present tense.
Hace **seis meses** que **vivo en Los Ángeles.**
You can also use:
present tense + **desde hace** + quantity of time
**Vivo en Los Ángeles** desde hace **seis meses.**

# VERBS

Verbs are the basic elements of a sentence. They tell us about the subject, the speaker's perception of an event or situation, and when the event or situation took place. Much of this information is found in the verb ending. For example, **llegarás** tells us that the subject is *you* (singular, familiar), that the action is *to arrive*, and that the speaker is referring to an action that will take place in the future.

## Person, Number, Tense, and Mood

Spanish assigns an ending to each verb according to person, number, tense, and mood.

There are three PERSONS: first, second, and third. For each person, there are two NUMBERS: singular and plural.

| Singular | Plural |
|---|---|
| **yo**<br>**tú**<br>**usted, él, ella** | **nosotros/as**<br>**vosotros/as**<br>**ustedes, ellos, ellas** |

There are three basic TENSES:

| |
|---|
| past<br>present<br>future |

Moods express a speaker's attitude toward or perception of an event or situation. The speaker may report (indicative); request or express doubt, disbelief, or denial (subjunctive); or give an order (imperative). The three MOODS are called:

| |
|---|
| indicative<br>subjunctive<br>imperative |

There are other forms of the verbs that do not reflect the subject or the attitude of the speaker. One of the forms is the infinitive. Dictionaries list verbs as infinitives, which end in **-ar, -er**, or **-ir**. The other two forms, present and past participles, often appear in dictionaries as well.

| Infinitive | | Present Participle | | Past Participle | |
|---|---|---|---|---|---|
| **hablar** | *to speak* | **hablando** | *speaking* | **hablado** | *spoken* |
| **comer** | *to eat* | **comiendo** | *eating* | **comido** | *eaten* |
| **vivir** | *to live* | **viviendo** | *living* | **vivido** | *lived* |

# INDICATIVE MOOD

## Present Tense

The present tense is used for an action taking place in the present or in general.

### Regular Verbs

To conjugate a regular verb, drop the **-ar, -er,** or **-ir** ending and add the endings in the following chart.

| -ar | -er | -ir |
|---|---|---|
| habl**o** | com**o** | viv**o** |
| habl**as** | com**es** | viv**es** |
| habl**a** | com**e** | viv**e** |
| habl**amos** | com**emos** | viv**imos** |
| habl**áis** | com**éis** | viv**ís** |
| habl**an** | com**en** | viv**en** |

### Verbs with Irregular *yo* Forms

| hacer | | poner | | saber | | salir | | traer | |
|---|---|---|---|---|---|---|---|---|---|
| **hago** | hacemos | **pongo** | ponemos | **sé** | sabemos | **salgo** | salimos | **traigo** | traemos |
| haces | hacéis | pones | ponéis | sabes | sabéis | sales | salís | traes | traéis |
| hace | hacen | pone | ponen | sabe | saben | sale | salen | trae | traen |

| tener | | venir | | ver | | conocer | |
|---|---|---|---|---|---|---|---|
| **tengo** | tenemos | **vengo** | venimos | **veo** | vemos | **conozco** | conocemos |
| tienes | tenéis | vienes | venís | ves | veis | conoces | conocéis |
| tiene | tienen | viene | vienen | ve | ven | conoce | conocen |

## Progressive Tenses

If you want to show that an action is or was in progress, use the present or past progressive. To do this, use the present or the imperfect or preterite indicative of the auxiliary verb **estar** with the present participle of the main verb: **hablando, comiendo, viviendo.** The present or past progressive can also be formed with the auxiliary verbs **andar** and **seguir.**

**Estábamos comiendo cuando llegó Tomás.**

**¿Sigues estudiando en México?**

**Maribel anda buscando trabajo.**

## Present Perfect

If the action has been completed, but still affects the present, use the present perfect. Form the present perfect by using the auxiliary form **haber** (**he, has, ha, hemos, habéis, han**) with the past participle of the main verb: **hablado, comido, vivido.**

Some verbs have irregular past participles:

| | | | | | | | |
|---|---|---|---|---|---|---|---|
| abrir | **abierto** | freír | **frito** | poner | **puesto** | ver | **visto** |
| decir | **dicho** | hacer | **hecho** | revolver | **revuelto** | volver | **vuelto** |
| escribir | **escrito** | morir | **muerto** | romper | **roto** | | |

Pronouns are always placed before the form of **haber** in the present perfect.

**El entrenador nos ha puesto a correr todos los días.**

## Past Perfect

The past perfect is used to talk about something that happened before a past action. It is formed by using the imperfect of the auxiliary verb **haber** with the past participle of the main verb. The past perfect is frequently used with words such as **cuando, ya, aún no,** or **todavía no.**

Síntesis gramatical

## Imperfect

The imperfect is used for ongoing or habitual actions in the past. It also describes the way things were, what used to happen or was going on, and mental and physical states in the past including age, clock time, and the way people felt in general. Only the verbs **ir, ser,** and **ver** are irregular in the imperfect.

| -ar | -er | -ir |
|---|---|---|
| habl**aba** | com**ía** | viv**ía** |
| habl**abas** | com**ías** | viv**ías** |
| habl**aba** | com**ía** | viv**ía** |
| habl**ábamos** | com**íamos** | viv**íamos** |
| habl**abais** | com**íais** | viv**íais** |
| habl**aban** | com**ían** | viv**ían** |

| ir | ser | ver |
|---|---|---|
| **iba** | **era** | **veía** |
| **ibas** | **eras** | **veías** |
| **iba** | **era** | **veía** |
| **íbamos** | **éramos** | **veíamos** |
| **ibais** | **erais** | **veíais** |
| **iban** | **eran** | **veían** |

## Preterite

The preterite is used to show that events began or were completed in the past and to view past actions as a completed whole. It also describes how a person reacted to a particular event.

| -ar | -er | -ir |
|---|---|---|
| habl**é** | com**í** | viv**í** |
| habl**aste** | com**iste** | viv**iste** |
| habl**ó** | com**ió** | viv**ió** |
| habl**amos** | com**imos** | viv**imos** |
| habl**asteis** | com**isteis** | viv**isteis** |
| habl**aron** | com**ieron** | viv**ieron** |

The preterite also gives special meaning to certain verbs:

| Verb | Preterite | Imperfect |
|---|---|---|
| **conocer** | *met*<br>*saw for the first time* | *knew (had familiarity with or knowledge of)* |
| **estar** | *was, were (for a specified period of time)* | *was, were (for an unspecified period of time)* |
| **poder** | *could (and did)* | *could (and may or may not have done)* |
| **no poder** | *couldn't (and didn't)* | *couldn't (was having trouble and may or may not have done)* |
| **querer** | *wanted (for the first time or for a specific length of time)*<br>*tried (sought to, meant to)* | *already wanted (when something else happened)* |
| **no querer** | *refused, wouldn't* | *already didn't want (when something else happened)* |
| **saber** | *knew (for the first time)*<br>*found out*<br>*first realized* | *already knew (when something else happened)* |
| **no saber** | *didn't find out (until something happened)* | *was already unaware (when something else happened)*<br>*didn't know (as a reaction to something)* |
| **ser** | *was (sums up a situation or event)* | *was (for an unspecified period of time)* |
| **tener** | *had or got (for the first time)* | *already had (when something else happened)* |
| **tener que** | *had to (and did)*<br>*had to (as a reaction to something)* | *had to (on a regular basis), already had to (when something else happened)* |

The following verbs are irregular in the preterite:

| | | |
|---|---|---|
| andar | **anduv-** | |
| estar | **estuv-** | |
| poder | **pud-** | |
| poner | **pus-** | **-e, -iste, -o** |
| querer | **quis-** | **-imos, -isteis** |
| saber | **sup-** | **-ieron** |
| tener | **tuv-** | |
| venir | **vin-** | |

| | | |
|---|---|---|
| decir | **dij-** | **-e, -iste, -o** |
| traer | **traj-** | **-imos, -isteis** |
| | | **-eron** |

**Dar, hacer, ser,** and **ir** are also irregular in the preterite.

| dar | hacer | ser/ir |
|---|---|---|
| **di** | **hice** | **fui** |
| **diste** | **hiciste** | **fuiste** |
| **dio** | **hizo** | **fue** |
| **dimos** | **hicimos** | **fuimos** |
| **disteis** | **hicisteis** | **fuisteis** |
| **dieron** | **hicieron** | **fueron** |

## Future

The future tense is used to describe what will take place. It can also be used to indicate probability about what's going on in the present. It is formed by adding the following endings to the future stem of the verb. The infinitive serves as the future stem for most verbs.

| REGULAR | | |
|---|---|---|
| **-ar** | **-er** | **-ir** |
| hablar**é** | comer**é** | vivir**é** |
| hablar**ás** | comer**ás** | vivir**ás** |
| hablar**á** | comer**á** | vivir**á** |
| hablar**emos** | comer**emos** | vivir**emos** |
| hablar**éis** | comer**éis** | vivir**éis** |
| hablar**án** | comer**án** | vivir**án** |

Some verbs have irregular stems in the future tense:

| | | | |
|---|---|---|---|
| haber | **habr-** | tener | **tendr-** |
| poder | **podr-** | valer | **valdr-** |
| querer | **querr-** | venir | **vendr-** |
| poner | **pondr-** | decir | **dir-** |
| salir | **saldr-** | hacer | **har-** |

Future actions can also be expressed with **ir a** + infinitive: **Voy a hablar con mi jefa.** You can also use **ir a** + infinitive in the **imperfect** to say what someone was going to do: **Yo iba a salir pero estaba cansada.**

## Conditional

The conditional is used to describe what *would happen* or what someone *would do* under certain circumstances. It is also used in expressions that tell what you *would like* or *not like,* and can be used to show probability about the past. It is formed by adding the following endings to the future stem of the verb. The infinitive serves as the future stem for most verbs.

| REGULAR | | |
|---|---|---|
| **-ar** | **-er** | **-ir** |
| hablar**ía** | comer**ía** | vivir**ía** |
| hablar**ías** | comer**ías** | vivir**ías** |
| hablar**ía** | comer**ía** | vivir**ía** |
| hablar**íamos** | comer**íamos** | vivir**íamos** |
| hablar**íais** | comer**íais** | vivir**íais** |
| hablar**ían** | comer**ían** | vivir**ían** |

The same verbs have irregular stems in the conditional as in the future tense.

# SUBJUNCTIVE MOOD

## Uses of the Subjunctive

The subjunctive is used in some sentences that have a main clause and a subordinate clause. The main clause has a subject and a verb and can stand on its own as a complete thought, while the subordinate clause cannot stand on its own and depends upon the main clause to give it meaning. The subjunctive is used in the following cases when there is a change in subject between the main and subordinate clauses:

1. when the main clause expresses hope, will, or wish

    **Yo quiero que Elena cante en el coro.**

2. when the person or thing being referred to is unknown or nonexistent

    **Busco un profesor que sepa inglés.**

3. with expressions that convey feelings or emotions such as **me alegra que, temo que, es triste que.**

    **Es triste que Paula esté enferma.**

4. when the main clause expresses uncertainty, negation, or denial

    **No es cierto que Roberto sea el hombre ideal.**

5. when the main clause expresses a suggestion or recommendation

    **Dámaso recomienda que practiquemos todos los días.**

6. when the main clause expresses doubt or disbelief

    **No creo que llueva hoy.**

The subjunctive is also used after the adverbial conjunctions **a menos (de) que, antes de que, con tal (de) que, en caso de que, para que,** and **sin que.** It is used after the adverbial conjunctions **en cuanto, hasta que, cuando, tan pronto como,** and **después de que** only when the sentence refers to an action that has not happened yet. When the sentence refers to habitual actions or actions in the past, use the indicative.

**En cuanto llego a casa siempre hago la tarea.**

**Juanito, en cuanto llegues a casa, haz tu tarea.**

**Tan pronto como llegaron a la playa empezó a llover.**

**Tan pronto como lleguen a la playa, llámenme.**

A fixed expression that always takes the subjunctive is **Ojalá que.**

When there is no change in subject between the main and subordinate clauses, omit **que** and use the infinitive.

**Yo quiero cantar en el coro.**

When the main clause expresses certainty or something that the speaker believes to be true, use the indicative.

**Me parece que Ángela tiene mucho trabajo.**

## Present Subjunctive

When the verb in the main clause of a sentence that requires the subjunctive is in the present or future, the present subjunctive is used in the subordinate clause. It is formed by adding the following endings to the first person singular form of the verb after removing **-o.**

| -ar | -er | -ir |
|---|---|---|
| habl**e** | com**a** | viv**a** |
| habl**es** | com**as** | viv**as** |
| habl**e** | com**a** | viv**a** |
| habl**emos** | com**amos** | viv**amos** |
| habl**éis** | com**áis** | viv**áis** |
| habl**en** | com**an** | viv**an** |

The following verbs are irregular in the subjunctive:

**dar: dé, des, dé, demos, deis, den**
**estar: esté, estés, esté, estemos, estéis, estén**
**haber: haya, hayas, haya, hayamos, hayáis, hayan**
**ir: vaya, vayas, vaya, vayamos, vayáis, vayan**
**saber: sepa, sepas, sepa, sepamos, sepáis, sepan**
**ser: sea, seas, sea, seamos, seáis, sean**

## Present Perfect Subjunctive

Use the present perfect subjunctive to express an emotion, judgment, doubt, or hope about something that has happened. It is formed with the subjunctive of **haber (haya, hayas, haya, hayamos, hayáis, hayan)** and the past participle of the main verb.

**Dudo que el avión haya llegado.**

**Es interesante que no hayan dicho nada.**

## Past Subjunctive

When the verb in the main clause of a sentence that requires the subjunctive is in the past or conditional, the past subjunctive is used in the subordinate clause. It is formed by adding the following endings to the third person plural preterite form of the verb after removing **-on.**

| -ar | -er | -ir |
|---|---|---|
| hablar**a** | comier**a** | vivier**a** |
| hablar**as** | comier**as** | vivier**as** |
| hablar**a** | comier**a** | vivier**a** |
| hablár**amos** | comiér**amos** | viviér**amos** |
| hablar**ais** | comier**ais** | vivier**ais** |
| hablar**an** | comier**an** | vivier**an** |

## IMPERATIVE MOOD

The imperative is used to get people to do things. Its forms are also called *commands.*

| | -ar | | -er | | -ir | |
|---|---|---|---|---|---|---|
| tú | habl**a** | no habl**es** | com**e** | no com**as** | viv**e** | no viv**as** |
| Ud. | habl**e** | no habl**e** | com**a** | no com**a** | viv**a** | no viv**a** |
| nosotros | habl**emos** | no habl**emos** | com**amos** | no com**amos** | viv**amos** | no viv**amos** |
| vosotros | habl**ad** | no habl**éis** | com**ed** | no com**áis** | viv**id** | no viv**áis** |
| Uds. | habl**en** | no habl**en** | com**an** | no com**an** | viv**an** | no viv**an** |

Several verbs have irregular **tú** imperative forms:

| | | |
|---|---|---|
| decir | **di** | **no digas** |
| hacer | **haz** | **no hagas** |
| ir | **ve** | **no vayas** |

| | | |
|---|---|---|
| poner | **pon** | **no pongas** |
| salir | **sal** | **no salgas** |
| ser | **sé** | **no seas** |

| | | |
|---|---|---|
| tener | **ten** | **no tengas** |
| venir | **ven** | **no vengas** |
| dar | **dé** | **no des** |

Negative **tú** and **vosotros(as)** commands are formed with the present subjunctive:

**No compres ese carro.** **No salgáis sin abrigo.**

Regular **nosotros** commands are also formed with the present subjunctive.

The verb **ir** has an irregular affirmative **nosotros** imperative form (**vamos**) and a regular negative form (**vayamos**).

**Vamos a la playa.** **No vayamos al cine.**

Another way to get a group of people to do something is to use **vamos a** + infinitive:

**¡Vamos a jugar!**

Pronouns are always connected to affirmative commands. When attaching pronouns to an affirmative command, regular rules of accentuation may call for written accents over the stressed syllable. Pronouns always come right before the verb in negative commands.

**¡Tráemelo!** **No me lo traigas.**

# MORE ABOUT VERBS

## Stem-changing Verbs

Stem-changing verbs have a spelling change in the stem's stressed syllable.

### THE -AR AND -ER STEM-CHANGING VERBS

Some verbs ending in **-ar** and **-er** change from **e** to **ie, u** to **ue,** and **o** to **ue.** These changes occur in all persons except the **nosotros** and **vosotros** forms.

| Infinitive | Present Indicative | Imperative | Present Subjunctive |
|---|---|---|---|
| **querer (ie)** *(to want)* | quiero<br>quieres<br>quiere<br>queremos<br>queréis<br>quieren | quiere (no quieras)<br>quiera (no quiera)<br>queramos (no queramos)<br>quered (no queráis)<br>quieran (no quieran) | quiera<br>quieras<br>quiera<br>queramos<br>queráis<br>quieran |
| **pensar (ie)** *(to think)* | pienso<br>piensas<br>piensa<br>pensamos<br>pensáis<br>piensan | piensa (no pienses)<br>piense (no piense)<br>pensemos (no pensemos)<br>pensad (no penséis)<br>piensen (no piensen) | piense<br>pienses<br>piense<br>pensemos<br>penséis<br>piensen |
| **probar (ue)** *(to try)* | pruebo<br>pruebas<br>prueba<br>probamos<br>probáis<br>prueban | prueba (no pruebes)<br>pruebe (no pruebe)<br>probemos (no probemos)<br>probad (no probéis)<br>prueben (no prueben) | pruebe<br>pruebes<br>pruebe<br>probemos<br>probéis<br>prueben |
| **volver (ue)** *(to return)* | vuelvo<br>vuelves<br>vuelve<br>volvemos<br>volvéis<br>vuelven | vuelve (no vuelvas)<br>vuelva (no vuelva)<br>volvamos (no volvamos)<br>volved (no volváis)<br>vuelvan (no vuelvan) | vuelva<br>vuelvas<br>vuelva<br>volvamos<br>volváis<br>vuelvan |

Verbs that follow the same pattern:

| | | | | |
|---|---|---|---|---|
| **acordar(se)** | **comenzar** | **doler** | **jugar** | **poder** |
| **acostarse** | **costar** | **empezar** | **llover** | **querer** |
| **almorzar** | **despertarse** | **encontrar** | **merendar** | **sentar** |

### THE -IR STEM-CHANGING VERBS

Stem-changing verbs ending in **-ir** may change from **e** to **ie,** from **e** to **i,** or from **o** to **ue** or **u.**

Such verbs also undergo a stem change in the preterite for the third persons singular and plural. The same stem change occurs in the **-ndo** form. For example: **pedir** → **pidió, pidieron, pidiendo; dormir** → **durmió, durmieron, durmiendo.**

Síntesis gramatical

| Infinitive | Indicative | | Imperative | Subjunctive | |
|---|---|---|---|---|---|
| | Present | Preterite | | Present | Past |
| **sentir (ie)(i)**<br>*(to feel)*<br><br>**-ndo** FORM<br>sintiendo | siento<br>sientes<br>siente<br>sentimos<br>sentís<br>sienten | sentí<br>sentiste<br>sintió<br>sentimos<br>sentisteis<br>sintieron | <br>siente (no sientas)<br>sienta (no sienta)<br>sintamos (no sintamos)<br>sentid (no sintáis)<br>sientan (no sientan) | sienta<br>sientas<br>sienta<br>sintamos<br>sintáis<br>sientan | sintiera<br>sintieras<br>sintiera<br>sintiéramos<br>sintierais<br>sintieran |
| **dormir (ue)(u)**<br>*(to sleep)*<br><br>**-ndo** FORM<br>durmiendo | duermo<br>duermes<br>duerme<br>dormimos<br>dormís<br>duermen | dormí<br>dormiste<br>durmió<br>dormimos<br>dormisteis<br>durmieron | <br>duerme (no duermas)<br>duerma (no duerma)<br>durmamos (no durmamos)<br>dormid (no durmáis)<br>duerman (no duerman) | duerma<br>duermas<br>duerma<br>durmamos<br>durmáis<br>duerman | durmiera<br>durmieras<br>durmiera<br>durmiéramos<br>durmierais<br>durmieran |

Other verbs that follow this pattern are **mentir, morir,** and **preferir.**

The verbs below are irregular in the same tenses as those above. The only difference is that they only have one change: **e** → **i.**

| Infinitive | Indicative | | Imperative | Subjunctive | |
|---|---|---|---|---|---|
| | Present | Preterite | | Present | Past |
| **pedir (i)**<br>*(to ask for, request)*<br><br>**-ndo** FORM<br>pidiendo | pido<br>pides<br>pide<br>pedimos<br>pedís<br>piden | pedí<br>pediste<br>pidió<br>pedimos<br>pedisteis<br>pidieron | <br>pide (no pidas)<br>pida (no pida)<br>pidamos (no pidamos)<br>pedid (no pidáis)<br>pidan (no pidan) | pida<br>pidas<br>pida<br>pidamos<br>pidáis<br>pidan | pidiera<br>pidieras<br>pidiera<br>pidiéramos<br>pidierais<br>pidieran |

Other verbs that follow this pattern are **seguir, servir, vestirse, repetir,** and **reír.**

## Gustar and Verbs Like It

**Gustar, encantar, fascinar, fastidiar, interesar, faltar,** and **tocar** are used to talk about things you like, love, dislike, are interested in, lack, or must do. The verb endings for **gustar** and verbs like it always agree with what is liked or disliked. The indirect object pronouns always precede the verb forms.

| If one thing is liked: | If more than one thing is liked: |
|---|---|
| **me**<br>**te**<br>**le**<br>**nos**<br>**os**<br>**les** } **gusta** | **me**<br>**te**<br>**le**<br>**nos**<br>**os**<br>**les** } **gustan** |

## *Saber* and *Conocer*

For the English verb *to know*, there are two verbs in Spanish, **saber** and **conocer.** See page R34 for how they are used in the preterite.

**Saber** means *to know* something or *to know how to* do something.
**¿Sabes que mañana no hay clase?** *Do you know that there is no school tomorrow?*
**¿Sabes chino?** *Do you know Chinese?*
**¿Sabes patinar?** *Do you know how to skate?*

**Conocer** means *to be acquainted with* somebody or something:
**¿Conoces a Alicia?** *Do you know Alicia?*
**¿Conoces Madrid?** *Do you know Madrid?*
**Conocer** is followed by the personal **a** when it takes a person as an object.

## The Verbs *Ser* and *Estar*

Both **ser** and **estar** mean *to be*, but they differ in their uses.

Use **ser:**

1. with nouns to identify and define the subject
   **La mejor estudiante de la clase es Katia.**
2. with **de** to indicate place of origin, ownership, or material
   **Carmen es de Venezuela.**
   **Este libro es de mi abuela.**
   **La blusa es de algodón.**
3. to describe identifying characteristics, such as physical and personality traits, nationality, religion, and profession
   **Mi tío es profesor. Es simpático e inteligente.**
4. to express the time, date, season, or where an event is taking place
   **Hoy es sábado y la fiesta es a las ocho en casa de Ana.**

Use **estar:**

1. to indicate location or position of the subject (except for events)
   **Lima está en Perú.**
2. to describe a condition that is subject to change
   **Maricarmen está triste.**
3. with the present participle (**-ndo** form) to describe an action in progress
   **Mario está escribiendo un poema.**
4. to convey the idea of *to look, to feel, to seem, to taste*
   **Tu hermano está muy guapo hoy.**
   **La sopa está deliciosa.**

## Passive

The passive voice is used to say that something *is done* or *has been done* to someone or something. There are two ways to express the passive voice in Spanish. The first way you can form it is with the pronoun **se** plus a verb in the third person singular or plural. The recipient of the action must agree in number with the verb.

**Se escribió la ópera en 1778.**

*The opera was written in 1778.*

**Se construyeron las torres en el siglo pasado.**

*The towers were built in the last century.*

You can also form the passive voice with **ser** plus the past participle. Both **ser** and the participle must agree in gender and number with the recipient of the action.

**La ópera fue escrita en 1778.**

**Las torres fueron construidas en el siglo pasado.**

## Haber

The verb **haber** is used in an impersonal form to mean *there is* or *there are.* It is always in the third person singular no matter how many items it refers to. The impersonal forms of **haber** are used in the present **(hay),** preterite **(hubo),** imperfect **(había),** and present subjunctive **(haya).**

## Verbs with Spelling Changes

Some verbs have a spelling change in some tenses in order to maintain the sound of the final consonant of the stem. The most common ones are those with stems ending in the consonants **g** and **c.** Remember that **g** and **c** have a soft sound in front of **e** or **i**, but a hard sound in front of **a, o,** or **u.** In order to maintain the soft sound in front of **a, o,** or **u,** the letters **g** and **c** change to **j** and **z,** respectively. In order to maintain the hard sound of **g** or **c** in front of **e** and **i, u** is added to the **g** (**gu**) and the **c** changes to **qu.**

1. Verbs ending in -**gar** change from **g** to **gu** before **e** in the first person of the preterite, in all persons of the present subjunctive, and in some persons of the imperative. Some verbs that follow the same pattern are **llegar** and **jugar.**

   **pagar** *to pay*
   Preterite: pag**ué**, pagaste, pagó, etc.
   Pres. Subj.: pa**gue**, pa**gue**s, pa**gue**, pa**gue**mos, pa**gué**is, pa**gue**n
   Imperative: paga (no pa**gue**s), pa**gue**, pa**gue**mos, pagad (no pa**gué**is), pa**gue**n

2. Verbs ending in -**ger** change from **g** to **j** before **o** and **a** in the first person of the present indicative, in all the persons of the present subjunctive, and in some persons of the imperative. Some verbs that follow the same pattern are **recoger** and **escoger.**

   **proteger** *to protect*
   Pres. Ind.: prote**jo**, proteges, protege, etc.
   Pres. Subj.: prote**ja**, prote**ja**s, prote**ja**, prote**ja**mos, prote**já**is, prote**ja**n
   Imperative: protege (no prote**ja**s), prote**ja**, prote**ja**mos, proteged (no prote**já**is), prote**ja**n

3. Verbs ending in -**guir** change from **gu** to **g** before **o** and **a** in the first person of the present indicative, in all persons of the present subjunctive, and in some persons of the imperative.

   **seguir** *to follow*
   Pres. Ind.: si**go**, sigues, sigue, etc.
   Pres. Subj.: si**ga**, si**ga**s, si**ga**, si**ga**mos, si**gá**is, si**ga**n
   Imperative: sigue (no si**ga**s), si**ga**, si**ga**mos, seguid (no si**gá**is), si**ga**n

4. Verbs ending in -**car** change from **c** to **qu** before **e** in the first person of the preterite, in all persons of the present subjunctive, and in some persons in the imperative. Some verbs that follow the same pattern are **buscar, practicar, sacar,** and **tocar.**

   **explicar** *to explain*
   Preterite: expli**qu**é, explicaste, explicó, etc.
   Pres. Subj.: expli**qu**e, expli**qu**es, expli**qu**e, expli**qu**emos, expli**qu**éis, expli**qu**en
   Imperative: explica (no expli**qu**es), expli**qu**e, expli**qu**emos, explicad (no expli**qu**éis), expli**qu**en

5. Verbs that end in -**cer** or -**cir** and are preceded by a consonant change from **c** to **zc** before **o** and **a.** This change occurs in the first person of the present indicative and in all persons of the present subjunctive. Some verbs that follow the same pattern are **parecer, pertenecer,** and **producir.**

   **conocer** *to know, to be acquainted with*
   Pres. Ind.: cono**zc**o, conoces, conoce, etc.
   Pres. Subj.: cono**zc**a, cono**zc**as, cono**zc**a, cono**zc**amos, cono**zc**áis, cono**zc**an

6. Verbs ending in -**zar** change from **z** to **c** before **e** in the first person of the preterite and in all persons of the present subjunctive. Some verbs that follow the same pattern are **almorzar** and **empezar.**

   **comenzar** *to start*
   Preterite: comen**c**é, comenzaste, comenzó, etc.
   Pres. Subj.: comien**c**e, comien**c**es, comien**c**e, comen**c**emos, comen**c**éis, comien**c**en

7. Verbs ending in -**aer** or -**eer** change from the unstressed **i** to **y** between vowels in the preterite third persons singular and plural, in all persons of the past subjunctive, and in the -**ndo** form. Note the accent marks over **i** in the **tú, nosotros,** and **vosotros** forms in the preterite. Some verbs that follow the same pattern are **leer** and **caer.**

   **creer** *to believe*
   Preterite: creí, creíste, cre**y**ó, creímos, creísteis, cre**y**eron
   Past Subj.: cre**y**era, cre**y**eras, cre**y**era, cre**y**éramos, cre**y**erais, cre**y**eran
   -**ndo** form: cre**y**endo
   Past Part.: creído

8. Verbs ending in -**uir** (except -**guir** and -**quir**) change from the unstressed **i** to **y** between vowels.

   **construir** *to build*
   Pres. Part.: constru**y**endo
   Pres. Ind.: constru**y**o, constru**y**es, constru**y**e, construimos, construís, constru**y**en
   Preterite: construí, construiste, constru**y**ó, construimos, construisteis, constru**y**eron
   Pres. Subj.: constru**y**a, constru**y**as, constru**y**a, constru**y**amos, constru**y**ais, constru**y**an
   Past. Subj.: constru**y**era, constru**y**eras, constru**y**era, constru**y**éramos, constru**y**erais, constru**y**eran
   Imperative: constru**y**e (no constru**y**as), constru**y**a, constru**y**amos, construid (no constru**y**áis), constru**y**an

## Irregular Verbs

These verbs have irregular forms in some tenses.

**abrir** *to open*
Past. Part.: abierto

**dar** *to give*
Pres. Ind.: doy, das, da, damos, dais, dan
Preterite: di, diste, dio, dimos, disteis, dieron

Imperative: da (no des), dé, demos, dad (no deis), den
Pres. Subj.: dé, des, dé, demos, deis, den
Past Subj.: diera, dieras, diera, diéramos, dierais, dieran

**decir** *to say, to tell*
Pres. Ind.: digo, dices, dice, decimos, decís, dicen
Preterite: dije, dijiste, dijo, dijimos, dijisteis, dijeron
Future: diré, dirás, dirá, diremos, diréis, dirán
Conditional: diría, dirías, diría, diríamos, diríais, dirían
Imperative: di (no digas), diga, digamos, decid (no digáis), digan
Pres. Subj.: diga, digas, diga, digamos, digáis, digan
Past Subj.: dijera, dijeras, dijera, dijéramos, dijerais, dijeran
Past Part.: dicho
-**ndo** Form: diciendo

**escribir** *to write*
Past Part.: escrito

**estar** *to be*
Pres. Ind.: estoy, estás, está, estamos, estáis, están
Preterite: estuve, estuviste, estuvo, estuvimos, estuvisteis, estuvieron
Imperative: está (no estés), esté, estemos, estad (no estéis), estén
Pres. Subj.: esté, estés, esté, estemos, estéis, estén
Past Subj.: estuviera, estuvieras, estuviera, estuviéramos, estuvierais, estuvieran

**haber** *to have*
Pres. Ind.: he, has, ha, hemos, habéis, han
Preterite: hube, hubiste, hubo, hubimos, hubisteis, hubieron
Future: habré, habrás, habrá, habremos, habréis, habrán
Conditional: habría, habrías, habría, habríamos, habríais, habrían
Pres. Subj.: haya, hayas, haya, hayamos, hayáis, hayan
Past Subj.: hubiera, hubieras, hubiera, hubiéramos, hubierais, hubieran

**hacer** *to do, to make*
Pres. Ind.: hago, haces, hace, hacemos, hacéis, hacen
Preterite: hice, hiciste, hizo, hicimos, hicisteis, hicieron
Future: haré, harás, hará, haremos, haréis, harán
Conditional: haría, harías, haría, haríamos, haríais, harían
Imperative: haz (no hagas), haga, hagamos, haced (no hagáis), hagan
Pres. Subj.: haga, hagas, haga, hagamos, hagáis, hagan
Past Part.: hecho

**ir** *to go*
Pres. Ind.: voy, vas, va, vamos, vais, van
Imp. Ind.: iba, ibas, iba, íbamos, ibais, iban
Preterite: fui, fuiste, fue, fuimos, fuisteis, fueron
Imperative: ve (no vayas), vaya, vamos, id (no vayáis), vayan
Pres. Subj.: vaya, vayas, vaya, vayamos, vayáis, vayan
Past Subj.: fuera, fueras, fuera, fuéramos, fuerais, fueran
-**ndo** Form: yendo

**mantener** *to maintain, to keep*
(See **tener** for pattern to follow.)

**poder** *to be able to, can*
Pres. Ind.: puedo, puedes, puede, podemos, podéis, pueden
Preterite: pude, pudiste, pudo, pudimos, pudisteis, pudieron
Future: podré, podrás, podrá, podremos, podréis, podrán

Conditional: podría, podrías, podría, podríamos, podríais, podrían
Pres. Subj.: pueda, puedas, pueda, podamos, podáis, puedan
Past Subj.: pudiera, pudieras, pudiera, pudiéramos, pudierais, pudieran

**poner** *to put, to set, to place*
Pres. Ind.: pongo, pones, pone, ponemos, ponéis, ponen
Preterite: puse, pusiste, puso, pusimos, pusisteis, pusieron
Future: pondré, pondrás, pondrá, pondremos, pondréis, pondrán
Conditional: pondría, pondrías, pondría, pondríamos, pondríais, pondrían
Imperative: pon (no pongas), ponga, pongamos, poned (no pongáis), pongan
Pres. Subj.: ponga, pongas, ponga, pongamos, pongáis, pongan
Past Part.: puesto

**romper(se)** *to break*
Past Part.: roto

**saber** *to know*
Pres. Ind.: sé, sabes, sabe, sabemos, sabéis, saben
Preterite: supe, supiste, supo, supimos, supisteis, supieron
Future: sabré, sabrás, sabrá, sabremos, sabréis, sabrán
Conditional: sabría, sabrías, sabría, sabríamos, sabríais, sabrían
Imperative: sabe (no sepas), sepa, sepamos, sabed (no sepáis), sepan
Pres. Subj.: sepa, sepas, sepa, sepamos, sepáis, sepan
Past Subj.: supiera, supieras, supiera, supiéramos, supierais, supieran

**salir** *to leave, to go out*
Pres. Ind.: salgo, sales, sale, salimos, salís, salen
Future: saldré, saldrás, saldrá, saldremos, saldréis, saldrán
Conditional: saldría, saldrías, saldría, saldríamos, saldríais, saldrían
Imperative: sal (no salgas), salga, salgamos, salid (no salgáis), salgan
Pres. Subj.: salga, salgas, salga, salgamos, salgáis, salgan

**ser** *to be*
Pres. Ind.: soy, eres, es, somos, sois, son
Imp. Ind.: era, eras, era, éramos, erais, eran
Preterite: fui, fuiste, fue, fuimos, fuisteis, fueron
Imperative: sé (no seas), sea, seamos, sed (no seáis), sean
Pres. Subj.: sea, seas, sea, seamos, seáis, sean
Past Subj.: fuera, fueras, fuera, fuéramos, fuerais, fueran

**tener** *to have*
Pres. Ind.: tengo, tienes, tiene, tenemos, tenéis, tienen
Preterite: tuve, tuviste, tuvo, tuvimos, tuvisteis, tuvieron
Future: tendré, tendrás, tendrá, tendremos, tendréis, tendrán
Conditional: tendría, tendrías, tendría, tendríamos, tendríais, tendrían
Imperative: ten (no tengas), tenga, tengamos, tened (no tengáis), tengan
Pres. Subj.: tenga, tengas, tenga, tengamos, tengáis, tengan
Past Subj.: tuviera, tuvieras, tuviera, tuviéramos, tuvierais, tuvieran

**traer** *to bring*
Pres. Ind.: traigo, traes, trae, traemos, traéis, traen
Preterite: traje, trajiste, trajo, trajimos, trajisteis, trajeron
Imperative: trae (no traigas), traiga, traigamos, traed (no traigáis), traigan
Pres. Subj.: traiga, traigas, traiga, traigamos, traigáis, traigan
Past Subj.: trajera, trajeras, trajera, trajéramos, trajerais, trajeran
Past Part.: traído
-**ndo** Form: trayendo

**valer** *to be worth*
Pres. Ind.: valgo, vales, vale, valemos, valéis, valen
Future: valdré, valdrás, valdrá, valdremos, valdréis, valdrán
Conditional: valdría, valdrías, valdría, valdríamos, valdríais, valdrían
Pres. Subj.: valga, valgas, valga, valgamos, valgáis, valgan

**venir** *to come*
Pres. Ind.: vengo, vienes, viene, venimos, venís, vienen
Preterite: vine, viniste, vino, vinimos, vinisteis, vinieron
Future: vendré, vendrás, vendrá, vendremos, vendréis, vendrán
Conditional: vendría, vendrías, vendría, vendríamos, vendríais, vendrían
Imperative: ven (no vengas), venga, vengamos, venid (no vengáis), vengan
Pres. Subj.: venga, vengas, venga, vengamos, vengáis, vengan
Past Subj.: viniera, vinieras, viniera, viniéramos, vinierais, vinieran
-**ndo** Form: viniendo

**ver** *to see*
Pres. Ind.: veo, ves, ve, vemos, veis, ven
Imp. Ind.: veía, veías, veía, veíamos, veíais, veían
Preterite: vi, viste, vio, vimos, visteis, vieron
Imperative: ve (no veas), vea, veamos, ved (no veáis), vean
Pres. Subj.: vea, veas, vea, veamos, veáis, vean
Past Subj.: viera, vieras, viera, viéramos, vierais, vieran
Past Part.: visto

# Vocabulario español-inglés

This vocabulary includes almost all words in the textbook, both active (for production) and passive (for recognition only). An entry in **boldface** type indicates that the word or phrase is active. Active words and phrases are practiced in the chapter and are listed on the **Repaso de gramática** and **Repaso de vocabulario** pages at the end of each chapter. You are expected to know and be able to use active vocabulary.

All other words are for recognition only. These words are found in exercises, in optional and visual material, in **Geocultura, Comparaciones, Lectura cultural/informativa, Leamos y escribamos, Novela en video,** and **También se puede decir.** You can usually understand the meaning of these words and phrases from the context or you can look them up in this vocabulary index. Many words have more than one definition; the definitions given here correspond to the way the words are used in ***¡Exprésate!***

Nouns are listed with definite articles and plural forms when the plural forms aren't formed according to general rules. The number after each entry refers to the chapter where the word or phrase first appears or where it becomes an active vocabulary word. Active words and phrases from Level I are indicated by the Roman numeral I; active words and phrases from Level II are indicated by the Roman numeral II. This vocabulary index follows the rules of the **Real Academia,** with **ch** and **ll** in the same sequence as in the English alphabet.

Stem changes are indicated in parentheses after the verb: **poder (ue).**

## A

***a*** *to, on, at,* I; *for, from,* II; a cada rato *every so often,* II; a fin de cuentas *in the end,* II; **a la derecha (de)** *to the right (of),* II; **a la izquierda (de)** *to the left (of),* II; **a la parrilla** *grilled,* II; **a la (última) moda** *in the (latest) style,* I; **a la vuelta** *around the corner,* I; a manera *in the manner of,* II; **a menudo** *often,* I; a partir de *as of, starting on,* II; **¿A qué se dedica...?** *What does . . . do?,* II; a solas *alone,* II; **a tiempo** *on time,* I; **a veces** *sometimes,* I; **llover a cántaros** *to rain cats and dogs,* I; a escondidas *hidden, secretly,* 4; **a todo dar** *great,* I; *flat-out,* 6; a menos (de) que *unless,* 7; **A mi parecer, no hay igualdad entre...** *The way I see it, there's no equality between . . .,* 3; a propósito *on purpose,* 4, **A decir verdad, me parece...** *To tell the truth, it strikes me as . . .,* 5; **A propósito, ¿qué has oído del/de la...?** *By the way, what have you heard about the...?,* 5; **a la vez** *at the same time,* 8; **A causa de esto...** *Because of this...,* 9; **A pesar de que hubo..., por otro lado...** *Although there was/were . . ., on the other hand . . .,* 10; **A que no va a bajar la tasa de...** *I bet that the rate of . . . won't go down.,* 10; **A lo mejor habrá** *Maybe there will be,* 10

abajo *below,* 1

**abarcar** *to include, to encompass,* II

**abierto(a)** *open,* II, 2

**el abogado, la abogada** *lawyer,* II

**abogar** *to advocate,* II

**abordar** *to board,* I

**abrazar(se)** *to hug (each other),* II

**el abrazo** *hug,* II; **Un abrazo de...** *A big hug from . . .,* II

el abrelatas *can opener,* 6

**el abrigo** *(over)coat,* I

**abril** *April,* I

**abrir** *to open,* I

absurdo(a) *absurd,* 6

**la abuela** *grandmother,* I

**el abuelo** *grandfather,* I

**los abuelos** *grandparents,* I

abundante *abundant,* 5, 9

**aburrido(a)** *bored, boring,* I

**aburrir** *to bore,* 2

**aburrirse** *to get bored,* II

**acá** *over here,* II; **¡Ven acá!** *Come over here!,* II

acabar *to end up,* 4

**acabar de** *to have just done something,* I

**acampar** *to camp,* I

el acceso *access,* 8

**el accidente** *accident,* 10

la acción *action;* **el Día de Acción de Gracias** *Thanksgiving Day,* I

el aceite *oil,* II; **el aceite de oliva** *olive oil,* II

**la acera** *sidewalk,* II

acerca de *about,* II

**el acero** *steel,* II

aclarar *to clarify,* II

acompañar *to accompany, to go with,* II

**aconsejar** *to advise:* **aconsejarle (a alguien)** *to advise (someone),* II

**el acontecimiento** *event,* 10

**acordarse (ue) de** *to remember,* II; **¿Te acordaste de...?** *Did you remember to . . .?,* II

**acordar (ue) la paz** *to make peace,* 9

el acordeón *accordion,* 5

**acostarse (ue)** *to go to bed,* I

**acostumbrarse** *to get accustomed to,* 7

la actitud *attitude,* II

**activo(a)** *active,* I

el acto *the act, action,* 4

el actor *actor,* II

los actores *actors,* 5

la actriz *actress,* II

**actualizar** *to update,* 8

actualmente *currently,* II

**la acuarela** *watercolor,* 5

**el acuario** *aquarium,* II

acuático(a) *aquatic,* II; **el esquí acuático** *water skiing,* II

el acueducto *aqueduct,* II

el acuerdo *agreement;* de acuerdo a *according to,* II; **Estoy de acuerdo.** *I agree.,* I
acuñar *to coin, to mint,* II
acusar *to accuse,* 3; acusar recibo de *to acknowledge receipt of,* 8
adecuado(a) *adequate, appropriate,* II
**adelante** *forward,* II; **seguir (i,i) adelante** *to go straight,* II
**los adelantos** *advances,* 8
adentrarse *to go deep into,* 9
**adentro** *inside,* II
**además** *besides,* I
adicionales *additional,* 5
**Adiós.** *Goodbye.,* I
adivinar *to guess,* II
adjunto *attached,* 8
**admitir un error** *to admit a mistake,* 3
la administración de empresas *business administration,* 7
el (la) adolescente *adolescent,* 3
**¿adónde?** *where?,* I; **¿Adónde fuiste?** *Where did you go?,* 1
adornado(a) *decorated, adorned,* 10
**los adornos** *decorations, ornaments,* II
adquirir (ie, i) *to acquire,* II
**la aduana** *customs,* I
la advertencia *warning,* 10
aéreo(a) *aerial,* II
**los aeróbicos** *aerobics,* II
**el aeropuerto** *airport,* I
afectar *to affect, to have an effect on,* II
**afeitarse** *to shave,* I
los aficionados *fans,* II
la afirmación *affirmation,* 3
afirmar *to affirm, to announce,* 6
**afortunadamente** *luckily,* II
**afuera** *outside,* II
**las afueras** *suburbs,* I; *outskirts,* II
**agarrar** *to get, to hold,* II
**la agenda electrónica** *electronic planner,* 8
**el agente, la agente** *agent,* I
**agosto** *August,* I
agradecer (zc) *to thank,* II
agregar *to add,* 8
agrícola *agricultural,* II
el agricultor *farmer,* 10
la agroindustria *agriculture industry,* 10
**el agua** (f.) *water,* I; **el agua** (f.) **mineral** *mineral water,* II; el agua potable *drinking water,* II; **tirarse al agua** *to dive in the water,* II; el agua (f.) de manantial *spring water,* 10
**el aguacate** *avocado,* 4
**aguado(a)** *watery, weak,* II
**aguantar** *to stand, to tolerate,* 2
**las aguas termales** *hot springs,* II
agudo(a) *acute,* II
**el águila** (f.) *eagle,* II
**¿Ah, sí? Pues, yo creo que son...** *Really? Well, I think . . .,* 2
ahí *there,* I
**ahora** *now,* I
**ahora bien** *nevertheless, well,* 9
**ahorrar** *to save money,* I; ahorrar tiempo *to save time,* 8
el aire *air;* **al aire libre** *open-air, outdoor,* II
**el ajedrez** *chess,* I
ajeno(a) *belonging to other people,* 10
**el ají** *chili pepper,* II
**al** (a + el) *to, to the,* I; **¡Al contrario!** *Not at all! As a matter of fact . . .,* II; *on the contrary,* II; **al final** *in the end,* II; **al gusto** *to (one's) taste,* II; **al lado de** *next to,* I; al vapor *steamed;* cocer al vapor *to steam,* II; al compás de *to the rhythm of,* 10; **¡Al contrario! No estoy de acuerdo.** *On the contrary! I disagree.,* 3; **Al (A la)... le falta sabor, pero no sé qué le falta.** *The . . . lacks flavor, but I don't know what's missing.,* 4; **Al final nos dimos cuenta de...** *In the end we realized . . .,* 9
el ala (f. las alas) *wing,* 6
el ala delta *hang-glider;* **volar (ue) con ala delta** *to go hang-gliding,* II
alabar *to praise,* 4
albergar *to put up,* II; *to shelter,* 5
**el albergue juvenil** *youth hostel,* II
**el álbum** *album, scrapbook,* II
la alcachofa *artichoke,* 2
el alcance *reach,* 3
alcanzar *to reach,* 7
la aldea *village,* 4
**alegrar** *to make happy,* 2
la alegría *happiness,* II; **Me dio (mucha) alegría.** *It made me (very) happy.,* II
la alergia *allergy,* 3 tener alergia a *to be allergic to,* 3
alérgico(a) *allergic,* 3
**el alemán** *German,* I
**el alfabeto** *alphabet,* I
**la alfombra** *carpet, rug,* II
el alga (f.) *alga, seaweed,* 9
**el álgebra** (f.) *algebra,* 3
**algo** *something, anything,* I; **¿Algo más?** *Anything else?,* II; **Es algo divertido.** *It's kind of fun.,* I
**el algodón** *cotton,* I; **de algodón** *made of cotton,* I
**alguien** *someone,* II; **hacerse amigo(a) de alguien** *to make friends with someone,* II
algún, alguna *some,* 1
**algún día** *some day,* I
**alguno(a) que otro(a) (cosa)** *the occasional (thing),* 6
la alianza *alliance,* 10
alimenticio(a) *pertaining to food,* II
el alimento *food, nourishment,* II
**aliviar** *to relieve,* II
**allá** *there (general area),* II
**allí** *there (specific place),* I; de allí *from there,* II
**el almacén** *department store,* I
**las almendras** *almonds,* II
**almorzar (ue)** *to have lunch,* I
**el almuerzo** *lunch,* I
**Aló.** *Hello. (telephone greeting),* I
alojar *to house,* II
**alquilar** *to rent,* I
alrededor de *around,* II
**las alternativas (a)** *alternatives (to),* 10; el altiplano *high plateau of the Andes,* 7
**alto(a)** *tall,* I
la altura *height,* II
alumbrar *to light up,* 4
**amable** *nice,* II
**amablemente** *nicely,* II
amar *to love,* II
**amarillo(a)** *yellow,* I
ambicioso(a) *ambitious,* 5
ambiental *environmental,* 10
**el ambiente** *environment,* 8; **el ambiente de trabajo** *work environment,* 8
amenazar *to threaten,* 10
americano(a) *American;* **el fútbol americano** *football,* I
amerindio *Amerindian,* 7
**la amiga, el amigo** *friend,* I
**amigable** *friendly,* 2
**la amistad** *friendship,* 2
el amor *love,* II; **de amor** *romance,* I
ampliar *to extend,* 3
amplio(a) *wide,* II; *spacious,* II
la analogía *analogy,* II
analizar *to analyze,* 2
**anaranjado(a)** *orange,* I
los ancianos *elderly,* II
**andar** *to walk,* II; **No, ando planeando...** *No, I'm planning on . . .,* II
el andén *sidewalk (Honduras),* II
andino(a) *of the Andes,* 7
el anfiteatro *amphitheater,* II
**el anillo** *ring,* I; **el (anillo de) compromiso** *engagement (ring),* 4
animado(a) *animated;* **los dibujos animados** *cartoons,* II
**el animador, la animadora** *cheerleader,* II
**el animal** *animal,* I; el animal de carga *pack animal,* II
**los animales de peluche** *stuffed animals,* II
**animar** *to cheer,* II; *to encourage,* 2
**el aniversario** *anniversary,* I
**anoche** *last night,* I
anotar *to jot down,* II
**anteayer** *day before yesterday,* I
los anteojos *glasses,* II
**los antepasados** *ancestors,* 7
anterior *previous,* II
**antes de** *before,* I; **Antes de que empiecen las clases quiero...** *Before classes start, I want to . . .,* 7

**antiguo(a)** *antique,* 5
**antipático(a)** *unfriendly,* I
antojarse *to take a fancy to something, to want something,* II
anunciar *to announce,* II
**los anuncios clasificados** *classified ads,* 6
**añadir** *to add,* I
el año *year;* **el Año Nuevo** *New Year's Day,* I; **el año pasado** *last year,* I; el año que viene *next year,* II; **Hace unos (muchos, cinco...) años** *A few (many, five . . .) years ago,* II; **los meses del año** *months of the year,* I; **todos los años** *every year,* II
**apagar** *to turn off,* II; *to put out,* II; **apagar incendios** *to put out fires,* II; **apagar la luz/las luces** *to turn off the light(s),* II
aparecer *to appear,* II
aparentemente *apparently,* II
**el apartamento** *apartment,* I
aparte *separate;* en una hoja aparte *on a separate sheet of paper,* II
el apellido *last name,* II; el apellido de soltera *maiden name,* 6
apetecer *to crave for,* 6
**el apio** *celery,* 4
aplaudir *to clap,* 5
aplicado(a) *applied, dedicated,* 4
apoderarse de *to seize,* II
**el aporte** *contribution,* 7
**apoyar** *to support,* 2, 7
**el apoyo** *support,* 7
**aprender (a)** *to learn (to),* II
el aprendizaje *learning,* 3
**apretado(a)** *tight,* II
**aprobar** *to pass,* 3; *to approve,* 6
apropiado(a) *appropriate,* II
**aprovechar** *to profit from,* 7
aproximadamente *approximately,* II
apuntar *to aim, to jot down,* 2
los apuntes *notes,* II; tomar apuntes *to take notes,* II
el apuro *difficult situation, tight spot,* 10
**aquél** *that (farther away)* (dem. pron.), II
**aquel** *that (farther away)* (dem. adj.), II; **en aquel entonces** *back then,* II; *in those days,* II
**aquella** *that (farther away),* II
**aquellas, aquellos** *those (farther away),* II
**aquí** *(right) here,* II; **por aquí** *around here,* II; **¡Ven aquí!** *Come (right) here!,* II
la araña *spider,* II
arar *to plough,* II
**el árbol** *tree,* II; **trepar a los árboles** *to climb trees,* II
el archipiélago *archipelago,* 9
arder *to burn,* 5
arduo(a) *arduous, tireless,* 3
**la arena** *sand,* II
**argentino(a)** *Argentine,* II
**árido(a)** *arid, dry,* II
el arqueólogo *archaeologist,* 10
**la arquitectura** *architecture,* 5
la armonía *harmony,* II
armonioso(a) *harmonious,* 9
arrancar *to pull out, tear off,* 9
el arrecife *reef,* II
**arreglar** *to clean up,* I; *to fix,* II
**arreglarse** *to get ready, to dress up,* II
arriba *up,* II
arrimarse *to come close, approach,* 10
**la arroba** @, I
la arrogancia *arrogance,* 3
arrojado(a) *thrown overboard,* 9
**el arroz** *rice,* I
**el arte** (f. las artes) *art,* I
el artefacto *artifact,* 7
**las artes dramáticas** *dramatic arts,* 5
**las artes marciales** *martial arts,* II, 2
**las artes plásticas** *plastic arts (sculpture, painting, architecture),* 5
la artesanía *crafts, artisanry,* II
el artesano *artisan, craftsman,* 7
**el artículo** *article,* 6; el artículo definido *definite article,* II
**los artículos de cuero** *leather goods,* II
artificial *artificial;* **los fuegos artificiales** *fireworks,* I
el artista, la artista *artist*
**artístico(a)** *artistic,* 5
las arvejas *peas,* 4
**asado(a)** *roasted,* II; **el lechón asado** *roast pork,* II; **el pollo asado** *roast chicken,* II; **la carne asada** *roast beef,* II; **el puerco asado** *roast pork,* 4
asar *to roast,* 2
la ascendencia *ancestry, descent,* II
el ascensor *elevator,* II
asegurar *to make sure,* 5
asentir *to agree,* 3
**los aseos** *public restrooms,* II
**así fue que** *so that's how,* II
**así que** *so,* II
asiático(a) *Asian,* 3
el asiento *seat,* II
asignar *to assign,* 3
**asimilar** *to assimilate,* 7
asimismo *likewise, also,* 6
**asistir a** *to attend,* I
el aspecto físico *physical appearance,* II; *side,* 9
**las aspiraciones** *aspirations,* 7
**la aspiradora** *vacuum cleaner,* II; **pasar la aspiradora** *to vacuum,* I
aspirar *to aspire,* 3
**la aspirina** *aspirin,* II
**el astronauta, la astronauta** *astronaut,* II
la astucia *cleverness, astuteness,* 9
el asunto *issue, matter,* 6
asustar *to scare,* 2
atar *to tie,* 2
la atención *attention*: **llamarle la atención** *to be interested in,* II
atender *to assist,* II
**atento(a)** *helpful,* 2; *courteous,* 8
**aterrador(a)** *terrifying,* 10
el atleta *athlete,* II
**atlético(a)** *athletic,* I
**el atletismo** *track and field,* II, 2
la atracción *attraction;* la atracción turística *tourist attraction,* II; el parque de atracciones *amusement park,* II
atraer *to attract,* II
atrapar *to catch,* II; *to trap,* 6
atravesar(ie) *to go through,* II
atreverse *to dare,* II
atrevido(a) *daring,* 2
atrevimiento *dare,* 2
**el atún** *tuna,* I
la audición *audition,* 5
**los audífonos** *headphones,* I
**el auditorio** *auditorium,* I
aumentar *to increase,* II
aún *still, yet,* II
**aunque** *although,* 9; **Aunque estoy de acuerdo..., creo que...** *Although I agree. . ., I think that. . .,* 10
la ausencia *absence*
auténtico(a) *authentic,* 4
el auto *car,* 10
**el autobús** *bus,* I; **la estación de autobuses** *bus station,* II
automático(a) *automatic*: **el cajero automático** *automatic teller machine,* I
el automóvil *car,* 10
**la autopista** *freeway, highway,* II
la autoridad *authority,* 9
el autorretrato *self-portrait,* II
**el (la) auxiliar administrativo(a)/ médico(a)/de laboratorio** *administrative/medical/laboratory assistant,* 8
el auxilio *help, aid*: los primeros auxilios *first aid,* II
los avances *advances,* 8
avanzar *to advance,* 4
el ave (f.) *bird,* II
**la avenida** *avenue,* II
**la aventura** *adventure,* I
**aventurero(a)** *adventurous,* II
**averiguar** *to find out,* II
la aviación *aviation,* 6
**el avión** *airplane,* I; **el boleto de avión** *plane ticket,* I
**¡Ay, no!** *Oh, no!,* I
**¡Ay, qué pesado!** *Oh, what a drag!,* II
**ayer** *yesterday,* I
el aymara *indigenous language of the Andes,* 7; los aymaras *indigenous people of the Andes,* 7
**la ayuda** *help,* I; **pedir ayuda** *to ask for help,* II
el (la) ayudante *helper,* 8
**ayudar** *to help,* I; *to assist,* II
**ayudarse** *to help each other,* II
**el azúcar** *sugar,* II
**azul** *blue,* I
**el ayuntamiento** *town hall,* II
azotar *to whip,* 2

Vocabulario español-inglés

# B

la bahía *bay,* II
el (la) bailador(a) *dancer,* 7
**bailar** *to dance,* I
**el baile** *dance,* I
**bajar** *to walk down (a street),* II; **bajar archivos** *to download files,* I; **bajar... hasta llegar a...** *to go down . . . until you get to . . .,* II
**bajar de peso** *to lose weight,* I
**bajarse de...** *to get off of . . .,* II
**bajo(a)** *short,* I; **la marea baja** *low tide,* II
**balanceado(a)** *balanced,* II; **llevar una dieta balanceada** *to eat a balanced diet,* II
el balazo *bullet,* 2
el balido *bleating,* 2
**las ballenas** *whales,* II
**el ballet** *ballet,* 5
**el balón de playa** *beachball,* II
el bambú *bamboo,* 5
**la banca** *park bench,* II
**el banco** *bank,* II
la banda *band,* II; **la banda escolar** *school band,* II
el (la) bandido(a) *bandit,* 9
**el (la) banquero(a) internacional** *international banker,* II
**bañarse** *to bathe,* I; **bañarse en el mar** *to swim in the sea,* II
**la bandera** *flag,* 9
**la bañera** *bathtub,* II
**el baño** *bathroom, restroom,* I; **el traje de baño** *swimsuit,* I
**barato(a)** *inexpensive,* I
**el barco** *boat,* I
la barraca *barrack,* II
**barrer** *to sweep,* II
el barril *barrel,* 6
**el barrio** *neighborhood,* II
**el barro** *clay,* II
barroco(a) *Baroque,* II
la base *base, basis:* con base en *based on,* II
basarse en *to be based on,* II
**el básquetbol** *basketball,* I
**bastante** + adj. *quite + adj.,* I; **bastante pequeño** *quite small,* I
**la basura** *trash,* I; *garbage,* II
**el basurero** *garbage can,* 10
**la batalla** *battle,* 5, 9
**el batido** *milkshake,* I
batir *to beat,* II; *to mix, to whisk,* II
**el bautizo** *baptism,* II
**bebé** *baby,* **tener un bebé,** *to have a baby,* 4
**beber (algo)** *to drink (something),* I
**las bebidas** *drinks,* II
la beca *scholarship,* II
**el béisbol** *baseball,* I
bellaco(a) *cunning,* 4
la belleza *beauty:* **el salón de belleza** *beauty parlor,* II
bello(a) *beautiful,* II
el benefactor *benefactor,* 3
beneficiado(a) *benefited,* 3
beneficiar *to benefit,* II
**los beneficios** *benefits,* 8
beneficioso(a) *beneficial,* II
**besar** *to kiss,* 3
**la biblioteca** *library,* I
**la bicicleta** *bike,* I; **montar en bicicleta** *to ride a bike,* I
**bien** *all right, fine,* I; *really,* I; **Espero que estés bien.** *I hope you're doing well.,* II; **Está bien.** *All right.,* I; **llevarse bien** *to get along well,* II; **Me caía muy bien.** *I really liked him/her.,* II; **Me fue muy bien.** *I did very well.,* II; **No te sienta bien.** *It doesn't look good on you.,* II; **Que te vaya bien.** *Hope things go well for you.,* I; **quedar bien** *to fit well,* I; **¡Te ves super bien!** *You look wonderful!,* II; **¿Vamos bien para...?** *Are we going the right way to . . .?,* II
los bienes raíces *real estate,* II
bifurcar *to split in two,* 2
**bilingüe: ser bilingüe** *to be bilingual,* 7
**el billete** *bill, money,* II
**la billetera** *wallet,* I
**los binóculos** *binoculars,* II
**la biología** *biology,* I
**biológico(a)** *organic,* 10
la bisnieta *great-granddaughter,* II
**el bistec** *steak,* II; **el bistec a la parrilla** *grilled steak,* II; **el bistec encebollado** *steak with onions,* II
**el bizcocho de chocolate** *chocolate cake,* 4
**blanco(a)** *white,* I; **en blanco** *blank,* I
blando(a) *soft, weak,* 10
**el bloque** *block,* II; **jugar con bloques** *to play with blocks,* II
el bloqueador *sunblock,* II
**la blusa** *blouse,* I
**la boca** *mouth,* I
**los bocadillos** *finger food,* II
**la boda** *wedding,* I
el boletín *bulletin,* 6
**el boleto de avión** *plane ticket,* I
**el boliche (jugar al boliche)** *bowling (to bowl),* 2
**el bolígrafo** *pen,* I
**la bolsa** *purse, bag,* I; *travel bag,* I
**la bomba** *bomb,* 10
**el bombero, la bombera** *firefighter,* II; **el camión de bomberos** *fire truck,* II; **la estación de bomberos** *fire station,* II
el bombón *bonbon,* 2
**bondadoso(a)** *generous,* 9
**bonito(a)** *pretty,* I
el borde *edge, border;* al borde *on the brink,* II
la bordona *sixth guitar string,* 10
el borrador *rough draft,* 3
**el bosque** *woods/forest,* II
**las botas** *boots,* I
**el bote** *boat,* II; **el bote de vela** *sailboat,* I; **pasear en bote** *to go boating,* II; **pasear en bote de vela** *to go out in a sailboat,* I
**el botones** *bellhop,* II
la brasa *hot coal,* 2
bravo(a) *brave, angry,* 2
**el brazo** *arm,* I
breve *short, brief,* II
brillante *bright,* II
brindar *to offer,* 6
**la brisa** *breeze,* II
la brocheta *skewer,* 7
**el bróculi** *broccoli,* I
la broma *joke,* 2
brotar *to bloom,* 10
bruto(a) *dumb,* II
**bucear** *to scuba dive,* II
**buen** *good,* I; **Hace buen tiempo.** *The weather is nice.,* I
**buenísimo(a)** *great,* II
**bueno(a)** *good,* I; **buena gente** *nice (person),* II; **Bueno,...** *Well/ Okay, . . .,* II; **Es buena idea que...** *It's a good idea for . . . to . . .,* II; **Bueno.** *Hello. (telephone greeting),* I; **sacar buenas notas** *to get good grades,* II
el buey *ox,* II
**la bufanda** *scarf,* II
**el búho** *owl,* II
**el buitre** *vulture,* II
burlarse *to make fun of,* 7
el burro *burro, mule,* 2
**buscar** *to look for,* I; **buscar un pasatiempo** *to find a hobby,* I
**Busco a alguien a quien le guste(n)... y que sepa algo de...** *I'm looking for someone who likes . . . and knows something about . . .,* 2
la búsqueda *search,* II

# C

la caballeriza *horse stable,* 2
**el caballo** *horse,* II; **montar a caballo** *to ride a horse,* II
la cabellera *head of hair,* 6
caber *to fit,* II; **No me cabe en la cabeza.** *I can't understand it.,* 8
**la cabeza** *head,* I; **un dolor de cabeza** *headache,* II
**la cabina telefónica** *phone booth,* II
el cachorro *cub,* 2
**el cactus** *cactus,* II
**cada** *each:* **cada uno(a)** *each, each one,* II; a cada rato *every so often,* II; cada noche *each night,* II

**la cadena** *chain,* II
**caer(se) (yo caigo)** *to fall (down),* II; **caerle bien/mal (a alguien)** *to make a good/bad impression (on someone),* II; *to like/dislike (someone),* II; **Me caía muy bien.** *I really liked him/her.,* II
**el café** *coffee,* I; *café, 2;* **el café con leche** *coffee with milk,* I; **de color café** *brown,* I; **tener los ojos de color café** *to have brown eyes,* II
**el café (Internet)** *(Internet) café,* II
el cafetal *coffee plantation,* II
**la cafetería** *cafeteria,* I; *coffee shop,* I
**la caja** *cash register,* II
**el cajero, la cajera** *cashier,* II
**el cajero automático** *automatic teller machine,* I
**el calabacín** *zucchini,* 4
la calabacita *squash,* 4
**el calambre** *cramp,* II; **darle un calambre** *to get a cramp,* II; **tener un calambre** *to have a cramp,* II
**los calcetines** *socks,* I; **un par de calcetines** *a pair of socks,* I
**la calculadora** *calculator,* I
**Calculo que van a implementar...** *I predict that they are going to implement . . .,* 10
**el cálculo** *calculus,* 3
**el caldo de pollo** *chicken soup,* II
**calentar (ie)** *to heat up,* I
**calentarse (ie)** *to warm up,* II
**la calidad del aire/agua** *air quality/water quality,* 10
**caliente** *hot,* I
**callado(a)** *quiet,* I
la calle *street,* II; **ir por la calle...** *to take . . . street,* II
calmar *to calm,* 2
el calor *heat;* **Hace calor.** *It's hot.,* I; **tener calor** *to be hot,* I
caluroso(a) *hot,* II
**la cama** *bed,* I; **quedarse en cama** *to stay in bed,* II
**la cámara** *camera,* I; la Cámara de Comercio *Chamber of Commerce,* II; **la cámara desechable** *disposable camera,* I; **la cámara digital** *digital camera,* II
los camareros *waiters,* II
**el camarón, los camarones** *shrimp,* 4
**cambiar** *to change,* 8; **cambiar (por)** *to exchange (for),* II; **Cambiando de tema, ¿qué me dices de...?** *Changing the subject, what do you have to say about . . .?,* 5
**caminar** *to walk,* I
**la caminata** *walk, hike:* **dar una caminata** *to go on a hike,* II
**el camión de bomberos** *fire truck,* II
**la camisa** *shirt,* I
**la camiseta** *T-shirt,* I
**el campeonato** *championship,* 10
los campesinos *peasants,* II
**el camping** *camping,* II; **hacer camping** *to go camping,* II
**el campo** *countryside,* I; *field (of work),* 8; **el campo de batalla** *battlefield,* 9
**los campos** *agricultural fields,* 7
**canadiense** *Canadian,* II
la cancha *court,* II; *playing field,* 10
la canción *song,* II
la canela *cinnamon,* II
el cántaro: **llover a cántaros** *to rain cats and dogs,* II
el canto *song,* II
**la canoa** *canoe,* I
**canoso(a)** *gray-haired,* I
**cansado(a)** *tired,* I
**cansarse de** *to get tired of,* 1
los cantantes *singers,* II
**cantar** *to sing,* I
la cantidad *amount,* II; *quantity,* II
el (la) cantor(a) *singer,* 10
la caña de azúcar *sugar cane,* 7
**la caña de pescar** *fishing rod,* II
el cáñamo *cattail reeds,* 7
el cañón (pl. los cañones) *canyon,* II
el caos *chaos,* 10
la capa de ozono *the ozone layer,* 6
capaz *capable,* 8
la capilla *chapel,* II
el capital *money,* 6
la capital *government capital,* 6
el capitán *captain,* 2
captar *to understand, to grasp,* 8
**la cara** *face,* I
**el caracol** *seashell,* II
el carácter (pl. los carácteres) *character, personality,* 4
la característica *characteristic,* 2
**los carbohidratos** *carbohydrates,* II
la cárcel *prison,* II
cargado(a) *loaded*
cargar *to carry,* 6
caribeño(a) *Caribbean,* II
las caricaturas *cartoons (Mexico),* II
el cariño *tenderness, affection;* **Con cariño,...** *Love, . . .,* II
**cariñoso(a)** *tender, affectionate,* II
**la carne** *meat, beef,* I; **la carne asada** *roast meat,* II
**el carnet de identidad** *ID,* I
**la carnicería** *butcher shop,* II
**caro(a)** *expensive,* I
**la carpeta** *folder,* I
**el carpintero, la carpintera** *carpenter,* II
**la carrera** *career,* 8; *race,* II; **echar carreras** *to run races,* II
**la carretera** *road,* II
el carril *lane,* II
**el carro** *car,* I; **el carro eléctrico/híbrido** *electric/hybrid car,* 10; **jugar con carritos** *to play with toy cars,* II
**la carta** *letter,* I; la carta de recomendación *letter of recommendation,* 8
**los carteles** *posters,* 5
**la cartera** *wallet,* II
**el cartero, la mujer cartero** *mail carrier,* II
**la casa** *house,* I; la casa natal *house where someone was born,* II; **jugar a la casita** *to play house,* II
el casabe *cassava bread,* 4
**casarse con** *to marry,* 4; **Fíjate que se ha casado.** *Get this: he/she got married,* 4
el caserío *hamlet, small village,* 9
**casi** *almost,* I; **casi nunca** *almost never,* I; **casi siempre** *almost always,* I
**castaño(a)** *dark brown,* I
el castellano *Castilian Spanish,* 1
**castigar** *to punish,* 9
**el castigo** *punishment,* 9
**el castillo** *castle,* II
**la catarata** *waterfall,* II
**el catarro** *cold,* I; **tener catarro** *to have a cold,* I
**la catedral** *cathedral,* II
**catorce** *fourteen,* I
**el CD** *CD,* II; **crear/grabar CDs** *to burn CDs,* II
**la cebolla** *onion,* II
**las cejas** *eyebrows,* II
**celebrar** *to celebrate,* I
el celo *zeal,* 3
**celoso(a)** *jealous,* 2
celular *cellular, cell,* I; **el teléfono celular** *cell phone,* II
**el cementerio** *cemetery,* II
**la cena** *dinner,* I
**cenar** *to eat dinner,* I
**la censura** *censorship,* 6
el centavo *cent,* 3
**centígrados** *Centigrade,* II
**el centro** *downtown,* I
**el centro comercial** *mall,* I
**el centro recreativo** *recreation center,* II
**cepillarse** *to brush,* II
**el cepillo de dientes** *toothbrush,* I
**la cerámica** *ceramic,* II
**la cerbatana** *hollow reed, blowgun,* 6
**cerca de** *close to, near,* I
el cerdo *pig,* I; **las chuletas de cerdo** *pork chops,* II
**los cereales** *cereal,* I
**el cerebro** *brain,* II
la ceremonia *ceremony,* 4
**la cereza** *cherry,* 4
cernerse *to hover,* 6
**cero** *zero,* I
**cerrar (ie)** *to close,* I; **cerrar la puerta con llave** *to lock the door,* II
la certeza *certainty,* 6
**el césped** *grass,* I
**la cesta** *basket,* II
el ceviche *raw fish marinated in lemon juice, chopped onions, salt and chili peppers,* 4
**las chancletas** *flip-flops,* II
**Chao.** *Bye.,* I
**la chaqueta** *jacket,* I

Vocabulario español-inglés

**charlar** *to talk, to chat,* I
**los cheques de viajero** *travelers' checks,* II
**los chícharos** *peas,* 4
el chico *boy,* II
el chile *pepper,* II
**chileno(a)** *Chilean,* II
la chimenea *chimney, hearth,* 2
chino(a) *Chinese:* **la comida china** *Chinese food,* I
el chisme *piece of gossip,* 2
**chismear** *to gossip,* 2
**el(la) chismoso(a)** *a gossip,* II, 2; **¡Qué chismoso(a)!** *What a gossip!,* II
**el chiste** *joke,* I; **contar(se) (ue) chistes** *to tell (each other) jokes,* II
**chistoso(a)** *funny,* II
**chocar** *to shock, to astonish,* 3
el choclo *corn,* 7
**el chocolate** *chocolate,* I; *hot chocolate,* I
**las chuletas de cerdo** *pork chops,* II
**el cibercafé** *cybercafé,* II
**el ciclismo (practicar ciclismo)** *biking (to bike),* 2
el ciclo *cycle,* II
**ciego(a)** *blind,* I
el cielo *sky,* II
**cien** *one hundred,* I
**la ciencia ficción** *science fiction,* I
**las ciencias** *science,* I; **las ciencias sociales** *social sciences,* 3
los científicos *scientists,* II
**ciento un(o)** *one hundred one,* I
cierto *true,* 1
ciertos(as) *certain,* II; hasta cierto punto *to some extent, in a way,* II
**cinco** *five,* I
**cincuenta** *fifty,* I
**el cine** *movie theater,* I
**la cinematografía** *cinematography,* 5
**el cinturón** *belt,* II; el cinturón de fuego *Ring of Fire,* II
el círculo *circle,* II
las circunstancias *circumstances,* 9
la ciruela *plum,* 10
la cirugía *surgery,* II
la cita *date,* II; *quote,* II
citar *to cite,* 3
**la ciudad** *city,* I; la ciudad natal *city where someone was born,* II; **el plano de la ciudad** *city map,* II
los ciudadanos *citizens,* II
la civilización *civilization,* 9
**claro** *of course,* II; **¡Claro que sí!** *Of course!,* I; **Sí, claro.** *Yes, of course.,* II
claro(a) *clear,* 6
la clase *kind, sort;* **¿Qué clase de trabajo realiza...?** *What kind of work does . . . do?,* II
la clase *class,* II; **el salón de clase** *classroom,* I; **tomar clases de...** *to take . . . lessons,* II
**clásico(a)** *classic,* 5; **la música clásica** *classical music,* II

clasificado(a) *classified;* los anuncios clasificados *classified ads,* II
la cláusula principal *main clause,* 9
la cláusula subordinada *subordinate clause,* 9
clave *key;* la palabra clave *key word,* II
**el cliente, la cliente** *client,* I
**el clima** *climate, weather,* II; **¿Cómo será el clima en...?** *I wonder what the weather is like at (in) . . .?,* II; **¡Qué clima tan seco!** *What a dry climate!,* II
**la clínica** *clinic,* II
**el club de debate** *debate club,* I
el cobalto *cobalt,* 10
**cobarde** *cowardly,* 9
**cobrar** *to charge,* II; **hacer una llamada por cobrar** *to make a collect call,* II
el cobre *copper,* II
la cocción *cooking time,* II
cocer(ue) *to cook,* II; cocer al vapor *to steam,* II
el coche *car,* 10
el cochinillo *pork,* II
**cocido(a)** *cooked,* II
**la cocina** *kitchen,* I
**cocinar** *to cook,* I
**el cocinero, la cocinera** *cook,* II
el coco *coconut,* II
el cocodrilo *crocodile,* II
el códice *codex, writing,* 3
**el codo** *elbow,* II
la cola *line,* I; *tail,* 6; **hacer cola** *to wait in line,* I
la colaboración *collaboration*
**coleccionar estampillas/pósters/monedas** *to collect stamps/posters/coins,* II
el colega *colleague,* II
**el colegio** *school,* I; **después del colegio** *after school,* II
**colgar (ue)** *to hang,* I
el colibrí cometa *red-tailed comet hummingbird,* 9
**el coliflor** *cauliflower,* 4
la colina *hill,* II
**el collar** *necklace,* II
colocar *to put, to place,* 6
**colombiano(a)** *Colombian,* II
**el color** *color,* I; **de color café** *brown,* I; **¿Qué te parece este color?** *What do you think of this color?,* II
la columna de consejos *advice column,* 3
**columpiarse** *to swing (on a swing),* II
**combatir** *to combat,* 3
**los combustibles** *fuels,* 10
**la comedia** *comedy or play,* 5
**el comedor** *dining room,* I
**comentar** *to comment,* 6
**el comentario** *commentary,* 6
**el (la) comentarista** *commentator,* 6
**comenzar (ie)** *to start,* I

**comer** *to eat,* I; **darle de comer al perro** *to feed the dog,* II; **¿Ha comido en...?** *Have you eaten at . . .?,* II
comercializado(a) *commercialized,* 7
**el comerciante, la comerciante** *merchant,* II
el comercio *trade,* II; *commerce,* II; la Cámara de Comercio *Chamber of Commerce,* II
**los comestibles** *food products, groceries,* II; **la tienda de comestibles** *grocery store,* II
**cometer (un crimen, un error)** *to commit (a crime), to make (a mistake),* 10
**cómico(a)** *funny,* I; **la revista de tiras cómicas** *comic book,* I; **las revistas cómicas** *comic books,* II
**la comida** *food, lunch,* I; *meal,* II; **la comida rápida** *fast food,* II; **la plaza de comida** *food court in a mall,* I
el comienzo *beginning,* 3
**la comisaría** *police department,* II
**como** *like, as,* II; como resultado *as a result,* II; **como siempre** *as always,* I; **tan... como** *as . . . as,* I; **tanto(a/os/as)... como...** *as much . . . as . . .,* II; **Como quieras.** *Whatever you want.,* 2
**¿cómo?** *how?, what?,* I; **¿Cómo eres (tú)?** *What are you like?,* I; **¿Cómo son...?** *What are . . . like?,* II; **¿Cómo eras?** *What were you like,* II; **¿Cómo debe ser un(a) buen(a) amigo(a)?** *What should a good friend be like?,* 2; **¿Cómo supiste el resultado?** *How did you find out the score?,* 6; **¿Cómo te enteraste de...?** *How did you find out about . . .?,* 6; **¿Cómo te fue en...?** *How did you do in . . .,* II
**Cómo no.** *Of course.,* II
**la cómoda** *chest of drawers, armoire,* II
cómodo(a) *comfortable,* II
el compañero, la compañera *friend, pal,* II
**el compañero de clase, la compañera de clase** *classmate,* I
**los compañeros de trabajo** *colleagues,* 8
la compañía *company,* 6
la comparación *comparison,* II
comparar *to compare,* II
**compartir** *to share,* II
**la compasión** *compassion,* 10
**la competencia** *competition,* II
**competente** *competent,* 8
competir (i, i) *to compete,* II
competitivo(a) *competitive,* 10
complejo(a) *complex,* II
el complemento directo *direct object,* II
el complemento indirecto *indirect object,* II
completar *to complete,* II

completo *complete,* II; **Se me olvidó por completo.** *I totally forgot.,* II
complicar *to complicate,* II
los compradores *buyers,* II
**comprar** *to buy,* I; **comprarle un regalo** *to buy (someone) a gift,* 3
las compras *purchases,* II; **ir de compras** *to go shopping,* II
**comprobar** *to verify, to check,* 8
**comprometerse** *to get engaged,* 4
comprometido(a) *engaged,* II
**el compromiso** *engagement,* 4; *commitment, obligation,* 7
compuesto(a) *composed,* II
**la computación** *computer science,* I
**la computadora** *computer,* I; **hacer diseño por computadora** *to do computer design,* II
común *common,* II
**la comunicación** *communication,* 3
**comunicarse** *to communicate,* 3
la comunidad *community,* II
**con** *with,* I; con base en *based on,* II; **Con cariño,...** *Love, . . .,* II; **¿Con qué frecuencia?** *How often?,* I; con razón *naturally,* II; contar con *to count on, to depend on,* II; **conmigo** *with me,* I; **contigo** *with you,* I; con tal (de) que *provided that,* 7; **Con el tiempo pude asimilar...** *With time I was able to assimilate . . .,* 7
concentrarse *to concentrate,* 5, 8
**el concierto** *concert,* I
**el concurso** *game show,* 6
el condado *county,* II
el cóndor *condor (bird),* 7
**conducir** *to drive,* II; **la licencia de conducir** *driver's license,* II
**el conductor, la conductora** *driver,* II
conectado(a) *connected,* II
el conejo *rabbit,* II
confeccionar *to make,* II
conferir (ie, i) *to confer upon, to give,* 3
confesar (ie) *to confess*
**confiable** *reliable,* 2
**confiar en** *to trust,* 2
la confianza *trust,* 2
confrontar *to confront,* 2
confundirse *to become confused,* 7
confuso(a) *mixed up,* 3
**congelado(a)** *frozen,* II
el congrí *rice and black beans,* 4
conjugar *to conjugate,* II
el conjunto *group,* II
**conmovedor(a)** *moving, ouching,* 10
**conocer (zc)** *to know (someone) or be familiar with a place,* I; **conocer el centro** *to get to know downtown,* II; **¿Conoces a...?** *Do you know . . .?,* II; dar a conocer *to introduce, to present,* II; **Quiero conocer...** *I want to see . . .,* I
**un(a) conocido(a)** *acquaintance,* 2
el conocimiento *knowledge,* II
el conquistador *conqueror,* 2
conquistar *to conquer,* II
la consecuencia *consequence,* 7
**conseguir (i, i)** *to obtain,* 7, 8
**el (la) consejero(a)** *guidance counselor,* 3; **El (La) consejero(a) insiste en que tome... ¡No me gusta para nada!** *The guidance counselor insists that I take . . . I don't like it at all!,* 3
**los consejos** *advice,* 3; **dar consejos** *to give advice,* II
**consentido(a)** *babied, spoiled,* II
el (la) conserje *janitor,* 8
conservador(a) *conservative,* 8
el conservador *curator,* II
**conservar** *to conserve,* 10
considerado(a) *respected, esteemed,* II
**considerarse** *to consider oneself,* 6
**constantemente** *constantly,* II
**construir** *to build,* II
el consultorio *doctor's office,* II
los consumidores *consumers,* II
el consumo *consumption,* II
el contacto *contact, touch:* **los lentes de contacto** *contact lenses,* II; ponerse en contacto *to contact, to get in touch,* II
contagioso(a) *contagious,* II
**la contaminación** *contamination/pollution,* 10
**contaminado(a)** *contaminated/polluted,* 10
**contar (ue) con** *to count on (someone),* 2
**contarse (ue)** *to tell each other,* II; **contar(se) (ue) chistes** *to tell (each other) jokes,* II
el contenido *content,* II
contemplar *to contemplate,* 2
**contemporáneo(a)** *contemporary,* 5
contener *to contain,* 2
**contento(a)** *happy,* I; **estar contento(a)** *to be happy,* I
**el contestador automático** *answering machine,* 8
contestar *to answer,* II
el contexto *context,* 1
**contra** *against,* 10
contradecir *to contradict,* 6
contraer *to enter into (marriage),* 4
contrario(a) *contrary;* **¡Al contrario!** *Not at all! As a matter of fact . . .,* II; *on the contrary,* II; el equipo contrario *opposing team,* II; lo contrario *opposite,* II
contratar *to hire,* 8
**contribuir** *to contribute,* 7
**el control de seguridad** *security checkpoint,* I
**controvertido(a)** *controversial,* 6
convencer *to convince,* II
conveniente *convenient,* 8
**conversador(a)** *talkative,* II
**conversar** *to converse,* 1
convertirse en + noun *to change into + noun, to turn into + noun,* 8
**la cooperación** *cooperation,* 10
copiar *to copy,* II
**el corazón** *heart,* II
**la corbata** *necktie,* II
la cordillera *mountain range,* 9
el coro *chorus,* 5
coronado(a) *crowned,* II
corporativo(a) *corporate,* 8
el corral *corral,* 6
el correcaminos *roadrunner,* II
corregir *to correct,* II
**el correo** *post office,* I; *mail,* I; **la oficina de correos** *post office,* I
**el correo electrónico** *e-mail (address),* I
**correr** *to run,* I
correspondiente *corresponding,* II
**cortado(a)** *cut,* II
**cortar** *to cut, to mow,* I
**cortarse** *to cut oneself,* II; **cortarse el pelo** *to get a haircut,* II
**corto(a)** *short (in length),* I; **los pantalones cortos** *shorts,* I
**la cosa** *thing,* I; **No es gran cosa.** *It's not a big deal.,* I
la cosecha *crop*
**coser** *to sew,* II
**la costa** *coast,* II
el costado *side,* 8
**costar (ue)** *to cost,* I
**costarricense** *Costa Rican,* II
**la costumbre** *custom,* II; *habit,* 7
**la creación** *creation,* 6, 9
**crear** *to create,* 5; **crear (quemar) CDs** *to make (burn) CDs,* II; **crear un álbum** *to create an album, scrapbook,* II
**creativo(a)** *creative,* 5
**crecer (zc)** *to grow,* 10
el crecimiento *growth,* II
el crédito *credit;* **la tarjeta de crédito** *credit card,* II
**Créeme que fue sin querer.** *Believe me, I didn't mean to do it.,* 3
**creer** *to believe, to think,* II; **Creo que sí.** *I think so.,* II; **¡No me lo puedo creer!** *I can't believe it!,* 4; **Creo que vale la pena acordarse de...** *I think it's worth remembering . . .,* 10
**creído(a)** *arrogant,* 2
**la crema** *cream,* II; **la crema protectora** *sunblock,* II; **la crema agria** *sour cream,* 4
la cría *breeding,* 9
los criadores *breeders,* 9
**criarse (en)** *to grow up (in),* 7
**el crimen** *crime,* 10
**la crisis ambiental/económica/política** *environmental/economic/political crisis,* 6

Vocabulario español-inglés

cristalino(a) *crystalline,* 4
criticar *to criticize,* 4
**criticón, criticona** *critical, judgmental,* 2
**el cruce** *intersection,* II; **el cruce de... con...** *the intersection of . . . and . . .,* II
el crucero *cruise,* II; **tomar un crucero** *to go on a cruise,* II
**el crucigrama** *crossword puzzle,* II; **hacer crucigramas** *to do crossword puzzles,* II
**crudo(a)** *raw,* II
cruzar *to cross,* II
**el cuaderno** *notebook,* I
**la cuadra** *block,* II
**el cuadro** *painting,* II; *box,* II
cual: lo cual *which,* II
cuál *which,* II
**¿cuál?** *what?, which?,* I; **¿Cuál de estas pinturas te gusta más, la de... o la de...?** *Which of these paintings do you like better, the one of (by) or the one of (by) . . .?,* 5
**¿cuáles?** *which (ones)?,* I
las cualidades *(personal) qualities,* 2
**cualquier** *any,* I
**cuando** *when,* I; **Cuando me enteré, no lo pude creer.** *When I found out,* I *couldn't believe it.,* II; **Cuando oí la noticia, no lo quise creer.** *When I heard the news,* I *didn't want to believe it.,* II; **fue cuando** *that was when,* II; **Cuando sea mayor me gustaría...** *When I'm older, I'd like to . . .,* 7
**¿cuándo?** *when?*
**¿cuánto(a)?** *how much?,* I; **¿Cuánto tiempo hace que tú...?** *How long have you been . . .?,* II; **¿Cuánto vale...?** *How much is . . .?,* II
**¿cuántos(as)?** *how many?,* I; **¿Cuántos años tiene...?** *How old is . . .?,* I
**cuarenta** *forty,* I
**cuarto** *quarter,* I; **menos cuarto** *quarter to (the hour),* I; **y cuarto** *quarter past (the hour),* I
**cuarto(a)** *fourth,* II
**el cuarto** *room,* I
**cuatro** *four,* I
**cuatrocientos(as)** *four hundred,* I
**cubrir** *to cover,* II
**la cuchara** *spoon,* I
**la cucharada** *tablespoon,* II
**la cucharadita** *teaspoon,* II
**el cuchillo** *knife,* I
**el cuello** *neck,* I
**la cuenta** *bill,* I; a fin de cuentas *in the end,* II
**el cuento** *story,* II, 9; **el cuento (de hadas)** *(fairy) tale,* 9; el cuento de viejas *old wives' tale,* 9
**la cuerda** *rope,* II; **saltar a la cuerda** *to jump rope,* II
el cuero *hide:* **los artículos de cuero** *leather goods,* II
el cuerpo *body,* 2
**cuesta(n)...** *costs . . .,* I
**la cueva** *cave,* II; **explorar cuevas** *to explore caves, to go spelunking,* II
el cuidado *care,* I; **tener cuidado** *to be careful,* II
**cuidar** *to take care of,* I; **cuidar a los enfermos** *to take care of sick people,* II; **cuidar a una mascota** *to take care of a pet,* II
**cuidarse** *to take care of oneself,* I; **cuidarse la salud** *to take care of one's health,* I
la culebra *snake,* II
culinario(a) *culinary,* II
la culpa *fault,* II
cultivar *to cultivate,* II
el cultivo *crop,* II
la cumbia *a type of Latin American music,* 5
**el cumpleaños** *birthday,* I; **la tarjeta de cumpleaños** *birthday card,* I
cumplir *to carry out, to serve,* II; cumplir con los requisitos *to meet the requirements,* 8
**la cuñada** *sister-in-law,* 4
**el cuñada** *brother-in-law,* 4
el cura *priest,* 6
la cura *cure,* 6
curar *to cure,* II
**curioso(a)** *curious,* II
**la curita** *adhesive bandage,* II
**el currículum (vitae)** *resume,* 8
**los cursos** *classes,* 3
cuyo(a) *whose,* II

## D

dado(a) *given,* II
la dama *lady,* II; **jugar a las damas** *to play checkers,* II
**la danza** *dance,* 5
dañino(a) *harmful,* 6
el daño *harm,* II
**dar (yo doy)** *to give,* I; **a todo dar** *great,* I; **Dale un saludo a... de mi parte.** *Say hi to . . . for me.,* II; **Me da igual.** *It's all the same to me.,* I; **dar una caminata** *to take a walk,* 1; **Me dio (alegría, tristeza, vergüenza, una rabia).** *It made me (happy, sad, embarrassed, angry).,* II; **dar consejos** *to give advice,* II; dar permiso *to give permission,* II; **dar una caminata** *to go for a walk, to hike,* II; **dar una vuelta por...** *to walk/drive around . . .,* II; **darle de comer al perro** *to feed the dog,* II; **Me dieron ganas de** + infinitive *I felt like . . .,* II; **me dieron un descuento** *they gave me a discount,* II; **darle miedo** *to scare,* II; **darle un calambre** *to get a cramp,* II; **darle un abrazo** *to give (someone) a hug,* 3
**dar a luz** *to give birth,* 4
**(no) darse por vencido** *to (not) give up,* 7
**darse prisa** *to hurry,* II
**darse un golpe en...** *to bump one's . . .,* II; **¡Uf! Me di un golpe en...** *Oh! I hit my . . .,* II
**Date tiempo para pensarlo.** *Give yourself time to think it over.,* 3
**de** *of, from, in, by,* I; de allí *from there,* II; **de amor** *romance . . .,* I; **de mi parte** *on my behalf, my regards;* **Dale un saludo a... de mi parte.** *Say hi to . . . for me.,* II; De nada. *You're welcome.,* II; de nuevo *again,* II; **¿De parte de quién?** *Who's calling?,* I; de paseo *out for a walk, going for a stroll,* II; **de pequeño(a)** *as a child,* II; **de repente** *suddenly,* II; **De repente, empezó a llover...** *Suddenly, it started to rain . . .,* II; ¿De veras? *Really?,* II; **de verdad** *honestly,* II; de vez en cuando *once in a while,* II; **de hecho,** *actually, in fact,* 3; de improviso *unexpectedly, suddenly,* 9; **de buen/mal gusto** *in good/bad taste,* 5; **De hoy en adelante** *from now on,* 1
**de cultivo biológico** *organic,* 10
**de modo...** *in a . . . way,* 6
**declarar la guerra** *to declare war,* 9
**debajo de** *underneath,* I
**el debate** *debate,* II
**deber** *should, ought to,* II; **deber** + infinitive *to need to, to have to do something,* II
debido(a) a *due to, because of,* II; *correct, proper, fitting,* 7
la década *decade,* 3
decidir *to decide,* II; decidirse a + infinitive *to decide to,* 8
**décimo(a)** *tenth,* II
**decir (yo digo)** *to say,* II; **¿Me dices dónde está...?** *Can you tell me where . . . is?,* II; **¿Me podría decir...?** *Could you tell me . . .?,* II; **¡No me digas!** *No way! You're kidding!,* II; **¿Puede repetir lo que dijo?** *Can you repeat what you said?,* II
declarar *to declare,* II; **declarar la guerra** *to declare war,* 9
**la decoración** *decoration,* I
**decorar** *to decorate,* I
**dedicarse a** *to devote/dedicate oneself to,* II; **¿A qué se dedica...?** *What does . . . do?,* II
**el dedo** *finger,* I; **el dedo del pie** *toe,* II
la defensa *defense,* 9

la deforestación *deforestation,* 10
las defunciones *obituaries,* 6
la degradación del suelo *soil degradation,* 10
**dejar** *to allow,* I; *to leave,* I; *to let,* II; dejar en paz *to leave somebody alone,* II; **dejar la propina** *to leave the tip,* II; **Se los dejo en...** *I'll let you have them for . . .,* II; **dejar plantado(a) a alguien** *to stand someone up,* 2
**dejar de** + infinitive *to stop doing something,* I; **dejar de hablarse** *to stop speaking to one another,* 3
**del (de + el)** *of the,* I
**delante de** *in front of,* I
**delgado(a)** *thin,* I
**delicioso(a)** *delicious,* I
**demasiado(a)** *too much,* I
demostrar (ue) *to demonstrate,* II
**el dentista, la dentista** *dentist,* II
dentro de *within,* II
**el dependiente, la dependiente** *salesclerk,* I
**los deportes** *sports,* I; **practicar deportes** *to play sports,* I
deportivo(a) *sports;* **la escalada deportiva** *rock-climbing,* II
el depósito *deposit,* 10
**la derecha** *right,* II; **a la derecha (de)** *to the right (of),* II; **doblar a la derecha en** *to turn right on,* II
**derecho** *straight,* II; **seguir adelante/derecho** *to go straight,* II; **seguir derecho hasta** *to keep going (straight) to,* II
**el derecho** *the right to,* 2
derramado(a) *spilled,* 9
derribar *to fell,* 2
**derretido(a)** *melted,* II
**derretir (i, i)** *to melt,* II
**la derrota** *defeat,* 5, 9
derrotar *to defeat,* II
el derrumbe *cave-in,* 10
desafiar *to challenge,* 7
**el desafío** *challenge,* 7
desafortunadamente *unfortunately,* 8
**desaparecer (zc)** *to disappear,* 8
**desarrollar** *to develop,* 10
**el desastre** *disaster,* 10
desastroso(a) *disastrous,* II
desatarse *to come undone,* 9
**desayunar** *to eat breakfast,* I
**el desayuno** *breakfast,* I
**descansar** *to rest,* I
descargar *to unload,* 2
el (la) descendiente *descendant,* 7
**desconocido(a)** *unknown,* 9
descortés *rude, discourteous,* 2
**describir** *to describe,* II
**el descubrimiento (de)** *discovery (of), 10*
**descubrir** *to discover,* 10
**el descuento** *discount,* II
desde luego *naturally, of course,* II
desde que *since,* 10
el desdén *disdain,* 3
**desear** *to want, to wish for, to desire,* I
**desechable** *disposable;* **la cámara desechable** *disposable camera,* I
**desembarcar** *to disembark, to deplane,* I
**desempeñar (el papel de...)** *to play (the role of . . .),* 5
**el desempleo** *unemployment,* 10
desensillar *to remove a saddle from,* 2
el deseo *desire,* II
desértico(a) *desert-like,* II
la desertificación *desertification,* 6
**desesperadamente** *frantically,* II
desesperado(a) *desperate,* 10, *exasperated*
el desfile *parade,* II
**desgraciadamente** *unfortunately,* II
**el desierto** *desert,* II
**desleal** *disloyal,* 2
**desperdiciar** *to waste,* 10
el despertador *alarm clock,* 1
**despertarse (ie)** *to wake,* I
el desprendimiento de tierras *landslide,* 10
**después** *after, afterwards,* I; **después de** *after,* I; **después de clases** *after class,* I; **después del colegio** *after school,* II; **que me llame después** *tell him/her to call me later,* I
destacarse *to stand out,* II
desterrado(a) *banished,* II
el destino *destination,* II; *destiny,* 3
las destrezas *skills,* II
**la destrucción** *destruction,* 10
los destructores *destroyers,* II
destruido(a) *destroyed,* II
destruir *to destroy,* II
la desventaja *disadvantage,* 8
**detallado(a)** *detailed,* 6
**el detalle** *detail,* 3
detener *to detain, to stop,* 4
**detrás de** *behind,* I
devolver (ue) *to return, to give back,* I
**di** *say, tell,* II
**el día** *day,* I; **algún día** *some day,* I; **Buenos días.** *Good morning.,* I; **el Día de Acción de Gracias** *Thanksgiving Day,* I; **el Día de la Independencia** *Independence Day,* I; **el Día de la Madre** *Mother's Day,* I; **el día de la semana** *day of the week,* I; **el Día de los Enamorados** *Valentine's Day,* I; **el día de tu santo** *your saint's day,* I; **el Día del Padre** *Father's Day,* I; **el día festivo** *holiday,* I; **el plato del día** *daily special,* II; hoy en día *nowadays,* II; **todos los días** *everyday,* I; **un día** *one day,* II; en esos días *in those days,* II; el día festivo *holiday,* 8
el diálogo *dialog,* 2
el diario *diary,* II
diario(a) *daily;* la rutina diaria *daily routine,* II
**dibujar** *to draw,* I
**el dibujo** *drawing,* 5
**los dibujos animados** *cartoons,* II
**el diccionario** *dictionary,* I
**dicho** *said (past participle of* **decir**), II
**diciembre** *December,* I
**el (la) dictador(a)** *dictator,* 9
**diecinueve** *nineteen,* I
**dieciocho** *eighteen,* I
**dieciséis** *sixteen,* I
**diecisiete** *seventeen,* I
**los dientes** *teeth,* I; **el cepillo de dientes** *toothbrush,* I; **la pasta de dientes** *toothpaste,* I; lavarse los dientes *to brush one's teeth,* II
**la dieta** *diet,* I; **la dieta balanceada** *balanced diet,* II; **seguir (i, i) una dieta sana** *to eat a balanced diet,* I
**diez** *ten,* I
**difícil** *difficult,* I
**Diga.** *Hello. (telephone greeting),* I
**las diligencias** *errands,* II; **hacer diligencias** *to run errands,* II
diligente *diligent,* 10
diminuto(a) *tiny, minute,* II
**el dinero** *money,* I; ganar dinero *to make money,* II; **sacar el dinero** *to get money,* I
**el (la) dios(a)** *god, goddess* 9
el (la) diplomático(a) *diplomat,* 7, 9
**la dirección** *address,* I
**el director, la directora** *principal,* 3, el/la director(a) de cine, *movie director,* 6
el dirigente de orquesta *orchestra conductor,* II
dirigido(a) *led,* 9
**dirigir** *to direct,* 8
dirigirse a *to address,* II
**el disco compacto** *compact disc,* I
**la discriminación** *discrimination,* 3
**discriminar** *to discriminate,* 7
**la disculpa** *apology,* 3
**disculparse** *to apologize,* 3
**Disculpe.** *Excuse me.,* II
el discurso *speech,* 7
**discutir** *to argue,* 3
diseñado(a) *designed,* 9
los diseñadores *designers,* II
**diseñar** *to design,* II; **diseñar páginas Web** *to design Web pages,* II
**el diseño** *design,* II; **hacer diseño por computadora** *to do computer design,* II; el diseño gráfico *graphic design,* 3
**disfrutar de** *to enjoy,* II
disparar *to shoot,* 2

Vocabulario español-inglés

disponer *to arrange,* 3
disponible *available,* II
distinto(a) *different,* 2
distraer *to distract,* II
distraerse *to entertain oneself, to relax,* II
la diversidad *diversity,* II
la diversión *amusement;* **el parque de diversiones** *amusement park,* I
diverso(a) *diverse,* II
**divertido(a)** *fun,* I
**divertirse (ie, i)** *to have fun,* II
**divorciado(a)(s)** *divorced,* 4
**divorciarse (de)** *to divorce,* 4
**el divorcio** *divorce,* 4
**doblar** *to turn,* II; **doblar a la derecha en** *to turn right on,* II; **doblar a la izquierda en** *to turn left on,* II
**doce** *twelve,* I
**el documental** *documentary,* 6
**doler (ue)** *to hurt,* I; **Me duele(n)...** *My . . . hurt(s).,* I; **¿Te duele algo?** *Does something hurt you?,* I
**el dolor de cabeza** *headache,* II
**el domingo** *Sunday,* I; **los domingos** *on Sundays,* I
dominicano(a) *Dominican,* 4
**el dominó** *dominoes,* 2
**donar tiempo a una causa** *to donate time to a cause,* 8
**¿dónde?** *where?,* I; **¿Dónde estabas y qué hacías cuando...?** *Where were you and what were you doing when . . .?,* 10
doña *title of respect used before a woman's Christian name,* 4
dorar *to brown,* 4
**dormir (ue, u)** *to sleep,* I; **dormir la siesta** *to take a nap,* I; **dormir lo suficiente** *to get enough sleep,* I
**dormirse (ue, u)** *to fall asleep,* II
**dos** *two,* I
**dos mil** *two thousand,* I
**dos millones (de)** *two million,* I
**doscientos(as)** *two hundred,* I
la dosis *dose,* 3
**el drama** *drama,* 5
dramático(a) *dramatic,* 5
dramatizar *to role-play,* II
el dramaturgo *playwright,* II
**la drogadicción** *drug addiction,* 10
**la ducha** *shower,* II
**ducharse** *to take a shower,* II
la duda *doubt;* sin duda *without a doubt,* II
dudar *to doubt,* 6
**Dudo que estés bien informado(a) sobre.../que sepas...** *I doubt that you're well informed about . . ./that you know . . .,* 6
el dueño *owner,* II
**dulce** *sweet,* I
**el dulce** *candy,* I; **el pan dulce** *pastry,* I; el dulce de leche *milk and sugar candy,* 4
**el dulce de coco** *coconut candy,* 4
**durante** *during,* I
durar *to last,* 2
**el durazno** *peach,* I
**el DVD** *DVD,* I

## E

**e** *and,* II
**echar** *to put in, to add,* II; *to grow, to put out,* 5, **echar carreras** *to run races,* II; **Está echado(a) a perder.** *It's spoiled.,* II; **Te echo mucho de menos.** *I miss you a lot.,* II
el eclipse *eclipse,* 3
los ecologistas *ecologists,* 9
**el ecoturismo** *ecotourism,* II; **hacer ecoturismo** *to go on an ecotour,* II
la edad *age,* II
**el edificio** *building,* I
el editor *editor,* 6
**los editoriales** *editorial section,* 6
**la educación física** *physical education,* I
**educativo(a)** *educational,* 6
efectivamente *actually, in effect,* 6
efectivo: **en efectivo** *in cash,* II
el efecto invernadero *greenhouse effect,* 10
eficaz *efficient,* 6
**egoísta** *selfish,* II
ejecutivo(a) *executive,* II
el ejemplo *example,* 2; por ejemplo *for example,* 2
ejercer *to practice,* II
el ejercicio *exercise;* **hacer ejercicios** *to exercise,* I; **los ejercicios aeróbicos** *aerobic exercises,* 1
**el** *the (masc. article),* I
**él** *he, him (after preposition),* I
**las elecciones** *elections,* 10
electrónico(a) *electronic;* **el correo electrónico** *e-mail address,* I
**elegante** *nice, elegant,* II
elegir *to choose,* 3
elevado(a) *elevated,* II
**ella** *she, her (after preposition),* I
**ellas** *they, them (after preposition),* I
**ellos** *they, them (after preposition),* I
**la embajada** *embassy,* II
el (la) embajador(a) *ambassador,* 7
la embarcación *boat, craft,* 9
el embarque *embarkation;* **la tarjeta de embarque** *boarding pass,* I
embravecido(a) *raging, wild,* 9
**la emisora** *radio/TV station,* 6
**emocionante** *moving, exciting,* 10
**la empanada** *turnover-like pastry,* I
emparejar *to match,* II
**empatar** *to tie a game,* II
**empeñarse en** *to insist on, be determined to,* 7
empeñoso(a) *persevering,* 10
**empezar (ie)** *to start, to begin,* I
la emigración *emigration,* 7
la emoción *emotion,* 2
**empeorar** *to make worse,* 8
el emperador *emperor,* 7, 9
**el (la) empleado(a)** *employee,* 8
emplear *to use,* II; *to hire,* II
el empleo *job,* II; **el empleo a medio tiempo** *part-time job,* 8; **el empleo a tiempo completo** *full-time job,* 8
**la empresa** *company,* 8
el (la) empresario(a) *businessman, businesswoman,* 10
**en** *on, in, at,* I; **en aquel entonces** *back then,* II; *in those days,* II; **en blanco** *blank,* I; **en efectivo** *cash,* II; en esa época *in those days,* II; en medio de *in the middle of,* II; **en oferta** *on sale,* II; en parejas *in pairs,* II; en particular *especially,* 1; **en punto** *on the dot,* I; **¿En qué le puedo servir?** *How can I help you?,* I; en realidad *in fact, really, actually,* II; en secreto *secretly,* II; **en seguida** *right away,* II; **en su punto** *just right,* II; en una hoja aparte *on a separate sheet of paper,* II; en vez de *instead of,* II; en esos días *in those days,* 2; en absoluto *not at all,* 2; en cuanto a *as to, in regards to,* 2; en vivo *live,* 2; **en tu lugar** *in your place,* 3; **en esa situación** *in that situation,* 3; en caso de que *in case,* 7; **En realidad, admiro...** *Actually, I admire . . .,* 5; **En cuanto cumpla los... años voy a...** *As soon as I turn . . . years old, I'm going to . . .,* 7; **en un santiamén** *instantly,* 8
los enamorados *lovers;* **el Día de los Enamorados** *Valentine's Day,* I
**enamorarse** *to fall in love,* 5, 9
el enano *dwarf,* II
**encajar (en)** *to fit in,* 7
**el encaje** *lace,* II
**Encantado(a).** *Delighted (to meet you).,* II
**encantado(a)** *enchanted,* 9
**encantar** *to really like, to love,* I; **Le encanta(n)...** *He/She/You love(s) . . .,* II
el encargo *order, task,* 5
encebollado(a) *cooked with onions;* **el bistec encebollado** *steak with onions,* II
las enchiladas *tortillas stuffed with meat or cheese (Mex.),* II
**encima de** *on top of, above,* I
la encina *oak tree,* 6
el encinal *oak grove,* 6
**encontrar (ue)** *to find,* I
**encontrarse (ue) con alguien** *to meet up with someone,* I
la encuesta *survey,* II
**el (la) enemigo(a)** *enemy,* 8

**la energía solar** *solar energy,* 10
**enero** *January,* I
enfadarse *to get angry,* II
**enfermarse** *to get sick,* II
**la enfermedad** *disease, sickness,* II, 10
**el enfermero, la enfermera** *nurse,* II
**enfermo(a)** *sick,* I; **estar enfermo(a)** *to be sick,* I
**los enfermos** *sick people,* II
**enfocarse en** *to focus on,* 7
**el enfoque local/nacional/mundial** *local/national/world perspective,* 6
**enfrentar** *to confront,* II
**enfrente de** *in front of, facing,* II
enfurecer *to infuriate,* 2
enmarañado(a) *tangled,* II
enojado(a) *angry,* 2
**enojarse** *to get angry,* II
**la ensalada** *salad,* I; **la ensalada mixta** *mixed salad,* II
ensangrentado(a) *bloody,* 2
ensayar *to rehearse,* 3
**el ensayo** *rehearsal,* I, *essay,* 2
**enseguida** *right away,* II, 8
**enseñar** *to teach, to show,* II
**entender (ie)** *to understand,* I
**enterarse** *to find out,* II
**entero(a)** *whole,* II; *entire,* II
enterrado(a) *buried,* II
enterrar (ie) *to bury,* 10
**Entiendo algo de..., pero nada de...** *I understand a little about . . ., but nothing about . . .,* 6
**entonces** *so, then,* II; **en aquel entonces** *back then,* II; *in those days,* II
**la entrada** *ticket,* II; *entrée, first course,* II; *entry (in a diary), entrance,* 4
los entrantes *appetizers,* II
las entrañas *entrails,* 2
**entre** *in between,* II
entregar *to give, to turn in,* II
**los entremeses** *appetizers,* II
**el entrenador, la entrenadora** *coach,* II
**el entrenamiento** *practice,* I
**entrenar(se)** *to work out,* I
**entretenido(a)** *entertaining,* 5
el entretenimiento *entertainment,* II
**la entrevista** *interview,* 8
**entrevistar** *to interview,* 6
entristecerse *to grow sad,* II
enumerar *to list,* II
envejecer (zc) *to grow old,* 10
en vivo *live,* 6
enviar *to send,* II; **enviar mensajes de texto** *to send text messages,* II
el episodio *episode, chapter,* II
la época: en esa época *in those days,* II
el equilibrio *balance, equilibrium*
el equinoccio *equinox,* 9
**el equipaje** *luggage,* I
**el equipo** *equipment,* II; *team,* II; el equipo contrario *opposing team,* II; el equipo de rescate *rescue equipment,* 10
**la equitación** *riding,* II
equivocado(a) *wrong,* II
equivocarse *to be wrong, to be mistaken,* II
**Eran como las dos cuando...** *It was around two when . . .,* II
**Érase una vez** *Once upon a time,* II; **Érase una vez en un lugar muy lejano...** *Once upon a time in a faraway place . . .,* 9
**Eres muy bueno(a) para..., ¿verdad?** *You're really good at . . ., aren't you?,* 2
el error *a mistake,* II; cometer un error *to make a mistake,* II
**la erupción (de un volcán)** *eruption (of a volcano),* 10
**Es...** *He/She/It is . . .,* I; **Es buena idea que...** *It's a good idea for . . . to . . .,* II; **Es importante que...** *It's important for . . . to . . .,* II; **¡Es increíble!** *It's incredible!,* II; **Es mejor que...** *It's better for . . . to . . .,* II; **Es que se me acabó...** *It's just that I ran out of . . .,* 4; **Es que se me olvidó ponerle...** *It's just that I forgot to add . . ..,* 4; es una lástima *it's a pity/shame,* 4; **Es mejor que veas la ópera. Es formidable.** *It's better for you to see the opera. It's great.,* 5; **Es evidente que...** *It's clear that . . .,* 6; **Es dudoso que...** *It's doubtful that . . .,* 6; **Es de esperar que...** *Hopefully . . .,* 9; **Es lamentable que...** *It's too bad that . . .,* 9; **Es muy posible que el tráfico aumente con...** *It's quite possible that traffic will increase with. . .,* 10; **Es de suponer que...** *I suppose that . . .,* 10
**la escalada deportiva** *rock-climbing,* II, 2
**escalar** *to climb,* 2
la escalera *staircase, stairs,* 9
la escena *scene,* II
**el escenario** *setting,* II; *stage, scenery,* 5
los esclavos *slaves,* II
la escoba *broom,* 8
**escoger** *to pick, to choose,* I
escolar *school (adj.);* **la banda escolar** *school band,* II; **los útiles escolares** *school supplies,* I
esconderse *to hide,* 6
el escondite *hiding place;* **jugar al escondite** *to play hide and seek,* II
**escribir** *to write,* I; **escribir poemas y cuentos** *to write poems and stories,* I; **Se escribe...** *It's spelled . . .,* I
**escrito(a)** *written (past participle of* **escribir**), II; *writings, manuscripts,* 7
los escritores *writers,* II
**el escritorio** *desk,* I
**escuchar** *to listen,* I
la escuela *school,* II
**esculpir** *to sculpt,* 5
**la escultura** *sculpture,* 5
**ése** *that (pron.),* II
**ese(a)** *that (adj.),* I
**esforzarse (ue)** *to strive, to make an effort,* 7
el esfuerzo *effort,* II
**la esgrima** *fencing,* 2
**esgrimir** *to fence,* 2
eso *that;* por eso *that's why,* II; **Eso me hace pensar en...** *That makes me think about . . .,* 5; **Eso me resulta fácil/bastante difícil.** *That's easy/pretty difficult for me.,* 8
**esos, esas** *those (adj.),* I
**ésos, ésas** *those (pron.),* II
el espacio *space,* II
**la espalda** *back,* I
espantar *to scare,* 2
**espantoso(a)** *frightening, terrible,* 10
**el español** *Spanish,* I
especial *special:* el plato especial *special dish,* II; **Qué hay de especial?** *What's the (daily) special?,* II
**las especialidades** *specialties,* II
los especialistas *specialists,* II
**las especias** *spices,* II
la especie *type,* II, *species,* 7
espectacular *spectacular,* 9
el espectáculo *show, performance,* II
los espectadores *spectators,* II
**el espejo** *mirror,* II
la espera *wait;* **la sala de espera** *waiting room,* I
la esperanza *hope,* 3
**esperar** *to wait, to hope, to expect,* I; **Espera un momento.** *Hold on a moment,* I; **Espero que el viaje sea divertido.** *I hope the trip is fun.,* II; **Espero que estés bien.** *I hope you're doing well.,* II; **Espero ver...** *I hope to see . . .,* I
**las espinacas** *spinach,* I
el esposo *husband,* II
el esquema *outline, sketch,* 7
**el esquí acuático** *water skiing,* II
**esquiar** *to ski,* I; **esquiar en el agua** *to water-ski,* I
**la esquina** *corner,* II
**esta** *this (adj.),* I
**ésta** *this (pron.),* I
**establecerse (zc)** *to get established,* 7
el establecimiento *establishment,* 2
**la estación** *station,* II; **la estación de bomberos** *fire station,* II; **la estación de trenes/autobuses** *train/bus station,* 1
**las estaciones** *seasons,* I
**el estacionamiento** *parking lot,* II
estacionarse *to park,* 8
**el estadio** *stadium,* I
las estadísticas *statistics,* II
el estado *state,* II
**estadounidense** *American,* II
**estallar** *to explode,* 10
**las estampillas** *stamps,* II; **coleccionar estampillas** *to collect stamps,* II
**el estante** *bookcase,* II
**estar** *to be,* I; **No está.** *He/She is not*

here., I; **Está a la vuelta.** *It's around the corner.*, I; **estar aburrido(a)** *to be bored*, I; **Está echado(a) a perder.** *It's spoiled.*, II; **Está (en su punto, exquisito(a), perfecto(a), quemado(a)).** *It's (just right, wonderful, perfect, burned).*, II; **Está (un poco) salado(a).** *It's (a little) salty.*, I; **Estoy harto(a) de...** *I'm fed up with . . .*, II; **Estoy loco(a) por...** *I'm crazy about . . .*, II; **¿Qué tal está...?** *How is the . . .?*, II; **Está bien.** *All right.*, I; **estar bien** *to be (doing) fine*, I; **Espero que estés bien.** *I hope you're doing well.*, II; **estar en oferta** *on sale*, II; **(no) estar de acuerdo** *to (not) agree*, I; **estar listo(a)** *to be ready*, I; **estar mal** *to be doing badly*, I; *to be sick*, II; **estar resfriado(a)** *to have a cold*, II; **estoy seguro(a) de** *I'm positive that*, II; **No estoy seguro(a).** *I'm not sure.*, II; **estar loco(a) por** *to be crazy about*, 2; **estar dolido** *to be upset*, 2, **Estoy regular.** *I'm all right.*, I; **estar resentido(a)** *to be resentful*, 3; **estar casado(a)(s)** *to be married*, 4; **Está para chuparse los dedos.** *It's good enough to lick your fingers.*, 4; **Está pasada la leche.** *The milk has gone bad.*, 4; **estar al tanto** *to be up-to-date*, 6; **estar bien/mal informado** *to be well/poorly informed*, 6; **estar actualizado** *to be up to date*, 6; **Está fuera de/a mi alcance** *It's outside/within my reach.*, 8; **Estaba en casa cuando...** *I was at home when . . .*, 10; **Estoy convencido(a) de que...** *I'm convinced that . . .*, 6; **Estoy seguro(a) (de) que...** *I'm sure that . . .*, 6; **Estaba en primera plana** *It was on the front page*, 6; **está claro que...**, *it's clear that . . .*, 6; **estar agradecido(a) por** *to be thankful for*, 7; **Estuvo a todo dar.** *It was great.*, I
**estas, estos** *these (adj.)*, I
**la estatua** *statue*, 5
**este(a)** *this (adj.)*, I; **Este retrato fue pintado por...** *This portrait was painted by . . .*, 5
**éste** *this (pron.)*, I
el este *east*, II
**el estereotipo** *stereotype*, 3
el estilo *style*, II
**el estilo de vida** *lifestyle*, 7
**estirarse** *to stretch*, I
el estofado *stew*, 4
**el estómago** *stomach*, I
**estornudar** *to sneeze*, II
**estos, estas** *these (adj.)*, I
**éstos, éstas** *these (pron.)*, II
la estrategia *strategy*, II
estrecho(a) *narrow*, II; estrechos *straits*, 9
la estrella *star*, II; la estrella solitaria *lone star*, II
**estrenar (una película)** *to open/premiere (a movie)*, 10
**el estreno** *opening/premiere*, 10
el estrés *stress*, II
**estricto(a)** *strict*, II
**estridente** *shrill*, 5
la estrofa *stanza*, 10
el estuario *estuary*, 10
**el estudiante, la estudiante** *student*, I
estudiantil *related to students*, 5; la orquesta estudiantil *student orchestra*, 5
**estudiar** *to study*, I
el estudio *study (room)*, II
los estudios *studies*, II
**la estufa** *stove*, II
**estupendo(a)** *marvelous*, I, 2
eterno(a) *eternal*, 2
**la etiqueta** *price tag*, II
europeo(a) *european*, II
evaluar *to evaluate, assess*, 2
evidente *obvious*, 6
**evitar** *to avoid*, II
exactamente *exactly*, 1
**el examen** *test*, I; **presentar el examen de...** *to take a . . . test*, I
**la excursión** *hike*, I; **ir de excursión** *to go on a hike*, I
la excusa *excuse*, II
exagerado(a) *exaggerated, dramatic*, 3
exagerar *to exaggerate*, 5
**el éxito** *success*, II
la expedición *expedition*, 9
experimentar *to experience*, 2
el experto *expert*, 6
la explicación *explanation*, II
explicar *to explain*, II
**los exploradores** *explorers*, 9
**explorar** *to explore*, II; **explorar cuevas** *to explore caves, to go spelunking*, II; **explorar la selva** *to explore the jungle*, II
la explotación *commercial use, exploitataion (of farmland)*, 9
explotar *to exploit*, II
la exportación *exportation*, 10
**la exposición** *exhibit*, 5
**expresarse** *to express (yourself)*, 7
**exquisito(a)** *wonderful*, II
extenso(a) *extensive*, 9
la extinción *extinction*, II
el extranjero, la extranjera *foreigner*, II
extranjero(a) *foreign*, II
extrañar *to miss*, II
extraño(a) *strange*, II
extremo(a) *extreme*, II
**extrovertido(a)** *outgoing*, I

## F

**la fábrica** *factory*, II
la fabricación *manufacture*, 8
los fabricantes *manufacturers*, II
la fábula *fable*, II
**fácil** *easy*, I
**facilitar** *to facilitate*, 8
**fácilmente** *easily*, II
**facturar** *to check*, I; **facturar el equipaje** *to check luggage*, I
**la falda** *skirt*, I; **la falda a media pierna** *mid-length skirt*, II; la falda de la montaña *the foot of the mountain*, II
fallecer *to pass away, die*, II
falso *false*, 1
**la falta de** *lack of*, 3
**faltar: Le falta no sé qué.** *It's missing something; I don't know what.*, II; **Le falta sabor.** *It's missing flavor.*, II; **Le falta sal.** *It's missing salt.*, II; **¿Qué te falta hacer?** *What do you still have to do?*, I; **Sólo me falta...** *I just need to . . .*, II; faltar el entrenamiento *to miss practice*, 2
**la fama** *reputation*, 3
**la familia** *family*, I
familiar *family-related*, 4; la foto familiar *family photo*, 4; los lazos familiares *family ties*, 4
los familiares *relatives*, II
famoso(a) *famous*, 2
**fanático(a)** *fan*, 2
**el fantasma** *ghost*, 9
fantástico(a) *fantastic*
**el farmacéutico, la farmacéutica** *pharmacist*, II
**la farmacia** *drugstore*, II
**fascinar** *to love*, II
**fastidiar** *to bother*, II
**fatal** *awful*, II
el favor *favor*; **Favor de** + infinitive *Please . . .*, II; **Haz el favor de** + infinitive *Please . . .*, II; **por favor** *please*, I
**febrero** *February*, I
**la fecha** *date*, I
¡Felicidades! *Congratulations!*, 2
**feliz (pl. felices): ¡Feliz...!** *Happy (Merry) . . .!*, I; **vivieron felices para siempre** *they lived happily ever after*, II
**fenomenal** *awesome*, I; *great*, II
**feo(a)** *ugly*, I
la feria *fair*, II
feroz *ferocious*, II
la ferretería *hardware store*, II
el ferrocarril *railroad*, II
**festejar** *to celebrate*, I
el festín *party*, 2

el festival *festival*, 6
**(poco) fiable** *(un)trustworthy*, 6
la ficción *fiction;* **la ciencia ficción** *science fiction*, I
ficticio(a) *fictitious*, 9
**los fideos** *noodles*, II; **la sopa de fideos** *noodle soup*, II
**la fiesta** *party*, I; **hacer una fiesta** *to have a party*, I; **la fiesta sorpresa** *surprise party*, I; las fiestas *holidays*, II
**la figura tallada** *carved figure*, II
**Fíjate que se ha casado.** *Get this: he/she got married.*, 4
el fin *end*; a fin de cuentas *in the end*, II; **por fin** *at last*, II; *finally*, II
**el fin de semana** *weekend*, I
el final *final:* **al final** *in the end*, II
financiar *to finance*, 3
la finca *territory*, II
fines de *the end of*, 2
fino(a) *fine, excellent*, II
**firmar** *to sign*, II
**la física** *physics*, 3
el flamenco *flamenco music*, 2
**el flan** *flan, custard*, I; **el flan de vainilla** *vanilla flan*, II
**flojo(a)** *baggy, loose*, II; *lazy*, 8
**la flor** *flower*, II
florecer *to bloom*, II
la floristería *flower shop*, II
fluir *to flow*, 6
**la fogata** *campfire*, II
el folleto *pamphlet, brochure*, II
el fomento *promotion, fostering*, 10
el fondo del mar *the bottom of the ocean*, 9
la forma *form;* **mantenerse en forma** *to stay in shape*, I
**formar** *to form*, 6
**formidable** *great, tremendous*, I, 5
formular *to formulate*, 3
**la fortuna** *fortune*, I
**la foto** *photo*, I
**la fotocopiadora** *photocopier*, 8
**la fotografía** *photography*, 5
**el fracaso** *failure*, II
la fragancia *fragrance*, 7
el fraile *friar*, 3
**francamente** *frankly*, II
**el francés** *French language*, I
el fray *friar*, 3
la frecuencia *frequency;* **¿Con qué frecuencia?** *How often?*, I
**frecuentemente** *frequently*, II
**el fregadero** *kitchen sink*, II
**freír (i, i)** *to fry*, II; **frito(a)** *fried (past participle of* **freír***)*, II
frenéticamente *frantically*, 9
frenético(a) *frantic, frenzied*, II
**las fresas (con crema)** *strawberries (and cream)*, II
**fresco(a)** *cool*, I
la frescura *freshness*, 6
**los frijoles** *beans*, 4
**frío(a)** *cold*, I; **tener frío** *to be cold*, II
**frito(a)** *fried (past participle of* **freír***)*, II; **las papas fritas** *French fries*, I
la frontera *border*, II
**frustrar** *to frustrate*, 2
**la fruta** *fruit*, I; **el surtido de frutas frescas** *assorted fresh fruit*, II
**la frutería** *fruit shop*, II
**fue cuando** *that was when*, II
**Fue todo un...** *It was a total . . .*, II
el fuego *fire*, II
**los fuegos artificiales** *fireworks*, I
**la fuente** *fountain*, II; *source*, II; **las fuentes de energía** *sources of energy*, 10
fuerte *strong*, II
fugaz *fleeting*, 2
**fumar** *to smoke*, I; **dejar de fumar** *to stop smoking*, I
**la función** *performance*, 5
funcionar *to work, to function*, 2
el (la) funcionario(a) *civil servant, public official*, 7
el fundador *founder*, II
fundar *to found*, II
fúnebre *mournful*, II
**el funeral** *funeral*, 4
el funicular *cable railway*, II
**furiosamente** *furiously*, II; *frantically*, II
**la fusión nuclear** *nuclear fusion*, 10
**el fútbol** *soccer*, I
**el fútbol americano** *football*, I
**el futuro** *future*, 10

## G

las gafas *glasses:* **las gafas de sol** *sunglasses*, II
**gala: los vestidos de gala** *fancy dresses, gowns*, II
**la galería** *gallery*, 5
**la galleta** *cookie*, I
el gallo *rooster*, II
la gamba *shrimp*, 2
la gana *desire:* **Me dieron ganas de** (+ infinitive) *I felt like . . .*, II; **tener ganas de...** *to feel like. . .*, II
el ganado *livestock*, 2
**ganar** *to win*, II; ganar dinero *to make money*, II
**los gandules** *pigeon peas*, II
**la ganga** *bargain*, I
**el garaje** *garage*, I
garantizar *to guarantee*, 10
**la garganta** *throat*, I
la gasolinera *gas station*, II
**gastar** *to spend*, I
**el gato, la gata** *cat*, I
el gaucho *Argentine cowboy*, 7, 9
**el gazpacho** *cold tomato soup*, II
la generación *generation*, 9
**generalmente** *generally*, II
generar *to generate*, 9
el género *genre*, II
**generoso(a)** *generous*, 2
**genial** *great*, 2
**la gente** *people*, II; **ayudar a la gente** *to help/assist people*, II; **buena gente** *nice (person)*, II
**la geografía** *geography*, 3
**la geometría** *geometry*, 3
**el gerente** *manager*, 8
el gigante *giant*, II
gigantesco(a) *gigantic*, 5
**la gimnasia** *gymnastics*, II
**el gimnasio** *gym*, I
la glorieta *traffic circle*, II
el (la) gobernador(a) *governor*, 3
el gobierno *government*, II
**el golf** *golf*, II
las golosinas *sweets, treats*, 2
**el golpe** *hit*, II; *bump*, II; **darse un golpe en...** *to bump one's . . .*, II; **¡Uf! Me di un golpe en...** *Oh! I hit my . . .*, II
golpear *to hit*, 9
**gordo(a)** *fat, overweight*, I
gótico(a) *gothic*, II
gozar de *to enjoy*, II
la grabación *recording*, II
**grabar CDs** *to burn CDs*, II
la gracia *humor*, II
**gracias** *thank you*, I; **el Día de Acción de Gracias** *Thanksgiving Day*, I; **Gracias por invitarme, pero ya lo/la he visto.** *Thanks for inviting me, but I've already seen it.*, 5; **Gracias, pero tengo mucho que hacer. La próxima vez iré.** *Thanks, but I have a lot to do. I'll go next time.*, 5; **Gracias al apoyo de... he podido superar...** *Thanks to the support of . . . I have been able to overcome . . .*, 7
**gracioso(a)** *witty*, I
**los grados Fahrenheit/centígrados** *degrees Fahrenheit/centrigrade*, 1
**la graduación** *graduation*, I
**graduarse (de)** *to graduate (from)*, 4
la gráfica *graph, diagram, chart*, II
**gran** *great, big, wide:* **Tenemos un gran surtido de regalos.** *We have a wide assortment of gifts.*, II; **No es gran cosa.** *It's not a big deal.*, I
la granada *pomegranate*, II
**grande** *big, large*, I
la grandeza *grandeur*, 2
el granero *granary*, II
**el granizo** *hail*, II
el grano *seed*, II, los granos, *grain*
**la grasa** *(dietary) fat*, I

Vocabulario español-inglés

**gratis** *free of charge,* II
gratuito(a) *free of charge,* 3
grave *serious,* II
el griego *Greek (language),* II
el (la) gringo(a) *American,* 2
**gris** *gray,* I
**gritar** *to shout,* II
el grito *shout,* II
**grosero(a)** *rude, vulgar,* 2
el grupero *a type of Mexican music,* 5
**el grupo étnico** *ethnic group,* 7
la guagua *baby,* 7
**los guantes** *gloves,* II
**guapísimo** *very handsome,* II; **¡Te ves guapísimo!** *You look very handsome!,* II
**guapo(a)** *good-looking,* I
el guardabosques *forest ranger,* II
**guardar los secretos** *to keep secrets,* 2
el guardia *guard;* el puesto de guardia *guard post,* II
**guatemalteco(a)** *Guatemalan,* II
la guayaba *guava,* 4
gubernamental *governmental,* 10
la guerra *war,* 9; la guerra civil *civil war,* 9
el guerrero *warrior,* II
el guía, la guía *guide:* el guía turístico *tour guide,* II; la guía telefónica *telephone book,* II; **la guía turística** *guide book,* II; la guía de ocio *entertainment guide*
los guineos *bananas (Puerto Rico, Dominican Republic),* II
los guisantes *peas,* II
el guiso *cooked dish,* II
**la guitarra** *guitar,* I
la gula *gluttony,* 4
**gustar: ¿Cuáles te gustan más...?** *Which do you like better . . ?,* II; **Me gustan más los cortos.** *I like the short ones better.,* II; **Me gustaría...** *I would like . . .,* I; **Me gustaría más...** *I would prefer . . .,* I; **¿ Te gustan más... o...?** *Do you like . . . or . . . more?,* II; **¿Qué te gustaba hacer?** *What did you like to do?,* II
**el gusto** *pleasure,* II; **al gusto** *to (one's) taste,* II; **El gusto es mío.** *The pleasure is mine.,* II; **Mucho gusto.** *Pleased/Nice to meet you.,* I; **¡Qué gusto verte!** *It's great to see you!,* I; **Tanto gusto.** *So nice to meet you.,* I
los gustos *likes,* II

## H

**haber** *to have (auxiliary verb),* II; **¿Ha comido en...?** *Have you eaten at . . .?,* II; haber publicado *having published,* II; **Hay algo que se me escapa.** *There's something I can't quite grasp.,* 8
**había** *there was, there used to be,* II; **Había una vez...** *There once was . . .,* II; **Había muchos desafíos en...** *There were many challenges in . . .,* 7
**las habichuelas** *beans (Puerto Rico),* II
la habilidad *ability,* 8
**la habitación** *bedroom,* I
el hábito *habit,* II
hablador(a) *chatty,* 3
**hablar** *to talk, to speak,* I; **Habla...** *. . . speaking (on the telephone),* I; **se habla** *is spoken,* II; **Hablando de arte, ¿qué me cuentas de...?** *Speaking of art, what can you tell me about . . .?,* 5; **Hablamos del tema; por consiguiente...** *We discussed the issue; consequently . . .,* 7
**¿Habrá...?** *(future tense of* **haber)** *Will there be . . .?,* II
**hacer (yo hago)** *to do, to make,* I; **¿Cuánto tiempo hace que tú...?** *How long have you been . . .?,* II; **Entonces, lo que tengo que hacer es...** *So, what I have to do is . . .,* II; **Hace mucho tiempo que yo...** *I've been . . . for a long time.,* II; **Hace poco tiempo que yo...** *I've been . . . for a little while.,* II; **Hace unos (muchos, cinco...) años** *A few (many, five . . .) years ago,* II; **¿Hará...?** *Will it be . . .?,* II; **Haz el favor de** + infinitive *Please . . .,* II; **hecho** *done (past participle of* **hacer**), II; **No hice nada.** *I didn't do anything.,* II; **¿Qué hacías de niño(a)?** *What did you use to do when you were a little boy/girl?,* II; **¿Qué harán ustedes en la playa?** *What will you do at the beach?,* II; **Se nos hace tarde.** *It's getting late.,* II; **Ya lo hice mil veces.** *I've already done it a thousand times.,* II; *to be (with weather expressions);* **Hace buen (mal) tiempo.** *The weather is nice (bad).,* I; **Hacer (calor, fresco, frío, sol, viento).** *to be (hot, cool, cold, sunny, windy).,* I; **¿Qué tiempo hace?** *What's the weather like?,* I; **hacer camping** *to go camping,* II; **hacer cola** *to wait in line,* I; **hacer crucigramas** *to do crossword puzzles,* II; **hacer diligencias** *to run errands,* II; **hacer diseño por computadora** *to do computer design,* II, 1; **hacer ecoturismo** *to go on an ecotour,* II; **hacer ejercicios aeróbicos** *to do aerobics,* II; **hacer juego** *to match, to go with,* II; **hacer la maleta** *to pack your suitcase,* I; **hacer preguntas** *to ask questions,* II; **hacer los quehaceres** *to do the chores,* I; **hacer senderismo** *to go hiking,* II; **hacer travesuras** *to play tricks,* II; **hacer un tour** *to take a guided tour,* II; **hacer un viaje** *to take a trip,* I; **hacer una fiesta** *to have a party,* I; **hacer una llamada por cobrar** *to make a collect call,* II; **hacer una reservación** *to make a reservation,* II; **hacer gimnasia** *to do gymnastics,* 1; **hacer windsurf** *to windsurf,* II; **hacer las paces** *to make up,* 3; **hacer(le) caso a** *to pay attention to,* 3, **Hace muchos años...** *Many years ago . . .,* 9; **Hace tiempo, vino un desconocido...** *Some time ago, a stranger came . . .,* 9
hacerse + adjective/noun *to become through personal effort,* 8
**hacerse amigo(a) de alguien** *to become friends with someone,* 1; hacerse arquitecto *to become an architect*
el hacha (f. las hachas) *hatchet, axe,* 6
hallar *to find*
**la hamaca** *hammock,* II
**el hambre** (f.) *hunger,* I, 10; **tener hambre** *to be hungry,* I
**la hamburguesa** *hamburger,* I
**el Hanukah** *Hanukkah,* I
la harina *flour,* II
harto(a) (de) *full (of):* **Estoy harto(a) de...** *I'm fed up with . . .,* II
**¿Has pensado en...?** *Have you thought about . . .?,* 3
**hasta** *until, up to,* I; hasta cierto punto *to some extent, in a way,* II; **Hasta luego.** *See you later.,* I; **Hasta mañana.** *See you tomorrow.,* I; **Hasta pronto.** *See you soon.,* I; **seguir derecho hasta** *to keep going (straight) to,* II; **subir/bajar... hasta llegar a** *to go up/down . . . until you get to,* II
**hay** *(present tense of* **haber**) *there is, there are,* I; **hay veces** *there are times,* I; **¿Qué hay de especial?** *What's the (daily) special?,* II; **¿Qué hay de nuevo?** *What's new?,* I
**hay que...** *one has to . . .,* 1; **¿Qué hay que hacer en la cocina?** *What needs to be done in the kitchen?,* II; **¿Y qué hay que hacer por aquí?** *And what is there to do around here?,* II; **Hay algo que se me escapa.** *There's something that I can't quite grasp.,* 8
**el (la) hechicero(a)** *sorcerer, sorceress,* 9
**el hecho** *deed, event, fact,* 9
**hecho(a) a mano** *handmade,* II
**la heladería** *ice cream shop,* I
helado(a) *frozen,* 2
**el helado** *ice cream,* I
el helicóptero *helicopter,* 10

la hembra *female,* 9
**la herencia** *heritage,* 7
**herido(a)** *hurt,* II
**herir (ie, i)** *to hurt (someone),* II, 3
**la hermana** *sister,* I
**la hermanastra** *stepsister,* 4
**el hermanastro** *stepbrother,* 4
**el hermano** *brother,* I
**los hermanos** *brothers, brothers and sisters,* I
**hermoso(a)** *beautiful,* 5
**el héroe** *hero,* 9
**la heroína** *heroine,* 9
las herramientas *tools,* 5
**hervido(a)** *boiled,* II
**hervir (ie, i)** *to boil,* II
**el hielo** *ice,* II; **el patinaje sobre hielo** *ice skating,* II
la hierba *grass,* II
el hierro *iron,* 10
**la hija** *daughter,* I
**el hijo** *son,* I
**los hijos** *sons, children,* I
el himno *anthem,* 5
**hinchado(a)** *swollen,* II
**hinchar** *to swell,* II
hipotético(a) *hypothetical,* 8
la histeria *hysteria,* 5
**la historia** *history,* I; *story,* II
los historiadores *historians,* II
histórico(a) *historical,* 9
el hocico *snout,* 2
el hogar *home, household,* 3
la hoja *sheet;* en una hoja aparte *on a separate sheet of paper,* II
**las hojas** *leaves,* II
hojear *to turn the pages of, to leaf through,* II
**hola** *hi, hello,* I
**el hombre** *man,* I; el hombre de nieve *snowman,* II; **el hombre/la mujer de negocios** *businessman/ businesswoman,* 8
**el hombro** *shoulder,* I
hondo(a) *deep;* **el plato hondo** *bowl,* I
**hondureño(a)** *Honduran,* II
**honesto(a)** *honest,* 2
**honrar** *to honor,* 9
la hora *hour,* II; **¿A qué hora...?** *At what time . . .?,* I; **¿Qué hora es?** *What time is it?,* I
**el horario** *schedule,* 3, 8
la hormiga *ant,* 8
**horneado(a)** *baked,* II
**hornear** *to bake,* II
**el horno** *oven,* I
**horrible** *horrible,* I
**hospedarse en...** *to stay at . . .,* II
**el hospital** *hospital,* II
hostelero(a): la industria hostelera *hospitality industry,* II
**el hotel** *hotel,* I
**hoy** *today,* I; hoy en día *nowadays,* II; **¿Qué fecha es hoy?** *What's today's date?,* I; **Hoy no, gracias. ¿Por qué no lo dejamos para la próxima semana?** *Not today, thanks. Why don't we wait and do it next week?,* 5; **hoy (en) día** *these days,* 8; **de hoy en adelante** *from now on,* 1
**hubo** (preterite tense of **haber**) *there was, there were,* II
**huele** (inf. **oler**) **a** *it smells like,* II
las huellas *traces,* II; *tracks,* II
**el hueso** *bone,* II
el huésped *guest;* el cuarto de huéspedes *guest room,* II
**el huevo** *egg,* I; **los huevos revueltos** *scrambled eggs,* II
**huir** *to flee, run away,* II
**húmedo(a)** *humid,* II
humilde *poor,* II
hundirse *to sink,* 9
**el huracán** *hurricane,* II

# I

**Iba a...** *(I) was going to . . .,* 2
los iberos *Iberians,* II
**la idea** *idea,* II; **Es buena idea que...** *It's a good idea for . . . to . . .,* II; **Ni idea.** *I have no idea.,* I
ideal *ideal,* 2
la identidad *identity;* **el carnet de identidad** *ID,* I
idílico(a) *idyllic,* 2
**los idiomas** *languages,* II
**la iglesia** *church,* I
**la ignorancia** *ignorance,* 3
igual *the same,* II; **Me da igual.** *It's all the same to me.,* I
**Igualmente.** *Likewise.,* I
**la imagen (positiva/negativa)** *(positive/negative) image,* 3
**imaginar** *to imagine,* 10; **Me imagino que...** *I imagine that . . .*
**imaginativo(a)** *imaginative,* 5
**impaciente** *impatient,* II
**imparcial** *unbiased, objective,* 6
**el imperio** *empire,* 7, 9
**el impermeable** *raincoat,* II
impreso(a) *printed,* 6
imponente *impressive,* II
imponer *to impose,* II
**importante** *important,* II; **Es importante que...** *It's important for . . . to . . .,* II
importar *to be important, to matter;* **no importa** *it doesn't matter,* II
imprescindible *indispensible,* II
**la impresión equivocada** *wrong impression,* 3
**impresionante** *impressive,* 5
**el impuesto** *tax,* II
incaico(a) *Incan,* II
incansable *tireless,* II
**el incendio** *fire,* II
la incertidumbre *uncertainty, doubt,* II
inclinado(a) *inclined, sloping,* II
**incluir** *to include,* II
incluso *even, actually,* II
incómodo(a) *uncomfortable,* II
**incomprensible** *incomprehensible,* 5
incorporarse *to join, become part of,* 7
la incredulidad *incredulousness, disbelief,* 6
**increíble** *incredible,* II
**la independencia** *independence,* 5, 9; **el Día de la Independencia** *Independence Day,* I
indicado(a) *indicated,* II
indicar *to indicate,* II
**la indiferencia** *indifference,* 10
indígena *indigenous,* II; *native,* 5
individualmente *individually,* 1
la industria *industry,* 8; la industria hostelera *hospitality industry,* II
industrial *industrial,* 10
inesperado(a) *unexpected,* 2
**infectado(a)** *infected,* II; **Ahora lo tengo infectado.** *Now it's infected.,* II
**infectar** *to infect,* II
influir *to influence, to have an influence,* 10
**informar** *to report,* 6
iniciar *to begin, to start,* 3
la inferencia *inference,* 7
influyente *influential,* II
**la información** *information,* II
**informar** *to inform,* 6
**informativo(a)** *informative,* 6
la ingeniería *engineering,* 7
**el ingeniero, la ingeniera** *engineer,* II
ingerir (ie, i) *to consume,* II
**el inglés** *English (language),* I
**los ingredientes** *ingredients,* II
ingresar *to join,* II
iniciado(a) *initiated, begun,* II
las iniciales *initials,* II
**injusto(a)** *unfair,* I; **Me parece injusto.** *It seems unfair to me.,* I
**inmediatamente** *immediately,* 8
inmensa *immense,* II
**los inmigrantes** *immigrants,* 10
**innovador(a)** *innovative,* 10
**el inodoro** *toilet,* II
inolvidable *unforgettable,* II
inscribirse *to sign up,* 3
**inseguro(a)** *insecure,* 2
insistir en *to insist,* 3
la insolencia *insolence,* 9
inspirado(a) *inspired,* II
**inspirarle confianza** *to inspire trust in (someone),* 6
las instrucciones *instructions*

Vocabulario español-inglés

**insultar** *to insult,* 3
integrarse *to integrate,* 7
**intelectual** *intellectual,* I
**inteligente** *intelligent,* I
intentar *to try,* II
la interacción *interaction,* II
**intercambiar** *to exchange, to trade,* II
el intercambio *exchange;* los programas de intercambio *exchange programs,* II
**el interés** (*pl.* **los intereses**) *interest,* II; **los lugares de interés** *places of interest,* I
**interesante** *interesting,* I
**interesar** *to interest,* II
**internacional** *international,* II; **banquero(a) internacional** *international banker,* II
**Internet** *Internet,* II; **el café Internet** *Internet café,* II
interrogante *interrogating, questioning,* 9
**interrumpir** *to interrupt,* I
íntimo(a) *intimate,* 3
la inundación *flood,* II
**el invento** *invention,* 10
el (la) inversionista *investor,* 9
invertir *to invest,* 6
la investigación *research,* II
**investigar** *to research,* 6
**el invierno** *winter,* I
**la invitación** *invitation,* I
**el invitado** *guest,* I
**invitar** *to invite,* I
involucrado(a) *involved,* 9
involuntario(a) *involuntary,* 10
**ir** *to go,* I; **Iré a/al...** *I'll go to . . .,* II; **Que te vaya bien.** *Hope things go well for you.,* I; **Fui a...** *I went to. . .,* 1, **Si todavía no ha ido a/al..., debe ir.** *If you haven't gone to . . . yet, you must go.,* II; **¿Vamos bien para...?** *Are we going the right way to . . .?,* II; **¡Ya voy!** *I'm coming!,* II; **ir a** + *infinitive* *to be going to (do something),* I; **ir a cafés** *to go to outdoor cafés,* II; **ir a un cibercafé** *to go to a cybercafé,* II; **ir al zoológico** *to go to the zoo,* II; **ir de compras** *to go shopping,* I; **ir de excursión** *to go hiking,* I; **ir de pesca** *to go fishing,* I; **ir de vacaciones** *to go on vacation,* II; **ir por la calle...** *to take . . . street,* II
irradiar *to irradiate, to radiate,* 9
irrecuperable *unrecoverable, irreversible,* 6
**irritar** *to irritate,* 2
**irse** *to leave,* I
**la isla** *island,* I; **la isla tropical** *tropical island,* II
el islote *isle,* II
italiano(a) *Italian;* **la comida italiana** *Italian food,* I
**el itinerario** *itinerary,* II
izado(a) *raised,* 9
**izquierdo(a)** *left,* II; **a la izquierda (de)** *to the left (of),* II; **doblar a la izquierda en** *to turn left on,* II

## J

el jabalí *wild boar,* 6
**el jabón** *soap,* I
**el jai alai** *jai-alai,* 2
**jamás** *never,* 1
**el jamón** *ham,* I
el japonés *Japanese,* II
**el jarabe** *cough syrup,* II
**el jardín** *garden,* I; **trabajar en el jardín** *to work in the garden,* II
el jefe *chief,* II; **el jefe, la jefa** *boss,* 8
el jinete *rider,* II
**joven** *young,* I
**el joven, la joven** *young person,* II
**los jóvenes** *young people,* I
la joya *jewel*
**las joyas** *jewelry,* II
**la joyería** *jewelry store,* I
los judíos *Jews,* II
**el juego** *game,* I; **el juego de mesa** *board game,* I; **hacer juego** *to match, to go with,* II; los Juegos Olímpicos *Olympic Games,* 2; **los juegos de computadora** *computer games,* 2
**el jueves** *Thursday,* I; **los jueves** *on Thursdays,* I
el(la) juez *judge,* 4
**el jugador, la jugadora** *player,* II
**jugar (ue)** *to play,* I; **jugar a la casita** *to play house,* II; **jugar a las damas** *to play checkers,* II; **jugar al ajedrez** *to play chess,* II; **jugar al escondite** *to play hide and seek,* II; **jugar al pilla-pilla** *to play tag,* II; **jugar al tenis** *to play tennis,* II; **jugar con bloques** *to play with blocks,* II; **jugar con carritos** *to play with toy cars,* II; **jugar naipes** *to play cards,* II; **Jugaremos con...** *We'll play with . . .,* II, **jugar al golf** *to play golf,* 1
**el jugo** *juice,* I; **el jugo de...** *. . . juice,* I
**el juguete** *toy,* I; **compartir los juguetes** *to share toys,* II
**la juguetería** *toy store,* I
**juguetón, juguetona** *playful,* II
**julio** *July,* I
el junco *reed,* II
**junio** *June,* I
juntarse *to get together,* 2
**juntos(as)** *together,* II; **trabajar juntos** *to work together,* II
justamente *precisely, exactly,* II
**la justicia** *justice,* 9
**justo(a)** *fair,* II; *right,* II; **¡No es justo!** *It's not fair!,* II
juvenil *youth,* II; **el albergue juvenil** *youth hostel,* II
la juventud *youth, childhood,* 2
**juzgar** *to judge,* 3

## K

**el kárate** *karate,* 2

## L

**la** *the (fem. article),* I
**la** *you, it, (pron.),* I; **Bueno, se la regalo por..., pero es mi última oferta.** *Okay, I'll give it to you for . . ., but that's my last offer.,* II; **Enseguida se la traigo.** *I'll bring it right away.,* II; **(No) te la recomiendo.** *I (don't) recommend it to you.,* II
el laberinto *labyrinth,* II
**los labios** *lips,* II
la labor *labor,* 6
labrado(a) *carved,* 6
el lado *side;* al lado *next door,* II; **al lado de** *next to,* I
el ladrillo *brick,* II
**el lagarto** *lizard,* II
**el lago** *lake,* I; **la orilla del lago** *lakeshore,* II
**lamentar** *to regret,* 9
**las láminas** *trading cards,* II
**la lámpara** *lamp,* II
**la lana** *wool,* I; **de lana** *made of wool,* I
**la lancha** *motorboat,* I; **pasear en lancha** *to go out in a motorboat,* I
**la langosta** *lobster,* 4
lanzar(se) *to throw,* II
el lanzamiento *launching,* 10
**el lápiz** (*pl.* **los lápices**) *pencil,* I; **el lápiz labial** *lipstick,* II
**largo(a)** *long,* I
**las** *the (pl. fem. article),* I
**las** *you, them (pron.),* I
la lástima *pity, compassion;* **¡Qué lástima!** *What a shame!,* I
**lastimarse** *to injure/hurt oneself,* II
**la lata** *can,* II; *nuisance;* **la lata de salsa de tomate** *can of tomato sauce,* II; **¡Qué lata!** *What a pain!,* I
**el lavabo** *bathroom sink,* II

el lavadero *kitchen sink (Peru),* II
**la lavadora** *washing machine,* II
el lavamanos *bathroom sink,* II
la lavandería *laundromat,* II
**el lavaplatos** *dishwasher,* II
**lavar** *to wash,* I; **lavar los platos** *to do the dishes,* I
**lavarse** *to wash,* I; **lavarse los dientes** *to brush one's teeth,* II
el lavatorio *bathroom sink (Peru, Texas),* II
**le** *to/for him, her, you (sing.),* I; **¿En qué le puedo servir?** *How can I help you?,* I; **Le aconsejo que...** *I recommend that you . . .,* II; **Le encanta(n)...** *He/she/you love(s) . . .,* II; **Le falta no sé qué.** *It's missing something; I don't know what.,* II; **Le falta sabor.** *It's missing flavor.,* II; **Le falta sal.** *It's missing salt.,* II; **Le gusta** + infinitive *He/She/It likes (to) . . .,* I; **Le presento a...** *This is (formal) . . .,* II; **Le voy a dar un precio especial.** *I'm going to give you a special price.,* II
**leal** *loyal,* 2
**la leche** *milk,* I; **el café con leche** *coffee with milk,* I
**el lechón** *piglet, pork,* II; **el lechón asado** *roasted pork,* II
**la lechuga** *lettuce,* II
la lechuza *owl,* II
el lector *reader,* 8
la lectura *reading,* II
**leer** *to read,* I
lejano(a) *far away, distant,* 5
lejos *far;* **lejos de** *far from,* I
el lema *motto,* II
la lengua *language,* II; *tongue,* II
**lentamente** *slowly,* II
**los lentes** *glasses,* I; **los lentes de contacto** *contact lenses,* II; **usar lentes** *to wear glasses,* I
**les** *to/for them, you,* I; **A ellos/ellas les gusta** + infinitive *They like to . . .,* I; **A ellos/ellas/ustedes les gusta(n)** + noun *They (emphatic) like . . .,* II; **Les presento a...** *I'd like you (pl.) to meet . . .,* II; **¿Se les ofrece algo más?** *Would you like anything else?,* II; **Le/Les adjunto un(a)...** *I'm enclosing a . . .,* 8; **les agradecieron a...** *they thanked them, you. . .,* 9
**la letra** *lyrics,* 5, *handwriting,* 8
el letrero *sign,* II
**levantar** *to lift,* I; **levantar pesas** *to lift weights,* I
**levantarse** *to get up,* I
**la ley (en contra/a favor de)** *law (against/in favor of),* 10
**la leyenda** *legend,* 9
**liberar** *to liberate,* 9
**la libertad** *liberty,* 9
el libertador *liberator,* 9
la libra *pound,* II
libre *free;* **al aire libre** *open-air, outdoor,* II; **el rato libre** *free time,* II; **la lucha libre** *wrestling,* II
**la librería** *bookstore,* I
**el libro** *book,* I; **el libro de amor** *romance book,* I; **el libro de aventuras** *adventure book,* I
**la licencia** *license,* II; **la licencia de conducir** *driver's license,* II; la licencia de maternidad *maternity leave,* 8
la licenciatura *bachelor's degree,* 8
el líder *leader,* 5, 9
la liebre *hare,* II
el lienzo *artist's canvas,* 5
la liga *league,* II
**la lima** *lime,* 4
**limpiar** *to clean,* I
la limpieza *cleaning,* 8
**el limón** *lemon,* 4
**lindo(a)** *pretty,* II; **lindísimo(a)** *really beautiful,* II
la línea *line;* **el patinaje en línea** *in-line skating,* II
**la linterna** *lantern, flashlight,* II
el lío *mess,* II
la liquidación *liquidation;* **la venta de liquidación** *clearance sale,* II
la lista *list,* II
**listo(a)** *ready,* I
listo(a)(s) *smart,* 1
**la literatura** *literature,* 3
la llama *flame,* II
la llamada *telephone call,* II; **hacer una llamada por cobrar** *to make a collect call,* II
**llamar** *to call,* I; **que me llame después** *tell him/her to call me later,* I
**llamarle la atención** *to be interested in,* II
**llamar la atención** *to attract one's attention,* 5
**llamarse** *to be named,* II
llamativo(a) *striking, attention-grabbing,* 5
el llano *plain, flat ground,* II
**la llave** *key,* II; **cerrar la puerta con llave** *to lock the door,* II
**la llegada** *arrival,* I
**llegar** *to arrive, to get there,* I; **¿Cómo puedo llegar a...?** *How can I get to . . .,* II; **subir/bajar... hasta llegar a** *to go up/down . . . until you get to,* II; **llegar a un acuerdo** *to reach an agreement,* 9
**llegar a ser** *to become,* 7; **llegar a ser** + adjective/noun *to become or to get to be (after a series of events or after a long time),* 7
llenar de *to fill up with,* II
lleno(a) *full,* II
**llevar** *to wear,* I; *to take,* I; *to take, to carry,* II; **llevar (a alguien)** *to take (someone),* II; llevar a cabo *to carry out,* II; **llevar una dieta balanceada** *to eat a balanced diet,* II; **¿Qué lleva el (la)...?** *What's in the . . .?,* II
llevarse *to carry off, to take away;* **llevarse bien** *to get along well,* II; **llevarse mal** *to get along badly,* II; llevarse una sorpresa *to have a surprise*
**llorar** *to cry,* II; **ponerse a llorar** *to start to cry,* II
**llover (ue)** *to rain,* I; **De repente, empezó a llover...** *Suddenly, it started to rain . . .,* II; **llover a cántaros** *to pour rain,* II
**la llovizna** drizzle, 1
**lloviznar** *to drizzle,* II
la lluvia de ideas *brainstorm,* 5
**lo** *him, it,* I; *you,* I; **Cuando me enteré, no lo pude creer.** *When I found out, I couldn't believe it.,* II; **No lo vas a creer, pero...** *You won't believe it, but . . .,* II; **Ya lo hice mil veces.** *I've already done it a thousand times.,* II; **Lo/La encontré muy interesante.** *I found it very interesting.,* 1; **Lo leí en la sección deportiva** *I read it in the sports section.,* 6; Lo que le cuesta trabajo..., *What is difficult . . .,* 7; **Lo puedo hacer.** *I can do it.,* 8; **Lo recuerdo como si fuera ayer...** *I remember it like it was yesterday.,* 10
lo contrario *opposite,* II
lo de *that matter of, that business about;* **¿Cómo te sentiste cuando supiste lo de...?** *How did you feel when you heard about . . .?,* II
**lo de siempre** *same as usual,* I
**lo que** *what,* II; *the thing that,* 10; **Cuéntame lo que pasó el día que...** *Tell me what happened the day that . . .,* II; **¿Encontraste lo que buscabas en...?** *Did you find what you were looking for at . . .?,* II; **Entonces, lo que tengo que hacer es...** *So, what I have to do is . . .,* II; lo que pasa *what is happening,* II; **¿Puede repetir lo que dijo?** *Can you repeat what you said?,* II, 2; **Lo que noto es que...** *What I notice is that . . .,* 10
**Lo siento.** *I'm sorry,* I
**lo siguiente** *the following,* I
lo suficiente *enough,* II; **dormir lo suficiente** *to get enough sleep,* I
**el lobo** *wolf,* II
localizado(a) *located,* II
**loco(a)** *crazy,* II; **Estoy loco(a) por...** *I'm crazy about . . .,* II
**el (la) locutor(a)** *announcer, newscaster,* 6
el lodo *mud,* 5
**lograr** *to achieve, to manage (to do something),* 7
el loro *parrot,* 9
**los** *the (pl. masc.),* I; **Los/Las... me dejan frío(a).** *The . . . don't do*

Vocabulario español-inglés

*anything for me (you, him, her).*, 2
**los** *you, them (pron.)*, I; **Enseguida se los traigo.** *I'll bring them to you right away.*, II; **Se los dejo en...** *I'll let you have them for . . .*, II
los cuales *which,* II
lozano(a) *leafy, robust,* 2
**la lucha libre** *wrestling,* II
lucir (zc) *to shine,* II; *to display,* 9
**luchar por** *to fight for,* 7
**luego** *then, later,* I; **Hasta luego.** *See you later.*, I; desde luego *naturally, of course,* II
el lugar *place,* II
**los lugares de interés** *places of interest,* I
la luminosidad *luminosity,* 9
luminoso(a) *bright, luminous,* II
la luna *moon,* II
**el lunes** *Monday,* I; **los lunes** *on Mondays,* I
**la luz** (*pl.* **las luces**) *light,* II; **apagar la luz/las luces** *to turn off the light(s),* II

## M

**la madera** *wood,* II
**la madrastra** *stepmother,* 4
**la madre** *mother,* I; **el Día de la Madre** *Mother's Day,* I
la madrina *godmother,* II
la madrugada *dusk,* 6
la maestra *teacher,* II
**mágico(a)** *magic,* 9
**el maíz** *corn,* I
majado(a) *mashed,* II
**mal** *bad;* **estar mal** *to be (doing) badly,* I; *to be sick,* II; **llevarse mal** *to get along badly,* II; **Me fue muy mal.** *I did very badly.*, II; **quedar mal** *to fit badly,* I; **Te veo mal.** *You don't look well.*, I
**maleducado(a)** *rude, ill-bred,* 2
**la maleta** *suitcase,* I; **hacer la maleta** *to pack your suitcase,* I
maliciosamente *maliciously,* 8
**malo(a)** *bad,* I; **sacar malas notas** *to get bad grades,* II
malsano(a) *unhealthy,* II
**maltratar** *to mistreat,* 3
**el (la) malvado(a)** *villain,* 9
**la mamá** *mom,* I
**mandar** *to send,* I
el mandato *command,* II
manejar *to drive,* II
la manera *way,* II; a manera *in the manner of,* II
las mangas *sleeves,* II
**las manifestaciones** *demonstrations,* 10
**la mano** *hand,* I; **hecho(a) a mano** *handmade,* II; pedir la mano *to ask for her hand in marriage,* II
**el mantel** *tablecloth,* II
**la mantequilla** *butter,* II
**mantener (ie)** *to maintain,* 7; *to support,* 7; mantener en equilibrio *to keep (something) balanced,* II
**mantenerse (me mantengo, ie)** *to maintain,* I; **mantenerse en forma** *to stay in shape,* I
**la manzana** *apple,* I; *block (Spain, Dominican Republic),* II
**el mañana** *tomorrow,* I; **Hasta mañana.** *See you tomorrow.*, I; **pasado mañana** *day after tomorrow,* I; **¿Mañana vamos a tener otra prueba en...? ¡Esto es el colmo!** *Tomorrow we're going to have another test in . . . This is the last straw!,* 3
**la mañana** *morning,* I; **de la mañana** *in the morning,* A.M., I; **por la mañana** *in the morning,* I
**el mapa** *map,* I
**el maquillaje** *makeup,* I
**maquillarse** *to put on makeup,* I
la máquina *car,* 10
**el mar** *sea,* II; **bañarse en el mar** *to swim in the sea,* II
la maravilla *wonder, marvel,* II
**maravilloso(a)** *marvelous,* 5
la marca *make, brand,* II
marcharse *to leave,* 6
marcial *martial;* **las artes marciales** *martial arts,* II
el maremoto *tidal wave, sea earthquake,* 10
el marinero *sailor,* 9
**los mariscos** *seafood,* II
marítimo(a) *maritime,* 6
**el martes** *Tuesday,* I; **los martes** *on Tuesdays,* I
**marzo** *March,* I
**más** *more,* I; **¿Algo más?** *Anything else?,* II; **¿Cuáles te gustan más, ... o ...?** *Which do you like better, . . . or . . .?,* II; **Esa corbata es la más elegante de todas.** *That tie is the nicest one.*, II; **Más o menos.** *So-so.*, I; *more or less,* II; **Me gustaría más...** *I would prefer to . . .,* I; **¿Qué más tengo que hacer?** *What else do I need to do?,* II; **¿Se les ofrece algo más?** *Would you like anything else?,* II; **más...que** *more . . . than,* I
la masa *mass,* II
el masaje *massage,* II
**la máscara** *mask,* II
**la mascota** *pet,* II; **cuidar a una mascota** *to take care of a pet,* II
**las matemáticas** *mathematics,* I
**la materia** *school subject,* I; *material,* II
matricularse *to register, to enroll,* II
el matrimonio *wedding,* II
**mayo** *May,* I
**la mayonesa** *mayonnaise,* II
**mayor** *older,* I; *greatest,* 7
la mayoría *majority,* II
**me** *me, to/for me,* I; **A mí (no) me gusta(n)** + noun *I (emphatic) (don't) like . . .,* II; **Me caía muy bien.** *I really liked him/her.*, II; **Me da igual.** *It's all the same to me.*, I; **Me di un golpe en...** *I hit my . . .,* II; **¿Me dices dónde está...?** *Can you tell me where . . . is?,* II; **Me dieron ganas de** + infinitive *I felt like . . .,* II; **Me dio (alegría, tristeza, vergüenza, una rabia).** *It made me (happy, sad, embarrassed, angry).*, II; **Me duele la garganta** *My throat hurts.*, II; **Me fue muy bien (mal).** *I did very well (badly).*, II; **Me gustaría...** *I would like . . .,* I; **Me gustaría más...** *I would prefer to . . .,* I; **Me levanto, me baño...** *I get up, I bathe . . .,* II; **¿Me podría decir...?** *Could you tell me . . .?,* II; **¿Me puede rebajar el precio de ese/esa...?** *Can you lower the price on that . . .?,* II; **Me puse** + adj. *I felt/became . . .,* II; **Me puse a** + infinitive *I started to . . .,* II; **Me quedan...** *They're . . .,* II; **Me reí mucho.** *I laughed a lot.*, II; **Me da lo mismo.** *It's all the same to me.*, 2; **Me choca la actitud de... hacia... ¡No aguanto más!** *I can't stand the attitude of . . . towards . . . I can't take it anymore!,* 3; me parece bien *it sounds good to me,* 4; me da gusto *it pleases me,* 4; **Me has dejado boquiabierto(a).** *You've left me speechless.*, 4; **¿Me acompañas a...?** *Do you want to come to . . . with me?,* 5; **Me cuesta trabajo (hacer)...** *It takes a lot of work for me (to do) . . .,* 8; **Me gustaría ser un(a)...** *I would like to be a . . .,* 8; **Me interesaría estudiar para ser un(a)** *I would be interested in studying to be a . . .,* 8; **Me parece que...** *It seems to me that . . .,* 10; **Me imagino que para el año ... habrá...,** *I imagine that by the year . . . there will be . . .,* 10
la mecánica *mechanics;* **trabajar en mecánica** *to work on cars,* II
**el mecánico, la mecánica** *mechanic,* II
la medalla *medal,* II
mediado(a) *mediated,* 10; a mediados de *in the middle of,* II
**la medianoche** *midnight,* I
mediante *through,* II
**el médico, la médica** *doctor,* II
las medidas necesarias *the necessary steps,* 10
medio(a) *half;* el Oriente Medio *Middle East,* II; en medio de *in the middle of,* II; **la falda a media pierna** *mid-length skirt,* II; **y media** *half past,* I

el medio ambiente *environment*, 10
la medio hermana *half sister*, 4
el medio hermano *half brother*, 4
el mediodía *midday, noon*, I
los medios de transporte *means of transportation*, I
medir (i, i) *to measure*, II; la taza de medir *measuring cup*, II
la mejilla *cheek*, II
mejor *better, best*, I; A lo mejor habrá... *Maybe there will be . . .*, 10; Es mejor que... *It's better for . . . to*, II; mejor que nadie *better than anyone*
mejorar *to improve*, 8
la melodía *melody*, 5
melodioso(a) *melodic*, 5
mencionar *to mention*, II
menor *younger*, I
menos *less*, I; Más o menos. *So-so.*, I; *more or less*, II; ...menos cuarto *quarter to (the hour)*, I; por/a lo menos *at least*, II; Te echo mucho de menos. *I miss you a lot.*, II, menos... que *less . . . than*, 1
el mensaje *message*, 6
mensual *monthly*, II
la mente *mind*, II
mentir (ie, i) *to lie*, 2
la mentira *lie*, II
el menú *menu*, II
el mercado *market*, II; el puesto del mercado *market stand*, II; ir de compras al mercado *to go shopping at the market*, II
la mercancía *merchandise*, II
merendar (ie) *to have a snack*, I
la mesa *table*, I; el juego de mesa *board game*, I
la meseta *highlands*, 2
el mesero, la mesera *server*, II
los meses del año *months of the year*, I
la mesita de noche *bedside table*, II
mestizo(a) *half-Caucasian, half-indigenous*, 7
la meta *goal*, 7
el método *method*, II
el metro *subway*, I; la parada del metro *subway stop*, II
mexicano(a) *Mexican*, II; la comida mexicana *Mexican food*, I
la mezcla *mixture*, II
mezclar *to mix*, I
mí *me (emphatic)*, I; A mí me gusta + infinitive *I like to . . .*, I; A mí siempre me toca... *I always have to . . .*, I; A mí (no) me gusta(n) + noun *I (emphatic) (don't) like . . .*, II
mi(s) *my*, I; Dale un saludo a... de mi parte. *Say hi to . . . for me.*, II; ¿Dónde estará(n) mi(s)...? *Where could my . . . be?*, II; Mis... enfrentaron obstáculos cuando... *My . . . faced obstacles when . . .*, 7; Mi éxito en... se debe a... *My success in . . . is due to . . .*, 7
el miedo *fear*, I; darle miedo *to scare*, II; tener miedo *to be scared*, I
la miel *honey*, II
los miembros *members*, II
mientras *while*, II
el miércoles *Wednesday*, I; los miércoles *on Wednesdays*, I
mil *one thousand*, I; dos mil *two thousand*, I; Ya lo hice mil veces. *I've already done it a thousand times.*, II
milagroso(a) *miraculous*, 10
el militar *military man*, 9
un millón (de) *one million*, I; dos millones (de) *two million*, I
el mimbre *willow*, II
la mina de cobre *copper mine*, 10
el mineral *mineral*; el agua *(f.)* mineral *mineral water*, II
el minero *miner*, 10
la minifalda *miniskirt*, II
mío(a) *mine*, II; El gusto es mío. *The pleasure is mine.*, II
míos, mías *mine*, II
mirar *to look*; Nada más estoy mirando. *I'm just looking.*, I; mirar las vitrinas *to window shop*, I
mi(s) *my*, I
la misa *Mass*, I
la misión *mission*, 3
los misioneros *missionaries*, II
mismo(a) *same*, II
el misterio *mystery*, I; la película de misterio *mystery movie*, I; las novelas de misterio *mystery novels*, II
misterioso(a) *mysterious*, 9
el mito *myth*, 9
mixto(a) *mixed*, II; la ensalada mixta *mixed salad*, II
la mochila *backpack*, I
la moda *style, fashion*, I; a la (última) moda *in the (latest) style*, I; pasado(a) de moda *out of style*, I
el modelo, la modelo *model*, II
moderno(a) *modern*, 5
el modo *way*, II; el modo de ser *way of being*, 7
el mojo *a type of sauce*, 4
moler *to grind*, 4
molestar *to bother*, II
el molino *mill*, 2; el molino de viento *windmill*, 2
el momento *moment*; Espera un momento. *Hold on a moment.*, I; en otro momento *at another time*, 2
la momia *mummy*, 10
las monedas *coins*, II; coleccionar monedas *to collect coins*, II
los monitos *comic strips (Texas)*, 6
el mono *monkey*, II
monstruoso(a) *monstrous*, 9
las montañas *mountains*, I; la falda de la montaña *the foot of the mountain*, II; subir a la montaña *to go up a mountain*, I
montañoso(a) *mountainous*, II
montar *to set up*, 7; montar a caballo *(to go) horseback riding*, II; montar en bicicleta *to ride a bike*, II
un montón *a ton*, I
la montura *saddle*, II
los monumentos *monuments*, II
morado(a) *purple*, I
moreno(a) *dark-haired; dark-skinned*, I
morirse (ue, u) *to die*, II
los moros *Moors*, II
el mortero *mortar*, II
la mosca *fly*, 10
la mostaza *mustard*, II
el mostrador *counter*, I
mostrar (ue) *to show*, II
la movida *night life, moving around*, 2
el movimiento *movement*, II
la muchacha *girl*, I
el muchacho *boy*, I
mucho(a) *a lot (of), much*, I; Hace mucho tiempo que... *I've been . . . for a long time.*, II; llueve mucho *it rains a lot*, I; Me reí mucho. *I laughed a lot.*, II; Mucho gusto. *Pleased/Nice to meet you.*, I; pasar mucho tiempo *to spend a lot of time*, II; Te echo mucho de menos. *I miss you a lot.*, II
muchos(as) *a lot of, many*, I; muchas veces *often*, II
mudarse *to move (houses)*, 2
la mueblería *furniture store*, II
los muebles *furniture*, II; sacudir los muebles *to dust the furniture*, II
la muerte *death*, II
muerto(a) *dead*, II
la mujer *woman*, I; la mujer cartero *mail carrier (f.)*, II; la mujer policía *policewoman*, II; para mujeres *for women*, I; la mujer de negocios *businesswoman*, 8, la mujer soldado *female soldier*, 9
la multa *fine*, II
el mundo *world*, II
la muñeca *wrist*, II
las muñecas *dolls*, II
la muralla *wall*, II
el mural *mural*, 5
el muro *wall*, II
musculoso(a) *muscular*, 9
el museo *museum*, I; visitar un museo *to visit a museum*, II
la música *music*, I; la música clásica

Vocabulario español-inglés

*classical music,* II; la música norteña *a type of Mexican music,* 5
los músicos *musicians,* II
**el muslo** *thigh,* II
mutuamente *mutually,* 8
**muy** + adjective *very,* I; **Me caía muy bien.** *I really liked him/her.,* II; **Me fue muy bien (mal).** *I did very well (badly).,* II; **Muy atentamente** *Most sincerely,* 8; **Muy estimado(a) Sr./Sra./Srta.:** *Dear Sir/Madam/Miss:,* 8

## N

**nacer (zc)** *to be born,* 4
nacido(a) *born,* II; recién nacido(a) *newborn,* II
**el nacimiento** *birth,* II
la nación *nation,* 6
**nacional** *national,* II; **el parque nacional** *national park,* II
**nada** *nothing, not anything,* I; **Nada más estoy mirando.** *I'm just looking.,* I; De nada. *You're welcome.,* II; **No hice nada.** *I didn't do anything.,* II; **para nada** *not at all,* II
**nadar** *to swim,* I
**nadie** *nobody, not anybody,* I; **mejor que nadie** *better than anyone,* II
**los naipes** *cards,* II; **jugar naipes** *to play cards,* II
**la naranja** *orange,* I
**la nariz** *nose,* I
narrado(a) *narrated,* II
**la natación** *swimming,* II
natal *native;* la casa natal *house where someone was born,* II; la ciudad natal *city where someone was born,* II
**la naturaleza** *nature,* II; **observar la naturaleza** *to nature watch,* II
**la navaja** *razor,* I
la nave *ship, vessel,* II; la nave espacial *space ship,* 6; **la nave hundida** *sunken ship,* 10
navegable *navigable,* 7
navegar *to sail, to navigate;* **navegar por Internet** *to surf the Internet,* I
**la Navidad** *Christmas,* I
las necesidades *needs,* II
**necesitar** *to need,* I; **¿Necesitas algo?** *Do you need anything?,* I
la negación *negation,* 3
negar (ie) *to deny,* 3
el negocio *business,* II; el hombre/la mujer de negocios *businessman/businesswoman,* I
**negro(a)** *black,* I
neoclásico(a) *neoclassical,* 10
**nervioso(a)** *nervous,* I
**nerviosamente** *nervously,* II
**nevar (ie)** *to snow,* I
**ni** *neither, nor,* I; **Ni idea.** *I have no idea.,* I
**nicaragüense** *Nicaraguan,* II
**la niebla** *fog,* II
**la nieta** *granddaughter,* I
**el nieto** *grandson,* I
**los nietos** *grandsons, grandchildren,* I
**nieva** *it snows,* I
**la nieve** *snow,* II; el hombre de nieve *snowman,* II
**ningún** *none, not (a single) one,* II
**ninguno(a)** *none, not (a single) one,* II; **No va a ninguna parte.** *He/She doesn't go anywhere.,* I
**la niña** *girl,* II; **¿Qué hacías de niña?** *What did you use to do when you were a little girl?,* II
la niñez *childhood,* II
**el niño** *boy,* II; **¿Qué hacías de niño?** *What did you use to do when you were a little boy?,* II
**los niños** *children,* I
el nivel *level,* 10
**no** *no,* I; *not, do not,* I; **Cómo no.** *Of course.,* II; **Ya no.** *Not anymore.,* II; **No, ando planeando...** *No, I'm planning . . .,* II; **¡No es justo!** *It's not fair!,* II; **No estoy seguro(a).** *I'm not sure.,* II; **No hice nada.** *I didn't do anything.,* II; **No lo vas a creer, pero...** *You won't believe it, but . . .,* II; **nomás** *just, only,* I; **¡No me digas!** *No way! You're kidding!,* II; **no sólo... sino... también** *not only . . . but . . . as well,* II; **No te lo/la recomiendo.** *I don't recommend it to you.,* II; **No te olvides de...** *Don't forget to . . .,* II; **No te preocupes.** *Don't worry.,* II; **¿no?** *right?,* I; **No cabe duda que...** *There's no doubt that . . .,* 6; no es cierto que... *it's not true that . . .,* 6; no intencional *unintentional,* 8; **No vayamos...** *Let's not go . . .,* 2; **No aguanto...** *I can't stand . . .,* 2; **No me parece que sea justo.** *I don't think it's fair.,* 3; **No te conviene...** *It's not good for you . . .,* 3; **No te olvides de...** *Don't forget to . . .,* 3; **No lo hice a propósito.** *I didn't do it on purpose.,* 3; **No quise hacerte daño/ofenderte.** *I didn't mean to hurt/offend you.,* 3; **¡No me digas!** *You don't say!,* 4; **¡No me lo puedo creer!** *I can't believe it!,* 4; **No te olvides de ir al ensayo de la banda.** *Don't forget to go to band practice.,* 5; **No creo que los periodistas/los noticieros sean...** *I don't think that journalists/newscasts are . . .,* 6; **No estoy seguro(a) (de) que tengas razón sobre...** *I'm not sure that you're right about . . .,* 6; **No tengo la menor idea si...** *I don't have the slightest idea if . . .,* 6; **No estudié así que...** *I didn't study, so . . .,* 7; **No logro entender...** *I can't seem to understand . . .,* 8; **No me cabe en la cabeza.** *I can't understand it.,* 8; **No me es nada difícil.** *It's not hard for me at all.,* 8; **No, no me acuerdo para nada.** *No, I don't remember at all.,* 10
**la noche** *night,* II; **esta noche** *tonight,* II; cada noche *each night,* II; **de la noche** *at night,* P.M., I; **la mesita de noche** *bedside table,* II; **por la noche** *at night, in the evening,* I
**la Nochebuena** *Christmas Eve,* I
**la Nochevieja** *New Year's Eve,* I
la noción *notion, idea,* 3
nocturno(a) *night,* II
nombrado(a) *named,* II
el norte *north,* II
**nos** *to/for us,* I; **Nos peleábamos** *We fought (would fight),* II; **¿Nos trae...?** *Would you bring us . . .?,* II; **¿Qué nos recomienda?** *What do you recommend?,* II; **Se nos hace tarde.** *It's getting late.,* II; **Nos costó trabajo acostumbrarnos a...** *It took a lot of work for us to get used to . . .,* 7; **Nos esforzamos en...** *We made a big effort at . . .,* 7
**nosotros(as)** *we, us (after preposition),* I
**la nota** *grade,* II; **sacar (buenas, malas) notas** *to get (good, bad) grades,* II
notar *to notice,* 2
**la noticia** *news,* II; **Cuando oí la noticia no lo quise creer.** *When I heard the news, I didn't want to believe it.,* II
**las noticias** *news,* II; **¿Qué noticias tienes de...?** *What news do you have of . . .?,* II; **las noticias (en línea)** *news (online),* 6
**el noticiero** *newscast,* 6
**novecientos(as)** *nine hundred,* I
**la novela** *novel,* I
**noveno(a)** *ninth,* II
**noventa** *ninety,* I
**noviembre** *November,* I
la novia *girlfriend,* II; *bride,* 4
el novio *boyfriend,* II; *groom,* 4
los novios *the bride and groom,* 4
las nubes *clouds,* II
**nublado(a)** *cloudy,* I; **Está nublado.** *It's cloudy.,* I
la nuca *nape of the neck,* 2

Vocabulario español-inglés

**nuestro(a)** *our,* I
**nueve** *nine,* I
**nuevo(a)** *new,* II; **el Año Nuevo** *New Year's Day,* I; *de nuevo* *again,* II; **¿Qué hay de nuevo?** *What's new?,* I
las nueces *nut(s),* I
**el número** *number,* I; *shoe size,* I
**nunca** *never,* I
**nutritivo(a)** *nutritious,* II

# O

**o** *or,* I
obedecer (zc) *to obey,* 7
**obediente** *obedient,* II
**los obituarios** *obituaries,* 6
**el objetivo** *objective,* 7
el objeto *object,* II
obligatorio(a) *obligatory,* 3
**la obra** *work,* 5; **(de teatro),** *play,* 5, la obra maestra *masterpiece,* 2
observar *to observe;* **observar la naturaleza** *to observe nature,* 1
obtener (-go, ie) *to obtain,* II
obvio(a) *obvious,* 6; Es obvio que *It's obvious that . . .,* 6
**ochenta** *eighty,* I
**ocho** *eight,* I
**ochocientos (as)** *eight hundred,* I
ocio *leisure, spare time,* 2; guía de ocio *entertainment guide,* 2
**octavo(a)** *eighth,* II
**octubre** *October,* I
**ocupado(a)** *busy,* II
ocupar *to occupy, fill, take up,* II
ocurrir *to occur,* II
**odiar** *to hate,* II
el oeste *west,* II
la oferta *special offer;* **estar en oferta** *to be on sale,* II; **la última oferta** *last offer,* II
**ofender** *to offend,* 3
**la oficina de...** *office of . . .,* II; **la oficina de cambio** *money exchange,* I; **la oficina de correos** *post office,* I; **la oficina de turismo** *tourism office,* II
**el oficio** *job, profession, occupation,* II
ofrecer (zc) *to offer,* II; **¿Se les ofrece algo más?** *Would you like anything else?,* II
**el oído** *(inner) ear,* I
**oír** *to hear,* II; **Cuando oí la noticia no lo quise creer.** *When I heard the news, I didn't want to believe it.,* II
**Ojalá que...** *I hope that . . .,* II; **Ojalá que los países aún en guerra...** *I hope that the countries still at war . . .,* 9
¡ojo! *careful!, look out!,* II
**los ojos** *eyes,* I; **tener los ojos azules** *to have blue eyes,* I; **tener ojos de color café** *to have brown eyes,* II
**las olas** *waves,* II
**oler (ue)** *to smell,* II; **huele a** *it smells like,* II
olímpico(a) *Olympic,* 2; los Juegos Olímpicos *Olympic Games,* 2
la oliva: **el aceite de oliva** *olive oil,* II
las ollas *pots, pans,* II
la ollita *little pot,* 2
el olor *odor, smell,* 2
oloroso(a) *good-smelling,* 2
**olvidar** *to forget,* 3
**olvidarse (de)** *to forget (about), to forget (to),* II; **No te olvides de...** *Don't forget to . . .,* II; **Se me olvidó por completo.** *I totally forgot.,* II
**once** *eleven,* I
la onda *wave,* 6; de onda corta *shortwave,* 6
ondular *to wave, to undulate,* 5
la opción *option, choice,* II
**opinar** *to think, to be of the opinion,* 6
la oportunidad *opportunity,* II
el opresor *oppressor,* 3
opuesto(a) *opposite,* 2
la oración *sentence,* II
**la oratoria** *speech (class),* 1
el orden *order, organization,* 6
la orden *command,* 6
el ordenador *computer,* II
ordinario(a) *ordinary,* 2
**la oreja** *(outer) ear,* II
**organizar** *to organize,* I; *to tidy up,* II
**el orgullo** *pride,* 7
**el origen** *origin,* 7
**original** *original,* 5
la orilla *edge, border;* **la orilla del lago** *lakeshore,* II; **la orilla del río** *riverbank,* II
**el oro** *gold,* II; el Siglo de Oro *Golden Age,* II; oros, copas y bastos *playing cards,* 10
orondo(a) *conceited,* 4
**la orquesta** *orchestra,* 5; el dirigente de orquesta *orchestra conductor,* II
la ortografía *spelling,* 2
**os** *to/for you (pl., Spain),* I
**el oso** *bear,* II
**el otoño** *autumn,* I
**otro(a)** *other, another:* **¿Otra vez, por favor?** *One more time, please?,* II
otros(as) *other, others,* II
la oveja *sheep,* 2
**Oye** *Hey,* II

# P

el pabellón *pavilion,* II; el pabellón nacional *flag,* 9
pacer (zc) *to graze on,* 2
la paciencia *patience,* II
**paciente** *patient,* II
el paciente, la paciente *patient,* II
**el padrastro** *stepfather,* 4
**el padre** *father,* I; *priest,* 5; **el Día del Padre** *Father's Day,* I
**los padres** *parents,* I
padrísimo(a) *really great, awesome,* 5
**pagar** *to pay,* I; **pagar con cheques de viajero** *to pay with traveler's checks,* II; **pagar con tarjeta de crédito** *to pay with a credit card,* II; **pagar en efectivo** *to pay cash,* II; **pagar la cuenta** *to pay the bill,* II
**la página** *page,* II; **páginas Web** *Web pages,* II
**el país** *country,* I
el paisaje *landscape,* 2
**la paja** *straw,* II
**el pájaro** *bird,* II
la palabra *word,* II; la palabra clave *key word,* II
el palacio *palace,* II
pálido(a) *pale,* 9
**el pan** *bread,* I; **el pan dulce** *pastry,* I; **el pan tostado** *toast,* I
**la panadería** *bakery,* II
**el pánico** *panic,* 10
**la pantalla** *monitor, screen,* I
**los pantalones (vaqueros)** *pants (jeans),* I; **los pantalones cortos** *shorts,* I
el panteón *cemetery,* II
**la pantorrilla** *calf,* I
el paño *cloth,* 8
**el papá** *dad,* I
**la papa** *potato,* I; **las papas fritas** *French fries,* I
**el papel** *paper,* I; *role,* II; hoja de papel *sheet of paper,* II
la papelería *stationer's shop,* II
**el par** *pair,* I
**para** *for, to, in order to,* I; **Estoy buscando un regalo para mi...** *I'm looking for a gift for my . . .,* II; **para nada** *not . . . a bit/at all,* II; Para servirle. *At your service.* **¿Tienes planes para el...?** *Do you have plans for . . .?,* II; **¿Vamos bien para...?** *Are we going the right way to . . .?,* II; para que *in order,* 7
el paracaídas *parachute;* **saltar en paracaídas** *to go skydiving,* II

**la parada del metro** *subway stop,* II
**el paraguas** *umbrella,* II
**paraguayo(a)** *Paraguayan,* II
el paraíso *paradise,* II
**parar** *to stop,* II
pararse *to stand up,* 2
**parcial** *biased,* 6
**Parece mentira que haya.../ que digan...** *It's hard to believe that there are . . ./that they say . . .,* 6
**parecer** *to seem, to think,* I; **Me parece bien.** *It's all right with me,* I; **Me parece injusto.** *It seems unfair to me.,* I; **¿Qué te parece este color?** *What do you think of this color?,* II; *to resemble,* 4; parecer que *in one's opinion,* 6
parecido(a) *similar,* II
**la pared** *wall,* II
la pareja *couple,* II; en parejas *in pairs,* II
**los parientes** *relatives,* II, el pariente lejano *distant relative,* 4
**el parque** *park,* I; el parque de atracciones *amusement park,* II; **el parque de diversiones** *amusement park,* I; **el parque nacional** *national park,* II
el párrafo *paragraph,* II
la parrilla *grill;* **el bistec a la parrilla** *grilled steak,* II
la parte *part;* **Dale un saludo a... de mi parte.** *Say hi to . . . for me.,* II
**participar** *to participate,* II
el participio pasado *past participle,* II
**la partida** *departure,* II
**el partido de...** *the . . . game,* I
partir *to start out on, to set off on;* a partir de *as of, starting on,* II; **A partir de entonces vivieron siempre felices.** *From then on they lived happily ever after.,* 9
el pasaboca *appetizer,* II
el pasadizo *corridor,* II
**pasado(a)** *last,* I; *past,* 10; **el año pasado** *last year,* I; **pasado(a) de moda** *out of style,* I; **pasado mañana** *day after tomorrow,* I
el pasaje *passage,* 3
pasajero(a) *temporary,* 6
**el pasajero, la pasajera** *passenger,* I
**el pasaporte** *passport,* I
**pasar** *to spend (time, occasion),* I; *to come in;* **Cuéntame lo que pasó el día que...** *Tell me what happened the day that . . .,* II; **pasar el rato solo** *to spend time alone,* I; **pasar mucho tiempo** *to spend a lot of time,* II; **¿Qué te pasó?** *What happened to you?,* II; **pasarlo bien/mal** *to have a good/bad time,* 2, **lo pasé de película/de maravilla** *I had a great time,* 1; **pasárselo bomba** *to have a great time,* 1; **pasar la aspiradora** *to vacuum,* I; **pasar por** *to stop at/by,* I; *to go through,* I; **pasar por alto** *to overlook,* 6; **pasártelo(la)** *to get someone for a telephone call,* I
**las pasas** *raisins,* 4
**el pasatiempo** *hobby,* I; **buscar un pasatiempo** *to look for a hobby,* I
el(la) paseante *walker, stroller,* II
**pasear** *to go for a walk,* I; **pasear en bote** *to go boating,* II; **pasear en bote de vela** *to go out in a sailboat,* I; **pasear en lancha** *to go out in a motorboat,* I
**pasearse** *to stroll, to take a walk,* II
el pasillo *hallway,* 5
pasivo(a) *passive,* 8
**la pasta de dientes** *toothpaste,* I
**el pastel** *cake,* I
**la pastelería** *pastry shop,* II
el(la) pastelero(a)(a) *pastry cook,* 4
**la pastilla** *pill,* II; **tomarse unas pastillas** *to take some pills,* II
el pasto *pasture,* 2
**el patinaje** *skating,* II; **el patinaje (en línea)** *(inline) skating,* II; **el patinaje sobre hielo** *ice-skating,* II
**patinar** *to skate,* I
**el patio** *patio, yard,* I
la patria *homeland, mother country,* 9
patrocinar *to sponsor,* II
el patrón *(pl. los patrones) pattern,* II; *master,* II
**el pavo (con relleno)** *turkey (with stuffing),* 4
la paz *peace;* dejar en paz *to leave somebody alone,* II
**peatonal** *pedestrian,* II; **la zona peatonal** *pedestrian zone,* II
los peatones *pedestrians,* II
**el pecho** *chest,* I
el pedazo *piece,* II
**pedir (i, i)** *to ask for, to order,* I; **pedir ayuda** *to ask for help,* II **pedir información** *to ask for information,* II; pedir la mano *to ask for her hand in marriage,* II; **pedir perdón** *to ask for forgiveness,* 3
**peinarse** *to comb your hair,* I; *to brush one's hair,* II
**el peine** *comb,* I
pelado(a) *peeled,* II
**pelearse** *to fight,* II, 3
**la película** *film, movie,* I; **(de ciencia ficción, de terror, de misterio)** *(science fiction, horror, mystery),* I; **el rollo de película** *roll of film,* II
el peligro *danger,* II
peligroso(a) *dangerous,* 2
**pelirrojo(a)** *red-headed,* I
**el pelo** *hair,* I; **cortarse el pelo** *to get a haircut,* II
la pelota *ball,* II
el peluche *felt;* **los animales de peluche** *stuffed animals,* II
**la peluquería** *hair salon,* II
**el peluquero, la peluquera** *hairstylist,* II
la pena *sorrow, grief,* 10
pendiente *pending,* 6
los pensamientos *thoughts,* II
**pensar (ie)** *to think,* I; **pensar** + infinitive *to plan to,* I; **pensar en** *to think about,* II
**la pensión** *boarding house, inn,* II
**peor(es)** *worse,* I
**el pepino** *cucumber,* 4
la pepita *kernel,* 4
**pequeño(a)** *small,* I; **de pequeño(a)** *as a child,* II
**la pera** *pear,* II
**perder (ie)** *to lose, to miss,* I; *to lose,* II; **Está echado(a) a perder.** *It's spoiled.,* II
**perderse (ie)** *to get lost,* II
el perdón *forgiveness,* II
**Perdón.** *Excuse me., Pardon me.,* II
**Perdóname. No sé en qué estaba pensando.** *Forgive me. I don't know what I was thinking.,* 3
**perdonar** *to forgive,* 3
**perezoso(a)** *lazy,* I
**perfecto(a)** *perfect,* II; **Está perfecto.** *It's perfect.,* II
**el periódico** *newspaper,* II; el periódico sensacionalista *tabloid newspaper,* 6
el periodismo *journalism,* 8
**el periodista, la periodista** *journalist,* 6
la perla *pearl,* II
permanecer (zc) *to stay, to remain,* II
el permiso *permission;* dar permiso *to give permission,* II
**permitir** *to allow,* II; **se permite** *is allowed,* II
**pero** *but, nevertheless,* I
**el perro, la perra** *dog,* I; **darle de comer al perro** *to feed the dog,* II
perseguido(a) *pursued,* 10
perseguir (i, i) *to chase,* 6
**la persona** *person,* I
el personaje *character,* 2
el personal *personnel, staff,* II
**pertenecer (zc) a** *to belong to,* 7
peruano(a) *Peruvian,* II
la pesadilla *nightmare,* 9
**pesado(a): ¡Ay, qué pesado!** *Oh, what a drag!,* II; **¡Qué pesado!** *How boring!,* II

**las pesas** *weights,* I
**la pesca** *fishing,* I
**la pescadería** *fish market,* II
**el pescado** *fish,* I
**pescar** *to fish,* I; **la caña de pescar** *fishing rod,* II
**pésimo(a)** *terrible,* I, 5
**el peso** *weight,* I
**los pesticidas** *pesticides,* 10
el petróleo *petroleum, oil,* 6
**el pez** (*pl.* **peces**) *fish (live),* II
**picado(a)** *diced,* II
**picante** *spicy,* I; **la salsa picante** *hot sauce,* I
el picadillo *dish of ground beef and vegetables,* 4
**picar** *to dice,* II; *to snack,* 2; *to sting,* 10; algo de picar *something to snack on*
**el picnic** *picnic,* I
**el pie** *foot,* I; **el dedo del pie** *toe,* II
**la piedra** *stone, rock,* II
**la piel** *skin,* II
**la pierna** *leg,* I; **la falda a media pierna** *mid-length skirt,* II
la pieza *piece,* II
la pila de heno *haystack,* 2
**pilla-pilla: jugar al pilla-pilla** *to play tag,* II
**la pimienta** *black pepper,* II
**pintar** *to paint,* II
**pintarse las uñas** *to paint one's nails,* II
**las pinturas** *paintings,* II
**la piña** *pineapple,* II
**la piñata** *piñata,* I
**la pirámide** *pyramid,* I; la pirámide alimenticia *food pyramid,* II
**la piscina** *swimming pool,* I
**el piso** *floor,* I; **el edificio de... pisos** *. . . story building,* I
el pisote *raccoon-like animal,* 6
la pista *clue,* II; *runway,* II
**el piyama** *pajamas,* I
la pizca *pinch,* II
**la pizza** *pizza,* I
la pizzería *pizza parlor,* 3
planchar *to iron*
**planear** *to plan,* II; **No, ando planeando...** *No, I'm planning . . .,* II
**los planes** *plans,* I; **¿Tienes planes para el...?** *Do you have plans for . . .?,* II
**el planeta** *planet,* 10
el plano *floorplan,* II; **el plano de la ciudad** *city map,* II
la planta *floor,* II
la planta hidroeléctrica *hydroelectric plant,* 8
la plantación bananera *banana plantation,* II

**las plantas** *plants,* I; **regar las plantas** *to water the plants,* II
**el plástico** *plastic,* II
**la plata** *silver,* II
**el plátano** *banana,* II
**platicar en línea** *to chat online,* I
el platillo *dish,* II
**el plato** *dish, plate,* I; **el plato del día** *daily special,* II; el plato especial *special dish,* II; **el plato hondo** *bowl,* I; **el plato principal** *main dish,* II; **lavar los platos** *to do the dishes,* I
**la playa** *beach,* I; **el balón de playa** *beachball,* II; **¿Qué harán ustedes en la playa?** *What will you all do at the beach?,* II
**la plaza** *town square, plaza,* II; **la plaza de comida** *food court in a mall,* I
el pluscuamperfecto *pluperfect, past perfect,* 5
la población *population,* II
**pobre** *poor,* II
**¡Pobrecito(a)!** *Poor thing!,* II
**poco(a)** *few, little, not much,* I; **Hace poco tiempo que yo...** *I've been . . . for a little while.,* II; **un poco** *a little,* I; **Poco a poco se adaptaron a...** *Little by little they adapted to . . .,* 7
**poco fiable** *untrustworthy,* 6
**pocos(as)** *few, not many,* I
**poder (ue, u)** *to be able to, can,* I; **¿Puedes dárme algún consejo?** *Can you give me some advice?,* 1; **Cómo puedo llegar a...?** *How can I get to . . .?,* II; **Cuando me enteré, no lo pude creer.** *When I found out, I couldn't believe it.,* II; **¿Me podría decir...?** *Could you tell me . . .?,* II; **¿Me puede rebajar el precio de ese/esa...?** *Can you lower the price on that . . .?,* II; **¿Puede repetir lo que dijo?** *Can you repeat what you said?,* II; **¿Puedo ayudarte?** *Can I help you?,* II; **¿Sabe usted dónde se puede...?** *Do you know where I can . . .?,* II; **¡No me lo puedo creer!** *I can't believe it!,*
los poderes *powers,* II
poderoso *powerful,* II
podrido(a) *rotten,* 6
**el poema** *poem,* II
la poesía *poetry,* II
**el policía** *police officer,* I; *policeman,* II; **la mujer policía** *policewoman,* II
el político *politician,* 6
la política *politics,* 6
**el pollo** *chicken,* I; **el caldo de pollo** *chicken soup,* II; **el pollo asado** *roast chicken,* II; **el pollo frito** *fried chicken,* 4
el polvo *dust:* quitar el polvo *to dust the furniture,* II
**el ponche** *punch,* I
**poner (pongo)** *to put,* I; **poner la mesa** *to set the table,* I
**ponerse (me pongo)** *to put on,* I; *to put something on,* II; **Me puse** + adjective *I got/became . . .,* II; **Me puse a** + infinitive *I started to . . .,* II; **ponerse a llorar** *to start to cry,* II; ponerse en contacto *to contact, to get in touch,* II; ponerse + adjective *to become (change in physical or mental state),* 8
popular *popular,* 2
**por** *in, by,* I; **cambiar (por)** *to exchange (for),* II; **dar una vuelta por...** *to walk/drive around,* II; **Estoy loco(a) por...** *I'm crazy about . . .,* II; **gritar por ayuda** *to yell for help,* II; **por el estilo** *of that sort,* I; **por la mañana** *in the morning,* I; **por la tarde** *in the afternoon,* I; **hablar por teléfono** *to talk on the phone,* I; **hacer diseño por computadora** *to do computer design,* II; **hacer una llamada por cobrar** *to make a collect call,* II; **ir por la calle...** *to take . . . street,* II; **llamar por teléfono** *to make a phone call,* I; **por aquí** *around here,* II; **¿Y qué hay que hacer por aquí?** *And what is there to do around here?,* II; **Se me olvidó por completo.** *I totally forgot.,* II; **por eso** *that's why,* II; **por favor** *please,* I; **por fin** *at last,* II; *finally,* II; por lo general *generally,* II; por lo menos *at least,* II; **por primera vez** *for the first time,* II; por ejemplo *for example,* 2; por medio de *by means of,* 2; por digna de *thanks to,* 3; **Por fin... logré...** *Finally . . . I managed to . . .,* 7; **Por medio de la presente...** *The purpose of this letter is . . .,* 8
**¿por qué?** *why?,* I; **¿Por qué no vamos a...?** *Why don't we go to . . .?,* 5
**Por supuesto.** *Of course.,* II
el porcentaje *percentage,* II
la porción *portion,* II
la porfía *persistence, struggle,* 4
los porotos *beans,* 7
**porque** *because,* I
el porteño *nickname given to people from Buenos Aires because of the port,* 10

poseer *to possess,* 9
el posgrado *postgraduate (program),* II
postal *postal;* la tarjeta postal *post card,* II
posteriormente *later, subsequently,* II
**los pósters** *posters,* II; **coleccionar pósters** *to collect posters,* II
**el postre** *dessert,* I
potable *drinkable;* el agua potable *drinking water,* II
**practicar** *to practice,* II; to play (a sport), II; **practicar atletismo** *to do track and field,* 1; **¿Sigues practicando...?** *Are you still practicing . . .?,* II; **practicar deportes** *to play sports,* I
práctico(a) *practical,* II
**el precio** *price,* II; **Le voy a dar un precio especial.** *I'm going to give you a special price.,* II; **¿Me puede rebajar el precio de ese/esa...?** *Can you lower the price on that . . .?,* II
preciso(a) *precise,* II
la predicción *prediction,* II
preferible *preferable,* 2
**preferido(a)** *favorite,* I
**preferir (ie, i)** *to prefer,* I
la pregunta *question,* II
preguntar *to ask,* II
**preguntarle a alguien** *ask someone,* II
**el prejuicio** *prejudice,* 3
premiado(a) *award-winning,* II
el premio *prize,* II
las prendas *jewelry,* II
**la prensa** *the press,* 6
**preocupar** *to worry*: **preocupar(le) (algo)** *to worry (about something),* 2; **preocuparse** *to worry,* I; **No te preocupes.** *Don't worry.,* I
**preparar** *to prepare,* I; **¿Cómo se prepara...?** *How do you make . . .? (How is . . . prepared?),* II
**los preparativos** *preparations,* I
presagiar *to forebode,* 9
la presencia *presence,* 4
**presentar** *to introduce,* II; *to present,* 5; **presentar el examen de...** *to take a . . . test,* I
el presidente *president,* 6
las prestaciones *benefits,* 8
**prestar** *to lend,* II
prever *to foresee,* 3
previo(a) *previous;* la experiencia previa *previous experience,* II
**la primavera** *spring,* I
**la primera plana** *front page,* 6
**el primero** *first,* I
**primero(a)** *first,* I
los primeros auxilios *first aid,* II
**el primo, la prima** *cousin,* I
**los primos** *cousins,* I
**la princesa** *princess,* 9
**principal: el plato principal** *main dish,* II
principalmente *mainly,* II
**el príncipe** *prince,* 9
**la prisa: darse prisa** *to hurry,* II; **tener prisa** *to be in a hurry,* I
probablemente *probably,* II
**el probador** *fitting room,* II
**probar (ue)** *to try, to taste,* I; **¿Probaste...?** *Did you try . . .?,* II
**probarse (ue)** *to try on,* II
el problema *problem,* 6
el proceso *process,* 10
la proclamación *proclamation,* 9
producido(a) *produced,* II
los productos lácteos *dairy products,* 4
**el profesor, la profesora** *teacher,* I
profundo(a) *deep,* II
el programa: los programas de intercambio *exchange programs,* II; **el programa de radio (a micrófono abierto)** *(call-in) radio show,* 6; **los programas (de)** *programs (for),* 10
**el programador, la programadora** *programmer,* II
**programar** *to program,* II
prohibir *to prohibit;* **se prohibe** *is prohibited,* II
prometer *to promise,* II
promocionar *to promote,* II
promover (ue) *to promote,* II
el pronombre: el pronombre de complemento directo *direct object pronoun,* II; el pronombre de complemento indirecto *indirect object pronoun,* II; el pronombre del objeto directo *direct object pronoun,* II; el pronombre posesivo *possessive pronoun,* II; el pronombre reflexivo *reflexive pronoun,* II; el pronombre demostrativo *demonstrative pronoun,* 1
pronosticar *to forecast,* II
pronto *soon;* **Hasta pronto.** *See you soon.,* I
**la propina** *tip,* II; **dejar la propina** *to leave the tip,* II
propio(a) *own,* II
proponer (-go) *to propose,* 2
el propósito *purpose,* II
la propuesta *proposal,* 8
la prosa *prose,* 3
próspero(a) *prosperous*
los (las) protagonistas *protagonists,* 9
protector(a): **la crema protectora** *sunblock,* II
proteger *to protect,* II
**las proteínas** *protein,* II
el proveedor *provider,* 6
la provincia *province,* 2
provocar *to provoke,* 10
**próximo(a)** *next,* I; **la próxima semana** *next week,* I; **el** (day of the week) **próximo** *next (day of the week),* I
el proyecto *project,* II
publicar *to publish,* II; haber publicado *having published,* II
la publicidad *publicity,* II
**el público** *audience,* 5
**el pueblo** *town, village,* II; el pueblo natal *home town,* 7
**el puente** *bridge,* 5
**el puerco asado** *roast pork,* 4
**la puerta** *door,* I; **cerrar (ie) la puerta con llave** *to lock the door,* II
**el puerto** *port,* II
puertorriqueño(a) *Puerto Rican,* 3
Pues,... *Well, . . .,* II; **Pues, la verdad es que...** *Well, the truth is that . . .,* 2; **Pues, sigue trabajando...** *Well, he's/she's still working . . .,* 4
el puesto de guardia *guard post,* II
**el puesto del mercado** *market stand,* II
**el puesto (de trabajo)** *position (for work),* 8
**el pulmón** (pl. los pulmones) *lung,* II
la pulpería *grocery store (Costa Rica),* II
**la pulsera** *bracelet,* I
la punta de lanza *spearhead,* 7
**el puntaje** *score,* II
**el punto** *dot,* I; *point,* II; **en punto** *on the dot,* I; **Está en su punto.** *It's just right.,* II; hasta cierto punto *to some extent, in a way,* II

## Q

**que: que me llame después** *(tell him/her to) call me later,* I; **Que te vaya bien.** *Hope things go well for you.,* I; **Que yo sepa, (no) hay...** *That I know of, there's (no) . . .,* 6
**¡Qué...!: ¡Ay, qué pesado!** *Oh, what a drag!,* II; **¡Qué bien!** *How great!,* I; **¡Qué chismoso(a)!** *What a gossip!,* II; **¡Qué clima tan seco!** *What a dry climate!,* II; **¡Qué divertido!** *What fun!,* I; **¡Qué fantástico!** *How fantastic!,* I; **¡Qué gusto verte!** *It's great to see you!,* I; **¡Qué lástima!** *What a shame!,* I; **¡Qué lata!** *What a pain!,* I; **¿Qué lleva el (la)...?** *What's in the . . .?,* II; **¡Qué mala suerte!** *What bad luck!,* I; **¡Qué pesado!**

*How boring!*, II; *What a drag.*, II; Qué raro. *That's strange.*, II; **¡Qué rico(a)!** *How delicious!*, II; ¡Qué ridículo! *How ridiculous!*, II; **¡Qué va! Eso no es cierto.** *No way! That's not true.*, 3; **Qué pena que se hayan...** *What a shame that they have . . .*, 4; **¡Qué sorpresa que se hayan...!** *What a surprise that they have . . .!*, 4; **¡Qué asco!** *That's disgusting!*, 4
**¿qué?** *what?*, I; **¿Qué hora es?** *What time is it?*, I; **¿A qué hora vas a...?** *What time are you going to . . .?*, I; **¿Qué me recomiendas?** *What do you recommend?*, 1; **¿Qué hiciste el verano pasado?** *What did you do last summer?*, 1; **¿A qué se dedica...?** *What does . . . do?*, II; **¿Qué clase de trabajo realiza...?** *What kind of work does . . . do?*, II; **¿Qué tal?** *How's it going?*, I; **¿Qué tal...?** *How is . . .?*, I; **¿Qué tal si...?** *How about if . . .?*, I; **¿Qué te parece...?** *What do you think of . . .?*, I; **¿Qué te pasa?** *What's wrong with you?*, I; **¿Qué te pasó?** *What happened to you?*, II; **¿Qué tiempo hace?** *What's the weather like?*, I; **¿Qué buscas en un(a) novio(a)?** *What do you look for in a boyfriend/ girlfriend?*, 2; **¿Qué te pasa? ¿Estás dolida?** *What's the matter? Are you upset?*, 2; **¿Qué anda haciendo...?** *What's . . . up to?*, 4; **¿Qué me cuentas de...?** *What can you tell me about . . .?*, 4; **¿Qué sabes de...?** *What do you know about . . .!*, 4; **¿Qué opinas de...?** *What do you think of . . .?*, 5; **¿Qué sé yo de...? No entiendo ni jota de...** *What do I know about . . .? I don't understand a thing about . . .*, 6; **Que yo sepa, (no) hay...** *That I know of, there is/are (isn't/aren't)*, 6; **¿Qué te gustaría hacer?** *What would you like to do?*, 8; **¿Qué tal lo pasaste?** *Did you have a good time?*, 1; **¿Qué te pareció...?** *How was . . .?*, 1; **¿Qué vas a hacer?** *What are you going to do?*, 1
quebrar (ie) *to break*, II
el quechua *indigenous language of the Andes*, 7; los quechuas *indigenous people of the Andes*
**quedar** *to fit, to look*, I; *to turn out (as in cooking)*, 4; **quedar bien/mal** *to fit well/poorly*, I
**quedarse** *to stay*, II; **quedarse +** adjective *to end up, to wind up, to be left a certain way*, 8
**los quehaceres** *household chores*, I; **hacer los quehaceres** *to do the chores*, I
la queja *complaint*, II
quejarse *to complain*, 7
**quemado(a)** *burned*, II; **Está quemado(a).** *It's burned.*, II
**quemar** *to burn*, II
**quemarse** *to get a sunburn, to get burned*, II
**querer (ie) a** *to love (someone)*, 2; **querer +** infinitive *to want to*, II; **quererse** *to love each other*, II; **¿Quieres ir a ver...?** *Do you want to go see . . .?*, 5
**querer (ie) que** *to want someone else to do something*, II
el (la) querido(a) *sweetheart*, 4
**Querido(a)...**, *Dear . . .*, II
**el queso** *cheese*, I
**¿quién?** *who?*, I; **¿De parte de quién?** *Who's calling?*, I
**¿quiénes?** *who? (pl.)*, I
**la química** *chemistry*, I
**quince** *fifteen*, I
**la quinceañera** *girl's fifteenth birthday*, I
**quinientos(as)** *five hundred*, I
**quinto(a)** *fifth*, II
**el quiosco de...** *. . . stand*, II
**Quisiera...** *I would like (to). . .*, I
quitar *to take away, remove*
**quitarse** *to take off*, I; **...que no se me quita** *. . . that won't go away*, II
quizás *perhaps, maybe*, II

## R

la rabia *anger:* **Me dio una rabia.** *It made me angry.*, II
**la radio** *radio (as a medium)*, 6
el radio *radio apparatus*, 6
**las raíces** *roots*, 7; bienes raíces *real estate*, II
la rama *branch*, 2
**rápidamente** *quickly*, II
rápido(a) *fast*, II; **la comida rápida** *fast food*, II
raro(a): Qué raro. *That's strange.*, II; *rare*, II
el rastro *trace*, II
**el rato** *time*, I; a cada rato *every so often*, II; **el rato libre** *free time*, II; **pasar el rato solo(a)** *to spend time alone*, I
el ratón *mouse*, II
**la razón** *reason*, I; **tener razón** *to be right*, I; con razón *naturally*, II
la reacción *reaction*, II
**reaccionar** *to react*, II
la realidad *reality:* En realidad, admiro *Actually, I admire . . .*, II
**realista** *realistic*, 5
**realizar (un sueño)** *to fulfull (a dream)* 7; **¿Qué clase de trabajo realiza...?** *What kind of work does . . . do?*, II
realmente *really*, 4
reanudar *to resume*, 2
la rebaja *discount*, II
**rebajar** *to lower*, II
**el recado** *message*, I; **dejar un recado** *to leave a message*, I
**el recepcionista, la recepcionista** *receptionist*, II
**la receta** *recipe*, II
recetar *to prescribe*, II
rechazar *to reject, turn down*, 2
**Reciba un cordial saludo** *Kind regards*, 8
**recibir** *to receive*, I
recién *just, recently;* recién nacido(a) *newborn*, II
**recientemente** *recently*, II
**el recibo** *receipt*, II
reciclable *recyclable*, 10
**reciclar** *to recycle*, 10
el recipiente *bowl*, II
reclamar *to claim*, 9
**el reclamo de equipaje** *baggage claim*, I
**recoger (a alguien)** *to pick up (someone)*, I
**recomendar (ie)** *to recommend*, II; **recomendarle (a alguien) que...** *to recommend that (someone) . . .*, II
la recompensa *payment*, 3
**la reconciliación** *reconciliation*, 3
**reconciliarse** *to reconcile*, 3
reconocer (zc) *to recognize*, II
recordar (ue) *to remind*, II; *to remember*, 3
**recorrer** *to tour*, I; *to go over, to look through*, II
el recorte *clipping*, 3
**recreativo: el centro recreativo** *recreation center*, II
el recuerdo *memory*, II; **comprar recuerdos** *to buy souvenirs*, II
recuperar *to retrieve*, II
los recursos *resources*, II; **los recursos naturales** *natural resources*, 10
la red *grid*, 2
reemplazar *to replace*, 2
referir (ie, i) *to refer;* se refiere a *refers to*, II
reflejar *to reflect*, II
refrescar *to refresh*, II
**el refresco** *soft drink*, I
**el refrigerador** *refrigerator*, I
**los refugiados** *refugees*, 10
refugiarse *to flee*, II; *to take refuge*, 10
los refugios *homeless shelters*, 10
**regalar** *to give*, II; **Bueno, se la regalo por..., pero es mi última oferta.** *Okay, I'll give it to you for . . ., but that's my last offer.*, II

Vocabulario español-inglés

**el regalo** *gift,* I
regular *to regulate,* 6
**regar (ie)** *to water,* II; **regar las plantas** *to water the plants,* II
**regatear** *to bargain,* II
registrarse para *to register for,* 7
**la regla** *ruler,* I
**regocijarse** *to rejoice,* 9
**regresar** *to return, to go back,* I
**regular** *all right,* I
**la reina** *queen,* 9
**reírse (i, i)** *to laugh,* II; **Me reí mucho.** *I laughed a lot.,* II
la relación *relationship,* II
relacionar *to relate,* II
**relajarse** *to relax,* I
**el relámpago** *lightning,* II
el relicario *locket,* II
religioso(a) *religious,* II
**el reloj** *watch, clock,* I
**el remo (remar)** *rowing (to row),* 2
los remos *oars,* 9
remolinar *to move around,* 2
el renacimiento *Renaissance,* II
**renovable/no renovable** *renewable/non-renewable,* 10
renunciar *to renounce, to reject,* 4
repartir *to deliver,* 7
repente: **de repente** *suddenly,* II; **De repente, empezó a llover...** *Suddenly, it started to rain . . .,* II
repentinamente *suddenly,* 9
el repertorio *repertoire,* II
**repetir (i, i)** *to repeat,* II; **¿Puede repetir lo que dijo?** *Can you repeat what you said?,* II
**el reportaje** *news report,* 6
reportar *to report,* 6
**el (la) reportero(a)** *reporter,* 6
la repostería *pastry shop (Dominican Republic),* II
la represa *dam,* II
representados *represented,* II
**requerir (ie, i)** *to require,* 8
**los requisitos** *requirements,* 8
la res *beef,* II
resbalar *to slide,* 7
**la reseña** *(critical) review,* 5
**reseñar** *to review, critique,* 6
la reserva natural *nature preserve,* 2
**la reservación** *reservation,* II; **hacer una reservación** *to make a reservation,* II
**resfriado(a)** *sick with a cold,* II; **estar resfriado(a)** *to have a cold,* II
**resfriarse** *to catch a cold,* II
la residencia *residence,* II
la resolución *solution (of a problem),* 2
resolver (ue) *to solve;* **resolver (ue) un problema** *to resolve a problem,* 2
respetado(a) *respected,* II
**respetar (a alguien)** *to respect (someone),* 3
**respetar los sentimientos de otros** *to respect others' feelings,* 2
**respetarse** *to respect each other,* II
**el respeto** *respect,* 3
responder *to answer, to reply, to respond,* II
el responsable *the one responsible for something,* 10
la respuesta *answer,* II
**el restaurante** *restaurant,* I
los restos *remains,* II
restringir *to restrict,* 6
el resultado: como resultado *as a result,* II
el resumen *summary,* 2
resumir *to summarize,* II
el reto *challenge,* 9
el retorno *return,* II
retumbar *to resound,* 2
**la reunión** *meeting,* I; *reunion,* I; **la reunión familiar** *family reunion,* 4; la reunión escolar, *class reunion,* 4
**reunirse** *to get together,* I
revelar *to reveal,* II
revisar *to examine,* II
la revisión *checking,* II
**la revista** *magazine,* I; **la revista de tiras cómicas** *comic book,* I; **las revistas cómicas** *comic books,* II
**la revolución** *revolution,* 5, 9
**revolver (ue)** *to stir,* II
**revuelto(a)** *stirred, scrambled, (past participle of* **revolver***),* II; **los huevos revueltos** *scrambled eggs,* II
**el rey** *king,* 9
la ribera *bank, shore,* 7
**rico(a)** *rich,* II; *tasty, delicious,* II; **¡Qué rico(a)!** *How delicious!,* II
ridículo(a): ¡Qué ridículo! *How ridiculous!,* II
la rima *rhyme,* 5
rimar *to rhyme,* 5
**el río** *river,* II; **la orilla del río** *riverbank,* II
la riqueza *richness,* 4
**riquísimo(a)** *delicious,* I
la risa *laughter, 2*
**el ritmo** *rhythm,* II, 5
robar *to steal,* 5; *to hold up,* 6
**el robo** *rip-off,* I; **¡Es un robo!** *It's a rip-off!,* I
**el robot** *robot,* 8
rociar *to baste, to sprinkle,* 4
el rococó *rococo (style),* 10
rocoso(a) *rocky,* II
rodear *to surround,* II
**la rodilla** *knee,* II
rogar (ue) *to beg,* II
**rojo(a)** *red,* I
**el rollo de película** *roll of film,* II
**romántico(a)** *romantic,* I
**el rompecabezas** *puzzle,* 2
**romper** to break, II; **roto** *broken (past participle of* **romper***),* II; **romper con** to break up with, 2
**romperse** + a body part *to break (one's body part),* II
**la ropa** *clothes,* I; la ropa vieja *a kind of beef stew,* 4
la rosa *rose,* 3
el rostro *face,* 3
**roto(a)** *broken (past participle of* **romper***),* II
rubicundo(a) *reddish,* 4
**rubio(a)** *blond,* I
rudo(a) *rough,* II
el ruido *noise,* II
**las ruinas** *ruins,* I; la ruina *decline, downfall,* 10
la runa *word used by the Quechua people to refer to themselves, the people,* 7
el ruso *Russian,* 5
la ruta *route,* II
la rutina *routine;* la rutina diaria *daily routine,* II

## S

**el sábado** *Saturday,* I; **los sábados** *on Saturdays,* I
**Sabe a...** *It tastes like . . .,* II; **Sabe delicioso(a).** *It tastes delicious!,* 4; **no sabe a nada** *doesn't taste like anything,* 4
**saber** *to know,* I; **No sé.** *I don't know.,* I; **saber de** *to know about,* I; **¿Sabes qué?** *You know what?,* I; **¿Sabe usted dónde se puede...?** *Do you know where I can . . .?,* II; **¿Ya sabías que...?** *Did you already know that . . .?,* II
**Que yo sepa, (no) hay...** *That I know, there is/are (isn't/aren't),* 6
**el (la) sabio(a)** *wise man/wise woman,* 9
**el sabor** *flavor,* II; **Le falta sabor.** *It's missing flavor.,* II
saborear *to savour,* II
**sabroso(a)** *tasty,* II
**sacar** *to take out,* I; **sacar buenas notas** *to get good grades,* II; **sacar el dinero** *to get money,* I; **sacar fotos** *to take photos,* I; **sacar malas notas** *to get bad grades,* II
**el saco** *jacket,* I
**el sacrificio** *sacrifice,* 7
**sacudir** *to dust,* II; **sacudir los muebles** *to dust the furniture,* II
sagrado(a) *sacred,* 4

sal *go out, leave,* I
**la sal** *salt,* II; **Le falta sal.** *It's missing salt.,* II
**la sala** *living room,* I
la sala de computadoras *computer room,* 6
**la sala de emergencias** *emergency room,* II
**la sala de espera** *waiting room,* I
**salado(a)** *salty,* I
**el salario** *salary,* 8
**la salchicha** *sausage,* 4
**la salida** *departure,* I; *exit,* I
**salir (salgo)** *to go out, to leave,* I; **¿Cómo salió la competencia de...?** *How did the . . . competition turn out?,* II; salir caro(a) *to end up costing a lot,* II; salir con alguien *to go out with someone;* salir mal *to turn out badly,* 8
el salón *room,* II; **el salón de belleza** *beauty parlor,* II; **el salón de clase** *classroom,* I
**la salsa** *sauce, gravy,* I; **la lata de salsa de tomate** *can of tomato sauce,* II; **la salsa picante** *hot sauce,* I
**saltar: saltar a la cuerda** *to jump rope,* II; **saltar en paracaídas** *to go skydiving,* II
**el salto de altura** *high jump,* 2
**la salud** *health,* I; **cuidarse la salud** *to take care of one's health,* I
el saludo *greeting:* **Dale un saludo a... de mi parte.** *Say hi to . . . for me.,* II; **Un saludo de,...** *Yours sincerely, . . .,* II
**salvadoreño(a)** *Salvadoran,* II
salvar *to save,* 9
el sancocho *Dominican vegetable and beef stew,* 4
**las sandalias** *sandals,* I
**la sandía** *watermelon,* 4
**el sándwich de...** *. . . sandwich,* I
la sangre *blood,* II
sano(a) *healthy:* **seguir (i, i) una dieta sana** *to eat a balanced diet,* I
el santo, la santa *saint,* II; **el día de tu santo** *your saint's day,* I; **la Semana Santa** *Holy Week,* I
la sardina *sardine,* 2
la sartén *frying pan,* 4
**satisfacer** *to satisfy,* 5
sazonar *to season,* 4
**se** se acostumbra *it is customary,* II; **Se escribe...** *It's spelled . . .,* I; **se habla** *is spoken,* II; **¿Se les ofrece algo más?** *Would you like anything else?,* II; **Se los dejo en...** *I'll let you have them for . . .,* II; **Se me olvidó por completo.** *I totally forgot.,* II; **Se nos hace tarde.** *It's getting late.,* II; **se permite** *is allowed,* II; **se prohibe** *is prohibited,* II; **se puede** *one can,* II; **¿Dónde se puede...?** *Where can I . . .?,* I; **¿Sabe usted dónde se puede...?** *Do you know where I can . . .?,* II; se refiere a *refers to,* II; **se trabaja** *one works,* II; **se vive** *one lives,* II; **Se me hace la boca agua.** *It makes my mouth water.,* 4; **Se me fue la mano con...** *I got carried away with . . .,* 4; **Se arrepiente de que...** *He/She regrets that . . .,* 9; **Se cuenta que de pronto...** *The story goes that all of a sudden . . .,* 9; **Se advierte que...** *They warn/advise that . . .,* 10
**la secadora** *dryer,* II; **la secadora de pelo** *hair dryer,* I
**secarse** *to dry oneself,* I; secarse el pelo *to dry one's hair,* II
**la sección: la sección de cocina** *cooking section,* 6; **la sección de moda** *fashion section,* 6; **la sección de ocio** *entertainment section,* 6; **la sección de sociedad** *society section,* 6; **la sección deportiva** *sports section,* 6; **la sección financiera** *finance section,* 6
**seco(a)** *cold, unfriendly (person),* 2; *dry;* **¡Qué clima tan seco!** *What a dry climate!,* II
**el secretario, la secretaria** *secretary,* II
el secreto *secret,* II; en secreto *secretly,* II
secuestrado(a) *kidnapped,* 9
la secundaria *high school,* 2
**la sed** *thirst,* I; **tener (tengo, ie) sed** *to be thirsty,* I
**la seda** *silk,* I; **de seda** *made of silk,* I
la sede *headquarters,* II
seguido(a) *continuous, straight:* **en seguida** *right away,* II
**seguir (i, i)** *to follow,* I; *to keep going,* II; **seguir** + gerund *to keep on doing something,* II; **seguir adelante/derecho** *to go straight,* II; **seguir derecho hasta** *to keep going (straight) to,* II; **seguir una dieta sana** *to eat well,* I; **¿Sigues pensando en...?** *Are you still thinking about . . .?,* II; **¿Sigues practicando...?** *Are you still practicing . . .?,* II; **seguir adelante** *to move forward,* 7; to keep going, II
según *according to,* II; **Según tengo entendido, ...** *From what I understand, . . .,* 4; **Según nos dicen, el malvado...** *From what they tell us, the villain . . .,* 9
el segundo *second,* II
**segundo(a)** *second,* II
la seguridad *security;* **el control de seguridad** *security checkpoint,* I
seguro *for sure, for certain,* II; de seguro *surely,* II; *safe,* 8; **estar seguro(a)** *to be sure,* II; **No estoy seguro(a).** *I'm not sure.,* II
**el seguro** *insurance,* 8; **el seguro (médico)** *(medical) insurance,* 8; seguro(a) *sure,* 9
**seis** *six,* I
**seiscientos(as)** *six hundred,* I
seleccionar *to select,* II
la selva *jungle,* II; **explorar la selva tropical** *to explore the tropical jungle,* II
**el semáforo** *traffic-light,* II
**la semana** *week,* I; **el día de la semana** *day of the week,* I; **esta semana** *this week,* I; **la próxima semana** *next week,* I
**la Semana Santa** *Holy Week,* I
**sembrar (ie)** *to plant,* 8, 10
semejante a *like, similar to,* II
la semejanza *similarity,* II
**el semestre** *semester,* 3
sencillez *simplicity,* II
sencillo(a) *simple,* II
el senado *senate,* 7
el (la) senador(a) *senator,* 6
**el senderismo (hacer senderismo)** *hiking (to hike),* II, 2
el sendero *path, track,* II
sensible *sensitive,* II
el sentido *meaning,* 2
**los sentimientos** *feelings,* 2
la señal *signal,* II
**el señor** *sir, Mr.,* I
**la señora** *ma'am, Mrs.,* I
**la señorita** *young lady, Miss,* I
la sensación *sensation, feeling,* II
sentado(a) *seated,* 2
sentar (ie): **De verdad, no te sienta bien.** *Honestly, it doesn't look good on you.,* II
**sentarse (ie)** *to sit down,* I
sentido del humor *sense of humor,* 3
los sentimientos *feelings,* II
sentir (ie, i) *to regret,* 2; **Lo siento, pero ya tengo otros planes/otro compromiso.** *I'm sorry, but I already have other plans/another engagement.,* 5
**sentirse (ie, i)** *to feel,* I; **¿Cómo te sentiste cuando...?** *How did you feel when . . .?,* II; **¿Cómo te sentiste cuando supiste lo de...?** *How did you feel when you heard about . . .?,* II
**separado(a)** *separated,* 4
**separarse (de)** *to separate,* 4
**septiembre** *September,* I
**séptimo(a)** *seventh,* II
la sequía *drought,* II
**ser** *to be,* I; **ser un rollo** *to be dead boring,* II; **somos... personas** *there are . . . people,* I; **Son...** *They are . . .,* II; **Son las...** *It's . . . o'clock.,* I; lo que sea *whatever it may be,* 2; **ser de ascendencia...** *to be of . . . descent,* 7; **ser (in)fiel** *to be (un)faithful,* 3
la serie *series,* 6
**Sería una buena/mala idea romper**

Vocabulario español-inglés

**con...** *It would be a good/bad idea to break up with . . .,* 3
**Sería buena idea ir al concierto de la sinfónica.** *It would be a good idea to go to the symphony.,* 5
**serio(a)** *serious,* I
**la serpiente** *snake,* II
**el servicio** *restroom,* I
**la servilleta** *napkin,* I
**servir (i, i)** *to serve,* I; **¿En qué le puedo servir?** *How can I help you?,* I
servir (i, i) para *to be used for,* II
**sesenta** *sixty,* I
**setecientos(as)** *seven hundred,* I
**setenta** *seventy,* I
**sexto(a)** *sixth,* II
**si** *if,* II; **si tengo suerte...** *if I'm lucky . . .,* I; **Si todavía no ha ido a/al..., debe ir.** *If you haven't gone to . . . yet, you must.,* II; **Si pudiera, iría a... a estudiar...** *If I could, I would go to . . . to study . . .,* 8; **Si tuvieras la oportunidad, ¿adónde irías?** *If you had the chance, where would you go?,* 8
**sí** *yes,* I; **¡Claro que sí!** *Of course!,* I; **Creo que sí.** *I think so.,* II; **Sí, claro.** *Yes, of course.,* II; **Sí, me la paso... Estoy loco(a) por...** *Yes, I'm always doing . . . I'm crazy about . . .,* 2; **Sí, estoy decepcionado(a) porque... Me dan ganas de llorar.** *Yes, I'm disappointed because . . . It makes me feel like crying.,* 2; **Sí, estoy entusiasmado(a) porque...** *Yes, I'm excited because . . .,* 2
sí mismo *him/herself,* II
**siempre** *always,* I; **casi siempre** *almost always,* I; **como siempre** *as always,* I; **Siempre he querido ser un(a)...** *I have always wanted to be a. . .,* 8
la siesta *nap,* 2
**siete** *seven,* I
el siglo *century,* 10; el Siglo de Oro *Golden Age,* II
el significado *meaning,* II
significar *to mean,* II
siguiente *following;* **lo siguiente** *the following,* I
silencioso(a) *silent,* 5
**la silla** *chair,* I
**la silla de ruedas** *wheelchair,* I; **estar en una silla de ruedas** *to be in a wheelchair,* I
**el sillón** *armchair,* II
el símbolo *symbol,* II
**simpático(a)** *friendly,* I
simplemente *simply,* 2
**sin** *without,* II; **¡Tanto tiempo sin verte!** *Long time, no see!,* I; sin que *without,* 7
sin duda *without a doubt,* II
sin embargo *however, nevertheless,* II
la sinfonía *symphony,* II
sinfónico(a) *symphonic,* II; **el concierto de la sinfónica** *concert symphony,* 5
siniestro(a) *sinister, evil,* II; *disaster, catastrophe,* II
**sino** *but (as in "Not this, but that instead."),* II; **no sólo... sino... también** *not only . . . but . . . as well,* II
**la sinagoga** *synagogue,* I
sincero(a) *sincere,* II
los movimientos sindicalistas *labor union movements,* 5
los síntomas *symptoms,* II
el sistema *system,* 7
el sitio *place,* II
los sitios de Internet *Internet sites,* 6
situado(a) *situated, located,* 10
la situación *circumstances,* 1
la soberanía *sovereignty,* 9
**sobre** *on top of, above, about,* 1; **el patinaje sobre hielo** *ice-skating,* II
sobre todo *especially,* II
sobresaliente *excellent,* II; *outstanding,* 5
sobrevivir *to survive,* II
**la sobrina** *niece,* I
**el sobrino** *nephew,* I
**los sobrinos** *nephews, nieces and nephews,* I
socializar *to socialize,* 2
la sociedad *society,* 7
el socio *partner, associate,* 10
**el sofá** *couch, sofa,* I
el sofrito *sautee of garlic, tomato, onion and other ingredients,* 4
**el sol** *sun,* II; **Hace sol.** *It's sunny.,* I; **las gafas de sol** *sunglasses,* II; **tomar el sol** *to sunbathe,* I
**solamente** *only,* II
**el soldado** *soldier,* 7, 9
**soleado(a)** *sunny,* II
**soler (ue)** + infinitive *to usually do something, to tend to do something,* II; **Solíamos** + infinitive *We usually + infinitive,* II
**Solía...** *I used to . . .,* II
**solicitar** *to apply,* 8
**la solicitud** *application,* 8
**la solidaridad** *solidarity, 10*
**solidario(a)** *supportive,* 2
**solitario(a)** *likes to be alone,* II; *lonely,* 1, la estrella solitaria *lone star,* II
**sólo** *only;* **no sólo... sino... también** *not only . . . but . . . as well,* II; **Sólo me falta...** *I just need to . . .,* II
**solo(a)** *alone,* I; *a solas alone,* II; **pasar el rato solo(a)** *to spend time alone,* I
la sombra *shadow,* 9
**el sombrero** *hat,* I
sonar *to ring,* 1
el sonido *sound,* II
**soñar (ue) con** *to dream of,* II; **Soñaba con ser...** *I dreamed of being . . .,* 7
**la sopa** *soup,* I; **la sopa de ajo** *garlic soup,* II; **la sopa de fideos** *noodle soup,* II; **la sopa de verduras** *vegetable soup,* I
soplar *to blow,* 10
soportar *to endure,* 10
**sordo(a)** *deaf,* I; *muffled,* 9
el soroche *altitude sickness,* 7
**sorprender(le)** *to surprise,* 2
**la sorpresa: la fiesta sorpresa** *surprise party,* I
sos: vos sos *you (informal) are,* II
sostenible *sustainable,* 6
el sótano *cellar,* II
**Soy bilingüe; por lo tanto tengo muchas oportunidades...** *I'm bilingual; therefore, I have many opportunities . . .,* 7
**Soy capaz de (hacer)...** *I'm capable of (doing) . . .,* 8
**Soy un(a) gran aficionado(a) a... ¿Qué deporte te gusta a ti?** *I'm a big . . . fan. What sport do you like?,* 2
**su(s)** *your, his, her, its, their,* I; **Está en su punto.** *It's just right.,* II
**subir** *to go up,* I; **subir a la montaña** *to go up the mountain,* I; **subir de peso** *to gain weight,* I; **subir... hasta llegar a** *to go up . . . until you get to,* II
**subirse a...** *to get on . . .,* II
subrayados(as) *underlined,* 9
subterráneo(a) *underground,* II
el subtexto *subtext*
suceder *to occur,* 1
el suceso *event*
sucio(a) *dirty,* II
la sucursal *branch,* II
**la suegra** *mother-in-law,* 4
**el suegro** *father-in-law,* 4
el sueldo *salary,* 8
**el sueño** *sleep,* I; **tener sueño** *to be sleepy,* I
**El sueño de mi vida es conmemorar a....** *My life-long dream is to commemorate . . .,* 9
**la suerte** *luck,* I; **¡Qué mala suerte!** *What bad luck!,* I; **Si tengo suerte...** *If I'm lucky . . .,* I; ¡Suerte! *Good luck!,* II; **tener suerte** *to be lucky,* I; **tuviste suerte** *you were lucky,* I
**el suéter** *sweater,* I
**suficiente** *enough,* I; **dormir (ue, u) lo suficiente** *to get enough sleep,* I
**sufrir** *to suffer,* 9
la sugerencia *suggestion,* 6

**sugerirle (ie, i) (a alguien) que...** *to suggest that (someone)...,* II
**Sugiero que no hagas caso a los rumores.** *I suggest that you not pay attention to rumors.,* 3
sujetar *to secure, to fasten, to hold,* 7
el sujeto *subject,* II
super *super;* **¡Te ves super bien!** *You look wonderful!,* II
superar *to exceed, to overcome,* 7
**superficial** *superficial,* 5
**el supermercado** *supermarket,* II
**supervisar** *to supervise,* 8
**suponer** *to suppose:* **Es de suponer que...** *I suppose that...,* 10; **Supongo que sí.** *I suppose so.,* 10
supuesto *supposed:* **Por supuesto.** *Of course.,* II
el sur *south,* 6
el suroeste *southwest,* 5
**surtido(a)** *assorted,* II; **el surtido de frutas frescas** *assorted fresh fruit,* II; **un gran surtido** *wide assortment,* II
suscitar *to awaken,* 4
**suscribirse a** *to subscribe to,* 6
**suspender** *to fail,* 3
el sustantivo *noun,* 2
sustituir *to substitute,* II
**suyo(a)** *yours (formal), his, hers, its, theirs,* II
**suyos(as)** *yours (formal), his, hers, its, theirs,* II

## T

la tabla *table, list, chart,* II
tachar *to cross off,* 4
**tal** *such:* **¿Qué tal?** *How's it going?,* I; **¿Qué tal...?** *How is...?,* I; **¿Qué tal está...?** *How is the...?,* II; **¿Qué tal estuvo?** *How was it?,* 1; **¿Qué tal si...?** *How about if...?,* I; tal vez *perhaps, maybe,* II
**el talento** *talent,* 8
**la talla** *(clothing) size,* I
**tallar en madera** *to do wood-carving,* 5
**tallado(a)** *carved, sculpted,* II; **la figura tallada** *carved figure,* II
**el taller** *shop (class), workshop,* I
los tamales *tamales,* I
**también** *also,* I; **no sólo... sino... también** *not only... but... as well,* II
el tambor *drum,* II
**tampoco** *neither, not either,* I
**tan... como** *as... as,* I
**Tan pronto como llegó...** *As soon as he/she arrived...,* 9
**Tan pronto como... pienso...** *As soon as... I plan on...,* 7
**tanto** *so long; so much,* II
**tantos(as)** *so many,* I; *so much,* II; **tantos(as)... como...** *as many... as...,* II
las tapas *Spanish finger food,* 2
el tapiz *tapestry,* 7
**tardar** *to take long, to be late,* II
**tardarse en** + infinitive *to take a long time (to),* II
**tarde** *late,* I; **Se nos hace tarde.** *It's getting late.,* II
**la tarde** *afternoon, evening* I; **Buenas tardes.** *Good afternoon,* I; **de la tarde** *in the afternoon, evening, P.M.,* I; **esta tarde** *this afternoon,* I; **por la tarde** *in the afternoon,* I
**la tarea** *homework,* II; **hacer la tarea** *to do homework,* I
**la tarjeta** *greeting card, card,* I; **la tarjeta de crédito** *credit card,* II; **la tarjeta de cumpleaños** *birthday card,* I; **la tarjeta de embarque** *boarding pass,* I; **la tarjeta postal** *post card,* II; **la tarjeta regalo** *gift card,* I
**el taxi** *taxi,* I; **tomar un taxi** *to take a taxi,* II
**el taxista, la taxista** *taxi driver,* II
**la taza de medir** *measuring cup,* II
**te** *to/for you,* I; **¿Te acordaste de...?** *Did you remember to...?,* II; **Te conocí** *I met you;* **Te echo mucho de menos.** *I miss you a lot.,* II; Te importa si...? *Do you mind if...?,* II; **Te presento a...** *I'd like you to meet...,* I; **Te aconsejo que...** *I advise you to...,* 1; **Te recomiendo que...** *I recommend that you...,* 1, **Te veo mal.** *You don't look well.,* I; **¡Te ves guapísimo!** *You look very handsome!,* II; **¡Te ves super bien!** *You look wonderful!,* II; **Te veo de buen humor.** *I see you're in a good mood.,* 2; **Te juro que no lo volveré a hacer.** *I swear I'll never do it again.,* 3; **Te aconsejo que vayas a la presentación de baile folclórico. Es muy...** *I recommend that you go to the folk dance performance. It's very...,* 5; **¿Te interesa ir a...?** *Are you interested in going to...?,* 5
**¿Te acuerdas (de) cuando sucedió...?** *Do you remember when... happened?,* 10; **Te apuesto que...** *I bet you that...,* 10
teatral *theatrical,* II
**el teatro** *theatre,* II
**el techo** *roof, ceiling,* II
la técnica *technique,* 5, 10
el (la) técnico *technician,* 5
**la tecnología** *technology,* 8
tejano(a) *Texan,* 10
**tejer** *to knit,* II; *to weave,* II
**los tejidos** *woven cloth, textiles,* II
la tejuela *shingle,* 9
la tela *fabric,* II
**la tele** *television (TV),* II
las telecomunicaciones *telecommunications,* 8
el teleférico *ski lift,* II
**telefónico(a)** *telephone;* **la cabina telefónica** *phone booth,* II, la guía telefónica *telephone book,* II
**el teléfono** *telephone number,* I; *telephone,* I; **hablar por teléfono** *to talk on the phone,* I; **llamar por teléfono** *to make a phone call,* I
**el teléfono celular** *cell phone,* II
**la telenovela** *soap opera,* 6
el televidente *TV viewer,* 6
**la televisión** *television (TV),* I; **ver televisión** *to watch TV,* I
**el televisor** *TV set,* II
el tema *theme, topic,* 6
temblar (ie) *to shake, to tremble,* 2
temer *to fear,* 2
el temor *fear,* 3
**la temperatura** *temperature,* II
**el templo** *temple,* I, 9
la temporada *season,* II
**temprano** *early,* I
**ten** *have,* I; **Ten en cuenta que...** *Keep in mind that...,* 10
las tendencias *tendencies,* II
**el tenedor** *fork,* I
**tener (tengo, ie)** *to have,* I; **tener... años** *to be... years old,* II; **tener (calor, frío, hambre, miedo, prisa, razón, sed, suerte, sueño)** *to be (hot, cold, hungry, afraid, in a hurry, right, thirsty, lucky, sleepy),* I; **tener catarro** *to have a cold,* I; **tener cuidado** *to be careful,* II; **tener el pelo...** *to have... hair,* II; **tener ganas de (hacer...)** *to feel like (doing)...,* I; **tener que** + infinitive *to have to (do something),* I; **tener tos** *to have a cough,* II; **tener un calambre** *to have a cramp,* II; **tener celos de** *to be jealous of,* 2; **tener fama de ser** *to be known to be,* 2; **tener un malentendido** *to have a misunderstanding,* 2; **tener mucho/algo/nada en común** *to have much/something/nothing in common,* 2; **tener éxito** *to be successful,* 7; **Tuvimos que hacer un gran esfuerzo para...** *We had to make a big effort to...,* 7; **Tengo la intención de...** *I intend to...,* 7; Tener el gusto de... *to have the pleasure of...,* 8; **Tenía muchas esperanzas de...** *I had many hopes of...,* 9
**el tenis** *tennis,* I; **los zapatos de tenis** *tennis shoes,* I
teñir (i, i) *to tint, to stain,* 9
**tercero(a)** *third,* II
**terco(a)** *stubborn,* 2

Vocabulario español-inglés

termal *thermal;* **las aguas termales** *hot springs,* II
la terminación *ending*
**terminar** *to finish,* I
los términos *words, expressions,* 3
la terraza *terrace,* II
**el terremoto** *earthquake,* II
el terreno *land,* II
el territorio *territory,* 9
**el terror** *horror,* I; **...de terror** *horror . . .,* I; **la película de terror** *horror film,* I
la tesis *thesis,* 8
el tesoro *treasure,* 2
el (la) testigo *witness,* 6
el testimonio *testimony,* II
**ti** *you (emphatic),* I
ti mismo *yourself,* II
**la tía** *aunt,* I
tibio(a) *lukewarm,* 4
**el tiburón** *shark,* II
**el tiempo** *weather,* I; *time,* II; **a tiempo** *on time,* I; **¿Cuánto tiempo hace que tú...?** *How long have you been . . .?,* II; **Hace buen (mal) tiempo.** *The weather is nice (bad).,* I; **Hace mucho tiempo que yo...** *I've been . . . for a long time.,* II; **Hace poco tiempo que yo...** *I've been . . . for a little while.,* II; **pasar mucho tiempo** *to spend a lot of time,* II; **¿Qué tiempo hace?** *What's the weather like?,* I; **¡Tanto tiempo sin verte!** *Long time, no see!,* I
**la tienda de...** *. . . store,* I; **la tienda de comestibles** *grocery store,* II
**la tienda de campaña** *tent,* II
el tiento *leather strap on a saddle,* 2
la tierra *land,* II
**tímido(a)** *shy,* I
**el tío** *uncle,* I
**los tíos** *uncles, uncles and aunts,* I
**típicamente** *typically,* II
**típico(a)** *typical,* II
el tipo *type,* II
tirar *to pull,* II; tirar a los leones, *to betray,* 9
**tirarse al agua** *to dive into the water,* II
**las tiras cómicas** *comic strips,* 6
**el tiro con arco** *archery,* 2
**los titulares** *headlines,* 6
el título *degree, title,* 8; el título universitario *college degree,* 3; el título académico *college degree,* 8
**la toalla** *towel,* I
**el tobillo** *ankle,* II
el tocadiscos *record player,* 6
**tocar** *to play (an instrument),* I; *to touch,* I; **tocarle (a alguien) +** infinitive *what someone has to do,* II
**el tocino** *bacon,* I
**todavía** *yet,* I; **todavía no** *not yet,* I; **¿Todavía no estás listo(a)?** *Aren't you ready yet?,* II

**todo(a)** *whole,* I; *all, every,* I; **a todo dar** *great,* I; sobre todo *especially,* II; todo el mundo *everybody,* 6
**todos(as)** *whole,* I; *all, every,* I; **todos los días** *every day,* I
**tolerante** *tolerant,* 2
**tomar** *to drink,* I; *to eat,* I; *to take,* I; *to accept,* I; **tomar clases de...** *to take . . . lessons,* II; **tomar el sol** *to sunbathe,* I; **tomar un batido** *to have a milkshake,* I; **tomar un crucero** *to go on a cruise,* II; **tomar un taxi** *to take a taxi,* II; **tomar apuntes** *to take notes,* 3; **tomar la iniciativa** *to take the initiative,* 7
**tomarse unas pastillas** *to take some pills,* II
**el tomate** *tomato,* I; **la lata de salsa de tomate** *can of tomato sauce,* II
el tono *tone,* II
**tonto(a)** *dumb,* I
topar *to run into,* 2
**torcer (ue)** *to twist,* II
**torcerse (ue)** + a body part *to sprain, to twist (one's body part),* II
**torcido(a)** *twisted,* II
**la tormenta** *storm,* II
tormentoso(a) *stormy,* 9
**el tornado** *tornado,* II
**la toronja** *grapefruit,* 4
**la torre** *tower,* 5
**la torta** *cake,* 4
**la tos** *cough,* II; **tener tos** *to have a cough,* II
**tostado(a)** *toasted,* II; **el pan tostado** *toast,* I
**tostar (ue)** *to toast,* II
**el tour** *guided tour,* II; **hacer un tour** *to take a guided tour,* II
**trabajador(a)** *hard-working,* I
**el trabajador social, la trabajadora social** *social worker,* II
**trabajar** *to work,* I; **trabajar en mecánica** *to work on cars,* II; **Pues, sigue trabajando...** *Well, he's/she's still working . . .,* 4; **Trabajo duro... y por eso...** *I work hard . . . and for that reason . . .,* 7
**el trabajo** *job, work,* I; **¿Qué clase de trabajo realiza...?** *What kind of work does . . . do?,* II
trabarse la lengua *to get tongue-tied,* 10
**la tradición** *tradition,* 7
**traer (traigo)** *to bring,* I
**la tragedia** *tragedy,* 5
**trágico(a)** *tragic,* 10
**traicionar** *to betray,* 7, 9
**el (la) traidor(a)** *traitor,* 9
**el traje** *suit,* II; **el traje de baño** *swimsuit,* I
la trama *plot (of a play),* II
la trampa *trap,* II
**tranquilamente** *calmly,* II

la tranquilidad *tranquility, peacefulness,* II
**Tranquilo(a).** *Relax.,* II; dejar tranquilo(a) *to leave (somebody) alone,* II
transcurrir *to take place,* II
el tránsito *traffic,* II
el transporte *transportation;* **los medios de transporte** *means of transportation,* I
trasero(a) *back, rear,* 8
trasladado(a) *moved,* II
tratar *to try,* II; *to be about,* II; **tratar de** + infinitive *to try to,* II
**tratar un tema a fondo** *to cover a topic in depth,* 6
través: a través de *through,* II
**las travesuras** *antics, mischief,* II; **hacer travesuras** *to play tricks,* II
**travieso(a)** *mischievous,* I
trazarse *to trace,* II
el trébol *clover,* 10
**trece** *thirteen,* I
**treinta** *thirty,* I
**treinta y cinco** *thirty-five,* I
**treinta y dos** *thirty-two,* I
**treinta y uno** *thirty-one,* I
**el tren** *train,* I; **la estación de tren** *train station,* II
**trepar** *to climb,* II
**tres** *three,* I
**trescientos(as)** *three hundred,* I
las tribus *tribes,* II
el trigo *wheat,* II
**triste** *sad,* I; **estar triste** *to be sad,* I
**la tristeza** *sadness:* **Me dio (mucha) tristeza.** *It made me (very) sad.,* II
**triunfar** *to triumph,* 7
**el trofeo** *trophy,* II
el tronco *trunk,* II
**las tropas** *troops,* 5, 9
**tropical** *tropical,* II; **explorar la selva tropical** *to explore the tropical jungle,* II; **la isla tropical** *tropical island,* II
**trotar** *to jog,* II
**el trozo** *passage,* II; *piece, chunk,* II
**el trueno** *thunder,* II
**tú** *you,* I
**tu(s)** *your (informal),* I
la tumba *tomb,* II
la tuna *traditional Spanish music group,* 2
turbar *to disturb,* 10
**el turismo** *tourism,* II; **la oficina de turismo** *tourism office,* II
**el turista, la turista** *tourist,* II
turístico(a) *tourist;* el guía turístico *tour guide,* II; la atracción turística *tourist attraction,* II; **la guía turística** *guide book,* II
turnarse *to take turns,* II
**tuyo(a)** *yours,* II

## U

ubicado(a) *located,* 9
**¡Uf! Me di un golpe en...** *Oh! I hit my . . .,* II
últimamente *lately,* 4
**último(a)** *latest,* I; *most remote,* 6; **a la (última) moda** *in the (latest) style,* I; **la última oferta** *last offer,* II
**un(a)** *a, an,* I; un rato *a while,* II; **Un(a) buen(a) amigo(a) debe apoyarme y... No debe...** *A good friend should support me and . . . He/She shouldn't . . .,* 2
**el ungüento** *ointment,* II
único(a) *only,* II
la unidad *unity,* 5
unir *to unite,* II
**la universidad** *university,* 3
**uno(a)** *one,* I; **Es la una.** *It is one o'clock.,* I
**unos(as)** *some,* I
**la uña** *nail,* II
**uruguayo(a)** *Uruguayan,* II
**usar** *to use, to wear,* I; **usar el/la...** *to wear size . . . in shoes/clothes,* I; **usar lentes** *to wear glasses,* I
**usted (Ud.)** *you (formal),* I
**ustedes (Uds.)** *you (pl.),* I
los usuarios *users,* II
útil *useful,* II
**los útiles escolares** *school supplies,* I
**utilizar** *utilize,* 8
las uvas *grapes,* II
**¡Uy!** *Oh!,* I

## V

**las vacaciones** *vacation,* I; **ir de vacaciones** *to go on vacation,* II
la vacante *vacancy,* 8
**la vainilla** *vanilla,* II; **el flan de vainilla** *vanilla flan,* II
**Vale.** *Okay.,* I
la valentía *courage, valour,* 9
valer (-go) *to cost, to be priced at;* **¿Cuánto vale(n)...?** *How much is (are) . . .?,* II; **(no) valer la pena** *to (not) be worth it,* 2
valerse (-go) de *to avail oneself of,* 3
**valiente** *brave,* 9
valioso(a) *valuable,* 3
el valle *valley,* 9
**vamos** *we are going,* II; **¿Vamos bien para...?** *Are we going the right way to . . .?,* II
cocer al vapor *to steam,* II
**los vaqueros** *jeans,* I
variar *to vary,* II
la variedad *variety,* II
varios(as) *various,* 1
la varita mágica *magic wand,* 9
el varón *male,* 4
las vasijas *containers,* II
**el vaso** *glass,* I
**¡Vaya! Por fin capto la idea.** *Aha! I finally get the idea.,* 8
la vecindad *area, neighborhood,* 5
**el vecindario** *neighborhood,* II
**el vecino, la vecina** *neighbor,* II
**los vegetales** *vegetables,* II; el aceite vegetal *vegetable oil,* II
**vegetariano(a)** *vegetarian,* II
**veinte** *twenty,* I
**veintiún** *twenty-one,* I
la vela *candle,* II; *sail;* **el bote de vela** *sailboat,* I; **pasear en bote de vela** *to go out in a sailboat,* I
**¡Ven acá!** *Come over here!,* II; **¡Ven aquí!** *Come (right) here!,* II
**vencer** *to defeat,* 9
**vendado(a)** *bandaged, wrapped,* II
**vendar** *to bandage, to wrap,* II
**vendarse** *to bandage, to wrap,* II
el vendedor *seller,* II
**vender** *to sell,* I; **vender de todo** *to sell everything,* I
**venezolano(a)** *Venezuelan,* II
**venir (vengo, ie)** *to come,* I; **¡Ven acá!** *Come over here!,* II; **¡Ven aquí!** *Come (right) here!,* II
**la venta** *sale,* II; **la venta de liquidación** *clearance sale,* II
**la ventaja** *advantage,* 8
**la ventana** *window,* I
**ver** *to watch, to see,* I; **Nos vemos.** *See you.,* I; **¡Qué gusto verte!** *It's great to see you!,* I; **¡Tanto tiempo sin verte!** *Long time, no see!,* I; **Te veo mal.** *You don't look well.,* I; **¿Cómo me veo con...?** *How do I look in . . .?,* II; **¡Te ves guapísimo!** *You look very handsome!,* II; **¡Te ves super bien!** *You look wonderful!,* II; nada que ver con *nothing to do with;* algo que ver con *something to do with,* 1
**el verano** *summer,* I
la verdad *truth,* II; **de verdad** *honestly,* II; **¿verdad?** *right?,* I
verdadero(a) *true,* II
**verde** *green,* I; **la zona verde** *green belt, park,* II
**las verduras** *vegetables,* I; **la sopa de verduras** *vegetable soup,* I
la vereda *sidewalk (Bolivia),* II
**la vergüenza** *embarrassment;* **Me dio (mucha) vergüenza.** *It made me (very) embarrassed.,* II
el verso *verse,* II
**el vestido** *dress,* I
el vestidor *fitting room,* II
**los vestidos de gala** *fancy dresses, gowns,* II
**vestirse (i, i)** *to get dressed,* I
la vez *(pl. veces) time;* **a veces** *sometimes,* I; en vez de *instead of,* II; **Érase una vez** *Once upon a time,* II; **Había una vez...** *There once was . . .,* II; **hay veces** *there are times,* I; tal vez *perhaps, maybe,* II; **Ya lo hice mil veces.** *I've already done it a thousand times.,* II
**viajar** *to travel,* 1; **viajé a...** *I traveled to . . .,* 1
**el viaje** *trip,* I; **Espero que el viaje sea divertido.** *I hope the trip is fun.,* II; **hacer un viaje** *to take a trip,* I
el viajero *traveler,* II; **los cheques de viajero** *travelers' checks,* II
**la víctima** *victim,* 9
**la victoria** *victory,* 5, 9
la vida *life,* II; la vida cotidiana *daily life,* 8; **la vida diaria** *daily life,* 8
**el video** *video,* I
**los videojuegos** *video games,* I
**el vidrio** *glass,* II
**viejo(a)** *old,* I
el vino *wine,* II
**el violín** *violin,* II
**el viento** *wind,* II; **Hace viento.** *It's windy.,* I
**el viernes** *Friday,* I
**el vinagre** *vinegar,* II
el visitante, la visitante *visitor,* II
**visitar** *to visit,* II
la víspera *eve,* II
la vista *view,* 2
el vistazo *glance,* II
**visto(a)** *seen (past participle of* **ver**), II
**las vitaminas** *vitamins,* II
**la vitrina** *shop window,* I; **mirar las vitrinas** *to window-shop,* I
**vivir** *to live,* I; **vivieron felices para siempre** *they lived happily ever after,* II
la vocación *vocation, calling,* 3
volar (ue) *to fly,* 6
**volar (ue) con ala delta** *to go hang gliding,* II
**el volcán** *volcano,* II
**el volibol** *volleyball,* I
voltearse *to turn around,* 8
**el voluntario** *volunteer,* 8
**volver (ue)** *to go/come back,* I; **vuelto** *returned (past participle of* **volver**), II
volverse (ue) + adjective *to become, to turn into (a gradual change),* 8; Me estoy volviendo loca. *I'm going crazy.,* 8
vos *you (informal),* II

**vosotros(as)** *you (pl., informal)*, I
votar *to vote*, 7
**Voy a... con la idea de...** *I'm going to . . . with the intention of . . .*, 7
la voz *voice*, 6
**el vuelo** *flight*, I; **perder el vuelo** *to miss the flight*, I
la vuelta *turn;* **a la vuelta** *around the corner*, I; **dar una vuelta por...** *to walk/drive around . . .*, II; **Está a la vuelta.** *It's around the corner.*, I
**vuestro(a)** *your (pl.)*, I
**vuestros(as)** *your (pl.)*, I

## W

el wáter *toilet (Peru)*, II
**el Web** *World Wide Web*, II; **diseñar páginas Web** *to design Web pages*, II; **páginas Web** *Web pages*, II
**el windsurf** *windsurf*, II; **hacer windsurf** *to windsurf*, II

## Y

**y** *and*, I
**ya** *already*, I; **Ya encontré mi(s)...** *I've already found my . . .*, II; **Ya lo hice mil veces.** *I've already done it a thousand times.*, II; **Ya no.** *Not anymore.*, II; **¿Ya sabías que...?** *Did you already know that . . .?*, II; **Ya te lo (la) paso.** *I'll get him/her.*, I; **¡Ya voy!** *I'm coming!*, II; **¡Ya caigo! Está más claro ahora.** *I get it! It's clearer now.*, 8; **Ya verás que van a promover...** *You'll see that they're going to promote . . .*, 10
la yapa *a small amount given in addition*, 7
el yeso *plaster*, II
**yo** *I*, I; **Yo que tú** *If I were you*, 3; **Yo te invito.** *My treat.*, 2
el yoga *yoga;* **hacer yoga** *to do yoga*, I
**el yogur** *yogurt*, 4
la yuca *yucca plant*, 4

## Z

**la zanahoria** *carrot*, I
**la zapatería** *shoe store*, I
**los zapatos** *shoes*, I
zapoteco(a) *related to the Zapotecs (Mexican civilization)*, 5
**la zona peatonal** *pedestrian zone*, II
**la zona verde** *green belt, park*, II
**el zoológico** *zoo*, I
el zopilote *vulture (Mexico, Central America)*, II
el zorro *fox*, 9

# Vocabulario inglés-español

This vocabulary includes all of the words presented in the **Vocabulario** sections of the chapters. These words are considered active—you are expected to know them and be able to use them. Expressions are listed under the English word you would be most likely to look up.

Spanish nouns are listed with the definite article and plural forms, when applicable. If a Spanish verb is stem-changing, the change is indicated in parentheses after the verb: **dormir (ue).** The number after each entry refers to the chapter in which the word or phrase is introduced. Words and phrases from Level I are indicated by the Roman numeral I. Words and phrases from Level II are indicated by the Roman numeral II.

To be sure you are using Spanish words and phrases in their correct context, refer to the chapters listed. You may also want to look up Spanish phrases in **Expresiones de ¡Exprésate!,** pp. R21–R24.

## A

**a,** *un(a)*, I
**A big hug from, . . .** *Un abrazo de,...*, II
**A few (many, five . . .) years ago** *Hace unos (muchos, cinco...) años*, II
**A good friend should support me and . . . He/she shouldn't . . .** *Un(a) buen(a) amigo(a) debe apoyarme y... No debe...*, 2
**a gossip** *chismoso(a)*, II; **What a gossip!** *¡Qué chismoso(a)!*, II
**a little** *un poco*, I
**a lot** *mucho*, I; **I laughed a lot.** *Me reí mucho.*, II; **I miss you a lot.** *Te echo mucho de menos.*, II; **to spend a lot of time** *pasar mucho tiempo*, II
**a lot of** *muchos(as)*, I
**a ton** *un montón*, I
**to achieve** *lograr*, 7
**accident** *el accidente*, 10
**accustomed: to get accustomed to** *acostumbrarse*, 7
**acquaintance** *un(a) conocido(a)*, 2
**active** *activo(a)*, I
**Actually, I admire . . .** *En realidad, admiro...*, 5
**to add** *añadir*, I; *echar*, II; **It's just that I forgot to add . . .** *Es que se me olvidó ponerle...*, 4
**address** *la dirección*, I; **My address is . . .** *Mi dirección es...*, I; **e-mail address** *el correo electrónico*, I
**adhesive bandage** *una curita*, II
**administrative assistant** *el (la) auxiliar administrativo(a)*, 8
**to admire: Actually, I admire . . .** *En realidad, admiro...*, 5
**to admit a mistake** *admitir un error*, 3
**advances** *los adelantos*, 8
**advantage** *la ventaja*, 8; **to take advantage of** *aprovechar*, 7
**adventure** *la aventura*, I; **adventure book** *el libro de aventura*, I
**adventurous** *aventurero(a)*, II
**advice** *el consejo*, II; **to give advice** *dar consejos*, II
**to advise** *aconsejar*, II; **They advise that . . .** *Se advierte que...*, 10
**to advise someone** *aconsejarle (a alguien)*, II
**aerobics** *los aeróbicos*, II; **to do aerobics** *hacer ejercicios aeróbicos*, II
**affectionate** *cariñoso(a)*, II
**after** *después*, I; *después de*, I; **after class** *después de clases*, I; **after school** *después del colegio*, II
**afternoon** *la tarde*, I; **in the afternoon, P.M.** *de la tarde*, I; *por la tarde*, I; **this afternoon** *esta tarde*, I
**afterwards** *después*, I
**agent** *el agente, la agente*, I
**agree: I agree.** *Estoy de acuerdo*, I; **I don't agree.** *No estoy de acuerdo.*, I
**Aha! I finally get the idea.** *¡Vaya! Por fin capto la idea.*, 8
**airplane** *el avión*, I; **by plane** *por avión*, I
**airport** *el aeropuerto*, I
**album** *el álbum*, II; **to create an album** *crear un álbum*, II
**algebra** *el álgebra*, 3
**all** *todo(a)(os)(as)*, I
**all right** *regular*, I
**to allow** *dejar*, I; *permitir*, II
**almonds** *las almendras*, II
**almost** *casi*, I; **almost always** *casi siempre*, I; **almost never** *casi nunca*, I
**alone** *solo(a)*, I
**alphabet** *el alfabeto*, I
**already** *ya*, I; **Thanks for inviting me, but I've already seen it.** *Gracias por invitarme, pero ya lo/la he visto.*, 5
**also** *también*, I
**alternatives (to)** *las alternativas (a)*, 10
**although** *aunque*, 9; **Although I agree . . ., I think that . . .** *Aunque estoy de acuerdo..., creo que...*, 10; **Although there was/were . . ., on the other hand . . .** *A pesar de que hubo..., por otro lado...*, 10
**always** *siempre*, I; **almost always** *casi siempre*, I; **as always** *como siempre*, I; **Yes, I'm always doing . . . I'm crazy about . . .** *Sí, me la paso... Estoy loco(a) por...*, 2; **I have always wanted to be a . . .** *Siempre he querido ser un(a)...*, 8
**American** *estadounidense*, II
**amusement park** *el parque de diversiones*, I
**an** *un(a)*, I
**ancestors** *los antepasados*, 7
**and** *y*, I; *e*, II; **And what is there to do around here?** *¿Y qué hay que hacer por aquí?*, II; **And your friends, what do they like to do?** *Y a tus amigos, ¿qué les gusta hacer?*, II
**ankle** *el tobillo*, II
**anniversary** *el aniversario*, I
**announcer** *el (la) locutor(a)*, 6
**answering machine** *el contestador automático*, 8
**antique** *antiguo(a)*, 5
**any** *cualquier*, I
**anything** *algo*, I; **Anything else?** *¿Algo más?*, II; **Would you like anything else?** *¿Se les ofrece algo más?*, II
**apartment** *el apartamento*, I
**apology** *la disculpa*, 3
**appetizers** *los entremeses*, II
**apple** *la manzana*, I
**application** *la solicitud*, 8
**to apply** *solicitar*, 8
**April** *abril*, I
**aquarium** *el acuario*, II
**archery** *el tiro con arco*, 2
**architecture** *la arquitectura*, 5
**Are you . . .?** *¿Eres...?*, I
**Are you interested in going to . . .?** *¿Te interesa ir a...?*, 5
**Are you still . . .?** *¿Sigues...?*, II; **Are you still practicing . . .?** *¿Sigues practicando...?*, II
**Aren't you ready yet?** *¿Todavía no estás listo(a)?*, II
**Argentine** *argentino(a)*, II
**to argue** *discutir*, 3
**arid** *árido(a)*, II
**arm** *el brazo*, I
**armchair** *el sillón*, II
**armoire** *la cómoda*, II
**around here** *por aquí*, II
**around the corner** *a la vuelta*, I
**arrival** *la llegada*, I
**to arrive** *llegar*, I; **As soon as he/she arrived . . .** *Tan pronto como llegó...*, 9
**arrogant** *creído(a)*, 2
**art** *el arte*, I; **plastic arts** *las artes plásticas*, 5; **dramatic arts** *las artes dramáticas*, 5; **Speaking of art, what can you tell me about . . .?** *Hablando de arte, ¿qué me cuentas de...?*, 5
**article** *el artículo*, 4
**artistic** *artístico(a)*, 5
**as** *como*, II
**as . . . as** *tan...como*, I

**as a child** *de pequeño(a)*, II
**as always** *como siempre*, I
**as much/many . . . as . . .** *tanto(a)/ tantos(as)... como...*, II
**As soon as . . . I plan on . . .** *Tan pronto como... pienso...*, 7
**As soon as he/she arrived . . .** *Tan pronto como llegó...*, 9
**As soon as I turn . . . years old, I'm going to . . .** *En cuanto cumpla los... años, voy a...*, 7
**to ask for** *pedir (i, i)*, I; *solicitar*, 8; **to ask for help** *pedir ayuda*, II; **to ask for information** *pedir información*, II; **to ask for forgiveness** *pedir perdón*, 3
**to ask questions** *hacer preguntas*, II
**to ask someone** *preguntarle a alguien*, II
**aspirations** *las aspiraciones*, 7
**aspirin** *la aspirina*, II
**to assimilate** *asimilar*, 7; **With time I was able to assimilate . . .** *Con el tiempo pude asimilar...*, 7
**assorted** *surtido(a)*, II; **assorted fresh fruit** *el surtido de frutas frescas*, II
**astronaut** *el astronauta, la astronauta*, II
**at** *a(l)*, I; **@** *la arroba*, I
**at all** *para nada*, II
**at last** *por fin*, II
**at the same time** *a la vez*, 8
**athletic** *atlético(a)*, I
**to attend** *asistir (a)*, I
**attitude: I can't stand the attitude of . . . towards . . . I can't take it anymore!** *Me choca la actitud de... hacia... ¡No aguanto más!*, 3
**to attract one's attention** *llamar la atención*, 5
**audience** *el público*, 5
**auditorium** *el auditorio*, I
**August** *agosto*, I
**aunt** *la tía*, I
**automatic teller machine** *el cajero automático*, I
**avocado** *el aguacate*, 4
**avenue** *la avenida*, II
**to avoid** *evitar*, II
**awesome** *fenomenal*, I
**awful** *fatal*, II

## B

**babied** *consentido(a)*, II
**back** *la espalda*, I
**back then** *en aquel entonces*, II
**backpack** *la mochila*, I
**bacon** *el tocino*, I
**bad** *malo(a)*, I; **to get bad grades** *sacar malas notas*, II; **in good/bad taste** *de buen/mal gusto*, 5; **It's too bad that . . .** *Es lamentable que...*, 9; **It would be a good/bad idea to break up with . . .** *Sería una buena/mala idea romper con...*, 3; **The milk has gone bad.** *Está pasada la leche.*, 4
**bag** *la bolsa*, I
**baggage** *el equipaje*, I; **baggage claim** *el reclamo de equipaje*, I
**baggy** *flojo(a)*, II
**to bake** *hornear*, II
**baked** *horneado(a)*, II
**bakery** *la panadería*, II
**balanced** *balanceado(a)*, II; **balanced diet** *la dieta balanceada*, II; **to eat a balanced diet** *llevar una dieta balanceada*, II; *seguir (i, i) una dieta sana*, I
**ballet** *el ballet*, 5
**banana** *el plátano*, II
**band: Don't forget to go to band practice.** *No te olvides de ir al ensayo de la banda.*, 5
**to bandage** *vendarse*, II
**bandaged** *vendado(a)*, II
**bank** *el banco*, II
**baptism** *el bautizo*, II
**bargain** *la ganga*, I
**to bargain** *regatear*, II
**baseball** *el béisbol*, I
**basket** *la cesta*, II
**basketball** *el básquetbol*, I
**to bathe** *bañarse*, I
**bathroom** *el baño*, I
**bathroom sink** *el lavabo*, II
**bathtub** *la bañera*, II
**battle** *la batalla*, 9
**battlefield** *el campo de batalla*, 9
**be** *sé*, I
**to be** *ser, estar*, I; **How are you?** *¿Cómo está(s)?*, I; **to be all right** *estar regular*, I; **to be bored** *estar aburrido(a)* I; **to be careful** *tener cuidado*, II; **to be dead boring** *ser un rollo*, II; **to be embroidered** *estar bordado(a)*, II; **to be familiar with (a place)** *conocer*, I; **to be fine** *estar bien*, I; **to be happy** *estar contento(a)* I; **to be hungry** *tener hambre*, I; **to be in a hurry** *tener prisa*, I; **to be in a wheelchair** *estar en una silla de ruedas*, I; **to be lucky** *tener suerte*, I; **to be nervous** *estar nervioso(a)* I; **to be ready** *estar listo(a)*, I; **to be right** *tener razón*, I; **to be sad** *estar triste*, I; **to be scared** *tener miedo*, I; **to be sick** *estar enfermo(a)* I; *estar mal*, II; **to be sleepy** *tener sueño*, I; **to be sure** *estar seguro(a)*, II; **to be thirsty** *tener sed*, I; **to be tired** *estar cansado(a)*, I; **to be . . . years old** *tener... años*, II; **What did you want to be?** *¿Qué querías ser?*, II; **to be crazy about** *estar loco(a) por*, 2; **to be a fanatic** *ser un(a) fanático(a)*, 2; **to be jealous of** *tener celos de*, 2; **to be known to be** *tener fama de ser*, 2; **to (not) be worth it** *(no) valer la pena*, 2; **to be resentful** *estar resentido(a)*, 3; **to be (un)faithful** *ser (in)fiel*, 3; **to be married** *estar casado(a)*, 4; **to be born** *nacer*, 4; **to be up-to-date** *estar al tanto*, 6; **to be of the opinion** *opinar*, 6; **to be of . . . descent** *ser de ascendencia...*, 7; **to be thankful for** *estar agradecido(a) por*, 7; **to insist on, be determined to** *empeñarse en*, 7
**to be able to** *poder (ue, u)*, I; **With time I was able to assimilate . . .** *Con el tiempo pude asimilar...*, 7; **I can do it.** *Lo puedo hacer.*, 8
**to be going to (do something)** *ir + a +* infinitive, I; **I'm going to give you a special price.** *Le voy a dar un precio especial.*, II; **I wasn't going to buy . . ., but they gave me a discount.** *No iba a comprar..., pero me dieron un descuento.*, II; **We're going to clean the rooms.** *Vamos a limpiar los cuartos.*, II; **We're going to go . . .** *Vamos a ir a/al...*, II
**to be interested in** *llamarle la atención*, II
**to be late** *tardar*, II
**to be named** *llamarse*, II; **His/Her name is . . .** *Se llama...*, II; **My . . .'s name is . . .** *Mi... se llama...*, II;
**beach** *la playa*, I
**beachball** *el balón de playa*, II
**beans** *las habichuelas*, II; *los frijoles*, 4
**bear** *el oso*, II
**beautiful** *hermoso(a)*, 5
**beauty parlor** *el salón de belleza*, II
**because** *porque*, I; **Because of this . . .** *A causa de esto...*, 9
**to become** *llegar a ser*, 7
**bed** *la cama*, I; **to go to bed** *acostarse*, I; **to make the bed** *hacer la cama*, I; **to stay in bed** *quedarse en cama*, II
**bedroom** *la habitación*, I
**bedside table** *la mesita de noche*, II
**beef** *la carne*, I
**before** *antes de*, I; **Before classes start, I want to . . .** *Antes de que empiecen las clases, quiero...*, 7
**to start crying** *ponerse a llorar*, II
**behind** *detrás de*, I
**to believe** *creer*, II; **When I found out, I couldn't believe it.** *Cuando me enteré, no lo pude creer.*, II; **When I heard the news, I didn't want to believe it.** *Cuando oí la noticia no lo quise creer.*, II; **Believe me, I didn't mean to do it.** *Créeme que fue sin querer.*, 3; **I can't believe it!** *¡No me lo puedo creer!*, 4; **It's hard to believe that there are . . ./that they say . . .** *Parece mentira que haya.../que digan...*, 6
**bellhop** *el botones*, II
**to belong to** *pertenecer(zc) a*, 7
**belt** *el cinturón*, II
**benefits** *los beneficios*, 8
**besides** *además*, I
**best** *mejor(es)*, I
**to bet: I bet that the rate of . . . won't go down.** *A que no va a bajar la tasa de...*, 10; **I bet you that . . .** *Te apuesto que...*, 10
**better** *mejor(es)*, I; **better than anyone** *mejor que nadie*, II; **It's better that . . .** *Es mejor que...*, II; **Which of these paintings do you like better, the one of (by) . . . or the one of (by) . . .?** *¿Cuál de estas pinturas te gusta más, la de... o la de...?*, 5
**to betray** *traicionar*, 9
**biased** *parcial*, 4
**big** *grande*, I; **I'm a big . . . fan. What sport do you like?** *Soy un(a) gran aficionado(a) a... ¿Qué deporte te gusta a ti?*, 2
**bike** *la bicicleta*, I; **to ride a bike** *montar en bicicleta*, I, **to bike** *practicar ciclismo*, 2
**biking** *el ciclismo*, 2
**bilingual: I'm bilingual; therefore, I have many opportunities . . .** *Soy bilingüe, por lo tanto, tengo muchas oportunidades...*, 7
**bill** *la cuenta*, I; *el billete*, II; **to pay the bill** *pagar la cuenta*, II
**binoculars** *los binóculos*, II
**biology** *la biología*, I
**bird** *el pájaro*, II
**birth** *el nacimiento*, II; **to give birth** *dar a luz*, 4
**birthday** *el cumpleaños*, I; **birthday card** *la tarjeta de cumpleaños*, I; **birthday of** *el cumpleaños de...*, I
**black** *negro(a)*, I

**blank** *en blanco*, I
**blind** *ciego(a)*, I
**block** *la cuadra*, II; *el bloque*, II; **to play with blocks** *jugar (ue) con bloques*, II
**blond** *rubio(a)*, I
**blouse** *la blusa*, I
**blue** *azul*, I
**to board** *abordar*, I
**board game** *el juego de mesa*, I
**boarding house** *la pensión*, II
**boarding pass** *la tarjeta de embarque*, I
**boat** *el barco*, I; *el bote*, II; **to go boating** *pasear en bote*, II
**to boil** *hervir (ie, i)*, II
**boiled** *hervido(a)*, II
**bomb** *la bomba*, 10
**bone** *el hueso*, II
**book** *el libro*, I; **adventure book** *el libro de aventura*, I; **romance book** *el libro de amor*, I
**bookcase** *el estante*, II
**bookstore** *la librería*, I
**boots** *las botas*, I
**boring** *aburrido(a)*, I; **to be bored** *estar aburrido*, I
**boss** *el jefe, la jefa*, 8
**to bother** *fastidiar, molestar*, II
**bowl** *el plato hondo*, I
**to bowl** *jugar al boliche*, 2
**bowling** *el boliche*, 2
**boy** *el muchacho*, I; *el niño*, II
**boyfriend: What do you look for in a boyfriend/girlfriend?** *¿Qué buscas en un(a) novio(a)?*, 2
**bracelet** *la pulsera*, I
**brain** *el cerebro*, II
**brave** *valiente*, 9
**bread** *el pan*, I
**to break** *romper*, II; **broken** *roto(a) (past participle of* **romper**), II
**to break (one's body part)** *romperse* + a body part, II
**to break up with** *romper con*, 2; **It would be a good/bad idea to break up with...** *Sería una buena/mala idea romper con...*, 3
**breakfast** *el desayuno*, I
**breeze** *la brisa*, II
**bridge** *el puente*, 5
**to bring** *traer (-igo)*, I; **Bring us the bill, please.** *Tráiganos la cuenta, por favor.*, II; **Did you bring your...?** *¿Trajiste tu...?*, II; **I'll bring it (them) right away.** *Enseguida se lo/la (los/las) traigo.*, II; **They bring movies to my house.** *Traen películas a mi casa.*, II; **Would you bring us...?** *¿Nos trae...?*, II
**broccoli** *el bróculi*, I
**broken** *roto(a) (past participle of* **romper**), II
**brother** *el hermano*, I
**brothers, brothers and sisters** *los hermanos*, I
**brother-in-law** *el cuñado*, 4
**brown** *castaño(a)*, I; *de color café*, I
**to brush** *cepillarse*, II
**to brush one's hair** *peinarse*, II; **to brush one's teeth** *lavarse los dientes*, I
**to build** *construir*, II
**building** *el edificio*, I; **... story building** *el edificio de... pisos*, I
**bump** *el golpe*, II; **to bump one's...** *darse un golpe en...*, II
**to bump one's...** *darse un golpe en...*, II
**to burn** *quemar*, II; **to burn CDs** *crear/grabar CDs*, II
**burned** *quemado(a)*, II; **It's burned.** *Está quemado(a).*, II
**bus** *el autobús*, I
**businessman** *el hombre de negocios*, 8
**businesswoman** *la mujer de negocios*, 8
**busy** *ocupado(a)*, II
**but** *pero*, I; **but (as in "Not this, but that instead.")** *sino*, II; **not only... but... as well** *no sólo... sino... también*, II
**butcher shop** *la carnicería*, II
**butter** *la mantequilla*, II
**to buy** *comprar*, I; **buy** *compre*, II; **don't buy** *no compre*, II; **I saw that... was (were) on sale, so I bought...** *Vi que... estaba(n) en oferta, así que compré...*, II; **I wasn't going to buy..., but they gave me a discount.** *No iba a comprar..., pero me dieron un descuento.*, II; **to buy souvenirs** *comprar recuerdos*, II; **you would buy** *comprarías*, I; **to buy (someone) a gift** *comprarle un regalo*, 3
**by plane** *por avion*, I
**By the way, what have you heard about the...?** *A propósito, ¿qué has oído de el/la...?*, 5
**Bye.** *Chao.* I

# C

**cactus** *el cactus*, II
**café** *el café*, II; **Internet café** *el café Internet*, II; **to get together at an Internet café** *reunirse en un café Internet*, II; **to go to outdoor cafés** *ir a cafés*, II
**cafeteria** *la cafetería*, I
**cake** *el pastel*, I
**calculator** *la calculadora*, I
**calculus** *el cálculo*, 3
**calf (of leg)** *la pantorrilla*, I
**to call** *llamar*, I; **I'll call back later.** *Llamo más tarde.*, I
**calmly** *tranquilamente*, II
**camera** *la cámara*, I; **disposable camera** *la cámara desechable*, I
**to camp** *acampar*, I
**campfire** *la fogata*, II
**camping** *camping*, II; **to go camping** *hacer camping*, II
**can** *la lata*, II; **can of tomato sauce** *la lata de salsa de tomate*, II
**can** *poder (ue, u)*, I; **Do you know where I can...?** *¿Sabe usted dónde se puede...?*, II; **How can I get to...?** *¿Cómo puedo llegar a...?*, II; **one can** *se puede*, II; **Can I...?** *¿Puedo...?*, I; **Can I help you?** *¿En qué le puedo servir?*, I; *¿Puedo ayudarte?*, II; **Can you lower the price on that...?** *¿Me puede rebajar el precio de ese/esa...?*, II; **Can you repeat what you said?** *¿Puede repetir lo que dijo?*, II; **Can you tell me where... is?** *¿Me dices dónde está...?*, II; **I can do it.** *Lo puedo hacer.*, 8
**Canadian** *canadiense*, II
**candy** *el dulce*, I
**canoe** *la canoa*, I
**capable: I am capable of (doing)...** *Soy capaz de (hacer)...*, 8
**car** *el carro*, I; **toy car** *el carrito*, II; **to work on cars** *trabaja en mecánica*, II
**carbohydrates** *los carbohidratos*, II
**card** *la tarjeta*, I
**cards** *los naipes*, II; **to play cards** *jugar naipes*, II
**career** *la carrera* , 8
**carpenter** *el carpintero, la carpintera*, II
**carpet** *la alfombra*, II
**carrot** *la zanahoria*, I
**to carry** *llevar*, II; **I got carried away with...** *Se me fue la mano con...*, 4
**cartoons** *los dibujos animados*, II
**carved figure** *la figura tallada*, II
**carving: to do woodcarving** *tallar en madera*, 5
**cash** *en efectivo*, II
**cash register** *la caja*, II
**cashier** *el cajero, la cajera*, II
**castle** *el castillo*, II
**cat** *el gato, la gata*, I; **to rain cats and dogs** *llover a cántaros*, II
**to catch a cold** *resfriarse*, II
**cathedral** *la catedral*, II
**cauliflower** *la coliflor*, 4
**cave** *la cueva*, II; **to explore caves, to go spelunking** *explorar cuevas*, II
**CD** *el CD*, II; **to burn CDs** *crear/grabar CDs*, II
**ceiling** *el techo*, II
**to celebrate** *celebrar, festejar*, I; **Tonight we're going to celebrate...** *Esta noche vamos a celebrar...*, II
**celery** *el apio*, 4
**cell phone** *el teléfono celular*, II
**cemetery** *el cementerio*, II
**censorship** *la censura*, 6
**Centigrade** *centígrados*, II
**ceramic** *la cerámica*, II
**cereal** *los cereales*, I
**chain** *la cadena*, II
**chair** *la silla*, I; **wheelchair** *la silla de ruedas*, I
**challenge** *el desafío*, 7; **There were many challenges in...** *Había muchos desafíos en...*, 7
**championship** *el campeonato*, 10
**chance: If you had the chance, where would you go?** *Si tuvieras la oportunidad, ¿adónde irías?*, 8
**to change** *cambiar*, 8; **Changing the subject, what do you have to say about...?** *Cambiando de tema, ¿qué me dices de...?*, 5
**channel** *el canal* , 6
**to charge** *cobrar*, II
**to chat** *charlar*, I; **to chat online** *platicar en línea*, I
**to check luggage** *facturar el equipaje*, I
**cheek** *la mejilla*, II
**to cheer** *animar*, II
**cheerleader** *el animador, la animadora*, II
**cheese** *el queso*, I
**chemistry** *la química*, I
**cherry** *la cereza*, 4
**chess** *el ajedrez*, I; **to play chess** *jugar al ajedrez*, II
**chest** *el pecho*, I
**chest of drawers** *la cómoda*, II
**chicken** *el pollo*, I; **roasted chicken** *el pollo asado*, II; **fried chicken** *el pollo frito*, 4
**chicken soup** *el caldo de pollo*, II
**children** *los hijos*, I
**chili pepper** *el ají*, II
**Chilean** *chileno(a)*, II

chocolate el chocolate, I; chocolate cake el bizcocho de chocolate, 4
chores los quehaceres, I
Christmas la Navidad, I
Christmas Eve la Nochebuena, I
chunk el trozo, II
church la iglesia, I
cinematography la cinematografía, 5
city la ciudad, I; city map el plano de la ciudad, II
class la clase, I; el curso, 3; after class después de clases, I
classic clásico(a), 5
classified ads los anuncios clasificados, 6
classmate el compañero de clase, I; la compañera de clase, I
clay el barro, II
to clean limpiar, I
to clean the room arreglar el cuarto, I; We're going to clean the rooms. Vamos a limpiar los cuartos., II
clear: I get it! It's clearer now. ¡Ya caigo! Está más claro ahora., 8
clearance sale la venta de liquidación, II
client el cliente, la cliente, I
climate el clima, II; What a dry climate! ¡Qué clima tan seco!, II
to climb subir, I; trepar, II; escalar, 2; to climb trees trepar a los árboles, II
clinic la clínica, II
to close cerrar (ie), I
close to cerca de, I
clothes la ropa, I
cloudy nublado(a), I
club el club de..., I
coach el entrenador, la entrenadora, II
coast la costa, II
coat el abrigo, I
coconut candy el dulce de coco, 4
coffee el café, I; coffee with milk el café con leche, I
coffee shop la cafetería, I
coins las monedas, II; to collect coins coleccionar monedas, II
cold frío(a), I; It's cold. Hace frío., I; to be cold tener frío, I; to have a cold tener catarro, I; cold, unfriendly seco(a), 2
cold tomato soup el gazpacho, II
colleagues los compañeros de trabajo, 8
to collect coleccionar, II; to collect coins coleccionar monedas, II; to collect posters coleccionar pósters, II; to collect stamps coleccionar estampillas, II
color el color, I
Colombian colombiano(a), II
comb el peine, I
to comb your hair peinarse, I
to combat combatir, 3
to come venir (-go, ie), I; come ven, I; Come over here! ¡Ven acá!, II; Come (right) here! ¡Ven aquí!, II; don't come no vengas, I; to come back volver, I; you're coming with me... vienes conmigo a..., I; Do you want to come to... with me? ¿Me acompañas a...?, 5
comedy la comedia, 5
comic book la revista de tiras cómicas, I
comic books las revistas cómicas, II
comic strips las tiras cómicas, 6
commemorate: My life-long dream is to commemorate... El sueño de mi vida es conmemorar a...., 9
commentary el comentario, 6
to commit (a crime) cometer (un crimen), 10
commitment el compromiso, 7
common: to have much/something/nothing in common tener mucho/algo/nada en común, 2
to communicate comunicarse, 3
communication la comunicación, 3
compact disc el disco compacto, I
company la empresa, 8
compassion la compasión, 10
competent competente, 8
competition la competencia, II
completely por completo, II; to cover a topic completely tratar un tema a fondo, 6
computer la computadora, I; to do computer design hacer diseño por computadora, II; computer games los juegos de computadora, 2
computer science la computación, I
concert el concierto, I
to confront enfrentar, II
consequently: We talked about the issue; consequently... Hablamos del tema; por consiguiente..., 7
to conserve conservar, 10
consider: to consider oneself considerarse, 6
constantly constantemente, II
contact lenses los lentes de contacto, II
contaminated/polluted contaminado(a), 10
contamination/pollution la contaminación, 10
contemporary contemporáneo(a), 5
contrary: On the contrary! I disagree. ¡Al contrario! No estoy de acuerdo., 3
to contribute contribuir, 7
contribution el aporte, 7
controversial controvertido(a), 6
convinced: I'm convinced that... Estoy convencido(a) de que..., 6
cook el cocinero, la cocinera, II
to cook cocinar, I
cooked cocido(a), II
cookie la galleta, I
cooking section la sección de cocina, 6
cool fresco(a), I; It's cool. Hace fresco., I
cooperation la cooperación, 10
corn el maíz, I
corner la esquina, II
to cost costar (ue), I; it will cost costará, I
Costa Rican costarricense, II
cotton el algodón, I; made of cotton de algodón, I
cough la tos, II; to have a cough tener tos, II
cough syrup el jarabe, II
Could you tell me...? ¿Me podría decir...?, II
counselor: guidance counselor el (la) consejero(a), 3
to count contar (ue), II
to count on contar (ue) con, 2
counter el mostrador, I
country el país, I
countryside el campo, I
cousin el primo, la prima, I
to cover cubrir, II; to cover a topic completely tratar un tema a fondo, 6
cowardly cobarde, 9
coyote el coyote, II
cramp el calambre, II; for someone to get a cramp darle un calambre, II; to have a cramp tener un calambre, II
crazy loco(a), II; I'm crazy about... Estoy loco(a) por..., II
cream la crema, II; la crema, II; strawberries (and cream) las fresas (con crema), II; sour cream la crema agria, 4
to create crear, 5
to create an album, scrapbook crear un álbum, II
creative creativo(a), 5
credit card la tarjeta de crédito, II
creation la creación, 9
crime el crimen, 10
crisis: environmental/economic/political crisis la crisis ambiental/económica/política, 6
critical criticón, criticona, 2; critical review la reseña, 5
to critique reseñar, 6
crossword puzzle el crucigrama, II; to do crossword puzzles hacer crucigramas, II
to cry llorar, II; to start crying ponerse a llorar, II; Yes, I'm disappointed because... It makes me feel like crying. Sí, estoy decepcionado(a) porque... Me dan ganas de llorar., 2
cucumber el pepino, 4
curious curioso(a), II
custard el flan, I
customs (airport) la aduana, I
customs (cultural) las costumbres, 7
cut cortado(a), II
to cut cortar, I; to cut the grass cortar el césped, I
to cut oneself cortarse, II
cybercafé el cibercafé, II; to go to a cybercafé ir a un cibercafé, II

## D

dad el papá, I
daily life la vida diaria, 8
daily special el plato del día, II
dance el baile, I; I recommend that you go to the folk dance performance. It's very... Te aconsejo que vayas a la presentación de baile folclórico. Es muy..., 5
to dance bailar, I; dancing bailando, I; to start dancing ponerse a bailar, I
dark-skinned; dark-haired moreno(a), I
date la fecha, I
daughter la hija, I
day el día, I; day of the week el día de la semana, I; Father's Day el Día del Padre, I; holiday el día festivo, I; Independence Day el Día de la Independencia, I; Mother's Day el Día de la Madre, I; some day algún día, I; Thanksgiving Day el Día de Acción de Gracias, I; Valentine's Day el Día de los Enamorados, I; What day is today? ¿Qué día es hoy?, I; your saint's day el día de tu santo, I; these days hoy (en) día, 8
day after tomorrow pasado mañana, I
day before yesterday anteayer, I
deaf sordo(a), I
Dear ..., Querido(a)..., II
Dear Sir/Madam/Miss: Muy estimado(a) Sr./Sra./Srta.:, 8
death la muerte, II
debate el debate, II
December diciembre, I

to decide *decidir*, II
to decide to *decidirse a* + infinitive, 8
to declare war *declarar la guerra*, 9
to decorate *decorar*, I; to decorate the patio. *decorar el patio.*, II
decoration *la decoración*, I
decorations *los adornos*, II
deed *el hecho*, 9
defeat *la derrota*, 9
to defeat *vencer*, 9
degrees Fahrenheit *los grados Fahrenheit*, II
delicious *delicioso(a)*, I; *riquísimo(a)*, I; *rico(a)*, II; How delicious! *¡Qué rico(a)!*, II; It tastes delicious. *Sabe delicioso(a).*, 4
to delight *encantar*, I
Delighted (to meet you) . . . *Encantado(a).*, II
demonstrations *las manifestaciones*, 10
dentist *el dentista, la dentista*, II
department store *el almacén*, I
departure *la salida*, I; *la partida*, II
descent: to be of (nationality) descent *ser de ascendencia*, 7
to describe *describir*, II; Describe . . . to me. *Descríbeme...*, II
desert *el desierto*, II
to design *diseñar*, II; to design Web pages *diseñar páginas Web*, II
design *el diseño*, II; to do computer design *hacer diseño por computadora*, II
desire *la gana*, I; to desire *desear*, I
desk *el escritorio*, I
dessert *el postre*, I
destination *el destino*, I
destined *destinado(a)*, I
destruction *la destrucción*, 10
detail *el detalle*, I
detailed *detallado(a)*, 6
to determine *determinar*, I
determined: to insist on, be determined to *empeñarse en*, 7
to develop *desarrollar*, 10
to dice *picar*, II
diced *picado(a)*, II
dictator *el (la) dictador(a)*, 9
dictionary *el diccionario*, I
Did you remember to . . .? *¿Te acordaste de...?*, II
Did you try . . .? *¿Probaste...?*, II
to die *morirse (ue, u)*, II
diet *la dieta*, I; to eat a balanced diet *llevar una dieta balanceada*, II; *seguir (i, i) una dieta sana*, I
difficult *difícil*, I; That's easy/pretty difficult for me. *Eso me resulta fácil/bastante difícil*, 8
digital camera *la cámara digital*, II
dining room *el comedor*, I
dinner *la cena*, I
to direct *dirigir*, 8
disadvantage *la desventaja*, 8
disagree: On the contrary! I disagree. *¡Al contrario! No estoy de acuerdo.*, 3
to disappear *desaparecer (zc)*, 9
disappointed: Yes, I'm disappointed because . . . It makes me feel like crying. *Sí, estoy decepcionado(a) porque... Me dan ganas de llorar.*, 2
disaster *el desastre*, 10
discount *el descuento*, II
to discover *descubrir*, 10
discovery (of) *el descubrimiento (de)*, 10
to discriminate *discriminar*, 7
discrimination *la discriminación*, 3
disease *la enfermedad*, 10
disgusting: That's disgusting! *¡Qué asco!*, 4
dish *el plato*, I
dishwasher *el lavaplatos*, II
disloyal *desleal*, 2
disposable *desechable*, I
to dive in the water *tirarse al agua*, II
divorce *el divorcio*, 4
to divorce *divorciarse (de)*, 4
divorced *divorciado(a)*, 4
to do *hacer (-go)*, I; And what is there to do around here? *¿Y qué hay que hacer por aquí?*, II; And your friends, what do they like to do? *Y a tus amigos, ¿qué les gusta hacer?*, II; do *haz*, I; doing *haciendo*, II; done *hecho (past participle of* hacer), II; don't do *no hagas*, I; I didn't do anything. *No hice nada.*, II; I've already done it a thousand times. *Ya lo hice mil veces.*, II; So, what I have to do is . . . *Entonces, lo que tengo que hacer es...*, II; we are doing *estamos haciendo*, I; What did you do? *¿Qué hiciste?*, I; What did you like to do when you were . . . years old? *¿Qué te gustaba hacer cuando tenías...?*, II; What did you use to do when you were a little boy/girl? *¿Qué hacías de niño(a)?*, II; What do you do every morning? *¿Qué haces todas las mañanas?*, II; What do you like to do on weekends? *¿Qué te gusta hacer los fines de semana?*, II; What do you want to do this afternoon? *¿Qué quieres hacer esta tarde?*, II; What do your friends do on weekends? *¿Qué hacen tus amigos los fines de semana?*, II; What else do I need to do? *¿Qué más tengo que hacer?*, II; What needs to be done in the kitchen? *¿Qué hay que hacer en la cocina?*, II; What will you all do at the beach? *¿Qué harán ustedes en la playa?*, II; to do aerobics *hacer ejercicios aeróbicos*, II; to do the chores *hacer los quehaceres*, I; to do computer design *hacer diseño por computadora*, II; to do crossword puzzles *hacer crucigramas*, II; to do homework *hacer la tarea*, I; to do woodcarving *tallar en madera*, 5; to do yoga *hacer yoga*, I; The . . . don't do anything for me. *Los/Las... me dejan frío(a).*, 2; Yes, I'm always doing . . . I'm crazy about . . . *Sí, me la paso... Estoy loco(a) por...*, 2; I can do it. *Lo puedo hacer.*, 8; What would you like to do? *¿Qué te gustaría hacer?*, 8; Where were you and what were you doing when . . .? *¿Dónde estabas y qué hacías cuando...?*, 10
Do you like . . .? *¿Te gusta(n)...?*, I
Do you remember when . . . happened? *¿Te acuerdas cuando sucedió...?*, 10
Do you want to come to . . . with me? *¿Me acompañas a...?*, 5
Do you want to go see . . . *¿Quieres ir a ver...?*, 5
doctor *el médico, la médica*, II
documentary *el documental*, 6
dog *el perro, la perra*, I; to feed the dog *darle de comer al perro*, II
dolls *las muñecas*, II
dominoes *el dominó*, 2
Don't forget to . . . *No te olvides de...*, II, 3; Don't forget to go to band practice. *No te olvides de ir al ensayo de la banda.*, 5
Don't worry. *No te preocupes.*, II
to donate time to a cause *donar tiempo a una causa*, 8
done *hecho(a) (past participle of* hacer), II
door *la puerta*, I; to lock the door *cerrar (ie) la puerta con llave*, II
dot *el punto*, I
doubt: I doubt that you're well-informed about . . ./that you know . . . *Dudo que estés bien informado(a) sobre.../que sepas...*, 6
doubtful: It's doubtful that . . . *Es dudoso que...*, 6
to download files *bajar archivos*, I
downtown *el centro*, I; to get to know downtown *conocer el centro*, II
drama *el drama*, 5
dramatic arts *las artes dramáticas*, 5
to draw *dibujar*, I
drawing *el dibujo*, 5
dream: My life-long dream is to commemorate . . . *El sueño de mi vida es conmemorar a....*, 9
to dream *soñar(ue)*, II; I dreamed of being . . . *Soñaba con ser...*, II; to dream of *soñar (ue) con*, 7
dress *el vestido*, I
to dress up *arreglarse*, II
to drink (something) *beber (algo)*, II; *tomar (algo)*, I
drinks *las bebidas*, II
to drive *conducir(zc)*, II
to drive around . . . *dar una vuelta por...*, II
driver *el conductor, la conductora*, II
driver's license *la licencia de conducir*, II
to drizzle *lloviznar*, II
drug addiction *la drogadicción*, 10
dry *árido(a)*, II; *seco(a)*, II; What a dry climate! *¡Qué clima tan seco!*, II; The . . . is dry/isn't very sweet. *El/La... está seco(a)/no está muy dulce.*, 4
to dry *secarse*, I
dryer *la secadora*, II
dumb *tonto(a)*, I
during *durante*, I
to dust *sacudir*, II; to dust the furniture *sacudir los muebles*, II
DVD *el DVD*, I; blank DVD *el DVD en blanco*, I

## E

each *cada:* each, each one *cada uno(a)*, II
eagle *el águila (f.)*, II
ear (inner) *el oído*, I; ear (outer) *la oreja*, II
early *temprano(a)*, I
earphones *los audífonos*, I
earrings *los aretes*, I
earthquake *el terremoto*, II
easily *fácilmente*, II
easy *fácil*, I; That's easy for me. *Eso me resulta fácil*, 8
to eat *comer*, I; *tomar*, I; don't eat *no coma*, II; *no comas*, II; eat *coma, come*, II; Have you eaten at . . .? *¿Ha comido en...?*, II; to eat a balanced diet *seguir (i, i) una dieta sana*, I; *llevar una dieta balanceada*, II; to eat breakfast

*desayunar*, I; **to eat dinner** *cenar*, I; **to eat lunch** *almorzar (ue)*, I
**economic crisis** *la crisis económica*, 6
**ecotourism** *el ecoturismo*, II; **to go on an ecotour** *hacer ecoturismo*, II
**editorial section** *los editoriales*, 6
**educational** *educativo(a)*, 6
**effort: to make an effort to** *esforzarse (ue) por*, 7; **We had to make a big effort to . . .** *Tuvimos que hacer un gran esfuerzo para...*, 7; **We made a big effort at . . .** *Nos esforzamos en...*, 7
**egg** *el huevo*, I; **scrambled eggs** *los huevos revueltos*, II
**eight** *ocho*, I
**eight hundred** *ochocientos*, I
**eighteen** *dieciocho*, I
**eighth** *octavo(a)*, II
**eighty** *ochenta*, I
**elbow** *el codo*, II
**elections** *las elecciones*, 10
**electric/hybrid car** *el carro eléctrico/híbrido*, 10
**electronic planner** *la agenda electrónica*, 8
**elegant** *elegante*, II
**eleven** *once*, I
**e-mail address** *el correo electrónico*, I
**embassy** *la embajada*, II
**embroidered** *bordado(a)*, II; **to be embroidered** *estar bordado(a)*, II
**emergency room** *la sala de emergencias*, II
**empire** *el imperio*, 9
**employee** *el (la) empleado(a)*, 8
**enchanted** *encantado(a)*, 9
**to enclose: I'm enclosing a . . .** *Le/Les adjunto un(a)...*, 8
**enemy** *el (la) enemigo(a)*, 9
**energy: solar energy** *la energía solar*, 10
**engaged: to get engaged** *comprometerse*, 4
**engagement** *el compromiso*, 4; **engagement ring** *el anillo de compromiso*, 4; **I'm sorry, but I already have other plans/another engagement.** *Lo siento, pero ya tengo otros planes/otro compromiso.*, 5
**engineer** *el ingeniero, la ingeniera*, II
**English** *el inglés*, I
**to enjoy** *disfrutar de*, II
**enough** *suficiente*, I; **to get enough sleep** *dormir (ue, u) lo suficiente*, I
**entertaining** *entretenido(a)*, 5
**entertainment section** *la sección de ocio*, 6
**environment** *el medio ambiente*, 10; **work environment** *el ambiente de trabajo*, 8
**environmental crisis** *la crisis ambiental*, 6
**equality: The way I see it, there's no equality between . . .** *A mi parecer, no hay igualdad entre...*, 3
**errands** *las diligencias*, II; **to run errands** *hacer diligencias*, II
**eruption (of a volcano)** *la erupción (de un volcán)*, 10
**established: to get established** *establecerse*, 7
**ethnic group** *el grupo étnico*, 7
**evening** *la tarde*, I; **in the evening, P.M.** *de la tarde*, I
**event** *el hecho*, 9; *el acontecimiento*, 10
**every day** *todos los días*, I
**every morning** *todas las mañanas*, II
**every year** *todos los años*, II
**everybody** *todos(as)*, I
**everything** *todo*, I
**evident: It's evident that . . .** *Es evidente que...*, 6
**to exchange** *intercambiar*, II; **to exchange (for)** *cambiar (por)*, II
**excited: Yes, I'm excited because . . .** *Sí, estoy entusiasmado(a) porque...*, 2
**exciting** *emocionante*, 10
**Excuse me.** *Perdón., Disculpe.*, II; **Excuse me, is there a . . . around here?** *Disculpe, ¿hay un(a)... por aquí?*, II
**to exercise** *hacer ejercicios*, I
**exhibit** *la exposición*, 5
**to expect** *esperar*, I
**expensive** *caro(a)*, I
**explode** *estallar*, 10
**to explore** *explorar*, II; **to explore caves** *explorar cuevas*, II; **to explore the tropical jungle** *explorar la selva tropical*, II
**explorers** *los exploradores*, 9
**to express (yourself)** *expresarse*, 7
**eyebrows** *las cejas*, II
**eyes** *los ojos*, I; **to have blue eyes** *tener ojos azules*, I; **to have brown eyes** *tener ojos de color café*, II

## F

**face** *la cara*, I
**to face: My . . . faced obstacles when . . .** *Mis... enfrentaron obstáculos cuando...*, 7
**to facilitate** *facilitar*, 8
**facing** *enfrente de*, II
**fact** *el hecho*, 9
**factory** *la fábrica*, II
**to fail (a test, a class)** *suspender*, 3
**failure** *el fracaso*, II
**fair** *justo(a)*, II; **It's not fair!** *¡No es justo!*, II; **I don't think it's fair.** *No me parece que sea justo.*, 3
**fairy tale** *el cuento de hadas*, 9
**faithful: to be (un)faithful** *ser (in)fiel*, 3
**to fall** *caer(se) (-igo)*, II; **to fall asleep** *dormirse (ue)*, II; **to fall in love** *enamorarse*, 9
**fall** *el otoño*, I
**family** *la familia*, I; **There are . . . people in my family.** *En mi familia somos...*, I
**family reunion** *la reunión familiar*, 4
**fan** *fanático(a)*, 2
**fancy dresses** *los vestidos de gala*, II
**fantastic: How fantastic!** *¡Qué fantástico(a)!*, I
**fashion section** *la sección de moda*, 6
**fast food** *la comida rápida*, II
**fat** *gordo(a)*, I; *la grasa*, I
**father** *el padre*, I; **Father's Day** *el Día del Padre*, I
**father-in-law** *el suegro*, 4
**favorite** *preferido(a)*, I
**February** *febrero*, I
**to feed the dog** *darle de comer al perro*, II
**to feel** *sentirse (ie, i)*, I; **to feel like doing something** *tener ganas de + infinitive*, I; **How did you feel when . . .?** *¿Cómo te sentiste cuando...?*, II; **How did you feel when you heard about . . .?** *¿Cómo te sentiste cuando supiste lo de...?*, II
**feelings** *los sentimientos*, 2
**to feel like** *querer (ie) + infinitive*, II; **Yes, I'm disappointed because . . . It makes me feel like crying.** *Sí, estoy decepcionado(a) porque... Me dan ganas de llorar.*, 2
**female soldier** *la mujer soldado*, 9
**to fence** *esgrimir*, 2
**fencing** *la esgrima*, 2
**few** *poco(a), pocos(as)*, I
**fifteen** *quince*, I
**fifth** *quinto(a)*, II
**fifty** *cincuenta*, I
**to fight** *pelearse*, 3; **to fight for** *luchar por*, 7
**film** *la película*, I
**finally** *por fin*, I; **Finally . . . managed to . . .** *Por fin... logró...*, 7
**financial section** *la sección financiera*, 6
**to find** *encontrar (ue)*, I; **Did you find what you were looking for at . . .?** *¿Encontraste lo que buscabas en...?*, II; **to find a hobby** *buscar un pasatiempo*, I; **I've already found my . . .** *Ya encontré mi(s)...*, II; **I find it to be very . . .** *Lo/La encuentro muy...*, 5
**to find out** *enterarse*, II; *averiguar*, II; **When I found out, I couldn't believe it.** *Cuando me enteré, no lo pude creer.*, II; **How did you find out about . . .?** *¿Cómo te enteraste de...?*, 6; **How did you find out the score?** *¿Cómo supiste el resultado?*, 6
**fine** *bien*, I
**finger** *el dedo*, I
**finger food** *los bocadillos*, II
**finish** *terminar*, I
**fire** *incendio*, II; **to put out fires** *apagar incendios*, II; **fire station** *la estación de bomberos*, II; **fire truck** *el camión de bomberos*, II; **firefighter** *el bombero, la bombera*, II; **fireworks** *los fuegos artificiales*, I
**first** *el primero*, I; *primero(a)*, I
**fish** *el pescado*, I; **fish (live)** *el pez*, II
**to fish** *pescar*, I
**fish market** *la pescadería*, II
**fishing** *la pesca*, I; **to go fishing** *ir de pesca*, I
**fishing rod** *la caña de pescar*, II
**to fit** *quedar*, I; **How do the . . . fit?** *¿Cómo te quedan...?*, II
**to fit in** *encajar (en)*, 7
**fitting room** *el probador*, II
**five** *cinco*, I
**five hundred** *quinientos*, I
**to fix** *arreglar*, II
**flag** *la bandera*, 9
**flan** *el flan*, I
**flashlight** *la linterna*, II
**flavor** *el sabor*, II; **It's missing flavor.** *Le falta sabor.*, II; **The . . . lacks flavor, but I don't know what's missing.** *Al (A la)... le falta sabor, pero no sé qué le falta.*, 4
**to flee** *huir*, II
**flight** *el vuelo*, I
**floor** *el piso*, I
**flower shop** *la floristería*, II
**to focus on** *enfocarse en*, 7
**fog** *la niebla*, II
**folder** *la carpeta*, I
**folk: I recommend that you go to the folk dance performance. It's very . . .** *Te aconsejo que vayas a la presentación de baile folclórico. Es muy...*, 5
**to follow** *seguir (i, i)*, I
**food** *la comida*, I; **Chinese (Italian,**

**Mexican) food** *la comida china (italiana, mexicana)*, I; **food court in a mall** *la plaza de comida*, I; **food products** *los comestibles*, II; **fast food** *la comida rápida*, II; **finger food** *los bocadillos*, II
**foot** *el pie*, I
**football** *el fútbol americano*, I
**for** *para*, I
**forest** *el bosque*, II
**to forget (about), to forget (to)** *olvidarse (de)*, II; **Don't forget to . . .** *No te olvides de...*, II; **I totally forgot.** *Se me olvidó por completo.*, II; **It's just that I forgot to add . . . .** *Es que se me olvidó ponerle...*, 4
**to forgive** *disculpar, perdonar*, 3; **Forgive me. I don't know what I was thinking.** *Perdóname. No sé en qué estaba pensando.*, 3
**forgiveness: to ask for forgiveness** *pedir perdón*, 3
**fork** *el tenedor*, I
**formidable** *formidable*, I
**fortune** *la fortuna*, I
**forty** *cuarenta*, I
**forward: to move forward** *seguir adelante*, 7
**fountain** *la fuente*, II
**four** *cuatro*, I
**four hundred** *cuatrocientos*, I
**fourteen** *catorce*, I
**fourth** *cuarto(a)*, II
**frankly** *francamente*, II
**frantically** *desesperadamente*, II
**free of charge** *gratis*, II
**free time** *el rato libre*, II
**freeway** *la autopista*, II
**French** *el francés*, I
**French fries** *las papas fritas*, I
**frequency** *la frecuencia*, I
**frequently** *frecuentemente*, II
**Friday** *el viernes*, I; **on Fridays** *los viernes*, I
**fried** *frito(a)*, II; **fried chicken** *el pollo frito*, 4
**friend** *el amigo, la amiga*, I; **to go out with his/her/their friends** *salir con sus amigos*, II; **to make friends with someone** *hacerse amigo(a) de alguien*, II; **A good friend should support me and . . . He/she shouldn't . . .** *Un(a) buen(a) amigo(a) debe apoyarme y... No debe...*, 2; **What should a good friend be like?** *¿Cómo debe ser un(a) buen(a) amigo(a)?*, 2
**friendly** *amigable*, 2
**friendship** *la amistad*, 2
**frightening** *espantoso(a)*, 10
**from** *de*, I
**From then on, they lived happily ever after.** *A partir de entonces, vivieron siempre felices.*, 9
**From what I understand . . .** *Según tengo entendido,...*, 4
**From what we've been told, the villain...** *Según nos dicen, el malvado...*, 9
**from where** *de dónde*, I
**front page** *la primera plana*, 6; **It was on the front page.** *Estaba en la primera plana.*, 6
**frozen** *congelado(a)*, II
**fruit** *la fruta*, I; **assorted fresh fruit** *el surtido de frutas frescas*, II
**fruit shop** *la frutería*, II
**to frustrate** *frustrar*, 2
**to fry** *freír (i, i)*, II; **fried** *frito (past participle of* **freír***)*, II
**fuels** *los combustibles*, 10
**to fulfill (a dream)** *realizar (un sueño)*, 7
**full-time job** *el empleo a tiempo completo*, 8
**fun** *divertido(a)*, I; **to have fun** *divertirse (ie, i)*, II
**funeral** *el funeral*, 4
**funny** *chistoso(a)*, II; *cómico(a)*, I
**furiously** *furiosamente*, II
**furniture** *los muebles*, II; **to dust the furniture** *sacudir los muebles*, II
**furniture store** *la mueblería*, II
**future** *el futuro*, 10

## G

**to gain weight** *subir de peso*, I
**gallery** *la galería*, 5
**game show** *el concurso*, 6
**garage** *el garaje*, I
**garbage** *la basura*, II
**garbage can** *el basurero*, 10
**garden** *el jardín*, I; **to work in the garden** *trabajar en el jardín*, II
**garlic** *el ajo*, II; **garlic soup** *la sopa de ajo*, II
**generally** *generalmente*, II
**generous** *bondadoso(a)*, II; *generoso(a)*, 2
**geography** *la geografía*, 3
**geometry** *la geometría*, 3
**German** *el alemán*, I
**to get** *conseguir (i, i)*, I; *agarrar*, II; **to get a haircut** *cortarse el pelo*, II; **to get a sunburn** *quemarse*, II; **to get along badly** *llevarse mal*, II; **to get along well** *llevarse bien*, II; **to get angry** *enojarse*, I; **to get bored** *aburrirse*, II; **to get burned** *quemarse*, II; **to get dressed** *vestirse (i, i)*, I; **to get lost** *perderse (ie)*, II; **to get off of . . .** *bajarse de...*, II; **to get on . . .** *subirse a...*, II; **to get ready** *arreglarse*, II; **to get sick** *enfermarse*, II; **to get someone for a telephone call** *pasártelo(la)*, I; **to get there** *llegar*, I; **How can I get to . . .** *¿Cómo puedo llegar a...?*, II; **to go up/down . . . until you get to** *subir/bajar... hasta llegar a*, II; **to get tired** *cansarse*, II; **to get together at an Internet café** *reunirse en un café Internet*, II; **to get up** *levantarse*, I; **to get engaged** *comprometerse*, 4; **to get accustomed to** *acostumbrarse*, 7; **to get established** *establecerse*, 7; **Aha! I finally get the idea.** *¡Vaya! Por fin capto la idea.*, 8; **I get it! It's clearer now.** *¡Ya caigo! Está más claro ahora.*, 8; **Get this: he/she got married.** *Fíjate que se ha casado.*, 4
**ghost** *el fantasma*, 9
**gift** *el regalo*, I; **to buy (someone) a gift** *comprarle un regalo*, 3
**gift card** *la tarjeta regalo*, I
**girl** *la muchacha*, I; *la niña*, II
**girl's fifteenth birthday** *la quinceañera*, I
**girlfriend: What do you look for in a boyfriend/girlfriend?** *¿Qué buscas en un(a) novio(a)?*, 2
**to give** *dar*, I; *regalar*, II; **don't give** *no des*, I; *no dé, no den*, II; **give** *da, dé, den*, II; **I'm going to give you a special price.** *Le voy a dar un precio especial.*, II; **I wasn't going to buy . . ., but they gave me a discount.** *No iba a comprar..., pero me dieron un descuento.*, II; **Okay, I'll give it to you for . . ., but that's my last offer.** *Bueno, se la regalo por..., pero es mi última oferta.*, II; **to give advice** *dar consejos*, II; **to give (someone) a hug** *darle un abrazo*, 3; **to give birth** *dar a luz*, 4; **to (not) give up** *(no) darse por vencido*, 7; **Give yourself time to think it over.** *Date tiempo para pensarlo.*, 3
**glass** *el vaso*, I; *el vidrio*, II
**glasses** *los lentes*, I; **to wear glasses** *usar lentes*, I
**gloves** *los guantes*, II
**to go** *ir*, I; **Are we going the right way to . . .?** *¿Vamos bien para...?*, II; **don't go** *no vayas*, I; *no vaya, no vayan*, II; **go** *ve*, I; *vaya, vayan*, II; *siga, sigue*, II; **gone** *ido (past participle of ir)*, II; **He/She doesn't go anywhere.** *No va a ninguna parte*, I; **If you haven't gone to . . . yet, you must.** *Si todavía no ha ido a/al..., debe ir.*, II; **I prefer to go to . . .** *Prefiero ir a/al...*, II; **I'll go to . . .** *Iré a/al...*, II; **I want to go to . . .** *Quiero ir a...*, II; **Tomorrow I'm going to . . .** *Mañana voy a...*, II; **Tonight we're going to celebrate . . .** *Esta noche vamos a celebrar...*, II; **Where do you intend to go tonight?** *¿Adónde piensan ir esta noche?*, II; **Where will you go this summer?** *¿Adónde irás este verano?*, II; **to go bad: The milk has gone bad.** *Está pasada la leche.*, 4; **to go boating** *pasear en bote*, II; **to go camping** *hacer camping*, II; **to go down . . . until you get to** *bajar... hasta llegar a*, II; **to go for a walk** *pasear*, I; *dar una caminata*, II; **to go hang gliding** *volar (ue) con ala delta*, II; **to go hiking** *ir de excursión*, I; *hacer senderismo*, II; **to go on a cruise** *tomar un crucero*, II; **to go on a hike** *dar una caminata*, II; **to go on an ecotour** *hacer ecoturismo*, II; **to go on vacation** *ir de vacaciones*, II; **to go shopping at the market** *ir de compras al mercado*, II; **to go skydiving** *saltar en paracaídas*, II; **to go spelunking** *explorar cuevas*, II; **to go straight** *seguir (i,i) adelante/derecho*, II; **to go to a cybercafé** *ir a un cibercafé*, II; **to go to bed** *acostarse (ue)*, I; **to go to outdoor cafés** *ir a cafés*, II; **to go to the zoo** *ir al zoológico*, II; **to go up** *subirse*, II; **to go up . . . until you get to** *subir... hasta llegar a*, II; **to go with** *hacer juego*, II; **I was going to . . .** *Iba a...*, 2; **Let's not go . . .** *No vayamos...*, 2; **I'm going to . . . with the intention of . . .** *Voy a... con la idea de...*, 7; **Why don't we go to . . .?** *¿Por qué no vamos a...?*, 5
**to go back** *regresar, volver (ue)*, I; **gone back** *vuelto (past participle of* **volver***)*, II
**go out** *sal*, I
**to go out** *salir (-go)*, I; **to go out with his/her/their friends** *salir con sus amigos*, II; **to go out in a sailboat (motorboat)** *pasear en bote de vela (lancha)*, I
**goal** *la meta*, 7
**god** *el dios*, 9
**goddess** *la diosa*, 9
**gold** *el oro*, II

golf *el golf*, II
gone *ido (past participle of* **ir**), II
good *bien*, II; **Honestly, it doesn't look good on you.** *De verdad, no te sienta bien*, II
good *bueno(a)*, I; **It's a good idea that . . .** *Es buena idea que...*, II; **to get good grades** *sacar buenas notas*, II; **You're really good at . . . aren't you?** *Eres muy bueno(a) para... ¿verdad?*, 2; **in good/bad taste** *de buen/mal gusto*, 5; **I see you're in a good mood.** *Te veo de buen humor.*, 2; **It would be a good/bad idea to break up with . . .** *Sería una buena/mala idea romper con...*, 3; **It's good enough to lick your fingers.** *Está para chuparse los dedos.*, 4; **It's not good for you . . .** *No te conviene...*, 3; **What should a good friend be like?** *¿Cómo debe ser un(a) buen(a) amigo(a)?*, 2
**Goodbye.** *Adiós.*, I
**good-looking** *guapo(a)*, I
**to gossip** *chismear*, 2
**gossip: What a gossip!** *¡Qué chismoso(a)!*, II
**gossipy** *chismoso(a)*, 2
**gowns** *los vestidos de gala*, II
**grade** *la nota*, II; **to get good grades** *sacar buenas notas*, II; **to get bad grades** *sacar malas notas*, II
**to graduate (from)** *graduarse (de)*, 4
**graduation** *la graduación*, I
**grandchildren** *los nietos*, I
**granddaughter** *la nieta*, I
**grandfather** *el abuelo*, I
**grandmother** *la abuela*, I
**grandparents** *los abuelos*, I
**grandson** *el nieto*, I
**grandsons** *los nietos*, I
**grapefruit** *la toronja*, 4
**grass** *el césped*, I
**gray** *gris*, I
**gray-haired** *canoso(a)*, I
**great** *estupendo(a)*, I; *a todo dar*, I; *buenísimo(a)*, II; *fenomenal*, II; *genial*, 2; *formidable*, 5; **It's better for you to see the opera. It's great.** *Es mejor que veas la ópera. Es formidable.*, 5
**green** *verde*, I
**green belt** *la zona verde*, II
**greeting card** *la tarjeta*, I
**grilled** *a la parrilla*, II; **grilled steak** *el bistec a la parrilla*, II
**groceries** *los comestibles*, II
**grocery store** *la tienda de comestibles*, II
**to grow** *crecer (zc)*, 10
**to grow up (in)** *criarse (en)*, 7
**group: ethnic group** *el grupo étnico*, 7
**Guatemalan** *guatemalteco(a)*, II
**guest** *el (la) invitado(a)*, I
**guidance counselor** *el (la) consejero(a)*, 3; **The guidance counselor insists that I take . . . I don't like it at all!** *El/La consejero(a) insiste en que tome... ¡No me gusta para nada!*, 3
**guide book** *la guía turística*, II
**guided tour** *el tour*, II; **to take a guided tour** *hacer un tour*, II
**guitar** *la guitarra*, I
**gym** *el gimnasio*, I
**gymnastics** *la gimnasia*, II

# H

**hail** *el granizo*, II
**hair** *el pelo*, I; **to comb your hair** *peinarse*, I; **to have . . . hair** *tener el pelo...*, II
**hair dryer** *la secadora de pelo*, I
**hair salon** *la peluquería*, II
**hairstylist** *el peluquero, la peluquera*, II
**half** *medio*, I; **half past** *y media*, I
**half brother** *el medio hermano*, 4
**half sister** *la medio hermana*, 4
**ham** *el jamón*, I
**hamburger** *la hamburguesa*, I
**hammock** *la hamaca*, II
**hand** *la mano*, I
**handmade** *hecho(a) a mano*, II
**to hang** *colgar (ue)*, I
**Hanukkah** *el Hanukah*, I
**happy** *contento(a)*, I; **to be happy** *estar contento(a)*, I
**Happy (Merry) . . .** *¡Feliz...!*, I
**hard** *difícil*, I; **I work hard . . . and for that reason . . .** *Trabajo duro... y por eso...*, 7; **It's not hard for me at all.** *No me es nada difícil.*, 8
**hardware store** *la ferretería*, II
**hard-working** *trabajador(a)*, I
**hat** *el sombrero*, I
**to hate** *odiar*, II
**have** *haber (auxiliary verb)*, II; **Have you eaten at . . .?** *¿Ha comido en...?*, II; *haya (present subjunctive of haber)*, II; **If you haven't gone to . . . yet, you must.** *Si todavía no ha ido a/al..., debe ir.*, II; **Have you thought about . . .?** *¿Has pensado en...?*, 3
**to have** *tener (-go, ie)*, I; **have** *ten*, I; **don't have** *no tengas*, I; **Do you have plans for . . .?** *¿Tienes planes para el...?*, II; **I always have to . . .** *A mí siempre me toca...*, I; **We have a wide assortment of gifts.** *Tenemos un gran surtido de regalos.*, II; **What news do you have of . . .?** *¿Qué noticias tienes de...?*, II; **to have . . . hair** *tener el pelo...*, II; **to have a cold** *tener catarro*, I; *estar resfriado(a)*, II; **to have a conversation** *conversar*, II; **to have a cough** *tener tos*, II; **to have a cramp** *tener un calambre*, II; **to have a milkshake** *tomar un batido*, I; **to have a party** *hacer una fiesta*, I; **to have a picnic** *tener un picnic*, I; **to have a snack** *merendar*, I; **to have brown eyes** *tener ojos de color café*, II; **to have fun** *divertirse (ie, i)*, II; **to have lunch** *almorzar*, I; **to have to (do something)** *tener que + infinitive*, I; *Deber + infinitive*, II; **So, what I have to do is . . .** *Entonces, lo que tengo que hacer es...*, II; **We have to put the dessert/the drinks in the refrigerator.** *Tenemos que poner el postre/los refrescos en el refrigerador.*, II; **We all have to help her.** *Todos tenemos que ayudarla.*, II; **to have a misunderstanding** *tener un malentendido*, 2; **to have much/something/nothing in common** *tener mucho/algo/nada en común*, 2; **I don't have the slightest idea if . . .** *No tengo la menor idea si...*, 6; **to have success** *tener éxito*, 7; **I had many hopes of . . .** *Tenía muchas esperanzas de...*, 9
**he** *él*, I; **He is . . .**, *Él es...*, I; **He (emphatic) likes . . .** *A él le gusta(n) + noun*, II
**He/She regrets that . . .** *Se arrepiente de que...*, 9
**He/She/You** *(emphatic)* **like(s) . . .** *A él/ella/usted le gusta(n) + noun*, II
**He/She/You like(s) to watch television.** *Le gusta ver la televisión.*, II
**He/She/You love(s) . . .** *Le encanta(n)...*, II
**head** *la cabeza*, I
**headache** *un dolor de cabeza*, II
**headlines** *los titulares*, 6
**health** *la salud*, I
**to hear** *oír(-go)*, II; **When I heard the news, I didn't want to believe it.** *Cuando oí la noticia no lo quise creer.*, II; **By the way, what have you heard about the . . .?** *A propósito, ¿qué has oído de el/la...?*, 5
**heart** *el corazón*, II
**heat** *el calor*, I
**to heat** *calentar (ie)*, I
**Hello.** *Aló., Bueno., Diga.*, I
**help** *la ayuda*, I; **to yell for help** *gritar por ayuda*, II
**to help** *ayudar*, I; **Can I help you?** *¿Puedo ayudarte?*, II; **We all have to help her.** *Todos tenemos que ayudarla.*, II; **to help at home** *ayudar en casa*, I; **to help each other** *ayudarse*, II; **to help people** *ayudar a la gente*, II
**helpful** *atento(a)*, 2
**here** *aquí*, II; **around here** *por aquí*, II; **Come (right) here!** *¡Ven aquí!*, II
**heritage** *la herencia*, 7
**hero** *el héroe*, 9
**heroine** *la heroína*, 9
**Hey** *Oye*, II
**Hi** *Hola*, I
**high jump** *el salto de altura*, 2
**highway** *la autopista*, II
**to hike** *dar una caminata*, II
**hiking** *el senderismo*, II; **to go hiking** *hacer senderismo*, II
**his** *su(s)*, I
**history** *la historia*, I
**hit** *el golpe*, II; **Oh! I hit my . . .** *¡Uf! Me di un golpe en...*, II
**hobby** *el pasatiempo*, I; **to look for a hobby** *buscar un pasatiempo*, I
**to hold** *agarrar*, II; **Hold on a moment.** *Espera un momento.*, I
**holiday** *el día festivo*, I
**Holy Week** *la Semana Santa*, I
**home: I was at home when . . .** *Estaba en casa cuando...*, 10
**homework** *la tarea*, I
**Honduran** *hondureño(a)*, II
**honest** *honesto(a)*, 2
**Honestly, it doesn't look good on you.** *De verdad, no te sienta bien.*, II
**to honor** *honrar*, 9
**hope: I had many hopes of . . .** *Tenía muchas esperanzas de...*, 9
**to hope (that) . . .** *esperar que + subj.*, II; **I hope the trip is fun.** *Espero que el viaje sea divertido.*, II; **I hope to see . . .** *Espero ver...*, I; **I hope you're doing well.** *Espero que estés bien.*, II; **I hope that . . .** *Ojalá que...*, II
**Hope things go well for you.** *Que te vaya bien.*, I

**Hopefully . . .** *Es de esperar que...,* 9
**Hopefully the war won't be . . .** *Ojalá que la guerra no sea...,* 9
**I hope that the countries still at war . . .** *Ojalá que los países aún en guerra...,* 9
**horrible** *horrible,* I
**horror** *el terror,* I
**horse** *el caballo,* II; **to ride a horse** *montar a caballo,* II
**hospital** *el hospital,* II
**hostel** *el albergue,* II; **youth hostel** *el albergue juvenil,* II
**hot** *caliente,* I; **hot sauce** *la salsa picante,* I; **hot chocolate** *el chocolate,* I; **hot springs** *las aguas termales,* II
**hotel** *el hotel,* I; **to stay in a hotel** *quedarse en un hotel,* I
**hour** *la hora,* I
**house** *la casa,* I; **to play house** *jugar a la casita,* II
**household chores** *los quehaceres,* I
**how?** *¿cómo?,* I; **How can I get to . . .?** *¿Cómo puedo llegar a...?,* II; **How did the . . . competition turn out?** *¿Cómo salió la competencia de...?,* II; **How did you do in . . .?** *¿Cómo te fue en...?,* II; **How did you feel when . . .?** *¿Cómo te sentiste cuando...?,* II; **How did you feel when you heard about . . .?** *¿Cómo te sentiste cuando supiste lo de...?,* II; **How did you react when . . .?** *¿Cómo reaccionaste cuando...?,* II; **How do I look in . . .?,** *¿Cómo me veo con...?,* II; **How do the . . . fit?** *¿Cómo te quedan...?,* II; **How do you make . . .?** *¿Cómo se prepara...?,* II; **How do you spell . . .** *¿Cómo se escribe...?,* I; **How does it fit?** *¿Cómo me queda?,* I; **How is . . . prepared?** *¿Cómo se prepara...?,* II; **How is the . . .?;** *¿Qué tal está...?,* II; **How long have you been . . .?** *¿Cuánto tiempo hace que tú...?,* II; **How many . . .?** *¿cuántos(as)?,* I; **how much?** *¿cuánto(a)?,* I; **How much is (are) . . .?** *¿Cuánto vale(n)...?,* II; **How often do you go . . .?** *¿Con qué frecuencia vas...?,* I; **How old are you?** *¿Cuántos años tienes?,* I; **How did you find out about . . .?** *¿Cómo te enteraste de...?,* 6; **How did you find out the score?** *¿Cómo supiste el resultado?,* 6
**How . . .! How boring!** *¡Qué pesado!,* II; **How delicious!** *¡Qué rico(a)!,* II; **How fantastic!** *¡Qué fantástico!,* I; **How great!** *¡Qué bien!,* I;
**hug** *el abrazo,* II; **A big hug from . . .** *Un abrazo de...,* II; **to give (someone) a hug** *darle un abrazo,* 3
**to hug each other** *abrazarse,* II
**humid** *húmedo(a),* II
**hunger** *el hambre,* I, 10
**hungry, to be** *tener hambre,* I
**hurricane** *el huracán,* II
**to hurry** *darse prisa,* II
**hurt** *herido(a),* II
**to hurt** *doler (ue),* I; *herir (ie, i),* II; **My . . . hurt(s)** *Me duele(n)...,* I; **Is something hurting you?** *¿Te duele algo?,* I; **I didn't mean to hurt/offend you.** *No quise hacerte daño/ofenderte.,* 3
**to hurt oneself** *lastimarse,* II
**husband** *el esposo,* II

# I

**I** *yo,* I; **I (emphatic) (don't) like . . .** *A mí (no) me gusta(n) + noun,* II; **I did very well (badly).** *Me fue muy bien (mal).,* II; **I didn't do anything.** *No hice nada.,* II; **I don't recommend it to you.** *No te lo/la (los/las) recomiendo.,* II; **I felt like . . .** *Me dieron ganas de + infinitive,* II; **I felt/became . . .** *Me puse + adj.,* II; **I have no idea.** *Ni idea.,* I; **I hope that** *ojalá que,* II; **I hope you're doing well.** *Espero que estés bien.,* II; **I just need to . . .** *Sólo me falta...,* II; **I laughed a lot.** *Me reí mucho.,* II; **I miss you a lot.** *Te echo mucho de menos.,* II; **I really liked him/her.** *Me caía muy bien.,* II; **I recommend that you . . .** *Le aconsejo que...,* II; **I saw that . . . was (were) on sale, so I bought . . .,** *Vi que... estaba(n) en oferta, así que compré...,* II; **I started to . . .** *Me puse a + infinitive,* II; **I totally forgot.** *Se me olvidó por completo.,* II; **I used to . . .** *Solía...,* II; **I wonder what the weather is like at (in) . . .?** *¿Cómo será el clima en...?,* II; **I would like . . .** *Quisiera...,* I; **I can't stand . . .** *No aguanto...,* 2; **I didn't study, so . . .** *No estudié, así que...,* 7; **I intend to . . .** *Tengo la intención de...,* 7; **I work hard . . . and for that reason . . .** *Trabajo duro... y por eso...,* 7; **I am capable of (doing) . . .** *Soy capaz de (hacer)...,* 8; **I bet that the rate of . . . won't go down.** *A que no va a bajar la tasa de...,* 10; **I bet you that . . .** *Te apuesto que...,* 10; **I can do it.** *Lo puedo hacer.,* 8; **I can't seem to understand . . .** *No logro entender...,* 8; **I can't understand it.** *No me cabe en la cabeza.,* 8; **I had many hopes of . . .** *Tenía muchas esperanzas de...,* 9; **I have always wanted to be a . . .** *Siempre he querido ser un(a)...,* 8; **I predict that they are going to implement . . .** *Calculo que van a implementar...,* 10; **I remember it like it was yesterday.** *Lo recuerdo como si fuera ayer.,* 10; **I think it's worth remembering . . .** *Creo que vale la pena acordarse de...,* 10; **I was at home when . . .** *Estaba en casa cuando...,* 10; **I would be interested in studying to be a . . .** *Me interesaría estudiar para ser un(a),* 8; **I would like to be a . . .** *Me gustaría ser un(a)...,* 8; **I can't believe it!** *¡No me lo puedo creer!,* 4; **I didn't do it on purpose.** *No lo hice a propósito.,* 3; **I didn't mean to hurt/offend you.** *No quise hacerte daño/ofenderte.,* 3; **I don't have the slightest idea if . . .** *No tengo la menor idea si...,* 6; **I don't think it's fair.** *No me parece que sea justo.,* 3; **I don't think that journalists/newscasts are . . .** *No creo que los periodistas/los noticieros sean...,* 6; **I doubt that you're well-informed about . . ./that you know . . .** *Dudo que estés bien informado(a) sobre.../que sepas...,* 6; **I find it to be very . . .** *Lo/La encuentro muy...,* 5; **I got carried away with . . .** *Se me fue la mano con...,* 4; **I read it in the sports section.** *Lo leí en la sección deportiva.,* 6; **I recommend that you go to the folk dance performance. It's very . . .** *Te aconsejo que vayas a la presentación de baile folclórico. Es muy...,* 5; **I see you're in a good mood.** *Te veo de buen humor.,* 2; **I suggest that you not pay attention to rumors.** *Sugiero que no hagas caso a los rumores.,* 3; **I swear I'll never do it again.** *Te juro que no lo volveré a hacer.,* 3; **I understand a little about . . ., but nothing about . . .** *Entiendo algo de..., pero nada de...,* 6
**I'd like you to meet . . . I'd like you (pl.) to meet . . .** *Les presento a...,* II
**I'll: I'll bring it (them) right away.** *Enseguida se lo/la (los/las) traigo.,* II; **I'll let you have them for . . .** *Se los dejo en...,* II
**I'm: I'm coming!** *¡Ya voy!,* II; **I'm fed up with . . .** *Estoy harto(a) de...,* II; **I'm going to give you a special price.** *Le voy a dar un precio especial.,* II; **I'm not sure.** *No estoy seguro(a).,* II; **I'm sorry.** *Lo siento.,* I; **I'm bilingual; therefore, I have many opportunities** *Soy bilingüe, por lo tanto, tengo muchas oportunidades...,* 7; **I'm going to . . . with the intention of . . .** *Voy a... con la idea de...,* 7; **I'm enclosing a . . .** *Le/Les adjunto un(a)...,* 8; **I'm convinced that . . .** *Estoy convencido(a) de que...,* 6; **I'm positive that . . .** *Estoy seguro(a) (de) que...,* 6; **I can't stand the attitude of . . . towards . . . I can't take it anymore!** *Me choca la actitud de... hacia... ¡No aguanto más!,* 3; **I've: I've been . . . for a little while.** *Hace poco tiempo que yo...,* II; **I've been . . . for a long time.** *Hace mucho tiempo que yo...,* II; **I'm not sure that you're right about . . .** *No estoy seguro(a) (de) que tengas razón sobre...,* 6; **I'm sorry, but I already have other plans/another engagement.** *Lo siento, pero ya tengo otros planes/otro compromiso.,* 5
**ice** *el hielo,* II
**ice cream** *el helado,* I
**ice cream shop** *la heladería,* I
**ice skating** *el patinaje sobre hielo,* II
**idea** *la idea,* II; **It's a good idea for . . . to . . .** *Es buena idea que...,* II; **I have no idea.** *Ni idea.,* I; **I don't have the slightest idea if . . .** *No tengo la menor idea si...,* 6; **Aha! I finally get the idea.** *¡Vaya! Por fin capto la idea.,* 8; **It would be a good idea to go to the symphony.** *Sería buena idea ir al concierto de la sinfónica.,* 5; **It would be a good/bad idea to break up with . . .** *Sería una buena/mala idea romper con...,* 3
**ID** *el carnet de identidad,* I
**if** *si,* II; **If you haven't gone to . . . yet, you must.** *Si todavía no ha ido a/al..., debe ir.,* II; **If I could, I would go to . . . to study . . .** *Si pudiera, iría a... para estudiar...,* 8; **If you had the chance, where would you go?** *Si tuvieras la oportunidad, ¿adónde irías?,* 8
**ignorance** *la ignorancia,* 3
**ill-mannered** *maleducado(a),* 2
**image: (positive/negative) image** *la imagen (positiva/negativa),* 3
**imaginative** *imaginativo(a),* 5

**to imagine: I imagine that by the year . . . there will be . . .** *Me imagino que para el año... habrá...,* 10
**immediately** *inmediatamente,* II, 8
**immigrants** *los inmigrantes,* 10
**impatient** *impaciente,* II
**implement: I predict that they are going to implement . . .** *Calculo que van a implementar...,* 10
**important** *importante,* II; **It's important for . . . to . . .** *Es importante que...,* II
**impression: wrong impression** *la impresión equivocada,* 3
**impressive** *impresionante,* 5
**to improve** *mejorar,* 8
**in a . . . way** *de modo...,* 6
**in between** *entre,* II
**in front of** *delante de,* I; *enfrente de,* II
**in the (latest) fashion** *a la (última) moda,* I
**in the end** *al final,* II; **In the end, we realized . . .** *Al final, nos dimos cuenta de...,* 9
**in those days** *en aquel entonces,* II
**in, by** *por,* I
**incomprehensible** *incomprensible,* 5
**to include** *incluir,* II
**incredible** *increíble,* II; **It's incredible!** *¡Es increíble!,* II
**independence** *la independencia,* 9
**Independence Day** *el Día de la Independencia,* I
**indifference** *la indiferencia,* 10
**inexpensive** *barato(a),* I
**to infect** *infectar,* II
**infected** *infectado(a),* II; **Now it's infected.** *Ahora lo tengo infectado.,* II
**to inform** *informar,* 6
**information** *la información,* II; **to ask for information** *pedir (i) información,* II
**informative** *informativo(a),* 6
**informed: to be well/poorly informed** *estar bien/mal informado,* 6; **I doubt that you're well-informed about . . . /that you know . . .** *Dudo que estés bien informado(a) sobre.../que sepas...,* 6
**ingredients** *los ingredientes,* II
**initiative: to take the initiative** *tomar la iniciativa,* 7
**to increase: It's quite possible that traffic will increase with . . .** *Es muy posible que el tráfico aumente con...,* 10
**to injure** *herir (ie, i),* II
**to injure oneself** *lastimarse,* II
**inn** *la pensión,* II
**innovative** *innovador(a),* 10
**insecure** *inseguro(a),* 2
**inside** *adentro,* II
**to insist: The guidance counselor insists that I take . . . I don't like it at all!** *El/La consejero(a) insiste en que tome... ¡No me gusta para nada!,* 3
**to insist on** *empeñarse en,* 7;
**to inspire trust in (someone)** *inspirarle confianza,* 6
**instantly** *en un santiamén,* 8
**to insult** *insultar,* 3
**insurance** *el seguro,* 8
**intellectual** *intelectual,* I
**intelligent** *inteligente,* I
**intend: I intend to . . .** *Tengo la intención de...,* 7
**intention: I'm going to . . . with the intention of . . .** *Voy a... con la idea de...,* 7
**to interest** *interesar,* II; **I would be interested in studying to be a . . .** *Me interesaría estudiar para ser un(a),* 8; **Are you interested in going to . . .?** *¿Te interesa ir a...?,* 5
**interest** *el interés,* I
**interesting** *interesante,* I
**international banker** *el (la) banquero(a) internacional,* II
**Internet** *el Internet,* II; **Internet café** *el café Internet,* II; **to get together at an Internet café** *reunirse en un café Internet,* II
**to interrupt** *interrumpir,* I
**intersection** *el cruce,* II
**interview** *la entrevista,* 8
**to interview** *entrevistar,* 6
**to introduce** *presentar,* I; **I want to introduce you to . . .** *Quiero presentarte a...,* II
**invention** *el invento,* 10
**invitation** *la invitación,* I
**to invite** *invitar,* I; **Thanks for inviting me, but I've already seen it.** *Gracias por invitarme, pero ya lo/la he visto.,* 5
**to irritate** *irritar,* 2
**is allowed** *se permite,* II
**is prohibited** *se prohibe,* II
**is spoken** *se habla,* II
**island** *la isla,* I; **tropical island** *la isla tropical,* II
**issue: We talked about the issue; consequently . . .** *Hablamos del tema; por consiguiente...,* 7
**it** *lo, la,* I; **it: It made me (very) embarrassed.** *Me dio (mucha) vergüenza.,* II; **It made me (very) happy.** *Me dio (mucha) alegría.,* II; **It made me (very) sad.** *Me dio (mucha) tristeza.,* II; **It made me angry.** *Me dio una rabia.,* II; **It's all right with me.** *Me parece bien.,* I; **It seems unfair to me** *Me parece injusto,* I; **it snows** *nieva,* I; **It started to rain.** *Empezó a llover.,* II **It tastes like . . .** *Sabe a...,* II; **It was a total . . .** *Fue todo un...,* II; **It was around two when . . .** *Eran como las dos cuando...,* II; **It took a lot of work for us to get used to . . .** *Nos costó trabajo acostumbrarnos a...,* 7; **It seems to me that . . .** *Me parece que...,* 10; **It takes a lot of work for me (to do) . . .** *Me cuesta trabajo (hacer)...,* 8; **It makes my mouth water.** *Se me hace la boca agua.,* 4; **It tastes delicious.** *Sabe delicioso(a).,* 4; **It was on the front page.** *Estaba en la primera plana.,* 6; **It would be a good idea to go to the symphony.** *Sería buena idea ir al concierto de la sinfónica.,* 5; **It would be a good/bad idea to break up with . . .** *Sería una buena/mala idea romper con...,* 3
**It's: It's a good idea for . . . to . . .** *Es buena idea que...,* II; **It's (a little) salty.** *Está (un poco) salado(a).,* I; **It's a rip-off!** *¡Es un robo!,* I; **It's all the same to me.** *Me da igual.,* I; **It's around the corner.** *Está a la vuelta.,* I; **It's awful.** *Es pésimo(a).,* I; **It's better for . . . to . . .** *Es mejor que...,* II; **It's clear that . . .** *está claro que...,* 6; **It's cold.** *Hace frío.,* I; **It's cool.** *Hace fresco.,* I; **It's delicious.** *Es delicioso(a).,* I; **It's getting late.** *Se nos hace tarde.,* II; **It's great to see you!** *¡Qué gusto verte!,* I; **It's hot.** *Hace calor.,* I; **It's important for . . . to . . .** *Es importante que...,* II; **It's incredible!** *¡Es increíble!,* II; **It's kind of fun.** *Es algo divertido.,* I; **It's missing flavor.** *Le falta sabor.,* II; **It's missing salt.** *Le falta sal.,* II; **It's missing something; I don't know what.** *Le falta no sé qué.,* II; **It's necessary to . . .** *Hay que + infinitive,* II; **It's not a big deal.** *No es gran cosa,* I; **It's not fair!** *¡No es justo!,* II; **It's okay.** *Está bien.,* I; **It's rather good.** *Es bastante bueno.,* I; **It's spelled . . .** *Se escribe...,* I; **It's spoiled.** *Está echado(a) a perder.,* II; **It's sunny.** *Hace sol.,* I; **It's windy.** *Hace viento.,* I; **It's all the same to me.** *Me da lo mismo.,* 2; **It's not hard for me at all.** *No me es nada difícil.,* 8; **It's outside/within my reach.** *Está fuera de/a mi alcance,* 8; **It's quite possible that traffic will increase with. . .** *Es muy posible que el tráfico aumente con...,* 10; **It's told that all of a sudden . . .** *Se cuenta que de pronto...,* 9; **It's too bad that . . .** *Es lamentable que...,* 9; **It's evident that . . .** *Es evidente que...,* 6; **It's good enough to lick your fingers.** *Está para chuparse los dedos.,* 4; **It's better for you to see the opera. It's great.** *Es mejor que veas la ópera. Es formidable.,* 5; **It's hard to believe that there are . . . /that they say . . .** *Parece mentira que haya.../que digan...,* 6; **It's just that I forgot to add . . . .** *Es que se me olvidó ponerle...,* 4; **It's just that I ran out of . . .** *Es que se me acabó...,* 4; **It's not good for you . . .** *No te conviene...,* 3

## J

**jacket** *la chaqueta,* I; *el saco,* I
**jai-alai** *el jai-alai,* 2
**January** *enero,* I
**jealous** *celoso(a),* 2; **to be jealous of** *tener (ie) celos de,* 2
**jeans** *los vaqueros,* I
**jewelry** *las joyas,* II
**jewelry store** *la joyería,* I
**job** *el trabajo,* I; *el oficio,* II; **full-time job** *el empleo a tiempo completo,* 8; **part-time job** *el empleo a medio tiempo,* 8
**to jog** *trotar,* II
**joke** *el chiste,* I; **to tell each other jokes** *contarse (ue) chistes,* II
**journalist** *el periodista, la periodista,* II; **I don't think that journalists/newscasts are . . .** *No creo que los periodistas/los noticieros sean...,* 6
**to judge** *juzgar,* 3
**judgmental** *criticón, criticona,* 2
**juice** *el jugo,* I
**July** *julio,* I
**to jump rope** *saltar a la cuerda,* II
**June** *junio,* I
**jungle** *la selva,* II
**just** *no más,* I; *sólo,* II; **I just need to . . .** *Sólo me falta...,* II; **to just have done something** *acabar de,* I; **just right** *en su punto,* II
**justice** *la justicia,* 9

## K

**karate** *el kárate*, 2
**Keep in mind that . . .** *Ten en cuenta que...*, 10
**to keep going** *seguir (i, i)*, II; **don't go/keep going** *no siga, no sigas*, II; **keep going** *siga, sigue*, II
**to keep going straight to** *seguir derecho hasta*, II
**to keep on doing something** *seguir + gerund*, II
**to (not) keep secrets** *(no) guardar los secretos*, 2
**key** *la llave*, II
**Kind of: It's kind of fun.** *Es algo divertido.*, I; **What kind of work does . . . do?** *¿Qué clase de trabajo realiza...?*, II
**Kind regards,** *Reciba un cordial saludo*, 8
**king** *el rey*, 9
**to kiss** *besar*, 3
**kitchen** *la cocina*, I
**kitchen sink** *el fregadero*, II
**knee** *la rodilla*, II
**knife** *el cuchillo*, I
**to knit** *tejer*, II
**to know** *saber*, I; **I don't know.** *No sé.*, I; **Did you already know that . . . ?** *¿Ya sabías que...?*, II; **Do you know where I can . . . ?** *¿Sabe usted dónde se puede...?*, II; **It needs something; I don't know what.** *Le falta no sé qué.*, II; **to be known to be** *tener fama de ser*; **I doubt that you're well-informed about . . ./that you know . . .** *Dudo que estés bien informado(a) sobre.../que sepas...*, 6; **That I know of, there is/are (isn't/aren't) . . .** *Que yo sepa, (no) hay...*, 6; **The . . . lacks flavor, but I don't know what's missing.** *Al (A la)... le falta sabor, pero no sé qué le falta.*, 4; **What do I know about . . . ? I don't understand a thing about . . .** *¿Qué sé yo de...? No entiendo ni jota de...?*, 6 **What do you know about . . . ?** *¿Qué sabes de...?*, 4
**to know (someone) or be familiar with a place** *conocer (zc)*, I; **Do you know . . . ?** *¿Conoces a...?*, II; **to get to know downtown** *conocer el centro*, II

## L

**laboratory assistant** *el (la) auxiliar de laboratorio*, 8
**lace** *el encaje*, II
**lack of** *la falta de*, 3
**to lack: The . . . lacks flavor, but I don't know what's missing.** *Al (A la)... le falta sabor, pero no sé qué le falta.*, 4
**lake** *el lago*, I
**lakeshore** *la orilla del lago*, II
**to lament** *lamentar*, 9
**lamp** *la lámpara*, II
**languages** *los idiomas*, II
**lantern** *la linterna*, II
**large** *grande*, I
**last** *pasado(a)*, I; **at last** *por fin*, II; **last night** *anoche*, I; **last offer** *la última oferta*, II
**late** *tarde*, I; **later** *más tarde*, I; **It's getting late.** *Se nos hace tarde.*, II
**latest** *último(a)*, I
**to laugh** *reírse (i, i)*, II; **I laughed a lot.** *Me reí mucho.*, II
**law (against/in favor of)** *la ley (en contra/a favor de)*, 10
**lawyer** *el abogado, la abogada*, II
**lazy** *perezoso(a)*, I
**to learn (to)** *aprender (a)*, II
**leather goods** *los artículos de cuero*, II
**to leave** *irse*, I; *dejar*, I; **don't leave** *no salgas*, I; **leave** *salir*, I; *sal*, I; **to leave a message** *dejar un recado*, I; **to leave the tip** *dejar la propina*, II
**leaves** *las hojas*, II
**left** *la izquierda*, II; **to the left (of)** *a la izquierda (de)*, II; **to turn left on** *doblar a la izquierda en*, II
**leg** *la pierna*, I
**legend** *la leyenda*, 9
**lemon** *el limón*, 4
**to lend** *prestar*, II
**letter** *la carta*, I; **The purpose of this letter is . . .** *Por medio de la presente...*, 8
**lettuce** *la lechuga*, II
**to liberate** *liberar*, 9
**liberty** *la libertad*, 9
**library** *la biblioteca*, I
**license** *la licencia*, II; **driver's license** *la licencia de conducir*, II
**to lie** *mentir (ie, i)*, 2
**lifestyle** *el estilo de vida*, 7
**lift** *levantar*, I; **to lift weights** *levantar pesas*, I
**light** *la luz*, II; **to turn off the light(s)** *apagar la luz/las luces*, II; **traffic light** *el semáforo*, II
**lightning** *el relámpago*, II
**like** *como*, II
**to like** *gustar*, I; **to like/dislike (someone)** *caerle bien/mal (a alguien)*; **I really liked him/her.** *Me caía muy bien.*, II; **And your friends, what do they like to do?** *Y a tus amigos, ¿qué les gusta hacer?*, II; **He/she/you** *(emphatic)* **like . . .** *A él/ella/usted le gusta(n) + noun*, II; **I would like . . .,** *Me gustaría...*, I; **What did you like to do when you were . . . years old?** *¿Qué te gustaba hacer cuando tenías...?*, II; **I'm a big . . . fan. What sport do you like?** *Soy un(a) gran aficionado(a) a... ¿Qué deporte te gusta a ti?*, 2; **When I'm older, I'd like to . . .** *Cuando sea mayor, me gustaría...*, 7; **I would like to be a . . .** *Me gustaría ser un(a)...*, 8; **What would you like to do?** *¿Qué te gustaría hacer?*, 8; **The guidance counselor insists that I take . . . I don't like it at all!** *El/La consejero(a) insiste en que tome... ¡No me gusta para nada!*, 3
**likes to be alone** *solitario(a)*, II
**Likewise.** *Igualmente.*, I
**lime** *la lima*, 4
**line** *la cola*, I; **to wait in line** *hacer cola*, I
**lips** *los labios*, II
**lipstick** *el lápiz labial*, II
**to listen** *escuchar*, I; **to listen to music** *escuchar música*, I
**literature** *la literatura*, 3
**little** *(adv.) poco*, I
**Little by little they adapted to . . .** *Poco a poco se adaptaron a...*, 7
**to live** *vivir*, I; **one lives** *se vive*, II; **they lived happily ever after** *vivieron felices para siempre*, II; **From then on, they lived happily ever after.** *A partir de entonces, vivieron siempre felices.*, 9
**living room** *la sala*, I
**lizard** *el lagarto*, II
**lobster** *la langosta*, 4
**local perspective** *enfoque local*, 6
**to lock the door** *cerrar la puerta con llave*, II
**long** *largo(a)*, I; **Long time no see.** *¡Tanto tiempo sin verte!*, I
**to look** *mirar*, I; **How do I look in . . . ?** *¿Cómo me veo en...?*, II; **It doesn't look good on you.** *No te sienta bien.*, II; **You look wonderful!** *¡Te ves super bien!*, II
**to look for** *buscar*, I; **Did you find what you were looking for at . . . ?** *¿Encontraste lo que buscabas en...?*, II; **don't look** *no busques*, II; **I'm looking for a gift for my . . .** *Estoy buscando un regalo para mi...*, II; **look** *busca*, II; **What do you look for in a boyfriend/girlfriend?** *¿Qué buscas en un(a) novio(a)?*, 2
**loose** *flojo(a)*, II
**to lose** *perder (ie)*, I; **to lose a game** *perder*, II
**to lose weight** *bajar de peso*, I
**to love** *encantar*, I; *fascinar*, II; **He/she/ you love(s) . . .** *Le encanta(n)...*, II; **to love (someone)** *querer a*, 2
**to love each other** *quererse (ie)*, II
**Love, . . .** *Con cariño,...*, II
**low tide** *la marea baja*, II
**to lower** *rebajar*, II; **Can you lower the price on that . . . ?** *¿Me puede rebajar el precio de ese/esa...?*, II
**loyal** *leal*, 2
**luck** *la suerte*, I
**luckily** *afortunadamente*, II
**luggage** *el equipaje*, I
**lunch** *el almuerzo*, I; *la comida*, I; **to have lunch** *almorzar(ue)*, I
**lung** *el pulmón*, II
**lyrics** *la letra*, 5

## M

**ma'am; Mrs.** *la señora, Sra.*, I
**made** *hecho (past participle of* **hacer**), II
**magazine** *la revista*, I
**magic** *mágico(a)*, 9
**mail** *el correo*, I
**mail carrier (f.)** *la mujer cartero*, II
**mail carrier (m.)** *el cartero*, II
**main dish** *el plato principal*, II
**to maintain** *mantenerse (ie)*, I, 7
**to make** *hacer (-go)*, I; **make** *haz*, I; **making** *haciendo*, II; **to make a (collect) call** *hacer una llamada (por cobrar)*, II; **to make a good/bad impression (on someone)** *caerle bien/mal a alguien*, II; **to make a reservation** *hacer una reservación*, II; **to make friends with someone** *hacerse amigo(a) de alguien*, II; **to make happy** *alegrar*, 2; **to make up** *hacer las paces*, 3; **to make a mistake** *cometer un error*, 3, 10; **to make an effort to** *esforzarse (ue) por*, 7; **to make worse** *empeorar*, 8; **to make peace** *acordar(ue) la paz*, 9
**makeup** *el maquillaje*, I
**mall** *el centro comercial*, I
**man** *el hombre*, I; **for men** *para hombres*, I

Vocabulario inglés-español

**to manage (to do something)** *lograr,* 7
**manager** *el (la) gerente,* 8
**many** *muchos(as),* I; **many years ago** *hace muchos años,* II; **not many** *pocos(as),* I; **Many years ago, . . .** *Hace muchos años,...,* 9
**map** *el mapa,* I
**March** *marzo,* I
**market** *el mercado,* II; **to go shopping at the market** *ir de compras al mercado,* II
**market stand** *el puesto del mercado,* II
**to marry** *casarse (con),* 4; **to be married** *estar casado(a),* 4; **Get this: he/she got married.** *Fíjate que se ha casado.,* 4
**martial arts** *las artes marciales,* II
**marvelous** *estupendo(a),* 2; *maravilloso,* 5
**mask** *la máscara,* II
**Mass** *la misa,* I
**to match** *hacer juego,* II
**mathematics** *las matemáticas,* I
**matter: What's the matter? Are you upset?** *¿Qué te pasa? ¿Estas dolido(a)?,* 2
**May** *mayo,* I
**maybe: Maybe there will be . . .** *A lo mejor habrá...,* 10
**mayonnaise** *la mayonesa,* II
**me** *mí,* I; *me,* I; **I** *(emphatic)* **(don't) like . . .** *A mí (no) me gusta(n)* + noun, II
**meal** *la comida,* I
**measuring cup** *la taza de medir,* II
**meat** *la carne,* I
**mechanic** *el mecánico, la mecánica,* II
**medical assistant** *el (la) auxiliar médico(a),* 8
**medical insurance** *el seguro médico,* 8
**to meet** *encontrarse (ue),* I
**meeting** *la reunión,* I
**melodic** *melodioso(a),* 5
**melody** *la melodía,* 5
**to melt** *derretir (i, i),* II
**melted** *derretido(a),* II
**memory** *el recuerdo,* II
**merchant** *el comerciante, la comerciante,* II
**Merry . . .** *¡Feliz...!,* I
**message** *el recado,* I
**Mexican** *mexicano(a),* II; **Mexican food** *la comida mexicana,* I
**midday** *el mediodía,* I
**mid-length skirt** *la falda a media pierna,* II
**midnight** *la medianoche,* I
**milk** *la leche,* I; **The milk has gone bad.** *Está pasada la leche.,* 4
**milkshake** *el batido,* I
**million** *un millón (de),* I
**mine** *mío(a), míos(as),* II; **The pleasure is mine.** *El gusto es mío.,* II
**mineral water** *el agua (f.) mineral,* II
**miniskirt** *la minifalda,* II
**mirror** *el espejo,* II
**mischievous** *travieso(a),* I
**Miss** *la señorita, Srta.,* I
**to miss** *perder(ie),* I; **The . . . lacks flavor, but I don't know what's missing.** *Al (A la)... le falta sabor, pero no sé qué le falta.,* 4
**mistake: to admit a mistake** *admitir un error,* 3; **to make a mistake** *cometer un error,* 3
**to mistreat** *maltratar,* 3
**misunderstanding: to have a misunderstanding** *tener un malentendido,* 2
**to mix** *mezclar,* I: **mixed** *mixto(a),* II;
**mixed salad** *la ensalada mixta,* II
**modern** *moderno(a),* 5
**mom** *la mamá,* I
**moment** *un momento,* I
**Monday** *el lunes,* I; **on Mondays** *los lunes,* I
**money** *el dinero,* I; *el billete,* II
**money exchange** *la oficina de cambio,* I
**monitor** *la pantalla,* I
**month** *el mes,* I
**months of the year** *los meses del año,* I
**monument** *el monumento,* II
**mood: I see you're in a good mood.** *Te veo de buen humor.,* 2
**more** *más,* I; **Not anymore.** *Ya no.,* II; **More or less.** *Más o menos.,*
**morning** *la mañana,* I; **in the morning, A.M.** *de la mañana,* I; *por la mañana,* I
**Most sincerely,** *Muy atentamente,* 8
**mother** *la madre,* I; **Mother's Day** *El Día de la Madre,* I
**mother-in-law** *la suegra,* 4
**motorboat** *la lancha,* I; **to go out in a motorboat** *pasear en lancha,* I
**mountain** *la montaña,* I
**mouth** *la boca,* I; **It makes my mouth water.** *Se me hace la boca agua.,* 4
**to move forward** *seguir adelante,* 7
**movie** *la película,* I
**movie theater** *el cine,* I
**moving** *conmovedor(a), emocionante,* 10
**museum** *el museo,* I; **to visit a museum** *visitar un museo,* II
**music** *la música,* I; **classical music** *la música clásica,* II; **music by . . .** *la música de,* I
**mustard** *la mostaza,* II
**my** mi(s), I; **My treat.** *Yo te invito,* 2; **My success in . . . is owed to . . .** *Mi éxito en... se debe a...,* 7; **My . . . faced obstacles when. . .** *Mis... enfrentaron obstáculos cuando...,* 7; **My life-long dream is to commemorate . . .** *El sueño de mi vida es conmemorar a....,* 9
**mystery** *el misterio,* I; **mystery novels** *novelas de misterio,* II
**mysterious** *misterioso(a),* 9
**myth** *el mito,* 9

## N

**nail** *la uña,* II
**napkin** *la servilleta,* I
**national park** *el parque nacional,* II
**national perspective** *enfoque nacional,* 6
**natural resources** *los recursos naturales,* 10
**nature** *la naturaleza,* II
**to nature watch** *observar la naturaleza,* II
**near** *cerca de,* I
**neck** *el cuello,* I
**necklace** *el collar,* II
**need** *necesitar,* I
**to need to** *deber* + infinitive, II; **You need to (should) . . .** *Debes* + infinitive, II; **You should wash the dishes/take out the garbage.** *Debes lavar los platos/sacar la basura.,* II
**neighbor** *el vecino, la vecina,* II
**neighborhood** *el vecindario, el barrio,* II
**neither, not either** *tampoco,* I; *ni,* I
**nephew** *el sobrino,* I
**nervous** *nervioso(a),* I
**nervously** *nerviosamente,* II
**never** *nunca,* I; **almost never** *casi nunca,* I; **I swear I'll never do it again.** *Te juro que no lo volveré a hacer.,* 3
**nevertheless** *ahora bien,* 9
**new** *nuevo(a),* II
**New Year's Eve** *la Nochevieja,* I
**news** *la noticia,* II; *las noticias,* II; **What news do you have of . . .?** *¿Qué noticias tienes de...?,* II; **When I heard the news, I didn't want to believe it.** *Cuando oí la noticia no lo quise creer.,* II; **news (online)** *las noticias (en linea),* 6; **news report** *el reportaje,* 6; **newscast** *el noticiero,* 4; **I don't think that journalists/newscasts are . . .** *No creo que los periodistas/los noticieros sean...,* 6
**newscaster** *el (la) locutor(a),* 6
**newspaper** *el periódico,* II
**next** *próximo(a),* I; **next to** *al lado de,* I; **Not today, thanks. Why don't we wait and do it next week?** *Hoy no, gracias. ¿Por qué no lo dejamos para la próxima semana?,* 5; **Thanks, but I have a lot to do. I'll go next time.** *Gracias, pero tengo mucho que hacer. La próxima vez iré.,* 5
**Nicaraguan** *nicaragüense,* II
**nice** *simpático(a),* I; *amable,* II; *elegante,* II; **nice (person)** *buena gente,* II; **Nice to meet you.** *Encantado(a),* I; *Mucho gusto.,* I
**nicely** *amablemente,* II
**niece** *la sobrina,* I
**night** *la noche,* II; **at night, P.M.** *de la noche,* I; *por la noche,* I
**nine** *nueve,* I
**nine hundred** *novecientos,* I
**nineteen** *diecinueve,* I
**ninety** *noventa,* I
**ninth** *noveno(a),* II
**no** *no,* I
**No way!** *¡Al contrario!; ¡No me digas!,* II; **No way! That's not true.** *¡Qué va! Eso no es cierto.,* 3
**nobody, not anybody** *nadie,* I
**none, not (a single) one** *ningún, ninguno(a),* II
**non-renewable** *no renovable,* 10
**noodle soup** *la sopa de fideos,* II
**noodles** *los fideos,* II
**noon** *mediodía,* I
**nor** *ni,* I
**nose** *la nariz,* I
**Not anymore.** *Ya no.,* II
**Not at all! As a matter of fact . . .** *¡Al contrario!,* II
**not only . . . but . . . as well** *no sólo... sino... también,* II
**Not today, thanks. Why don't we wait and do it next week?** *Hoy no, gracias. ¿Por qué no lo dejamos para la próxima semana?,* 5
**not yet** *todavía no,* I
**notes: to take notes** *tomar apuntes,* 3
**notebook** *el cuaderno,* I
**nothing** *nada,* I; **to have much/something/nothing in common** *tener mucho/algo/nada en común,* 2
**notice: What I notice is that . . .** *Lo que noto es que...,* 10
**novel** *la novela,* I
**November** *noviembre,* I
**now** *ahora,* I

nowhere *ninguna parte*, I
nuclear fusion *la fusión nuclear*, 10
number *el número*, I
nurse *el enfermero, la enfermera*, II
nutritious *nutritivo(a)*, II

## O

obituaries *los obituarios*, 6
objective *imparcial*, 6
objective *el objetivo*, 7
obligation *el compromiso*, 7
obstacles: My . . . faced obstacles when . . . *Mis... enfrentaron obstáculos cuando...*, 7
to obtain *conseguir (i, i)*, 8
occasional: the occasional (thing) *alguno(a) que otro(a) (cosa)*, 6
occupation *el oficio*, II
October *octubre*, I
of *de*, I
of course *claro*, II; Of course! *¡Claro que sí!*, I; Of course. *Cómo no.*, II, *Por supuesto.*, II; Yes, of course. *Sí, claro.*, II
of the *del, de la*, I
to offend *ofender*, 3; I didn't mean to hurt/offend you. *No quise hacerte daño/ofenderte.*, 3
office of . . . *la oficina de...*, II
often *a menudo*, I
Oh! I hit my . . . *¡Uf! Me di un golpe en...*, II
Oh, no! *¡Ay, no!*, I
Oh, what a drag! *¡Ay, qué pesado!*, II
oil *el aceite*, II; olive oil *el aceite de oliva*, II
ointment *el ungüento*, II
Okay, I'll give it to you for . . ., but that's my last offer. *Bueno, se la regalo por..., pero es mi última oferta.*, II
Okay. *Vale.*, I
old *viejo(a)*, I
older *mayor(es)*, I; When I'm older, I'd like to . . . *Cuando sea mayor, me gustaría...*, 7
olive: olive oil *el aceite de oliva*, II
on *en*, I; on sale *estar en oferta*, II; I saw that . . . was (were) on sale, so I bought . . . *Vi que... estaba(n) en oferta, así que compré...*, II; on the dot *en punto*, I; on time *a tiempo*, I; on top of, above *encima de*, I
Once upon a time *Érase una vez*, II; Once upon a time, in a faraway place . . . *Érase una vez, en un lugar muy lejano...*, 9
one *uno*, I
one can *se puede*, II
one day *un día*, II
one hundred *cien*, I
one hundred one *ciento uno*, I
one lives *se vive*, II
one million *un millón (de)*, I
One more time, please? *¿Otra vez, por favor?*, II
one must . . . *hay que...*, II
one thousand *mil*, I; I've already done it a thousand times. *Ya lo hice mil veces.*, II
one works *se trabaja*, II
onion *la cebolla*, II
only *solo*, I; *no más*, I; *solamente*, II
to open *abrir*, I; don't open *no abra*, II; open *abra*, II; open *abierto (past participle of abrir)*, II; to open gifts *abrir regalos*, I; to open (a movie) *estrenar (una película)*, 10
open *abierto (past participle of* abrir*)*, II
open-air *al aire libre*, II
opening *el estreno*, 10
opera: It's better for you to see the opera. It's great. *Es mejor que veas la ópera. Es formidable.*, 5
opinion: to be of the opinion *opinar*, 6
opportunities: I'm bilingual; therefore, I have many opportunities *Soy bilingüe, por lo tanto, tengo muchas oportunidades...*, 7
or *o*, I
orange *la naranja*, I; *anaranjado(a)*, I
orchestra *la orquesta*, 5
to order *pedir (i, i)*, I
organic *orgánico(a)*, 10
to organize *organizar*, I; don't organize *no organice, no organices*, II; organize *organice, organiza*, II
origin *el origen*, 7
original *original*, 5
ornaments *los adornos*, II
ought to *deber*, II
our *nuestro(a), nuestros(as)*, I
out of style *pasado(a) de moda*, I
outdoor *al aire libre*, II
outgoing *extrovertido(a)*, I
outside *afuera*, II
oven *el horno*, I
over here *acá*, II; Come over here! *¡Ven acá!*, II
overcoat *el abrigo*, I
overcome: Thanks to the support of . . . I have been able to overcome . . . *Gracias al apoyo de..., he podido superar...*, 7
to overlook *pasar por alto*, 6
owe: My success in . . . is owed to . . . *Mi éxito en... se debe a...*, 7
owl *el búho*, II

## P

to pack your suitcase *hacer la maleta*, I
page *la página*, II; to design Web pages *diseñar páginas Web*, II; Web pages *páginas Web*, II; front page *la primera plana*, 6
pain: What a pain! *¡Qué lata!*, I
to paint *pintar*, II; This portrait was painted by . . . What do you think of it? *Este retrato fue pintado por... ¿Qué te parece?*, 5
to paint one's nails *pintarse las uñas*, II
painting *el cuadro*, II;
paintings *las pinturas*, II; Which of these paintings do you like better, the one of (by) . . . or the one of (by) . . .? *¿Cuál de estas pinturas te gusta más, la de... o la de...?*, 5
pair *el par*, I
pajamas *el piyama*, I
palace *el palacio*, 9
panic *el pánico*, 10
pants (jeans) *los pantalones (vaqueros)*, I
paper *el papel*, I
Paraguayan *paraguayo(a)*, II
Pardon me. *Perdón.*, II
parents *los padres*, I
park *el parque*, I; *la zona verde*, II; amusement park *el parque de diversiones*, I; national park *el parque nacional*, II
park bench *la banca*, II
parking lot *el estacionamiento*, II
part-time job *el empleo a medio tiempo*, 8
to participate *participar*, II
party, to have a *hacer una fiesta*, I; surprise party *la fiesta sorpresa*, I
pass *boarding pass*
to pass (a test, class) *aprobar (ue)*, 3
passenger *el pasajero, la pasajera*, I
passport *el pasaporte*, I
pastry *el pan dulce*, I
pastry shop *la pastelería*, II
patient *paciente*, II
patio *el patio*, I
to pay *pagar*, I; to pay the bill *pagar la cuenta*, II
to pay attention: I suggest that you not pay attention to rumors. *Sugiero que no hagas caso a los rumores.*, 3
peach *el durazno*, I
pear *la pera*, II
peas *los chícharos*, 4
pedestrian *peatonal*, II; pedestrian zone *la zona peatonal*, II
pen *el bolígrafo*, I
pencil *el lápiz*, I
people *la gente*, II; to help/assist people *ayudar a la gente*, II
pepper *la pimienta*, II
perfect *perfecto(a)*, II; It's perfect. *Está perfecto.*, II
performance *la función*, 5; I recommend that you go to the folk dance performance. It's very . . . *Te aconsejo que vayas a la presentación de baile folclórico. Es muy...*, 5
person *la persona*, I
perspective: local/national/world perspective *enfoque local/nacional/mundial*, 6
Peruvian *peruano(a)*, II
pesticides *los pesticidas*, 10
pet *la mascota*, II; to take care of a pet *cuidar a una mascota*, II
pharmacist *el farmacéutico, la farmacéutica*, II
phone booth *la cabina telefónica*, II
photo *la foto*, I; to show photos *enseñar fotos*, I; to take photos *sacar fotos*, I
photocopier *la fotocopiadora*, 8
photography *la fotografía*, 5
physical education *la educación física*, I
physics *la física*, 3
to pick up (someone) *recoger (a alguien)*, I; don't pick up *no recoja, no recojas*, II; pick up *recoge, recoja*, II; to pick someone up *recoger a alguien*, II
picnic *el picnic*, I
piece *el trozo*, II
pill *la pastilla*, II; to take some pills *tomarse unas pastillas*, II
pineapple *la piña*, II
piñata *la piñata*, I
pizza *la pizza*, I
place *el lugar*, I; Once upon a time, in a faraway place . . . *Érase una vez, en un lugar muy lejano...*, 9

**to plan** *planear,* II; **No, I'm planning on . . .** *No, ando planeando...,* II
**plane ticket** *el boleto de avión,* I
**planet** *el planeta,* 10
**plans** *los planes,* I; **Do you have plans for . . .?** *¿Tienes planes para el...?,* II; **I'm sorry, but I already have other plans/another engagement.** *Lo siento, pero ya tengo otros planes/otro compromiso.,* 5
**to plant** *sembrar (ie),* 8, 10
**plantain** *el plátano,* II
**plants** *las plantas,* I; **to water the plants** *regar las plantas,* II
**plastic** *el plástico,* II; **plastic arts** *las artes plásticas,* 5
**plate** *el plato,* I
**play** *la obra (de teatro),* 5
**to play: to play a game or sport** *jugar (ue) (a),* I; **to play cards** *jugar naipes,* II; **to play checkers** *jugar a las damas,* II; **to play chess** *jugar al ajedrez,* II; **to play hide and seek** *jugar al escondite,* II; **to play house** *jugar a la casita,* II; **to play tag** *jugar al pilla-pilla,* II; **to play tennis** *jugar al tenis,* II; **to play with blocks** *jugar con bloques,* II; **to play with toy cars** *jugar con carritos,* II; **We'll play with . . .** *Jugaremos con...,* II; **to play (an instrument)** *tocar,* I; **don't play** *no toques,* II; **play it** *tócalo,* II; **to play the piano** *tocar el piano,* I; **to play sports** *practicar deportes,* I; **to play tricks** *hacer travesuras,* II; **to play (the role of . . .)** *desempeñar el papel de...,* 5
**player** *el jugador, la jugadora,* II
**playful** *juguetón, juguetona,* II
**plaza** *la plaza,* II
**please** *por favor,* I; **Please . . .** *Favor de + infinitive, Haz el favor de + infinitive,* II
**Pleased to meet you.** *Encantado(a).,* I; *Mucho gusto.,* I
**pleasure** *el gusto,* II; **The pleasure is mine.** *El gusto es mío.,* II
**poem** *el poema,* II
**police department** *la comisaría,* II
**police officer** *el policía,* I
**policeman** *el policía,* II
**policewoman** *la mujer policía,* II
**political crisis** *la crisis política,* 6
**pool** *la piscina,* I
**poor** *pobre,* II
**Poor thing!** *¡Pobrecito(a)!,* II
**poorly: to be poorly-informed** *estar mal informado(a),* 6
**porch** *el patio,* I
**pork** *el lechón,* II; **roasted pork** *el lechón asado,* II; *el puerco asado,* 4
**pork chops** *las chuletas de cerdo,* II
**port** *el puerto,* II
**portrait: This portrait was painted by . . . What do you think of it?** *Este retrato fue pintado por... ¿Qué te parece?,* 5
**position (for work)** *el puesto (de trabajo),* 8
**positive: I'm positive that . . .** *Estoy seguro(a) (de) que...,* 6
**possible: It's quite possible that traffic will increase with . . .** *Es muy posible que el tráfico aumente con...,* 10
**post office** *la oficina de correos,* I
**posters** *los pósters,* II; **to collect posters** *coleccionar pósters,* II
**potato** *la papa,* I; **potato chips** *las papitas,* I
**powers** *los poderes,* 9
**to practice** *practicar,* II; **Are you still practicing . . .?** *¿Sigues practicando...?,* II
**practice** *el entrenamiento,* I; **Don't forget to go to band practice.** *No te olvides de ir al ensayo de la banda.,* 5
**to predict: I predict that they are going to implement . . .** *Calculo que van a implementar...,* 10
**to prefer** *preferir (ie, i),* I
**prejudice** *el prejuicio,* 3
**premiere** *el estreno,* 10
**to premiere (a movie)** *estrenar (una película),* 10
**preparations** *los preparativos,* I
**to prepare** *preparar,* I; **How is . . . prepared?** *¿Cómo se prepara...?,* II
**to present** *presentar,* 5
**the press** *la prensa,* 6
**pretty** *bonito(a),* I; *lindo(a),* II
**price** *el precio,* II
**price tag** *la etiqueta,* II
**pride** *el orgullo,* 7
**prince** *el príncipe,* 9
**princess** *la princesa,* 9
**principal** *el (la) director(a),* 3
**profession** *el oficio,* II
**to program** *programar,* II
**programmer** *el programador, la programadora,* II
**programs for** *los programas de,* 10
**to promote: You will see that they're going to promote . . .** *Ya verás que van a promover (ue)...,* 10
**protein** *las proteínas,* II
**public restrooms** *los aseos, los baños,* II
**public speaking** *la oratoria,* II
**punch** *el ponche,* I
**to punish** *castigar,* 9
**punishment** *el castigo,* 9
**purple** *morado(a),* I
**purpose: I didn't do it on purpose.** *No lo hice a propósito.,* 3; **The purpose of this letter is . . .** *Por medio de la presente...,* 8
**purse** *la bolsa,* I
**put** *puesto (past participle of poner),* II
**to put** *poner (-go),* I; **don't put** *no pongas,* I; **put** *pon,* I; **put** *puesto (past participle of* **poner***),* II
**to put in** *echar,* II
**to put on** *ponerse,* I
**to put on makeup** *maquillarse,* I
**to put out** *apagar,* II; **to put out fires** *apagar incendios,* II
**to put something on** *ponerse,* II
**puzzle** *el rompecabezas,* 2
**pyramid** *la pirámide,* I

## Q

**air quality/water quality** *la calidad del aire/agua,* 10
**quarter past (the hour)** *y cuarto,* I
**quarter to (the hour)** *menos cuarto,* I
**queen** *la reina,* 9
**quickly** *rápidamente,* II
**quiet** *callado(a),* I
**quite** + adjective *bastante* + adjective, I

## R

**radio (as a medium)** *la radio,* 6; **radio station** *la emisora,* 6; **(call-in) radio program** *programa de radio (a micrófono abierto),* 6
**to rain** *llover (ue),* I; **it rains a lot** *llueve mucho,* I; **to rain cats and dogs** *llover a cántaros,* II; **Suddenly, it started to rain . . .** *De repente, empezó a llover...,* II
**raincoat** *el impermeable,* II
**raisins** *las pasas,* 4
**rate: I bet that the rate of . . . won't go down.** *A que no va a bajar la tasa de...,* 10;
**rather** *bastante* + adjective, I
**raw** *crudo(a),* II
**razor** *la navaja,* I
**reach: It's outside/within my reach.** *Está fuera de/a mi alcance,* 8
**to reach** *alcanzar,* 7
**to react** *reaccionar,* II; **How did you react when . . .?** *¿Cómo reaccionaste cuando...?,* II
**to read** *leer,* I; **reading** *leyendo,* II; **I read it in the sports section.** *Lo leí en la sección deportiva.,* 6
**ready** *listo(a),* I; **to be ready** *estar listo(a),* I; **Aren't you ready yet?** *¿Todavía no estás listo(a)?,* II
**realistic** *realista,* 5
**to realize: In the end, we realized . . .** *Al final, nos dimos cuenta de...,* 9
**Really? Well, I think . . .** *¿Ah, sí? Pues, yo creo que...,* 2
**really beautiful** *lindísimo(a),* II
**reason: I work hard . . . and for that reason . . .** *Trabajo duro... y por eso...,* 7
**receipt** *el recibo,* II
**to receive** *recibir,* I; **to receive gifts** *recibir regalos,* I
**recently** *recientemente,* II
**receptionist** *el recepcionista, la recepcionista,* II
**recipe** *la receta,* II
**to recommend** *recomendar (ie),* II; **I (don't) recommend it to you.** *(No) te la recomiendo.,* II; **I recommend that you . . .** *Le aconsejo que...,* II; **What do you recommend?** *¿Qué nos recomienda?,* II; **What restaurant do you recommend to me?** *¿Qué restaurante me recomienda usted?,* II; **I recommend that you go to the folk dance performance. It's very . . .** *Te aconsejo que vayas a la presentación de baile folclórico. Es muy...,* 5
**to recommend that someone . . .** *recomendarle (a alguien) que...,* II
**to reconcile** *reconciliarse,* 3
**reconciliation** *la reconciliación,* 3
**recreation center** *el centro recreativo,* II
**to recycle** *reciclar,* 10
**red** *rojo(a),* I
**red-headed** *pelirrojo(a),* I
**refrigerator** *el refrigerador,* I
**refugees** *los refugiados,* 10
**regret: He/She regrets that . . .** *Se arrepiente de que...,* 9
**rehearsal** *el ensayo,* I
**to rejoice** *regocijarse,* 9
**relatives** *los parientes,* II; **to stay with**

**relatives** *quedarse con parientes*, II
**relax** *relajarse*, I; **Relax.** *Tranquilo(a).*, II
**reliable** *confiable*, 2
**to remember** *acordarse (ue) de*, II; **Did you remember to . . .?** *¿Te acordaste de...?*, II; **Do you remember when . . . happened?** *¿Te acuerdas (de) cuando sucedió...?*, 10; **I remember it like it was yesterday.** *Lo recuerdo como si fuera ayer.*, 10; **I think it's worth remembering . . .** *Creo que vale la pena acordarse de...*, 10; **No, I don't remember it at all.** *No, no me acuerdo para nada.*, 10
**renewable** *renovable*, 10
**to rent** *alquilar*, I; **to rent videos** *alquilar videos*, I
**to repeat** *repetir (i, i)*, II; **Can you repeat what you said?** *¿Puede repetir lo que dijo?*, II
**reporter** *el (la) reportero(a)*, 6
**reputation** *la fama*, 3
**to require** *requerir (ie, i)*, 8
**requirements** *los requisitos*, 8
**resentful: to be resentful** *estar resentido(a)*, 3
**reservation** *la reservación*, II; **to make a reservation** *hacer una reservación*, II
**to resolve a problem** *resolver (ue) un problema*, 2
**resource: natural resources** *los recursos naturales*, 10
**respect** *el respeto*, 3
**to respect (someone)** *respetar (a alguien)*, 3
**to respect each other** *respetarse*, II
**to respect others' feelings** *respetar los sentimientos de otros*, 2
**to research** *investigar*, 6
**to rest** *descansar*, I
**restaurant** *el restaurante*, II; **What restaurant do you recommend to me?** *¿Qué restaurante me recomienda usted?*, II
**restroom** *el baño, el servicio*, I
**resume** *el currículum (vitae)*, 8
**to return, to go back** *regresar*, I
**returned, gone back** *vuelto (past participle of* **volver**), II
**reunion: family reunion** *la reunión familiar*, 4
**review** *la reseña*, 5
**to review** *reseñar*, 6
**revolution** *la revolución*, 9
**rhythm** *el ritmo*, 5
**rice** *el arroz*, I
**to ride horseback** *montar a caballo*, II
**to ride a bike** *montar en bicicleta*, I
**riding** *la equitación*, II
**right** *la derecha*, II; **to the right (of)** *a la derecha (de)*, II; **to turn right on** *doblar a la derecha en*, II
**right away** *en seguida*, II, 8
**right?** *¿no?*, I; *¿verdad?*, I; **to be right** *tener razón*, I
**ring** *el anillo*, I
**rip off** *el robo*, I
**river** *el río*, II
**riverbank** *la orilla del río*, II
**road** *la carretera*, II
**roast beef** *la carne asada*, II
**roast meat** *la carne asada*, II
**roasted** *asado(a)*, II; **roasted chicken** *el pollo asado*, II; **roasted pork** *el lechón asado*, II; *el puerco asado*, 4
**robot** *el robot*, 8
**rock** *la piedra*, II
**rock-climbing** *la escalada deportiva*, II
**roll of film** *el rollo de película*, II
**romance book** *el libro de amor*, I
**romantic** *romántico(a)*, I
**roof** *el techo*, II
**room** *el cuarto*, I
**roots** *las raíces*, 7
**rope** *la cuerda*, II; **to jump rope** *saltar a la cuerda*, II
**to row** *remar*, II
**rowing** *el remo*, 2
**rude** *grosero(a)*, 2
**rug** *la alfombra*, II
**ruins** *las ruinas*, I
**ruler** *la regla*, I
**rumor: I suggest that you not pay attention to rumors.** *Sugiero que no hagas caso a los rumores.*, 3
**to run** *correr*, I; **to run away** *huir*, II; **to run errands** *hacer diligencias*, II; **to run races** *echar carreras*, II
**to run out of: It's just that I ran out of . . .** *Es que se me acabó...*, 4

## S

**sacrifice** *el sacrificio*, 7
**sad** *triste*, I
**sailboat** *el bote de vela*, I; **to go out in a sailboat** *pasear en bote de vela*, I
**salad** *la ensalada*, I
**salary** *el salario*, 8
**sale** *la venta*, II; **clearance sale** *la venta de liquidación*, II
**salesclerk** *el dependiente, la dependiente*, I
**salt** *la sal*, II; **It's missing salt.** *Le falta sal.*, II
**salty** *salado(a)*, I; **The... is salty/spicy.** *El/La... está salado(a)/picante.*, 4
**Salvadoran** *salvadoreño(a)*, II
**same: It's all the same to me.** *Me da lo mismo.*, 2
**same as usual** *lo de siempre*, I
**sand** *la arena*, II
**sandals** *las sandalias*, I
**sandwich** *el sándwich*, I
**Saturday** *el sábado*, I; **on Saturdays** *los sábados*, I
**sauce, gravy** *la salsa*, I; **tomato sauce** *la salsa de tomate*, II; **hot sauce** *la salsa picante*, I
**sausage** *la salchicha*, 4
**to save money** *ahorrar*, I
**to say** *decir (yo digo)*, II; **Can you repeat what you said?** *¿Puede repetir lo que dijo?*, II; **said** *dicho (past participle of* **decir**), II; **say** *di*, II; **You don't say!** *¡No me digas!*, II, 4; **Changing the subject, what do you have to say about . . .?** *Cambiando de tema, ¿qué me dices de...?*, 5
**Say hi to . . . for me.** *Dale un saludo a... de mi parte.*, II
**to scare** *darle miedo*, II
**scarf** *la bufanda*, II
**scenery** *el escenario*, 5
**schedule** *el horario*, 3, 8
**school** *el colegio*, I; **after school** *después del colegio*, II; **school band** *la banda escolar*, II; **school supplies** *los útiles escolares*, I
**science** *las ciencias*, I; **science fiction** *la ciencia ficción*, I; **computer science** *la computación*, I; **social sciences** *las ciencias sociales*, 3
**score** *el puntaje*, II
**scrambled** *revuelto(a)*, II; **scrambled eggs** *los huevos revueltos*, II
**scrapbook** *el álbum*, II; **to create a scrapbook** *crear un álbum*, II
**to scuba dive** *bucear*, II
**to sculpt** *esculpir*, 5
**sea** *el mar*, II; **to swim in the sea** *bañarse en el mar*, II
**seafood** *los mariscos*, II
**second** *segundo(a)*, II
**secretary** *el secretario, la secretaria*, II
**secrets: to (not) keep secrets** *(no) guardar los secretos*, 2
**security checkpoint** *el control de seguridad*, I
**to see** *ver*, I; **I saw that . . . was (were) on sale, so I bought . . .** *Vi que... estaba(n) en oferta, así que compré...*, II; **seen** *visto (past participle of ver)*, II; **See you tomorrow.** *Hasta mañana.*, I; **See you.** *Nos vemos.*, I; **Do you want to go see . . .** *¿Quieres ir a ver...?*, 5; **I see you're in a good mood.** *Te veo de buen humor.*, 2; **The way I see it, there's no equality between . . .** *A mi parecer, no hay igualdad entre...*, 3
**to seem** *parecer (zc)*, I; **It seems to be that . . .** *Me parece que...*, 10
**seen** *visto(a) (past participle of* **ver**), II
**selfish** *egoísta*, II
**to sell** *vender*, I
**semester** *el semestre*, 3
**to send** *mandar*, I; **to send text messages** *enviar mensajes de texto*, II
**separated** *separado(a)*, 4
**September** *septiembre*, I
**serious** *serio(a)*, I
**to serve** *servir (i, i)*, I
**server** *el mesero, la mesera*, II
**to set** *poner (-go)*, I; **to set the table** *poner la mesa*, I
**seven** *siete*, I
**seven hundred** *setecientos*, I
**seventeen** *diecisiete*, I
**seventh** *séptimo(a)*, II
**seventy** *setenta*, I
**to sew** *coser*, II
**shame: What a shame that they have . . .** *Qué pena que se hayan...*, 4
**to share** *compartir*, II; **to share toys** *compartir los juguetes*, II
**to shave** *afeitarse*, I
**she** *ella*, I; **She** *(emphatic)* **likes . . .** *A ella le gusta(n) + noun*, II
**shell** *el caracol*, II
**ship: sunken ship** *la nave hundida*, 10
**shirt** *la camisa*, I
**shoe size** *el número*, I
**shoe store** *la zapatería*, I
**shoes** *los zapatos*, I; **tennis shoes** *los zapatos de tenis*, I
**shop window** *la vitrina*, I; **to window shop** *mirar las vitrinas*, I;
**shopping** *las compras*, II; **I like to go shopping.** *Me gusta ir de compras.*, II; **to go shopping at the market** *ir de compras al mercado*, II
**short** *(height) bajo(a)*, I; *(length) corto(a)*, I
**shorts** *los pantalones cortos*, I

Vocabulario inglés-español

**should** *deber*, I; **A good friend should support me and . . . He/she shouldn't . . .** *Un(a) buen(a) amigo(a) debe apoyarme y... No debe...*, 2
**shoulder** *el hombro*, I
**to shout** *gritar*, II
**show: game show** *el concurso*, 4
**to show** *enseñar*, I; **Show me . . .** *Enséñame...*, II; **to show photos** *enseñar fotos*, I
**shower** *la ducha*, II
**shrill** *estridente*, 5
**shrimp** *el camarón, los camarones*, 4
**shy** *tímido(a)*, I
**sick people** *los enfermos*, II; **to take care of sick people** *cuidar a los enfermos*, II
**sick with a cold** *resfriado(a)*, II
**sick: to be sick** *estar enfermo(a)*, I; *estar mal*, II
**sickness** *la enfermedad*, II, 10
**sidewalk** *la acera*, II
**to sign** *firmar*, II
**silk** *la seda*, I
**silly** *tonto(a)*
**silver** *la plata*, II
**to sing** *cantar*, I
**sink: bathroom sink** *el lavabo*, II; **kitchen sink** *el fregadero*, II
**sir, Mr.** *el señor, Sr.*, I
**sister** *la hermana*, I
**sister-in-law** *la cuñada*, 4
**to sit down** *sentarse (ie)*, I
**six** *seis*, I
**six hundred** *seiscientos*, I
**sixteen** *dieciséis*, I
**sixth** *sexto(a)*, II
**sixty** *sesenta*, I
**size** *la talla*, I
**to skate** *patinar*, I
**skating** *el patinaje*, II; **in-line skating** *el patinaje en línea*, II; **ice-skating** *el patinaje sobre hielo*, II
**to ski** *esquiar*, I; **to water ski** *esquiar en el agua*, I
**skin** *la piel*, II
**skirt** *la falda*, I
**to sleep** *dormir (ue, u)*, I; **sleeping** *durmiendo*, II; **to get enough sleep** *dormir lo suficiente*, I
**slowly** *lentamente*, II
**small** *pequeño(a)*, I; **pretty small** *bastante pequeño*, I
**to smell** *oler(ue)*, II
**smells like** *huele a*, II
**to smoke** *fumar*, I; **to stop smoking** *dejar de fumar*, I
**to snack** *merendar (ie)*, I
**snake** *la serpiente*, II
**to sneeze** *estornudar*, II
**to snow** *nevar (ie)*, I
**snow** *la nieve*, II
**so** *así que*, II
**so** *entonces*, II; **So, what I have to do is . . .** *Entonces, lo que tengo que hacer es...*, II
**so much; so many** *tanto*, I; *tanto(a), tantos(as)*, II
**so that's how** *así fue que*, II
**soap** *el jabón*, I
**soap opera** *la telenovela*, 6
**society section** *la sección de sociedad*, 6
**soccer** *el fútbol*, I
**social sciences** *las ciencias sociales*, 3
**social worker** *el trabajador social, la trabajadora social*, II
**socks** *los calcetines*, I; **a pair of socks** *un par de calcetines*, I
**sofa** *el sofá*, I
**soft drink** *el refresco*, I
**solar energy** *la energía solar*, 10
**soldier** *el soldado*, 9
**solidarity** *la solidaridad*, 10
**some** *unos(as)*, I
**some day** *algún día*, I
**Some time ago, a stranger came . . .** *Hace tiempo, vino un desconocido...*, 9
**someone** *alguien*, II; **to advise someone to . . .** *aconsejarle (a alguien) que...*, II; **to ask someone** *preguntarle a alguien*, II; **to pick someone up** *recoger a alguien*, II; **to recommend that someone . . .** *recomendarle (a alguien) que...*, II; **to suggest that someone . . .** *sugerirle (a alguien) que...*, II; **to take someone** *llevar a alguien*, II
**something** *algo*, I; **to have much/something/nothing in common** *tener mucho/algo/nada en común*, 2; **There's something I can't quite grasp.** *Hay algo que se me escapa.*, 8
**sometimes** *a veces*, I
**son** *el hijo*, I
**sorcerer, sorceress** *el (la) hechicero(a)*, 9
**sorry: I'm sorry, but I already have other plans/another engagement.** *Lo siento, pero ya tengo otros planes/otro compromiso.*, 5
**so-so** *más o menos*, I
**soup** *la sopa*, I; **garlic soup** *la sopa de ajo*, II; **noodle soup** *la sopa de fideos*, II; **vegetable soup** *la sopa de verduras*, I
**sources of energy** *las fuentes de energía*, 10
**Spanish** *el español*, I
**to speak** *hablar*, I; **is spoken** *se habla*, II; **to stop speaking to one another** *dejar de hablarse*, 3; **Speaking of art, what can you tell me about . . .?** *Hablando de arte, ¿qué me cuentas de...?*, 5
**specialties** *las especialidades*, II
**speech** *la oratoria*, II
**speechless: You've left me speechless.** *Me has dejado boquiabierto(a).*, 4
**to spend** *(money) gastar*, I; *(time) pasar*, I; **to spend a lot of time** *pasar mucho tiempo*, II; **to spend time alone** *pasar el rato solo(a)*, I
**spices** *las especias*, II
**spicy** *picante*, I; **The . . . is salty/spicy.** *El/La... está salado(a)/picante.*, 4
**spinach** *las espinacas*, I
**split peas** *los gandules*, II
**spoiled** *consentido(a)*, II
**spoon** *la cuchara*, I
**sports** *los deportes*, I; **I'm a big . . . fan. What sport do you like?** *Soy un(a) gran aficionado(a) a... ¿Qué deporte te gusta a ti?*, 2
**sports cards** *las láminas*, II
**sports section** *la sección deportiva*, 6; **I read it in the sports section.** *Lo leí en la sección deportiva.*, 6
**to sprain (one's body part)** *torcerse (ue)* + a body part, II
**spring** *la primavera*, I
**stadium** *el estadio*, I
**stage** *el escenario*, 5
**stamps** *las estampillas*, II; **to collect stamps** *coleccionar estampillas*, II
**stand** *el quiosco de...*, II
**to stand** *aguantar*, 2
**to stand someone up** *dejar plantado(a) a alguien*, 2
**to start** *empezar (ie)*, I; *comenzar (ie)*, I; **don't start** *no empieces*, II; **Suddenly, it started to rain . . .** *De repente, empezó a llover...*, II; **to start crying** *ponerse a llorar*, II
**station** *la estación*, II; **fire station** *la estación de bomberos*, II; **train station** *la estación de tren*, II
**statue** *la estatua*, 5
**to stay** *quedarse*, I; **to stay in bed** *quedarse en cama*, II; **to stay with relatives** *quedarse con parientes*, II; **to stay at . . .** *hospedarse en...*, II; **to stay in shape** *mantenerse (mantengo, ie) en forma*, I
**steak** *el bistec*, II; **grilled steak** *el bistec a la parrilla*, II; **steak with onions** *el bistec encebollado*, II
**steel** *el acero*, II
**stepbrother** *el hermanastro*, 4
**stepfather** *el padrastro*, 4
**stepsister** *la hermanastra*, 4
**stepmother** *la madrastra*, 4
**stereotype** *el estereotipo*, 3
**still: Well, he's/she's still working . . .** *Pues, sigue trabajando...*, 4
**to stir** *revolver(ue)*, II; **stirred** *revuelto (past participle of revolver)*, II
**stirred** *revuelto (past participle of revolver)*, II
**stomach** *el estómago*, I
**stone** *la piedra*, II
**to stop** *parar*, II; **to stop doing something** *dejar de + infinitive*, I; **to stop speaking to one another** *dejar de hablarse*, 3
**store** *la tienda de...*, I; **grocery store** *la tienda de comestibles*, II
**storm** *la tormenta*, II
**story** *el piso*, I; **. . . story building** *el edificio de . . .pisos*, I
**story** *el cuento*, II; **to tell each other stories** *contarse cuentos*, II
**stove** *la estufa*, II
**straight** *derecho*, II; **to go straight** *seguir (i, i) adelante/derecho*, II; **to keep going (straight) to** *seguir derecho hasta*, II
**stranger: Some time ago, a stranger came . . .** *Hace tiempo, vino un desconocido...*, 9
**straw** *la paja*, II; **We're going to have another test in . . . tomorrow? This is the last straw!** *¿Mañana vamos a tener otra prueba en...? ¡Esto es el colmo!*, 3
**strawberries (and cream)** *las fresas (con crema)*, II
**to stretch** *estirarse*, I
**strict** *estricto(a)*, II
**strike: To tell the truth, it strikes me as . . .** *A decir verdad, me parece...*, 5
**to stroll** *pasearse*, II
**stubborn** *terco(a)*, 2
**student** *el estudiante, la estudiante*, I
**to study** *estudiar*, I; **I didn't study, so . . .** *No estudié, así que...*, 7; **I would be interested in studying to be a . . .** *Me interesaría estudiar para ser un(a)*, 8; **If I could, I would go to . . . to study . . .** *Si pudiera, iría a... para estudiar...*, 8
**stuffed animals** *los animales de peluche*, II
**style** *la moda*, I; **in the latest style** *a la última moda*, I; **out of style** *pasado de moda*, I

subject *la materia*, I; **Changing the subject, what do you have to say about . . .?** *Cambiando de tema, ¿qué me dices de...?*, 5
**success: to have success** *tener éxito*, 7; **My success in . . . is owed to . . .** *Mi éxito en... se debe a...*, 7
**to subscribe to** *suscribirse a*, 6
**suburbs** *las afueras*, I
**subway** *el metro*, I
**subway stop** *la parada del metro*, II
**success** *el éxito*, II
**suddenly** *de repente*, II; **Suddenly, it started to rain . . .** *De repente, empezó a llover...*, II; **It's told that all of a sudden . . .** *Se cuenta que de pronto...*, 9
**to suffer** *sufrir*, 9
**sugar** *el azúcar*, II
**to suggest: I suggest that you not pay attention to rumors.** *Sugiero que no hagas caso a los rumores.*, 3
**to suggest that someone . . .** *sugerirle (ie, i) (a alguien) que...*, II
**suit** *el traje*, II
**suitcase** *la maleta*, I
**summer** *el verano*, I
**sun** *el sol*, II
**to sunbathe** *tomar el sol*, I
**sunblock** *la crema protectora*, II
**Sunday** *el domingo*, I; **on Sundays** *los domingos*, I
**sunglasses** *las gafas de sol*, II
**sunken ship** *la nave hundida*, 10
**sunny** *soleado(a)*, II
**superficial** *superficial*, 5
**supermarket** *el supermercado*, II
**to supervise** *supervisar*, 8
**to suppose: I suppose that . . .** *Es de suponer que...*, 10; **I suppose so.** *Supongo que sí*, 10
**support** *el apoyo*, 7; **Thanks to the support of . . . I have been able to overcome . . .** *Gracias al apoyo de..., he podido superar...*, 7; **A good friend should support me and . . . He/She shouldn't . . .** *Un(a) buen(a) amigo(a) debe apoyarme y... No debe...*, 2
**to support** *apoyar*, 2, 7
**supportive** *solidario(a)*, 2
**sure: I'm not sure that you're right about . . .** *No estoy seguro(a) (de) que tengas razón sobre...*, 6
**to surf the Internet** *navegar por Internet*, I
**to surprise** *sorprender*, 2; **surprise: What a surprise that they have . . .!** *¡Qué sorpresa que se hayan...!*, 4
**surprise party** *la fiesta sorpresa*, I
**to swear: I swear I'll never do it again.** *Te juro que no lo volveré a hacer.*, 3
**sweater** *el suéter*, I
**to sweep** *barrer*, II
**sweet** *dulce*, I; **The . . . is dry/isn't very sweet.** *El/La... está seco(a)/no está muy dulce.*, 4
**to swell** *hinchar*, II
**to swim** *nadar*, I; **to swim in the sea** *bañarse en el mar*, II
**swimming (swim class)** *la natación*, II
**swimsuit** *el traje de baño*, I
**to swing (on a swing)** *columpiarse*, II
**swollen** *hinchado(a)*, II
**symphony: It would be a good idea to go to the symphony.** *Sería buena idea ir al concierto de la sinfónica.*, 5
**synagogue** *la sinagoga*, I

# T

**table** *la mesa*, I
**tablecloth** *el mantel*, II
**tablespoon** *la cucharada*, II
**to take: to take . . . lessons** *tomar clases de...*, II; **to take a taxi** *tomar un taxi*, II; **to take a test** *presentar un examen*, I; **to take photos** *sacar photos*, I; **to take (someone)** *llevar (a alguien)*, II; **to take . . . street** *ir por la calle...*, II; **to take a guided tour** *hacer un tour*, II; **to take a long time (to)** *tardarse en* + infinitive, II; **to take a nap** *dormir la siesta*, I; **to take a shower** *ducharse*, II; **to take a walk** *pasearse*, II; **to take notes** *tomar apuntes*, 3; **It took a lot of work for us to get used to . . .** *Nos costó trabajo acostumbrarnos a...*, 7; **to take advantage of** *aprovechar*, 7; **to take the initiative** *tomar la iniciativa*, 7; **I can't stand the attitude of . . . towards . . . I can't take it anymore!** *Me choca la actitud de... hacia... ¡No aguanto más!*, 3; **to take care of** *cuidar*, I; **Take care.** *Cuídate.*, I; **to take care of a pet** *cuidar a una mascota*, II; **to take care of oneself** *cuidarse*, I; **to take care of sick people** *cuidar a los enfermos*, II; **to take long** *tardar*, II; **The guidance counselor insists that I take . . . I don't like it at all!** *El/La consejero(a) insiste en que tome... ¡No me gusta para nada!*, 3
**to take off** *quitarse*, I
**to take out** *sacar*, I; **don't take out** *no saque*, II; **take out** *saque*, II; **You should take out the garbage.** *Debes sacar la basura.*, II
**to take some pills** *tomarse unas pastillas*, II
**tale** *el cuento*, 9
**talent** *el talento*, 8
**to talk** *hablar*, I; *charlar*, I; *conversar*, II; **don't talk** *no hables*, II; **talking** *hablando*, II; **We talked about the issue; consequently...** *Hablamos del tema; por consiguiente...*, 7
**talkative** *conversador(a)*, II
**tall** *alto(a)*, I
**tamales** *los tamales*, I
**to taste** *probar (ue)*, I; *al gusto*, II; **It tastes delicious.** *Sabe delicioso(a).*, 4; **The . . . doesn't taste like anything.** *El/La... no sabe a nada.*, 4
**taste** *el gusto*, II; **to taste** *al gusto*, II; **in good/bad taste** *de buen/mal gusto*, 5
**tasty** *rico(a), sabroso(a)*, II
**tax** *el impuesto*, II
**taxi** *el taxi*, I; **to take a taxi** *tomar un taxi*, II
**taxi driver** *el taxista, la taxista*, II
**tea** *el té*, II
**to teach** *enseñar*, II
**teacher** *la profesora, el profesor*, I
**team** *el equipo*, II
**teaspoon** *la cucharadita*, II
**technology** *la tecnología*, 8
**teeth** *los dientes*, I
**telephone number** *el teléfono*, I
**telephones** *los teléfonos*, II
**television** *la televisión*, I; **to watch television** *ver la televisión*, I; **TV** *la tele*, II; **TV station** *la emisora*, 6

**to tell** *contar (ue)*, II; **Tell me what happened the day that . . .** *Cuéntame lo que pasó el día que...*, II; **to tell jokes** *contar chistes*, I; **It's told that all of a sudden . . .** *Se cuenta que de pronto...*, 9; **Speaking of art, what can you tell me about . . .?** *Hablando de arte, ¿qué me cuentas de...?*, 5; **What can you tell me about . . .?** *¿Qué me cuentas de...?*, 4
**to tell** *decir (yo digo)*, II; **don't tell** *no digas*, II; **Can you tell me where . . . is?** *¿Me dices dónde está...?*, II; **Could you tell me . . .?** *¿Me podría decir...?*, II; **tell** *di*, II; **To tell the truth, it strikes me as . . .** *A decir verdad, me parece...*, 5
**to tell each other** *contarse (ue)*, II; **to tell each other jokes** *contarse chistes*, II; **to tell each other stories** *contarse cuentos*, II
**temperature** *la temperatura*, II
**temple** *el templo*, I, 9
**ten** *diez*, I
**tender** *cariñoso(a)*, II
**tennis** *el tenis*, I; **tennis shoes** *los zapatos de tenis*, I; **to play tennis** *jugar al tenis*, II
**tent** *la tienda de campaña*, II
**tenth** *décimo(a)*, II
**terrible** *pésimo(a)*, 5; *espantoso(a)*, 10
**terrifying** *aterrador(a)*, 10
**test** *el examen*, I; **to take a . . . test** *presentar el examen de...*, I; **We're going to have another test in . . . tomorrow? This is the last straw!** *¿Mañana vamos a tener otra prueba en...? ¡Esto es el colmo!*, 3
**textiles** *los tejidos*, II
**to thank: They thanked . . .** *Les agradecieron a...*, 9
**thank you** *gracias*, I
**thankful: to be thankful for** *estar agradecido(a) por*, 7
**thanks: Thanks to the support of . . . I have been able to overcome . . .** *Gracias al apoyo de..., he podido superar...*, 7; **Not today, thanks. Why don't we wait and do it next week?** *Hoy no, gracias. ¿Por qué no lo dejamos para la próxima semana?*, 5; **Thanks for inviting me, but I've already seen it.** *Gracias por invitarme, pero ya lo/la he visto.*, 5; **Thanks, but I have a lot to do. I'll go next time.** *Gracias, pero tengo mucho que hacer. La próxima vez iré.*, 5
**Thanksgiving Day** *el Día de Acción de Gracias*, I
**that** *ese(a)*, I; *ése*, II; **that** *(farther away) aquél, aquel, aquella*, II; **that was when** *fue cuando*, II; **that won't go away** *...que no se me quita ...*, II; **That I know of, there's (no) . . .** *Que yo sepa, (no) hay...*, 6; **That makes me think about . . .** *Eso me hace pensar en...*, 5
**That's disgusting!** *¡Qué asco!*, 4
**That's easy/pretty difficult for me.** *Eso me resulta fácil/bastante difícil.*, 8
**the** *el, la, los, las*, I; **The pleasure is mine.** *El gusto es mío.*, I; **The purpose of this letter is . . .** *Por medio de la presente...*, 8; **The milk has gone bad.** *Está pasada la leche.*, 4; **The way I see it, there's no equality between . . .** *A mi parecer, no hay igualdad entre...*, 3; **The . . . doesn't taste like anything.** *El/La... no sabe a nada.*, 4; **The . . . is**

**dry/isn't very sweet.** *El/La... está seco(a)/no está muy dulce.*, 4; **The . . . is salty/spicy.** *El/La... está salado(a)/picante.*, 4; **The . . . lacks flavor, but I don't know what's missing.** *Al (A la)... le falta sabor, pero no sé qué le falta.*, 4
**to the left of** *a la izquierda (de)*, II
**to the right of** *a la derecha (de)*, II
**theatre** *el teatro*, II
**their** *su(s)*, I
**them** *los, las*, I
**then** *entonces*, II; **back then** *en aquel entonces*, II
**then** *luego*, I
**there** *allí*, I; **there** *(general area) allá*, II; **there is, there are** *hay*, I; **there used to be** *había*, II; **there was** *había*, II; **There once was . . .** *Había una vez...*, II; **There were many challenges in . . .** *Había muchos desafíos en...*, 7; **I imagine that by the year . . . there will be . . .** *Me imagino que para el año... habrá...*, 10; **There's something I can't quite grasp.** *Hay algo que se me escapa.*, 8
**these** *éstos, éstas, estos, estas*, I; **these days** *hoy (en) día*, 8
**they** *ellas, ellos*, I; **They** (emphatic) **like . . .** *A ellos/ellas/ustedes les gusta(n)* + noun, II; **they lived happily ever after** *vivieron felices*, II; **They're . . .** *Me quedan...*, II; **They advise that . . .** *Se advierte que...*, 10; **They thanked . . .** *Les agradecieron a...*, 9
**thigh** *el muslo*, II
**thin** *delgado(a)*, I
**thing** *la cosa*, I; **the occasional (thing)** *alguno(a) que otro(a) (cosa)*, 6
**to think** *pensar (ie)*, I; **don't think** *no pienses*, II; **think** *piensa*, II; *creer*, II; **I think so.** *Creo que sí.*, II; **What do you think of this color?** *¿Qué te parece este color?*, II; **Really? Well, I think . . .** *¿Ah, sí? Pues, yo creo que son...*, 2; **Forgive me. I don't know what I was thinking.** *Perdóname. No sé en qué estaba pensando.*, 3; **Give yourself time to think it over.** *Date tiempo para pensarlo.*, 3; **Have you thought about . . .?** *¿Has pensado en...?*, 3; **I don't think it's fair.** *No me parece que sea justo.*, 3; **I don't think that journalists/newscasts are . . .** *No creo que los periodistas/ los noticieros sean...*, 6; **to think, to be of the opinion** *opinar*, 6; **I think it's worth remembering . . .** *Creo que vale la pena acordarse de...*, 10; **That makes me think about...** *Eso me hace pensar en...*, 5; **This portrait was painted by . . . What do you think of it?** *Este retrato fue pintado por... ¿Qué te parece?*, 5; **What do you think of...?** *¿Qué opinas de...?*, 5
**third** *tercero(a)*, II
**thirst** *la sed*, I
**thirteen** *trece*, I
**thirty** *treinta*, I
**this** *ésta, éste*, I; *este(a)*, I; **This is . . .** *Le presento a... (formal)*, II; *Te presento a... (informal)*, II; **This portrait was painted by . . . What do you think of it?** *Este retrato fue pintado por... ¿Qué te parece?*, 5
**those** *ésos, ésas, esos, esas*, I; **those** *(farther away) aquellos, aquellas, aquéllos, aquéllas*, II
**three** *tres*, I
**three hundred** *trescientos*, I
**throat** *la garganta*, I
**thunder** *el trueno*, II
**Thursday** *el jueves*, I; **on Thursdays** *los jueves*, I
**ticket** *el boleto*, I
**ticket** *la entrada*, II
**tide** *la marea*, II; **low tide** *la marea baja*, II
**tie** *la corbata*, II
**to tie a game** *empatar*, II
**tight** *apretado(a), estrecho(a)*, II
**time: I've been . . . for a long time.** *Hace mucho tiempo que...*, II; **to spend a lot of time** *pasar mucho tiempo*, II; **free time** *el rato libre*, II; **time(s)** *vez (pl. veces)*, II; **Once upon a time** *Érase una vez*, II; **One more time, please?** *¿Otra vez, por favor?*, II; **I've already done it a thousand times.** *Ya lo hice mil veces.*, II; **at the same time** *a la vez*, 8; **Once upon a time, in a faraway place . . .** *Érase una vez, en un lugar muy lejano...*, 9; **Some time ago, a stranger came . . .** *Hace tiempo, vino un desconocido...*, 9; **Give yourself time to think it over.** *Date tiempo para pensarlo.*, 3; **Thanks, but I have a lot to do. I'll go next time.** *Gracias, pero tengo mucho que hacer. La próxima vez iré.*, 5
**tip** *la propina*, II; **to leave the tip** *dejar la propina*, II
**tired** *cansado(a)*, I
**to/for me** *me*, I; **you** *te*, I; **us** *nos*, I; **him, her, you, them** *le(s)*, I
**toast** *el pan tostado*, I
**toasted** *tostado(a)*, II
**today** *hoy*, I; **Not today, thanks. Why don't we wait and do it next week?** *Hoy no, gracias. ¿Por qué no lo dejamos para la próxima semana?*, 5
**toe** *el dedo del pie*, II
**together** *juntos(as)*, II; **to work together** *trabajar juntos*, II
**toilet** *el inodoro*, II
**tolerant** *tolerante*, 2
**to tolerate** *aguantar*, 2
**tomato** *el tomate*, I; **can of tomato sauce** *la lata de salsa de tomate*, II
**tomorrow** *mañana*, I; **We're going to have another test in . . . tomorrow? This is the last straw!** *¿Mañana vamos a tener otra prueba en...? ¡Esto es el colmo!*, 3
**tonight** *esta noche*, II
**too much** *demasiado(a)*, I
**toothbrush** *el cepillo de dientes*, I
**toothpaste** *la pasta de dientes*, I
**topic: to cover a topic completely** *tratar un tema a fondo*, 6
**tornado** *el tornado*, II
**totally** *por completo*, II; **I totally forgot.** *Se me olvidó por completo.*, II
**touching** *conmovedor(a)*, 10
**to tour** *recorrer*, I
**tourism** *el turismo*, II; **tourism office** *la oficina de turismo*, II
**tourism office** *la oficina de turismo*, II
**tourist** *el turista, la turista*, II
**towel** *la toalla*, I
**tower** *la torre*, 5
**town** *el pueblo*, II; **town hall** *el ayuntamiento*, II; **town square** *la plaza*, II
**toy** *el juguete*, I; **to share toys** *compartir los juguetes*, II; **toy car** *el carrito*, II; **to play with toy cars** *jugar (ue) con carritos*, II; **toy store** *la juguetería*, I
**track and field** *el atletismo*, II
**to trade** *intercambiar*, II
**tradition** *la tradición*, 7
**traffic: It's quite possible that traffic will increase with . . .** *Es muy posible que el tráfico aumente con...*, 10
**traffic light** *el semáforo*, II
**tragedy** *la tragedia*, 5
**tragic** *trágico(a)*, 10
**train station** *la estación de tren*, II
**traitor** *el (la) traidor(a)*, 9
**trash** *la basura*, I
**traveler's checks** *los cheques de viajero*, II
**treat: My treat.** *Yo te invito*, 2
**tree** *el árbol*, II; **to climb trees** *trepar a los árboles*, II
**tricks** *las travesuras*, II; **to play tricks** *hacer travesuras*, II
**trip** *el viaje*, I
**to triumph** *triunfar*, 7
**troops** *las tropas*, 9
**trophy** *el trofeo*, II
**tropical** *tropical*, II; **to explore the tropical jungle** *explorar la selva tropical*, II; **tropical island** *la isla tropical*, II
**true: No way! That's not true.** *¡Qué va! Eso no es cierto.*, 3
**trust: to inspire trust in** *inspirarle confianza*, 6
**to trust** *confiar en*, 2
**trustworthy** *fiable*, 6
**truth: To tell the truth, it strikes me as . . .** *A decir verdad, me parece...*, 5
**to try on** *probarse (ue)*, II
**to try, taste** *probar (ue)*, I
**to try to** *tratar de + infinitive*, 8
**T-shirt** *la camiseta*, I
**Tuesday** *el martes*, I; **on Tuesdays** *los martes*, I
**tuna fish** *el atún*, I
**turkey (with stuffing)** *el pavo (con relleno)*, 4
**to turn** *doblar*, II
**to turn left on** *doblar a la izquierda en*, II
**to turn off** *apagar*, II; **to turn off the light(s)** *apagar la luz/las luces*, II
**to turn right on** *doblar a la derecha en*, II
**turnover-like pastry** *la empanada*, I
**TV set** *el televisor*, II
**twelve** *doce*, I
**twenty** *veinte*, I
**to twist (one's body part)** *torcer (ue) + a body part*, II
**twisted** *torcido(a)*, II
**two** *dos*, I
**two hundred** *doscientos*, I
**two thousand** *dos mil*, I
**typically** *típicamente*, II

## U

**ugly** *feo(a)*, I
**umbrella** *el paraguas*, II
**unbiased** *imparcial*, 6
**uncle** *el tío*, I

**under, underneath** *debajo (de)*, I

**to understand: I can't seem to understand . . .** *No logro entender...*, 8; **I can't understand it.** *No me cabe en la cabeza.*, 8; **From what I understand . . .** *Según tengo entendido,...*, 4; **I understand a little about . . ., but nothing about . . .** *Entiendo algo de..., pero nada de...*, 6; **What do I know about . . .? I don't understand a thing about . . .** *¿Qué sé yo de...? No entiendo ni jota de...?*, 6

**unemployment** *el desempleo*, 10

**unfair** *injusto(a)*, I

**unfaithful: to be (un)faithful** *ser (in)fiel*, 3

**unfortunately** *desgraciadamente*, II

**unfriendly** *antipático(a)*, I; *seco(a)*, 2

**university** *la universidad*, 3

**unknown** *desconocido(a)*, 9

**until** *hasta*, I; **See you later.** *Hasta luego.*, I; **See you tomorrow.** *Hasta mañana.*, I; **See you soon.** *Hasta pronto.*, I

**untrustworthy** *poco fiable*, 6

**up to** *hasta*, I; **What's . . . up to?** *¿Qué anda haciendo...?*, 4

**up-to-date: to be up-to-date** *estar al tanto*, 6

**to update** *actualizar*, 8

**upset: What's the matter? Are you upset?** *¿Qué te pasa? ¿Estás dolido(a)?*, 2

**Uruguayan** *uruguayo(a)*, II

**us** *nos*, I

**usually: to usually do something, to tend to do something** *soler (ue) + infinitive*, II; **We usually** + infinitive *Solíamos + infinitive*, II

**to utilize** *utilizar*, 8

## V

**vacation** *las vacaciones*, I; **to go on vacation** *ir de vacaciones*, II

**to vacuum** *pasar la aspiradora*, I; **vacuum cleaner** *la aspiradora*, II

**Valentine's Day** *el Día de los Enamorados*, I

**vanilla** *la vainilla*, II; **vanilla flan** *el flan de vainilla*, II

**vegetables** *las verduras*, I; *los vegetales*, II; **vegetable soup** *la sopa de verduras*, I

**vegetarian** *vegetariano(a)*, II

**Venezuelan** *venezolano(a)*, II

**very** *muy + adjective*, I; **I did very well (badly).** *Me fue muy bien (mal).*, II; **very bad** *pésimo(a)*, I; **very handsome** *guapísimo*, II

**victim** *la víctima*, 9

**victory** *la victoria*, 9

**video** *el video*, I

**video games** *los videojuegos*, I

**village** *el pueblo*, II

**villain** *el (la) malvado(a)*, 9; **From what they tell us, the villain . . .** *Según nos dicen, el malvado...*, 9

**vinegar** *vinagre*, II

**violin** *el violín*, II

**to visit** *visitar*, II; **to visit a museum** *visitar un museo*, II

**vitamins** *las vitaminas*, II

**volcano** *el volcán*, II

**volleyball** *el volibol*, I

**volunteer** *el (la) voluntario(a)*, 8

**vulture** *el buitre*, II

## W

**to wait** *esperar*, I; **Not today, thanks. Why don't we wait and do it next week?** *Hoy no, gracias. ¿Por qué no lo dejamos para la próxima semana?*, 5

**waiting room** *la sala de espera*, I

**to wake** *despertarse (ie)*, I

**to walk** *caminar*, I; *andar*, II; **to go for a walk** *pasear*, I

**to walk . . .** *dar una vuelta por...*, II

**to walk down (a street)** *bajar*, II; **to go down . . . until you get to** *bajar... hasta llegar a*, II

**wall** *la pared*, II

**wallet** *la billetera*, I; *la cartera*, II

**to want** *querer (ie)*, I; **I want to go to . . .** *Quiero ir a...*, II; **I want to introduce you to . . .** *Quiero presentarte a...*, II; **I want to see . . .** *Quiero conocer...*, I; **I wanted . . ., but there weren't any in my size.** *Quería..., pero no había en mi número.*, II; **What did you want to be?** *¿Qué querías ser?*, II; **What do you want to do this afternoon?** *¿Qué quieres hacer esta tarde?*, II; **When I heard the news, I didn't want to believe it.** *Cuando oí la noticia no lo quise creer.*, II; **Whatever you want.** *Como quieras.*, 2; **I have always wanted to be a . . .** *Siempre he querido ser un(a)...*, 8; **Do you want to come to . . . with me?** *¿Me acompañas a...?*, 5; **Do you want to go see . . .** *¿Quieres ir a ver...?*, 5

**to want someone else to do something** *querer que*, II

**to warm up** *calentarse (ie)*, II

**to warn: They warn that . . .** *Se advierte que...*, 10

**to wash** *lavar*, I; **to wash the dishes** *lavar los platos*, I; *lavarse*, I

**washing machine** *la lavadora*, II

**to waste** *desperdiciar*, 10

**to watch** *ver*, I; **to watch television** *ver televisión*, I

**watch, clock** *el reloj*, I

**to water** *regar (ie)*, II; **to water the plants** *regar las plantas*, II; **It makes my mouth water.** *Se me hace la boca agua.*, 4

**water** *el agua (f.)*, I; **mineral water** *el agua (f.) mineral*, II; **to dive in the water** *tirarse al agua*, II

**water skiing** *el esquí acuático*, II

**watercolor** *la acuarela*, 5

**waterfall** *la catarata*, II

**watermelon** *la sandía*, 4

**watery** *aguado(a)*, II

**waves** *las olas*, II

**way: in a . . . way** *de modo...*, 6; **way of being** *el modo de ser*, 7; **No way! That's not true.** *¡Qué va! Eso no es cierto.*, 3; **The way I see it, there's no equality between . . .** *A mi parecer, no hay igualdad entre...*, 3

**we** *nosotros(as)*, I; **We** (emphatic) **like . . .** *A nosotros nos gusta(n) + noun*, II; **We had to make a big effort to . . .** *Tuvimos que hacer un gran esfuerzo para...*, 7; **We made a big effort at . . .** *Nos esforzamos en...*, 7; **We talked about the issue; consequently . . .** *Hablamos del tema; por consiguiente...*, 7

**we are going** *vamos*, II; **We're going to . . .** *Vamos a ir a/al...*, II; **Are we going the right way to . . .?** *¿Vamos bien para...?*, II

**we fought (would fight)** *nos peleábamos*, II

**weak** *aguado(a)*, II

**to wear** *llevar*, I; **to wear glasses** *usar lentes*, I

**weather** *el tiempo*, I; **The weather is nice (bad).** *Hace buen (mal) tiempo.*, I; *el clima*, II; **I wonder what the weather is like at (in) . . .?** *¿Cómo será el clima en...?*, II

**wedding** *la boda*, I

**Wednesday** *el miércoles*, I; **on Wednesdays** *los miércoles*, I

**week** *la semana*, I; **Not today, thanks. Why don't we wait and do it next week?** *Hoy no, gracias. ¿Por qué no lo dejamos para la próxima semana?*, 5

**weekend** *el fin de semana*, I; **weekends** *los fines de semana*, I

**weight** *el peso*, I

**weights** *las pesas*, I; **to lift weights** *levantar pesas*, I

**well** *bien*, II; *ahora bien*, 9; **I did very well.** *Me fue muy bien.*, II; **I hope you're doing well.** *Espero que estés bien.*, II; **to get along well** *llevarse bien*, II; **to be well-informed** *estar bien informado*, 6

**Well, . . .** *Bueno,...*, II; **Really? Well, I think . . .** *¿Ah, sí? Pues, yo creo que son...*, 2; **Well, the truth is that . . .** *Pues, la verdad es que...*. 2; **Well, he's/she's still working . . .** *Pues, sigue trabajando...*, 4

**We're going to have another test in . . . tomorrow? This is the last straw!** *¿Mañana vamos a tener otra prueba en...? ¡Esto es el colmo!*, 3

**whales** *las ballenas*, II

**what** *lo que*, II; **So, what I have to do is . . .** *Entonces, lo que tengo que hacer es...*, II; **What I notice is that . . .** *Lo que noto es que...*, 10

**What . . .!** *¡Qué...!*, II; **What a dry climate!** *¡Qué clima tan seco!*, II; **What a gossip!** *¡Qué chismoso(a)!*, II; **What a pain!** *¡Qué lata!*, I; **What a shame!** *¡Qué lástima!*, I; **What bad luck!** *¡Qué mala suerte!*, I; **What a shame that they have . . .** *Qué pena que se hayan...*, 4; **What a surprise that they have . . .!** *¡Qué sorpresa que se hayan...!*, 4

**What . . .?** *¿Qué...?*, II; **What are you like?** *¿Cómo eres tú?*, I; **What are your parents/brothers and sisters/ friends like?** *¿Cómo son tus padres/ hermanos/amigos?*, II; **What did you like to do when you were . . . years old?** *¿Qué te gustaba hacer cuando tenías...?*, II; **What did you use to do when you were a little boy/girl?** *¿Qué hacías de niño(a)?*, II; **What did you want to be?** *¿Qué querías ser?*, II; **What do you do every morning?** *¿Qué haces todas las mañanas?*, II; **What do you like to do**

**on weekends?** *¿Qué te gusta hacer los fines de semana?*, II; **What do you recommend?** *¿Qué nos recomienda?*, II; **What do you still have to do?** *¿Qué te falta hacer?*, I; **What do you think of this color?** *¿Qué te parece este color?*, II; **What do you want to do this afternoon?** *¿Qué quieres hacer esta tarde?*, II; **What do your friends do on weekends?** *¿Qué hacen tus amigos los fines de semana?*, II; **What does . . . do?** *¿A qué se dedica...?*, II; **What else do I need to do?** *¿Qué más tengo que hacer?*, II; **What happened to you?** *¿Qué te pasó?*, II; **What kind of work does . . . do?** *¿Qué clase de trabajo realiza...?*, II; **What needs to be done in the kitchen?** *¿Qué hay que hacer en la cocina?*, II; **What news do you have of . . .?** *¿Qué noticias tienes de...?*, II; **What restaurant do you recommend to me?** *¿Qué restaurante me recomienda usted?*, II; **what someone has to do** *(me/te/le/nos/les) toca + infinitive*, II; **What were you like . . .?** *¿Cómo eras...?*, II; **What will you all do at the beach?** *¿Qué harán ustedes en la playa?*, II; **What's in the . . .?** *¿Qué lleva el (la)...?*, II; **What's new?** *¿Qué hay de nuevo?*, I; **What's the (daily) special?** *¿Qué hay de especial?*, II; **What's wrong with you?** *¿Qué te pasa?*, I; What would you like to do? *¿Qué te gustaría hacer?*, 8; **Where were you and what were you doing when . . .?** *¿Dónde estabas y qué hacías cuando...?*, 10; **What can you tell me about . . .?** *¿Qué me cuentas de...?*, 4; **What do I know about . . .? I don't understand a thing about . . .** *¿Qué sé yo de...? No entiendo ni jota de...?*, 6; **What do you know about . . .?** *¿Qué sabes de...?*, 4; **What do you look for in a boyfriend/girlfriend?** *¿Qué buscas en un(a) novio(a)?*, 2; **What do you think of . . .?** *¿Qué opinas de...?*, 5; **What should a good friend be like?** *¿Cómo debe ser un(a) buen(a) amigo(a)?*, 2

**What!** *¿Cómo?, ¿Qué?*, I

**what?, which?** *¿cuál?*, I

**What's the matter? Are you upset?** *¿Qué te pasa? ¿Estas dolido(a)?*, 2

**What's . . . up to?** *¿Qué anda haciendo...?*, 4

**Whatever you want.** *Como quieras.*, 2

**wheelchair** *la silla de ruedas*, I; **I use a wheelchair.** *Estoy en una silla de ruedas.*, II

**when** *cuando*, I; **When I found out, I couldn't believe it.** *Cuando me enteré, no lo pude creer.*, II; **When I heard the news, I didn't want to believe it.** *Cuando oí la noticia no lo quise creer.*, II; **that was when** *fue cuando*, II; **When I'm older, I'd like to . . .** *Cuando sea mayor, me gustaría...*, 7

**when?** *¿cuándo?*, I

**where?** *¿adónde?, ¿dónde?*, I; **Where did you go on vacation during the winter?** *¿Adónde fuiste de vacaciones durante el invierno?*, II; **Where will you go this summer?** *¿Adónde irás este verano?*, II; **Where do you intend to go tonight?** *¿Adónde piensan ir esta noche?*, II; **Can you tell me where . . . is?** *¿Me dices dónde está...?*, II; **Do you know where I can . . .?** *¿Sabe usted dónde se puede...?*, II; **Where could my . . . be?** *¿Dónde estará(n) mi(s)...?*, II; **Where were you and what were you doing when . . .?** *¿Dónde estabas y qué hacías cuando...?*, 10

**which?** *¿cuál?, ¿cuáles?*, I; **Which of these paintings do you like better, the one of (by) . . . or the one of (by) . . .?** *¿Cuál de estas pinturas te gusta más, la de... o la de...?*, 5

**while** *mientras*, II

**white** *blanco(a)*, I

**Who's calling?** *¿De parte de quién?*, I

**whole** *todo(a)*, I; *entero(a)*, II

**why** *¿por qué?*, I; **Why don't we go to . . .?** *¿Por qué no vamos a...?*, 5

**wide assortment** *un gran surtido*, II

**Will it be . . .?** *¿Hará...?*, II

**Will there be . . .?** *¿Habrá...?*, II

**to win** *ganar*, II

**wind** *el viento*, II

**window** *la ventana*, I; **to window shop** *mirar las vitrinas*, I

**windsurf** *el windsurf*, II; **to windsurf** *hacer windsurf*, II

**winter** *el invierno*, I

**wise man/woman** *el (la) sabio(a)*, 9

**to wish for** *desear*, I

**with** *con*, I; **with me** *conmigo*, I; **with you** *contigo*, I; **With time I was able to assimilate . . .** *Con el tiempo pude asimilar...*, 7

**witty** *gracioso(a)*, I

**wolf** *el lobo*, II

**woman** *la mujer*, I

**wood** *la madera*, II; **to do woodcarving** *tallar en madera*, 5

**wool** *la lana*, I

**to work** *trabajar*, I; **one works** *se trabaja*, II; **to work in the garden** *trabajar en el jardín*, II; **to work on cars** *trabajar en mecánica*, II; **to work together** *trabajar juntos*, II; **I work hard . . . and for that reason . . .** *Trabajo duro... y por eso...*, 7; **Well, he's/she's still working . . .** *Pues, sigue trabajando...*, 4

**work** *el trabajo*, I; **It took a lot of work for us to get used to . . .** *Nos costó trabajo acostumbrarnos a...*, 7; **It takes a lot of work for me (to do) . . .** *Me cuesta trabajo (hacer)...*, 8

**work environment** *el ambiente de trabajo*, 8

**to work out** *entrenar(se)*, I

**workshop** *el taller*, I

**world perspective** *el enfoque mundial*, 6

**World Wide Web** *el Web*, II; **Web pages** *páginas Web*, II

**to worry** *preocuparse*, I; **Don't worry.** *No te preocupes.*, I; *to worry*, 2

**worse** *peor(es)*, I; **to make worse** *empeorar*, 8

**worth: to (not) be worth it** *(no) valer la pena*, 2; **I think it's worth remembering . . .** *Creo que vale la pena acordarse de...*, 10

**Would you bring us . . .?** *¿Nos trae...?*, II

**Would you like anything else?** *¿Se les ofrece algo más?*, II

**woven cloth** *los tejidos*, II

**to wrap** *vendarse*, II

**wrapped** *vendado(a)*, II

**wrestling** *la lucha libre*, II

**wrist** *la muñeca*, II

**to write** *escribir*, I; **don't write** *no escribas*, II; **write** *escribe*, II; **writing** *escribiendo*, II; **written** *escrito (past participle of escribir)*, II

**wrong impression** *la impresión equivocada*, 3

# Y

**yard** *el patio*, I

**year** *el año*, I; **A few (many, five . . .) years ago** *Hace unos (muchos, cinco...) años*, II; **every year** *todos los años*, II; **last year** *el año pasado*, I; **New Year** *el Año Nuevo* I; **Many years ago, . . .** *Hace muchos años,...*, 9; **I imagine that by the year . . . there will be . . .** *Me imagino que para el año... habrá...*, 10

**to yell** *gritar*, II

**yellow** *amarillo(a)*, I

**yes** *sí*, I; **Yes, of course.** *Sí, claro.*, II; **Yes, I'm disappointed because . . . It makes me feel like crying.** *Sí, estoy decepcionado(a) porque... Me dan ganas de llorar.*, 2; **Yes, I'm excited because . . .** *Sí, estoy entusiasmado(a) porque...*, 2

**yesterday** *ayer*, I; **I remember it like it was yesterday.** *Lo recuerdo como si fuera ayer.*, 10

**yoga: to do yoga** *hacer yoga*, I

**yogurt** *el yogur*, 4

**you** *usted, (Ud.) ustedes, (Uds.) (formal)* I; *tú, vosotros(as), (informal)* I; **You were lucky!** *Ah, ¡tuviste suerte!*, I; **You're kidding** *No me digas*, II; **You're really good at . . . aren't you?** *Eres muy bueno(a) para... ¿verdad?*, 2; **You've left me speechless.** *Me has dejado boquiabierto(a).*, 4;

**You** *(emphatic)* **like . . .** *A ti te gusta(n) + noun*, II; *A vosotros os gusta(n) + noun, (pl., informal)*, II

**You don't say!** *¡No me digas!*, II, 4

**You look great!** *¡Te ves super bien!*, II

**You look very handsome!** *¡Te ves guapísimo!*, II

**You will see that they're going to promote . . .** *Ya verás que van a promover...*, 10

**You won't believe it, but . . .** *No lo vas a creer, pero...*, II

**young** *joven*, I

**young people** *los jóvenes*, I

**young person** *el joven, la joven*, II

**younger** *menor(es)*, I

**your** *tu(s), su(s), vuestro(a)(s)*, I

**Yours sincerely, . . .** *Un saludo de,...*, II

**yours** *tuyo(a), tuyos(as)*, II

**yours (formal), his, hers, its, theirs** *suyo(a), suyos(as)*, II

**youth hostel** *el albergue juvenil*, II

# Z

**zero** *cero*, I

**zoo** *el zoológico*, I; **to go to the zoo** *ir al zoológico*, II

**zucchini** *el calabacín*, 4

# Índice gramatical

Page numbers in boldface type refer to the first presentation of the topic. Other page numbers refer to the grammar topic in subsequent presentations or in the ***¡Exprésate!*** features. The Roman numeral I preceding page numbers indicates Level 1; the Roman numeral II indicates Level 2; the Roman numeral III indicates Level 3. Page numbers beginning with R refer to the **Síntesis gramatical** in this Reference Section (pages R25–R46).

## A



## B



## C

## D



## E

## F



## G



## H



## I

Índice gramatical

## Q



## R



Índice gramatical

## S



## T



## U



Índice gramatical

## V



## W



## Y

# Agradecimientos

## STAFF CREDITS

**Editorial**
Priscilla Blanton, Barbara Kristof, Amber P. Nichols, Douglas Ward

**Editorial Development Team**
Marion Bermondy, Konstanze Alex Brown, Lynda Cortez, Janet Welsh Crossley, Jean Miller, Beatriz Malo Pojman, Paul Provence, Jaishree Venkatesan, J. Elisabeth Wright

**Editorial Staff**
Sara Anbari, Hubert W. Bays, Yamilé Dewailly, Milagros Escamilla, Rebecca Jordan, Rita Ricardo, Glenna Scott, Géraldine Touzeau-Patrick

**Editorial Permissions**
Ann B. Farrar, Yuri Muñoz

**Book Design**
Kay Selke, Marta Kimball, José Garza, Sally Bess, Liann Lech, Lana Cox

**Image Acquisitions**
Curtis Riker, Jeannie Taylor, Cindy Verheyden, Michelle Dike, Sam Dudgeon, Victoria Smith

**Media Design**
Richard Metzger, Chris Smith

**Cover Design**
Marc Cooper, Kay Selke

**eMedia**
Edwin Blake, Kimberly Cammerata, Grant Davidson, Nina Degollado, Lydia Doty, Cathy Kuhles, Jamie Lane, Sean McCormick, Robert Moorhead, Beth Sample, Annette Saunders, Dakota Smith, Kenneth Whiteside

**Production, Manufacturing, and Inventory**
Marleis Roberts, Rose Degollado, Jevara Jackson, Rhonda Fariss

## ACKNOWLEDGMENTS

**For permission to reprint copyrighted material, grateful acknowledgment is made to the following sources:**

***Agencia Literaria Carmen Balcells:*** "Oda al presente" from *Nuevas odas elementales* by Pablo Neruda. Copyright © 2003 by Random House Mondadori, S.A.

***Agencia Literaria Carmen Balcells, S.A.:*** "El árbol de oro" from *Historias de la Artámila* by Ana María Matute. Copyright © 1961 by Ana María Matute.

***BBC World Service:*** From "Educación sin fronteras" from *BBC Mundo* web site, November 14, 2002, accessed October 2, 2003, at http://news.bbc.co.uk/hi/spanish/specials/newsid_2411517.stm. Copyright © 2002 BBC World Service.

***Bilingual Press/Editorial Bilingüe, Arizona State University:*** "Un oso y un amor" from *Primeros encuentros* by Sabine Ulibarrí. Copyright © 1982 by Bilingual Press/Editorial Bilingüe.

***Editorial de la Universidad de Puerto Rico:*** "Danza Negra" by Luis Palés Matos from *Aproximaciones al estudio de la literatura hispánica* by Carmelo Virgillo, L. Teresa Valdivieso, and Edward H. Friedman. Copyright © by Editorial de la Universidad de Puerto Rico.

***Fondo de Cultura Económica:*** From "Epístola" from *Donde nacen las aguas: Antología* by Nicolás Guillén. Copyright © 2002 by Fondo de Cultura Económica. Chapter 11 from *Popol Vuh: Las antiguas historias del Quiché,* translated by Adrián Recinos. Copyright © 1952, 1986 by Fondo de Cultura Económica.

***Houghton Mifflin Company:*** From "Senderos fronterizos" from *Senderos fronterizos: Continuación de Cajas de cartón* by Francisco Jiménez. Copyright © 2001 by Francisco Jiménez; Spanish translation copyright © 2002 by Francisco Jiménez. All rights reserved.

***International Editors Agency:*** "El eclipse" from *Obras Completas (y otros cuentos)* by Augusto Monterroso. Copyright © 1998 by Editorial Anagrama, S.A. and Augusto Monterroso.

***La Insignia:*** From "Recuperar la Tierra" by María José Atiénzar from *La Insignia* web site, accessed January 5, 2004, at http://www.lainsignia.org/2003/junio/ecol_003.htm. Copyright © 2003 by La Insignia.

***Medios Digitales Copesa:*** "El Caleuche" adapted by Carlos Ducci Claro from *Fiestas Patrias 2001* web site; accessed January 14, 2004, at http://docs.tercera.cl/especiales/2001/fonda2001/tradiciones/LEYENDAS/sur.html. Copyright © 2001 by Medio Digitales Copesa. All rights reserved.

## PHOTOGRAPHY CREDITS

Abbreviations used: c-center, b-bottom, t-top, l-left, r-right, bkgd-background. Others indicate image label.

**Teacher Edition**

All photos by Don Couch/HRW except: page T5 (r) ©Comstock; T6 (b) ©Jeremy Woodhouse, Digital Vision; (cl) John Langford/HRW; T8 (cl) ©Zefa Visual Media-Germany/Index Stock Imagery; T9 (cr) ©Owen Franken/Corbis; T10 (cl) ©Art Wolfe/Getty Images; T11 (cr) ©Jerry Alexander/Lonely Planet Images; T12 (cl) ©D. Boone/Corbis; T13 (cr) ©Bruce Dale/National Geographic Image Collection; T14 (cl) ©Paul Harris/Getty Images; T15 (condor) ©Frank Schreider/Photo Researchers; (cr) ©Grant Dixon/Lonely Planet Images; T17 (cr) ©Hubert Stadler/Corbis; T19 (tr) HRW Photo; T22 (cl) John Langford/HRW; (tl) Alvaro Ortiz/HRW; T23 (tl) Gary Russ/HRW; T24 (bl) Sam Dudgeon/HRW; T25 (cl) PhotoDisc/Getty Images; (tl) John Langford/HRW; T26 (cl) ©Philip Coblentz, Brand X Pictures; T27 (cl) Sam Dudgeon/HRW; (tl) John Langford/HRW; T28 (cl) John Langford/HRW; T29 (tl) Gary Russ/HRW; T30 (tl) Alvaro Ortiz/HRW; T31 (bl) Gary Russ/HRW; (tl) John Langford/HRW; T34 (bl) ©Philip Coblentz, Brand X Pictures; (cl) ©Danny Lehman/Corbis; T35 (bl) Art Resource, NY; (cl) ©Rob Lewine/Corbis; (tl) ©Robert Landau/Corbis; T36 (bl) Instituto Salvadoreño de Turismo; (cl) ©M. Timothy O'Keefe/Bruce Coleman; (tl) ©2003 Brian A. Vikander; T37 (bl) ©Robert Francis/South American Pictures; (cl) Christine Galida/HRW; (tl) Chip & Rosa María de la Cueva Peterson; T38 (bl) ©Galen Rowell/Odyssey Productions; (cl) ©Bob Daemmrich/Stock Boston; (tl) SuperStock; T39 (bl) ©2003 Estate of Pablo Picasso/Artists Rights Society (ARS), New York, Scala/Art Resource, New York; (cl) SuperStock; (tl) painting ©2004 Banco de México Diego Rivera & Frida Kahlo Museums Trust. Av. Cinco de Mayo No. 2, Col. Centro, Del. Cuauhtémoc 06059, México, D. F.; photo source The Granger Collection, New York; T50 (bl) ©Dennis Galante/Taxi/Stone; (br) ©Luc Beziat/Getty Images/Stone; (Chaco) ©Royalty-Free/Corbis; T51 (#1–#4) Martha Granger/Edge Video Productions/HRW; (Chisos) ©David Muench/Corbis; (GeoVision) ©Robert Francis/South American Pictures; (mundillo) John Langford/HRW; (Video Novela) John Langford/HRW; T53 (cr) PhotoDisc/Getty Images; T55 (br) John Langford/HRW; T56 (cr) PhotoDisc/Getty Images; T59 (Sandrock) Photographer: Mark Ibach, courtesy Paul Sandrock; T60 (Beers) courtesy Kylene Beers; T61 (Strickland) courtesy Cindy Strickland; T61 (Tomlinson) Photographer Gitchell's Studio, courtesy Carol Ann Tomlinson; T62 (LeLoup) R Kaussner Photo, courtesy Jean W. LeLoup; (Ponterio) R Kaussner Photo, courtesy Robert Ponterio; T63 (Humbach) courtesy Nancy Humbach; T64–T67 (border) PhotoDisc/Getty Images; T64 (br) ©Comstock; T65 (br) PhotoDisc/Getty Images; (clock) ©Royalty-Free/Corbis; (cr) PhotoDisc/Getty Images; (tr) Sam Dudgeon/HRW/SCRABBLE® is a trademark of Hasbro in the United States and Canada. ©2002 Hasbro, Inc. All Rights Reserved; T66 (boards) PhotoDisc/Getty Images; (cr) John Langford/HRW; T67 (br) Sam Dudgeon/HRW; (cr) ©Bill Truslow/Getty Images/Stone; 5C (tr) ©Swim Ink/Corbis; 5D (bl) Alvaro Ortiz; (tr) ©Philadelphia Museum of Art, Pennsylvania/Giraudon, Paris/SuperStock; 10 (Lord) courtesy Christine Lord; 47C (tr) ©Hugh Sitton/Image Bank/Getty Images; 47D (bl) Sam Dudgeon/HRW; (tr) ©Adam Woolfitt/CORBIS ; 65 (Rhymes) courtesy Angie Rhymes; 66 (Harshman) courtesy Kassie Harshman; 73 (Avendaño) courtesy Alejandro Avendaño; 95C (tr) HIRB/Index Stock Imagery; 95D (bl) Sam Dudgeon/HRW; (tr) Suzanne Murphy-Larronde/D. Donne Bryant Photography; 108 (Bassi) courtesy Clementina Bassi; 134 (Phillips) HRW Photo; 137C (tr) Sam Dudgeon/HRW; 137D (bl) Scott Vallance/VIP Photo/HRW; (tr) ©Stockbyte; 145 (Peters) courtesy Kim Peters; 174 (Conlon) courtesy Kristine Conlon; 176 (Furillos) courtesy Maritza and Robert Furillo; 185C (tr) painting ©2004 Banco de México Diego Rivera & Frida Kahlo Museums Trust. Av. Cinco de Mayo No. 2, Col. Centro, Del. Cuauhtémoc 06059, México, D. F.; photo ©Schalkwijk/Art Resource, NY; Reproduction Authorized by the National Institute of Fine Arts and Literature, Mexico City; 185D (bl) Sam Dudgeon/HRW; (tr) Joe Jaworski/HRW; 207 (Cole) courtesy Aura Cole; 227C (tr) Gary Russ/HRW; 227D (bl) Sam Dudgeon/HRW; (tr) Miwako Ikeda/International Stock Photography; 234 (Hale) courtesy Linda Hale; 246 (Calhoun) courtesy Wayne Calhoun; 275C (tr) ©Amy Etra/PhotoEdit; 275D (bl) Scott Vallance/VIP Photo/HRW; (tr) Jeremy Horner/CORBIS; 285 (Meegan) courtesy Marsha Meegan; 316 (Martyny) courtesy Gudrun U. Martyny; 317C (tr) ©Bill Aron/PhotoEdit; 317D (bl) Scott Vallance/VIP Photo/HRW; (tr) Suzanne Murphy-Larronde; 356 (Bromley) courtesy Kimberly Bromley; 365C (tr) ©Richard T. Nowitz/Corbis; 365D (bl) Sam Dudgeon/HRW; (tr) ©Abbie Enock/Travel Ink/CORBIS; 371 (Haedo) courtesy Meruchy Haedo; 407C (tr) ©Dorling Kindersley LTD Picture Library; 407D (bl) Scott Vallance/VIP Photo/HRW; 426 (Reina) courtesy Luisa Reina; 431 (Gaddess) courtesy Jack Gaddess.

ICONS: e-community, PhotoDisc/Getty Images; Fine Art Connection ©Stockbyte; Game Bank, PhotoDisc/Getty Images; Holt Online Learning, PhotoDisc/Getty Images; Pacing Tips, PhotoDisc/Getty Images; Partner Class Project, Steve Ewert Photography; Projects, Victoria Smith/HRW; Tradition, HRW photo.

**Student Edition**

COVERS: FRONT (bl) Don Couch/HRW; (br) John Langford/HRW; (tl) ©LOOK Die Bildagentur der Fotografen GmbH/Alamy; (tr) ©Robert Frerck/Odyssey. BACK Don Couch/HRW.

AUTHORS: Page iii (Humbach) courtesy Nancy Humbach; (Madrigal Velasco) courtesy Sylvia Madrigal.

TABLE OF CONTENTS: Page vi (cl) ©Zefa Visual Media-Germany/Index Stock Imagery; vii (cr) ©Owen Franken/Corbis; viii (cl) ©Art Wolfe/Getty Images; ix (cr) ©Jerry Alexander/Lonely Planet Images; x (cl) ©D. Boone/Corbis; xi (cr) ©Bruce Dale/National Geographic Image Collection; xii (cl) ©Paul Harris/Getty Images; xiii (cr) ©Grant Dixon/Lonely Planet Images; xiii (inset) ©Harvey Lloyd/Getty Images/Taxi; xiv (cr) Don Couch/HRW; xv (cr) ©Hubert Stadler/Corbis; xvi (tr) Don Couch/HRW; xvii (cl) John Langford/HRW; (tr) Don Couch/HRW.

CAPÍTULO 1 All photos by Don Couch/HRW except: Page xviii (t) ©Robert Frerck/Odyssey Productions; 1 (ave, Daimiel) ©Sincronia Audiovisuals; (b) ©Zefa Visual Media-Germany/Index Stock Imagery; (flor, tl, tr) ©Owen Franken/Corbis; (Yebes) ©Centro Astronómico de Yebes; 2 (bl) ©Index Fototeca; (br) ©Cathedral of Santiago de Compostela/Dagli Orti/Art Archive; (tl) ©Giraudon/Art Resource, NY; (tr) ©Robert Frerck/Odyssey Productions; 3 (bc) ©AP/Wide World Photos; (bl) PhotoDisc/Getty Images; (tl) ©AKG Images; (tr) ©The Stapleton Collection/Bridgeman Art Library; 4 (bl, tl) Alvaro Ortiz/HRW; (br) ©Francesc Muntada/Corbis; (tr) ©Robert Frerck/Odyssey Productions; 5 (b) ©Metropolitan Museum of Art, New York, USA/Bridgeman Art Library; (tc) ©Museum of Fine Arts, Budapest, Hungary/Bridgeman Art Library; (tl) ©Hermitage, St. Petersburg, Russia/Bridgeman Art Library; (tr) ©Robert Frerck/Odyssey Productions; 8 (bl, l, tc, tr) Alvaro Ortiz/HRW; (br) ©Royalty Free/Corbis; 9 (c) Alvaro Ortiz/HRW; (r) ©Robert Frerck/Odyssey Productions; 10 (A) PhotoDisc/Getty Images; (B) ©Bob Krist/Corbis; (bl) ©Francesc Muntada/Corbis; (C) Victoria Smith/HRW; (D) ©Archivo Iconográfico, S.A./Corbis; 11 (bl) Nancy Black/Mercury Press International; (br) ©David Young-Wolff/PhotoEdit; (c) Alvaro Ortiz/HRW; (cl) Heinz Hebeisen/Iberimage; (cr, t) ©Robert Frerck/Odyssey Productions; 12 (cl) Alvaro Ortiz/HRW; 13 (r) ©Archivo Iconografico, S.A./Corbis; 15 (1) ©Michael Keller/Index Stock Imagery; (2) ©David Young-Wolff/PhotoEdit; (3) ©Bob Winsett/Index Stock Imagery; (Adriana) ©Tom Rosenthal/SuperStock; 17 (1, 2) PhotoDisc/Getty Images; (3) ©Comstock Images; (4) Royalty Free/Brand X Pictures; 18 (l) John Langford/HRW; 20 (t) ©Gonzalez/Laif/Aurora Photos; 21 (b) ©Jeff Greenberg/PhotoEdit; 22 (l) ©Ellen Senisi/Photo Researchers; (r) PhotoDisc/Getty Images; 23 (tr) PhotoDisc/Getty Images; 24 (cl) ©Robert Frerck/Odyssey Productions; 25 (1) Victoria Smith/HRW; (2, 3, 4) Sam Dudgeon/HRW; 26 (all) Alvaro Ortiz/HRW; 27 (2) Victoria Smith/HRW; (3) Sam Dudgeon/HRW; (4) PhotoDisc/Getty Images; (golf bag) ©Royalty Free/Corbis; (t) ©Jean Dominique Dallet/SuperStock; 28 (l) Gary Russ/HRW; 29 (cl) ©Royalty Free Rubberball Productions; (cr, l) PhotoDisc/Getty Images; (r) Victoria Smith/HRW; 30 (cl) John Langford/HRW; 31 (r) ©Bob Daemmrich/PhotoEdit; 32 (l) Sam Dudgeon/HRW; 33 (bc) ©SW Productions/Brand X Pictures/PictureQuest; (bl) ©John A. Rizzo/Photodisc/PictureQuest; (br, tr) ©Royalty Free/Corbis; (c, cl, cr) PhotoDisc/Getty Images; 36 (b) ©Mark Antman/The Image Works; (t) ©Owen Franken/Corbis; 37 (tl) ©Godo-Foto; 41 (br) ©Chris Collins/zefa/Corbis; 42 (A) ©Steve Timewell/Iberian Image; (B) PhotoDisc/Getty Images; (C) ©Image Ideas; (D) ©Royalty Free/Corbis; 46 (A) ©Image Source/PictureQuest; (B, C, D) ©Royalty Free/Corbis.

CAPÍTULO 2 All photos by Don Couch/HRW except: Page 48–49 (all) Alvaro Ortiz/HRW; 50 (bl) ©Elena Rooraid/The Image Works; (b, l) Alvaro Ortiz/HRW; (tc) ©Valentí Zapater/V&W/The Image Works; (tr) ©Michael S Yamashita/Corbis; 51 (br, r) Alvaro Ortiz/HRW; (cl) ©Ingram Publishing; (cr) PhotoDisc/Getty Images; (tl) ©Jeff Greenberg/PhotoEdit; (tr) ©Royalty Free/Corbis; 52 (A) ©Werran/Ochsner/Imagestate; (B) ©Pablo Corral Vega/Corbis; (bl) ©Francesc Muntada/Getty Images; (C) ©Dann Tardif/Corbis; (D) ©Rachel Epstein/PhotoEdit; (E) Randy M. Ury/Corbis; (F, G) PhotoDisc/Getty Images; (H) ©Brooke Slezak/Getty Images; 54 (t) Alvaro Ortiz/HRW; 55 (r) ©AP/Wide World Photos; 56 (l) John Langford/HRW; 60 (l) Sam Dudgeon/HRW; 61 (r) ©Owen Franken/Corbis; 62 (t) ©Enrique Carrascal/Alfaqui Fotografía; 63 (b) ©AP/Wide World Photos; (t) John Langford/HRW; 64 (all) Alvaro Ortiz/HRW; 65 (all) Alvaro Ortiz/HRW; 66 (tl) ©Robert Fried Photography; 68 (tl) Alvaro Ortiz/HRW; 69 (r) Alvaro Ortiz/HRW; 71 (r) ©Stuart Cohen/The Image Works; 72 (l) Gary Russ/HRW; 74 (bl) PhotoDisc/Getty Images; 78 (bl) ©Enrique Carrascal/Alfaqui Fotografía; 79 (tl) ©Eising/StockFood America; 83 (br) ©Lawrence Manning/Corbis; 84 (c) ©George D. Lepp/Corbis; (l) ©Lawrence Manning/Corbis; (r) ©Darama/Corbis; 88 (cl, l) PhotoDisc/Getty Images; (cr) ©Mike Powell/Allsport Concepts/Getty Images; (r) ©Royalty Free/Corbis.

CAPÍTULO 3 All photos by John Langford/HRW except: Page 90 (b) ©H. Rodgers/Art Directors & TRIP Photo Library; (c) ©Art Wolfe/Getty Images; (t) ©David Parker/Science Photo Library/Photo Researchers; 91 (bc) ©NOAA; (bl) ©AP/Wide World Photos; (br) ©Jerry Alexander/Lonely Planet Images; (c) ©Martjan Lammertink; 92 (br) ©North Wind Picture Archives; (cl) ©Ayuntamiento de Coruña, Spain/Bridgeman Art Library; (cr) ©Ira Block/National Geographic Image Collection; (tl) ©Robert Fried Photography; (tr) ©North Wind Picture Archives; 93 (bl) ©U.S. Naval Historical Center; (br) Catalog # 16399, Object #5162 in the Collection of the San Juan National Historic Site, San Juan, Puerto Rico. Photograph courtesy of the National Park Service; (cr) ©Getty Images; (tl) ©Bernard Boutrit/Woodfin Camp & Associates; 94 (b) From the collection of the Museum of History, Anthropology and Art of the University of Puerto Rico; (cr) ©Christie's Images; (t) ©AKG Images; 95 (bc) ©AP/Wide World Photos; (bl) ©The Solomon R. Guggenheim Foundation, New York/Guggenheim Museum; (br) ©AP/Wide World Photos; (c) ©Nicole Marie Sanchez/Courtesy of Fundación Ramón Oviedo; (tl) The Cock, 1941 by Mariano (Mariano Rodríguez). Oil on canvas, 29 1/4 X 25 1/8". Gift of the Comisión Cubana de Cooperación Intelectual Digital Image ©The Museum of Modern Art/Licensed by SCALA/Art Resource, NY; (tr) Cuatro Vientos, 2000 by Ramón Oviedo. Acrylic on canvas, 50 x 70 inches. Private collection of Antonio Ocaña; 98 (all) Nathan Keay/HRW; 99 (r) Sam Dudgeon/HRW; 100 (bl) ©Robert Fried Photography; 103 (1) ©Sean Murphy/Getty Images; (3) ©David White/Index Stock Imagery; (bc) Mary Kate Denny/PhotoEdit; 104 (l) Sam Dudgeon/HRW; 105 (all) Sam Dudgeon/HRW; 106 (cr) ©P. Treanor/Art Directors & TRIP Photo Library; 110 (t) ©Jeff Greenberg/PhotoEdit; 111 (br) ©D. Donne Bryant/DDB Stock Photography; (br) Sam Dudgeon/HRW; (t) Don Couch/HRW; 114 (A, D, E, F) Sam Dudgeon/HRW; (C) Nathan Keay/HRW; 115 (tr) ©Robert Fried Photography; 117 (r) ©Keith Dannemiller/Corbis/SABA; 119 (all) Sam Dudgeon/HRW; 120 (l) Sam Dudgeon/HRW; 122 (A, B, C, E) Sam Dudgeon/HRW; (D, F) Victoria Smith/HRW; 126 (r) ©Michael Newman/PhotoEdit; (tl) PhotoDisc/Getty Images; 127 (tl) ©Ariel Skelley/Corbis; 131 (b) ©David Young-Wolff/PhotoEdit; 136 (all) Sam Dudgeon/HRW.

CAPÍTULO 4 All photos by John Langford/HRW except: Page 140–141 (all) David Pou/HRW; 143 (cr) ©Martha Cooper/Viesti Associates; 144 (tl) David Pou/HRW; 145 (1) Michael Newman/PhotoEdit; (2) ©David Lok/SuperStock; (3) ©Royalty Free/Corbis; (4) Don Couch/HRW; (tr) Rudi Von Briel/PhotoEdit; 149 (1, 3, 4) David Pou/HRW; (yo) ©Michael Newman/PhotoEdit; 150 (cl) David Pou/HRW; 151 (cr) Robert Frerck/Odyssey Productions; 152 (tl) ©Rob Lewine/Corbis; 153 (br) ©Rudi Von Briel/PhotoEdit; (t) Sam Dudgeon/HRW; 154 (all) David Pou/HRW; 155 (bl, tl, tr) David Pou/HRW; (cl) Victoria Smith/HRW; (cr) William Koechling/HRW; 156 (a., c., d.) David Pou/HRW; (b.) Victoria Smith/HRW; (e., f.) William Koechling/HRW; 157 (cr) David Pou/HRW; 158 (tl) David Pou/HRW; 159 (a., b., d., e., f.) William Koechling/HRW; (c.) Sam Dudgeon/HRW; 160 (bl, l) Gary Russ/HRW; 163 (1, 2, 3, 5, 6) William Koechling/HRW; (4) Sam Dudgeon/HRW; 168 (b, tl) David Pou/HRW; 169 (tl) David Pou/HRW; 170–171 (all) William Koechling/HRW; 172 (1) Mary Ellen Bartley/Foodpix; (2) Dorling Kindersley LTD Picture Library; (3, 6) PhotoDisc/Getty Images; (4) ©Royalty Free/Corbis; (5) Scott Vallance/VIP Photo/HRW; (tr) William Koechling/HRW; 173 (br) ©Jeff Greenberg/Alamy; 174 (A) ©Stockbyte/SuperStock; (B) ©Chuck Savage/Corbis; (C) ©David Young-Wolff/PhotoEdit; 178 (all) William Koechling/HRW.

CAPÍTULO 5 All photos by Don Couch/HRW except: Page 180–181 (t) ©David Muench/GETTY; 180 (br) ©Raymond Watt/Albuquerque International Balloon Fiesta; (c) ©NASA Human Space Flight Gallery; 181 (bl) ©Anthony Cooper/Ecoscene/Corbis; (br) ©Royalty Free/Corbis; (c) ©Bettmann/Corbis; (tl) ©Goldberg Diego/Corbis/Sygma; (tr) ©Bruce Dale/National Geographic Image Collection; 182 (bl) ©Collection of Moody Medical Library, The University of Texas Medical Branch, Galveston/Adair Margo Gallery; (br) ©Jose Luis Soto/Museum of National Independence, Dolores Hidalgo, México/©Doranne Jacobson/International Images; (tl) ©David Frazier/Getty Images; (tr) ©Philip James Corwin/Corbis; 183 (b) ©D. Boone/Corbis; (c) ©Corbis; (tl) ©North Wind Picture Archives; (tr) All trademarks and copyrights used herein are properties of the United States Postal Service and are used under license to Holt Rinehart and Winston All rights reserved; 184 (bl) ©Robert Frerck/Getty Images; (br) ©John Loengard/Time Life Pictures/Getty Images; (tl) ©Dewitt Jones/Corbis; (tr) ©Chuck Place Photography; 185 (alfombra) ©George H. H. Huey/Corbis; (bc, br) ©Mario Torero; (cl) Sandia/Watermelon ©1986 by Carmen Lomas Garza. Gouache painting on paper, 20 x 28 inches. Collection of Dudley D. Brooks & Tomas Ybarra-Frausto, New York, NY/Courtesy of Carmen Lomas Garza; (cr) ©David W. Hamilton/Getty Images; (tl) ©David Tineo; 186–187 (c) Gary Russ/HRW; 188 (br) Martha Granger/Edge Video Productions/HRW; (tl) Victoria Smith/HRW; (tr) Gary Russ/HRW; 189 (c) Gary Russ/HRW; 190 (A) ©Robert Emmett Bright/Photo Researchers; (B) ©Robert Fried Photography; (C) ©Virginia Historical Society, Richmond, Virginia; (D) ©Albright-Knox Art Gallery/Corbis; (E) ©New York Historical Society; (F) ©Mary Heller/Mira; 191 (bc) ©Marilee Whitehouse-Holm/SuperStock; (bl) ©Dennie Cody/Getty Images; (br) ©National Anthropological Museum Mexico/Dagli Orti/Art Archive; (br) ©Buddy Mays/Corbis; 193 (r) ©Robert Frerck/Odyssey Productions; 194 (br) ©Jeff Greenberg/Alamy; (l) Sam Dudgeon/HRW; 195 (1) PhotoDisc/Getty Images; (2) ©SuperStock; (3) ©Steve Vidler/SuperStock; (4) ©ARS, NY/©The Museum of Modern Art/Licensed by SCALA/Art Resource, NY; (tr) ©Royalty Free/Corbis; 196 (l) ©El Paso Museum of Archaeology; 197 (r) ©Bob Daemmrich Photography; 198

(l) Sam Dudgeon/HRW; 199 (tr) ©Joel Salcido/Bob Daemmrich Photography; 200 (tl) painting ©2004 Banco de México Diego Rivera & Frida Kahlo Museums Trust. Av. Cinco de Mayo No. 2, Col. Centro, Del. Cuauhtémoc 06059, México, D. F.; photo source ©Robert Frerck/Odyssey Productions; Reproduction Authorized by the National Institute of Fine Arts and Literature, Mexico City; 201 (br) Cindy Bland Verheyden/HRW; 202 (l) Gary Russ/HRW; 204 (A) ©A. Tovy/Art Directors & TRIP Photo Library; (B) ©BSIP Agency/Index Stock Imagery; (C) ©AP/Wide World Photos; (D) PhotoDisc/Getty Images; (E) ©Odile Noel/Lebrecht Collection; (F) ©Wolfgang Kaehler Photography; 205 (cr) ©Bob Daemmrich/Stock Boston; 207 (r) Leonel Monroy/Latin Focus; 209 (tr) ©Richard Hutchings/PhotoEdit; 212 (l) John Langford/HRW; 216 (l) ©Bettmann/Corbis; 221 (br) ©David Young-Wolff/PhotoEdit; 222 (1) ©Michael S. Yamashita/Corbis; (2) ©Susan Ruggles/Index Stock Imagery; (3) ©Michael Newman/PhotoEdit; 226 (A) ©Greg Williams/Latin Focus; (B) ©Robert Fried/DDB Stock Photography; (C) ©Jeff Greenberg/PhotoEdit; (D) ©Jay Syverson/Corbis.

CAPÍTULO 6 All photos by Sam Dudgeon/HRW except: Page 228–229 (all) Gary Russ/HRW; 230 (bc) ©Shelley Gazin/Corbis; (bl) ©Larry Kolvoord/The Image Works; (br) ©Wesley Boxce/Getty Images; 231 (cl) ©Spencer Grant/PhotoEdit; (cr) Keith Dannemiller/Corbis/SABA; (tl) ©Luis Diez Solano/COVER/The Image Works; (tr) STR/AFP/Getty Images; 232 (desierto) Paul McCormick/Image Bank/Getty Images; (tv) PhotoDisc/Getty Images; 233 (tr) Don Couch/HRW; 234 (t) Don Couch/HRW; 235 (cr) ©Robert Frerck/Odyssey Productions; 236 (cl) ©Robert Fried Photography; 237 (cr) ©Bob Daemmrich/The Image Works; 238 (l) John Langford/HRW; 240 (l) John Langford/HRW; 241 (cr) ©Robert Frerck/Odyssey Productions; 242 (b) Gary Russ/HRW; (t) ©Robert Fried Photography; 243 (br) ©Tony Arruza Photography; (t) Don Couch/HRW; 244, 245 (all) Victoria Smith/HRW; 246 (tl) ©Action Images/Icon Sports Media; 247 (1, 7, 8) Victoria Smith/HRW; 248 (tl) Victoria Smith/HRW; 249 (cr) ©Robert Frerck/Odyssey Productions; 251 (cr) ©Royalty Free/Corbis; 252 (bl) ©Despotovic Dusko/Corbis/Sygma; 253 (cr) ©DigitalVision; 258 (l, tr) ©Reuters NewMedia/Corbis; 259 (tl) ©AFP/Corbis; 263 (br) ©Bob Daemmrich Photo; 264 (B) ©Larry Kolvoord/The Image Works; (C) ©Robert E. Daemmrich/Getty Images; (D) ©Quin Llenas/COVER/The Image Works; (E) ©Jose Luis Pelaez/Corbis; 268 (A) ©Peter Beck/Corbis; (B) ©STL/Icon Sports Media; (C) ©Davis Barber/PhotoEdit; (D) ©Len Kaufman.

CAPÍTULO 7: All photos by Don Couch/HRW except: Page 270 (t) PhotoDisc/Getty Images; 271 (b) ©Francois Gohier/Photo Researchers; (condor) ©Frank Schreider/Photo Researchers; (tr) ©Grant Dixon/Lonely Planet Images; 272 (bl) ©North Wind Picture Archives; (tl) Atahualpa, Fourteenth Inca, 1 of 14 Portraits of Inca Kings, Colonial Period, mid 18th century, Peru, South America. Oil on canvas, 23 5/8 x 21 3/4 in., ©Brooklyn Museum of Art. 1995.29.14; (tr) ©Pablo Corral Vega/Corbis; 273 (bc) ©AP/Wide World Photos; (cl) ©Hippenmeyer/AFP/Getty Images; (cr) ©Bettmann/Corbis; (tl) ©Museo Nacional de Bellas Artes/Kactus Foto/SuperStock; 274 (bl) ©Paul Harris/Getty Images; (br) La Santusa, 1928, José Sabogal, Cajabamba, Cajamarca, 1888 - Lima, 1956, óleo sobre lienzo sobre nórdex, 65 x 56 cm. Museo de Arte de Lima, donación Manuel Cisneros Sánchez, cód. V-2.0-401/© Museo de Arte de Lima; (tl) ©Ronald Sheridan/Ancient Art & Architecture Collection, Ltd; 74 (tr) ©Photo by Paul Maeyaert/Cuzco Cathedral, Cuzco, Peru/Bridgeman Art Library; 275 (br) Columbine Galleries, Loveland CO; (c) ©Miguel Andrango; (tl) ©Guayasamín Foundation Collection/Fundacion Guayasamín; 279 (tl) ©Robert Fried Photography; 282 (t) ©Todd Wolf; 284 (l) John Langford/HRW; 285 (r) ©Jeremy Horner/Corbis; 287 (1) ©A. Ramey/PhotoEdit; (2, 3) ©David Young-Wolff/PhotoEdit; (4) ©Vanessa Vick/Photo Researchers; 288 (1) ©Bob Daemmrich/PhotoEdit; (2) ©David Young-Wolff/PhotoEdit; (3) ©Kindra Clineff/Index Stock Imagery; (4) ©Bill Aron/PhotoEdit; 289 (r) ©Robert Frerck/Odyssey Productions; 291 (br) Richard Michael Pruitt/NewsCom; 293 (tl) ©Mark Scott/Alamy; 294 (2) ©SuperStock; (3) ©Bob Daemmrich Photography; (A) ©Rob Lewine/Corbis; (D) ©Michelle D. Bridwell/PhotoEdit; 297 (cr) ©Robert Frerck/Odyssey Productions; 298 (bl) ©Robert Frerck/Odyssey Productions; 300 (bl) ©Pablo Coral Vega/Corbis; 302 (cl) ©Loren McIntyre/Woodfin Camp & Associates; 306 (br) ©Len Kaufman; (tl) ©Steve Vidler/SuperStock; 307 (cl, tl) ©Robert Frerck/Odyssey Productions; 311 (br) ©Tibor Bognár/Corbis; 312 (A) ©Daniel Zheng/Corbis; (B) ©Myrleen Ferguson Cate/PhotoEdit; (C) ©Charles Gupton/Corbis; (D) ©Jay Thomas/Imagestate; 316 (A) ©J. Highet/Art Directors & TRIP Photo Library; (B) ©Michelle D. Bridwell/PhotoEdit; (C) ©Susan Van Etten/PhotoEdit; (D) ©Anton Vengo/SuperStock.

CAPÍTULO 8 All photos by Don Couch/HRW except: Page 320 (computer) Sam Dudgeon/HRW; 321 (tc) ©Fujifotos/The Image Works; 323 (1) Peter Van Steen/HRW; (2-boy) Victoria Smith/HRW; (2-screen, 3, 4-boy) Sam Dudgeon/HRW; (4-robot) ©Fujifotos/The Image Works; 325 (cr) ©Robert Fried Photography; 326 (l) Sam Dudgeon/HRW; 328 (cl) John Langford/HRW; 331 (1) Victoria Smith/HRW; (2, 3, 4, 5, 6) Sam Dudgeon/HRW; 332 (tl) ©Bob Daemmrich/Bob Daemmrich Photography; 333 (br) ©Patrick Zachmann/Magnum Photos; 340 (l) John Langford/HRW; 341 (cl) ©Robert Frerck/Odyssey Productions; 343 (1) Sam Dudgeon/HRW; (2) ©DigitalVision; (3, yo) PhotoDisc/Getty Images; (4) ©G.K. & Vikki Hart/PhotoDisc/Getty Images; 344 (l) John Langford/HRW; 345 (tr) ©Marcel & Eva Malherbe/The Image Works; 348 (br) ©Patrick Zachmann/Magnum Photos; (cl) ©Jeff Greenberg/The Image Works; 349 (tl) ©Melanie Carr/Imagestate; 353 (br) ©David Young-Wolff/PhotoEdit; 354 (a., b., c.) PhotoDisc/Getty Images; (d.) ©Fujifotos/The Image Works; 358 (all) Sam Dudgeon/HRW.

CAPÍTULO 9 All photos by Don Couch/HRW except: Page 360 (t) ©Victor Englebert Photography; 361 (b) ©Hubert Stadler/Corbis; (chaco) ©R. Cinti/Focus; (Houssay, Leloir) ©Mary Evans Picture Library; (Montevideo) ©Daniel Rivademar/Odyssey Productions; 362 (bc) ©Museo Nacional de Bellas Artes Buenos Aires/Dagli Orti/Art Archive; (tl) Biblioteca Nacional de Chile; 363 (br) ©AFP/Corbis; (cl) ©Norman Tomalin/Alamy; (tl) ©Bettmann/Corbis; (tr) ©Peter Marlow/Magnum Photos; 364 (br) ©Museo Histórico Nacional, Buenos Aires, Argentina/Index/Bridgeman Art Library; (tl) ©Chris Sharp/DDB Stock Photography; (tr) ©Hubert Stadler/Corbis; 365 (cl) ©ARS, NY/Giraudon/Art Resource, NY; (tr) ©Mercedes Ulloa Reyes; 370 (cl) ©AP/Wide World Photos; 374 (bl) ©Kenneth W. Fink/Photo Researchers; 376 (l) Gary Russ/HRW; 377 (cr) ©John Gefrom/Latin Focus; 379 (cr) ©Robert Holmes/Robert Holmes Photography; 381 (br) ©Stock Montage; 382 (br) ©Index/Bridgeman Art Library; (tr) ©SuperStock; 383 (bl) ©Museo Nacional de Historia Lima/Dagli Orti/Art Archive; (cr) ©Mary Evans Picture Library; (tl) ©Corbis; 384 (A) ©DigitalVision; (B) ©Robert Fried Photography; (bl) ©Pablo Corral Vega/Corbis; (C) ©Steve Casimiro/Getty Images; (D) ©Clarin/Corbis/Sygma; 385 (tr) ©Robert Frerck/Odyssey Productions; 387 (1) ©Bettmann/Corbis; (2) ©AP/Wide World Photos; (2) ©Pablo Corral Vega/Corbis; (4) ©Daniel Aguilar/Reuters/Time Life Pictures/Getty Images; 388 (l) Sam Dudgeon/HRW; 390 (cl) Azul y Blanco afiche gentileza del director Sebastián Araya, Chile; 391 (cr) PhotoDisc/Getty Images; 392 1/8 Pg. ©Patrick Ward/Corbis; 397 (tl) Peter Marlow/Magnum Photos; 401 (br) ©Felix Stenson/f1/Alamy; 406 (1, 4) Peter Van Steen/HRW; (2) Victoria Smith/HRW; (3) Sam Dudgeon/HRW.

CAPÍTULO 10 All photos by Don Couch/HRW; except: Page 410 (bc) ©Nik Wheeler/Corbis; (c) ©Diego Giudice/AP/Wide World Photos; (cl) ©Stephen Frink/Getty Images; (cr) ©Daniel Luna/AP/Wide World Photos; 411 (tl) ©Victor Englebert Photography; (tr) Rogerio Reis/Tyba/BrazilPhotos; (tr-inset) Francois Gohier/Photo Researchers; 412 (A) ©Vo Trung Dung/Corbis/Sygma; (B) ©Stephen Frink/Index Stock Imagery; (bl) ©Topical Press Agency/Hulton Archive/Getty Images; (C) ©Popperfoto/Alamy; (D) ©G. H. Harrison/Bruce Coleman; 413 (cr) ©AFP/Corbis; 415 (cr) ©Walter Bibikow/Index Stock Imagery; 416 (bl, l) Sam Dudgeon/HRW; 417 (1) Victoria Smith/HRW; (2, 3, 4) Sam Dudgeon/HRW; 418 (bl) ©Topham/The Image Works; 419 (r) David Phillips/HRW; 420 (bl) ©Robert Frerck/Odyssey Productions; (cl) John Langford/HRW; 422 (tl) ©AFP/Corbis; 423 (br) ©Heidi Jo Brady/Odyssey Productions; 424 (bc) ©Alex Ocampo/The Photoworks/DDB Stock Photography; (bl) ©Tony Freeman/PhotoEdit; (cl) ©Francesc Muntada/Corbis; (cr) ©Neil Beer/Corbis; 425 (cl) ©Joseph Sohm/Visions of America/Corbis; (tl) ©Rob Crandall/The Image Works; (tr) ©Photographer 9074/Imagestate; 426 (bl) ©Carlos Goldin/DDB Stock Photography; 431 (1, 2) Sam Dudgeon/HRW; (3) Peter Van Steen/HRW; (4) Peter Chartrand/DDB Stock Photography; (cr) ©Bruce Clarke/Index Stock Imagery; 432 (bl) ©Jeremy Woodhouse/Pixelchrome; 433 (1) ©SuperStock; (2) ©WP Wittman Photography; (3) ©Carlos Reyes-Manzo/Andes Press Agency; (4) ©Inga Spence/Visuals Unlimited; (5) ©Bill Varie/Corbis; (6) Charles Philip/Photri-Microstock; 435 (cr) ©Luis Padilla/Getty Images; 439 (tl) ©Frank Kletschkus/Imagestate; 443 ©Strauss/Curtis/Corbis; 444 (A) ©Ian Cartwright/PhotoDisc/Getty Images; (B) ©Bettmann/Corbis; (C) ©Reuters NewMedia/Corbis; (D) ©AFP/Corbis; 448 (A, D) Victoria Smith/HRW; (B, C) Sam Dudgeon/HRW.

REPASO DE VOCABULARIO: Page R9 (br) ©David Young-Wolff/PhotoEdit; (c) PhotoDisc/Getty Images; R10 (bc) PhotoDisc/Getty Images; (br) ©Robert Fried Photography; (br-screen) Paul McCormick/Image Bank/Getty Images; (tc) John Langford/HRW; R11 (bc) ©Stockbyte; (c) ©Royalty Free/Corbis; (cr) David Pou/HRW; R12 (bc, br) William Koechling/HRW; (cr) David Pou/HRW; (tc) ©Ingram Publishing; R13 (br) ©Victor Englebert Photography; (c) PhotoDisc/Getty Images; (tc) William Koechling/HRW; R14 (bl) ©Bob Winsett/Index Stock Imagery; (cr) ©Jeff Greenberg/PhotoEdit.

VOCABULARIO ADICIONAL: Page R15 (all) PhotoDisc/Getty Images; R16 (bl) PhotoDisc/Getty Images; (br) John Langford/HRW; R17 (bc) PhotoDisc/Getty Images; (tl) ©Royalty Free/Corbis; R18 (Chac Mool) ©Royalty Free/Corbis; (cl) Ryan McVay/PhotoDisc/Getty Images; (computer) ©Thinkstock/Fotosearch; R19 (cr) PhotoDisc/Getty Images.

NOVELA STILL PHOTOS: Puerto Rico - John Langford/HRW; Spain, Mexico, Costa Rica, Peru, Chile, Argentina - Don Couch/HRW. VIDEOCULTURA ICON: Don Couch/HRW.